# THE BEST OF
# LOUISA MAY ALCOTT

They all drew to the fire, mother in the big chair, with Beth at her feet.

# THE BEST OF
# LOUISA MAY ALCOTT

## Edited by Claire Booss

### LITTLE WOMEN
### LITTLE MEN

AND

### TWENTY-FOUR
### SHORT STORIES

*Illustrated by Frank T. Merrill, Reginald B. Birch,*
*Addie Ledyard, and others*

GRAMERCY BOOKS
NEW YORK • AVENEL

## Acknowledgments

In gathering this anthology and the illustrations for it, several people were consulted and were very helpful. I would particularly like to thank Madeleine Stern, Milton Reissman of the Victoria Bookshop, Madelon Bedell, and Martha Saxton.

C.B.

*Publishers Note:* This book was originally published under the title *Works of Louisa May Alcott.*

Copyright © 1982 by Crown Publishers, Inc.
All rights reserved.

This 1994 edition is published by Gramercy Books,
distributed by Outlet Book Company, Inc.,
a Random House Company, 40 Engelhard Avenue, Avenel, New Jersey 07001.

**Library of Congress Cataloging in Publication Data**

Alcott, Louisa May, 1832–1888.
  [Selections.   1994]
  The best of Louisa May Alcott / edited by Claire Booss.
      p.   cm.
  Originally published: Works of Louisa May Alcott. New York:
Avenel Books, 1982.
  ISBN: 0-517-10034-7
  I. Booss, Claire.   II. Title.
PS1016.B6   1994
813'.4—dc20                                            92–37538
                                                        CIP

Manufactured in the United States of America

10  9  8  7  6  5  4  3  2  1

# CONTENTS

# INTRODUCTION

THE very first words of *Little Women*, spoken by a plaintive Jo, "Christmas won't be Christmas without any presents," herald Louisa May Alcott's preoccupation with holidays, and Christmas in particular. She loved them because they bring out, or should, the values she exalted: kindness, generosity, family warmth, joy, and humor. And she would have been gratified to know that, more than a century later, her stories are like gifts to us—gifts of special moments and special qualities—whose force and freshness offer the surprise and delight of unexpected presents.

For these tales, long and short, have been carefully selected from the author's golden period, which began in the 1860s, a few years before the publication of *Little Women* made her famous. Prior to that, she had gone through two stages of development as a writer. Her earliest work was overly and sweetly sentimental, designed to please a public that relished virtuous heroines and good and stalwart children who melted the hearts of sour elders. Next was her period of lurid and sensational pot-boilers, cooked up expressly to keep the family pot boiling. But whatever her style of prose, she was constantly and eagerly engaged in writing. It was her connection to life, her genius, as well as a very practical necessity. Rarely have need and natural inclination met so well.

Then came Louisa May Alcott's mature period, represented here, in which she began to write tellingly and movingly about real people and their lives. It began with *Hospital Sketches*, published in 1863, a compassionate collection based on her experiences as a Civil War nurse tending the sick and wounded. "A Night," the most touching of those pieces, is included in this book.

In 1868 she published *Little Women*. It was in this novel that she fully demonstrated her warmth and her perception and her gift for drawing her audience irresistibly into her story. The reader feels as if he or she is the fifth child in the March family and lives the story with them—because of Louisa's great warmth for her characters and theirs for one another: not a goody-goody, simpering warmth but a joyous, down-to-earth affection, full of humor and bounce. Along with this went a strong appreciation of her characters' unique foibles and eccentricities, perhaps because she herself had a father, who, though brilliant, was eccentric in the extreme. It was also here that the value and emphasis she put on independence became evident. In a day when most women were content to passively accept the support and protection of whatever male figure society provided for them (whether husband, father, or brother), she became self-supporting at a very young age, later contributing to, and finally taking over, the major support of her family.

In *Little Men,* based on her nephews, she went on to narrate the further adventures of Jo March, the Louisa-like figure of *Little Women,* after her marriage to Professor Bhaer. Although Louisa herself never married, she was so deeply involved in her sisters' families that she writes with intimate understanding of family relationships. The dedication to the book read: "To Freddy and Johnny, The Little Men, to whom she owes some of the best and happiest hours of her life, this book is gratefully dedicated by their loving 'Aunt Weedy.' "

Most of the short stories here have been culled from *Aunt Jo's Scrap-Bag,* a six-volume series published from 1872 to 1882, which is perhaps her most versatile creation in its appeal to young and old. One will be reading along, charmed by the words meant to beguile a child, when suddenly one runs across a nugget of adult wit or insight that is sly and surprising.

In the autobiographical "My Boys," she confesses:

> I like boys and oysters raw; so, though good manners are always pleasing, I don't mind the rough outside burr which repels most people, and perhaps that is the reason why the burrs open and let me see the soft lining and taste the sweet nut hidden inside.

And later she goes on to describe a teen-aged conquest:

> With the amiable Augustus at my feet, gallantly supplying me with bushes to strip while we talked about books and poetry, I really felt as if I had got into a novel, and enjoyed it immensely. I believe a dim idea that Gus was sentimental hovered in my mind, but I would not encourage it, though I laughed in my sleeve when he was spouting Latin for my benefit, and was uncertain whether to box his ears or simper later in the day, when he languished over the gate, and said he thought chestnut hair the loveliest in the world.

This series was another of her presents to her family. Her preface, written during the Christmas holidays of 1871–72, said:

As grandmothers rummage their piece-bags and bundles in search of gay odds and ends to make gifts with which to fill the little stockings that hang all in a row on Christmas Eve, so I have gathered together some stories, old and new, to amuse the large family that has so rapidly and beautifully grown up about me.

I hope that when they promenade in night-caps and gowns to rifle the plump stockings, the little "dears" will utter an "Oh!" of pleasure, and give a prance of satisfaction, as they pull out this small gift from Aunt Jo's scrap-bag.

And this was truly a scrap-bag, displaying Louisa May Alcott's immense diversity of interests and subjects. Besides the romances she recounted in "My Boys," there are other delicious boy/girl stories like "Cupid and Chow-Chow," which is relevant today because it deals with sexism in the nursery and the issues of courage and guilt.

There is comedy and suspense in "Clams," a rattling good ghost story. And there are stories in which animals are the most important characters: the horse in "Rosa's Tale," a description of a day at the zoo in "My May-Day Among Curious Birds and Beasts," the gentle humor of "Buzz," a fly, and even "The Whale's Story," which anticipates modern interest in this unique mammal.

Of course, Louisa did love holidays, and so there are holiday stories here—"An Old-Fashioned Thanksgiving" and two Christmas tales, "How It All Happened" and "Tessa's Surprise." The author also had a special feeling for old people. "A Happy Birthday" is a sweet story about an old lady's birthday celebration, and a nice contrast to all the stories about youngsters.

In addition to the *Scrap-Bag* stories, there is also "Little Button-Rose," which was long enough to be published as a separate book, and "Onawandah," from *Spinning Wheel Stories,* a poignant tale of a young Indian who lives for a time in a white settlement and grows deeply attached to his adopted family.

The editions that were chosen for this collection are, in all cases, the early or first ones. The modern reader may be surprised to discover old-fashioned styles of punctuation and spelling, but these have been retained in order to convey the flavor and quaintness of the originals.

It is no wonder that some of the best and most humanistic illustrators chose to portray Louisa May Alcott's work. None was better suited to this than Frank T. Merrill, who captured the essential Alcott charm so variously and so profusely. The illustrations for *Little Women* selected here appeared in the first illustrated edition of her work, in the 1880s, which contained 200 drawings! Louisa herself was captivated by them, and Merrill went on to illustrate *Little Men* and many of her short stories.

The artist who brought an entirely different but equally vivid look to *Little Men* was Reginald Birch, whose art dominates that story in this book, with supplemental pictures by Merrill. The short stories include illustrations by Addie Ledyard and Jessie McDermott, as well as several by the redoubtable Frank T. Merrill, and other artists unknown.

This collection reminds us of how timeless Louisa May Alcott's work is. The drawings of her earliest illustrators, which should have been as immortal as her prose, have happily been revived here, and they enhance the stories from her golden period, which, like that sparkling element, have beauty, universal appeal, and lasting value.

CLAIRE BOOSS

# LITTLE WOMEN

## OR MEG, JO, BETH AND AMY.

### BY LOUISA M. ALCOTT.

*Illustrated by Frank T. Merrill*

# PREFACE

*"Go then, my little Book, and show to all*
*That entertain and bid thee welcome shall,*
*What thou dost keep close shut up in thy breast;*
*And wish what thou dost show them may be blest*
*To them for good, may make them choose to be*
*Pilgrims better, by far, than thee or me.*
*Tell them of Mercy; she is one*
*Who early hath her pilgimage begun.*
*Yea, let young damsels learn of her to prize*
*The world which is to come, and so be wise;*
*For little tripping maids may follow God*
*Along the ways which saintly feet have trod."*

Adapted from JOHN BUNYAN.

*Overleaf:* Title page design from original illustrated edition, illustrated by
Frank T. Merrill.

# CHAPTER I

### PLAYING PILGRIMS

"CHRISTMAS won't be Christmas without any presents," grumbled Jo, lying on the rug.

"It's so dreadful to be poor!" sighed Meg, looking down at her old dress.

"I don't think it's fair for some girls to have plenty of pretty things, and other girls nothing at all," added little Amy, with an injured sniff.

"We've got father and mother and each other," said Beth contentedly, from her corner.

The four young faces on which the firelight shone brightened at the cheerful words, but darkened again as Jo said sadly,—

"We haven't got father, and shall not have him for a long time." She didn't say "perhaps never," but each silently added it, thinking of father far away, where the fighting was.

Nobody spoke for a minute; then Meg said in an altered tone,—

"You know the reason mother proposed not having any presents this Christmas was because it is going to be a hard winter for every one; and she thinks we ought not to spend money for pleasure, when our men are suffering so in the army. We can't do much, but we can make our little sacrifices, and ought to do it gladly. But I am afraid I don't." And Meg shook her head, as she thought regretfully of all the pretty things she wanted.

"But I don't think the little we should spend would do any good. We've each got a dollar, and the army wouldn't be much helped by our giving that. I agree not to expect anything from mother or you, but I do want to buy Undine and Sintram for myself; I've wanted it *so* long," said Jo, who was a bookworm.

"I planned to spend mine in new music," said Beth, with a little sigh, which no one heard but the hearth-brush and kettle-holder.

"I shall get a nice box of Faber's drawing-pencils; I really need them," said Amy decidedly.

"Mother didn't say anything about our money, and she won't wish us to give up everything. Let's each buy what we want, and have a little fun; I'm sure we work hard enough to earn it," cried Jo, examining the heels of her shoes in a gentlemanly manner.

"I know *I* do,—teaching those tiresome children nearly all day, when I'm longing to enjoy myself at home," began Meg, in the complaining tone again.

"You don't have half such a hard time as I do," said Jo. "How would you like to be shut up for hours with a nervous, fussy old lady, who keeps you trotting, is never satisfied, and worries you till you're ready to fly out of the window or cry?"

"It's naughty to fret; but I do think washing dishes and keeping things tidy is the worst work in the world. It makes me cross; and my hands get so stiff, I can't practice well at all;" and Beth looked at her rough hands with a sigh that any one could hear that time.

"I don't believe any of you suffer as I do," cried Amy; "for you don't have to go to school with impertinent girls, who plague you if you don't know your lessons, and laugh at your dresses, and label your father if he isn't rich, and insult you when your nose isn't nice."

"If you mean *libel*, I'd say so, and not talk about *labels*, as if papa was a pickle-bottle," advised Jo, laughing.

"I know what I mean, and you needn't be *statirical* about it. It's proper to use good words, and improve your *vocabilary*," returned Amy, with dignity.

"Don't peck at one another, children. Don't you wish we had the money papa lost when we were little, Jo? Dear me! How happy and good we'd be, if we had no worries!" said Meg, who could remember better times.

"You said, the other day, you thought we were a deal happier than the King children, for they were fighting and fretting all the time, in spite of their money."

"So I did, Beth. Well, I think we are; for, though we do have to work, we make fun for ourselves, and are a pretty jolly set, as Jo would say."

"Jo does use such slang words!" observed Amy, with a reproving look at the long figure stretched on the rug. Jo immediately sat up, put her hands in her pockets, and began to whistle.

"Don't, Jo; it's so boyish!"

"That's why I do it."

"I detest rude, unlady-like girls!"

"I hate affected, niminy-piminy chits!"

" 'Birds in their little nests agree,' " sang Beth, the peace-maker, with such a funny face that both sharp voices softened to a laugh, and the "pecking" ended for that time.

"Really, girls, you are both to be blamed," said Meg, beginning to lecture in her elder-sisterly fashion. "You are old enough to leave off boyish tricks, and to behave better, Josephine. It didn't matter so much when you were a little girl; but now you are so tall, and turn up your hair, you should remember that you are a young lady."

"I'm not! And if turning up my hair makes me one, I'll wear it in two tails till I'm twenty," cried Jo, pulling off her net, and shaking down a chestnut mane. "I hate to think I've got to grow up, and be Miss March, and wear long gowns, and look as prim as a China-aster! It's bad enough to be a girl, anyway, when I like boys' games and work and manners! I can't get over my disappointment in not being a boy; and it's worse than ever now, for I'm dying to go and fight with papa, and I can only stay at home and knit, like a poky old woman!" And Jo shook the blue army-sock till the needles rattled like castanets, and her ball bounded across the room.

"Poor Jo! It's too bad, but it can't be helped; so you must try to be contented with making your name boyish, and playing brother to us girls," said Beth, stroking the rough head at her knee with a hand that all the dish-washing and dusting in the world could not make ungentle in its touch.

"As for you, Amy," continued Meg, "you are altogether too particular and prim. Your airs are funny now; but you'll grow up an affected little goose, if you don't take care. I like your nice manners and refined ways of speaking, when you don't try to be elegant; but your absurd words are as bad as Jo's slang."

"If Jo is a tom-boy and Amy a goose, what am I, please?" asked Beth, ready to share the lecture.

"You're a dear, and nothing else," answered Meg warmly; and no one contradicted her, for the "Mouse" was the pet of the family.

As young readers like to know "how people look," we will take this moment to give them a little sketch of the four sisters, who sat knitting away in the twilight, while the December snow fell quietly without, and the fire crackled cheerfully within. It was a comfortable old room, though the carpet was faded and the furniture very plain; for a good picture or two hung on the walls, books filled the recesses, chrysanthemums and Christmas roses bloomed in the windows, and a pleasant atmosphere of home-peace pervaded it.

Margaret, the eldest of the four, was sixteen, and very pretty, being plump and fair, with large eyes, plenty of soft, brown hair, a sweet mouth, and white hands, of which she was rather vain. Fifteen-year-old Jo was very tall, thin, and brown, and reminded one of a colt; for she never seemed to know what to do with her long limbs, which were very much in her way. She had a decided mouth, a comical nose, and sharp, gray eyes, which appeared to see everything, and were by turns fierce, funny, or thoughtful. Her long, thick hair was her one beauty; but it was usually bundled into a net, to be out of her way. Round shoulders had Jo, big hands and feet, a fly-away look to her clothes, and the uncomfortable appearance of a girl who was rapidly shooting up into a woman, and didn't like it. Elizabeth—or Beth, as everyone called her—was a rosy, smooth-haired, bright-eyed girl of thirteen, with a shy manner, a timid voice, and a peaceful expression, which was seldom disturbed. Her father called her "Little Tranquillity," and the name suited her excellently; for she seemed to live in a happy world of her own, only venturing out to meet the few whom she trusted and loved. Amy, though the youngest, was a most important person,—in her own opinion at least. A regular snow-maiden, with blue eyes, and yellow hair, curling on her shoulders, pale and slender, and always carrying herself like a young lady mindful of her manners. What the characters of the four sisters were we will leave to be found out.

The clock struck six; and, having swept up the hearth, Beth put a pair of slippers down to warm. Somehow the sight of the old shoes had a good effect upon the girls; for mother was coming, and every one brightened to welcome her. Meg stopped lecturing, and lighted the lamp, Amy got out of the easy-chair without being asked, and Jo forgot how tired she was as she sat up to hold the slippers nearer to the blaze.

"They are quite worn out; Marmee must have a new pair."

"I thought I'd get her some with my dollar," said Beth.

"No, I shall!" cried Amy.

"I'm the oldest," began Meg, but Jo cut in with a decided—

"I'm the man of the family now papa is away, and *I* shall provide the slippers, for he told me to take special care of mother while he was gone."

"I'll tell you what we'll do," said Beth; "let's each get her something for Christmas, and not get anything for ourselves."

"That's like you, dear! What will we get?" exclaimed Jo.

Every one thought soberly for a minute; then Meg announced, as if the idea was suggested by the sight of her own pretty hands, "I shall give her a nice pair of gloves."

"Army shoes, best to be had," cried Jo.

"Some handkerchiefs, all hemmed," said Beth.

"I'll get a little bottle of cologne; she likes it, and it won't cost much, so I'll have some left to buy my pencils," added Amy.

"How will we give the things?" asked Meg.

"Put them on the table, and bring her in and see her open the bundles.

Don't you remember how we used to do on our birthdays?" answered Jo.

"I used to be *so* frightened when it was my turn to sit in the big chair with the crown on, and see you all come marching round to give the presents, with a kiss. I liked the things and the kisses, but it was dreadful to have you sit looking at me while I opened the bundles," said Beth, who was toasting her face and the bread for tea, at the same time.

"Let Marmee think we are getting things for ourselves, and then surprise her. We must go shopping tomorrow afternoon, Meg; there is so much to do about the play for Christmas night," said Jo, marching up and down, with her hands behind her back and her nose in the air.

"I don't mean to act any more after this time; I'm getting too old for such things," observed Meg, who was as much a child as ever about "dressing-up" frolics.

"You won't stop, I know, as long as you can trail round in a white gown with your hair down, and wear gold-paper jewelry. You are the best actress we've got, and there'll be an end of everything if you quit the boards." said Jo. "We ought to rehearse tonight. Come here, Amy, and do the fainting scene, for you are as stiff as a poker in that."

"I can't help it; I never saw anyone faint, and I don't choose to make myself all black and blue, tumbling flat as you do. If I can go down easily, I'll drop; if I can't, I shall fall into a chair and be graceful; I don't care if Hugo does come at me with a pistol," returned Amy, who was not gifted with dramatic power, but was chosen because she was small enough to be borne out shrieking by the villain of the piece.

"Do it this way; clasp your hands so, and stagger across the room, crying frantically, 'Roderigo! Save me! Save me!' " and away went Jo, with a melodramatic scream which was truly thrilling.

Amy followed, but she poked her hands out stiffly before her, and jerked herself along as if she went by machinery; and her "Ow!" was more suggestive of pins being run into her than of fear and anguish. Jo gave a despairing groan, and Meg laughed outright, while Beth let her bread burn as she watched the fun, with interest.

"It's no use! Do the best you can when the time comes, and if the audience laughs, don't blame me. Come on, Meg."

Then things went smoothly, for Don Pedro defied the world in a speech of two pages without a single break; Hagar, the witch, chanted an awful incantation over her kettleful of simmering toads, with weird effect; Roderigo rent his chains asunder manfully, and Hugo died in agonies of remorse and arsenic, with a wild "Ha! ha!"

"It's the best we've had yet," said Meg, as the dead villain sat up and rubbed his elbows.

"I don't see how you can write and act such splendid things, Jo. You're a regular Shakespeare!" exclaimed Beth, who firmly believed that her sisters were gifted with wonderful genius in all things.

"Not quite," replied Jo modestly. "I do think, 'The Witch's Curse, an Operatic Tragedy,' is rather a nice thing; but I'd like to try Macbeth, if we only had a trap-door for Banquo. I always wanted to do the killing part. 'Is that a dagger that I see before me?' " muttered Jo, rolling her eyes and clutching at the air, as she had seen a famous tragedian do.

"No it's the toasting fork, with mother's shoe on it instead of the bread.

Beth's stage-struck!" cried Meg, and the rehearsal ended in a general burst of laughter.

"Glad to find you so merry, my girls," said a cheery voice at the door, and actors and audience turned to welcome a tall, motherly lady, with a "can-I-help-you" look about her which was truly delightful. She was not elegantly dressed, but a noble-looking woman, and the girls thought the gray cloak and unfashionable bonnet covered the most splendid mother in the world.

"Well, dearies, how have you got on today? There was so much to do, getting the boxes ready to go tomorrow, that I didn't come home to dinner. Has any one called, Beth? How is your cold, Meg? Jo, you look tired to death. Come and kiss me, baby."

While making these maternal inquiries Mrs. March got her wet things off, her warm slippers on, and sitting down in the easy-chair, drew Amy to her lap, preparing to enjoy the happiest hour of her busy day. The girls flew about, trying to make things comfortable, each in her own way. Meg arranged the tea-table; Jo brought wood and set chairs, dropping, overturning, and clattering everything she touched; Beth trotted to and fro between parlor and kitchen, quiet and busy; while Amy gave directions to every one, as she sat with her hands folded.

As they gathered about the table, Mrs. March said, with a particularly happy face, "I've got a treat for you after supper."

A quick, bright smile went round like a streak of sunshine. Beth clapped her hands, regardless of the biscuit she held, and Jo tossed up her napkin, crying, "A letter! A letter! Three cheers for father!"

"Yes, a nice long letter. He is well, and thinks he shall get through the cold season better than we feared. He sends all sorts of loving wishes for Christmas, and an especial message to you girls," said Mrs. March, patting her pocket as if she had got a treasure there.

"Hurry and get done! Don't stop to quirk your little finger, and simper over your plate, Amy," cried Jo, choking in her tea, and dropping her bread, butter side down, on the carpet, in her haste to get at the treat.

Beth ate no more, but crept away, to sit in her shadowy corner and brood over the delight to come, till the others were ready.

"I think it was so splendid in father to go as a chaplain when he was too old to be drafted, and not strong enough for a soldier," said Meg warmly.

"Don't I wish I could go as a drummer, a *vivan*—what's its name? or a nurse, so I could be near him and help him," exclaimed Jo, with a groan.

"It must be very disagreeable to sleep in a tent, and eat all sorts of bad-tasting things, and drink out of a tin mug," sighed Amy.

"When will he come home, Marmee?" asked Beth, with a little quiver in her voice.

"Not for many months, dear, unless he is sick. He will stay and do his work faithfully as long as he can, and we won't ask for him back a minute sooner than he can be spared. Now come and hear the letter."

They all drew to the fire, mother in the big chair with Beth at her feet, Meg and Amy perched on either arm of the chair, and Jo leaning on the back, where no one would see any sign of emotion if the letter should happen to be touching. Very few letters were written in those hard times that were not touching, especially those which fathers sent home. In this one little was said of the hardships endured, the dangers faced, or the homesickness conquered; it was a cheerful, hopeful letter, full of lively descriptions of camp life, marches, and military news; and only at the end did the writer's heart overflow with fatherly love and longing for the little girls at home.

"Give them all my dear love and a kiss. Tell them I think of them by day, pray for them by night, and find my best comfort in their affection at all times. A year seems very long to wait before I see them, but remind them that while we wait we may all work, so that these hard days need not be wasted. I know they will remember all I said to them, that they will be loving children to you, will do their duty faithfully, fight their bosom enemies bravely, and conquer themselves so beautifully, that when I come back to them I may be fonder and prouder than ever of my little women."

Everybody sniffed when they came to that part; Jo wasn't ashamed of the great tear that dropped off the end of her nose, and Amy never minded the rumpling of her curls as she hid her face on her mother's shoulder and sobbed out, "I *am* a selfish girl! But I'll truly try to be better, so he mayn't be disappointed in me by and by."

"We all will!" cried Meg. "I think too much of my looks, and hate to work, but won't any more, if I can help it."

"I'll try and be what he loves to call me, 'a little woman,' and not be rough and wild; but do my duty here instead of wanting to be somewhere else," said Jo, thinking that keeping her temper at home was a much harder task than facing a rebel or two down South.

Beth said nothing, but wiped away her tears with the blue army-sock, and began to knit with all her might, losing no time in doing the duty that lay nearest her, while she resolved in her quiet little soul to be all that father hoped to find her when the year brought round the happy coming home.

Mrs. March broke the silence that followed Jo's words, by saying in her cheery voice, "Do you remember how you used to play Pilgrim's Progress when you were little things? Nothing delighted you more than to have me tie my piece-bags on your backs for burdens, give you hats and sticks and rolls of paper, and let you travel through the house from the cellar, which was the City of Destruction, up, up, to the house-top, where you had all the lovely things you could collect to make a Celestial City."

"What fun it was, especially going by the lions, fighting Apollyon, and passing through the Valley where the hobgoblins were!" said Jo.

"I liked the place where the bundles fell off and tumbled downstairs," said Meg.

"My favorite part was when we came out on the flat roof where our flowers and arbors and pretty things were, and all stood and sang for joy up there in the sunshine," said Beth, smiling, as if that pleasant moment had come back to her.

"I don't remember much about it, except that I was afraid of the cellar and the dark entry, and always liked the cake and milk we had up at the top. If I wasn't too old for such things, I'd rather like to play it over again," said Amy, who began to talk of renouncing childish things at the mature age of twelve.

"We never are too old for this, my dear, because it is a play we are playing all the time in one way or another. Our burdens are here, our road is before us, and the longing for goodness and happiness is the guide that leads us through many troubles and mistakes to the peace which is a true Celestial City. Now, my little pilgrims, suppose you begin again, not in play, but in earnest, and see how far on you can get before father comes home."

"Really, mother? Where are our bundles?" asked Amy, who was a very literal young lady.

"Each of you told what your burden was just now, except Beth; I rather think she hasn't got any," said her mother.

"Yes, I have; mine is dishes and dusters, and envying girls with nice pianos, and being afraid of people."

Beth's bundle was such a funny one that everybody wanted to laugh; but nobody did, for it would have hurt her feelings very much.

"Let us do it," said Meg thoughtfully. "It is only another name for trying to be good, and the story may help us; for though we do want to be good, it's hard work, and we forget, and don't do our best."

"We were in the Slough of Despond tonight, and mother came and pulled us out as Help did in the book. We ought to have our roll of directions, like Christian. What shall we do about that?" asked Jo, delighted with the fancy which lent a little romance to the very dull task of doing her duty.

"Look under your pillows, Christmas morning, and you will find your guide-book," replied Mrs. March.

They talked over the new plan while old Hannah cleared the table; then out came the four little work-baskets, and the needles flew as the girls made sheets for Aunt March. It was uninteresting sewing, but tonight no one grumbled. They adopted Jo's plan of dividing the long seams into four parts, and calling the quarters Europe, Asia, Africa, and America, and in that way got on capitally, especially when they talked about the different countries as they stitched their way through them.

At nine they stopped work, and sung, as usual, before they went to bed. No one but Beth could get much music out of the old piano; but she had a way of softly touching the yellow keys, and making a pleasant accompaniment to the simple songs they sang. Meg had a voice like a flute, and she and her mother led the little choir. Amy chirped like a cricket, and Jo wandered through the airs at her own sweet will, always coming out at the wrong place with a croak or a quaver that spoilt the most pensive tune. They had always done this from the time they could lisp

*"Crinkle, crinkle, 'ittle 'tar,"*

and it had become a household custom, for the mother was a born singer. The first sound in the morning was her voice, as she went about the house singing like a lark; and the last sound at night was the same cheery sound, for the girls never grew too old for that familiar lullaby.

No one but Beth could get much music out of the old piano.

# CHAPTER II

## A MERRY CHRISTMAS

Jo was the first to wake in the gray dawn of Christmas morning. No stockings hung at the fireplace, and for a moment she felt as much disappointed as she did long ago when her little sock fell down because it was so crammed with goodies. Then she remembered her mother's promise, and, slipping her hand under her pillow, drew out a little crimson-covered book. She knew it very well, for it was that beautiful old story of the best life ever lived, and Jo felt that it was a true guide-book for any pilgrim going the long journey. She woke Meg with a "Merry Christmas," and bade her see what was under her pillow. A green-covered book appeared, with the same picture inside, and a few words written by their mother, which made their one present very precious in their eyes. Presently Beth and Amy woke, to rummage and find their little books also,—one dove-colored, the other blue; and all sat looking at and talking about them, while the east grew rosy with the coming day.

In spite of her small vanities, Margaret had a sweet and pious nature, which unconsciously influenced her sisters, especially Jo, who loved her very tenderly, and obeyed her because her advice was so gently given.

"Girls," said Meg seriously, looking from the tumbled head beside her to the two little night-capped ones in the room beyond, "mother wants us to read and love and mind these books, and we must begin at once. We used to be faithful about it; but since father went away, and all this war trouble unsettled us, we have neglected many things. You can do as you please; but I shall keep my book on the table here, and read a little every morning as soon as I wake, for I know it will do me good, and help me through the day."

Then she opened her new book and began to read. Jo put her arm round her, and, leaning cheek to cheek, read also, with the quiet expression so seldom seen on her restless face.

"How good Meg is! Come, Amy, let's do as they do. I'll help you with the hard words, and they'll explain things if we don't understand," whispered Beth, very much impressed by the pretty books and her sisters' example.

"I'm glad mine is blue," said Amy; and then the rooms were very still while the pages were softly turned, and the winter sunshine crept in to touch the bright heads and serious faces with a Christmas greeting.

"Where is mother?" asked Meg, as she and Jo ran down to thank her for their gifts, half an hour later.

"Goodness only knows. Some poor creeter come a-beggin', and your ma went straight off to see what was needed. There never *was* such a woman for givin' away vittles and drink, clothes and firin'," replied Hannah, who had lived with the family since Meg was born, and was considered by them all more as a friend than a servant.

"She will be back soon, I think; so fry your cakes, and have everything ready," said Meg, looking over the presents which were collected in a basket and kept under the sofa, ready to be produced at the proper time. "Why, where is Amy's bottle of cologne?" she added, as the little flask did not appear.

"She took it out a minute ago, and went off with it to put a ribbon on it, or some such notion," replied Jo, dancing about the room to take the first stiffness off the new army-slippers.

"How nice my handkerchiefs look, don't they? Hannah washed and ironed them for me, and I marked them all myself," said Beth, looking proudly at the somewhat uneven letters which had cost her such labor.

"Bless the child! She's gone and put 'Mother' on them instead of 'M. March.' How funny!" cried Jo, taking up one.

"Isn't it right? I thought it was better to do it so, because Meg's initials are 'M. M.,' and I don't want anyone to use these but Marmee," said Beth, looking troubled.

"It's all right, dear, and a very pretty idea,—quite sensible, too, for no one can ever mistake now. It will please her very much, I know," said Meg, with a frown for Jo and a smile for Beth.

"There's mother. Hide the basket, quick!" cried Jo, as a door slammed, and steps sounded in the hall.

Amy came in hastily, and looked rather abashed when she saw her sisters all waiting for her.

"Where have you been, and what are you hiding behind you?" asked Meg, surprised to see, by her hood and cloak, that lazy Amy had been out so early.

"Don't laugh at me, Jo! I didn't mean anyone should know till the time came. I only meant to change the little bottle for a big one, and I gave *all* my money to get it, and I'm truly trying not to be selfish any more."

As she spoke, Amy showed the handsome flask which replaced the cheap one; and looked so earnest and humble in her little effort to forget herself that Meg hugged her on the spot, and Jo pronounced her "a trump," while Beth ran to the window, and picked her finest rose to ornament the stately bottle.

"You see I felt ashamed of my present, after reading and talking about being good this morning, so I ran round the corner and changed it the minute I was up! And I'm *so* glad, for mine is the handsomest now."

Another bang of the street-door sent the basket under the sofa, and the girls to the table, eager for breakfast.

"Merry Christmas, Marmee! Many of them! Thank you for our books; we read some, and mean to every day," they cried, in chorus.

"Merry Christmas, little daughters! I'm glad you began at once, and hope you will keep on. But I want to say one word before we sit down. Not far away from here lies a poor woman with a little new-born baby. Six children are huddled into one bed to keep from freezing, for they have no fire. There is nothing to eat over there; and the oldest boy came to tell me they were suffering hunger and cold. My girls, will you give them your breakfast as a Christmas present?"

They were all unusually hungry, having waited nearly an hour, and for a minute no one spoke; only a minute, for Jo exclaimed impetuously,—

"I'm so glad you came before we began!"

"May I go and help carry the things to the poor little children?" asked Beth eagerly.

"*I* shall take the cream and the muffins," added Amy, heroically giving up the articles she most liked.

Meg was already covering the buckwheats, and piling the bread into one big plate.

"I thought you'd do it," said Mrs. March, smiling as if satisfied. "You shall all go and help me, and when we come back we will have bread and milk for breakfast, and make it up at dinner-time."

They were soon ready, and the procession set out. Fortunately it was early, and they went through back streets, so few people saw them, and no one laughed at the queer party.

A poor, bare, miserable room it was, with broken windows, no fire, ragged bed-clothes, a sick mother, wailing baby, and a group of pale, hungry children cuddled under one old quilt, trying to keep warm.

How the big eyes stared and the blue lips smiled as the girls went in!

"Ach, mein Gott! It is good angels come to us!" said the poor woman, crying for joy.

"Funny angels in hoods and mittens," said Jo, and set them laughing.

In a few minutes it really did seem as if kind spirits had been at work there. Hannah, who had carried wood, made a fire, and stopped up the broken panes with old hats and her own cloak. Mrs. March gave the mother tea and gruel, and comforted her with promises of help, while she dressed the little baby as tenderly as if it had been her own. The girls, meantime, spread the table, set the children round the fire, and fed them like so many hungry birds,—laughing, talking, and trying to understand the funny broken English.

"Das ist gut!" "Die Engel-kinder!" cried the poor things, as they ate, and warmed their purple hands at the comfortable blaze.

The girls had never been called angel children before, and thought it very agreeable, especially Jo, who had been considered a "Sancho" ever since she was born. That was a very happy breakfast, though they didn't get any of it; and when they went away, leaving comfort behind, I think there were not in all the city four merrier people than the hungry little girls who gave away their breakfasts and contented themselves with bread and milk on Christmas morning.

"That's loving our neighbor better than ourselves, and I like it," said Meg, as they set out their presents, while their mother was upstairs collecting clothes for the poor Hummels.

Not a very splendid show, but there was a great deal of love done up in the few little bundles; and the tall vase of red roses, white chrysanthemums, and trailing vines, which stood in the middle, gave quite an elegant air to the table.

"She's coming! Strike up, Beth! Open the door, Amy! Three cheers for Marmee!" cried Jo, prancing about, while Meg went to conduct mother to the seat of honor.

Beth played her gayest march, Amy threw open the door, and Meg enacted escort with great dignity. Mrs. March was both surprised and touched; and smiled with her eyes full as she examined her presents, and read the little notes which accompanied them. The slippers went on at once, a new handkerchief was slipped into her pocket, well scented with Amy's cologne, the rose was fastened in her bosom, and the nice gloves were pronounced a "perfect fit."

There was a good deal of laughing and kissing and explaining, in the simple, loving fashion which makes these home-festivals so pleasant at the time, so sweet to remember long afterward, and then all fell to work.

The morning charities and ceremonies took so much time that the rest of the day was devoted to preparations for the evening festivities. Being still too young to go often to the theatre, and not rich enough to afford any great outlay for private performances, the girls put their wits to work, and—necessity being the mother of invention—made whatever they needed. Very clever were some of their productions,—pasteboard guitars, antique lamps made of old-fashioned butter-boats covered with silver paper, gorgeous robes of old cotton, glittering with tin spangles from a pickle factory, and armor covered with the same useful diamond-shaped bits, left in sheets when the lids of tin preserve-pots were cut out. The furniture was used to being turned topsy-turvy, and the big chamber was the scene of many innocent revels.

No gentlemen were admitted; so Jo played male parts to her heart's content, and took immense satisfaction in a pair of russet-leather boots given her by a friend, who knew a lady who knew an actor. These boots, an old foil, and a slashed doublet once used by an artist for some picture, were Jo's chief treasures, and appeared on all occasions. The smallness of the company made it necessary for the two principal actors to take several parts apiece; and they certainly deserved some credit for the hard work they did in learning three or four different parts, whisking in and out of various costumes, and managing the stage besides. It was excellent drill for their memories, a harmless amusement, and employed many hours which otherwise would have been idle, lonely, or spent in less profitable society.

On Christmas night, a dozen girls piled on to the bed which was the dress-circle, and sat before the blue and yellow chintz curtains in a most flattering state of expectancy. There was a good deal of rustling and whispering behind the curtain, a trifle of lamp-smoke, and an occasional giggle from Amy, who was apt to get hysterical in the excitement of the moment. Presently a bell sounded, the curtains flew apart, and the Operatic Tragedy began.

"A gloomy wood," according to the one play-bill, was represented by a few shrubs in pots, green baize on the floor, and a cave in the distance. This cave was made with a clothes-horse for a roof, bureaus for walls; and in it was a small furnace in full blast, with a black pot on it, and an old witch bending over it. The stage was dark, and the glow of the furnace had a fine effect, especially as real steam issued from the kettle when the witch took off the cover. A moment was allowed for the first thrill to subside; then Hugo, the villain, stalked in with a clanking sword at his side, a slouched hat, black beard, mysterious cloak, and the boots. After pacing to and fro in much agitation, he struck his forehead, and burst out in a wild strain, singing of his hatred to Roderigo, his love for Zara, and his pleasing resolution to kill the one and win the other. The gruff tones of Hugo's voice, with an occasional shout when his feelings overcame him, were very impressive, and the audience applauded the moment he paused for breath. Bowing with the air of one accustomed to public praise, he stole to the cavern, and ordered Hagar to come forth with a commanding "What ho, minion! I need thee!"

Out came Meg, with gray horse-hair hanging about her face, a red and black robe, a staff, and cabalistic signs upon her cloak. Hugo demanded a potion to make Zara adore him, and one to destroy Roderigo. Hagar, in a fine dramatic melody, promised both, and proceeded to call up the spirit who would bring the love philter:—

> *"Hither, hither, from thy home,*
> *Airy sprite, I bid thee come!*
> *Born of roses, fed on dew,*
> *Charms and potions canst thou brew?*
> *Bring me here, with elfin speed,*
> *The fragrant philter which I need;*
> *Make it sweet and swift and strong,*
> *Spirit, answer now my song!"*

A soft strain of music sounded, and then at the back of the cave appeared a little figure in cloudy white, with glittering wings, golden hair, and a garland of roses on its head. Waving a wand, it sang,—

> *"Hither I come,*
> *From my airy home,*
> *Afar in the silver moon.*
> *Take the magic spell,*
> *And use it well,*
> *Or its power will vanish soon!"*

And, dropping a small, gilded bottle at the witch's feet, the spirit vanished. Another chant from Hagar produced another apparition,—not a lovely one; for, with a bang, an ugly black imp appeared, and, having croaked a reply, tossed a dark bottle at Hugo, and disappeared with a mocking laugh. Having warbled his thanks and put the potions in his boots, Hugo departed; and Hagar informed the audience that, as he had killed a few of her friends in times past, she has cursed him, and intends to thwart his plans, and be revenged on him. Then the curtain fell, and the audience reposed and ate candy while discussing the merits of the play.

A good deal of hammering went on before the curtain rose again; but when it became evident what a masterpiece of stage-carpentering had been got up, no one murmured at the delay. It was truly superb! A tower rose to the ceiling; half-way up appeared a window, with a lamp burning at it, and behind the white curtain appeared Zara in a lovely blue and silver dress, waiting for Roderigo. He came in gorgeous array, with plumed cap, red cloak, chestnut love-locks, a guitar, and the boots, of course. Kneeling at the foot of the tower, he sang a serenade in melting tones. Zara replied, and, after a musical dialogue, consented to fly. Then came the grand effect of the play. Roderigo produced a rope-ladder, with five steps to it, threw up one end, and invited Zara to descend. Timidly she crept from her lattice, put her hand on Roderigo's shoulder, and was about to leap gracefully down when "Alas! Alas for Zara!" she forgot her train,—it caught in the window; the tower tottered, leaned forward, fell with a crash, and buried the unhappy lovers in the ruins!

A universal shriek arose as the russet boots waved wildly from the wreck, and a golden head emerged, exclaiming, "I told you so! I told you so!" With wonderful presence of mind, Don Pedro, the cruel sire, rushed in, dragged out his daughter, with a hasty aside,—

"Don't laugh! Act as if it was all right!"—and, ordering Roderigo up, banished him from the kingdom with wrath and scorn. Though decidedly shaken by the fall of the tower upon him, Roderigo defied the old gentleman, and refused to stir. This dauntless example fired Zara: she also defied her sire, and he ordered them both to the deepest dungeons of the castle. A stout little retainer came in with chains, and led them away, looking very much frightened, and evidently forgetting the speech he ought to have made.

Act third was the castle hall; and here Hagar appeared, having come to free the lovers and finish Hugo. She hears him coming, and hides; sees him put the potions into two cups of wine, and bid the timid little servant "Bear them to the captives in their cells, and tell them I shall come anon." The servant takes Hugo aside to tell him something, and Hagar changes the cups for two others which are harmless. Ferdinando, the "minion," carries them away, and Hagar puts back the cup which holds the poison meant for Roderigo. Hugo, getting thirsty after a long warble, drinks it, loses his wits, and, after a good deal of clutching and stamping, falls flat and dies; while Hagar informs him what she has done in a song of exquisite power and melody.

This was a truly thrilling scene, though some persons might have thought that the sudden tumbling down of a quantity of long hair rather marred the effect of the villain's death. He was called before the curtain, and with great propriety appeared, leading Hagar, whose singing was considered more wonderful than all the rest of the performance put together.

Act fourth displayed the despairing Roderigo on the point of stabbing himself, because he has been told that Zara has deserted him. Just as the dagger is at his heart, a lovely song is sung under his window, informing him that Zara is true, but in danger, and he can save her, if he will. A key is thrown in, which unlocks the door, and in a spasm of rapture he tears off his chains, and rushes away to find and rescue his lady-love.

Act fifth opened with a stormy scene between Zara and Don Pedro. He wishes her to go into a convent, but she won't hear of it; and, after a touching appeal, is about to faint, when Roderigo dashes in and demands her hand. Don Pedro refuses, because he is not rich. They shout and gesticulate tremendously, but cannot agree, and Roderigo is about to bear away the exhausted Zara, when the timid servant enters with a letter and a bag from Hagar, who has mysteriously disappeared. The latter informs the party that she bequeaths untold wealth to the young pair, and an awful doom to Don Pedro, if he doesn't make them happy. The bag is opened, and several quarts of tin money shower down upon the stage, till it is quite glorified with the glitter. This entirely softens the "stern sire": he consents without a murmur, all join in a joyful chorus, and the curtain falls upon the lovers kneeling to receive Don Pedro's blessing in attitudes of the most romantic grace.

Tumultuous applause followed, but received an unexpected check; for the cot-bed, on which the "dress-circle" was built, suddenly shut up, and extinguished the enthusiastic audience. Roderigo and Don Pedro flew to the rescue, and all were taken out unhurt, though many were speechless with laughter. The excitement had hardly subsided, when Hannah appeared, with "Mrs. March's compliments, and would the ladies walk down to supper."

This was a surprise, even to the actors; and, when they saw the table, they looked at one another in rapturous amazement. It was like Marmee to get up a little treat for them; but anything so fine as this was unheard-of since the departed days of plenty. There was ice-cream,—actually two dishes of it, pink and white,—and cake and fruit and distracting French bonbons, and, in the middle of the table, four great bouquets of hot-house flowers!

It quite took their breath away; and they stared first at the table and then at their mother, who looked as if she enjoyed it immensely.

"Is it fairies?" asked Amy.

"It's Santa Claus," said Beth.

"Mother did it;" and Meg smiled her sweetest, in spite of her gray beard and white eyebrows.

"Aunt March had a good fit, and sent the supper," cried Jo, with a sudden inspiration.

"All wrong. Old Mr. Laurence sent it," replied Mrs. March.

"The Laurence boy's grandfather! What in the world put such a thing into his head? We don't know him!" exclaimed Meg.

"Hannah told one of his servants about your breakfast party. He is an odd old gentleman, but that pleased him. He knew my father, years ago; and he sent me a polite note this afternoon, saying he hoped I would allow him to express his friendly feeling toward my children by sending them a few trifles in honor of the day. I could not refuse; and so you have a little feast at night to make up for the bread-and-milk breakfast."

"That boy put it into his head, I know he did! He's a capital fellow, and I wish we could get acquainted. He looks as if he'd like to know us; but he's bashful, and Meg is so prim she won't let me speak to him when we pass," said Jo, as the plates went round, and the ice began to melt out of sight, with "Ohs!" and "Ahs!" of satisfaction.

"You mean the people who live in the big house next door, don't you?" asked one of the girls. "My mother knows old Mr. Laurence; but says he's very proud, and doesn't like to mix with his neighbors. He keeps his grandson shut up, when he isn't riding or walking with his tutor, and makes him study very hard. We invited him to our party, but he didn't come. Mother says he's very nice, though he never speaks to us girls."

"Our cat ran away once, and he brought her back, and we talked over the fence, and were getting on capitally,—all about cricket, and so on,—when he saw Meg coming, and walked off. I mean to know him some day; for he needs fun, I'm sure he does," said Jo decidedly.

"I like his manners, and he looks like a little gentleman; so I've no

The lovers kneeling to receive Don Pedro's blessing.

objection to your knowing him, if a proper opportunity comes. He brought the flowers himself; and I should have asked him in, if I had been sure what was going on upstairs. He looked so wistful as he went away, hearing the frolic, and evidently having none of his own."

"It's a mercy you didn't, mother!" laughed Jo, looking at her boots. "But we'll have another play, some time, that he *can* see. Perhaps he'll help act; wouldn't that be jolly?"

"I never had such a fine bouquet before! How pretty it is!" And Meg examined her flowers with great interest.

"They *are* lovely! But Beth's roses are sweeter to me," said Mrs. March, smelling the half-dead posy in her belt.

Beth nestled up to her, and whispered softly, "I wish I could send my bunch to father. I'm afraid he isn't having such a merry Christmas as we are."

# CHAPTER III

## THE LAURENCE BOY

"Jo! Jo! Where are you?" cried Meg, at the foot of the garret stairs.

"Here!" answered a husky voice from above; and, running up, Meg found her sister eating apples and crying over the "Heir of Redclyffe," wrapped up in a comforter on an old three-legged sofa by the sunny window. This was Jo's favorite refuge; and here she loved to retire with half a dozen russets and a nice book, to enjoy the quiet and the society of a pet rat who lived near by, and didn't mind her a particle. As Meg appeared, Scrabble whisked into his hole. Jo shook the tears off her cheeks, and waited to hear the news.

"Such fun! Only see! A regular note of invitation from Mrs. Gardiner for tomorrow night!" cried Meg, waving the precious paper, and then proceeding to read it, with girlish delight.

" 'Mrs. Gardiner would be happy to see Miss March and Miss Josephine at a little dance on New-Year's Eve.' Marmee is willing we should go; now what *shall* we wear?"

"What's the use of asking that, when you know we shall wear our poplins, because we haven't got anything else?" answered Jo, with her mouth full.

"If I only had a silk!" sighed Meg. "Mother says I may when I'm eighteen, perhaps; but two years is an everlasting time to wait."

"I'm sure our pops look like silk, and they are nice enough for us. Yours is as good as new, but I forgot the burn and the tear in mine. Whatever shall I do? The burn shows badly, and I can't take any out."

"You must sit still all you can, and keep your back out of sight; the front is all right. I shall have a new ribbon for my hair, and Marmee will lend me her little pearl pin, and my new slippers are lovely, and my gloves will do, though they aren't as nice as I'd like."

"Mine are spoilt with lemonade, and I can't get any new ones, so I shall have to go without," said Jo, who never troubled herself much about dress.

"You *must* have gloves, or I won't go," cried Meg decidedly. "Gloves are more important than anything else; you can't dance without them, and if you don't I should be so mortified."

"Then I'll stay still. I don't care much for company dancing; it's no fun to go sailing round; I like to fly about and cut capers."

"You can't ask mother for new ones, they are so expensive, and you are so careless. She said, when you spoilt the others, that she shouldn't get you any more this winter. Can't you make them do?" asked Meg anxiously.

"I can hold them crumpled up in my hand, so no one will know how stained they are; that's all I can do. No! I'll tell you how we can manage— each wear one good one and carry a bad one; don't you see?"

"Your hands are bigger than mine, and you will stretch my glove dreadfully," began Meg, whose gloves were a tender point with her.

"Then I'll go without. I don't care what people say!" cried Jo, taking up her book.

"You may have it, you may! Only don't stain it, and do behave nicely. Don't put your hands behind you, or stare, or say 'Christopher Columbus!' will you?"

"Don't worry about me; I'll be as prim as I can, and not get into any scrapes, if I can help it. Now go and answer your note, and let me finish this splendid story."

So Meg went away to "accept with thanks," look over her dress, and sing blithely as she did up her one real lace frill; while Jo finished her story, her four apples, and had a game of romps with Scrabble.

On New-Year's Eve the parlor was deserted, for the two younger girls played dressing-maids, and the two elder were absorbed in the all-important business of "getting ready for the party." Simple as the toilets were, there was a great deal of running up and down, laughing and talking, and at one time a strong smell of burnt hair pervaded the house. Meg wanted a few curls about her face, and Jo undertook to pinch the papered locks with a pair of hot tongs.

"Ought they to smoke like that?" asked Beth, from her perch on the bed.

"It's the dampness drying," replied Jo.

"What a queer smell! It's like burnt feathers," observed Amy, smoothing her own pretty curls with a superior air.

"There, now I'll take off the papers and you'll see a cloud of little ringlets," said Jo, putting down the tongs.

She did take off the papers, but no cloud of ringlets appeared, for the hair came with the papers, and the horrified hair-dresser laid a row of little scorched bundles on the bureau before her victim.

"Oh, oh, oh! What *have* you done? I'm spoilt! I can't go! My hair, oh, my hair!" wailed Meg, looking with despair at the uneven frizzle on her forehead.

"Just my luck! You shouldn't have asked me to do it; I always spoil everything. I'm so sorry, but the tongs were too hot, and so I've made a mess," groaned poor Jo, regarding the black pancakes with tears of regret.

"It isn't spoilt; just frizzle it, and tie your ribbon so the ends come on your forehead a bit, and it will look like the last fashion. I've seen many girls do it so," said Amy consolingly.

"Serves me right for trying to be fine. I wish I'd let my hair alone," cried Meg petulantly.

"So do I, it was so smooth and pretty. But it will soon grow out again," said Beth, coming to kiss and comfort the shorn sheep.

After various lesser mishaps, Meg was finished at last, and by the united exertions of the family Jo's hair was got up and her dress on. They looked very well in their simple suits,—Meg in silvery drab, with a blue velvet snood, lace frills, and the pearl pin; Jo in maroon, with a stiff, gentlemanly linen collar, and a white chrysanthemum or two for her only ornament. Each put on one nice light glove, and carried one soiled one, and all pronounced the effect "quite easy and fine." Meg's high-heeled slippers were very tight, and hurt her, though she would not own it, and Jo's nineteen hair-pins all seemed stuck straight into her head, which was not exactly comfortable; but, dear me, let us be elegant or die!

"Have a good time, dearies!" said Mrs. March, as the sisters went daintily down the walk. "Don't eat much supper, and come away at eleven, when I send Hannah for you." As the gate clashed behind them, a voice cried from a window,—

"Girls, girls! *Have* you both got nice pocket-handkerchiefs?"

"Yes, yes, spandy nice, and Meg has cologne on hers," cried Jo, adding, with a laugh, as they went on, "I do believe Marmee would ask that if we were all running away from an earthquake."

"It is one of her aristocratic tastes, and quite proper, for a real lady is always known by neat boots, gloves, and handkerchief," replied Meg, who had a good many little "aristocratic tastes" of her own.

"Now don't forget to keep the bad breadth out of sight, Jo. Is my sash right? And does my hair look *very* bad?" said Meg, as she turned from the glass in Mrs. Gardiner's dressing-room, after a prolonged prink.

"I know I shall forget. If you see me doing anything wrong, just remind me by a wink, will you?" returned Jo, giving her collar a twitch and her head a hasty brush.

"No, winking isn't lady-like; I'll lift my eyebrows if anything is wrong, and nod if you are all right. Now hold your shoulders straight, and take short steps, and don't shake hands if you are introduced to any one: it isn't the thing."

"How *do* you learn all the proper ways? I never can. Isn't that music gay?"

Down they went, feeling a trifle timid, for they seldom went to parties, and, informal as this little gathering was, it was an event to them. Mrs. Gardiner, a stately old lady, greeted them kindly, and handed them over to the eldest of her six daughters. Meg knew Sallie, and was at her ease very soon; but Jo, who didn't care much for girls or girlish gossip, stood about, with her back carefully against the wall, and felt as much out of place as a colt in a flower-garden. Half a dozen jovial lads were talking about skates in another part of the room, and she longed to go and join them, for skating was one of the joys of her life. She telegraphed her wish to Meg, but the eyebrows went up so alarmingly that she dared not stir. No one came to talk to her, and one by one the group near her dwindled away, till she was left alone. She could not roam about and amuse herself, for the burnt breadth would show, so she stared at people rather forlornly till the dancing began. Meg was asked at once, and the tight slippers tripped about so briskly that none would have guessed the pain their wearer suffered smilingly. Jo saw a big red-headed youth approaching her corner, and fearing he meant to engage her, she slipped into a curtained recess, intending to peep and enjoy herself in peace. Unfortunately, another bashful person had chosen the same refuge; for, as the curtain fell behind her, she found herself face to face with the "Laurence boy."

"Dear me, I didn't know any one was here!" stammered Jo, preparing to back out as speedily as she had bounced in.

But the boy laughed, and said pleasantly, though he looked a little startled,—

"Don't mind me; stay, if you like."

"Sha'n't I disturb you?"

"Not a bit; I only came here because I don't know many people, and felt rather strange at first, you know."

"So did I. Don't go away, please, unless you'd rather."

The boy sat down again and looked at his pumps, till Jo said, trying to be polite and easy,—

"I think I've had the pleasure of seeing you before; you live near us, don't you?"

"Next door." And he looked up and laughed outright, for Jo's prim manner was rather funny when he remembered how they had chatted about cricket when he brought the cat home.

That put Jo at her ease; and she laughed too, as she said, in her heartiest way,—

"We did have such a good time over your nice Christmas present."

"Grandpa sent it."

"But you put it into his head, didn't you, now?"

"How is your cat, Miss March?" asked the boy, trying to look sober, while his black eyes shone with fun.

"Nicely, thank you, Mr. Laurence; but I am not Miss March, I'm only Jo," returned the young lady.

"I'm not Mr. Laurence, I'm only Laurie,"

"Laurie Laurence,—what an odd name!"

"My first name is Theodore, but I don't like it, for the fellows called me Dora, so I made them say Laurie instead."

"I hate my name, too—so sentimental! I wish every one would say Jo, instead of Josephine. How did you make the boys stop calling you Dora?"

"I thrashed 'em."

"I can't thrash Aunt March, so I suppose I shall have to bear it;" and Jo resigned herself with a sigh.

"Don't you like to dance, Miss Jo?" asked Laurie, looking as if he thought the name suited her.

"I like it well enough if there is plenty of room, and every one is lively. In a place like this I'm sure to upset something, tread on people's toes, or do something dreadful, so I keep out of mischief, and let Meg sail about. Don't you dance?"

"Sometimes; you see I've been abroad a good many years, and haven't been into company enough yet to know how you do things here."

"Abroad!" cried Jo. "Oh, tell me about it! I love dearly to hear people describe their travels."

Laurie didn't seem to know where to begin; but Jo's eager questions soon set him going, and he told her how he had been at school in Vevey, where the boys never wore hats, and had a fleet of boats on the lake, and for holiday fun went walking trips about Switzerland with their teachers.

"Don't I wish I'd been there!" cried Jo. "Did you go to Paris?"

"We spent last winter there."

"Can you talk French?"

"We were not allowed to speak anything else at Vevey."

"Do say some! I can read it, but can't pronounce."

"Quel nom a cette jeune demoiselle en les pantoufles jolis?" said Laurie good-naturedly.

"How nicely you do it! Let me see,—you said, 'Who is the young lady in the pretty slippers,' didn't you?"

"Oui, mademoiselle."

"It's my sister Margaret, and you knew it was! Do you think she is pretty?"

"Yes; she makes me think of the German girls, she looks so fresh and quiet, and dances like a lady."

Jo quite glowed with pleasure at this boyish praise of her sister, and stored it up to repeat to Meg. Both peeped and criticised and chatted, till they felt like old acquaintances. Laurie's bashfulness soon wore off; for Jo's gentlemanly demeanor amused and set him at his ease, and Jo was her merry self again, because her dress was forgotten, and nobody lifted their eyebrows at her. She liked the "Laurence boy" better than ever, and took several good looks at him, so that she might describe him to the girls; for they had no brothers, very few male cousins, and boys were almost unknown creatures to them.

"Curly black hair; brown skin; big, black eyes; handsome nose; fine teeth; small hands and feet; taller than I am; very polite, for a boy, and altogether jolly. Wonder how old he is?"

It was on the tip of Jo's tongue to ask; but she checked herself in time, and, with unusual tact, tried to find out in a roundabout way.

"I suppose you are going to college soon? I see you pegging away at your books,—no, I mean studying hard;" and Jo blushed at the dreadful "pegging" which had escaped her.

Laurie smiled, but didn't seem shocked, and answered, with a shrug,—

"Not for a year or two; I won't go before seventeen, anyway."

"Aren't you but fifteen?" asked Jo, looking at the tall lad, whom she had imagined seventeen already.

"Sixteen, next month."

"How I wish I was going to college! You don't look as if you liked it."

"I hate it! Nothing but grinding or skylarking. And I don't like the way fellows do either, in this country."

"What do you like?"

"To live in Italy, and to enjoy myself in my own way."

Jo wanted very much to ask what his own way was; but his black brows looked rather threatening as he knit them; so she changed the subject by saying, as her foot kept time, "That's a splendid polka! Why don't you go and try it?"

"If you will come too," he answered, with a gallant little bow.

"I can't; for I told Meg I wouldn't, because—" There Jo stopped, and looked undecided whether to tell or to laugh.

"Because what?" asked Laurie curiously.

"You won't tell?"

"Never!"

"Well, I have a bad trick of standing before the fire, and so I burn my frocks, and I scorched this one; and, though it's nicely mended, it shows, and Meg told me to keep still, so no one would see it. You may laugh, if you want to; it is funny, I know."

But Laurie didn't laugh; he only looked down a minute, and the expression of his face puzzled Jo, when he said very gently,—

"Never mind that; I'll tell you how we can manage: there's a long hall out there, and we can dance grandly, and no one will see us. Please come?"

Jo thanked him, and gladly went, wishing she had two neat gloves, when she saw the nice, pearl-colored ones her partner wore. The hall was empty, and they had a grand polka; for Laurie danced well, and taught her the German step, which delighted Jo, being full of swing and spring. When the music stopped, they sat down on the stairs to get their breath; and Laurie was in the midst of an account of a students' festival at Heidelberg, when Meg appeared in search of her sister. She beckoned, and Jo reluctantly followed her into a side room, where she found her on a sofa, holding her foot, and looking pale.

"I've sprained my ankle. That stupid high heel turned, and gave me a sad wrench. It aches so, I can hardly stand, and I don't know how I'm ever going to get home," she said, rocking to and fro in pain.

"I knew you'd hurt your feet with those silly shoes. I'm sorry. But I don't see what you can do, except get a carriage, or stay here all night," answered Jo, softly rubbing the poor ankle as she spoke.

"I can't have a carriage, without its costing ever so much. I dare say I can't get one at all; for most people come in their own, and it's a long way to the stable, and no one to send."

"I'll go."

"No, indeed! It's past nine, and dark as Egypt. I can't stop here, for the house is full. Sallie has some girls staying with her. I'll rest till Hannah comes, and then do the best I can."

"I'll ask Laurie; he will go," said Jo, looking relieved as the idea occurred to her.

"Mercy, no! Don't ask or tell any one. Get me my rubbers, and put these slippers with our things. I can't dance anymore; but as soon as supper is over, watch for Hannah, and tell me the minute she comes."

"They are going out to supper now. I'll stay with you; I'd rather."

"No, dear, run along, and bring me some coffee. I'm so tired, I can't stir!"

So Meg reclined, with rubbers well hidden, and Jo went blundering away to the dining-room, which she found after going into a china-closet, and opening the door of a room where old Mr. Gardiner was taking a little private refreshment. Making a dart at the table, she secured the coffee, which she immediately spilt, thereby making the front of her dress as bad as the back.

"Oh, dear, what a blunderbuss I am!" exclaimed Jo, finishing Meg's glove by scrubbing her gown with it.

"Can I help you?" said a friendly voice; and there was Laurie, with a full cup in one hand and a plate of ice in the other.

"I was trying to get something for Meg, who is very tired, and some one shook me; and here I am, in a nice state," answered Jo, glancing dismally from the stained skirt to the coffee-colored glove.

"Too bad! I was looking for some one to give this to. May I take it to your sister?"

"Oh, thank you! I'll show you where she is. I don't offer to take it myself, for I should only get into another scrape if I did."

They sat down on the stairs.

Jo led the way; and, as if used to waiting on ladies, Laurie drew up a little table, brought a second instalment of coffee and ice for Jo, and was so obliging that even particular Meg pronounced him a "nice boy." They had a merry time over the bonbons and mottoes, and were in the midst of a quiet game of "Buzz," with two or three other young people who had strayed in, when Hannah appeared. Meg forgot her foot, and rose so quickly that she was forced to catch hold of Jo, with an exclamation of pain.

"Hush! Don't say anything," she whispered, adding aloud, "It's nothing. I turned my foot a little, that's all"; and limped upstairs to put her things on.

Hannah scolded, Meg cried, and Jo was at her wits' end, till she decided to take things into her own hands. Slipping out, she ran down, and, finding a servant, asked if he could get her a carriage. It happened to be a hired waiter, who knew nothing about the neighborhood; and Jo was looking round for help, when Laurie, who had heard what she said, came up, and offered his grandfather's carriage, which had just come for him, he said.

"It's so early! You can't mean to go yet?" began Jo, looking relieved, but hesitating to accept the offer.

"I always go early,—I do, truly! Please let me take you home? It's all on my way, you know, and it rains, they say."

That settled it; and, telling him of Meg's mishap, Jo gratefully accepted, and rushed up to bring down the rest of the party. Hannah hated rain as much as a cat does; so she made no trouble, and they rolled away in the luxurious close carriage, feeling very festive and elegant. Laurie went on the box; so Meg could keep her foot up, and the girls talked over their party in freedom.

"I had a capital time. Did you?" asked Jo, rumpling up her hair, and making herself comfortable.

"Yes, till I hurt myself. Sallie's friend, Annie Moffat, took a fancy to me, and asked me to come and spend a week with her, when Sallie does. She is going in the spring, when the opera comes; and it will be perfectly splendid, if mother only lets me go," answered Meg, cheering up at the thought.

"I saw you dancing with the red-headed man I ran away from. Was he nice?"

"Oh, very! His hair is auburn, not red; and he was very polite, and I had a delicious redowa with him."

"He looked like a grasshopper in a fit, when he did the new step. Laurie and I couldn't help laughing. Did you hear us?"

"No; but it was very rude. What *were* you about all that time, hidden away there?"

Jo told her adventures, and, by the time she had finished, they were at home. With many thanks, they said "Good-night" and crept in, hoping to disturb no one; but the instant their door creaked, two little night-caps bobbed up, and two sleepy but eager voices cried out,—

"Tell about the party! Tell about the party!"

With what Meg called "a great want of manners," Jo had saved some bonbons for the little girls; and they soon subsided, after hearing the most thrilling events of the evening.

"I declare, it really seems like being a fine young lady, to come home from the party in a carriage, and sit in my dressing-gown, with a maid to wait on me," said Meg, as Jo bound up her foot with arnica, and brushed her hair.

"I don't believe fine young ladies enjoy themselves a bit more than we do, in spite of our burnt hair, old gowns, one glove apiece, and tight slippers that sprain our ankles when we are silly enough to wear them." And I think Jo was quite right.

# CHAPTER IV

## BURDENS

"OH dear, how hard it does seem to take up our packs and go on," sighed Meg, the morning after the party; for, now the holidays were over, the week of merry-making did not fit her for going on easily with the task she never liked.

"I wish it was Christmas or New-Year all the time; wouldn't it be fun?" answered Jo, yawning dismally.

"We shouldn't enjoy ourselves half so much as we do now. But it does seem so nice to have little suppers and bouquets, and go to parties, and drive home, and read and rest, and not work. It's like other people, you know, and I always envy girls who do such things; I'm so fond of luxury," said Meg, trying to decide which of two shabby gowns was the least shabby.

"Well, we can't have it, so don't let us grumble, but shoulder our bundles and trudge along as cheerfully as Marmee does. I'm sure Aunt March is a regular Old Man of the Sea to me, but I suppose when I've learned to carry her without complaining, she will tumble off, or get so light that I sha'n't mind her."

This idea tickled Jo's fancy, and put her in good spirits; but Meg didn't brighten, for her burden, consisting of four spoilt children, seemed heavier than ever. She hadn't heart enough even to make herself pretty, as usual, by putting on a blue neck-ribbon, and dressing her hair in the most becoming way.

"Where's the use of looking nice, when no one sees me but those cross midgets, and no one cares whether I'm pretty or not?" she muttered, shutting her drawer with a jerk. "I shall have to toil and moil all my days, with only little bits of fun now and then, and get old and ugly and sour, because I'm poor, and can't enjoy my life as other girls do. It's a shame!"

So Meg went down, wearing an injured look, and wasn't at all agreeable at breakfast-time. Every one seemed rather out of sorts, and inclined to croak. Beth had a headache, and lay on the sofa, trying to comfort herself with the cat and three kittens; Amy was fretting because her lessons were not learned, and she couldn't find her rubbers; Jo *would* whistle and make a great racket getting ready; Mrs. March was very busy trying to finish a letter, which must go at once; and Hannah had the grumps, for being up late didn't suit her.

"There never *was* such a cross family!" cried Jo, losing her temper when she had upset an inkstand, broken both boot-lacings, and sat down upon her hat.

"You're the crossest person in it!" returned Amy, washing out the sum, that was all wrong, with the tears that had fallen on her slate.

"Beth, if you don't keep these horrid cats down cellar I'll have them drowned," exclaimed Meg angrily, as she tried to get rid of the kitten, which had scrambled up her back, and stuck like a burr just out of reach.

Jo laughed, Meg scolded, Beth implored, and Amy wailed, because she couldn't remember how much nine times twelve was.

"Girls, girls, do be quiet one minute! I *must* get this off by the early mail, and you drive me distracted with your worry," cried Mrs. March, crossing out the third spoilt sentence in her letter.

There was a momentary lull, broken by Hannah, who stalked in, laid two hot turn-overs on the table, and stalked out again. These turn-overs were an institution; and the girls called them "muffs," for they had no others, and found the hot pies very comforting to their hands on cold mornings. Hannah never forgot to make them, no matter how busy or grumpy she might be, for the walk was long and bleak; the poor things got no other lunch, and were seldom home before two.

"Cuddle your cats, and get over your headache, Bethy. Good-by, Marmee; we are a set of rascals this morning, but we'll come home regular angels. Now then, Meg!" and Jo tramped away, feeling that the pilgrims were not setting out as they ought to do.

They always looked back before turning the corner, for their mother was always at the window, to nod and smile, and wave her hand to them. Somehow it seemed as if they couldn't have got through the day without that; for, whatever their mood might be, the last glimpse of that motherly face was sure to affect them like sunshine.

"If Marmee shook her fist instead of kissing her hand to us, it would serve us right, for more ungrateful wretches than we are were never seen," cried Jo, taking a remorseful satisfaction in the snowy walk and bitter wind.

"Don't use such dreadful expressions," said Meg, from the depths of the veil in which she had shrouded herself like a nun sick of the world.

"I like good strong words, that mean something," replied Jo, catching her hat as it took a leap off her head, preparatory to flying away altogether.

"Call yourself any names you like; but *I* am neither a rascal nor a wretch, and I don't choose to be called so."

"You're a blighted being, and decidedly cross today because you can't sit in the lap of luxury all the time. Poor dear, just wait till I make my fortune, and you shall revel in carriages and ice-cream and high-heeled slippers and posies and red-headed boys to dance with."

"How ridiculous you are, Jo!" but Meg laughed at the nonsense, and felt better in spite of herself.

"Lucky for you I am; for if I put on crushed airs, and tried to be dismal, as you do, we should be in a nice state. Thank goodness, I can always find something funny to keep me up. Don't croak any more, but come home jolly, there's a dear."

Jo gave her sister an encouraging pat on the shoulder as they parted for the day, each going a different way, each hugging her little warm turn-over, and each trying to be cheerful in spite of wintry weather, hard work, and the unsatisfied desires of pleasure-loving youth.

When Mr. March lost his property in trying to help an unfortunate friend, the two oldest girls begged to be allowed to do something toward their own support, at least. Believing that they could not begin too early to cultivate energy, industry, and independence, their parents consented, and both fell to work with the hearty good-will which in spite of all obstacles, is sure to succeed at last. Margaret found a place as nursery governess, and felt rich with her small salary. As she said, she *was* "fond of luxury," and her chief trouble was poverty. She found it harder to bear than the others, because she could remember a time when home was beautiful, life full of ease and pleasure, and want of any kind unknown. She tried not to be envious or discontented, but it was very natural that the young girl should long for pretty things, gay friends, accomplishments, and a happy life. At the Kings' she daily saw all she wanted, for the children's older sisters were just out, and Meg caught frequent glimpses of dainty ball-dresses and bouquets, heard lively gossip about theatres, concerts, sleighing parties, and merry-makings of all kinds, and saw money lavished on trifles which would have been so precious to her. Poor Meg seldom complained, but a sense of injustice made her feel bitter toward everyone sometimes, for she had not yet learned to know how rich she was in the blessings which alone can make life happy.

Jo happened to suit Aunt March, who was lame, and needed an active person to wait upon her. The childless old lady had offered to adopt one of the girls when the troubles came, and was much offended because her offer was declined. Other friends told the Marches that they had lost all chance of being remembered in the rich old lady's will; but the unworldly Marches only said,—

"We can't give up our girls for a dozen fortunes. Rich or poor, we will keep together and be happy in one another."

The old lady wouldn't speak to them for a time, but happening to meet Jo at a friend's, something in her comical face and blunt manners struck the old lady's fancy, and she proposed to take her for a companion. This did not suit Jo at all; but she accepted the place since nothing better appeared, and, to every one's surprise, got on remarkably well with her irascible relative. There was an occasional tempest, and once Jo had marched home, declaring she couldn't bear it any longer; but Aunt March always cleared up quickly, and sent for her back again with such urgency that she could not refuse, for in her heart she rather liked the peppery old lady.

I suspect that the real attraction was a large library of fine books, which was left to dust and spiders since Uncle March died. Jo remembered the kind old gentleman, who used to let her build railroads and bridges with his big dictionaries, tell her stories about the queer pictures in his Latin books, and buy her cards of gingerbread whenever he met her in the street. The dim, dusty room, with the busts staring down from the tall bookcases, the cozy chairs, the globes, and, best of all, the wilderness of books, in which she could wander where she liked, made the library a region of bliss to her. The moment Aunt March took her nap, or was busy with company, Jo hurried to this quiet place, and, curling herself up in the easy-chair, devoured poetry, romance, history, travels, and pictures, like a regular book-worm. But, like all happiness, it did not last long; for as sure as she had just reached the heart of the story, the sweetest verse of the song, or the most perilous adventure of her traveller, a shrill voice called, "Josy-phine! Josy-phine!" and she had to leave her paradise to wind yarn, wash the poodle, or read Belsham's Essays by the hour together.

Jo's ambition was to do something very splendid; what it was she had no idea, as yet, but left it for time to tell her; and, meanwhile, found her greatest affliction in the fact that she couldn't read, run, and ride as much as she liked. A quick temper, sharp tongue, and restless spirit were always getting her into scrapes, and her life was a series of ups and downs, which were both comic and pathetic. But the training she received at Aunt March's was just what she needed; and the thought that she was doing something to support herself made her happy, in spite of the perpetual "Josy-phine!"

Beth was too bashful to go to school; it had been tried, but she suffered so much that it was given up, and she did her lessons at home, with her father. Even when he went away, and her mother was called to devote her skill and energy to Soldiers' Aid Societies, Beth went faithfully on by herself, and did the best she could. She was a housewifely little creature, and helped Hannah keep home neat and comfortable for the workers, never thinking of any reward but to be loved. Long, quiet days she spent, not lonely nor idle, for her little world was peopled with imaginary friends, and she was by nature a busy bee. There were six dolls to be taken up and dressed every morning, for Beth was a child still, and loved her pets as well as ever. Not one whole or handsome one among them; all were outcasts till Beth took them in; for, when her sisters outgrew these idols, they passed to her, because Amy would have nothing old or ugly. Beth cherished them all the more tenderly for that very reason, and set up a hospital for infirm dolls. No pins were ever stuck into their cotton vitals; no harsh words or blows were ever given them; no neglect ever saddened the heart of the most repulsive: but all were fed and clothed, nursed and caressed, with an affection which never failed. One forlorn fragment of *dollanity* had belonged to Jo; and, having led a tempestuous life, was left a wreck in the ragbag, from which dreary poorhouse it was rescued by Beth, and taken to her refuge. Having no top to its head, she tied on a neat little cap, and, as both arms and legs were gone, she hid these deficiencies by folding it in a blanket, and devoting her best bed to this chronic invalid. If any one had known the care lavished on that dolly, I think it would have touched their hearts, even while they laughed. She brought it bits of bouquets; she read to it, took it out to breathe the air, hidden under her coat; she sung it lullabys, and never went to bed without kissing its dirty face, and whispering tenderly, "I hope you'll have a good night, my poor dear."

Beth had her troubles as well as the others; and not being an angel, but a very human little girl, she often "wept a little weep," as Jo said, because she couldn't take music lessons and have a fine piano. She loved music so dearly, tried so hard to learn, and practiced away so patiently at the jingling old instrument, that it did seem as if someone (not to hint Aunt March) ought to help her. Nobody did, however, and nobody saw Beth wipe the tears off the yellow keys, that wouldn't keep in tune, when she was all alone. She sang like a little lark about her work, never was too tired to play for Marmee and the girls, and day after day said hopefully to herself, "I know I'll get my music some time, if I'm good."

There are many Beths in the world, shy and quiet, sitting in corners till needed, and living for others so cheerfully that no one sees the sacrifices till the little cricket on the hearth stops chirping, and the sweet, sunshiny presence vanishes, leaving silence and shadow behind.

If anybody had asked Amy what the greatest trial of her life was, she would have answered at once, "My nose." When she was a baby, Jo had accidentally dropped her into the coal-hod, and Amy insisted that the fall had ruined her nose forever. It was not big, nor red, like poor "Petrea's"; it was only rather flat, and all the pinching in the world could not give it an aristocratic point. No one minded it but herself, and it was doing its best to grow, but Amy felt deeply the want of a Grecian nose, and drew whole sheets of handsome ones to console herself.

"Little Raphael," as her sisters called her, had a decided talent for drawing, and was never so happy as when copying flowers, designing fairies, or illustrating stories with queer specimens of art. Her teachers complained that, instead of doing her sums, she covered her slate with animals; the blank pages of her atlas were used to copy maps on; and caricatures of the most ludicrous description came flutteriag out of all her books at unlucky moments. She got through her lessons as well as she could, and managed to escape reprimands by being a model of deportment. She was a great favorite with her mates, being good-tempered, and possessing the happy art of pleasing without effort. Her little airs and graces were much admired, so were her accomplishments; for beside her drawing, she could play twelve tunes, crochet, and read French without mispronouncing more than two thirds of the words. She had a plaintive way of saying, "When papa was rich we did so-and-so," which was very touching; and her long words were considered "perfectly elegant" by the girls.

Amy was in a fair way to be spoilt; for every one petted her, and her small vanities and selfishnesses were growing nicely. One thing, however, rather quenched the vanities; she had to wear her cousin's clothes. Now Florence's mamma hadn't a particle of taste, and Amy suffered deeply at having to wear a red instead of a blue bonnet, unbecoming gowns, and fussy aprons that did not fit. Everything was good, well made, and little worn; but Amy's artistic eyes were much afflicted, especially this winter, when her school dress was a dull purple, with yellow dots, and no trimming.

"My only comfort," she said to Meg, with tears in her eyes, "is, that mother don't take tucks in my dresses whenever I'm naughty, as Maria Parks' mother does. My dear, it's really dreadful; for sometimes she is so bad her frock is up to her knees, and she can't come to school. When I think of this *deggerredation,* I feel that I can bear even my flat nose and purple gown, with yellow sky-rockets on it."

Meg was Amy's confidant and monitor, and, by some strange attraction of opposites, Jo was gentle Beth's. To Jo alone did the shy child tell her thoughts; and over her big, harum-scarum sister, Beth unconsciously exercised more influence than any one in the family. The two older girls were a great deal to one another, but each took one of the younger into her keeping, and watched over her in her own way; "playing mother" they called it, and put their sisters in the places of discarded dolls, with the maternal instinct of little women.

"Has anybody got anything to tell? It's been such a dismal day I'm really dying for some amusement," said Meg, as they sat sewing together that evening.

"I had a queer time with aunt today, and, as I got the best of it, I'll tell you about it," began Jo, who dearly loved to tell stories. "I was reading that everlasting Belsham, and droning away as I always do, for aunt soon drops off, and then I take out some nice book, and read like fury till she wakes up. I actually made myself sleepy; and, before she began to nod, I gave such a gape that she asked me what I meant by opening my mouth wide enough to take the whole book in at once.

" 'I wish I could, and be done with it,' said I, trying not to be saucy.

"Then she gave me a long lecture on my sins, and told me to sit and think them over while she just 'lost' herself for a moment. She never finds herself very soon; so the minute her cap began to bob, like a top-heavy dahlia, I whipped the 'Vicar of Wakefield' out of my pocket, and read away, with one eye on him, and one on aunt. I'd just got to where they all tumbled into the water, when I forgot, and laughed out loud. Aunt woke up; and, being more good-natured after her nap, told me to read a bit, and show what frivolous work I preferred to the worthy and instructive Belsham. I did my very best, and she liked it, though she only said,—

" 'I don't understand what it's all about. Go back and begin it, child.'

"Back I went, and made the Primroses as interesting as ever I could. Once I was wicked enough to stop in a thrilling place, and say meekly, 'I'm afraid it tires you, ma'am; sha'n't I stop now?'

"She caught up her knitting, which had dropped out of her hands, gave me a sharp look through her specs, and said, in her short way,—

" 'Finish the chapter, and don't be impertinent, miss.' "

"Did she own she liked it?" asked Meg.

"Oh, bless you, no! But she let old Belsham rest; and, when I ran back after my gloves this aftenoon, there she was, so hard at the Vicar that she didn't hear me laugh as I danced a jig in the hall, because of the good time coming. What a pleasant life she might have, if she only chose. I don't envy her much, in spite of her money, for after all rich people have about as many worries as poor ones, I think," added Jo.

"That reminds me," said Meg, "that I've got something to tell. It isn't funny, like Jo's story, but I thought about it a good deal as I came home. At the Kings' today I found everybody in a flurry, and one of the children said that her oldest brother had done something dreadful, and papa had sent him away. I heard Mrs. King crying and Mr. King talking very loud, and Grace and Ellen turned away their faces when they passed me, so I shouldn't see how red their eyes were. I didn't ask any questions, of course; but I felt so sorry for them, and was rather glad I hadn't any wild brothers to do wicked things and disgrace the family."

"I think being disgraced in school is a great deal try*inger* than anything bad boys can do," said Amy, shaking her head, as if her experience of life had been a deep one. "Susie Perkins came to school today with a lovely red carnelian ring; I wanted it dreadfully, and wished I was her with all my might. Well, she drew a picture of Mr. Davis, with a monstrous nose and a hump, and the words, 'Young ladies, my eye is upon you!' coming out of his mouth in a balloon thing. We were laughing over it, when all of a sudden his eye *was* on us, and he ordered Susie to bring up her slate. She was *parry*lized with fright, but she went, and oh, what *do* you think he did? He took her by the ear,—the ear! Just fancy how horrid!—and led her to the recitation platform, and made her stand there half an hour, holding that slate so every one could see."

"Didn't the girls laugh at the picture?" asked Jo, who relished the scrape.

"Laugh? Not one! They sat as still as mice; and Susie cried quarts, I know she did. I didn't envy her then; for I felt that millions of carnelian rings wouldn't have made me happy, after that. I never, never should have got over such a agonizing mortification." And Amy went on with her work, in the proud consciousness of virtue, and the successful utterance of two long words in a breath.

"I saw something that I liked this morning, and I meant to tell it at dinner, but I forgot," said Beth, putting Jo's topsy-turvy basket in order as she talked. "When I went to get some oysters for Hannah, Mr. Laurence was in the fish-shop; but he didn't see me, for I kept behind a barrel, and he was busy with Mr. Cutter, the fish-man. A poor woman came in, with a pail and a mop, and asked Mr. Cutter if he would let her do some scrubbing for a bit of fish, because she hadn't any dinner for her children, and had been disappointed of a day's work. Mr. Cutter was in a hurry, and said 'No,' rather crossly; so she was going away, looking hungry and sorry, when Mr. Laurence hooked up a big fish with the crooked end of his cane, and held it out to her. She was so glad and surprised, she took it right in her arms, and thanked him over and over. He told her to 'go along and cook it,' and she hurried off, so happy! Wasn't it good of him? Oh, she did look so funny, hugging the big, slippery fish, and hoping Mr. Laurence's bed in heaven would be 'aisy.'"

When they had laughed at Beth's story, they asked their mother for one; and, after a moment's thought, she said soberly,—

"As I sat cutting out blue flannel jackets today, at the rooms, I felt very anxious about father, and thought how lonely and helpless we should be, if anything happened to him. It was not a wise thing to do; but I kept on worrying, till an old man came in, with an order for some clothes. He sat down near me, and I began to talk to him; for he looked poor and tired and anxious.

"'Have you sons in the army?' I asked; for the note he brought was not to me.

"'Yes, ma'am. I had four, but two were killed, one is a prisoner, and I'm going to the other, who is very sick in a Washington hospital,' he answered quietly.

"'You have done a great deal for your country, sir,' I said, feeling respect now, instead of pity.

"'Not a mite more than I ought, ma'am. I'd go myself, if I was any use; as I ain't, I give my boys, and give 'em free.'

"He spoke so cheerfully, looked so sincere, and seemed so glad to give his all, that I was ashamed of myself. I'd given one man, and thought it too much, while he gave four, without grudging them. I had all my girls to comfort me at home; and his last son was waiting, miles away, to say 'good-by' to him, perhaps! I felt so rich, so happy, thinking of my blessings, that I made him a nice bundle, gave him some money, and thanked him heartily for the lesson he had taught me."

"Tell another story, mother,—one with a moral to it, like this. I like to think about them afterwards, if they are real, and not too preachy," said Jo, after a minute's silence.

Mrs. March smiled, and began at once; for she had told stories to this little audieuce for many years, and knew how to please them.

Mr. Laurence hooked up a big fish.

"Once upon a time, there were four girls, who had enough to eat and drink and wear, a good many comforts and pleasures, kind friends and parents, who loved them dearly, and yet they were not contented." (Here the listeners stole sly looks at one another, and began to sew diligently.) "These girls were anxious to be good, and made many excellent resolutions; but they did not keep them very well, and were constantly saying, 'If we only had this,' or 'If we could only do that,' quite forgetting how much they already had, and how many pleasant things they actually could do. So they asked an old woman what spell they could use to make them happy, and she said, 'When you feel discontented, think over your blessings, and be grateful.' " (Here Jo looked up quickly, as if about to speak, but changed her mind, seeing that the story was not done yet.)

"Being sensible girls, they decided to try her advice, and soon were surprised to see how well off they were. One discovered that money couldn't keep shame and sorrow out of rich people's houses; another that, though she was poor, she was a great deal happier, with her youth, health, and good spirits, than a certain fretful, feeble old lady, who couldn't enjoy her comforts; a third that, disagreeable as it was to help get dinner, it was harder still to have to go begging for it; and the fourth, that even carnelian rings were not so valuable as good behavior. So they agreed to stop complaining, to enjoy the blessings already possessed, and try to deserve them, lest they should be taken away entirely, instead of increased; and I believe they were never disappointed, or sorry that they took the old woman's advice."

"Now, Marmee, that is very cunning of you to turn our own stories against us, and give us a sermon instead of a romance!" cried Meg.

"I like that kind of sermon. It's the sort father used to tell us," said Beth thoughtfully, putting the needles straight on Jo's cushion.

"I don't complain near as much as the others do, and I shall be more careful than ever now; for I've had warning from Susie's downfall," said Amy morally.

"We needed that lesson, and we won't forget it. If we do, you just say to us, as old Chloe did in 'Uncle Tom,' 'Tink ob yer marcies, chillen! tink ob yer marcies!' " added Jo, who could not, for the life of her, help getting a morsel of fun out of the little sermon, though she took it to heart as much as any of them.

# CHAPTER V

## BEING NEIGHBORLY

"WHAT in the world are you going to do now, Jo?" asked Meg, one snowy afternoon, as her sister came tramping through the hall, in rubber boots, old sack and hood, with a broom in one hand and a shovel in the other.

"Going out for exercise," answered Jo, with a mischievous twinkle in her eyes.

"I should think two long walks this morning would have been enough! It's cold and dull out; and I advise you to stay, warm and dry, by the fire, as I do," said Meg, with a shiver.

"Never take advice! Can't keep still all day, and, not being a pussy-cat, I don't like to doze by the fire. I like adventures, and I'm going to find some."

Meg went back to toast her feet and read "Ivanhoe"; and Jo began to dig paths with great energy. The snow was light, and with her broom she soon swept a path all round the garden, for Beth to walk in when the sun came out; and the invalid dolls needed air. Now, the garden separated the Marches' house from that of Mr. Laurence. Both stood in a suburb of the city, which was still country-like, with groves and lawns, large gardens, and quiet streets. A low hedge parted the two estates. On one side was an old, brown house, looking rather bare and shabby, robbed of the vines that in summer covered its walls, and the flowers which then surrounded it. On the other side was a stately stone mansion, plainly betokening every sort of comfort and luxury from the big coach-house and well-kept grounds to the conservatory and the glimpses of lovely things one caught between the rich curtains. Yet it seemed a lonely, lifeless sort of house; for no children frolicked on the lawn, no motherly face ever smiled at the windows, and few people went in and out, except the old gentleman and his grandson.

To Jo's lively fancy, this fine house seemed a kind of enchanted palace, full of splendors and delights, which no one enjoyed. She had long wanted to behold these hidden glories, and to know the "Laurence boy," who looked as if he would like to be known, if he only knew how to begin. Since the party, she had been more eager than ever, and had planned many ways of making friends with him; but he had not been seen lately, and Jo began to think he had gone away, when she one day spied a brown face at an upper window, looking wistfully down into their garden, where Beth and Amy were snowballing one another.

"That boy is suffering for society and fun," she said to herself. "His grandpa does not know what's good for him, and keeps him shut up all alone. He needs a party of jolly boys to play with, or somebody young and lively. I've a great mind to go over and tell the old gentleman so!"

The idea amused Jo, who liked to do daring things, and was always scandalizing Meg by her queer performances. The plan of "going over" was not forgotten; and when the snowy afternoon came, Jo resolved to try what could be done. She saw Mr. Laurence drive off, and then sallied out to dig her way down to the hedge, where she paused, and took a survey. All quiet,—curtains down at the lower windows; servants out of sight, and nothing human visible but a curly black head leaning on a thin hand at the upper window.

"There he is," thought Jo, "poor boy! All alone and sick this dismal day." It's a shame! I'll toss up a snowball and make him look out, and then say a kind word to him."

Up went a handful of soft snow, and the head turned at once, showing a face which lost its listless look in a minute, as the big eyes brightened and the mouth began to smile. Jo nodded and laughed, and flourished her broom as she called out,—

"How do you do? Are you sick?"

Laurie opened the window, and croaked out as hoarsely as a raven,—

"Better, thank you. I've had a bad cold, and been shut up a week."

"I'm sorry. What do you amuse yourself with?"

"Nothing; it's as dull as tombs up here."

"Don't you read?"

"Not much; they won't let me."

"Can't somebody read to you?"

"Grandpa does, sometimes; but my books don't interest him, and I hate to ask Brooke all the time."

"Have some one come and see you, then."

"There isn't any one I'd like to see. Boys make such a row, and my head is weak."

"Isn't there some nice girl who'd read and amuse you? Girls are quiet, and like to play nurse."

"Don't know any."

"You know us," began Jo, then laughed, and stopped.

"So I do! Will you come, please?" cried Laurie.

"I'm not quiet and nice; but I'll come, if mother will let me. I'll go ask her. Shut that window, like a good boy, and wait till I come."

With that, Jo shouldered her broom and marched into the house, wondering what they would all say to her. Laurie was in a flutter of excitement at the idea of having company, and flew about to get ready; for, as Mrs. March said, he was "a little gentleman," and did honor to the coming guest by brushing his curly pate, putting on a fresh collar, and trying to tidy up the room, which, in spite of half a dozen servants, was anything but neat. Presently there came a loud ring, then a decided voice, asking for "Mr. Laurie," and a surprised-looking servant came running up to announce a young lady.

"All right, show her up, it's Miss Jo," said Laurie, going to the door of his little parlor to meet Jo, who appeared, looking rosy and kind and quite at her ease, with a covered dish in one hand and Beth's three kittens in the other.

"Here I am, bag and baggage," she said briskly. "Mother sent her love, and was glad if I could do anything for you. Meg wanted me to bring some of her blanc-mange; she makes it very nicely, and Beth thought her cats would be comforting. I knew you'd laugh at them, but I couldn't refuse, she was so anxious to do something."

It so happened that Beth's funny loan was just the thing; for, in laughing over the kits, Laurie forgot his bashfulness, and grew sociable at once.

"That looks too pretty to eat," he said, smiling with pleasure, as Jo uncovered the dish, and showed the blanc-mange, surrounded by a garland of green leaves, and the scarlet flowers of Amy's pet geranium.

"It isn't anything, only they all felt kindly, and wanted to show it. Tell the girl to put it away for your tea: it's so simple, you can eat it; and, being soft, it will slip down without hurting your sore throat. What a cozy room this is!"

"It might be if it was kept nice; but the maids are lazy, and I don't know how to make them mind. It worries me, though."

"I'll right it up in two minutes; for it only needs to have the hearth brushed, so,—and the things made straight on the mantel-piece, so,— and the books put here, and the bottles there, and your sofa turned from the light, and the pillows plumped up a bit. Now, then, you're fixed."

And so he was; for, as she laughed and talked, Jo had whisked things into place, and given quite a different air to the room. Laurie watched her in respectful silence; and when she beckoned him to his sofa, he sat down with a sigh of satisfaction, saying gratefully,—

"How kind you are! Yes, that's what it wanted. Now please take the big chair, and let me do something to amuse my company."

"No; I came to amuse you. Shall I read aloud?" and Jo looked affectionately toward some inviting books near by.

"Thank you; I've read all those, and if you don't mind, I'd rather talk," answered Laurie.

"Not a bit; I'll talk all day if you'll only set me going. Beth says I never know when to stop."

"Is Beth the rosy one, who stays at home a good deal, and sometimes goes out with a little basket?" asked Laurie, with interest.

"Yes, that's Beth; she's my girl, and a regular good one she is, too."

"The pretty one is Meg, and the curly-haired one is Amy, I believe?"

"How did you find that out?"

Laurie colored up, but answered frankly, "Why, you see, I often hear you calling to one another, and when I'm alone up here, I can't help looking over at your house, you always seem to be having such good times. I beg your pardon for being so rude, but sometimes you forget to put down the curtain at the window where the flowers are; and when the lamps are lighted, it's like looking at a picture to see the fire, and you all round the table with your mother; her face is right opposite, and it looks so sweet behind the flowers, I can't help watching it. I haven't got any mother, you know;" and Laurie poked the fire to hide a little twitching of the lips that he could not control.

The solitary, hungry look in his eyes went straight to Jo's warm heart. She had been so simply taught that there was no nonsense in her head, and at fifteen she was as innocent and frank as any child. Laurie was sick and lonely; and, feeling how rich she was in home-love and happiness, she gladly tried to share it with him. Her face was very friendly and her sharp voice unusually gentle as she said,—

"We'll never draw that curtain any more, and I give you leave to look as much as you like. I just wish, though, instead of peeping, you'd come over and see us. Mother is so splendid, she'd do you heaps of good, and Beth would sing to you if *I* begged her to, and Amy would dance; Meg and I would make you laugh over our funny stage properties, and we'd have jolly times. Wouldn't your grandpa let you?"

"I think he would, if your mother asked him. He's very kind, though he does not look so; and he lets me do what I like, pretty much, only he's afraid I might be a bother to strangers," began Laurie, brightening more and more.

"We are not strangers, we are neighbors, and you needn't think you'd be a bother. We *want* to know you, and I've been trying to do it this ever so long. We haven't been here a great while, you know, but we have got acquainted with all our neighbors but you."

"You see grandpa lives among his books, and doesn't mind much what happens outside. Mr. Brooke, my tutor, doesn't stay here, you know, and I have no one to go about with me, so I just stop at home and get on as I can."

"That's bad. You ought to make an effort, and go visiting everywhere you are asked; then you'll have plenty of friends, and pleasant places to go to. Never mind being bashful; it won't last long if you keep going."

Laurie turned red again, but wasn't offended at being accused of bashfulness; for there was so much good-will in Jo, it was impossible not to take her blunt speeches as kindly as they were meant.

"Do you like your school?" asked the boy, changing the subject, after a little pause, during which he stared at the fire, and Jo looked about her, well pleased.

"Don't go to school; I'm a business man—girl, I mean. I go to wait on my great-aunt, and a dear, cross old soul she is, too," answered Jo.

Laurie opened his mouth to ask another question; but remembering just in time that it wasn't manners to make too many inquiries into people's afairs, he shut it again, and looked uncomfortable. Jo liked his good breeding, and didn't mind having a laugh at Aunt March, so she gave him a lively description of the fidgety old lady, her fat poodle, the parrot that talked Spanish, and the library where she revelled. Laurie enjoyed that immensely; and when she told about the prim old gentleman who came once to woo Aunt March, and, in the middle of a fine speech, how Poll had tweaked his wig off to his great dismay, the boy lay back and laughed till the tears ran down his cheeks, and a maid popped her head in to see what was the matter.

"Oh! That does me no end of good. Tell on, please," he said, taking his face out of the sofa-cushion, red and shining with merriment.

Much elated with her success, Jo did "tell on," all about their plays and plans, their hopes and fears for father, and the most interesting events of the little world in which the sisters lived. Then they got to talking about books; and to Jo's delight, she found that Laurie loved them as well as she did, and had read even more than herself.

"If you like them so much, come down and see ours. Grandpa is out, so you needn't be afraid," said Laurie, getting up.

"I'm not afraid of anything," returned Jo, with a toss of the head.

"I don't believe you are!" exclaimed the boy, looking at her with much admiration, though he privately thought she would have good reason to be a trifle afraid of the old gentleman, if she met him in some of his moods.

The atmosphere of the whole house being summer-like, Laurie led the way from room to room, letting Jo stop to examine whatever struck her fancy; and so at last they came to the library, where she clapped her hands, and pranced, as she always did when especially delighted. It was lined with books, and there were pictures and statues, and distracting little cabinets full of coins and curiosities, and sleepy-hollow chairs, and queer tables, and bronzes; and, best of all, a great open fireplace, with quaint tiles all round it.

"What richness!" sighed Jo, sinking into the depth of a velvet chair, and gazing about her with an air of intense satisfaction. "Theodore Laurence, you ought to be the happiest boy in the world," she added impressively.

"A fellow can't live on books," said Laurie, shaking his head, as he perched on a table opposite.

Before he could say more, a bell rung, and Jo flew up, exclaiming with alarm, "Mercy me! It's your grandpa!"

"Well, what if it is? You are not afraid of anything, you know," returned the boy, looking wicked.

"I think I am a little bit afraid of him, but I don't know why I should be. Marmee said I might come, and I don't think you're any the worse for it," said Jo, composing herself, though she kept her eyes on the door.

"I'm a great deal better for it, and ever so much obliged. I'm only afraid you are very tired talking to me; it was *so* pleasant, I couldn't bear to stop," said Laurie gratefully.

"The doctor to see you, sir," and the maid beckoned as she spoke.

"Would you mind if I left you for a minute? I suppose I must see him," said Laurie.

"Don't mind me. I'm as happy as a cricket here," answered Jo.

Laurie went away, and his guest amused herself in her own way. She was standing before a fine portrait of the old gentleman, when the door opened again, and, without turning, she said decidedly, "I'm sure now that I shouldn't be afraid of him, for he's got kind eyes, though his mouth is grim, and he looks as if he had a tremendous will of his own. He isn't as handsome as *my* grandfather, but I like him."

"Thank you, ma'am," said a gruff voice behind her; and there, to her great dismay, stood old Mr. Laurence.

Poor Jo blushed till she couldn't blush any redder, and her heart began to beat uncomfortably fast as she thought what she had said. For a minute a wild desire to run away possessed her; but that was cowardly, and the girls would laugh at her; so she resolved to stay, and get out of the scrape as she could. A second look showed her that the living eyes, under the bushy gray eyebrows, were kinder even than the painted ones; and there was a sly twinkle in them, which lessened her fear a good deal. The gruff voice was gruffer than ever, as the old gentleman said abruptly, after that dreadful pause, "So you're not afraid of me, hey?"

"Not much, sir."

"And you don't think me as handsome as your grandfather?"

"Not quite, sir."

"And I've got a tremendous will, have I?"

"I only said I thought so."

"But you like me, in spite of it?"

"Yes, I do, sir."

That answer pleased the old gentleman; he gave a short laugh, shook hands with her, and, putting his finger under her chin, turned up her face, examined it gravely, and let it go, saying, with a nod, "You've got your grandfather's spirit, if you haven't his face. He *was* a fine man, my dear; but, what is better, he was a brave and an honest one, and I was proud to be his friend."

"Thank you, sir;" and Jo was quite comfortable after that, for it suited her exactly.

"What have you been doing to this boy of mine, hey?" was the next question, sharply put.

"Only trying to be neighborly, sir;" and Jo told how her visit came about.

"You think he needs cheering up a bit, do you?"

"Yes, sir; he seems a little lonely, and young folks would do him good perhaps. We are only girls, but we should be glad to help if we could, for we don't forget the spendid Christmas present you sent us," said Jo eagerly.

"Tut, tut, tut! That was the boy's affair. How is the poor woman?"

"Doing nicely, sir;" and off went Jo, talking very fast, as she told all about the Hummels, in whom her mother had interested richer friends than they were.

"Just her father's way of doing good. I shall come and see your mother some fine day. Tell her so. There's the tea-bell; we have it early, on the boy's account. Come down, and go on being neighborly."

"If you'd like to have me, sir."

"Shouldn't ask you, if I didn't;" and Mr. Laurence offered her his arm with old-fashioned courtesy.

"What *would* Meg say to this?" thought Jo, as she was marched away, while her eyes danced with fun as she imagined herself telling the story at home.

"Hey! Why, what the dickens has come to the fellow?" said the old gentleman, as Laurie came running down stairs, and brought up with a start of surprise at the astonishing sight of Jo arm-in-arm with his redoubtable grandfather.

"I didn't know you'd come, sir," he began, as Jo gave him a triumphant little glance.

"That's evident, by the way you racket downstairs. Come to your tea, sir, and behave like a gentleman;" and having pulled the boy's hair by way of a caress, Mr. Laurence walked on, while Laurie went through a series of comic evolutions behind their backs, which nearly produced an explosion of laughter from Jo.

The old gentleman did not say much as he drank his four cups of tea, but he watched the young people, who soon chatted away like old friends, and the change in his grandson did not escape him. There was color, light, and life in the boy's face now, vivacity in his manner, and genuine merriment in his laugh.

"She's right; the lad *is* lonely. I'll see what these little girls can do for him," thought Mr. Laurence, as he looked and listened. He liked Jo, for her odd, blunt ways suited him; and she seemed to understand the boy almost as well as if she had been one herself.

If the Laurences had been what Jo called "prim and poky," she would not have got on at all, for such people always made her shy and awkward; but finding them free and easy, she was so herself, and made a good impression. When they rose she proposed to go, but Laurie said he had something more to show her, and took her away to the conservatory, which had been lighted for her benefit. It seemed quite fairylike to Jo,

Putting his finger under her chin.

as she went up and down the walks, enjoying the blooming walls on either side, the soft light, the damp sweet air, and the wonderful vines and trees that hung above her,—while her new friend cut the finest flowers till his hands were full; then he tied them up, saying, with the happy look Jo liked to see, "Please give these to your mother, and tell her I like the medicine she sent me very much."

They found Mr. Laurence standing before the fire in the great drawing-room, but Jo's attention was entirely absorbed by a grand piano, which stood open.

"Do you play?" she asked, turning to Laurie with a respectful expression.

"Sometimes," he answered modestly.

"Please do now. I want to hear it, so I can tell Beth."

"Won't you first?"

"Don't know how; too stupid to learn, but I love music dearly."

So Laurie played, and Jo listened, with her nose luxuriously buried in heliotrope and tea-roses. Her respect and regard for the "Laurence boy" increased very much, for he played remarkably well, and didn't put on any airs. She wished Beth could hear him, but she did not say so; only praised him till he was quite abashed, and his grandfather came to the rescue. "That will do, that will do, young lady. Too many sugar-plums are not good for him. His music isn't bad, but I hope he will do as well in more important things. Going? Well, I'm much obliged to you, and I hope you'll come again. My respects to your mother. Good-night, Doctor Jo."

He shook hands kindly, but looked as if something did not please him. When they got into the hall, Jo asked Laurie if she had said anything amiss. He shook his head.

"No, it was me; he doesn't like to hear me play."

"Why not?"

"I'll tell you some day. John is going home with you, as I can't."

"No need of that; I am not a young lady, and it's only a step. Take care of yourself, won't you?"

"Yes; but you will come again, I hope?"

"If you promise to come and see us after you are well."

"I will."

"Good-night, Laurie!"

"Good-night, Jo, good-night!"

When all the afternoon's adventures had been told, the family felt inclined to go visiting in a body, for each found something very attractive in the big house on the other side of the hedge. Mrs. March wanted to talk of her father with the old man who had not forgotten him; Meg longed to walk in the conservatory; Beth sighed for the grand piano; and Amy was eager to see the fine pictures and statues.

"Mother, why didn't Mr. Laurence like to have Laurie play?" asked Jo, who was of an inquiring disposition.

"I am not sure, but I think it was because his son, Laurie's father, married an Italian lady, a musician, which displeased the old man, who is very proud. The lady was good and lovely and accomplished, but he did not like her, and never saw his son after he married. They both died when Laurie was a little child, and then his grandfather took him home.

I fancy the boy, who was born in Italy, is not very strong, and the old man is afraid of losing him, which makes him so careful. Laurie comes naturally by his love of music, for he is like his mother, and I dare say his grandfather fears that he may want to be a musician; at any rate, his skill reminds him of the woman he did not like, and so he 'glowered,' as Jo said."

"Dear me, how romantic!" exclaimed Meg.

"How silly!" said Jo. "Let him be a musician, if he wants to, and not plague his life out sending him to college, when he hates to go."

"That's why he has such handsome black eyes and pretty manners, I suppose. Italians are always nice," said Meg, who was a little sentimental.

"What do you know about his eyes and his manners? You never spoke to him, hardly," cried Jo, who was *not* sentimental.

"I saw him at the party, and what you tell shows that he knows how to behave. That was a nice little speech about the medicine mother sent him."

"He meant the blanc-mange, I suppose."

"How stupid you are, child! He meant you, of course."

"Did he?" and Jo opened her eyes as if it had never occurred to her before.

"I never saw such a girl! You don't know a compliment when you get it," said Meg, with the air of a young lady who knew all about the matter.

"I think they are great nonsense, and I'll thank you not to be silly, and spoil my fun. Laurie's a nice boy, and I like him, and I won't have any sentimental stuff about compliments and such rubbish. We'll all be good to him, because he hasn't got any mother, and he *may* come over and see us, mayn't he, Marmee?"

"Yes, Jo, your little friend is very welcome, and I hope Meg will remember that children should be children as long as they can."

"I don't call myself a child, and I'm not in my teens yet," observed Amy. "What do you say, Beth?"

"I was thinking about our 'Pilgrim's Progress,'" answered Beth, who had not heard a word. "How we got out of the Slough and through the Wicket Gate by resolving to be good, and up the steep hill by trying; and that may be the house over there, full of splendid things, is going to be our Palace Beautiful."

"We have got to get by the lions, first," said Jo, as if she rather liked the prospect.

# CHAPTER VI

## BETH FINDS THE PALACE BEAUTIFUL

THE big house did prove a Palace Beautiful, though it took some time for all to get in, and Beth found it very hard to pass the lions. Old Mr. Laurence was the biggest one; but after he had called, said something funny or kind to each one of the girls, and talked over old times with their mother, nobody felt much afraid of him, except timid Beth. The other lion was the fact that they were poor and Laurie rich; for this made them shy of accepting favors which they could not return. But, after a while, they found that he considered them the benefactors, and could not do enough to show how grateful he was for Mrs. March's motherly welcome, their cheerful society, and the comfort he took in that humble home of theirs. So they soon forgot their pride, and interchanged kindnesses without stopping to think which was the greater.

All sorts of pleasant things happened about that time; for the new friendship flourished like grass in spring. Everyone liked Laurie, and he privately informed his tutor that "the Marches were regularly splendid girls." With the delightful enthusiasm of youth, they took the solitary boy into their midst, and made much of him, and he found something very charming in the innocent companionship of these simple-hearted girls. Never having known mother or sisters, he was quick to feel the influences they brought about him; and their busy, lively ways made him ashamed of the indolent life he led. He was tired of books, and found people so interesting now that Mr. Brooke was obliged to make very unsatisfactory reports; for Laurie was always playing truant, and running over to the Marches'.

"Never mind; let him take a holiday, and make it up afterwards," said the old gentleman. "The good lady next door says he is studying too hard, and needs young society, amusement, and exercise. I suspect she is right, and that I've been coddling the fellow as if I'd been his grandmother. Let him do what he likes, as long as he is happy. He can't get into mischief in that little nunnery over there; and Mrs. March is doing more for him than we can."

What good times they had, to be sure! Such plays and tableaux, such sleigh-rides and skating frolics, such pleasant evenings in the old parlor, and now and then such gay little parties at the great house. Meg could walk in the conservatory whenever she liked, and revel in bouquets; Jo browsed over the new library voraciously, and convulsed the old gentleman with her criticisms; Amy copied pictures, and enjoyed beauty to her heart's content; and Laurie played "lord of the manor" in the most delightful style.

But Beth, though yearning for the grand piano, could not pluck up courage to go to the "Mansion of Bliss," as Meg called it. She went once with Jo; but the old gentleman, not being aware of her infirmity, stared at her so hard from under his heavy eyebrows, and said "Hey!" so loud, that he frightened her so much her "feet chattered on the floor," she told her mother; and she ran away, declaring she would never go there any more, not even for the dear piano. No persuasions or enticements could overcome her fear, till, the fact coming to Mr. Laurence's ear in some mysterious way, he set about mending matters. During one of the brief calls he made, he artfully led the conversation to music, and talked away about great singers whom he had seen, fine organs he had heard, and told such charming anecdotes that Beth found it impossible to stay in her distant corner, but crept nearer and nearer, as if fascinated. At the back of his chair she stopped, and stood listening, with her great eyes wide open, and her cheeks red with the excitement of this unusual performance. Taking no more notice of her than if she had been a fly, Mr. Laurence talked on about Laurie's lessons and teachers; and presently, as if the idea had just occurred to him, he said to Mrs. March,—

"The boy neglects his music now, and I'm glad of it, for he was getting too fond of it. But the piano suffers for want of use. Wouldn't some of your girls like to run over, and practice on it now and then, just to keep it in tune, you know, ma'am?"

Beth took a step forward, and pressed her hands tightly together to keep from clapping them, for this was an irresistible temptation; and the thought of practicing on that splendid instrument quite took her breath away. Before Mrs. March could reply, Mr. Laurence went on with an odd little nod and smile,—

"They needn't see or speak to any one, but run in at any time; for I'm shut up in my study at the other end of the house, Laurie is out a great deal, and the servants are never near the drawing-room after nine o'clock."

Here he rose, as if going, and Beth made up her mind to speak, for that last arrangement left nothing to be desired. "Please tell the young ladies what I say; and if they don't care to come, why, never mind." Here a little hand slipped into his, and Beth looked up at him with a face full of gratitude, as she said, in her earnest yet timid way,—

"O sir, they do care, very, very much!"

"Are you the musical girl?" he asked, without any startling "Hey!" as he looked down at her very kindly.

"I'm Beth. I love it dearly, and I'll come, if you are quite sure nobody will hear me—and be disturbed," she added, fearing to be rude, and trembling at her own boldness as she spoke.

"Not a soul, my dear. The house is empty half the day; so come, and drum away as much as you like, and I shall be obliged to you."

"How kind you are, sir!"

Beth blushed like a rose under the friendly look he wore; but she was not frightened now, and gave the big hand a grateful squeeze, because she had no words to thank him for the precious gift he had given her. The old gentleman softly stroked the hair off her forehead, and, stooping down, he kissed her, saying, in a tone few people ever heard,—

"I had a little girl once, with eyes like these. God bless you, my dear! Good day, madam;" and away he went, in a great hurry.

Beth had a rapture with her mother, and then rushed up to impart the glorious news to her family of invalids, as the girls were not at home. How blithely she sang that evening, and how they all laughed at her, because she woke Amy in the night by playing the piano on her face in her sleep. Next day, having seen both the old and young gentleman out of the house, Beth, after two or three retreats, fairly got in at the side-door, and made her way, as noiselessly as any mouse, to the drawing-room, where her idol stood. Quite by accident, of course, some pretty, easy music lay on the piano; and, with trembling fingers, and frequent stops to listen and look about, Beth at last touched the great instrument, and straightway forgot her fear, herself, and everything else but the unspeakable delight which the music gave her, for it was like the voice of a beloved friend.

She stayed till Hannah came to take her home to dinner; but she had no appetite, and could only sit and smile upon every one in a general state of beatitude.

After that, the little brown hood slipped through the hedge nearly every day, and the great drawing-room was haunted by a tuneful spirit that came and went unseen. She never knew that Mr. Laurence often opened his study-door to hear the old-fashioned airs he liked; she never saw Laurie mount guard in the hall to warn the servants away; she never suspected that the exercise-books and new songs which she found in the rack were put there for her especial benefit; and when he talked to her about music at home, she only thought how kind he was to tell things that helped her so much. So she enjoyed herself heartily, and found, what isn't always the case, that her granted wish was all she had hoped. Perhaps it was because she was so grateful for this blessing that a greater was given her; at any rate, she deserved both.

"Mother, I'm going to work Mr. Laurence a pair of slippers. He is so kind to me, I must thank him, and I don't know any other way. Can I do it?" asked Beth, a few weeks after that eventful call of his.

"Yes, dear. It will please him very much, and be a nice way of thanking him. The girls will help you about them, and I will pay for the making up," replied Mrs. March, who took peculiar pleasure in granting Beth's requests, because she so seldom asked anything for herself.

After many serious discussions with Meg and Jo, the pattern was chosen, the materials bought, and the slippers begun. A cluster of grave yet cheerful pansies, on a deeper purple ground, was pronounced very appropriate and pretty; and Beth worked away early and late, with occasional lifts over hard parts. She was a nimble little needle-woman, and they were finished before any one got tired of them. Then she wrote a very short, simple note, and, with Laurie's help, got them smuggled onto the study-table one morning before the old gentleman was up.

When this excitement was over, Beth waited to see what would happen. All that day passed, and a part of the next, before any acknowledgment arrived, and she was beginning to fear she had offended her crotchety friend. On the afternoon of the second day, she went out to do an errand, and give poor Joanna, the invalid doll, her daily exercise. As she came up the street, on her return, she saw three, yes, four, heads popping in and out of the parlor windows, and the moment they saw her, several hands were waved, and several joyful voices screamed,—

"Here's a letter from the old gentleman! Come quick, and read it!"

"O Beth, he's sent you—" began Amy, gesticulating with unseemly energy; but she got no further, for Jo quenched her by slamming down the window.

Beth hurried on in a flutter of suspense. At the door, her sisters seized and bore her to the parlor in a triumphal procession, all pointing, and all saying at once, "Look there! Look there!" Beth did look, and turned pale with delight and surprise; for there stood a little cabinet-piano, with a letter lying on the glossy lid, directed, like a sign-board, to "Miss Elizabeth March."

"For me?" gasped Beth, holding onto Jo, and feeling as if she should tumble down, it was such an overwhelming thing altogether.

"O, sir, they do care very much."

"Yes; all for you, my precious! Isn't it splendid of him? Don't you think he's the dearest old man in the world? Here's the key in the letter. We didn't open it, but we are dying to know what he says," cried Jo, hugging her sister, and offering the note.

"You read it! I can't, I feel so queer! Oh, it is too lovely!" and Beth hid her face in Jo's apron, quite upset by her present.

Jo opened the paper, and began to laugh, for the first words she saw were,—

"MISS MARCH:
   *"Dear Madam,—"*
   "How nice it sounds! I wish some one would write to me so!" said Amy, who thought the old-fashioned address very elegant.
   " 'I have had many pairs of slippers in my life, but I never had any that suited me so well as yours,' " continued Jo. " 'Heart's-ease is my favorite flower, and these will always remind me of the gentle giver. I like to pay my debts; so I know you will allow "the old gentleman" to send you something which once belonged to the little granddaughter he lost. With hearty thanks and best wishes, I remain
   " 'Your grateful friend and humble servant,
                              " 'JAMES LAURENCE.' "

"There, Beth, that's an honor to be proud of, I'm sure! Laurie told me how fond Mr. Laurence used to be of the child who died, and how he kept all her little things carefully. Just think, he's given you her piano. That comes of having big blue eyes and loving music," said Jo, trying to soothe Beth, who trembled, and looked more excited than she had ever been before.

"See the cunning brackets to hold candles, and the nice green silk, puckered up, with a gold rose in the middle, and the pretty rack and stool, all complete," added Meg, opening the instrument and displaying its beauties.

" 'Your humble servant, James Laurence'; only think of his writing that to you. I'll tell the girls. They'll think it's splendid," said Amy, much impressed by the note.

"Try it, honey. Let's hear the sound of the baby-pianny," said Hannah, who always took a share in the family joys and sorrows.

So Beth tried it; and every one pronounced it the most remarkable piano ever heard. It had evidently been newly tuned and put in apple-pie order; but, perfect as it was, I think the real charm of it lay in the happiest of all happy faces which leaned over it, as Beth lovingly touched the beautiful black and white keys and pressed the bright pedals.

"You'll have to go and thank him," said Jo, by way of a joke; for the idea of the child's really going never entered her head.

"Yes, I mean to. I guess I'll go now, before I get frightened thinking about it." And, to the utter amazement of the assembled family, Beth walked deliberately down the garden, through the hedge, and in at the Laurences' door.

"Well, I wish I may die if it ain't the queerest thing I ever see! The pianny has turned her head! She'd never have gone in her right mind," cried Hannah, staring after her, while the girls were rendered quite speechless by the miracle.

They would have been still more amazed if they had seen what Beth did afterward. If you will believe me, she went and knocked at the study-door before she gave herself time to think; and when a gruff voice called out, "Come in!" she did go in, right up to Mr. Laurence, who looked quite taken aback, and held out her hand, saying, with only a small quaver in her voice, "I came to thank you, sir, for—" But she didn't finish; for he looked so friendly that she forgot her speech, and, only remembering that he had lost the little girl he loved, she put both arms round his neck, and kissed him.

If the roof of the house had suddenly flown off, the old gentleman wouldn't have been more astonished; but he liked it,—oh, dear, yes, he liked it amazingly!—and was so touched and pleased by that confiding little kiss that all his crustiness vanished; and he just set her on his knee, and laid his wrinkled cheek against her rosy one, feeling as if he had got his own little granddaughter back again. Beth ceased to fear him from that moment, and sat there talking to him as cozily as if she had known him all her life; for love casts out fear, and gratitude can conquer pride. When she went home, he walked with her to her own gate, shook hands cordially, and touched his hat as he marched back again, looking very stately and erect, like a handsome, soldierly old gentleman, as he was.

When the girls saw that performance, Jo began to dance a jig, by way of expressing her satisfaction; Amy nearly fell out of the window in her surprise; and Meg exclaimed, with uplifted hands, "Well, I do believe the world is coming to an end!"

# CHAPTER VII

## AMY'S VALLEY OF HUMILIATION

That boy is a perfect Cyclops, isn't he?" said Amy, one day, as Laurie clattered by on horseback, with a flourish of his whip as he passed.

"How dare you say so, when he's got both his eyes? And very handsome ones they are, too," cried Jo, who resented any slighting remarks about her friend.

"I didn't say anything about his eyes, and I don't see why you need fire up when I admire his riding."

"Oh, my goodness! That little goose means a centaur, and she called him a Cyclops," exclaimed Jo, with a burst of laughter.

"You needn't be so rude; it's only a 'lapse of lingy,' as Mr. Davis says," retorted Amy, finishing Jo with her Latin. "I just wish I had a little of the money Laurie spends on that horse," she added, as if to herself, yet hoping her sisters would hear.

"Why?" asked Meg kindly, for Jo had gone off in another laugh at Amy's second blunder.

"I need it so much; I'm dreadfully in debt, and it won't be my turn to have the rag-money for a month."

"In debt, Amy? What do you mean?" and Meg looked sober.

"Why, I owe at least a dozen pickled limes, and I can't pay them, you know, till I have money, for Marmee forbade my having anything charged at the shop."

"Tell me all about it. Are limes the fashion now? It used to be pricking bits of rubber to make balls;" and Meg tried to keep her countenance, Amy looked so grave and important.

"Why, you see, the girls are always buying them, and unless you want to be thought mean, you must do it, too. It's nothing but limes now, for every one is sucking them in their desks in school-time, and trading them off for pencils, bead-rings, paper dolls, or something else, at recess. If one girl likes another, she gives her a lime; if she's mad with her, she eats one before her face, and don't offer even a suck. They treat by turns; and I've had ever so many, but haven't returned them; and I ought, for they are debts of honor, you know."

"How much will pay them off, and restore your credit?" asked Meg, taking out her purse.

"A quarter would more than do it, and leave a few cents over for a treat for you. Don't you like limes?"

"Not much; you may have my share. Here's the money. Make it last as long as you can, for it isn't very plenty, you know."

"Oh, thank you! It must be so nice to have pocket-money! I'll have a grand feast, for I haven't tasted a lime this week. I felt delicate about taking any, as I couldn't return them, and I'm actually suffering for one."

Next day Amy was rather late at school; but could not resist the temptation of displaying, with pardonable pride, a moist brown-paper parcel, before she consigned it to the inmost recesses of her desk. During the next few minutes the rumor that Amy March had got twenty-four delicious limes (she ate one on the way), and was going to treat, circulated through her "set," and the attentions of her friends became quite overwhelming. Katy Brown invited her to her next party on the spot; Mary Kingsley insisted on lending her her watch till recess; and Jenny Snow, a satirical young lady, who had basely twitted Amy upon her limeless state, promptly buried the hatchet, and offered to furnish answers to certain appalling sums. But Amy had not forgotten Miss Snow's cutting remarks about "some persons whose noses were not too flat to smell other people's limes, and stuck-up people, who were not too proud to ask for them;" and she instantly crushed "that Snow girl's" hopes by the withering telegram, "You needn't be so polite all of a sudden, for you won't get any."

A distinguished personage happened to visit the school that morning, and Amy's beautifully drawn maps received praise, which honor to her foe rankled in the soul of Miss Snow, and caused Miss March to assume the airs of a studious young peacock. But, alas, alas! Pride goes before a fall, and the revengeful Snow turned the tables with disastrous success. No sooner had the guest paid the usual stale compliments, and bowed himself out, than Jenny, under pretence of asking an important question, informed Mr. Davis, the teacher, that Amy March had pickled limes in her desk.

Now Mr. Davis had declared limes a contraband article, and solemnly vowed to publicly ferrule the first person who was found breaking the law. This much-enduring man had succeeded in banishing chewing-gum after a long and stormy war, had made a bonfire of the confiscated novels and newspapers, had suppressed a private post-office, had forbidden distortions of the face, nicknames, and caricatures, and done all that one man could do to keep half a hundred rebellious girls in order. Boys are trying enough to human patience, goodness knows! But girls are infinitely more so, especially to nervous gentlemen, with tyrannical tempers, and no more talent for teaching than Dr. Blimber. Mr. Davis knew any quantity of Greek, Latin, Algebra, and ologies of all sorts, so he was called a fine teacher; and manners, morals, feelings, and examples were not considered of any particular importance. It was a most unfortunate moment for denouncing Amy, and Jenny knew it. Mr. Davis had evidently taken his coffee too strong that morning; there was an east wind, which always affected his neuralgia; and his pupils had not done him the credit which he felt he deserved: therefore, to use the expressive, if not elegant, language of a school-girl, "he was as nervous as a witch and as cross as a bear." The word "limes" was like fire to powder; his yellow face flushed, and he rapped on his desk with an energy which made Jenny skip to her seat with unusual rapidity.

"Young ladies, attention, if you please!"

At the stern order the buzz ceased, and fifty pairs of blue, black, gray, and brown eyes were obediently fixed upon his awful countenance.

"Miss March, come to the desk."

Amy rose to comply with outward composure, but a secret fear oppressed her, for the limes weighed upon her conscience.

"Bring with you the limes you have in your desk," was the unexpected command which arrested her before she got out of her seat.

"Don't take all," whispered her neighbor, a young lady of great presence of mind.

Amy hastily shook out half a dozen, and laid the rest down before Mr. Davis, feeling that any man possessing a human heart would relent when that delicious perfume met his nose. Unfortunately, Mr. Davis particularly detested the odor of the fashionable pickle, and disgust added to his wrath.

"Is that all?"

"Not quite," stammered Amy.

"Bring the rest immediately."

With a despairing glance at her set, she obeyed.

"You are sure there are no more?"

"I never lie, sir."

"So I see. Now take these disgusting things two by two, and throw them out of the window."

There was a simultaneous sigh, which created quite a little gust, as the last hope fled, and the treat was ravished from their longing lips. Scarlet with shame and anger, Amy went to and fro six dreadful times; and as each doomed couple—looking oh! so plump and juicy—fell from her reluctant hands, a shout from the street completed the anguish of the girls, for it told them that their feast was being exulted over by the little Irish children, who were their sworn foes. This—this was too much; all flashed indignant or appealing glances at the inexorable Davis, and one passionate lime-lover burst into tears.

As Amy returned from her last trip, Mr. Davis gave a portentous "Hem!" and said in his most impressive manner,—

"Young ladies you remember what I said to you a week ago. I am sorry this has happened; but I never allow my rules to be infringed, and I *never* break my word. Miss March, hold out your hand."

Amy started, and put both hands behind her, turning on him an imploring look which pleaded for her better than the words she could not utter. She was rather a favorite with "old Davis," as, of course, he was called, and it's my private belief that he *would* have broken his word if the indignation of one irrepressible young lady had not found vent in a hiss. That hiss, faint as it was, irritated the irascible gentleman, and sealed the culprit's fate .

"Your hand, Miss March!" was the only answer her mute appeal received; and, too proud to cry or beseech, Amy set her teeth, threw back her head defiantly, and bore without flinching several tingling blows on her little palm. They were neither many nor heavy, but that made no difference to her. For the first time in her life she had been struck; and the disgrace, in her eyes, was as deep as if he had knocked her down.

"You will now stand on the platform till recess," said Mr. Davis, resolved to do the thing thoroughly, since he had begun.

That was dreadful. It would have been bad enough to go to her seat, and see the pitying faces of her friends, or the satisfied ones of her few enemies; but to face the whole school, with that shame fresh upon her, seemed impossible, and for a second she felt as if she could only drop down where she stood, and break her heart with crying. A bitter sense of wrong, and the thought of Jenny Snow, helped her to bear it; and, taking the ignominious place, she fixed her eyes on the stove-funnel above what now seemed a sea of faces, and stood there, so motionless and white that the girls found it very hard to study, with that pathetic figure before them.

During the fifteen minutes that followed, the proud and sensitive little girl suffered a shame and pain which she never forgot. To others it might seem a ludicrous or trivial affair, but to her it was a hard experience; for during the twelve years of her life she had been governed by love alone, and a blow of that sort had never touched her before. The smart of her hand and the ache of her heart were forgotten in the sting of the thought,—

"I shall have to tell at home, and they will be so disappointed in me!"

The fifteen minutes seemed an hour; but they came to an end at last, and the word "Recess!" had never seemed so welcome to her before.

"You can go, Miss March," said Mr. Davis, looking, as he felt, uncomfortable.

He did not soon forget the reproachful glance Amy gave him, as she went, without a word to any one, straight into the ante-room, snatched her things, and left the place "forever," as she passionately declared to

Amy bore without flinching several tingling blows.

herself. She was in a sad state when she got home; and when the older girls arrived, some time later, an indignation meeting was held at once. Mrs. March did not say much, but looked disturbed, and comforted her afflicted little daughter in her tenderest manner. Meg bathed the insulted hand with glycerine and tears; Beth felt that even her beloved kittens would fail as a balm for griefs like this; Jo wrathfully proposed that Mr. Davis be arrested without delay; and Hannah shook her fist at the "villain," and pounded potatoes for dinner as if she had him under her pestle.

No notice was taken of Amy's flight, except by her mates; but the sharp-eyed demoiselles discovered that Mr. Davis was quite benignant in the afternoon, also unusually nervous. Just before school closed, Jo appeared, wearing a grim expression, as she stalked up to the desk, and delivered a letter from her mother; then collected Amy's property and departed, carefully scraping the mud from her boots on the door-mat, as if she shook the dust of the place off her feet.

"Yes, you can have a vacation from school, but I want you to study a little every day, with Beth," said Mrs. March, that evening. "I don't approve of corporal punishment, especially for girls. I dislike Mr. Davis's manner of teaching, and don't think the girls you associate with are doing you any good, so I shall ask your father's advice before I send you anywhere else."

"That's good! I wish all the girls would leave, and spoil his old school. It's perfectly maddening to think of those lovely limes," sighed Amy, with the air of a martyr.

"I am not sorry you lost them, for you broke the rules, and deserved some punishment for disobedience," was the severe reply, which rather disappointed the young lady, who expected nothing but sympathy.

"Do you mean you are glad I was disgraced before the whole school?" cried Amy.

"I should not have chosen that way of mending a fault," replied her mother; "but I'm not sure that it won't do you more good than a milder method. You are getting to be rather conceited, my dear, and it is quite time you set about correcting it. You have a good many little gifts and virtues, but there is no need of parading them, for conceit spoils the finest genius. There is not much danger that real talent or goodness will be overlooked long; even if it is, the consciousness of possessing and using it well should satisfy one, and the great charm of all power is modesty."

"So it is!" cried Laurie, who was playing chess in a corner with Jo. "I knew a girl, once, who had a really remarkable talent for music, and she didn't know it; never guessed what sweet little things she composed when she was alone, and wouldn't have believed it if any one had told her."

"I wish I'd known that nice girl; maybe she would have helped me, I'm so stupid," said Beth, who stood beside him, listening eagerly.

"You do know her, and she helps you better than any one else could," answered Laurie, looking at her with such mischievous meaning in his merry black eyes, that Beth suddenly turned very red, and hid her face in the sofa-cushion, quite overcome by such an unexpected discovery.

Jo let Laurie win the game, to pay for that praise of her Beth, who could not be prevailed upon to play for them after her compliment. So

Laurie did his best, and sang delightfully, being in a particularly lively humor, for to the Marches he seldom showed the moody side of his character. When he was gone, Amy, who had been pensive all the evening, said suddenly, as if busy over some new idea,—

"Is Laurie an accomplished boy?"

"Yes; he has had an excellent education, and has much talent; he will make a fine man, if not spoilt by petting," replied her mother.

"And he isn't conceited, is he?" asked Amy.

"Not in the least; that is why he is so charming, and we all like him so much."

"I see; it's nice to have accomplishments, and be elegant; but not to show off or get perked up," said Amy thoughtfully.

"These things are always seen and felt in a person's manner and conversation, if modestly used; but it is not necessary to display them," said Mrs. March.

"Any more than it's proper to wear all your bonnets and gowns and ribbons at once, that folks may know you've got them," added Jo; and the lecture ended in a laugh.

# CHAPTER VIII

## JO MEETS APOLLYON

"GIRLS, where are you going?" asked Amy, coming into their room one Saturday afternoon, and finding them getting ready to go out, with an air of secrecy which excited her curiosity.

"Never mind; little girls shouldn't ask questions," returned Jo sharply.

Now if there *is* anything mortifying to our feelings, when we are young, it is to be told that; and to be bidden to "run away, dear," is still more trying to us. Amy bridled up at this insult, and determined to find out the secret, if she teased for an hour. Turning to Meg, who never refused her anything very long, she said coaxingly, "Do tell me! I should think you might let me go, too; for Beth is fussing over her piano, and I haven't got anything to do, and am *so* lonely."

"I can't, dear, because you aren't invited," began Meg; but Jo broke in impatiently, "Now, Meg, be quiet, or you will spoil it all. You can't go, Amy; so don't be a baby, and whine about it."

"You are going somewhere with Laurie, I know you are; you were whispering and laughing together, on the sofa, last night, and you stopped when I came in. Aren't you going with him?"

"Yes, we are; now do be still, and stop bothering."

Amy held her tongue, but used her eyes, and saw Meg slip a fan into her pocket.

"I know! I know! You're going to the theatre to see the 'Seven Castles!' " she cried; adding resolutely, "and I *shall* go, for mother said I might see it; and I've got my rag-money, and it was mean not to tell me in time."

"Just listen to me a minute, and be a good child," said Meg soothingly.

"Mother doesn't wish you to go this week, because your eyes are not well enough yet to bear the light of this fairy piece. Next week you can go with Beth and Hannah, and have a nice time."

"I don't like that half as well as going with you and Laurie. Please let me; I've been sick with this cold so long, and shut up, I'm dying for some fun. Do, Meg! I'll be ever so good," pleaded Amy, looking as pathetic as she could.

"Suppose we take her. I don't believe mother would mind, if we bundle her up well," began Meg.

"If *she* goes *I* sha'n't; and if 1 don't, Laurie won't like it; and it will be very rude, after he invited only us, to go and drag in Amy. I should think she'd hate to poke herself where she isn't wanted," said Jo crossly, for she disliked the trouble of overseeing a fidgety child, when she wanted to enjoy herself.

Her tone and manner angered Amy, who began to put her boots on, saying, in her most aggravating way, "I *shall* go; Meg says I may; and if I pay for myself, Laurie hasn't anything to do with it."

"You can't sit with us, for our seats are reserved, and you mustn't sit alone; so Laurie will give you his place, and that will spoil our pleasure; or he'll get another seat for you, and that isn't proper, when you weren't asked. You sha'n't stir a step; so you may just stay where you are," scolded Jo, crosser than ever, having just pricked her finger in her hurry.

Sitting on the floor, with one boot on, Amy began to cry, and Meg to reason with her, when Laurie called from below, and the two girls hurried down, leaving their sister wailing; for now and then she forgot her grown-up ways, and acted like a spoilt child. Just as the party was setting out, Amy called over the banisters, in a threatening tone, "You'll be sorry for this, Jo March; see if you ain't."

"Fiddlesticks!" returned Jo, slamming the door.

They had a charming time, for "The Seven Castles of the Diamond Lake" were as brilliant and wonderful as heart could wish. But, in spite of the comical red imps, sparkling elves, and gorgeous princes and princesses, Jo's pleasure had a drop of bitterness in it; the fairy queen's yellow curls reminded her of Amy; and between the acts she amused herself with wondering what her sister would do to make her "sorry for it." She and Amy had had many lively skirmishes in the course of their lives, for both had quick tempers, and were apt to be violent when fairly roused. Amy teased Jo, and Jo irritated Amy, and semioccasional explosions occurred, of which both were much ashamed afterward. Although the oldest, Jo had the least self-control, and had hard times trying to curb the fiery spirit which was continually getting her into trouble; her anger never lasted long, and, having humbly confessed her fault, she sincerely repented, and tried to do better. Her sisters used to say that they rather liked to get Jo into a fury, because she was such an angel afterward. Poor Jo tried desperately to be good, but her bosom enemy was always ready to flame up and defeat her; and it took years of patient effort to subdue it.

When they got home, they found Amy reading in the parlor. She assumed an injured air as they came in; never lifted her eyes from her book, or asked a single question. Perhaps curiosity might have conquered

"Girls, where are you going?"

resentment, if Beth had not been there to inquire, and receive a glowing description of the play. On going up to put away her best hat, Jo's first look was toward the bureau; for, in their last quarrel, Amy had soothed her feelings by turning Jo's top drawer upside down on the floor. Everything was in its place, however; and after a hasty glance into her various closets, bags, and boxes, Jo decided that Amy had forgiven and forgotten her wrongs.

There Jo was mistaken; for next day she made a discovery which produced a tempest. Meg, Beth, and Amy were sitting together, late in the afternoon, when Jo burst into the room, looking excited, and demanding breathlessly, "Has any one taken my book?"

Meg and Beth said "No," at once, and looked surprised; Amy poked the fire, and said nothing. Jo saw her color rise, and was down upon her in a minute.

"Amy, you've got it!"

"No, I haven't."

"You know where it is, then!"

"No, I don't."

"That's a fib!" cried Jo, taking her by the shoulders, and looking fierce enough to frighten a much braver child than Amy.

"It isn't. I haven't got it, don't know where it is now, and don't care."

"You know something about it, and you'd better tell at once, or I'll make you," and Jo gave her a slight shake.

"Scold as much as you like, you'll never see your silly old book again," cried Amy, getting excited in her turn.

"Why not?"

"I burnt it up."

"What! My little book I was so fond of, and worked over and meant to finish before father got home? Have you really burnt it?" said Jo, turning very pale, while her eyes kindled and her hands clutched Amy nervously.

"Yes, I did! I told you I'd make you pay for being so cross yesterday, and I have, so—"

Amy got no farther, for Jo's hot temper mastered her, and she shook Amy till her teeth chattered in her head; crying, in a passion of grief and anger,—

"You wicked, wicked girl! I never can write it again, and I'll never forgive you as long as I live."

Meg flew to rescue Amy, and Beth to pacify Jo, but Jo was quite beside herself; and, with a parting box on her sister's ear, she rushed out of the room up to the old sofa in the garret, and finished her fight alone.

The storm cleared up below, for Mrs. March came home, and, having heard the story, soon brought Amy to a sense of the wrong she had done her sister. Jo's book was the pride of her heart, and was regarded by her family as a literary sprout of great promise. It was only half a dozen little fairy tales, but Jo had worked over them patiently, putting her whole heart into her work, hoping to make something good enough to print. She had just copied them with great care, and had destroyed the old manuscript, so that Amy's bonfire had consumed the loving work of several years. It seemed a small loss to others, but to Jo it was a dreadful calamity, and she felt that it never could be made up to her. Beth mourned as for a departed kitten, and Meg refused to defend her pet; Mrs. March looked grave and grieved, and Amy felt that no one would love her till she had asked pardon for the act which she now regretted more than any of them.

When the tea-bell rang, Jo appeared, looking so grim and unapproachable that it took all Amy's courage to say meekly,—

"Please forgive me Jo; I'm very, very sorry."

"I never shall forgive you," was Jo's stern answer; and from that moment, she ignored Amy entirely.

No one spoke of the great trouble,—not even Mrs. March,—for all had learned by experience that when Jo was in that mood words were wasted; and the wisest course was to wait till some little accident, or her own generous nature, softened Jo's resentment, and healed the breach. It was not a happy evening; for, though they sewed as usual, while their mother read aloud from Bremer, Scott, or Edgeworth, something was wanting, and the sweet home-peace was disturbed. They felt this most when singing-time came; for Beth could only play, Jo stood dumb as a stone, and Amy broke down, so Meg and mother sang alone. But, in spite of their efforts to be as cheery as larks, the flute-like voices did not seem to chord as well as usual, and all felt out of tune.

As Jo received her good-night kiss, Mrs. March whispered gently,—

"My dear, don't let the sun go down upon your anger; forgive each other, help each other, and begin again tomorrow."

Jo wanted to lay her head down on that motherly bosom, and cry her grief and anger all away; but tears were an unmanly weakness, and she felt so deeply injured that she really *couldn't* quite forgive yet. So she winked hard, shook her head, and said, gruffly because Amy was listening, —

"It was an abominable thing, and she don't deserve to be forgiven."

With that she marched off to bed, and there was no merry or confidential gossip that night.

Amy was much offended that her overtures of peace had been repulsed, and began to wish she had not humbled herself, to feel more injured than ever, and to plume herself on her superior virtue in a way which was particularly exasperating. Jo still looked like a thundercloud, and nothing went well all day. It was bitter cold in the morning; she dropped her precious turn-over in the gutter, Aunt March had an attack of fidgets, Meg was pensive, Beth *would* look grieved and wistful when she got home, and Amy kept making remarks about people who were always talking about being good, and yet wouldn't try, when other people set them a virtuous example.

"Everybody is so hateful, I'll ask Laurie to go skating. He is always kind and jolly, and will put me to rights, I know," said Jo to herself, and off she went.

Amy heard the clash of skates, and looked out with an impatient exclamation,—

"There! She promised I should go next time, for this is the last ice we shall have. But it's no use to ask such a cross-patch to take me."

"Don't say that; you *were* very naughty, and it *is* hard to forgive the loss of her precious little book; but I think she might do it now, and I guess she will, if you try her at the right minute," said Meg. "Go after them; don't say anything till Jo has got good-natured with Laurie, then take a quiet minute, and just kiss her, or do some kind thing, and I'm sure she'll be friends again, with all her heart."

"I'll try," said Amy, for the advice suited her; and, after a flurry to get ready, she ran after the friends, who were just disappearing over the hill.

It was not far to the river, but both were ready before Amy reached them. Jo saw her coming, and turned her back; Laurie did not see, for he was carefully skating along the shore, sounding the ice, for a warm spell had preceded the cold snap.

"I'll go on to the first bend, and see if it's all right, before we begin to race," Amy heard him say, as he shot away, looking like a young Russian, in his fur-trimmed coat and cap.

Jo heard Amy panting after her run, stamping her feet and blowing her fingers as she tried to put her skates on; but Jo never turned, and went slowly zigzagging down the river taking a bitter, unhappy sort of satisfaction in her sister's troubles. She had cherished her anger till it grew strong, and took possession of her, as evil thoughts and feelings always do, unless cast out at once. As Laurie turned the bend, he shouted back,—

"Keep near the shore; it isn't safe in the middle."

Jo heard, but Amy was just struggling to her feet, and did not catch a word. Jo glanced over her shoulder, and the little demon she was harboring said in her ear,—

"No matter whether she heard or not, let her take care of herself."

Laurie had vanished round the bend; Jo was just at the turn, and Amy, far behind, striking out toward the smoother ice in the middle of the river. For a minute Jo stood still, with a strange feeling at her heart; then she resolved to go on, but something held and turned her round, just in time to see Amy throw up her hands and go down, with the sudden crash of rotten ice, the splash of water, and a cry that made Jo's heart stand still with fear. She tried to call Laurie, but her voice was gone; she tried to rush forward, but her feet seemed to have no strength in them; and, for a second, she could only stand motionless, staring, with a terror-stricken face, at the little blue hood above the black water. Something rushed swiftly by her, and Laurie's voice cried out,—

"Bring a rail; quick, quick!"

How she did it, she never knew; but for the next few minutes she worked as if possessed, blindly obeying Laurie, who was quite self-possessed, and, lying flat, held Amy up by his arm and hockey till Jo dragged a rail from the fence, and together they got the child out, more frightened than hurt.

"Now then, we must walk her home as fast as we can; pile our things on her, while I get off these confounded skates," cried Laurie, wrapping his coat round Amy, and tugging away at the straps, which never seemed so intricate before.

Shivering, dripping, and crying, they got Amy home; and, after an exciting time of it, she fell asleep, rolled in blankets, before a hot fire.

During the bustle Jo had scarcely spoken; but flown about, looking pale and wild, with her things half off, her dress torn, and her hands cut and bruised by ice and rails, and refractory buckles. When Amy was comfortably asleep, the house quiet, and Mrs. March sitting by the bed, she called Jo to her, and began to bind up the hurt hands.

"Are you sure she is safe?" whispered Jo, looking remorsefully at the golden head, which might have been swept away from her sight forever under the treacherous ice.

"Quite safe, dear; she is not hurt, and won't even take cold, I think, you were so sensible in covering and getting her home quickly," replied her mother cheerfully.

"Laurie did it all; I only let her go. Mother, if she *should* die, it would be my fault"; and Jo dropped down beside the bed, in a passion of penitent tears, telling all that had happened, bitterly condemning her hardness of heart, and sobbing out her gratitude for being spared the heavy punishment which might have come upon her.

"It's my dreadful temper! I try to cure it; I think I have, and then it breaks out worse than ever. O mother, what shall I do? What shall I do?" cried poor Jo, in despair.

"Watch and pray, dear; never get tired of trying; and never think it is impossible to conquer your fault," said Mrs. March, drawing the blowzy head to her shoulder, and kissing the wet cheek so tenderly that Jo cried harder than ever.

"You don't know, you can't guess how bad it is! It seems as if I could do anything when I'm in a passion; I get so savage, I could hurt any one, and enjoy it. I'm afraid I *shall* do something dreadful some day, and spoil my life, and make everybody hate me. O mother, help me, do help me!"

"I will, my child, I will. Don't cry so bitterly, but remember this day, and resolve, with all your soul, that you will never know another like it. Jo, dear, we all have our temptations, some far greater than yours, and it often takes us all our lives to conquer them. You think your temper is the worst in the world; but mine used to be just like it."

"Yours, mother? Why, you are never angry!" and, for the moment Jo forgot remorse in surprise.

"I've been trying to cure it for forty years, and have only succeeded in controlling it. I am angry nearly every day of my life, Jo; but I have learned not to show it; and I still hope to learn not to feel it, though it may take me another forty years to do so."

The patience and the humility of the face she loved so well was a better lesson to Jo than the wisest lecture, the sharpest reproof. She felt comforted at once by the sympathy and confidence given her; the knowledge that her mother had a fault like hers, and tried to mend it, made her own easier to bear and strengthened her resolution to cure it; though forty years seemed rather a long time to watch and pray, to a girl of fifteen.

"Mother, are you angry when you fold your lips tight together, and go out of the room sometimes, when Aunt March scolds, or people worry you?" asked Jo, feeling nearer and dearer to her mother than ever before.

"Yes, I've learned to check the hasty words that rise to my lips; and when I feel that they mean to break out against my will, I just go away a minute, and give myself a little shake, for being so weak and wicked," answered Mrs. March, with a sigh and a smile, as she smoothed and fastened up Jo's dishevelled hair.

"How did you learn to keep still? That is what troubles me—for the sharp words fly out before I know what I'm about; and the more I say the worse I get, till it's a pleasure to hurt people's feelings, and say dreadful things. Tell me how you do it, Maramee dear."

"My good mother used to help me—"

"As you do us—" interrupted Jo, with a grateful kiss.

"But I lost her when I was a little older than you are, and for years had to struggle on alone, for I was too proud to confess my weakness to any one else. I had a hard time, Jo, and shed a good many bitter tears over my failures; for, in spite of my efforts, I never seemed to get on. Then your father came, and I was so happy that I found it easy to be good. But by and by, when I had four little daughters round me, and we were poor, then the old trouble began again; for I am not patient by nature, and it tried me very much to see my children wanting anything."

"Poor mother! What helped you then?"

"Your father, Jo. He never loses patience,—never doubts or complains,—but always hopes, and works and waits so cheerfully, that one is ashamed to do otherwise before him. He helped and comforted me, and showed me that I must try to practise all the virtues I would have my little girls possess, for I was their example. It was easier to try for your sakes than for my own; a startled or surprised look from one of you, when I spoke sharply, rebuked me more than any words could have done; and the love, respect, and confidence of my children was the sweetest reward I could receive for my efforts to be the woman I would have them copy."

"O mother, if I'm ever half as good as you, I shall be satisfied," cried Jo, much touched.

"I hope you will be a great deal better, dear; but you must keep watch over your 'bosom enemy,' as father calls it, or it may sadden, if not spoil your life. You have had a warning; remember it, and try with heart and soul to master this quick temper, before it brings you greater sorrow and regret than you have known today."

"I will try, mother; I truly will. But you must help me, remind me, and keep me from flying out. I used to see father sometimes put his finger on his lips, and look at you with a very kind, but sober face, and you always folded your lips tight or went away: was he reminding you then?" asked Jo softly.

"Yes; I asked him to help me so, and he never forgot it, but saved me from many a sharp word by that little gesture and kind look."

Jo saw that her mother's eyes filled and her lips trembled, as she spoke; and, fearing that she had said too much, she whispered anxiously, "Was it wrong to watch you, and to speak of it? I didn't mean to be rude, but it's so comfortable to say all I think to you, and feel so safe and happy here."

"My Jo, you may say anything to your mother, for it is my greatest happiness and pride to feel that my girls confide in me, and know how much I love them."

"I thought I'd grieved you."

"No, dear; but speaking of father reminded me how much I miss him, how much I owe him, and how faithfully I should watch and work to keep his little daughters safe and good for him."

"Yet you told him to go, mother, and didn't cry when he went, and never complain now, or seem as if you needed any help," said Jo, wondering.

"I gave my best to the country I love, and kept my tears till he was gone. Why should I complain, when we both have merely done our duty and will surely be the happier for it in the end? If I don't seem to need help, it is because I have a better friend, even than father, to comfort and sustain me. My child, the troubles and temptations of your life are beginning, and may be many; but you can overcome and outlive them all if you learn to feel the strength and tenderness of your Heavenly Father as you do that of your earthly one. The more you love and trust Him, the nearer you will feel to Him, and the less you will depend on human power and wisdom. His love and care never tire or change, can never be taken from you, but may become the source of life-long peace, happiness, and strength. Believe this heartily, and go to God with all your little cares, and hopes, and sins, and sorrows, as freely and confidingly as you come to your mother."

Jo's only answer was to hold her mother close, and, in the silence which followed, the sincerest prayer she had ever prayed left her heart without words; for in that sad, yet happy hour, she had learned not only the bitterness of remorse and despair, but the sweetness of self-denial and self-control; and, led by her mother's hand, she had drawn nearer to the Friend who welcomes every child with a love stronger than that of any father, tenderer than that of any mother.

Amy stirred, and sighed in her sleep; and, as if eager to begin at once to mend her fault, Jo looked up with an expression on her face which it had never worn before.

"I let the sun go down on my anger; I wouldn't forgive her, and today, if it hadn't been for Laurie, it might have been too late! How could I be so wicked?" said Jo, half aloud, as she leaned over her sister, softly stroking the wet hair scattered on the pillow.

As if she heard, Amy opened her eyes, and held out her arms, with a smile that went straight to Jo's heart. Neither said a word, but they hugged one another close, in spite of the blankets, and everything was forgiven and forgotten in one hearty kiss.

# CHAPTER IX

## MEG GOES TO VANITY FAIR

"I DO think it was the most fortunate thing in the world that those children should have the measles just now," said Meg, one April day, as she stood packing the "go abroady" trunk in her room, surrounded by her sisters.

"And so nice of Annie Moffat not to forget her promise. A whole fortnight of fun will be regularly splendid," replied Jo, looking like a windmill, as she folded skirts with her long arms.

"And such lovely weather; I'm so glad of that," added Beth, tidily sorting neck and hair ribbons in her best box, lent for the great occasion.

"I wish I was going to have a fine time, and wear all these nice things," said Amy, with her mouth full of pins, as she artistically replenished her sister's cushion.

"I wish you were all going; but, as you can't, I shall keep my adventures to tell you when I come back. I'm sure it's the least I can do, when you have been so kind, lending me things, and helping me get ready," said Meg, glancing round the room at the very simple outfit, which seemed nearly perfect in their eyes.

"What did mother give you out of the treasure-box?" asked Amy, who had not been present at the opening of a certain cedar chest, in which Mrs. March kept a few relics of past splendor, as gifts for her girls when the proper time came.

"A pair of silk stockings, that pretty carved fan, and a lovely blue sash. I wanted the violet silk; but there isn't time to make it over, so I must be contented with my old tarlatan."

"It will look nicely over my new muslin skirt, and the sash will set it off beautifully. I wish I hadn't smashed my coral bracelet, for you might have had it," said Jo, who loved to give and lend, but whose possessions were usually too dilapidated to be of much use.

Packing the go abroady trunk.

"There is a lovely old-fashioned pearl set in the treasure-box; but mother said real flowers were the prettiest ornament for a young girl, and Laurie promised to send me all I want," replied Meg. "Now, let me see; there's my new gray walking-suit—just curl up the feather in my hat, Beth,—then my poplin, for Sunday, and the small party,—it looks heavy for spring, doesn't it? The violet silk would be so nice; oh, dear!"

"Never mind; you've got the tarlatan for the big party, and you always look like an angel in white," said Amy, brooding over the little store of finery in which her soul delighted.

"It isn't low-necked, and it doesn't sweep enough, but it will have to do. My blue house-dress looks so well, turned and freshly trimmed, that I feel as if I'd got a new one. My silk sacque isn't a bit the fashion, and my bonnet doesn't look like Sallie's; I didn't like to say anything, but I was sadly disappointed in my umbrella. I told mother black, with a white handle, but she forgot, and bought a green one, with a yellowish handle. It's strong and neat, so I ought not to complain, but I know I shall feel ashamed of it beside Annie's silk one with a gold top," sighed Meg, surveying the little umbrella with great disfavor.

"Change it," advised Jo.

"I won't be so silly, or hurt Marmee's feelings, when she took so much pains to get my things. It's a nonsensical notion of mine, and I'm not going to give up to it. My silk stockings and two pairs of new gloves are my comfort. You are a dear, to lend me yours, Jo. I feel so rich, and sort of elegant, with two new pairs, and the old ones cleaned up for common;" and Meg took a refreshing peep at her glove-box.

"Annie Moffat has blue and pink bows on her nightcaps; would you put some on mine?" she asked, as Beth brought up a pile of snowy muslins, fresh from Hannah's hands.

"No, I wouldn't; for the smart caps won't match the plain gowns, without any trimming on them. Poor folks shouldn't rig," said Jo decidedly.

"I wonder if I shall *ever* be happy enough to have real lace on my clothes, and bows on my caps?" said Meg impatiently.

"You said the other day that you'd be perfectly happy if you could only go to Annie Moffat's," observed Beth, in her quiet way.

"So I did! Well, I *am* happy, and I *won't* fret; but it does seem as if the more one gets the more one wants, doesn't it? There, now, the trays are ready, and everything in but my ball-dress, which I shall leave for mother to pack," said Meg, cheering up, as she glanced from the half-filled trunk to the many-times pressed and mended white tarlatan, which she called her "ball-dress," with an important air.

The next day was fine, and Meg departed, in style, for a fortnight of novelty and pleasure. Mrs. March had consented to the visit rather reluctantly, fearing that Margaret would come back more discontented than she went. But she had begged so hard, and Sallie had promised to take good care of her, and a little pleasure seemed so delightful after a winter of irksome work, that the mother yielded, and the daughter went to take her first taste of fashionable life.

The Moffats *were* very fashionable, and simple Meg was rather daunted, at first, by the splendor of the house and the elegance of its occupants. But they were kindly people, in spite of the frivolous life they led, and soon put their guest at her ease. Perhaps Meg felt, without understanding why, that they were not particularly cultivated or intelligent people, and that all their gilding could not quite conceal the ordinary material of which they were made. It certainly was agreeable to fare sumptuously, drive in a fine carriage, wear her best frock every day, and do nothing but enjoy herself. It suited her exactly; and soon she began to imitate the manners and conversation of those about her; to put on little airs and graces, use French phrases, crimp her hair, take in her dresses, and talk about the fashions as well as she could. The more she saw of Annie Moffat's pretty things, the more she envied her, and sighed to be rich. Home now looked bare and dismal as she thought of it, work grew harder than ever, and she felt that she was a very destitute and much-injured girl, in spite of the new gloves and silk stockings.

She had not much time for repining, however, for the three young girls were busily employed in "having a good time." They shopped, walked, rode, and called all day; went to theatres and operas, or frolicked at home in the evening; for Annie had many friends, and knew how to entertain them. Her older sisters were very fine young ladies, and one was engaged, which was extremely interesting and romantic, Meg thought. Mr. Moffat was a fat, jolly old gentleman, who knew her father; and Mrs. Moffat, a fat, jolly old lady, who took as great a fancy to Meg as her daughter had done. Every one petted her; and "Daisy," as they called her, was in a fair way to have her head turned.

When the evening for the "small party" came, she found that the poplin wouldn't do at all, for the other girls were putting on thin dresses, and making themselves very fine indeed; so out came the tarlatan, looking older, limper, and shabbier than ever beside Sallie's crisp new one. Meg saw the girls glance at it and then at one another, and her cheeks began to burn, for, with all her gentleness, she was very proud. No one said a word about it, but Sallie offered to dress her hair, and Annie to tie her sash, and Belle, the engaged sister, praised her white arms; but in their kindness Meg saw only pity for her poverty, and her heart felt very heavy as she stood by herself, while the others laughed, chattered, and flew about like gauzy butterflies. The hard, bitter feeling was getting pretty bad, when the maid brought in a box of flowers. Before she could speak, Annie had the cover off and all were exclaiming at the lovely roses, heath, and fern within.

"It's for Belle, of course; George always sends her some, but these are altogether ravishing," cried Annie, with a great sniff.

"They are for Miss March, the man said. And here's a note," put in the maid, holding it to Meg.

"What fun! Who are they from? Didn't know you had a lover," cried the girls, fluttering about Meg in a high state of curiosity and surprise.

"The note is from mother, and the flowers from Laurie," said Meg simply, yet much gratified that he had not forgotten her.

"Oh, indeed!" said Annie, with a funny look, as Meg slipped the note into her pocket, as a sort of talisman against envy, vanity, and false pride; for the few loving words had done her good, and the flowers cheered her up by their beauty.

Feeling almost happy again, she laid by a few ferns and roses for herself, and quickly made up the rest in dainty bouquets for the breasts, hair, or skirts of her friends, offering them so prettily that Clara, the elder sister, told her she was "the sweetest little thing she ever saw;" and they looked quite charmed with her small attention. Somehow the kind act finished her despondency; and when all the rest went to show themselves to Mrs. Moffat, she saw a happy, bright-eyed face in the mirror, as she laid her ferns against her rippling hair, and fastened the roses in the dress that didn't strike her as so *very* shabby now.

She enjoyed herself very much that evening, for she danced to her heart's content; every one was very kind, and she had three compliments. Annie made her sing, and someone said she had a remarkably fine voice; Major Lincoln asked who "the fresh little girl, with the beautiful eyes," was; and Mr. Moffat insisted on dancing with her, because she "didn't dawdle, but had some spring in her," as he gracefully expressed it. So, altogether, she had a very nice time, till she overheard a bit of a conversation, which disturbed her extremely. She was sitting just inside the conservatory, waiting for her partner to bring her an ice, when she heard a voice ask, on the other side of the flowery wall,—

"How old is he?"

"Sixteen or seventeen, I should say," replied another voice.

"It would be a grand thing for one of those girls, wouldn't it? Sallie says they are very intimate now, and the old man quite dotes on them."

"Mrs. M. has made her plans, I dare say, and will play her cards well, early as it is. The girl evidently doesn't think of it yet," said Mrs. Moffat.

"She told that fib about her mamma, as if she did know, and colored up when the flowers came, quite prettily. Poor thing! She'd be so nice if she was only got up in style. Do you think she'd be offended if we offered to lend her a dress for Thursday?" asked another voice.

"She's proud, but I don't believe she'd mind, for that dowdy tarlatan is all she has got. She may tear it tonight, and that will be a good excuse for offering a decent one."

"We'll see. I shall ask young Laurence, as a compliment to her, and we'll have fun about it afterward."

Here Meg's partner appeared, to find her looking much flushed and rather agitated. She *was* proud, and her pride was useful just then, for it helped her hide her mortification, anger, and disgust at what she had just heard; for, innocent and unsuspicious as she was, she could not help understanding the gossip of her friends. She tried to forget it, but could not, and kept repeating to herself, "Mrs. M. has made her plans," "that fib about her mamma," and "dowdy tarlatan," till she was ready to cry, and rush home to tell her troubles and ask for advice. As that was impossible, she did her best to seem gay; and, being rather excited, she succeeded so well that no one dreamed what an effort she was making. She was very glad when it was all over, and she was quiet in her bed, where she could think and wonder and fume till her head ached and her hot cheeks were cooled by a few natural tears. Those foolish, yet well-meant words, had opened a new world to Meg, and much disturbed the peace of the old one, in which, till now, she had lived as happily as a child. Her innocent friendship with Laurie was spoilt by the silly speeches she had overheard; her faith in her mother was a little shaken by the worldly plans attributed to her by Mrs. Moffat, who judged others by herself; and the sensible resolution to be contented with the simple wardrobe which suited a poor man's daughter, was weakened by the unnecessary pity of girls who thought a shabby dress one of the greatest calamities under heaven.

Poor Meg had a restless night, and got up heavy-eyed, unhappy, half resentful toward her friends, and half ashamed of herself for not speaking out frankly, and setting everything right. Everybody dawdled that morning, and it was noon before the girls found energy enough even to take up their worsted work. Something in the manner of her friends struck Meg at once; they treated her with more respect, she thought; took quite a tender interest in what she said, and looked at her with eyes that plainly betrayed curiosity. All this surprised and flattered her, though she did not understand it till Miss Belle looked up from her writing, and said, with a sentimental air,—

"Daisy, dear, I've sent an invitation to your friend, Mr. Laurence, for Thursday. We should like to know him, and it's only a proper compliment to you."

Meg colored, but a mischievous fancy to tease the girls made her reply demurely,—

"You are very kind, but I'm afraid he won't come."

"Why not, *chérie?*" asked Miss Belle.

"He's too old."

"My child, what do you mean? What is his age, I beg to know!" cried Miss Clara.

"Nearly seventy, I believe," answered Meg, counting stitches, to hide the merriment in her eyes.

"You sly creature! Of course we meant the young man," exclaimed Miss Belle, laughing.

"There isn't any; Laurie is only a little boy," and Meg laughed also at the queer look which the sisters exchanged as she thus described her supposed lover.

"About your age," Nan said.

"Nearer my sister Jo's; I am seventeen in August," returned Meg, tossing her head.

"It's very nice of him to send you flowers, isn't it?" said Annie, looking wise about nothing.

"Yes, he often does, to all of us; for their house is full, and we are so fond of them. My mother and old Mr. Laurence are friends, you know, so it is quite natural that we children should play together;" and Meg hoped they would say no more.

"It's evident Daisy isn't out yet," said Miss Clara to Belle, with a nod.

"Quite a pastoral state of innocence all round," returned Miss Belle, with a shrug.

"I'm going out to get some little matters for my girls; can I do anything for you, young ladies?" asked Mrs. Moffat, lumbering in, like an elephant, in silk and lace.

"No, thank you, ma'am," replied Sallie. "I've got my new pink silk for Thursday, and don't want a thing."

"Nor I,—" began Meg, but stopped, because it occurred to her that she did want several things, and could not have them.

"What shall you wear?" asked Sallie.

"My old white one again if I can mend it fit to be seen; it got sadly torn last night," said Meg, trying to speak quite easily but feeling very uncomfortable.

"Why don't you send home for another?" said Sallie, who was not an observing young lady.

"I haven't got any other." It cost Meg an effort to say that but Sallie did not see it, and exclaimed, in amiable surprise,—

"Only that? How funny—" She did not finish her speech, for Belle shook her head at her, and broke in, saying kindly,—

"Not at all; where is the use of having a lot of dresses when she isn't out? There's no need of sending home, Daisy, even if you had a dozen, for I've got a sweet blue silk laid away, which I've outgrown, and you shall wear it, to please me, won't you, dear?"

"You are very kind, but I don't mind my old dress, if you don't; it does well enough for a little girl like me," said Meg.

"Now do let me please myself by dressing you up in style. I admire to do it, and you'd be a regular little beauty, with a touch here and there. I sha'n't let any one see you till you are done, and then we'll burst upon them like Cinderella and her godmother, going to the ball," said Belle, in her persuasive tone.

Meg couldn't refuse the offer so kindly made, for a desire to see if she would be "a little beauty" after touching up, caused her to accept, and forget all her former uncomfortable feelings towards the Moffats.

On the Thursday evening, Belle shut herself up with her maid; and, between then, they turned Meg into a fine lady. They crimped and curled her hair, they polished her neck and arms with some fragrant powder, touched her lips with coralline salve, to make them redder, and Hortense would have added "a *soupçon* of rouge," if Meg had not rebelled. They laced her into a sky-blue dress, which was so tight she could hardly breathe, and so low in the neck that modest Meg blushed at herself in the mirror. A set of silver filagree was added, bracelets, necklace, brooch, and even ear-rings, for Hortense tied them on, with a bit of pink silk, which did not show. A cluster of tea-rosebuds at the bosom, and a *ruche*, reconciled Meg to the display of her pretty white shoulders, and a pair of high-heeled blue silk boots satisfied the last wish of her heart. A laced handkerchief, a plumy fan, and a bouquet in a silver holder finished her off; and Miss Belle surveyed her with the satisfaction of a little girl with a newly dressed doll.

"Mademoiselle is charmante, très jolie, is she not?" cried Hortense, clasping her hands in an affected rapture.

"Come and show yourself," said Miss Belle, leading the way to the room where the others were waiting.

As Meg went rustling after, with her long skirts trailing, her ear-rings tinkling, her curls waving, and her heart beating, she felt as if her "fun" had really begun at last, for the mirror had plainly told her that she *was* "a little beauty." Her friends repeated the pleasing phrase enthusiastically;

and, for several minutes, she stood, like the jackdaw in the fable, enjoying her borrowed plumes, while the rest chattered like a party of magpies.

"While I dress, do you drill her, Nan, in the management of her skirt, and those French heels, or she will trip herself up. Take your silver butterfiy, and catch up that long curl on the left side of her head, Clara, and don't any of you disturb the charming work of my hands," said Belle, as she hurried away, looking well pleased with her success.

"I'm afraid to go down, I feel so queer and stiff and half-dressed," said Meg to Sallie, as the bell rang, and Mrs. Moffat sent to ask the young ladies to appear at once.

"You don't look a bit like yourself, but you are very nice. I'm nowhere beside you, for Belle has heaps of taste, and you're quite French, I assure you. Let your flowers hang; don't be so careful of them, and be sure you don't trip," returned Sallie, trying not to care that Meg was prettier than herself.

Keeping that warning carefully in mind, Margaret got safely down stairs, and sailed into the drawing-rooms, where the Moffats and a few early guests were assembled. She very soon discovered that there is a charm about fine clothes which attracts a certain class of people, and secures their respect. Several young ladies, who had taken no notice of her before, were very affectionate all of a sudden; several young gentlemen, who had only stared at her at the other party, now not only stared, but asked to be introduced, and said all manner of foolish but agreeable things to her; and several old ladies, who sat on sofas, and criticised the rest of the party, inquired who she was, with an air of interest. She heard Mrs. Moffat reply to one of them,—

"Daisy March—father a colonel in the army—one of our first families, but reverses of fortune, you know; intimate friends of the Laurences; sweet creature, I assure you; my Ned is quite wild about her."

"Dear me!" said the old lady, putting up her glass for another observation of Meg, who tried to look as if she had not heard, and been rather shocked at Mrs. Moffat's fibs.

The "queer feeling" did not pass away, but she imagined herself acting the new part of fine lady, and so got on pretty well, though the tight dress gave her a side-ache, the train kept getting under her feet, and she was in constant fear lest her ear-rings should fly off and get lost or broken. She was flirting her fan, and laughing at the feeble jokes of a young gentleman who tried to be witty, when she suddenly stopped laughing, and looked confused; for, just opposite, she saw Laurie. He was staring at her with undisguised surprise, and disapproval also, she thought; for, though he bowed and smiled, yet something in his honest eyes made her blush, and wish she had her old dress on. To complete her confusion, she saw Belle nudge Annie, and both glance from her to Laurie, who, she was happy to see, looked unusually boyish and shy.

"Silly creatures, to put such thoughts into my head! I won't care for it, or let it change me a bit," thought Meg, and rustled across the room to shake hands with her friend.

"I'm glad you came, I was afraid you wouldn't," she said, with her most grown-up air.

"Jo wanted me to come, and tell her how you looked, so I did;" answered

Laurie, without turning his eyes upon her, though he half smiled at her maternal tone.

"What shall you tell her?" asked Meg, full of curiosity to know his opinion of her, yet feeling ill at ease with him, for the first time.

"I shall say I didn't know you; for you look so grown-up, and unlike yourself, I'm quite afraid of you," he said, fumbling at his glove-button.

"How absurd of you! The girls dressed me up for fun, and I rather like it. Wouldn't Jo stare if she saw me?" said Meg, bent on making him say whether he thought her improved or not.

"Yes, I think she would," returned Laurie gravely.

"Don't you like me so?" asked Meg.

"No, I don't," was the blunt reply.

"Why not?" in an anxious tone.

He glanced at her frizzled head, bare shoulders, and fantastically trimmed dress, with an expression that abashed her more than his answer, which had not a particle of his usual politeness about it.

"I don't like fuss and feathers."

That was altogether too much from a lad younger than herself; and Meg walked away, saying petulantly,—

"You are the rudest boy I ever saw."

Feeling very much ruffled, she went and stood at a quiet window, to cool her cheeks, for the tight dress gave her an uncomfortably brilliant color. As she stood there, Major Lincoln passed by; and, a minute after, she heard him saying to his mother,—

"They are making a fool of that little girl; I wanted you to see her, but they have spoilt her entirely; she's nothing but a doll, tonight."

"Oh, dear!" sighed Meg; "I wish I'd been sensible, and worn my own things; then I should not have disgusted other people, or felt so uncomfortable and ashamed myself."

She leaned her forehead on the cool pane, and stood half hidden by the curtains, never minding that her favorite waltz had begun, till some one touched her; and, turning, she saw Laurie, looking penitent, as he said, with his very best bow, and his hand out,—

"Please forgive my rudeness, and come and dance with me."

"I'm afraid it will be too disagreeable to you," said Meg, trying to look offended, and failing entirely.

"Not a bit of it; I'm dying to do it. Come, I'll be good; I don't like your gown, but I do think you are—just splendid;" and he waved his hands, as if words failed to express his admiration.

Meg smiled and relented, and whispered, as they stood waiting to catch the time,—

"Take care my skirt don't trip you up; it's the plague of my life, and I was a goose to wear it."

"Pin it round your neck, and then it will be useful," said Laurie, looking down at the little blue boots, which he evidently approved of.

Away they went, fleetly and gracefully; for, having practised at home, they were well matched, and the blithe young couple were a pleasant sight to see, as they twirled merrily round and round, feeling more friendly than ever after their small tiff.

"Laurie, I want you to do me a favor; will you?" said Meg, as he stood

Asked to be introduced.

fanning her, when her breath gave out, which it did very soon, though she would not own why.

"Won't I!" said Laurie, with alacrity.

"Please don't tell them at home about my dress tonight. They won't understand the joke, and it will worry mother."

"Then why did you do it?" said Laurie's eyes, so plainly that Meg hastily added,—

"I shall tell them, myself, all about it, and 'fess' to mother how silly I've been. But I'd rather do it myself; so you'll not tell, will you?"

"I give you my word I won't; only what shall I say when they ask me?"

"Just say I looked pretty well, and was having a good time."

"I'll say the first, with all my heart; but how about the other? You don't look as if you were having a good time; are you?" and Laurie looked at her with an expression which made her answer, in a whisper,— "No; not just now. Don't think I'm horrid; I only wanted a little fun, but this sort doesn't pay, I find, and I'm getting tired of it."

"Here comes Ned Moffat; what does he want?" said Laurie, knitting his black brows, as if he did not regard his young host in the light of a pleasant addition to the party.

"He put his name down for three dances, and I suppose he's coming for them. What a bore!" said Meg, assuming a languid air, which amused Laurie immensely.

He did not speak to her again till supper-time, when he saw her drinking champagne with Ned and his friend Fisher, who were behaving "like a pair of fools," as Laurie said to himself, for he felt a brotherly sort of right to watch over the Marches, and fight their battles whenever a defender was needed.

"You'll have a splitting headache tomorrow, if you drink much of that. I wouldn't, Meg; your mother doesn't like it, you know," he whispered, leaning over her chair, as Ned turned to refill her glass, and Fisher stooped to pick up her fan.

"I'm not Meg, tonight; I'm 'a doll,' who does all sorts of crazy things. Tomorrow I shall put away my 'fuss and feathers,' and be desperately good again," she answered, with an affected little laugh.

"Wish tomorrow was here, then," muttered Laurie, walking off ill-pleased at the change he saw in her.

Meg danced and flirted, chattered and giggled, as the other girls did; after supper she undertook the German, and blundered through it, nearly upsetting her partner with her long skirt, and romping in a way that scandalized Laurie, who looked on and meditated a lecture. But he got no chance to deliver it, for Meg kept away from him till he came to say good-night.

"Remember!" she said, trying to smile, for the splitting headache had already begun.

"Silence à la mort,' replied Laurie, with a melodramatic flourish, as he went away.

This little bit of by-play excited Annie's curiosity; but Meg was too tired for gossip, and went to bed, feeling as if she had been to a masquerade, and hadn't enjoyed herself as much as she expected. She was sick all the next day, and on Saturday went home, quite used up with her fortnight's fun, and feeling that she had "sat in the lap of luxury" long enough.

"It does seem pleasant to be quiet, and not have company manners on all the time. Home is a nice place, though it isn't splendid," said Meg, looking about her with a restful expression, as she sat with her mother and Jo on the Sunday evening.

"I'm glad to hear you say so, dear, for I was afraid home would seem dull and poor to you, after your fine quarters," replied her mother, who had given her many anxious looks that day; for motherly eyes are quick to see any change in children's faces.

Meg had told her adventures gayly, and said over and over what a charming time she had had; but something still seemed to weigh upon her spirits, and, when the younger girls were gone to bed, she sat thoughtfully staring at the fire, saying little, and looking worried. As the clock struck nine, and Jo proposed bed, Meg suddenly left her chair, and, taking Beth's stool, leaned her elbows on her mother's knee, saying bravely,—

"Marmee, I want to ' 'fess.' "

"I thought so; what is it, dear?"

"Shall I go away?" asked Jo discreetly.

"Of course not; don't I always tell you everything? I was ashamed to speak of it before the children, but I want you to know all the dreadful things I did at the Moffats'."

"We are prepared," said Mrs. March, smiling, but looking a little anxious.

"I told you they dressed me up, but I didn't tell you that they powdered and squeezed and frizzled, and made me look like a fashion-plate. Laurie thought I wasn't proper; I know he did, though he didn't say so, and one man called me 'a doll.' I knew it was silly, but they flattered me, and said I was a beauty, and quantities of nonsense, so I let them make a fool of me."

"Is that all?" asked Jo, as Mrs. March looked silently at the downcast face of her pretty daughter, and could not find it in her heart to blame her little follies.

"No; I drank champagne and romped and tried to flirt, and was altogether abominable," said Meg self-reproachfully.

"There is something more, I think;" and Mrs. March smoothed the soft cheek, which suddenly grew rosy, as Meg answered slowly,—

"Yes; it's very silly, but I want to tell it, because I hate to have people say and think such things about us and Laurie."

Then she told the various bits of gossip she had heard at the Moffats'; and, as she spoke, Jo saw her mother fold her lips tightly, as if ill pleased that such ideas should be put into Meg's innocent mind.

"Well, if that isn't the greatest rubbish I ever heard," cried Jo indignantly. "Why didn't you pop out and tell them so, on the spot?"

"I couldn't, it was so embarrassing for me. I couldn't help hearing, at first, and then I was so angry and ashamed, I didn't remember that I ought to go away."

"Just wait till I see Annie Moffat, and I'll show you how to settle such ridiculous stuff. The idea of having 'plans,' and being kind to Laurie, because he's rich, and may marry us by and by! Won't he shout, when

I tell him what those silly things say about us poor children?" and Jo laughed, as if, on second thoughts, the thing struck her as a good joke.

"If you tell Laurie, I'll never forgive you! She mustn't, must she, mother?" said Meg, looking distressed.

"No; never repeat that foolish gossip, and forget it as soon as you can," said Mrs. March gravely. "I was very unwise to let you go among people of whom I know so little,—kind, I dare say, but worldly, ill-bred, and full of these vulgar ideas about young people. I am more sorry than I can express for the mischief this visit may have done you, Meg."

"Don't be sorry, I won't let it hurt me; I'll forget all the bad, and remember only the good; for I did enjoy a great deal, and thank you very much for letting me go. I'll not be sentimental or dissatisfied, mother; I know I'm a silly little girl, and I'll stay with you till I'm fit to take care of myself. But it *is* nice to be praised and admired, and I can't help saying I like it," said Meg, looking half ashamed of the confession.

"That is perfectly natural, and quite harmless, if the liking does not become a passion, and lead one to do foolish or unmaidenly things. Learn to know and value the praise which is worth having, and to excite the admiration of excellent people by being modest as well as pretty, Meg."

Margaret sat thinking a moment, while Jo stood with her hands behind her, looking both interested and a little perplexed; for it was a new thing to see Meg blushing and talking about admiration, lovers, and things of that sort; and Jo felt as if, during that fortnight, her sister had grown up amazingly, and was drifting away from her into a world where she could not follow.

"Mother, do you have 'plans,' as Mrs. Moffat said?" asked Meg bashfully.

"Yes, my dear, I have a great many; all mothers do, but mine differ somewhat from Mrs. Moffat's, I suspect. I will tell you some of them, for the time has come when a word may set this romantic little head and heart of yours right, on a very serious subject. You are young, Meg, but not too young to understand me; and mothers' lips are the fittest to speak of such things to girls like you. Jo, your turn will come in time, perhaps, so listen to my 'plans,' and help me carry them out, if they are good."

Jo went and sat on one arm of the chair, looking as if she thought they were about to join in some very solemn affair. Holding a hand of each, and watching the two young faces wistfully, Mrs. March said, in her serious yet cheery way,—

"I want my daughters to be beautiful, accomplished, and good; to be admired, loved, and respected; to have a happy youth, to be well and wisely married, and to lead useful, pleasant lives, with as little care and sorrow to try them as God sees fit to send. To be loved and chosen by a good man is the best and sweetest thing which can happen to a woman; and I sincerely hope my girls may know this beautiful experience. It is natural to think of it, Meg; right to hope and wait for it, and wise to prepare for it; so that, when the happy time comes, you may feel ready for the duties and worthy of the joy. My dear girls, I *am* ambitious for you, but not to have you make a dash in the world,—marry rich men merely because they are rich, or have splendid houses, which are not homes because love is wanting. Money is a needful and precious thing,— and, when well used, a noble thing,—but I never want you to think it is the first or only prize to strive for. I'd rather see you poor men's wives, if you were happy, beloved, contented, than queens on thrones, without self-respect and peace."

"Poor girls don't stand any chance, Belle says, unless they put themselves forward," sighed Meg.

"Then we'll be old maids," said Jo stoutly.

"Right, Jo; better be happy old maids than unhappy wives, or unmaidenly girls, running about to find husbands," said Mrs. March decidedly. "Don't be troubled, Meg; poverty seldom daunts a sincere lover. Some of the best and most honored women I know were poor girls, but so love-worthy that they were not allowed to be old maids. Leave these things to time; make this home happy, so that you may be fit for homes of your own, if they are offered you, and contented here if they are not. One thing remember, my girls: mother is always ready to be your confidant, father to be your friend; and both of us trust and hope that our daughters, whether married or single, will be the pride and comfort of our lives."

"We will, Marmee, we will!" cried both, with all their hearts, as she bade them good-night.

# CHAPTER X

## THE P. C. AND P. O.

As spring came on, a new set of amusements became the fashion, and the lengthening days gave long afternoons for work and play of all sorts. The garden had to be put in order, and each sister had a quarter of the little plot to do what she liked with. Hannah used to say, "I'd know which each of them gardings belonged to, ef I see'em in Chiny;" and so she might, for the girls' tastes differed as much as their characters. Meg's had roses and heliotrope, myrtle, and a little orange-tree in it. Jo's bed was never alike two seasons, for she was always trying experiments; this year it was to be a plantation of sun-flowers, the seeds of which cheerful and aspiring plant were to feed "Aunt Cockle-top" and her family of chicks. Beth had old-fashioned, fragrant flowers in her garden,—sweet peas and mignonette, larkspur, pinks, pansies, and southernwood, with chickweed for the bird, and catnip for the pussies. Amy had a bower in hers,—rather small and earwiggy, but very pretty to look at,—with honeysuckles and morning-glories hanging their colored horns and bells in graceful wreaths all over it; tall, white lilies, delicate ferns, and as many brilliant, picturesque plants as would consent to blossom there.

Gardening, walks, rows on the river, and flower-hunts employed the fine days; and for rainy ones, they had house diversions,—some old, some new,—all more or less original. One of these was the "P. C."; for, as secret societies were the fashion, it was thought proper to have one; and, as all of the girls admired Dickens, they called themselves the Pickwick

Club. With a few interruptions, they had kept this up for a year, and met every Saturday evening in the big garret, on which occasions the ceremonies were as follows: Three chairs were arranged in a row before a table, on which was a lamp, also four white badges, with a big "P. C." in different colors on each, and the weekly newspaper, called "The Pickwick Portfolio," to which all contributed something; while Jo, who revelled in pens and ink, was the editor. At seven o'clock, the four members ascended to the club-room, tied their badges round their heads, and took their seats with great solemnity. Meg, as the eldest, was Samuel Pickwick; Jo, being of a literary turn, Augustus Snodgrass; Beth, because she was round and rosy, Tracy Tupman; and Amy, who was always trying to do what she couldn't, was Nathaniel Winkle. Pickwick, the president, read the paper, which was filled with original tales, poetry, local news, funny advertisements, and hints, in which they goodnaturedly reminded each other of their faults and short-comings. On one occasion, Mr. Pickwick put on a pair of spectacles without any glasses, rapped upon the table, hemmed, and, having stared hard at Mr. Snodgrass, who was tilting back in his chair, till he arranged himself properly, began to read:—

# "The Pickwick Portfolio."

## MAY 20, 18—

### ANNIVERSARY ODE.

Again we meet to celebrate
  With badge and solemn rite,
Our fifty-second anniversary,
  In Pickwick Hall, to-night.

We all are here in perfect health,
  None gone from our small band;
Again we see each well-known face,
  And press each friendly hand.

Our Pickwick, always at his post,
  With reverence we greet,
As, spectacles on nose, he reads
  Our well-filled weekly sheet.

Although he suffers from a cold,
  We joy to hear him speak,
For words of wisdom from him fall,
  In spite of croak or squeak.

Old six-foot Snodgrass looms on high,
  With elephantine grace,
And beams upon the company,
  With brown and jovial face.

Poetic fire lights up his eye,
  He struggles 'gainst his lot.
Behold ambition on his brow,
  And on his nose a blot!

Next our peaceful Tupman comes,
  So rosy, plump, and sweet,
Who chokes with laughter at the puns,
  And tumbles off his seat.

Prim little Winkle too is here,
  With every hair in place,
A model of propriety,
  Though he hates to wash his face.

The year is gone, we still unite
  To joke and laugh and read,
And tread the path of literature
  That doth to glory lead.

Long may our paper prosper well,
  Our club unbroken be,
And coming years their blessings pour
  On the useful, gay " P. C."
                          A. SNODGRASS.

---◆---

### THE MASKED MARRIAGE.

#### A TALE OF VENICE.

---

Gondola after gondola swept up to the marble steps, and left its lovely load to swell the brilliant throng that filled the stately halls of Count de Adelon. Knights and ladies, elves and pages, monks and flower-girls, all mingled gayly in the dance. Sweet voices and rich melody filled the air; and so with mirth and music the masquerade went on.

"Has your Highness seen the Lady Viola to-night?" asked a gallant troubadour of the fairy queen who floated down the hall upon his arm.

"Yes; is she not lovely, though so sad! Her dress is well chosen, too, for in a week she weds Count Antonio, whom she passionately hates."

"By my faith, I envy him. Yonder he comes, arrayed like a bridegroom, except the black mask. When that is off we shall see how he regards the fair maid whose heart he cannot win, though her stern father bestows her hand," returned the troubadour.

"'T is whispered that she loves the young English artist who haunts her steps, and is spurned by the old count," said the lady, as they joined the dance.

The revel was at its height when a priest appeared, and, withdrawing the young pair to an alcove hung with purple velvet, he motioned them to kneel. Instant silence fell upon the gay throng; and not a sound, but the dash of fountains or the rustle of orange-groves sleeping in the moonlight, broke the hush, as Count de Adelon spoke thus : —

"My lords and ladies, pardon the ruse by which I have gathered you here to witness the marriage of my daughter. Father, we wait your services."

All eyes turned toward the bridal party, and a low murmur of amazement went through the throng, for neither bride nor groom removed their masks. Curiosity and wonder possessed all hearts, but respect restrained all tongues till the holy rite was over. Then the eager spectators gathered round the count, demanding an explanation.

"Gladly would I give it if I could; but I only know that it was the whim of my timid Viola, and I yielded to it. Now, my children, let the play end. Unmask, and receive my blessing."

But neither bent the knee; for the young bridegroom replied, in a tone that startled all listeners, as the mask fell, disclosing the noble face of Ferdinand Devereux, the artist lover; and, leaning on the breast where now flashed the star of an English earl, was the lovely Viola, radiant with joy and beauty.

"My lord, you scornfully bade me claim your daughter when I could boast as high a name and vast a fortune as the Count Antonio. I can do more; for even your ambitious soul cannot refuse the Earl of Devereux and De Vere, when he gives his ancient name and boundless wealth in return for the beloved hand of this fair lady, now my wife."

The count stood like one changed to stone; and, turning to the bewildered crowd, Ferdinand added, with a gay smile of triumph, "To you, my gallant friends, I can only wish that your wooing may prosper as mine has done; and that you may all win as fair a bride as I have, by this masked marriage."

S. PICKWICK.

❖

Why is the P. C. like the Tower of Babel? It is full of unruly members.

❖

## THE HISTORY OF A SQUASH.

Once upon a time a farmer planted a little seed in his garden, and after a while it sprouted and became a vine, and bore many squashes. One day in October, when they were ripe, he picked one and took it to market. A grocer-man bought and put it in his shop. That same morning, a little girl, in a brown hat and blue dress, with a round face and snub nose, went and bought it for her mother. She lugged it home, cut it up, and boiled it in the big pot; mashed some of it, with salt and butter, for dinner; and to the rest she added a pint of milk, two eggs, four spoons of sugar, nutmeg, and some crackers; put it in a deep dish, and baked it till it was brown and nice; and next day it was eaten by a family named March.

T. TUPMAN.

———◆———

MR. PICKWICK, *Sir:* —

I address you upon the subject of sin the sinner I mean is a man named Winkle who makes trouble in his club by laughing and sometimes won't write his piece in this fine paper I hope you will pardon his badness and let him send a French fable because he can't write out of his head as he has so many lessons to do and no brains in future I will try to take time by the fetlock and prepare some work which will be all *commy la fo* that means all right I am in haste as it is nearly school time

Yours respectably,      N. WINKLE.

[The above is a manly and handsome acknowledgment of past misdemeanors. If our young friend studied punctuation, it would be well.]

———◆———

## A SAD ACCIDENT.

On Friday last, we were startled by a violent shock in our basement, followed by cries of distress. On rushing, in a body, to the cellar, we discovered our beloved President prostrate upon the floor, having tripped and fallen while getting wood for domestic purposes. A perfect scene of ruin met our eyes; for in his fall Mr. Pickwick had plunged his head and shoulders into a tub of water, upset a keg of soft soap upon his manly form, and torn his garments badly. On being removed from this perilous situation, it was discovered that he had suffered no injury but several bruises; and, we are happy to add, is now doing well.

ED.

## THE PUBLIC BEREAVEMENT.

It is our painful duty to record the sudden and mysterious disappearance of our cherished friend, Mrs. Snowball Pat Paw. This lovely and beloved cat was the pet of a large circle of warm and admiring friends; for her beauty attracted all eyes, her graces and virtues endeared her to all hearts, and her loss is deeply felt by the whole community.

When last seen, she was sitting at the gate, watching the butcher's cart; and it is feared that some villain, tempted by her charms, basely stole her. Weeks have passed, but no trace of her has been discovered; and we relinquish all hope, tie a black ribbon to her basket, set aside her dish, and weep for her as one lost to us forever.

———◆———

A sympathizing friend sends the following gem: —

## A LAMENT

### FOR S. B. PAT PAW.

We mourn the loss of our little pet,
  And sigh o'er her hapless fate,
For never more by the fire she 'll sit,
  Nor play by the old green gate.

The little grave where her infant sleeps,
  Is 'neath the chestnut tree;
But o'er *her* grave we may not weep,
  We know not where it may be.

Her empty bed, her idle ball,
  Will never see her more;
No gentle tap, no loving purr
  Is heard at the parlor-door.

Another cat comes after her mice,
  A cat with a dirty face;
But she does not hunt as our darling did,
  Nor play with her airy grace.

Her stealthy paws tread the very hall
  Where Snowball used to play,
But she only spits at the dogs our pet
  So gallantly drove away.

She is useful and mild, and does her best,
  But she is not fair to see;
And we cannot give her your place, dear,
  Nor worship her as we worship thee.
                                    A. S.

## ADVERTISEMENTS.

Miss Oranthy Bluggage, the accomplished Strong-Minded Lecturer, will deliver her famous Lecture on "Woman and Her Position," at Pickwick Hall, next Saturday Evening, after the usual performances.

A Weekly Meeting will be held at Kitchen Place, to teach young ladies how to cook. Hannah Brown will preside; and all are invited to attend.

The Dustpan Society will meet on Wednesday next, and parade in the upper story of the Club House. All members to appear in uniform and shoulder their brooms at nine precisely.

Mrs. Beth Bouncer will open her new assortment of Doll's Millinery next week. The latest Paris Fashions have arrived, and orders are respectfully solicited.

A New Play will appear at the Barnville Theatre, in the course of a few weeks, which will surpass anything ever seen on the American stage. "The Greek Slave, or Constantine the Avenger," is the name of this thrilling drama!!!

### HINTS.

If S. P. didn't use so much soap on his hands, he wouldn't always be late at breakfast. A. S. is requested not to whistle in the street. T. T. please don't forget Amy's napkin. N. W. must not fret because his dress has not nine tucks.

### WEEKLY REPORT.

Meg — Good.
Jo — Bad.
Beth — Very good.
Amy — Middling.

As the President finished reading the paper (which I beg leave to assure my readers is a *bona fide* copy of one written by *bona fide* girls once upon a time), a round of applause followed, and then Mr. Snodgrass rose to make a proposition.

"Mr. President and gentlemen," he began, assuming a parliamentary attitude and tone, "I wish to propose the admission of a new member,—one who highly deserves the honor, would be deeply grateful for it, and would add immensely to the spirit of the club, the literary value of the paper, and be no end jolly and nice. I propose Mr. Theodore Laurence as an honorary member of the P. C. Come now, do have him."

Jo's sudden change of tone made the girls laugh; but all looked rather anxious, and no one said a word, as Snodgrass took his seat.

"We'll put it to vote," said the President. "All in favor of this motion please to manifest it by saying 'Ay.'"

A loud response from Snodgrass, followed, to everybody's surprise, by a timid one from Beth.

"Contrary minded say 'No.'"

Meg and Amy were contrary minded; and Mr. Winkle rose to say, with great elegance, "We don't wish any boys; they only joke and bounce about. This is a ladies' club, and we wish to be private and proper."

"I'm afraid he'll laugh at our paper, and make fun of us afterward," observed Pickwick, pulling the little curl on her forehead, as she always did when doubtful.

Up rose Snodgrass, very much in earnest. "Sir, I give you my word as a gentleman, Laurie won't do anything of the sort. He likes to write, and he'll give a tone to our contributions, and keep us from being sentimental, don't you see? We can do so little for him, and he does so much for us, I think the least we can do is to offer him a place here, and make him welcome if he comes."

This artful allusion to benefits conferred brought Tupman to his feet, looking as if he had quite made up his mind.

"Yes, we ought to do it, even if we *are* afraid. I say he *may* come and his grandpa, too, if he likes."

This spirited burst from Beth electrified the club, and Jo left her seat to shake hands approvingly. "Now then, vote again. Everybody remember it's our Laurie, and say 'Ay!'" cried Snodgrass excitedly.

"Ay! Ay! Ay!" replied three voices at once.

"Good! Bless you. Now, as there's nothing like 'taking time by the *fetlock*,' as Winkle characteristically observes, allow me to present the new member;" and, to the dismay of the rest of the club, Jo threw open the door of the closet, and displayed Laurie sitting on a rag-bag, flushed and twinkling with suppressed laughter.

"You rogue! You traitor! Jo, how could you?" cried the three girls, as Snodgrass led her friend triumphantly forth; and, producing both a chair and a badge, installed him in a jiffy.

"The coolness of you two rascals is amazing," began Mr. Pickwick, trying to get up an awful frown, and only succeeding in producing an amiable smile. But the new member was equal to the occasion; and, rising, with a grateful salutation to the Chair, said, in the most engaging manner, "Mr. President and ladies,—I beg pardon, gentlemen,—allow me to introduce myself as Sam Weller, the very humble servant of the club."

"Good! good!" cried Jo, pounding with the handle of the old warming-pan on which she leaned.

"My faithful friend and noble patron," continued Laurie, with a wave of the hand, "who has so flatteringly presented me, is not to be blamed for the base stratagem of tonight. I planned it, and she only gave in after lots of teasing."

"Come now, don't lay it all on yourself; you know I proposed the cupboard," broke in Snodgrass, who was enjoying the joke amazingly.

"Never you mind what she says. I'm the wretch that did it, sir," said the new member, with a Welleresque nod to Mr. Pickwick. "But on my honor, I never will do so again, and henceforth *dewote* myself to the interest of this immortal club.

"Hear! Hear!" cried Jo, clashing the lid of the warming-pan like a cymbal.

"Go on, go on!" added Winkle and Tupman, while the President bowed benignly.

"I merely wish to say, that as a slight token of my gratitude for the honor done me, and as a means of promoting friendly relations between adjoining nations, I have set up a post-office in the hedge in the lower corner of the garden; a fine, spacious building, with padlocks on the doors, and every convenience for the mails,—also the females, if I may be allowed the expression. It's the old martin-house; but I've stopped up the door, and made the roof open, so it will hold all sorts of things, and save our valuable time. Letters, manuscripts, books, and bundles can be passed in there; and, as each nation has a key, it will be uncommonly nice, I fancy. Allow me to present the club key; and, with many thanks for your favor, take my seat."

Great applause as Mr. Weller deposited a little key on the table, and subsided; the warming-pan clashed and waved wildly, and it was some time before order could be restored. A long discussion followed, and every one came out surprising, for every one did her best; so it was an unusually lively meeting, and did not adjourn till a late hour, when it broke up with three shrill cheers for the new member. No one ever regretted the admittance of Sam Weller, for a more devoted, well-behaved, and jovial member no club could have. He certainly did add "spirit" to the meetings, and "a tone" to the paper; for his orations convulsed his hearers, and his contributions were excellent, being patriotic, classical, comical, or dramatic, but never sentimental. Jo regarded them as worthy of Bacon, Milton, or Shakespeare; and remodelled her own works with good effect, she thought.

The P. O. was a capital little institution, and flourished wonderfully, for nearly as many queer things passed through it as through the real office. Tragedies and cravats, poetry and pickles, garden-seeds and long letters, music and gingerbread, rubbers, invitations, scoldings and puppies. The old gentleman liked the fun, and amused himself by sending odd bundles, mysterious messages, and funny telegrams; and his gardener, who was smitten with Hannah's charms, actually sent a love-letter to Jo's care. How they laughed when the secret came out, never dreaming how many love-letters that little post-office would hold in the years to come!

# CHAPTER XI

## EXPERIMENTS

"THE first of June! The Kings are off to the sea-shore tomorrow, and I'm free. Three months' vacation,—how I shall enjoy it!" exclaimed Meg, coming home one warm day to find Jo laid upon the sofa in an unusual state of exhaustion, while Beth took of her dusty boots, and Amy made lemonade for the refreshnment of the whole party.

"Aunt March went today, for which, oh, be joyful!" said Jo. "I was mortally afraid she'd ask me to go with her; if she had, I should have felt as if I ought to do it; but Plumfield is about as gay as a churchyard, you know, and I'd rather be excused. We had a flurry getting the old lady off, and I had a fright every time she spoke to me, for I was in such a hurry to be through that I was uncommonly helpful and sweet, and feared she'd find it impossible to part from me. I quaked till she was fairly in the carriage, and had a final fright, for, as it drove off, she popped out her head, saying, 'Josyphine, won't you—?' I didn't hear any more, for I basely turned aud fled; I did actually run, and whisked round the corner, where I felt safe."

"Poor old Jo! She came in looking as if bears were after her," said Beth, as she cuddled her sister's feet with a motherly air.

"Aunt March is a regular samphire, is she not?" observed Amy, tasting her mixture critically.

"She means *vampire*, not sea-weed; but it doesn't matter; it's too warm to be particular about one's parts of speech," murmured Jo.

"What shall you do all your vacation?" asked Amy, changing the subject, with tact.

"I shall lie abed late, and do nothing," replied Meg, from the depths of the rocking-chair. "I've been routed up early all winter, and had to spend my days working for other people; so now I'm going to rest and revel to my heart's content."

"No," said Jo; "that dozy way wouldn't suit me. I've laid in a heap of books, and I'm going to improve my shining hours reading on my perch in the old appletree, when I'm not having l—"

"Don't say 'larks!' " implored Amy, as a return snub for the "samphire" correction.

"I'll say 'nightingales,' then, with Laurie; that's proper and appropriate, since he's a warbler."

"Don't let us do any lessons, Beth, for a while, but play all the time, and rest, as the girls mean to," proposed Amy.

"Well, I will, if mother doesn't mind. I want to learn some new songs, and my children need fitting up for the summer; they are dreadfully out of order, and really suffering for clothes."

"May we, mother?" asked Meg, turning to Mrs. March, who sat sewing, in what they called "Marmee's corner."

"You may try your experiment for a week, and see how you like it. I think by Saturday night you will find that all play and no work is as bad as all work and no play."

"Oh, dear, no! it will be delicious, I'm sure," said Meg complacently.

"I now propose a toast, as my 'friend and pardner, Sairy Gamp,' says. Fun forever, and no grubbing!" cried Jo, rising, glass in hand, as the lemonade went round.

They all drank it merrily, and began the experment by lounging for the rest of the day. Next morning, Meg did not appear till ten o'clock; her solitary breakfast did not taste nice, and the room seemed lonely and untidy; for Jo had not filled the vases, Beth had not dusted, and Amy's books lay scattered about. Nothing was neat and pleasant but "Marmee's corner," which looked as usual; and there Meg sat, to "rest and read," which meant yawn, and imagine what pretty summer dresses she would get with her salary. Jo spent the morning on the river, with Laurie, and the afternoon reading and crying over "The Wide, Wide World," up in the apple-tree. Beth began by rummaging everything out of the big closet, where her family resided, but, getting tired before half done, she left her establishment topsy-turvy, and went to her music, rejoicing that she had no dishes to wash. Amy arranged her bower, put on her best white frock, smoothed her curls, and sat down to draw, under the honeysuckles, hoping some one would see and inquire who the young artist was. As no one appeared but an inquisitive daddy-long-legs, who examined her work with interest, she went to walk, got caught in a shower, and came home dripping.

At tea-time they compared notes, and all agreed that it had been a delightful, though unusually long day. Meg, who went shopping in the afternoon, and got a "sweet blue muslin," had discovered, after she had cut the breadths off, that it wouldn't wash, which mishap made her slightly cross. Jo had burnt the skin off her nose boating, and got a raging headache by reading too long. Beth was worried by the confusion of her closet, and the difficulty of learning three or four songs at once; and Amy deeply regretted the damage done her frock, for Katy Brown's party was to be the next day; and now, like Flora McFlimsey, she had "nothing to wear." But these were mere trifles; and they assured their mother that the experiment was working finely. She smiled, said nothing, and, with Hannah's help, did their neglected work, keeping home pleasant, and the domestic machinery running smoothly. It was astonishing what a peculiar and uncomfortable state of things was produced by the "resting and revelling" process. The days kept getting longer and longer, the weather was unusually variable, and so were tempers; an unsettled feeling possessed everyone, and Satan found plenty of mischief for the idle hands to do. As the height of luxury, Meg put out some of her sewing and then found time hang so heavily that she fell to snipping and spoiling her clothes, in her attempts to furbish them up à la Moffat. Jo read till her eyes gave out, and she was sick of books; got so fidgety that even good-natured Laurie had a quarrel with her, and so reduced in spirits that she desperately wished she had gone with Aunt March. Beth got on pretty well, for she was constantly forgetting that it was to be *all play, and no work*, and fell back into her old ways now and then; but something in the air affected her, and more than once, her tranquillity was much disturbed; so much so, that on one occasion, she actually shook poor dear Joanna, and told her she was "a fright." Amy fared worst of all, for her resources were small; and when her sisters left her to amuse and care for herself, she soon found that accomplished and important little self a great burden. She didn't like dolls, fairy-tales were childish, and one couldn't draw all the time; tea-parties didn't amount to much, neither did picnics, unless very well conducted. "If one could have a fine house, full of nice girls, or go travelling, the summer would be delightful, but to stay at home with three selfish sisters and a grown-up boy was enough to try the patience of a Boaz," complained Miss Malaprop, after several days devoted to pleasure, fretting, and *ennui*.

No one would own that they were tired of the experiment; but, by Friday night, each acknowledged to herself that she was glad the week was nearly done. Hoping to impress the lesson more deeply, Mrs. March, who had a good deal of humor, resolved to finish off the trial in an appropriate manner, so she gave Hannah a holiday, and let the girls enjoy the full effect of the play system.

When they got up on Saturday morning, there was no fire in the kitchen, no breakfast in the dining-room, and no mother anywhere to be seen.

"Mercy on us! what *has* happened?" cried Jo, staring about her in dismay.

Meg ran upstairs, and soon came back again, looking relieved, but rather bewildered, and a little ashamed.

"Mother isn't sick, only very tired, and she says she is going to stay quietly in her room all day, and let us do the best we can. It's a very queer thing for her to do, she doesn't act a bit like herself, but she says it has been a hard week for her, so we mustn't grumble, but take care of ourselves."

"That's easy enough, and I like the idea; I'm aching for something to do—that is, some new amusement, you know," added Jo quickly.

In fact it *was* an immense relief to them all to have a little work, and they took hold with a will, but soon realized the truth of Hannah's saying, "Housekeeping ain't no joke." There was plenty of food in the larder, and, while Beth and Amy set the table, Meg and Jo got breakfast, wondering, as they did so, why servants ever talked about hard work.

"I shall take some up to mother, though she said we were not to think of her, for she'd take care of herself," said Meg, who presided, and felt quite matronly behind the teapot.

So a tray was fitted out before anyone began, and taken up, with the cook's compliments. The boiled tea was very bitter, the omelette scorched, and the biscuits speckled with saleratus; but Mrs. March received her repast with thanks, and laughed heartily over it after Jo was gone.

"Poor little souls, they will have a hard time, I'm afraid; but they won't suffer, and it will do them good," she said, producing the more palatable viands with which she had provided herself, and disposing of the bad breakfast, so that their feelings might not be hurt,—a motherly little deception, for which they were grateful.

Many were the complaints below, and great the chagrin of the head cook at her failures. "Never mind, I'll get the dinner, and be servant; you be mistress, keep your hands nice, see company, and give orders," said Jo, who knew still less than Meg about culinary affairs.

This obliging offer was gladly accepted; and Margaret retired to the parlor, which she hastily put in order by whisking the litter under the sofa, and shutting the blinds, to save the trouble of dusting. Jo, with perfect faith in her own powers, and a friendly desire to make up the quarrel, immediately put a note in the office, inviting Laurie to dinner.

"You'd better see what you have got before you think of having company," said Meg, when informed of the hospitable but rash act.

"Oh, there's corned beef and plenty of potatoes; and I shall get some asparagus, and a lobster, 'for a relish,' as Hannah says. We'll have lettuce, and make a salad. I don't know how, but the book tells. I'll have blanc-mange and strawberries for dessert; and coffee, too, if you want to be elegant."

"Don't try too many messes, Jo, for you can't make anything but gingerbread and molasses candy, fit to eat. I wash my hands of the dinner-party; and, since you have asked Laurie on your own responsibility, you may just take care of him."

"I don't want you to do anything but be civil to him, and help to the pudding. You'll give me your advice if I get in a muddle, won't you?" asked Jo, rather hurt.

"Yes; but I don't know much, except about bread, and a few trifles. You had better ask mother's leave before you order anything," returned Meg prudently.

"Of course I shall; I'm not a fool," and Jo went off in a huff at the doubts expressed of her powers.

"Get what you like, and don't disturb me; I'm going out to dinner, and can't worry about things at home," said Mrs. March, when Jo spoke to her. "I never enjoyed housekeeping, and I'm going to take a vacation today, and read, write, go visiting, and amuse myself."

The unusual spectacle of her busy mother rocking comfortably, and reading, early in the morning, made Jo feel as if some natural phenomenon had occurred; for an eclipse, an earthquake, or a volcanic eruption would hardly have seemed stranger.

"Everything is out of sorts, somehow," she said to herself, going down stairs. "There's Beth crying; that's a sure sign that something is wrong with this family. If Amy is bothering, I'll shake her."

Feeling very much out of sorts herself, Jo hurried into the parlor to find Beth sobbing over Pip, the canary, who lay dead in the cage, with his little claws pathetically extended, as if imploring the food for want of which he had died.

"It's all my fault—I forgot him—there isn't a seed or a drop left. O Pip! O Pip! how could I be so cruel to you?" cried Beth, taking the poor thing in her hands, and trying to restore him.

Jo peeped into his half-open eye, felt his little heart, and finding him stiff and cold, shook her head, and offered her domino-box for a coffin.

"Put him in the oven, and maybe he will get warm and revive," said Amy hopefully.

"He's been starved, and he sha'n't be baked, now he's dead. I'll make him a shroud, and he shall be buried in the garden; and I'll never have another bird, never, my Pip! For I am too bad to own one," murmured Beth, sitting on the floor with her pet folded in her hands.

"The funeral shall be this afternoon, and we will all go. Now, don't cry, Bethy; it's a pity, but nothing goes right this week, and Pip has had the worst of the experiment. Make the shroud, and lay him in my box; and, after the dinner-party, we'll have a nice little funeral," said Jo, beginning to feel as if she had undertaken a good deal.

Leaving the others to console Beth, she departed to the kitchen, which was in a most discouraging state of confusion. Putting on a big apron, she fell to work, and got the dishes piled up ready for washing, when she discovered that the fire was out.

"Here's a sweet prospect!" muttered Jo, slamming the stove-door open, and poking vigorously among the cinders.

Having rekindled the fire, she thought she would go to market while the water heated. The walk revived her spirits; and, flattering herself that she had made good bargains, she trudged home again, after buying a very young lobster, some very old asparagus, and two boxes of acid strawberries. By the time she got cleared up, the dinner arrived, and the stove was red-hot. Hannah had left a pan of bread to rise, Meg had worked it up early, set it on the hearth for a second rising, and forgotten it. Meg was entertaining Sallie Gardiner in the parlor, when the door flew open, and a floury, crocky, flushed, and dishevelled figure appeared, demanding tartly,—

"I say, isn't bread 'riz' enough when it runs over the pans?"

Sallie began to laugh; but Meg nodded, and lifted her eyebrows as high as they would go, which caused the apparition to vanish, and put the sour bread into the oven without further delay. Mrs. March went out, after peeping here and there to see how matters went, also saying a word of comfort to Beth, who sat making a winding-sheet, while the dear departed lay in state in the domino-box. A strange sense of help-lessness fell upon the girls as the gray bonnet vanished round the corner; and despair seized them, when, a few minutes later, Miss Crocker appeared, and said she'd come to dinner. Now, this lady was a thin, yellow spinster, with a sharp nose and inquisitive eyes, who saw everything, and gossiped about all she saw. They disliked her, but had been taught to be kind to her, simply because she was old and poor, and had few friends. So Meg gave her the easy-chair, and tried to entertain her, while she asked questions, criticised everything, and told stories of the people whom she knew.

Language cannot describe the anxieties, experiences, and exertions which Jo underwent that morning; and the dinner she served up became a standing joke. Fearing to ask any more advice, she did her best alone, and discovered that something more than energy and good-will is necessary to make a cook. She boiled the asparagus for an hour, and was grieved to find the heads cooked off and the stalks harder than ever. The bread burnt black; for the salad-dressing so aggravated her, that she let everything else go till she had convinced herself that she could not make it fit to eat. The lobster was a scarlet mystery to her, but she hammered and poked, till it was unshelled, and its meagre proportions concealed in a grove of lettuce-leaves. The potatoes had to be hurried, not to keep the asparagus waiting, and were not done at last. The blanc-mange was lumpy, and the strawberries not as ripe as they looked, having been skillfully "deaconed."

"Well, they can eat beef, and bread and butter, if they are hungry; only it's mortifying to have to spend your whole morning for nothing," thought Jo, as she rang the bell half an hour later than usual, and stood, hot, tired, and dispirited, surveying the feast spread for Laurie, accustomed to all sorts of elegance, and Miss Crocker, whose curious eyes would mark all failures, and whose tattling tongue would report them far and wide.

Poor Jo would gladly have gone under the table, as one thing after another was tasted and left; while Amy giggled, Meg looked distressed, Miss Crocker pursed up her lips, and Laurie talked and laughed with all his might, to give a cheerful tone to the festive scene. Jo's one strong point was the fruit, for she had sugared it well, and had a pitcher of rich cream to eat with it. Her hot cheeks cooled a trifle, and she drew a long breath, as the pretty glass plates went round, and every one looked graciously at the little rosy islands floating in a sea of cream. Miss Crocker tasted first, made a wry face, and drank some water hastily. Jo, who had refused, thinking there might not be enough, for they dwindled sadly after the picking over, glanced at Laurie, but he was eating away manfully, though there was a slight pucker about his mouth, and he kept his eye fixed on his plate. Amy, who was fond of delicate fare, took a heaping spoonful, choked, hid her face in her napkin, and left the table precipitately.

"Oh, what is it?" exclaimed Jo, trembling.

"Salt instead of sugar, and the cream is sour," replied Meg, with a tragic gesture.

Jo uttered a groan, and fell back in her chair; remembering that she had given a last hasty powdering to the berries out of one of the two boxes on the kitchen table, and had neglected to put the milk in the refrigerator. She turned scarlet, and was on the verge of crying, when she met Laurie's eyes, which *would* look merry in spite of his heroic efforts; the comical side of the affair suddenly struck her, and she laughed till the tears ran down her cheeks. So did every one else, even "Croaker," as the girls called the old lady; and the unfortunate dinner ended gayly, with bread and butter, olives and fun.

"I haven't strength of mind enough to clear up now, so we will sober ourselves with a funeral," said Jo, as they rose; and Miss Crocker made ready to go, being eager to tell the new story at another friend's dinner-table.

They did sober themselves, for Beth's sake; Laurie dug a grave under the ferns in the grove, little Pip was laid in, with many tears, by his tender-hearted mistress, and covered with moss, while a wreath of violets and chickweed was hung on the stone which bore his epitaph, composed by Jo, while she struggled with the dinner:—

> "Here lies Pip March,
> Who died the 7th of June;
> Loved and lamented sore,
> And not forgotten soon."

At the conclusion of the ceremonies, Beth retired to her room, overcome with emotion and lobster; but there was no place of repose, for the beds were not made, and she found her grief much assuaged by beating up pillows and putting things in order. Meg helped Jo clear away the remains of the feast, which took half the afternoon, and left them so tired that they agreed to be contented with tea and toast for supper. Laurie took Amy to drive, which was a deed of charity, for the sour cream seemed to have had a bad effect upon her temper. Mrs. March came home to find the three older girls hard at work in the middle of the afternoon; and a glance at the closet gave her an idea of the success of one part of the experiment.

Before the housewives could rest, several people called, and there was a scramble to get ready to see them; then tea must be got, errands done; and one or two necessary bits of sewing neglected till the last minute. As twilight fell, dewy and still, one by one they gathered in the porch where the June roses were budding beautifully, and each groaned or sighed as she sat down, as if tired or troubled.

"What a dreadful day this has been!" begun Jo, usually the first to speak.

"It has seemed shorter than usual, but so uncomfortable," said Meg.

"Not a bit like home," added Amy.

"It can't seem so without Marmee and little Pip," sighed Beth, glancing, with full eyes, at the empty cage above her head.

"Here's mother, dear, and you shall have another bird tomorrow, if you want it."

As she spoke, Mrs. March came and took her place among them, looking as if her holiday had not been much pleasanter than theirs.

"Are you satisfied with your experiment, girls, or do you want another week of it?" she asked, as Beth nestled up to her, and the rest turned toward her with brightening faces, as flowers turn toward the sun.

"I don't!" cried Jo decidedly.

"Nor I," echoed the others.

"You think, then, that it is better to have a few duties, and live a little for others, do you?"

"Lounging and larking doesn't pay," observed Jo, shaking her head. "I'm tired of it, and mean to go to work at something right off."

"Suppose you learn plain cooking; that's a useful accomplishment, which no woman should be without," said Mrs. March, laughing inaudibly at the recollection of Jo's dinner-party; for she had met Miss Crocker, and heard her account of it.

"Mother, did you go away and let everything be, just to see how we'd get on?" cried Meg, who had had suspicions all day.

"Yes; I wanted you to see how the comfort of all depends on each doing her share faithfully. While Hannah and I did your work, you got on pretty well, though I don't think you were very happy or amiable; so I thought, as a little lesson, I would show you what happens when every one thinks only of herself. Don't you feel that it is pleasanter to help one another, to have daily duties which make leisure sweet when it comes, and to bear and forbear, that home may be comfortable and lovely to us all?"

"We do, mother, we do!" cried the girls.

"Then let me advise you to take up your little burdens again; for though they seem heavy sometimes, they are good for us, and lighten as we learn to carry them. Work is wholesome, and there is plenty for every one; it keeps us from *ennui* and mischief, is good for health and spirits, and gives us a sense of power and independence better than money or fashion."

"We'll work like bees, and love it too; see if we don't!" said Jo. "I'll learn plain cooking for my holiday task; and the next dinner-party I have shall be a success."

"I'll make the set of shirts for father, instead of letting you do it, Marmee. I can and I will, though I'm not fond of sewing; that will be better than fussing over my own things, which are plenty nice enough as they are," said Meg.

"I'll do my lessons every day, and not spend so much time with my music and dolls. I am a stupid thing, and ought to be studying, not playing," was Beth's resolution; while Amy followed their example by heroically declaring, "I shall learn to make buttonholes, and attend to my parts of speech."

"Very good! Then I am quite satisfied with the experiment, and fancy that we shall not have to repeat it; only don't go to the other extreme, and delve like slaves. Have regular hours for work and play; make each day both useful and pleasant, and prove that you understand the worth of time by employing it well. Then youth will be delightful, old age will bring few regrets, and life become a beautiful success, in spite of poverty."

"We'll remember, mother!" and they did.

# CHAPTER XII

## CAMP LAURENCE

BETH was post-mistress, for, being most at home, she could attend to it regularly, and dearly liked the daily task of unlocking the little door and distributing the mail. One July day she came in with her hands full, and went about the house leaving letters and parcels, like the penny post.

"Here's your posy, mother! Laurie never forgets that," she said, putting the fresh nosegay in the vase that stood in "Marmee's corner," and was kept supplied by the affectionate boy.

"Miss Meg March, one letter and a glove," continued Beth, delivering the articles to her sister, who sat near her mother, stitching wristbands.

"Why, I left a pair over there, and here is only one," said Meg, looking at the gray cotton glove.

"Didn't you drop the other in the garden?"

"No, I'm sure I didn't; for there was only one in the office."

"I hate to have odd gloves! Never mind, the other may be found. My letter is only a translation of the German song I wanted; I think Mr. Brooke did it, for this isn't Laurie's writing."

Mrs. March glanced at Meg, who was looking very pretty in her gingham morning-gown, with the little curls blowing about her forehead, and very womanly, as she sat sewing at her little work-table, full of tidy white rolls; so unconscious of the thought in her mother's mind as she sewed and sang, while her fingers flew, and her thoughts were busied with girlish fancies as innocent and fresh as the pansies in her belt, that Mrs. March smiled, and was satisfied.

"Two letters for Doctor Jo, a book, and a funny old hat, which covered the whole post-office, stuck outside," said Beth, laughing, as she went into the study, where Jo sat writing.

"What a sly fellow Laurie is! I said I wished bigger hats were the fashion, because I burn my face every hot day. He said, 'Why mind the fashion? Wear a big hat, and be comfortable!' I said I would if I had one, and he has sent me this, to try me. I'll wear it, for fun, and show him I *don't* care for the fashion;" and, hanging the antique broad-brim on a bust of Plato, Jo read her letters.

One from her mother made her cheeks glow and her eyes fill, for it said to her,—

> "MY DEAR:
> "I write a little word to tell you with how much satisfaction I watch your efforts to control your temper. You say nothing about your trials, failures, or successes, and think, perhaps, that no one sees them but the Friend whose help you daily ask, if I may trust the well-worn cover of your guide-book. *I*, too, have seen them all, and heartily believe in the sincerity of your resolution, since it begins to

bear fruit. Go on, dear, patiently and bravely, and always believe that no one sympathizes more tenderly with you than your loving

"MOTHER."

"That does me good! That's worth millions of money and pecks of praise. O Marmee, I do try! I will keep on trying, and not get tired, since I have you to help me."

Laying her head on her arms, Jo wet her little romance with a few happy tears, for she *had* thought that no one saw and appreciated her efforts to be good; and this assurance was doubly precious, doubly encouraging, because unexpected, and from the person whose commendation she most valued. Feeling stronger than ever to meet and subdue her Apollyon, she pinned the note inside her frock, as a shield and a reminder, lest she be taken unaware, and proceeded to open her other letter, quite ready for either good or bad news. In a big, dashing hand, Laurie wrote,—

"DEAR JO,
What ho!

Some English girls and boys are coming to see me tomorrow and I want to have a jolly time. If it's fine, I'm going to pitch my tent in Longmeadow, and row up the whole crew to lunch and croquet,— have a fire, make messes, gypsy fashion, and all sorts of larks. They are nice people, and like such things. Brooke will go, to keep us boys steady, and Kate Vaughn will play propriety for the girls. I want you all to come; can't let Beth off, at any price, and nobody shall worry her. Don't bother about rations,—I'll see to that, and everything else,—only do come, there's a good fellow!

"In a tearing hurry,
Yours ever, LAURIE."

"Here's richness!" cried Jo, flying in to tell the news to Meg.

"Of course we can go, mother? It will be such a help to Laurie, for I can row, and Meg see to the lunch, and the children be useful in some way."

"I hope the Vaughns are not fine, grown-up people. Do you know anything about them, Jo?" asked Meg.

"Only that there are four of them. Kate is older than you, Fred and Frank (twins) about my age, and a little girl (Grace), who is nine or ten. Laurie knew them abroad, and liked the boys; I fancied, from the way he primmed up his mouth in speaking of her, that he didn't admire Kate much."

"I'm so glad my French print is clean; it's just the thing, and so becoming!" observed Meg complacently. "Have you anything decent, Jo?"

"Scarlet and gray boating suit, good enough for me. I shall row and tramp about, so I don't want any starch to think of. You'll come, Betty?"

"If you won't let any of the boys talk to me."

"Not a boy!"

"I like to please Laurie; and I'm not afraid of Mr. Brooke, he is so kind; but I don't want to play, or sing, or say anything. I'll work hard, and not trouble anyone; and you'll take care of me, Jo, so I'll go."

"That's my good girl; you do try to fight off your shyness, and I love you for it. Fighting faults isn't easy, as I know; and a cheery word kind of gives a lift. Thank you, mother," and Jo gave the thin cheek a grateful kiss, more precious to Mrs. March than if it had given back the rosy roundness of her youth.

"I had a box of chocolate drops, and the picture I wanted to copy," said Amy, showing her mail.

"And I got a note from Mr. Laurence, asking me to come over and play to him tonight, before the lamps are lighted, and I shall go," added Beth, whose friendship with the old gentleman prospered finely.

"Now let's fly round, and do double duty today, so that we can play tomorrow with free minds," said Jo, preparing to replace her pen with a broom.

When the sun peeped into the girls' room early next morning, to promise them a fine day, he saw a comical sight. Each had made such preparation for the fête as seemed necessary and proper. Meg had an extra row of little curl-papers across her forehead, Jo had copiously anointed her afflicted face with cold cream, Beth had taken Joanna to bed with her to atone for the approaching separation, and Amy had capped the climax by putting a clothes-pin on her nose, to uplift the offending feature. It was one of the kind artists use to hold the paper on their drawing-boards, therefore quite appropriate and effective for the purpose to which it was now put. This funny spectacle appeared to amuse the sun, for he burst out with such radiance that Jo woke up, and roused all her sisters by a hearty laugh at Amy's ornament.

Sunshine and laughter were good omens for a pleasure party, and soon a lively bustle began in both houses. Beth, who was ready first, kept reporting what went on next door, and enlivened her sisters' toilets by frequent telegrams from the window.

"There goes the man with the tent! I see Mrs. Barker doing up the lunch in a hamper and a great basket. Now Mr. Laurence is looking up at the sky, and the weathercock; I wish he would go, too. There's Laurie, looking like a sailor,—nice boy . Oh, mercy me! Here's a carriage full of people—a tall lady, a little girl, and two dreadful boys. One is lame; poor thing, he's got a crutch. Laurie didn't tell us that. Be quick, girls! It's getting late. Why, there is Ned Moffat, I do declare. Look, Meg, isn't that the man who bowed to you one day, when we were shopping?"

"So it is. How queer that he should come. I thought he was at the Mountains. There is Sallie; I'm glad she got back in time. Am I all right, Jo?" cried Meg, in a flutter.

"A regular daisy. Hold up your dress and put your hat straight; it looks sentimental tipped that way, and will fly off at the first puff. Now, then, come on!"

"O Jo, you are not going to wear that awful hat? It's too absurd! You shall *not* make a guy of yourself," remonstrated Meg, as Jo tied down, with a red ribbon, the broad-brimmed, old-fashioned Leghorn Laurie had sent for a joke.

"I just will, though, for it's capital,—so shady, light, and big. It will

make fun; and I don't mind being a guy if I'm comfortable." With that
Jo marched straight away, and the rest followed,—a bright little band
of sisters, all looking their best, in summer suits, with happy faces under
the jaunty hat-brims.

Laurie ran to meet, and present them to his friends, in the most cordial
manner. The lawn was the/reception room, and for several minutes a
lively scene was enacted there. Meg was grateful to see that Miss Kate,
though twenty, was dressed with a simplicity which American girls would
do well to imitate; and she was much flattered by Mr. Ned's assurances
that he came especially to see her. Jo understood why Laurie "primmed
up his mouth" when speaking of Kate, for that young lady had a stand-
off-don't-touch-me air, which contrasted strongly with the free and easy
demeanor of the other girls. Beth took an observation of the new boys,
and decided that the lame one was not "dreadful," but gentle and feeble,
and she would be kind to him on that account. Amy found Grace a well-
mannered, merry little person; and after staring dumbly at one another
for a few minutes, they suddenly became very good friends.

Tents, lunch, and croquet utensils having been sent on beforehand,
the party was soon embarked, and the two boats pushed off together,
leaving Mr. Laurence waving his hat on the shore. Laurie and Jo rowed
one boat; Mr. Brooke and Ned the other; while Fred Vaughn, the riotous
twin, did his best to upset both by paddling about in a wherry like a
disturbed water-bug. Jo's funny hat deserved a vote of thanks, for it was
of general utility; it broke the ice in the beginning, by producing a laugh;
it created quite a refreshing breeze, flapping to and fro, as she rowed,
and would make an excellent umbrella for the whole party, if a shower
came up, she said. Kate looked rather amazed at Jo's proceedings, especially

as she exclaimed "Christopher Columbus!" when she lost her oar; and Laurie said, "My dear fellow, did I hurt you?" when he tripped over her feet in taking his place. But after putting up her glass to examine the queer girl several times, Miss Kate decided that she was "odd, but rather clever," and smiled upon her from afar.

Meg, in the other boat, was delightfully situated, face to face with the rowers, who both admired the prospect, and feathered their oars with uncommon "skill and dexterity." Mr. Brooke was a grave, silent young man, with handsome brown eyes and a pleasant voice. Meg liked his quiet manners, and considered him a walking encyclopedia of useful knowledge. He never talked to her much; but he looked at her a good deal, and she felt sure that he did not regard her with aversion. Ned, being in college, of course put on all the airs which Freshmen think it their bounden duty to assume; he was not very wise, but very good-natured, and altogether an excellent person to carry on a picnic. Sallie Gardiner was absorbed in keeping her white piqué dress clean, and chattering with the ubiquitous Fred, who kept Beth in constant terror by his pranks.

It was not far to Longmeadow; but the tent was pitched and the wickets down by the time they arrived. A pleasant green field, with three wide-spreading oaks in the middle, and a smooth strip of turf for croquet.

"Welcome to Camp Laurence!" said the young host, as they landed, with exclamations of delight.

"Brooke is commander-in-chief; I am commissary-general; the other fellows are staff-officers; and you, ladies, are company. The tent is for your especial benefit, and that oak is your drawing-room; this is the mess-room, and the third is the camp-kitchen. Now, let's have a game before it gets hot, and then we'll see about dinner."

Frank, Beth, Amy, and Grace sat down to watch the game played by the other eight. Mr. Brooke chose Meg, Kate, and Fred; Laurie took Sallie, Jo, and Ned. The Englishers played well; but the Americans played better, and contested every inch of the ground as strongly as if the spirit of '76 inspired them. Jo and Fred had several skirmishes, and once narrowly escaped high words. Jo was through the last wicket, and had missed the stroke, which failure ruffled her a good deal. Fred was close behind her, and his turn came before hers; he gave a stroke, his ball hit the wicket, and stopped an inch on the wrong side. No one was very near; and running up to examine, he gave it a sly nudge with his toe, which put it just an inch on the right side.

"I'm through! Now, Miss Jo, I'll settle you, and get in first," cried the young gentleman, swinging his mallet for another blow.

"You pushed it; I saw you; it's my turn now," said Jo sharply.

"Upon my word, I didn't move it; it rolled a bit, perhaps, but that is allowed; so stand off please, and let me have a go at the stake."

"We don't cheat in America, but you can, if you choose," said Jo angrily.

"Yankees are a deal the most tricky, everybody knows. There you go!" returned Fred, croqueting her ball far away.

Jo opened her lips to say something rude, but checked herself in time, colored up to her forehead, and stood a minute, hammering down a wicket with all her might, while Fred hit the stake, and declared himself out with much exultation. She went off to get her ball, and was a long time finding it, among the bushes; but she came back, looking cool and quiet, and waited her turn patiently. It took several strokes to regain the place she had lost; and, when she got there, the other side had nearly won, for Kate's ball was the last but one, and lay near the stake.

"By George, it's all up with us! Good-by, Kate. Miss Jo owes me one, so you are finished," cried Fred excitedly, as they all drew near to see the finish.

"Yankees have a trick of being generous to their enemies," said Jo, with a look that made the lad redden, "especially when they beat them," she added, as, leaving Kate's ball untouched, she won the game by a clever stroke.

Laurie threw up his hat; then remembered that it wouldn't do to exult over the defeat of his guests, and stopped in the middle of a cheer to whisper to his friend,—

"Good for you, Jo! He did cheat, I saw him; we can't tell him so, but he won't do it again, take my word for it."

Meg drew her aside, under pretence of pinning up a loose braid, and said approvingly,—

"It was dreadfully provoking; but you kept your temper, and I'm so glad, Jo."

"Don't praise me, Meg, for I could box his ears this minute. I should certainly have boiled over if I hadn't stayed among the nettles till I got my rage under enough to hold my tongue. It's simmering now, so I hope he'll keep out of my way," returned Jo, biting her lips, as she glowered at Fred from under her big hat.

"Time for lunch," said Mr. Brooke, looking at his watch. "Commissary-general, will you make the fire and get water, while Miss March, Miss Sallie, and I spread the table? Who can make good coffee?"

"Jo can," said Meg, glad to recommnend her sister. So Jo, feeling that her late lessons in cookery were to do her honor, went to preside over the coffee-pot, while the children collected dry sticks, and the boys made a fire, and got water from a spring near by. Miss Kate sketched, and Frank talked to Beth, who was making little mats of braided rushes to serve as plates.

The commander-in-chief and his aids soon spread the table-cloth with an inviting array of eatables and drinkables, prettily decorated with green leaves. Jo announced that the coffee was ready, and every one settled themselves to a hearty meal; for youth is seldom dyspeptic, and exercise develops wholesome appetites. A very merry lunch it was; for everything seemed fresh and funny, and frequent peals of laughter startled a venerable horse who fed near by. There was a pleasing inequality in the table, which produced many mishaps to cups and plates; acorns dropped into the milk, little black ants partook of the refreshnments without being invited, and fuzzy caterpillars swung down from the tree, to see what was going on. Three white-headed children peeped over the fence, and an objectionable dog barked at them from the other side of the river with all his might and main.

"Now, Miss Jo, I'll settle you."

"There's salt here, if you prefer it," said Laurie, as he handed Jo a saucer of berries.

"Thank you, I prefer spiders," she replied, fishing up two unwary little ones who had gone to a creamy death. "How dare you remind me of that horrid dinner-party, when yours is so nice in every way?" added Jo, as they both laughed, and ate out of one plate, the china having run short.

"I had an uncommonly good time that day, and haven't got over it yet. This is no credit to me, you know; I don't do anything; it's you and Meg and Brooke who make it go, and I'm no end obliged to you. What shall we do when we can't eat any more?" asked Laurie, feeling that his trump card had been played when lunch was over.

"Have games, till it's cooler. I brought 'Authors,' and I dare say Miss Kate knows something new and nice. Go and ask her; she's company, and you ought to stay with her more."

"Aren't you company too? I thought she'd suit Brooke; but he keeps talking to Meg, and Kate just stares at them through that ridiculous glass of hers. I'm going, so you needn't try to preach propriety, for you can't do it, Jo."

Miss Kate did know several new games; and as the girls would not, and the boys could not, eat any more, they all adjourned to the drawing-room to play "Rigmarole."

"One person begins a story, any nonsense you like, and tells as long as he pleases, only taking care to stop short at some exciting point, when the next takes it up and does the same. It's very funny when well done, and makes a perfect jumble of tragical comical stuff to laugh over. Please start it, Mr. Brooke," said Kate, with a commanding air, which surprised Meg, who treated the tutor with as much respect as any other gentleman.

Lying on the grass at the feet of the two young ladies, Mr. Brooke obediently began the story, with the handsome brown eyes steadily fixed upon the sunshiny river.

"Once on a time, a knight went out into the world to seek his fortune, for he had nothing but his sword and his shield. He travelled a long while, nearly eight-and-twenty years, and had a hard time of it, till he came to the palace of a good old king, who had offered a reward to any one who would tame and train a fine but unbroken colt, of which he was very fond. The knight agreed to try, and got on slowly but surely; for the colt was a gallant fellow, and soon learned to love his new master, though he was freakish and wild. Every day, when he gave his lessons to this pet of the king's, the knight rode him through the city; and, as he rode, he looked everywhere for a certain beautiful face, which he had seen many times in his dreams, but never found. One day, as he went prancing down a quiet street, he saw at the window of a ruinous castle the lovely face. He was delighted, inquired who lived in this old castle, and was told that several captive princesses were kept there by a spell, and spun all day to lay up money to buy their liberty. The knight wished intensely that he could free them; but he was poor, and could only go by each day, watching for the sweet face, and longing to see it out in the sunshine. At last he resolved to get into the castle and ask how he could help them. He went and knocked; the great door flew open, and he beheld—"

"A ravishingly lovely lady, who exclaimed, with a cry of rapture, 'At last! At last!' " continued Kate, who had read French novels, and admired the style. " ' 'Tis she!' cried Count Gustave, and fell at her feet in an ecstasy of joy. 'Oh, rise !' she said, extending a hand of marble fairness. 'Never! Till you tell me how I mày rescue you,' swore the knight, still kneeling. 'Alas, my cruel fate condemns me to remain here till my tyrant is destroyed.' 'Where is the villain?' 'In the mauve salon. Go, brave heart, and save me from despair.' 'I obey, and return victorious or dead!' With these thrilling words he rushed away, and flinging open the door of the mauve salon, was about to enter, when he received—"

"A stunning blow from the big Greek lexicon, which an old fellow in a black gown fired at him," said Ned. "Instantly Sir What's-his-name recovered himself, pitched the tyrant out of the window, and turned to join the lady, victorious, but with a bump on his brow; found the door locked, tore up the curtains, made a rope ladder, got half-way down when the ladder broke, and he went head first into the moat, sixty feet below. Could swim like a duck, paddled round the castle till he came to a little door guarded by two stout fellows; knocked their heads together till they cracked like a couple of nuts, then, by a trifling exertion of his prodigious strength, he smashed in the door, went up a pair of stone steps covered with dust a foot thick, toads as big as your fist, and spiders that would frighten you into hysterics, Miss March. At the top of these steps he came plump upon a sight that took his breath away and chilled his blood—"

"A tall figure, all in white with a veil over its face and a lamp in its wasted hand," went on Meg. "It beckoned, gliding noiselessly before him down a corridor as dark and cold as any tomb. Shadowy effigies in armor stood on either side, a dead silence reigned, the lamp burned blue, and the ghostly figure ever and anon turned its face toward him, showing the glitter of awful eyes through its white veil. They reached a curtained door, behind which sounded lovely music; he sprang forward to enter, but the spectre plucked him back, and waved threateningly before him a—"

"Snuff-box," said Jo, in a sepulchral tone, which convulsed the audience. " 'Thankee,' said the knight politely, as he took a pinch, and sneezed seven times so violently that his head fell off. 'Ha! ha!' laughed the ghost; and having peeped through the key-hole at the princesses spinning away for dear life, the evil spirit picked up her victim and put him in a large tin box, where there were eleven other knights packed together without their heads, like sardines, who all rose and began to—"

"Dance a hornpipe," cut in Fred, as Jo paused for breath; "and, as they danced, the rubbishy old castle turned to a man-of-war in full sail. 'Up with the jib, reef the tops'l halliards, helm hard a lee, and man the guns!' roared the captain, as a Portuguese pirate hove in sight, with a flag black as ink flying from her foremast. 'Go in and win, my hearties!' says the captain; and a tremendous fight begun. Of course the British beat; they always do."

"No they don't!" cried Jo, aside.

"Having taken the pirate captain prisoner, sailed slap over the schooner, whose decks were piled with dead, and whose lee-scuppers ran blood, for the order had been 'Cutlasses, and die hard!' 'Bosen's mate, take a bight of the flying-jib sheet, and start this villain if he don't confess his sins double quick,' said the British captain. The Portuguese held his tongue like a brick, and walked the plank, while the jolly tars cheered like mad. But the sly dog dived, came up under the man-of-war, scuttled her, and down she went, with all sail set, 'To the bottom of the sea, sea, sea,' where—"

"Oh, gracious! What *shall* I say?" cried Sallie, as Fred ended his rigmarole, in which he had jumbled together, pell-mell, nautical phrases and facts, out of one of his favorite books. "Well, they went to the bottom, and a nice mermaid welcomed them, but was much grieved on finding the box of headless knights, and kindly pickled them in brine, hoping to discover the mystery about them; for, being a woman, she was curious. By and by a diver came down, and the mermaid said, 'I'll give you this box of pearls if you can take it up;' for she wanted to restore the poor things to life, and couldn't raise the heavy load herself. So the diver hoisted it up, and was much disappointed, on opening it, to find no pearls. He left it in a great lonely field, where it was found by a—"

"Little goose-girl, who kept a hundred fat geese in the field," said Amy, when Sallie's invention gave out. "The little girl was sorry for them, and asked an old woman what she should do to help them. 'Your geese will tell you, they know everything,' said the old woman. So she asked what she should use for new heads, since the old ones were lost, and all the geese opened their hundred mouths and screamed—"

" 'Cabbages!' " continued Laurie promptly. " 'Just the thing,' said the girl, and ran to get twelve fine ones from her garden. She put them on, the knights revived at once, thanked her, and went on their way rejoicing, never knowing the difference, for there were so many other heads like them in the world that no one thought anything of it. The knight in whom I'm interested went back to find the pretty face, and learned that the princesses had spun themselves free, and all gone to be married, but one. He was in a great state of mind at that; and mounting the colt, who stood by him through thick and thin, rushed to the castle to see which was left. Peeping over the hedge, he saw the queen of his affections picking flowers in her garden. 'Will you give me a rose?' said he. 'You must come and get it. I can't come to you; it isn't proper,' said she, as sweet as honey. He tried to climb over the hedge, but it seemed to grow higher and higher; then he tried to push through, but it grew thicker and thicker, and he was in despair. So he patiently broke twig after twig, till he had made a little hole, through which he peeped, saying imploringly, 'Let me in! Let me in!' But the pretty princess did not seem to understand, for she picked her roses quietly, and left him to fight his way in. Whether he did or not, Frank will tell you."

"I can't; I'm not playing, I never do," said Frank, dismayed at the sentimental predicament out of which he was to rescue the absurd couple. Beth had disappeared behind Jo, and Grace was asleep.

"So the poor knight is to be left sticking in the hedge, is he?" asked

Mr. Brooke, still watching the river, and playing with the wild rose in his button-hole.

"I guess the princess gave him a posy, and opened the gate, after a while," said Laurie, smiling to himself, as he threw acorns at his tutor.

"What a piece of nonsense we have made! With practice we might do something quite clever. Do you know 'Truth'?" asked Sallie, after they had laughed over their story.

"I hope so," said Meg soberly.

"The game, I mean?"

"What is it?" said Fred.

"Why, you pile up your hands, choose a number, and draw out in turn, and the person who draws at the number has to answer truly any questions put by the rest, It's great fun."

"Let's try it," said Jo, who liked new experiments.

Miss Kate and Mr. Brooke, Meg, and Ned declined, but Fred, Sallie, Jo, and Laurie piled and drew; and the lot fell to Laurie.

"Who are your heroes?" asked Jo.

"Grandfather and Napoleon."

"Which lady here do you think prettiest?" said Sallie.

"Margaret."

"Which do you like best?" from Fred.

"Jo, of course."

"What silly questions you ask!" and Jo gave a disdainful shrug as the rest laughed at Laurie's matter-of-fact tone.

"Try again; truth isn't a bad game," said Fred.

"It's a very good one for you," retorted Jo, in a low voice.

Her turn came next.

"What is your greatest fault?" asked Fred, by way of testing in her the virtue he lacked himself.

"A quick temper."

"What do you most wish for?" said Laurie.

"A pair of boot-lacings," returned Jo, guessing and defeating his purpose.

"Not a true answer; you must say what you really do want most."

"Genius; don't you wish you could give it to me, Laurie?" and she slyly smiled in his disappointed face.

"What virtues do you most admire in a man?" asked Sallie.

"Courage and honesty."

"Now my turn," said Fred, as his hand came last.

"Let's give it to him," whispered Laurie to Jo, who nodded, and asked at once,—

"Didn't you cheat at croquet?"

"Well, yes, a little bit."

"Good! Didn't you take your story out of 'The Sea-Lion'?" said Laurie.

"Rather."

"Don't you think the English nation perfect in every respect?" asked Sallie.

"I should be ashamed of myself if I didn't."

"He's a true John Bull. Now, Miss Sallie, you shall have a chance without waiting to draw. I'll harrow up your feelings first, by asking if you don't think you are something of a flirt," said Laurie, as Jo nodded to Fred, as a sign that peace was declared.

"You impertinent boy! Of course I'm not," exclaimed Sallie, with an air that proved the contrary.

"What do you hate most?" asked Fred.

"Spiders and rice-pudding."

"What do you like best?" asked Jo.

"Dancing and French gloves."

"Well, *I* think Truth is a very silly play; let's have a sensible game of Authors, to refresh our minds," proposed Jo.

Ned, Frank, and the little girls joined in this, and, while it went on, the three elders sat apart, talking. Miss Kate took out her sketch again, and Margaret watched her, while Mr. Brooke lay on the grass, with a book, which he did not read.

"How beautifully you do it! I wish I could draw,' said Meg, with mingled admiration and regret in her voice.

"Why don't you learn? I should think you had taste and talent for it," replied Miss Kate graciously.

"I haven't time."

"Your mamma prefers other accomplishments, I fancy. So did mine; but I proved to her that I had talent, by taking a few lessons privately, and then she was quite willing I should go on. Can't you do the same with your governess?"

"I have none."

"I forgot; young ladies in America go to school more than with us. Very fine schools they are, too, papa says. You go to a private one, I suppose?"

"I don't go at all; I am a governess myself."

"Oh, indeed!" said Miss Kate; but she might as well have said, "Dear me, how dreadful!" for her tone implied it, and something in her face made Meg color, and wish she had not been so frank.

Mr. Brooke looked up, and said quickly, "Young ladies in America love independence as much as their ancestors did, and are admired and respected for supporting themselves."

"Oh, yes; of course it's very nice and proper in them to do so. We have many most respectable and worthy young women, who do the same and are employed by the nobility, because, being the daughters of gentlemen, they are both well-bred and accomplished, you know," said Miss Kate, in a patronizing tone, that hurt Meg's pride, and made her work seem not only more distasteful, but degrading.

"Did the German song suit, Miss March?" inquired Mr. Brooke, breaking an awkward pause.

"Oh, yes! It was very sweet, and I'm much obliged to whoever translated it for me;" and Meg's downcast face brightened as she spoke.

"Don't you read German?" asked Miss Kate, with a look of surprise.

"Not very well. My father, who taught me, is away, and I don't get on very fast alone, for I've no one to correct my pronunciation."

"Try a little now; here is Schiller's 'Mary Stuart,' and a tutor who loves to teach," and Mr. Brooke laid his book on her lap, with an inviting smile.

"It's so hard I'm afraid to try," said Meg, grateful, but bashful in the presence of the accomplished young lady beside her.

"I'll read a bit to encourage you;" and Miss Kate read one of the most beautiful passages, in a perfectly correct but perfectly expressionless manner.

Mr. Brooke made no comment, as she returned the book to Meg, who said innocently,—

"I thought it was poetry."

"Some of it is. Try this passage."

There was a queer smile about Mr. Brooke's mouth as he opened at poor Mary's lament.

Meg obediently following the long grass-blade which her new tutor used to point with, read slowly and timidly, unconsciously making poetry of the hard words by the soft intonation of her musical voice. Down the page went the green guide, and presently, forgetting her listener in the beauty of the sad scene, Meg read as if alone, giving a little touch of tragedy to the words of the unhappy queen. If she had seen the brown eyes then, she would have stopped short; but she never looked up, and the lesson was not spoiled for her.

"Very well indeed!" said Mr. Brooke, as she paused, quite ignoring her many mistakes, and looking as if he did, indeed, "love to teach."

Miss Kate put up her glass, and, having taken a survey of the little tableau before her, shut her sketch-book, saying, with condescension,—

"You've a nice accent, and, in time, will be a clever reader. I advise you to learn, for German is a valuable accomplishment to teachers. I must look after Grace, she is romping;" and Miss Kate strolled away, adding to herself, with a shrug, "I didn't come to chaperone a governess, though she *is* young and pretty. What odd people these Yankees are; I'm afraid Laurie will be quite spoilt among them."

"I forgot that English people rather turn up their noses at governesses, and don't treat them as we do," said Meg, looking after the retreating figure with an annoyed expression.

"Tutors, also, have rather a hard time of it there, as I know to my sorrow. There's no place like America for us workers, Miss Margaret;" and Mr. Brooke looked so contented and cheerful, that Meg was ashamed to lament her hard lot.

"I'm glad I live in it then. I don't like my work, but I get a good deal of satisfaction out of it after all, so I won't complain; I only wish I liked teaching as you do."

"I think you would if you had Laurie for a pupil. I shall be very sorry to lose him next year," said Mr. Brooke, busily punching holes in the turf.

"Going to college, I suppose?" Meg's lips asked that question, but her eyes added, "And what becomes of you?"

"Yes; it's high time he went, for he is ready; and as soon as he is off, I shall turn soldier. I am needed."

"I am glad of that!" exclaimed Meg. "I should think every young man would want to go; though it is hard for the mothers and sisters who stay at home," she added sorrowfully.

"I have neither, and very few friends, to care whether I live or die," said Mr. Brooke, rather bitterly, as he absently put the dead rose in the hole he had made and covered it up, like a little grave.

"Laurie and his grandfather would care a great deal, and we should all be very sorry to have any harm happen to you," said Meg heartily.

"Thank you; that sounds pleasant," began Mr. Brooke, looking cheerful again; but before he could finish his speech, Ned, mounted on the old horse, came lumbering up to display his equestrian skill before the young ladies, and there was no more quiet that day.

"Don't you love to ride?" asked Grace of Amy, as they stood resting, after a race round the field with the others, led by Ned.

"I dote upon it; my sister Meg used to ride when papa was rich, but we don't keep any horses now, except Ellen Tree," added Amy, laughing.

"Tell me about Ellen Tree; is it a donkey?" asked Grace, curiously.

"Why, you see, Jo is crazy about horses, and so am I, but we've only got an old side-saddle, and no horse. Out in our garden is an apple-tree, that has a nice low branch; so Jo put the saddle on it, fixed some reins on the part that turns up, and we bounce away on Ellen Tree whenever we like."

"How funny!" laughed Grace. "I have a pony at home, and ride nearly every day in the park, with Fred and Kate; it's very nice, for my friends go too, and the Row is full of ladies and gentlemen."

"Dear, how charming! I hope I shall go abroad some day; but I'd rather go to Rome than the Row," said Amy who had not the remotest idea what the Row was, and wouldn't have asked for the world.

Frank, sitting just behind the little girls, heard what they were saying, and pushed his crutch away from him with an impatient gesture as he watched the active lads going through all sorts of comical gymnastics. Beth, who was collecting the scattered Author-cards, looked up, and said, in her shy yet friendly way,—

"I'm afraid you are tired; can I do anything for you?"

"Talk to me, please; it's dull, sitting by myself," answered Frank, who had evidently been used to being made much of at home.

If he had asked her to deliver a Latin oration, it would not have seemed a more impossible task to bashful Beth; but there was no place to run to, no Jo to hide behind now, and the poor boy looked so wistfully at her, that she bravely resolved to try.

"What do you like to talk about?" she asked, fumbling over the cards, and dropping half as she tried to tie them up.

"Well, I like to hear about cricket and boating and hunting," said Frank, who had not yet learned to suit his amusements to his strength.

"My heart! What shall I do? I don't know anything about them," thought Beth; and, forgetting the boy's misfortune in her flurry, she said, hoping to make him talk, "I never saw any hunting, but I suppose you know all about it."

"I did once; but I can never hunt again, for I got hurt leaping a confounded five-barred gate; so there are no more horses and hounds for me," said Frank, with a sigh that made Beth hate herself for her innocent blunder.

"Your deer are much prettier than our ugly buffaloes," she said, turning to the prairies for help, and feeling glad that she had read one of the boys' books in which Jo delighted.

Buffaloes proved soothing and satisfactory; and, in her eagerness to amuse another, Beth forgot herself, and was quite unconscious of her sisters' surprise and delight at the unusual spectacle of Beth talking away to one of the dreadful boys, against whom she had begged protection.

"Bless her heart! She pities him, so she is good to him," said Jo, beaming at her from the croquet-ground.

"I always said she was a little saint," added Meg, as if there could be no further doubt of it.

"I haven't heard Frank laugh so much for ever so long," said Grace to Amy, as they sat discussing dolls, and making tea-sets out of the acorn-cups.

"My sister Beth is a very *fastidious* girl, when she likes to be," said Amy, well pleased at Beth's success. She meant "fascinating," but as Grace didn't know the exact meaning of either word, "fastidious" sounded well, and made a good impression.

An impromptu circus, fox and geese, and an amicable game of croquet, finished the afternoon. At sunset the tent was struck, hampers packed, wickets pulled up, boats loaded, and the whole party floated down the river, singing at the tops of their voices. Ned, getting sentimental, warbled a serenade with the pensive refrain,—

*"Alone, alone, ah! woe, alone,"*

and at the lines —

> *"We each are young, we each have a heart,*
> *Oh, why should we stand thus coldly apart?"*

He looked at Meg with such a lackadaisical expression that she laughed outright and spoilt his song.

"How can you be so cruel to me?" he whispered, under cover of a lively chorus. "You've kept close to that starched-up Englishwoman all day, and now you snub me."

"I didn't mean to; but you looked so funny I really couldn't help it," replied Meg, passing over the first part of his reproach; for it was quite true that she *had* shunned him, remembering the Moffat party and the talk after it.

Ned was offended, and turned to Sallie for consolation, saying to her rather pettishly, "There isn't a bit of flirt in that girl, is there?"

"Not a particle; but she's a dear," returned Sallie, defending her friend even while confessing her short-comings.

"She's not a stricken deer, anyway," said Ned, trying to be witty, and succeeding as well as very young gentlemen usually do.

On the lawn, where it had gathered, the little party separated with cordial good-nights and good-byes, for the Vaughns were going to Canada. As the four sisters went home through the garden, Miss Kate looked after them, saying, without the patronizing tone in her voice, "In spite of their demonstrative manners, American girls are very nice when one knows them."

"I quite agree with you," said Mr. Brooke.

# CHAPTER XIII

## CASTLES IN THE AIR

LAURIE lay luxuriously swinging to and fro in his hammock, one warm September afternoon, wondering what his neighbors were about, but too lazy to go and find out. He was in one of his moods; for the day had been both unprofitable and unsatisfactory, and he was wishing he could live it over again. The hot weather made him indolent, and he had shirked his studies, tried Mr. Brooke's patience to the utmost, displeased his grandfather by practicing half the afternoon, frightened the maid-servants half out of their wits, by mischievously hinting that one of his dogs was going mad, and, after high words with the stable-man about some fancied neglect of his horse, he had flung himself into his hammock, to fume over the stupidity of the world in general, till the peace of the lovely day quieted him in spite of himself. Staring up into the green gloom of the horse-chestnut trees above him, he dreamed dreams of all sorts, and was just imagining himself tossing on the ocean, in a voyage round the world, when the sound of voices brought him ashore in a flash. Peeping through the meshes of the hammock, he saw the Marches coming out, as if bound on some expedition.

"What in the world are those girls about now?" thought Laurie, opening his sleepy eyes to take a good look, for there was something rather peculiar in the appearance of his neighbors. Each wore a large, flapping hat, a brown linen pouch slung over one shoulder, and carried a long staff. Meg had a cushion, Jo a book, Beth a basket, and Amy a portfolio. All walked quietly through the garden, out at the little back gate, and began to climb the hill that lay between the house and river.

"Well, that's cool!" said Laurie to himself, "to have a picnic and never ask me. They can't be going in the boat, for they haven't got the key. Perhaps they forgot it; I'll take it to them, and see what's going on."

Though possessed of half a dozen hats, it took him some time to find one; then there was a hunt for the key, which was at last discovered in his pocket; so that the girls were quite out of sight when he leaped the fence and ran after them. Taking the shortest way to the boathouse, he waited for them to appear: but no one came, and he went up the hill to take an observation. A grove of pines covered one part of it, and from the heart of this green spot came a clearer sound than the soft sigh of the pines or the drowsy chirp of the crickets.

"Here's a landscape!" thought Laurie, peeping through the bushes, and looking wide-awake and good-natured already.

It *was* rather a pretty little picture; for the sisters sat together in the shady nook, with sun and shadow flickering over them, the aromatic wind lifting their hair and cooling their hot cheeks, and all the little wood-people going on with their affairs as if these were no strangers, but old friends. Meg sat upon her cushion, sewing daintily with her white hands, and looking as fresh and sweet as a rose, in her pink dress, among the green. Beth was sorting the cones that lay thick under the hemlock near by, for she made pretty things of them. Amy was sketching a group of ferns, and Jo was knitting as she read aloud. A shadow passed over the boy's face as he watched them, feeling that he ought to go away, because uninvited; yet lingering, because home seemed very lonely, and this quiet party in the woods most attractive to his restless spirit. He stood so still that a squirrel, busy with its harvesting, ran down a pine close beside him, saw him suddenly and skipped back, scolding so shrilly that Beth looked up, espied the wistful face behind the birches, and beckoned with a reassuring smile.

"May I come in, please? Or shall I be a bother?" he asked, advancing slowly.

Meg lifted her eyebrows, but Jo scowled at her defiantly, and said, at once, "Of course you may. We should have asked you before, only we thought you wouldn't care for such a girl's game as this."

"I always liked your games; but if Meg doesn't want me, I'll go away."

"I've no objection, if you do something; it's against the rules to be idle here," replied Meg, gravely but graciously.

"Much obliged; I'll do anything if you'll let me stop a bit, for it's as dull as the Desert of Sahara down there. Shall I sew, read, cone, draw, or do all at once? Bring on your bears; I'm ready," and Laurie sat down, with a submissive expression delightful to behold.

"Finish this story while I set my heel," said Jo, handing him the book.

"Yes'm," was the meek answer, as he began, doing his best to prove his gratitude for the favor of an admission into the "Busy Bee Society."

The story was not a long one, and, when it was finished, he ventured to ask a few questions as a reward of merit.

"Please, ma'am, could I inquire if this highly instructive and charming institution is a new one?"

"Would you tell him?" asked Meg of her sisters.

"He'll laugh," said Amy warningly.

"Who cares?" said Jo.

"I guess he'll like it," added Beth.

"Of course I shall! I give you my word I won't laugh. Tell away, Jo, and don't be afraid."

"The idea of being afraid of you! Well, you see we used to play 'Pilgrim's Progress,' and we have been going on with it in earnest, all winter and summer."

"Yes, I know," said Laurie, nodding wisely.

"Who told you?" demanded Jo.

"Spirits."

"No, I did; I wanted to amuse him one night when you were all away, and he was rather dismal. He did like it, so don't scold, Jo," said Beth meekly.

"You can't keep a secret. Never mind; it saves trouble now."

"Go on, please," said Laurie, as Jo became absorbed in her work, looking a trifle displeased.

"Oh, didn't she tell you about this new plan of ours? Well, we have tried not to waste our holiday, but each has had a task, and worked at it with a will. The vacation is nearly over, the stints are all done, and we are ever so glad that we didn't dawdle."

"Yes, I should think so;" and Laurie thought regretfully of his own idle days.

"Mother likes to have us out of doors as much as possible; so we bring our work here, and have nice times. For the fun of it we bring our things in these bags, wear the old hats, use poles to climb the hill, and play pilgrims, as we used to do years ago. We call this hill the 'Delectable Mountain,' for we can look far away and see the country where we hope to live some time."

Jo pointed, and Laurie sat up to examine; for through an opening in the wood one could look across the wide, blue river, the meadows on the other side, far over the outskirts of the great city, to the green hills that rose to meet the sky. The sun was low, and the heavens glowed with the splendor of an autumn sunset. Gold and purple clouds lay on the hill-tops; and rising high into the ruddy light were silvery white peaks, that shone like the airy spires of some Celestial City.

"How beautiful that is!" said Laurie softly, for he was quick to see and feel beauty of any kind.

"It's often so; and we like to watch it, for it is never the same, but always splendid," replied Amy, wishing she could paint it.

"Jo talks about the country where we hope to live some time,—the real country, she means, with pigs and chickens and haymaking. It would be nice, but I wish the beautiful country up there was real, and we could ever go to it," said Beth musingly.

"There is a lovelier country even than that, where we *shall* go, by and by, when we are good enough," answered Meg, with her sweet voice.

"It seems so long to wait, so hard to do; I want to fly away at once, as those swallows fly, and go in at that splendid gate."

"You'll get there, Beth, sooner or later; no fear of that," said Jo; "I'm the one that will have to fight and work, and climb and wait, and maybe never get in after all."

"You'll have me for company, if that's any comfort. I shall have to do a deal of travelling before I come in sight of your Celestial City. If I arrive late, you'll say a good word for me, won't you, Beth?"

Something in the boy's face troubled his little friend; but she said cheerfully, with her quiet eyes on the changing clouds, "If people really want to go, and really try all their lives, I think they will get in; for I don't believe there are any locks on that door, or any guards at the gate. I always imagine it is as it is in the picture, where the shining ones stretch out their hands to welcome poor Christian as he comes up from the river."

"Wouldn't it be fun if all the castles in the air which we make could come true, and we could live in them?" said Jo, after a little pause.

"I've made such quantities it would be hard to choose which I'd have," said Laurie, lying flat, and throwing cones at the squirrel who had betrayed him.

"You'd have to take your favorite one. What is it?" asked Meg.

"If I tell mine, will you tell yours?"

"Yes, if the girls will too."

"We will. Now, Laurie."

"After I'd seen as much of the world as I want to, I'd like to settle in Germany, and have just as much music as I choose. I'm to be a famous musician myself, and all creation is to rush to hear me; and I'm never to be bothered about money or business, but just enjoy myself, and live for what I like. That's my favorite castle. What's yours, Meg?"

Margaret seemed to find it a little hard to tell hers, and waved a brake before her face, as if to disperse imaginary gnats, while she said slowly, "I should like a lovely house, full of all sorts of luxurious things,— nice food, pretty clothes, handsome furniture, pleasant people, and heaps of money. I am to be mistress of it, and manage it as I like, with plenty of servants, so I never need work a bit. How I should enjoy it! For I wouldn't be idle, but do good, and make every one love me dearly."

"Wouldn't you have a master for your castle in the air?" asked Laurie slyly.

"I said 'pleasant people,' you know;" and Meg carefully tied up her shoe as she spoke, so that no one saw her face.

"Why don't you say you'd have a splendid, wise, good husband, and some angelic little children? You know your castle wouldn't be perfect without," said blunt Jo, who had no tender fancies yet, and rather scorned romance, except in books.

"You'd have nothing but horses, inkstands, and novels in yours," answered Meg petulantly.

"Wouldn't I, though? I'd have a stable full of Arabian steeds, rooms piled with books, and I'd write out of a magic inkstand, so that my works should be as famous as Laurie's music. I want to do something splendid before I go into my castle,—something heroic or wonderful, that won't be forgotten after I'm dead. I don't know what, but I'm on the watch for it, and mean to astonish you all, some day. I think I shall write books, and get rich and famous: that would suit me, so that is *my* favorite dream."

"Mine is to stay at home safe with father and mother, and help take care of the family," said Beth contentedly.

"Don't you wish for anything else?" asked Laurie.

"Since I had my little piano, I am perfectly satisfied. I only wish we may all keep well and be together; nothing else."

"I have ever so many wishes; but the pet one is to be an artist, and go to Rome, and do fine pictures, and be the best artist in the whole world," was Amy's modest desire.

"We're an ambitious set, aren't we? Every one of us, but Beth, wants to be rich and famous, and gorgeous in every respect. I do wonder if any of us will ever get our wishes," said Laurie, chewing grass, like a meditative calf.

"I've got the key to my castle in the air; but whether I can unlock the door remains to be seen," observed Jo mysteriously.

"I've got the key to mine, but I'm not allowed to try it. Hang college!" muttered Laurie, with an impatient sigh.

"Here's mine!" and Amy waved her pencil.

"I haven't got any," said Meg forlornly.

"Yes, you have," said Laurie at once.

"Where?"

"In your face."

"Nonsense; that's of no use."

"Wait and see if it doesn't bring you something worth having," replied the boy, laughing at the thought of a charming little secret which he fancied he knew.

Meg colored behind the brake, but asked no questions, and looked across the river with the same expectant expression which Mr. Brooke had worn when he told the story of the knight.

"If we are all alive ten years hence, let's meet, and see how many of us have got our wishes, or how much nearer we are then than now," said Jo, always ready with a plan.

"Bless me! How old I shall be,—twenty-seven!" exclaimed Meg, who felt grown up already, having just reached seventeen.

"You and I will be twenty-six, Teddy, Beth twenty-four, and Amy twenty-two. What a venerable party!" said Jo.

"I hope I shall have done something to be proud of by that time; but I'm such a lazy dog, I'm afraid I shall 'dawdle,' Jo."

"You need a motive, mother says; and when you get it, she is sure you'll work splendidly."

"Is she? By Jupiter I will, if I only get the chance!" cried Laurie, sitting up with sudden energy. "I ought to be satisfied to please grandfather, and I do try, but it's working against the grain, you see, and comes hard. He wants me to be an India merchant, as he was, and I'd rather be shot. I hate tea and silk and spices, and every sort of rubbish his old ships bring, and I don't care how soon they go to the bottom when I own them. Going to college ought to satisfy him, for if I give him four years he ought to let me off from the business; but he's set, and I've got to do just as he did, unless I break away and please myself, as my father did. If there was any one left to stay with the old gentleman, I'd do it tomorrow."

Laurie spoke excitedly, and looked ready to carry his threat into execution on the slightest provocation; for he was growing up very fast, and, in spite of his indolent ways, had a young man's hatred of subjection, a young man's restless longing to try the world for himself.

"I advise you to sail away in one of your ships, and never come home again till you have tried your own way," said Jo, whose imagination was fired by the thought of such a daring exploit, and whose sympathy was excited by what she called "Teddy's wrongs."

"That's not right, Jo; you mustn't talk in that way, and Laurie mustn't take your bad advice. You should do just what your grandfather wishes, my dear boy," said Meg, in her most maternal tone. "Do your best at college, and, when he sees that you try to please him, I'm sure he won't be hard or unjust to you. As you say, there is no one else to stay with and love him, and you'd never forgive yourself if you left him without his permission. Don't be dismal or fret, but do your duty; and you'll get your reward, as good Mr. Brooke has, by being respected and loved."

"What do you know about him?" asked Laurie, grateful for the good advice, but objecting to the lecture, and glad to turn the conversation from himself after his unusual outbreak.

"Only what your grandpa told us about him,—how he took good care of his own mother till she died, and wouldn't go abroad as tutor to some nice person, because he wouldn't leave her; and how he provides now for an old woman who nursed his mother; and never tells any one, but is just as generous and patient and good as he can be."

"So he is, dear old fellow!" said Laurie heartily, as Meg paused, looking flushed and earnest with her story. "It's like grandpa to find out all about him, without letting him know, and to tell all his goodness to others, so that they might like him. Brooke couldn't understand why your mother was so kind to him, asking him over with me, and treating him in her beautiful friendly way. He thought she was just perfect, and talked about it for days and days, and went on about you all in flaming style. If ever I do get my wish, you see what I'll do for Brooke."

"Begin to do something now, by not plaguing his life out," said Meg sharply.

"How do you know I do, miss?"

"I can always tell by his face, when he goes away. If you have been good, he looks satisfied and walks briskly; if you have plagued him, he's sober and walks slowly, as if he wanted to go back and do his work better."

"Well, I like that! So you keep an account of my good and bad marks in Brooke's face, do you? I see him bow and smile as he passes your window, but I didn't know you'd got up a telegraph."

"We haven't; don't be angry, and oh, don't tell him I said anything! It was only to show that I cared how you get on, and what is said here is said in confidence, you know," cried Meg, much alarmed at the thought of what might follow from her careless speech.

"*I* don't tell tales," replied Laurie, with his "high and mighty" air, as Jo called a certain expression which he occasionally wore. "Only if Brooke is going to be a thermometer, I must mind and have fair weather for him to report."

"Please don't be offended. I didn't mean to preach or tell tales or be silly; I only thought Jo was encouraging you in a feeling which you'd be sorry for, by and by. You are so kind to us, we feel as if you were our brother, and say just what we think. Forgive me, I meant it kindly." And Meg offered her hand with a gesture both affectionate and timid.

Ashamed of his momentary pique, Laurie squeezed the kind little hand, and said frankly, "I'm the one to be forgiven; I'm cross, and have been out of sorts all day. I like to have you tell me my faults and be sisterly, so don't mind if I am grumpy sometimes; I thank you all the same."

Bent on showing that he was not offended, he made himself as agreeable as possible,—wound cotton for Meg, recited poetry to please Jo, shook down cones for Beth, and helped Amy with her ferns, proving himself a fit person to belong to the "Busy Bee Society." In the midst of an animated discussion on the domestic habits of turtles (one of those amiable creatures having strolled up from the river), the faint sound of a bell warned them that Hannah had put the tea "to draw," and they would just have time to get home to supper.

"May I come again?" asked Laurie.

"Yes, if you are good, and love your book, as the boys in the primer are told to do," said Meg, smiling.

"I'll try."

"Then you may come, and I'll teach you to knit as the Scotchmen do; there's a demand for socks just now," added Jo, waving hers, like a big blue worsted banner, as they parted at the gate.

That night, when Beth played to Mr. Laurence in the twilight, Laurie, standing in the shadow of the curtain, listened to the little David, whose simple music always quieted his moody spirit, and watched the old man, who sat with his gray head on his hand, thinking tender thoughts of the dead child he had loved so much. Remembering the conversation of the afternoon, the boy said to himself, with the resolve to make the sacrifice cheerfully, "I'll let my castle go, and stay with the dear old gentleman while he needs me, for I am all he has."

# CHAPTER XIV

## SECRETS

JO was very busy in the garret, for the October days began to grow chilly, and the afternoons were short. For two or three hours the sun lay warmly in the high window, showing Jo seated on the old sofa, writing busily, with her papers spread out upon a trunk before her, while Scrabble, the pet rat, promenaded the beams overhead, accompanied by his oldest son, a fine young fellow, who was evidently very proud of his whiskers. Quite absorbed in her work, Jo scribbled away till the last page was filled, when she signed her name with a flourish, and threw down her pen, exclaiming,—

"There, I've done my best! If this won't suit I shall have to wait till I can do better."

Lying back on the sofa, she read the manuscript carefully through, making dashes here and there, and putting in any exclamation points, which looked like little balloons; then she tied it up with a smart red ribbon, and sat a minute looking at it with a sober, wistful expression, which plainly showed how earnest her work had been. Jo's desk up here was an old tin kitchen, which hung against the wall. In it she kept her papers and a few books, safely shut away from Scrabble, who, being likewise of a literary turn, was fond of making a circulating library of such books as were left in his way, by eating the leaves. From this tin receptacle Jo produced another manuscript; and, putting both in her pocket, crept quietly down stairs, leaving her friends to nibble her pens and taste her ink.

She put on her hat and jacket as noiselessly as possible, and, going to the back entry window, got out upon the roof of a low porch, swung herself down to the grassy bank, and took a roundabout way to the road. Once there, she composed herself, hailed a passing omnibus, and rolled away to town, looking very merry and mysterious.

If anyone had been watching her, he would have thought her movements decidedly peculiar; for, on alighting, she went off at a great pace till she reached a certain number in a certain busy street; having found the place with some difficulty, she went into the door-way, looked up the dirty stairs, and, after standing stock still a minute, suddenly dived into the street, and walked away as rapidly as she came. This manoeuvre she repeated several times, to the great amusement of a black-eyed young gentleman lounging in the window of a building opposite. On returning for the third time, Jo gave herself a shake, pulled her hat over her eyes, and walked up the stairs, looking as if she were going to have all her teeth out.

There was a dentist's sign, among others, which adorned the entrance, and, after staring a moment at the pair of artificial jaws which slowly opened and shut to draw attention to a fine set of teeth, the young gentleman put on his coat, took his hat, and went down to post himself in the opposite doorway, saying, with a smile and a shiver,—

"It's like her to come alone, but if she has a bad time she'll need some one to help her home."

In ten minutes Jo came running down stairs with a very red face, and the general appearance of a person who had just passed through a trying ordeal of some sort. When she saw the young gentleman she looked anything but pleased, and passed him with a nod; but he followed, asking, with an air of sympathy,—

"Did you have a bad time?"

"Not very."

"You got through quickly."

"Yes, thank goodness!"

"Why did you go alone?"

"Didn't want anyone to know."

"You're the oddest fellow I ever saw. How many did you have out?"

Jo looked at her friend as if she did not understand him; then began to laugh, as if mightily amused at something.

"There are two which I want to have come out, but I must wait a week."

"What are you laughing at? You are up to some mischief, Jo," said Laurie, looking mystified.

"So are you. What were you doing, sir, up in that billiard saloon?"

"Begging your pardon, ma'am, it wasn't a billiard saloon, but a gymnasium, and I was taking a lesson in fencing."

"I'm glad of that."

"Why?"

"You can teach me, and then when we play Hamlet, you can be Laertes, and we'll make a fine thing of the fencing scene."

Laurie burst out with a hearty boy's laugh, which made several passers-by smile in spite of themselves.

"I'll teach you whether we play Hamlet or not; it's grand fun, and will straighten you up capitally. But I don't believe that was your only reason for saying 'I'm glad,' in that decided way; was it, now?"

"No, I was glad that you were not in the saloon, because I hope you never go to such places. Do you?"

"Not often."

"I wish you wouldn't."

"It's no harm, Jo. I have billiards at home, but it's no fun unless you have good players; so, as I'm fond of it, I come sometimes and have a game with Ned Moffat or some of the other fellows."

"Oh dear, I'm so sorry, for you'll get to liking it better and better, and will waste time and money, and grow like those dreadful boys. I did hope you'd stay respectable, and be a satisfaction to your friends," said Jo, shaking her head.

"Can't a fellow take a little innocent amusement now and then without losing his respectability?" asked Laurie, looking nettled.

"That depends upon how and where he takes it. I don't like Ned and his set, and wish you'd keep out of it. Mother won't let us have him at our house, though he wants to come; and if you grow like him she won't be willing to have us frolic together as we do now."

"Won't she?" asked Laurie anxiously.

"No, she can't bear fashionable young men, and she'd shut us all up in bandboxes rather than have us associate with them."

"Well, she needn't get out her bandboxes yet; I'm not a fashionable party, and don't mean to be; but I do like harmless larks now and then, don't you?"

"Yes, nobody minds them, so lark away, but don't get wild, will you? Or there will be an end of all our good times."

"I'll be a double-distilled saint."

"I can't bear saints: just be a simple, honest, respectable boy, and we'll never desert you. I don't know what I *should* do if you acted like Mr. King's son; he had plenty of money, but didn't know how to spend it, and got tipsy and gambled, and ran away, and forged his father's name, I believe, and was altogether horrid."

"You think I'm likely to do the same? Much obliged."

"No, I don't—oh, *dear*, no!—but I hear people talking about money being such a temptation, and I sometimes wish you were poor; I shouldn't worry then."

"Do you worry about me, Jo?"

"A little, when you look moody or discontented, as you sometimes do; for you've got such a strong will, if you once get started wrong, I'm afraid it would be hard to stop you."

Laurie walked in silence a few minutes, and Jo watched him, wishing she had held her tongue, for his eyes looked angry, though his lips still smiled as if at her warnings.

"Are you going to deliver lectures all the way home?" he asked presently.

"Of course not; why?"

"Because if you are, I'll take a 'bus; if you are not, I'd like to walk with you, and tell you something very interesting."

"I won't preach any more, and I'd like to hear the news immensely."

"Very well, then; come on. It's a secret, and if I tell you, you must tell me yours."

"I haven't got any," began Jo, but stopped suddenly, remembering that she had.

"You know you have,—you can't hide anything; so up and 'fess, or I won't tell," cried Laurie.

"Is your secret a nice one?"

"Oh, isn't it! All about people you know, and such fun! You ought to hear it, and I've been aching to tell it this long time. Come, you begin."

"You'll not say anything about it at home, will you?"

"Not a word."

"And you won't tease me in private?"

"I never tease."

"Yes, you do; you get everything you want out of people. I don't know how you do it, but you are a born wheedler."

"Thank you; fire away."

"Well, I've left two stories with a newspaper man, and he's to give his answer next week," whispered Jo, in her confidant's ear.

"Hurrah for Miss March, the celebrated American authoress!" cried Laurie throwing up his hat and catching it again, to the great delight of two ducks, four cats, five hens, and half a dozen Irish children; for they were out of the city now.

"Hush! It won't come to anything, I dare say; but I couldn't rest till I had tried, and I said nothing about it, because I didn't want any one else to be disappointed."

"It won't fail. Why, Jo, your stories are works of Shakespeare, compared to half the rubbish that is published every day. Won't it be fun to see them in print; and sha'n't we feel proud of our authoress?"

Jo's eyes sparkled, for it is always pleasant to be believed in; and a friend's praise is always sweeter than a dozen newspaper puffs.

"Where's *your* secret? Play fair, Teddy, or I'll never believe you again," she said, trying to extinguish the brilliant hopes that blazed up at a word of encouragement.

"I may get into a scrape for telling; but I didn't promise not to, so I will, for I never feel easy in my mind till I've told you any plummy bit of news I get. I know where Meg's glove is."

"Is that all?" said Jo, looking disappointed, as Laurie nodded and twinkled, with a face full of mysterious intelligence.

"It's quite enough for the present, as you'll agree when I tell you where it is."

"Tell, then."

Laurie bent, and whispered three words in Jo's ear, which produced a comical change. She stood and stared at him for a minute, looking both surprised and displeased, then walked on, saying sharply, "How do you know?"

"Saw it."

"Where?"

"Pocket."

"All this time?"

"Yes; isn't that romantic?"

"No, it's horrid."

"Don't you like it?"

"Of course I don't. It's ridiculous; it won't be allowed. My patience! What would Meg say?"

"You are not to tell any one; mind that."

"I didn't promise."

"That was understood, and I trusted you."

"Well, I won't for the present, any way; but I'm disgusted, and wish you hadn't told me."

"I thought you'd be pleased."

"At the idea of anybody coming to take Meg away? No, thank you."

"You'll feel better about it when somebody comes to take you away."

"I'd like to see anyone try it," cried Jo fiercely.

"So should I!" and Laurie chuckled at the idea.

"I don't think secrets agree with me; I feel rumpled up in my mind since you told me that," said Jo, rather ungratefully.

"Race down this hill with me, and you'll be all right," suggested Laurie.

No one was in sight; the smooth road sloped invitingly before her; and finding the temptation irresistible, Jo darted away, soon leaving hat and comb behind her, and scattering hair-pins as she ran. Laurie reached the goal first, and was quite satisfied with the success of his treatment; for his Atalanta came panting up, with flying hair, bright eyes, ruddy cheeks, and no signs of dissatisfaction in her face.

"I wish I was a horse; then I could run for miles in this splendid air, and not lose my breath. It was capital; but see what a guy it's made me. Go, pick up my things, like a cherub as you are," said Jo, dropping down under a maple-tree, which was carpeting the bank with crimson leaves.

Laurie leisurely departed to recover the lost property, and Jo bundled up her braids, hoping no one would pass by till she was tidy again. But some one did pass, and who should it be but Meg, looking particularly ladylike in her state and festival suit, for she had been making calls.

"What in the world are you doing here?" she asked, regarding her dishevelled sister with well-bred surprise.

"Getting leaves," meekly answered Jo, sorting the rosy handful she had just swept up.

"And hair-pins," added Laurie, throwing half a dozen into Jo's lap. "They grow on this road, Meg; so do combs and brown straw hats."

"You have been running, Jo; how could you? When *will* you stop such romping ways?" said Meg reprovingly, as she settled her cuffs, and smoothed her hair, with which the wind had taken liberties.

"Never till I'm stiff and old, and have to use a crutch. Don't try to make me grow up before my time, Meg: it's hard enough to have you change all of a sudden; let me be a little girl as long as I can."

As she spoke, Jo bent over the leaves to hide the trembling of her lips; for lately she had felt that Margaret was fast getting to be a woman, and Laurie's secret made her dread the separation which must surely come some time, and now seemed very near. He saw the trouble in her face, and drew Meg's attention from it by asking quickly, "Where have you been calling, all so fine?"

"At the Gardiners', and Sallie has been telling me all about Belle Moffat's wedding. It was very splendid, and they have gone to spend the winter in Paris. Just think how delightful that must be!"

"Do you envy her, Meg?" said Laurie.

"I'm afraid I do."

"I'm glad of it!" muttered Jo, tying on her hat with a jerk.

"Why?" asked Meg, looking surprised.

"Because if you care much about riches, you will never go and marry a poor man," said Jo, frowning at Laurie, who was mutely warning her to mind what she said.

"I shall never 'go and marry' any one," observed Meg, walking on with great dignity, while the others followed, laughing, whispering, skipping stones, and "behaving like children," as Meg said to herself, though she might have been tempted to join them if she had not had her best dress on.

For a week or two, Jo behaved so queerly that her sisters were quite bewildered. She rushed to the door when the postman rang; was rude to Mr. Brooke whenever they met; would sit looking at Meg with a woebegone face, occasionally jumping up to shake, and then to kiss her, in a very mysterious manner; Laurie and she were always making signs to one another, and talking about "Spread Eagles," till the girls declared they had both lost their wits. On the second Saturday after Jo got out of the window, Meg, as she sat sewing at her window, was scandalized by the sight of Laurie chasing Jo all over the garden, and finally capturing her in Amy's bower. What went on there, Meg could not see; but shrieks of laughter were heard, followed by the murmur of voices and a great flapping of newspapers.

"What shall we do with that girl? She never *will* behave like a young lady," sighed Meg, as she watched the race with a disapproving face.

"I hope she won't; she is so funny and dear as she is," said Beth, who had never betrayed that she was a little hurt at Jo's having secrets with anyone but her.

"It's very trying, but we never can make her *commy la fo*," added Amy, who sat making some new frills for herself, with her curls tied up in a very becoming way,—two agreeable things, which made her feel unusually elegant and ladylike.

In a few minutes Jo bounced in, laid herself on the sofa, and affected to read.

"Have you anything interesting there?" asked Meg, with condescension.

"Nothing but a story; won't amount to much, I guess," returned Jo, carefully keeping the name of the paper out of sight.

"You'd better read it aloud; that will amuse us and keep you out of mischief," said Amy, in her most grown-up tone.

"What's the name?" asked Beth, wondering why Jo kept her face behind the sheet.

"The Rival Painters."

"That sounds well; read it," said Meg.

With a loud "Hem!" and a long breath, Jo began to read very fast. The girls listened with interest, for the tale was romantic, and somewhat pathetic, as most of the characters died in the end.

"I like that about the splendid picture," was Amy's approving remark, as Jo paused.

"I prefer the lovering part. Viola and Angelo are two of our favorite names; isn't that queer?" said Meg, wiping her eyes, for the "lovering part" was tragical.

"Who wrote it?" asked Beth, who had caught a glimpse of Jo's face.

The reader suddenly sat up, cast away the paper, displaying a flushed countenance, and, with a funny mixture of solemnity and excitement, replied in a loud voice, "Your sister."

"You?" cried Meg, dropping her work.

"It's very good," said Amy critically.

"I knew it! I knew it! O my Jo, I *am* so proud!" and Beth ran to hug her sister, and exult over this splendid success.

Dear me, how delighted they all were, to be sure! How Meg wouldn't believe it till she saw the words, "Miss Josephine March," actually printed in the paper; how graciously Amy criticized the artistic parts of the story, and offered hints for a sequel, which unfortunately couldn't be carried out, as the hero and heroine were dead; how Beth got excited, and skipped and sang with joy; how Hannah came in to exclaim "Sakes alive, well I never!" in great astonishment at "that Jo's doin's;" how proud Mrs. March was when she knew it; how Jo laughed, with tears in her eyes, as she declared she might as well be a peacock and done with it; and how the "Spread Eagle" might be said to flap his wings triumphantly over the House of March, as the paper passed from hand to hand.

"Tell us all about it." "When did it come?" "How much did you get for it?" "What *will* father say?" "Won't Laurie laugh?" cried the family, all in one breath, as they clustered about Jo; for these foolish, affectionate people made a jubilee of every little household joy.

"Stop jabbering, girls, and I'll tell you everything," said Jo, wondering if Miss Burney felt any grander over her "Evelina" than she did over her "Rival Painters." Having told how she disposed of her tales, Jo added, "And when I went to get my answer, the man said he liked them both, but didn't pay beginners, only let them print in his paper, and noticed the stories. It was good practice, he said; and when the beginners improved, anyone would pay. So I let him have the two stories, and today this was sent to me, and Laurie caught me with it, and insisted on seeing it, so I let him; and he said it was good, and I shall write more, and he's going to get the next paid for, and I *am* so happy, for in time I may be able to support myself and help the girls."

Jo's breath gave out here; and, wrapping her head in the paper, she bedewed her little story with a few natural tears; for to be independent, and earn the praise of those she loved were the dearest wishes of her heart, and this seemed to be the first step toward that happy end.

# CHAPTER XV

## A TELEGRAM

NOVEMBER is the most disagreeable month in the whole year," said Margaret, standing at the window one dull afternoon, looking out at the frost-bitten garden.

"That's the reason I was born in it," observed Jo pensively, quite unconscious of the blot on her nose.

"If something very pleasant should happen now, we should think it a delightful month," said Beth, who took a hopeful view of everything, even November.

"I dare say; but nothing pleasant ever *does* happen in this family," said Meg, who was out of sorts. "We go grubbing along day after day, without a bit of change, and very little fun. We might as well be in a treadmill."

"My patience, how blue we are!" cried Jo. "I don't much wonder, poor dear, for you see other girls having splendid times, while you grind, grind, year in and year out. Oh, don't I wish I could manage things for you as I do for my heroines! You're pretty enough and good enough already, so I'd have some rich relation leave you a fortune unexpectedly; then you'd dash out as an heiress, scorn every one who has slighted you, go abroad, and come home my Lady Something, in a blaze of splendor and elegance."

"People don't have fortunes left them in that style now-a-days; men have to work, and women to marry for money. It's a dreadfully unjust world," said Meg bitterly.

"Jo and I are going to make fortunes for you all; just wait ten years, and see if we don't," said Amy, who sat in a corner, making mud pies, as Hannah called her little clay models of birds, fruit, and faces.

"Can't wait, and I'm afraid I haven't much faith in ink and dirt, though I'm grateful for your good intentions."

Meg sighed, and turned to the frost-bitten garden again; Jo groaned, and leaned both elbows on the table in a despondent attitude, but Amy spatted away energetically; and Beth, who sat at the other window, said, smiling, "Two pleasant things are going to happen right away: Marmee is coming down the street, and Laurie is tramping through the garden as if he had something nice to tell."

In they both came, Mrs. March with her usual question, "Any letter from father, girls?" and Laurie to say in his persuasive way, "Won't some of you come for a drive? I've been working away at mathematics till my head is in a muddle, and I'm going to freshen my wits by a brisk turn. It's a dull day, but the air isn't bad, and I'm going to take Brooke home, so it will be gay inside, if it isn't out. Come, Jo, you and Beth will go, won't you?"

"Of course we will."

"Much obliged, but I'm busy;" and Meg whisked out her work-basket, for she had agreed with her mother that it was best, for her at least, not to drive often with the young gentleman.

"We three will be ready in a minute," cried Amy, running away to wash her hands.

"Can I do anything for you, Madam Mother?" asked Laurie, leaning over Mrs. March's chair, with the affectionate look and tone he always gave her.

"No, thank you, except call at the office, if you'll be so kind, dear. It's our day for a letter, and the postman hasn't been. Father is as regular as the sun, but there's some delay on the way, perhaps."

A sharp ring interrupted her, and a minute after Hannah came in with a letter.

"It's one of them horrid telegraph things, mum," she said, handing it as if she was afraid it would explode and do some damage.

At the word "telegraph," Mrs. March snatched it, read the two lines it contained, and dropped back into her chair as white as if the little paper had sent a bullet to her heart. Laurie dashed down stairs for water, while Meg and Hannah supported her, and Jo read aloud, in a frightened voice,—

> "MRS. MARCH:
> "Your husband is very ill. Come at once.
> > "S. HALE,
> > "Blank Hospital, Washington."

How still the room was as they listened breathlessly, how strangely the day darkened outside, and how suddenly the whole world seemed to change as the girls gathered about their mother, feeling as if all the happiness and support of their lives was about to be taken from them. Mrs. March was herself again directly; read the message over, and stretched out her arms to her daughters, saying, in a tone they never forgot, "I shall go at once, but it may be too late. O children, children, help me to bear it!"

For several minutes there was nothing but the sound of sobbing in the room, mingled with broken words of comfort, tender assurances of help, and hopeful whispers that died away in tears. Poor Hannah was the first to recover, and with unconscious wisdom she set all the rest a good example; for, with her, work was the panacea for most afflictions.

"The Lord keep the dear man! I won't waste no time a cryin', but git your things ready right away, mum," she said heartily, as she wiped her face on her apron, gave her mistress a warm shake of the hand with her own hard one, and went away, to work like three women in one.

"She's right; there's no time for tears now. Be calm, girls, and let me think."

They tried to be calm, poor things, as their mother sat up, looking pale, but steady, and put away her grief to think and plan for them.

"Where's Laurie?" she asked presently, when she had collected her thoughts, and decided on the first duties to be done.

"Here, ma'am. Oh, let me do something!" cried the boy, hurrying from the next room, whither he had withdrawn, feeling that their first sorrow was too sacred for even his friendly eyes to see.

"Send a telegram saying I will come at once. The next train goes early in the morning. I'll take that."

"What else? The horses are ready; I can go anywhere, do anything," he said, looking ready to fly to the ends of the earth.

"Leave a note at Aunt March's. Jo, give me that pen and paper."

Tearing off the blank side of one of her newly copied pages, Jo drew the table before her mother, well knowing that money for the long, sad journey must be borrowed, and feeling as if she could do anything to add a little to the sum for her father.

"Now go, dear; but don't kill yourself driving at a desperate pace; there is no need of that."

Mrs. March's warning was evidently thrown away; for five minutes later Laurie tore by the window on his own fleet horse, riding as if for his life.

"Jo, run to the rooms, and tell Mrs. King that I can't come. On the way get these things. I'll put them down; they'll be needed, and I must go prepared for nursing. Hospital stores are not always good. Beth, go and ask Mr. Laurence for a couple of bottles of old wine: I'm not too proud to beg for father; he shall have the best of everything. Amy, tell Hannah to get down the black trunk; and, Meg, come and help me find my things, for I'm half bewildered."

Writing, thinking, and directing, all at once, might well bewilder the poor lady, and Meg begged her to sit quietly in her room for a little while, and let them work. Everyone scattered like leaves before a gust of wind; and the quiet, happy household was broken up as suddenly as if the paper had been an evil spell.

Mr. Laurence came hurrying back with Beth, bringing every comfort the kind old gentleman could think of for the invalid, and friendliest promises of protection for the girls during the mother's absence, which comforted her very much. There was nothing he didn't offer, from his own dressing-gown to himself as escort. But that last was impossible. Mrs. March would not hear of the old gentleman's undertaking the long journey; yet an expression of relief was visible when he spoke of it, for anxiety ill fits one for travelling. He saw the look, knit his heavy eyebrows, rubbed his hands, and marched abruptly away, saying he'd be back directly. No one had time to think of him again till, as Meg ran through the entry, with a pair of rubbers in one hand and a cup of tea in the other, she came suddenly upon Mr. Brooke.

"I'm very sorry to hear of this, Miss March," he said, in the kind, quiet tone which sounded very pleasantly to her perturbed spirit. "I came to offer myself as escort to your mother. Mr. Laurence has commissions for me in Washington and it will give me real satisfaction to be of service to her there."

Down dropped the rubbers, and the tea was very near following, as Meg put out her hand, with a face so full of gratitude, that Mr. Brooke would have felt repaid for a much greater sacrifice than the trifling one of time and comfort which he was about to make.

"How kind you all are! Mother will accept, I'm sure; and it will be

She came suddenly upon Mr. Brooke.

such a relief to know that she has someone to take care of her. Thank you very, very much!"

Meg spoke earnestly, and forgot herself entirely till something in the brown eyes looking down at her made her remember the cooling tea, and lead the way into the parlor, saying she would call her mother.

Everything was arranged by the time Laurie returned with a note from Aunt March, enclosing the desired sum, and a few lines repeating what she had often said before,—that she had always told them it was absurd for March to go into the army, always predicted that no good would come of it, and she hoped they would take her advice next time. Mrs. March put the note in the fire, the money in her purse, and went on with her preparations, with her lips folded tightly, in a way which Jo would have understood if she had been there.

The short afternoon wore away; all the other errands were done, and Meg and her mother busy at some necessary needlework, while Beth and Amy got tea, and Hannah finished her ironing with what she called a "slap and a bang," but still Jo did not come. They began to get anxious; and Laurie went off to find her, for no one ever knew what freak Jo might take into her head. He missed her, however, and she came walking in with a very queer expression of countenance, for there was a mixture of fun and fear, satisfaction and regret, in it, which puzzled the family as much as did the roll of bills she laid before her mother, saying, with a little choke in her voice, "That's my contribution towards making father comfortable and bringing him home!"

"My dear, where did you get it? Twenty-five dollars! Jo, I hope you haven't done anything rash?"

"No, it's mine honestly; I didn't beg, borrow, or steal it. I earned it; and I don't think you'll blame me, for I only sold what was my own."

As she spoke, Jo took off her bonnet, and a general outcry arose, for all her abundant hair was cut short.

"Your hair! Your beautiful hair!" "O Jo, how could you? Your one beauty." "My dear girl, there was no need of this." "She doesn't look like my Jo any more, but I love her dearly for it!"

As every one exclaimed, and Beth hugged the cropped head tenderly, Jo assumed an indifferent air, which did not deceive anyone a particle, and said, rumpling up the brown bush, and trying to look as if she liked it, "It doesn't affect the fate of the nation, so don't wail, Beth. It will be good for my vanity; I was getting too proud of my wig. It will do my brains good to have that mop taken off; my head feels deliciously light and cool, and the barber said I could soon have a curly crop, which will be boyish, becoming, and easy to keep in order. I'm satisfied; so please take the money, and let's have supper."

"Tell me all about it, Jo. *I* am not quite satisfied, but I can't blame you, for I know how willingly you sacrificed your vanity, as you call it, to your love. But, my dear, it was not necessary, and I'm afraid you will regret it, one of these days," said Mrs. March.

"No, I won't!" returned Jo stoutly, feeling much relieved that her prank was not entirely condemned.

"What made you do it?" asked Amy, who would as soon have thought of cutting of her head as her pretty hair.

"Well, I was wild to do something for father," replied Jo, as they gathered about the table, for healthy young people can eat even in the midst of trouble. "I hate to borrow as much as mother does, and I knew Aunt March would croak; she always does, if you ask for a ninepence. Meg gave all her quarterly salary toward the rent, and I only got some clothes with mine, so I felt wicked, and was bound to have some money, if I sold the nose off my face to get it."

"You needn't feel wicked, my child: you had no winter things, and got the simplest with your own hard earnings," said Mrs. March, with a look that warmed Jo's heart.

"I hadn't the least idea of selling my hair at first, but as I went along I kept thinking what I could do, and feeling as if I'd like to dive into some of the rich stores and help myself. In a barber's window I saw tails of hair with the prices marked; and one black tail, not so thick as mine, was forty dollars. It came over me all of a sudden that I had one thing to make money out of, and without stopping to think, I walked in, asked if they bought hair, and what they would give for mine."

"I don't see how you dared to do it," said Beth, in a tone of awe.

"Oh, he was a little man who looked as if he merely lived to oil his hair. He rather stared, at first, as if he wasn't used to having girls bounce into his shop and ask him to buy their hair. He said he didn't care about mine, it wasn't the fashionable color, and he never paid much for it in the first place; the work put into it made it dear, and so on. It was getting late, and I was afraid, if it wasn't done right away, that I shouldn't have it done at all, and you know when I start to do a thing, I hate to give it up; so I begged him to take it, and told him why I was in such a hurry. It was silly, I dare say, but it changed his mind, for I got rather excited, and told the story in my topsy-turvy way, and his wife heard, and said so kindly,—

" 'Take it, Thomas, and oblige the young lady; I'd do as much for our Jimmy any day if I had a spire of hair worth selling.' "

"Who was Jimmy?" asked Amy, who liked to have things explained as they went along.

"Her son, she said, who was in the army. How friendly such things make strangers feel, don't they? She talked away all the time the man chopped, and diverted my mind nicely."

"Didn't you feel dreadfully when the first cut came?" asked Meg, with a shiver.

"I took a last look at my hair while the man got his things, and that was the end of it. I never snivel over trifles like that; I will confess, though, I felt queer when I saw the dear old hair laid out on the table, and felt only the short, rough ends on my head. It almost seemed as if I'd an arm or a leg off. The woman saw me look at it, and picked out a long lock for me to keep. I'll give it to you, Marmee, just to remember past glories by; for a crop is so comfortable I don't think I shall ever have a mane again."

Mrs. March folded the wavy chestnut lock, and laid it away with a short gray one in her desk. She only said "Thank you, deary," but something in her face made the girls change the subject, and talk as cheerfully as they could about Mr. Brooke's kindness, the prospect of a fine day tomorrow, and the happy times they would have when father came home to be nursed.

No one wanted to go to bed, when, at ten o'clock, Mrs. March put by the last finished job, and said, "Come, girls." Beth went to the piano and played the father's favorite hymn; all began bravely, but broke down one by one, till Beth was left alone, singing with all her heart, for to her music was always a sweet consoler.

"Go to bed and don't talk, for we must be up early, and shall need all the sleep we can get. Good-night, my darlings," said Mrs. March, as the hymn ended, for no one cared to try another.

They kissed her quietly, and went to bed as silently as if the dear invalid lay in the next room. Beth and Amy soon fell asleep in spite of the great trouble, but Meg lay awake, thinking the most serious thoughts she had ever known in her short life. Jo lay motionless, and her sister fancied that she was asleep, till a stifled sob made her exclaim, as she touched a wet cheek,—

"Jo, dear, what is it? Are you crying about father?"

"No, not now."

"What then?"

"My—my hair!" burst out poor Jo, trying vainly to smother her emotion in the pillow.

It did not sound at all comical to Meg, who kissed and caressed the afflicted heroine in the tenderest manner.

"I'm not sorry," protested Jo, with a choke. "I'd do it again tomorrow, if I could. It's only the vain, selfish part of me that goes and cries in this silly way. Don't tell any one, it's all over now. I thought you were asleep, so I just made a little private moan for my one beauty. How came you to be awake?"

"I can't sleep, I'm so anxious," said Meg.

"Think about something pleasant, and you'll soon drop off."

"I tried it, but felt wider awake than ever."

"What did you think of?"

"Handsome faces,—eyes particularly," answered Meg, smiling to herself, in the dark.

"What color do you like best?"

"Brown—that is, sometimes; blue are lovely."

Jo laughed, and Meg sharply ordered her not to talk, then amiably promised to make her hair curl, and fell asleep to dream of living in her castle in the air.

The clocks were striking midnight, and the rooms were very still, as a figure glided quietly from bed to bed, smoothing a coverlid here, settling a pillow there, and pausing to look long and tenderly at each unconscious face, to kiss each with lips that mutely blessed, and to pray the fervent prayers which only mothers utter. As she lifted the curtain to look out into the dreary night, the moon broke suddenly from behind the clouds, and shone upon her like a bright, benignant face, which seemed to whisper in the silence, "Be comforted, dear soul! There is always light behind the clouds."

# CHAPTER XVI

## LETTERS

IN the cold gray dawn the sisters lit their lamp, and read their chapter with an earnestness never felt before; for now the shadow of a real trouble had come, the little books were full of help and comfort; and, as they dressed, they agreed to say good-by cheerfully and hopefully, and send their mother on her anxious journey unsaddened by tears or complaints from them. Everything seemed very strange when they went down,—so dim and still outside, so full of light and bustle within. Breakfast at that early hour seemed odd, and even Hannah's familiar face looked unnatural as she flew about her kitchen with her night-cap on. The big trunk stood ready in the hall, mother's cloak and bonnet lay on the sofa, and mother herself sat trying to eat, but looking so pale and worn with sleeplessness and anxiety that the girls found it very hard to keep their resolution. Meg's eyes kept filling in spite of herself; Jo was obliged to hide her face in the kitchen roller more than once; and the little girls' wore a grave, troubled expression, as if sorrow was a new experience to them.

Nobody talked much, but as the time drew very near, and they sat waiting for the carriage, Mrs. March said to the girls, who were all busied about her, one folding her shawl, another smoothing out the strings of her bonnet, a third putting on her overshoes, and a fourth fastening up her travelling bag,—

"Children, I leave you to Hannah's care and Mr. Laurence's protection. Hannah is faithfulness itself, and our good neighbor will guard you as if you were his own. I have no fears for you, yet I am anxious that you should take this trouble rightly. Don't grieve and fret when I am gone, or think that you can comfort yourselves by being idle and trying to forget. Go on with your work as usual, for work is a blessed solace. Hope and keep busy; and whatever happens, remember that you never can be fatherless."

"Yes, mother."

"Meg, dear, be prudent, watch over your sisters, consult Hannah, and, in any perplexity, go to Mr. Laurence. Be patient, Jo, don't get despondent or do rash things; write to me often, and be my brave girl, ready to help and cheer us all. Beth, comfort yourself with your music, and be faithful to the little home duties; and you, Amy, help all you can, be obedient, and keep happy safe at home."

"We will, mother! We will!"

The rattle of an approaching carriage made them all start and listen. That was the hard minute, but the girls stood it well: no one cried, no one ran away or uttered a lamentation, though their hearts were very heavy as they sent loving messages to father, remembering, as they spoke, that it might be too late to deliver them. They kissed their mother quietly, clung about her tenderly, and tried to wave their hands cheerfully when she drove away.

Laurie and his grandfather came over to see her off, and Mr. Brooke looked so strong and sensible and kind that the girls christened him "Mr. Greatheart" on the spot.

"Good-by, my darlings! God bless and keep us all!" whispered Mrs. March, as she kissed one dear little face after the other, and hurried into the carriage.

As she rolled away, the sun came out, and, looking back, she saw it shining on the group at the gate, like a good omen. They saw it also, and smiled and waved their hands; and the last thing she beheld, as she turned the corner, was the four bright faces, and behind them, like a body-guard, old Mr. Laurence, faithful Hannah, and devoted Laurie.

"How kind every one is to us!" she said, turning to find fresh proof of it in the respectful sympathy of the young man's face.

"I don't see how they can help it," returned Mr. Brooke, laughing so infectiously that Mrs. March could not help smiling; and so the long journey began with the good omens of sunshine, smiles, and cheerful words.

"I feel as if there had been an earthquake," said Jo, as their neighbors went home to breakfast, leaving them to rest and refresh themselves.

"It seems as if half the house was gone," added Meg forlornly.

Beth opened her lips to say something, but could only point to the pile of nicely-mended hose which lay on mother's table, showing that even in her last hurried moments she had thought and worked for them. It was a little thing, but it went straight to their hearts; and, in spite of their brave resolutions, they all broke down, and cried bitterly.

Hannah wisely allowed them to relieve their feelings, and, when the shower showed signs of clearing up, she came to the rescue, armed with a coffee-pot.

"Now, my dear young ladies, remember what your ma said, and don't fret. Come and have a cup of coffee all round, and then let's fall to work, and be a credit to the family."

Coffee was a treat, and Hannah showed great tact in making it that morning. No one could resist her persuasive nods, or the fragrant invitation issuing from the nose of the coffee-pot. They drew up to the table, exchanged their handkerchiefs for napkins, and in ten minutes were all right again.

" 'Hope and keep busy;' that's the motto for us, so let's see who will remember it best. I shall go to Aunt March, as usual. Oh, won't she lecture though!" said Jo, as she sipped with returning spirit.

"I shall go to my Kings, though I'd much rather stay at home and attend to things here," said Meg, wishing she hadn't made her eyes so red.

"No need of that; Beth and I can keep house perfectly well," put in Amy, with an important air.

"Hannah will tell us what to do; and we'll have everything nice when you come home," added Beth, getting out her mop and dish-tub without delay.

"I think anxiety is very interesting," observed Amy, eating sugar, pensively.

The girls couldn't help laughing, and felt better for it, though Meg shook her head at the young lady who could find consolation in a sugar-bowl.

The sight of the turnovers made Jo sober again; and when the two went out to their daily tasks, they looked sorrowfully back at the window where they were accustomed to see their mother's face. It was gone; but Beth had remembered the little household ceremony, and there she was, nodding away at them like a rosy-faced mandarin.

"That's so like my Beth!" said Jo, waving her hat, with a grateful face. "Good-by, Meggy; I hope the Kings won't train today. Don't fret about father, dear," she added, as they parted.

"And I hope Aunt March won't croak. Your hair *is* becoming, and it looks very boyish and nice," returned Meg, trying not to smile at the curly head, which looked comically small on her tall sister's shoulders.

"That's my only comfort;" and, touching her hat *à la* Laurie, away went Jo, feeling like a shorn sheep on a wintry day.

News from their father comforted the girls very much; for, though dangerously ill, the presence of the best and tenderest of nurses had already done him good. Mr. Brooke sent a bulletin every day, and, as the head of the family, Meg insisted on reading the despatches, which grew more and more cheering as the week passed. At first, everyone was eager to write, and plump envelopes were carefully poked into the letter-box by one or other of the sisters, who felt rather important with their Washington correspondence. As one of these packets contained characteristic notes from the party, we will rob an imaginary mail, and read them:—

"MY DEAREST MOTHER,—

"It is impossible to tell you how happy your last letter made us, for the news was so good we couldn't help laughing and crying over it. How very kind Mr. Brooke is, and how fortunate that Mr. Laurence's business detains him near you so long, since he is so useful to you and father. The girls are all as good as gold. Jo helps me with the sewing, and insists on doing all sorts of hard jobs. I should be afraid she might overdo, if I didn't know that her 'moral fit' wouldn't last long. Beth is as regular about her tasks as a clock, and never forgets what you told her. She grieves about father, and looks sober except when she is at her little piano. Amy minds me nicely, and I take great care of her. She does her own hair, and I am teaching her to make button-holes and mend her stockings. She tries very hard, and I know you will be pleased with her improvement when you come. Mr. Laurence watches over us like a motherly old hen, as Jo says; and Laurie is very kind and neighborly. He and Jo keep us merry, for we get pretty blue sometimes, and feel like orphans, with you so far away. Hannah is a perfect saint; she does not scold at all, and always calls me Miss 'Margaret,' which is quite proper, you know, and treats me with respect. We are all well and busy; but we long, day and night, to have you back. Give my dearest love to father, and believe me, ever your own.

"MEG."

This note, prettily written on scented paper, was a great contrast to the next, which was scribbled on a big sheet of thin foreign paper, ornamented with blots and all manner of flourishes and curly-tailed letters:—

"MY PRECIOUS MARMEE,—

"Three cheers for dear father! Brooke was a trump to telegraph right off, and let us know the minute he was better. I rushed up garret when the letter came, and tried to thank God for being so good to us; but I could only cry, and say, 'I'm glad! I'm glad!' Didn't that do as well as a regular prayer? For I felt a great many in my heart. We have such funny times; and now I can enjoy them, for everyone is so desperately good, it's like living in a nest of turtle-doves. You'd laugh to see Meg head the table and try to be motherish. She gets prettier every day, and I'm in love with her sometimes. The children are regular archangels, and I—well, I'm Jo, and never shall be anything else. Oh, I must tell you that I came near having a quarrel with Laurie. I freed my mind about a silly little thing, and he was offended. I was right, but didn't speak as I ought, and he marched home, saying he wouldn't come again till I begged pardon. I declared I wouldn't, and got mad. It lasted all day; I felt bad, and wanted you very much. Laurie and I are both so proud, it's hard to beg pardon; but I thought he'd come to it, for I *was* in the right. He didn't come; and just at night I remembered what you said when Amy fell into the river. I read my little book, felt better, resolved not to let the sun set on *my* anger, and ran over to tell Laurie I was sorry. I met him at the gate, coming for the same thing. We both laughed, begged each other's pardon, and felt all good and comfortable again.

"I made a 'pome' yesterday, when I was helping Hannah wash; and, as father likes my silly little things, I put it in to amuse him. Give him the lovingest hug that ever was, and kiss yourself a dozen times for your

"TOPSY-TURVY JO."

### "A SONG FROM THE SUDS

*"Queen of my tub, I merrily sing,*
*While the white foam rises high;*
*And sturdily wash and rinse and wring,*
*And fasten the clothes to dry;*
*Then out in the free fresh air they swing,*
*Under the sunny sky.*

*"I wish we could wash from our hearts and souls*
*The stains of the week away,*
*And let water and air by their magic make*

> *Ourselves as pure as they;*
> *Then on the earth there would be indeed*
> *A glorious washing-day!*

> "*Along the path of a useful life,*
> *Will heart's-ease ever bloom;*
> *The busy mind has no time to think*
> *Of sorrow or care or gloom;*
> *And anxious thoughts may be swept away,*
> *As we bravely wield a broom.*

> "*I am glad a task to me is given,*
> *To labor at day by day;*
> *For it brings me health and strength and hope,*
> *And I cheerfully learn to say,—*
> '*Head, you may think, Heart, you may feel,*
> *But, Hand, you shall work away!*' "

"DEAR MOTHER,—

"There is only room for me to send my love, and some pressed pansies from the root I have been keeping safe in the house for father to see. I read every morning, try to be good all day, and sing myself to sleep with father's tune. I can't sing 'Land of the Leal' now; it makes me cry. Everyone is very kind, and we are as happy as we can be without you. Amy wants the rest of the page, so I must stop. I didn't forget to cover the holders, and I wind the clock and air the rooms every day.

"Kiss dear father on the cheek he calls mine. Oh, do come soon to your loving

"LITTLE BETH."

"MA CHERE MAMMA,—

"We are all well I do my lessons always and never corroberate the girls—Meg says I mean contradick so I put in both words and you can take the properest. Meg is a great comfort to me and lets me have jelly every night at tea its so good for me Jo says because it keeps me sweet tempered. Laurie is not as respeckful as he ought to be now I am almost in my teens, he calls me Chick and hurts my feelings by talking French to me very fast when I say Merci or Bon jour as Hattie King does. The sleeves of my blue dress were all worn out, and Meg put in new ones, but the full front came wrong and they are more blue than the dress. I felt bad but did not fret I bear my troubles well but I do wish Hannah would put more starch in my aprons and have buckwheats every day. Can't she? Didn't I make that interrigation point nice? Meg says my punchtuation and spelling are disgraceful and I am mortyfied but dear me I have so many things to do, I can't stop. Adieu, I send heaps of love to Papa.

"Your affectionate daughter,
"AMY CURTIS MARCH."

"DEAR MIS MARCH,—

"I jes drop a line to say we git on fust rate. The girls is clever and fly round right smart. Miss Meg is going to make a proper good housekeeper; she hes the liking for it, and gits the hang of things surprisin quick. Jo doos beat all for goin ahead, but she don't stop to cal'k'late fust, and you never know where she's like to bring up. She done out a tub of clothes on Monday, but she starched em afore they was wrenched, and blued a pink calico dress till I thought I should a died a laughin. Beth is the best of little creeters, and a sight of help to me, bein so forehanded and dependable. She tries to learn everything, and really goes to market beyond her years; likewise keeps accounts, with my help, quite wonderful. We have got on very economical so fur; I don't let the girls hev coffee only once a week, accordin to your wish, and keep em on plain wholesome vittles. Amy does well about frettin, wearin her best clothes and eatin sweet stuff. Mr. Laurie is as full of didoes as usual, and turns the house upside down frequent; but he heartens up the girls, and so I let em hev full swing. The old gentleman sends heaps of things, and is rather wearin, but means wal, and it aint my place to say nothin. My bread is riz, so no more at this time. I send my duty to Mr. March, and hope he's seen the last of his Pewmonia.

"Yours Respectful,

"HANNAH MULLET."

"HEAD NURSE OF WARD NO. 2,—

"All serene on the Rappahannock, troops in fine condition, commissary department well conducted, the Home Guard under Colonel Teddy always on duty, Comander-in-chief General Laurence reviews the army daily, Quartermaster Mullett keeps order in camp, and Major Lion does picket duty at night. A salute of twenty-four guns was fired on receipt of good news from Washington, and a dress parade took place at head-quarters. Commander-in-chief sends best wishes, in which he is heartily joined by

"COLONEL TEDDY."

"DEAR MADAM,—

"The little girls are all well; Beth and my boy report daily; Hannah is a model servant, and guards pretty Meg like a dragon. Glad the fine weather holds; pray make Brooke useful, and draw on me for funds if expenses exceed your estimate. Don't let your husband want anything. Thank God he is mending.

"Your sincere friend and servant,

"JAMES LAURENCE."

"I wind the clock."

# CHAPTER XVII

## LITTLE FAITHFUL

FOR a week the amount of virtue in the old house would have supplied the neighborhood. It was really amazing, for everyone seemed in a heavenly frame of mind, and self-denial was all the fashion. Relieved of their first anxiety about their father, the girls insensibly relaxed their praiseworthy efforts a little, and began to fall back into the old ways. They did not forget their motto, but hoping and keeping busy seemed to grow easier; and after such tremendous exertions, they felt that Endeavor deserved a holiday, and gave it a good many.

Jo caught a bad cold through neglect to cover the shorn head enough, and was ordered to stay at home till she was better, for Aunt March didn't like to hear people read with colds in their heads. Jo liked this, and after an energetic rummage from garret to cellar, subsided on the sofa to nurse her cold with arsenicum and books. Amy found that house-work and art did not go well together, and returned to her mud pies. Meg went daily to her pupils, and sewed, or thought she did, at home, but much time was spent in writing long letters to her mother, or reading the Washington despatches over and over. Beth kept on, with only slight relapses into idleness or grieving.

All the little duties were faithfully done each day, and many of her sisters' also, for they were forgetful, and the house seemed like a clock whose pendulum was gone a-visiting. When her heart got heavy with longings for mother or fears for father, she went away into a certain closet, hid her face in the folds of a certain dear old gown, and made her little moan and prayed her little prayer quietly by herself. Nobody knew what cheered her up after a sober fit, but every one felt how sweet and helpful Beth was, and fell into a way of going to her for comfort or advice in their small affairs.

All were unconscious that this experience was a test of character; and, when the first excitement was over, felt that they had done well, and deserved praise. So they did; but their mistake was in ceasing to do well, and they learned this lesson through much anxiety and regret.

"Meg, I wish you'd go and see the Hummels; you know mother told us not to forget them," said Beth, ten days after Mrs. March's departure.

"I'm too tired to go this afternoon," replied Meg, rocking comfortably as she sewed.

"Can't you, Jo?" asked Beth.

"Too stormy for me with my cold."

"I thought it was almost well."

"It's well enough for me to go out with Laurie, but not well enough to go to the Hummels'," said Jo, laughing, but looking a little ashamed of her inconsistency.

"Why don't you go yourself?" asked Meg.

"I *have* been every day, but the baby is sick, and I don't know what to do for it. Mrs. Hummel goes away to work, and Lottchen takes care of it; but it gets sicker and sicker and I think you or Hannah ought to go."

Beth spoke earnestly, and Meg promised she would go tomorrow.

"Ask Hannah for some nice little mess, and take it round, Beth; the air will do you good," said Jo, adding apologetically, "I'd go, but I want to finish my writing."

"My head aches and I'm tired, so I thought maybe some of you would go," said Beth.

"Amy will be in presently, and she will run down for us," suggested Meg.

"Well, I'll rest a little and wait for her."

So Beth lay down on the sofa, the others returned to their work, and the Hummels were forgotten. An hour passed: Amy did not come; Meg went to her room to try on a new dress; Jo was absorbed in her story, and Hannah was sound asleep before the kitchen fire, when Beth quietly put on her hood, filled her basket with odds and ends for the poor children, and went out into the chilly air, with a heavy head, and a grieved look in her patient eyes. It was late when she came back, and no one saw her creep upstairs and shut herself into her mother's room. Half an hour after Jo went to "mother's closet" for something, and there found Beth sitting on the medicine chest, looking very grave, with red eyes, and a camphor-bottle in her hand.

"Christopher Columbus! What's the matter?" cried Jo, as Beth put out her hand as if to warn her off, and asked quickly,—

"You've had the scarlet fever, haven't you?"

"Years ago, when Meg did. Why?"

"Then I'll tell you. Oh, Jo, the baby's dead!"

"What baby?"

"Mrs. Hummel's; it died in my lap before she got home," cried Beth, with a sob.

"My poor dear, how dreadful for you! I ought to have gone," said Jo, taking her sister in her arms as she sat down in her mother's big chair, with a remorseful face.

"It wasn't dreadful, Jo, only so sad! I saw in a minute that it was sicker, but Lottchen said her mother had gone for a doctor, so I took baby and let Lotty rest. It seemed asleep, but all of a sudden it gave a little cry, and trembled, and then lay very still. I tried to warm its feet, and Lotty gave it some milk, but it didn't stir, and I knew it was dead."

"Don't cry, dear! What did you do?"

"I just sat and held it softly till Mrs. Hummel came with the doctor. He said it was dead, and looked at Heinrich and Minna, who have got sore throats. 'Scarlet fever, ma'am. Ought to have called me before,' he said crossly. Mrs. Hummel told him she was poor, and had tried to cure baby herself, but now it was too late, and she could only ask him to help the others, and trust to charity for his pay. He smiled then, and was kinder; but it was very sad, and I cried with them till he turned round, all of a sudden, and told me to go home and take belladonna right away, or I'd have the fever."

"No, you won't!" cried Jo, hugging her close, with a frightened look.

"O Beth, if you should be sick I never could forgive myself. What *shall* we do?"

"Don't be frightened, I guess I shan't have it badly. I looked in mother's book, and saw that it begins with headache, sore throat, and queer feelings like mine, so I did take some belladonna, and I feel better," said Beth, laying her cold hands on her hot forehead, and trying to look well.

"If mother was only at home!" exclaimed Jo, seizing the book, and feeling that Washington was an immense way off. She read a page, looked at Beth, felt her head, peeped into her throat, and then said gravely, "You've been over the baby every day for more than a week, and among the others who are going to have it; so I'm afraid *you* are going to have it, Beth. I'll call Hannah, she knows all about sickness."

"Don't let Amy come; she never had it, and I should hate to give it to her. Can't you and Meg have it over again?" asked Beth, anxiously.

"I guess not; don't care if I do; serve me right, selfish pig, to let you go, and stay writing rubbish myself!" muttered Jo, as she went to consult Hannah.

The good soul was wide awake in a minute, and took the lead at once, assuring Jo that there was no need to worry; everyone had scarlet fever, and, if rightly treated, nobody died,—all of which Jo believed, and felt much relieved as they went up to call Meg.

"Now I'll tell you what we'll do," said Hannah, when she had examined and questioned Beth; "we will have Dr. Bangs, just to take a look at you, dear, and see that we start right; then we'll send Amy off to Aunt March's, for a spell, to keep her out of harm's way, and one of you girls can stay at home and amuse Beth for a day or two."

"I shall stay, of course; I'm oldest," began Meg, looking anxious and self-reproachful.

"*I* shall, because it's my fault she is sick; I told mother I'd do the errands, and I haven't," said Jo decidedly.

"Which will you have, Beth? There ain't no need of but one," said Hannah.

"Jo, please;" and Beth leaned her head against her sister, with a contented look, which effectually settled that point.

"I'll go and tell Amy," said Meg, feeling a little hurt, yet rather relieved, on the whole, for she did not like nursing, and Jo did.

Amy rebelled outright, and passionately declared that she had rather have the fever than go to Aunt March. Meg reasoned, pleaded, and commanded: all in vain. Amy protested that she would *not* go; and Meg left her in despair, to ask Hannah what should be done. Before she came back, Laurie walked into the parlor to find Amy sobbing, with her head in the sofa-cushions. She told her story, expecting to be consoled; but Laurie only put his hands in his pockets and walked about the room, whistling softly, as he knit his brows in deep thought. Presently he sat down beside her, and said, in his most wheedlesome tone, "Now be a sensible little woman, and do as they say. No, don't cry, but hear what a jolly plan I've got. You go to Aunt March's, and I'll come and take you out every day, driving or walking, and we'll have capital times. Won't that be better than moping here?"

"I don't wish to be sent off as if I was in the way," began Amy, in an injured voice.

"Bless your heart, child, it's to keep you well. You don't want to be sick, do you?"

"No, I'm sure I don't; but I dare say I shall be, for I've been with Beth all the time."

"That's the very reason you ought to go away at once, so that you may escape it. Change of air and care will keep you well, I dare say; or, if it does not entirely, you will have the fever more lightly. I advise you to be off as soon as you can, for scarlet fever is no joke, miss."

"But it's dull at Aunt March's, and she is so cross," said Amy, looking rather frightened.

"It won't be dull with me popping in every day to tell you how Beth is, and take you out gallivanting. The old lady likes me, and I'll be as sweet as possible to her, so she won't peck at us, whatever we do."

"Will you take me out in the trotting wagon with Puck?"

"On my honor as a gentleman."

"And come every single day?"

"See if I don't."

"And bring me back the minute Beth is well?"

"The identical minute."

"And go to the theatre, truly?"

"A dozen theatres, if we may."

"Well—I guess—I will," said Amy slowly.

"Good girl! Call Meg, and tell her you'll give in," said Laurie, with an approving pat, which annoyed Amy more than the "giving in."

Meg and Jo came running down to behold the miracle which had been wrought; and Amy, feeling very precious and self-sacrificing, promised to go, if the doctor said Beth was going to be ill.

"How is the little dear?" asked Laurie; for Beth was his especial pet, and he felt more anxious about her than he liked to show.

"She is lying down on mother's bed, and feels better. The baby's death troubled her, but I dare say she has only got cold. Hannah *says* she thinks so; but she *looks* worried, and that makes me fidgety," answered Meg.

"What a trying world it is!" said Jo, rumpling up her hair in a fretful sort of way. "No sooner do we get out of one trouble than down comes another. There doesn't seem to be anything to hold on to when mother's gone; so I'm all at sea."

"Well, don't make a porcupine of yourself, it isn't becoming. Settle your wig, Jo, and tell me if I shall telegraph to your mother, or do anything?" asked Laurie, who never had been reconciled to the loss of his friend's one beauty.

"That is what troubles me," said Meg. "I think we ought to tell her if Beth is really ill, but Hannah says we mustn't, for mother can't leave father, and it will only make them anxious. Beth won't be sick long, and Hannah knows just what to do, and mother said we were to mind her, so I suppose we must, but it doesn't seem quite right to me."

"Hum, well, I can't say; suppose you ask grandfather after the doctor has been."

"We will. Jo, go and get Dr. Bangs at once," commanded Meg; "we can't decide anything till he has been."

"Stay where you are, Jo; I'm errand-boy to this establishment," said Laurie, taking up his cap.

"I'm afraid you are busy," began Meg.

"No, I've done my lessons for the day."

"Do you study in vacation time?" asked Jo.

"I follow the good example my neighbors set me," was Laurie's answer, as he swung himself out of the room.

"I have great hopes of my boy," observed Jo, watching him fly over the fence with an approving smile.

"He does very well—for a boy," was Meg's somewhat ungracious answer, for the subject did not interest her.

Dr. Bangs came, said Beth had symptoms of the fever, but thought she would have it lightly, though he looked sober over the Hummel story. Amy was ordered off at once, and provided with something to ward off danger, she departed in great state, with Jo and Laurie as escort.

Aunt March received them with her usual hospitality.

"What do you want now?" she asked, looking sharply over her spectacles, while the parrot, sitting on the back of her chair, called out,—

"Go away. No boys allowed here."

Laurie retired to the window, and Jo told her story.

"No more than I expected, if you are allowed to go poking about among poor folks. Amy can stay and make herself useful if she isn't sick, which I've no doubt she will be,—looks like it now. Don't cry, child, it worries me to hear people sniff."

Amy *was* on the point of crying, but Laurie slyly pulled the parrot's tail, which caused Polly to utter an astonished croak, and call out,—

"Bless my boots!" in such a funny way, that she laughed instead.

"What do you hear from your mother?" asked the old lady gruffly.

"Father is much better," replied Jo, trying to keep sober.

"Oh, is he? Well, that won't last long, I fancy; March never had any stamina," was the cheerful reply.

"Ha, ha! Never say die, take a pinch of snuff, good by, good by!" squalled Polly, dancing on her perch, and clawing at the old lady's cap as Laurie tweaked him in the rear.

"Hold your tongue, you disrespectful old bird! And, Jo, you'd better go at once; it isn't proper to be gadding about so late with a rattle-pated boy like—"

"Hold your tongue, you disrespectful old bird!" cried Polly, tumbling off the chair with a bounce, and running to peck the "rattle-pated" boy, who was shaking with laughter at the last speech.

"I don't think I *can* bear it, but I'll try," thought Amy, as she was left alone with Aunt March.

"Get along, you fright!" screamed Polly and at that rude speech Amy could not restrain a sniff.

# CHAPTER XVIII

## DARK DAYS

BETH did have the fever, and was much sicker than anyone but Hannah and the doctor suspected. The girls knew nothing about illness, and Mr. Laurence was not allowed to see her, so Hannah had everything all her own way, and busy Dr. Bangs did his best, but left a good deal to the excellent nurse. Meg stayed at home, lest she should infect the Kings, and kept house, feeling very anxious and a little guilty when she wrote letters in which no mention was made of Beth's illness. She could not think it right to deceive her mother, but she had been bidden to mind Hannah, and Hannah wouldn't hear of "Mrs. March bein' told, and worried just for sech a trifle." Jo devoted herself to Beth day and night; not a hard task, for Beth was very patient, and bore her pain uncomplainingly as long as she could control herself. But there came a time when during the fever fits she began to talk in a hoarse, broken voice, to play on the coverlet, as if on her beloved little piano, and try to sing with a throat so swollen that there was no music left; a time when she did not know the familiar faces round her, but addressed them by wrong names, and called imploringly for her mother. Then Jo grew frightened, Meg begged to be allowed to write the truth, and even Hannah said she "would think of it, though there was no danger *yet*." A letter from Washington added to their trouble, for Mr. March had had a relapse, and could not think of coming home for a long while.

How dark the days seemed now, how sad and lonely the house, and how heavy were the hearts of the sisters as they worked and waited, while the shadow of death hovered over the once happy home! Then it was that Margaret, sitting alone with tears dropping often on her work, felt how rich she had been in things more precious than any luxuries money could buy,—in love, protection, peace, and health, the real blessings of life. Then it was that Jo, living in the darkened room, with that suffering little sister always before her eyes, and that pathetic voice sounding in her ears, learned to see the beauty and the sweetness of Beth's nature, to feel how deep and tender a place she filled in all hearts, and to acknowledge the worth of Beth's unselfish ambition to live for others, and make home happy by the exercise of those simple virtues which all may possess, and which all should love and value more than talent, wealth, or beauty. And Amy, in her exile, longed eagerly to be at home, that she might work for Beth, feeling now that no service would be hard or irksome, and remembering, with regretful grief, how many neglected tasks those willing hands had done for her. Laurie haunted the house like a restless ghost, and Mr. Laurence locked the grand piano, because he could not bear to be reminded of the young neighbor who used to make the twilight pleasant for him. Everyone missed Beth. The milkman, baker, grocer, and butcher inquired how she did; poor Mrs. Hummel came to beg pardon for her thoughtlessness, and to get a shroud for Minna; the neighbors sent all sorts of comforts and good wishes, and even those who knew her best were surprised to find how many friends shy little Beth had made.

Meanwhile she lay on her bed with old Joanna at her side, for even in her wanderings she did not forget her forlorn *protégé*. She longed for her cats, but would not have them brought, lest they should get sick; and, in her quiet hours, she was full of anxiety about Jo. She sent loving messages to Amy, bade them tell her mother that she would write soon; and often begged for pencil and paper to try to say a word, that father might not think she had neglected him. But soon even these intervals of consciousness ended, and she lay hour after hour, tossing to and fro, with incoherent words on her lips, or sank into a heavy sleep which brought her no refreshment. Dr. Bangs came twice a day, Hannah sat up at night, Meg kept a telegram in her desk all ready to send off at any minute, and Jo never stirred from Beth's side.

The first of December was a wintry day indeed to them, for a bitter wind blew, snow fell fast, and the year seemed getting ready for its death. When Dr. Bangs came that morning, he looked long at Beth, held the hot hand in both his own a minute, and laid it gently down, saying, in a low tone, to Hannah,—

"If Mrs. March *can* leave her husband, she'd better be sent for."

Hannah nodded without speaking, for her lips twitched nervously; Meg dropped down into a chair as the strength seemed to go out of her limbs at the sound of those words; and Jo, after standing with a pale face for a minute, ran to the parlor, snatched up the telegram, and, throwing on her things, rushed out into the storm. She was soon back, and, while noiselessly taking off her cloak, Laurie came in with a letter, saying that Mr. March was mending again. Jo read it thankfully, but the heavy weight did not seem lifted off her heart, and her face was so full of misery that Laurie asked quickly,—

"What is it? Is Beth worse?"

"I've sent for mother," said Jo, tugging at her rubber boots with a tragical expression.

"Good for you, Jo! Did you do it on your own responsibility?" asked Laurie, as he seated her in the hall chair, and took off the rebellious boots, seeing how her hands shook.

"No, the doctor told us to."

"O Jo, it's not so bad as that?" cried Laurie, with a startled face.

"Yes, it is; she doesn't know us, she doesn't even talk about the flocks of green doves, as she calls the vine-leaves on the wall; she doesn't look like my Beth, and there's nobody to help us bear it; mother and father both gone, and God seems so far away I can't find Him."

As the tears streamed fast down poor Jo's cheeks, she stretched out her hand in a helpless sort of way, as if groping in the dark, and Laurie took it in his, whispering, as well as he could, with a lump in his throat,—

"I'm here. Hold on to me, Jo, dear!"

She could not speak, but she did "hold on," and the warm grasp of the friendly human hand comforted her sore heart, and seemed to lead her nearer to the Divine arm which alone could uphold her in her trouble. Laurie longed to say something tender and comfortable, but no fitting words came to him, so he stood silent, gently stroking her bent head as her mother used to do. It was the best thing he could have done; far more soothing than the most eloquent words, for Jo felt the unspoken sympathy, and, in the silence, learned the sweet solace which affection administers to sorrow. Soon she dried the tears which had relieved her, and looked up with a grateful face.

"Thank you, Teddy, I'm better now; I don't feel so forlorn, and will try to bear it if it comes."

"Keep hoping for the best; that will help you, Jo. Soon your mother will be here, and then everything will be right."

"I'm so glad father is better; now she won't feel so bad about leaving him. Oh, me! It does seem as if all the troubles came in a heap, and I got the heaviest part on my shoulders," sighed Jo, spreading her wet handkerchief over her knees to dry.

"Doesn't Meg pull fair?" asked Laurie, looking indignant.

"Oh, yes; she tries to, but she can't love Bethy as I do; and she won't miss her as I shall. Beth is my conscience, and I *can't* give her up. I can't! I can't!"

Down went Jo's face into the wet handkerchief, and she cried despairingly; for she had kept up bravely till now, and never shed a tear. Laurie drew his hand across his eyes, but could not speak till he had subdued the choky feeling in his throat and steadied his lips. It might be unmanly, but he couldn't help it, and I am glad of it. Presently, as Jo's sobs quieted, he said hopefully, "I don't think she will die; she's so good, and we all love her so much, I don't believe God will take her away yet."

"The good and dear people always do die," groaned Jo, but she stopped crying, for her friend's words cheered her up, in spite of her own doubts and fears.

"Poor girl, you're worn out. It isn't like you to be forlorn. Stop a bit; I'll hearten you up in a jiffy."

Laurie went off two stairs at a time, and Jo laid her wearied head down on Beth's little brown hood, which no one had thought of moving from the table where she left it. It must have possessed some magic, for the submissive spirit of its gentle owner seemed to enter into Jo; and, when Laurie came running down with a glass of wine, she took it with a smile, and said bravely, "I drink—Health to my Beth! You are a good doctor, Teddy, and *such* a comfortable friend; how can I ever pay you?" she added, as the wine refreshed her body, as the kind words had done her troubled mind.

"I'll send in my bill, by and by; and tonight I'll give you something that will warm the cockles of your heart better than quarts of wine," said Laurie, beaming at her with a face of suppressed satisfaction at something.

"What is it?" cried Jo, forgetting her woes for a minute, in her wonder.

"I telegraphed to your mother yesterday, and Brooke answered she'd come at once, and she'll be here tonight, and everything will be all right. Aren't you glad I did it?"

Laurie spoke very fast, and turned red and excited all in a minute, for he had kept his plot a secret, for fear of disappointing the girls or harming Beth. Jo grew quite white, flew out of her chair, and the moment

Gently stroking her head as her mother used to do.

he stopped speaking she electrified him by throwing her arms round his neck, and crying out, with a joyful cry, "O Laurie! O mother! I *am* so glad!" She did not weep again, but laughed hysterically, and trembled and clung to her friend as if she was a little bewildered by the sudden news.

Laurie, though decidedly amazed, behaved with great presence of mind; he patted her back soothingly, and, finding that she was recovering, followed it up by a bashful kiss or two, which brought Jo round at once. Holding on to the banisters, she put him gently away, saying breathlessly, "Oh, don't! I didn't mean to; it was dreadful of me; but you were such a dear to go and do it in spite of Hannah that I couldn't help flying at you. Tell me all about it, and don't give me wine again; it makes me act so."

"I don't mind," laughed Laurie, as he settled his tie. "Why, you see I got fidgety, and so did grandpa. We thought Hannah was overdoing the authority business, and your mother ought to know. She'd never forgive us if Beth—well, if anything happened, you know. So I got grandpa to say it was high time we did something, and off I pelted to the office yesterday, for the doctor looked sober and Hannah most took my head off when I proposed a telegram. I never *can* bear to be 'lorded over;' so that settled my mind, and I did it. Your mother will come, I know, and the late train is in at two, A.M. I shall go for her; and you've only got to bottle up your rapture, and keep Beth quiet, till that blessed lady gets here."

"Laurie, you're an angel! How shall I ever thank you?"

"Fly at me again; I rather like it," said Laurie, looking mischievous,—a thing he had not done for a fortnight.

"No, thank you. I'll do it by proxy, when your grandpa comes. Don't tease, but go home and rest, for you'll be up half the night. Bless you, Teddy, bless you!"

Jo had backed into a corner; and, as she finished her speech, she vanished precipitately into the kitchen, where she sat down upon a dresser, and told the assembled cats that she was "happy, oh, *so* happy!" while Laurie departed, feeling that he had made rather a neat thing of it.

"That's the interferingest chap I ever see; but I forgive him, and do hope Mrs. March is coming on right away," said Hannah, with an air of relief, when Jo told the good news.

Meg had a quiet rapture, and then brooded over the letter, while Jo set the sick-room in order, and Hannah "knocked up a couple of pies in case of company unexpected." A breath of fresh air seemed to blow through the house, and something better than sunshine brightened the quiet rooms. Everything appeared to feel the hopeful change; Beth's bird began to chirp again, and a half-blown rose was discovered on Amy's bush in the window; the fires seemed to burn with unusual cheeriness; and every time the girls met, their pale faces broke into smiles as they hugged one another, whispering encouragingly, "Mother's coming, dear! Mother's coming!" Everyone rejoiced but Beth; she lay in that heavy stupor, alike unconscious of hope and joy, doubt and danger. It was a piteous sight,—the once rosy face so changed and vacant, the once busy hands so weak and wasted, the once smiling lips quite dumb, and the once pretty, well-kept hair scattered rough and tangled on the pillow. All day she lay so, only rousing now and then to mutter, "Water!" with lips so parched they could hardly shape the word; all day Jo and Meg hovered over her, watching, waiting, hoping, and trusting in God ad mother; and all day the snow fell, the bitter wind raged, and the hours dragged slowly by. But night came at last; and every time the clock struck, the sisters, still sitting on either side the bed, looked at each other with brightening eyes, for each hour brought help nearer. The doctor had been in to say that some change, for better or worse, would probably take place about midnight, at which time he would return.

Hannah, quite worn out, lay down on the sofa at the bed's foot, and fell fast asleep; Mr. Laurence marched to and fro in the parlor, feeling that he would rather face a rebel battery than Mrs. March's anxious countenance as she entered; Laurie lay on the rug, pretending to rest, but staring into the fire with the thoughtful look which made his black eyes beautifully soft and clear.

The girls never forgot that night, for no sleep came to them as they kept their watch, with that dreadful sense of powerlessness which comes to us in hours like those.

"If God spares Beth I never will complain again," whispered Meg earnestly.

"If God spares Beth I'll try to love and serve Him all my life," answered Jo, with equal fervor.

"I wish I had no heart, it aches so," sighed Meg, after a pause.

"If life is often as hard as this, I don't see how we ever shall get through it," added her sister despondently.

Here the clock struck twelve, and both forgot themselves in watching Beth, for they fancied a change passed over her wan face. The house was still as death, and nothing but the wailing of the wind broke the deep hush. Weary Hannah slept on, and no one but the sisters saw the pale shadow which seemed to fall upon the little bed. An hour went by, and nothing happened except Laurie's quiet departure for the station. Another hour,—still no one came; and anxious fears of delay in the storm, or accidents by the way, or, worst of all, a great grief at Washington, haunted the poor girls.

It was past two, when Jo, who stood at the window thinking how dreary the world looked in its winding-sheet of snow, heard a movement by the bed, and, turning quickly, saw Meg kneeling before their mother's easy-chair, with her face hidden. A dreadful fear passed coldly over Jo, as she thought, "Beth is dead, and Meg is afraid to tell me."

She was back at her post in an instant, and to her excited eyes a great change seemed to have taken place. The fever flush and the look of pain were gone, and the beloved little face looked so pale and peaceful in its utter repose, that Jo felt no desire to weep or to lament. Leaning low over this dearest of her sisters, she kissed the damp forehead with her heart on her lips, and softly whispered, "Good-by, my Beth; good-by!"

As if waked by the stir, Hannah started out of her sleep, hurried to the bed, looked at Beth, felt her hands, listened at her lips, and then, throwing her apron over her head, sat down to rock to and fro, exclaiming, under her breath, "The fever's turned; she's sleepin' nat'ral; her skin's damp, and she breathes easy. Praise be given! Oh, my goodness me!"

Before the girls could believe the happy truth, the doctor came to confirm it. He was a homely man, but they thought his face quite heavenly when he smiled, and said, with a fatherly look at them, "Yes, my dears, I think the little girl will pull through this time. Keep the house quiet; let her sleep, and when she wakes, give her—"

What they were to give, neither heard; for both crept into the dark hall, and, sitting on the stairs, held each other close, rejoicing with hearts too full for words. When they went back to be kissed and cuddled by faithful Hannah, they found Beth lying, as she used to do, with her cheek pillowed on her hand, the dreadful pallor gone, and breathing quietly, as if just fallen asleep.

"If mother would only come now!" said Jo, as the winter night began to wane.

"See," said Meg, coming up with a white, half-opened rose, "I thought this would hardly be ready to lay in Beth's hand tomorrow if she—went away from us. But it has blossomed in the night, and now I mean to put it in my vase here, so that when the darling wakes, the first thing she sees will be the little rose, and mother's face."

Never had the sun risen so beautifully, and never had the world seemed so lovely, as it did to the heavy eyes of Meg and Jo, as they looked out in the early morning, when their long, sad vigil was done.

"It looks like a fairy world," said Meg, smiling to herself, as she stood behind the curtain, watching the dazzling sight.

"Hark!" cried Jo, starting to her feet.

Yes, there was a sound of bells at the door below, a cry from Hannah, and then Laurie's voice saying, in a joyful whisper, "Girls, she's come! She's come!"

# CHAPTER XIX

## AMY'S WILL

WHILE these things were happening at home, Amy was having hard times at Aunt March's. She felt her exile deeply, and, for the first time in her life, realized how much she was beloved and petted at home. Aunt March never petted anyone; she did not approve of it; but she meant to be kind, for the well-behaved little girl pleased her very much, and Aunt March had a soft place in her old heart for her nephew's children, though she didn't think proper to confess it. She really did her best to make Amy happy, but, dear me, what mistakes she made! Some old people keep young at heart in spite of wrinkles and gray hairs, can sympathize with children's little cares and joys, make them feel at home, and can hide wise lessons under pleasant plays, giving and receiving friendship in the sweetest way. But Aunt March had not this gift, and she worried Amy very much with her rules and orders, her prim ways, and long, prosy talks. Finding the child more docile and amiable than her sister, the old lady felt it her duty to try and counteract, as far as possible, the bad effects of home freedom and indulgence. So she took Amy in hand, and taught her as she herself had been taught sixty years ago,—a process which carried dismay to Amy's soul, and made her feel like a fly in the web of a very strict spider.

She had to wash the cups every morning, and polish up the old-fashioned spoons, the fat silver teapot, and the glasses, till they shone. Then she must dust the room, and what a trying job that was! Not a speck escaped Aunt March's eye, and all the furniture had claw legs, and much carving, which was never dusted to suit. Then Polly must be fed, the lap-dog combed, and a dozen trips upstairs and down, to get things, or deliver orders, for the old lady was very lame, and seldom left her big chair. After these tiresome labors, she must do her lessons, which was a daily trial of every virtue she possessed. Then she was allowed one hour for exercise or play, and didn't she enjoy it? Laurie came every day, and wheedled Aunt March, till Amy was allowed to go out with him, when they walked and rode, and had capital times. After dinner, she had to read aloud, and sit still while the old lady slept, which she usually did for an hour, as she dropped off over the first page. Then patchwork or towels appeared, and Amy sewed with outward meekness and inward rebellion till dusk, when she was allowed to amuse herself as she liked till tea-time. The evenings were the worst of all, for Aunt March fell to telling long stories about her youth, which were so unutterably dull that Amy was always ready to go to bed, intending to cry over her hard fate, but usually going to sleep before she had squeezed out more than a tear or two.

If it had not been for Laurie, and old Esther, the maid, she felt that she never could have got through that dreadful time. The parrot alone was enough to drive her distracted, for he soon felt that she did not admire him, and revenged himself by being as mischievous as possible. He pulled her hair whenever she came near him, upset his bread and milk to plague her when she had newly cleaned his cage, made Mop bark by pecking at him while Madam dozed; called her names before company, and behaved in all respects like a reprehensible old bird. Then she could not endure the dog,—a fat, cross beast, who snarled and yelped at her when she made his toilet, and who lay on his back, with all his legs in the air and a most idiotic expression of countenance when he wanted something to eat, which was about a dozen times a day. The cook was bad-tempered, the old coachman deaf, and Esther the only one who ever took any notice of the young lady.

Esther was a Frenchwoman, who had lived with "Madame," as she called her mistress, for many years, and who rather tyrannized over the old lady, who could not get along without her. Her real name was Estelle, but Aunt March ordered her to change it, and she obeyed, on condition that she was never asked to change her religion. She took a fancy to Mademoiselle, and amused her very much, with odd stories of her life in France, when Amy sat with her while she got up Madame's laces. She also allowed her to roam about the great house, and examine the curious and pretty things stored away in the big wardrobes and the ancient chests;

for Aunt March hoarded like a magpie. Amy's chief delight was an Indian cabinet, full of queer drawers, little pigeon-holes, and secret places, in which were kept all sorts of ornaments, some precious, some merely curious, all more or less antique. To examine and arrange these things gave Amy great satisfaction, especially the jewel-cases, in which, on velvet cushions, reposed the ornaments which had adorned a belle forty years ago. There was the garnet set which Aunt March wore when she came out, the pearls her father gave her on her wedding-day, her lover's diamonds, the jet mourning rings and pins, the queer lockets, with portraits of dead friends, and weeping willows made of hair inside; the baby bracelets her one little daughter had worn; Uncle March's big watch, with the red seal so many childish hands had played with, and in a box, all by itself, lay Aunt March's wedding-ring, too small now for her fat finger, but put carefully away, like the most precious jewel of them all.

"Which would Mademoiselle choose if she had her will?" asked Esther, who always sat near to watch over and lock up the valuables.

"I like the diamonds best, but there is no necklace among them, and I'm fond of necklaces, they are so becoming. I should choose this if I might," replied Amy, looking with great admiration at a string of gold and ebony beads, from which hung a heavy cross of the same.

"I, too, covet that, but not as a necklace; ah, no! To me it is a rosary, and as such I should use it like a good Catholic," said Esther, eying the handsome thing wistfully.

"Is it meant to use as you use the string of good-smelling wooden beads hanging over your glass?" asked Amy.

"Truly, yes, to pray with. It would be pleasing to the saints if one used so fine a rosary as this, instead of wearing it as a vain bijou."

"You seem to take a great deal of comfort in your prayers, Esther, and always come down looking quiet and satisfied. I wish I could."

"If Mademoiselle was a Catholic, she would find true comfort; but, as that is not to be, it would be well if you went apart each day, to meditate and pray, as did the good mistress whom I served before Madame. She had a little chapel, and in it found solacement for much trouble."

"Would it be right for me to do so too?" asked Amy, who, in her loneliness, felt the need of help of some sort, and found that she was apt to forget her little book, now that Beth was not there to remind her of it.

"It would be excellent and charming; and I shall gladly arrange the little dressing-room for you if you like it. Say nothing to Madame, but when she sleeps go you and sit alone a while to think good thoughts, and pray the dear God to preserve your sister."

Esther was truly pious, and quite sincere in her advice; for she had an affectionate heart, and felt much for the sisters in their anxiety. Amy liked the idea, and gave her leave to arrange the light closet next her room, hoping it would do her good.

"I wish I knew where all these pretty things would go when Aunt March dies," she said, as she slowly replaced the shining rosary, and shut the jewel-cases one by one.

"To you and your sisters. I know it; Madame confides in me; I witnessed her will, and it is to be so," whispered Esther, smiling.

"How nice! But I wish she'd let us have them now. Pro-cras-ti-nation is not agreeable," observed Amy, taking a last look at the diamonds.

"It is too soon yet for the young ladies to wear these things. The first one who is affianced will have the pearls—Madame has said it; and I have a fancy that the little turquoise ring will be given to you when you go, for Madame approves your good behavior and charming manners."

"Do you think so? Oh, I'll be a lamb, if I can only have that lovely ring! It's ever so much prettier than Kitty Bryant's. I do like Aunt March, after all;" and Amy tried on the blue ring with a delighted face, and a firm resolve to earn it.

From that day she was a model of obedience, and the old lady complacently admired the success of her training. Esther fitted up the closet with a little table, placed a footstool before it, and over it a picture taken from one of the shut-up rooms. She thought it was of no great value, but, being appropriate, she borrowed it, well knowing that Madame would never know it, nor care if she did. It was, however, a very valuable copy of one of the famous pictures of the world, and Amy's beauty-loving eyes were never tired of looking up at the sweet face of the divine mother, while tender thoughts of her own were busy at her heart. On the table she laid her little Testament and hymn-book, kept a vase always full of the best flowers Laurie brought her, and came every day to "sit alone, thinking good thoughts, and praying the dear God to preserve her sister." Esther had given her a rosary of black beads, with a silver cross, but Amy hung it up and did not use it, feeling doubtful as to its fitness for Protestant prayers.

The little girl was very sincere in all this, for, being left alone outside the safe home-nest, she felt the need of some kind hand to hold by so sorely, that she instinctively turned to the strong and tender Friend, whose fatherly love most closely surrounds his little children. She missed her mother's help to understand and rule herself, but having been taught where to look, she did her best to find the way, and walk in it confidingly. But Amy was a young pilgrim, and just now her burden seemed very heavy. She tried to forget herself, to keep cheerful, and be satisfied with doing right, though no one saw or praised her for it. In her first effort at being very, very good, she decided to make her will, as Aunt March had done; so that if she *did* fall ill and die, her possessions might be justly and generously divided. It cost her a pang even to think of giving up the little treasures which in her eyes were as precious as the old lady's jewels.

During one of her play-hours she wrote out the important document as well as she could, with some help from Esther as to certain legal terms, and, when the good-natured Frenchwoman had signed her name, Amy felt relieved, and laid it by to show Laurie, whom she wanted as a second witness. As it was a rainy day, she went upstairs to amuse herself in one of the large chambers, and took Polly with her for company. In this room there was a wardrobe full of old-fashioned costumes, with which Esther allowed her to play, and it was her favorite amusement to array herself in the faded brocades, and parade up and down before the long mirror, making stately courtesies, and sweeping her train about, with a rustle which delighted her ears. So busy was she on this day that she did not hear Laurie's ring, nor see his face peeping in at her, as she gravely promenaded to and fro, flirting her fan and tossing her head, on which she wore a great pink turban, contrasting oddly with her blue brocade dress and yellow quilted petticoat. She was obliged to walk carefully, for she had on high-heeled shoes, and, as Laurie told Jo afterward, it was a comical sight to see her mince along in her gay suit, with Polly sidling and bridling just behind her, imitating her as well as he could, and occasionally stopping to laugh or exclaim, "Ain't we fine? Get along, you fright! Hold your tongue! Kiss me, dear! Ha! Ha!"

Having with difficulty restrained an explosion of merriment, lest it should offend her majesty, Laurie tapped, and was graciously received.

"Sit down and rest while I put these things away; then I want to consult you about a very serious matter," said Amy, when she had shown her splendor, and driven Polly into a corner. "That bird is the trial of my life," she continued, removing the pink mountain from her head, while Laurie seated himself astride of a chair. "Yesterday, when aunt was asleep, and I was trying to be as still as a mouse, Polly began to squall and flap about in his cage; so I went to let him out, and found a big spider there. I poked it out, and it ran under the bookcase; Polly marched straight after it, stooped down and peeped under the bookcase, saying, in his funny way, with a cock of his eye, 'Come out and take a walk, my dear.' I *couldn't* help laughing, which made Poll swear, and aunt woke up and scolded us both."

"Did the spider accept the old fellow's invitation?" asked Laurie, yawning.

"Yes; out it came, and away ran Polly, frightened to death, and scrambled up on aunt's chair, calling out, 'Catch her! Catch her! Catch her!' as I chased the spider."

"That's a lie! Oh lor!" cried the parrot, pecking at Laurie's toes.

"I'd wring your neck if you were mine, you old torment," cried Laurie, shaking his fist at the bird, who put his head on one side, and gravely croaked, "Allyluyer! Bless your buttons, dear!"

"Now I'm ready," said Amy, shutting the wardrobe, and taking a paper out of her pocket. "I want you to read that, please, and tell me if it is legal and right. I felt that I ought to do it, for life is uncertain and I don't want any ill-feeling over my tomb."

Laurie bit his lips, and turning a little from the pensive speaker, read the following document, with praiseworthy gravity, considering the spelling:—

### "MY LAST WILL AND TESTIMENT

"I, Amy Curtis March, being in my sane mind, do give and bequeethe all my earthly property—viz. to wit:—namely

"To my father, my best pictures, sketches, maps, and works of art, including frames. Also my $100, to do what he likes with.

"To my mother, all my clothes, except the blue apron with pockets,— also my likeness, and my medal, with much love.

"To my dear sister Margaret, I give my turkquoise ring (if I get it), also my green box with the doves on it, also my piece of real lace for her neck, and my sketch of her as a memorial of her 'little girl.'

"To Jo I leave my breast-pin, the one mended with sealing wax, also my bronze inkstand—she lost the cover—and my most precious plaster rabbit, because I am sorry I burnt up her story.

"To Beth (if she lives after me) I give my dolls and the little bureau, my fan, my linen collars and my new slippers if she can wear them being thin when she gets well. And I herewith also leave her my regret that I ever made fun of old Joanna.

"To my friend and neighbor Theodore Laurence I bequeethe my paper marshay portfolio, my clay model of a horse though he did say it hadn't any neck. Also in return for his great kindness in the hour of affliction any one of my artistic works he likes, Noter Dame is the best.

"To our venerable benefactor Mr. Laurence I leave my purple box with a looking glass in the cover which will be nice for his pens and remind him of the departed girl who thanks him for his favors to her family, specially Beth.

"I wish my favorite playmate Kitty Bryant to have the blue silk apron and my gold-bead ring with a kiss.

"To Hannah I give the bandbox she wanted and all the patch work I leave hoping she 'will remember me, when it you see.'

"And now having disposed of my most valuable property I hope all will be satisfied and not blame the dead. I forgive everyone, and trust we may all meet when the trump shall sound. Amen.

"To this will and testament I set my hand and seal on this 20th day of Nov. Anni Domino 1861.

"AMY CURTIS MARCH"

"*Witnesses:* ESTELLE VALNOR THEODORE LAURENCE"

The last name was written in pencil, and Amy explained that he was to rewrite it in ink, and seal it up for her properly.

"What put it into your head? Did anyone tell you about Beth's giving away her things?" asked Laurie soberly, as Amy laid a bit of red tape, with sealing-wax, a taper, and a standish before him.

She explained; and then asked anxiously, "What about Beth?"

"I'm sorry I spoke; but as I did, I'll tell you. She felt so ill one day that she told Jo she wanted to give her piano to Meg, her cats to you, and the poor old doll to Jo, who would love it for her sake. She was sorry she had so little to give, and left locks of hair to the rest of us, and her best love to grandpa. *She* never thought of a will."

Laurie was signing and sealing as he spoke, and did not look up till a great tear dropped on the paper. Amy's face was full of trouble; but she only said, "Don't people put sort of postscripts to their wills, sometimes?"

"Yes; 'codicils,' they call them."

"Put one in mine then—that I wish *all* my curls cut off, and given round to my friends. I forgot it; but I want it done, though it will spoil my looks."

Laurie added it, smiling at Amy's last and greatest sacrifice. Then he amused her for an hour, and was much interested in all her trials. But when he came to go, Amy held him back to whisper, with trembling lips, "Is there really any danger about Beth?"

"I'm afraid there is; but we must hope for the best, so don't cry, dear;" and Laurie put his arm about her with a brotherly gesture which was very comforting.

When he had gone, she went to her little chapel, and, sitting in the twilight, prayed for Beth, with streaming tears and an aching heart, feeling that a million turquoise rings would not console her for the loss of her gentle little sister.

# CHAPTER XX

## CONFIDENTIAL

I DON'T think I have any words in which to tell the meeting of the mother and daughters; such hours are beautiful to live, but very hard to describe, so I will leave it to the imagination of my readers, merely saying that the house was full of genuine happiness, and that Meg's tender hope was realized; for when Beth woke from that long, healing sleep, the first objects on which her eyes fell *were* the little rose and mother's face. Too weak to wonder at anything, she only smiled, and nestled close into the loving arms about her, feeling that the hungry longing was satisfied at last. Then she slept again, and the girls waited upon their mother, for she would not unclasp the thin hand which clung to hers even in sleep.

Hannah had "dished up" an astonishing breakfast for the traveller, finding it impossible to vent her excitement in any other way; and Meg and Jo fed their mother like dutiful young storks, while they listened to her whispered account of father's state, Mr. Brooke's promise to stay and nurse him, the delays which the storm occasioned on the homeward journey, and the unspeakable comfort Laurie's hopeful face had given her when she arrived, worn out with fatigue, anxiety, and cold.

What a strange, yet pleasant day that was! So brilliant and gay without,

Amy's Will

for all the world seemed abroad to welcome the first snow; so quiet and reposeful within, for everyone slept, spent with watching, and a Sabbath stillness reigned through the house, while nodding Hannah mounted guard at the door. With a blissful sense of burdens lifted off, Meg and Jo closed their weary eyes, and lay at rest, like storm-beaten boats, safe at anchor in a quiet harbor. Mrs. March would not leave Beth's side, but rested in the big chair, waking often to look at, touch, and brood over her child, like a miser over some recovered treasure.

Laurie, meanwhile, posted off to comfort Amy, and told his story so well that Aunt March actually "sniffed" herself, and never once said, "I told you so." Amy came out so strong on this occasion that I think the good thoughts in the little chapel really began to bear fruit. She dried her tears quickly, restrained her impatience to see her mother, and never even thought of the turquoise ring, when the old lady heartily agreed in Laurie's opinion, that she behaved "like a capital little woman." Even Polly seemed impressed, for he called her "good girl," blessed her buttons, and begged her to "come and take a walk, dear," in his most affable tone. She would very gladly have gone out to enjoy the bright wintry weather; but, discovering that Laurie was dropping with sleep in spite of manful efforts to conceal the fact, she persuaded him to rest on the sofa, while she wrote a note to her mother. She was a long time about it; and, when she returned, he was stretched out, with both arms under his head, sound asleep, while Aunt March had pulled down the curtains, and sat doing nothing in an unusual fit of benignity.

After a while, they began to think he was not going to wake till night, and I'm not sure that he would, had he not been effectually roused by Amy's cry of joy at sight of her mother. There probably were a good many happy little girls in and about the city that day, but it is my private opinion that Amy was the happiest of all, when she sat in her mother's lap and told her trials, receiving consolation and compensation in the shape of approving smiles and fond caresses. They were alone together in the chapel, to which her mother did not object when its purpose was explained to her.

"On the contrary, I like it very much, dear," looking from the dusty rosary to the well-worn little book, and the lovely picture with its garland of evergreen. "It is an excellent plan to have some place where we can go to be quiet, when things vex or grieve us. There are a good many hard times in this life of ours, but we can always bear them if we ask help in the right way. I think my little girl is learning this?"

"Yes, mother; and when I go home I mean to have a corner in the big closet to put my books, and the copy of that picture which I've tried to make. The woman's face is not good,—it's too beautiful for me to draw,—but the baby is done better, and I love it very much. I like to think He was a little child once, for then I don't seem so far away, and that helps me."

As Amy pointed to the smiling Christ-child on his mother's knee, Mrs. March saw something on the lifted hand that made her smile. She said nothing, but Amy understood the look, and, after a minute's pause, she added gravely,—

"I wanted to speak to you about this, but I forgot it. Aunt gave me the ring today; she called me to her and kissed me, and put it on my finger, and said I was a credit to her, and she'd like to keep me always. She gave that funny guard to keep the turquoise on, as it's too big. I'd like to wear them, mother; can I?"

"They are very pretty, but I think you're rather too young for such ornaments, Amy," said Mrs. March, looking at the plump little hand, with the band of sky-blue stones on the forefinger, and the quaint guard, formed of two tiny, golden hands clasped together.

"I'll try not to be vain," said Amy. "I don't think I like it only because it's so pretty; but I want to wear it as the girl in the story wore her bracelet, to remind me of something."

"Do you mean Aunt March?" asked her mother, laughing.

"No, to remind me not to be selfish." Amy looked so earnest and sincere about it, that her mother stopped laughing, and listened respectfully to the little plan.

"I've thought a great deal lately about my 'bundle of naughties,' and being selfish is the largest one in it; so I'm going to try hard to cure it, if I can. Beth isn't selfish, and that's the reason everyone loves her and feels so bad at the thoughts of losing her. People wouldn't feel half so bad about me if I was sick, and I don't deserve to have them; but I'd like to be loved and missed by a great many friends, so I'm going to try and be like Beth all I can. I'm apt to forget my resolutions; but if I had something always about me to remind me, I guess I should do better. May I try this way?"

"Yes; but I have more faith in the corner of the big closet. Wear your ring, dear, and do your best; I think you will prosper, for the sincere wish to be good is half the battle. Now I must go back to Beth. Keep up your heart, little daughter, and we will soon have you home again."

That evening, while Meg was writing to her father, to report the traveller's safe arrival, Jo slipped upstairs into Beth's room, and, finding her mother in her usual place, stood a minute twisting her fingers in her hair, with a worried gesture and an undecided look.

"What is it, deary?" asked Mrs. March, holding out her hand, with a face which invited confidence.

"I want to tell you something, mother."

"About Meg?"

"How quickly you guessed! Yes, it's about her, and though it's a little thing, it fidgets me."

"Beth is asleep; speak low, and tell me all about it. That Moffat hasn't been here, I hope?" asked Mrs. March rather sharply.

"No, I should have shut the door in his face if he had," said Jo, settling herself on the floor at her mother's feet. "Last summer Meg left a pair of gloves over at the Laurences', and only one was returned. We forgot all about it, till Teddy told me that Mr. Brooke had it. He kept it in his waistcoat pocket, and once it fell out, and Teddy joked him about it, and Mr. Brooke owned that he liked Meg, but didn't dare say so, she was so young and he so poor. Now, isn't it a *dread*ful state of things?"

"Do you think Meg cares for him?" asked Mrs. March, with an anxious look.

"Mercy me! I don't know anything about love and such nonsense!"

cried Jo, with a funny mixture of interest and contempt. "In novels, the girls show it by starting and blushing, fainting away, growing thin, and acting like fools. Now Meg does not do anything of the sort: she eats and drinks and sleeps, like a sensible creature; she looks straight in my face when I talk about that man, and only blushes a little bit when Teddy jokes about lovers. I forbid him to do it, but he doesn't mind me as he ought."

"Then you fancy that Meg is *not* interested in John?"

"Who?" cried Jo, staring.

"Mr. Brooke. I call him 'John' now; we fell into the way of doing so at the hospital, and he likes it."

"Oh, dear! I know you'll take his part: he's been good to father, and you won't send him away, but let Meg marry him, if she wants to. Mean thing! To go petting papa and helping you, just to wheedle you into liking him;" and Jo pulled her hair again with a wrathful tweak.

"My dear, don't get angry about it, and I will tell you how it happened. John went with me at Mr. Laurence's request, and was so devoted to poor father that we couldn't help getting fond of him. He was perfectly open and honorable about Meg, for he told us he loved her, but would earn a comfortable home before he asked her to marry him. He only wanted our leave to love her and work for her, and the right to make her love him if he could. He is a truly excellent young man, and we could not refuse to listen to him; but I will not consent to Meg's engaging herself so young."

"Of course not; it would be idiotic! I knew there was mischief brewing; I felt it; and now it's worse than I imagined. I just wish I could marry Meg myself, and keep her safe in the family."

This odd arrangement made Mrs. March smile; but she said gravely, "Jo, I confide in you, and don't wish you to say anything to Meg yet. When John comes back, and I see them together, I can judge better of her feelings toward him."

"She'll see his in those handsome eyes that she talks about, and then it will be all up with her. She's got such a soft heart, it will melt like butter in the sun if anyone looks sentimentally at her. She read the short reports he sent more than she did your letters, and pinched me when I spoke of it, and likes brown eyes, and doesn't think John an ugly name, and she'll go and fall in love, and there's an end of peace and fun, and cozy times together. I see it all! They'll go lovering around the house, and we shall have to dodge; Meg will be absorbed, and no good to me any more; Brooke will scratch up a fortune somehow, carry her off, and make a hole in the family; and I shall break my heart, and everything will be abominably uncomfortable. Oh, dear me! Why weren't we all boys, then there wouldn't be any bother."

Jo leaned her chin on her knees, in a disconsolate attitude, and shook her fist at the reprehensible John. Mrs. March sighed, and Jo looked up with an air of relief.

"You don't like it, mother? I'm glad of it. Let's send him about his business, and not tell Meg a word of it, but all be happy together as we always have been."

"I did wrong to sigh, Jo. It is natural and right you should all go to homes of your own, in time; but I do want to keep my girls as long as I can; and I am sorry that this happened so soon, for Meg is only seventeen, and it will be some years before John can make a home for her. Your father and I have agreed that she shall not bind herself in any way, nor be married, before twenty. If she and John love one another, they can wait, and test the love by doing so. She is conscientious, and I have no fear of her treating him unkindly. My pretty, tender-hearted girl! I hope things will go happily with her."

"Hadn't you rather have her marry a rich man?" asked Jo, as her mother's voice faltered a little over the last words.

"Money is a good and useful thing, Jo; and I hope my girls will never feel the need of it too bitterly, nor be tempted by too much. I should like to know that John was firmly established in some good business, which gave him an income large enough to keep free from debt and make Meg comfortable. I'm not ambitious for a splendid fortune, a fashionable position, or a great name for my girls. If rank and money come with love and virtue, also, I should accept them gratefully, and enjoy your good fortune; but I know, by experience, how much genuine happiness can be had in a plain little house, where the daily bread is earned, and some privations give sweetness to the few pleasures. I am content to see Meg begin humbly, for, if I am not mistaken, she will be rich in the possession of a good man's heart, and that is better than a fortune."

"I understand, mother, and quite agree; but I'm disappointed about Meg, for I'd planned to have her marry Teddy by and by, and sit in the lap of luxury all her days. Wouldn't it be nice?" asked Jo, looking up, with a brighter face.

"He is younger than she, you know," began Mrs. March; but Jo broke in,—

"Only a little; he's old for his age, and tall; and can be quite grown-up in his manners if he likes. Then he's rich and generous and good, and loves us all; and *I* say it's a pity my plan is spoilt."

"I'm afraid Laurie is hardly grown up enough for Meg, and altogether too much of a weathercock, just now, for anyone to depend on. Don't make plans, Jo; but let time and their own hearts mate your friends. We can't meddle safely in such matters, and had better not get 'romantic rubbish,' as you call it, into our heads, lest it spoil our friendship."

"Well, I won't; but I hate to see things going all criss-cross and getting snarled up, when a pull here and a snip there would straighten it out. I wish wearing flat-irons on our heads would keep us from growing up. But buds will be roses, and kittens, cats,—more's the pity!"

"What's that about flat-irons and cats?" asked Meg, as she crept into the room, with the finished letter in her hand.

"Only one of my stupid speeches. I'm going to bed; come, Peggy," said Jo, unfolding herself, like an animated puzzle.

"Quite right, and beautifully written. Please add that I send my love to John," said Mrs. March, as she glanced over the letter, and gave it back.

"Do you call him 'John'?" asked Meg, smiling, with her innocent eyes looking down into her mother's.

"Yes; he has been like a son to us, and we are very fond of him," replied Mrs. March, returning the look with a keen one.

"I'm glad of that, he is so lonely. Good-night, mother, dear. It is so inexpressibly comfortable to have you here," was Meg's quiet answer.

The kiss her mother gave her was a very tender one; and, as she went away, Mrs. March said, with a mixture of satisfaction and regret, "She does not love John yet, but will soon learn to."

# CHAPTER XXI

## LAURIE MAKES MISCHIEF, AND JO MAKES PEACE

JO'S face was a study next day, for the secret rather weighed upon her, and she found it hard not to look mysterious and important. Meg observed it, but did not trouble herself to make inquiries, for she had learned that the best way to manage Jo was by the law of contraries, so she felt sure of being told everything if she did not ask. She was rather surprised, therefore, when the silence remained unbroken, and Jo assumed a patronizing air, which decidedly aggravated Meg, who in her turn assumed an air of dignified reserve, and devoted herself to her mother. This left Jo to her own devices; for Mrs. March had taken her place as nurse, and bade her rest, exercise, and amuse herself after her long confinement. Amy being gone, Laurie was her only refuge; and, much as she enjoyed his society, she rather dreaded him just then, for he was an incorrigible tease, and she feared he would coax her secret from her.

She was quite right; for the mischief-loving lad no sooner suspected a mystery than he set himself to find it out, and led Jo a trying life of it. He wheedled, bribed, ridiculed, threatened, and scolded; affected indifference, that he might surprise the truth from her; declared he knew, then that he didn't care; and, at last, by dint of perseverance, he satisfied himself that it concerned Meg and Mr. Brooke. Feeling indignant that he was not taken into his tutor's confidence, he set his wits to work to devise some proper retaliation for the slight.

Meg meanwhile had apparently forgotten the matter, and was absorbed in preparations for her father's return; but all of a sudden a change seemed to come over her, and, for a day or two, she was quite unlike herself. She started when spoken to, blushed when looked at, was very quiet, and sat over her sewing, with a timid, troubled look on her face. To her mother's inquiries she answered that she was quite well, and Jo's she silenced by begging to be let alone.

"She feels it in the air—love, I mean—and she's going very fast. She's got most of the symptoms,—is twittery and cross, doesn't eat, lies awake, and mopes in corners. I caught her singing that song he gave her, and once she said 'John,' as you do, and then turned as red as a poppy. Whatever shall we do?" said Jo, looking ready for any measures, however violent.

"Nothing but wait. Let her alone, be kind and patient, and father's coming will settle everything," replied her mother.

"Here's a note to you, Meg, all sealed up. How odd! Teddy never seals mine," said Jo, next day, as he distributed the contents of the little post-office.

Mrs. March and Jo were deep in their own affairs, when a sound from Meg made them look up to see her staring at her note, with a frightened face.

"My child, what is it?" cried her mother, running to her, while Jo tried to take the paper which had done the mischief.

"It's all a mistake—he didn't send it. O Jo, how could you do it?" and Meg hid her face in her hands, crying as if her heart was quite broken.

"Me! I've done nothing! What's she talking about?" cried Jo, bewildered.

Meg's mild eyes kindled with anger as she pulled a crumpled note from her pocket, and threw it at Jo, saying reproachfully,—

"You wrote it, and that bad boy helped you. How could you be so rude, so mean, and cruel to us both?"

Jo hardly heard her, for she and her mother were reading the note, which was written in a peculiar hand.

"MY DEAREST MARGARET,—

"I can no longer restrain my passion, and must know my fate before I return. I dare not tell your parents yet, but I think they would consent if they knew that we adored one another. Mr. Laurence will help me to some good place, and then, my sweet girl, you will make me happy. I implore you to say nothing to your family yet, but to send one word of hope through Laurie to

"Your devoted JOHN."

"Oh, the little villain! That's the way he meant to pay me for keeping my word to mother. I'll give him a hearty scolding, and bring him over to beg pardon," cried Jo, burning to execute immediate justice. But her mother held her back, saying, with a look she seldom wore,—

"Stop, Jo, you must clear yourself first. You have played so many pranks, that I am afraid you have had a hand in this."

"On my word, mother, I haven't! I never saw that note before, and don't know anything about it, as true as I live!" said Jo, so earnestly that they believed her. "If I *had* taken a part in it I'd have done it better than this, and have written a sensible note. I should think you'd have known Mr. Brooke wouldn't write such stuff as that," she added, scornfully tossing down the paper.

"It's like his writing," faltered Meg, comparing it with the note in her hand.

"O Meg, you didn't answer it?" cried Mrs. March quickly.

"Yes, I did !" and Meg hid her face again, overcome with shame.

"Here's a scrape! *Do* let me bring that wicked boy over to explain, and be lectured. I can't rest till I get hold of him;" and Jo made for the door again.

"Hush! Let me manage this, for it is worse than I thought. Margaret, tell me the whole story," commanded Mrs. March, sitting down by Meg, yet keeping hold of Jo, lest she should fly off.

"I received the first letter from Laurie, who didn't look as if he knew anything about it," began Meg, without looking up. "I was worried at first, and meant to tell you; then I remembered how you liked Mr. Brooke, so I thought you wouldn't mind if I kept my little secret for a few days. I'm so silly that I liked to think no one knew; and, while I was deciding what to say, I felt like the girls in books, who have such things to do. Forgive me, mother, I'm paid for my silliness now; I never can look him in the face again."

"What did you say to him?" asked Mrs. March.

"I only said I was too young to do anything about it yet; that I didn't wish to have secrets from you, and he must speak to father. I was very grateful for his kindness, and would be his friend, but nothing more, for a long while."

Mrs. March smiled, as if well pleased, and Jo clapped her hands, exclaiming, with a laugh,—

"You are almost equal to Caroline Percy, who was a pattern of prudence! Tell on, Meg. What did he say to that?"

"He writes in a different way entirely, telling me that he never sent any love-letter at all, and is very sorry that my roguish sister, Jo, should take such liberties with our names. It's very kind and respectful, but think how dreadful for me!"

Meg leaned against her mother, looking the image of despair, and Jo tramped about the room, calling Laurie names. All of a sudden she stopped, caught up the two notes, and, after looking at them closely, said decidedly, "I don't believe Brooke ever saw either of these letters. Teddy wrote both, and keeps yours to crow over me with, because I wouldn't tell him my secret."

"Don't have any secrets, Jo; tell it to mother, and keep out of trouble, as I should have done," said Meg warningly.

"Bless you, child! Mother told me."

"That will do, Jo. I'll comfort Meg while you go and get Laurie. I shall sift the matter to the bottom, and put a stop to such pranks at once."

Away ran Jo, and Mrs. March gently told Meg Mr. Brooke's real feelings. "Now, dear, what are your own? Do you love him enough to wait till he can make a home for you, or will you keep yourself quite free for the present?"

"I've been so scared and worried, I don't want to have anything to do with lovers for a long while,—perhaps never," answered Meg petulantly. "If John *doesn't* know anything about this nonsense, don't tell him, and make Jo and Laurie hold their tongues. I won't be deceived and plagued and made a fool of,—it's a shame!"

Seeing that Meg's usually gentle temper was roused and her pride hurt by this mischievous joke, Mrs. March soothed her by promises of entire silence, and great discretion for the future. The instant Laurie's step was heard in the hall, Meg fled into the study, and Mrs. March received the culprit alone. Jo had not told him why he was wanted, fearing he wouldn't come; but he knew the minute he saw Mrs. March's face, and stood twirling his hat, with a guilty air which convicted him at

Jo and her mother were reading the note.

once. Jo was dismissed, but chose to march up and down the hall like a sentinel, having some fear that the prisoner might bolt. The sound of voices in the parlor rose and fell for half an hour; but what happened during that interview the girls never knew.

When they were called in, Laurie was standing by their mother, with such a penitent face that Jo forgave him on the spot, but did not think it wise to betray the fact. Meg received his humble apology, and was much comforted by the assurance that Brooke knew nothing of the joke.

"I'll never tell him to my dying day,—wild horses sha'n't drag it out of me; so you'll forgive me, Meg, and I'll do anything to show how out-and-out sorry I am," he added, looking very much ashamed of himself.

"I'll try; but it was a very ungentlemanly thing to do. I didn't think you could be so sly and malicious, Laurie," replied Meg, trying to hide her maidenly confusion under a gravely reproachful air.

"It was altogether abominable, and I don't deserve to be spoken to for a month; but you will, though, won't you?" and Laurie folded his hands together with such an imploring gesture, as he spoke in his irresistibly persuasive tone, that it was impossible to frown upon him, in spite of his scandalous behavior. Meg pardoned him, and Mrs. March's grave face relaxed, in spite of her efforts to keep sober, when she heard him declare that he would atone for his sins by all sorts of penances, and abase himself like a worm before the injured damsel.

Jo stood aloof, meanwhile, trying to harden her heart against him, and succeeding only in primming up her face into an expression of entire disapprobation. Laurie looked at her once or twice, but, as she showed no sign of relenting, he felt injured, and turned his back on her till the others were done with him, when he made her a low bow, and walked off without a word.

As soon as he had gone, she wished she had been more forgiving; and when Meg and her mother went upstairs, she felt lonely, and longed for Teddy. After resisting for some time, she yielded to the impulse, and, armed with a book to return, went over to the big house.

"Is Mr. Laurence in?" asked Jo, of a housemaid, who was coming downstairs.

"Yes, miss; but I don't believe he's seeable just yet."

"Why not? Is he ill?"

"La, no, miss, but he's had a scene with Mr. Laurie, who is in one of his tantrums about something, which vexes the old gentleman, so I dursn't go nigh him."

"Where is Laurie?"

"Shut up in his room, and he won't answer, though I've been a-tapping. I don't know what's to become of the dinner, for it's ready, and there's no one to eat it."

"I'll go and see what the matter is. I'm not afraid of either of them."

Up went Jo, and knocked smartly on the door of Laurie's little study.

"Stop that, or I'll open the door and make you!" called out the young gentleman, in a threatening tone.

Jo immediately knocked again; the door flew open, and in she bounced, before Laurie could recover from his surprise. Seeing that he really *was* out of temper, Jo, who knew how to manage him, assumed a contrite expression, and going artistically down upon her knees, said meekly, "Please forgive me for being so cross. I came to make it up, and can't go away till I have."

"It's all right. Get up, and don't be a goose, Jo," was the cavalier reply to her petition.

"Thank you; I will. Could I ask what's the matter? You don't look exactly easy in your mind."

"I've been shaken, and I won't bear it!" growled Laurie indignantly.

"Who did it?" demanded Jo.

"Grandfather; if it had been anyone else I'd have—" and the injured youth finished his sentence by an energetic gesture of the right arm.

"That's nothing; I often shake you, and you don't mind," said Jo soothingly.

"Pooh! You're a girl, and it's fun; but I'll allow no man to shake *me*."

"I don't think anyone would care to try it, if you looked as much like a thunder-cloud as you do now. Why were you treated so?"

"Just because I wouldn't say what your mother wanted me for. I'd promised not to tell, and of course I wasn't going to break my word."

"Couldn't you satisfy your grandpa in any other way?"

"No; he *would* have the truth, the whole truth, and nothing but the truth. I'd have told my part of the scrape, if I could without bringing Meg in. As I couldn't, I held my tongue, and bore the scolding till the old gentleman collared me. Then I got angry, and bolted, for fear I should forget myself."

"It wasn't nice, but he's sorry, I know; so go down and make up. I'll help you."

"Hanged if I do! I'm not going to be lectured and pummelled by every one, just for a bit of a frolic. I *was* sorry about Meg, and begged pardon like a man; but I won't do it again, when I wasn't in the wrong."

"He didn't know that."

"He ought to trust me, and not act as if I was a baby. It's no use, Jo; he's got to learn that I'm able to take care of myself, and don't need anyone's apron-string to hold on by."

"What pepper-pots you are!" sighed Jo. "How do you mean to settle this affair?"

"Well, he ought to beg pardon, and believe me when I say I can't tell him what the fuss's about."

"Bless you! He won't do that."

"I won't go down till he does."

"Now, Teddy, be sensible; let it pass, and I'll explain what I can. You can't stay here, so what's the use of being melodramatic?"

"I don't intend to stay here long, any way. I'll slip off and take a journey somewhere, and when grandpa misses me he'll come round fast enough."

"I dare say; but you ought not to go and worry him."

"Don't preach. I'll go to Washington and see Brooke; it's gay there, and I'll enjoy myself after the troubles."

"What fun you'd have! I wish I could run off too," said Jo, forgetting her part of Mentor in lively visions of martial life at the capital.

"Come on, then! Why not? You go and surprise your father, and I'll stir up old Brooke. It would be a glorious joke; let's do it, Jo. We'll leave a letter saying we are all right, and trot off at once. I've got money enough; it will do you good, and be no harm, as you go to your father."

For a moment Jo looked as if she would agree; for, wild as the plan was, it just suited her. She was tired of care and confinement, longed for change, and thoughts of her father blended temptingly with the novel charms of camps and hospitals, liberty and fun. Her eyes kindled as they turned wistfully toward the window, but they fell on the old house opposite, and she shook her head with sorrowful decision.

"If I was a boy, we'd run away together, and have a capital time; but as I'm a miserable girl, I must be proper, and stop at home. Don't tempt me, Teddy, it's a crazy plan."

"That's the fun of it," began Laurie, who had got a wilful fit on him, and was possessed to break out of bounds in some way.

"Hold your tongue!" cried Jo, covering her ears. " 'Prunes and prisms' are my doom, and I may as well make up my mind to it. I came here to moralize, not to hear about things that make me skip to think of."

"I know Meg would wet-blanket such a proposal, but I thought you had more spirit," began Laurie insinuatingly.

"Bad boy, be quiet! Sit down and think of your own sins, don't go making me add to mine. If I get your grandpa to apologize for the shaking, will you give up running away?" asked Jo seriously.

"Yes, but you won't do it," answered Laurie, who wished "to make up," but felt that his outraged dignity must be appeased first.

"If I can manage the young one I can the old one," muttered Jo, as she walked away, leaving Laurie bent over a railroad map, with his head propped up on both hands.

"Come in!" and Mr. Laurence's gruff voice sounded gruffer than ever, as Jo tapped at his door.

"It's only me, sir, come to return a book," she said blandly, as she entered.

"Want any more?" asked the old gentleman, looking grim and vexed, but trying not to show it.

"Yes, please. I like old Sam so well, I think I'll try the second volume," returned Jo, hoping to propitiate him by accepting a second dose of Boswell's "Johnson," as he had recommended that lively work.

The shaggy eyebrows unbent a little, as he rolled the steps toward the shelf where the Johnsonian literature was placed. Jo skipped up, and, sitting on the top step, affected to be searching for her book, but was really wondering how best to introduce the dangerous object of her visit. Mr. Laurence seemed to suspect that something was brewing in her mind; for, after taking several brisk turns about the room, he faced round on her, speaking so abruptly that "Rasselas" tumbled face downward on the floor.

"What has that boy been about? Don't try to shield him. I know he has been in mischief by the way he acted when he came home. I can't get a word from him; and when I threatened to shake the truth out of him he bolted upstairs, and locked himself into his room."

"He did do wrong, but we forgave him, and all promised not to say a word to anyone," began Jo reluctantly.

"That won't do; he shall not shelter himself behind a promise from you soft-hearted girls. If he's done anything amiss, he shall confess, beg pardon, and be punished. Out with it, Jo, I won't be kept in the dark."

Mr. Laurence looked so alarming and spoke so sharply that Jo would have gladly run away, if she could, but she was perched aloft on the steps, and he stood at the foot, a lion in the path, so she had to stay and brave it out.

"Indeed, sir, I cannot tell; mother forbade it. Laurie has confessed, asked pardon, and been punished quite enough. We don't keep silence to shield him, but someone else, and it will make more trouble if you interfere. Please don't; it was partly my fault, but it's all right now; so let's forget it, and talk about the 'Rambler,' or something pleasant."

"Hang the 'Rambler!' Come down and give me your word that this harum-scarum boy of mine hasn't done anything ungrateful or impertinent. If he has, after all your kindness to him, I'll thrash him with my own hands."

The threat sounded awful, but did not alarm Jo, for she knew the irascible old gentleman would never lift a finger against his grandson, whatever he might say to the contrary. She obediently descended, and made as light of the prank as she could without betraying Meg or forgetting the truth.

"Hum—ha—well, if the boy held his tongue because he promised, and not from obstinacy, I'll forgive him. He's a stubborn fellow, and hard to manage," said Mr. Laurence, rubbing up his hair till it looked as if he had been out in a gale, and smoothing the frown from his brow with an air of relief.

"So am I; but a kind word will govern me when all the king's horses and all the king's men couldn't," said Jo, trying to say a kind word for her friend, who seemed to get out of one scrape only to fall into another.

"You think I'm not kind to him, hey?" was the sharp answer.

"Oh, dear, no, sir; you are rather too kind sometimes, and then just a trifle hasty when he tries your patience. Don't you think you are?"

Jo was determined to have it out now, and tried to look quite placid, though she quaked a little after her bold speech. To her great relief and surprise, the old gentleman only threw his spectacles on to the table with a rattle, and exclaimed frankly,—

"You're right, girl, I am! I love the boy, but he tries my patience past bearing, and I don't know how it will end, if we go on so."

"I'll tell you, he'll run away." Jo was sorry for that speech the minute it was made; she meant to warn him that Laurie would not bear much restraint, and hoped he would be more forbearing with the lad.

Mr. Laurence's ruddy face changed suddenly, and he sat down, with a troubled glance at the picture of a handsome man, which hung over his table. It was Laurie's father, who *had* run away in his youth, and married against the imperious old man's will. Jo fancied he remembered and regretted the past, and she wished she had held her tongue.

"He won't do it unless he is very much worried, and only threatens it sometimes, when he gets tired of studying. I often think I should like to, especially since my hair was cut; so, if you ever miss us, you may advertise for two boys, and look among the ships bound for India."

She laughed as she spoke, and Mr. Laurence looked relieved, evidently taking the whole as a joke.

"You hussy, how dare you talk in that way? Where's your respect for me, and your proper bringing up? Bless the boys and girls! What torments they are; yet we can't do without them," he said, pinching her cheeks good-humoredly. "Go and bring that boy down to his dinner, tell him it's all right, and advise him not to put on tragedy airs with his grandfather. I won't bear it."

"He won't come, sir; he feels badly because you didn't believe him when he said he couldn't tell. I think the shaking hurt his feelings very much."

Jo tried to look pathetic, but must have failed, for Mr. Laurence began to laugh, and she knew the day was won.

"I'm sorry for that, and ought to thank him for not shaking *me*, I suppose. What the dickens does the fellow expect?" and the old gentleman looked a trifle ashamed of his own testiness.

"If I were you, I'd write him an apology, sir. He says he won't come down till he has one, and talks about Washington, and goes on in an absurd way. A formal apology will make him see how foolish he is, and bring him down quite amiable. Try it; he likes fun, and this way is better than talking. I'll carry it up, and teach him his duty."

Mr. Laurence gave her a sharp look, and put on his spectacles, saying slowly, "You're a sly puss, but I don't mind being managed by you and Beth. Here, give me a bit of paper, and let us have done with this nonsense."

The note was written in the terms which one gentleman would use to another after offering some deep insult. Jo dropped a kiss on the top of Mr. Laurence's bald head, and ran up to slip the apology under Laurie's door, advising him, through the key-hole, to be submissive, decorous, and a few other agreeable impossibilities. Finding the door locked again, she left the note to do its work, and was going quietly away, when the young gentleman slid down the banisters, and waited for her at the bottom, saying, with his most virtuous expression of countenance, "What a good fellow you are, Jo! Did you get blown up?" he added, laughing.

"No; he was pretty mild, on the whole."

"Ah! I got it all round; even you cast me off over there, and I felt just ready to go to the deuce," he began apologetically.

"Don't talk in that way; turn over a new leaf and begin again, Teddy, my son."

"I keep turning over new leaves, and spoiling them, as I used to spoil my copy-books; and I make so many beginnings there never will be an end," he said dolefully.

"Go and eat your dinner; you'll feel better after it. Men always croak when they are hungry," and Jo whisked out at the front door after that.

"That's a 'label' on my 'sect,'" answered Laurie, quoting Amy, as he went to partake of humble-pie dutifully with his grandfather, who was quite saintly in temper and overwhelmingly respectful in manner all the rest of the day.

Everyone thought the matter ended and the little cloud blown over;

He stood at the foot, like a lion in the path.

but the mischief was done, for, though others forgot it, Meg remembered. She never alluded to a certain person, but she thought of him a good deal, dreamed dreams more than ever; and once Jo, rummaging her sister's desk for stamps, found a bit of paper scribbled over with the words, "Mrs. John Brooke;" whereat she groaned tragically, and cast it into the fire, feeling that Laurie's prank had hastened the evil day for her.

# CHAPTER XXII

## PLEASANT MEADOWS

LIKE sunshine after storm were the peaceful weeks which followed. The invalids improved rapidly, and Mr. March began to talk of returning early in the new year. Beth was soon able to lie on the study sofa all day, amusing herself with the well-beloved cats, at first, and, in time, with doll's sewing, which had fallen sadly behindhand. Her once active limbs were so stiff and feeble that Jo took her a daily airing about the house in her strong arms. Meg cheerfully blackened and burnt her white hands cooking delicate messes for "the dear;" while Amy, a loyal slave of the ring, celebrated her return by giving away as many of her treasures as she could prevail on her sisters to accept.

As Christmas approached, the usual mysteries began to haunt the house, and Jo frequently convulsed the family by proposing utterly impossible or magnificently absurd ceremonies, in honor of this unusually merry Christmas. Laurie was equally impracticable, and would have had bonfires, sky-rockets, and triumphal arches, if he had had his own way. After many skirmishes and snubbings, the ambitious pair were considered effectually quenched, and went about with forlorn faces, which were rather belied by explosions of laughter when the two got together.

Several days of unusually mild weather fitly ushered in a splendid Christmas Day. Hannah "felt in her bones" that it was going to be an unusually fine day, and she proved herself a true prophetess, for everybody and everything seemed bound to produce a grand success. To begin with, Mr. March wrote that he should soon be with them; then Beth felt uncommonly well that morning, and, being dressed in her mother's gift,—a soft crimson merino wrapper,—was borne in triumph to the window to behold the offering of Jo and Laurie. The Unquenchables had done their best to be worthy of the name, for, like elves, they had worked by night, and conjured up a comical surprise. Out in the garden stood a stately snow-maiden, crowned with holly, bearing a basket of fruit and flowers in one hand, a great roll of new music in the other, a perfect rainbow of an Afghan round her chilly shoulders, and a Christmas carol issuing from her lips, on a pink paper streamer:—

*"THE JUNGFRAU TO BETH*

*"God bless you, dear Queen Bess!*
*May nothing you dismay,*

> *But health and peace and happiness*
> *Be yours, this Christmas Day.*

> "*Here's fruit to feed our busy bee,*
> *And flowers for her nose;*
> *Here's music for her pianee,*
> *An Afghan for her toes.*

> "*A portrait of Joanna, see,*
> *By Raphael No. 2,*
> *Who labored with great industry*
> *To make it fair and true.*

> "*Accept a ribbon red, I beg,*
> *For Madam Purrer's tail;*
> *And ice-cream made by lovely Peg,—*
> *A Mont Blanc in a pail.*

> "*Their dearest love my makers laid*
> *Within my breast of snow:*
> *Accept it, and the Alpine maid,*
> *From Laurie and from Jo.*"

How Beth laughed when she saw it, how Laurie ran up and down to bring in the gifts, and what ridiculous speeches Jo made as she presented them!

"I'm so full of happiness, that, if father was only here, I couldn't hold one drop more," said Beth, quite sighing with contentment as Jo carried her off to the study to rest after the excitement, and to refresh herself with some of the delicious grapes the "Jungfrau" had sent her.

"So am I," added Jo, slapping the pocket wherein reposed the long-desired Undine and Sintram.

"I'm sure I am," echoed Amy, poring over the engraved copy of the Madonna and Child, which her mother had given her, in a pretty frame.

"Of course I am!" cried Meg, smoothing the silvery folds of her first silk dress; for Mr. Laurence had insisted on giving it.

"How can *I* be otherwise?" said Mrs. March gratefully, as her eyes went from her husband's letter to Beth's smiling face, and her hand caressed the brooch made of gray and golden, chestnut and dark brown hair, which the girls had just fastened on her breast.

Now and then, in this work-a-day world, things do happen in the delightful story-book fashion, and what a comfort that is. Half an hour after everyone had said they were so happy they could only hold one drop more, the drop came. Laurie opened the parlor door, and popped his head in very quietly. He might just as well have turned a somersault and uttered an Indian war-whoop; for his face was so full of suppressed excitement and his voice so treacherously joyful, that everyone jumped up, though he only said, in a queer, breathless voice, "Here's another Christmas present for the March family."

Before the words were well out of his mouth, he was whisked away somehow, and in his place appeared a tall man, muffled up to the eyes, leaning on the arm of another tall man, who tried to say something and couldn't. Of course there was a general stampede; and for several minutes everybody seemed to lose their wits, for the strangest things were done, and no one said a word. Mr. March became invisible in the embrace of four pairs of loving arms; Jo disgraced herself by nearly fainting away, and had to be doctored by Laurie in the china-closet; Mr. Brooke kissed Meg entirely by mistake, as he somewhat incoherently explained; and Amy, the dignified, tumbled over a stool, and, never stopping to get up, hugged and cried over her father's boots in the most touching manner. Mrs. March was the first to recover herself, and held up her hand with a warning, "Hush! Remember Beth!"

But it was too late; the study door flew open, the little red wrapper appeared on the threshold,—joy put strength into the feeble limbs,—and Beth ran straight into her father's arms. Never mind what happened just after that; for the full hearts overflowed, washing away the bitterness of the past, and leaving only the sweetness of the present.

It was not at all romantic, but a hearty laugh set everybody straight again, for Hannah was discovered behind the door, sobbing over the fat turkey, which she had forgotten to put down when she rushed up from the kitchen. As the laugh subsided, Mrs. March began to thank Mr. Brooke for his faithful care of her husband, at which Mr. Brooke suddenly remembered that Mr. March needed rest, and, seizing Laurie, he precipitately retired. Then the two invalids were ordered to repose, which they did, by both sitting in one big chair, and talking hard.

Mr. March told how he had longed to surprise them, and how, when the fine weather came, he had been allowed by his doctor to take advantage of it; how devoted Brooke had been, and how he was altogether a most estimable and upright young man. Why Mr. March paused a minute just there, and, after a glance at Meg, who was violently poking the fire, looked at his wife with an inquiring lift of the eyebrows, I leave you to imagine; also why Mrs. March gently nodded her head, and asked, rather abruptly, if he wouldn't have something to eat. Jo saw and understood the look; and she stalked grimly away to get wine and beef-tea, muttering to herself, as she slammed the door, "I hate estimable young men with brown eyes!"

There never *was* such a Christmas dinner as they had that day. The fat turkey was a sight to behold, when Hannah sent him up, stuffed, browned, and decorated; so was the plum-pudding, which quite melted in one's mouth; likewise the jellies, in which Amy revelled like a fly in a honey-pot. Everything turned out well, which was a mercy, Hannah said, "For my mind was that flustered, mum, that it's a merrycle I didn't roast the pudding, and stuff the turkey with raisins, let alone bilin' of it in a cloth."

Mr. Laurence and his grandson dined with them, also Mr. Brooke,—at whom Jo glowered darkly, to Laurie's infinite amusement. Two easy-chairs stood side by side at the head of the table, in which sat Beth and her father, feasting modestly on chicken and a little fruit. They drank healths, told stories, sung songs, "reminisced," as the old folks say, and had a thoroughly good time. A sleigh-ride had been planned, but the girls would not leave their father; so the guests departed early, and, as twilight gathered, the happy family sat together round the fire.

"Just a year ago we were groaning over the dismal Christmas we expected to have. Do you remember?" asked Jo, breaking a short pause which had followed a long conversation about many things.

"Rather a pleasant year on the whole!" said Meg, smiling at the fire, and congratulating herself on having treated Mr. Brooke with dignity.

"I think it's been a pretty hard one," observed Amy, watching the light shine on her ring with thoughtful eyes.

"I'm glad it's over, because we've got you back," whispered Beth, who sat on her father's knee.

"Rather a rough road for you to travel, my little pilgrims, especially the latter part of it. But you have got on bravely; and I think the burdens are in a fair way to tumble off very soon," said Mr. March, looking with fatherly satisfaction at the four young faces gathered round him.

"How do you know? Did mother tell you?" asked Jo.

"Not much; straws show which way the wind blows, and I've made several discoveries today."

"Oh, tell us what they are!" cried Meg, who sat beside him.

"Here is one;" and taking up the hand which lay on the arm of his chair, he pointed to the roughened forefinger, a burn on the back, and two or three little hard spots on the palm. "I remember a time when this hand was white and smooth, and your first care was to keep it so. It was very pretty then, but to me it is much prettier now,—for in these seeming blemishes I read a little history. A burnt-offering has been made of vanity; this hardened palm has earned something better than blisters; and I'm sure the sewing done by these pricked fingers will last a long time, so much good-will went into the stitches. Meg, my dear, I value the womanly skill which keeps home happy more than white hands or fashionable accomplishments. I'm proud to shake this good, industrious little hand, and hope I shall not soon be asked to give it away."

If Meg had wanted a reward for hours of patient labor, she received it in the hearty pressure of her father's hand and the approving smile he gave her.

"What about Jo? Please say something nice; for she has tried so hard, and been so very, very good to me," said Beth, in her father's ear.

He laughed, and looked across at the tall girl who sat opposite, with an unusually mild expression in her brown face.

"In spite of the curly crop, I don't see the 'son Jo' whom I left a year ago," said Mr. March. "I see a young lady who pins her collar straight, laces her boots neatly and neither whistles, talks slang, nor lies on the rug as she used to do. Her face is rather thin and pale, just now, with watching and anxiety; but I like to look at it, for it has grown gentler, and her voice is lower; she doesn't bounce, but moves quietly, and takes care of a certain little person in a motherly way which delights me. I rather miss my wild girl; but if I get a strong, helpful, tender-hearted woman in her place, I shall feel quite satisfied. I don't know whether the shearing sobered our black sheep, but I do know that in all Washington I couldn't find anything beautiful enough to be bought with the five-and-twenty dollars which my good girl sent me."

Jo's keen eyes were rather dim for a minute, and her thin face grew rosy in the firelight, as she received her father's praise, feeling that she did deserve a portion of it.

"Now Beth," said Amy, longing for her turn, but ready to wait.

"There's so little of her, I'm afraid to say much, for fear she will slip away altogether, though she is not so shy as she used to be," began their father cheerfully; but recollecting how nearly he *had* lost her, he held her close, saying tenderly, with her cheek against his own, "I've got you safe, my Beth, and I'll keep you so, please God."

After a minute's silence, he looked down at Amy, who sat on the cricket at his feet, and said, with a caress of the shining hair,—

"I observed that Amy took drumsticks at dinner, ran errands for her mother all the afternoon, gave Meg her place tonight, and has waited on everyone with patience and good-humor. I also observe that she does not fret much nor look in the glass, and has not even mentioned a very pretty ring which she wears; so I conclude that she has learned to think of other people more and of herself less, and has decided to try and mould her character as carefully as she moulds her little clay figures. I am glad of this; for though I should be very proud of a graceful statue made by her, I shall be infinitely prouder of a lovable daughter, with a talent for making life beautiful to herself and others."

"What are you thinking of, Beth?" asked Jo, when Amy had thanked her father and told about her ring.

"I read in 'Pilgrim's Progress' today, how, after many troubles, Christian and Hopeful came to a pleasant green meadow, where lilies bloomed all the year round, and there they rested happily, as we do now, before they went on to their journey's end," answered Beth; adding, as she slipped out of her father's arms, and went slowly to the instrument, "It's singing time now, and I want to be in my old place. I'll try to sing the song of the shepherdboy which the Pilgrims heard. I made the music for father, because he likes the verses."

So, sitting at the dear little piano, Beth softly touched the keys, and, in the sweet voice they had never thought to hear again, sung to her own accompaniment the quaint hymn, which was a singularly fitting song for her:—

*"He that is down need fear no fall,*
 *He that is low no pride;*
*He that is humble ever shall*
 *Have God to be his guide.*

*"I am content with what I have,*
 *Little be it or much;*
*And, Lord! contentment still I crave,*
 *Because Thou savest such.*

*"Fulness to them a burden is,*
 *That go on pilgrimage;*
*Here little, and hereafter bliss,*
 *Is best from age to age!"*

# CHAPTER XXIII

## AUNT MARCH SETTLES THE QUESTION

LIKE bees swarming after their queen, mother and daughters hovered about Mr. March the next day neglecting everything to look at, wait upon, and listen to the new invalid, who was in a fair way to be killed by kindness. As he sat propped up in a big chair by Beth's sofa, with the other three close by, and Hannah popping in her head now and then, "to peek at the dear man," nothing seemed needed to complete their happiness. But something *was* needed, and the elder ones felt it, though none confessed the fact. Mr. and Mrs. March looked at one another with an anxious expression, as their eyes followed Meg. Jo had sudden fits of sobriety, and was seen to shake her fist at Mr. Brooke's umbrella, which had been left in the hall; Meg was absent-minded, shy, and silent, started when the bell rang, and colored when John's name was mentioned; Amy said, "Everyone seemed waiting for something, and couldn't settle down, which was queer, since father was safe at home," and Beth innocently wondered why their neighbors didn't run over as usual.

Laurie went by in the afternoon, and, seeing Meg at the window, seemed suddenly possessed with a melodramatic fit, for he fell down upon one knee in the snow, beat his breast, tore his hair, and clasped his hands imploringly, as if begging some boon; and when Meg told him to behave himself and go away, he wrung imaginary tears out of his handkerchief, and staggered round the corner as if in utter despair.

"What does the goose mean?" said Meg, laughing, and trying to look unconscious.

"He's showing you how your John will go on by and by. Touching, isn't it?" answered Jo scornfully.

"Don't say *my John*, it isn't proper or true;" but Meg's voice lingered over the words as if they sounded pleasant to her. "Please don't plague me, Jo; I've told you I don't care *much* about him, and there isn't to be anything said, but we are all to be friendly, and go on as before."

"We can't, for something has been said, and Laurie's mischief has spoilt you for me. I see it, and so does mother; you are not like your old self a bit, and seem ever so far away from me. I don't mean to plague you, and will bear it like a man, but I do wish it was all settled. I hate to wait; so if you mean ever to do it, make haste and have it over quickly," said Jo pettishly.

"*I* can't say or do anything till he speaks, and he won't, because father said I was too young," began Meg, bending over her work, with a queer little smile, which suggested that she did not quite agree with her father on that point.

"If he did speak, you wouldn't know what to say, but would cry or blush, or let him have his own way, instead of giving a good, decided, No."

"I'm not so silly and weak as you think. I know just what I should say, for I've planned it all, so I needn't be taken unawares; there's no knowing what may happen, and I wished to be prepared."

Jo couldn't help smiling at the important air which Meg had unconsciously assumed, and which was as becoming as the pretty color varying in her cheeks.

"Would you mind telling me what you'd say?" asked Jo more respectfully.

"Not at all; you are sixteen now, quite old enough to be my confidant, and my experience will be useful to you by and by, perhaps, in your own affairs of this sort."

"Don't mean to have any; it's fun to watch other people philander, but I should feel like a fool doing it myself," said Jo, looking alarmed at the thought.

"I think not, if you liked anyone very much, and he liked you." Meg spoke as if to herself, and glanced out at the lane, where she had often seen lovers walking together in the summer twilight.

"I thought you were going to tell your speech to that man," said Jo, rudely shortening her sister's little reverie.

"Oh, I should merely say, quite calmly and decidedly, 'Thank you, Mr. Brooke, you are very kind, but I agree with father that I am too young to enter into any engagement at present; so please say no more, but let us be friends as we were.' "

"Hum! That's stiff and cool enough. I don't believe you'll ever say it, and I know he won't be satisfied if you do. If he goes on like the rejected lovers in books, you'll give in, rather than hurt his feelings."

"No, I won't. I shall tell him I've made up my mind, and shall walk out of the room with dignity."

Meg rose as she spoke, and was just going to rehearse the dignified exit, when a step in the hall made her fly into her seat, and begin to sew as if her life depended on finishing that particular seam in a given time. Jo smothered a laugh at the sudden change, and, when someone gave a modest tap, opened the door with a grim aspect, which was anything but hospitable.

"Good afternoon. I came to get my umbrella,—that is, to see how your father finds himself today," said Mr. Brooke, getting a trifle confused as his eye went from one tell-tale face to the other.

"It's very well, he's in the rack, I'll get him, and tell it you are here," and having jumbled her father and the umbrella well together in her reply, Jo slipped out of the room to give Meg a chance to make her speech and air her dignity. But the instant she vanished, Meg began to sidle towards the door, murmuring,—

"Mother will like to see you. Pray sit down, I'll call her."

"Don't go; are you afraid of me, Margaret?" and Mr. Brooke looked so hurt that Meg thought she must have done something very rude. She blushed up to the little curls on her forehead, for he had never called her Margaret before, and she was surprised to find how natural and sweet it seemed to hear him say it. Anxious to appear friendly and at her ease, she put out her hand with a confiding gesture, and said gratefully,—

He sat in the big chair by Beth's sofa.

"How can I be afraid when you have been so kind to father? I only wish I could thank you for it."

"Shall I tell you how?" asked Mr. Brooke, holding the small hand fast in both his own, and looking down at Meg with so much love in the brown eyes, that her heart began to flutter, and she both longed to run away and to stop and listen.

"Oh no, please don't—I'd rather not," she said, trying to withdraw her hand, and looking frightened in spite of her denial.

"I won't trouble you, I only want to know if you care for me a little, Meg. I love you so much, dear," added Mr. Brooke tenderly.

This was the moment for the calm, proper speech, but Meg didn't make it; she forgot every word of it, hung her head, and answered, "I don't know," so softly, that John had to stoop down to catch the foolish little reply.

He seemed to think it was worth the trouble, for he smiled to himself as if quite satisfied, pressed the plump hand gratefully, and said, in his most persuasive tone, "Will you try and find out? I want to know *so* much; for I can't go to work with any heart until I learn whether I am to have my reward in the end or not."

"I'm too young," faltered Meg, wondering why she was so fluttered, yet rather enjoying it.

"I'll wait; and in the meantime, you could be learning to like me. Would it be a very hard lesson, dear?"

"Not if I chose to learn it, but—"

"Please choose to learn, Meg. I love to teach, and this is easier than German," broke in John, getting possession of the other hand, so that she had no way of hiding her face, as he bent to look into it.

His tone was properly beseeching; but, stealing a shy look at him, Meg saw that his eyes were merry as well as tender, and that he wore the satisfied smile of one who had no doubt of his success. This nettled her; Annie Moffat's foolish lessons in coquetry came into her mind, and the love of power, which sleeps in the bosoms of the best of little women, woke up all of a sudden and took possession of her. She felt excited and strange, and, not knowing what else to do, followed a capricious impulse, and, withdrawing her hands, said petulantly, "I *don't* choose. Please go away and let me be!"

Poor Mr. Brooke looked as if his lovely castle in the air was tumbling about his ears, for he had never seen Meg in such a mood before, and it rather bewildered him.

"Do you really mean that?" he asked anxiously, following her as she walked away.

"Yes, I do; I don't want to be worried about such things. Father says I needn't; it's too soon and I'd rather not."

"Mayn't I hope you'll change your mind by and by? I'll wait, and say nothing till you have had more time. Don't play with me, Meg. I didn't think that of you."

"Don't think of me at all. I'd rather you wouldn't," said Meg, taking a naughty satisfaction in trying her lover's patience and her own power.

He was grave and pale now, and looked decidedly more like the novel heroes whom she admired; but he neither slapped his forehead nor

"Shall I tell you how?"

tramped about the room, as they did; he just stood looking at her so wistfully, so tenderly, that she found her heart relenting in spite of her. What would have happened next I cannot say, if Aunt March had not come hobbling in at this interesting minute.

The old lady couldn't resist her longing to see her nephew; for she had met Laurie as she took her airing, and, hearing of Mr. March's arrival, drove straight out to see him. The family were all busy in the back part of the house, and she had made her way quietly in, hoping to surprise them. She did surprise two of them so much that Meg started as if she had seen a ghost, and Mr. Brooke vanished into the study.

"Bless me, what's all this?" cried the old lady, with a rap of her cane, as she glanced from the pale young gentleman to the scarlet young lady.

"It's father's friend. I'm *so* surprised to see you!" stammered Meg, feeling that she was in for a lecture now.

"That's evident," returned Aunt March, sitting down. "But what is father's friend saying to make you look like a peony? There's mischief going on, and I insist upon knowing what it is," with another rap.

"We were merely talking. Mr. Brooke came for his umbrella," began Meg, wishing that Mr. Brooke and the umbrella were safely out of the house.

"Brooke? That boy's tutor? Ah! I understand now. I know all about it. Jo blundered into a wrong message in one of your father's letters, and I made her tell me. You haven't gone and accepted him, child?" cried Aunt March, looking scandalized.

"Hush! He'll hear. Sha'n't I call mother?" said Meg, much troubled.

"Not yet. I've something to say to you, and I must free my mind at once. Tell me, do you mean to marry this Cook? If you do, not one penny of my money ever goes to you. Remember that, and be a sensible girl," said the old lady impressively.

Now Aunt March possessed in perfection the art of rousing the spirit of opposition in the gentlest people, and enjoyed doing it. The best of us have a spice of perversity in us, especially when we are young and in love. If Aunt March had begged Meg to accept John Brooke, she would probably have declared she couldn't think of it; but as she was peremptorily ordered *not* to like him, she immediately made up her mind that she would. Inclination as well as perversity made the decision easy, and, being already much excited, Meg opposed the old lady with unusual spirit.

"I shall marry whom I please, Aunt March, and you can leave your money to anyone you like," she said, nodding her head with a resolute air.

"Highty tighty! Is that the way you take my advice, miss? You'll be sorry for it, by and by, when you've tried love in a cottage, and found it a failure."

"It can't be a worse one than some people find in big houses," retorted Meg.

Aunt March put on her glasses and took a look at the girl, for she did not know her in this new mood. Meg hardly knew herself, she felt so brave and independent,—so glad to defend John, and assert her right to love him, if she liked. Aunt March saw that she had begun wrong, and, after a little pause, made a fresh start, saying, as mildly as she could, "Now, Meg, my dear, be reasonable, and take my advice. I mean it kindly, and don't want you to spoil your whole life by making a mistake at the beginning. You ought to marry well, and help your family; it's your duty to make a rich match, and it ought to be impressed upon you."

"Father and mother don't think so; they like John, though he *is* poor."

"Your parents, my dear, have no more worldly wisdom than two babies."

"I'm glad of it," cried Meg stoutly.

Aunt March took no notice, but went on with her lecture. "This Rook is poor, and hasn't got any rich relations, has he?"

"No; but he has many warm friends."

"You can't live on friends; try it, and see how cool they'll grow. He hasn't any business, has he?"

"Not yet; Mr. Laurence is going to help him."

"That won't last long. James Laurence is a crotchety old fellow, and not to be depended on. So you intend to marry a man without money, position, or business, and go on working harder than you do now, when you might be comfortable all your days by minding me and doing better? I thought you had more sense, Meg."

"I couldn't do better if I waited half my life! John is good and wise; he's got heaps of talent; he's willing to work, and sure to get on, he's so energetic and brave. Everyone likes and respects him, and I'm proud to think he cares for me, though I'm so poor and young and silly," said Meg, looking prettier than ever in her earnestness.

"He knows *you* have got rich relations, child; that's the secret of his liking, I suspect."

"Aunt March, how dare you say such a thing? John is above such meanness, and I won't listen to you a minute if you talk so," cried Meg indignantly, forgetting everything but the injustice of the old lady's suspicions. "My John wouldn't marry for money, any more than I would. We are willing to work, and we mean to wait. I'm not afraid of being poor, for I've been happy so far, and I know I shall be with him, because he loves me, and I—"

Meg stopped there, remembering all of a sudden that she hadn't made up her mind; that she had told "her John" to go away, and that he might be overhearing her inconsistent remarks.

Aunt March was very angry, for she had set her heart on having her pretty niece make a fine match, and something in the girl's happy young face made the lonely old woman feel both sad and sour.

"Well, I wash my hands of the whole affair! You are a wilful child, and you've lost more than you know by this piece of folly. No, I won't stop; I'm disappointed in you, and haven't spirits to see your father now. Don't expect anything from me when you are married; your Mr. Book's friends must take care of you. I'm done with you forever."

And, slamming the door in Meg's face, Aunt March drove off in high dudgeon. She seemed to take all the girl's courage with her; for, when left alone, Meg stood a moment, undecided whether to laugh or cry. Before she could make up her mind, she was taken possession of by Mr. Brooke, who said, all in one breath, "I couldn't help hearing, Meg. Thank you for defending me, and Aunt March for proving that you *do* care for me a little bit."

"I didn't know how much, till she abused you," began Meg.

"And I needn't go away, but may stay and be happy, may I, dear?"

Here was another fine chance to make the crushing speech and the stately exit, but Meg never thought of doing either, and disgraced herself forever in Jo's eyes by meekly whispering, "Yes, John," and hiding her face on Mr. Brooke's waistcoat.

Fifteen minutes after Aunt March's departure, Jo came softly downstairs, paused an instant at the parlor door, and, hearing no sound within, nodded and smiled, with a satisfied expression, saying to herself, "She has sent him away as we planned, and that affair is settled. I'll go and hear the fun, and have a good laugh over it."

But poor Jo never got her laugh, for she was transfixed upon the threshold by a spectacle which held her there, staring with her mouth nearly as wide open as her eyes. Going in to exult over a fallen enemy, and to praise a strong-minded sister for the banishment of an objectionable lover, it certainly *was* a shock to behold the aforesaid enemy serenely sitting on the sofa, with the strong-minded sister enthroned upon his knee, and wearing an expression of the most abject submission. Jo gave a sort of gasp, as if a cold shower-bath had suddenly fallen upon her,— for such an unexpected turning of the tables actually took her breath away. At the odd sound, the lovers turned and saw her. Meg jumped up, looking both proud and shy; but "that man," as Jo called him, actually laughed, and said coolly, as he kissed the astonished new-comer, "Sister Jo, congratulate us!"

That was adding insult to injury,—it was altogether too much,—and, making some wild demonstration with her hands, Jo vanished without a word. Rushing upstairs, she startled the invalids by exclaiming tragically, as she burst into the room, "Oh, *do* somebody go down quick; John Brooke is acting dreadfully, and Meg likes it!"

Mr. and Mrs. March left the room with speed; and, casting herself upon the bed, Jo cried and scolded tempestuously as she told the awful news to Beth and Amy. The little girls however, considered it a most agreeable and interesting event, and Jo got little comfort from them; so she went up to her refuge in the garret, and confided her troubles to the rats.

Nobody ever knew what went on in the parlor that afternoon; but a great deal of talking was done, and quiet Mr. Brooke astonished his friends by the eloquence and spirit with which he pleaded his suit, told his plans, and persuaded them to arrange everything just as he wanted it.

The tea-bell rang before he had finished describing the paradise which he meant to earn for Meg, and he proudly took her in to supper, both looking so happy that Jo hadn't the heart to be jealous or dismal. Amy was very much impressed by John's devotion and Meg's dignity, Beth beamed at them from a distance, while Mr. and Mrs. March surveyed the young couple with such tender satisfaction that it was perfectly evident Aunt March was right in calling them as "unworldly as a pair of babies." No one ate much, but everyone looked very happy, and the old room seemed to brighten up amazingly when the first romance of the family began there.

"You can't say nothing pleasant ever happens now, can you, Meg?" said Amy, trying to decide how she would group the lovers in the sketch she was planning to take.

"No, I'm sure I can't. How much has happened since I said that! It seems a year ago," answered Meg, who was in a blissful dream, lifted far above such common things as bread and butter.

"The joys come close upon the sorrows this time, and I rather think the changes have begun," said Mrs. March. "In most families there comes, now and then, a year full of events; this has been such a one, but it ends well, after all."

"Hope the next will end better," muttered Jo, who found it very hard to see Meg absorbed in a stranger before her face; for Jo loved a few persons very dearly, and dreaded to have their affection lost or lessened in any way.

"I hope the third year from this *will* end better; I mean it shall, if I live to work out my plans," said Mr. Brooke, smiling at Meg, as if everything had become possible to him now.

"Doesn't it seem very long to wait?" asked Amy, who was in a hurry for the wedding.

"I've got so much to learn before I shall be ready, it seems a short time to me," answered Meg, with a sweet gravity in her face, never seen there before.

"You have only to wait; *I* am to do the work," said John, beginning his labors by picking up Meg's napkin, with an expression which caused Jo to shake her head, and then say to herself, with an air of relief, as the front door banged, "Here comes Laurie. Now we shall have a little sensible conversation."

But Jo was mistaken; for Laurie came prancing in, overflowing with spirits, bearing a great bridal-looking bouquet for "Mrs. John Brooke," and evidently laboring under the delusion that the whole affair had been brought about by his excellent management.

"I knew Brooke would have it all his own way, he always does; for when he makes up his mind to accomplish anything, it's done, though the sky falls," said Laurie, when he had presented his offering and his congratulations.

"Much obliged for that recommendation. I take it as a good omen for the future, and invite you to my wedding on the spot," answered Mr. Brooke, who felt at peace with all mankind, even his mischievous pupil.

"I'll come if I'm at the ends of the earth; for the sight of Jo's face alone, on that occasion, would be worth a long journey. You don't look festive, ma'am; what's the matter?" asked Laurie, following her into a corner of the parlor, whither all had adjourned to greet Mr. Laurence.

"I don't approve of the match, but I've made up my mind to bear it, and shall not say a word against it," said Jo solemnly. "You can't know how hard it is for me to give up Meg," she continued, with a little quiver in her voice.

"You don't give her up. You only go halves," said Laurie consolingly.

"It never can be the same again. I've lost my dearest friend," sighed Jo.

"You've got me, anyhow. I'm not good for much, I know; but I'll stand by you, Jo, all the days of my life; upon my word I will!" and Laurie meant what he said.

"I know you will, and I'm ever so much obliged; you are always a great comfort to me, Teddy," returned Jo, gratefully shaking hands.

"Well, now, don't be dismal, there's a good fellow. It's all right, you see. Meg is happy; Brooke will fly round and get settled immediately; grandpa will attend to him, and it will be very jolly to see Meg in her own little house. We'll have capital times after she is gone, for I shall be through college before long, and then we'll go abroad, or some nice trip or other. Wouldn't that console you?"

"I rather think it would; but there's no knowing what may happen in three years," said Jo thoughtfully.

"That's true. Don't you wish you could take a look forward, and see where we shall all be then? I do," returned Laurie.

"I think not, for I might see something sad; and everyone looks so happy now, I don't believe they could be much improved,"and Jo's eyes went slowly round the room, brightening as they looked, for the prospect was a pleasant one.

Father and mother sat together, quietly re-living the first chapter of the romance which for them began some twenty years ago. Amy was drawing the lovers, who sat apart in a beautiful world of their own, the light of which touched their faces with a grace the little artist could not copy. Beth lay on her sofa, talking cheerily with her old friend, who held her little hand as if he felt that it possessed the power to lead him along the peaceful way she walked. Jo lounged in her favorite low seat, with the grave, quiet look which best became her; and Laurie, leaning on the back of her chair, his chin on a level with her curly head, smiled with his friendliest aspect, and nodded at her in the long glass which reflected them both.

So grouped, the curtain falls upon Meg, Jo, Beth, and Amy. Whether it ever rises again, depends upon the reception given to the first act of the domestic drama called "LITTLE WOMEN."

# Little Women · PART II

### or *Good Wives*

*Overleaf:* "O, Jo, can't you?"

# CHAPTER XXIV

## GOSSIP

In order that we may start afresh, and go to Meg's wedding with free minds, it will be well to begin with a little gossip about the Marches. And here let me premise, that if any of the elders think there is too much "lovering" in the story, as I fear they may (I'm not afraid the young folks will make that objection), I can only say with Mrs. March, "What *can* you expect when I have four gay girls in the house, and a dashing young neighbor over the way?"

The three years that have passed have brought but few changes to the quiet family. The war is over, and Mr. March safely at home, busy with his books and the small parish which found in him a minister by nature as by grace,—a quiet, studious man, rich in the wisdom that is better than learning, the charity which calls all mankind "brother," the piety that blossoms into character, making it august and lovely.

These attributes, in spite of poverty and the strict integrity which shut him out from the more worldly successes, attracted to him many admirable persons, as naturally as sweet herbs draw bees, and as naturally he gave them the honey into which fifty years of hard experience had distilled no bitter drop. Earnest young men found the gray-headed scholar as young at heart as they; thoughtful or troubled women instinctively brought their doubts and sorrows to him, sure of finding the gentlest sympathy, the wisest counsel; sinners told their sins to the pure-hearted old man, and were both rebuked and saved; gifted men found a companion in him; ambitious men caught glimpses of nobler ambitions than their own; and even worldlings confessed that his beliefs were beautiful and true, although "they wouldn't pay."

To outsiders, the five energetic women seemed to rule the house, and so they did in many things; but the quiet scholar, sitting among his books, was still the head of the family, the household conscience, anchor, and comforter; for to him the busy, anxious women always turned in troublous times, finding him, in the truest sense of those sacred words, husband and father.

The girls gave their hearts into their mother's keeping, their souls into their father's; and to both parents, who lived and labored so faithfully for them, they gave a love that grew with their growth, and bound them tenderly together by the sweetest tie which blesses life and outlives death.

Mrs. March is as brisk and cheery, though rather grayer, than when we saw her last, and just now so absorbed in Meg's affairs that the hospitals and homes, still full of wounded "boys" and soldiers' widows, decidedly miss the motherly missionary's visits.

John Brooke did his duty manfully for a year, got wounded, was sent home, and not allowed to return. He received no stars or bars, but he deserved them, for he cheerfully risked all he had; and life and love are very precious when both are in full bloom. Perfectly resigned to his discharge, he devoted himself to getting well, preparing for business, and earning a home for Meg. With the good sense and sturdy independence that characterized him, he refused Mr. Laurence's more generous offers, and accepted the place of book-keeper, feeling better satisfied to begin with an honestly-earned salary than by running any risks with borrowed money.

Meg had spent the time in working as well as waiting, growing womanly in character, wise in housewifely arts, and prettier than ever; for love is a great beautifier. She had her girlish ambitions and hopes, and felt some disappointment at the humble way in which the new life must begin. Ned Moffat had just married Sallie Gardiner, and Meg couldn't help contrasting their fine house and carriage, many gifts, and splendid outfit, with her own, and secretly wishing she could have the same. But somehow envy and discontent soon vanished when she thought of all the patient love and labor John had put into the little home awaiting her; and when they sat together in the twilight, talking over their small plans, the future always grew so beautiful and bright that she forgot Sallie's splendor, and felt herself the richest, happiest girl in Christendom.

Jo never went back to Aunt March, for the old lady took such a fancy to Amy that she bribed her with the offer of drawing lessons from one of the best teachers going; and for the sake of this advantage, Amy would have served a far harder mistress. So she gave her mornings to duty, her afternoons to pleasure, and prospered finely. Jo, meantime, devoted herself to literature and Beth, who remained delicate long after the fever was a thing of the past. Not an invalid exactly, but never again the rosy, healthy creature she had been; yet always hopeful, happy, and serene, busy with the quiet duties she loved, everyone's friend, and an angel in the house, long before those who loved her most had learned to know it.

As long as "The Spread Eagle" paid her a dollar a column for her "rubbish," as she called it, Jo felt herself a woman of means, and spun her little romances diligently. But great plans fermented in her busy brain and ambitious mind, and the old tin kitchen in the garret held a slowly increasing pile of blotted manuscript, which was one day to place the name of March upon the roll of fame.

Laurie, having dutifully gone to college to please his grandfather, was now getting through it in the easiest possible manner to please himself. A universal favorite, thanks to money, manners, much talent, and the kindest heart that ever got its owner into scrapes by trying to get other people out of them, he stood in great danger of being spoilt, and probably would have been, like many another promising boy, if he had not possessed a talisman against evil in the memory of the kind old man who was bound up in his success, the motherly friend who watched over him as if he were her son, and last, but not least by any means, the knowledge that four innocent girls loved, admired, and believed in him with all their hearts.

Being only "a glorious human boy," of course he frolicked and flirted, grew dandified, aquatic, sentimental, or gymnastic, as college fashions ordained; hazed and was hazed, talked slang, and more than once came perilously near suspension and expulsion. But as high spirits and the love of fun were the causes of these pranks, he always managed to save himself by frank confession, honorable atonement, or the irresistible power of persuasion, which he possessed in perfection. In fact, he rather prided himself on his narrow escapes, and liked to thrill the girls with graphic accounts of his triumphs over wrathful tutors, dignified professors, and vanquished enemies. The "men of my class" were heroes in the eyes of the girls, who never wearied of the exploits of "our fellows," and were frequently allowed to bask in the smiles of these great creatures, when Laurie brought them home with him.

Amy especially enjoyed this high honor, and became quite a belle among them; for her ladyship early felt and learned to use the gift of fascination with which she was endowed. Meg was too much absorbed in her private and particular John to care for any other lords of creation, and Beth too shy to do more than peep at them, and wonder how Amy dared to order them about so; but Jo felt quite in her element, and found it very difficult to refrain from imitating the gentlemanly attitudes, phrases, and feats, which seemed more natural to her than the decorums prescribed for young ladies. They all liked Jo immensely, but never fell in love with her, though very few escaped without paying the tribute of a sentimental sigh or two at Amy's shrine. And speaking of sentiment brings us very naturally to the "Dove-cote."

That was the name of the little brown house which Mr. Brooke had prepared for Meg's first home. Laurie had christened it, saying it was highly appropriate to the gentle lovers, who "went on together like a pair of turtle-doves, with first a bill and then a coo." It was a tiny house, with a little garden behind, and a lawn about as big as a pocket-handkerchief in front. Here Meg meant to have a fountain, shrubbery, and a profusion of lovely flowers; though just at present, the fountain was represented by a weather-beaten urn, very like a dilapidated slop-bowl; the shrubbery consisted of several young larches, undecided whether to live or die; and the profusion of flowers was merely hinted by regiments of sticks, to show where seeds were planted. But inside, it was altogether charming, and the happy bride saw no fault from garret to cellar. To be sure, the hall was so narrow, it was fortunate that they had no piano, for one never could have been got in whole; the dining-room was so small that six people were a tight fit; and the kitchen stairs seemed built for the express purpose of precipitating both servants and china pell-mell into the coal-bin. But once get used to these slight blemishes, and nothing could be more complete, for good sense and good taste had presided over the furnishing, and the result was highly satisfactory. There were no marble-topped tables, long mirrors, or lace curtains in the little parlor, but simple furniture, plenty of books, a fine picture or two, a stand of flowers in the bay-window, and, scattered all about, the pretty gifts which came from friendly hands, and were the fairer for the loving messages they brought.

I don't think the Parian Psyche Laurie gave lost any of its beauty because John put up the bracket it stood upon; that any upholsterer could have draped the plain muslin curtains more gracefully than Amy's artistic hand; or that any store-room was ever better provided with good wishes, merry words, and happy hopes, than that in which Jo and her mother put away Meg's few boxes, barrels, and bundles; and I am morally certain that the spandy-new kitchen never *could* have looked so cozy and neat if Hannah had not arranged every pot and pan a dozen times over, and laid the fire all ready for lighting, the minute "Mis. Brooke came home." I also doubt if any young matron ever began life with so rich a supply of dusters, holders, and piece-bags; for Beth made enough to last till the silver wedding came round, and invented three different kinds of dishcloths for the express service of the bridal china.

People who hire all these things done for them never know what they lose; for the homeliest tasks get beautified if loving hands do them, and Meg found so many proofs of this, that everything in her small nest, from the kitchen roller to the silver vase on her parlor table, was eloquent of home love and tender forethought.

What happy times they had planning together, what solemn shopping excursions; what funny mistakes they made, and what shouts of laughter arose over Laurie's ridiculous bargains. In his love of jokes, this young gentleman, though nearly through college, was as much of a boy as ever. His last whim had been to bring with him, on his weekly visits, some new, useful, and ingenious article for the young housekeeper. Now a bag of remarkable clothes-pins; next, a wonderful nutmeg-grater, which fell to pieces at the first trial; a knife-cleaner that spoilt all the knives; or a sweeper that picked the nap neatly off the carpet, and left the dirt; labor-saving soap that took the skin off one's hands; infallible cements which stuck firmly to nothing but the fingers of the deluded buyer; and every kind of tin-ware, from a toy savings-bank for odd pennies, to a wonderful boiler which would wash articles in its own steam, with every prospect of exploding in the process.

In vain Meg begged him to stop. John laughed at him, and Jo called him "Mr. Toodles." He was possessed with a mania for patronizing Yankee ingenuity, and seeing his friends fitly furnished forth. So each week beheld some fresh absurdity.

Everything was done at last, even to Amy's arranging different colored soaps to match the different colored rooms, and Beth's setting the table for the first meal.

"Are you satisfied? Does it seem like home, and do you feel as if you should be happy here?" asked Mrs. March, as she and her daughter went through the new kingdom, arm-in-arm; for just then they seemed to cling together more tenderly than ever.

"Yes, mother, perfectly satisfied, thanks to you all, and *so* happy that I can't talk about it," answered Meg, with a look that was better than words.

"If she only had a servant or two it would be all right," said Amy, coming out of the parlor, where she had been trying to decide whether the bronze Mercury looked best on the whatnot or the mantel-piece.

"Mother and I have talked that over, and I have made up my mind to try her way first. There will be so little to do, that, with Lotty to run my errands and help me here and there, I shall only have enough work to keep me from getting lazy or homesick," answered Meg tranquilly.

"Sallie Moffat has four," began Amy.

"If Meg had four the house wouldn't hold them, and master and missis would have to camp in the garden," broke in Jo, who, enveloped in a big blue pinafore, was giving the last polish to the door-handles.

"Sallie isn't a poor man's wife, and many maids are in keeping with her fine establishment. Meg and John begin humbly, but I have a feeling that there will be quite as much happiness in the little house as in the big one. It's a great mistake for young girls like Meg to leave themselves nothing to do but dress, give orders, and gossip. When I was first married, I used to long for my new clothes to wear out or get torn, so that I might have the pleasure of mending them; for I got heartily sick of doing fancy work and tending my pocket-handkerchief."

"Why didn't you go into the kitchen and make messes, as Sallie says she does, to amuse herself, though they never turn out well, and the servants laugh at her," said Meg.

"I did, after a while; not to 'mess,' but to learn of Hannah how things should be done, that my servants need *not* laugh at me. It was play then; but there came a time when I was truly grateful that I not only possessed the will but the power to cook wholesome food for my little girls, and help myself when I could no longer afford to hire help. You begin at the other end, Meg, dear; but the lessons you learn now will be of use to you by and by, when John is a richer man, for the mistress of a house, however splendid, should know how work ought to be done, if she wishes to be well and honestly served."

"Yes, mother, I'm sure of that," said Meg, listening respectfully to the little lecture; for the best of women will hold forth upon the all-absorbing subject of housekeeping. "Do you know I like this room most of all in my baby-house," added Meg, a minute after, as they went upstairs, and she looked into her well-stored linen-closet.

Beth was there, laying the snowy piles smoothly on the shelves, and exulting over the goodly array. All three laughed as Meg spoke; for that linen-closet was a joke. You see, having said that if Meg married "that Brooke" she shouldn't have a cent of her money, Aunt March was rather in a quandary, when time had appeased her wrath and made her repent her vow. She never broke her word, and was much exercised in her mind how to get round it, and at last devised a plan whereby she could satisfy herself. Mrs. Carrol, Florence's mamma, was ordered to buy, have made, and marked, a generous supply of house and table linen, and send it as *her* present, all of which was faithfully done; but the secret leaked out, and was greatly enjoyed by the family; for Aunt March tried to look utterly unconscious, and insisted that she could give nothing but the old-fashioned pearls, long promised to the first bride.

"That's a housewifely taste which I am glad to see. I had a young friend who set up housekeeping with six sheets, but she had finger bowls for company, and that satisfied her," said Mrs. March, patting the damask tablecloths, with a truly feminine appreciation of their fineness.

"I haven't a single finger bowl, but this is a 'set out' that will last me all my days, Hannah says;" and Meg looked quite contented, as well she might.

"Toodles is coming," cried Jo from below; and they all went down to meet Laurie, whose weekly visit was an important event in their quiet lives.

A tall, broad-shouldered young fellow, with a cropped head, a felt-basin of a hat, and a fly-away coat, came tramping down the road at a great pace, walked over the low fence without stopping to open the gate, straight up to Mrs. March, with both hands out, and a hearty—

"Here I am, mother! Yes, it's all right."

The last words were in answer to the look the elder lady gave him; a kindly questioning look, which the handsome eyes met so frankly that the little ceremony closed, as usual, with a motherly kiss.

"For Mrs. John Brooke, with the maker's congratulations and compliments. Bless you, Beth! What a refreshing spectacle you are, Jo. Amy, you are getting altogether too handsome for a single lady."

As Laurie spoke, he delivered a brown paper parcel to Meg, pulled Beth's hair-ribbon, stared at Jo's big pinafore, and fell into an attitude of mock rapture before Amy, then shook hands all round, and everyone began to talk.

"Where is John?" asked Meg anxiously.

"Stopped to get the license for tomorrow, ma'am."

"Which side won the last match, Teddy?" inquired Jo, who persisted in feeling an interest in manly sports despite her nineteen years.

"Ours, of course. Wish you'd been there to see."

"How is the lovely Miss Randal?" asked Amy, with a significant smile.

"More cruel than ever; don't you see how I'm pining away?" and Laurie gave his broad chest a sounding slap and heaved a melodramatic sigh.

"What's the last joke? Undo the bundle and see, Meg," said Beth, eying the knobby parcel with curiosity.

"It's a useful thing to have in the house in case of fire or thieves," observed Laurie, as a watchman's rattle appeared, amid the laughter of the girls.

"Any time when John is away, and you get frightened, Mrs. Meg, just swing that out of the front window, and it will rouse the neighborhood in a jiffy. Nice thing, isn't it?" and Laurie gave them a sample of its powers that made them cover up their ears.

"There's gratitude for you! And speaking of gratitude reminds me to mention that you may thank Hannah for saving your wedding-cake from destruction. I saw it going into your house as I came by, and if she hadn't defended it manfully I'd have had a pick at it, for it looked like a remarkably plummy one."

"I wonder if you will ever grow up, Laurie," said Meg, in a matronly tone.

"I'm doing my best, ma'am, but can't get much higher, I'm afraid, as six feet is about all men can do in these degenerate days," responded the young gentleman, whose head was about level with the little chandelier.

"I suppose it would be profanation to eat anything in this spick and span new bower, so, as I'm tremendously hungry, I propose an adjournment," he added presently.

"Mother and I are going to wait for John. There are some last things to settle," said Meg, bustling away.

"Beth and I are going over to Kitty Bryant's to get more flowers for tomorrow," added Amy, tying a picturesque hat over her picturesque curls, and enjoying the effect as much as anybody.

"Come, Jo, don't desert a fellow. I'm in such a state of exhaustion I can't get home without help. Don't take off your apron, whatever you do; it's peculiarly becoming," said Laurie, as Jo bestowed his especial aversion in her capacious pocket, and offered him her arm to support his feeble steps.

"Now, Teddy, I want to talk seriously to you about tomorrow," began Jo, as they strolled away together. "You *must* promise to behave well, and not cut up any pranks, and spoil our plans."

"Not a prank."

"And don't say funny things when we ought to be sober."

"I never do; you are the one for that."

"And I implore you not to look at me during the ceremony; I shall certainly laugh if you do."

"You won't see me; you'll be crying so hard that the thick fog round you will obscure the prospect."

"I never cry unless for some great affliction."

"Such as fellows going to college, hey?" cut in Laurie, with a suggestive laugh.

"Don't be a peacock. I only moaned a trifle to keep the girls company."

"Exactly. I say, Jo, how is grandpa this week; pretty amiable?"

"Very; why, have you got into a scrape, and want to know how he'll take it?" asked Jo rather sharply.

"Now, Jo, do you think I'd look your mother in the face, and say 'All right,' if it wasn't?" and Laurie stopped short, with an injured air.

"No, I don't."

"Then don't go and be suspicious; I only want some money," said Laurie, walking on again, appeased by her hearty tone.

"You spend a great deal, Teddy."

"Bless you, *I* don't spend it; it spends itself, somehow, and is gone before I know it."

"You are so generous and kind-hearted that you let people borrow, and can't say 'No' to anyone. We heard about Henshaw, and all you did for him. If you always spent money in that way, no one would blame you," said Jo warmly.

"Oh, he made a mountain out of a mole-hill. You wouldn't have me let that fine fellow work himself to death, just for the want of a little help, when he is worth a dozen of us lazy chaps, would you?"

"Of course not; but I don't see the use of your having seventeen waistcoats, endless neckties, and a new hat every time you come home. I thought you'd got over the dandy period; but every now and then it breaks out in a new spot. Just now it's the fashion to be hideous,—to make your head look like a scrubbing-brush, wear a strait-jacket, orange gloves, and clumping, square-toed boots. If it was cheap ugliness, I'd say nothing; but it costs as much as the other, and I don't get any satisfaction out of it."

Laurie threw back his head, and laughed so heartily at this attack, that the felt-basin fell off, and Jo walked on it, which insult only afforded him an opportunity for expatiating on the advantages of a rough-and-ready costume, as he folded up the maltreated hat, and stuffed it into his pocket.

"Don't lecture any more, there's a good soul! I have enough all through the week, and like to enjoy myself when I come home. I'll get myself up regardless of expense, tomorrow, and be a satisfaction to my friends."

"I'll leave you in peace if you'll *only* let your hair grow. I'm not aristocratic, but I do object to being seen with a person who looks like a young prize-fighter," observed Jo severely.

"This unassuming style promotes study; that's why we adopt it," returned Laurie, who certainly could not be accused of vanity, having voluntarily sacrificed a handsome curly crop to the demand for quarter-of-an-inch-long stubble.

"By the way, Jo, I think that little Parker is really getting desperate about Amy. He talks of her constantly, writes poetry, and moons about in a most suspicious manner. He'd better nip his little passion in the bud, hadn't he?" added Laurie, in a confidential, elder-brotherly tone, after a minute's silence.

"Of course he had; we don't want any more marrying in this family for years to come. Mercy on us, what *are* the children thinking of?" and Jo looked as much scandalized as if Amy and little Parker were not yet in their teens.

"It's a fast age, and I don't know what we are coming to, ma'am. You are a mere infant, but you'll go next, Jo, and we'll be left lamenting," said Laurie, shaking his head over the degeneracy of the times.

"Don't be alarmed; I'm not one of the agreeable sort. Nobody will want me, and it's a mercy, for there should always be one old maid in a family."

"You won't give anyone a chance," said Laurie, with a sidelong glance and a little more color than before in his sunburnt face. "You won't show the soft side of your character; and if a fellow gets a peep at it by accident, and can't help showing that he likes it, you treat him as Mrs. Gummidge did her sweetheart,—throw cold water over him,—and get so thorny no one dares touch or look at you."

"I don't like that sort of thing; I'm too busy to be worried with nonsense, and I think it's dreadful to break up families so. Now don't say any more about it; Meg's wedding has turned all our heads, and we talk of nothing but lovers and such absurdities. I don't wish to get cross, so let's change the subject;" and Jo looked quite ready to fling cold water on the slightest provocation.

Whatever his feelings might have been, Laurie found a vent for them in a long low whistle, and the fearful prediction, as they parted at the gate, "Mark my words, Jo, you'll go next."

# CHAPTER XXV

## THE FIRST WEDDING

THE June roses over the porch were awake bright and early on that morning, rejoicing with all their hearts in the cloudless sunshine, like friendly little neighbors, as they were. Quite flushed with excitement were their ruddy faces, as they swung in the wind, whispering to one another what they had seen; for some peeped in at the dining-room windows, where the feast was spread, some climbed up to nod and smile at the sisters as they dressed the bride, others waved a welcome to those who came and went on various errands in garden, porch, and hall, and all, from the rosiest full-blown flower to the palest baby-bud, offered their tribute of beauty and fragrance to the gentle mistress who had loved and tended them so long.

Meg looked very like a rose herself; for all that was best and sweetest in heart and soul seemed to bloom into her face that day, making it fair and tender, with a charm more beautiful than beauty. Neither silk, lace, nor orange-flowers would she have. "I don't want to look strange or fixed up today," she said. "I don't want a fashionable wedding, but only those about me whom I love, and to them I wish to look and be my familiar self."

So she made her wedding gown herself, sewing into it the tender hopes and innocent romances of a girlish heart. Her sisters braided up her pretty hair, and the only ornaments she wore were the lilies of the valley, which "her John" liked best of all the flowers that grew.

"You *do* look just like our own dear Meg, only so very sweet and lovely that I should hug you if it wouldn't crumple your dress," cried Amy, surveying her with delight, when all was done.

"Then I am satisfied. But please hug and kiss me, everyone, and don't mind my dress; I want a great many crumples of this sort put into it today;" and Meg opened her arms to her sisters, who clung about her with April faces for a minute, feeling that the new love had not changed the old.

"Now I'm going to tie John's cravat for him, and then to stay a few minutes with father quietly in the study;" and Meg ran down to perform these little ceremonies, and then to follow her mother wherever she went, conscious that, in spite of the smiles on the motherly face, there was a secret sorrow hid in the motherly heart at the flight of the first bird from the nest.

As the younger girls stand together, giving the last touches to their simple toilet, it may be a good time to tell of a few changes which three years have wrought in their appearance; for all are looking their best just now.

Jo's angles are much softened; she has learned to carry herself with ease, if not grace. The curly crop has lengthened into a thick coil, more becoming to the small head atop the tall figure. There is a fresh color in her brown cheeks, a soft shine in her eyes, and only gentle words fall from her sharp tongue today.

Beth has grown slender, pale, and more quiet than ever; the beautiful, kind eyes are larger, and in them lies an expression that saddens one, although it is not sad itself. It is the shadow of pain which touches the young face with such pathetic patience; but Beth seldom complains, and always speaks hopefully of "being better soon."

Amy is with truth considered "the flower of the family;" for at sixteen she has the air and bearing of a full-grown woman—not beautiful, but possessed of that indescribable charm called grace. One saw it in the lines of her figure, the make and motion of her hands, the flow of her dress, the droop of her hair,—unconscious, yet harmonious, and as attractive to many as beauty itself. Amy's nose still afflicted her, for it never *would* grow Grecian; so did her mouth, being too wide, and having a decided chin. These offending features gave character to her whole face, but she never could see it, and consoled herself with her wonderfully fair complexion, keen blue eyes, and curls, more golden and abundant than ever.

All three wore suits of thin silver gray (their best gowns for the summer), with blush-roses in hair and bosom; and all three looked just what they were,—fresh-faced, happy-hearted girls, pausing a moment in their busy lives to read with wistful eyes the sweetest chapter in the romance of womanhood.

There were to be no ceremonious performances, everything was to be as natural and homelike as possible; so when Aunt March arrived, she was scandalized to see the bride come running to welcome and lead her in, to find the bridegroom fastening up a garland that had fallen down, and to catch a glimpse of the paternal minister marching upstairs with a grave countenance, and a wine-bottle under each arm.

"Upon my word, here's a state of things!" cried the old lady, taking the seat of honor prepared for her, and settling the folds of her lavender *moire* with a great rustle. "You oughtn't to be seen till the last minute, child."

"I'm not a show, aunty, and no one is coming to stare at me, to criticize my dress, or count the cost of my luncheon. I'm too happy to care what anyone says or thinks, and I'm going to have my little wedding just as I like it. John, dear, here's your hammer;" and away went Meg to help "that man" in his highly improper employment.

Mr. Brooke didn't even say "Thank you," but as he stooped for the unromantic tool, he kissed his little bride behind the folding-door, with a look that made Aunt March whisk out her pocket-handkerchief, with a sudden dew in her sharp old eyes.

A crash, a cry, and a laugh from Laurie, accompanied by the indecorous exclamation, "Jupiter Ammon! Jo's upset the cake again!" caused a momentary flurry, which was hardly over when a flock of cousins arrived, aud "the party came in," as Beth used to say when a child.

"Don't let that young giant come near me; he worries me worse than mosquitoes," whispered the old lady to Amy, as the rooms filled, and Laurie's black head towered above the rest.

"He has promised to be very good today, and he *can* be perfectly elegant if he likes," returned Amy, gliding away to warn Hercules to beware of the dragon, which warning caused him to haunt the old lady with a devotion that nearly distracted her.

There was no bridal procession, but a sudden silence fell upon the room as Mr. March and the young pair took their places under the green arch. Mother and sisters gathered close, as if loath to give Meg up; the fatherly voice broke more than once, which only seemed to make the service more beautiful and solemn; the bridegroom's hand trembled visibly, and no one heard his replies; but Meg looked straight up in her husband's eyes, and said, "I will!" with such tender trust in her own face and voice that her mother's heart rejoiced, and Aunt March sniffed audibly.

Jo did *not* cry, though she was very near it once, and was only saved from a demonstration by the consciousness that Laurie was staring fixedly at her, with a comical mixture of merriment and emotion in his wicked black eyes. Beth kept her face hidden on her mother's shoulder, but Amy stood like a graceful statue, with a most becoming ray of sunshine touching her white forehead and the flower in her hair.

It wasn't at all the thing, I'm afraid, but the minute she was fairly married, Meg cried, "The first kiss for Marmee!" and, turning, gave it with her heart on her lips. During the next fifteen minutes she looked more like a rose than ever, for everyone availed themselves of their privileges to the fullest extent, from Mr. Laurence to old Hannah, who, adorned with a head-dress fearfully and wonderfully made, fell upon her in the hall, crying, with a sob and a chuckle, "Bless you, deary, a hundred times! The cake ain't hurt a mite, and everything looks lovely."

Everybody cleared up after that, and said something brilliant, or tried to, which did just as well, for laughter is ready when hearts are light. There was no display of gifts, for they were already in the little house, nor was there an elaborate breakfast, but a plentiful lunch of cake and fruit, dressed with flowers. Mr. Laurence and Aunt March shrugged and smiled at one another when water, lemonade, and coffee were found to be the only sorts of nectar which the three Hebes carried round. No one said anything, however, till Laurie, who insisted on serving the bride, appeared before her, with a loaded salver in his hand and a puzzled expression on his face.

"Has Jo smashed all the bottles by accident?" he whispered, "or am I merely laboring under a delusion that I saw some lying about loose this morning?"

"No; your grandfather kindly offered us his best, and Aunt March actually sent some, but father put away a little for Beth, and despatched the rest to the Soldiers' Home. You know he thinks that wine should be used only in illness, and mother says that neither she nor her daughters will ever offer it to any young man under her roof."

Meg spoke seriously, and expected to see Laurie frown or laugh; but he did neither, for after a quick look at her, he said, in his impetuous way, "I like that! For I've seen enough harm done to wish other women would think as you do."

"You are not made wise by experience, I hope?" and there was an anxious accent in Meg's voice.

"No; I give you my word for it. Don't think too well of me, either; this is not one of my temptations. Being brought up where wine is as common as water, and almost as harmless, I don't care for it; but when a pretty girl offers it, one doesn't like to refuse, you see."

"But you will, for the sake of others, if not for your own. Come, Laurie, promise, and give me one more reason to call this the happiest day of my life."

A demand so sudden and so serious made the young man hesitate a moment, for ridicule is often harder to bear than self-denial. Meg knew that if he gave the promise he would keep it at all costs; and, feeling her power, used it as a woman may for her friend's good. She did not speak, but she looked up at him with a face made very eloquent by happiness, and a smile which said, "No one can refuse me anything today." Laurie certainly could not; and, with an answering smile, he gave her his hand, saying heartily, "I promise, Mrs. Brooke!"

"I thank you, very, very much."

"And I drink 'long life to your resolution,' Teddy," cried Jo, baptizing him with a splash of lemonade, as she waved her glass, and beamed approvingly upon him.

So the toast was drunk, the pledge made, and loyally kept, in spite of many temptations; for, with instinctive wisdom, the girls had seized a happy moment to do their friend a service, for which he thanked them all his life.

After lunch, people strolled about, by twos and threes, through house and garden, enjoying the sunshine without and within. Meg and John happened to be standing together in the middle of the grass-plot, when Laurie was seized with an inspiration which put the finishing touch to this unfashionable wedding.

"All the married people take hands and dance round the new-made husband and wife, as the Germans do, while we bachelors and spinsters prance in couples outside!" cried Laurie, promenading down the path with Amy, with such infectious spirit and skill that everyone else followed their example without a murmur. Mr. and Mrs. March, Aunt and Uncle Carrol, began it; others rapidly joined in; even Sallie Moffat, after a moment's hesitation, threw her train over her arm, and whisked Ned into the ring. But the crowning joke was Mr. Laurence and Aunt March; for when the stately old gentleman *chasséed* solemnly up to the old lady, she just tucked her cane under her arm, and hopped briskly away to join hands with the rest, and dance about the bridal pair, while the young folks pervaded the garden, like butterflies on a midsummer day.

Want of breath brought the impromptu ball to a close, and then people began to go.

"I wish you well, my dear, I heartily wish you well; but I think you'll be sorry for it," said Aunt March to Meg, adding to the bridegroom, as he led her to the carriage, "You've got a treasure, young man, see that you deserve it."

"That is the prettiest wedding I've been to for an age, Ned, and I don't see why, for there wasn't a bit of style about it," observed Mrs. Moffat to her husband, as they drove away.

"Laurie, my lad, if you ever want to indulge in this sort of thing, get one of those little girls to help you, and I shall be perfectly satisfied," said Mr. Laurence, settling himself in his easy-chair to rest, after the excitement of the morning.

"I'll do my best to gratify you, sir," was Laurie's unusually dutiful reply, as he carefully unpinned the posy Jo had put in his button-hole.

The little house was not far away, and the only bridal journey Meg had was the quiet walk with John, from the old home to the new. When she came down, looking like a pretty Quakeress in her dove-colored suit and straw bonnet tied with white, they all gathered about her to say "good-by," as tenderly as if she had been going to make the grand tour.

"Don't feel that I am separated from you, Marmee dear, or that I love you any the less for loving John so much," she said, clinging to her mother, with full eyes, for a moment. "I shall come every day, father, and expect to keep my old place in all your hearts, though I *am* married. Beth is going to be with me a great deal, and the other girls will drop in now and then to laugh at my housekeeping struggles. Thank you all for my happy wedding-day. Good-by, good-by!"

They stood watching her, with faces full of love and hope and tender pride, as she walked away, leaning on her husband's arm, with her hands full of flowers, and the June sunshine brightening her happy face,—and so Meg's married life began.

# CHAPTER XXVI

## ARTISTIC ATTEMPTS

IT takes people a long time to learn the difference between talent and genius, especially ambitious young men and women. Amy was learning this distinction through much tribulation; for, mistaking enthusiasm for inspiration, she attempted every branch of art with youthful audacity. For a long time there was a lull in the "mud-pie" business, and she devoted herself to the finest pen-and-ink drawing, in which she showed such taste and skill that her graceful handiwork proved both pleasant and profitable. But overstrained eyes soon caused pen and ink to be laid aside for a bold attempt at poker-sketching.

While this attack lasted, the family lived in constant fear of a conflagration; for the odor of burning wood pervaded the house at all hours;

smoke issued from attic and shed with alarming frequency, red-hot pokers lay about promiscuously, and Hannah never went to bed without a pail of water and the dinner-bell at her door, in case of fire. Raphael's face was found boldly executed on the under side of the molding-board, and Bacchus on the head of a beer-barrel; a chanting cherub adorned the cover of the sugar-bucket, and attempts to portray Romeo and Juliet supplied kindlings for some time.

From fire to oil was a natural transition for burnt fingers, and Amy fell to painting with undiminished ardor. An artist friend fitted her out with his cast-off palettes, brushes, and colors; and she daubed away, producing pastoral and marine views such as were never seen on land or sea. Her monstrosities in the way of cattle would have taken prizes at an agricultural fair; and the perilous pitching of her vessels would have produced sea-sickness in the most nautical observer, if the utter disregard to all known rules of shipbuilding and rigging had not convulsed him with laughter at the first glance. Swarthy boys and dark-eyed Madonnas, staring at you from one corner of the studio, suggested Murillo; oily-brown shadows of faces, with a lurid streak in the wrong place, meant Rembrandt; buxom ladies and dropsical infants, Rubens; and Turner appeared in tempests of blue thunder, orange lightning, brown rain, and purple clouds, with a tomato-colored splash in the middle, which might be the sun or a buoy, a sailor's shirt or a king's robe, as the spectator pleased.

Charcoal portraits came next; and the entire family hung in a row, looking as wild and crocky as if just evoked from a coal-bin. Softened into crayon sketches, they did better; for the likenesses were good, and Amy's hair, Jo's nose, Meg's mouth, and Laurie's eyes were pronounced "wonderfully fine." A return to clay and plaster followed, and ghostly casts of her acquaintances haunted corners of the house, or tumbled off closet-shelves onto people's heads. Children were enticed in as models, till their incoherent accounts of her mysterious doings caused Miss Amy to be regarded in the light of a young ogress. Her efforts in this line, however, were brought to an abrupt close by an untoward accident, which quenched her ardor. Other models failing her for a time, she undertook to cast her own pretty foot, and the family were one day alarmed by an unearthly bumping and screaming, and running to the rescue, found the young enthusiast hopping wildly about the shed, with her foot held fast in a pan-full of plaster, which had hardened with unexpected rapidity. With much difficulty and some danger she was dug out; for Jo was so overcome with laughter while she excavated, that her knife went too far, cut the poor foot, and left a lasting memorial of one artistic attempt, at least.

After this Amy subsided, till a mania for sketching from nature set her to haunting river, field, and wood, for picturesque studies, and sighing for ruins to copy. She caught endless colds sitting on damp grass to book "a delicious bit," composed of a stone, a stump, one mushroom, and a broken mullein-stalk, or "a heavenly mass of clouds," that looked like a choice display of featherbeds when done. She sacrificed her complexion floating on the river in the midsummer sun, to study light and

Her foot held fast in a panful of plaster.

shade, and got a wrinkle over her nose, trying after "points of sight," or whatever the squint-and-string performance is called.

If "genius is eternal patience," as Michelangelo affirms, Amy certainly had some claim to the divine attribute, for she persevered in spite of all obstacles, failures, and discouragements, firmly believing that in time she should do something worthy to be called "high art."

She was learning, doing, and enjoying other things, meanwhile, for she had resolved to be an attractive and accomplished woman, even if she never became a great artist. Here she succeeded better; for she was one of those happily created beings who please without effort, make friends everywhere, and take life so gracefully and easily that less fortunate souls are tempted to believe that such are born under a lucky star. Everybody liked her, for among her good gifts was tact. She had an instinctive sense of what was pleasing and proper, always said the right thing to the right person, did just what suited the time and place, and was so self-possessed that her sisters used to say, "If Amy went to court without any rehearsal beforehand, she'd know exactly what to do."

One of her weaknesses was a desire to move in "our best society," without being quite sure what the *best* really was. Money, position, fashionable accomplishments, and elegant manners were most desirable things in her eyes, and she liked to associate with those who possessed them, often mistaking the false for the true, and admiring what was not admirable. Never forgetting that by birth she was a gentlewoman, she cultivated her aristocratic tastes and feelings, so that when the opportunity came she might be ready to take the place from which poverty now excluded her.

"My lady," as her friends called her, sincerely desired to be a genuine lady, and was so at heart, but had yet to learn that money cannot buy refinement of nature, that rank does not always confer nobility, and that true breeding makes itself felt in spite of external drawbacks.

"I want to ask a favor of you, mamma," Amy said, coming in, with an important air, one day.

"Well, little girl, what is it?" replied her mother, in whose eyes the stately young lady still remained "the baby."

"Our drawing class breaks up next week, and before the girls separate for the summer, I want to ask them out here for a day. They are wild to see the river, sketch the broken bridge, and copy some of the things they admire in my book. They have been very kind to me in many ways, and I am grateful, for they are all rich, and know I am poor, yet they never made any difference."

"Why should they?" and Mrs. March put the question with what the girls called her "Maria Theresa air."

"You know as well as I that it *does* make a difference with nearly everyone, so don't ruffle up, like a dear, motherly hen, when your chickens get pecked by smarter birds; the ugly duckling turned out a swan, you know;" and Amy smiled without bitterness, for she possessed a happy temper and hopeful spirit.

Mrs. March laughed, and smoothed down her maternal pride as she asked,—

"Well, my swan, what is your plan?"

"I should like to ask the girls out to lunch next week, to take them a drive to the places they want to see, a row on the river, perhaps, and make a little artistic *fête* for them."

"That looks feasible. What do you want for lunch? Cake, sandwiches, fruit, and coffee will be all that is necessary, I suppose?"

"Oh dear, no! We must have cold tongue and chicken, French chocolate and ice-cream, besides. The girls are used to such things, and I want my lunch to be proper and elegant, though I *do* work for my living."

"How many young ladies are there?" asked her mother, beginning to look sober.

"Twelve or fourteen in the class, but I dare say they won't all come."

"Bless me, child, you will have to charter an omnibus to carry them about."

"Why, mother, how *can* you think of such a thing? Not more than six or eight will probably come, so I shall hire a beach-wagon, and borrow Mr. Laurence's cherry-bounce." (Hannah's pronunciatioin of *char-à-banc*.)

"All this will be expensive, Amy."

"Not very; I've calculated the cost, and I'll pay for it myself."

"Don't you think, dear, that as these girls are used to such things, and the best we can do will be nothing new, that some simpler plan would be pleasanter to them, as a change, if nothing more, and much better for us than buying or borrowing what we don't need, and attempting a style not in keeping with our circumstances?"

"If I can't have it as I like, I don't care to have it at all. I know that I can carry it out perfectly well, if you and the girls will help a little; and I don't see why I can't if I'm willing to pay for it," said Amy, with the decision which opposition was apt to change into obstinacy.

Mrs. March knew that experience was an excellent teacher, and when it was possible she left her children to learn alone the lessons which she would gladly have made easier, if they had not objected to taking advice as much as they did salts and senna.

"Very well, Amy; if your heart is set upon it, and you see your way through without too great an outlay of money, time, and temper, I'll say no more. Talk it over with the girls, and whichever way you decide, I'll do my best to help you."

"Thanks, mother; you are always *so* kind;" and away went Amy to lay her plan before her sisters.

Meg agreed at once, and promised her aid, gladly offering anything she possessed, from her little house itself to her very best salt-spoons. But Jo frowned upon the whole project, and would have nothing to do with it at first.

"Why in the world should you spend your money, worry your family, and turn the house upside down for a parcel of girls who don't care a sixpence for you? I thought you had too much pride and sense to truckle to any mortal woman just because she wears French boots and rides in a *coupé*," said Jo, who, being called from the tragical climax of her novel, was not in the best mood for social enterprises.

"I *don't* truckle, and I hate being patronized as much as you do!" returned Amy indignantly, for the two still jangled when such questions arose. "The girls do care for me, and I for them, and there's a great deal of kindness and sense and talent among them, in spite of what you call fashionable nonsense. You don't care to make people like you, to go into good society, and cultivate your manners and tastes. I do, and I mean to make the most of every chance that comes. *You* can go through the world with your elbows out and your nose in the air, and call it independence, if you like. That's not my way."

When Amy whetted her tongue and freed her mind she usually got the best of it, for she seldom failed to have common sense on her side, while Jo carried her love of liberty and hate of conventionalities to such an unlimited extent that she naturally found herself worsted in an argument. Amy's definition of Jo's idea of independence was such a good hit that both burst out laughing, and the discussion took a more amiable turn. Much against her will, Jo at length consented to sacrifice a day to Mrs. Grundy, and help her sister through what she regarded as "a nonsensical business."

The invitations were sent, nearly all accepted, and the following Monday was set apart for the grand event. Hannah was out of humor because her week's work was deranged, and prophesied that "ef the washin' and ironin' warn't done reg'lar nothin' would go well anywheres." This hitch in the mainspring of the domestic machinery had a bad effect upon the whole concern; but Amy's motto was "Nil desperandum," and having made up her mind what to do, she proceeded to do it in spite of all obstacles. To begin with, Hannah's cooking didn't turn out well: the chicken was tough, the tongue too salt, and the chocolate wouldn't froth properly. Then the cake and ice cost more than Amy expected, so did the wagon; and various other expenses, which seemed trifling at the outset, counted up rather alarmingly afterward. Beth got cold and took to her bed, Meg had an unusual number of callers to keep her at home, and Jo was in such a divided state of mind that her breakages, accidents, and mistakes were uncommonly numerous, serious, and trying.

"If it hadn't been for mother I never should have got through," as Amy declared afterward, and gratefully remembered when "the best joke of the season" was entirely forgotten by everybody else.

If it was not fair on Monday, the young ladies were to come on Tuesday,—an arrangement which aggravated Jo and Hannah to the last degree. On Monday morning the weather was in that undecided state which is more exasperating than a steady pour. It drizzled a little, shone a little, blew a little, and didn't make up its mind till it was too late for anyone else to make up theirs. Amy was up at dawn, hustling people out of their beds and through their breakfasts, that the house might be got in order. The parlor struck her as looking uncommonly shabby; but without stopping to sigh for what she had not, she skilfully made the best of what she had, arranging chairs over the worn places in the carpet, covering stains on the walls with pictures framed in ivy, and filling up empty corners with home-made statuary, which gave an artistic air to the room, as did the lovely vases of flowers Jo scattered about.

The lunch looked charmingly; and as she surveyed it, she sincerely hoped it would taste well, and that the borrowed glass, china, and silver would get safely home again. The carriages were promised, Meg and mother were all ready to do the honors, Beth was able to help Hannah behind the scenes, Jo had engaged to be as lively and amiable as an absent mind, an aching head, and a very decided disapproval of everybody and everything would allow, and, as she wearily dressed, Amy cheered herself with anticipations of the happy moment, when, lunch safely over, she should drive away with her friends for an afternoon of artistic delights; for the "cherry-bounce" and the broken bridge were her strong points.

Then came two hours of suspense, during which she vibrated from parlor to porch, while public opinion varied like the weathercock. A smart shower at eleven had evidently quenched the enthusiasm of the young ladies who were to arrive at twelve, for nobody came; and at two the exhausted family sat down in a blaze of sunshine to consume the perishable portions of the feast, that nothing might be lost.

"No doubt about the weather today; they will certainly come, so we must fly round and be ready for them," said Amy, as the sun woke her next morning. She spoke briskly, but in her secret soul she wished she had said nothing about Tuesday, for her interest, like her cake, was getting a little stale.

"I can't get any lobsters, so you will have to do without salad today," said Mr. March, coming in half an hour later, with an expression of placid despair.

"Use the chicken, then; the toughness won't matter in a salad," advised his wife.

"Hannah left it on the kitchen-table a minute, and the kittens got at it. I'm very sorry, Amy," added Beth, who was still a patroness of cats.

"Then I *must* have a lobster, for tongue alone won't do," said Amy decidedly.

"Shall I rush into town and demand one?" asked Jo, with the magnanimity of a martyr.

"You'd come bringing it home under your arm, without any paper, just to try me. I'll go myself," answered Amy, whose temper was beginning to fail.

Shrouded in a thick veil and armed with a genteel traveling-basket, she departed, feeling that a cool drive would soothe her ruffled spirit, and fit her for the labors of the day. After some delay, the object of her desire was procured, likewise a bottle of dressing, to prevent further loss of time at home, and off she drove again, well pleased with her own forethought.

As the omnibus contained only one other passenger, a sleepy old lady, Amy pocketed her veil, and beguiled the tedium of the way by trying to find out where all her money had gone to. So busy was she with her card full of refractory figures that she did not observe a new-comer, who entered without stopping the vehicle, till a masculine voice said, "Good-morning, Miss March," and, looking up, she beheld one of Laurie's most elegant college friends. Fervently hoping that he would get out before she did, Amy utterly ignored the basket at her feet, and, congratulating herself that she had on her new travelling dress, returned the young man's greeting with her usual suavity and spirit.

They got on excellently; for Amy's chief care was soon set at rest by learning that the gentleman would leave first, and she was chatting away in a peculiarly lofty strain, when the old lady got out. In stumbling to the door, she upset the basket, and—oh, horror!—the lobster, in all its vulgar size and brilliancy, was revealed to the high-born eyes of a Tudor.

"By Jove, she's forgotten her dinner!" cried the unconscious youth, poking the scarlet monster into its place with his cane, and preparing to hand out the basket after the old lady.

"Please don't—it's—it's mine," murmured Amy, with a face nearly as red as her fish.

"Oh, really, I beg pardon; it's an uncommonly fine one, isn't it?" said Tudor, with great presence of mind, and an air of sober interest that did credit to his breeding.

Amy recovered herself in a breath, set her basket boldly on the seat, and said, laughing,—

"Don't you wish you were to have some of the salad he's to make, and to see the charming young ladies who are to eat it?"

Now that was tact, for two of the ruling foibles of the masculine mind were touched: the lobster was instantly surrounded by a halo of pleasing reminiscences, and curiosity about "the charming young ladies" diverted his mind from the comical mishap.

"I suppose he'll laugh and joke over it with Laurie, but I sha'n't see them; that's a comfort," thought Amy, as Tudor bowed and departed.

She did not mention this meeting at home (though she discovered that, thanks to the upset, her new dress was much damaged by the rivulets of dressing that meandered down the skirt), but went through with the preparations which now seemed more irksome than before; and at twelve o'clock all was ready again. Feeling that the neighbors were interested in her movements, she wished to efface the memory of yesterday's failure by a grand success today; so she ordered the "cherry-bounce," and drove away in state to meet and escort her guests to the banquet.

"There's the rumble, they're coming! I'll go into the porch to meet them; it looks hospitable, and I want the poor child to have a good time after all her trouble," said Mrs. March, suiting the action to the word. But after one glance, she retired, with an indescribable expression, for, looking quite lost in the big carriage, sat Amy and one young lady.

"Run, Beth, and help Hannah clear half the things off the table; it will be too absurd to put a luncheon for twelve before a single girl," cried Jo, hurrying away to the lower regions, too excited to stop even for a laugh.

In came Amy, quite calm, and delightfully cordial to the one guest who had kept her promise; the rest of the family, being of a dramatic turn, played their parts equally well, and Miss Eliott found them a most hilarious set; for it was impossible to entirely control the merriment which possessed them. The remodeled lunch being gayly partaken of, the studio and garden visited, and art discussed with enthusiasm, Amy ordered a buggy (alas for the elegant cherry-bounce!) and drove her friend quietly about the neighborhood till sunset, when "the party went out."

As she came walking in, looking very tired, but as composed as ever, she observed that every vestige of the unfortunate *fête* had disappeared, except a suspicious pucker about the corners of Jo's mouth.

"You've had a lovely afternoon for your drive, dear," said her mother, as respectfully as if the whole twelve had come.

"Miss Eliott is a very sweet girl, and seemed to enjoy herself, I thought," observed Beth, with unusual warmth.

"Could you spare me some of your cake? I really need some, I have so much company, and I can't make such delicious stuff as yours," asked Meg soberly.

"Take it all; I'm the only one here who likes sweet things, and it will mould before I can dispose of it," answered Amy, thinking with a sigh of the generous store she had laid in for such an end as this.

"It's a pity Laurie isn't here to help us," began Jo, as they sat down to ice-cream and salad for the second time in two days.

A warning look from her mother checked any further remarks, and the whole family ate in heroic silence, till Mr. March mildly observed, "Salad was one of the favorite dishes of the ancients, and Evelyn"—here a general explosion of laughter cut short the "history of sallets," to the great surprise of the learned gentleman.

"Bundle everything into a basket and send it to the Hummels: Germans like messes. I'm sick of the sight of this; and there's no reason you should all die of a surfeit because I've been a fool," cried Amy, wiping her eyes.

"I thought I *should* have died when I saw you two girls rattling about in the what-you-call-it, like two little kernels in a very big nut-shell, and mother waiting in state to receive the throng," sighed Jo, quite spent with laughter.

"I'm very sorry you were disappointed, dear, but we all did our best to satisfy you," said Mrs. March, in a tone full of motherly regret.

"I *am* satisfied; I've done what I undertook, and it's not my fault that it failed; I comfort myself with that," said Amy, with a little quiver in her voice. "I thank you all very much for helping me, and I'll thank you still more if you won't allude to it for a month, at least."

No one did for several months; but the word *"fête"* always produced a general smile, and Laurie's birthday gift to Amy was a tiny coral lobster in the shape of a charm for her watch-guard.

# CHAPTER XXVII

## LITERARY LESSONS

FORTUNE suddenly smiled upon Jo, and dropped a good-luck penny in her path. Not a golden penny, exactly, but I doubt if half a million would have given more real happiness than did the little sum that came to her in this wise.

Every few weeks she would shut herself up in her room, put on her scribbling suit, and "fall into a vortex," as she expressed it, writing away at her novel with all her heart and soul, for till that was finished she could find no peace. Her "scribbling suit" consisted of a black woolen pinafore on which she could wipe her pen at will, and a cap of the same material, adorned with a cheerful red bow, into which she bundled her hair when the decks were cleared for action. This cap was a beacon to the inquiring eyes of her family, who during these periods kept their distance, merely popping in their heads semi-occasionally, to ask, with interest, "Does genius burn, Jo?" They did not always venture even to ask this question, but took an observation of the cap, and judged accordingly. If this expressive article of dress was drawn low upon the forehead, it was a sign that hard work was going on; in exciting moments it was pushed rakishly askew; and when despair seized the author it was plucked wholly off, and cast upon the floor. At such times the intruder silently withdrew; and not until the red bow was seen gayly erect upon the gifted brow, did anyone dare address Jo.

She did not think herself a genius by any means; but when the writing fit came on, she gave herself up to it with entire abandon, and led a blissful life, unconscious of want, care, or bad weather, while she sat safe and happy in an imaginary world, full of friends almost as real and dear to her as any in the flesh. Sleep forsook her eyes, meals stood untasted, day and night were all too short to enjoy the happiness which blessed her only at such times, and made these hours worth living, even if they bore no other fruit. The divine afflatus usually lasted a week or two, and then she emerged from her "vortex," hungry, sleepy, cross, or despondent.

She was just recovering from one of these attacks when she was prevailed upon to escort Miss Crocker to a lecture, and in return for her virtue was rewarded with a new idea. It was a People's Course, the lecture on the Pyramids, and Jo rather wondered at the choice of such a subject for such an audience, but took it for granted that some great social evil would be remedied or some great want supplied by unfolding the glories of the Pharaohs to an audience whose thoughts were busy with the price of coal and flour, and whose lives were spent in trying to solve harder riddles than that of the Sphinx.

They were early; and while Miss Crocker set the heel of her stocking, Jo amused herself by examining the faces of the people who occupied the seat with them. On her left were two matrons, with massive foreheads, and bonnets to match, discussing Woman's Rights and making tatting. Beyond sat a pair of humble lovers, artlessly holding each other by the hand, a somber spinster eating peppermints out of a paper bag, and an old gentleman taking his preparatory nap behind a yellow bandanna. On her right, her only neighbor was a studious-looking lad absorbed in a newspaper.

It was a pictorial sheet, and Jo examined the work of art nearest her, idly wondering what unfortuitous concatenation of circumstances needed the melodramatic illustration of an Indian in full war costume, tumbling over a precipice with a wolf at his throat, while two infuriated young gentlemen, with unnaturally small feet and big eyes, were stabbing each other close by, and a disheveled female was flying away in the background with her mouth wide open. Pausing to turn a page, the lad saw her looking, and, with boyish good-nature, offered half his paper, saying bluntly, "Want to read it? That's a first-rate story."

Jo accepted it with a smile, for she had never outgrown her liking for

Jo's "scribbling suit."

lads, and soon found herself involved in the usual labyrinth of love, mystery, and murder, for the story belonged to that class of light literature in which the passions have a holiday, and when the author's invention fails, a grand catastrophe clears the stage of one half the *dramatis personæ*, leaving the other half to exult over their downfall.

"Prime, isn't it?" asked the boy, as her eye went down the last paragraph of her portion.

"I think you and I could do as well as that if we tried," returned Jo, amused at his admiration of the trash.

"I should think I was a pretty lucky chap if I could. She makes a good living out of such stories, they say"; and he pointed to the name of Mrs. S. L. A. N. G. Northbury, under the title of the tale.

"Do you know her?" asked Jo, with sudden interest.

"No; but I read all her pieces, and I know a fellow who works in the office where this paper is printed."

"Do you say she makes a good living out of stories like this?" And Jo looked more respectfully at the agitated group and thickly-sprinkled exclamation-points that adorned the page.

"Guess she does! She knows just what folks like, and gets paid well for writing it."

Here the lecture began, but Jo heard very little of it, for while Prof. Sands was prosing away about Belzoni, Cheops, scarabei, and hieroglyphics, she was covertly taking down the address of the paper, and boldly resolving to try for the hundred-dollar prize offered in its columns for a sensational story. By the time the lecture ended and the audience awoke, she had built up a splendid fortune for herself (not the first founded upon paper), and was already deep in the concoction of her story, being unable to decide whether the duel should come before the elopement or after the murder.

She said nothing of her plan at home, but fell to work next day, much to the disquiet of her mother, who always looked a little anxious when "genius took to burning." Jo had never tried this style before, contenting herself with very mild romances for the "Spread Eagle." Her theatrical experience and miscellaneous reading were of service now, for they gave her some idea of dramatic effect, and supplied plot, language, and costumes. Her story was as full of desperation and despair as her limited acquaintance with those uncomfortable emotions enabled her to make it, and, having located it in Lisbon, she wound up with an earthquake, as a striking and appropriate *dénouement*. The manuscript was privately despatched, accompanied by a note, modestly saying that if the tale didn't get the prize, which the writer hardly dared expect, she would be very glad to receive any sum it might be considered worth.

Six weeks is a long time to wait, and a still longer time for a girl to keep a secret; but Jo did both, and was just beginning to give up all hope of ever seeing her manuscript again, when a letter arrived which almost took her breath away; for on opening it, a check for a hundred dollars fell into her lap. For a minute she stared at it as if it had been a snake, then she read her letter and began to cry. If the amiable gentleman who wrote that kindly note could have known what intense happiness he was giving a fellow-creature, I think he would devote his leisure hours, if he has any, to that amusement; for Jo valued the letter more than the money, because it was encouraging; and after years of effort it was *so* pleasant to find that she had learned to do something, though it was only to write a sensation story.

A prouder young woman was seldom seen than she, when, having composed herself, she electrified the family by appearing before them with the letter in one hand, the check in the other, announcing that she had won the prize. Of course there was a great jubilee, and when the story came everyone read and praised it; though after her father had told her that the language was good, the romance fresh and hearty, and the tragedy quite thrilling, he shook his head, and said in his unworldly way,—

"You can do better than this, Jo. Aim at the highest, and never mind the money."

"*I* think the money is the best part of it. What *will* you do with such a fortune?" asked Amy, regarding the magic slip of paper with a reverential eye.

"Send Beth and mother to the seaside for a month or two," answered Jo promptly.

"Oh, how splendid! No, I can't do it, dear, it would be so selfish," cried Beth, who had clapped her thin hands, and taken a long breath, as if pining for fresh ocean-breezes; then stopped herself, and motioned away the check which her sister waved before her.

"Ah, but you shall go, I've set my heart on it; that's what I tried for, and that's why I succeeded. I never get on when I think of myself alone, so it will help me to work for you, don't you see? Besides, Marmee needs the change, and she won't leave you, so you *must* go. Won't it be fun to see you come home plump and rosy again? Hurrah for Dr. Jo, who always cures her patients!"

To the seaside they went, after much discussion; and though Beth didn't come home as plump and rosy as could be desired, she was much better, while Mrs. March declared she felt ten years younger; so Jo was satisfied with the investment of her prize money, and fell to work with a cheery spirit, bent on earning more of those delightful checks. She did earn several that year, and began to feel herself a power in the house; for by the magic of a pen, her "rubbish" turned into comforts for them all. "The Duke's Daughter" paid the butcher's bill, "A Phantom Hand" put down a new carpet, and the "Curse of the Coventrys" proved the blessing of the Marches in the way of groceries and gowns.

Wealth is certainly a most desirable thing, but poverty has its sunny side, and one of the sweet uses of adversity is the genuine satisfaction which comes from hearty work of head or hand; and to the inspiration of necessity, we owe half the wise, beautiful, and useful blessings of the world. Jo enjoyed a taste of this satisfaction, and ceased to envy richer girls, taking great comfort in the knowledge that she could supply her own wants, and need ask no one for a penny.

Little notice was taken of her stories, but they found a market; and, encouraged by this fact, she resolved to make a bold stroke for fame and fortune. Having copied her novel for the fourth time, read it to all her confidential friends, and submitted it with fear and trembling to three publishers, she at last disposed of it, on condition that she would cut it down one third, and omit all the parts which she particularly admired.

"Now I must either bundle it back into my tin-kitchen to mould, pay for printing it myself, or chop it up to suit purchasers, and get what I can for it. Fame is a very good thing to have in the house, but cash is more convenient; so I wish to take the sense of the meeting on this important subject," said Jo, calling a family council.

"Don't spoil your book, my girl, for there is more in it than you know, and the idea is well worked out. Let it wait and ripen," was her father's advice; and he practiced as he preached, having waited patiently thirty years for fruit of his own to ripen, and being in no haste to gather it, even now, when it was sweet and mellow.

"It seems to me that Jo will profit more by making the trial than by waiting," said Mrs. March. "Criticism is the best test of such work, for it will show her both unsuspected merits and faults, and help her to do better next time. We are too partial; but the praise and blame of outsiders will prove useful, even if she gets but little money."

"Yes," said Jo, knitting her brows, "that's just it; I've been fussing over the thing so long, I really don't know whether it's good, bad, or indifferent. It will be a great help to have cool, impartial persons take a look at it, and tell me what they think of it."

"I wouldn't leave out a word of it; you'll spoil it if you do, for the interest of the story is more in the minds than in the actions of the people, and it will be all a muddle if you don't explain as you go on," said Meg, who firmly believed that this book was the most remarkable novel ever written.

"But Mr. Allen says, 'Leave out the explanations, make it brief and dramatic, and let the characters tell the story,'" interrupted Jo, turning to the publisher's note.

"Do as he tells you; he knows what will sell, and we don't. Make a good, popular book, and get as much money as you can. By and by, when you've got a name, you can afford to digress, and have philosophical and metaphysical people in your novels," said Amy, who took a strictly practical view of the subject.

"Well," said Jo, laughing, "if my people *are* 'philosophical and meta-physical,' it isn't my fault, for I know nothing about such things, except what I hear father say, sometimes. If I've got some of his wise ideas jumbled up with my romance, so much the better for me. Now, Beth, what do you say?"

"I should so like to see it printed *soon*," was all Beth said, and smiled in saying it; but there was an unconscious emphasis on the last word, and a wistful look in the eyes that never lost their childlike candor, which chilled Jo's heart, for a minute, with a foreboding fear, and decided her to make her little venture "soon."

So, with Spartan firmness, the young authoress laid her first-born on her table, and chopped it up as ruthlessly as any ogre. In the hope of pleasing everyone, she took everyone's advice; and, like the old man and his donkey in the fable, suited nobody.

Her father liked the metaphysical streak which had unconsciously got into it; so that was allowed to remain, though she had her doubts about it. Her mother thought that there *was* a trifle too much description; out, therefore, it nearly all came, and with it many necessary links in the story. Meg admired the tragedy; so Jo piled up the agony to suit her, while Amy objected to the fun, and, with the best intentions in life, Jo quenched the sprightly scenes which relieved the somber character of the story. Then, to complete the ruin, she cut it down one third, and confidingly sent the poor little romance, like a picked robin, out into the big, busy world, to try its fate.

Well, it was printed, and she got three hundred dollars for it; likewise plenty of praise and blame, both so much greater than she expected that she was thrown into a state of bewilderment, from which it took her some time to recover.

"You said, mother, that criticism would help me; but how can it, when it's so contradictory that I don't know whether I've written a promising book or broken all the ten commandments?" cried poor Jo, turning over a heap of notices, the perusal of which filled her with pride and joy one minute, wrath and dire dismay the next. "This man says 'An exquisite book, full of truth, beauty, and earnestness; all is sweet, pure, and healthy,' " continued the perplexed authoress. "The next, 'The theory of the book is bad, full of morbid fancies, spiritualistic ideas, and unnatural characters.' Now, as I had no theory of any kind, don't believe in Spiritualism, and copied my characters from life, I don't see how this critic *can* be right. Another says, 'It's one of the best American novels which has appeared for years' (I know better than that); and the next asserts that 'though it is original, and written with great force and feeling, it is a dangerous book.' 'Tisn't! Some make fun of it, some over-praise, and nearly all insist that I had a deep theory to expound, when I only wrote it for the pleasure and the money. I wish I'd printed it whole or not at all, for I do hate to be so misjudged."

Her family and friends administered comfort and commendation liberally; yet it was a hard time for sensitive, high-spirited Jo, who meant so well, and had apparently done so ill. But it did her good, for those whose opinion had real value gave her the criticism which is an author's best education; and when the first soreness was over, she could laugh at her poor little book, yet believe in it still, and feel herself the wiser and stronger for the buffeting she had received.

"Not being a genius, like Keats, it won't kill me," she said stoutly; "and I've got the joke on my side, after all; for the parts that were taken straight out of real life are denounced as impossible and absurd, and the scenes that I made up out of my own silly head are pronounced 'charmingly natural, tender, and true.' So I'll comfort myself with that; and when I'm ready, I'll up again and take another."

# CHAPTER XXVIII

## DOMESTIC EXPERIENCES

LIKE most other young matrons, Meg began her married life with the determination to be a model housekeeper. John should find home a paradise; he should always see a smiling face, should fare sumptuously every day, and never know the loss of a button. She brought so much love, energy, and cheerfulness to the work that she could not but succeed, in spite of some obstacles. Her paradise was not a tranquil one; for the little woman fussed, was over-anxious to please, and bustled about like a true Martha, cumbered with many cares. She was too tired, sometimes, even to smile; John grew dyspeptic after a course of dainty dishes, and ungratefully demanded plain fare. As for buttons, she soon learned to wonder where they went, to shake her head over the carelessness of men, and to threaten to make him sew them on himself, and then see if *his* work would stand impatient tugs and clumsy fingers any better than hers.

They were very happy, even after they discovered that they couldn't live on love alone. John did not find Meg's beauty diminished, though she beamed at him from behind the familiar coffee-pot; nor did Meg miss any of the romance from the daily parting, when her husband followed up his kiss with the tender inquiry, "Shall I send home veal or mutton for dinner, darling?" The little house ceased to be a glorified bower, but it became a home, and the young couple soon felt that it was a change for the better. At first they played keep-house, and frolicked over it like children; then John took steadily to business, feeling the cares of the head of a family upon his shoulders; and Meg laid by her cambric wrappers, put on a big apron, and fell to work, as before said, with more energy than discretion.

While the cooking mania lasted she went through Mrs. Cornelius's Receipt Book as if it were a mathematical exercise, working out the problems with patience and care. Sometimes her family were invited in to help eat up a too bounteous feast of successes, or Lotty would be privately despatched with a batch of failures, which were to be concealed from all eyes in the convenient stomachs of the little Hummels. An evening with John over the account-books usually produced a temporary lull in the culinary enthusiasm, and a frugal fit would ensue, during which the poor man was put through a course of bread-pudding, hash, and warmed-over coffee, which tried his soul, although he bore it with praiseworthy fortitude. Before the golden mean was found, however, Meg added to her domestic possessions what young couples seldom get on long without,—a family jar.

Fired with a housewifely wish to see her store-room stocked with home-made preserves, she undertook to put up her own currant jelly. John was requested to order home a dozen or so of little pots, and an extra quantity of sugar, for their own currants were ripe, and were to be attended to at once. As John firmly believed that "my wife" was equal to anything, and took a natural pride in her skill, he resolved that she should be gratified, and their only crop of fruit laid by in a most pleasing form for winter use. Home came four dozen delightful little pots, half a barrel of sugar, and a small boy to pick the currants for her. With her pretty hair tucked into a little cap, arms bared to the elbow, and a checked apron which had a coquettish look in spite of the bib, the young housewife fell to work, feeling no doubts about her success; for hadn't she seen Hannah do it hundreds of times? The array of pots rather amazed her at first, but John was so fond of jelly, and the nice little jars would look so well on the top shelf, that Meg resolved to fill them all, and spent a long day picking, boiling, straining, and fussing over her jelly. She did her best; she asked advice of Mrs. Cornelius; she racked her brain to remember what Hannah did that she had left undone; she reboiled, resugared, and restrained, but that dreadful stuff wouldn't *"jell."*

She longed to run home, bib and all, and ask mother to lend a hand, but John and she had agreed that they would never annoy anyone with their private worries, experiments, or quarrels. They had laughed over that last word as if the idea it suggested was a most preposterous one; but they had held to their resolve, and whenever they could get on without help they did so, and no one interfered, for Mrs. March had advised the plan. So Meg wrestled alone with the refractory sweetmeats all that hot summer day, and at five o'clock sat down in her topsy-turvy kitchen, wrung her bedaubed hands, lifted up her voice and wept.

Now, in the first flush of the new life, she had often said,—

"My husband shall always feel free to bring a friend home whenever he likes. I shall always be prepared; there shall be no flurry, no scolding, no discomfort, but a neat house, a cheerful wife, and a good dinner. John, dear, never stop to ask my leave, invite whom you please, and be sure of a welcome from me."

How charming that was, to be sure! John quite glowed with pride to hear her say it, and felt what a blessed thing it was to have a superior wife. But, although they had had company from time to time, it never happened to be unexpected, and Meg had never had an opportunity to distinguish herself till now. It always happens so in this vale of tears; there is an inevitability about such things which we can only wonder at, deplore, and bear as we best can.

If John had not forgotten all about the jelly, it really would have been unpardonable in him to choose that day, of all the days in the year, to bring a friend home to dinner unexpectedly. Congratulating himself that a handsome repast had been ordered that morning, feeling sure that it would be ready to the minute, and indulging in pleasant anticipations of the charming effect it would produce, when his pretty wife came running out to meet him, he escorted his friend to his mansion, with the irrepressible satisfaction of a young host and husband.

It is a world of disappointments, as John discovered when he reached the Dove-cote. The front door usually stood hospitably open; now it was not only shut, but locked, and yesterday's mud still adorned the steps. The parlor-windows were closed and curtained, no picture of the pretty wife sewing on the piazza, in white, with a distracting little bow in her hair, or a bright-eyed hostess, smiling a shy welcome as she greeted her guest. Nothing of the sort, for not a soul appeared, but a sanguinary-looking boy asleep under the currant-bushes.

"I'm afraid something has happened. Step into the garden, Scott, while I look up Mrs. Brooke," said John, alarmed at the silence and solitude.

Round the house he hurried, led by a pungent smell of burnt sugar, and Mr. Scott strolled after him, with a queer look on his face. He paused discreetly at a distance when Brooke disappeared; but he could both see and hear, and, being a bachelor, enjoyed the prospect mightily.

In the kitchen reigned confusion and despair; one edition of jelly was trickled from pot to pot, another lay upon the floor, and a third was burning gayly on the stove. Lotty, with Teutonic phlegm, was calmly eating bread and currant wine, for the jelly was still in a hopelessly liquid state, while Mrs. Brooke, with her apron over her head, sat sobbing dismally.

"My dearest girl, what is the matter?" cried John, rushing in, with awful visions of scalded hands, sudden news of affliction, and secret consternation at the thought of the guest in the garden.

"O John, I *am* so tired and hot and cross and worried! I've been at it till I'm all worn out. Do come and help me or I *shall* die!" and the exhausted housewife cast herself upon his breast, giving him a sweet welcome in every sense of the word, for her pinafore had been baptized at the same time as the floor.

"What worries you, dear? Has anything dreadful happened?" asked the anxious John, tenderly kissing the crown of the little cap, which was all askew.

"Yes," sobbed Meg despairingly.

"Tell me quick, then. Don't cry, I can bear anything better than that. Out with it, love."

"The—the jelly won't jell and I don't know what to do!"

John Brooke laughed then as he never dared to laugh afterward; and the derisive Scott smiled involuntarily as he heard the hearty peal, which put the finishing stroke to poor Meg's woe.

"Is that all? Fling it out of the window, and don't bother any more about it. I'll buy you quarts if you want it; but for heaven's sake don't have hysterics, for I've brought Jack Scott home to dinner, and—"

John got no further, for Meg cast him off, and clasped her hands with a tragic gesture as she fell into a chair, exclaiming in a tone of mingled indignation, reproach, and dismay,—

"A man to dinner, and everything in a mess! John Brooke, how *could* you do such a thing?"

"Hush, he's in the garden! I forgot the confounded jelly, but it can't be helped now," said John, surveying the prospect with an anxious eye.

"You ought to have sent word, or told me this morning, and you ought to have remembered how busy I was," continued Meg petulantly; for even turtle-doves will peck when ruffled.

"I didn't know it this morning, and there was no time to send word, for I met him on the way out. I never thought of asking leave, when you have always told me to do as I liked. I never tried it before, and hang me if I ever do again!" added John, with an aggrieved air.

"I should hope not! Take him away at once; I can't see him, and there isn't any dinner."

"Well, I like that! Where's the beef and vegetables I sent home, and the pudding you promised?" cried John, rushing to the larder.

"I hadn't time to cook anything; I meant to dine at mother's. I'm sorry, but I was *so* busy;" and Meg's tears began again.

John was a mild man, but he was human; and after a long day's work, to come home tired, hungry, and hopeful, to find a chaotic house, an empty table, and a cross wife was not exactly conducive to repose of mind or manner. He restrained himself, however, and the little squall would have blown over, but for one unlucky word.

"It's a scrape, I acknowledge; but if you will lend a hand, we'll pull through, and have a good time yet. Don't cry, dear, but just exert yourself a bit, and knock us up something to eat. We're both as hungry as hunters, so we sha'n't mind what it is. Give us the cold meat, and bread and cheese; we won't ask for jelly."

He meant it for a good-natured joke; but that one word sealed his fate. Meg thought it was *too* cruel to hint about her sad failure, and the last atom of patience vanished as he spoke.

"You must get yourself out of the scrape as you can; I'm too used up to 'exert' myself for anyone. It's like a man to propose a bone and vulgar bread and cheese for company. I won't have anything of the sort in my house. Take that Scott up to mother's, and tell him I'm away, sick, dead,—anything. I won't see him, and you two can laugh at me and my jelly as much as you like; you won't have anything else here;" and having delivered her defiance all in one breath, Meg cast away her pinafore, and precipitately left the field to bemoan herself in her own room.

What those two creatures did in her absence, she never knew; but Mr. Scott was not taken "up to mother's," and when Meg descended, after they had strolled away together, she found traces of a promiscuous lunch which filled her with horror. Lotty reported that they had eaten "a much, and greatly laughed, and the master bid her throw away all the sweet stuff, and hide the pots."

Meg longed to go and tell mother; but a sense of shame at her own shortcomings, of loyalty to John, "who might be cruel, but nobody should know it," restrained her; and after a summary clearing up, she dressed herself prettily, and sat down to wait for John to come and be forgiven.

Unfortunately, John didn't come, not seeing the matter in that light. He had carried it off as a good joke with Scott, excused his little wife as well as he could, and played the host so hospitably that his friend enjoyed the impromptu dinner, and promised to come again. But John was angry, though he did not show it; he felt that Meg had got him into a scrape, and then deserted him in his hour of need. "It wasn't fair to tell a man to bring folks home any time, with perfect freedom, and when he took you at your word, to flame up and blame him, and leave him in the lurch, to be laughed at or pitied. No, by George, it wasn't! And Meg must know it." He had fumed inwardly during the feast, but when the flurry was over, and he strolled home, after seeing Scott off, a milder mood came over him. "Poor little thing! It was hard upon her when she tried so heartily to please me. She was wrong, of course, but then she was young. I must be patient and teach her." He hoped she had not gone home—he hated gossip and interference. For a minute he was ruffled again at the mere thought of it; and then the fear that Meg would cry herself sick softened his heart, and sent him on at a quicker pace, resolving to be calm and kind, but firm, quite firm, and show her where she had failed in her duty to her spouse.

Meg likewise resolved to be "calm and kind, but firm," and show *him* his duty. She longed to run to meet him, and beg pardon, and be kissed and comforted, as she was sure of being; but, of course, she did nothing of the sort, and when she saw John coming, began to hum quite naturally, as she rocked and sewed, like a lady of leisure in her best parlor.

John was a little disappointed not to find a tender Niobe; but, feeling that his dignity demanded the first apology, he made none, only came leisurely in, and laid himself upon the sofa, with the singularly relevant remark,—

"We are going to have a new moon, my dear."

"I've no objection," was Meg's equally soothing remark.

A few other topics of general interest were introduced by Mr. Brooke, and wet-blanketed by Mrs. Brooke, and conversation languished. John went to one window, unfolded his paper, and wrapped himself in it, figuratively speaking. Meg went to the other window, and sewed as if new rosettes for her slippers were among the necessaries of life. Neither spoke; both looked quite "calm and firm," and both felt desperately uncomfortable.

"Oh dear," thought Meg, "married life is very trying, and does need infinite patience, as well as love, as mother says." The word "mother" suggested other maternal counsels, given long ago, and received with unbelieving protests.

"John is a good man, but he has his faults, and you must learn to see and bear with them, remembering your own. He is very decided, but never will be obstinate, if you reason kindly, not oppose impatiently. He is very accurate, and particular about the truth—a good trait, though you call him 'fussy.' Never deceive him by look or word, Meg, and he will give you the confidence you deserve, the support you need. He has a temper, not like ours,—one flash, and then all over,—but the white, still anger, that is seldom stirred, but once kindled, is hard to quench. Be careful, very careful, not to wake this anger against yourself, for peace and happiness depend on keeping his respect. Watch yourself, be the first to ask pardon if you both err, and guard against the little piques, misunderstandings, and hasty words that often **pave the way** for bitter sorrow and regret."

These words came back to Meg, as she sat sewing in the sunset, especially the last. This was the first serious disagreement; her own hasty speeches sounded both silly and unkind, as she recalled them, her own anger looked childish now, and thoughts of poor John coming home to such a scene quite melted her heart. She glanced at him with tears in her eyes, but he did not see them; she put down her work and got up, thinking, "I *will* be the first to say, 'Forgive me,'" but he did not seem to hear her; she went very slowly across the room, for pride was hard to swallow, and stood by him, but he did not turn his head. For a minute she felt as if she really couldn't do it; then came the thought, "This is the beginning, I'll do my part, and have nothing to reproach myself with," and stooping down, she softly kissed her husband on the forehead. Of course that settled it; the penitent kiss was better than a world of words, and John had her on his knee in a minute, saying tenderly,—

"It was too bad to laugh at the poor little jelly-pots. Forgive me, dear, I never will again!"

But he did, oh bless you, yes, hundreds of times, and so did Meg, both declaring that it was the sweetest jelly they ever made; for family peace was preserved in that little family jar.

After this, Meg had Mr. Scott to dinner by special invitation, and served him up a pleasant feast without a cooked wife for the first course; on which occasion she was so gay and gracious, and made everything go off so charmingly, that Mr. Scott told John he was a happy fellow, and shook his head over the hardships of bachelorhood all the way home.

In the autumn, new trials and experiences came to Meg. Sallie Moffat renewed her friendship, was always running out for a dish of gossip at the little house, or inviting "that poor dear" to come in and spend the day at the big house. It was pleasant, for in dull weather Meg often felt lonely; all were busy at home, John absent till night, and nothing to do but sew, or read, or potter about. So it naturally fell out that Meg got into the way of gadding and gossiping with her friend. Seeing Sallie's pretty things made her long for such, and pity herself because she had not got them. Sallie was very kind, and often offered her the coveted trifles; but Meg declined them, knowing that John wouldn't like it; and then this foolish little woman went and did what John disliked infinitely worse.

She knew her husband's income, and she loved to feel that he trusted her, not only with his happiness, but what some men seem to value more,—his money. She knew where it was, was free to take what she liked, and all he asked was that she should keep account of every penny, pay bills once a month, and remember that she was a poor man's wife. Till now, she had done well, been prudent and exact, kept her little account-books neatly, and showed them to him monthly without fear. But that autumn the serpent got into Meg's paradise, and tempted her, like many a modern Eve, not with apples, but with dress. Meg didn't like to be pitied and made to feel poor; it irritated her, but she was ashamed to confess it, and now and then she tried to console herself by buying something pretty, so that Sallie needn't think she had to economize. She always felt wicked after it, for the pretty things were seldom necessaries; but then they cost so little, it wasn't worth worrying about; so the trifles increased unconsciously, and in the shopping excursions she was no longer a passive looker-on.

But the trifles cost more than one would imagine; and when she cast up her accounts at the end of the month, the sum total rather scared her. John was busy that month, and left the bills to her; the next month he was absent; but the third he had a grand quarterly settling up, and Meg never forgot it. A few days before she had done a dreadful thing, and it weighed upon her conscience. Sallie had been buying silks, and Meg longed for a new one,—just a handsome light one for parties, her black silk was so common, and thin things for evening wear were only proper for girls. Aunt March usually gave the sisters a present of twenty-five dollars apiece at New Year; that was only a month to wait, and here was a lovely violet silk going at a bargain, and she had the money, if she only dared to take it. John always said what was his was hers; but would he think it right to spend not only the prospective five-and-twenty, but another five-and-twenty out of the household fund? That was the question. Sallie had urged her to do it, had offered to loan the money, and with the best intentions in life, had tempted Meg beyond her strength. In an evil moment the shopman held up the lovely, shimmering folds, and said, "A bargain, I assure you, ma'am." She answered, "I'll take it;" and it was cut off and paid for, and Sallie had exulted, and she had laughed as if it were a thing of no consequence, and driven away, feeling as if she had stolen something, and the police were after her.

When she got home, she tried to assuage the pangs of remorse by spreading forth the lovely silk; but it looked less silvery now, didn't become her, after all, and the words "fifty dollars" seemed stamped like a pattern down each breadth. She put it away; but it haunted her, not delightfully, as a new dress should, but dreadfully, like the ghost of a folly that was not easily laid. When John got out his books that night, Meg's heart sank, and, for the first time in her married life, she was afraid of her husband. The kind, brown eyes looked as if they could be stern; and though he was unusually merry, she fancied he had found her out, but didn't mean to let her know it. The house-bills were all paid, the books all in order. John had praised her, and was undoing the old pocketbook which they called the "bank," when Meg, knowing that it was quite empty, stopped his hand, saying nervously,—

"You haven't seen my private expense book yet."

John never asked to see it; but she always insisted on his doing so, and used to enjoy his masculine amazement at the queer things women wanted, and made him guess what "piping" was, demand fiercely the meaning of a "hug-me-tight," or wonder how a little thing composed of three rosebuds, a bit of velvet, and a pair of strings, could possibly be a bonnet, and cost five or six dollars. That night he looked as if he would like the fun of quizzing her figures and pretending to be horrified at her extravagance, as he often did, being particularly proud of his prudent wife.

The little book was brought slowly out, and laid down before him. Meg got behind his chair under pretence of smoothing the wrinkles out of his tired forehead, and standing there, she said, with her panic increasing with every word,—

"John, dear, I'm ashamed to show you my book, for I've really been dreadfully extravagant lately. I go about so much I must have things, you know, and Sallie advised my getting it, so I did; and my New-Year's money will partly pay for it: but I was sorry after I'd done it, for I knew you'd think it wrong in me."

John laughed, and drew her round beside him, saying good-humoredly, "Don't go and hide. I won't beat you if you *have* got a pair of killing boots; I'm rather proud of my wife's feet, and don't mind if she does pay eight or nine dollars for her boots, if they are good ones."

That had been one of her last "trifles," and John's eye had fallen on it as he spoke. "Oh, what *will* he say when he comes to that awful fifty dollars!" thought Meg, with a shiver.

"It's worse than boots, it's a silk dress," she said, with the calmness of desperation, for she wanted the worst over.

"Well, dear, what is the 'dem'd total,' as Mr. Mantalini says?"

That didn't sound like John, and she knew he was looking up at her with the straightforward look that she had always been ready to meet and answer with one as frank till now. She turned the page and her head at the same time, pointing to the sum which would have been bad enough without the fifty, but which was appalling to her with that added. For a minute the room was very still; then John said slowly,—but she could feel it cost him an effort to express no displeasure,—

"Well, I don't know that fifty is much for a dress, with all the furbelows and notions you have to have to finish it off these days."

"It isn't made or trimmed," sighed Meg faintly, for a sudden recollection of the cost still to be incurred quite overwhelmed her.

"Twenty-five yards of silk seems a good deal to cover one small woman, but I've no doubt my wife will look as fine as Ned Moffat's when she gets it on," said John dryly.

"I know you are angry, John, but I can't help it. I don't mean to waste your money, and I didn't think those little things would count up so. I can't resist them when I see Sallie buying all she wants, and pitying me because I don't. I try to be contented, but it is hard, and I'm tired of being poor."

The last words were spoken so low she thought he did not hear them, but he did, and they wounded him deeply, for he had denied himself many pleasures for Meg's sake. She could have bitten her tongue out the minute she had said it, for John pushed the books away, and got up, saying, with a little quiver in his voice, "I was afraid of this; I do my best, Meg." If he had scolded her, or even shaken her, it would not have broken her heart like those few words. She ran to him and held him close, crying, with repentant tears, "O John, my dear, kind, hard-working boy, I didn't mean it! It was so wicked, so untrue and ungrateful, how could I say it! Oh, how could I say it!"

He was very kind, forgave her readily, and did not utter one reproach; but Meg knew that she had done and said a thing which would not be forgotten soon, although he might never allude to it again. She had promised to love him for better for worse; and then she, his wife, had reproached him with his poverty, after spending his earnings recklessly. It was dreadful; and the worst of it was John went on so quietly afterward, just as if nothing had happened, except that he stayed in town later, and worked at night when she had gone to cry herself to sleep. A week of remorse nearly made Meg sick; and the discovery that John had countermanded the order for his new great-coat reduced her to a state of despair which was pathetic to behold. He had simply said, in answer to her surprised inquiries as to the change, "I can't afford it, my dear."

Meg said no more, but a few minutes after he found her in the hall, with her face buried in the old great-coat, crying as if her heart would break.

They had a long talk that night, and Meg learned to love her husband better for his poverty, because it seemed to have made a man of him, given him the strength and courage to fight his own way, and taught him a tender patience with which to bear and comfort the natural longings and failures of those he loved.

Next day she put her pride in her pocket, went to Sallie, told the truth, and asked her to buy the silk as a favor. The good-natured Mrs. Moffat willingly did so, and had the delicacy not to make her a present of it immediately afterward. Then Meg ordered home the great-coat, and, when John arrived, she put it on, and asked him how he liked her new silk gown. One can imagine what answer he made, how he received his present, and what a blissful state of things ensued. John came home early, Meg gadded no more; and that great-coat was put on in the morning by a very happy husband, and taken off at night by a most devoted little wife. So the year rolled round, and at midsummer there came to Meg a new experience,—the deepest and tenderest of a woman's life.

Laurie came sneaking into the kitchen of the Dove-cote, one Saturday, with an excited face, and was received with the clash of cymbals; for Hannah clapped her hands with a saucepan in one and the cover in the other.

"How's the little mamma? Where is everybody? Why didn't you tell me before I came home?" began Laurie, in a loud whisper.

"Happy as a queen, the dear! Every soul of 'em is upstairs a worshipin'; we didn't want no hurrycanes round. Now you go into the parlor, and

I'll send 'em down to you," with which somewhat involved reply Hannah vanished, chuckling ecstatically.

Presently Jo appeared, proudly bearing a flannel bundle laid forth upon a large pillow. Jo's face was very sober, but her eyes twinkled, and there was an odd sound in her voice of repressed emotion of some sort.

"Shut your eyes and hold out your arms," she said invitingly.

Laurie backed precipitately into a corner, and put his hands behind him with an imploring gesture: "No, thank you, I'd rather not. I shall drop it or smash it, as sure as fate."

"Then you sha'n't see your nevvy," said Jo decidedly, turning as if to go.

"I will, I will! Only you must be responsible for damages;" and, obeying orders, Laurie heroically shut his eyes while something was put into his arms. A peal of laughter from Jo, Amy, Mrs. March, Hannah, and John caused him to open them the next minute, to find himself invested with two babies instead of one.

No wonder they laughed, for the expression of his face was droll enough to convulse a Quaker, as he stood and stared wildly from the unconscious innocents to the hilarious spectators, with such dismay that Jo sat down on the floor and screamed.

"Twins, by Jupiter!" was all he said for a minute; then, turning to the women with an appealing look that was comically piteous, he added, "Take 'em quick, somebody. I'm going to laugh, and I shall drop 'em."

John rescued his babies, and marched up and down, with one on each arm, as if already initiated into the mysteries of baby-tending, while Laurie laughed till the tears ran down his cheeks.

"It's the best joke of the season, isn't it? I wouldn't have you told, for I set my heart on surprising you, and I flatter myself I've done it," said Jo, when she got her breath.

"I never was more staggered in my life. Isn't it fun? Are they boys? What are you going to name them? Let's have another look. Hold me up, Jo; for upon my life it's one too many for me," returned Laurie, regarding the infants with the air of a big, benevolent Newfoundland looking at a pair of infantile kittens.

"Boy and girl. Aren't they beauties?" said the proud papa, beaming upon the little, red squirmers as if they were unfledged angels.

"Most remarkable children I ever saw. Which is which?" and Laurie bent like a well-sweep to examine the prodigies.

"Amy put a blue ribbon on the boy and a pink on the girl, French fashion, so you can always tell. Besides, one has blue eyes and one brown. Kiss them, Uncle Teddy," said wicked Jo.

"I'm afraid they mightn't like it," began Laurie, with unusual timidity in such matters.

"Of course they will; they are used to it now. Do it this minute, sir!" commanded Jo, fearing he might propose a proxy.

Laurie screwed up his face, and obeyed with a gingerly peck at each little cheek that produced another laugh, and made the babies squeal.

"There, I knew they didn't like it! That's the boy; see him kick; he hits out with his fists like a good one. Now then, young Brooke, pitch into a man of your own size, will you?" cried Laurie, delighted with a poke in the face from a tiny fist, flapping aimlessly about.

"He's to be named John Laurence, and the girl Margaret, after mother and grandmother. We shall call her Daisy, so as not to have two Megs, and I suppose the mannie will be Jack, unless we find a better name," said Amy, with aunt-like interest.

"Name him Demijohn, and call him 'Demi' for short," said Laurie.

"Daisy and Demi,—just the thing! I *knew* Teddy would do it," cried Jo, clapping her hands.

Teddy certainly had done it that time, for the babies were "Daisy" and "Demi" to the end of the chapter.

# CHAPTER XXIX

## CALLS

"Come, Jo, it's time."

"For what?"

"You don't mean to say you have forgotten that you promised to make half a dozen calls with me today?"

"I've done a good many rash and foolish things in my life, but I don't think I ever was mad enough to say I'd make six calls in one day, when a single one upsets me for a week."

"Yes, you did; it was a bargain between us. I was to finish the crayon of Beth for you, and you were to go properly with me, and return our neighbors' visits."

"If it was fair—that was in the bond; and I stand to the letter of my bond, Shylock. There is a pile of clouds in the east; it's *not* fair, and I don't go."

"Now, that's shirking. It's a lovely day, no prospect of rain, and you pride yourself on keeping promises; so be honorable; come and do your duty, and then be at peace for another six months."

At that minute Jo was particularly absorbed in dress-making; for she was mantua-maker general to the family, and took especial credit to herself because she could use a needle as well as a pen. It was very provoking to be arrested in the act of a first trying-on, and ordered out to make calls in her best array, on a warm July day. She hated calls of the formal sort, and never made any till Amy compelled her with a bargain, bribe, or promise. In the present instance, there was no escape; and having clashed her scissors rebelliously, while protesting that she smelt thunder, she gave in, put away her work, and taking up her hat and gloves with an air of resignation, told Amy the victim was ready.

"Jo March, you are perverse enough to provoke a saint! You don't intend to make calls in that state, I hope," cried Amy, surveying her with amazement.

"Why not? I'm neat and cool and comfortable; quite proper for a dusty walk on a warm day. If people care more for my clothes than they do for me, I don't wish to see them. You can dress for both, and be as elegant as you please: it pays for you to be fine; it doesn't for me, and furbelows only worry me."

"Oh dear!" sighed Amy; "now she's in a contrary fit, and will drive me distracted before I can get her properly ready. I'm sure it's no pleasure to me to go today, but it's a debt we owe society, and there's no one to pay it but you and me. I'll do anything for you, Jo, if you'll only dress yourself nicely, and come and help me do the civil. You can talk so well, look so aristocratic in your best things, and behave so beautifully, if you try, that I'm proud of you. I'm afraid to go alone; do come and take care of me."

"You're an artful little puss to flatter and wheedle your cross old sister in that way. The idea of my being aristocratic and well-bred, and your being afraid to go anywhere alone! I don't know which is the most absurd. Well, I'll go if I must, and do my best. You shall be commander of the expedition, and I'll obey blindly; will that satisfy you?" said Jo, with a sudden change from perversity to lamb-like submission.

"You're a perfect cherub! Now put on all your best things, and I'll tell you how to behave at each place, so that you will make a good impression. I want people to like you, and they would if you'd only try to be a little more agreeable. Do your hair the pretty way, and put the pink rose in your bonnet; it's becoming, and you look too sober in your plain suit. Take your light gloves and the embroidered handkerchief. We'll stop at Meg's, and borrow her white sunshade, and then you can have my dove-colored one."

While Amy dressed, she issued her orders, and Jo obeyed them; not without entering her protest, however, for she sighed as she rustled into her new organdie, frowned darkly at herself as she tied her bonnet strings in an irreproachable bow, wrestled viciously with pins as she put on her collar, wrinkled up her features generally as she shook out the handkerchief, whose embroidery was as irritating to her nose as the present mission was to her feelings; and when she had squeezed her hands into tight gloves with three buttons and a tassel, as the last touch of elegance, she turned to Amy with an imbecile expression of countenance, saying meekly,—

"I'm perfectly miserable; but if you consider me presentable, I die happy."

"You are highly satisfactory; turn slowly round, and let me get a careful view." Jo revolved, and Amy gave a touch here and there, then fell back, with her head on one side, observing graciously, "Yes, you'll do; your head is all I could ask, for that white bonnet *with* the rose is quite ravishing. Hold back your shoulders, and carry your hands easily, no matter if your gloves do pinch. There's one thing you can do well, Jo, that is, wear a shawl—I can't; but it's very nice to see you, and I'm so glad Aunt March gave you that lovely one; it's simple, but handsome, and those folds over the arm are really artistic. Is the point of my mantle in the middle, and have I looped my dress evenly? I like to show my boots, for my feet *are* pretty, though my nose isn't."

"You are a thing of beauty and a joy forever," said Jo, looking through her hand with the air of a connoisseur at the blue feather against the gold hair. "Am I to drag my best dress through the dust, or loop it up, please, ma'am?"

"Hold it up when you walk, but drop it in the house; the sweeping style suits you best, and you must learn to trail your skirts gracefully. You haven't half buttoned one cuff; do it at once. You'll never look finished if you are not careful about the little details, for they make up the pleasing whole."

Jo sighed, and proceeded to burst the buttons off her glove, in doing up her cuff; but at last both were ready, and sailed away, looking as "pretty as picters," Hannah said, as she hung out of the upper window to watch them.

"Now, Jo dear, the Chesters consider themselves very elegant people, so I want you to put on your best deportment. Don't make any of your abrupt remarks, or do anything odd, will you? Just be calm, cool, and quiet,—that's safe and ladylike; and you can easily do it for fifteen minutes," said Amy, as they approached the first place, having borrowed the white parasol and been inspected by Meg, with a baby on each arm.

"Let me see. 'Calm, cool, and quiet,'—yes, I think I can promise that. I've played the part of a prim young lady on the stage, and I'll try it off. My powers are great, as you shall see; so be easy in your mind, my child."

Amy looked relieved, but naughty Jo took her at her word; for, during the first call, she sat with every limb gracefully composed, every fold correctly draped, calm as a summer sea, cool as a snow-bank, and as silent as a sphinx. In vain Mrs. Chester alluded to her "charming novel," and the Misses Chester introduced parties, picnics, the opera, and the fashions; each and all were answered by a smile, a bow, and a demure "Yes" or "No," with the chill on. In vain Amy telegraphed the word "Talk," tried to draw her out, and administered covert pokes with her foot. Jo sat as if blandly unconscious of it all, with deportment like Maud's face, "icily regular, splendidly null."

"What a haughty, uninteresting creature that oldest Miss March is!" was the unfortunately audible remark of one of the ladies, as the door closed upon their guests. Jo laughed noiselessly all through the hall, but Amy looked disgusted at the failure of her instructions, and very naturally laid the blame upon Jo.

"How could you mistake me so? I merely meant you to be properly dignified and composed, and you made yourself a perfect stock and stone. Try to be sociable at the Lambs', gossip as other girls do, and be interested in dress and flirtations and whatever nonsense comes up. They move in the best society, are valuable persons for us to know, and I wouldn't fail to make a good impression there for anything."

"I'll be agreeable; I'll gossip and giggle, and have horrors and raptures over any trifle you like. I rather enjoy this, and now I'll imitate what is called 'a charming girl;' I can do it, for I have May Chester as a model, and I'll improve upon her. See if the Lambs don't say, 'What a lively, nice creature that Jo March is!' "

Amy felt anxious, as well she might, for when Jo turned freakish there was no knowing where she would stop. Amy's face was a study when she saw her sister skim into the next drawing-room, kiss all the young ladies with effusion, beam graciously upon the young gentlemen, and join in the chat with a spirit which amazed the beholder. Amy was taken possession of by Mrs. Lamb, with whom she was a favorite, and forced to hear a long account of Lucretia's last attack, while three delightful young gentlemen hovered near, waiting for a pause when they might rush in and rescue her. So situated, she was powerless to check Jo, who seemed possessed by a spirit of mischief, and talked away as volubly as the old lady. A knot of heads gathered about her, and Amy strained her ears to hear what was going on; for broken sentences filled her with alarm, round eyes and uplifted hands tormented her with curiosity, and frequent peals of laughter made her wild to share the fun. One may imagine her suffering on overhearing fragments of this sort of conversation:—

"She rides splendidly,—who taught her?"

"No one; she used to practice mounting, holding the reins, and sitting straight on an old saddle in a tree. Now she rides anything, for she doesn't know what fear is, and the stable-man lets her have horses cheap, because she trains them to carry ladies so well. She has such a passion for it, I often tell her if everything else fails she can be a horse-breaker, and get her living so."

At this awful speech Amy contained herself with difficulty, for the impression was being given that she was rather a fast young lady, which was her especial aversion. But what could she do? For the old lady was in the middle of her story, and long before it was done Jo was off again, making more droll revelations, and committing still more fearful blunders.

"Yes, Amy was in despair that day, for all the good beasts were gone, and of three left, one was lame, one blind, and the other so balky that you had to put dirt in his mouth before he would start. Nice animal for a pleasure party, wasn't it?"

"Which did she choose?" asked one of the laughing gentlemen, who enjoyed the subject.

"None of them; she heard of a young horse at the farmhouse over the river, and, though a lady had never ridden him, she resolved to try, because he was handsome and spirited. Her struggles were really pathetic; there was no one to bring the horse to the saddle, so she took the saddle to the horse. My dear creature, she actually rowed it over the river, put it on her head, and marched up to the barn to the utter amazement of the old man!"

"Did she ride the horse?"

"Of course she did, and had a capital time. I expected to see her brought home in fragments, but she managed him perfectly, and was the life of the party."

"Well, I call that plucky!" and young Mr. Lamb turned an approving glance upon Amy, wondering what his mother could be saying to make the girl look so red and uncomfortable.

She was still redder and more uncomfortable a moment after, when a sudden turn in the conversation introduced the subject of dress. One of the young ladies asked Jo where she got the pretty drab hat she wore to the picnic; and stupid Jo, instead of mentioning the place where it was bought two years ago, must needs answer, with unnecessary frankness, "Oh, Amy painted it; you can't buy those soft shades, so we paint ours any color we like. It's a great comfort to have an artistic sister."

"Isn't that an original idea?" cried Miss Lamb, who found Jo great fun.

"That's nothing compared to some of her brilliant performances. There's nothing the child can't do. Why, she wanted a pair of blue boots for Sallie's party, so she just painted her soiled white ones the loveliest shade of sky-blue you ever saw, and they looked exactly like satin," added Jo, with an air of pride in her sister's accomplishments that exasperated Amy till she felt that it would be a relief to throw her card-case at her.

"We read a story of yours the other day, and enjoyed it very much," observed the elder Miss Lamb, wishing to compliment the literary lady, who did not look the character just then, it must be confessed.

Any mention of her "works" always had a bad effect upon Jo, who either grew rigid and looked offended, or changed the subject with a *brusque* remark, as now. "Sorry you could find nothing better to read. I write that rubbish because it sells, and ordinary people like it. Are you going to New York this winter?"

As Miss Lamb had "enjoyed" the story, this speech was not exactly grateful or complimentary. The minute it was made Jo saw her mistake; but, fearing to make the matter worse, suddenly remembered that it was for her to make the first move toward departure, and did so with an abruptness that left three people with half-finished sentences in their mouths.

"Amy, we *must* go. *Good*-by, dear; *do* come and see us; we are *pining* for a visit. I don't dare to ask *you*, Mr. Lamb; but if you *should* come, I don't think I shall have the heart to send you away."

Jo said this with such a droll imitation of May Chester's gushing style that Amy got out of the room as rapidly as possible, feeling a strong desire to laugh and cry at the same time.

"Didn't I do that well?" asked Jo, with a satisfied air, as they walked away.

"Nothing could have been worse," was Amy's crushing reply. "What possessed you to tell those stories about my saddle, and the hats and boots, and all the rest of it?"

"Why, it's funny, and amuses people. They know we are poor, so it's no use pretending that we have grooms, buy three or four hats a season, and have things as easy and fine as they do."

"You needn't go and tell them all our little shifts, and expose our poverty in that perfectly unnecessary way. You haven't a bit of proper pride, and never will learn when to hold your tongue and when to speak," said Amy despairingly.

Poor Jo looked abashed, and silently chafed the end of her nose with the stiff handkerchief, as if performing a penance for her misdemeanors.

"How shall I behave here?" she asked, as they approached the third mansion.

"Just as you please; I wash my hands of you," was Amy's short answer.

"Then I'll enjoy myself. The boys are at home, and we'll have a comfortable time. Goodness knows I need a little change, for elegance has a bad effect upon my constitution," returned Jo gruffly, being disturbed by her failures to suit.

An enthusiastic welcome from three big boys and several pretty children speedily soothed her ruffled feelings; and, leaving Amy to entertain the hostess and Mr. Tudor, who happened to be calling likewise, Jo devoted herself to the young folks, and found the change refreshing. She listened to college stories with deep interest, caressed pointers and poodles without a murmur, agreed heartily that "Tom Brown was a brick," regardless of the improper form of praise; and when one lad proposed a visit to his turtle-tank, she went with an alacrity which caused mamma to smile upon her, as that motherly lady settled the cap which was left in a ruinous condition by filial hugs, bearlike but affectionate, and dearer to her than the most faultless *coiffure* from the hands of an inspired Frenchwoman.

Leaving her sister to her own devices, Amy proceeded to enjoy herself to her heart's content. Mr. Tudor's uncle had married an English lady who was third cousin to a living lord, and Amy regarded the whole family with great respect; for, in spite of her American birth and breeding, she possessed that reverence for titles which haunts the best of us,—that unacknowledged loyalty to the early faith in kings which set the most democratic nation under the sun in a ferment at the coming of a royal yellow-haired laddie, some years ago, and which still has something to do with the love the young country bears the old, like that of a big son for an imperious little mother, who held him while she could, and let him go with a farewell scolding when he rebelled. But even the satisfaction of talking with a distant connection of the British nobility did not render Amy forgetful of time; and when the proper number of minutes had passed, she reluctantly tore herself from this aristocratic society, and looked about for Jo, fervently hoping that her incorrigible sister would not be found in any position which should bring disgrace upon the name of March.

It might have been worse, but Amy considered it bad; for Jo sat on the grass, with an encampment of boys about her, and a dirty-footed dog reposing on the skirt of her state and festival dress, as she related one of Laurie's pranks to her admiring audience. One small child was poking turtles with Amy's cherished parasol, a second was eating gingerbread over Jo's best bonnet, and a third playing ball with her gloves. But all were enjoying themselves; and when Jo collected her damaged property to go, her escort accompanied her, begging her to come again, "it was such fun to hear about Laurie's larks."

"Capital boys, aren't they? I feel quite young and brisk again after that," said Jo, strolling along with her hands behind her, partly from habit, partly to conceal the bespattered parasol.

"Why do you always avoid Mr. Tudor?" asked Amy, wisely refraining from any comment upon Jo's dilapidated appearance.

"Don't like him; he puts on airs, snubs his sisters, worries his father, and doesn't speak respectfully of his mother. Laurie says he is fast, and *I* don't consider him a desirable acquaintance; so I let him alone."

"You might treat him civilly, at least. You gave him a cool nod; and just now you bowed and smiled in the politest way to Tommy Chamberlain, whose father keeps a grocery store. If you had just reversed the nod and the bow, it would have been right," said Amy reprovingly.

"No, it wouldn't," returned perverse Jo; "I neither like, respect, nor admire Tudor, though his grandfather's uncle's nephew's niece *was* third cousin to a lord. Tommy is poor and bashful and good and very clever; I think well of him, and like to show that I do, for he *is* a gentleman in spite of the brown-paper parcels."

"It's no use trying to argue with you," began Amy.

"Not the least, my dear," interrupted Jo; "so let us look amiable, and drop a card here, as the Kings are evidently out, for which I'm deeply grateful."

The family card-case having done its duty, the girls walked on, and Jo uttered another thanksgiving on reaching the fifth house, and being told that the young ladies were engaged.

"Now let us go home, and never mind Aunt March today. We can run down there any time, and it's really a pity to trail through the dust in our best bibs and tuckers, when we are tired and cross."

"Speak for yourself, if you please. Aunt likes to have us pay her the compliment of coming in style, and making a formal call; it's a little thing to do, but it gives her pleasure, and I don't believe it will hurt your things half so much as letting dirty dogs and clumping boys spoil them. Stoop down, and let me take the crumbs off of your bonnet."

"What a good girl you are, Amy!" said Jo, with a repentant glance from her own damaged costume to that of her sister, which was fresh and spotless still. "I wish it was as easy for me to do little things to please people as it is for you. I think of them, but it takes too much time to do them; so I wait for a chance to confer a great favor, and let the small ones slip; but they tell best in the end, I fancy."

Amy smiled, and was mollified at once, saying with a maternal air,—

"Women should learn to be agreeable, particularly poor ones; for they have no other way of repaying the kindnesses they receive. If you'd remember that, and practice it, you'd be better liked than I am, because there is more of you."

"I'm a crotchety old thing, and always shall be, but I'm willing to own that you are right; only it's easier for me to risk my life for a person than to be pleasant to him when I don't feel like it. It's a great misfortune to have such strong likes and dislikes, isn't it?"

"It's a greater not to be able to hide them. I don't mind saying that I don't approve of Tudor any more than you do; but I'm not called upon to tell him so; neither are you, and there is no use in making yourself disagreeable because he is."

"But I think girls ought to show when they disapprove of young men; and how can they do it except by their manners? Preaching does not do any good, as I know to my sorrow, since I've had Teddy to manage; but there are many little ways in which I can influence him without a word, and I say we *ought* to do it to others if we can."

"Teddy is a remarkable boy, and can't be taken as a sample of other boys," said Amy, in a tone of solemn conviction, which would have convulsed the "remarkable boy," if he had heard it. "If we were belles, or women of wealth and position, we might do something, perhaps; but for us to frown at one set of young gentlemen because we don't approve of them, and smile upon another set because we do, wouldn't have a particle of effect, and we should only be considered odd and puritanical."

"So we are to countenance things and people which we detest, merely because we are not belles and millionaires, are we? That's a nice sort of morality."

"I can't argue about it, I only know that it's the way of the world; and people who set themselves against it only get laughed at for their pains. I don't like reformers, and I hope you will never try to be one."

"I do like them, and I shall be one if I can; for, in spite of the laughing, the world would never get on without them. We can't agree about that, for you belong to the old set, and I to the new: you will get on the best, but I shall have the liveliest time of it. I should rather enjoy the brickbats and hooting, I think."

"Well, compose yourself now, and don't worry aunt with your new ideas."

"I'll try not to, but I'm always possessed to burst out with some particularly blunt speech or revolutionary sentiment before her; it's my doom, and I can't help it."

They found Aunt Carrol with the old lady, both absorbed in some very interesting subject; but they dropped it as the girls came in, with a conscious look which betrayed that they had been talking about their nieces. Jo was not in a good humor, and the perverse fit returned; but Amy, who had virtuously done her duty, kept her temper, and pleased everybody, was in a most angelic frame of mind. This amiable spirit was felt at once, and both the aunts "my deared" her affectionately, looking what they afterwards said emphatically,—"That child improves every day."

"Are you going to help about the fair, dear?" asked Mrs. Carrol, as

Amy sat down beside her with the confiding air elderly people like so well in the young.

"Yes, aunt. Mrs. Chester asked me if I would, and I offered to tend a table, as I have nothing but my time to give."

"I'm not," put in Jo decidedly. "I hate to be patronized, and the Chesters think it's a great favor to allow us to help with their highly connected fair. I wonder you consented, Amy: they only want you to work."

"I am willing to work: it's for the freedmen as well as the Chesters, and I think it very kind of them to let me share the labor and the fun. Patronage does not trouble me when it is well meant."

"Quite right and proper. I like your grateful spirit, my dear; it's a pleasure to help people who appreciate our efforts: some do not, and that is trying," observed Aunt March, looking over her spectacles at Jo, who sat apart, rocking herself, with a somewhat morose expression.

If Jo had only known what a great happiness was wavering in the balance for one of them, she would have turned dovelike in a minute; but, unfortunately, we don't have windows in our breasts, and cannot see what goes on in the minds of our friends; better for us that we cannot as a general thing, but now and then it would be such a comfort, such a saving of time and temper. By her next speech, Jo deprived herself of several years of pleasure, and received a timely lesson in the art of holding her tongue.

"I don't like favors; they oppress and make me feel like a slave. I'd rather do everything for myself, and be perfectly independent."

"Ahem!" coughed Aunt Carrol softly, with a look at Aunt March.

"I told you so," said Aunt March, with a decided nod to Aunt Carrol. Mercifully unconscious of what she had done, Jo sat with her nose in the air, and a revolutionary aspect which was anything but inviting.

"Do you speak French, dear?" asked Mrs. Carrol, laying her hand on Amy's.

"Pretty well, thanks to Aunt March, who lets Esther talk to me as often as I like," replied Amy, with a grateful look, which caused the old lady to smile affably.

"How are you about languages?" asked Mrs. Carrol of Jo.

"Don't know a word; I'm very stupid about studying anything; can't bear French, it's such a slippery, silly sort of language," was the *brusque* reply.

Another look passed between the ladies, and Aunt March said to Amy, "You are quite strong and well, now, dear, I believe? Eyes don't trouble you any more, do they?"

"Not at all, thank you, ma'am. I'm very well, and mean to do great things next winter, so that I may be ready for Rome, whenever that joyful time arrives."

"Good girl! You deserve to go, and I'm sure you will some day," said Aunt March, with an approving pat on the head, as Amy picked up her ball for her.

> "Cross-patch, draw the latch,
> Sit by the fire and spin,"

squalled Polly, bending down from his perch on the back of her chair to peep into Jo's face, with such a comical air of impertinent inquiry that it was impossible to help laughing.

"Most observing bird," said the old lady.

"Come and take a walk, my dear?" cried Polly, hopping toward the china-closet, with a look suggestive of lump-sugar.

"Thank you, I will. Come, Amy;" and Jo brought the visit to an end, feeling more strongly than ever that calls did have a bad effect upon her constitution. She shook hands in a gentlemanly manner, but Amy kissed both the aunts, and the girls departed, leaving behind them the impression of shadow and sunshine; which impression caused Aunt March to say, as they vanished,—

"You'd better do it, Mary; I'll supply the money," and Aunt Carrol to reply decidedly, "I certainly will, if her father and mother consent."

# CHAPTER XXX

## CONSEQUENCES

MRS. CHESTER'S fair was so very elegant and select that it was considered a great honor by the young ladies of the neighborhood to be invited to take a table, and everyone was much interested in the matter. Amy was asked, but Jo was not, which was fortunate for all parties, as her elbows were decidedly akimbo at this period of her life, and it took a good many hard knocks to teach her how to get on easily. The "haughty, uninteresting creature" was let severely alone; but Amy's talent and taste were duly complimented by the offer of the art-table, and she exerted herself to prepare and secure appropriate and valuable contributions to it.

Everything went on smoothly till the day before the fair opened; then there occurred one of the little skirmishes which it is almost impossible to avoid, when some five-and-twenty women, old and young, with all their private piques and prejudices, try to work together.

May Chester was rather jealous of Amy because the latter was a greater favorite than herself; and, just at this time, several trifling circumstances occurred to increase the feeling. Amy's dainty pen-and-ink work entirely eclipsed May's painted vases,—that was one thorn; then the all-conquering Tudor had danced four times with Amy, at a late party, and only once with May,—that was thorn number two; but the chief grievance that rankled in her soul, and gave her an excuse for her unfriendly conduct, was a rumor which some obliging gossip had whispered to her, that the March girls had made fun of her at the Lambs'. All the blame of this should have fallen upon Jo, for her naughty imitation had been too lifelike to escape detection, and the frolicsome Lambs had permitted the joke to escape. No hint of this had reached the culprits, however, and Amy's dismay can be imagined, when, the very evening before the fair, as she was putting the last touches to her pretty table, Mrs. Chester, who, of course, resented the supposed ridicule of her daughter, said, in a bland tone, but with a cold look,—

"I find, dear, that there is some feeling among the young ladies about my giving this table to anyone but my girls. As this is the most prominent, and some say the most attractive table of all, and they are the chief getters-up of the fair, it is thought best for them to take this place. I'm sorry, but I know you are too sincerely interested in the cause to mind a little personal disappointment, and you shall have another table if you like."

Mrs. Chester had fancied beforehand that it would be easy to deliver this little speech; but when the time came, she found it rather difficult to utter it naturally, with Amy's unsuspicious eyes looking straight at her, full of surprise and trouble.

Amy felt that there was something behind this, but could not guess what, and said quietly, feeling hurt, and showing that she did,—

"Perhaps you had rather I took no table at all?"

"Now, my dear, don't have any ill feeling, I beg; it's merely a matter of expediency, you see; my girls will naturally take the lead, and this table is considered their proper place. *I* think it very appropriate to you, and feel very grateful for your efforts to make it so pretty; but we must give up our private wishes, of course, and I will see that you have a good place elsewhere. Wouldn't you like the flower-table? The little girls undertook it, but they are discouraged. You could make a charming thing of it, and the flower-table is always attractive, you know."

"Especially to gentlemen," added May, with a look which enlightened Amy as to one cause of her sudden fall from favor. She colored angrily, but took no other notice of that girlish sarcasm, and answered, with unexpected amiability,—

"It shall be as you please, Mrs. Chester. I'll give up my place here at once, and attend to the flowers, if you like."

"You can put your own things on your own table, if you prefer," began May, feeling a little conscience-stricken, as she looked at the pretty racks, the painted shells, and quaint illuminations Amy had so carefully made and so gracefully arranged. She meant it kindly, but Amy mistook her meaning, and said quickly,—

"Oh, certainly, if they are in your way;" and sweeping her contributions into her apron, pell-mell, she walked off, feeling that herself and her works of art had been insulted past forgiveness.

"Now she's mad. Oh, dear, I wish I hadn't asked you to speak, mamma," said May, looking disconsolately at the empty spaces on her table.

"Girls' quarrels are soon over," returned her mother, feeling a trifle ashamed of her own part in this one, as well she might.

The little girls hailed Amy and her treasures with delight, which cordial reception somewhat soothed her perturbed spirit, and she fell to work, determined to succeed florally, if she could not artistically. But everything seemed against her: it was late, and she was tired; everyone was too busy with their own affairs to help her; and the little girls were only hindrances, for the dears fussed and chattered like so many magpies, making a great deal of confusion in their artless efforts to preserve the most perfect order. The evergreen arch wouldn't stay firm after she got it up, but wiggled and threatened to tumble down on her head when the hanging baskets were filled; her best tile got a splash of water, which left a sepia tear on the Cupid's cheek; she bruised her hands with hammering, and got cold working in a draught, which last affliction filled her with apprehensions for the morrow. Any girl-reader who has suffered like afflictions will sympathize with poor Amy, and wish her well through with her task.

There was great indignation at home when she told her story that evening. Her mother said it was a shame, but told her she had done right; Beth declared she wouldn't go to the fair at all; and Jo demanded why she didn't take all her pretty things and leave those mean people to get on without her.

"Because they are mean is no reason why I should be. I hate such things, and though I think I've a right to be hurt, I don't intend to show it. They will feel that more than angry speeches or huffy actions, won't they, Marmee?"

"That's the right spirit, my dear; a kiss for a blow is always best, though it's not very easy to give it sometimes," said her mother, with the air of one who had learned the difference between preaching and practicing.

In spite of various very natural temptations to resent and retaliate, Amy adhered to her resolution all the next day, bent on conquering her enemy by kindness. She began well, thanks to a silent reminder that came to her unexpectedly, but most opportunely. As she arranged her table that morning, while the little girls were in an ante-room filling the baskets, she took up her pet production,—a little book, the antique cover of which her father had found among his treasures, and in which, on leaves of vellum, she had beautifully illuminated different texts. As she turned the pages, rich in dainty devices, with very pardonable pride, her eye fell upon one verse that made her stop and think. Framed in a brilliant scroll-work of scarlet, blue, and gold, with little spirits of good-will helping one another up and down among the thorns and flowers, were the words, "Thou shalt love thy neighbor as thyself."

"I ought, but I don't," thought Amy, as her eye went from the bright page to May's discontented face behind the big vases, that could not hide the vacancies her pretty work had once filled. Amy stood a minute, turning the leaves in her hand, reading on each some sweet rebuke for all heart-burnings and uncharitableness of spirit. Many wise and true sermons are preached us every day by unconscious ministers in street, school, office, or home; even a fair-table may become a pulpit, if it can offer the good and helpful words which are never out of season. Amy's conscience preached her a little sermon from that text, then and there; and she did what many of us do not always do,—took the sermon to heart, and straightway put it in practice.

A group of girls were standing about May's table, admiring the pretty things, and talking over the change of saleswomen. They dropped their voices, but Amy knew they were speaking of her, hearing one side of the story, and judging accordingly. It was not pleasant, but a better spirit had come over her, and presently a chance offered for proving it. She heard May say sorrowfully,—

"It's too bad, for there is no time to make other things, and I don't want to fill up with odds and ends. The table was just complete then: now it's spoilt."

"I dare say she'd put them back if you asked her," suggested someone.

"How could I after all the fuss?" began May, but she did not finish, for Amy's voice came across the hall, saying pleasantly,—

"You may have them, and welcome, without asking, if you want them. I was just thinking I'd offer to put them back, for they belong to your table rather than mine. Here they are; please take them, and forgive me if I was hasty in carrying them away last night."

As she spoke, Amy returned her contribution, with a nod and a smile, and hurried away again, feeling that it was easier to do a friendly thing than it was to stay and be thanked for it.

"Now, I call that lovely of her, don't you?" cried one girl.

May's answer was inaudible; but another young lady, whose temper was evidently a little soured by making lemonade, added, with a disagreeable laugh, "Very lovely; for she knew she wouldn't sell them at her own table."

Now, that was hard; when we make little sacrifices we like to have them appreciated, at least; and for a minute Amy was sorry she had done it, feeling that virtue was not always its own reward. But it is,—as she presently discovered; for her spirits began to rise, and her table to blossom under her skilful hands; the girls were very kind, and that one little act seemed to have cleared the atmosphere amazingly.

It was a very long day, and a hard one to Amy, as she sat behind her table, often quite alone, for the little girls deserted very soon: few cared to buy flowers in summer, and her bouquets began to droop long before night.

The art-table *was* the most attractive in the room; there was a crowd about it all day long, and the tenders were constantly flying to and fro with important faces and rattling money-boxes. Amy often looked wistfully across, longing to be there, where she felt at home and happy, instead of in a corner with nothing to do. It might seem no hardship to some of us; but to a pretty, blithe young girl, it was not only tedious, but very trying; and the thought of being found there in the evening by her family, and Laurie and his friends, made it a real martyrdom.

She did not go home till night, and then she looked so pale and quiet that they knew the day had been a hard one, though she made no complaint, and did not even tell what she had done. Her mother gave her an extra cordial cup of tea, Beth helped her dress, and made a charming little wreath for her hair, while Jo astonished her family by getting herself up with unusual care, and hinting darkly that the tables were about to be turned.

"Don't do anything rude, pray, Jo. I won't have any fuss made, so let it all pass, and behave yourself," begged Amy, as she departed early, hoping to find a reinforcement of flowers to refresh her poor little table.

"I merely intend to make myself entrancingly agreeable to everyone I know, and to keep them in your corner as long as possible. Teddy and his boys will lend a hand, and we'll have a good time yet," returned Jo, leaning over the gate to watch for Laurie. Presently the familiar tramp was heard in the dusk, and she ran out to meet him.

"Is that my boy?"

"As sure as this is my girl!" and Laurie tucked her hand under his arm, with the air of a man whose every wish was gratified.

"O Teddy, such doings!" and Jo told Amy's wrongs with sisterly zeal.

"A flock of our fellows are going to drive over by and by, and I'll be hanged if I don't make them buy every flower she's got, and camp down before her table afterward," said Laurie, espousing her cause with warmth.

"The flowers are not at all nice, Amy says, and the fresh ones may not arrive in time. I don't wish to be unjust or suspicious, but I shouldn't wonder if they never came at all. When people do one mean thing they are very likely to do another," observed Jo, in a disgusted tone.

"Didn't Hayes give you the best out of our gardens? I told him to."

"I didn't know that; he forgot, I suppose; and, as your grandpa was poorly, I didn't like to worry him by asking, though I did want some."

"Now, Jo, how could you think there was any need of asking! They are just as much yours as mine. Don't we always go halves in everything?" began Laurie, in the tone that always made Jo turn thorny.

"Gracious, I hope not! Half of some of your things wouldn't suit me at all. But we mustn't stand philandering here; I've got to help Amy, so you go and make yourself splendid; and if you'll be so very kind as to let Hayes take a few nice flowers up to the Hall, I'll bless you forever."

"Couldn't you do it now?" asked Laurie, so suggestively that Jo shut the gate in his face with inhospitable haste, and called through the bars, "Go away, Teddy; I'm busy."

Thanks to the conspirators, the tables *were* turned that night; for Hayes sent up a wilderness of flowers, with a lovely basket, arranged in his best manner, for a centrepiece; then the March family turned out *en masse*, and Jo exerted herself to some purpose, for people not only came but stayed, laughing at her nonsense, admiring Amy's taste, and apparently enjoying themselves very much. Laurie and his friends gallantly threw themselves into the breach, bought up the bouquets, encamped before the table, and made that corner the liveliest spot in the room. Amy was in her element now, and, out of gratitude, if nothing more, was as sprightly and gracious as possible,—coming to the conclusion, about that time, that virtue *was* its own reward, after all.

Jo behaved herself with exemplary propriety; and when Amy was happily surrounded by her guard of honor, Jo circulated about the hall, picking up various bits of gossip, which enlightened her upon the subject of the Chester change of base. She reproached herself for her share of the ill-feeling, and resolved to exonerate Amy as soon as possible; she also discovered what Amy had done about the things in the morning, and considered her a model of magnanimity. As she passed the art-table, she glanced over it for her sister's things, but saw no signs of them. "Tucked away out of sight, I dare say," thought Jo, who could forgive her own wrongs, but hotly resented any insult offered to her family.

"Good evening, Miss Jo. How does Amy get on?" asked May, with a conciliatory air, for she wanted to show that she also could be generous.

"She has sold everything she had that was worth selling, and now she is enjoying herself. The flower-table is always attractive, you know, 'especially to gentlemen.' "

Jo *couldn't* resist giving that little slap, but May took it so meekly she regretted it a minute after, and fell to praising the great vases, which still remained unsold.

"Is Amy's illumination anywhere about? I took a fancy to buy that for father," said Jo, very anxious to learn the fate of her sister's work.

"Everything of Amy's sold long ago; I took care that the right people saw them, and they made a nice little sum of money for us," returned May, who had overcome sundry small temptations, as well as Amy, that day.

Much gratified, Jo rushed back to tell the good news; and Amy looked both touched and surprised by the report of May's words and manner.

"Now, gentlemen, I want you to go and do your duty by the other tables as generously as you have by mine—especially the art-table," she said, ordering out "Teddy's Own," as the girls called the college friends.

" ' Charge, Chester, charge!' is the motto for that table; but do your duty like men, and you'll get your money's worth of *art* in every sense of the word," said the irrepressible Jo, as the devoted phalanx prepared to take the field.

"To hear is to obey, but March is fairer far than May," said little Parker, making a frantic effort to be both witty and tender, and getting promptly quenched by Laurie, who said, "Very well, my son, for a small boy!" and walked him off, with a paternal pat on the head.

"Buy the vases," whispered Amy to Laurie, as a final heaping of coals of fire on her enemy's head.

To May's great delight, Mr. Laurence not only bought the vases, but pervaded the hall with one under each arm. The other gentlemen speculated with equal rashness in all sorts of frail trifles, and wandered helplessly about afterward burdened with wax flowers, painted fans, filigree portfolios, and other useful and appropriate purchases.

Aunt Carrol was there, heard the story, looked pleased, and said something to Mrs. March in a corner, which made the latter lady beam with satisfaction, and watch Amy with a face full of mingled pride and anxiety, though she did not betray the cause of her pleasure till several days later.

The fair was pronounced a success; and when May bade Amy good night, she did not "gush" as usual, but gave her an affectionate kiss, and a look which said, "Forgive and forget." That satisfied Amy; and when she got home she found the vases paraded on the parlor chimney-piece, with a great bouquet in each. "The reward of merit for a magnanimous March," as Laurie announced with a flourish.

"You've a deal more principle and generosity and nobleness of character than I ever gave you credit for, Amy. You've behaved sweetly, and I respect you with all my heart," said Jo warmly, as they brushed their hair together late that night.

"Yes, we all do, and love her for being so ready to forgive. It must have been dreadfully hard, after working so long, and setting your heart on selling your own pretty things. I don't believe I could have done it as kindly as you did," added Beth from her pillow.

"Why, girls, you needn't praise me so; I only did as I'd be done by. You laugh at me when I say I want to be a lady, but I mean a true gentlewoman in mind and manners, and I try to do it as far as I know how. I can't explain exactly, but I want to be above the little meannesses and follies and faults that spoil so many women. I'm far from it now, but I do my best, and hope in time to be what mother is."

Amy spoke earnestly, and Jo said, with a cordial hug,—

"I understand now what you mean, and I'll never laugh at you again. You are getting on faster than you think, and I'll take lessons of you in true politeness, for you've learned the secret, I believe. Try away, deary; you'll get your reward some day, and no one will be more delighted than I shall."

A week later Amy did get her reward, and poor Jo found it hard to be delighted. A letter came from Aunt Carrol, and Mrs. March's face was illuminated to such a degree, when she read it, that Jo and Beth, who were with her, demanded what the glad tidings were.

"Aunt Carrol is going abroad next month, and wants—"

"Me to go with her!" burst in Jo, flying out of her chair in an uncontrollable rapture.

"No, dear, not you; it's Amy."

"0 mother! She's too young; it's my turn first. I've wanted it so long— it would do me so much good, and be so altogether splendid—I *must* go."

"I'm afraid it's impossible, Jo. Aunt says Amy, decidedly, and it is not for us to dictate when she offers such a favor."

"It's always so. Amy has all the fun and I have all the work. It isn't fair, oh, it isn't fair!" cried Jo passionately.

"I'm afraid it is partly your own fault, dear. When Aunt spoke to me the other day, she regretted your blunt manners and too independent spirit; and here she writes, as if quoting something you had said,—'I planned at first to ask Jo; but as "favors burden her," and she "hates French," I think I won't venture to invite her. Amy is more docile, will make a good companion for Flo, and receive gratefully any help the trip may give her.' "

"Oh, my tongue, my abominable tongue! Why can't I learn to keep it quiet?" groaned Jo, remembering words which had been her undoing. When she had heard the explanation of the quoted phrases, Mrs. March said sorrowfully,—

"I wish you could have gone, but there is no hope of it this time; so try to bear it cheerfully, and don't sadden Amy's pleasure by reproaches or regrets."

"I'll try," said Jo, winking hard, as she knelt down to pick up the basket she had joyfully upset. "I'll take a leaf out of her book, and try not only to seem glad, but to be so, and not grudge her one minute of happiness; but it won't be easy, for it is a dreadful disappointment;" and poor Jo bedewed the little fat pincushion she held with several very bitter tears.

"Jo, dear, I'm very selfish, but I couldn't spare you, and I'm glad you are not going quite yet," whispered Beth, embracing her, basket and all, with such a clinging touch and loving face, that Jo felt comforted in spite of the sharp regret that made her want to box her own ears, and humbly beg Aunt Carrol to burden her with this favor, and see how gratefully she would bear it.

By the time Amy came in, Jo was able to take her part in the family jubilation; not quite as heartily as usual, perhaps, but without repinings at Amy's good fortune. The young lady herself received the news as tidings of great joy, went about in a solemn sort of rapture, and began to sort her colors and pack her pencils that evening, leaving such trifles as clothes, money, and passports to those less absorbed in visions of art than herself.

"It isn't a mere pleasure trip to me, girls," she said impressively, as she scraped her best palette. "It will decide my career; for if I have any genius, I shall find it out in Rome, and will do something to prove it."

"Suppose you haven't?" said Jo, sewing away, with red eyes, at the new collars which were to be handed over to Amy.

"Then I shall come home and teach drawing for my living," replied the aspirant for fame, with philosophic composure; but she made a wry face at the prospect, and scratched away at her palette as if bent on vigorous measures before she gave up her hopes.

"No, you won't; you hate hard work, and you'll marry some rich man, and come home to sit in the lap of luxury all your days," said Jo.

"Your predictions sometimes come to pass, but I don't believe that one will. I'm sure I wish it would, for if I can't be an artist myself, I should like to be able to help those who are," said Amy, smiling, as if the part of Lady Bountiful would suit her better than that of a poor drawing-teacher.

"Hum!" said Jo, with a sigh; "if you wish it you'll have it, for your wishes are always granted—mine never."

"Would you like to go?" asked Amy, thoughtfully patting her nose with her knife.

"Rather!"

"Well, in a year or two I'll send for you, and we'll dig in the Forum for relics, and carry out all the plans we've made so many times."

"Thank you; I'll remind you of your promise when that joyful day comes, if it ever does," returned Jo, accepting the vague but magnificent offer as gratefully as she could.

There was not much time for preparation, and the house was in a ferment till Amy was off. Jo bore up very well till the last flutter of blue ribbon vanished, when she retired to her refuge, the garret, and cried till she couldn't cry any more. Amy likewise bore up stoutly till the steamer sailed; then, just as the gangway was about to be withdrawn, it suddenly came over her that a whole ocean was soon to roll between her and those who loved her best, and she clung to Laurie, the last lingerer, saying with a sob,—

"Oh, take care of them for me; and if anything should happen—"

"I will, dear, I will; and if anything happens, I'll come and comfort you," whispered Laurie, little dreaming that he would be called upon to keep his word.

So Amy sailed away to find the old world, which is always new and beautiful to young eyes, while her father and friend watched her from the shore, fervently hoping that none but gentle fortunes would befall the happy-hearted girl, who waved her hand to them till they could see nothing but the summer sunshine dazzling on the sea.

# CHAPTER XXXI

## OUR FOREIGN CORRESPONDENT

"LONDON.

"DEAREST PEOPLE,—

"Here I really sit at a front window of the Bath Hotel, Piccadilly. It's not a fashionable place, but uncle stopped here years ago, and won't go anywhere else; however, we don't mean to stay long, so it's no great matter. Oh, I can't begin to tell you how I enjoy it all! I never can, so I'll only give you bits out of my note-book, for I've done nothing but sketch and scribble since I started.

"I sent a line from Halifax, when I felt pretty miserable, but after that I got on delightfully, seldom ill, on deck all day, with plenty of pleasant people to amuse me. Everyone was very kind to me, especially the officers. Don't laugh, Jo; gentlemen really are very necessary aboard ship, to hold on to, or to wait upon one; and as they have nothing to do, it's a mercy to make them useful, otherwise they would smoke themselves to death, I'm afraid.

"Aunt and Flo were poorly all the way, and liked to be let alone, so when I had done what I could for them, I went and enjoyed myself. Such walks on deck, such sunsets, such splendid air and waves! It was almost as exciting as riding a fast horse, when we went rushing on so grandly. I wish Beth could have come, it would have done her so much good; as for Jo, she would have gone up and sat on the main-top jib, or whatever the high thing is called, made friends with the engineers, and tooted on the captain's speaking-trumpet, she'd have been in such a state of rapture.

"It was all heavenly, but I was glad to see the Irish coast and found it very lovely, so green and sunny, with brown cabins here and there, ruins on some of the hills, and gentlemen's country-seats in the valleys, with deer feeding in the parks. It was early in the morning, but I didn't regret getting up to see it, for the bay was full of little boats, the shore *so* picturesque, and a rosy sky overhead. I never shall forget it.

"At Queenstown one of my new acquaintances left us,—Mr. Lennox,—and when I said something about the Lakes of Killarney, he sighed and sung, with a look at me,—

> 'Oh, have you e'er heard of Kate Kearney?
> She lives on the banks of Killarney;
> From the glance of her eye,
> Shun danger and fly,
> For fatal's the glance of Kate Kearney.'

Wasn't that nonsensical?

"We only stopped at Liverpool a few hours. It's a dirty, noisy place, and I was glad to leave it. Uncle rushed out and bought a pair of dog-skin gloves, some ugly, thick shoes, and an umbrella, and got shaved *à la* mutton-chop, the first thing. Then he flattered himself that he looked like a true Briton; but the first time he had the mud cleaned off his shoes, the little bootblack knew that an American stood in them, and said, with a grin, 'There yer har, sir. I've give 'em the latest Yankee shine.' It amused uncle immensely. Oh, I *must* tell you what that absurd Lennox did! He got his friend Ward, who came on with us, to order a bouquet for me, and the first thing I saw in my room was a lovely one, with 'Robert Lennox's compliments,' on the card. Wasn't that fun, girls? I like travelling.

"I never *shall* get to London if I don't hurry. The trip was like riding through a long picture-gallery, full of lovely landscapes. The

"Every one was very kind, especially the officers."

farmhouses were my delight; with thatched roofs, ivy up to the eaves, latticed windows, and stout women with rosy children at the doors. The very cattle looked more tranquil than ours, as they stood knee-deep in clover, and the hens had a contented cluck, as if they never got nervous, like Yankee biddies. Such perfect color I never saw,—the grass so green, sky so blue, grain so yellow, woods so dark,—I was in a rapture all the way. So was Flo; and we kept bouncing from one side to the other, trying to see everything while we were whisking along at the rate of sixty miles an hour. Aunt was tired and went to sleep, but uncle read his guide-book, and wouldn't be astonished at anything. This is the way we went on: Amy, flying up,—'Oh, that must be Kenilworth, that gray place among the trees!' Flo, darting to my window,—'How sweet! We must go there some time, won't we, papa?' Uncle, calmly admiring his boots,—'No, my dear, not unless you want beer; that's a brewery.'

"A pause,—then Flo cried out,'Bless me, there's a gallows and a man going up.' 'Where, where?' shrieks Amy, staring out at two tall posts with a cross-beam and some dangling chains. 'A colliery,' remarks uncle, with a twinkle of the eye. 'Here's a lovely flock of lambs all lying down,' says Amy. 'See, papa, aren't they pretty!' added Flo sentimentally. 'Geese, young ladies,' returns uncle, in a tone that keeps us quiet till Flo settles down to enjoy 'The Flirtations of Capt. Cavendish,' and I have the scenery all to myself.

"Of course it rained when we got to London, and there was nothing to be seen but fog and umbrellas. We rested, unpacked, and shopped a little between the showers. Aunt Mary got me some new things, for I came off in such a hurry I wasn't half ready. A white hat and blue feather, a muslin dress to match, and the loveliest mantle you ever saw. Shopping in Regent Street is perfectly splendid; things seem so cheap—nice ribbons only sixpence a yard. I laid in a stock, but shall get my gloves in Paris. Doesn't that sound sort of elegant and rich?

"Flo and I, for the fun of it, ordered a hansom cab, while aunt and uncle were out, and went for a drive, though we learned afterward that it wasn't the thing for young ladies to ride in them alone. It was so droll! For when we were shut in by the wooden apron, the man drove so fast that Flo was frightened, and told me to stop him. But he was up outside behind somewhere, and I couldn't get at him. He didn't hear me call, nor see me flap my parasol in front, and there we were, quite helpless, rattling away, and whirling around corners at a break-neck pace. At last, in my despair, I saw a little door in the roof, and on poking it open, a red eye appeared, and a beery voice said,—

" 'Now then, mum?'

"I gave my order as soberly as I could, and slamming down the door, with an 'Aye, aye, mum,' the man made his horse walk, as if going to a funeral. I poked again, and said, 'A little faster;' then off he went, helter-skelter, as before, and we resigned ourselves to our fate.

"Today was fair, and we went to Hyde Park, close by, for we are more aristocratic than we look. The Duke of Devonshire lives near. I often see his footmen lounging at the back gate; and the Duke of Wellington's house is not far off. Such sights as I saw, my dear! It was as good as Punch, for there were fat dowagers rolling about in their red and yellow coaches, with gorgeous Jeameses in silk stockings and velvet coats, up behind, and powdered coachmen in front. Smart maids, with the rosiest children I ever saw; handsome girls, looking half asleep; dandies, in queer English hats and lavender kids, lounging about, and tall soldiers, in short red jackets and muffin caps stuck on one side, looking so funny I longed to sketch them.

"Rotten Row means '*Route de Roi*,' or the king's way; but now it's more like a riding-school than anything else. The horses are splendid, and the men, especially the grooms, ride well; but the women are stiff, and bounce, which isn't according to our rules. I longed to show them a tearing American gallop, for they trotted solemnly up and down, in their scant habits and high hats, looking like the women in a toy Noah's Ark. Everyone rides,—old men, stout ladies, little children,—and the young folks do a deal of flirting here; I saw a pair exchange rosebuds, for it's the thing to wear one in the button-hole, and I thought it rather a nice little idea.

"In the P.M. to Westminster Abbey; but don't expect me to describe it, that's impossible—so I'll only say it was sublime! This evening we are going to see Fechter, which will be an appropriate end to the happiest day of my life.

"MIDNIGHT.

"It's very late, but I can't let my letter go in the morning without telling you what happened last evening. Who do you think came in, as we were at tea? Laurie's English friends, Fred and Frank Vaughn! I was *so* surprised, for I shouldn't have known them but for the cards. Both are tall fellows, with whiskers; Fred handsome in the English style, and Frank much better, for he only limps slightly, and uses no crutches. They had heard from Laurie where we were to be, and came to ask us to their house; but uncle won't go, so we shall return the call, and see them as we can. They went to the theatre with us, and we did have *such* a good time, for Frank devoted himself to Flo, and Fred and I talked over past, present, and future fun as if we had known each other all our days. Tell Beth Frank asked for her, and was sorry to hear of her ill health. Fred laughed when I spoke of Jo, and sent his 'respectful compliments to the big hat.' Neither of them had forgotten Camp Laurence, or the fun we had there. What ages ago it seems, doesn't it?

"Aunt is tapping on the wall for the third time, so I *must* stop. I really feel like a dissipated London fine lady, writing here so late, with my room full of pretty things, and my head a jumble of parks, theatres, new gowns, and gallant creatures who say 'Ah!' and twirl their blond mustaches with the true English lordliness. I long to see you all, and in spite of my nonsense am, as ever, your loving

AMY."

"PARIS.

"DEAR GIRLS,—

"In my last I told you about our London visit,—how kind the Vaughns were, and what pleasant parties they made for us. I enjoyed the trips to Hampton Court and the Kensington Museum more than anything else,—for at Hampton I saw Raphael's cartoons, and, at the Museum, rooms full of pictures by Turner, Lawrence, Reynolds, Hogarth, and the other great creatures. The day in Richmond Park was charming, for we had a regular English picnic, and I had more splendid oaks and groups of deer than I could copy; also heard a nightingale, and saw larks go up. We 'did' London to our hearts' content, thanks to Fred and Frank, and were sorry to go away; for, though English people are slow to take you in, when they once make up their minds to do it they cannot be outdone in hospitality, *I* think. The Vaughns hope to meet us in Rome next winter, and I shall be dreadfully disappointed if they don't, for Grace and I are great friends, and the boys very nice fellows,—especially Fred.

"Well, we were hardly settled here, when he turned up again, saying he had come for a holiday, and was going to Switzerland. Aunt looked sober at first, but he was so cool about it she couldn't say a word; and now we get on nicely, and are very glad he came, for he speaks French like a native, and I don't know what we should do without him. Uncle doesn't know ten words, and insists on talking English very loud, as if that would make people understand him. Aunt's pronunciation is old-fashioned, and Flo and I, though we flattered ourselves that we knew a good deal, find we don't, and are very grateful to have Fred do the *'parley vooing,'* as uncle calls it.

"Such delightful times as we are having! Sight-seeing from morning till night, stopping for nice lunches in the gay *cafés*, and meeting with all sorts of droll adventures. Rainy days I spend in the Louvre, revelling in pictures. Jo would turn up her naughty nose at some of the finest, because she has no soul for art; but *I* have, and I'm cultivating eye and taste as fast as I can. She would like the relics of great people better, for I've seen her Napoleon's cocked hat and gray coat, his baby's cradle and his old toothbrush; also Marie Antoinette's little shoe, the ring of Saint Denis, Charlemagne's sword, and many other interesting things. I'll talk for hours about them when I come, but haven't time to write.

"The Palais Royale is a heavenly place,—so full of *bijouterie* and lovely things that I'm nearly distracted because I can't buy them. Fred wanted to get me some, but of course I didn't allow it. Then the Bois and the Champs Elysées are *très magnifique*. I've seen the imperial family several times,—the emperor an ugly, hard-looking man, the empress pale and pretty, but dressed in bad taste, *I* thought,— purple dress, green hat, and yellow gloves. Little Nap. is a handsome boy, who sits chatting to his tutor, and kisses his hand to the people as he passes in his four-horse barouche, with postilions in red satin jackets, and a mounted guard before and behind.

"We often walk in the Tuileries Gardens, for they are lovely, though the antique Luxembourg Gardens suit me better. Père la Chaise is very curious, for many of the tombs are like small rooms, and, looking in, one sees a table with images or pictures of the dead, and chairs for the mourners to sit in when they come to lament. That is so Frenchy.

"Our rooms are on the Rue de Rivoli, and, sitting in the balcony, we look up and down the long, brilliant street. It is so pleasant that we spend our evenings talking there, when too tired with our day's work to go out. Fred is very entertaining, and is altogether the most agreeable young man I ever knew,—except Laurie, whose manners are more charming. I wish Fred was dark, for I don't fancy light men; however, the Vaughns are very rich, and come of an excellent family, so I won't find fault with their yellow hair, as my own is yellower.

"Next week we are off to Germany and Switzerland; and, as we shall travel fast, I shall only be able to give you hasty letters. I keep my diary, and try to 'remember correctly and describe clearly all that I see and admire,' as father advised. It is good practice for me, and, with my sketch-book, will give you a better idea of my tour than these scribbles.

"Adieu; I embrace you tenderly.

"Votre Amie."


"Heidelberg.

"My dear Mamma,—

"Having a quiet hour before we leave for Berne, I'll try to tell you what has happened, for some of it is very important, as you will see.

"The sail up the Rhine was perfect, and I just sat and enjoyed it with all my might. Get father's old guide-books, and read about it; I haven't words beautiful enough to describe it. At Coblentz we had a lovely time, for some students from Bonn, with whom Fred got acquainted on the boat, gave us a serenade. It was a moonlight night, and, about one o'clock, Flo and I were waked by the most delicious music under our windows. We flew up, and hid behind the curtains; but sly peeps showed us Fred and the students singing away down below. It was the most romantic thing I ever saw,—the river, the bridge of boats, the great fortress opposite, moonlight everywhere, and music fit to melt a heart of stone.

"When they were done we threw down some flowers, and saw them scramble for them, kiss their hands to the invisible ladies, and go laughing away,—to smoke and drink beer, I suppose. Next morning Fred showed me one of the crumpled flowers in his vest-pocket, and looked very sentimental. I laughed at him, and said I didn't throw it, but Flo, which seemed to disgust him, for he tossed it out of the window, and turned sensible again. I'm afraid I'm going to have trouble with that boy, it begins to look like it.

"The baths at Nassau were very gay, so was Baden-Baden, where Fred lost some money, and I scolded him. He needs someone to look after him when Frank is not with him. Kate said once she hoped he'd marry soon, and I quite agree with her that it would be well for him. Frankfort was delightful; I saw Goethe's house, Schiller's statue, and Dannecker's famous 'Ariadne.' It was very lovely, but I should have enjoyed it more if I had known the story better. I didn't like to ask, as everyone knew it or pretended they did. I wish Jo would tell me all about it; I ought to have read more, for I find I don't know anything, and it mortifies me.

"Now comes the serious part,—for it happened here, and Fred is just gone. He has been so kind and jolly that we all got quite fond of him; I never thought of anything but a travelling friendship, till the serenade night. Since then I've begun to feel that the moonlight walks, balcony talks, and daily adventures were something more to him than fun. I haven't flirted, mother, truly, but remembered what you said to me, and have done my very best. I can't help it if people like me; I don't try to make them, and it worries me if I don't care for them, though Jo says I haven't got any heart. Now I know mother will shake her head, and the girls say, 'Oh, the mercenary little wretch!' but I've made up my mind, and, if Fred asks me, I shall accept him, though I'm not madly in love. I like him, and we get on comfortably together. He is handsome, young, clever enough, and very rich,—ever so much richer than the Laurences. I don't think his family would object, and I should be very happy, for they are all kind, well-bred, generous people, and they like me. Fred, as the eldest twin, will have the estate, I suppose, and such a splendid one as it is! A city house in a fashionable street, not so showy as our big houses, but twice as comfortable, and full of solid luxury, such as English people believe in. I like it, for it's genuine. I've seen the plate, the family jewels, the old servants, and pictures of the country place, with its park, great house, lovely grounds, and fine horses. Oh, it would be all I should ask! And I'd rather have it than any title such as girls snap up so readily, and find nothing behind. I may be mercenary, but I hate poverty, and don't mean to bear it a minute longer than I can help. One of us *must* marry well; Meg didn't, Jo won't, Beth can't yet, so I shall, and make everything cozy all round. I wouldn't marry a man I hated or despised. You may be sure of that; and, though Fred is not my model hero, he does very well, and, in time, I should get fond enough of him if he was very fond of me, and let me do just as I liked. So I've been turning the matter over in my mind the last week, for it was impossible to help seeing that Fred liked me. He said nothing, but little things showed it; he never goes with Flo, always gets on my side of the carriage, table, or promenade, looks sentimental when we are alone, and frowns at anyone else who ventures to speak to me. Yesterday, at dinner, when an Austrian officer stared at us, and then said something to his friend,— a rakish-looking baron,—about *'ein wonderschönes Blöndchen,'* Fred looked as fierce as a lion, and cut his meat so savagely, it nearly flew off his plate. He isn't one of the cool, stiff Englishmen, but is rather peppery, for he has Scotch blood in him, as one might guess from his bonnie blue eyes.

"Well, last evening we went up to the castle about sunset,—at least all of us but Fred, who was to meet us there, after going to the Post

Restante for letters. We had a charming time poking about the ruins, the vaults where the monster tun is, and the beautiful gardens made by the elector, long ago, for his English wife. I liked the great terrace best, for the view was divine; so, while the rest went to see the rooms inside, I sat there trying to sketch the gray stone lion's head on the wall, with scarlet woodbine sprays hanging round it. I felt as if I'd got into a romance, sitting there, watching the Neckar rolling through the valley, listening to the music of the Austrian band below, and waiting for my lover, like a real story-book girl. I had a feeling that something was going to happen, and I was ready for it. I didn't feel blushy or quakey, but quite cool, and only a little excited.

"By and by I heard Fred's voice, and then he came hurrying through the great arch to find me. He looked so troubled that I forgot all about myself, and asked what the matter was. He said he'd just got a letter begging him to come home, for Frank was very ill; so he was going at once, in the night train, and only had time to say good-by. I was very sorry for him, and disappointed for myself, but only for a minute, because he said, as he shook hands,—and said it in a way that I could not mistake,—'I shall soon come back; you won't forget me, Amy?'

"I didn't promise, but I looked at him, and he seemed satisfied, and there was no time for anything but messages and good-byes, for he was off in an hour, and we all miss him very much. I know he wanted to speak, but I think, from something he once hinted, that he had promised his father not to do anything of the sort yet awhile, for he is a rash boy, and the old gentleman dreads a foreign daughter-in-law. We shall soon meet in Rome; and then, if I don't change my mind, I'll say 'Yes, thank you,' when he says 'Will you, please?'

"Of course this is all *very private,* but I wished you to know what was going on. Don't be anxious about me; remember I am your 'prudent Amy,' and be sure I will do nothing rashly. Send me as much advice as you like; I'll use it if I can. I wish I could see you for a good talk, Marmee. Love and trust me.

"Ever your                               Amy."

# CHAPTER XXXII

### TENDER TROUBLES

"Jo, I'm anxious about Beth."

"Why, mother, she has seemed unusually well since the babies came."

"It's not her health that troubles me now; it's her spirits. I'm sure there is something on her mind, and I want you to discover what it is."

"What makes you think so, mother?"

"She sits alone a good deal, and doesn't talk to her father as much as she used. I found her crying over the babies the other day. When she sings, the songs are always sad ones, and now and then I see a look in her face that I don't understand. This isn't like Beth, and it worries me."

"Have you asked her about it?"

"I have tried once or twice; but she either evaded my questions, or looked so distressed that I stopped. I never force my children's confidence, and I seldom have to wait for it long."

Mrs. March glanced at Jo as she spoke, but the face opposite seemed quite unconscious of any secret disquietude but Beth's; and, after sewing thoughtfully for a minute, Jo said,—

"I think she is growing up, and so begins to dream dreams, and have hopes and fears and fidgets, without knowing why, or being able to explain them. Why, mother, Beth's eighteen, but we don't realize it, and treat her like a child, forgetting she's a woman."

"So she is. Dear heart, how fast you do grow up," retuned her mother, with a sigh and a smile.

"Can't be helped, Marmee, so you must resign yourself to all sorts of worries, and let your birds hop out of the nest, one by one. I promise never to hop very far, if that is any comfort to you."

"It is a great comfort, Jo; I always feel strong when you are at home, now Meg is gone. Beth is too feeble and Amy too young to depend upon; but when the tug comes, you are always ready."

"Why, you know I don't mind hard jobs much, and there must always be one scrub in a family. Amy is splendid in fine works, and I'm not; but I feel in my element when all the carpets are to be taken up, or half the family fall sick at once. Amy is distinguishing herself abroad; but if anything is amiss at home, I'm your man."

"I leave Beth to your hands, then, for she will open her tender little heart to her Jo sooner than to anyone else. Be very kind, and don't let her think anyone watches or talks about her. If she only would get quite strong and cheerful again, I shouldn't have a wish in the world."

"Happy woman! I've got heaps."

"My dear, what are they?"

"I'll settle Bethy's troubles, and then I'll tell you mine. They are not very wearing, so they'll keep;" and Jo stitched away, with a wise nod which set her mother's heart at rest about her, for the present at least.

While apparently absorbed in her own affairs, Jo watched Beth; and, after many conflicting conjectures, finally settled upon one which seemed to explain the change in her. A slight incident gave Jo the clue to the mystery, she thought, and lively fancy, loving heart did the rest. She was affecting to write busily one Saturday afternoon, when she and Beth were alone together; yet as she scribbled, she kept her eye on her sister, who seemed unusually quiet. Sitting at the window, Beth's work often dropped into her lap, and she leaned her head upon her hand, in a dejected attitude, while her eyes rested on the dull, autumnal landscape. Suddenly someone passed below, whistling like an operatic blackbird, and a voice called out,—

"All serene! Coming in tonight."

Beth started, leaned forward, smiled and nodded, watched the passer-by till his quick tramp died away, then said softly, as if to herself,—

"How strong and well and happy that dear boy looks."

She leaned her head upon her hand.

"Hum!" said Jo, still intent upon her sister's face; for the bright color faded as quickly as it came, the smile vanished, and presently a tear lay shining on the window-ledge. Beth whisked it off, and glanced apprehensively at Jo; but she was scratching away at a tremendous rate, apparently engrossed in "Olympia's Oath." The instant Beth turned, Jo began her watch again, saw Beth's hand go quietly to her eyes more than once, and, in her half-averted face, read a tender sorrow that made her own eyes fill. Fearing to betray herself, she slipped away, murmuring something about needing more paper.

"Mercy on me, Beth loves Laurie!" she said, sitting down in her own room, pale with the shock of the discovery which she believed she had just made. "I never dreamt of such a thing. What *will* mother say? I wonder if he—" there Jo stopped, and turned scarlet with a sudden thought. "If he shouldn't love back again, how dreadful it would be. He must; I'll make him!" And she shook her head threateningly at the picture of the mischievous-looking boy laughing at her from the wall. "Oh dear, we *are* growing up with a vengeance. Here's Meg married and a mamma, Amy flourishing away at Paris, and Beth in love. I'm the only one that has sense enough to keep out of mischief." Jo thought intently for a minute, with her eyes fixed on the picture; then she smoothed out her wrinkled forehead, and said, with a decided nod at the face opposite, "No, thank you, sir; you're very charming, but you've no more stability than a weathercock; so you needn't write touching notes, and smile in that insinuating way, for it won't do a bit of good, and I won't have it."

Then she sighed, and fell into a reverie, from which she did not wake till the early twilight sent her down to take new observations, which only confirmed her suspicion. Though Laurie flirted with Amy and joked with Jo, his manner to Beth had always been peculiarly kind and gentle, but so was everybody's; therefore, no one thought of imagining that he cared more for her than for the others. Indeed, a general impression had prevailed in the family, of late, that "our boy" was getting fonder than ever of Jo, who, however, wouldn't hear a word upon the subject, and scolded violently if anyone dared to suggest it. If they had known the various tender passages of the past year, or rather attempts at tender passages which had been nipped in the bud, they would have had the immense satisfaction of saying, "I told you so." But Jo hated "philandering," and wouldn't allow it, always having a joke or a smile ready at the least sign of impending danger.

When Laurie first went to college, he fell in love about once a month; but these small flames were as brief as ardent, did no damage, and much amused Jo, who took great interest in the alternations of hope, despair, and resignation, which were confided to her in their weekly conferences. But there came a time when Laurie ceased to worship at many shrines, hinted darkly at one all-absorbing passion, and indulged occasionally in Byronic fits of gloom. Then he avoided the tender subject altogether, wrote philosophical notes to Jo, turned studious, and gave out that he was going to "dig," intending to graduate in a blaze of glory. This suited the young lady better than twilight confidences, tender pressures of the hand, and eloquent glances of the eye; for with Jo, brain developed earlier than heart, and she preferred imaginary heroes to real ones, because, when tired of them, the former could be shut up in the tin-kitchen till called for, and the latter were less manageable.

Things were in this state when the grand discovery was made, and Jo watched Laurie that night as she had never done before. If she had not got the new idea into her head, she would have seen nothing unusual in the fact that Beth was very quiet, and Laurie very kind to her. But having given the rein to her lively fancy, it galloped away with her at a great pace; and common sense, being rather weakened by a long course of romance writing, did not come to the rescue. As usual, Beth lay on the sofa, and Laurie sat in a low chair close by, amusing her with all sorts of gossip; for she depended on her weekly "spin," and he never disappointed her. But that evening, Jo fancied that Beth's eyes rested on the lively, dark face beside her with peculiar pleasure, and that she listened with intense interest to an account of some exciting cricket-match, though the phrases, "caught off a tice," "stumped off his ground," and "the leg hit for three," were as intelligible to her as Sanscrit. She also fancied, having set her heart upon seeing it, that she saw a certain increase of gentleness in Laurie's manner, that he dropped his voice now and then, laughed less than usual, was a little absent-minded, and settled the afghan over Beth's feet with an assiduity that was really almost tender.

"Who knows? Stranger things have happened," thought Jo, as she fussed about the room. "She will make quite an angel of him, and he will make life delightfully easy and pleasant for the dear, if they only love each other. I don't see how he can help it; and I do believe he would if the rest of us were out of the way."

As everyone *was* out of the way but herself, Jo began to feel that she ought to dispose of herself with all speed. But where should she go? And burning to lay herself upon the shrine of sisterly devotion, she sat down to settle that point.

Now, the old sofa was a regular patriarch of a sofa,—long, broad, well-cushioned, and low; a trifle shabby, as well it might be, for the girls had slept and sprawled on it as babies, fished over the back, rode on the arms, and had menageries under it as children, and rested tired heads, dreamed dreams, and listened to tender talk on it as young women. They all loved it, for it was a family refuge, and one corner had always been Jo's favorite lounging-place. Among the many pillows that adorned the venerable couch was one, hard, round, covered with prickly horsehair, and furnished with a knobby button at each end; this repulsive pillow was her especial property, being used as a weapon of defence, a barricade, or a stern preventive of too much slumber.

Laurie knew this pillow well, and had cause to regard it with deep aversion, having been unmercifully pummelled with it in former days when romping was allowed, and now frequently debarred by it from taking the seat he most coveted, next to Jo in the sofa corner. If "the sausage" as they called it, stood on end, it was a sign that he might approach and repose; but if it lay flat across the sofa, woe to the man, woman, or child who dared disturb it! That evening Jo forgot to barricade her corner, and had not been in her seat five minutes, before a massive form appeared beside her, and, with both arms spread over the sofa-back, both long legs stretched out before him, Laurie exclaimed, with a sigh of satisfaction,—

"Now, *this* is filling at the price."

"No slang," snapped Jo, slamming down the pillow. But it was too late, there was no room for it; and, coasting on to the floor, it disappeared in a most mysterious manner.

"Come, Jo, don't be thorny. After studying himself to a skeleton all the week, a fellow deserves petting, and ought to get it."

"Beth will pet you; I'm busy."

"No, she's not to be bothered with me; but you like that sort of thing, unless you've suddenly lost your taste for it. Have you? Do you hate your boy, and want to fire pillows at him?"

Anything more wheedlesome than that touching appeal was seldom heard, but Jo quenched "her boy" by turning on him with the stern query,—

"How many bouquets have you sent Miss Randal this week?"

"Not one, upon my word. She's engaged. Now then."

"I'm glad of it; that's one of your foolish extravagances,—sending flowers and things to girls for whom you don't care two pins," continued Jo reprovingly.

"Sensible girls, for whom I do care whole papers of pins, won't let me send them 'flowers and things,' so what can I do? My feelings must have a *went*."

"Mother doesn't approve of flirting, even in fun; and you do flirt desperately, Teddy."

"I'd give anything if I could answer, 'So do you.' As I can't, I'll merely say that I don't see any harm in that pleasant little game, if all parties understand that it's only play."

"Well, it does look pleasant, but I can't learn how it's done. I've tried, because one feels awkward in company, not to do as everybody else is doing; but I don't seem to get on," said Jo, forgetting to play Mentor.

"Take lessons of Amy; she has a regular talent for it."

"Yes, she does it very prettily, and never seems to go too far. I suppose it's natural to some people to please without trying, and others to always say and do the wrong thing in the wrong place."

"I'm glad you can't flirt; it's really refreshing to see a sensible, straight-forward girl, who can be jolly and kind without making a fool of herself. Between ourselves, Jo, some of the girls I know really do go on at such a rate I'm ashamed of them. They don't mean any harm, I'm sure; but if they knew how we fellows talked about them afterward, they'd mend their ways, I fancy."

"They do the same; and, as their tongues are the sharpest, you fellows get the worst of it, for you are as silly as they, every bit. If you behaved properly, they would; but, knowing you like their nonsense, they keep it up, and then you blame them."

"Much you know about it, ma'am," said Laurie, in a superior tone. "We don't like romps and flirts, though we may act as if we did sometimes. The pretty, modest girls are never talked about, except respectfully, among gentlemen. Bless your innocent soul! If you could be in my place for a month you'd see things that would astonish you a trifle. Upon my word, when I see one of those harum-scarum girls, I always want to say with our friend Cock Robin,—

> " 'Out upon you, fie upon you,
> Bold-faced jig!' "

It was impossible to help laughing at the funny conflict between Laurie's chivalrous reluctance to speak ill of womankind, and his very natural dislike of the unfeminine folly of which fashionable society showed him many samples. Jo knew that "young Laurence" was regarded as a most eligible *parti* by worldly mammas, was much smiled upon by their daughters, and flattered enough by ladies of all ages to make a coxcomb of him; so she watched him rather jealously, fearing he would be spoilt, and rejoiced more than she confessed to find that he still believed in modest girls. Returning suddenly to her admonitory tone, she said, dropping her voice, "If you *must* have a 'went,' Teddy, go and devote yourself to one of the 'pretty, modest girls' whom you do respect, and not waste your time with the silly ones."

"You really advise it?" and Laurie looked at her with an odd mixture of anxiety and merriment in his face.

"Yes, I do; but you'd better wait till you are through college, on the whole, and be fitting yourself for the place meantime. You're not half good enough for—well, whoever the modest girl may be," and Jo looked a little queer likewise, for a name had almost escaped her.

"That I'm not!" acquiesced Laurie, with an expression of humility quite new to him, as he dropped his eyes, and absently wound Jo's apron-tassel round his finger.

"Mercy on us, this will never do," thought Jo; adding aloud, "Go and sing to me. I'm dying for some music, and always like yours."

"I'd rather stay here, thank you."

"Well, you can't; there isn't room. Go and make yourself useful, since you are too big to be ornamental. I thought you hated to be tied to a woman's apron-string?" retorted Jo, quoting certain rebellious words of his own.

"Ah, that depends on who wears the apron!" and Laurie gave an audacious tweak at the tassel.

"Are you going?" demanded Jo, diving for the pillow.

He fled at once, and the minute it was well "Up with the bonnets of bonnie Dundee," she slipped away, to return no more till the young gentleman had departed in high dudgeon.

Jo lay long awake that night, and was just dropping off when the sound of a stifled sob made her fly to Beth's bedside, with the anxious inquiry, "What is it, dear?"

"I thought you were asleep," sobbed Beth.

"Is it the old pain, my precious?"

"No; it's a new one; but I can bear it," and Beth tried to check her tears.

"Tell me all about it, and let me cure it as I often did the other."

"You can't; there is no cure." There Beth's voice gave way, and, clinging to her sister, she cried so despairingly that Jo was frightened.

"Where is it? Shall I call mother?"

Beth did not answer the first question; but in the dark one hand went involuntarily to her heart, as if the pain were there; with the other she held Jo fast, whispering eagerly, "No, no, don't call her, don't tell her. I shall be better soon. Lie down here and 'poor' my head. I'll be quiet, and go to sleep; indeed I will."

Jo obeyed; but as her hand went softly to and fro across Beth's hot forehead and wet eyelids, her heart was very full, and she longed to speak. But young as she was, Jo had learned that hearts, like flowers, cannot be rudely handled, but must open naturally; so, though she believed she knew the cause of Beth's new pain, she only said, in her tenderest tone, "Does anything trouble you, deary?"

"Yes, Jo," after a long pause.

"Wouldn't it comfort you to tell me what it is?"

"Not now, not yet."

"Then I won't ask; but remember, Bethy, that mother and Jo are always glad to hear and help you, if they can."

"I know it. I'll tell you by and by."

"Is the pain better now?"

"Oh, yes, much better; you are so comfortable, Jo!"

"Go to sleep, dear; I'll stay with you."

So cheek to cheek they fell asleep, and on the morrow Beth seemed quite herself again; for at eighteen, neither heads nor hearts ache long, and a loving word can medicine most ills.

But Jo had made up her mind, and, after pondering over a project for some days, she confided it to her mother.

"You asked me the other day what my wishes were. I'll tell you one of them, Marmee," she began, as they sat alone together. "I want to go away somewhere this winter for a change."

"Why, Jo?" and her mother looked up quickly, as if the words suggested a double meaning.

With her eyes on her work, Jo answered soberly, "I want something new; I feel restless, and anxious to be seeing, doing, and learning more than I am. I brood too much over my own small affairs, and need stirring up, so, as I can be spared this winter, I'd like to hop a little way, and try my wings."

"Where will you hop?"

"To New York. I had a bright idea yesterday, and this is it. You know Mrs. Kirke wrote to you for some respectable young person to teach her children and sew. It's rather hard to find just the thing, but I think I should suit if I tried."

"My dear, go out to service in that great boarding-house!" and Mrs. March looked surprised, but not displeased.

"It's not exactly going out to service; for Mrs. Kirke is your friend,— the kindest soul that ever lived,—and would make things pleasant for me, I know. Her family is separate from the rest, and no one knows me there. Don't care if they do; it's honest work, and I'm not ashamed of it."

"Up with the Bonnets of Bonnie Dundee."

"Nor I; but your writing?"

"All the better for the change. I shall see and hear new things, get new ideas, and, even if I haven't much time there, I shall bring home quantities of material for my rubbish."

"I have no doubt of it; but are these your only reasons for this sudden fancy?"

"No, mother."

"May I know the others?"

Jo looked up and Jo looked down, then said slowly, with sudden color in her cheeks, "It may be vain and wrong to say it, but—I'm afraid—Laurie is getting too fond of me."

"Then you don't care for him in the way it is evident he begins to care for you?" and Mrs. March looked anxious as she put the question.

"Mercy, no! I love the dear boy, as I always have, and am immensely proud of him; but as for anything more, it's out of the question."

"I'm glad of that, Jo."

"Why, please?"

"Because, dear, I don't think you suited to one another. As friends you are very happy, and your frequent quarrels soon blow over; but I fear you would both rebel if you were mated for life. You are too much alike and too fond of freedom, not to mention hot tempers and strong wills, to get on happily together, in a relation which needs infinite patience and forbearance, as well as love."

"That's just the feeling I had, though I couldn't express it. I'm glad you think he is only beginning to care for me. It would trouble me sadly to make him unhappy; for I couldn't fall in love with the dear old fellow merely out of gratitude, could I?"

"You are sure of his feeling for you?"

The color deepened in Jo's cheeks, as she answered, with the look of mingled pleasure, pride, and pain which young girls wear when speaking of first lovers,—

"I'm afraid it is so, mother; he hasn't said anything, but he looks a great deal. I think I had better go away before it comes to anything."

"I agree with you, and if it can be managed you shall go."

Jo looked relieved, and, after a pause, said, smiling, "How Mrs. Moffat would wonder at your want of management, if she knew; and how she will rejoice that Annie still may hope."

"Ah, Jo, mothers may differ in their management, but the hope is the same in all,—the desire to see their children happy. Meg is so, and I am content with her success. You I leave to enjoy your liberty till you tire of it; for only then will you find that there is something sweeter. Amy is my chief care now, but her good sense will help her. For Beth, I indulge no hopes except that she may be well. By the way, she seems brighter this last day or two. Have you spoken to her?"

"Yes; she owned she had a trouble, and promised to tell me by and by. I said no more, for I think I know it;" and Jo told her little story.

Mrs. March shook her head, and did not take so romantic a view of the case, but looked grave, and repeated her opinion that, for Laurie's sake, Jo should go away for a time.

"Let us say nothing about it to him till the plan is settled; then I'll run away before he can collect his wits and be tragical. Beth must think I'm going to please myself, as I am, for I can't talk about Laurie to her; but she can pet and comfort him after I'm gone, and so cure him of this romantic notion. He's been through so many little trials of the sort, he's used to it, and will soon get over his love-lornity."

Jo spoke hopefully, but could not rid herself of the foreboding fear that this "little trial" would be harder than the others, and that Laurie would not get over his "love-lornity" as easily as heretofore.

The plan was talked over in a family council, and agreed upon; for Mrs. Kirke gladly accepted Jo, and promised to make a pleasant home for her. The teaching would render her independent; and such leisure as she got might be made profitable by writing, while the new scenes and society would be both useful and agreeable. Jo liked the prospect and was eager to be gone, for the home-nest was growing too narrow for her restless nature and adventurous spirit. When all was settled, with fear and trembling she told Laurie; but to her surprise he took it very quietly. He had been graver than usual of late, but very pleasant; and, when jokingly accused of turning over a new leaf, he answered soberly, "So I am; and I mean this one shall stay turned."

Jo was very much relieved that one of his virtuous fits should come on just then, and made her preparations with a lightened heart,—for Beth seemed more cheerful,—and hoped she was doing the best for all.

"One thing I leave to your especial care," she said, the night before she left.

"You mean your papers?" asked Beth.

"No, my boy. Be very good to him, won't you?"

"Of course I will; but I can't fill your place, and he'll miss you sadly."

"It won't hurt him; so remember, I leave him in your charge, to plague, pet, and keep in order."

"I'll do my best, for your sake," promised Beth, wondering why Jo looked at her so queerly.

When Laurie said "Good-by," he whispered significantly, "It won't do a bit of good, Jo. My eye is on you; so mind what you do, or I'll come and bring you home."

# CHAPTER XXXIII

## JO'S JOURNAL

"NEW YORK, November.

"DEAR MARMEE AND BETH,—

"I'm going to write you a regular volume, for I've got heaps to tell, though I'm not a fine young lady traveling on the continent. When I lost sight of father's dear old face, I felt a trifle blue, and might have shed a briny drop or two, if an Irish lady with four small children, all crying more or less, hadn't diverted my mind; for I amused myself by dropping gingerbread nuts over the seat every time they opened their mouths to roar.

"Soon the sun came out, and taking it as a good omen, I cleared up likewise, and enjoyed my journey with all my heart.

"Mrs. Kirke welcomed me so kindly I felt at home at once, even in that big house full of strangers. She gave me a funny little sky-parlor—all she had; but there is a stove in it, and a nice table in a sunny window, so I can sit here and write whenever I like. A fine view and a church-tower opposite atone for the many stairs, and I took a fancy to my den on the spot. The nursery, where I am to teach and sew, is a pleasant room next Mrs. Kirke's private parlor, and the two little girls are pretty children,—rather spoilt, I fancy, but they took to me after telling them 'The Seven Bad Pigs;' and I've no doubt I shall make a model governess.

"I am to have my meals with the children, if I prefer it to the great table, and for the present I do, for I *am* bashful, though no one will believe it.

" 'Now, my dear, make yourself at home,' said Mrs. K. in her motherly way; 'I'm on the drive from morning to night, as you may suppose with such a family; but a great anxiety will be off my mind if I know the children are safe with you. My rooms are always open to you, and your own shall be as comfortable as I can make it. There are some pleasant people in the house if you feel sociable, and your evenings are always free. Come to me if anything goes wrong, and be as happy as you can. There's the tea-bell; I must run and change my cap;' and off she bustled, leaving me to settle myself in my new nest.

"As I went downstairs, soon after, I saw something I liked. The flights are very long in this tall house, and as I stood waiting at the head of the third one for a little servant-girl to lumber up, I saw a gentleman come along behind her, take the heavy hod of coal out of her hand, carry it all the way up, put it down at a door near by, and walk away, saying, with a kind nod and a foreign accent,—

" 'It goes better so. The little back is too young to haf such heaviness.'

"Wasn't it good of him? I like such things, for, as father says, trifles show character. When I mentioned it to Mrs. K., that evening, she laughed, and said,—

" 'That must have been Professor Bhaer; he's always doing things of that sort.'

"Mrs. K. told me he was from Berlin; very learned and good, but poor as a church-mouse, and gives lessons to support himself and two little orphan nephews whom he is educating here, according to the wishes of his sister, who married an American. Not a very romantic story, but it interested me; and I was glad to hear that Mrs. K. lends him her parlor for some of his scholars. There is a glass door between it and the nursery, and I mean to peep at him, and then I'll tell you how he looks. He's almost forty, so it's no harm, Marmee.

"After tea and a go-to-bed romp with the little girls, I attacked the big work-basket, and had a quiet evening chatting with my new friend. I shall keep a journal-letter, and send it once a week; so good-night, and more tomorrow."

*"Tuesday Eve.*

"Had a lively time in my seminary, this morning, for the children acted like Sancho; and at one time I really thought I should shake them all round. Some good angel inspired me to try gymnastics, and I kept it up till they were glad to sit down and keep still. After luncheon, the girl took them out for a walk, and I went to my needlework, like little Mabel, 'with a willing mind.' I was thanking my stars that I'd learned to make nice button-holes, when the parlor-door opened and shut, and someone began to hum,—

*'Kennst du das Land,'*

like a big bumble-bee. It was dreadfully improper, I know, but I couldn't resist the temptation; and lifting one end of the curtain before the glass door, I peeped in. Professor Bhaer was there; and while he arranged his books, I took a good look at him. A regular German,—rather stout, with brown hair tumbled all over his head, a bushy beard, good nose, the kindest eyes I ever saw, and a splendid big voice that does one's ears good, after our sharp or slipshod American gabble. His clothes were rusty, his hands were large, and he hadn't a really handsome feature in his face, except his beautiful teeth; yet I liked him, for he had a fine head; his linen was very nice, and he looked like a gentleman, though two buttons were off his coat, and there was a patch on one shoe. He looked sober in spite of his humming, till he went to the window to turn the hyacinth bulbs toward the sun, and stroke the cat, who received him like an old friend. Then he smiled; and when a tap came at the door, called out in a loud, brisk tone,—

" 'Herein!'

"I was just going to run, when I caught sight of a morsel of a child carrying a big book, and stopped to see what was going on.

" 'Me wants my Bhaer,' said the mite, slamming down her book, and running to meet him.

" 'Thou shalt haf thy Bhaer; come, then, and take a goot hug from him, my Tina,' said the Professor, catching her up, with a laugh, and holding her so high over his head that she had to stoop her little face to kiss him.

" 'Now me mus tuddy my lessin,' went on the funny little thing; so he put her up at the table, opened the great dictionary she had brought, and gave her a paper and pencil, and she scribbled away, turning a leaf now and then, and passing her little fat finger down the page, as if finding a word, so soberly that I nearly betrayed myself by a laugh, while Mr. Bhaer stood stroking her pretty hair, with a fatherly look, that made me think she must be his own, though she looked more French than German.

"Another knock and the appearance of two young ladies sent me back to my work, and there I virtuously remained through all the noise and gabbling that went on next door. One of the girls kept laughing affectedly, and saying 'Now Professor,' in a coquettish tone, and the other pronounced her German with an accent that must have made it hard for him to keep sober.

"Both seemed to try his patience sorely; for more than once I heard him say emphatically, 'No, no, it is *not* so; you haf not attend to what I say;' and once there was a loud rap, as if he struck the table with his book, followed by the despairing exclamation, 'Prut! It all goes bad this day.'

"Poor man, I pitied him; and when the girls were gone, took just one more peep, to see if he survived it. He seemed to have thrown himself back in his chair, tired out, and sat there with his eyes shut till the clock struck two, when he jumped up, put his books in his pocket, as if ready for another lesson, and, taking little Tina, who had fallen asleep on the sofa, in his arms, he carried her quietly away. I fancy he has a hard life of it.

"Mrs. Kirke asked me if I wouldn't go down to the five o'clock dinner; and, feeling a little bit homesick, I thought I would, just to see what sort of people are under the same roof with me. So I made myself respectable, and tried to slip in behind Mrs. Kirke; but as she is short, and I'm tall, my efforts at concealment were rather a failure. She gave me a seat by her, and after my face cooled off, I plucked up courage, and looked about me. The long table was full, and every-one intent on getting their dinner,—the gentlemen especially, who seemed to be eating on time, for they *bolted* in every sense of the word, vanishing as soon as they were done. There was the usual assortment of young men absorbed in themselves; young couples absorbed in each other; married ladies in their babies, and old gentle-men in politics. I don't think I shall care to have much to do with any of them, except one sweet-faced maiden lady, who looks as if she had something in her.

"Cast away at the very bottom of the table was the Professor, shouting answers to the questions of a very inquisitive, deaf old gentleman on one side, and talking philosophy with a Frenchman on the other. If Amy had been here, she'd have turned her back on him forever, because, sad to relate, he had a great appetite, and shovelled in his dinner in a manner which would have horrified 'her ladyship.' I didn't mind, for I like 'to see folks eat with a relish,' as Hannah says, and the poor man must have needed a deal of food after teaching idiots all day.

"As I went upstairs after dinner, two of the young men were settling their hats before the hall-mirror, and I heard one say low to the other, 'Who's the new party?'

" 'Governess, or something of that sort.'

" 'What the deuce is she at our table for?'

" 'Friend of the old lady's.'

" 'Handsome head, but no style.'

" 'Not a bit of it. Give us a light and come on.'

"I felt angry at first; and then I didn't care, for a governess is as good as a clerk, and I've got sense, if I haven't style, which is more than some people have, judging from the remarks of the elegant beings who clattered away, smoking like bad chimneys. I hate ordinary people!"

*"Thursday.*

"Yesterday was a quiet day, spent in teaching, sewing, and writing in my little room, which is very cozy, with a light and fire. I picked up a few bits of news, and was introduced to the Professor. It seems that Tina is the child of the Frenchwoman who does the fine ironing in the laundry here. The little thing has lost her heart to Mr. Bhaer, and follows him about the house like a dog whenever he is at home, which delights him, as he is very fond of children, though a 'bacheldore.' Kitty and Minnie Kirke likewise regard him with affection, and tell all sorts of stories about the plays he invents, the presents he brings, and the splendid tales he tells. The young men quiz him, it seems, call him Old Fritz, Lager Beer, Ursa Major, and make all manner of jokes on his name. But he enjoys it like a boy, Mrs. K. says, and takes it so good-naturedly that they all like him, in spite of his foreign ways.

"The maiden lady is a Miss Norton,—rich, cultivated, and kind. She spoke to me at dinner today (for I went to table again, it's such fun to watch people), and asked me to come and see her at her room. She has fine books and pictures, knows interesting persons, and seems friendly; so I shall make myself agreeable, for I *do* want to get into good society, only it isn't the same sort that Amy likes.

"I was in our parlor last evening, when Mr. Bhaer came in with some newspapers for Mrs. Kirke. She wasn't there, but Minnie, who is a little old woman, introduced me very prettily: 'This is mamma's friend, Miss March.'

" 'Yes; and she's jolly and we like her lots,' added Kitty, who is an *enfant terrible.*

"We both bowed, and then we laughed, for the prim introduction and the blunt addition were rather a comical contrast.

" 'Ah, yes, I hear these naughty ones go to vex you, Mees Marsch. If so again, call at me and I come,' he said, with a threatening frown that delighted the little wretches.

"I promised I would, and he departed; but it seems as if I was doomed to see a good deal of him, for today, as I passed his door on my way out, by accident I knocked against it with my umbrella. It flew open, and there he stood in his dressing gown, with a big blue sock on one hand, and a darning-needle in the other; he didn't seem at all ashamed of it, for when I explained and hurried on, he waved his hand, sock and all, saying in his loud, cheerful way,—

" 'You haf a fine day to make your walk. *Bon voyage, mademoiselle.'*

"I laughed all the way downstairs; but it was a little pathetic, also, to think of the poor man having to mend his own clothes. The German gentlemen embroider, I know; but darning hose is another thing, and not so pretty."

*"Saturday.*

"Nothing has happened to write about, except a call on Miss Norton, who has a room full of lovely things, and who was very charming, for she showed me all her treasures, and asked me if I would sometimes go with her to lectures and concerts, as her escort,—if I enjoyed them. She put it as a favor, but I'm sure Mrs. Kirke has told her about us, and she does it out of kindness to me. I'm as proud as Lucifer, but such favors from such people don't burden me, and I accepted gratefully.

"When I got back to the nursery there was such an uproar in the parlor that I looked in; and there was Mr. Bhaer down on his hands and knees, with Tina on his back, Kitty leading him with a jump-rope, and Minnie feeding two small boys with seed-cakes, as they roared and ramped in cages built of chairs.

" 'We are playing *nargerie*,' explained Kitty.

" 'Dis is mine effalunt!' added Tina, holding on by the Professor's hair.

" 'Mamma always allows us to do what we like Saturday afternoon, when Franz and Emil come, doesn't she, Mr. Bhaer?' said Minnie.

"The 'effalunt' sat up, looking as much in earnest as any of them, and said soberly to me,—

" 'I gif you my wort it is so. If we make too large a noise you shall say "Hush!" to us, and we go more softly.'

"I promised to do so, but left the door open, and enjoyed the fun as much as they did,—for a more glorious frolic I never witnessed. They played tag and soldiers, danced and sung, and when it began to grow dark they all piled on to the sofa about the Professor, while he told charming fairy stories of the storks on the chimney-tops, and the little 'kobolds,' who ride the snow-flakes as they fall. I wish Americans were as simple and natural as Germans, don't you?

"I'm so fond of writing, I should go spinning on forever if motives of economy didn't stop me; for though I've used thin paper and written fine, I tremble to think of the stamps this long letter will need. Pray forward Amy's as soon as you can spare them. My small news will sound very flat after her splendors, but you will like them, I know. Is Teddy studying so hard that he can't find time to write to his friends? Take good care of him for me, Beth, and tell me all about the babies, and give heaps of love to everyone.

"From your faithful

Jo.

"P.S. On reading over my letter it strikes me as rather Bhaery; but I am always interested in odd people, and I really had nothing else to write about. Bless you!"

"DECEMBER.

"MY PRECIOUS BETSEY,—

"As this is to be a scribble-scrabble letter, I direct it to you, for it may amuse you, and give you some idea of my goings on; for, though quiet, they are rather amusing, for which, oh, be joyful! After what Amy would call Herculaneum efforts, in the way of mental and moral agriculture, my young ideas begin to shoot and my little twigs to bend as I could wish. They are not so interesting to me as Tina and the boys, but I do my duty by them, and they are fond of me. Franz and Emil are jolly little lads, quite after my own heart; for the mixture of German and American spirit in them produces a constant state of effervescence. Saturday afternoons are riotous times, whether spent in the house or out; for on pleasant days they all go to walk, like a seminary, with the Professor and myself to keep order; and then such fun!

"We are very good friends now, and I've begun to take lessons. I really couldn't help it, and it all came about in such a droll way that I must tell you. To begin at the beginning, Mrs. Kirke called to me, one day, as I passed Mr. Bhaer's room, where she was rummaging.

" 'Did you ever see such a den, my dear? Just come and help me put these books to rights, for I've turned everything upside down, trying to discover what he has done with the six new handkerchiefs I gave him not long ago.'

"I went in, and while we worked I looked about me, for it was 'a den,' to be sure. Books and papers everywhere; a broken meerschaum, and an old flute over the mantel-piece as if done with; a ragged bird, without any tail, chirped on one window-seat, and a box of white mice adorned the other; half-finished boats and bits of string lay among the manuscripts; dirty little boots stood drying before the fire; and traces of the dearly beloved boys, for whom he makes a slave of himself, were to be seen all over the room. After a grand rummage three of the missing articles were found,—one over the bird-cage, one covered with ink, and a third burnt brown, having been used as a holder.

" 'Such a man!' laughed good-natured Mrs. K., as she put the relics in the rag-bag. 'I suppose the others are torn up to rig ships, bandage cut fingers, or make kite-tails. It's dreadful, but I can't scold him: he's so absent-minded and good-natured, he lets those boys ride over him rough-shod. I agreed to do his washing and mending, but he forgets to give out his things and I forget to look them over, so he comes to a sad pass sometimes.'

" 'Let me mend them,' said I. 'I don't mind it, and he needn't know. I'd like to,—he's so kind to me about bringing my letters and lending books.'

"So I have got his things in order, and knit heels into two pairs of the socks,—for they were boggled out of shape with his queer darns. Nothing was said, and I hoped he wouldn't find it out, but one day last week he caught me at it. Hearing the lessons he gives to others has interested and amused me so much that I took a fancy to learn; for Tina runs in and out, leaving the door open, and I can hear. I had been sitting near this door, finishing off the last sock, and trying to understand what he said to a new scholar, who is as stupid as I am. The girl had gone, and I thought he had also, it was so still, and I was busily gabbling over a verb, and rocking to and fro in a most absurd way, when a little crow made me look up, and there was Mr. Bhaer looking and laughing quietly, while he made signs to Tina not to betray him.

" 'So!' he said, as I stopped and stared like a goose, 'you peep at me, I peep at you, and that is not bad; but see, I am not pleasanting when I say, haf you a wish for German?'

" 'Yes; but you are too busy. I am too stupid to learn,' I blundered out, as red as a peony.

" 'Prut! We will make the time, and we fail not to find the sense. At efening I shall gif a little lesson with much gladness; for, look you, Mees Marsch, I haf this debt to pay,' and he pointed to my work. "Yes," they say to one another, these so kind ladies, "he is a stupid old fellow; he will see not what we do; he will never opserve that his sock-heels go not in holes any more, he will think his buttons grow out new when they fall, and believe that strings make theirselves." Ah! But I haf an eye, and I see much. I haf a heart, and I feel the thanks for this. Come, a little lesson then and now, or no more good fairy works for me and mine.'

"Of course I couldn't say anything after that, and as it really is a splendid opportunity, I made the bargain, and we began. I took four lessons, and then I stuck fast in a grammatical bog. The Professor was very patient with me, but it must have been torment to him, and now and then he'd look at me with such an expression of mild despair that it was a toss-up with me whether to laugh or cry. I tried both ways; and when it came to a sniff of utter mortification and woe, he just threw the grammar on to the floor, and marched out of the room. I felt myself disgraced and deserted forever, but didn't blame him a particle, and was scrambling my papers together, meaning to rush upstairs and shake myself hard, when in he came, as brisk and beaming as if I'd covered myself with glory.

" 'Now we shall try a new way. You and I will read these pleasant little märchen together, and dig no more in that dry book, that goes in the corner for making us trouble.'

"He spoke so kindly, and opened Hans Andersen's fairy tales so invitingly before me, that I was more ashamed than ever, and went at my lesson in a neck-or-nothing style that seemed to amuse him immensely. I forgot my bashfulness, and pegged away (no other word will express it) with all my might, tumbling over long words, pronouncing according to the inspiration of the minute, and doing my very best. When I finished reading my first page, and stopped for breath, he clapped his hands and cried out, in his hearty way, 'Das ist gut! Now we go well! My turn. I do him in German; gif me your ear.' And away he went, rumbling out the words with his strong voice, and a relish which was good to see as well as hear. Fortunately the story was the 'Constant Tin Soldier,' which is droll, you know, so I could laugh,—and I did,—though I didn't understand half he read, for I couldn't help it, he was so earnest, I so excited, and the whole thing so comical.

"After that we got on better, and now I read my lessons pretty well; for this way of studying suits me, and I can see that the grammar gets tucked into the tales and poetry as one gives pills in jelly. I like it very much, and he doesn't seem tired of it yet,—which is very good of him, isn't it? I mean to give him something on Christmas, for I dare not offer money. Tell me something nice, Marmee.

"I'm glad Laurie seems so happy and busy, that he has given up smoking, and lets his hair grow. You see Beth manages him better than I did. I'm not jealous, dear; do your best, only don't make a saint of him. I'm afraid I couldn't like him without a spice of human naughtiness. Read him bits of my letters. I haven't time to write much, and that will do just as well. Thank Heaven Beth continues so comfortable."

"JANUARY.

"A Happy New Year to you all, my dearest family, which of course includes Mr. L. and a young man by the name of Teddy. I can't tell you how much I enjoyed your Christmas bundle, for I didn't get it till night, and had given up hoping. Your letter came in the morning, but you said nothing about a parcel, meaning it for a surprise; so I was disappointed, for I'd had a 'kind of a feeling' that you wouldn't forget me. I felt a little low in my mind, as I sat up in my room, after tea; and when the big, muddy, battered-looking bundle was brought to me, I just hugged it, and pranced. It was so *homey* and refreshing, that I sat down on the floor and read and looked and ate and laughed and cried, in my usual absurd way. The things were just what I wanted, and all the better for being made instead of bought. Beth's new 'ink-bib' was capital; and Hannah's box of hard gingerbread will be a treasure. I'll be sure and wear the nice flannels you sent, Marmee, and read carefully the books father has marked. Thank you all, heaps and heaps!

"Speaking of books reminds me that I'm getting rich in that line, for, on New Year's Day, Mr. Bhaer gave me a fine Shakespeare. It is one he values much, and I've often admired it, set up in the place of honor, with his German Bible, Plato, Homer, and Milton; so you may imagine how I felt when he brought it down, without its cover, and showed me my name in it, 'from my friend Friedrich Bhaer.'

" 'You say often you wish a library: here I gif you one; for between these lids (he meant covers), is many books in one. Read him well, and he will help you much; for the study of character in this book will help you to read it in the world and paint it with your pen.'

"I thanked him as well as I could, and talk now about 'my library,' as if I had a hundred books. I never knew how much there was in Shakespeare before; but then I never had a Bhaer to explain it to me. Now *don't* laugh at his horrid name; it isn't pronounced either Bear or Beer, as people *will* say it, but something between the two, as only Germans can give it. I'm glad you both like what I tell you about him, and hope you will know him some day. Mother would admire his warm heart, father his wise head. I admire both, and feel rich in my new 'friend Friedrich Bhaer.'

"Not having much money, or knowing what he'd like, I got several little things, and put them about the room, where he would find them unexpectedly. They were useful, pretty, or funny,—a new standish on his table, a little vase for his flower,—he always has one, or a bit of green in a glass, to keep him fresh, he says,—and a holder for his blower, so that he needn't burn up what Amy calls 'mouchoirs.' I made it like those Beth invented,—a big butterfly with a fat body, and black and yellow wings, worsted feelers, and bead eyes. It took his fancy immensely, and he put it on his mantel-piece as an article of *vertu;* so it was rather a failure after all. Poor as he is, he didn't forget a servant or a child in the house; and not a soul here, from the French laundry-woman to Miss Norton, forgot him. I was so glad of that.

"They got up a masquerade, and had a gay time New Year's Eve. I didn't mean to go down, having no dress; but at the last minute, Mrs. Kirke remembered some old brocades, and Miss Norton lent me lace and feathers; so I dressed up as Mrs. Malaprop, and sailed in with a mask on. No one knew me, for I disguised my voice, and no one dreamed of the silent, haughty Miss March (for they think I am very stiff and cool, most of them; and so I am to whipper-snappers) could dance and dress, and burst out into a 'nice derangement of epitaphs, like an allegory on the banks of the Nile.' I enjoyed it very much; and when we unmasked, it was fun to see them stare at me. I heard one of the young men tell another that he knew I'd been an actress; in fact, he thought he remembered seeing me at one of the minor theatres. Meg will relish that joke. Mr. Bhaer was Nick Bottom, and Tina was Titania,—a perfect little fairy in his arms. To see them dance was 'quite a landscape,' to use a Teddyism.

"I had a very happy New Year, after all; and when I thought it over in my room, I felt as if I was getting on a little in spite of my many failures; for I'm cheerful all the time now, work with a will, and take more interest in other people than I used to, which is satisfactory. Bless you all! Ever your loving

Jo."

# CHAPTER XXXIV

## A FRIEND

THOUGH very happy in the social atmosphere about her, and very busy with the daily work that earned her bread, and made it sweeter for the effort, Jo still found time for literary labors. The purpose which now took possession of her was a natural one to a poor and ambitious girl; but the means she took to gain her end were not the best. She saw that money conferred power: money and power, therefore, she resolved to have; not to be used for herself alone, but for those whom she loved more than self.

The dream of filling home with comforts, giving Beth everything she wanted, from strawberries in winter to an organ in her bedroom; going abroad herself, and always having *more* than enough, so that she might indulge in the luxury of charity, had been for years Jo's most cherished castle in the air.

The prize-story experience had seemed to open a way which might, after long travelling and much up-hill work lead to this delightful *château en Espagne*. But the novel disaster quenched her courage for a time, for public opinion is a giant which has frightened stouter-hearted Jacks on bigger bean-stalks than hers. Like that immortal hero, she reposed awhile after the first attempt, which resulted in a tumble, and the least lovely of the giant's treasures, if I remember rightly. But the "up again and take another" spirit was as strong in Jo as in Jack; so she scrambled up, on the shady side this time, and got more booty, but nearly left behind her what was far more precious than the money-bags.

She took to writing sensation stories; for in those dark ages, even all-perfect America read rubbish. She told no one, but concocted a "thrilling tale," and boldly carried it herself to Mr. Dashwood, editor of the "Weekly Volcano." She had never read "Sartor Resartus," but she had a womanly instinct that clothes possess an influence more powerful over many than the worth of character or the magic of manners. So she dressed herself in her best, and, trying to persuade herself that she was neither excited nor nervous, bravely climbed two pairs of dark and dirty stairs to find herself in a disorderly room, a cloud of cigar-smoke, and the presence of three gentlemen, sitting with their heels rather higher than their hats, which articles of dress none of them took the trouble to remove on her appearance. Somewhat daunted by this reception, Jo hesitated on the threshold, murmuring in much embarrassment,—

"Excuse me, I was looking for the 'Weekly Volcano' office; I wished to see Mr. Dashwood."

Down went the highest pair of heels, up rose the smokiest gentleman, and, carefully cherishing his cigar between his fingers, he advanced, with a nod, and a countenance expressive of nothing but sleep. Feeling that she must get through the matter somehow, Jo produced her manuscript, and, blushing redder and redder with each sentence, blundered out fragments of the little speech carefully prepared for the occasion.

"A friend of mine desired me to offer—a story—just as an experiment—would like your opinion—be glad to write more if this suits."

While she blushed and blundered, Mr. Dashwood had taken the manuscript, and was turning over the leaves with a pair of rather dirty fingers, and casting critical glances up and down the neat pages.

"Not a first attempt, I take it?" observing that the pages were numbered, covered only on one side, and not tied up with a ribbon,—sure sign of a novice.

"No, sir; she has had some experience, and got a prize for a tale in the 'Blarneystone Banner.' "

"Oh, did she?" and Mr. Dashwood gave Jo a quick look, which seemed to take note of everything she had on, from the bow in her bonnet to the buttons on her boots. "Well, you can leave it, if you like. We've more of this sort of thing on hand than we know what to do with at present; but I'll run my eye over it, and give you an answer next week."

Now, Jo did *not* like to leave it, for Mr. Dashwood didn't suit her at all; but, under the circumstances, there was nothing for her to do but bow and walk away, looking particularly tall and dignified, as she was apt to do when nettled or abashed. Just then she was both; for it was perfectly evident, from the knowing glances exchanged among the gentlemen, that her little fiction of "my friend" was considered a good joke; and a laugh, produced by some inaudible remark of the editor, as he closed the door, completed her discomfiture. Half resolving never to return, she went home, and worked off her irritation by stitching pinafores vigorously; and in an hour or two was cool enough to laugh over the scene, and long for next week.

When she went again, Mr. Dashwood was alone, whereat she rejoiced; Mr. Dashwood was much wider awake than before, which was agreeable; and Mr. Dashwood was not too deeply absorbed in a cigar to remember his manners: so the second interview was much more comfortable than the first.

"We'll take this" (editors never say I), "if you don't object to a few alterations. It's too long, but omitting the passages I've marked will make it just the right length," he said, in a business-like tone.

Jo hardly knew her own MS. again, so crumpled and underscored were its pages and paragraphs; but, feeling as a tender parent might on being asked to cut off her baby's legs in order that it might fit into a new cradle, she looked at the marked passages, and was surprised to find that all the moral reflections—which she had carefully put in as ballast for much romance—had been stricken out.

"But, sir, I thought every story should have some sort of a moral, so I took care to have a few of my sinners repent."

Mr. Dashwood's editorial gravity relaxed into a smile, for Jo had forgotten her "friend," and spoken as only an author could.

"People want to be amused, not preached at, you know. Morals don't sell nowadays;" which was not quite a correct statement, by the way.

"You think it would do with these alterations, then?"

"Yes; it's a new plot, and pretty well worked up—language good, and so on," was Mr. Dashwood's affable reply.

"What do you—that is, what compensation—" began Jo, not exactly knowing how to express herself.

"Oh, yes, well, we give from twenty-five to thirty for things of this sort. Pay when it comes out," returned Mr. Dashwood, as if that point had escaped him; such trifles often do escape the editorial mind, it is said.

"Very well; you can have it," said Jo, handing back the story, with a satisfied air; for, after the dollar-a-column work, even twenty-five seemed good pay.

"Shall I tell my friend you will take another if she has one better than this?" asked Jo, unconscious of her little slip of the tongue, and emboldened by her success.

"Well, we'll look at it; can't promise to take it. Tell her to make it short and spicy, and never mind the moral. What name would your friend like to put to it?" in a careless tone.

"None at all, if you please; she doesn't wish her name to appear, and has no *nom de plume*," said Jo, blushing in spite of herself.

"Just as she likes, of course. The tale will be out next week; will you call for the money, or shall I send it?" asked Mr. Dashwood, who felt a natural desire to know who his new contributor might be.

"I'll call. Good morning, sir."

As she departed, Mr. Dashwood put up his feet, with the graceful remark, "Poor and proud, as usual, but she'll do."

Following Mr. Dashwood's directions, and making Mrs. Northbury her model, Jo rashly took a plunge into the frothy sea of sensational literature; but, thanks to the life-preserver thrown her by a friend, she came up again, not much the worse for her ducking.

Like most young scribblers, she went abroad for her characters and scenery; and banditti, counts, gypsies, nuns, and duchesses appeared upon her stage, and played their parts with as much accuracy and spirit as could be expected. Her readers were not particular about such trifles as grammar, punctuation, and probability, and Mr. Dashwood graciously permitted her to fill his columns at the lowest prices, not thinking it necessary to tell her that the real cause of his hospitality was the fact that one of his hacks, on being offered higher wages, had basely left him in the lurch.

She soon became interested in her work, for her emaciated purse grew stout, and the little hoard she was making to take Beth to the mountains next summer grew slowly but surely as the weeks passed. One thing disturbed her satisfaction, and that was that she did not tell them at home. She had a feeling that father and mother would not approve, and preferred to have her own way first, and beg pardon afterward. It was easy to keep her secret, for no name appeared with her stories; Mr. Dashwood had, of course, found it out very soon, but promised to be dumb; and, for a wonder, kept his word.

She thought it would do her no harm, for she sincerely meant to write nothing of which she should be ashamed, and quieted all pricks of conscience by anticipations of the happy minute when she should show her earnings and laugh over her well-kept secret.

But Mr. Dashwood rejected any but thrilling tales; and, as thrills could not be produced except by harrowing up the souls of the readers, history and romance, land and sea, science and art, police records and lunatic asylums, had to be ransacked for the purpose. Jo soon found that her innocent experience had given her but few glimpses of the tragic world which underlies society; so, regarding it in a business light, she set about supplying her deficiencies with characteristic energy. Eager to find material for stories, and bent on making them original in plot, if not masterly in execution, she searched newspapers for accidents, incidents, and crimes; she excited the suspicions of public librarians by asking for works on poisons; she studied faces in the street, and characters, good, bad, and indifferent, all about her; she delved in the dust of ancient times for facts or fictions so old that they were as good as new, and introduced herself to folly, sin, and misery, as well as her limited opportunities allowed. She thought she was prospering finely; but, unconsciously, she was beginning to desecrate some of the womanliest attributes of a woman's character. She was living in bad society; and, imaginary though it was, its influence affected her, for she was feeding heart and fancy on dangerous and unsubstantial food, and was fast brushing the innocent bloom from her nature by a premature acquaintance with the darker side of life, which comes soon enough to all of us.

She was beginning to feel rather than see this, for much describing of other people's passions and feelings set her to studying and speculating about her own,—a morbid amusement, in which healthy young minds do not voluntarily indulge. Wrong-doing always brings its own punishment; and, when Jo most needed hers, she got it.

I don't know whether the study of Shakespeare helped her to read character, or the natural instinct of a woman for what was honest, brave, and strong; but while endowing her imaginary heroes with every perfection under the sun, Jo was discovering a live hero, who interested her in spite of many human imperfections. Mr. Bhaer, in one of their conversations, had advised her to study simple, true, and lovely characters, wherever she found them, as good training for a writer. Jo took him at his word, for she coolly turned round and studied him,—a proceeding which would have much surprised him, had he known it, for the worthy Professor was very humble in his own conceit.

Why everybody liked him was what puzzled Jo, at first. He was neither rich nor great, young nor handsome; in no respect what is called fascinating, imposing, or brilliant; and yet he was as attractive as a genial fire, and people seemed to gather about him as naturally as about a warm hearth. He was poor, yet always appeared to be giving something away; a stranger, yet everyone was his friend; no longer young, but as happy-hearted as a boy; plain and peculiar, yet his face looked beautiful to many, and his oddities were freely forgiven for his sake. Jo often watched him, trying to discover the charm, and, at last, decided that it was benevolence which worked the miracle. If he had any sorrow, "it sat with its head under its wing," and he turned only his sunny side to the world. There were lines upon his forehead, but Time seemed to have touched him gently, re-membering how kind he was to others. The pleasant curves about his mouth were the memorials of many friendly words and cheery laughs; his eyes were never cold or hard, and his big hand had a warm, strong grasp that was more expressive than words.

His very clothes seemed to partake of the hospitable nature of the wearer. They looked as if they were at ease, and liked to make him comfortable; his capacious waistcoat was suggestive of a large heart un-derneath; his rusty coat had a social air, and the baggy pockets plainly proved that little hands often went in empty and came out full; his very boots were benevolent, and his collars never stiff and raspy like other people's.

"That's it!" said Jo to herself, when she at length discovered that genuine good-will towards one's fellowmen could beautify and dignify even a stout German teacher, who shovelled in his dinner, darned his own socks, and was burdened with the name of Bhaer.

Jo valued goodness highly, but she also possessed a most feminine respect for intellect, and a little discovery which she made about the Professor added much to her regard for him. He never spoke of himself, and no one ever knew that in his native city he had been a man much honored and esteemed for learning and integrity, till a countryman came to see him, and, in a conversation with Miss Norton, divulged the pleasing fact. From her Jo learned it, and liked it all the better because Mr. Bhaer had never told it. She felt proud to know that he was an honored Professor in Berlin, though only a poor language-master in America; and his homely, hard-working life was much beautified by the spice of romance which this discovery gave it.

Another and a better gift than intellect was shown her in a most unexpected manner. Miss Norton had the *entrée* into literary society, which Jo would have had no chance of seeing but for her. The solitary woman felt an interest in the ambitious girl, and kindly conferred many favors of this sort both on Jo and the Professor. She took them with her, one night, to a select symposium, held in honor of several celebrities.

Jo went prepared to bow down and adore the mighty ones whom she had worshipped with youthful enthusiasm afar off. But her reverence for genius received a severe shock that night, and it took her some time to recover from the discovery that the great creatures were only men and women after all. Imagine her dismay, on stealing a glance of timid admiration at the poet whose lines suggested an ethereal being fed on "spirit, fire, and dew," to behold him devouring his supper with an ardor which flushed his intellectual countenance. Turning as from a fallen idol, she made other discoveries which rapidly dispelled her romantic illusions. The great novelist vibrated between two decanters with the regularity of a pendulum; the famous divine flirted openly with one of the Madame de Staëls of the age, who looked daggers at another Corinne, who was amiably satirizing her, after out-manœuvring her in efforts to absorb the profound philosopher, who imbibed tea Johnsonianly and appeared to slumber, the loquacity of the lady rendering speech impossible. The scientific celebrities, forgetting their mollusks and glacial periods, gossiped about art, while devoting themselves to oysters and ices with characteristic energy; the young musician, who was charming the city like a second Orpheus, talked horses; and the specimen of the British nobility present happened to be the most ordinary man of the party.

Before the evening was half over, Jo felt so completely *désillusionnée*, that she sat down in a corner to recover herself. Mr. Bhaer soon joined her, looking rather out of his element, and presently several of the philosophers, each mounted on his hobby, came ambling up to hold an intellectual tournament in the recess. The conversation was miles beyond Jo's comprehension, but she enjoyed it, though Kant and Hegel were unknown gods, the Subjective and Objective unintelligible terms; and the only thing "evolved from her inner consciousness," was a bad headache after it was all over. It dawned upon her gradually that the world was being picked to pieces, and put together on new, and, according to the talkers, on infinitely better principles than before; that religion was in a fair way to be reasoned into nothingness, and intellect was to be the only God. Jo knew nothing about philosophy or metaphysics of any sort, but a curious excitement, half pleasurable, half painful, came over her, as she listened with a sense of being turned adrift into time and space, like a young balloon out on a holiday.

She looked round to see how the Professor liked it, and found him looking at her with the grimmest expression she had ever seen him wear. He shook his head, and beckoned her to come away; but she was fascinated, just then, by the freedom of Speculative Philosophy, and kept her seat, trying to find out what the wise gentlemen intended to rely upon after they had annihilated all the old beliefs.

Now, Mr. Bhaer was a diffident man, and slow to offer his own opinions, not because they were unsettled, but too sincere and earnest to be lightly spoken. As he glanced from Jo to several other young people, attracted by the brilliancy of the philosophic pyrotechnics, he knit his brows, and

longed to speak, fearing that some inflammable young soul would be
led astray by the rockets, to find, when the display was over, that they
had only an empty stick or a scorched hand.

He bore it as long as he could; but when he was appealed to for an
opinion, he blazed up with honest indignation, and defended religion
with all the eloquence of truth,—an eloquence which made his broken
English musical, and his plain face beautiful. He had a hard fight, for
the wise men argued well; but he didn't know when he was beaten, and
stood to his colors like a man. Somehow, as he talked, the world got
right again to Jo; the old beliefs, that had lasted so long, seemed better
than the new; God was not a blind force, and immortality was not a
pretty fable, but a blessed fact. She felt as if she had solid ground under
her feet again; and when Mr. Bhaer paused, out-talked, but not one
whit convinced, Jo wanted to clap her hands and thank him.

She did neither; but she remembered this scene, and gave the Professor
her heartiest respect, for she knew it cost him an effort to speak out
then and there, because his conscience would not let him be silent. She
began to see that character is a better possession than money, rank,
intellect, or beauty; and to feel that if greatness is what a wise man has
defined it to be, "truth, reverence, and good-will," then her friend Friedrich
Bhaer was not only good, but great.

This belief strengthened daily. She valued his esteem, she coveted his
respect, she wanted to be worthy of his friendship; and, just when the
wish was sincerest, she came near losing everything. It all grew out of a
cocked hat; for one evening the Professor came in to give Jo her lesson,
with a paper soldier-cap on his head, which Tina had put there, and he
had forgotten to take off.

"It's evident he doesn't look in his glass before coming down," thought
Jo, with a smile, as he said "Goot efening," and sat soberly down, quite
unconscious of the ludicrous contrast between his subject and his head-
gear, for he was going to read her the "Death of Wallenstein."

She said nothing at first, for she liked to hear him laugh out his big,
hearty laugh, when anything funny happened, so she left him to discover
it for himself, and presently forgot all about it; for to hear a German
read Schiller is rather an absorbing occupation. After the reading came
the lesson, which was a lively one, for Jo was in a gay mood that night,
and the cocked-hat kept her eyes dancing with merriment. The Professor
didn't know what to make of her, and stopped at last, to ask, with an
air of mild surprise that was irresistible,—

"Mees Marsch, for what do you laugh in your master's face? Haf you
no respect for me, that you go on so bad?"

"How can I be respectful, sir, when you forget to take your hat off?"
said Jo.

Lifting his hand to his head, the absent-minded Professor gravely felt
and removed the little cocked-hat, looked at it a minute, and then threw
back his head, and laughed like a merry bass-viol.

"Ah! I see him now; it is that imp Tina who makes me a fool with my
cap. Well, it is nothing: but see you, if this lesson goes not well, you too
shall wear him."

But the lesson did not go at all for a few minutes, because Mr. Bhaer caught sight of a picture on the hat, and, unfolding it, said, with an air of great disgust,—

"I wish these papers did not come in the house; they are not for children to see, nor young people to read. It is not well, and I haf no patience with those who make this harm."

Jo glanced at the sheet, and saw a pleasing illustration composed of a lunatic, a corpse, a villain, and a viper. She did not like it; but the impulse that made her turn it over was not one of displeasure, but fear, because, for a minute, she fancied the paper was the "Volcano." It was not, however, and her panic subsided as she remembered that, even if it had been, and one of her own tales in it, there would have been no name to betray her. She had betrayed herself, however, by a look and a blush; for, though an absent man, the Professor saw a good deal more than people fancied. He knew that Jo wrote, and had met her down among the newspaper offices more than once; but as she never spoke of it, he asked no questions, in spite of a strong desire to see her work. Now it occurred to him that she was doing what she was ashamed to own, and it troubled him. He did not say to himself, "It is none of my business; I've no right to say anything," as many people would have done; he only remembered that she was young and poor, a girl far away from mother's love and father's care; and he was moved to help her with an impulse as quick and natural as that which would prompt him to put out his hand to save a baby from a puddle. All this flashed through his mind in a minute, but not a trace of it appeared in his face; and by the time the paper was turned, and Jo's needle threaded, he was ready to say quite naturally, but very gravely,—

"Yes, you are right to put it from you. I do not like to think that good young girls should see such things. They are made pleasant to some, but I would more rather give my boys gunpowder to play with than this bad trash."

"All may not be bad, only silly, you know; and if there is a demand for it, I don't see any harm in supplying it. Many very respectable people make an honest living out of what are called sensation stories," said Jo, scratching gathers so energetically that a row of little slits followed her pin.

"There is a demand for whiskey, but I think you and I do not care to sell it. If the respectable people knew what harm they did, they would not feel that the living *was* honest. They haf no right to put poison in the sugar-plum, and let the small ones eat it. No; they should think a little, and sweep mud in the street before they do this thing."

Mr. Bhaer spoke warmly, and walked to the fire, crumpling the paper in his hands. Jo sat still, looking as if the fire had come to her; for her cheeks burned long after the cocked hat had turned to smoke, and gone harmlessly up the chimney.

"I should like much to send all the rest after him," muttered the Professor, coming back with a relieved air.

Jo thought what a blaze her pile of papers upstairs would make, and her hard-earned money lay rather heavily on her conscience at that minute. Then she thought consolingly to herself, "Mine are not like that;

He doesn't prink at his glass before coming.

they are only silly, never bad, so I won't be worried;" and taking up her book, she said, with a studious face,—

"Shall we go on, sir? I'll be very good and proper now."

"I shall hope so," was all he said, but he meant more than she imagined; and the grave, kind look he gave her made her feel as if the words "Weekly Volcano" were printed in large type on her forehead.

As soon as she went to her room, she got out her papers, and carefully re-read every one of her stories. Being a little short-sighted, Mr. Bhaer sometimes used eye-glasses, and Jo had tried them once, smiling to see how they magnified the fine print of her book; now she seemed to have got on the Professor's mental or moral spectacles also; for the faults of these poor stories glared at her dreadfully, and filled her with dismay.

"They *are* trash, and will soon be worse than trash if I go on; for each is more sensational than the last. I've gone blindly on, hurting myself and other people, for the sake of money; I know it's so, for I can't read this stuff in sober earnest without being horribly ashamed of it; and what *should* I do if they were seen at home, or Mr. Bhaer got hold of them?"

Jo turned hot at the bare idea, and stuffed the whole bundle into her stove, nearly setting the chimney afire with the blaze.

"Yes, that's the best place for such inflammable nonsense; I'd better burn the house down, I suppose, than let other people blow themselves up with my gunpowder," she thought, as she watched the "Demon of the Jura" whisk away, a little black cinder with fiery eyes.

But when nothing remained of all her three months' work except a heap of ashes, and the money in her lap, Jo looked sober, as she sat on the floor, wondering what she ought to do about her wages.

"I think I haven't done much harm *yet*, and may keep this to pay for my time," she said, after a long meditation, adding impatiently, "I almost wish I hadn't any conscience, it's so inconvenient. If I didn't care about doing right, and didn't feel uncomfortable when doing wrong, I should get on capitally. I can't help wishing sometimes, that father and mother hadn't been so particular about such things."

Ah, Jo, instead of wishing that, thank God that "father and mother *were* particular," and pity from your heart those who have no such guardians to hedge them round with principles which may seem like prison-walls to impatient youth, but which will prove sure foundations to build character upon in womanhood.

Jo wrote no more sensational stories, deciding that the money did not pay for her share of the sensation; but, going to the other extreme, as is the way with people of her stamp, she took a course of Mrs. Sherwood, Miss Edgeworth, and Hannah More; and then produced a tale which might have been more properly called an essay or a sermon, so intensely moral was it. She had her doubts about it from the beginning; for her lively fancy and girlish romance felt as ill at ease in the new style as she would have done masquerading in the stiff and cumbrous costume of the last century. She sent this didactic gem to several markets, but it found no purchaser; and she was inclined to agree with Mr. Dashwood, that morals didn't sell.

Then she tried a child's story, which she could easily have disposed of if she had not been mercenary enough to demand filthy lucre for it. The only person who offered enough to make it worth her while to try juvenile literature was a worthy gentleman who felt it his mission to convert all the world to his particular belief. But much as she liked to write for children, Jo could not consent to depict all her naughty boys as being eaten by bears or tossed by mad bulls, because they did not go to a particular Sabbath-school, nor all the good infants, who did go, as rewarded by every kind of bliss, from gilded gingerbread to escorts of angels, when they departed this life with psalms or sermons on their lisping tongues. So nothing came of these trials; and Jo corked up her inkstand, and said, in a fit of very wholesome humility,—

"I don't know anything; I'll wait till I do before I try again, and, meantime, 'sweep mud in the street,' if I can't do better; that's honest, at least;" which decision proved that her second tumble down the bean-stalk had done her some good.

While these internal revolutions were going on, her external life had been as busy and uneventful as usual; and if she sometimes looked serious or a little sad no one observed it but Professor Bhaer. He did it so quietly that Jo never knew he was watching to see if she would accept and profit by his reproof; but she stood the test, and he was satisfied; for, though no words passed between them, he knew that she had given up writing. Not only did he guess it by the fact that the second finger of her right hand was no longer inky, but she spent her evenings downstairs now, was met no more among newspaper offices, and studied with a dogged patience, which assured him that she was bent on occupying her mind with something useful, if not pleasant.

He helped her in many ways, proving himself a true friend, and Jo was happy; for, while her pen lay idle, she was learning other lessons besides German, and laying a foundation for the sensation story of her own life.

It was a pleasant winter and a long one, for she did not leave Mrs. Kirke till June. Everyone seemed sorry when the time came; the children were inconsolable, and Mr. Bhaer's hair stuck straight up all over his head, for he always rumpled it wildly when disturbed in mind.

"Going home? Ah, you are happy that you haf a home to go in," he said, when she told him, and sat silently pulling his beard, in the corner, while she held a little levee on that last evening.

She was going early, so she bade them all good-by over night; and when his turn came, she said warmly,—

"Now, sir, you won't forget to come and see us, if you ever travel our way, will you? I'll never forgive you if you do, for I want them all to know my friend."

"Do you? Shall I come?" he asked, looking down at her with an eager expression which she did not see.

"Yes, come next month; Laurie graduates then, and you'd enjoy Commencement as something new."

"That is your best friend, of whom you speak?" he said, in an altered tone.

"Yes, my boy Teddy; I'm very proud of him, and should like you to see him."

Jo looked up then, quite unconscious of anything but her own pleasure in the prospect of showing them to one another. Something in Mr. Bhaer's face suddenly recalled the fact that she might find Laurie more than a "best friend," and, simply because she particularly wished not to look as if anything was the matter, she involuntarily began to blush; and the more she tried not to, the redder she grew. If it had not been for Tina on her knee, she didn't know what would have become of her. Fortunately, the child was moved to hug her; so she managed to hide her face an instant, hoping the Professor did not see it. But he did, and his own changed again from that momentary anxiety to its usual expression, as he said cordially,—

"I fear I shall not make the time for that, but I wish the friend much success, and you all happiness. Gott bless you!" and with that, he shook hands warmly, shouldered Tina, and went away.

But after the boys were abed, he sat long before his fire, with the tired look on his face, and the *"heimweh,"* or homesickness, lying heavy at his heart. Once, when he remembered Jo, as she sat with the little child in her lap and that new softness in her face, he leaned his head on his hands a minute, and then roamed about the room, as if in search of something that he could not find.

"It is not for me; I must not hope it now," he said to himself, with a sigh that was almost a groan; then, as if reproaching himself for the longing that he could not repress, he went and kissed the two towzled heads upon the pillow, took down his seldom-used meerschaum, and opened his Plato.

He did his best, and did it manfully; but I don't think he found that a pair of rampant boys, a pipe, or even the divine Plato, were very satisfactory substitutes for wife and child and home.

Early as it was, he was at the station, next morning, to see Jo off; and, thanks to him, she began her solitary journey with the pleasant memory of a familiar face smiling its farewell, a bunch of violets to keep her company, and, best of all, the happy thought,—

"Well, the winter's gone, and I've written no books, earned no fortune; but I've made a friend worth having, and I'll try to keep him all my life."

# CHAPTER XXXV

## HEARTACHE

WHATEVER his motive might have been, Laurie studied to some purpose that year, for he graduated with honor, and gave the Latin oration with the grace of a Phillips and the eloquence of a Demosthenes, so his friends said. They were all there, his grandfather,—oh, so proud!—Mr. and Mrs. March, John and Meg, Jo and Beth, and all exulted over him with the sincere admiration which boys make light of at the time, but fail to win from the world by any after-triumphs.

"I've got to stay for this confounded supper, but I shall be home early tomorrow; you'll come and meet me as usual, girls?" Laurie said, as he put the sisters into the carriage after the joys of the day were over. He said "girls," but he meant Jo, for she was the only one who kept up the old custom; she had not the heart to refuse her splendid, successful boy anything, and answered warmly,—

"I'll come, Teddy, rain or shine, and march before you, playing 'Hail the conquering hero comes,' on a jews-harp."

Laurie thanked her with a look that made her think, in a sudden panic, "Oh, deary me! I know he'll say something, and then what shall I do?"

Evening meditation and morning work somewhat allayed her fears, and having decided that she wouldn't be vain enough to think people were going to propose when she had given them every reason to know what her answer would be, she set forth at the appointed time, hoping Teddy wouldn't do anything to make her hurt his poor little feelings. A call at Meg's, and a refreshing sniff and sip at the Daisy and Demijohn, still further fortified her for the *tête-à-tête,* but when she saw a stalwart figure looming in the distance, she had a strong desire to turn about and run away.

"Where's the jews-harp, Jo?" cried Laurie, as soon as he was within speaking distance.

"I forgot it;" and Jo took heart again, for that salutation could not be called lover-like.

She always used to take his arm on these occasions; now she did not, and he made no complaint, which was a bad sign, but talked on rapidly about all sorts of far-away subjects, till they turned from the road into the little path that led homeward through the grove. Then he walked more slowly, suddenly lost his fine flow of language, and, now and then, a dreadful pause occurred. To rescue the conversation from one of the wells of silence into which it kept falling, Jo said hastily,—

"Now you must have a good long holiday!"

"I intend to."

Something in his resolute tone made Jo look up quickly to find him looking down at her with an expression that assured her the dreaded moment had come, and made her put out her hand with an imploring,—

"No, Teddy, please don't!"

"I will, and you *must* hear me. It's no use, Jo; we've got to have it out, and the sooner the better for both of us," he answered, getting flushed and excited all at once.

"Say what you like, then; I'll listen," said Jo, with a desperate sort of patience.

Laurie was a young lover, but he was in earnest, and meant to "have it out," if he died in the attempt; so he plunged into the subject with characteristic impetuosity, saying in a voice that *would* get choky now and then, in spite of manful efforts to keep it steady,—

"I've loved you ever since I've known you, Jo; couldn't help it, you've been so good to me. I've tried to show it, but you wouldn't let me; now I'm going to make you hear, and give me an answer, for I *can't* go on so any longer."

"I wanted to save you this; I thought you'd understand—" began Jo, finding it a great deal harder than she expected.

"I know you did; but girls are so queer you never know what they mean. They say No when they mean Yes, and drive a man out of his wits just for the fun of it," returned Laurie, entrenching himself behind an undeniable fact.

"*I* don't. I never wanted to make you care for me so, and I went away to keep you from it if I could."

"I thought so; it was like you, but it was no use. I only loved you all the more, and I worked hard to please you, and I gave up billiards and everything you didn't like, and waited and never complained, for I hoped you'd love me, though I'm not half good enough—" here there was a choke that couldn't be controlled, so he decapitated buttercups while he cleared his "confounded throat."

"Yes, you are; you're a great deal too good for me, and I'm so grateful to you, and so proud and fond of you, I don't see why I can't love you as you want me to. I've tried, but I can't change the feeling, and it would be a lie to say I do when I don't."

"Really, truly, Jo?"

He stopped short, and caught both her hands as he put his question with a look that she did not soon forget.

"Really, truly, dear."

They were in the grove now, close by the stile; and when the last words fell reluctantly from Jo's lips, Laurie dropped her hands and turned as if to go on, but for once in his life that fence was too much for him; so he just laid his head down on the mossy post, and stood so still that Jo was frightened.

"O Teddy, I'm so sorry, so desperately sorry, I could kill myself if it would do any good! I wish you wouldn't take it so hard. I can't help it; you know it's impossible for people to make themselves love other people if they don't," cried Jo inelegantly but remorsefully, as she softly patted his shoulder, remembering the time when he had comforted her so long ago.

"They do sometimes," said a muffled voice from the post.

"I don't believe it's the right sort of love, and I'd rather not try it," was the decided answer.

There was a long pause, while a blackbird sung blithely on the willow by the river, and the tall grass rustled in the wind. Presently Jo said very soberly, as she sat down on the step of the stile,—

"Laurie, I want to tell you something."

He started as if he had been shot, threw up his head, and cried out, in a fierce tone—

"*Don't* tell me that, Jo; I can't bear it now!"

"Tell what?" she asked, wondering at his violence.

"That you love that old man."

"What old man?" demanded Jo, thinking he must mean his grandfather.

"That devilish Professor you were always writing about. If you say you love him, I know I shall do something desperate;" and he looked as if he would keep his word, as he clenched his hands, with a wrathful spark in his eyes.

He laid his head down on the mossy post.

Jo wanted to laugh, but restrained herself, and said warmly, for she, too, was getting excited with all this,—

"Don't swear, Teddy! He isn't old, nor anything bad, but good and kind, and the best friend I've got, next to you. Pray, don't fly into a passion; I want to be kind, but I know I shall get angry if you abuse my Professor. I haven't the least idea of loving him or anybody else."

"But you will after a while, and then what will become of me?"

"You'll love someone else too, like a sensible boy, and forget all this trouble."

"I *can't* love anyone else; and I'll never forget you, Jo, never! Never!" with a stamp to emphasize his passionate words.

"What *shall* I do with him?" sighed Jo, finding that emotions were more unmanageable than she expected. "You haven't heard what I wanted to tell you. Sit down and listen; for indeed I want to do right and make you happy," she said, hoping to soothe him with a little reason, which proved that she knew nothing about love.

Seeing a ray of hope in that last speech, Laurie threw himself down on the grass at her feet, leaned his arm on the lower step of the stile, and looked up at her with an expectant face. Now that arrangement was not conducive to calm speech or clear thought on Jo's part; for how *could* she say hard things to her boy while he watched her with eyes full of love and longing, and lashes still wet with the bitter drop or two her hardness of heart had wrung from him? She gently turned his head away, saying, as she stroked the wavy hair which had been allowed to grow for her sake,—how touching that was, to be sure!—

"I agree with mother that you and I are not suited to each other, because our quick tempers and strong wills would probably make us very miserable, if we were so foolish as to—" Jo paused a little over the last word, but Laurie uttered it with a rapturous expression,—

"Marry,—no, we shouldn't! If you loved me, Jo, I should be a perfect saint, for you could make me anything you like."

"No, I can't. I've tried it and failed, and I won't risk our happiness by such a serious experiment. We don't agree and we never shall; so we'll be good friends all our lives, but we won't go and do anything rash."

"Yes, we will if we get the chance," muttered Laurie rebelliously.

"Now do be reasonable, and take a sensible view of the case," implored Jo, almost at her wit's end.

"I won't be reasonable; I don't want to take what you call 'a sensible view;' it won't help me, and it only makes you harder. I don't believe you've got any heart."

"I wish I hadn't!"

There was a little quiver in Jo's voice, and, thinking it a good omen, Laurie turned round, bringing all his persuasive powers to bear as he said, in the wheedlesome tone that had never been so dangerously wheedlesome before,—

"Don't disappoint us, dear! Everyone expects it. Grandpa has set his heart upon it, your people like it, and I can't get on without you. Say you will, and let's be happy. Do, do!"

Not until months afterward did Jo understand how she had the strength of mind to hold fast to the resolution she had made when she decided that she did not love her boy, and never could. It was very hard to do, but she did it, knowing that delay was both useless and cruel.

"I can't say 'Yes' truly, so I won't say it at all. You'll see that I'm right, by and by, and thank me for it"—she began solemnly.

"I'll be hanged if I do!" and Laurie bounced up off the grass, burning with indignation at the bare idea.

"Yes, you will!" persisted Jo; "you'll get over this after a while, and find some lovely, accomplished girl, who will adore you, and make a fine mistress for your fine house. I shouldn't. I'm homely and awkward and odd and old, and you'd be ashamed of me, and we should quarrel,— we can't help it even now, you see,—and I shouldn't like elegant society and you would, and you'd hate my scribbling, and I couldn't get on without it, and we should be unhappy, and wish we hadn't done it, and everything would be horrid!"

"Anything more?" asked Laurie, finding it hard to listen patiently to this prophetic burst.

"Nothing more, except that I don't believe I shall ever marry. I'm happy as I am, and love my liberty too well to be in any hurry to give it up for any mortal man."

"I know better!" broke in Laurie. "You think so now; but there'll come a time when you *will* care for somebody, and you'll love him tremendously, and live and die for him. I know you will, it's your way, and I shall have to stand by and see it;" and the despairing lover cast his hat upon the ground with a gesture that would have seemed comical, if his face had not been so tragical.

"Yes, I *will* live and die for him, if he ever comes and makes me love him in spite of myself, and you must do the best you can!" cried Jo, losing patience with poor Teddy. "I've done my best, but you *won't* be reasonable, and it's selfish of you to keep teasing for what I can't give. I shall always be fond of you, very fond indeed, as a friend, but I'll never marry you; and the sooner you believe it the better for both of us,—so now!"

That speech was like fire to gunpowder. Laurie looked at her a minute as if he did not quite know what to do with himself, then turned sharply away, saying, in a desperate sort of tone,—

"You'll be sorry some day, Jo."

"Oh, where are you going?" she cried, for his face frightened her.

"To the devil!" was the consoling answer.

For a minute Jo's heart stood still, as he swung himself down the bank, toward the river; but it takes much folly, sin, or misery to send a young man to a violent death, and Laurie was not one of the weak sort who are conquered by a single failure. He had no thought of a melodramatic plunge, but some blind instinct led him to fling hat and coat into his boat, and row away with all his might, making better time up the river than he had done in many a race. Jo drew a long breath and unclasped her hands as she watched the poor fellow trying to outstrip the trouble which he carried in his heart.

"That will do him good, and he'll come home in such a tender, penitent state of mind, that I sha'n't dare to see him," she said; adding, as she went slowly home, feeling as if she had murdered some innocent thing, and buried it under the leaves,—

"Now I must go and prepare Mr. Laurence to be very kind to my poor boy. I wish he'd love Beth; perhaps he may, in time, but I begin to think I was mistaken about her. Oh dear! How can girls like to have lovers and refuse them. I think it's dreadful."

Being sure that no one could do it so well as herself, she went straight to Mr. Laurence, told the hard story bravely through, and then broke down, crying so dismally over her own insensibility that the kind old gentleman, though sorely disappointed, did not utter a reproach. He found it difficult to understand how any girl could help loving Laurie, and hoped she would change her mind, but he knew even better than Jo that love cannot be forced, so he shook his head sadly, and resolved to carry his boy out of harm's way; for Young Impetuosity's parting words to Jo disturbed him more than he would confess.

When Laurie came home, dead tired, but quite composed, his grandfather met him as if he knew nothing, and kept up the delusion very successfully for an hour or two. But when they sat together in the twilight, the time they used to enjoy so much, it was hard work for the old man to ramble on as usual, and harder still for the young one to listen to praises of the last year's success, which to him now seemed love's labor lost. He bore it as long as he could, then went to his piano, and began to play. The windows were open; and Jo, walking in the garden with Beth, for once understood music better than her sister, for he played the "Sonata Pathétique," and played it as he never did before.

"That's very fine, I dare say, but it's sad enough to make one cry; give us something gayer, lad," said Mr. Laurence, whose kind old heart was full of sympathy, which he longed to show, but knew not how.

Laurie dashed into a livelier strain, played stormily for several minutes, and would have got through bravely, if, in a momentary lull, Mrs. March's voice had not been heard calling,—

"Jo, dear, come in; I want you."

Just what Laurie longed to say, with a different meaning! As he listened, he lost his place; the music ended with a broken chord, and the musician sat silent in the dark.

"I can't stand this," muttered the old gentleman. Up he got, groped his way to the piano, laid a kind hand on either of the broad shoulders, and said, as gently as a woman,—

"I know, my boy, I know."

No answer for an instant; then Laurie asked sharply,—

"Who told you?"

"Jo herself."

"Then there's an end of it!" and he shook off his grandfather's hands with an impatient motion; for, though grateful for the sympathy, his an's pride could not bear a man's pity.

"Not quite; I want to say one thing, and then there shall be an end of it," returned Mr. Laurence, with unusual mildness. "You won't care to stay at home just now, perhaps?"

"I don't intend to run away from a girl. Jo can't prevent my seeing her, and I shall stay and do it as long as I like," interrupted Laurie, in a defiant tone.

"Not if you are the gentleman I think you. I'm disappointed, but the girl can't help it; and the only thing left for you to do is to go away for a time. Where will you go?"

"Anywhere. I don't care what becomes of me;" and Laurie got up, with a reckless laugh, that grated on his grandfather's ear.

"Take it like a man, and don't do anything rash, for God's sake. Why not go abroad, as you planned, and forget it?"

"I can't."

"But you've been wild to go, and I promised you should when you got through college."

"Ah, but I didn't mean to go alone!" and Laurie walked fast through the room, with an expression which it was well his grandfather did not see.

"I don't ask you to go alone; there's someone ready and glad to go with you, anywhere in the world."

"Who, sir?" stopping to listen.

"Myself."

Laurie came back as quickly as he went, and put out his hand, saying huskily,—

"I'm a selfish brute; but—you know—grandfather—"

"Lord help me, yes, I do know, for I've been through it all before, once in my own young days, and then with your father. Now, my dear boy, just sit quietly down, and hear my plan. It's all settled, and can be carried out at once," said Mr. Laurence, keeping hold of the young man, as if fearful that he would break away, as his father had done before him.

"Well, sir, what is it?" and Laurie sat down, without a sign of interest in face or voice.

"There is business in London that needs looking after; I meant you should attend to it; but I can do it better myself, and things here will get on very well with Brooke to manage them. My partners do almost everything; I'm merely holding on till you take my place, and can be off at any time."

"But you hate travelling, sir; I can't ask it of you at your age," began Laurie, who was grateful for the sacrifice, but much preferred to go alone, if he went at all.

The old gentleman knew that perfectly well, and particularly desired to prevent it; for the mood in which he found his grandson assured him that it would not be wise to leave him to his own devices. So, stifling a natural regret at the thought of the home comforts he would leave behind him, he said stoutly,—

"Bless your soul, I'm not superannuated yet. I quite enjoy the idea; it will do me good, and my old bones won't suffer, for travelling nowadays is almost as easy as sitting in a chair."

A restless movement from Laurie suggested that *his* chair was not easy, or that he did not like the plan, and made the old man add hastily,—

"I don't mean to be a marplot or a burden; I go because I think you'd feel happier than if I was left behind. I don't intend to gad about with you, but leave you free to go where you like, while I amuse myself in my own way. I've friends in London and Paris, and should like to visit them; meantime you can go to Italy, Germany, Switzerland, where you will, and enjoy pictures, music, scenery, and adventures to your heart's content."

Now, Laurie felt just then that his heart was entirely broken, and the world a howling wilderness; but at the sound of certain words which the old gentleman artfully introduced into his closing sentence, the broken heart gave an unexpected leap, and a green oasis or two suddenly appeared in the howling wilderness. He sighed, and then said, in a spiritless tone,—

"Just as you like, sir; it doesn't matter where I go or what I do."

"It does to me, remember that, my lad; I give you entire liberty, but I trust you to make an honest use of it. Promise me that, Laurie."

"Anything you like, sir."

"Good," thought the old gentleman. "You don't care now, but there'll come a time when that promise will keep you out of mischief, or I'm much mistaken."

Being an energetic individual, Mr. Laurence struck while the iron was hot; and before the blighted being recovered spirit enough to rebel, they were off. During the time necessary for preparation, Laurie bore himself as young gentlemen usually do in such cases. He was moody, irritable, and pensive by turns; lost his appetite, neglected his dress, and devoted much time to playing tempestuously on his piano; avoided Jo, but consoled himself by staring at her from his window, with a tragical face that haunted her dreams by night, and oppressed her with a heavy sense of guilt by day. Unlike some sufferers, he never spoke of his unrequited passion, and would allow no one, not even Mrs. March, to attempt consolation or offer sympathy. On some accounts, this was a relief to his friends; but the weeks before his departure were very uncomfortable, and everyone rejoiced that the "poor, dear fellow was going away to forget his trouble, and come home happy." Of course, he smiled darkly at their delusion, but passed it by, with the sad superiority of one who knew that his fidelity, like his love, was unalterable.

When the parting came he affected high spirits, to conceal certain inconvenient emotions which seemed inclined to assert themselves. This gayety did not impose upon anybody, but they tried to look as if it did, for his sake, and he got on very well till Mrs. March kissed him, with a whisper full of motherly solicitude; then, feeling that he was going very fast, he hastily embraced them all round, not forgetting the afflicted Hannah, and ran downstairs as if for his life. Jo followed a minute after to wave her hand to him if he looked round. He did look round, came back, put his arms about her, as she stood on the step above him, and looked up at her with a face that made his short appeal both eloquent and pathetic.

"O Jo, can't you?"

"Teddy, dear, I wish I could!"

That was all, except a little pause; then Laurie straightened himself up, said "It's all right, never mind," and went away without another word. Ah, but it wasn't all right, and Jo *did* mind; for while the curly head lay on her arm a minute after her hard answer, she felt as if she had stabbed her dearest friend; and when he left her without a look behind him, she knew that the boy Laurie never would come again.

# CHAPTER XXXVI

## BETH'S SECRET

WHEN Jo came home that spring, she had been struck with the change in Beth. No one spoke of it or seemed aware of it, for it had come too gradually to startle those who saw her daily; but to eyes sharpened by absence, it was very plain; and a heavy weight fell on Jo's heart as she saw her sister's face. It was no paler and but little thinner than in the autumn; yet there was a strange, transparent look about it, as if the mortal was being slowly refined away, and the immortal shining through the frail flesh with an indescribably pathetic beauty. Jo saw and felt it, but said nothing at the time, and soon the first impression lost much of its power; for Beth seemed happy, no one appeared to doubt that she was better; and, presently, in other cares, Jo for a time forgot her fear.

But when Laurie was gone, and peace prevailed again, the vague anxiety returned and haunted her. She had confessed her sins and been forgiven; but when she showed her savings and proposed the mountain trip, Beth had thanked her heartily, but begged not to go so far away from home. Another little visit to the seashore would suit her better, and, as grandma could not be prevailed upon to leave the babies, Jo took Beth down to the quiet place, where she could live much in the open air, and let the fresh sea-breezes blow a little color into her pale cheeks.

It was not a fashionable place, but, even among the pleasant people there, the girls made few friends, preferring to live for one another. Beth was too shy to enjoy society, and Jo too wrapped up in her to care for anyone else; so were all in all to each other, and came and went, quite unconscious of the interest they excited in those about them, who watched with sympathetic eyes the strong sister and the feeble one, always together, as if they felt instinctively that a long separation was not far away.

They did feel it, yet neither spoke of it; for often between ourselves and those nearest and dearest to us there exists a reserve which it is very hard to overcome. Jo felt as if a veil had fallen between her heart and Beth's; but when she put out her hand to lift it up, there seemed something sacred in the silence, and she waited for Beth to speak. She wondered, and was thankful also, that her parents did not seem to see what she saw; and, during the quiet weeks, when the shadow grew so plain to her, she said nothing of it to those at home, believing that it would tell itself when Beth came back no better. She wondered still more if her sister really guessed the hard truth, and what thoughts were passing through her mind during the long hours when she lay on the warm rocks, with her head in Jo's lap, while the winds blew healthfully over her, and the sea made music at her feet.

One day Beth told her. Jo thought she was asleep, she lay so still; and, putting down her book, sat looking at her with wistful eyes, trying to see signs of hope in the faint color on Beth's cheeks. But she could not find enough to satisfy her, for the cheeks were very thin, and the hands seemed too feeble to hold even the rosy little shells they had been gathering. It came to her then more bitterly than ever that Beth was slowly drifting away from her, and her arms instinctively tightened their hold upon the dearest treasure she possessed. For a minute her eyes were too dim for seeing, and, when they cleared, Beth was looking up at her so tenderly that there was hardly any need for her to say,—

"Jo, dear, I'm glad you know it. I've tried to tell you, but I couldn't."

There was no answer except her sister's cheek against her own, not even tears; for when most deeply moved, Jo did not cry. She was the weaker, then, and Beth tried to comfort and sustain her, with her arms about her, and the soothing words she whispered in her ear.

"I've known it for a good while, dear, and, now I'm used to it, it isn't hard to think of or to bear. Try to see it so, and don't be troubled about me, because it's best; indeed it is."

"Is this what made you so unhappy in the autumn, Beth? You did not feel it then, and keep it to yourself so long, did you?" asked Jo, refusing to see or say that it *was* best, but glad to know that Laurie had no part in Beth's trouble.

"Yes, I gave up hoping then, but I didn't like to own it. I tried to think it was a sick fancy, and would not let it trouble anyone. But when I saw you all so well and strong, and full of happy plans, it was hard to feel that I could never be like you, and then I was miserable, Jo."

"O Beth, and you didn't tell me, didn't let me comfort and help you! How could you shut me out, and bear it all alone?"

Jo's voice was full of tender reproach, and her heart ached to think of the solitary struggle that must have gone on while Beth learned to say good-by to health, love, and life, and take up her cross so cheerfully.

"Perhaps it was wrong, but I tried to do right; I wasn't sure, no one said anything, and I hoped I was mistaken. It would have been selfish to frighten you all when Marmee was so anxious about Meg, and Amy away, and you so happy with Laurie,—at least, I thought so then."

"And I thought that you loved him, Beth, and I went away because I couldn't," cried Jo, glad to say all the truth.

Beth looked so amazed at the idea that Jo smiled in spite of her pain, and added softly,—

"Then you didn't, deary? I was afraid it was so, and imagined your poor little heart full of love-lornity all that while."

"Why, Jo, how could I, when he was so fond of you?" asked Beth, as innocently as a child. "I do love him dearly; he is so good to me, how can I help it? But he never could be anything to me but my brother. I hope he truly will be, sometime."

"Not through me," said Jo decidedly. "Amy is left for him, and they would suit excellently; but I have no heart for such things, now. I don't care what becomes of anybody but you, Beth. You *must* get well."

With her head in Jo's lap, while the wind blew healthfully over her.

"I want to, oh, so much! I try, but every day I lose a little, and feel more sure that I shall never gain it back. It's like the tide, Jo, when it turns, it goes slowly, but it can't be stopped."

"It *shall* be stopped, your tide must noᵗ turn so soon, nineteen is too young. Beth, I can't let you go. I'll work and pray and fight against it. I'll keep you in spite of everything; there must be ways, it can't be too late. God won't be so cruel as to take you from me," cried poor Jo rebelliously, for her spirit was far less piously submissive than Beth's.

Simple, sincere people seldom speak much of their piety; it shows itself in acts, rather than in words, and has more influence than homilies or protestations. Beth could not reason upon or explain the faith that gave her courage and patience to give up life, and cheerfully wait for death. Like a confiding child, she asked no questions, but left everything to God and nature, Father and mother of us all, feeling sure that they, and they only, could teach and strengthen heart and spirit for this life and the life to come. She did not rebuke Jo with saintly speeches, only loved her better for her passionate affection, and clung more closely to the dear human love, from which our Father never means us to be weaned, but through which He draws us closer to Himself. She could not say, "I'm glad to go," for life was very sweet to her; she could only sob out, "I try to be willing," while she held fast to Jo, as the first bitter wave of this great sorrow broke over them together.

By and by Beth said, with recovered serenity,—

"You'll tell them this when we go home?"

"I think they will see it without words," sighed Jo; for now it seemed to her that Beth changed every day.

"Perhaps not; I've heard that the people who love best are often blindest to such things. If they don't see it, you will tell them for me. I don't want any secrets, and it's kinder to prepare them. Meg has John and the babies to comfort her, but you must stand by father and mother, won't you, Jo?"

"If I can; but, Beth, I don't give up yet; I'm going to believe that it *is* a sick fancy, and not let you think it's true," said Jo, trying to speak cheerfully.

Beth lay a minute thinking, and then said in her quiet way,—

"I don't know how to express myself, and shouldn't try to anyone but you, because I can't speak out, except to my Jo. I only mean to say that I have a feeling that it never was intended I should live long. I'm not like the rest of you; I never made any plans about what I'd do when I grew up; I never thought of being married, as you all did. I couldn't seem to imagine myself anything but stupid little Beth, trotting about at home, of no use anywhere but there. I never wanted to go away, and the hard part now is the leaving you all. I'm not afraid, but it seems as if I should be homesick for you even in heaven."

Jo could not speak; and for several minutes there was no sound but the sigh of the wind and the lapping of the tide. A white-winged gull flew by, with the flash of sunshine on its silvery breast; Beth watched it till it vanished, and her eyes were full of sadness. A little gray-coated sand-bird came tripping over the beach, "peeping" softly to itself, as if enjoying the sun and sea; it came quite close to Beth, looked at her with a friendly eye, and sat upon a warm stone, dressing its wet feathers, quite at home. Beth smiled, and felt comforted, for the tiny thing seemed to offer its small friendship, and remind her that a pleasant world was still to be enjoyed.

"Dear little bird! See, Jo, how tame it is. I like peeps better than the gulls: they are not so wild and handsome, but they seem happy, confiding little things. I used to call them my birds, last summer; and mother said they reminded her of me,—busy, quaker-colored creatures, always near the shore, and always chirping that contented little song of theirs. You are the gull, Jo, strong and wild, fond of the storm and the wind, flying far out to sea, and happy all alone. Meg is the turtle-dove, and Amy is like the lark she writes about, trying to get up among the clouds, but always dropping down into its nest again. Dear little girl! She's so ambitious, but her heart is good and tender; and no matter how high she flies, she never will forget home. I hope I shall see her again, but she seems *so* far away."

"She is coming in the spring, and I mean that you shall be all ready to see and enjoy her. I'm going to have you well and rosy by that time," began Jo, feeling that of all the changes in Beth, the talking change was the greatest, for it seemed to cost no effort now, and she thought aloud in a way quite unlike bashful Beth.

"Jo, dear, don't hope any more; it won't do any good, I'm sure of that. We won't be miserable, but enjoy being together while we wait. We'll have happy times, for I don't suffer much, and I think the tide will go out easily, if you help me."

Jo leaned down to kiss the tranquil face; and with that silent kiss, she dedicated herself soul and body to Beth.

She was right: there was no need of any words when they got home, for father and mother saw plainly, now, what they had prayed to be saved from seeing. Tired with her short journey, Beth went at once to bed, saying how glad she was to be at home; and when Jo went down, she found that she would be spared the hard task of telling Beth's secret. Her father stood leaning his head on the mantel-piece, and did not turn as she came in; but her mother stretched out her arms as if for help, and Jo went to comfort her without a word.

# CHAPTER XXXVII

## NEW IMPRESSIONS

AT three o'clock in the afternoon, all the fashionable world at Nice may be seen on the Promenade des Anglais,—a charming place; for the wide walk, bordered with palms, flowers, and tropical shrubs, is bounded on one side by the sea, on the other by the grand drive, lined with hotels and villas, while beyond lie orange-orchards and the hills. Many nations are represented, many languages spoken, many costumes worn; and, on a sunny day, the spectacle is as gay and brilliant as a carnival. Haughty

English, lively French, sober Germans, handsome Spaniards, ugly Russians, meek Jews, free-and-easy Americans, all drive, sit, or saunter here, chatting over the news, and criticizing the latest celebrity who has arrived,— Ristori or Dickens, Victor Emmanuel or the Queen of the Sandwich Islands. The equipages are as varied as the company, and attract as much attention, especially the low basket-barouches in which ladies drive themselves, with a pair of dashing ponies, gay nets to keep their voluminous flounces from overflowing the diminutive vehicles, and little grooms on the perch behind.

Along this walk, on Christmas Day, a tall young man walked slowly, with his hands behind him, and a somewhat absent expression of coun- tenance. He looked like an Italian, was dressed like an Englishman, and had the independent air of an American,—a combination which caused sundry pairs of feminine eyes to look approvingly after him, and sundry dandies in black velvet suits, with rose-colored neckties, buff gloves, and orange-flowers in their button-holes, to shrug their shoulders, and then envy him his inches. There were plenty of pretty faces to admire, but the young man took little notice of them, except to glance, now and then, at some blonde girl, or lady in blue. Presently he strolled out of the promenade, and stood a moment at the crossing, as if undecided whether to go and listen to the band in the Jardin Publique, or to wander along the beach toward Castle Hill. The quick trot of ponies' feet made him look up, as one of the little carriages, containing a single lady, came rapidly down the street. The lady was young, blonde, and dressed in blue. He stared a minute, then his whole face woke up, and, waving his hat like a boy, he hurried forward to meet her.

"O Laurie, is it really you? I thought you'd never come!" cried Amy, dropping the reins, and holding out both hands, to the great scandalization of a French mamma, who hastened her daughter's steps, lest she should be demoralized by beholding the free manners of these "mad English."

"I was detained by the way, but I promised to spend Christmas with you, and here I am."

"How is your grandfather? When did you come? Where are you staying?"

"Very well—last night—at the Chauvain. I called at your hotel, but you were all out."

"I have so much to say, I don't know where to begin! Get in, and we can talk at our ease; I was going for a drive, and longing for company. Flo's saving up for tonight."

"What happens then, a ball?"

"A Christmas party at our hotel. There are many Americans there, and they give it in honor of the day. You'll go with us, of course? Aunt will be charmed."

"Thank you. Where now?" asked Laurie, leaning back and folding his arms, a proceeding which suited Amy, who preferred to drive; for her parasol-whip and blue reins over the white ponies' backs, afforded her infinite satisfaction.

"I'm going to the banker's first, for letters, and then to Castle Hill; the view is so lovely, and I like to feed the peacocks. Have you ever been there?"

"Often, years ago; but I don't mind having a look at it."

"Now tell me all about yourself. The last I heard of you, your grandfather wrote that he expected you from Berlin."

"Yes, I spent a month there, and then joined him in Paris, where he has settled for the winter. He has friends there, and finds plenty to amuse him; so I go and come, and we get on capitally."

"That's a sociable arrangement," said Amy, missing something in Laurie's manner, though she couldn't tell what.

"Why, you see he hates to travel, and I hate to keep still; so we each suit ourselves, and there is no trouble. I am often with him, and he enjoys my adventures, while I like to feel that someone is glad to see me when I get back from my wanderings. Dirty old hole, isn't it?" he added, with a look of disgust, as they drove along the boulevard to the Place Napoleon, in the old city.

"The dirt is picturesque, so I don't mind. The river and the hills are delicious, and these glimpses of the narrow cross-streets are my delight. Now we shall have to wait for that procession to pass; it's going to the Church of St. John."

While Laurie listlessly watched the procession of priests under their canopies, white-veiled nuns bearing lighted tapers, and some brotherhood in blue, chanting as they walked, Amy watched him, and felt a new sort of shyness steal over her; for he was changed, and she could not find the merry-faced boy she left in the moody-looking man beside her. He was handsomer than ever, and greatly improved, she thought; but now that the flush of pleasure at meeting her was over, he looked tired and spiritless,—not sick, nor exactly unhappy, but older and graver than a year or two of prosperous life should have made him. She couldn't understand it, and did not venture to ask questions; so she shook her head, and touched up her ponies, as the procession wound away across the arches of the Paglioni bridge, and vanished in the church.

"*Que pensez vous?*" she said, airing her French, which had improved in quantity, if not in quality, since she came abroad.

"That mademoiselle has made good use of her time, and the result is charming," replied Laurie, bowing, with his hand on his heart, and an admiring look.

She blushed with pleasure, but somehow the compliment did not satisfy her like the blunt praises he used to give her at home, when he promenaded round her on festival occasions, and told her she was "altogether jolly," with a hearty smile and an approving pat on the head. She didn't like the new tone; for, though not *blasé*, it sounded indifferent in spite of the look.

"If that's the way he's going to grow up, I wish he'd stay a boy," she thought, with a curious sense of disappointment and discomfort, trying meantime to seem quite easy and gay.

At Avigdor's she found the precious home-letters, and, giving the reins to Laurie, read them luxuriously as they wound up the shady road between green hedges, where tea-roses bloomed as freshly as in June.

"Beth is very poorly, mother says. I often think I ought to go home, but they all say 'stay;' so I do, for I shall never have another chance like this," said Amy, looking sober over one page.

"I think you are right, there; you could do nothing at home, and it is a great comfort to them to know that you are well and happy, and enjoying so much, my dear."

He drew a little nearer, and looked more like his old self, as he said that; and the fear that sometimes weighed on Amy's heart was lightened, for the look, the act, the brotherly "my dear," seemed to assure her that if any trouble did come, she would not be alone in a strange land. Presently she laughed, and showed him a small sketch of Jo in her scribbling-suit, with the bow rampantly erect upon her cap, and issuing from her mouth the words, "Genius burns!"

Laurie smiled, took it, put it in his vest-pocket, "to keep it from blowing away," and listened with interest to the lively letter Amy read him.

"This will be a regularly merry Christmas to me, with presents in the morning, you and letters in the afternoon, and a party at night," said Amy, as they alighted among the ruins of the old fort, and a flock of splendid peacocks came trooping about them, tamely waiting to be fed. While Amy stood laughing on the bank above him as she scattered crumbs to the brilliant birds, Laurie looked at her as she had looked at him, with a natural curiosity to see what changes time and absence had wrought. He found nothing to perplex or disappoint, much to admire and approve; for, overlooking a few little affectations of speech and manner, she was as sprightly and graceful as ever, with the addition of that indescribable something in dress and bearing which we call elegance. Always mature for her age, she had gained a certain *aplomb* in both carriage and conversation, which made her seem more of a woman of the world than she was; but her old petulance now and then showed itself, her strong will still held its own, and her native frankness was unspoiled by foreign polish.

Laurie did not read all this while he watched her feed the peacocks, but he saw enough to satisfy and interest him, and carried away a pretty little picture of a bright-faced girl standing in the sunshine, which brought out the soft hue of her dress, the fresh color of her cheeks, the golden gloss of her hair, and made her a prominent figure in the pleasant scene.

As they came up on to the stone plateau that crowns the hill, Amy waved her hand as if welcoming him to her favorite haunt, and said, pointing here and there,—

"Do you remember the Cathedral and the Corso, the fishermen dragging their nets in the bay, and the lovely road to Villa Franca, Schubert's Tower, just below, and, best of all, that speck far out to sea which they say is Corsica?"

"I remember; it's not much changed," he answered, without enthusiasm.

"What Jo would give for a sight of that famous speck!" said Amy, feeling in good spirits, and anxious to see him so also.

"Yes," was all he said, but he turned and strained his eyes to see the island which a greater usurper than even Napoleon now made interesting in his sight.

"Take a good look at it for her sake, and then come and tell me what you have been doing with yourself all this while," said Amy, seating herself, ready for a good talk.

But she did not get it; for, though he joined her, and answered all her questions freely, she could only learn that he had roved about the continent and been to Greece. So, after idling away an hour, they drove home again; and, having paid his respects to Mrs. Carrol, Laurie left them, promising to return in the evening.

It must be recorded of Amy that she deliberately "prinked" that night. Time and absence had done its work on both the young people; she had seen her old friend in a new light, not as "our boy," but as a handsome and agreeable man, and she was conscious of a very natural desire to find favor in his sight. Amy knew her good points, and made the most of them, with the taste and skill which is a fortune to a poor and pretty woman.

Tarlatan and tulle were cheap at Nice, so she enveloped herself in them on such occasions, and, following the sensible English fashion of simple dress for young girls, got up charming little toilettes with fresh flowers, a few trinkets, and all manner of dainty devices, which were both inexpensive and effective. It must be confessed that the artist sometimes got possession of the woman, and indulged in antique *coiffures*, statuesque attitudes, and classic draperies. But, dear heart, we all have our little weaknesses, and find it easy to pardon such in the young, who satisfy our eyes with their comeliness, and keep our hearts merry with their artless vanities.

"I do want him to think I look well, and tell them so at home," said Amy to herself, as she put on Flo's old white silk ball-dress, and covered it with a cloud of fresh illusion, out of which her white shoulders and golden head emerged with a most artistic effect. Her hair she had the sense to let alone, after gathering up the thick waves and curls into a Hebe-like knot at the back of her head.

"It's not the fashion, but it's becoming, and I can't afford to make a fright of myself," she used to say, when advised to frizzle, puff, or braid, as the latest style commanded.

Having no ornaments fine enough for this important occasion, Amy looped her fleecy skirts with rosy clusters of azalea, and framed the white shoulders in delicate green vines. Remembering the painted boots, she surveyed her white satin slippers with girlish satisfaction, and *chasséed* down the room, admiring her aristocratic feet all by herself.

"My new fan just matches my flowers, my gloves fit to a charm, and the real lace on aunt's *mouchoir* gives an air to my whole dress. If I only had a classical nose and mouth I should be perfectly happy," she said, surveying herself with a critical eye, and a candle in each hand.

In spite of this affliction, she looked unusually gay and graceful as she glided away; she seldom ran,—it did not suit her style, she thought, for, being tall, the stately and Junoesque was more appropriate than the sportive or piquante. She walked up and down the long saloon while waiting for Laurie, and once arranged herself under the chandelier, which had a good effect upon her hair; then she thought better of it, and went away to the other end of the room, as if ashamed of the girlish desire to have the first view a propitious one. It so happened that she could not have done a better thing, for Laurie came in so quietly she did not hear him; and, as she stood at the distant window, with her head half turned, and one hand gathering up her dress, the slender, white figure against the red curtains was as effective as a well-placed statue.

"Good evening, Diana!" said Laurie, with the look of satisfaction she liked to see in his eyes when they rested on her.

"Good evening, Apollo!" she answered, smiling back at him, for he, too, looked unusually *debonnaire,* and the thought of entering the ball-room on the arm of such a personable man caused Amy to pity the four plain Misses Davis from the bottom of her heart.

"Here are your flowers; I arranged them myself, remembering that you didn't like what Hannah calls a 'sot-bookay,' " said Laurie, handing her a delicate nosegay, in a holder that she had long coveted as she daily passed it in Cardiglia's window.

"How kind you are!" she exclaimed gratefully. "If I'd known you were coming I'd have had something ready for you today, though not as pretty as this, I'm afraid."

"Thank you; it isn't what it should be, but you have improved it," he added, as she snapped the silver bracelet on her wrist.

"Please don't."

"I thought you liked that sort of thing?"

"Not from you; it doesn't sound natural, and I like your old bluntness better."

"I'm glad of it," he answered, with a look of relief; then buttoned her gloves for her, and asked if his tie was straight, just as he used to do when they went to parties together, at home.

The company assembled in the long *salle à manger,* that evening, was such as one sees nowhere but on the Continent. The hospitable Americans had invited every acquaintance they had in Nice, and, having no prejudice against titles, secured a few to add lustre to their Christmas ball.

A Russian prince condescended to sit in a corner for an hour, and talk with a massive lady, dressed like Hamlet's mother, in black velvet, with a pearl bridle under her chin. A Polish count, aged eighteen, devoted himself to the ladies, who pronounced him "a fascinating dear," and a German Serene Something, having come for the supper alone, roamed vaguely about, seeking what he might devour. Baron Rothschild's private secretary, a large-nosed Jew, in tight boots, affably beamed upon the world, as if his master's name crowned him with a golden halo; a stout Frenchman, who knew the Emperor, came to indulge his mania for dancing, and Lady de Jones, a British matron, adorned the scene with her little family of eight. Of course, there were many light-footed, shrill-voiced American girls, handsome, lifeless-looking English ditto, and a few plain but piquante French demoiselles; likewise the usual set of travelling young gentlemen, who disported themselves gayly, while mammas of all nations lined the walls, and smiled upon them benignly when they danced with their daughters.

Any young girl can imagine Amy's state of mind when she "took the stage" that night, leaning on Laurie's arm. She knew she looked well, she loved to dance, she felt that her foot was on her native heath in a ball-room, and enjoyed the delightful sense of power which comes when young girls first discover the new and lovely kingdom they are born to rule by virtue of beauty, youth, and womanhood. She did pity the Davis girls, who were awkward, plain, and destitute of escort, except a grim papa and three grimmer maiden aunts, and she bowed to them in her

"Here are your flowers."

friendliest manner as she passed; which was good of her, as it permitted them to see her dress, and burn with curiosity to know who her distinguished-looking friend might be. With the first burst of the band, Amy's color rose, her eyes began to sparkle, and her feet to tap the floor impatiently; for she danced well, and wanted Laurie to know it: therefore the shock she received can better be imagined than described, when he said, in a perfectly tranquil tone,—

"Do you care to dance?"

"One usually does at a ball."

Her amazed look and quick answer caused Laurie to repair his error as fast as possible.

"I meant the first dance. May I have the honor?"

"I can give you one if I put off the Count. He dances divinely; but he will excuse me, as you are an old friend," said Amy, hoping that the name would have a good effect, and show Laurie that she was not to be trifled with.

"Nice little boy, but rather a short Pole to support

> " 'A daughter of the gods,
>    Divinely tall, and most divinely fair,' "

was all the satisfaction she got, however.

The set in which they found themselves was composed of English, and Amy was compelled to walk decorously through a cotillon, feeling all the while as if she could dance the Tarantula with a relish. Laurie resigned her to the "nice little boy," and went to do his duty to Flo, without securing Amy for the joys to come, which reprehensible want of forethought was properly punished, for she immediately engaged herself till supper, meaning to relent if he then gave any signs of penitence. She showed him her ball-book with demure satisfaction when he strolled, instead of rushing, up to claim her for the next, a glorious polka-redowa; but his polite regrets didn't impose upon her, and when she gallopaded away with the Count, she saw Laurie sit down by her aunt with an actual expression of relief.

That was unpardonable; and Amy took no more notice of him for a long while, except a word now and then, when she came to her chaperon, between the dances, for a necessary pin or a moment's rest. Her anger had a good effect, however, for she hid it under a smiling face, and seemed unusually blithe and brilliant. Laurie's eyes followed her with pleasure, for she neither romped nor sauntered, but danced with spirit and grace, making the delightsome pastime what it should be. He very naturally fell to studying her from this new point of view; and, before the evening was half over, had decided that "little Amy was going to make a very charming woman."

It was a lively scene, for soon the spirit of the social season took possession of everyone, and Christmas merriment made all faces shine, hearts happy, and heels light. The musicians fiddled, tooted, and banged as if they enjoyed it; everybody danced who could, and those who couldn't admired their neighbors with uncommon warmth. The air was dark with Davises, and many Joneses gambolled like a flock of young giraffes. The golden secretary darted through the room like a meteor, with a dashing Frenchwoman, who carpeted the floor with her pink satin train. The Serene Teuton found the supper-table, and was happy, eating steadily through the bill of fare, and dismayed the *garçons* by the ravages he committed. But the Emperor's friend covered himself with glory, for he danced everything, whether he knew it or not, and introduced impromptu pirouettes when the figures bewildered him. The boyish abandon of that stout man was charming to behold; for, though he "carried weight," he danced like an india-rubber ball. He ran, he flew, he pranced; his face glowed, his bald head shone; his coat-tails waved wildly, his pumps actually twinkled in the air, and when the music stopped, he wiped the drops from his brow, and beamed upon his fellow-men like a French Pickwick without glasses.

Amy and her Pole distinguished themselves by equal enthusiasm, but more graceful agility; and Laurie found himself involuntarily keeping time to the rhythmic rise and fall of the white slippers as they flew by as indefatigably as if winged. When little Vladimir finally relinquished her, with assurances that he was "desolated to leave so early," she was ready to rest, and see how her recreant knight had borne his punishment.

It had been successful; for, at three-and-twenty, blighted affections find a balm in friendly society, and young nerves will thrill, young blood dance, and healthy young spirits rise, when subjected to the enchantment of beauty, light, music, and motion. Laurie had a waked-up look as he rose to give her his seat; and when he hurried away to bring her some supper, she said to herself, with a satisfied smile,—

"Ah, I thought that would do him good!"

"You look like Balzac's 'Femme peinte par elle-même,' " he said, as he fanned her with one hand, and held her coffee-cup in the other.

"My rouge won't come off;" and Amy rubbed her brilliant cheek, and showed him her white glove with a sober simplicity that made him laugh outright.

"What do you call this stuff?" he asked, touching a fold of her dress that had blown over his knee.

"Illusion."

"Good name for it; it's very pretty—new thing, isn't it?"

"It's as old as the hills; you have seen it on dozens of girls, and you never found out that it was pretty till now—*stupide!*"

"I never saw it on you before, which accounts for the mistake, you see,"

"None of that, it is forbidden; I'd rather take coffee than compliments just now. No, don't lounge, it makes me nervous."

Laurie sat bolt upright, and meekly took her empty plate, feeling an odd sort of pleasure in having "little Amy" order him about; for she had lost her shyness now, and felt an irresistible desire to trample on him, as girls have a delightful way of doing when lords of creation show any signs of subjection.

"Where did you learn all this sort of thing?" he asked, with a quizzical look.

"As 'this sort of thing' is rather a vague expression, would you kindly explain?" returned Amy, knowing perfectly well what he meant, but wickedly leaving him to describe what is indescribable.

"Well—the general air, the style, the self-possession, the—the—illusion—you know," laughed Laurie, breaking down, and helping himself out of his quandary with the new word.

Amy was gratified, but, of course, didn't show it, and demurely answered, "Foreign life polishes one in spite of one's self; I study as well as play; and as for this"—with a little gesture toward her dress—"why, tulle is cheap, posies to be had for nothing, and I am used to making the most of my poor little things."

Amy rather regretted that last sentence, fearing it wasn't in good taste; but Laurie liked her the better for it, and found himself both admiring and respecting the brave patience that made the most of opportunity, and the cheerful spirit that covered poverty with flowers. Amy did not know why he looked at her so kindly, nor why he filled up her book with his own name, and devoted himself to her for the rest of the evening, in the most delightful manner; but the impulse that wrought this agreeable change was the result of one of the new impressions which both of them were unconsciously giving and receiving.

# CHAPTER XXXVIII

## ON THE SHELF

IN France the young girls have a dull time of it till they are married, when *"Vive la liberté"* becomes their motto. In America, as everyone knows, girls early sign the declaration of independence, and enjoy their freedom with republican zest; but the young matrons usually abdicate with the first heir to the throne, and go into a seclusion almost as close as a French nunnery, though by no means as quiet. Whether they like it or not, they are virtually put upon the shelf as soon as the wedding excitement is over, and most of them might exclaim, as did a very pretty woman the other day, "I'm as handsome as ever, but no one takes any notice of me because I'm married."

Not being a belle or even a fashionable lady, Meg did not experience this affliction till her babies were a year old, for in her little world primitive customs prevailed, and she found herself more admired and beloved than ever.

As she was a womanly little woman, the maternal instinct was very strong, and she was entirely absorbed in her children, to the utter exclusion of everything and everybody else. Day and night she brooded over them with tireless devotion and anxiety, leaving John to the tender mercies of the help, for an Irish lady now presided over the kitchen department. Being a domestic man, John decidedly missed the wifely attentions he had been accustomed to receive; but, as he adored his babies, he cheerfully relinquished his comfort for a time, supposing, with masculine ignorance, that peace would soon be restored. But three months passed, and there was no return of repose; Meg looked worn and nervous, the babies absorbed every minute of her time, the house was neglected, and Kitty, the cook, who took life "aisy," kept him on short commons. When he went out in the morning he was bewildered by small commissions for the captive mamma; if he came gayly in at night, eager to embrace his family, he was quenched by a "Hush! They are just asleep after worrying all day." If he proposed a little amusement at home, "No, it would disturb the babies." If he hinted at a lecture or concert, he was answered with a reproachful look, and a decided "Leave my children for pleasure, never!" His sleep was broken by infant wails and visions of a phantom figure pacing noiselessly to and fro in the watches of the night; his meals were interrupted by the frequent flight of the presiding genius, who deserted him, half-helped, if a muffled chirp sounded from the nest above; and when he read his paper of an evening, Demi's colic got into the shipping-list, and Daisy's fall affected the price of stocks, for Mrs. Brooke was only interested in domestic news.

The poor man was very uncomfortable, for the children had bereft him of his wife; home was merely a nursery, and the perpetual "hushing" made him feel like a brutal intruder whenever he entered the sacred precincts of Babyland. He bore it very patiently for six months, and, when no signs of amendment appeared, he did what other paternal exiles do,—tried to get a little comfort elsewhere. Scott had married and gone to housekeeping not far off, and John fell into the way of running over for an hour or two of an evening, when his own parlor was empty, and his own wife singing lullabies that seemed to have no end. Mrs. Scott was a lively, pretty girl, with nothing to do but be agreeable, and she performed her mission most successfully. The parlor was always bright and attractive, the chess-board ready, the piano in tune, plenty of gay gossip, and a nice little supper set forth in tempting style.

John would have preferred his own fireside if it had not been so lonely; but as it was, he gratefully took the next best thing, and enjoyed his neighbor's society.

Meg rather approved of the new arrangement at first, and found it a relief to know that John was having a good time instead of dozing in the parlor, or tramping about the house and waking the children. But by and by, when the teething worry was over, and the idols went to sleep at proper hours, leaving mamma time to rest, she began to miss John, and find her work basket dull company, when he was not sitting opposite in his old dressing gown, comfortably scorching his slippers on the fender. She would not ask him to stay at home, but felt injured because he did not know that she wanted him without being told, entirely forgetting the many evenings he had waited for her in vain. She was nervous and worn out with watching and worry, and in that unreasonable frame of mind which the best of mothers occasionally experience when domestic cares oppress them. Want of exercise robs them of cheerfulness, and too much devotion to that idol of American women, the teapot, makes them feel as if they were all nerve and no muscle.

"Yes," she would say, looking in the glass, "I'm getting old and ugly; John doesn't find me interesting any longer, so he leaves his faded wife and goes to see his pretty neighbor, who has no incumbrances. Well, the babies love me; they don't care if I am thin and pale, and haven't time to crimp my hair; they are my comfort, and some day John will see what I've gladly sacrificed for them, won't he, my precious?"

To which pathetic appeal Daisy would answer with a coo, or Demi with a crow, and Meg would put by her lamentations for a maternal revel, which soothed her solitude for the time being. But the pain increased as politics absorbed John, who was always running over to discuss interesting points with Scott, quite unconscious that Meg missed him. Not a word did she say, however, till her mother found her in tears one day, and insisted on knowing what the matter was, for Meg's drooping spirits had not escaped her observation.

"I wouldn't tell anyone except you, mother; but I really do need advice, for, if John goes on so much longer I might as well be widowed," replied Mrs. Brooke, drying her tears on Daisy's bib, with an injured air.

"Goes on how, my dear?" asked her mother anxiously.

"He's away all day, and at night, when I want to see him, he is continually going over to the Scotts'. It isn't fair that I should have the hardest work, and never any amusement. Men are very selfish, even the best of them."

"So are women; don't blame John till you see where you are wrong yourself."

"But it can't be right for him to neglect me."

"Don't you neglect him?"

"Why, mother, I thought you'd take my part!"

"So I do, as far as sympathizing goes; but I think the fault is yours, Meg."

"I don't see how."

"Let me show you. Did John ever neglect you, as you call it, while you made it a point to give him your society of an evening, his only leisure time?"

"No; but I can't do it now, with two babies to tend."

"I think you could, dear; and I think you ought. May I speak quite freely, and will you remember that it's mother who blames as well as mother who sympathizes?"

"Indeed I will! Speak to me as if I were little Meg again. I often feel as if I needed teaching more than ever since these babies look to me for everything."

Meg drew her low chair beside her mother's, and, with a little interruption in either lap, the two women rocked and talked lovingly together, feeling that the tie of motherhood made them more one than ever.

"You have only made the mistake that most young wives make,— forgotten your duty to your husband in your love for your children. A very natural and forgivable mistake, Meg, but one that had better be remedied before you take to different ways; for children should draw you nearer than ever, not separate you, as if they were all yours, and John had nothing to do but support them. I've seen it for some weeks, but have not spoken, feeling sure it would come right in time."

"I'm afraid it won't. If I ask him to stay, he'll think I'm jealous; and I wouldn't insult him by such an idea. He doesn't see that I want him, and I don't know how to tell him without words."

"Make it so pleasant he won't want to go away. My dear, he's longing for his little home; but it isn't home without you, and you are always in the nursery."

"Oughtn't I to be there?"

"Not all the time; too much confinement makes you nervous, and then you are unfitted for everything. Besides, you owe something to John as well as to the babies; don't neglect husband for children, don't shut him out of the nursery, but teach him how to help in it. His place is there as well as yours, and the children need him; let him feel that he has his part to do, and he will do it gladly and faithfully, and it will be better for you all."

"You really think so, mother?"

"I know it, Meg, for I've tried it; and I seldom give advice unless I've proved its practicability. When you and Jo were little, I went on just as you are, feeling as if I didn't do my duty unless I devoted myself wholly to you. Poor father took to his books, after I had refused all offers of help, and left me to try my experiment alone. I struggled along as well as I could, but Jo was too much for me. I nearly spoilt her by indulgence. You were poorly, and I worried about you till I fell sick myself. Then father came to the rescue, quietly managed everything, and made himself so helpful that I saw my mistake, and never have been able to get on without him since. That is the secret of our home happiness: he does not let business wean him from the little cares and duties that affect us all, and I try not to let domestic worries destroy my interest in his pursuits. Each do our part alone in many things, but at home we work together, always."

"It is so, mother; and my great wish is to be to my husband and children what you have been to yours. Show me how; I'll do anything you say."

"You always were my docile daughter. Well, dear, if I were you, I'd let John have more to do with the management of Demi, for the boy needs training, and it's none too soon to begin. Then I'd do what I have often proposed, let Hannah come and help you; she is a capital nurse, and you may trust the precious babies to her while you do more housework. You need the exercise, Hannah would enjoy the rest, and John would find his wife again. Go out more; keep cheerful as well as busy, for you are the sunshine-maker of the family, and if you get dismal there is no fair weather. Then I'd try to take an interest in whatever John likes,— talk with him, let him read to you, exchange ideas, and help each other in that way. Don't shut yourself up in a bandbox because you are a woman, but understand what is going on, and educate yourself to take your part in the world's work, for it all affects you and yours."

"John is so sensible, I'm afraid he will think I'm stupid if I ask questions about politics and things."

"I don't believe he would; love covers a multitude of sins, and of whom could you ask more freely than of him? Try it, and see if he doesn't find your society far more agreeable than Mrs. Scott's suppers."

"I will. Poor John! I'm afraid I *have* neglected him sadly, but I thought I was right, and he never said anything."

"He tried not to be selfish, but he *has* felt rather forlorn, I fancy. This is just the time, Meg, when young married people are apt to grow apart, and the very time when they ought to be most together; for the first tenderness soon wears off, unless care is taken to preserve it; and no time is so beautiful and precious to parents as the first years of the little lives given them to train. Don't let John be a stranger to the babies, for they will do more to keep him safe and happy in this world of trial and temptation than anything else, and through them you will learn to know and love one another as you should. Now, dear, good-by; think over mother's preachment, act upon it if it seems good, and God bless you all!"

Meg did think it over, found it good, and acted upon it, though the first attempt was not made exactly as she planned to have it. Of course the children tyrannized over her, and ruled the house as soon as they found out that kicking and squalling brought them whatever they wanted. Mamma was an abject slave to their caprices, but papa was not so easily subjugated, and occasionally afflicted his tender spouse by an attempt at paternal discipline with his obstreperous son. For Demi inherited a trifle of his sire's firmness of character,—we won't call it obstinacy,— and when he made up his little mind to have or to do anything, all the king's horses and all the king's men could not change that pertinacious little mind. Mamma thought the dear too young to be taught to conquer his prejudices, but papa believed that it never was too soon to learn obedience; so Master Demi early discovered that when he undertook to "wrastle" with "parpar," he always got the worst of it; yet, like the Eng- lishman, Baby respected the man who conquered him, and loved the father whose grave "No, no," was more impressive than all mamma's love-pats.

A few days after the talk with her mother, Meg resolved to try a social evening with John; so she ordered a nice supper, set the parlor in order, dressed herself prettily, and put the children to bed early, that nothing should interfere with her experiment. But, unfortunately, Demi's most unconquerable prejudice was against going to bed, and that night he decided to go on a rampage; so poor Meg sung and rocked, told stories and tried every sleep-provoking wile she could devise, but all in vain, the big eyes wouldn't shut; and long after Daisy had gone to byelow, like the chubby little bunch of good-nature she was, naughty Demi lay staring at the light, with the most discouragingly wide-awake expression of countenance.

"Will Demi lie still like a good boy, while mamma runs down and gives poor papa his tea?" asked Meg, as the hall-door softly closed, and the well-known step went tiptoeing into the dining-room.

"Me has tea!" said Demi, preparing to join in the revel.

"No; but I'll save you some little cakies for breakfast, if you'll go bye-by like Daisy. Will you, lovey?"

"Iss!" and Demi shut his eyes tight, as if to catch sleep and hurry the desired day.

Taking advantage of the propitious moment, Meg slipped away, and ran down to greet her husband with a smiling face, and the little blue bow in her hair which was his especial admiration. He saw it at once, and said, with pleased surprise,—

"Why, little mother, how gay we are tonight. Do you expect company?"

"Only you, dear."

"Is it a birthday, anniversary, or anything?"

"No; I'm tired of being a dowdy, so I dressed up as a change. You always make yourself nice for table, no matter how tired you are; so why shouldn't I when I have the time?"

"I do it out of respect to you, my dear," said old-fashioned John.

"Ditto, ditto, Mr. Brooke," laughed Meg, looking young and pretty again, as she nodded to him over the teapot.

"Well, it's altogether delightful, and like old times. This tastes right. I drink your health, dear." And John sipped his tea with an air of reposeful rapture, which was of very short duration, however; for, as he put down his cup, the door-handle rattled mysteriously, and a little voice was heard, saying impatiently,—

"Opy doy; me's tummin!"

"It's that naughty boy. I told him to go to sleep alone, and here he is, downstairs, getting his death a-cold pattering over that canvas," said Meg, answering the call.

"Mornin' now," announced Demi, in a joyful tone, as he entered, with his long night-gown gracefully festooned over his arm, and every curl bobbing gayly as he pranced about the table, eying the "cakies" with loving glances.

"No, it isn't morning yet. You must go to bed, and not trouble poor mamma; then you can have the little cake with sugar on it."

"Me loves parpar," said the artful one, preparing to climb the paternal knee, and revel in forbidden joys. But John shook his head, and said to Meg,—

"If you told him to stay up there, and go to sleep alone, make him do it, or he will never learn to mind you."

"Yes, of course. Come, Demi;" and Meg led her son away, feeling a strong desire to spank the little marplot who hopped beside her, laboring under the delusion that the bribe was to be administered as soon as they reached the nursery.

Nor was he disappointed; for that short-sighted woman actually gave him a lump of sugar, tucked him into his bed, and forbade any more promenades till morning.

"Iss!" said Demi the perjured, blissfully sucking his sugar, and regarding his first attempt as eminently successful.

Meg returned to her place, and supper was progressing pleasantly, when the little ghost walked again, and exposed the maternal delinquencies by boldly demanding,—

"More sudar, marmar."

"Now this won't do," said John, hardening his heart against the engaging little sinner. "We shall never know any peace till that child learns to go to bed properly. You have made a slave of yourself long enough; give him one lesson, and then there will be an end of it. Put him in his bed and leave him, Meg."

"He won't stay there; he never does, unless I sit by him."

"I'll manage him. Demi, go upstairs, and get into your bed, as mamma bids you."

"S'ant!" replied the young rebel, helping himself to the coveted "cakie," and beginning to eat the same with calm audacity.

"You must never say that to papa; I shall carry you if you don't go yourself."

"Go 'way; me don't love parpar;" and Demi retired to his mother's skirts for protection.

But even that refuge proved unavailing, for he was delivered over to the enemy, with a "Be gentle with him, John," which struck the culprit with dismay; for when mamma deserted him, then the judgment-day was at hand. Bereft of his cake, defrauded of his frolic, and borne away by a strong hand to that detested bed, poor Demi could not restrain his wrath, but openly defied papa, and kicked and screamed lustily all the way upstairs. The minute he was put into bed on one side, he rolled out on the other, and made for the door, only to be ignominiously caught up by the tail of his little toga, and put back again, which lively performance was kept up till the young man's strength gave out, when he devoted himself to roaring at the top of his voice. This vocal exercise usually conquered Meg; but John sat as unmoved as the post which is popularly believed to be deaf. No coaxing, no sugar, no lullaby, no story; even the light was put out, and only the red glow of the fire enlivened the "big dark" which Demi regarded with curiosity rather than fear. This new order of things disgusted him, and he howled dismally for "marmar," as his angry passions subsided, and recollections of his tender bondwoman returned to the captive autocrat. The plaintive wail which succeeded the passionate roar went to Meg's heart, and she ran up to say beseechingly,—

"Let me stay with him; he'll be good, now, John."

"No, my dear, I've told him he must go to sleep, as you bid him; and he must, if I stay here all night."

"But he'll cry himself sick," pleaded Meg, reproaching herself for deserting her boy.

"No, he won't, he's so tired he will soon drop off, and then the matter is settled; for he will understand that he has got to mind. Don't interfere; I'll manage him."

"He's my child, and I can't have his spirit broken by harshness."

"He's my child, and I won't have his temper spoilt by indulgence. Go down, my dear, and leave the boy to me."

When John spoke in that masterful tone, Meg always obeyed, and never regretted her docility.

"Please let me kiss him once, John?"

"Certainly. Demi, say 'good-night' to mamma, and let her go and rest, for she is very tired with taking care of you all day."

Meg always insisted upon it that the kiss won the victory; for after it was given, Demi sobbed more quietly, and lay quite still at the bottom of the bed, whither he had wriggled in his anguish of mind.

"Poor little man, he's worn out with sleep and crying. I'll cover him up, and then go and set Meg's heart at rest," thought John, creeping to the bedside, hoping to find his rebellious heir asleep.

But he wasn't; for the moment his father peeped at him, Demi's eyes opened, his little chin began to quiver, and he put up his arms, saying, with a penitent hiccough, "Me's dood, now."

Sitting on the stairs, outside, Meg wondered at the long silence which followed the uproar; and, after imagining all sorts of impossible accidents, she slipped into the room, to set her fears at rest. Demi lay fast asleep; not in his usual spread-eagle attitude, but in a subdued bunch, cuddled close in the circle of his father's arm and holding his father's finger, as if he felt that justice was tempered with mercy, and had gone to sleep a sadder and a wiser baby. So held, John had waited with womanly patience till the little hand relaxed its hold; and, while waiting, had fallen asleep, more tired by that tussle with his son than with his whole day's work.

As Meg stood watching the two faces on the pillow, she smiled to herself, and then slipped away again, saying, in a satisfied tone,—

"I never need fear that John will be too harsh with my babies: he *does* know how to manage them, and will be a great help, for Demi *is* getting too much for me."

When John came down at last, expecting to find a pensive or reproachful wife, he was agreeably surprised to find Meg placidly trimming a bonnet, and to be greeted with the request to read something about the election, if he was not too tired. John saw in a minute that a revolution of some kind was going on, but wisely asked no questions, knowing that Meg was such a transparent little person, she couldn't keep a secret to save her life, and therefore the clew would soon appear. He read a long debate with the most amiable readiness and then explained it in his most lucid manner, while Meg tried to look deeply interested, to ask intelligent questions, and keep her thoughts from wandering from the state of the nation to the state of her bonnet. In her secret soul, however, she decided that politics were as bad as mathematics, and that the mission of politicians seemed to be calling each other names; but she kept these feminine ideas to herself, and when John paused, shook her head, and said with what she thought diplomatic ambiguity,—

"Well, I really don't see what we are coming to."

John laughed, and watched her for a minute, as she poised a pretty little preparation of lace and flowers on her hand, and regarded it with the genuine interest which his harangue had failed to waken.

"She is trying to like politics for my sake, so I'll try and like millinery for hers, that's only fair," thought John the Just, adding aloud,—

"That's very pretty; is it what you call a breakfast-cap?"

"My dear man, it's a bonnet! My very best go-to-concert-and-theatre bonnet."

"I beg your pardon; it was so small, I naturally mistook it for one of the fly-away things you sometimes wear. How do you keep it on?"

"These bits of lace are fastened under the chin with a rosebud, so;" and Meg illustrated by putting on the bonnet, and regarding him with an air of calm satisfaction that was irresistible.

"It's a love of a bonnet, but I prefer the face inside, for it looks young and happy again;" and John kissed the smiling face, to the great detriment of the rosebud under the chin.

"I'm glad you like it, for I want you to take me to one of the new concerts some night; I really need some music to put me in tune. Will you, please?"

"Of course I will, with all my heart, or anywhere else you like. You have been shut up so long, it will do you no end of good, and I shall enjoy it, of all things. What put it into your head, little mother?"

"Well, I had a talk with Marmee the other day, and told her how nervous and cross and out of sorts I felt, and she said I needed change and less care; so Hannah is to help me with the children, and I'm to see to things about the house more, and now and then have a little fun, just to keep me from getting to be a fidgety, broken-down old woman before my time. It's only an experiment, John, and I want to try it for your sake as much as for mine, because I've neglected you shamefully lately, and I'm going to make home what it used to be, if I can. You don't object, I hope?"

Never mind what John said, or what a very narrow escape the little bonnet had from utter ruin; all that we have any business to know is that John did *not* appear to object, judging from the changes which gradually took place in the house and its inmates. It was not all Paradise by any means, but everyone was better for the division of labor system; the children throve under the paternal rule, for accurate, steadfast John brought order and obedience into Babydom, while Meg recovered her spirits and composed her nerves by plenty of wholesome exercise, a little pleasure, and much confidential conversation with her sensible husband. Home grew home-like again, and John had no wish to leave it, unless he took Meg with him. The Scotts came to the Brookes' now, and everyone found the little house a cheerful place, full of happiness, content, and family love. Even gay Sallie Moffatt liked to go there. "It is always so quiet and pleasant here; it does me good, Meg," she used to say, looking about her with wistful eyes, as if trying to discover the charm, that she might use it in her great house, full of splendid loneliness; for there were no riotous, sunny-faced babies there, and Ned lived in a world of his own, where there was no place for her.

This household happiness did not come all at once, but John and Meg had found the key to it, and each year of married life taught them how to use it, unlocking the treasuries of real home-love and mutual helpfulness, which the poorest may possess, and the richest cannot buy. This is the sort of shelf on which young wives and mothers may consent to be laid, safe from the restless fret and fever of the world, finding loyal lovers in the little sons and daughters who cling to them, undaunted by sorrow, poverty, or age; walking side by side, through fair and stormy weather, with a faithful friend, who is, in the true sense of the good old Saxon word, the "house-band," and learning, as Meg learned, that a woman's happiest kingdom is home, her highest honor the art of ruling it, not as a queen, but a wise wife and mother.

"My dear man, it's a bonnet."

# CHAPTER XXXIX

## LAZY LAURENCE

LAURIE went to Nice intending to stay a week, and remained a month. He was tired of wandering about alone, and Amy's familiar presence seemed to give a home-like charm to the foreign scenes in which she bore a part. He rather missed the "petting" he used to receive, and enjoyed a taste of it again; for no attentions, however flattering, from strangers, were half so pleasant as the sisterly adoration of the girls at home. Amy never would pet him like the others, but she was very glad to see him now, and quite clung to him, feeling that he was the representative of the dear family for whom she longed more than she would confess. They naturally took comfort in each other's society, and were much together, riding, walking, dancing, or dawdling, for, at Nice, no one can be very industrious during the gay season. But, while apparently amusing themselves in the most careless fashion, they were half-consciously making discoveries and forming opinions about each other. Amy rose daily in the estimation of her friend, but he sunk in hers, and each felt the truth before a word was spoken. Amy tried to please, and succeeded, for she was grateful for the many pleasures he gave her, and repaid him with the little services to which womanly women know how to lend an indescribable charm. Laurie made no effort of any kind, but just let himself drift along as comfortably as possible, trying to forget, and feeling that all women owed him a kind word because one had been cold to him. It cost him no effort to be generous, and he would have given Amy all the trinkets in Nice if she would have taken them; but, at the same time, he felt that he could not change the opinion she was forming of him, and he rather dreaded the keen blue eyes that seemed to watch him with such half-sorrowful, half-scornful surprise.

"All the rest have gone to Monaco for the day; I preferred to stay at home and write letters. They are done now, and I am going to Valrosa to sketch; will you come?" said Amy, as she joined Laurie one lovely day when he lounged in as usual, about noon.

"Well, yes; but isn't it rather warm for such a long walk?" he answered slowly, for the shaded *salon* looked inviting, after the glare without.

"I'm going to have the little carriage, and Baptiste can drive, so you'll have nothing to do but hold your umbrella and keep your gloves nice," returned Amy, with a sarcastic glance at the immaculate kids, which were a weak point with Laurie.

"Then I'll go with pleasure;" and he put out his hand for her sketch-book. But she tucked it under her arm with a sharp—

"Don't trouble yourself; it's no exertion to me, but *you* don't look equal to it."

Laurie lifted his eyebrows, and followed at a leisurely pace as she ran downstairs; but when they got into the carriage he took the reins himself, and left little Baptiste nothing to do but fold his arms and fall asleep on his perch.

The two never quarrelled,—Amy was too well-bred, and just now Laurie was too lazy; so, in a minute he peeped under her hat-brim with an inquiring air; she answered with a smile, and they went on together in the most amicable manner.

It was a lovely drive, along winding roads rich in the picturesque scenes that delight beauty-loving eyes. Here an ancient monastery, whence the solemn chanting of the monks came down to them. There a bare-legged shepherd, in wooden shoes, pointed hat, and rough jacket over one shoulder, sat piping on a stone, while his goats skipped among the rocks or lay at his feet. Meek, mouse-colored donkeys, laden with panniers of freshly cut grass, passed by, with a pretty girl in a *capaline* sitting between the green piles, or an old woman spinning with a distaff as she went. Brown, soft-eyed children ran out from the quaint stone hovels to offer nosegays, or bunches of oranges still on the bough. Gnarled olive-trees covered the hills with their dusky foliage, fruit hung golden in the orchard, and great scarlet anemones fringed the roadside; while beyond green slopes and craggy heights, the Maritime Alps rose sharp and white against the blue Italian sky.

Valrosa well deserved its name, for, in that climate of perpetual summer, roses blossomed everywhere. They overhung the archway, thrust themselves between the bars of the great gate with a sweet welcome to passersby, and lined the avenue, winding through lemon-trees and feathery palms up to the villa on the hill. Every shadowy nook, where seats invited one to stop and rest, was a mass of bloom; every cool grotto had its marble nymph smiling from a veil of flowers, and every fountain reflected crimson, white, or pale pink roses, leaning down to smile at their own beauty. Roses covered the walls of the house, draped the cornices, climbed the pillars, and ran riot over the balustrade of the wide terrace, whence one looked down on the sunny Mediterranean, and the white-walled city on its shore.

"This is a regular honeymoon Paradise, isn't it? Did you ever see such roses?" asked Amy, pausing on the terrace to enjoy the view, and a luxurious whiff of perfume that came wandering by.

"No, nor felt such thorns," returned Laurie, with his thumb in his mouth, after a vain attempt to capture a solitary scarlet flower that grew just beyond his reach.

"Try lower down, and pick those that have no thorns," said Amy, gathering three of the tiny cream-colored ones that starred the wall behind her. She put them in his button-hole, as a peace-offering, and he stood a minute looking down at them with a curious expression, for in the Italian part of his nature there was a touch of superstition, and he was just then in that state of half-sweet, half-bitter melancholy, when imaginative young men find significance in trifles, and food for romance everywhere. He had thought of Jo in reaching after the thorny red rose, for vivid flowers became her, and she had often worn ones like that from the greenhouse at home. The pale roses Amy gave him were the sort that the Italians lay in dead hands, never in bridal wreaths, and, for a moment, he wondered if the omen was for Jo or for himself; but

the next instant his American common-sense got the better of senti-
mentality, and he laughed a heartier laugh than Amy had heard since
he came.

"It's good advice; you'd better take it and save your fingers," she said,
thinking her speech amused him.

"Thank you, I will," he answered in jest, and a few months later he
did it in earnest.

"Laurie, when are you going to your grandfather?" she asked presently,
as she settled herself on a rustic seat.

"Very soon."

"You have said that a dozen times within the last three weeks."

"I dare say; short answers save trouble."

"He expects you, and you really ought to go."

"Hospitable creature! I know it."

"Then why don't you do it?"

"Natural depravity, I suppose."

"Natural indolence, you mean. It's really dreadful!" and Amy looked
severe.

"Not so bad as it seems, for I should only plague him if I went, so I
might as well stay, and plague you a little longer, you can bear it better;
in fact, I think it agrees with you excellently;" and Laurie composed
himself for a lounge on the broad ledge of the balustrade.

Amy shook her head, and opened her sketch-book with an air of
resignation; but she had made up her mind to lecture "that boy," and
in a minute she began again.

"What are you doing just now?"

"Watching lizards."

"No, no; I mean what do you intend and wish to do?"

"Smoke a cigarette, if you'll allow me."

"How provoking you are! I don't approve of cigars, and I will only
allow it on condition that you let me put you into my sketch; I need a
figure."

"With all the pleasure in life. How will you have me,—full-length or
three-quarters, on my head or my heels? I should respectfully suggest
a recumbent posture, then put yourself in also, and call it 'Dolce far
niente.'"

"Stay as you are, and go to sleep if you like. *I* intend to work hard,"
said Amy, in her most energetic tone.

"What delightful enthusiasm!" And he leaned against a tall urn with
an air of entire satisfaction.

"What would Jo say if she saw you now?" asked Amy impatiently,
hoping to stir him up by the mention of her still more energetic sister's
name.

"As usual, 'Go away, Teddy, I'm busy!' " He laughed as he spoke, but
the laugh was not natural, and a shade passed over his face, for the
utterance of the familiar name touched the wound that was not healed
yet. Both tone and shadow struck Amy, for she had seen and heard
them before, and now she looked up in time to catch a new expression
on Laurie's face,—a hard, bitter look, full of pain, dissatisfaction, and
regret. It was gone before she could study it, and the listless expression

back again. She watched him for a moment with artistic pleasure, thinking how like an Italian he looked, as he lay basking in the sun with uncovered head, and eyes full of southern dreaminess; for he seemed to have forgotten her, and fallen into a reverie.

"You look like the effigy of a young knight asleep on his tomb," she said, carefully tracing the well-cut profile defined against the dark stone.

"Wish I was!"

"That's a foolish wish, unless you have spoilt your life. You are so changed, I sometimes think—" there Amy stopped, with a half-timid, half-wistful look, more significant than her unfinished speech.

Laurie saw and understood the affectionate anxiety which she hesitated to express, and looking straight into her eyes, said, just as he used to say it to her mother,—

"It's all right, ma'am."

That satisfied her and set at rest the doubts that had begun to worry her lately. It also touched her, and she showed that it did, by the cordial tone in which she said,—

"I'm glad of that! I didn't think you'd been a very bad boy, but I fancied you might have wasted money at that wicked Baden-Baden, lost your heart to some charming Frenchwoman with a husband, or got into some of the scrapes that young men seem to consider a necessary part of a foreign tour. Don't stay out there in the sun; come and lie on the grass here, and 'let us be friendly,' as Jo used to say when we got in the sofa-corner and told secrets."

Laurie obediently threw himself down on the turf, and began to amuse himself by sticking daisies into the ribbons of Amy's hat, that lay there.

"I'm all ready for the secrets;" and he glanced up with a decided expression of interest in his eyes.

"I've none to tell; you may begin."

"Haven't one to bless myself with. I thought perhaps you'd had some news from home."

"You have heard all that has come lately. Don't you hear often? I fancied Jo would send you volumes."

"She's very busy; I'm roving about so, it's impossible to be regular, you know. When do you begin your great work of art, Raphaella?" he asked, changing the subject abruptly after another pause, in which he had been wondering if Amy knew his secret, and wanted to talk about it.

"Never," she answered, with a despondent but decided air. "Rome took all the vanity out of me; for after seeing the wonders there, I felt too insignificant to live, and gave up all my foolish hopes in despair."

"Why should you, with so much energy and talent?"

"That's just why,—because talent isn't genius, and no amount of energy can make it so. I want to be great, or nothing. I won't be a commonplace dauber, so I don't intend to try any more."

"And what are you going to do with yourself now, if I may ask?"

"Polish up my other talents, and be an ornament to society, if I get the chance."

It was a characteristic speech, and sounded daring; but audacity becomes young people, and Amy's ambition had a good foundation. Laurie smiled, but he liked the spirit with which she took up a new purpose when a long-cherished one died, and spent no time lamenting.

"Good! And here is where Fred Vaughn comes in, I fancy."

Amy preserved a discreet silence, but there was a conscious look in her downcast face, that made Laurie sit up and say gravely,—

"Now I'm going to play brother, and ask questions. May I?"

"I don't promise to answer."

"Your face will, if your tongue won't. You aren't woman of the world enough yet to hide your feelings, my dear. I heard rumors about Fred and you last year, and it's my private opinion that, if he had not been called home so suddenly and detained so long, something would have come of it—hey?"

"That's not for me to say," was Amy's prim reply; but her lips would smile, and there was a traitorous sparkle of the eye, which betrayed that she knew her power and enjoyed the knowledge.

"You are not engaged, I hope?" and Laurie looked very elder-brotherly and grave all of a sudden.

"No."

"But you will be, if he comes back and goes properly down upon his knees, won't you?"

"Very likely."

"Then you are fond of old Fred?"

"I could be, if I tried."

"But you don't intend to try till the proper moment? Bless my soul, what unearthly prudence! He's a good fellow, Amy, but not the man I fancied you'd like."

"He is rich, a gentleman, and has delightful manners," began Amy, trying to be quite cool and dignified, but feeling a little ashamed of herself, in spite of the sincerity of her intentions.

"I understand; queens of society can't get on without money, so you mean to make a good match, and start in that way? Quite right and proper, as the world goes, but it sounds odd from the lips of one of your mother's girls."

"True, nevertheless."

A short speech, but the quiet decision with which it was uttered contrasted curiously with the young speaker. Laurie felt this instinctively, and laid himself down again, with a sense of disappointment which he could not explain. His look and silence, as well as a certain inward self-disapproval, ruffled Amy, and made her resolve to deliver her lecture without delay.

"I wish you'd do me the favor to rouse yourself a little," she said sharply.

"Do it for me, there's a dear girl."

"I could, if I tried;" and she looked as if she would like doing it in the most summary style.

"Try, then; I give you leave," returned Laurie, who enjoyed having someone to tease, after his long abstinence from his favorite pastime.

"You'd be angry in five minutes."

"I'm never angry with you. It takes two flints to make a fire: you are as cool and soft as snow."

"You don't know what I can do; snow produces a glow and a tingle, if applied rightly. Your indifference is half affectation, and a good stirring up would prove it."

"Stir away; it won't hurt me and it may amuse you, as the big man said when his little wife beat him. Regard me in the light of a husband or a carpet, and beat till you are tired, if that sort of exercise agrees with you."

Being decidedly nettled herself, and longing to see him shake off the apathy that so altered him, Amy sharpened both tongue and pencil, and began:—

"Flo and I have got a new name for you; it's 'Lazy Laurence.' How do you like it?"

She thought it would annoy him; but he only folded his arms under his head, with an imperturbable "That's not bad. Thank you, ladies."

"Do you want to know what I honestly think of you?"

"Pining to be told."

"Well, I despise you."

If she had even said "I hate you," in a petulant or coquettish tone, he would have laughed, and rather liked it; but the grave, almost sad, accent of her voice made him open his eyes, and ask quickly,—

"Why, if you please?"

"Because, with every chance for being good, useful, and happy, you are faulty, lazy, and miserable."

"Strong language, mademoiselle."

"If you like it, I'll go on."

"Pray, do; it's quite interesting."

"I thought you'd find it so; selfish people always like to talk about themselves."

"Am *I* selfish?" The question slipped out involuntarily and in a tone of surprise, for the one virtue on which he prided himself was generosity.

"Yes, very selfish," continued Amy, in a calm, cool voice, twice as effective, just then, as an angry one. "I'll show you how, for I've studied you while we have been frolicking, and I'm not at all satisfied with you. Here you have been abroad nearly six months, and done nothing but waste time and money and disappoint your friends."

"Isn't a fellow to have any pleasure after a four-years grind?"

"You don't look as if you'd had much; at any rate, you are none the better for it, as far as I can see. I said, when we first met, that you had improved. Now I take it all back, for I don't think you half so nice as when I left you at home. You have grown abominably lazy; you like gossip, and waste time on frivolous things; you are contented to be petted and admired by silly people, instead of being loved and respected by wise ones. With money, talent, position, health, and beauty,—ah, you like that, Old Vanity! But it's the truth, so I can't help saying it,—with all these splendid things to use and enjoy, you can find nothing to do but dawdle; and, instead of being the man you might and ought to be, you are only—" There she stopped, with a look that had both pain and pity in it.

"Saint Laurence on a gridiron," added Laurie, blandly finishing the sentence. But the lecture began to take effect, for there was a wide-awake sparkle in his eyes now, and a half-angry, half-injured expression replaced the former indifference.

"I supposed you'd take it so. You men tell us we are angels, and say we can make you what we will; but the instant we honestly try to do you good, you laugh at us, and won't listen, which proves how much your flattery is worth." Amy spoke bitterly, and turned her back on the exasperating martyr at her feet.

In a minute a hand came down over the page, so that she could not draw, and Laurie's voice said, with a droll imitation of a penitent child,—

"I will be good, oh, I will be good!"

But Amy did not laugh, for she was in earnest; and, tapping on the outspread hand with her pencil, said soberly,—

"Aren't you ashamed of a hand like that? It's as soft and white as a woman's, and looks as if it never did anything but wear Jouvin's best gloves, and pick flowers for ladies. You are not a dandy, thank Heaven! So I'm glad to see there are no diamonds or big seal-rings on it, only the little old one Jo gave you so long ago. Dear soul, I wish she was here to help me!"

"So do I!"

The hand vanished as suddenly as it came, and there was energy enough in the echo of her wish to suit even Amy. She glanced down at him with a new thought in her mind; but he was lying with his hat half over his face, as if for shade, and his mustache hid his mouth. She only saw his chest rise and fall, with a long breath that might have been a sigh, and the hand that wore the ring nestled down into the grass, as if to hide something too precious or too tender to be spoken of. All in a minute various hints and trifles assumed shape and significance in Amy's mind, and told her what her sister never had confided to her. She remembered that Laurie never spoke voluntarily of Jo; she recalled the shadow on his face just now, the change in his character, and the wearing of the little old ring, which was no ornament to a handsome hand. Girls are quick to read such signs and feel their eloquence. Amy had fancied that perhaps a love trouble was at the bottom of the alteration, and now she was sure of it. Her keen eyes filled, and, when she spoke again, it was in a voice that could be beautifully soft and kind when she chose to make it so.

"I know I have no right to talk so to you, Laurie; and if you weren't the sweetest-tempered fellow in the world, you'd be very angry with me. But we are all so fond and proud of you, I couldn't bear to think they should be disappointed in you at home as I have been, though, perhaps, they would understand the change better than I do."

"I think they would," came from under the hat, in a grim tone, quite as touching as a broken one.

"They ought to have told me, and not let me go blundering and scolding, when I should have been more kind and patient than ever. I never did like that Miss Randal, and now I hate her!" said artful Amy, wishing to be sure of her facts this time.

"Hang Miss Randal!" And Laurie knocked the hat off his face with a look that left no doubt of his sentiments toward that young lady.

"I beg pardon; I thought—" and there she paused diplomatically.

"No, you didn't; you knew perfectly well I never cared for anyone but Jo." Laurie said that in his old, impetuous tone, and turned his face away as he spoke.

"I did think so; but as they never said anything about it, and you came away, I supposed I was mistaken. And Jo wouldn't be kind to you? Why, I was sure she loved you dearly."

"She *was* kind, but not in the right way; and it's lucky for her she didn't love me, if I'm the good-for-nothing fellow you think me. It's her fault, though, and you may tell her so."

The hard, bitter look came back again as he said that, and it troubled Amy, for she did not know what balm to apply.

"I was wrong, I didn't know. I'm very sorry I was so cross, but I can't help wishing you'd bear it better, Teddy, dear."

"Don't, that's her name for me!" And Laurie put up his hand with a quick gesture to stop the words spoken in Jo's half-kind, half-reproachful tone. "Wait till you've tried it yourself," he added, in a low voice, as he pulled up the grass by the handful.

"I'd take it manfully, and be respected if I couldn't be loved," said Amy, with the decision of one who knew nothing about it.

Now, Laurie flattered himself that he *had* borne it remarkably well, making no moan, asking no sympathy, and taking his trouble away to live it down alone. Amy's lecture put the matter in a new light, and for the first time it did look weak and selfish to lose heart at the first failure, and shut himself up in moody indifference. He felt as if suddenly shaken out of a pensive dream, and found it impossible to go to sleep again. Presently he sat up, and asked slowly,—

"Do you think Jo would despise me as you do?"

"Yes, if she saw you now. She hates lazy people. Why don't you do something splendid, and *make* her love you?"

"I did my best, but it was no use."

"Graduating well, you mean? That was no more than you ought to have done, for your grandfather's sake. It would have been shameful to fail after spending so much time and money, when everyone knew you *could* do well."

"I did fail, say what you will, for Jo wouldn't love me," began Laurie, leaning his head on his hand in a despondent attitude.

"No, you didn't, and you'll say so in the end, for it did you good, and proved that you could do something if you tried. If you'd only set about another task of some sort, you'd soon be your hearty, happy self again, and forget your trouble."

"That's impossible."

"Try it and see. You needn't shrug your shoulders, and think 'Much she knows about such things.' I don't pretend to be wise, but I *am* observing, and I see a great deal more than you'd imagine. I'm interested in other people's experiences and inconsistencies; and, though I can't explain, I remember and use them for my own benefit. Love Jo all your days, if you choose, but don't let it spoil you, for it's wicked to throw away so many good gifts because you can't have the one you want. There, I won't lecture any more, for I know you'll wake up and be a man in spite of that hardhearted girl."

Neither spoke for several minutes. Laurie sat turning the little ring on his finger, and Amy put the last touches to the hasty sketch she had been working at while she talked. Presently she put it on his knee, merely saying,—

"How do you like that?"

He looked and then he smiled, as he could not well help doing, for it was capitally done,—the long, lazy figure on the grass, with listless face, half-shut eyes, and one hand holding a cigar, from which came the little wreath of smoke that encircled the dreamer's head.

"How well you draw!" he said, with genuine surprise and pleasure at her skill, adding, with a half-laugh,—

"Yes, that's me."

"As you are: this is as you were;" and Amy laid another sketch beside the one he held.

It was not nearly so well done, but there was a life and spirit in it which atoned for many faults, and it recalled the past so vividly that a sudden change swept over the young man's face as he looked. Only a rough sketch of Laurie taming a horse; hat and coat were off, and every line of the active figure, resolute face, and commanding attitude, was full of energy and meaning. The handsome brute, just subdued, stood arching his neck under the tightly drawn rein, with one foot impatiently pawing the ground, and ears pricked up as if listening for the voice that had mastered him. In the ruffled mane, the rider's breezy hair and erect attitude, there was a suggestion of suddenly arrested motion, of strength, courage, and youthful buoyancy, that contrasted sharply with the supine grace of the *"Dolce far niente"* sketch. Laurie said nothing; but, as his eye went from one to the other, Amy saw him flush up and fold his lips together as if he read and accepted the little lesson she had given him. That satisfied her; and, without waiting for him to speak, she said, in her sprightly way,—

"Don't you remember the day you played Rarey with Puck, and we all looked on? Meg and Beth were frightened, but Jo clapped and pranced, and I sat on the fence and drew you. I found that sketch in my portfolio the other day, touched it up, and kept it to show you."

"Much obliged. You've improved immensely since then, and I congratulate you. May I venture to suggest in 'a honeymoon Paradise' that five o'clock is the dinner-hour at your hotel?"

Laurie rose as he spoke, returned the pictures with a smile and a bow, and looked at his watch, as if to remind her that even moral lectures should have an end. He tried to resume his former easy, indifferent air, but it *was* an affectation now, for the rousing had been more efficacious than he would confess. Amy felt the shade of coldness in his manner, and said to herself,—

"Now I've offended him. Well, if it does him good, I'm glad; if it makes him hate me, I'm sorry; but it's true, and I can't take back a word of it."

They laughed and chatted all the way home; and little Baptiste, up behind, thought that monsieur and mademoiselle were in charming spirits. But both felt ill at ease; the friendly frankness was disturbed, the sunshine had a shadow over it, and, despite their apparent gayety, there was a secret discontent in the heart of each.

"Shall we see you this evening, *mon frère?*" asked Amy, as they parted at her aunt's door.

"Unfortunately I have an engagement. *Au revoir, mademoiselle,*" and Laurie bent as if to kiss her hand, in the foreign fashion, which became him better than many men. Something in his face made Amy say quickly and warmly,—

"No; be yourself with me, Laurie, and part in the good old way. I'd rather have a hearty English hand-shake than all the sentimental salutations in France."

"Good-by, dear," and with these words, uttered in the tone she liked, Laurie left her, after a hand-shake almost painful in its heartiness.

Next morning, instead of the usual call, Amy received a note which made her smile at the beginning and sigh at the end:—

"MY DEAR MENTOR,—

"Please make my adieux to your aunt, and exult within yourself, for 'Lazy Laurence' has gone to his grandpa, like the best of boys. A pleasant winter to you, and may the gods grant you a blissful honeymoon at Valrosa! I think Fred would be benefited by a rouser. Tell him so, with my congratulations.

"Yours gratefully,

TELEMACHUS."

"Good boy! I'm glad he's gone," said Amy, with an approving smile; the next minute her face fell as she glanced about the empty room, adding, with an involuntary sigh,—

"Yes, I *am* glad, but how I shall miss him!"

# CHAPTER XL

## THE VALLEY OF THE SHADOW

WHEN the first bitterness was over, the family accepted the inevitable, and tried to bear it cheerfully, helping one another by the increased affection which comes to bind households tenderly together in times of trouble. They put away their grief, and each did his or her part toward making that last year a happy one.

The pleasantest room in the house was set apart for Beth, and in it was gathered everything that she most loved,—flowers, pictures, her piano, the little work-table, and the beloved pussies. Father's best books found their way there, mother's easy-chair, Jo's desk, Amy's finest sketches; and every day Meg brought her babies on a loving pilgrimage, to make sunshine for Aunty Beth. John quietly set apart a little sum, that he might enjoy the pleasure of keeping the invalid supplied with the fruit she loved and longed for; old Hannah never wearied of concocting dainty dishes to tempt a capricious appetite, dropping tears as she worked;

and from across the sea came little gifts and cheerful letters, seeming to bring breaths of warmth and fragrance from lands that know no winter.

Here, cherished like a household saint in its shrine, sat Beth, tranquil and busy as ever; for nothing could change the sweet, unselfish nature, and even while preparing to leave life, she tried to make it happier for those who should remain behind. The feeble fingers were never idle, and one of her pleasures was to make little things for the school-children daily passing to and fro,—to drop a pair of mittens from her window for a pair of purple hands, a needle-book for some small mother of many dolls, pen-wipers for young penmen toiling through forests of pot-hooks, scrap-books for picture-loving eyes, and all manner of pleasant devices, till the reluctant climbers up the ladder of learning found their way strewn with flowers, as it were, and came to regard the gentle giver as a sort of fairy godmother, who sat above there, and showered down gifts miraculously suited to their tastes and needs. If Beth had wanted any reward, she found it in the bright little faces always turned up to her window, with nods and smiles, and the droll little letters which came to her, full of blots and gratitude.

The first few months were very happy ones, and Beth often used to look round, and say "How beautiful this is!" as they all sat together in her sunny room, the babies kicking and crowing on the floor, mother and sisters working near, and father reading, in his pleasant voice, from the wise old books which seemed rich in good and comfortable words, as applicable now as when written centuries ago; a little chapel, where a paternal priest taught his flock the hard lessons all must learn, trying to show them that hope can comfort love, and faith make resignation possible. Simple sermons, that went straight to the souls of those who listened; for the father's heart was in the minister's religion, and the frequent falter in the voice gave a double eloquence to the words he spoke or read.

It was well for all that this peaceful time was given them as preparation for the sad hours to come; for, by and by, Beth said the needle was "so heavy," and put it down forever; talking wearied her, faces troubled her, pain claimed her for its own, and her tranquil spirit was sorrowfully perturbed by the ills that vexed her feeble flesh. Ah me! Such heavy days, such long, long nights, such aching hearts and imploring prayers, when those who loved her best were forced to see the thin hands stretched out to them beseechingly, to hear the bitter cry, "Help me, help me!" and to feel that there was no help. A sad eclipse of the serene soul, a sharp struggle of the young life with death; but both were mercifully brief, and then, the natural rebellion over, the old peace returned more beautiful than ever. With the wreck of her frail body, Beth's soul grew strong; and, though she said little, those about her felt that she was ready, saw that the first pilgrim called was likewise the fittest, and waited with her on the shore, trying to see the Shining Ones coming to receive her when she crossed the river.

Jo never left her for an hour since Beth had said, "I feel stronger when you are here." She slept on a couch in the room, waking often to renew the fire, to feed, lift, or wait upon the patient creature who seldom asked for anything, and "tried not to be a trouble." All day she haunted the room, jealous of any other nurse, and prouder of being chosen then than of any honor her life ever brought her. Precious and helpful hours to Jo, for now her heart received the teaching that it needed; lessons in patience were so sweetly taught her that she could not fail to learn them; charity for all, the lovely spirit that can forgive and truly forget unkindness, the loyalty to duty that makes the hardest easy, and the sincere faith that fears nothing, but trusts undoubtingly.

Often, when she woke, Jo found Beth reading in her well-worn little book, heard her singing softly, to beguile the sleepless night, or saw her lean her face upon her hands, while slow tears dropped through the transparent fingers; and Jo would lie watching her, with thoughts too deep for tears, feeling that Beth, in her simple, unselfish way, was trying to wean herself from the dear old life, and fit herself for the life to come, by sacred words of comfort, quiet prayers, and the music she loved so well.

Seeing this did more for Jo than the wisest sermons, the saintliest hymns, the most fervent prayers that any voice could utter; for, with eyes made clear by many tears, and a heart softened by the tenderest sorrow, she recognized the beauty of her sister's life,—uneventful, unambitious, yet full of the genuine virtues which "smell sweet, and blossom in the dust," the self-forgetfulness that makes the humblest on earth remembered soonest in heaven, the true success which is possible to all.

One night, when Beth looked among the books upon her table, to find something to make her forget the mortal weariness that was almost as hard to bear as pain, as she turned the leaves of her old favorite Pilgrim's Progress, she found a little paper, scribbled over in Jo's hand. The name caught her eye, and the blurred look of the lines made her sure that tears had fallen on it.

"Poor Jo! She's fast asleep, so I won't wake her to ask leave; she shows me all her things, and I don't think she'll mind if I look at this," thought Beth, with a glance at her sister, who lay on the rug, with the tongs beside her, ready to wake up the minute the log fell apart.

### "MY BETH

"Sitting patient in the shadow
  Till the blessed light shall come,
A serene and saintly presence
  Sanctifies our troubled home.
Earthly joys and hopes and sorrows
  Break like ripples on the strand
Of the deep and solemn river
  Where her willing feet now stand.

"O my sister, passing from me,
  Out of human care and strife,
Leave me, as a gift, those virtues
  Which have beautified your life.
Dear, bequeath me that great patience
  Which has power to sustain

*A cheerful, uncomplaining spirit*
*In its prison-house of pain.*

*"Give me, for I need it sorely,*
*Of that courage, wise and sweet,*
*Which has made the path of duty*
*Green beneath your willing feet.*
*Give me that unselfish nature,*
*That with charity divine*
*Can pardon wrong for love's dear sake—*
*Meek heart, forgive me mine!*

*"Thus our parting daily loseth*
*Something of its bitter pain,*
*And while learning this hard lesson,*
*My great loss becomes my gain.*
*For the touch of grief will render*
*My wild nature more serene,*
*Give to life new aspirations,*
*A new trust in the unseen.*

*"Henceforth, safe across the river,*
*I shall see forevermore*
*A beloved, household spirit*
*Waiting for me on the shore.*
*Hope and faith, born of my sorrow,*
*Guardian angels shall become,*
*And the sister gone before me*
*By their hands shall lead me home."*

Blurred and blotted, faulty and feeble, as the lines were, they brought a look of inexpressible comfort to Beth's face, for her one regret had been that she had done so little; and this seemed to assure her that her life had not been useless, that her death would not bring the despair she feared. As she sat with the paper folded between her hands, the charred log fell asunder. Jo started up, revived the blaze, and crept to the bedside, hoping Beth slept.

"Not asleep, but so happy, dear. See, I found this and read it; I knew you wouldn't care. Have I been all that to you, Jo?" she asked, with wistful, humble earnestness.

"O Beth, so much, so much!" and Jo's head went down upon the pillow, beside her sister's.

"Then I don't feel as if I'd wasted my life. I'm not so good as you make me, but I *have* tried to do right; and now, when it's too late to begin even to do better, it's such a comfort to know that someone loves me so much, and feels as if I'd helped them."

"More than anyone in the world, Beth. I used to think I couldn't let you go; but I'm learning to feel that I don't lose you; that you'll be more to me than ever, and death can't part us, though it seems to."

"I know it cannot, and I don't fear it any longer, for I'm sure I shall be your Beth still, to love and help you more than ever. You must take my place, Jo, and be everything to father and mother when I'm gone. They will turn to you, don't fail them; and if it's hard to work alone, remember that I don't forget you, and that you'll be happier in doing that than writing splendid books or seeing all the world; for love is the only thing that we can carry with us when we go, and it makes the end so easy."

"I'll try, Beth;" and then and there Jo renounced her old ambition, pledged herself to a new and better one, acknowledging the poverty of other desires, and feeling the blessed solace of a belief in the immortality of love.

So the spring days came and went, the sky grew clearer, the earth greener, the flowers were up fair and early, and the birds came back in time to say good-by to Beth, who, like a tired but trustful child, clung to the hands that had led her all her life, as father and mother guided her tenderly through the Valley of the Shadow, and gave her up to God.

Seldom, except in books, do the dying utter memorable words, see visions, or depart with beatified countenances; and those who have sped many parting souls know that to most the end comes as naturally and simply as sleep. As Beth had hoped, the "tide went out easily;" and in the dark hour before the dawn, on the bosom where she had drawn her first breath, she quietly drew her last, with no farewell but one loving look, one little sigh.

With tears and prayers and tender hands, mother and sisters made her ready for the long sleep that pain would never mar again, seeing with grateful eyes the beautiful serenity that soon replaced the pathetic patience that had wrung their hearts so long, and feeling, with reverent joy, that to their darling death was a benignant angel, not a phantom full of dread.

When morning came, for the first time in many months the fire was out, Jo's place was empty, and the room was very still. But a bird sang blithely on a budding bough, close by, the snow-drops blossomed freshly at the window, and the spring sunshine streamed in like a benediction over the placid face upon the pillow,—a face so full of painless peace that those who loved it best smiled through their tears, and thanked God that Beth was well at last.

# CHAPTER XLI

## LEARNING TO FORGET

AMY'S lecture did Laurie good, though, of course, he did not own it till long afterward; men seldom do, for when women are the advisers, the lords of creation don't take the advice till they have persuaded themselves that it is just what they intended to do; then they act upon it, and, if it succeeds, they give the weaker vessel half the credit of it; if it fails, they generously give her the whole. Laurie went back to his grandfather, and was so dutifully devoted for several weeks that the old gentleman declared the climate of Nice had improved him wonderfully, and he had better try it again. There was nothing the young gentleman would have liked better, but elephants could not have dragged him back after the scolding he had received; pride forbid, and whenever the longing grew very strong, he fortified his resolution by repeating the words that had made the deepest impression, "I despise you"; "Go and do something splendid that will *make* her love you."

Laurie turned the matter over in his mind so often that he soon brought himself to confess that he *had* been selfish and lazy; but then when a man has a great sorrow, he should be indulged in all sorts of vagaries till he has lived it down. He felt that his blighted affections were quite dead now; and, though he should never cease to be a faithful mourner, there was no occasion to wear his weeds ostentatiously. Jo *wouldn't* love him, but he might *make* her respect and admire him by doing something which should prove that a girl's "No" had not spoilt his life. He had always meant to do something, and Amy's advice was quite unnecessary. He had only been waiting till the aforesaid blighted affections were decently interred; that being done, he felt that he was ready to "hide his stricken heart, and still toil on."

As Goethe, when he had a joy or a grief, put it into a song, so Laurie resolved to embalm his love-sorrow in music, and compose a Requiem which should harrow up Jo's soul and melt the heart of every hearer. Therefore the next time the old gentleman found him getting restless and moody, and ordered him off, he went to Vienna, where he had musical friends, and fell to work with the firm determination to distinguish himself. But, whether the sorrow was too vast to be embodied in music, or music too ethereal to uplift a mortal woe, he soon discovered that the Requiem was beyond him, just at present. It was evident that his mind was not in working order yet, and his ideas needed clarifying; for often in the middle of a plaintive strain, he would find himself humming a dancing tune that vividly recalled the Christmas ball at Nice, especially the stout Frenchman, and put an effectual stop to tragic composition for the time being.

Then he tried an Opera, for nothing seemed impossible in the beginning; but here, again, unforeseen difficulties beset him. He wanted Jo for his heroine, and called upon his memory to supply him with tender recollections and romantic visions of his love. But memory turned traitor; and, as if possessed by the perverse spirit of the girl, would only recall Jo's oddities, faults, and freaks, would only show her in the most unsentimental aspects,—beating mats with her head tied up in a bandanna, barricading herself with the sofa-pillow, or throwing cold water over his passion *à la* Gummidge,—and an irresistible laugh spoilt the pensive picture he was endeavoring to paint. Jo wouldn't be put into the Opera at any price, and he had to give her up with a "Bless that girl, what a torment she is!" and a clutch at his hair, as became a distracted composer.

When he looked about him for another and a less intractable damsel to immortalize in melody, memory produced one with the most obliging readiness. This phantom wore many faces, but it always had golden hair, was enveloped in a diaphanous cloud, and floated airily before his mind's eye in a pleasing chaos of roses, peacocks, white ponies, and blue ribbons. He did not give the complacent wraith any name, but he took her for his heroine, and grew quite fond of her, as well he might; for he gifted her with every gift and grace under the sun, and escorted her, unscathed, through trials which would have annihilated any mortal woman.

Thanks to this inspiration, he got on swimmingly for a time, but gradually the work lost its charm, and he forgot to compose, while he sat musing, pen in hand, or roamed about the gay city to get new ideas and refresh his mind, which seemed to be in a somewhat unsettled state that winter. He did not do much, but he thought a great deal and was conscious of a change of some sort going on in spite of himself. "It's genius simmering, perhaps. I'll let it simmer, and see what comes of it," he said, with a secret suspicion, all the while, that it wasn't genius, but something far more common. Whatever it was, it simmered to some purpose, for he grew more and more discontented with his desultory life, began to long for some real and earnest work to go at, soul and body, and finally came to the wise conclusion that everyone who loved music was not a composer. Returning from one of Mozart's grand operas, splendidly performed at the Royal Theatre, he looked over his own, played a few of the best parts, sat staring up at the busts of Mendelssohn, Beethoven, and Bach, who stared benignly back again; then suddenly he tore up his music-sheets, one by one, and, as the last fluttered out of his hand, he said soberly to himself,—

"She is right! Talent isn't genius, and you can't make it so. That music has taken the vanity out of me as Rome took it out of her, and I won't be a humbug any longer. Now what shall I do?"

That seemed a hard question to answer, and Laurie began to wish he had to work for his daily bread. Now, if ever, occurred an eligible opportunity for "going to the devil," as he once forcibly expressed it, for he had plenty of money and nothing to do, and Satan is proverbially fond of providing employment for full and idle hands. The poor fellow had temptations enough from without and from within, but he withstood them pretty well; for, much as he valued liberty, he valued good faith and confidence more, so his promise to his grandfather, and his desire to be able to look honestly into the eyes of the women who loved him, and say "All's well," kept him safe and steady.

Very likely some Mrs. Grundy will observe, "I don't believe it; boys will be boys, young men must sow their wild oats, and women must not expect miracles." I dare say *you* don't, Mrs. Grundy, but it's true nevertheless. Women work a good many miracles, and I have a persuasion that they may perform even that of raising the standard of manhood by refusing to echo such sayings. Let the boys be boys, the longer the better, and let the young men sow their wild oats if they must; but mothers, sisters, and friends may help to make the crop a small one, and keep many tares from spoiling the harvest, by believing, and showing that they believe, in the possibility of loyalty to the virtues which make men manliest in good women's eyes. If it *is* a feminine delusion, leave us to enjoy it while we may, for without it half the beauty and the romance of life is lost, and sorrowful forebodings would embitter all our hopes of the brave, tender-hearted little lads, who still love their mothers better than themselves, and are not ashamed to own it.

Laurie thought that the task of forgetting his love for Jo would absorb all his powers for years; but, to his great surprise, he discovered it grew easier every day. He refused to believe it at first, got angry with himself, and couldn't understand it; but these hearts of ours are curious and contrary things, and time and nature work their will in spite of us. Laurie's heart *wouldn't* ache; the wound persisted in healing with a rapidity that astonished him, and, instead of trying to forget, he found himself trying to remember. He had not foreseen this turn of affairs, and was not prepared for it. He was disgusted with himself, surprised at his own fickleness, and full of a queer mixture of disappointment and relief that he could recover from such a tremendous blow so soon. He carefully stirred up the embers of his lost love, but they refused to burst into a blaze: there was only a comfortable glow that warmed and did him good without putting him into a fever, and he was reluctantly obliged to confess that the boyish passion was slowly subsiding into a more tranquil sentiment, very tender, a little sad and resentful still, but that was sure to pass away in time, leaving a brotherly affection which would last unbroken to the end.

As the word "brotherly" passed through his mind in one of these reveries, he smiled, and glanced up at the picture of Mozart that was before him:—

"Well, he was a great man; and when he couldn't have one sister he took the other, and was happy."

Laurie did not utter the words, but he thought them; and the next instant kissed the little old ring, saying to himself,—

"No, I won't! I haven't forgotten, I never can. I'll try again, and if that fails, why, then—"

Leaving his sentence unfinished, he seized pen and paper and wrote to Jo, telling her that he could not settle to anything while there was the least hope of her changing her mind. Couldn't she, wouldn't she, and let him come home and be happy? While waiting for an answer he did nothing, but he did it energetically, for he was in a fever of impatience. It came at last, and settled his mind effectually on one point, for Jo decidedly couldn't and wouldn't. She was wrapped up in Beth, and never wished to hear the word "love" again. Then she begged him to be happy with somebody else, but always to keep a little corner of his heart for his loving sister Jo. In a postscript she desired him not to tell Amy that Beth was worse; she was coming home in the spring, and there was no need of saddening the remainder of her stay. That would be time enough, please God, but Laurie must write to her often, and not let her feel lonely, homesick, or anxious.

"So I will, at once. Poor little girl; it will be a sad going home for her, I'm afraid;" and Laurie opened his desk, as if writing to Amy had been the proper conclusion of the sentence left unfinished some weeks before.

But he did not write the letter that day; for, as he rummaged out his best paper, he came across something which changed his purpose. Tumbling about in one part of the desk, among bills, passports, and business documents of various kinds were several of Jo's letters, and in another compartment were three notes from Amy, carefully tied up with one of her blue ribbons, and sweetly suggestive of the little dead roses put away inside. With a half-repentant, half-amused expression, Laurie gathered up all Jo's letters, smoothed, folded, and put them neatly into a small drawer of the desk, stood a minute turning the ring thoughtfully on his finger, then slowly drew it off, laid it with the letters, locked the drawer, and went out to hear High Mass at Saint Stefan's, feeling as if there had been a funeral; and, though not overwhelmed with affliction, this seemed a more proper way to spend the rest of the day than in writing letters to charming young ladies.

The letter went very soon, however, and was promptly answered, for Amy *was* homesick, and confessed it in the most delightfully confiding manner. The correspondence flourished famously, and letters flew to and fro, with unfailing regularity, all through the early spring. Laurie sold his busts, made allumettes of his opera, and went back to Paris, hoping somebody would arrive before long. He wanted desperately to go to Nice, but would not till he was asked; and Amy would not ask him, for just then she was having little experiences of her own, which made her rather wish to avoid the quizzical eyes of "our boy."

Fred Vaughn had returned, and put the question to which she had once decided to answer, "Yes, thank you;" but now she said, "No, thank you," kindly but steadily; for, when the time came, her courage failed her, and she found that something more than money and position was needed to satisfy the new longing that filled her heart so full of tender hopes and fears. The words, "Fred is a good fellow, but not at all the man I fancied you would ever like," and Laurie's face when he uttered them, kept returning to her as pertinaciously as her own did when she said in look, if not in words, "I shall marry for money." It troubled her to remember that now, she wished she could take it back, it sounded so unwomanly. She didn't want Laurie to think her a heartless, worldly creature; she didn't care to be a queen of society now half so much as she did to be a lovable woman; she was so glad he didn't hate her for the dreadful things she said, but took them so beautifully, and was kinder than ever. His letters were such a comfort, for the home letters were very irregular, and were not half so satisfactory as his when they did come. It was not only a pleasure, but a duty to answer them, for the poor fellow was forlorn, and needed petting, since Jo persisted in being stony-hearted. She ought to have made an effort, and tried to love him; it couldn't be very hard, many people would be proud and glad to have such a dear boy care for them; but Jo never would act like other girls, so there was nothing to do but be very kind, and treat him like a brother.

If all brothers were treated as well as Laurie was at this period, they would be a much happier race of beings than they are. Amy never lectured now; she asked his opinion on all subjects; she was interested in everything he did, made charming little presents for him, and sent him two letters a week, full of lively gossip, sisterly confidences, and captivating sketches of the lovely scenes about her. As few brothers are complimented by having their letters carried about in their sisters' pockets, read and reread diligently, cried over when short, kissed when long, and treasured carefully, we will not hint that Amy did any of these fond and foolish things. But she certainly did grow a little pale and pensive that spring, lost much of her relish for society, and went out sketching alone a good deal. She never had much to show when she came home, but was studying nature, I dare say, while she sat for hours, with her hands folded, on the terrace at Valrosa, or absently sketched any fancy that occurred to her,—a stalwart knight carved on a tomb, a young man asleep in the grass, with his hat over his eyes, or a curly-haired girl in gorgeous array, promenading down a ball-room on the arm of a tall gentleman, both faces being left a blur according to the last fashion in art, which was safe, but not altogether satisfactory.

Her aunt thought that she regretted her answer to Fred; and, finding denials useless and explanations impossible, Amy left her to think what she liked, taking care that Laurie should know that Fred had gone to Egypt. That was all, but he understood it, and looked relieved, as he said to himself, with a venerable air,—

"I was sure she would think better of it. Poor old fellow! I've been through it all, and I can sympathize."

With that he heaved a great sigh, and then, as if he had discharged his duty to the past, put his feet up on the sofa, and enjoyed Amy's letter luxuriously.

While these changes were going on abroad, trouble had come at home; but the letter telling that Beth was failing never reached Amy, and when the next found her, the grass was green above her sister. The sad news met her at Vevay, for the heat had driven them from Nice in May, and they had travelled slowly to Switzerland, by way of Genoa and the Italian lakes. She bore it very well, and quietly submitted to the family decree that she should not shorten her visit, for, since it was too late to say good-by to Beth, she had better stay, and let absence soften her sorrow. But her heart was very heavy; she longed to be at home, and every day looked wistfully across the lake, waiting for Laurie to come and comfort her.

He did come very soon; for the same mail brought letters to them both, but he was in Germany, and it took some days to reach him. The moment he read it, he packed his knapsack, bade adieu to his fellow-pedestrians, and was off to keep his promise, with a heart full of joy and sorrow, hope and suspense.

He knew Vevay well; and as soon as the boat touched the little quay, he hurried along the shore to La Tour, where the Carrols were living *en pension*. The *garçon* was in despair that the whole family had gone to take a promenade on the lake; but no, the blond mademoiselle might be in the chateau garden. If monsieur would give himself the pain of sitting down, a flash of time should present her. But monsieur could not wait even "a flash of time," and, in the middle of the speech, departed to find mademoiselle himself.

A pleasant old garden on the borders of the lovely lake, with chestnuts rustling overhead, ivy climbing everywhere, and the black shadow of the tower falling far across the sunny water. At one corner of the wide, low wall was a seat, and here Amy often came to read or work, or console herself with the beauty all about her. She was sitting here that day, leaning her head on her hand, with a homesick heart and heavy eyes,

Turning the ring thoughtfully upon his finger.

thinking of Beth, and wondering why Laurie did not come. She did not hear him cross the court-yard beyond, nor see him pause in the archway that led from the subterranean path into the garden. He stood a minute, looking at her with new eyes, seeing what no one had ever seen before,— the tender side of Amy's character. Everything about her mutely suggested love and sorrow,—the blotted letters in her lap, the black ribbon that tied up her hair, the womanly pain and patience in her face; even the little ebony cross at her throat seemed pathetic to Laurie, for he had given it to her, and she wore it as her only ornament. If he had any doubts about the reception she would give him, they were set at rest the minute she looked up and saw him; for, dropping everything, she ran to him, exclaiming, in a tone of unmistakable love and longing,—

"O Laurie, Laurie, I knew you'd come to me!"

I think everything was said and settled then; for, as they stood together quite silent for a moment, with the dark head bent down protectingly over the light one, Amy felt that no one could comfort and sustain her so well as Laurie, and Laurie decided that Amy was the only woman in the world who could fill Jo's place, and make him happy. He did not tell her so; but she was not disappointed, for both felt the truth, were satisfied, and gladly left the rest to silence.

In a minute Amy went back to her place; and, while she dried her tears, Laurie gathered up the scattered papers, finding in the sight of sundry well-worn letters and suggestive sketches good omens for the future. As he sat down beside her, Amy felt shy again, and turned rosy red at the recollection of her impulsive greeting.

"I couldn't help it; I felt so lonely and sad, and was so very glad to see you. It was such a surprise to look up and find you, just as I was beginning to fear you wouldn't come," she said, trying in vain to speak quite naturally.

"I came the minute I heard. I wish I could say something to comfort you for the loss of dear little Beth; but I can only feel, and—" He could not get any further, for he, too, turned bashful all of a sudden, and did not quite know what to say. He longed to lay Amy's head down on his shoulder, and tell her to have a good cry, but he did not dare; so took her hand instead, and gave it a sympathetic squeeze that was better than words.

"You needn't say anything; this comforts me," she said softly. "Beth is well and happy, and I mustn't wish her back; but I dread the going home, much as I long to see them all. We won't talk about it now, for it makes me cry, and I want to enjoy you while you stay. You needn't go right back, need you?"

"Not if you want me, dear."

"I do, so much. Aunt and Flo are very kind; but you seem like one of the family, and it would be so comfortable to have you for a little while."

Amy spoke and looked so like a homesick child, whose heart was full, that Laurie forgot his bashfulness all at once, and gave her just what she wanted,—the petting she was used to and the cheerful conversation she needed.

"Poor little soul, you look as if you'd grieved yourself half-sick! I'm going to take care of you, so don't cry any more, but come and walk about with me; the wind is too chilly for you to sit still," he said, in the half-caressing, half-commanding way that Amy liked, as he tied on her hat, drew her arm through his, and began to pace up and down the sunny walk, under the new-leaved chestnuts. He felt more at ease upon his legs; and Amy found it very pleasant to have a strong arm to lean upon, a familiar face to smile at her, and a kind voice to talk delightfully for her alone.

The quaint old garden had sheltered many pairs of lovers, and seemed expressly made for them, so sunny and secluded was it, with nothing but the tower to overlook them, and the wide lake to carry away the echo of their words, as it rippled by below. For an hour this new pair walked and talked, or rested on the wall, enjoying the sweet influences which gave such a charm to time and place; and when an unromantic dinner-bell warned them away, Amy felt as if she left her burden of loneliness and sorrow behind her in the chateau garden.

The moment Mrs. Carrol saw the girl's altered face, she was illuminated with a new idea, and exclaimed to herself, "Now I understand it all,— the child has been pining for young Laurence. Bless my heart, I never thought of such a thing!"

With praiseworthy discretion, the good lady said nothing, and betrayed no sign of enlightenment; but cordially urged Laurie to stay, and begged Amy to enjoy his society, for it would do her more good than so much solitude. Amy was a model of docility; and, as her aunt was a good deal occupied with Flo, she was left to entertain her friend, and did it with more than her usual success.

At Nice, Laurie had lounged and Amy had scolded; at Vevey, Laurie was never idle, but always walking, riding, boating, or studying, in the most energetic manner, while Amy admired everything he did, and followed his example as far and as fast as she could. He said the change was owing to the climate, and she did not contradict him, being glad of a like excuse for her own recovered health and spirits.

The invigorating air did them both good, and much exercise worked wholesome changes in minds as well as bodies. They seemed to get clearer views of life and duty up there among the everlasting hills; the fresh winds blew away desponding doubts, delusive fancies, and moody mists; the warm spring sunshine brought out all sorts of aspiring ideas, tender hopes, and happy thoughts; the lake seemed to wash away the troubles of the past, and the grand old mountains to look benignly down upon them, saying, "Little children, love one another."

In spite of the new sorrow, it was a very happy time, so happy that Laurie could not bear to disturb it by a word. It took him a little while to recover from his surprise at the rapid cure of his first, and, as he had firmly believed, his last and only love. He consoled himself for the seeming disloyalty by the thought that Jo's sister was almost the same as Jo's self, and the conviction that it would have been impossible to love any other woman but Amy so soon and so well. His first wooing had been of the tempestuous order, and he looked back upon it as if through a long vista of years, with a feeling of compassion blended with regret. He was not ashamed of it, but put it away as one of the bitter-sweet experiences of his life, for which he could be grateful when the pain was over. His second wooing he resolved should be as calm and simple as possible; there was no need of having a scene, hardly any need of telling Amy that he loved her; she knew it without words, and had given him his answer long ago. It all came about so naturally that no one could complain, and he knew that everybody would be pleased, even Jo. But when our first little passion has been crushed, we are apt to be wary and slow in making a second trial; so Laurie let the days pass, enjoying every hour, and leaving to chance the utterance of the word that would put an end to the first and sweetest part of his new romance.

He had rather imagined that the *dénouement* would take place in the chateau garden by moonlight, and in the most graceful and decorous manner; but it turned out exactly the reverse, for the matter was settled on the lake, at noonday, in a few blunt words. They had been floating about all the morning, from gloomy St. Gingolf to sunny Montreux, with the Alps of Savoy on one side, Mont St. Bernard and the Dent du Midi on the other, pretty Vevey in the valley, and Lausanne upon the hill beyond, a cloudless blue sky overhead, and the bluer lake below, dotted with the picturesque boats that look like white-winged gulls.

They had been talking of Bonnivard, as they glided past Chillon, and of Rousseau, as they looked up at Clarens, where he wrote his "*Héloise.*" Neither had read it, but they knew it was a love-story, and each privately wondered if it was half as interesting as their own. Amy had been dabbling her hand in the water during the little pause that fell between them, and, when she looked up, Laurie was leaning on his oars, with an expression in his eyes that made her say hastily, merely for the sake of saying something,—

"You must be tired; rest a little, and let me row; it will do me good; for, since you came, I have been altogether lazy and luxurious."

"I'm not tired; but you may take an oar, if you like. There's room enough, though I have to sit nearly in the middle, else the boat won't trim," returned Laurie, as if he rather liked the arrangement.

Feeling that she had not mended matters much, Amy took the offered third of a seat, shook her hair over her face, and accepted an oar. She rowed as well as she did many other things; and, though she used both hands, and Laurie but one, the oars kept time, and the boat went smoothly through the water.

"How well we pull together, don't we?" said Amy, who objected to silence just then.

"So well that I wish we might always pull in the same boat. Will you, Amy?" very tenderly.

"Yes, Laurie," very low.

Then they both stopped rowing, and unconsciously added a pretty little *tableau* of human love and happiness to the dissolving views reflected in the lake.

# CHAPTER XLII

## ALL ALONE

IT was easy to promise self-abnegation when self was wrapped up in another, and heart and soul were purified by a sweet example; but when the helpful voice was silent, the daily lesson over, the beloved presence gone, and nothing remained but loneliness and grief, then Jo found her promise very hard to keep. How could she "comfort father and mother," when her own heart ached with a ceaseless longing for her sister; how could she "make the house cheerful," when all its light and warmth and beauty seemed to have deserted it when Beth left the old home for the new; and where in all the world could she "find some useful, happy work to do," that would take the place of the loving service which had been its own reward? She tried in a blind, hopeless way to do her duty, secretly rebelling against it all the while, for it seemed unjust that her few joys should be lessened, her burdens made heavier, and life get harder and harder as she toiled along. Some people seemed to get all sunshine, and some all shadow; it was not fair, for she tried more than Amy to be good, but never got any reward, only disappointment, trouble, and hard work.

Poor Jo, these were dark days to her, for something like despair came over her when she thought of spending all her life in that quiet house, devoted to humdrum cares, a few small pleasures, and the duty that never seemed to grow any easier. "I can't do it. I wasn't meant for a life like this, and I know I shall break away and do something desperate if somebody don't come and help me," she said to herself, when her first efforts failed, and she fell into the moody, miserable state of mind which often comes when strong wills have to yield to the inevitable.

But someone did come and help her, though Jo did not recognize her good angels at once, because they wore familiar shapes, and used the simple spells best fitted to poor humanity. Often she started up at night, thinking Beth called her; and when the sight of the little empty bed made her cry with the bitter cry of an unsubmissive sorrow, "O Beth, come back! Come back!" She did not stretch out her yearning arms in vain; for, as quick to hear her sobbing as she had been to hear her sister's faintest whisper, her mother came to comfort her, not with words only, but the patient tenderness that soothes by a touch, tears that were mute reminders of a greater grief than Jo's, and broken whispers, more eloquent than prayers, because hopeful resignation went hand-in-hand with natural sorrow. Sacred moments, when heart talked to heart in the silence of the night, turning affliction to a blessing, which chastened grief and strengthened love. Feeling this, Jo's burden seemed easier to bear, duty grew sweeter, and life looked more endurable, seen from the safe shelter of her mother's arms.

When aching heart was a little comforted, troubled mind likewise found help; for one day she went to the study, and, leaning over the good gray head lifted to welcome her with a tranquil smile, she said, very humbly,—

"Father, talk to me as you did to Beth. I need it more than she did, for I'm all wrong."

"My dear, nothing can comfort me like this," he answered, with a falter in his voice, and both arms round her, as if he, too, needed help, and did not fear to ask it.

Then, sitting in Beth's little chair close beside him, Jo told her troubles,— the resentful sorrow for her loss, the fruitless efforts that discouraged her, the want of faith that made life look so dark, and all the sad bewilderment which we call despair. She gave him entire confidence, he gave her the help she needed, and both found consolation in the act; for the time had come when they could talk together not only as father and daughter, but as man and woman, able and glad to serve each other with mutual sympathy as well as mutual love. Happy, thoughtful times there in the old study which Jo called "the church of one member," and from which she came with fresh courage, recovered cheerfulness, and a more submissive spirit; for the parents who had taught one child to meet death without fear, were trying now to teach another to accept life without despondency or distrust, and to use its beautiful opportunities with gratitude and power.

Other helps had Jo,—humble, wholesome duties and delights that would not be denied their part in serving her, and which she slowly learned to see and value. Brooms and dishcloths never could be as distasteful as they once had been, for Beth had presided over both; and something of her housewifely spirit seemed to linger round the little mop and the old brush, that was never thrown away. As she used them, Jo found herself humming the songs Beth used to hum, imitating Beth's orderly ways, and giving the little touches here and there that kept everything fresh and cozy, which was the first step toward making home happy, though she didn't know it, till Hannah said with an approving squeeze of the hand,—

"You thoughtful creter, you're determined we sha'n't miss that dear lamb ef you can help it. We don't say much, but we see it, and the Lord will bless you for't, see ef He don't."

As they sat sewing together, Jo discovered how much improved her sister Meg was; how well she could talk, how much she knew about good, womanly impulses, thoughts, and feelings, how happy she was in husband and children, and how much they were all doing for each other.

"Marriage is an excellent thing, after all. I wonder if I should blossom out half as well as you have, if I tried it?" said Jo, as she constructed a kite for Demi, in the topsy-turvy nursery.

"It's just what you need to bring out the tender, womanly half of your nature, Jo. You are like a chestnut-burr, prickly outside, but silky-soft within, and a sweet kernel, if one can only get at it. Love will make you show your heart some day, and then the rough burr will fall off."

"Frost opens chestnut-burrs, ma'am, and it takes a good shake to bring them down. Boys go nutting, and I don't care to be bagged by them," returned Jo, pasting away at the kite which no wind that blows would ever carry up, for Daisy had tied herself on as a bob.

Meg laughed, for she was glad to see a glimmer of Jo's old spirit, but she felt it her duty to enforce her opinion by every argument in her power; and the sisterly chats were not wasted, especially as two of Meg's most effective arguments were the babies, whom Jo loved tenderly. Grief is the best opener for some hearts, and Jo's was nearly ready for the bag: a little more sunshine to ripen the nut, then, not a boy's impatient shake, but a man's hand reached up to pick it gently from the burr, and find the kernel sound and sweet. If she had suspected this, she would have shut up tight, and been more prickly than ever; fortunately she wasn't thinking about herself, so, when the time came, down she dropped.

Now, if she had been the heroine of a moral story-book, she ought at this period of her life to have become quite saintly, renounced the world, and gone about doing good in a mortified bonnet, with tracts in her pocket. But, you see, Jo wasn't a heroine; she was only a struggling human girl, like hundreds of others, and she just acted out her nature, being sad, cross, listless, or energetic, as the mood suggested. It's highly virtuous to say we'll be good, but we can't do it all at once, and it takes a long pull, a strong pull, and a pull all together, before some of us even get our feet set in the right way. Jo had got so far, she was learning to do her duty, and to feel unhappy if she did not; but to do it cheerfully— ah, that was another thing! She had often said she wanted to do something splendid, no matter how hard; and now she had her wish, for what could be more beautiful than to devote her life to father and mother, trying to make home as happy to them as they had to her? And, if difficulties were necessary to increase the splendor of the effort, what could be harder for a restless, ambitious girl than to give up her own hopes, plans, and desires, and cheerfully live for others?

Providence had taken her at her word; here was the task, not what she had expected, but better, because self had no part in it: now, could she do it? She decided that she would try; and, in her first attempt, she found the helps I have suggested. Still another was given her, and she took it, not as a reward, but as a comfort, as Christian took the refreshment afforded by the little arbor where he rested, as he climbed the hill called Difficulty.

"Why don't you write? That always used to make you happy," said her mother, once, when the desponding fit overshadowed Jo.

"I've no heart to write, and if I had, nobody cares for my things."

"We do; write something for us, and never mind the rest of the world. Try it, dear; I'm sure it would do you good, and please us very much."

"Don't believe I can;" but Jo got out her desk, and began to overhaul her half-finished manuscripts.

An hour afterward her mother peeped in, and there she was, scratching away, with her black pinafore on, and an absorbed expression, which caused Mrs. March to smile, and slip away, well pleased with the success of her suggestion. Jo never knew how it happened, but something got into that story that went straight to the hearts of those who read it; for, when her family had laughed and cried over it, her father sent it, much against her will, to one of the popular magazines, and, to her utter surprise, it was not only paid for, but others requested. Letters from several persons, whose praise was honor, followed the appearance of the little story, newspapers copied it, and strangers as well as friends admired it. For a small thing it was a great success; and Jo was more astonished than when her novel was commended and condemned all at once.

"I don't understand it. What *can* there be in a simple little story like that, to make people praise it so?" she said, quite bewildered.

"There is truth in it, Jo, that's the secret; humor and pathos make it alive, and you have found your style at last. You wrote with no thought of fame or money, and put your heart into it, my daughter; you have had the bitter, now comes the sweet. Do your best, and grow as happy as we are in your success."

"If there *is* anything good or true in what I write, it isn't mine; I owe it all to you and mother and to Beth," said Jo, more touched by her father's words than by any amount of praise from the world.

So, taught by love and sorrow, Jo wrote her little stories, and sent them away to make friends for themselves and her, finding it a very charitable world to such humble wanderers; for they were kindly welcomed, and sent home comfortable tokens to their mother, like dutiful children whom good fortune overtakes.

When Amy and Laurie wrote of their engagement, Mrs. March feared that Jo would find it difficult to rejoice over it, but her fears were soon set at rest; for, though Jo looked grave at first, she took it very quietly, and was full of hopes and plans for "the children" before she read the letter twice. It was a sort of written duet, wherein each glorified the other in lover-like fashion, very pleasant to read and satisfactory to think of, for no one had any objection to make.

"You like it, mother?" said Jo, as they laid down the closely written sheets, and looked at one another.

"Yes, I hoped it would be so, ever since Amy wrote that she had refused Fred. I felt sure then that something better than what you call the 'mercenary spirit' had come over her, and a hint here and there in her letters made me suspect that love and Laurie would win the day."

"How sharp you are, Marmee, and how silent! You never said a word to me."

"Mothers have need of sharp eyes and discreet tongues when they have girls to manage. I was half afraid to put the idea into your head, lest you should write and congratulate them before the thing was settled."

"I'm not the scatter-brain I was; you may trust me, I'm sober and sensible enough for anyone's *confidante* now."

"So you are, dear, and I should have made you mine, only I fancied it might pain you to learn that your Teddy loved anyone else."

"Now, mother, did you really think I could be so silly and selfish, after I'd refused his love, when it was freshest, if not best?"

"I knew you were sincere then, Jo, but lately I have thought that if he came back, and asked again, you might, perhaps, feel like giving another answer. Forgive me, dear, I can't help seeing that you are very lonely, and sometimes there is a hungry look in your eyes that goes to my heart; so I fancied that your boy might fill the empty place if he tried now."

"No, mother, it is better as it is, and I'm glad Amy has learned to love him. But you are right in one thing: I *am* lonely, and perhaps if Teddy had tried again, I might have said 'Yes,' not because I love him any more, but because I care more to be loved than when he went away."

"I'm glad of that, Jo, for it shows that you are getting on. There are plenty to love you, so try to be satisfied with father and mother, sisters and brothers, friends and babies, till the best lover of all comes to give you your reward."

"Mothers are the *best* lovers in the world; but I don't mind whispering to Marmee that I'd like to try all kinds. It's very curious, but the more I try to satisfy myself with all sorts of natural affections, the more I seem to want. I'd no idea hearts could take in so many; mine is so elastic, it never seems full now, and I used to be quite contented with my family. I don't understand it."

"I do;" and Mrs. March smiled her wise smile, as Jo turned back the leaves to read what Amy said of Laurie.

"It is so beautiful to be loved as Laurie loves me; he isn't sentimental, doesn't say much about it, but I see and feel it in all he says and does, and it makes me so happy and so humble that I don't seem to be the same girl I was. I never knew how good and generous and tender he was till now, for he lets me read his heart, and I find it full of noble impulses and hopes and purposes, and am so proud to know it's mine. He says he feels as if he 'could make a prosperous voyage now with me aboard as mate, and lots of love for ballast.' I pray he may, and try to be all he believes me, for I love my gallant captain with all my heart and soul and might, and never will desert him, while God lets us be together. O mother, I never knew how much like heaven this world could be, when two people love and live for one another!"

"And that's our cool, reserved, and worldly Amy! Truly, love does work miracles. How very, very happy they must be!" And Jo laid the rustling sheets together with a careful hand, as one might shut the covers of a lovely romance, which holds the reader fast till the end comes, and he finds himself alone in the work-a-day world again.

By and by Jo roamed away upstairs, for it was rainy, and she could not walk. A restless spirit possessed her, and the old feeling came again, not bitter as it once was, but a sorrowfully patient wonder why one sister should have all she asked, the other nothing. It was not true; she knew that, and tried to put it away, but the natural craving for affection was strong, and Amy's happiness woke the hungry longing for someone to "love with heart and soul, and cling to while God let them be together."

Up in the garret, where Jo's unquiet wanderings ended, stood four little wooden chests in a row, each marked with its owner's name, and each filled with relics of the childhood and girlhood ended now for all. Jo glanced into them, and when she came to her own, leaned her chin on the edge, and stared absently at the chaotic collection, till a bundle of old exercise-books caught her eye. She drew them out, turned them over, and re-lived that pleasant winter at kind Mrs. Kirke's. She had smiled at first, then she looked thoughtful, next sad, and when she came to a little message written in the Professor's hand, her lips began to tremble, the books slid out of her lap, and she sat looking at the friendly words, as if they took a new meaning, and touched a tender spot in her heart.

"Wait for me, my friend. I may be a little late, but I shall surely come."

"Oh, if he only would! So kind, so good, so patient with me always; my dear old Fritz, I didn't value him half enough when I had him, but now how I should love to see him, for everyone seems going away from me, and I'm all alone."

And holding the little paper fast, as if it were a promise yet to be fulfilled, Jo laid her head down on a comfortable rag-bag, and cried, as if in opposition to the rain pattering on the roof.

Was it all self-pity, loneliness, or low spirits? Or was it the waking up of a sentiment which had bided its time as patiently as its inspirer? Who shall say?

# CHAPTER XLIII

## SURPRISES

Jo was alone in the twilight, lying on the old sofa, looking at the fire, and thinking. It was her favorite way of spending the hour of dusk; no one disturbed her, and she used to lie there on Beth's little red pillow, planning stories, dreaming dreams, or thinking tender thoughts of the sister who never seemed far away. Her face looked tired, grave, and rather sad; for tomorrow was her birthday, and she was thinking how fast the years went by, how old she was getting, and how little she seemed to have accomplished. Almost twenty-five, and nothing to show for it.

Jo was mistaken in that; there was a good deal to show, and by and by she saw, and was grateful for it.

"An old maid, that's what I'm to be. A literary spinster, with a pen for a spouse, a family of stories for children, and twenty years hence a morsel of fame, perhaps; when, like poor Johnson, I'm old, and can't enjoy it, solitary, and can't share it, independent, and don't need it. Well, I needn't be a sour saint nor a selfish sinner; and, I dare say, old maids are very comfortable when they get used to it; but—" and there Jo sighed, as if the prospect was not inviting.

It seldom is, at first, and thirty seems the end of all things to five-and-twenty; but it's not so bad as it looks, and one can get on quite happily if one has something in one's self to fall back upon. At twenty-five, girls begin to talk about being old maids, but secretly resolve that they never will be; at thirty they say nothing about it, but quietly accept the fact, and, if sensible, console themselves by remembering that they have twenty more useful, happy years, in which they may be learning to grow old gracefully. Don't laugh at the spinsters, dear girls, for often very tender, tragical romances are hidden away in the hearts that beat so quietly under the sober gowns, and many silent sacrifices of youth, health, ambition, love itself, make the faded faces beautiful in God's sight. Even the sad, sour sisters should be kindly dealt with, because they have missed the sweetest part of life, if for no other reason; and, looking at them with compassion, not contempt, girls in their bloom should remember that they too may miss the blossom time; that rosy cheeks don't last forever, that silver threads will come in the bonnie brown hair, and that, by and by, kindness and respect will be as sweet as love and admiration now.

Gentlemen, which means boys, be courteous to the old maids, no matter how poor and plain and prim, for the only chivalry worth having is that which is the readiest to pay deference to the old, protect the feeble, and serve womankind, regardless of rank, age, or color. Just recollect the good aunts who have not only lectured and fussed, but nursed and petted, too often without thanks; the scrapes they have helped you out of, the "tips" they have given you from their small store, the stitches the patient old fingers have set for you, the steps the willing old feet have taken, and gratefully pay the dear old ladies the little attentions that women love to receive as long as they live. The bright-eyed girls are quick to see such traits, and will like you all the better for them; and if death, almost the only power that can part mother and son, should rob you of yours, you will be sure to find a tender welcome and maternal cherishing from some Aunt Priscilla, who has kept the warmest corner of her lonely old heart for "the best nevvy in the world."

Jo must have fallen asleep (as I dare say my reader has during this little homily), for suddenly Laurie's ghost seemed to stand before her,— a substantial, lifelike ghost,—leaning over her, with the very look he used to wear when he felt a good deal and didn't like to show it. But, like Jenny in the ballad,—

> *"She could not think it he,"*

and lay staring up at him in startled silence, till he stooped and kissed her. Then she knew him, and flew up, crying joyfully,—

"O my Teddy! O my Teddy!"

"Dear Jo, you are glad to see me, then?"

"Glad! My blessed boy, words can't express my gladness. Where's Amy?"

"Your mother has got her down at Meg's. We stopped there by the way, and there was no getting my wife out of their clutches."

"Your what?" cried Jo, for Laurie uttered those two words with an unconscious pride and satisfaction which betrayed him.

"Oh, the dickens! Now I've done it;" and he looked so guilty that Jo was down upon him like a flash.

"You've gone and got married!"

"Yes, please, but I never will again;" and he went down upon his knees, with a penitent clasping of hands, and a face full of mischief, mirth, and triumph.

"Actually married?"

"Very much so, thank you."

"Mercy on us! What dreadful thing will you do next?" and Jo fell into her seat, with a gasp.

"A characteristic, but not exactly complimentary, congratulation," returned Laurie, still in an abject attitude, but beaming with satisfaction.

"What can you expect, when you take one's breath away, creeping in like a burglar, and letting cats out of bags like that? Get up, you ridiculous boy, and tell me all about it."

"Not a word, unless you let me come in my old place, and promise not to barricade."

Jo laughed at that as she had not done for many a long day, and patted the sofa invitingly, as she said, in a cordial tone,—

"The old pillow is up garret, and we don't need it now; so, come and 'fess, Teddy."

"How good it sounds to hear you say 'Teddy'! No one ever calls me that but you;" and Laurie sat down, with an air of great content.

"What does Amy call you?"

"My lord."

"That's like her. Well, you look it;" and Jo's eyes plainly betrayed that she found her boy comelier than ever.

The pillow was gone, but there *was* a barricade, nevertheless,—a natural one, raised by time, absence, and change of heart. Both felt it, and for a minute looked at one another as if that invisible barrier cast a little shadow over them. It was gone directly, however, for Laurie said, with a vain attempt at dignity,—

"Don't I look like a married man and the head of a family?"

"Not a bit, and you never will. You've grown bigger and bonnier, but you are the same scapegrace as ever."

"Now, really, Jo, you ought to treat me with more respect," began Laurie, who enjoyed it all immensely.

"How can I, when the mere idea of you, married and settled, is so irresistibly funny that I can't keep sober!" answered Jo, smiling all over her face, so infectiously that they had another laugh, and then settled down for a good talk, quite in the pleasant old fashion.

"It's no use your going out in the cold to get Amy, for they are all coming up presently. I couldn't wait; I wanted to be the one to tell you the grand surprise, and have 'first skim,' as we used to say when we squabbled about the cream."

"Of course you did, and spoilt your story by beginning at the wrong end. Now, start right, and tell me how it all happened; I'm pining to know."

"Well, I did it to please Amy," began Laurie, with a twinkle that made Jo exclaim,—

"Fib number one; Amy did it to please you. Go on, and tell the truth, if you can, sir."

"Now she's beginning to marm it; isn't it jolly to hear her?" said Laurie to the fire, and the fire glowed and sparkled as if it quite agreed. "It's all the same, you know, she and I being one. We planned to come home with the Carrols, a month or more ago, but they suddenly changed their minds, and decided to pass another winter in Paris. But grandpa wanted to come home; he went to please me, and I couldn't let him go alone, neither could I leave Amy; and Mrs. Carrol had got English notions about chaperons and such nonsense, and wouldn't let Amy come with us. So I just settled the difficulty by saying, 'Let's be married, and then we can do as we like.' "

"Of course you did; you always have things to suit you."

"Not always;" and something in Laurie's voice made Jo say hastily,—

"How did you ever get aunt to agree?"

"It was hard work; but, between us, we talked her over, for we had heaps of good reasons on our side. There wasn't time to write and ask leave, but you all liked it, had consented to it by and by, and it was only 'taking Time by the fetlock,' as my wife says."

"Aren't we proud of those two words, and don't we like to say them?" interrupted Jo, addressing the fire in her turn, and watching with delight the happy light it seemed to kindle in the eyes that had been so tragically gloomy when she saw them last.

"A trifle, perhaps; she's such a captivating little woman I can't help being proud of her. Well, then, uncle and aunt were there to play propriety; we were so absorbed in one another we were of no mortal use apart, and that charming arrangement would make everything easy all round; so we did it."

"When, where, how?" asked Jo, in a fever of feminine interest and curiosity, for she could not realize it a particle.

"Six weeks ago, at the American consul's, in Paris; a very quiet wedding, of course, for even in our happiness we didn't forget dear little Beth."

Jo put her hand in his as he said that, and Laurie gently smoothed the little red pillow, which he remembered well.

"Why didn't you let us know afterward?" asked Jo, in a quieter tone, when they had sat quite still a minute.

"We wanted to surprise you; we thought we were coming directly home, at first; but the dear old gentleman, as soon as we were married, found he couldn't be ready under a month, at least, and sent us off to spend our honeymoon wherever we liked. Amy had once called Valrosa a regular honeymoon home, so we went there, and were as happy as people are but once in their lives. My faith! Wasn't it love among the roses!"

Laurie seemed to forget Jo for a minute, and Jo was glad of it; for the fact that he told her these things so freely and naturally assured her that he had quite forgiven and forgotten. She tried to draw away her hand; but, as if he guessed the thought that prompted the half-involuntary impulse, Laurie held it fast, and said, with a manly gravity she had never seen in him before,—

"Jo, dear, I want to say one thing, and then we'll put it by forever. As I told you in my letter, when I wrote that Amy had been so kind to me, I never shall stop loving you; but the love is altered, and I have learned to see that it is better as it is. Amy and you change places in my heart, that's all. I think it was meant to be so, and would have come about naturally, if I had waited, as you tried to make me; but I never could be patient, and so I got a heartache. I was a boy then, headstrong and violent; and it took a hard lesson to show me my mistake. For it *was* one, Jo, as you said, and I found it out, after making a fool of myself. Upon my word, I was so tumbled up in my mind, at one time, that I didn't know which I loved best, you or Amy, and tried to love both alike; but I couldn't, and when I saw her in Switzerland, everything seemed to clear up all at once. You both got into your right places, and I felt sure that it was well off with the old love before it was on with the new; that I could honestly share my heart between sister Jo and wife Amy, and love them both dearly. Will you believe it, and go back to the happy old times when we first knew one another?"

"I'll believe it, with all my heart; but, Teddy, we never can be boy and girl again: the happy old times can't come back, and we mustn't expect it. We are man and woman now, with sober work to do, for playtime is over, and we must give up frolicking. I'm sure you feel this; I see the change in you, and you'll find it in me. I shall miss my boy, but I shall love the man as much, and admire him more, because he means to be what I hoped he would. We can't be little playmates any longer, but we will be brother and sister, to love and help one another all our lives, won't we, Laurie?"

He did not say a word, but took the hand she offered him, and laid his face down on it for a minute, feeling that out of the grave of a boyish passion, there had risen a beautiful, strong friendship to bless them both. Presently Jo said cheerfully, for she didn't want the coming home to be a sad one,—

"I can't make it true that you children are really married, and going to set up housekeeping. Why, it seems only yesterday that I was buttoning Amy's pinafore, and pulling your hair when you teased. Mercy me, how time does fly!"

"As one of the children is older than yourself, you needn't talk so like a grandma. I flatter myself I'm a 'gentleman growed,' as Peggotty said of David; and when you see Amy, you'll find her rather a precocious infant," said Laurie, looking amused at her maternal air.

"You may be a little older in years, but I'm ever so much older in feeling, Teddy. Women always are; and this last year has been such a hard one that I feel forty."

"Poor Jo! We left you to bear it alone, while we went pleasuring. You *are* older; here's a line, and there's another; unless you smile, your eyes look sad, and when I touched the cushion, just now, I found a tear on it. You've had a great deal to bear, and had to bear it all alone. What a selfish beast I've been!" and Laurie pulled his own hair, with a remorseful look.

But Jo only turned over the traitorous pillow, and answered, in a tone which she tried to make quite cheerful,—

"No, I had father and mother to help me, the dear babies to comfort me, and the thought that you and Amy were safe and happy, to make the troubles here easier to bear. I *am* lonely, sometimes, but I dare say it's good for me, and—"

"You never shall be again," broke in Laurie, putting his arm about her, as if to fence out every human ill. "Amy and I can't get on without you, so you must come and teach 'the children' to keep house, and go halves in everything, just as we used to do, and let us pet you, and all be blissfully happy and friendly together."

"If I shouldn't be in the way, it would be very pleasant. I begin to feel quite young already; for, somehow, all my troubles seemed to fly away when you came. You always were a comfort, Teddy;" and Jo leaned her head on his shoulder, just as she did years ago, when Beth lay ill, and Laurie told her to hold on to him.

He looked down at her, wondering if she remembered the time, but Jo was smiling to herself, as if, in truth, her troubles *had* all vanished at his coming.

"You are the same Jo still, dropping tears about one minute, and laughing the next. You look a little wicked now; what is it, grandma?"

"I was wondering how you and Amy get on together."

"Like angels!"

"Yes, of course, at first; but which rules?"

"I don't mind telling you that she does, now; at least I let her think so,—it pleases her, you know. By and by we shall take turns, for marriage, they say, halves one's rights and doubles one's duties."

"You'll go on as you begin, and Amy will rule you all the days of your life."

"Well, she does it so imperceptibly that I don't think I shall mind much. She is the sort of woman who knows how to rule well; in fact, I rather like it, for she winds one round her finger as softly and prettily as a skein of silk, and makes you feel as if she was doing you a favor all the while."

"That ever I should live to see you a henpecked husband and enjoying it!" cried Jo, with uplifted hands.

It was good to see Laurie square his shoulders, and smile with masculine scorn at that insinuation, as he replied, with his "high and mighty" air,—

"Amy is too well-bred for that, and I am not the sort of man to submit to it. My wife and I respect ourselves and one another too much ever to tyrannize or quarrel."

Jo liked that, and thought the new dignity very becoming, but the boy seemed changing very fast into the man, and regret mingled with her pleasure.

"I am sure of that; Amy and you never did quarrel as we used to. She is the sun and I the wind, in the fable, and the sun managed the man best, you remember."

"She can blow him up as well as shine on him," laughed Laurie. "Such a lecture as I got at Nice! I give you my word it was a deal worse than any of your scoldings,—a regular rouser. I'll tell you all about it sometime,— *she* never will, because, after telling me that she despised and was ashamed of me, she lost her heart to the despicable party and married the good-for-nothing."

"What baseness! Well, if she abuses you, come to me, and I'll defend you."

"I look as if I needed it, don't I?" said Laurie, getting up and striking an attitude which suddenly changed from the imposing to the rapturous, as Amy's voice was heard calling,—

"Where is she? Where's my dear old Jo?"

In trooped the whole family, and everyone was hugged and kissed all over again, and, after several vain attempts, the three wanderers were set down to be looked at and exulted over. Mr. Laurence, hale and hearty as ever, was quite as much improved as the others by his foreign tour, for the crustiness seemed to be nearly gone, and the old-fashioned courtliness had received a polish which made it kindlier than ever. It was good to see him beam at "my children," as he called the young pair; it was better still to see Amy pay him the daughterly duty and affection which completely won his old heart; and best of all, to watch Laurie revolve about the two, as if never tired of enjoying the pretty picture they made.

The minute she put her eyes upon Amy, Meg became conscious that her own dress hadn't a Parisian air, that young Mrs. Moffat would be entirely eclipsed by young Mrs. Laurence, and that "her ladyship" was altogether a most elegant and graceful woman. Jo thought, as she watched the pair, "How well they look together! I was right, and Laurie has found the beautiful, accomplished girl who will become his home better than clumsy old Jo, and be a pride, not a torment to him." Mrs. March and her husband smiled and nodded at each other with happy faces, for they saw that their youngest had done well, not only in worldly things, but the better wealth of love, confidence, and happiness.

For Amy's face was full of the soft brightness which betokens a peaceful heart, her voice had a new tenderness in it, and the cool, prim carriage was changed to a gentle dignity, both womanly and winning. No little affectations marred it, and the cordial sweetness of her manner was more charming than the new beauty or the old grace, for it stamped her at once with the unmistakable sign of the true gentlewoman she had hoped to become.

"Love has done much for our little girl," said her mother softly.

"She has had a good example before her all her life, my dear," Mr. March whispered back, with a loving look at the worn face and gray head beside him.

Daisy found it impossible to keep her eyes off her "pitty aunty," but attached herself like a lap-dog to the wonderful châtelaine full of delightful charms. Demi paused to consider the new relationship before he compromised himself by the rash acceptance of a bribe, which took the tempting form of a family of wooden bears from Berne. A flank movement produced an unconditional surrender, however, for Laurie knew where to have him.

"Young man, when I first had the honor of making your acquaintance you hit me in the face: now I demand the satisfaction of a gentleman;" and with that the tall uncle proceeded to toss and tousle the small nephew in a way that damaged his philosophical dignity as much as it delighted his boyish soul.

"Blest if she ain't in silk from head to foot? Ain't it a relishin' sight to see her settin' there as fine as a fiddle, and hear folks calling little Amy, Mis. Laurence?" muttered old Hannah, who could not resist frequent "peeks" through the slide as she set the table in a most decidedly promiscuous manner.

Mercy on us, how they did talk! First one, then the other, then all burst out together, trying to tell the history of three years in half an hour. It was fortunate that tea was at hand, to produce a lull and provide refreshment, for they would have been hoarse and faint if they had gone on much longer. Such a happy procession as filed away into the little dining-room! Mr. March proudly escorted "Mrs. Laurence;" Mrs. March as proudly leaned on the arm of "my son;" the old gentleman took Jo, with a whispered "You must be my girl now," and a glance at the empty corner by the fire, that made Jo whisper back, with trembling lips, "I'll try to fill her place, sir."

The twins pranced behind, feeling that the millennium was at hand, for everyone was so busy with the newcomers that they were left to revel at their own sweet will, and you may be sure they made the most of the opportunity. Didn't they steal sips of tea, stuff gingerbread *ad libitum*, get a hot biscuit apiece, and, as a crowning trespass, didn't they each whisk a captivating little tart into their tiny pockets, there to stick and crumble treacherously, teaching them that both human nature and pastry are frail? Burdened with the guilty consciousness of the sequestered tarts, and fearing that Dodo's sharp eyes would pierce the thin disguise of cambric and merino which hid their booty, the little sinners attached themselves to "Dranpa," who hadn't his spectacles on. Amy, who was handed about like refreshments, returned to the parlor on Father Laurence's arm; the others paired off as before, and this arrangement left Jo companionless. She did not mind it at the minute, for she lingered to answer Hannah's eager inquiry,—

"Will Miss Amy ride in her coop (*coupé*), and use all them lovely silver dishes that's stored away over yander?"

"Shouldn't wonder if she drove six white horses, ate off gold plate, and wore diamonds and point-lace every day. Teddy thinks nothing too good for her," returned Jo with infinite satisfaction.

"No more there is! Will you have hash or fish-balls for breakfast?" asked Hannah, who wisely mingled poetry and prose.

"I don't care"; and Jo shut the door, feeling that food was an uncongenial topic just then. She stood a minute looking at the party vanishing above, and, as Demi's short plaid legs toiled up the last stair, a sudden sense of loneliness came over her so strongly that she looked about her with dim eyes, as if to find something to lean upon, for even Teddy had deserted her. If she had known what birthday gift was coming every minute nearer and nearer, she would not have said to herself, "I'll weep a little weep when I go to bed; it won't do to be dismal now." Then she drew her hand over her eyes,—for one of her boyish habits was never to know where her handkerchief was,—and had just managed to call up a smile when there came a knock at the porch-door.

She opened it with hospitable haste, and started as if another ghost had come to surprise her; for there stood a tall, bearded gentleman, beaming on her from the darkness like a midnight sun.

"O Mr. Bhaer, I *am* so glad to see you!" cried Jo, with a clutch, as if she feared the night would swallow him up before she could get him in.

"And I to see Miss Marsch,—but no, you haf a party—" and the Professor paused as the sound of voices and the tap of dancing feet came down to them.

"No, we haven't, only the family. My sister and friends have just come home, and we are all very happy. Come in, and make one of us."

Though a very social man, I think Mr. Bhaer would have gone decorously away, and come again another day; but how could he, when Jo shut the door behind him, and bereft him of his hat? Perhaps her face had something to do with it, for she forgot to hide her joy at seeing him, and showed it with a frankness that proved irresistible to the solitary man, whose welcome far exceeded his boldest hopes.

"If I shall not be Monsieur de Trop, I will so gladly see them all. You haf been ill, my friend?"

He put the question abruptly, for, as Jo hung up his coat, the light fell on her face, and he saw a change in it.

"O Mr. Bhaer, I am so glad to see you."

"Not ill, but tired and sorrowful. We have had trouble since I saw you last."

"Ah, yes, I know. My heart was sore for you when I heard that;" and he shook hands again, with such a sympathetic face that Jo felt as if no comfort could equal the look of the kind eyes, the grasp of the big, warm hand.

"Father, mother, this is my friend, Professor Bhaer," she said, with a face and tone of such irrepressible pride and pleasure that she might as well have blown a trumpet and opened the door with a flourish.

If the stranger had had any doubts about his reception, they were set at rest in a minute by the cordial welcome he received. Everyone greeted him kindly, for Jo's sake at first, but very soon they liked him for his own. They could not help it, for he carried the talisman that opens all hearts, and these simple people warmed to him at once, feeling even the more friendly because he was poor; for poverty enriches those who live above it, and is a sure passport to truly hospitable spirits. Mr. Bhaer sat looking about him with the air of a traveller who knocks at a strange door, and, when it opens, finds himself at home. The children went to him like bees to a honey-pot; and, establishing themselves on each knee, proceeded to captivate him by rifling his pockets, pulling his beard, and investigating his watch, with juvenile audacity. The women telegraphed their approval to one another, and Mr. March, feeling that he had got a kindred spirit, opened his choicest stores for his guest's benefit, while silent John listened and enjoyed the talk, but said not a word, and Mr. Laurence found it impossible to go to sleep.

If Jo had not been otherwise engaged, Laurie's behavior would have amused her; for a faint twinge, not of jealousy, but something like suspicion, caused that gentleman to stand aloof at first, and observe the new-comer with brotherly circumspection. But it did not last long. He got interested in spite of himself, and, before he knew it, was drawn into the circle; for Mr. Bhaer talked well in this genial atmosphere, and did himself justice. He seldom spoke to Laurie, but he looked at him often, and a shadow would pass across his face, as if regretting his own lost youth, as he watched the young man in his prime. Then his eye would turn to Jo so wistfully that she would have surely answered the mute inquiry if she had seen it; but Jo had her own eyes to take care of, and, feeling that they could not be trusted, she prudently kept them on the little sock she was knitting, like a model maiden aunt.

A stealthy glance now and then refreshed her like sips of fresh water after a dusty walk, for the sidelong peeps showed her several propitious omens. Mr. Bhaer's face had lost the absent-minded expression, and looked all alive with interest in the present moment, actually young and handsome, she thought, forgetting to compare him with Laurie, as she usually did strange men, to their great detriment. Then he seemed quite inspired, though the burial customs of the ancients, to which the conversation had strayed, might not be considered an exhilarating topic. Jo quite glowed with triumph when Teddy got quenched in an argument, and thought to herself, as she watched her father's absorbed face, "How he would enjoy having such a man as my Professor to talk with every day!" Lastly, Mr. Bhaer was dressed in a new suit of black, which made him look more like a gentleman than ever. His bushy hair had been cut and smoothly brushed, but didn't stay in order long, for, in exciting moments, he rumpled it up in the droll way he used to do; and Jo liked it rampantly erect better than flat, because she thought it gave his fine forehead a Jove-like aspect. Poor Jo, how she did glorify that plain man, as she sat knitting away so quietly, yet letting nothing escape her, not even the fact that Mr. Bhaer actually had gold sleeve-buttons in his immaculate wrist-bands!

"Dear old fellow! He couldn't have got himself up with more care if he'd been going a-wooing," said Jo to herself; and then a sudden thought, born of the words, made her blush so dreadfully that she had to drop her ball, and go down after it to hide her face.

The manœuvre did not succeed as well as she expected, however; for, though just in the act of setting fire to a funeral-pile, the Professor dropped his torch, metaphorically speaking, and made a dive after the little blue ball. Of course they bumped their heads smartly together, saw stars, and both came up flushed and laughing, without the ball, to resume their seats, wishing they had not left them.

Nobody knew where the evening went to; for Hannah skilfully abstracted the babies at an early hour, nodding like two rosy poppies, and Mr. Laurence went home to rest. The others sat around the fire, talking away, utterly regardless of the lapse of time, till Meg, whose maternal mind was impressed with a firm conviction that Daisy had tumbled out of bed, and Demi set his night-gown afire studying the structure of matches, made a move to go.

"We must have our sing, in the good old way, for we are all together again once more," said Jo, feeling that a good shout would be a safe and pleasant vent for the jubilant emotions of her soul.

They were not *all* there. But no one found the words thoughtless or untrue; for Beth still seemed among them, a peaceful presence, invisible, but dearer than ever, since death could not break the household league that love made indissoluble. The little chair stood in its old place; the tidy basket, with the bit of work she left unfinished when the needle grew "so heavy," was still on its accustomed shelf; the beloved instrument, seldom touched now, had not been moved; and above it Beth's face, serene and smiling, as in the early days, looked down upon them, seeming to say, "Be happy. I am here."

"Play something, Amy. Let them hear how much you have improved," said Laurie, with pardonable pride in his promising pupil.

But Amy whispered, with full eyes, as she twirled the faded stool,—

"Not tonight, dear. I can't show off tonight."

But she did show something better than brilliancy or skill; for she sung Beth's songs with a tender music in her voice which the best master could not have taught, and touched the listeners' hearts with a sweeter power than any other inspiration could have given her. The room was very still, when the clear voice failed suddenly at the last line of Beth's favorite hymn. It was hard to say,—

*"Earth hath no sorrow that heaven cannot heal;"*

and Amy leaned against her husband, who stood behind her, feeling that her welcome home was not quite perfect without Beth's kiss.

"Now, we must finish with Mignon's song; for Mr. Bhaer sings that," said Jo, before the pause grew painful. And Mr. Bhaer cleared his throat with a gratified "Hem!" as he stepped into the corner where Jo stood, saying,—

"You will sing with me? We go excellently well together."

A pleasing fiction, by the way; for Jo had no more idea of music than a grasshopper. But she would have consented if he had proposed to sing a whole opera, and warbled away, blissfully regardless of time and tune. It didn't much matter; for Mr. Bhaer sang like a true German, heartily and well; and Jo soon subsided into a subdued hum, that she might listen to the mellow voice that seemed to sing for her alone.

*"Know'st thou the land where the citron blooms,"*

used to be the Professor's favorite line, for "das land" meant Germany to him; but now he seemed to dwell, with peculiar warmth and melody, upon the words,—

*"There, oh there, might I with thee,*
*O my beloved, go!"*

and one listener was so thrilled by the tender invitation that she longed to say she did know the land, and would joyfully depart thither whenever he liked.

The song was considered a great success, and the singer retired covered with laurels. But a few minutes afterward, he forgot his manners entirely, and stared at Amy putting on her bonnet; for she had been introduced simply as "my sister," and no one had called her by her new name since he came. He forgot himself still further when Laurie said, in his most gracious manner, at parting,—

"My wife and I are very glad to meet you, sir. Please remember that there is always a welcome waiting for you over the way."

Then the Professor thanked him so heartily, and looked so suddenly illuminated with satisfaction, that Laurie thought him the most delightfully demonstrative old fellow he ever met.

"I too shall go; but I shall gladly come again, if you will gif me leave, dear madame, for a little business in the city will keep me here some days."

He spoke to Mrs. March, but he looked at Jo; and the mother's voice gave as cordial an assent as did the daughter's eyes; for Mrs. March was not so blind to her children's interest as Mrs. Moffat supposed.

"I suspect that is a wise man," remarked Mr. March, with placid satisfaction, from the hearth-rug, after the last guest had gone.

"I know he is a good one," added Mrs. March, with decided approval, as she wound up the clock.

"I thought you'd like him," was all Jo said, as she slipped away to her bed.

She wondered what the business was that brought Mr. Bhaer to the city, and finally decided that he had been appointed to some great honor, somewhere, but had been too modest to mention the fact. If she had seen his face when, safe in his own room, he looked at the picture of a severe and rigid young lady, with a good deal of hair, who appeared to be gazing darkly into futurity, it might have thrown some light upon the subject, especially when he turned off the gas, and kissed the picture in the dark.

# CHAPTER XLIV

## MY LORD AND LADY

"PLEASE, Madam Mother, could you lend me my wife for half an hour? The luggage has come, and I've been making hay of Amy's Paris finery, trying to find some things I want," said Laurie, coming in the next day to find Mrs. Laurence sitting in her mother's lap, as if being made "the baby" again.

"Certainly. Go, dear; I forget that you have any home but this," and Mrs. March pressed the white hand that wore the wedding-ring, as if asking pardon for her maternal covetousness.

"I shouldn't have come over if I could have helped it; but I can't get on without my little woman any more than a—"

"Weathercock can without wind," suggested Jo, as he paused for a simile; Jo had grown quite her own saucy self again since Teddy came home.

"Exactly; for Amy keeps me pointing due west most of the time, with only an occasional whiffle round to the south, and I haven't had an easterly spell since I was married; don't know anything about the north, but am altogether salubrious and balmy, hey, my lady?"

"Lovely weather so far; I don't know how long it will last, but I'm not afraid of storms, for I'm learning how to sail my ship. Come home, dear, and I'll find your bootjack; I suppose that's what you are rummaging after among my things. Men are *so* helpless, mother," said Amy, with a matronly air, which delighted her husband.

"What are you going to do with yourselves after you get settled?" asked Jo, buttoning Amy's cloak as she used to button her pinafores.

"We have our plans; we don't mean to say much about them yet, because we are such very new brooms, but we don't intend to be idle. I'm going into business with a devotion that shall delight grandfather, and prove to him that I'm not spoilt. I need something of the sort to keep me steady. I'm tired of dawdling, and mean to work like a man."

"And Amy, what is she going to do?" asked Mrs. March, well pleased at Laurie's decision, and the energy with which he spoke.

"After doing the civil all round, and airing our best bonnet, we shall astonish you by the elegant hospitalities of our mansion, the brilliant society we shall draw about us, and the beneficial influence we shall exert

over the world at large. That's about it, isn't it, Madame Récamier?"
asked Laurie, with a quizzical look at Amy.

"Time will show. Come away, Impertinence, and don't shock my family
by calling me names before their faces," answered Amy, resolving that
there should be a home with a good wife in it before she set up a *salon*
as a queen of society.

"How happy those children seem together!" observed Mr. March,
finding it difficult to become absorbed in his Aristotle after the young
couple had gone.

"Yes, and I think it will last," added Mrs. March, with the restful
expression of a pilot who has brought a ship safely into port.

"I know it will. Happy Amy!" and Jo sighed, then smiled brightly as
Professor Bhaer opened the gate with an impatient push.

Later in the evening, when his mind had been set at rest about the
bootjack, Laurie said suddenly to his wife, who was flitting about, arranging
her new art treasures,—

"Mrs. Laurence."

"My lord!"

"That man intends to marry our Jo!"

"I hope so; don't you, dear?"

"Well, my love, I consider him a trump, in the fullest sense of that
expressive word, but I do wish he was a little younger and a good deal
richer."

"Now, Laurie, don't be too fastidious and worldly-minded. If they love
one another it doesn't matter a particle how old they are nor how poor.
Women *never* should marry for money—" Amy caught herself up short
as the words escaped her, and looked at her husband, who replied, with
malicious gravity,—

"Certainly not, though you do hear charming girls say that they intend
to do it sometimes. If my memory serves me, you once thought it your
duty to make a rich match; that accounts, perhaps, for your marrying
a good-for-nothing like me."

"O my dearest boy, don't, don't say that! I forgot you were rich when
I said 'Yes.' I'd have married you if you hadn't a penny, and I sometimes
wish you *were* poor that I might show how much I love you;" and Amy,
who was very dignified in public and very fond in private, gave convincing
proofs of the truth of her words.

"You don't really think I am such a mercenary creature as I tried to
be once, do you? It would break my heart if you didn't believe that I'd
gladly pull in the same boat with you, even if you had to get your living
by rowing on the lake."

"Am I an idiot and a brute? How could I think so, when you refused
a richer man for me, and won't let me give you half I want to now, when
I have the right? Girls do it every day, poor things, and are taught to
think it is their only salvation; but you had better lessons, and, though
I trembled for you at one time, I was not disappointed, for the daughter
was true to the mother's teaching. I told mamma so yesterday, and she
looked as glad and grateful as if I'd given her a check for a million, to
be spent in charity. You are not listening to my moral remarks, Mrs.

Mrs. Laurence sitting in her mother's lap.

Laurence;" and Laurie paused, for Amy's eyes had an absent look, though fixed upon his face.

"Yes, I am, and admiring the dimple in your chin at the same time. I don't wish to make you vain, but I must confess that I'm prouder of my handsome husband than of all his money. Don't laugh, but your nose is *such* a comfort to me;" and Amy softly caressed the well-cut feature with artistic satisfaction.

Laurie had received many compliments in his life, but never one that suited him better, as he plainly showed, though he did laugh at his wife's peculiar taste, while she said slowly,—

"May I ask you a question, dear?"

"Of course you may."

"Shall you care if Jo does marry Mr. Bhaer?"

"Oh, that's the trouble, is it? I thought there was something in the dimple that didn't suit you. Not being a dog in the manger, but the happiest fellow alive, I assure you I can dance at Jo's wedding with a heart as light as my heels. Do you doubt it, my darling?"

Amy looked up at him, and was satisfied; her last little jealous fear vanished forever, and she thanked him, with a face full of love and confidence.

"I wish we could do something for that capital old Professor. Couldn't we invent a rich relation, who shall obligingly die out there in Germany, and leave him a tidy little fortune?" said Laurie, when they began to pace up and down the long drawing-room, arm-in-arm, as they were fond of doing, in memory of the chateau garden.

"Jo would find us out, and spoil it all; she is very proud of him, just as he is, and said yesterday that she thought poverty was a beautiful thing."

"Bless her dear heart! She won't think so when she has a literary husband, and a dozen little professors and professorins to support. We won't interfere now, but watch our chance, and do them a good turn in spite of themselves. I owe Jo for a part of my education, and she believes in people's paying their honest debts, so I'll get round her in that way."

"How delightful it is to be able to help others, isn't it? That was always one of my dreams, to have the power of giving freely; and, thanks to you, the dream has come true."

"Ah! We'll do quantities of good, won't we? There's one sort of poverty that I particularly like to help. Out-and-out beggars get taken care of, but poor gentlefolks fare badly, because they won't ask, and people don't dare to offer charity; yet there are a thousand ways of helping them, if one only knows how to do it so delicately that it does not offend. I must say, I like to serve a decayed gentleman better than a blarneying beggar; I suppose it's wrong, but I do, though it is harder."

"Because it takes a gentleman to do it," added the other member of the domestic admiration society.

"Thank you, I'm afraid I don't deserve that pretty compliment. But I was going to say that while I was dawdling about abroad, I saw a good many talented young fellows making all sorts of sacrifices, and enduring real hardships, that they might realize their dreams. Splendid fellows, some of them, working like heroes, poor and friendless, but so full of

They began to pace up and down.

courage, patience, and ambition, that I was ashamed of myself, and longed to give them a right good lift. Those are people whom it's a satisfaction to help, for if they've got genius, it's an honor to be allowed to serve them, and not let it be lost or delayed for want of fuel to keep the pot boiling; if they haven't, it's a pleasure to comfort the poor souls, and keep them from despair when they find it out."

"Yes, indeed; and there's another class who can't ask, and who suffer in silence. I know something of it, for I belonged to it before you made a princess of me, as the king does the beggar-maid in the old story. Ambitious girls have a hard time, Laurie, and often have to see youth, health, and precious opportunities go by, just for want of a little help at the right minute. People have been very kind to me; and whenever I see girls struggling along, as we used to do, I want to put out my hand and help them, as I was helped."

"And so you shall, like an angel as you are!" cried Laurie, resolving, with a glow of philanthropic zeal, to found and endow an institution for the express benefit of young women with artistic tendencies. "Rich people have no right to sit down and enjoy themselves, or let their money accumulate for others to waste. It's not half so sensible to leave legacies when one dies as it is to use the money wisely while alive, and enjoy making one's fellow-creatures happy with it. We'll have a good time ourselves, and add an extra relish to our own pleasure by giving other people a generous taste. Will you be a little Dorcas, going about emptying a big basket of comforts, and filling it up with good deeds?"

"With all my heart, if you will be a brave St. Martin, stopping, as you ride gallantly through the world, to share your cloak with the beggar."

"It's a bargain, and we shall get the best of it!"

So the young pair shook hands upon it, and then paced happily on again, feeling that their pleasant home was more home-like because they hoped to brighten other homes, believing that their own feet would walk more uprightly along the flowery path before them, if they smoothed rough ways for other feet, and feeling that their hearts were more closely knit together by a love which could tenderly remember those less blest than they.

# CHAPTER XLV

## DAISY AND DEMI

I CANNOT feel that I have done my duty as humble historian of the March family, without devoting at least one chapter to the two most precious and important members of it. Daisy and Demi had now arrived at years of discretion; for in this fast age babies of three or four assert their rights, and get them, too, which is more than many of their elders do. If there ever were a pair of twins in danger of being utterly spoilt by adoration, it was these prattling Brookes. Of course they were the most remarkable children ever born, as will be shown when I mention that they walked at eight months, talked fluently at twelve months, and at two years they took their places at table, and behaved with a propriety which charmed all beholders. At three, Daisy demanded a "needler," and actually made a bag with four stitches in it; she likewise set up housekeeping in the sideboard, and managed a microscopic cooking-stove with a skill that brought tears of pride to Hannah's eyes, while Demi learned his letters with his grandfather, who invented a new mode of teaching the alphabet by forming the letters with his arms and legs, thus uniting gymnastics for head and heels. The boy early developed a mechanical genius which delighted his father and distracted his mother, for he tried to imitate every machine he saw, and kept the nursery in a chaotic condition, with his "sewin-sheen,"—a mysterious structure of string, chairs, clothes-pins, and spools, for wheels to go "wound and wound;" also a basket hung over the back of a big chair, in which he vainly tried to hoist his too confiding sister, who, with feminine devotion, allowed her little head to be bumped till rescued, when the young inventor indignantly remarked, "Why, marmar, dat's my lellywaiter, and me's trying to pull her up."

Though utterly unlike in character, the twins got on remarkably well together, and seldom quarreled more than thrice a day. Of course, Demi tyrannized over Daisy, and gallantly defended her from every other aggressor; while Daisy made a galley-slave of herself, and adored her brother as the one perfect being in the world. A rosy, chubby, sunshiny little soul was Daisy, who found her way to everybody's heart, and nestled there. One of the captivating children, who seem made to be kissed and cuddled, adorned and adored like little goddesses, and produced for general approval on all festive occasions. Her small virtues were so sweet that she would have been quite angelic if a few small naughtinesses had not kept her delightfully human. It was all fair weather in her world, and every morning she scrambled up to the window in her little night-gown to look out, and say, no matter whether it rained or shone, "Oh, pitty day, oh, pitty day!" Everyone was a friend, and she offered kisses to a stranger so confidingly that the most inveterate bachelor relented, and baby-lovers became faithful worshippers.

"Me loves evvybody," she once said, opening her arms, with her spoon in one hand, and her mug in the other, as if eager to embrace and nourish the whole world.

As she grew, her mother began to feel that the Dove-cote would be blest by the presence of an inmate as serene and loving as that which had helped to make the old house home, and to pray that she might be spared a loss like that which had lately taught them how long they had entertained an angel unawares. Her grandfather often called her "Beth," and her grandmother watched over her with untiring devotion, as if trying to atone for some past mistake, which no eye but her own could see.

Demi, like a true Yankee, was of an inquiring turn, wanting to know everything, and often getting much disturbed because he could not get satisfactory answers to his perpetual "What for?"

He also possessed a philosophic bent, to the great delight of his grand-father, who used to hold Socratic conversations with him, in which the precocious pupil occasionally posed his teacher, to the undisguised satisfaction of the womenfolk.

"What makes my legs go, dranpa?" asked the young philosopher, surveying those active portions of his frame with a meditative air, while resting after a go-to-bed frolic one night.

"It's your little mind, Demi," replied the sage, stroking the yellow head respectfully.

"What is a little mine?"

"It is something which makes your body move, as the spring made the wheels go in my watch when I showed it to you."

"Open me; I want to see it go wound."

"I can't do that any more than you could open the watch. God winds you up, and you go till He stops you."

"Does I?" and Demi's brown eyes grew big and bright as he took in the new thought. "Is I wounded up like the watch?"

"Yes; but I can't show you how; for it is done when we don't see."

Demi felt of his back, as if expecting to find it like that of the watch, and then gravely remarked,—

"I dess Dod does it when I's asleep."

A careful explanatioin followed, to which he listened so attentively that his anxious grandmother said,—

"My dear, do you think it wise to talk about such things to that baby? He's getting great bumps over his eyes, and learning to ask the most unanswerable questions."

"If he is old enough to ask the questions he is old enough to receive true answers. I am not putting the thoughts into his head, but helping him unfold those already there. These children are wiser than we are, and I have no doubt the boy understands every word I have said to him. Now, Demi, tell me where you keep your mind?"

If the boy had replied like Alcibiades, "By the gods, Socrates, I cannot tell," his grandfather would not have been surprised; but when, after standing a moment on one leg, like a meditative young stork, he answered, in a tone of calm conviction, "In my little belly," the old gentleman could only join in grandma's laugh, and dismiss the class in metaphysics.

There might have been cause for maternal anxiety, if Demi had not given convincing proofs that he was a true boy, as well as a budding philosopher; for, often, after a discussion which caused Hannah to prophesy, with ominous nods, "That child ain't long for this world," he would turn about and set her fears at rest by some of the pranks with which dear, dirty, naughty little rascals distract and delight their parents' souls.

Meg made many moral rules, and tried to keep them; but what mother was ever proof against the winning wiles, the ingenious evasions, or the tranquil audacity of the miniature men and women who so early show themselves accomplished Artful Dodgers?

"No more raisins, Demi, they'll make you sick," says mamma to the young person who offers his services in the kitchen with unfailing regularity on plum-pudding day.

"Me likes to be sick."

"I don't want to have you, so run away and help Daisy make patty-cakes."

He reluctantly departs, but his wrongs weigh upon his spirit; and, by and by, when an opportunity comes to redress them, he outwits mamma by a shrewd bargain.

"Now you have been good children, and I'll play anything you like," says Meg, as she leads her assistant cooks upstairs, when the pudding is safely bouncing in the pot.

"Truly, marmar?" asks Demi, with a brilliant idea in his well-powdered head.

"Yes, truly; anything you say," replies the short-sighted parent, preparing herself to sing "The Three Little Kittens" half a dozen times over, or to take her family to "Buy a penny bun," regardless of wind or limb. But Demi corners her by the cool reply,—

"Then we'll go and eat up all the raisins."

Aunt Dodo was chief playmate and *confidante* of both children, and the trio turned the little house topsy-turvy. Aunt Amy was as yet only a name to them, Aunt Beth soon faded into a pleasantly vague memory, but Aunt Dodo was a living reality, and they made the most of her, for which compliment she was deeply grateful. But when Mr. Bhaer came, Jo neglected her playfellows, and dismay and desolation fell upon their little souls. Daisy, who was fond of going about peddling kisses, lost her best customer and became bankrupt; Demi, with infantile penetration, soon discovered that Dodo liked to play with "the bear-man" better than she did with him; but, though hurt, he concealed his anguish, for he hadn't the heart to insult a rival who kept a mine of chocolate-drops in his waistcoat-pocket, and a watch that could be taken out of its case and freely shaken by ardent admirers.

Some persons might have considered these pleasing liberties as bribes; but Demi didn't see it in that light, and continued to patronize the "bear-man" with pensive affability, while Daisy bestowed her small affections upon him at the third call, and considered his shoulder her throne, his arm her refuge, his gifts treasures of surpassing worth.

Gentlemen are sometimes seized with sudden fits of admiration for the young relatives of ladies whom they honor with their regard; but this counterfeit philoprogenitiveness sits uneasily upon them, and does not deceive anybody a particle. Mr. Bhaer's devotion was sincere, however likewise effective,—for honesty is the best policy in love as in law; he was one of the men who are at home with children, and looked particularly well when little faces made a pleasant contrast with his manly one. His business, whatever it was, detained him from day to day, but evening seldom failed to bring him out to see—well, he always asked for Mr. March, so I suppose *he* was the attraction. The excellent papa labored under the delusion that he was, and reveled in long discussions with the kindred spirit, till a chance remark of his more observing grandson suddenly enlightened him.

Mr. Bhaer came in one evening to pause on the threshold of the study, astonished by the spectacle that met his eye. Prone upon the floor lay Mr. March, with his respectable legs in the air, and beside him, likewise prone, was Demi, trying to imitate the attitude with his own short, scarletstockinged legs, both grovelers so seriously absorbed that they were unconscious of spectators, till Mr. Bhaer laughed his sonorous laugh, and Jo cried out, with a scandalized face,—

"Father, father, here's the Professor!"

Down went the black legs and up came the gray head, as the preceptor said, with undisturbed dignity,—

"Good evening, Mr. Bhaer. Excuse me for a moment; we are just finishing our lesson. Now, Demi, make the letter and tell its name."

"I knows him!" and, after a few convulsive efforts, the red legs took the shape of a pair of compasses, and the intelligent pupil triumphantly shouted, "It's a We, dranpa, it's a We!"

"He's a born Weller," laughed Jo, as her parent gathered himself up, and her nephew tried to stand on his head, as the only mode of expressing his satisfaction that school was over.

"What have you been at today, bübchen?" asked Mr. Bhaer, picking up the gymnast.

"Me went to see little Mary."

"And what did you there?"

"I kissed her," began Demi, with artless frankness.

"Prut! Thou beginnest early. What did the little Mary say to that?" asked Mr. Bhaer, continuing to confess the young sinner, who stood upon his knee, exploring the waistcoat-pocket.

"Oh, she liked it, and she kissed me, and I liked it. *Don't* little boys like little girls?" added Demi, with his mouth full, and an air of bland satisfaction.

"You precocious chick! Who put that into your head?" said Jo, enjoying the innocent revelations as much as the Professor.

" 'Tisn't in mine head; it's in mine mouf," answered literal Demi, putting out his tongue, with a chocolate-drop on it, thinking she alluded to confectionery, not ideas.

"Thou shouldst save some for the little friend: sweets to the sweet, mannling;" and Mr. Bhaer offered Jo some, with a look that made her wonder if chocolate was not the nectar drunk by the gods. Demi also saw the smile, was impressed by it, and artlessly inquired,—

"Do great boys like great girls, too, 'Fessor?"

Like young Washington, Mr. Bhaer "couldn't tell a lie"; so he gave the somewhat vague reply that he believed they did sometimes, in a tone that made Mr. March put down his clothes-brush, glance at Jo's retiring face, and then sink into his chair, looking as if the "precocious chick" had put an idea into *his* head that was both sweet and sour.

Why Dodo, when she caught him in the china-closet half an hour afterward, nearly squeezed the breath out of his little body with a tender embrace, instead of shaking him for being there, and why she followed up this novel perfomance by the unexpected gift of a big slice of bread and jelly, remained one of the problems over which Demi puzzled his small wits, and was forced to leave unsolved forever.

"Dranpa, it's a We."

# CHAPTER XLVI

## UNDER THE UMBRELLA

WHILE Laurie and Amy were taking conjugal strolls over velvet carpets, as they set their house in order, and planned a blissful future, Mr. Bhaer and Jo were enjoying promenades of a different sort, along muddy roads and sodden fields.

"I always do take a walk toward evening, and I don't know why I should give it up, just because I often happen to meet the Professor on his way out," said Jo to herself, after two or three encounters; for, though there were two paths to Meg's, whichever one she took she was sure to meet him, either going or returning. He was always walking rapidly, and never seemed to see her till quite close, when he would look as if his short-sighted eyes had failed to recognize the approaching lady till that moment. Then, if she was going to Meg's, he always had something for the babies; if her face was turned homeward, he had merely strolled down to see the river, and was just about returning, unless they were tired of his frequent calls.

Under the circumstances, what could Jo do but greet him civilly, and invite him in? If she *was* tired of his visits, she concealed her weariness with perfect skill, and took care that there should be coffee for supper, "as Friedrich—I mean Mr. Bhaer—doesn't like tea."

By the second week, everyone knew perfectly well what was going on, yet everyone tried to look as if they were stone-blind to the changes in Jo's face. They never asked why she sang about her work, did up her hair three times a day, and got so blooming with her evening exercise; and no one seemed to have the slightest suspicion that Professor Bhaer, while talking philosophy with the father, was giving the daughter lessons in love.

Jo couldn't even lose her heart in a decorous manner, but sternly tried to quench her feelings; and, failing to do so, led a somewhat agitated life. She was mortally afraid of being laughed at for surrendering, after her many and vehement declarations of independence. Laurie was her especial dread; but, thanks to the new manager, he behaved with praiseworthy propriety, never called Mr. Bhaer "a capital old fellow" in public, never alluded, in the remotest manner, to Jo's improved appearance, or expressed the least surprise at seeing the Professor's hat on the Marches' hall-table nearly every evening. But he exulted in private and longed for the time to come when he could give Jo a piece of plate, with a bear and a ragged staff on it as an appropriate coat-of-arms.

For a fortnight, the Professor came and went with lover-like regularity; then he stayed away for three whole days, and made no sign,—a proceeding which caused everybody to look sober, and Jo to become pensive, at first, and then—alas for romance!—very cross.

"Disgusted, I dare say, and gone home as suddenly as he came. It's nothing to me, of course; but I *should* think he would have come and bid us good-by, like a gentleman," she said to herself, with a despairing look at the gate, as she put on her things for the customary walk, one dull afternoon.

"You'd better take the little umbrella, dear; it looks like rain," said her mother, observing that she had on her new bonnet, but not alluding to the fact.

"Yes, Marmee; do you want anything in town? I've got to run in and get some paper," returned Jo, pulling out the bow under her chin before the glass as an excuse for not looking at her mother.

"Yes; I want some twilled silesia, a paper of number nine needles, and two yards of narrow lavender ribbon. Have you got your thick boots on, and something warm under your cloak?"

"I believe so," answered Jo absently.

"If you happen to meet Mr. Bhaer, bring him home to tea. I quite long to see the dear man," added Mrs. March.

Jo heard *that*, but made no answer, except to kiss her mother, and walk rapidly away, thinking with a glow of gratitude, in spite of her heartache,—

"How good she is to me! What *do* girls do who haven't any mothers to help them through their troubles?"

The dry-goods stores were not down among the counting-houses, banks, and wholesale warerooms, where gentlemen most do congregate; but Jo found herself in that part of the city before she did a single errand, loitering along as if waiting for someone, examining engineering instruments in one window and samples of wool in another, with most unfeminine interest; tumbling over barrels, being half-smothered by descending bales, and hustled unceremoniously by busy men who looked as if they wondered "how the deuce she got there." A drop of rain on her cheek recalled her thoughts from baffled hopes to ruined ribbons; for the drops continued to fall, and, being a woman as well as a lover, she felt that, though it was too late to save her heart, she might her bonnet. Now she remembered the little umbrella, which she had forgotten to take in her hurry to be off; but regret was unavailing, and nothing could be done but borrow one or submit to a drenching. She looked up at the lowering sky, down at the crimson bow already flecked with black, forward along the muddy street, then one long, lingering look behind, at a certain grimy warehouse, with "Hoffmann, Swartz, & Co." over the door, and said to herself, with a sternly reproachful air,—

"It serves me right! What business had I to put on all my best things and come philandering down here, hoping to see the Professor? Jo, I'm ashamed of you! No, you shall *not* go there to borrow an unmbrella, or find out where he is, from his friends. You shall trudge away, and do your errands in the rain; and if you catch your death and ruin your bonnet, it's no more than you deserve. Now then!"

With that she rushed across the street so impetuously that she narrowly escaped annihilation from a passing truck, and precipitated herself into the arms of a stately old gentleman, who said, "I beg pardon, ma'am," and looked mortally offended. Somewhat daunted, Jo righted herself, spread her handkerchief over the devoted ribbons, and, putting temptation behind her, hurried on, with increasing dampness about the ankles, and much clashing of umbrellas overhead. The fact that a somewhat dilapidated blue one remained stationary above the unprotected bonnet, attracted her attention; and, looking up, she saw Mr. Bhaer looking down.

"I feel to know the strong-minded lady who goes so bravely under many horse-noses, and so fast through much mud. What do you down here, my friend?"

"I'm shopping."

Mr. Bhaer smiled, as he glanced from the pickle-factory on one side, to the wholesale hide and leather concern on the other; but he only said politely,—

"You haf no unmbrella. May I go also, and take for you the bundles?"

"Yes, thank you."

Jo's cheeks were as red as her ribbon, and she wondered what he thought of her; but she didn't care, for in a minute she found herself walking away arm-in-arm with her Professor, feeling as if the sun had suddenly burst out with uncommon brilliancy, that the world was all right again, and that one thoroughly happy woman was paddling through the wet that day.

"We thought you had gone," said Jo hastily, for she knew he was looking at her. Her bonnet wasn't big enough to hide her face, and she feared he might think the joy it betrayed unmaidenly.

"Did you believe that I should go with no farewell to those who haf been so heavenly kind to me?" he asked so reproachfully that she felt as if she had insulted him by the suggestion, and answered heartily,—

"No, *I* didn't; I knew you were busy about your own affairs, but we rather missed you,—father and mother especially."

"And you?"

"I'm always glad to see you, sir."

In her anxiety to keep her voice quite calm, Jo made it rather cool, and the frosty little monosyllable at the end seemed to chill the Professor, for his smile vanished, as he said gravely,—

"I thank you, and come one time more before I go."

"You *are* going, then?"

"I haf no longer any business here; it is done."

"Successfully, I hope?" said Jo, for the bitterness of disappointment was in that short reply of his.

"I ought to think so, for I haf a way opened to me by which I can make my bread and gif my Jünglings much help."

"Tell me, please! I like to know all about the—the boys," said Jo eagerly.

"That is so kind, I gladly tell you. My friends find for me a place in a college, where I teach as at home, and earn enough to make the way smooth for Franz and Emil. For this I should be grateful, should I not?"

"Indeed you should. How splendid it will be to have you doing what you like, and be able to see you often, and the boys!" cried Jo, clinging to the lads as an excuse for the satisfaction she could not help betraying.

"Ah! But we shall not meet often, I fear; this place is at the West."

"So far away!" and Jo left her skirts to their fate, as if it didn't matter now what became of her clothes or herself.

Mr. Bhaer could read several languages, but he had not learned to

Looking up she saw Mr. Bhaer.

read women yet. He flattered himself that he knew Jo pretty well, and was, therefore, much amazed by the contradictions of voice, face, and manner, which she showed him in rapid succession that day, for she was in half a dozen different moods in the course of half an hour. When she met him she looked surprised, though it was impossible to help suspecting that she had come for that express purpose. When he offered her his arm, she took it with a look that filled him with delight; but when he asked if she missed him, she gave such a chilly, formal reply that despair fell upon him. On learning his good fortune she almost clapped her hands: was the joy all for the boys? Then, on hearing his destination, she said, "So far away!" in a tone of despair that lifted him onto a pinnacle of hope; but the next minute she tumbled him down again by observing, like one entirely absorbed in the matter,—

"Here's the place for my errands; will you come in? It won't take long."

Jo rather prided herself upon her shopping capabilities, and particularly wished to impress her escort with the neatness and despatch with which she would accomplish the business. But, owing to the flutter she was in, everything went amiss; she upset the tray of needles, forgot the silesia was to be "twilled" till it was cut off, gave the wrong change, and covered herself with confusion by asking for lavender ribbon at the calico counter. Mr. Bhaer stood by, watching her blush and blunder; and, as he watched, his own bewilderment seemed to subside, for he was beginning to see that on some occasions women, like dreams, go by contraries.

When they came out, he put the parcel under his arm with a more cheerful aspect, and splashed through the puddles as if he rather enjoyed it, on the whole.

"Should we not do a little what you call shopping for the babies, and haf a farewell feast tonight if I go for my last call at your so pleasant home?" he asked, stopping before a window full of fruit and flowers.

"What will we buy?" said Jo, ignoring the latter part of his speech, and sniffing the mingled odors with an affectation of delight as they went in.

"May they haf oranges and figs?" asked Mr. Bhaer, with a paternal air.

"They eat them when they can get them."

"Do you care for nuts?"

"Like a squirrel."

"Hamburg grapes; yes, we shall surely drink to the Fatherland in those?"

Jo frowned upon that piece of extravagance, and asked why he didn't buy a frail of dates, a cask of raisins, and a bag of almonds, and done with it? Whereat Mr. Bhaer confiscated her purse, produced his own, and finished the marketing by buying several pounds of grapes, a pot of rosy daisies, and a pretty jar of honey, to be regarded in the light of a demijohn. Then, distorting his pockets with the knobby bundles, and giving her the flowers to hold, he put up the old umbrella, and they travelled on again.

"Miss Marsch, I haf a great favor to ask of you," began the Professor, after a moist promenade of half a block.

"Yes, sir;" and Jo's heart began to beat so hard she was afraid he would hear it.

"I am bold to say it in spite of the rain, because so short a time remains to me."

"Yes, sir;" and Jo nearly crushed the small flower-pot with the sudden squeeze she gave it.

"I wish to get a little dress for my Tina, and I am too stupid to go alone. Will you kindly gif me a word of taste and help?"

"Yes, sir;" and Jo felt as calm and cool, all of a sudden, as if she had stepped into a refrigerator.

"Perhaps also a shawl for Tina's mother, she is so poor and sick, and the husband is such a care. Yes, yes, a thick, warm shawl would be a friendly thing to take the little mother."

"I'll do it with pleasure, Mr. Bhaer." "I'm going very fast and he's getting dearer every minute," added Jo to herself; then, with a mental shake, she entered into the business with an energy which was pleasant to behold.

Mr. Bhaer left it all to her, so she chose a pretty gown for Tina, and then ordered out the shawls. The clerk, being a married man, condescended to take an interest in the couple, who appeared to be shopping for their family.

"Your lady may prefer this; it's a superior article, a most desirable color, quite chaste and genteel," he said, shaking out a comfortable gray shawl, and throwing it over Jo's shoulders.

"Does this suit you, Mr. Bhaer?" she asked, turning her back to him, and feeling deeply grateful for the chance of hiding her face.

"Excellently well; we will haf it," answered the Professor, smiling to himself as he paid for it, while Jo continued to rummage the counters like a confirmed bargain-hunter.

"Now shall we go home?" he asked, as if the words were very pleasant to him.

"Yes; it's late, and I'm *so* tired." Jo's voice was more pathetic than she knew; for now the sun seemed to have gone in as suddenly as it came out, the world grew muddy and miserable again, and for the first time she discovered that her feet were cold, her head ached, and that her heart was colder than the former, fuller of pain than the latter. Mr. Bhaer was going away; he only cared for her as a friend; it was all a mistake, and the sooner it was over the better. With this idea in her head, she hailed an approaching omnibus with such a hasty gesture that the daisies flew out of the pot and were badly damaged.

"This is not our omniboos," said the Professor, waving the loaded vehicle away, and stopping to pick up the poor little flowers.

"I beg your pardon, I didn't see the name distinctly. Never mind, I can walk. I'm used to plodding in the mud," returned Jo, winking hard, because she would have died rather than openly wipe her eyes.

Mr. Bhaer saw the drops on her cheeks, though she turned her head away; the sight seemed to touch him very much, for, suddenly stooping down, he asked in a tone that meant a great deal,—

"Heart's dearest, why do you cry?"

Now, if Jo had not been new to this sort of thing she would have said she wasn't crying, had a cold in her head, or told any other feminine fib proper to the occasion; instead of which that undignified creature answered, with an irrepressible sob,—

"Because you are going away."

"Ach, mein Gott, that is *so* good!" cried Mr. Bhaer, managing to clasp his hands in spite of the umbrella and the bundles. "Jo, I haf nothing but much love to gif you; I came to see if you could care for it, and I waited to be sure that I was something more than a friend. Am I? Can you make a little place in your heart for old Fritz?" he added, all in one breath.

"Oh, yes!" said Jo; and he was quite satisfied, for she folded both hands over his arm, and looked up at him with an expression that plainly showed how happy she would be to walk through life beside him, even though she had no better shelter than the old umbrella, if he carried it.

It was certainly proposing under difficulties, for, even if he had desired to do so, Mr. Bhaer could not go down upon his knees, on account of the mud; neither could he offer Jo his hand, except figuratively, for both were full; much less could he indulge in tender demonstrations in the open street, though he was near it: so the only way in which he could express his rapture was to look at her, with an expression which glorified his face to such a degree that there actually seemed to be little rainbows in the drops that sparkled on his beard. If he had not loved Jo very much, I don't think he could have done it *then*, for she looked far from lovely, with her skirts in a deplorable state, her rubber boots splashed to the ankle, and her bonnet a ruin. Fortunately, Mr. Bhaer considered her the most beautiful woman living, and she found him more "Jove-like" than ever, though his hat-brim was quite limp with the little rills trickling thence upon his shoulders (for he held the umbrella all over Jo), and every finger of his gloves needed mending.

Passers-by probably thought them a pair of harmless lunatics, for they entirely forgot to hail a 'bus, and strolled leisurely along, oblivious of deepening dusk and fog. Little they cared what anybody thought, for they were enjoying the happy hour that seldom comes but once in any life, the magical moment which bestows youth on the old, beauty on the plain, wealth on the poor, and gives human hearts a foretaste of heaven. The Professor looked as if he had conquered a kingdom, and the world had nothing more to offer him in the way of bliss; while Jo trudged beside him, feeling as if her place had always been there, and wondering how she ever could have chosen any other lot. Of course, she was the first to speak—intelligibly, I mean, for the emotional remarks which followed her impetuous "Oh, yes!" were not of a coherent or reportable character.

"Friedrich, why didn't you—"

"Ah, heaven, she gifs me the name that no one speaks since Minna died!" cried the Professor, pausing in a puddle to regard her with grateful delight.

"I always call you so to myself—I forgot; but I won't, unless you like it."

"Like it? It is more sweet to me than I can tell. Say 'thou,' also, and I shall say your language is almost as beautiful as mine."

"Isn't 'thou' a little sentimental?" asked Jo, privately thinking it a lovely monosyllable.

"Sentimental? Yes. Thank Gott, we Germans believe in sentiment, and keep ourselves young mit it. Your English 'you' is so cold, say 'thou,' heart's dearest, it means so much to me," pleaded Mr. Bhaer, more like a romantic student than a grave professor.

"Well, then, why didn't thou tell me all this sooner?" asked Jo bashfully.

"Now I shall haf to show thee all my heart, and I so gladly will, because thou must take care of it hereafter. See, then, my Jo,—ah, the dear, funny little name!—I had a wish to tell something the day I said good-by, in New York; but I thought the handsome friend was betrothed to thee, and so I spoke not. Wouldst thou have said 'Yes,' then, if I *had* spoken?"

"I don't know; I'm afraid not, for I didn't have any heart just then."

"Prut! That I do not believe. It was asleep till the fairy prince came through the wood, and waked it up. Ah, well, 'Die erste Liebe ist die beste;' but that I should not expect."

"Yes, the first love *is* the best; so be contented, for I never had another. Teddy was only a boy, and soon got over his little fancy," said Jo, anxious to correct the Professor's mistake.

"Good! Then I shall rest happy, and be sure that thou givest me all. I haf waited so long, I am grown selfish, as thou wilt find, Professorin."

"I like that," cried Jo, delighted with her new name. "Now tell me what brought you, at last, just when I most wanted you?"

"This"; and Mr. Bhaer took a little worn paper out of his waistcoat-pocket.

Jo unfolded it, and looked much abashed, for it was one of her own contributions to a paper that paid for poetry, which accounted for her sending it an occasional attempt.

"How could that bring you?" she asked, wondering what he meant.

"I found it by chance; I knew it by the names and the initials, and in it there was one little verse that seemed to call me. Read and find him; I will see that you go not in the wet."

Jo obeyed, and hastily skimmed through the lines which she had christened—

### "IN THE GARRET

"Four little chests all in a row,
  Dim with dust, and worn by time,
All fashioned and filled, long ago,
  By children now in their prime.
Four little keys hung side by side,
  With faded ribbons, brave and gay
When fastened there, with childish pride,
    Long ago, on a rainy day.
Four little names, one on each lid,
    Carved out by a boyish hand,
And underneath there lieth hid
    Histories of the happy band

*Once playing here, and pausing oft*
    *To hear the sweet refrain,*
*That came and went on the roof aloft,*
    *In the falling summer rain.*

" '*Meg*' *on the first lid, smooth and fair.*
    *I look in with loving eyes,*
*For folded here, with well-known care,*
    *A goodly gathering lies,*
*The record of a peaceful life,—*
    *Gifts to gentle child and girl,*
*A bridal gown, lines to a wife,*
    *A tiny shoe, a baby curl.*
*No toys in this first chest remain,*
    *For all are carried away,*
*In their old age, to join again*
    *In another small Meg's play.*
*Ah, happy mother! Well I know*
    *You hear, like a sweet refrain,*
*Lullabies ever soft and low*
    *In the falling summer rain.*

" '*Jo*' *on the next lid, scratched and worn,*
    *And within a motley store*
*Of headless dolls, of school-books torn,*
    *Birds and beasts that speak no more;*
*Spoils brought home from the fairy ground*
    *Only trod by youthful feet,*
*Dreams of a future never found,*
    *Memories of a past still sweet;*
*Half-writ poems, stories wild,*
    *April letters, warm and cold,*
*Diaries of a wilful child,*
    *Hints of a woman early old;*
*A woman in a lonely home,*
    *Hearing, like a sad refrain,—*
'*Be worthy love, and love will come,*'
    *In the falling summer rain.*

"*My Beth! The dust is always swept*
    *From the lid that bears your name,*
*As if by loving eyes that wept,*
    *By careful hands that often came.*
*Death canonized for us one saint,*
    *Ever less human than divine,*
*And still we lay, with tender plaint,*
    *Relics in this household shrine,—*
*The silver bell, so seldom rung,*
    *The little cap which last she wore,*
*The fair, dead Catherine that hung*

*By angels borne above her door;*
*The songs she sang, without lament,*
*In her prison-house of pain,*
*Forever are they sweetly blent*
*With the falling summer rain.*

*"Upon the last lid's polished field—*
*Legend now both fair and true—*
*A gallant knight bears on his shield,*
*'Amy,' in letters gold and blue.*
*Within lie snoods that bound her hair,*
*Slippers that have danced their last,*
*Faded flowers laid by with care,*
*Fans whose airy toils are past;*
*Gay valentines, all ardent flames,*
*Trifles that have borne their part*
*In girlish hopes and fears and shames,—*
*The record of a maiden heart*
*Now learning fairer, truer spells,*
*Hearing, like a blithe refrain,*
*The silver sound of bridal bells*
*In the falling summer rain.*

*"Four little chests all in a row,*
*Dim with dust, and worn by time,*
*Four women, taught by weal and woe*
*To love and labor in their prime.*
*Four sisters, parted for an hour,*
*None lost, one only gone before,*
*Made by love's immortal power,*
*Nearest and dearest evermore.*
*Oh, when these hidden stores of ours*
*Lie open to the Father's sight,*
*May they be rich in golden hours,*
*Deeds that show fairer for the light,*
*Lives whose brave music long shall ring,*
*Like a spirit-stirring strain,*
*Souls that shall gladly soar and sing*
*In the long sunshine after rain.*

"J.M."

"It's very bad poetry, but I felt it when I wrote it, one day when I was very lonely, and had a good cry on a ragbag. I never thought it would go where it could tell tales," said Jo, tearing up the verses the Professor had treasured so long.

"Let it go, it has done its duty, and I will haf a fresh one when I read all the brown book in which she keeps her little secrets," said Mr. Bhaer, with a smile, as he watched the fragments fly away on the wind. "Yes," he added earnestly, "I read that, and I think to myself, She has a sorrow, she is lonely, she would find comfort in true love. I haf a heart full, full for her; shall I not go and say, 'If this is not too poor a thing to gif for what I shall hope to receive, take it in Gott's name?' "

"And so you came to find that it was not too poor, but the one precious thing I needed," whispered Jo.

"I had no courage to think that at first, heavenly kind as was your welcome to me. But soon I began to hope, and then I said, 'I will haf her if I die for it,' and so I will!" cried Mr. Bhaer, with a defiant nod, as if the walls of mist closing round them were barriers which he was to surmount or valiantly knock down.

Jo thought that was splendid, and resolved to be worthy of her knight, though he did not come prancing on a charger in gorgeous array.

"What made you stay away so long?" she asked presently, finding it so pleasant to ask confidential questions and get delightful answers that she could not keep silent.

"It was not easy, but I could not find the heart to take you from that so happy home until I could haf a prospect of one to give you, after much time, perhaps, and hard work. How could I ask you to gif up so much for a poor old fellow, who has no fortune but a little learning?"

"I'm glad you *are* poor; I couldn't bear a rich husband," said Jo decidedly, adding, in a softer tone, "Don't fear poverty; I've known it long enough to lose my dread, and be happy working for those I love; and don't call yourself old,—forty is the prime of life. I couldn't help loving you if you were seventy!"

The Professor found that so touching that he would have been glad of his handkerchief, if he could have got at it; as he couldn't, Jo wiped his eyes for him, and said, laughing, as she took away a bundle or two,—

"I may be strong-minded, but no one can say I'm out of my sphere now, for woman's special mission is supposed to be drying tears and bearing burdens. I'm to carry my share, Friedrich, and help to earn the home. Make up your mind to that, or I'll never go," she added resolutely, as he tried to reclaim his load.

"We shall see. Haf you patience to wait a long time, Jo? I must go away and do my work alone. I must help my boys first, because, even for you, I may not break my word to Minna. Can you forgif that, and be happy while we hope and wait?"

"Yes, I know I can; for we love one another, and that makes all the rest easy to bear. I have my duty, also, and my work. I couldn't enjoy myself if I neglected them even for you, so there's no need of hurry or impatience. You can do your part out West, I can do mine here, and both be happy hoping for the best, and leaving the future to be as God wills."

"Ah! Thou gifest me such hope and courage, and I haf nothing to gif back but a full heart and these empty hands," cried the Professor, quite overcome.

Jo never, never would learn to be proper; for when he said that as they stood upon the steps, she just put both hands into his, whispering tenderly, "Not empty now;" and, stooping down, kissed her Friedrich under the umbrella. It was dreadful, but she would have done it if the flock of draggle-tailed sparrows on the hedge had been human beings, for she was very far gone indeed, and quite regardless of everything but

Under the umbrella.

her own happiness. Though it came in such a very simple guise, that was the crowning moment of both their lives, when, turning from the night and storm and loneliness to the household light and warmth and peace waiting to receive them, with a glad "Welcome home!" Jo led her lover in, and shut the door.

# CHAPTER XLVII

## HARVEST TIME

FOR a year Jo and her Professor worked and waited, hoped and loved, met occasionally, and wrote such voluminous letters that the rise in the price of paper was accounted for, Laurie said. The second year began rather soberly, for their prospects did not brighten, and Aunt March died suddenly. But when their first sorrow was over,—for they loved the old lady in spite of her sharp tongue,—they found they had cause for rejoicing, for she had left Plumfield to Jo, which made all sorts of joyful things possible.

"It's a fine old place, and will bring a handsome sum; for of course you intend to sell it," said Laurie, as they were all talking the matter over, some weeks later.

"No, I don't," was Jo's decided answer, as she petted the fat poodle, whom she had adopted, out of respect to his former mistress.

"You don't mean to live there?"

"Yes, I do."

"But, my dear girl, it's an immense house, and will take a power of money to keep it in order. The garden and orchard alone need two or three men, and farming isn't in Bhaer's line, I take it."

"He'll try his hand at it there, if I propose it."

"And you expect to live on the produce of the place? Well, that sounds paradisiacal, but you'll find it desperate hard work."

"The crop we are going to raise is a profitable one;" and Jo laughed.

"Of what is this fine crop to consist, ma'am?"

"Boys. I want to open a school for little lads,—a good, happy, homelike school, with me to take care of them, and Fritz to teach them."

"There's a truly Joian plan for you! Isn't that just like her?" cried Laurie, appealing to the family, who looked as much surprised as he.

"I like it," said Mrs. March decidedly.

"So do I," added her husband, who welcomed the thought of a chance for trying the Socratic method of education on modern youth.

"It will be an immense care for Jo," said Meg, stroking the head of her one all-absorbing son.

"Jo can do it, and be happy in it. It's a splendid idea. Tell us all about it," cried Mr. Laurence, who had been longing to lend the lovers a hand, but knew that they would refuse his help.

"I knew you'd stand by me, sir. Amy does too—I see it in her eyes, though she prudently waits to turn it over in her mind before she speaks.

Now, my dear people," continued Jo earnestly, "just understand that this isn't a new idea of mine, but a long-cherished plan. Before my Fritz came, I used to think how, when I'd made my fortune, and no one needed me at home, I'd hire a big house, and pick up some poor, forlorn little lads, who hadn't any mothers, and take care of them, and make life jolly for them before it was too late. I see so many going to ruin, for want of help at the right minute; I love so to do anything for them; I seem to feel their wants, and sympathize with their troubles, and, oh, I should *so* like to be a mother to them!"

Mrs. March held out her hand to Jo, who took it, smiling, with tears in her eyes, and went on in the old enthusiastic way, which they had not seen for a long while.

"I told my plan to Fritz once, and he said it was just what he would like, and agreed to try it when we got rich. Bless his dear heart, he's been doing it all his life,—helping poor boys, I mean, not getting rich; that he'll never be; money doesn't stay in his pocket long enough to lay up any. But now, thanks to my good old aunt, who loved me better than I ever deserved, *I'm* rich, at least I feel so, and we can live at Plumfield perfectly well, if we have a flourishing school. It's just the place for boys, the house is big, and the furniture strong and plain. There's plenty of room for dozens inside, and splendid grounds outside. They could help in the garden and orchard: such work is healthy, isn't it, sir? Then Fritz can train and teach in his own way, and father will help him. I can feed and nurse and pet and scold them; and mother will be my stand-by. I've always longed for lots of boys, and never had enough; now I can fill the house full, and revel in the little dears to my heart's content. Think what luxury,—Plumfield my own, and a wilderness of boys to enjoy it with me!"

As Jo waved her hands, and gave a sigh of rapture, the family went off into a gale of merriment, and Mr. Laurence laughed till they thought he'd have an apoplectic fit.

"I don't see anything funny," she said gravely, when she could be heard. "Nothing could be more natural or proper than for my Professor to open a school, and for me to prefer to reside on my own estate."

"She is putting on airs already," said Laurie, who regarded the idea in the light of a capital joke. "But may I inquire how you intend to support the establishment? If all the pupils are little ragamuffins, I'm afraid your crop won't be profitable in a worldly sense, Mrs. Bhaer."

"Now don't be a wet-blanket, Teddy. Of course I shall have rich pupils, also,—perhaps begin with such altogether; then, when I've got a start, I can take a ragamuffin or two, just for a relish. Rich people's children often need care and comfort, as well as poor. I've seen unfortunate little creatures left to servants, or backward ones pushed forward, when it's real cruelty. Some are naughty through mismanagement or neglect, and some lose their mothers. Besides, the best have to get through the hobbledehoy age, and that's the very time they need most patience and kindness. People laugh at them, and hustle them about, try to keep them out of sight, and expect them to turn, all at once, from pretty children into fine young men. They don't complain much,—plucky little souls,— but they feel it. I've been through something of it, and I know all about it. I've a special interest in such young bears, and like to show them that I see the warm, honest, well-meaning boys' hearts, in spite of the clumsy arms and legs and the topsy-turvy heads. I've had experience, too, for haven't I brought up one boy to be a pride and honor to his family?"

"I'll testify that you tried to do it," said Laurie, with a grateful look.

"And I've succeeded beyond my hopes; for here you are, a steady, sensible business man, doing heaps of good with your money, and laying up the blessings of the poor, instead of dollars. But you are not merely a business man: you love good and beautiful things, enjoy them yourself, and let others go halves, as you always did in the old times. I *am* proud of you, Teddy, for you get better every year, and everyone feels it, though you won't let them say so. Yes, and when I have my flock, I'll just point to you, and say, 'There's your model, my lads.' "

Poor Laurie didn't know where to look; for, man though he was, something of the old bashfulness came over him as this burst of praise made all faces turn approvingly upon him.

"I say, Jo, that's rather too much," he began, just in his old boyish way. "You have all done more for me than I can ever thank you for, except by doing my best not to disappoint you. You have rather cast me off lately, Jo, but I've had the best of help, nevertheless; so, if I've got on at all you may thank these two for it;" and he laid one hand gently on his grandfather's white head, the other on Amy's golden one, for the three were never far apart.

"I do think that families are the most beautiful things in all the world!" burst out Jo, who was in an unusually uplifted frame of mind just then. "When I have one of my own, I hope it will be as happy as the three I know and love the best. If John and my Fritz were only here, it would be quite a little heaven on earth," she added more quietly. And that night, when she went to her room, after a blissful evening of family counsels, hopes, and plans, her heart was so full of happiness that she could only calm it by kneeling beside the empty bed always near her own, and thinking tender thoughts of Beth.

It was a very astonishing year altogether, for things seemed to happen in an unusually rapid and delightful manner. Almost before she knew where she was, Jo found herself married and settled at Plumfield. Then a family of six or seven boys sprung up like mushrooms, and flourished surprisingly, poor boys as well as rich; for Mr. Laurence was continually finding some touching case of destitution, and begging the Bhaers to take pity on the child, and he would gladly pay a trifle for its support. In this way the sly old gentleman got round proud Jo, and furnished her with the style of boy in which she most delighted.

Of course it was up-hill work at first, and Jo made queer mistakes; but the wise Professor steered her safely into calmer waters, and the most rampant ragamuffin was conquered in the end. How Jo did enjoy her "wilderness of boys," and how poor, dear Aunt March would have lamented had she been there to see the sacred precincts of prim, well-ordered Plumfield overrun with Toms, Dicks, and Harrys! There was a sort of poetic justice about it, after all, for the old lady had been the terror of the boys for miles round; and now the exiles feasted freely on forbidden plums, kicked up the gravel with profane boots unreproved, and played cricket in the big field where the irritable "cow with a crumpled horn" used to invite rash youths to come and be tossed. It became a sort of boys' paradise, and Laurie suggested that it should be called the "Bhaer-garten," as a compliment to its master and appropriate to its inhabitants.

It never was a fashionable school, and the Professor did not lay up a fortune; but it *was* just what Jo intended it to be,—"a happy, homelike place for boys, who needed teaching, care, and kindness." Every room in the big house was soon full; every little plot in the garden soon had its owner; a regular menagerie appeared in barn and shed, for pet animals were allowed; and, three times a day, Jo smiled at her Fritz from the head of a long table lined on either side with rows of happy young faces, which all turned to her with affectionate eyes, confiding words, and grateful hearts, full of love for "Mother Bhaer." She had boys enough now, and did not tire of them, though they were not angels, by any means, and some of them caused both Professor and Professorin much trouble and anxiety. But her faith in the good spot which exists in the heart of the naughtiest, sauciest, most tantalizing little ragamuffin gave her patience, skill, and, in time, success; for no mortal boy could hold out long with Father Bhaer shining on him as benevolently as the sun, and Mother Bhaer forgiving him seventy times seven. Very precious to Jo was the friendship of the lads; their penitent sniffs and whispers after wrong-doing; their droll or touching little confidences; their pleasant enthusiasms, hopes, and plans; even their misfortunes, for they only endeared them to her all the more. There were slow boys and bashful boys; feeble boys and riotous boys; boys that lisped and boys that stuttered; one or two lame ones; and a merry little quadroon, who could not be taken in elsewhere, but who was welcome to the "Bhaer-garten," though some people predicted that his admission would ruin the school.

Yes; Jo was a very happy woman there, in spite of hard work, much anxiety, and a perpetual racket. She enjoyed it heartily, and found the applause of her boys more satisfying than any praise of the world; for now she told no stories except to her flock of enthusiastic believers and admirers. As the years went on, two little lads of her own came to increase her happiness,—Rob, named for grandpa, and Teddy, a happy-go-lucky baby, who seemed to have inherited his papa's sunshiny temper as well as his mother's lively spirit. How they ever grew up alive in that whirlpool of boys was a mystery to their grandma and aunts; but they flourished like dandelions in spring, and their rough nurses loved and served them well.

There were a great many holidays at Plumfield, and one of the most delightful was the yearly apple-picking; for then the Marches, Laurences, Brookes, and Bhaers turned out in full force, and made a day of it. Five years after Jo's wedding, one of these fruitful festivals occurred,—a mellow October day, when the air was full of an exhilarating freshness which made the spirits rise, and the blood dance healthily in the veins. The old orchard wore its holiday attire; golden-rod and asters fringed the mossy walls; grasshoppers skipped briskly in the sere grass, and crickets chirped like fairy pipers at a feast; squirrels were busy with their small harvesting; birds twittered their adieux from the alders in the lane;

and every tree stood ready to send down its shower of red or yellow apples at the first shake. Everybody was there; everybody laughed and sang, climbed up and tumbled down; everybody declared that there never had been such a perfect day or such a jolly set to enjoy it; and everyone gave themselves up to the simple pleasures of the hour as freely as if there were no such things as care or sorrow in the world.

Mr. March strolled placidly about, quoting Tusser, Cowley, and Columella to Mr. Laurence, while enjoying—

*"The gentle apple's winey juice."*

The Professor charged up and down the green aisles like a stout Teutonic knight, with a pole for a lance, leading on the boys, who made a hook and ladder company of themselves, and performed wonders in the way of ground and lofty tumbling. Laurie devoted himself to the little ones, rode his small daughter in a bushel-basket, took Daisy up among the birds' nests, and kept adventurous Rob from breaking his neck. Mrs. March and Meg sat among the apple piles like a pair of Pomonas, sorting the contributions that kept pouring in; while Amy, with a beautiful motherly expression in her face, sketched the various groups, and watched over one pale lad, who sat adoring her with his little crutch beside him.

Jo was in her element that day, and rushed about, with her gown pinned up, her hat anywhere but on her head, and her baby tucked under her arm, ready for any lively adventure which might turn up. Little Teddy bore a charmed life, for nothing ever happened to him, and Jo never felt any anxiety when he was whisked up into a tree by one lad, galloped off on the back of another, or supplied with sour russets by his indulgent papa, who labored under the Germanic delusion that babies could digest anything, from pickled cabbage to buttons, nails, and their own small shoes. She knew that little Ted would turn up again in time, safe and rosy, dirty and serene, and she always received him back with a hearty welcome, for Jo loved her babies tenderly.

At four o'clock a lull took place, and baskets remained empty, while the apple-pickers rested, and compared rents and bruises. Then Jo and Meg, with a detachment of the bigger boys, set forth the supper on the grass, for an out-of-door tea was always the crowning joy of the day. The land literally flowed with milk and honey on such occasions, for the lads were not required to sit at table, but allowed to partake of refreshment as they liked,—freedom being the sauce best beloved by the boyish soul. They availed themselves of the rare privilege to the fullest extent, for some tried the pleasing experiment of drinking milk while standing on their heads, others lent a charm to leap-frog by eating pie in the pauses of the game, cookies were sown broadcast over the field, and apple-turnovers roosted in the trees like a new style of bird. The little girls had a private tea-party, and Ted roved among the edibles at his own sweet will.

When no one could eat any more, the Professor proposed the first regular toast, which was always drunk at such times,—"Aunt March, God bless her!" A toast heartily given by the good man, who never forgot how much he owed her, and quietly drunk by the boys, who had been taught to keep her memory green.

"Now, grandma's sixtieth birthday! Long life to her, with three times three!"

That was given with a will, as you may well believe; and the cheering once begun, it was hard to stop it. Everybody's health was proposed, from Mr. Laurence, who was considered their special patron, to the astonished guinea-pig, who had strayed from its proper sphere in search of its young master. Demi, as the oldest grandchild, then presented the queen of the day with various gifts, so numerous that they were transported to the festive scene in a wheelbarrow. Funny presents, some of them, but what would have been defects to other eyes were ornaments to grandma's,—for the children's gifts were all their own. Every stitch Daisy's patient little fingers had put into the handkerchiefs she hemmed was better than embroidery to Mrs. March; Demi's shoe-box was a miracle of mechanical skill, though the cover wouldn't shut; Rob's footstool had a wiggle in its uneven legs, that she declared was very soothing; and no page of the costly book Amy's child gave her was so fair as that on which appeared, in tipsy capitals, the words,—"To dear Grandma, from her little Beth."

During this ceremony the boys had mysteriously disappeared; and, when Mrs. March had tried to thank her children, and broken down, while Teddy wiped her eyes on his pinafore, the Professor suddenly began to sing. Then, from above him, voice after voice took up the words, and from tree to tree echoed the music of the unseen choir, as the boys sung, with all their hearts, the little song Jo had written, Laurie set to music, and the Professor trained his lads to give with the best effect. This was something altogether new, and it proved a grand success; for Mrs. March couldn't get over her surprise, and insisted on shaking hands with every one of the featherless birds, from tall Franz and Emil to the little quadroon, who had the sweetest voice of all.

After this, the boys dispersed for a final lark, leaving Mrs. March and her daughters under the festival tree.

"I don't think I ever ought to call myself 'Unlucky Jo' again, when my greatest wish has been so beautifully gratified," said Mrs. Bhaer, taking Teddy's little fist out of the milk-pitcher, in which he was rapturously churning.

"And yet your life is very different from the one you pictured so long ago. Do you remember our castles in the air?" asked Amy, smiling as she watched Laurie and John playing cricket with the boys.

"Dear fellows! It does my heart good to see them forget business, and frolic for a day," answered Jo, who now spoke in a maternal way of all mankind. "Yes, I remember; but the life I wanted then seems selfish, lonely, and cold to me now. I haven't given up the hope that I may write a good book yet, but I can wait, and I'm sure it will be all the better for such experiences and illustrations as these;" and Jo pointed from the lively lads in the distance to her father, leaning on the Professor's arm, as they walked to and fro in the sunshine, deep in one of the conversations which both enjoyed so much, and then to her mother, sitting enthroned among her daughters, with their children in her lap and at her feet, as if all found help and happiness in the face which never could grow old to them.

"My castle was the most nearly realized of all. I asked for splendid things, to be sure, but in my heart I knew I should be satisfied, if I had a little home, and John, and some dear children like these. I've got them all, thank God, and am the happiest woman in the world;" and Meg laid her hand on her tall boy's head, with a face full of tender and devout content.

"My castle is very different from what I planned, but I would not alter it, though, like Jo, I don't relinquish all my artistic hopes, or confine myself to helping others fulfil their dreams of beauty. I've begun to model a figure of baby, and Laurie says it is the best thing I've ever done. I think so myself, and mean to do it in marble, so that, whatever happens, I may at least keep the image of my little angel."

As Amy spoke, a great tear dropped on the golden hair of the sleeping child in her arms; for her one well-beloved daughter was a frail little creature and the dread of losing her was the shadow over Amy's sunshine. This cross was doing much for both father and mother, for one love and sorrow bound them closely together. Amy's nature was growing sweeter, deeper, and more tender; Laurie was growing more serious, strong, and firm; and both were learning that beauty, youth, good fortune, even love itself, cannot keep care and pain, loss and sorrow, from the most blest; for—

> *"Into each life some rain must fall,*
> *Some days must be dark and sad and dreary."*

"She is growing better, I am sure of it, my dear. Don't despond, but hope and keep happy," said Mrs. March, as tender-hearted Daisy stooped from her knee, to lay her rosy cheek against her little cousin's pale one.

"I never ought to, while I have you to cheer me up, Marmee, and Laurie to take more than half of every burden," replied Amy warmly. "He never lets me see his anxiety, but is so sweet and patient with me, so devoted to Beth, and such a stay and comfort to me always, that I can't love him enough. So, in spite of my one cross, I can say with Meg, 'Thank God, I'm a happy woman.' "

"There's no need for me to say it, for everyone can see that I'm far happier than I deserve," added Jo, glancing from her good husband to her chubby children, tumbling on the grass beside her. "Fritz is getting gray and stout; I'm growing as thin as a shadow, and am thirty; we never shall be rich, and Plumfield may burn up any night, for that incorrigible Tommy Bangs *will* smoke sweet-fern cigars under the bed-clothes, though he's set himself afire three times already. But in spite of these unromantic facts, I have nothing to complain of, and never was so jolly in my life. Excuse the remark, but living among boys, I can't help using their expressions now and then."

"Yes, Jo, I think your harvest will be a good one," began Mrs. March, frightening away a big black cricket that was staring Teddy out of countenance.

"Not half so good as yours, mother. Here it is, and we never can thank

Leaving Mrs. March and her daughters under the festival tree.

you enough for the patient sowing and reaping you have done," cried Jo, with the loving impetuosity which she never could outgrow.

"I hope there will be more wheat and fewer tares every year," said Amy softly.

"A large sheaf, but I know there's room in your heart for it, Marmee dear," added Meg's tender voice.

Touched to the heart, Mrs. March could only stretch out her arms, as if to gather children and grandchildren to herself, and say, with face and voice full of motherly love, gratitude, and humility,—

"O my girls, however long you may live, I never can wish you a greater happiness than this!"

# Little Men
## Life at Plumfield with Jo's Boys

*Illustrated by*

*Reginald B. Birch and Frank T. Merrill*

*Overleaf:* Half hidden by the bouquet of laughing young faces.

# CHAPTER I

## NAT

"PLEASE, sir, is this Plumfield?" asked a ragged boy of the man who opened the great gate at which the omnibus left him.

"Yes; who sent you?"

"Mr. Laurence. I have got a letter for the lady."

"All right; go up to the house, and give it to her; she'll see to you, little chap."

The man spoke pleasantly, and the boy went on, feeling much cheered by the words. Through the soft spring rain that fell on sprouting grass and budding trees, Nat saw a large square house before him—a hospitable-looking house, with an old-fashioned porch, wide steps, and lights shining in many windows. Neither curtains nor shutters hid the cheerful glimmer; and, pausing a moment before he rang, Nat saw many little shadows dancing on the walls, heard the pleasant hum of young voices, and felt that it was hardly possible that the light and warmth and comfort within could be for a homeless "little chap" like him.

"I hope the lady *will* see to me," he thought; and gave a timid rap with the great bronze knocker, which was a jovial griffin's head.

A rosy-faced servant-maid opened the door, and smiled as she took the letter which he silently offered. She seemed used to receiving strange boys, for she pointed to a seat in the hall, and said, with a nod,—

"Sit there and drip on the mat a bit, while I take this in to missis."

Nat found plenty to amuse him while he waited, and stared about him curiously, enjoying the view, yet glad to do so unobserved in the dusky recess by the door.

The house seemed swarming with boys, who were beguiling the rainy twilight with all sorts of amusements. There were boys everywhere, "upstairs and down-stairs and in the lady's chamber," apparently, for various open doors showed pleasant groups of big boys, little boys, and middle-sized boys in all stages of evening relaxation, not to say effervescence. Two large rooms on the right were evidently school-rooms, for desks, maps, blackboards, and books were scattered about. An open fire burned on the hearth, and several indolent lads lay on their backs before it, discussing a new cricket-ground, with such animation that their boots waved in the air. A tall youth was practicing on the flute in one corner, quite undisturbed by the racket all about him. Two or three others were jumping over the desks, pausing, now and then, to get their breath, and laugh at the droll sketches of a little wag who was caricaturing the whole household on a blackboard.

In the room on the left a long supper-table was seen, set forth with great pitchers of new milk, piles of brown and white bread, and perfect stacks of the shiny gingerbread so dear to boyish souls. A flavor of toast was in the air, also suggestions of baked apples, very tantalizing to one hungry little nose and stomach.

The hall, however, presented the most inviting prospect of all, for a brisk game of tag was going on in the upper entry. One landing was devoted to marbles, the other to checkers, while the stairs were occupied by a boy reading, a girl singing lullaby to her doll, two puppies, a kitten, and a constant succession of small boys sliding down the banisters, to the great detriment of their clothes, and danger to their limbs.

So absorbed did Nat become in this exciting race, that he ventured farther and farther out of his corner; and when one very lively boy came down so swiftly that he could not stop himself, but fell off the banisters, with a crash that would have broken any head but one rendered nearly as hard as a cannon-ball by eleven years of constant bumping, Nat forgot himself, and ran up to the fallen rider, expecting to find him half-dead. The boy, however, only winked rapidly for a second, then lay calmly looking up at the new face with a surprised "Hullo!"

"Hullo!" returned Nat, not knowing what else to say, and thinking that form of reply both brief and easy.

"Are you a new boy?" asked the recumbent youth, without stirring.

"Don't know yet."

"What's your name?"

"Nat Blake."

"Mine's Tommy Bangs; come up and have a go, will you?" and Tommy got upon his legs like one suddenly remembering the duties of hospitality.

"Guess I won't, till I see whether I'm going to stay or not," returned Nat, feeling the desire to stay increase every moment.

"I say, Demi, here's a new one. Come and see to him;" and the lively Thomas returned to his sport with unabated relish.

At his call, the boy reading on the stairs looked up with a pair of big brown eyes, and after an instant's pause, as if a little shy, he put the book under his arm, and came soberly down to greet the new-comer, who found something very attractive in the pleasant face of this slender, mild-eyed boy.

"Have you seen Aunt Jo?" he asked, as if that was some sort of important ceremony.

The boy . . . lay calmly looking up at the new face with a
surprised "Hullo!"

"I haven't seen anybody yet but you boys; I'm waiting," answered Nat.

"Did Uncle Laurie send you?" proceeded Demi, politely, but gravely.

"Mr. Laurence did."

"He is Uncle Laurie; and he always sends nice boys."

Nat looked gratified at the remark, and smiled, in a way that made his thin face very pleasant. He did not know what to say next, so the two stood staring at one another in friendly silence, till the little girl came up with her doll in her arms. She was very like Demi, only not so tall, and had a rounder, rosier face, and blue eyes.

"This is my sister Daisy," announced Demi, as if presenting a rare and precious creature.

The children nodded to one another; and the little girl's face dimpled with pleasure, as she said, affably,—"I hope you'll stay. We have such good times here; don't we, Demi?"

"Of course, we do; that's what Aunt Jo has Plumfield for."

"It seems a very nice place indeed," observed Nat, feeling that he must respond to these amiable young persons.

"It's the nicest place in the world; isn't it Demi?" said Daisy, who evidently regarded her brother as authority on all subjects.

"No; I think Greenland, where the icebergs and seals are, is more interesting. But I'm fond of Plumfield, and it *is* a very nice place to be in," returned Demi, who was interested just now in a book on Greenland. He was about to offer to show Nat the pictures and explain them, when the servant returned, saying, with a nod toward the parlor-door,—

"All right; you are to stop."

"I'm glad; now come to Aunt Jo." And Daisy took him by the hand with a pretty protecting air, which made Nat feel at home at once.

Demi returned to his beloved book, while his sister led the new-comer into a back room, where a stout gentleman was frolicking with two little boys on the sofa, and a thin lady was just finishing the letter which she seemed to have been re-reading.

"Here he is, Aunty!" cried Daisy.

"So this is my new boy? I am glad to see you, my dear, and hope you'll be happy here," said the lady, drawing him to her, and stroking back the hair from his forehead with a kind hand and a motherly look, which made Nat's lonely little heart yearn toward her.

She was not at all handsome, but she had a merry sort of face, that never seemed to have forgotten certain childish ways and looks, any more than her voice and manner had; and these things, hard to describe but very plain to see and feel, made her a genial, comfortable kind of person, easy to get on with, and generally "jolly," as boys would say. She saw the little tremble of Nat's lips as she smoothed his hair, and her keen eyes grew softer, but she only drew the shabby figure nearer and said, laughing,—

"I am Mother Bhaer, that gentleman is Father Bhaer, and these are the two little Bhaers.—Come here, boys, and see Nat."

The three wrestlers obeyed at once; and the stout man, with a chubby child on each shoulder, came up to welcome the new boy. Rob and Teddy merely grinned at him, but Mr. Bhaer shook hands, and pointing to a low chair near the fire, said, in a cordial voice,—

"There is a place all ready for thee, my son; sit down and dry thy wet feet at once."

"Wet? so they are! My dear, off with your shoes this minute, and I'll have some dry things ready for you in a jiffy," cried Mrs. Bhaer, bustling about so energetically, that Nat found himself in the cosy little chair, with dry socks and warm slippers on his feet, before he would have had time to say Jack Robinson, if he had wanted to try. He said "Thank you, ma'am," instead; and said it so gratefully, that Mrs. Bhaer's eyes grew soft again, and she said something merry, because she felt so tender, which was a way she had.

"These are Tommy Bang's slippers; but he never will remember to put them on in the house; so he shall not have them. They are too big; but that's all the better; you can't run away from us so fast as if they fitted."

"I don't want to run away, ma'am." And Nat spread his grimy little hands before the comfortable blaze, with a long sigh of satisfaction.

"That's good! Now I am going to toast you well, and try to get rid of that ugly cough. How long have you had it, dear?" asked Mrs. Bhaer, as she rummaged in her big basket for a strip of flannel.

"All winter. I got cold, and it wouldn't get better, somehow."

"No wonder, living in that damp cellar with hardly a rag to his poor dear back!" said Mrs. Bhaer, in a low tone to her husband, who was looking at the boy with a skilful pair of eyes, that marked the thin temples and feverish lips, as well as the hoarse voice and frequent fits of coughing that shook the bent shoulders under the patched jacket.

"Robin, my man, trot up to Nursey, and tell her to give thee the cough-bottle and the liniment," said Mr. Bhaer, after his eyes had exchanged telegrams with his wife's.

Nat looked a little anxious at the preparations, but forgot his fears, in a hearty laugh, when Mrs. Bhaer whispered to him, with a droll look,—

"Hear my rogue Teddy try to cough. The syrup I'm going to give you has honey in it; and he wants some."

Little Ted was red in the face with his exertions by the time the bottle came, and was allowed to suck the spoon, after Nat had manfully taken a dose, and had the bit of flannel put about his throat.

These first steps toward a cure were hardly completed, when a great bell rang, and a loud tramping through the hall announced supper. Bashful Nat quaked at the thought of meeting many strange boys, but Mrs. Bhaer held out her hand to him, and Rob said, patronizingly, "Don't be 'fraid; I'll take care of you."

Twelve boys, six on a side, stood behind their chairs, prancing with impatience to begin, while the tall flute-playing youth was trying to curb their ardor. But no one sat down, till Mrs. Bhaer was in her place behind the teapot, with Teddy on her left, and Nat on her right.

"This is our new boy, Nat Blake. After supper you can say, How do you do? Gently, boys, gently."

As she spoke every one stared at Nat, and then whisked into their seats, trying to be orderly, and failing utterly. The Bhaers did their best to have the lads behave well at meal times, and generally succeeded pretty well, for their rules were few and sensible, and the boys, knowing that they tried to make things easy and happy, did their best to obey. But there *are* times when hungry boys cannot be repressed without real cruelty, and Saturday evening, after a half-holiday, was one of those times.

"Dear little souls, do let them have one day in which they can howl and racket and frolic, to their hearts' content. A holiday isn't a holiday, without plenty of freedom and fun; and they shall have full swing once a week," Mrs. Bhaer used to say, when prim people wondered why banister-sliding, pillow-fights and all manner of jovial games were allowed under the once decorous roof of Plumfield.

It did seem at times as if the aforesaid roof was in danger of flying off; but it never did, for a word from Father Bhaer could at any time produce a lull, and the lads had learned that liberty must not be abused. So, in spite of many dark predictions, the school flourished, and manners and morals were insinuated, without the pupils exactly knowing how it was done.

Nat found himself very well off behind the tall pitchers, with Tommy Bangs just round the corner, and Mrs. Bhaer close by, to fill up plate and mug as fast as he could empty them.

"Who is that boy next the girl down at the other end?" whispered Nat to his young neighbor under cover of a general laugh.

"That's Demi Brooke. Mr. Bhaer is his uncle."

"What a queer name!"

"His real name is John, but they call him Demi-John, because his father is John too. That's a joke, don't you see?" said Tommy, kindly explaining. Nat did not see, but politely smiled, and asked, with interest,—

"Isn't he a very nice boy?"

"I bet you he is; knows lots and reads like anything."

"Who is the fat one next him?"

"Oh, that's Stuffy Cole. His name is George, but we call him Stuffy 'cause he eats so much. The little fellow next Father Bhaer is his boy Rob, and then there's big Franz his nephew; he teaches some, and kind of sees to us."

"He plays the flute, doesn't he?" asked Nat as Tommy rendered himself speechless by putting a whole baked apple into his mouth at one blow.

Tommy nodded, and said, sooner than one would have imagined possible under the circumstances, "Oh, don't he, though? And we dance sometimes, and do gymnastics to music. I like a drum myself, and mean to learn as soon as ever I can."

"I like a fiddle best; I can play one too," said Nat, getting confidential on this attractive subject.

"Can you?" and Tommy stared over the rim of his mug with round eyes, full of interest. "Mr. Bhaer's got an old fiddle, and he'll let you play on it if you want to."

"Could I? Oh, I would like it ever so much. You see I used to go round fiddling with my father, and another man, till he died."

"Wasn't that fun?" cried Tommy, much impressed.

"No, it was horrid; so cold in winter, and hot in summer. And I got tired; and they were cross sometimes; and I didn't have enough to eat." Nat paused to take a generous bite of gingerbread, as if to assure himself that the hard times were over; and then he added regretfully,—"But I did love my little fiddle, and I miss it. Nicolo took it away when father died, and wouldn't have me any longer, 'cause I was sick."

"You'll belong to the band if you play good. See if you don't."

"Do you have a band here?" And Nat's eyes sparkled.

"Guess we do; a jolly band, all boys; and they have concerts and things. You just see what happens tomorrow night."

After this pleasantly exciting remark, Tommy returned to his supper, and Nat sank into a blissful reverie over his full plate.

Mrs. Bhaer had heard all they said, while apparently absorbed in filling mugs, and overseeing little Ted, who was so sleepy that he put his spoon in his eye, nodded like a rosy poppy, and finally fell fast asleep, with his cheek pillowed on a soft bun. Mrs. Bhaer had put Nat next to Tommy, because that roly-poly boy had a frank and social way with him, very attractive to shy persons. Nat felt this, and had made several small confidences during supper, which gave Mrs. Bhaer the key to the new boy's character, better than if she had talked to him herself.

In the letter which Mr. Laurence had sent with Nat, he had said—

"DEAR JO,—

Here is a case after your own heart. This poor lad is an orphan now, sick and friendless. He has been a street-musician; and I found him in a cellar, mourning for his dead father, and his lost violin. I think there is something in him, and have a fancy that between us we may give this little man a lift. You cure his overtasked body, Fritz help his neglected mind, and when he is ready I'll see if he is a genius or only a boy with a talent which may earn his bread for him. Give him a trial, for the sake of your own boy,

"TEDDY."

"Of course we will!" cried Mrs. Bhaer, as she read the letter; and when she saw Nat, she felt at once that whether he was a genius or not, here was a lonely, sick boy, who needed just what she loved to give, a home, and motherly care. Both she and Mr. Bhaer observed him quietly; and in spite of ragged clothes, awkward manners, and a dirty face, they saw much about Nat that pleased them. He was a thin, pale boy, of twelve, with blue eyes, and a good forehead under the rough, neglected hair; an anxious, scared face, at times, as if he expected hard words, or blows; and a sensitive mouth, that trembled when a kind glance fell on him; while a gentle speech called up a look of gratitude, very sweet to see. "Bless the poor dear, he shall fiddle all day long if he likes," said Mrs. Bhaer to herself, as she saw the eager, happy expression on his face when Tommy talked of the band.

So, after supper, when the lads flocked into the school-room for more "high jinks," Mrs. Jo appeared with a violin in her hand, and after a word with her husband, went to Nat, who sat in a corner watching the scene with intense interest.

"Now, my lad, give us a little tune. We want a violin in our band, and I think you will do it nicely."

She expected that he would hesitate; but he seized the old fiddle at once, and handled it with such loving care, it was plain to see that music was his passion.

"I'll do the best I can, ma'am," was all he said; and then drew the bow across the strings, as if eager to hear the dear notes again.

There was a great clatter in the room, but as if deaf to any sounds but those he made, Nat played softly to himself, forgetting every thing in his delight. It was only a simple negro melody, such as street-musicians play, but it caught the ears of the boys at once, and silenced them, till they stood listening with surprise and pleasure. Gradually they got nearer and nearer, and Mr. Bhaer came up to watch the boy; for, as if he was in his element now, Nat played away and never minded any one, while his eyes shone, his cheeks reddened, and his thin fingers flew, as he hugged the old fiddle and made it speak to all their hearts the language that he loved.

A hearty round of applause rewarded him better than a shower of pennies, when he stopped and glanced about him, as if to say—

"I've done my best; please like it."

"I say, you do that first rate," cried Tommy, who considered Nat his *protégé*.

"You shall be first fiddle in my band," added Franz, with an approving smile.

Mrs. Bhaer whispered to her husband—

"Teddy is right. There's something in the child." And Mr. Bhaer nodded his head emphatically, as he clapped Nat on the shoulder, saying, heartily—

"You play well, my son. Come now and play something which we can sing."

It was the proudest, happiest minute of the poor boy's life when he was led to the place of honor by the piano, and the lads gathered round, never heeding his poor clothes, but eying him respectfully, and waiting eagerly to hear him play again.

They chose a song he knew; and after one or two false starts they got going, and violin, flute, and piano led a chorus of boyish voices that made the old roof ring again. It was too much for Nat, more feeble than he knew; and as the final shout died away, his face began to work, he dropped the fiddle, and turning to the wall, sobbed like a little child.

"My dear, what is it?" asked Mrs. Bhaer, who had been singing with all her might, and trying to keep little Rob from beating time with his boots.

"You are all so kind—and it's so beautiful—I can't help it," sobbed Nat, coughing till he was breathless.

"Come with me, dear; you must go to bed and rest; you are worn out, and this is too noisy a place for you," whispered Mrs. Bhaer; and took him away to her own parlor, where she let him cry himself quiet.

Then she won him to tell her all his troubles, and listened to the little story with tears in her own eyes, though it was not a new one to her.

"My child, you *have* got a father and a mother now, and this is home. Don't think of those sad times any more, but get well and happy; and be sure you shall never suffer again, if we can help it. This place is made for all sorts of boys to have a good time in, and to learn how to help themselves and be useful men, I hope. You shall have as much music as you want, only you must get strong first. Now come up to Nursey and have a bath, and then go to bed, and tomorrow we will lay some nice little plans together."

Nat held her hand fast in his, but had not a word to say, and let his grateful eyes speak for him, as Mrs. Bhaer led him up to a big room, where they found a stout German woman with a face so round and cheery, that it looked like a sort of sun, with the wide frill of her cap for rays.

"This is Nursey Hummel, and she will give you a nice bath, and cut your hair, and make you all 'comfy, as Rob says. That's the bath-room in there; and on Saturday nights we scrub all the little lads first, and pack them away in bed before the big ones get through singing. Now then, Rob, in with you."

As she talked, Mrs. Bhaer had whipped off Rob's clothes and popped him into a long bath-tub in the little room opening into the nursery.

There were two tubs, besides foot-baths, basins, douche-pipes, and all manner of contrivances for cleanliness. Nat was soon luxuriating in the other bath; and while simmering there, he watched the performances of the two women, who scrubbed, clean night-gowned, and bundled into bed four or five small boys, who, of course, cut up all sorts of capers during the operation, and kept every one in a gale of merriment till they were extinguished in their beds.

By the time Nat was washed and done up in a blanket by the fire, while Nursey cut his hair, a new detachment of boys arrived and were shut into the bath-room, where they made as much splashing and noise as a school of young whales at play.

"Nat had better sleep here, so that if his cough troubles him in the night you can see that he takes a good draught of flax-seed tea," said Mrs. Bhaer, who was flying about like a distracted hen with a large brood of lively ducklings.

Nursey approved the plan, finished Nat off with a flannel night-gown, a drink of something warm and sweet, and then tucked him into one of the three little beds standing in the room, where he lay looking like a contented mummy, and feeling that nothing more in the way of luxury could be offered him. Cleanliness in itself was a new and delightful sensation; flannel gowns were unknown comforts in his world; sips of "good stuff" soothed his cough as pleasantly as kind words did his lonely heart; and the feeling that somebody cared for him made that plain room seem a sort of heaven to the homeless child. It was like a cosy dream; and he often shut his eyes to see if it would not vanish when he opened them again. It was too pleasant to let him sleep, and he could not have done so if he had tried, for in a few minutes one of the peculiar institutions of Plumfield was revealed to his astonished but appreciative eyes.

A momentary lull in the aquatic exercises was followed by the sudden appearance of pillows flying in all directions, hurled by white goblins, who came rioting out of their beds. The battle raged in several rooms, all down the upper hall, and even surged at intervals into the nursery, when some hard-pressed warrior took refuge there. No one seemed to mind this explosion in the least; no one forbade it, or even looked surprised. Nursey went on hanging up towels, and Mrs. Bhaer looked out clean clothes, as calmly as if the most perfect order reigned. Nay, she even chased one daring boy out of the room, and fired after him the pillow he had slyly thrown at her.

"Won't they hurt 'em?" asked Nat, who lay laughing with all his might.

"Oh dear, no! We always allow one pillow-fight Saturday night. The cases are changed to-morrow; and it gets up a glow after the boys' baths; so I rather like it myself," said Mrs. Bhaer, busy again among her dozen pairs of socks.

"What a very nice school this is!" observed Nat, in a burst of admiration.

"It's an odd one," laughed Mrs. Bhaer; "but you see we don't believe in making children miserable by too many rules, and too much study. I forbade night-gown parties at first; but, bless you, it was of no use. I could no more keep those boys in their beds, than so many jacks in the box. So I made an agreement with them: I was to allow a fifteen-minute pillow-fight, every Saturday night; and they promised to go properly to bed, every other night. I tried it, and it worked well. If they don't keep their word, no frolic; if they do, I just turn the glasses round, put the lamps in safe places, and let them rampage as much as they like."

"It's a beautiful plan," said Nat, feeling that he should like to join in the fray, but not venturing to propose it the first night. So he lay enjoying the spectacle, which certainly was a lively one.

Tommy Bangs led the assailing party, and Demi defended his own room with a dogged courage, fine to see, collecting pillows behind him as fast as they were thrown, till the besiegers were out of ammunition, when they would charge upon him in a body, and recover their arms. A few slight accidents occurred, but nobody minded, and gave and took sounding thwacks with perfect good humor, while pillows flew like big snow flakes, till Mrs. Bhaer looked at her watch, and called out—

"Time is up, boys. Into bed, every man Jack, or pay the forfeit!"

"What is the forfeit?" asked Nat, sitting up in his eagerness to know what happened to those wretches who disobeyed this most peculiar, but public-spirited school-ma'am.

"Lose their fun next time," answered Mrs. Bhaer. "I give them five minutes to settle down, then put out the lights, and expect order. They are honorable lads, and they keep their word."

That was evident, for the battle ended as abruptly as it began—a parting shot or two, a final cheer, as Demi fired the seventh pillow at the retiring foe, a few challenges for next time, then order prevailed; and nothing but an occasional giggle, or a suppressed whisper, broke the quiet which followed the Saturday-night frolic, as Mother Bhaer kissed her new boy, and left him to happy dreams of life at Plumfield.

# CHAPTER II

## THE BOYS

WHILE Nat takes a good long sleep, I will tell my little readers something about the boys, among whom he found himself when he woke up.

To begin with our old friends. Franz was a tall lad, of sixteen now, a regular German, big, blond, and bookish, also very domestic, amiable, and musical. His uncle was fitting him for college, and his aunt for a happy home of his own hereafter, because she carefully fostered in him gentle manners, love of children, respect for women, old and young, and helpful ways about the house. He was her right-hand man on all occasions, steady, kind, and patient; and he loved his merry aunt like a mother, for such she had tried to be to him.

Emil was quite different, being quick-tempered, restless, and enterprising, bent on going to sea, for the blood of the old vikings stirred in his veins, and could not be tamed. His uncle promised that he should go when he was sixteen, and set him to studying navigation, gave him stories of good and famous admirals and heroes to read, and let him lead the life of a frog in river, pond, and brook, when lessons were done. His room looked like the cabin of a man-of-war, for everything was nautical, military, and ship shape. Captain Kyd was his delight, and his favorite amusement was to rig up like that piratical gentleman, and roar out sanguinary sea-songs at the top of his voice. He would dance nothing but sailors' hornpipes, rolled in his gait, and was as nautical in conversation as his uncle would permit. The boys called him "Commodore," and took great pride in his fleet, which whitened the pond and suffered disasters that would have daunted any commander but a sea-struck boy.

Demi was one of the children who show plainly the effect of intelligent love and care, for soul and body worked harmoniously together. The natural refinement which nothing but home influence can teach, gave him sweet and simple manners: his mother had cherished an innocent and loving heart in him; his father had watched over the physical growth of his boy, and kept the little body straight and strong on wholesome food and exercise and sleep, while Grandpa March cultivated the little mind with the tender wisdom of a modern Pythagoras,—not tasking it with long, hard lessons, parrot-learned, but helping it to unfold as naturally and beautifully as sun and dew help roses bloom. He was not a perfect child, by any means, but his faults were of the better sort; and being early taught the secret of self-control, he was not left at the mercy of appetites and passions, as some poor little mortals are, and then punished for yielding to the temptations against which they have no armor. A quiet, quaint boy was Demi, serious, yet cheery, quite unconscious that he was unusually bright and beautiful, yet quick to see and love intelligence or beauty in other children. Very fond of books, and full of lively fancies, born of a strong imagination and a spiritual nature, these traits made his parents anxious to balance them with useful knowledge and healthful society, lest they should make him one of those pale precocious children who amaze and delight a family sometimes, and fade away like hot-house flowers, because the young soul blooms too soon, and has not a hearty body to root it firmly in the wholesome soil of this world.

So Demi was transplanted to Plumfield, and took so kindly to the life there, that Meg and John and grandpa felt satisfied that they had done well. Mixing with other boys brought out the practical side of him, roused his spirit, and brushed away the pretty cobwebs he was so fond of spinning in that little brain of his. To be sure, he rather shocked his mother when he came home, by banging doors, saying "by George" emphatically, and demanding tall thick boots "that clumped like papa's." But John rejoiced over him, laughed at his explosive remarks, got the boots, and said contentedly, "He is doing well; so let him clump. I want my son to be a manly boy, and this temporary roughness won't hurt him. We can polish him up by and by; and as for learning, he will pick that up as pigeons do peas. So don't hurry him."

Daisy was as sunshiny and charming as ever, with all sorts of little womanlinesses budding in her, for she was like her gentle mother, and delighted in domestic things. She had a family of dolls, whom she brought up in the most exemplary manner; she could not get on without her little work-basket and bits of sewing, which she did so nicely, that Demi frequently pulled out his handkerchief to display her neat stitches, and Baby Josy had a flannel petticoat beautifully made by Sister Daisy. She liked to quiddle about the china-closet, prepare the salt-cellars, put the spoons straight on the table; and every day went round the parlor with her brush, dusting chairs and tables. Demi called her a "Betty," but was very glad to have her keep his things in order, lend him her nimble fingers in all sorts of work, and help him with his lessons, for they kept abreast there, and had no thought of rivalry.

The love between them was as strong as ever; and no one could laugh Demi out of his affectionate ways with Daisy. He fought her battles valiantly, and never could understand why boys should be ashamed to say "right out," that they loved their sisters. Daisy adored her twin, thought "my brother" the most remarkable boy in the world, and every morning, in her little wrapper, trotted to tap at his door with a motherly— "Get up, my dear, it's 'most breakfast time; and here's your clean collar."

Rob was an energetic morsel of a boy, who seemed to have discovered the secret of perpetual motion, for he never was still. Fortunately, he was not mischievous, nor very brave; so he kept out of trouble pretty well, and vibrated between father and mother like an affectionate little pendulum with a lively tick, for Rob was a chatterbox.

Teddy was too young to play a very important part in the affairs of Plumfield, yet he had his little sphere, and filled it beautifully. Everyone felt the need of a pet at times, and Baby was always ready to accommodate, for kissing and cuddling suited him excellently, Mrs. Jo seldom stirred without him; so he had his little finger in all the domestic pies, and every one found them all the better for it, for they believed in babies at Plumfield.

Dick Brown, and Adolphus or Dolly Pettingill, were two eight-years olds. Dolly stuttered badly, but was gradually getting over it, for no one was allowed to mock him and Mr. Bhaer tried to cure it, by making him talk slowly. Dolly was a good little lad, quite uninteresting and ordinary, but he flourished here, and went through his daily duties and pleasures with placid content and propriety.

Dick Brown's affliction was a crooked back, yet he bore his burden so cheerfully, that Demi once asked in his queer way, "Do humps make people good-natured? I'd like one if they do." Dick was always merry, and did his best to be like other boys, for a plucky spirit lived in the feeble little body. When he first came, he was very sensitive about his misfortune, but soon learned to forget it, for no one dared remind him of it, after Mr. Bhaer had punished one boy for laughing at him.

"God don't care; for my soul is straight if my back isn't," sobbed Dick to his tormentor on that occasion; and, by cherishing this idea, the Bhaers soon led him to believe that people also loved his soul, and did not mind his body, except to pity and help him to bear it.

Playing menagerie once with the others, someone said, "What animal will you be, Dick?"

"Oh, I'm the dromedary; don't you see the hump on my back?" was the laughing answer.

"So you are, my nice little one that don't carry loads, but marches by the elephant first in the procession," said Demi, who was arranging the spectacle.

"I hope others will be as kind to the poor dear as my boys have learned to be," said Mrs. Jo, quite satisfied with the success of her teaching, as Dick ambled past her, looking like a very happy, but a very feeble little dromedary, beside stout Stuffy, who did the elephant with ponderous propriety.

Jack Ford was a sharp, rather a sly lad, who was sent to this school, because it was cheap. Many men would have thought him a smart boy, but Mr. Bhaer did not like his way of illustrating that Yankee word, and thought his unboyish keenness and money-loving as much of an affliction as Dolly's stutter, or Dick's hump.

Ned Barker was like a thousand other boys of fourteen, all legs, blunder, and bluster. Indeed the family called him the "Blunderbuss," and always expected to see him tumble over the chairs, bump against the tables, and knock down any small articles near him. He bragged a good deal about what he could do, but seldom did anything to prove it, was not brave, and a little given to tale-telling. He was apt to bully the small boys, and flatter the big ones, and without being at all bad, was just the sort of fellow who could very easily be led astray.

George Cole had been spoilt by an over-indulgent mother, who stuffed him with sweetmeats till he was sick, and then thought him too delicate to study, so that at twelve years old, he was a pale, puffy boy, dull, fretful, and lazy. A friend persuaded her to send him to Plumfield, and there he soon got waked up, for sweet things were seldom allowed, much exercise required, and study made so pleasant, that Stuffy was gently lured along, till he quite amazed his anxious mamma by his improvement, and convinced her that there was really something remarkable in Plumfield air.

Billy Ward was what the Scotch tenderly call an "innocent," for though thirteen years old, he was like a child of six. He had been an unusually intelligent boy, and his father had hurried him on too fast, giving him all sorts of hard lessons, keeping him at his books six hours a day, and expecting him to absorb knowledge as a Strasburg goose does the food crammed down its throat. He thought he was doing his duty, but he nearly killed the boy, for a fever gave the poor child a sad holiday, and when he recovered, the overtasked brain gave out, and Billy's mind was like a slate over which a sponge has passed, leaving it blank.

It was a terrible lesson to his ambitious father; he could not bear the sight of his promising child, changed to a feeble idiot, and he sent him away to Plumfield, scarcely hoping that he could be helped, but sure that he would be kindly treated. Quite docile and harmless was Billy, and it was pitiful to see how hard he tried to learn, as if groping dimly after the lost knowledge which had cost him so much. Day after day, he pored over the alphabet, proudly said A and B, and thought that he knew them, but on the morrow they were gone, and all the work was to be done over again. Mr. Bhaer had infinite patience with him, and kept on in spite of the apparent hopelessness of the task, not caring for book lessons, but trying gently to clear away the mists from the darkened mind, and give it back intelligence enough to make the boy less a burden and an affliction.

Mrs. Bhaer strengthened his health by every aid she could invent, and the boys all pitied and were kind to him. He did not like their active plays, but would sit for hours watching the doves, would dig holes for Teddy till even that ardent grubber was satisfied, or follow Silas, the man, from place to place seeing him work, for honest Si was very good to him, and though he forgot his letters Billy remembered friendly faces.

Tommy Bangs was the scapegrace of the school, and the most trying little scapegrace that ever lived. As full of mischief as a monkey, yet so good-hearted that one could not help forgiving his tricks; so scatter-brained that words went by him like the wind, yet so penitent for every misdeed, that it was impossible to keep sober when he vowed tremendous vows of reformation, or proposed all sorts of queer punishments to be inflicted upon himself. Mr. and Mrs. Bhaer lived in a state of preparation for any mishap, from the breaking of Tommy's own neck, to the blowing up of the entire family with gunpowder; and Nursey had a particular drawer in which she kept bandages, plasters, and salves for his especial use, for Tommy was always being brought in half dead; but nothing ever killed him, and he rose from every downfall with redoubled vigor.

The first day he came, he chopped the top off one finger in the hay-cutter, and during the week, fell from the shed roof, was chased by an angry hen who tried to pick his eyes out because he examined her chickens, got run away with, and had his ears boxed violently by Asia, who caught him luxuriously skimming a pan of cream with half a stolen pie. Undaunted, however, by any failures or rebuffs, this indomitable youth went on amusing himself with all sorts of tricks till no one felt safe. If he did not know his lessons, he always had some droll excuse to offer, and as he was usually clever at his books, and as bright as a button in composing answers when he did not know them, he got on pretty well at school. But out of school,—Ye gods and little fishes! How Tommy did carouse!

He wound fat Asia up in her own clothesline against the post, and left her there to fume and scold for half an hour one busy Monday morning. He dropped a hot cent down Mary Ann's back as that pretty maid was waiting at table one day when there were gentlemen to dinner, whereat the poor girl upset the soup and rushed out of the room in dismay, leaving the family to think that she had gone mad. He fixed a pail of water up in a tree, with a bit of ribbon fastened to the handle, and when Daisy, attracted by the gay streamer, tried to pull it down, she got a douche bath that spoiled her clean frock and hurt her little feelings very much. He put rough white pebbles in the sugar-bowl when his grandmother came to tea, and the poor old lady wondered why they didn't melt in her cup, but was too polite to say anything. He passed round snuff in church so that five of the boys sneezed with such violence they had to go out. He dug paths in winter time, and then privately watered them so that people should tumble down. He drove poor Silas nearly wild by hanging his big boots in conspicuous places, for his feet were enormous, and he was very much ashamed of them. He persuaded confiding little Dolly to tie a thread to one of his loose teeth, and leave the string hanging from his mouth when he went to sleep, so that Tommy could pull it out without his feeling the dreaded operation. But the tooth wouldn't come at the first tweak, and poor Dolly woke up in great anguish of spirit, and lost all faith in Tommy from that day forth. The last prank had been to give the hens bread soaked in rum, which made them tipsy and scandalized all the other fowls, for the respectable old biddies went staggering about, pecking and clucking in the most maudlin manner, while the family were convulsed with laughter at their antics, till Daisy took pity on them and shut them up in the hen-house to sleep off their intoxication.

These were the boys, and they lived together as happily as twelve lads could, studying and playing, working and squabbling, fighting faults and cultivating virtues in the good old-fashioned way. Boys at other schools probably learned more from books, but less of that better wisdom which makes good men. Latin, Greek, and mathematics were all very well, but in Professor Bhaer's opinion, self-knowledge, self-help, and self-control were more important, and he tried to teach them carefully. People shook their heads sometimes at his ideas, even while they owned that the boys improved wonderfully in manners and morals. But then, as Mrs. Jo said to Nat, it was an "odd school."

# CHAPTER III

## SUNDAY

THE moment the bell rang next morning Nat flew out of bed, and dressed himself with great satisfaction in the suit of clothes he found on the chair. They were not new, being half-worn garments of one of the well to-do boys; but Mrs. Bhaer kept all such cast-off feathers for the picked robins who strayed into her nest. They were hardly on when Tommy appeared in a high state of clean collar, and escorted Nat down to breakfast.

The sun was shining into the dining-room on the well-spread table, and the flock of hungry, hearty lads who gathered round it. Nat observed that they were much more orderly than they had been the night before, and every one stood silently behind his chair while little Rob, standing beside his father at the head of the table, folded his hands, reverently bent his curly head, and softly repeated a short grace in the devout German fashion, which Mr. Bhaer loved and taught his little son to honor. Then they all sat down to enjoy the Sunday-morning breakfast of coffee, steak, and baked potatoes, instead of the bread and milk fare with which they usually satisfied their young appetites. There was much pleasant talk while the knives and forks rattled briskly, for certain Sunday lessons were to be learned, the Sunday walk settled, and plans for the week discussed. As he listened, Nat thought it seemed as if this day must be a very pleasant one, for he loved quiet, and there was a cheerful sort of hush over everything that pleased him very much; because, in spite of his rough life, the boy possessed the sensitive nerves which belong to a music-loving nature.

"Now, my lads, get your morning jobs done, and let me find you ready for church when the 'bus comes round," said Father Bhaer, and set the example by going into the school-room to get books ready for the morrow.

Every one scattered to his or her task, for each had some little daily duty, and was expected to perform it faithfully. Some brought wood and water, brushed the steps, or ran errands for Mrs. Bhaer. Others fed the pet animals, and did chores about the barn with Franz. Daisy washed the cups, and Demi wiped them, for the twins liked to work together, and Demi had been taught to make himself useful in the little house at home. Even baby Teddy had his small job to do, and trotted to and fro, putting napkins away, and pushing chairs into their places. For half an hour the lads buzzed about like a hive of bees, then the 'bus drove round, Father Bhaer and Franz with the eight older boys piled in, and away they went for a three mile drive to church in town.

Because of the troublesome cough Nat preferred to stay at home with the four small boys, and spent a happy morning in Mrs. Bhaer's room, listening to the stories she read them, learning the hymn she taught them, and then quietly employing himself pasting pictures into an old ledger.

"This is my Sunday closet," she said, showing him shelves filled with picture-books, paint-boxes, architect ural blocks, little diaries, and materials for letter-writing. "I want my boys to love Sunday, to find it a peaceful, pleasant day, when they can rest from common study and play, yet enjoy quiet pleasures, and learn, in simple ways, lessons more important than any taught in school. Do you understand me?" she asked, watching Nat's attentive face.

"You mean to be good?" he said, after hesitating a minute.

"Yes; to be good, and to love to be good. It is hard work sometimes, I know very well; but we all help one another, and so we get on. This is one of the ways in which I try to help my boys," and she took down a thick book, which seemed half-full of writing, and opened at a page on which there was one word at the top.

"Why, that's my name!" cried Nat, looking both surprised and interested.

"Yes; I have a page for each boy. I keep a little account of how he gets on through the week, and Sunday night I show him the record. If it is bad I am sorry and disappointed, if it is good I am glad and proud; but, whichever it is, the boys know I want to help them, and they try to do their best for love of me and Father Bhaer."

"I should think they would," said Nat, catching a glimpse of Tommy's name opposite his own, and wondering what was written under it.

Mrs. Bhaer saw his eye on the words, and shook her head, saying, as she turned a leaf—

"No, I don't show my records to any but the one to whom each belongs. I call this my conscience book; and only you and I will ever know what is to be written on the page below your name. Whether you will be pleased or ashamed to read it next Sunday depends on yourself. I think it will be a good report; at any rate, I shall try to make things easy for you in this new place, and shall be quite contented if you keep our few rules, live happily with the boys, and learn something."

"I'll try, ma'am;" and Nat's thin face flushed up with the earnestness of his desire to make Mrs. Bhaer "glad and proud," not "sorry and disappointed." "It must be a great deal of trouble to write about so many," he added, as she shut her book with an encouraging pat on the shoulder.

"Not to me, for I really don't know which I like best, writing or boys," she said, laughing to see Nat stare with astonishment at the last item. "Yes, I know many people think boys are a nuisance, but that is because they don't understand them. I do; and I never saw the boy yet whom I could not get on capitally with after I had once found the soft spot in his heart. Bless me, I couldn't get on at all without my flock of dear, noisy, naughty, harum-scarum little lads, could I, my Teddy?" and Mrs. Bhaer hugged the young rogue, just in time to save the big inkstand from going into his pocket.

Nat, who had never heard any thing like this before, really did not know whether Mother Bhaer was a trifle crazy, or the most delightful woman he had ever met. He rather inclined to the latter opinion, in spite of her peculiar tastes, for she had a way of filling up a fellow's plate before he asked, of laughing at his jokes, gently tweaking him by the ear, or clapping him on the shoulder, that Nat found very engaging.

"Now, I think you would like to go into the school-room and practise some of the hymns we are to sing tonight," she said, rightly guessing the thing of all others that he wanted to do.

Alone with the beloved violin and the music-book propped up before him in the sunny window, while Spring beauty filled the world outside, and Sabbath silence reigned within, Nat enjoyed an hour or two of genuine happiness, learning the sweet old tunes, and forgetting the hard past in the cheerful present.

When the church-goers came back and dinner was over, everyone read, wrote letters home, said their Sunday lessons, or talked quietly to one another, sitting here and there about the house. At three o'clock the entire family turned out to walk, for all the active young bodies must

have exercise; and in these walks the active young minds were taught
to see and love the providence of God in the beautiful miracles which
Nature was working before their eyes. Mr. Bhaer always went with them,
and in his simple, fatherly way, found for his flock "Sermons in stones,
books in the running brooks, and good in everything."

Mrs. Bhaer with Daisy and her own two boys drove into town, to pay
the weekly visit to Grandma, which was busy Mother Bhaer's one holiday
and greatest pleasure. Nat was not strong enough for the long walk, and
asked to stay at home with Tommy, who kindly offered to do the honors
of Plumfield. "You've seen the house, so come out and have a look at
the garden, and the barn, and the menagerie," said Tommy, when they
were left alone with Asia, to see that they didn't get into mischief; for,
though Tommy was one of the best meaning boys who ever adorned
knickerbockers, accidents of the most direful nature were always happening
to him, no one could exactly tell how.

"What is your menagerie?" asked Nat, as they trotted along the drive
that encircled the house.

"We all have pets you see, and we keep 'em in the corn-barn, and call
it the menagerie. Here you are. Isn't my guinea-pig a beauty?" And
Tommy proudly presented one of the ugliest specimens of that pleasing
animal that Nat ever saw.

"I know a boy with a dozen of 'em, and he said he'd give me one, only
I hadn't any place to keep it, so I couldn't have it. It was white, with
black spots, a regular rouser, and maybe I could get it for you if you'd
like it," said Nat, feeling it would be a delicate return for Tommy's
attentions.

"I'd like it ever so much, and I'll give you this one, and they can live
together if they don't fight. Those white mice are Rob's, Franz gave 'em
to him. The rabbits are Ned's, and the bantams outside are Stuffy's. That
box thing is Demi's turtle-tank, only he hasn't begun to get 'em yet. Last
year he had sixty-two, whackers some of 'em. He stamped one of 'em
with his name and the year, and let it go; and he says maybe he will find
it ever so long after and know it. He read about a turtle being found
that had a mark on it that showed it must be hundreds of years old.
Demi's such a funny chap."

"What is in this box?" asked Nat, stopping before a large deep one,
half-full of earth.

"Oh, that's Jack Ford's worm-shop. He digs heaps of 'em and keeps
'em here, and when we want any to go a fishing with, we buy some of
him. It saves lots of trouble, only he charged too much for 'em. Why,
last time we traded I had to pay two cents a dozen, and then got little
ones. Jack's mean sometimes, and I told him I'd dig for myself if he
didn't lower his prices. Now, I own two hens, those gray ones with top
knots, first-rate ones they are too, and I sell Mrs. Bhaer the eggs, but I
never ask her more than twenty-five cents a dozen, never! I'd be ashamed
to do it," cried Tommy with a glance of scorn at the worm-shop.

"Who owns the dogs?" asked Nat, much interested in these commercial
transactions, and feeling that T. Bangs was a man whom it would be a
privilege and a pleasure to patronize.

"The big dog is Emil's. His name is Christopher Columbus. Mrs. Bhaer named him because she likes to say Christopher Columbus, and no one minds it if she means the dog," answered Tommy, in the tone of a showman displaying his menagerie. "The white pup is Rob's, and the yellow one is Teddy's. A man was going to drown them in our pond and Pa Bhaer wouldn't let him. They do well enough for the little chaps, I don't think much of 'em myself. Their names are Castor and Pollux."

"I'd like Toby the donkey best, if I could have anything, it's so nice to ride, and he's so little and good," said Nat, remembering the weary tramps he had taken on his own tired feet.

"Mr. Laurie sent him out to Mrs. Bhaer, so she shouldn't carry Teddy on her back when we go to walk. We're all fond of Toby, and he's a first-rate donkey, sir. Those pigeons belong to the whole lot of us, we each have our pet one, and go shares in all the little ones as they come along. Squabs are great fun; there ain't any now, but you can go up and take a look at the old fellows, while I see if Cockletop and Granny have laid any eggs."

Nat climbed up a ladder, put his head through a trap door and took a long look at the pretty doves billing and cooing in their spacious loft. Some on their nests, some bustling in and out, and some sitting at their doors, while many went flying from the sunny housetop to the straw-strewn farmyard, where six sleek cows were placidly ruminating.

"Everybody has got something but me. I wish I had a dove, or a hen, or even a turtle, all my own," thought Nat, feeling very poor as he saw the interesting treasures of the other boys. "How do you get these things?" he asked, when he joined Tommy in the barn.

"We find 'em, or buy 'em, or folks give 'em to us, My father sends me mine; but as soon as I get egg money enough, I'm going to buy a pair of ducks. There's a nice little pond for 'em behind the barn, and people pay well for duck-eggs, and the little duckies are pretty, and it's fun to see 'em swim," said Tommy, with the air of a millionaire.

Nat sighed, for he had neither father nor money, nothing in the wide world but an old empty pocket-book, and the skill that lay in his ten finger tips. Tommy seemed to understand the question and the sigh which followed his answer, for after a moment of deep thought, he suddenly broke out—

"Look here, I'll tell you what I'll do. If you will hunt eggs for me, I hate it, I'll give you one egg out of every dozen. You keep account, and when you've had twelve, Mother Bhaer will give you twenty-five cents for 'em, and then you can buy what you like, don't you see?"

"I'll do it! What a kind feller you are, Tommy!" cried Nat, quite dazzled by this brilliant offer.

"Pooh! That is not any thing. You begin now and rummage the barn, and I'll wait here for you. Granny is cackling, so you're sure to find one somewhere," and Tommy threw himself down on the hay with a luxurious sense of having made a good bargain, and done a friendly thing.

Nat joyfully began his search, and went rustling from loft to loft till he found two fine eggs, one hidden under a beam, and the other in an old peck measure, which Mrs. Cockletop had appropriated.

"You may have one and I'll have the other, that will just make up my last dozen, and to-morrow we'll start fresh. Here, you chalk your accounts up near mine, and then we'll be all straight," said Tommy, showing a row of mysterious figures on the smooth side of an old winnowing machine.

With a delightful sense of importance, the proud possessor of one egg opened his account with his friend, who laughingly wrote above the figures these imposing words,

"T. Bangs & Co."

Poor Nat found them so fascinating that he was with difficulty persuaded to go and deposit his first piece of portable property in Asia's store-room. Then they went on again, and having made the acquaintance of the two horses, six cows, three pigs, and one Alderney "Bossy," as calves are called in New England, Tommy took Nat to a certain old willow-tree that overhung a noisy little brook. From the fence it was an easy scramble into a wide niche between the three big branches, which had been cut off to send out from year to year a crowd of slender twigs, till a green canopy rustled overhead. Here little seats had been fixed, and in a hollow place a closet made big enough to hold a book or two, a dismantled boat, and several half-finished whistles.

"This is Demi's and my private place; we made it, and nobody can come up unless we let 'em, except Daisy, we don't mind her," said Tommy, as Nat looked with delight from the babbling brown water below to the green arch above, where bees were making a musical murmur as they feasted on the long yellow blossoms that filled the air with sweetness.

"Oh, it's just beautiful!" cried Nat. "I do hope you'll let me up sometimes. I never saw such a nice place in all my life. I'd like to be a bird, and live here always."

"It is pretty nice. You can come if Demi don't mind, and I guess he won't, because he said last night that he liked you."

"Did he?" and Nat smiled with pleasure, for Demi's regard seemed to be valued by all the boys, partly because he was Father Bhaer's nephew, and partly because he was such a sober, conscientious little fellow.

"Yes; Demi likes quiet chaps, and I guess he and you will get on if you care about reading as he does."

Poor Nat's flush of pleasure deepened to a painful scarlet at those last words, and he stammered out—

"I can't read very well; I never had any time; I was always fiddling round, you know."

"I don't love it myself, but I can do it well enough when I want to," said Tommy, after a surprised look, which said as plainly as words, "A boy twelve years old and can't read!"

"I can read music, anyway," added Nat, rather ruffled at having to confess his ignorance.

"I can't;" and Tommy spoke in a respectful tone, which emboldened Nat to say firmly—

"I mean to study real hard and learn everything I can, for I never had a chance before. Does Mr. Bhaer give hard lessons?"

"No, he isn't a bit cross; he sort of explains and gives you a boost over the hard places. Some folks don't; my other master didn't. If we missed a word, didn't we get raps on the head!" and Tommy rubbed his own pate as if it tingled yet with the liberal supply of raps, the memory of which was the only thing he brought away after a year with his "other master."

"I think I could read this," said Nat, who had been examining the books.

"Read a bit, then; I'll help you," resumed Tommy, with a patronizing air.

So Nat did his best, and floundered through a page with many friendly "boosts" from Tommy, who told him he would soon "go it" as well as anybody. Then they sat and talked boy-fashion about all sorts of things, among others, gardening; for Nat, looking down from his perch, asked what was planted in the many little patches lying below them on the other side of the brook.

"These are our farms," said Tommy. "We each have our own patch, and raise what we like in it, only we have to choose different things, and can't change till the crop is in, and we must keep it in order all summer."

"What are you going to raise this year?"

"Wal, I *cattlea*ted to hev beans, as they are about the easiest crop a-goin'."

Nat could not help laughing, for Tommy had pushed back his hat, put his hands in his pockets, and drawled out his words in unconscious imitation of Silas, the man who managed the place for Mr. Bhaer.

"Come, you needn't laugh; beans *are* ever so much easier than corn or potatoes. I tried melons last year, but the bugs were a bother, and the old things wouldn't get ripe before the frost, so I didn't have but one good water and two little 'mush mellions,' " said Tommy, relapsing into a "Silasism" with the last word.

"Corn looks pretty growing," said Nat, politely, to atone for his laugh.

"Yes, but you have to hoe it over and over again. Now, six weeks' beans only have to be done once or so, and they get ripe soon. I'm going to try 'em, for I spoke first. Stuffy wanted 'em, but he's got to take peas; they only have to be picked, and he ought to do it, he eats such a lot."

"I wonder if I shall have a garden?" said Nat, thinking that even corn hoeing must be pleasant work.

"Of course you will," said a voice from below, and there was Mr. Bhaer returned from his walk, and come to find them, for he managed to have a little talk with every one of the lads sometime during the day, and found that these chats gave them a good start for the coming week.

Sympathy is a sweet thing, and it worked wonders here, for each boy knew that Father Bhaer was interested in him, and some were readier to open their hearts to him than to a woman, especially the older ones, who liked to talk over their hopes and plans, man to man. When sick or in trouble they instinctively turned to Mrs. Jo, while the little ones made her their mother-confessor on all occasions.

In descending from their nest, Tommy fell into the brook; being used to it he calmly picked himself out and retired to the house to be dried. This left Nat to Mr. Bhaer, which was just what he wished, and, during the stroll they took among the garden plots, he won the lad's heart by giving him a little "farm," and discussing crops with him as gravely as if the food for the family depended on the harvest. From this pleasant topic they went to others, and Nat had many new and helpful thoughts put into a mind that received them as gratefully as the thirsty earth had received the warm spring rain. All supper time he brooded over them, often fixing his eyes on Mr. Bhaer with an inquiring look, that seemed to say,—"I like that, do it again, sir." I don't know whether the man understood the child's mute language or not, but when the boys were all gathered together in Mrs. Bhaer's parlor for the Sunday evening talk, he chose a subject which might have been suggested by the walk in the garden.

As he looked about him Nat thought it seemed more like a great family than a school, for the lads were sitting in a wide half-circle round the fire, some on chairs, some on the rug, Daisy and Demi on the knees of uncle Fritz, and Rob snugly stowed away in the back of his mother's easy-chair, where he could nod unseen if the talk got beyond his depth. Every one looked quite comfortable, and listened attentively, for the long walk made rest agreeable, and as every boy there knew that he would be called upon for his views, he kept his wits awake to be ready with an answer.

"Once upon a time," began Mr. Bhaer in the dear old-fashioned way, "there was a great and wise gardener who had the largest garden ever seen. A wonderful and lovely place it was, and he watched over it with the greatest skill and care, and raised all manner of excellent and useful things. But weeds would grow even in this fine garden; often the ground was bad and the good seeds sown in it would not spring up. He had many under gardeners to help him. Some did their duty and earned the rich wages he gave them; but others neglected their parts and let them run to waste, which displeased him much. But he was very patient, and for thousands and thousands of years he worked and waited for his great harvest."

"He must have been pretty old," said Demi; who was looking straight into uncle Fritz's face, as if to catch every word.

"Hush, Demi, it's a fairy story," whispered Daisy.

"No, I think it's a arrygory," said Demi.

"What is a arrygory?" called out Tommy, who was of an inquiring turn.

"Tell him, Demi, if you can, and don't use words unless you are quite sure you know what they mean," said Mr. Bhaer.

"I do know, grandpa told me! A fable is a arrygory; it's a story that means something. My 'Story without an end' is one, because the child in it means a soul; don't it, aunty?" cried Demi, eager to prove himself right.

"That's it, dear; and uncle's story is an allegory, I am quite sure; so listen and see what it means," returned Mrs. Jo, who always took part in whatever was going on, and enjoyed it as much as any boy among them.

Demi composed himself, and Mr. Bhaer went on in his best English, for he had improved much in the last five years, and said the boys did it.

"This great gardener gave a dozen or so of little plots to one of his servants, and told him to do his best and see what he could raise. Now this servant was not rich, nor wise, nor very good, but he wanted to help because the gardener had been very kind to him in many ways. So he gladly took the little plots and fell to work. They were all sorts of shapes and sizes, and some were very good soil, some rather stony, and all of them needed much care, for in the rich soil the weeds grew fast, and in the poor soil there were many stones."

"What was growing in them besides the weeds and stones?" asked Nat; so interested, he forgot his shyness and spoke before them all.

"Flowers," said Mr. Bhaer, with a kind look. "Even the roughest, most neglected little bed had a bit of heart's-ease or a sprig of mignonette in it. One had roses, sweet peas, and daisies in it,"—here he pinched the plump cheek of the little girl leaning on his arm. "Another had all sorts of curious plants in it, bright pebbles, a vine that went climbing up like Jack's bean-stalk, and many good seeds just beginning to sprout; for, you see, *this* bed had been taken fine care of by a wise old man, who had worked in gardens of this sort all his life."

At this part of the "arrygory," Demi put his head on one side like an inquisitive bird, and fixed his bright eye on his uncle's face, as if he suspected something and was on the watch. But Mr. Bhaer looked perfectly innocent, and went on glancing from one young face to another, with a grave, wistful look, that said much to his wife, who knew how earnestly he desired to do his duty in these little garden plots.

"As I tell you, some of these beds were easy to cultivate,—that means to take care of, Daisy,—and others were very hard. There was one particularly sunshiny little bed, that might have been full of fruits and vegetables as well as flowers, only it wouldn't take any pains, and when the man sowed, well, we'll say melons in this bed, they came to nothing, because the little bed neglected them. The man was sorry, and kept on trying, though every time the crop failed, all the bed said, was, 'I forgot.' "

Here a general laugh broke out and every one looked at Tommy, who had pricked up his ears at the word "melons," and hung down his head at the sound of his favorite excuse.

"I knew he meant us!" cried Demi, clapping his hands. "You are the man, and we are the little gardens; aren't we, Uncle Fritz?"

"You have guessed it. Now each of you tell me what crop I shall try to sow in you this spring, so that next autumn I may get a good harvest out of my twelve, no, thirteen, plots," said Mr. Bhaer, nodding at Nat as he corrected himself.

"You can't sow corn and beans and peas in us. Unless you mean we are to eat a great many and get fat," said Stuffy, with a sudden brightening of his round, dull face as the pleasing idea occurred to him.

"He don't mean that kind of seeds. He means things to make us good; and the weeds are faults," cried Demi, who usually took the lead in these talks, because he was used to this sort of thing, and liked it very much.

"Yes, each of you think what you need most, and tell me, and I will help you to grow it; only, you must do your best, or you will turn out like Tommy's melons—all leaves and no fruit. I will begin with the oldest, and ask the mother what she will have in her plot, for we are all parts of the beautiful garden, and may have rich harvests for our Master if we love Him enough," said Father Bhaer.

"I shall devote the whole of *my* plot to the largest crop of patience I can get, for that is what I need most," said Mrs. Jo, so soberly that the lads fell to thinking in good earnest what they should say when their turns came, and some among them felt a twinge of remorse, that they had helped to use up Mother Bhaer's stock of patience so fast.

Franz wanted perseverance, Tommy steadiness, Ned went in for good temper, Daisy for industry, Demi for "as much wiseness as grandpa," and Nat timidly said he wanted so many things he would let Mr. Bhaer choose for him. The others chose much the same things, and patience, good temper, and generosity seemed the favorite crops. One boy wished to like to get up early, but did not know what name to give that sort of seed; and poor Stuffy sighed out—

"I wish I loved my lessons as much as I do my dinner, but I can't."

"We will plant self-denial, and hoe it and water it, and make it grow so well that next Christmas no one will get ill by eating too much dinner. If you exercise your mind, George, it will get hungry just as your body does, and you will love books almost as much as my philosopher here," said Mr. Bhaer; adding, as he stroked the hair off Demi's fine forehead, "You are greedy also, my son, and you like to stuff your little mind full of fairy tales and fancies, as well as George likes to fill his little stomach with cake and candy. Both are bad, and I want you to try something better. Arithmetic is not half so pleasant as 'Arabian Nights,' I know, but it is a very useful thing, and now is the time to learn it, else you will be ashamed and sorry by and by."

"But, 'Harry and Lucy,' and 'Frank,' are not fairy books, and they are all full of barometers, and bricks, and shoeing horses, and useful things, and I'm fond of them; ain't I, Daisy?" said Demi, anxious to defend himself.

"So they are; but I find you reading 'Roland and Maybird' a great deal oftener than 'Harry and Lucy,' and I think you are not half as fond of 'Frank' as you are of 'Sinbad.' Come, I shall make a little bargain with you both,—George shall eat but three times a day, and you shall read but one story book a week, and I will give you the new cricket-ground; only, you must promise to play in it," said Uncle Fritz in his persuasive way, for Stuffy hated to run about, and Demi was always reading in play hours.

"But we don't like cricket," said Demi.

"Perhaps not *now,* but you will when you know it. Besides, you do like to be generous, and the other boys want to play, and you can give them the new ground if you choose."

This was taking them both on the right side, and they agreed to the bargain, to the great satisfaction of the rest.

There was a little more talk about the gardens, and then they all sang together. The band delighted Nat, for Mrs. Bhaer played the piano, Franz the flute, Mr. Bhaer a bass viol, and he himself the violin. A very simple little concert, but all seemed to enjoy it, and old Asia, sitting in the corner, joined at times with the sweetest voice of any, for in this family, master and servant, old and young, black and white, shared in the Sunday song, which went up to the Father of them all. After this they each shook hands with Father Bhaer; Mother Bhaer kissed them every one from sixteen-year old Franz to little Rob, who kept the tip of her nose for his own particular kisses, and then they trooped up to bed.

The light of the shaded lamp that burned in the nursery shone softly on a picture hanging at the foot of Nat's bed. There were several others on the walls, but the boy thought there must be something peculiar about this one, for it had a graceful frame of moss and cones about it, and on a little bracket underneath stood a vase of wild flowers freshly gathered from the spring woods. It was the most beautiful picture of them all, and Nat lay looking at it dimly feeling what it meant, and wishing he knew all about it.

"That's my picture," said a little voice in the room. Nat popped up his head, and there was Demi in his night-gown pausing on his way back from Aunt Jo's chamber, whither he had gone to get a cot for a cut finger.

"What is he doing to the children?" asked Nat.

"That is Christ, the Good Man, and He is blessing the children. Don't you know about Him?" said Demi, wondering.

"Not much, but I'd like to. He looks so kind," answered Nat, whose chief knowledge of the Good Man consisted in hearing His name taken in vain.

"I know all about it, and I like it very much, because it is true," said Demi.

"Who told you?"

"My Grandpa, he knows *everything*, and tells the best stories in the world. I used to play with his big books, and make bridges, and railroads, and houses, when I was a little boy," began Demi.

"How old are you now?" asked Nat, respectfully.

"'Most ten."

"You know a lot of things, don't you?"

"Yes; you see my head is pretty big, and Grandpa says it will take a good deal to fill it, so I keep putting pieces of wisdom into it as fast as I can," returned Demi, in his quaint way.

Nat laughed, and then said soberly—

"Tell on, please."

And Demi gladly told on without pause or punctuation. "I found a very pretty book one day and wanted to play with it, but Grandpa said I mustn't, and showed me the pictures, and told me about them, and I liked the stories very much, all about Joseph and his bad brothers, and the frogs that came up out of the sea, and dear little Moses in the water, and ever so many more lovely ones, but I liked about the Good Man best of all, and Grandpa told it to me so many times that I learned it by heart, and he gave me this picture so I shouldn't forget, and it was put up here once when I was sick, and I left it for other sick boys to see."

"What makes Him bless the children?" asked Nat, who found something very attractive in the chief figure of the group.

"Because He loved them."

"Were they poor children?" asked Nat, wistfully.

"Yes, I think so; you see some haven't got hardly any clothes on, and the mothers don't look like rich ladies. He liked poor people, and was very good to them. He made them well, and helped them, and told rich people they must not be cross to them, and they loved Him dearly, dearly," cried Demi with enthusiasm.

"Was He rich?"

"Oh no! He was born in a barn, and was so poor He hadn't any house to live in when He grew up, and nothing to eat sometimes, but what people gave Him, and He went round preaching to everybody, and trying to make them good, till the bad men killed Him."

"What for?" and Nat sat up in his bed to look and listen, so interested was he in this man who cared for the poor so much.

"I'll tell you all about it; Aunt Jo won't mind;" and Demi settled himself on the opposite bed, glad to tell his favorite story to so good a listener.

Nursey peeped in to see if Nat was asleep, but when she saw what was going on, she slipped away again, and went to Mrs. Bhaer, saying with her kind face full of motherly emotion—

"Will the dear lady come and see a pretty sight? It's Nat listening with all his heart to Demi telling the story of the Christ-child, like a little white angel as he is."

Mrs. Bhaer had meant to go and talk with Nat a moment before he slept, for she had found that a serious word spoken at this time often did much good. But when she stole to the nursery door, and saw Nat eagerly drinking in the words of his little friend, while Demi told the sweet and solemn story as it had been taught him, speaking softly as he sat with his beautiful eyes fixed on the tender face above them, her own filled with tears, and she went silently away, thinking to herself—

"Demi is unconsciously helping the poor boy better than I can; I will not spoil it by a single word."

The murmur of the childish voice went on for a long time, as one innocent heart preached that great sermon to another, and no one hushed it. When it ceased at last, and Mrs. Bhaer went to take away the lamp, Demi was gone and Nat fast asleep, lying with his face toward the picture, as if he had already learned to love the Good Man who loved little children, and was a faithful friend to the poor. The boy's face was very placid, and as she looked at it she felt that if a single day of care and kindness had done so much, a year of patient cultivation would surely bring a grateful harvest from this neglected garden, which was already sown with the best of all seed by the little missionary in the night-gown.

# CHAPTER IV

## STEPPING-STONES

WHEN Nat went into school on Monday morning, he quaked inwardly, for now he thought he should have to display his ignorance before them all. But Mr. Bhaer gave him a seat in the deep window where he could turn his back on the others, and Franz heard him say his lessons there, so no one could hear his blunders or see how he blotted his copy-book.

Nat eagerly drinking in the words of his little friend.

He was truly grateful for this, and toiled away so diligently that Mr. Bhaer said, smiling, when he saw his hot face and inky fingers—

"Don't work so hard, my boy; you will tire yourself out, and there is time enough."

"But I *must* work hard, or I can't catch up with the others. They know heaps, and I don't know anything," said Nat, who had been reduced to a state of despair by hearing the boys recite their grammar, history, and geography with what he thought amazing ease and accuracy.

"You know a good many things which they don't," said Mr. Bhaer, sitting down beside him, while Franz led a class of small students through the intricacies of the multiplication table.

"Do I?" and Nat looked utterly incredulous.

"Yes; for one thing, you can keep your temper, and Jack, who is quick at numbers, cannot; that is an excellent lesson, and I think you have learned it well. Then, you can play the violin, and not one of the lads can, though they want to do it very much. But, best of all, Nat, you really care to learn something, and that is half the battle. It seems hard at first, and you will feel discouraged, but plod away, and things will get easier and easier as you go on."

Nat's face had brightened more and more as he listened, for, small as the list of his learning was, it cheered him immensely to feel that he had anything to fall back upon. "Yes, I can keep my temper—father's beating taught me that; and I can fiddle, though I don't know where the Bay of Biscay is," he thought, with a sense of comfort impossible to express. Then he said aloud, and so earnestly that Demi heard him—

"I *do* want to learn, and I *will* try. I never went to school, but I couldn't help it; and if the fellows don't laugh at me, I guess I'll get on first rate—you and the lady are so good to me."

"They shan't laugh at you; if they do, I'll—I'll—tell them not to," cried Demi, quite forgetting where he was.

The class stopped in the middle of 7 times 9, and every one looked up to see what was going on.

Thinking that a lesson in learning to help one another was better than arithmetic just then, Mr. Bhaer told them about Nat, making such an interesting and touching little story out of it that the good-hearted lads all promised to lend him a hand, and felt quite honored a be called upon to impart their stores of wisdom to the chap who fiddled so capitally. This appeal established the right feeling among them, and Nat had few hindrances to struggle against, for everyone was glad to give him a "boost" up the ladder of learning.

Till he was stronger, much study was not good for him, however, and Mrs. Jo found various amusements in the house for him while others were at their books. But his garden was his best medicine, and he worked away like a beaver, preparing his little farm, sowing his beans, watching eagerly to see them grow, and rejoicing over each green leaf and slender stalk that shot up and flourished in the warm spring weather. Never was a garden more faithfully hoed; Mr. Bhaer really feared that nothing would find time to grow, Nat kept up such a stirring of the soil; so he gave him easy jobs in the flower garden or among the strawberries, where he worked and hummed as busily as the bees booming all about him.

"This is the crop I like best," Mrs. Bhaer used to say, as she pinched the once thin cheeks now getting plump and ruddy, or stroked the bent shoulders that were slowly straightening up with healthful work, good food, and the absence of that heavy burden, poverty.

Demi was his little friend, Tommy his patron, and Daisy the comforter of all his woes; for, though the children were younger than he, his timid spirit found a pleasure in their innocent society, and rather shrunk from the rough sports of the elder lads. Mr. Laurence did not forget him, but sent clothes and books, music and kind messages, and now and then came out to see how his boy was getting on, or took him into town to a concert; on which occasions Nat felt himself translated into the seventh heaven of bliss, for he went to Mr. Laurence's great house, saw his pretty wife and little fairy of a daughter, had a good dinner, and was made so comfortable, that he talked and dreamed of it for days and nights afterward.

It takes so little to make a child happy, that it is a pity in a world full of sunshine and pleasant things, that there should be any wistful faces, empty hands, or lonely little hearts. Feeling this, the Bhaers gathered up all the crumbs they could find to feed their flock of hungry sparrows, for they were not rich, except in charity. Many of Mrs. Jo's friends who had nurseries sent her the toys of which their children so soon tired, and in mending these Nat found an employment that just suited him. He was very neat and skilful with those slender fingers of his, and passed many a rainy afternoon with his gum-bottle, paint-box, and knife, repairing furniture, animals, and games, while Daisy was dressmaker to the dilapidated dolls. As fast as the toys were mended, they were put carefully away in a certain drawer which was to furnish forth a Christmas tree for all the poor children of the neighborhood, that being the way the Plumfield boys celebrated the birthday of Him who loved the poor and blessed the little ones.

Demi was never tired of reading and explaining his favorite books, and many a pleasant hour did they spend in the old willow, revelling over "Robinson Crusoe," "Arabian Nights," "Edgeworth's Tales," and the other dear immortal stories that will delight children for centuries to come. This opened a new world to Nat, and his eagerness to see what came next in the story helped him on till he could read as well as anybody, and felt so rich and proud with his new accomplishment, that there was danger of his being as much of a bookworm as Demi.

Another helpful thing happened in a most unexpected and agreeable manner. Several of the boys were "in business," as they called it, for most of them were poor, and knowing that they would have their own way to make by and by, the Bhaers encouraged any efforts at independence. Tommy sold his eggs; Jack speculated in live stock; Franz helped in the teaching, and was paid for it; Ned had a taste for carpentry, and a turning-lathe was set up for him in which he turned all sorts of useful or pretty things, and sold them; while Demi constructed water-mills, whirligigs, and unknown machines of an intricate and useless nature, and disposed of them to the boys.

"Let him be a mechanic if he likes," said Mr. Bhaer. "Give a boy a trade, and he is independent. Work is wholesome, and whatever talent these lads possess, be it for poetry or ploughing, it shall be cultivated and made useful to them if possible."

So when Nat came running to him one day to ask with an excited face—

"Can I go and fiddle for some people who are to have a picnic in our woods? They will pay me, and I'd like to earn some money as the other boys do, and fiddling is the only way I know how to do it,"—

Mr. Bhaer answered readily—

"Go, and welcome. It is an easy and a pleasant way to work, and I am glad it is offered you."

Nat went, and did so well, that when he came home he had two dollars in his pocket, which he displayed with intense satisfaction, as he told how much he had enjoyed the afternoon, how kind the young people were, and how they had praised his dance-music, and promised to have him again.

"It is so much nicer than fiddling in the street, for then I got none of the money, and now I have it all, and a good time besides. I'm in business now as well as Tommy and Jack, and I like it ever so much," said Nat, proudly patting the old pocket-book, and feeling like a millionaire already.

He *was* in business truly, for pic-nics were plenty as summer opened, and Nat's skill was in great demand. He was always at liberty to go if lessons were not neglected, and if the pic-nics were respectable young people. For Mr. Bhaer explained to him that a good plain education is necessary for everyone, and that no amount of money should hire him to go where he might be tempted to do wrong. Nat quite agreed to this, and it was a pleasant sight to see the innocent hearted lad go driving away in the gay wagons that stopped at the gate for him, or to hear him come fiddling home tired but happy, with his well-earned money in one pocket, and some "goodies" from the feast for Daisy or little Ted, whom he never forgot.

"I'm going to save up till I get enough to buy a violin for myself, and then I can earn my own living, can't I?" he used to say, as he brought his dollars to Mr. Bhaer to keep.

"I hope so, Nat; but we must get you strong and hearty first, and put a little more knowledge into this musical head of yours. Then Mr. Laurie will find you a place somewhere, and in a few years we will all come to hear you play in public."

With much congenial work, encouragement and hope, Nat found life getting easier and happier every day, and made such progress in his music lessons, that his teacher forgave his slowness in some other things, knowing very well that where the heart is the mind works best. The only punishment the boy ever needed for neglect of more important lessons was to hang up the fiddle and the bow for a day. The fear of losing his bosom friend entirely made him go at his books with a will; and having proved that *he could* master the lessons, what was the use of saying "I can't?"

Daisy had a great love of music, and a great reverence for any one who could make it, and she was often found sitting on the stairs outside Nat's door while he was practicing. This pleased him very much, and he played his best for that one quiet little listener; for she never would come in, but preferred to sit sewing her gay patchwork, or tending one of her many dolls, with an expression of dreamy pleasure on her face that made Aunt Jo say, with tears in her eyes,—

"So like my Beth," and go softly by, lest even her familiar presence mar the child's sweet satisfaction.

Nat was very fond of Mrs. Bhaer; but found something even more attractive in the good professor, who took fatherly care of the shy feeble boy, who had barely escaped with his life from the rough sea on which his little boat had been tossing rudderless for twelve years. Some good angel must have watched over him, for, though his body had suffered, his soul seemed to have taken little harm, and came ashore as innocent as a shipwrecked baby. Perhaps his love of music kept it sweet in spite of the discord all about him; Mr. Laurie said so, and he ought to know. However that might be, Father Bhaer took real pleasure in fostering poor Nat's virtues, and in curing his faults, finding his new pupil as docile and affectionate as a girl. He often called Nat his "daughter" when speaking of him to Mrs. Joe, and she used to laugh at his fancy, for Madame liked manly boys, and thought Nat amiable but weak, though you never would have guessed it, for she petted him as she did Daisy, and he thought her a very delightful woman.

One fault of Nat's gave the Bhaers much anxiety, although they saw how it had been strengthened by fear and ignorance. I regret to say that Nat sometimes told lies. Not very black ones, seldom getting deeper than gray, and often the mildest of white fibs; but that did not matter, a lie is a lie, and though we all tell many polite untruths in this queer world of ours, it is not right, and everybody knows it.

"You cannot be too careful; watch your tongue, and eyes, and hands, for it is easy to tell, and look, and act untruth," said Mr. Bhaer, in one of the talks he had with Nat about his chief temptation.

"I know it, and I don't mean to, but it's so much easier to get along if you ain't very fussy about being exactly true. I used to tell 'em because I was afraid of father and Nicolo, and now I do sometimes because the boys laugh at me. I know it's bad, but I forget," and Nat looked much depressed by his sins.

"When I was a little lad I used to tell lies! Ach! What fibs they were, and my old grandmother cured me of it—how, do you think? My parents had talked, and cried, and punished, but still did I forget as you. Then said the dear old grandmother, 'I shall help you to remember, and put a check on this unruly part,' with that she drew out my tongue and snipped the end with her scissors till the blood ran. That was terrible, you may believe, but it did me much good, because it was sore for days, and every word I said came so slowly that I had time to think. After that I was more careful, and got on better, for I feared the big scissors. Yet the dear grandmother was most kind to me in all things, and when she lay dying far away in Nuremburg, she prayed that little Fritz might love God and tell the truth."

"I never had any grandmothers, but if you think it will cure me, I'll let you snip my tongue," said Nat heroically, for he dreaded pain, yet did wish to stop fibbing.

Mr. Bhaer smiled, but shook his head.

"I have a better way than that, I tried it once before and it worked well. See now, when you tell a lie I will not punish you, but you shall punish me."

"How?" asked Nat, startled at the idea.

"You shall ferule me in the good old-fashioned way; I seldom do it myself, but it may make you remember better to give me pain than to feel it yourself."

"Strike you? Oh, I couldn't!" cried Nat.

"Then mind that tripping tongue of thine. I have no wish to be hurt, but I would gladly bear much pain to cure this fault."

This suggestion made such an impression on Nat, that for a long time he set a watch upon his lips, and was desperately accurate, for Mr. Bhaer judged rightly, that love of him would be more powerful with Nat than fear for himself. But alas! One sad day Nat was off his guard, and when peppery Emil threatened to thrash him, if it was he who had run over his garden and broken down his best hills of corn, Nat declared he didn't, and then was ashamed to own up that he did do it, when Jack was chasing him the night before.

He thought no one would find it out, but Tommy happened to see him, and when Emil spoke of it a day or two later, Tommy gave his evidence, and Mr. Bhaer heard it. School was over, and they were all standing about in the hall, and Mr. Bhaer had just sat down on the straw settee, to enjoy his frolic with Teddy; but when he heard Tommy, and saw Nat turn scarlet, and look at him with a frightened face, he put the little boy down, saying, "Go to thy mother, bübchen, I will come soon," and taking Nat by the hand led him into the school, and shut the door.

The boys looked at one another in silence for a minute, then Tommy slipped out and peeping in at the half-closed blinds, beheld a sight that quite bewildered him. Mr. Bhaer had just taken down the long rule that hung over his desk, so seldom used that it was covered with dust.

"My eye! he's going to come down heavy on Nat this time. Wish I hadn't told," thought good-natured Tommy, for to be feruled was the deepest disgrace at this school.

"You remember what I told you last time?" said Mr. Bhaer, sorrowfully, not angrily.

"Yes; but please don't make me, I can't bear it," cried Nat backing up against the door with both hands behind him, and a face full of distress.

"Why don't he up and take it like a man? I would," thought Tommy, though his heart beat fast at the sight.

"I shall keep my word, and you must remember to tell the truth. Obey me, Nat, take this and give me six good strokes."

Tommy was so staggered by this last speech that he nearly tumbled down the bank, but saved himself, and hung on to the window ledge, staring in with eyes as round as the stuffed owl's on the chimney-piece.

Nat took the rule, for when Mr. Bhaer spoke in that tone every one obeyed him, and, looking as scared and guilty as if about to stab his master, he gave two feeble blows on the broad hand held out to him. Then he stopped and looked up half-blind with tears, but Mr. Bhaer said steadily,—

"Go on, and strike harder."

As if seeing that it must be done, and eager to have the hard task soon over, Nat drew his sleeve across his eyes and gave two more quick hard strokes that reddened the hand, yet hurt the giver more.

"Isn't that enough?" he asked in a breathless sort of tone.

"Two more," was all the answer, and he gave them, hardly seeing where they fell, then threw the rule all across the room, and hugging the kind hand in both his own, laid his face down on it sobbing out in a passion of love, and shame, and penitence—

"I will remember! Oh! I will!"

Then Mr. Bhaer put an arm about him, and said in a tone as compassionate as it had just now been firm—

"I think you will. Ask the dear God to help you, and try to spare us both another scene like this."

Tommy saw no more, for he crept back to the hall, looking so excited and sober that the boys crowded round him to ask what was being done to Nat.

In a most impressive whisper Tommy told them, and they looked as if the sky was about to fall, for this reversing the order of things almost took their breath away.

"He made me do the same thing once," said Emil, as if confessing a crime of the deepest dye.

"And you hit him? Dear old Father Bhaer? By thunder, I'd just like to see you do it now!" said Ned, collaring Emil in a fit of righteous wrath.

"It was ever so long ago. I'd rather have my head cut off than do it now," and Emil mildly laid Ned on his back instead of cuffing him, as he would have felt it his duty to do on any less solemn occasion.

"How could you?" said Demi, appalled at the idea.

"I was hopping mad at the time, and thought I shouldn't mind a bit, rather like it perhaps. But when I'd hit Uncle one good crack, everything he had ever done for me came into my head all at once somehow, and I couldn't go on. No, sir! If he'd laid me down and walked on me, I wouldn't have minded, I felt so mean;" and Emil gave himself a good thump in the chest to express his sense of remorse for the past.

"Nat's crying like anything, and feels no end sorry, so don't let's say a word about it; will we?" said tender-hearted Tommy.

"Of course we won't, but it's awful to tell lies," and Demi looked as if he found the awfulness much increased when the punishment fell not upon the sinner, but his best Uncle Fritz.

"Suppose we all clear out, so Nat can cut up-stairs if he wants to," proposed Franz, and led the way to the barn, their refuge in troublous times.

Nat did not come to dinner, but Mrs. Jo took some up to him, and said a tender word, which did him good, though he could not look at her. By and by the lads playing outside heard the violin, and said among themselves: "He's all right now." He was all right, but felt shy about going down, till, opening his door to slip away into the woods, he found Daisy sitting on the stairs with neither work nor doll, only her little handkerchief in her hand, as if she had been mourning for her captive friend.

"I'm going to walk; want to come?" asked Nat, trying to look as if nothing was the matter, yet feeling very grateful for her silent sympathy, because he fancied everyone must look upon him as a wretch.

"Oh yes!" and Daisy ran for her hat, proud to be chosen as a companion by one of the big boys.

The others saw them go, but no one followed, for boys have a great deal more delicacy than they get credit for, and the lads instinctively felt that, when in disgrace, gentle little Daisy was their most congenial friend.

The walk did Nat good, and he came home quieter than usual, but looking cheerful again, and hung all over with daisy-chains, made by his little playmate while he lay on the grass and told her stories.

No one said a word about the scene of the morning, but its effect was all the more lasting for that reason, perhaps. Nat tried his very best, and found much help, not only from the earnest little prayers he prayed to his Friend in heaven, but also in the patient care of the earthly friend, whose kind hand he never touched without remembering that it had willingly borne pain for his sake.

# CHAPTER V

## PATTY PANS

"WHAT'S the matter, Daisy?"

"The boys won't let me play with them."

"Why not?"

"They say girls can't play foot-ball."

"They can, for I've done it!" and Mrs. Bhaer laughed at the remem-berance of certain youthful frolics.

"I know I can play; Demi and I used to, and have nice times, but he won't let me now because the other boys laugh at him," and Daisy looked deeply grieved at her brother's hardness of heart.

"On the whole, I think he is right, deary. It's all very well when you two are alone, but it is too rough a game for you with a dozen boys; so I'd find some nice little play for myself."

"I'm tired of playing alone!" and Daisy's tone was very mournful.

"I'll play with you by and by, but just now I must fly about and get things ready for a trip into town. You shall go with me and see mamma, and if you like you can stay with her."

"I should like to go and see her and baby Josy, but I'd rather come back, please. Demi would miss me, and I love to be here, Aunty."

"You can't get on without your Demi, can you?" and Aunt Jo looked as if she quite understood the love of the little girl for her only brother.

" 'Course I can't; we're twins, and so we love each other more than other people," answered Daisy, with a brightening face, for she considered being a twin one of the highest honors she could ever receive.

"Now, what will you do with your little self while I fly round?" asked

"I will remember! Oh! I will!"

Mrs. Bhaer, who was whisking piles of linen into a wardrobe with great rapidity.

"I don't know, I'm tired of dolls and things; I wish you'd make up a new play for me, Aunty Jo," said Daisy, swinging listlessly on the door.

"I shall have to think of a bran new one, and it will take me some time; so suppose you go down and see what Asia has got for your lunch," suggested Mrs. Bhaer, thinking that would be a good way in which to dispose of the little hindrance for a time.

"Yes, I think I'd like that, if she isn't cross," and Daisy slowly departed to the kitchen, where Asia, the black cook, reigned undisturbed.

In five minutes Daisy was back again, with a wide-awake face, a bit of dough in her hand and a dab of flour on her little nose.

"O Aunty! Please could I go and make gingersnaps and things? Asia isn't cross, and she says I may, and it would be such fun, please do," cried Daisy, all in one breath.

"Just the thing, go and welcome, make what you like, and stay as long as you please," answered Mrs. Bhaer, much relieved, for sometimes the one little girl was harder to amuse than the dozen boys.

Daisy ran off, and while she worked, Aunt Jo racked her brain for a new play. All of a sudden she seemed to have an idea for she smiled to herself, slammed the doors of the wardrobe, and walked briskly away, saying, "I'll do it, if it's a possible thing!"

What it was no one found out that day, but Aunt Jo's eyes twinkled so when she told Daisy she had thought of a new play, and was going to buy it, that Daisy was much excited and asked questions all the way into town, without getting answers that told her anything. She was left at home to play with the new baby, and delight her mother's eyes, while Aunt Jo went off shopping. When she came back with all sorts of queer parcels in corners of the carry-all, Daisy was so full of curiosity, that she wanted to go back to Plumfield at once. But her aunt would not be hurried, and made a long call in mamma's room, sitting on the floor with baby in her lap, making Mrs. Brooke laugh at the pranks of the boys, and all sorts of droll nonsense.

How her aunt told the secret Daisy could not imagine, but her mother evidently knew it, for she said, as she tied on the little bonnet and kissed the rosy little face inside, "Be a good child, my Daisy, and learn the nice new play Aunty has got for you. It's a most useful and interesting one, and it is very kind of her to play it with you, because she does not like it very well herself."

This last speech made the two ladies laugh heartily, and increased Daisy's bewilderment. As they drove away something rattled in the back of the carriage.

"What's that?" asked Daisy, pricking up her ears.

"The new play," answered Mrs. Jo, solemnly.

"What is it made of?" cried Daisy.

"Iron, tin, wood, brass, sugar, salt, coal, and a hundred other things."

"How strange! What color is it?"

"All sorts of colors."

"Is it large?"

"Part of it is, and a part isn't."

"Did I ever see one?"

"Ever so many, but never one so nice as this."

"Oh! What can it be? I can't wait. When *shall* I see it?" and Daisy bounced up and down with impatience.

"Tomorrow morning, after lessons."

"Is it for the boys too?"

"No, all for you and Bess. The boys will like to see it, and want to play one part of it. But you can do as you like about letting them."

"I'll let Demi, if he wants to."

"No fear that they won't all want to, especially Stuffy," and Mrs. Bhaer's eyes twinkled more than ever, as she patted a queer knobby bundle in her lap.

"Let me feel just once," prayed Daisy.

"Not a feel; you'd guess in a minute and spoil the fun."

Daisy groaned and then smiled all over her face, for through a little hole in the paper she caught a glimpse of something bright.

"How *can* I wait so long? Couldn't I see it today?"

"Oh dear, no! it has got to be arranged, and ever so many parts fixed in their places. I promised Uncle Teddy that you shouldn't see it till it was all in apple-pie order."

"If Uncle knows about it then it *must* be splendid!" cried Daisy, clapping her hands; for this kind, rich, jolly uncle of hers was as good as a fairy god-mother to the children, and was always planning merry surprises, pretty gifts, and droll amusements for them.

"Yes; Teddy went and bought it with me, and we had such fun in the shop choosing the different parts. He would have everything fine and large, and my little plan got regularly splendid when he took hold. You must give him your very best kiss when he comes, for he is the kindest uncle that ever went and bought a charming little coo— Bless me! I nearly told you what it was!" and Mrs. Bhaer cut that most interesting word short off in the middle, and began to look over her bills as if afraid she would let the cat out of the bag if she talked anymore. Daisy folded her hands with an air of resignation, and sat quite still trying to think what play had a "coo" in it.

When they got home she eyed every bundle that was taken out, and one large heavy one, which Franz took straight up-stairs and hid in the nursery, filled her with amazement and curiosity. Something very mysterious went on up there that afternoon, for Franz was hammering, and Asia trotting up and down, and Aunt Jo flying around like a will-o'-the-wisp, with all sorts of things under her apron, while little Ted, who was the only child admitted, because he couldn't talk plain, babbled and laughed, and tried to tell what the "sumpin pitty" was.

All this made Daisy half wild, and her excitement spread among the boys, who quite overwhelmed Mother Bhaer with offers of assistance, which she declined by quoting their own words to Daisy—

"Girls can't play with boys. This is for Daisy, and Bess and me so we don't want you." Whereupon the young gentlemen meekly retired, and invited Daisy to a game of marbles, horse, foot-ball, anything she liked, with a sudden warmth and politeness which astonished her innocent little soul.

Thanks to these attentions, she got through the afternoon went early to bed, and next morning did her lessons with an energy which made Uncle Fritz wish that a new game could be invented every day. Quite a thrill pervaded the school-room when Daisy was dismissed at eleven o'clock, for every one knew that *now* she was going to have the new and mysterious play.

Many eyes followed her as she ran away, and Demi's mind was so distracted by this event that when Franz asked him where the desert of Sahara was, he mournfully replied, "In the nursery," and the whole school laughed at him.

"Aunt Jo, I've done all my lessons, and I can't wait one single minute more!" cried Daisy, flying into Mrs. Bhaer's room.

"It's all ready, come on;" and tucking Ted under one arm, and her work-basket under the other, Aunt Jo promptly led the way up-stairs.

"I don't see any thing," said Daisy, staring about her as she got inside the nursery door.

"Do you hear anything?" asked Aunt Jo, catching Ted back by his little frock as he was making straight for one side of the room.

Daisy did hear an odd crackling, and then a purry little sound as of a kettle singing. These noises came from behind a curtain drawn before a deep bay window. Daisy snatched it back, gave one joyful "Oh!" and then stood gazing with delight at—what do you think?

A wide seat ran round the three sides of the window; on one side hung and stood all sorts of little pots and pans, gridirons, and skillets; on the other side a small dinner and tea set, and on the middle part a cooking-stove. Not a tin one, that was of no use, but a real iron stove, big enough to cook for a large family of very hungry dolls. But the best of it was that a real fire burned in it, real steam came out of the nose of the little tea-kettle, and the lid of the little boiler actually danced a jig, the water inside bubbled so hard. A pane of glass had been taken out and replaced by a sheet of tin, with a hole for the small funnel, and real smoke went sailing away outside so naturally, that it did one's heart good to see it. The box of wood with a hod of charcoal stood near by; just above hung dustpan, brush and broom; a little market basket was on the low table at which Daisy used to play, and over the back of her little chair hung a white apron with a bib, and a droll mob cap. The sun shone in as if he enjoyed the fun, the little stove roared beautifully, the kettle steamed, the new tins sparkled on the walls, the pretty china stood in tempting rows, and it was altogether as cheery and complete a kitchen as any child could desire.

Daisy stood quite still after the first glad "Oh!" but her eyes went quickly from one charming object to an other, brightening as they looked, till they came to Aunt Jo's merry face; there they stopped as the happy little girl hugged her, saying gratefully—

"O Aunty, it's a splendid new play! Can I really cook at the dear stove, and have parties and mess, and sweep, and make fires that truly burn? I like it *so* much! What made you think of it?"

"Your liking to make gingersnaps with Asia made me think of it," said Mrs. Bhaer, holding Daisy, who frisked as if she would fly. "I knew Asia wouldn't let you mess in her kitchen very often, and it wouldn't be safe at this fire up here, so I thought I'd see if I could find a little stove for you, and teach you to cook; that would be fun, and useful too. So I travelled round among the toy shops, but everything large cost too much and I was thinking I should have to give it up, when I met Uncle Teddy. As soon as he knew what I was about, he said he wanted to help, and insisted on buying the biggest toy stove we could find. I scolded, but he only laughed, and teased me about my cooking when we were young, and said I must teach Bess as well as you, and went on buying all sorts of nice little things for my 'cooking class' as he called it."

"I'm so glad you met him!" said Daisy, as Mrs. Jo stopped to laugh at the memory of the funny time she had with Uncle Teddy.

"You must study hard and learn to make all kinds of things, for he says he shall come out to tea very often, and expects something uncommonly nice."

"It's the sweetest, dearest kitchen in the world, and I'd rather study with it than do any thing else. Can't I learn pies, and cake, and maccaroni, and everything?" cried Daisy, dancing round the room with a new saucepan in one hand and the tiny poker in the other.

"All in good time. This is to be a useful play, I am to help you, and you are to be my cook, so I shall tell you what to do, and show you how. Then we shall have things fit to eat, and you will be really learning how to cook on a small scale. I'll call you Sally, and say you are a new girl just come," added Mrs. Jo, settling down to work, while Teddy sat on the floor sucking his thumb, and staring at the stove as if it was a live thing, whose appearance deeply interested him.

"That will be *so* lovely! What shall I do first?" asked Sally, with such a happy face and willing air that Aunt Jo wished all new cooks were half as pretty and pleasant.

"First of all, put on this clean cap and apron. I am rather old-fashioned, and I like my cook to be very tidy."

Sally tucked her curly hair into the round cap, and put on the apron without a murmur, though usually she rebelled against bibs.

"Now, you can put things in order, and wash up the new china. The old set needs washing also, for my last girl was apt to leave it in a sad state after a party."

Aunt Jo spoke quite soberly, but Sally laughed, for she knew who the untidy girl was who had left the cups sticky. Then she turned up her cuffs, and with a sigh of satisfaction began to stir about her kitchen, having little raptures now and then over the "sweet rolling-pin," the "darling dish-tub," or the "cunning pepperpot."

"Now, Sally, take your basket and go to market; here is the list of things I want for dinner," said Mrs. Jo, giving her a bit of paper when the dishes were all in order.

"Where is the market?" asked Daisy, thinking that the new play got more and more interesting every minute.

"Asia is the market."

Away went Sally, causing another stir in the school room as she passed the door in her new costume, and whispered to Demi, with a face full of delight—"It's a perfectly splendid play!"

Old Asia enjoyed the joke as much as Daisy, and laughed jollily as the little girl came flying into the room with her cap all on one side, the lids of her basket rattling like castanets, and looking like a very crazy little cook.

"Mrs. Aunt Jo wants these things, and I must have them right away," said Daisy, importantly.

"Let's see, honey; here's two pounds of steak, potatoes, squash, apples, bread and butter. The meat ain't come yet; when it does I'll send it up. The other things are all handy."

Then Asia packed one potato, one apple, a bit of squash, a little pat of butter, and a roll, into the basket, telling Sally to be on the watch for the butcher's boy, because he sometimes played tricks.

"Who is he?" and Daisy hoped it would be Demi.

"You'll see," was all Asia would say; and Sally went off in great spirits, singing a verse from dear Mary Howitt's sweet story in rhyme,—

> *"Away went little Mabel,*
> *With the wheaten cake so fine,*
> *The new made pot of butter,*
> *And the little flask of wine."*

"Put every thing but the apple into the store-closet for the present," said Mrs. Jo, when the cook got home.

There was a cupboard under the middle shelf, and on opening the door fresh delights appeared. One half was evidently the cellar, for wood, coal, and kindlings were piled there. The other half was full of little jars, boxes, and all sorts of droll contrivances for holding small quantities of flour, meal, sugar, salt, and other household stores. A pot of jam was there, a little tin box of gingerbread, a cologne bottle full of currant wine, and a tiny canister of tea. But the crowning charm was two doll's pans of new milk, with cream actually rising on it, and a wee skimmer all ready to skim it with. Daisy clasped her hands at this delicious spectacle, and wanted to skim immediately. But Aunt Jo said—

"Not yet; you will want the cream to eat on your apple-pie at dinner, and must not disturb it till then."

"Am I going to have pie?" cried Daisy, hardly believing that such bliss could be in store for her.

"Yes; if your oven does well we will have two pies—one apple and one strawberry," said Mrs. Jo, who was nearly as much interested in the new play as Daisy herself.

"Oh, what next?" asked Sally, all impatience to begin.

"Shut the lower draught of the stove, so that the oven may heat. Then wash your hands and get out the flour, sugar, salt, butter, and cinnamon. See if the pieboard is clean, and pare your apple ready to put in."

Daisy got things together with as little noise and spilling as could be expected, from so young a cook.

"I really don't know how to measure for such tiny pies; I must guess at it, and if these don't succeed, we must try again," said Mrs. Jo, looking rather perplexed, and very much amused with the small concern before her. "Take that little pan full of flour, put in a pinch of salt, and then rub in as much butter as will go on that plate. Always remember to put your dry things together first, and then the wet. It mixes better so."

"I know how; I saw Asia do it. Don't I butter the pie plates too? She did, the first thing," said Daisy, whisking the flour about at a great rate.

"Quite right! I do believe you have a gift for cooking, you take to it so cleverly," said Aunt Jo, approvingly. "Now a dash of cold water, just enough to wet it; then scatter some flour on the board, work in a little, and roll the paste out; yes, that's the way. Now put dabs of butter all over it, and roll it out again. We won't have our pastry very rich, or the dolls will get dyspeptic."

Daisy laughed at the idea, and scattered the dabs with a liberal hand. Then she rolled and rolled with her delightful little pin, and having got her paste ready proceeded to cover the plates with it. Next the apple was sliced in, sugar and cinnamon lavishly sprinkled over it, and then the top crust put on with breathless care.

"I always wanted to cut them round, and Asia never would let me. How nice it is to do it all my ownty donty self," said Daisy, as the little knife went clipping round the doll's plate poised on her hand.

All cooks, even the best, meet with mishaps sometimes, and Sally's first one occurred then, for the knife went so fast that the plate slipped, turned a somersault in the air, and landed the dear little pie upside down on the floor. Sally screamed, Mrs. Jo laughed, Teddy scrambled to get it, and for a moment confusion reigned in the new kitchen.

"It didn't spill or break, because I pinched the edges together so hard; it isn't hurt a bit, so I'll prick holes in it, and then it will be ready," said Sally, picking up the capsized treasure and putting it into shape with a child-like disregard of the dust it had gathered in its fall.

"My new cook has a good temper I see, and that is such a comfort," said Mrs. Jo. "Now open the jar of strawberry jam, fill the uncovered pie, and put some strips of paste over the top as Asia does."

"I'll make a D in the middle, and have zigzags all round, that will be so interesting when I come to eat it," said Sally, loading her pie with quirls and flourishes that would have driven a real pastry cook wild. "*Now* I put them in!" she exclaimed; when the last grimy knob had been carefully planted in the red field of jam, and with an air of triumph she shut them into the little oven.

"Clear up your things; a good cook never lets her utensils collect. Then pare your squash and potatoes."

"There is only one potato," giggled Sally.

"Cut it in four pieces, so it will go into the little kettle, and put the bits into cold water till it is time to cook them."

"Do I soak the squash too?"

"No, indeed! Just pare it and cut it up, and put it into the steamer over the pot. It is drier so, though it takes longer to cook."

Here a scratching at the door caused Sally to run and open it, when Kit appeared with a covered basket in his mouth.

"Here's the butcher's boy!" cried Daisy, much tickled at the idea, as she relieved him of his load, whereat he licked his lips and began to beg, evidently thinking that it was his own dinner, for he often carried it to his master in that way. Being undeceived, he departed in great wrath and barked all the way downstairs, to ease his wounded feelings.

In the basket were two bits of steak (doll's pounds), a baked pear, a small cake, and paper with them on which Asia had scrawled, "For Missy's lunch, if her cookin' don't turn out well."

"I don't want any of her old pears and things; my cooking *will* turn out well, and I'll have a splendid dinner; see if I don't!" cried Daisy, indignantly.

"We may like them if company should come. It is always well to have something in the store-room," said Aunt Jo, who had been taught this valuable fact by a series of domestic panics.

"Me is hundry," announced Teddy, who began to think what with so much cooking going on it was about time for somebody to eat something. His mother gave him her work-basket to rummage, hoping to keep him quiet till dinner was ready, and returned to her housekeeping.

"Put on your vegetables, set the table, and then have some coals kindling ready for the steak."

What a thing it was to see the potatoes bobbing about in the little pot; to peep at the squash getting soft so fast in the tiny steamer; to whisk open the oven door every five minutes to see how the pies got on, and at last when the coals were red and glowing, to put two real steaks on a finger-long gridiron and proudly turn them with a fork. The potatoes were done first, and no wonder, for they had boiled frantically all the while. They were pounded up with a little pestle, had much butter and no salt put in (cook forgot it in the excitement of the moment), then it was made into a mound in a gay red dish, smoothed over with a knife dipped in milk, and put in the oven to brown.

So absorbed in these last performances had Sally been, that she forgot her pastry till she opened the door to put in the potato, then a wail arose, for, alas! Alas! The little pies were burnt black!

"Oh, my pies! My darling pies! They are all spoilt!" cried poor Sally, wringing her dirty little hands as she surveyed the ruin of her work. The tart was especially pathetic, for the quirls and zigzags stuck up in all directions from the blackened jelly, like the walls and chimney of a house after a fire.

"Dear, dear, I forgot to remind you to take them out; it's just my luck," said Aunt Jo, remorsefully. "Don't cry, darling, it was my fault; we'll try again after dinner," she added, as a great tear dropped from Sally's eyes and sizzled on the hot ruins of the tart.

More would have followed, if the steak had not blazed up just then, and so occupied the attention of cook, that she quickly forgot the lost pastry.

"Put the meat-dish and your own plates down to warm, while you mash the squash with butter, salt, and a little pepper on the top," said Mrs. Jo, devoutly hoping that the dinner would meet with no further disasters.

The "cunning pepper-pot" soothed Sally's feelings, and she dished up her squash in fine style. The dinner was safely put upon the table; the six dolls were seated three on a side; Teddy took the bottom, and Sally the top. When all were settled, it was a most imposing spectacle, for one

Kit appeared with a covered basket in his mouth.

doll was in full ball costume, another in her night-gown; Jerry, the worsted boy, wore his red winter suit, while Annabella, the noseless darling, was airily attired in nothing but her own kid skin. Teddy, as father of the family, behaved with great propriety, for he smilingly devoured every thing offered him, and did not find a single fault. Daisy beamed upon her company like the weary, warm, but hospitable hostess, so often to be seen at larger tables than this, and did the honors with an air of innocent satisfaction, which we do *not* often see elsewhere.

The steak was so tough, that the little carving-knife would not cut it; the potato did not go round, and the squash was very lumpy; but the guests appeared politely unconscious of these trifles; and the master and mistress of the house cleared the table with appetites that any one might envy them. The joy of skimming a jug-full of cream mitigated the anguish felt for the loss of the pies, and Asia's despised cake proved a treasure in the way of dessert.

"That is the nicest lunch I ever had; can't I do it every day?" asked Daisy as she scraped up and ate the leavings all round.

"You can cook things every day after lessons, but I prefer that you should eat your dishes at your regular meals, and only have a bit of gingerbread for lunch. Today, being the first time, I don't mind, but we must keep our rules. This afternoon you can make some thing for tea if you like," said Mrs. Jo, who had enjoyed the dinner-party very much, though no one had invited her to partake.

"Do let me make flapjacks for Demi, he loves them so, and it's such fun to turn them and put sugar in between," cried Daisy, tenderly wiping a yellow stain off Annabella's broken nose, for Bella had refused to eat squash when it was pressed upon her as good for "lumatism," a complaint which it is no wonder she suffered from, considering the lightness of her attire.

"But if you give Demi goodies, all the others will expect some also, and then you will have your hands full."

"Couldn't I have Demi come up to tea alone just this one time, and after that I could cook things for the others if they were good," proposed Daisy, with a sudden inspiration.

"That is a capital idea, Posy! We will make your little messes rewards for the good boys, and I don't know one among them who would not like something nice to eat more than almost anything else. If little men are like big ones, good cooking will touch their hearts and soothe their tempers delightfully," added Aunt Jo, with a merry nod toward the door, where stood Papa Bhaer, surveying the scene with a face full of amusement.

"That last hit was for me, sharp woman. I accept it, for it is true; but if I had married thee for thy cooking, heart's dearest, I should have fared badly all these years," answered the professor, laughing, as he tossed Teddy, who became quite apoplectic in his endeavors to describe the feast he had just enjoyed.

Daisy proudly showed her kitchen, and rashly promised Uncle Fritz as many flapjacks as he could eat. She was just telling about the new rewards when the boys, headed by Demi, burst into the room snuffing the air like a pack of hungry hounds, for school was out, dinner was not ready, and the fragrance of Daisy's steak led them straight to the spot.

A prouder little damsel was never seen than Sally as she displayed her treasures and told the lads what was in store for them. Several rather scoffed at the idea of her cooking anything fit to eat, but Stuffy's heart was won at once, Nat and Demi had firm faith in her skill, and the others said they would wait and see. All admired the kitchen, however, and examined the stove with deep interest. Demi offered to buy the boiler on the spot, to be used in a steam-engine which he was constructing; and Ned declared that the best and biggest saucepan was just the thing to melt his lead in when he ran bullets, hatchets, and such trifles.

Daisy looked so alarmed at these proposals, that Mrs. Jo then and there made and proclaimed a law that no boy should touch, use, or even approach the sacred stove without a special permit from the owner thereof. This increased its value immensely in the eyes of the gentlemen, especially as any infringement of the law would be punished by the forfeiture of all right to partake of the delicacies promised to the virtuous.

At this point the bell rang, and the entire population went down to dinner, which meal was enlivened by each of the boy's giving Daisy a list of things he would like to have cooked for him as fast as he earned them. Daisy, whose faith in her stove was unlimited, promised everything, if Aunt Jo would tell her how to make them. This suggestion rather alarmed Mrs. Jo, for some of the dishes were quite beyond her skill— wedding-cake for instance, bull's-eye candy, and cabbage soup with herrings and cherries in it, which Mr. Bhaer proposed as his favorite, and immediately reduced his wife to despair, for German cookery was beyond her.

Daisy wanted to begin again the minute dinner was done, but she was only allowed to clear up, fill the kettle ready for tea, and wash out her apron, which looked as if she had cooked a Christmas feast. She was then sent out to play till five o'clock, for Uncle Fritz said that too much study, even at cooking stoves, was bad for little minds and bodies, and Aunt Jo knew by long experience how soon new toys lose their charm if they are not prudently used.

Everyone was very kind to Daisy that afternoon. Tommy promised her the first fruits of his garden, though the only visible crop just then was pigweed; Nat offered to supply her with wood, free of charge; Stuffy quite worshipped her; Ned immediately fell to work on a little refrigerator for her kitchen; and Demi, with a punctuality beautiful to see in one so young, escorted her to the nursery just as the clock struck five. It was not time for the party to begin, but he begged so hard to come in and help that he was allowed privileges few visitors enjoy, for he kindled the fire, ran errands, and watched the progress of his supper with intense interest. Mrs. Jo directed the affair as she came and went, being very busy putting up clean curtains all over the house.

"Ask Asia for a cup of sour cream, then your cakes will be light without much soda, which I don't like," was the first order.

Demi tore down-stairs, and returned with the cream, also a puckered-up face, for he had tasted it on his way, and found it so sour that he predicted the cakes would be uneatable. Mrs. Jo took this occasion to deliver a short lecture from the step-ladder on the chemical properties of soda, to which Daisy did not listen, but Demi did, and understood it, as he proved by the brief but comprehensive reply—

"Yes, I see, soda turns sour things sweet, and the fizzling up makes them light. Let's see you do it, Daisy."

"Fill that bowl nearly full of flour and add a little salt to it," continued Mrs. Jo.

"Oh dear, everything has to have salt in it, seems to me," said Sally, who was tired of opening the pill-box in which it was kept.

"Salt is like good-humor, and nearly everything is better for a pinch of it, Posy," and Uncle Fritz stopped as he passed, hammer in hand, to drive up two or three nails for Sally's little pans to hang on.

"You are not invited to tea, but I'll give you some cakes, and I won't be cross," said Daisy, putting up her floury little face to thank him with a kiss.

"Fritz, you must not interrupt my cooking class, or I'll come in and moralize when you are teaching Latin. How would you like that?" said Mrs. Jo, throwing a great chintz curtain down on his head.

"Very much, try it and see," and the amiable Father Bhaer went singing and tapping about the house like a mammoth woodpecker.

"Put the soda into the cream, and when it 'fizzles,' as Demi says, stir it into the flour, and beat it up as hard as ever you can. Have your griddle hot, butter it well, and then fry away till I come back," and Aunt Jo vanished also.

Such a clatter as the little spoon made, and such a beating as the batter got, it quite foamed I assure you; and when Daisy poured some on to the griddle, it rose like magic into a puffy flapjack, that made Demi's mouth water. To be sure the first one stuck and scorched, because she forgot the butter, but after that first failure all went well, and six capital little cakes were safely landed in a dish.

"I think I'd like maple-syrup better than sugar," said Demi from his arm-chair, where he had settled himself after setting the table in a new and peculiar manner.

"Then go and ask Asia for some," answered Daisy, going into the bath-room to wash her hands.

While the nursery was empty something dreadful happened. You see, Kit had been feeling hurt all day because he had carried meat safely and yet got none to pay him. He was not a bad dog, but he had his little faults like the rest of us, and could not always resist temptation. Happening to stroll into the nursery at that moment, he smelt the cakes, saw them unguarded on the low table, and never stopping to think of consequences, swallowed all six at one mouthful. I am glad to say that they were very hot, and burned him so badly that he could not repress a surprised yelp. Daisy heard it, ran in, saw the empty dish, also the end of a yellow tail disappearing under the bed. Without a word she seized that tail, pulled out the thief, and shook him till his ears flapped wildly, then bundled him down-stairs to the shed, where he spent a lonely evening in the coal-bin."

Cheered by the sympathy which Demi gave her, Daisy made another bowl full of batter, and fried a dozen cakes, which were even better than the others. Indeed, Uncle Fritz after eating two sent up word that he had never tasted any so nice, and every boy at the table below envied Demi at the flapjack party above.

It was a truly delightful supper, for the little teapot lid only fell off three times, and the milk jug upset but once; the cakes floated in syrup, and the toast had a delicious beef-steak flavor, owing to cook's using the gridiron to make it on. Demi forgot philosophy, and stuffed like any carnal boy, while Daisy planned sumptuous banquets, and the dolls looked on smiling affably.

"Well, dearies, have you had a good time?" asked Mrs. Jo, coming up with Teddy on her shoulder.

"A *very* good time. I shall come again *soon*," answered Demi, with emphasis.

"I'm afraid you have eaten too much, by the look of that table."

"No, I haven't, I only ate fifteen cakes, and they were very little ones," protested Demi, who had kept his sister busy supplying his plate.

"They won't hurt him, they are so nice," said Daisy, with such a funny mixture of maternal fondness, and housewifely pride, that Aunt Jo could only smile, and say—

"Well, on the whole, the new game is a success then?"

"*I* like it," said Demi, as if his approval was all that was necessary.

"It is the dearest play ever made!" cried Daisy, hugging her little dish-tub as she proposed to wash up the cups. "I just wish everybody had a sweet cooking stove like mine," she added, regarding it with affection.

"This play ought to have a name," said Demi, gravely removing the syrup from his countenance with his tongue.

"It has."

"Oh, what?" asked both children, eagerly.

"Well, I think we will call it Patty-pans," and Aunt Jo retired, satisfied with the success of her last trap to catch a sunbeam.

# CHAPTER VI

## A FIRE BRAND

"PLEASE, ma'am, could I speak to you? It is something *very* important," said Nat, popping his head in at the door of Mrs. Bhaer's room.

It was the fifth head which had popped in during the last half-hour; but Mrs. Jo was used to it, so she looked up, and said briskly—

"What is it, my lad?"

Nat came in, shut the door carefully behind him, and said in an eager, anxious tone—

"Dan has come."

"Who is Dan?"

"He's a boy I used to know when I fiddled round the streets. He sold papers, and he was kind to me, and I saw him the other day in town, and told him how nice it was here, and he's come."

"But, my dear boy, that is rather a sudden way to pay a visit."

"Oh, it isn't a visit, he wants to stay if you will let him!" said Nat, innocently.

"Well, but I don't know about that," began Mrs. Bhaer, rather startled by the coolness of the proposition.

"Why, I thought you liked to have poor boys come and live with you, and be kind to 'em as you were to me," said Nat, looking surprised and alarmed.

"So I do, but I like to know something about them first. I have to choose them, because there are so many. I have not room for all. I wish I had."

"I told him to come because I thought you'd like it, but if there isn't room he can go away again," said Nat, sorrowfully.

The boy's confidence in her hospitality touched Mrs. Bhaer, and she could not find the heart to disappoint his hope, and spoil his kind little plan, so she said—

"Tell me about this Dan."

"I don't know anything, only he hasn't got any folks, and he's poor, and he was good to me, so I'd like to be good to him if I could."

"Excellent reasons every one; but really, Nat, the house is full, and I don't know where I could put him," said Mrs. Bhaer, more and more inclined to prove herself the haven of refuge he seemed to think her.

"He could have my bed, and I could sleep in the barn. It isn't cold now, and I don't mind, I used to sleep anywhere with father," said Nat, eagerly.

Something in his speech and face made Mrs. Jo put her hand on his shoulder, and say in her kindest tone :

"Bring in your friend, Nat; I think we must find room for him without giving him your place."

Nat joyfully ran off, and soon returned followed by a most unprepossessing boy, who slouched in and stood looking about him, with a half bold, half sullen look, which made Mrs. Bhaer say to herself, after one glance :

"A bad specimen, I am afraid."

"This is Dan," said Nat, presenting him as if sure of his welcome.

"Nat tells me you would like to come and stay with us," began Mrs. Jo, in a friendly tone.

"Yes," was the gruff reply.

"Have you no friends to take care of you?"

"No."

"Say, 'No, ma'am,' " whispered Nat.

"Shan't neither," muttered Dan.

"How old are you?"

"About fourteen."

"You look older. What can you do?"

"Most anything."

"If you stay here we shall want you to do as the others do, work and study as well as play. Are you willing to agree to that?"

"Don't mind trying."

"Well, you can stay a few days, and we will see how we get on together. Take him out, Nat, and amuse him till Mr. Bhaer comes home, when we will settle about the matter," said Mrs. Jo, finding it rather difficult to get on with this cool young person, who fixed his big black eyes on her with a hard, suspicious expression, sorrowfully unboyish.

"Come on, Nat," he said, and slouched out again.

"Thank you, ma'am," added Nat, as he followed him, feeling without quite understanding the difference in the welcome given to him and to his ungracious friend.

"The fellows are having a circus out in the barn; don't you want to come and see it?" he asked, as they came down the wide steps on to the lawn.

"Are they big fellows?" said Dan.

"No; the big ones are gone fishing."

"Fire away then," said Dan.

Nat led him to the great barn and introduced him to his set, who were disporting themselves among the half empty lofts. A large circle was marked out with hay on the wide floor, and in the middle stood Demi with a long whip, while Tommy, mounted on the much enduring Toby, pranced about the circle playing being a monkey.

"You must pay a pin a-piece, or you can't see the show," said Stuffy, who stood by the wheel-barrow in which sat the band, consisting of a pocket-comb blown upon by Ned, and a toy drum beaten spasmodically by Rob.

"He's company, so I'll pay for both," said Nat, handsomely, as he stuck two crooked pins in the dried mushroom which served as money-box.

With a nod to the company they seated themselves on a couple of boards, and the performance went on. After the monkey act, Ned gave them a fine specimen of his agility by jumping over an old chair, and runing up and down ladders, sailor fashion. Then Demi danced a jig with a gravity beautiful to behold. Nat was called upon to wrestle with Stuffy, and speedily laid that stout youth upon the ground. After this, Tommy proudly advanced to turn a somersault, an accomplishment which he had acquired by painful perseverance, practising in private till every joint of his little frame was black and blue. His feats were received with great applause, and he was about to retire, flushed with pride and a rush of blood to the head, when a scornful voice in the audience was heard to say—

"Ho! that ain't anything!"

"Say that again, will you?" and Tommy bristled up like an angry turkey-cock.

"Do you want to fight," said Dan, promptly descending from the barrel and doubling up his fists in a business-like manner.

"No, I don't;" and the candid Thomas retired a step, rather taken aback by the proposition.

"Fighting isn't allowed!" cried the others, much excited.

"You're a nice lot," sneered Dan.

"Come, if you don't behave, you shan't stay," said Nat, firing up at that insult to his friends.

"I'd like to see him do better than I did, that's all," observed Tommy, with a swagger.

"Clear the way, then," and without the slightest preparation Dan turned three somersaults one after the other and came up on his feet.

"You can't beat that, Tom; you always hit your head and tumble flat," said Nat, pleased at his friend's success.

Before he could say any more the audience were electrified by three more somersaults backwards, and a short promenade on the hands, head down, feet up. This brought down the house, and Tommy joined in the admiring cries which greeted the accomplished gymnast as he righted himself, and looked at them with an air of calm superiority.

"Do you think I could learn to do it without its hurting me very much?" Tom meekly asked, as he rubbed the elbows which still smarted after the last attempt.

"What will you give me if I'll teach you?" said Dan.

"My new jack-knife; it's got five blades, and only one is broken."

"Give it here then."

Tommy handed it over with an affectionate look at its smooth handle. Dan examined it carefully, then putting it into his pocket, walked off, saying with a wink—

"Keep it up till you learn, that's all."

A howl of wrath from Tommy was followed by a general uproar, which did not subside till Dan, finding himself in a minority, proposed that they should play stick-knife, and whichever won should have the treasure. Tommy agreed, and the game was played in a circle of excited faces, which all wore an expression of satisfaction, when Tommy won and secured the knife in the depth of his safest pocket.

"You come off with me, and I'll show you round," said Nat, feeling that he must have a little serious conversation with his friend in private.

What passed between them no one knew, but when they appeared again, Dan was more respectful to everyone, though still gruff in his speech, and rough in his manner; and what else could be expected of the poor lad who had been knocking about the world all his short life with no one to teach him any better?

The boys had decided that they did not like him, and so they left him to Nat, who soon felt rather oppressed by the responsibility, but was too kind-hearted to desert him.

Tommy, however, felt that in spite of the jack-knife transaction, there was a bond of sympathy between them, and longed to return to the interesting subject of somersaults. He soon found an opportunity, for Dan, seeing how much he admired him, grew more amiable, and by the end of the first week was quite intimate with the lively Tom.

Mr. Bhaer when he heard the story and saw Dan, shook his head, but only said quietly—

"The experiment may cost us something, but we will try it."

If Dan felt any gratitude for his protection, he did not show it, and took without thanks all that was given him. He was ignorant, but very quick to learn when he chose; had sharp eyes to watch what went on about him; a saucy tongue, rough manners, and a temper that was fierce and sullen by turns. He played with all his might, and played well at almost all the games. He was silent and gruff before grown people, and only now and then was thoroughly social among the lads. Few of them really liked him, but few could help admiring his courage and strength, for nothing daunted him, and he knocked tall Franz flat on one occasion with an ease that caused all the others to keep at a respectful distance from his fists. Mr. Bhaer watched him silently, and did his best to tame the "Wild Boy," as they called him, but in private the worthy man shook his head, and said soberly, "I *hope* the experiment will turn out well, but I am a little afraid it may cost too much."

Mrs. Bhaer lost her patience with him half a dozen times a day, yet never gave him up, and always insisted that there was something good in the lad after all; for he was kinder to animals than to people, he liked to rove about in the woods, and, best of all, little Ted was fond of him. What the secret was no one could discover, but Baby took to him at once—gabbled and crowed whenever he saw him—preferred his strong back to ride on to any of the others—and called him "My Danny" out of his own little head. Teddy was the only creature to whom Dan showed any affection, and this was only manifested when he thought no one else could see it; but mothers' eyes are quick, and motherly hearts instinctively divine who love their babies. So Mrs. Jo soon saw and felt that there *was* a soft spot in rough Dan, and bided her time to touch and win him.

But an unexpected and decidedly alarming event upset all their plans, and banished Dan from Plumfield.

Tommy, Nat, and Demi began by patronizing Dan, because the other lads rather slighted him; but soon they each felt there was a certain fascination about the bad boy, and from looking down upon him they came to looking up, each for a different reason. Tommy admired his skill and courage; Nat was grateful for past kindness; and Demi regarded him as a sort of animated story book, for when he chose Dan could tell his adventures in a most interesting way. It pleased Dan to have the three favorites like him, and he exerted himself to be agreeable, which was the secret of his success.

The Bhaers were surprised, but hoped the lads would have a good influence over Dan, and waited with some anxiety, trusting that no harm would come of it.

Dan felt they did not quite trust him, and never showed them his best side, but took a wilful pleasure in trying their patience and thwarting their hopes as far as he dared.

Mr. Bhaer did not approve of fighting, and did not think it a proof of either manliness or courage for two lads to pommel one another for the amusement of the rest. All sorts of hardy games and exercises were encouraged, and the boys were expected to take hard knocks and tumbles without whining; but black eyes and bloody noses given for the fun of it were forbidden as a foolish and a brutal play.

Dan laughed at this rule, and told such exciting tales of his own valor, and the many frays that he had been in, that some of the lads were fired with a desire to have a regular good "mill."

"Don't tell, and I'll show you how," said Dan; and, getting half a dozen of the lads together behind the barn, he gave them a lesson in boxing, which quite satisfied the ardor of most of them. Emil, however, could not submit to be beaten by a fellow younger than himself,—for Emil was past fourteen, and a plucky fellow,—so he challenged Dan to a fight. Dan accepted at once, and the others looked on with intense interest.

What little bird carried the news to head-quarters no one ever knew, but, in the very hottest of the fray, when Dan and Emil were fighting like a pair of young bull-dogs, and the others with fierce, excited faces were cheering them on, Mr. Bhaer walked into the ring, plucked the combatants apart with a strong hand, and said in the voice they seldom heard—

"I can't allow this, boys! Stop it at once; and never let me see it again. I keep a school for boys, not for wild beasts. Look at each other and be ashamed of yourselves."

"You let me go, and I'll knock him down again," shouted Dan, sparring away in spite of the grip on his collar.

"Come on, come on, I ain't thrashed yet!" cried Emil, who had been down five times, but did not know when he was beaten.

"They are playing be gladdy—what-you-call-'ems, like the Romans, Uncle Fritz," called out Demi, whose eyes were bigger than ever with the excitement of this new pastime.

"They were a fine set of brutes; but we have learned something since then I hope, and I cannot have you make my barn a Colosseum. Who proposed this?" asked Mr. Bhaer.

"Dan," answered several voices.

"Don't you know that it is forbidden?"

"Yes," growled Dan, sullenly.

"Then why break the rule?"

"They'll all be molly-coddles, if they don't know how to fight."

"Have you found Emil a molly-coddle? He doesn't look much like one," and Mr. Bhaer brought the two face to face. Dan had a black eye, and his jacket was torn to rags; but Emil's face was covered with blood from a cut lip and a bruised nose, while a bump on his forehead was already as purple as a plum. In spite of his wounds however, he still glared upon his foe, and evidently panted to renew the fight.

"He'd make a first-rater if he was taught," said Dan, unable to withhold the praise from the boy who made it necessary for him to do his best.

"He'll be taught to fence and box by and by, and till then I think he will do very well without any lessons in mauling. Go and wash your faces; and remember, Dan, if you break any more of the rules again, you will be sent away. That was the bargain; do your part and we will do ours."

The lads went off, and after a few more words to the spectators, Mr. Bhaer followed to bind up the wounds of the young gladiators. Emil went to bed sick, and Dan was an unpleasant spectacle for a week.

But the lawless lad had no thought of obeying, and soon transgressed again.

One Saturday afternoon as a party of the boys went out to play, Tommy said—

"Let's go down to the river, and cut a lot of new fish-poles."

"Take Toby to drag them back, and one of us can ride him down," proposed Stuffy, who hated to walk.

"That means *you*, I suppose; well, hurry up, lazy-bones," said Dan.

Away they went, and having got the poles were about to go home, when Demi unluckily said to Tommy, who was on Toby with a long rod in his hand—

"You look like the picture of the man in the bullfight, only you haven't got a red cloth, or pretty clothes on."

"I'd like to see one; wouldn't you?" said Tommy shaking his lance.

"Let's have one; there's old Buttercup in the big meadow, ride at her Tom, and see her run," proposed Dan, bent on mischief.

"No, you mustn't," began Demi, who was learning to distrust Dan's propositions.

"Why not, little fuss-button?" demanded Dan.

"I don't think Uncle Fritz would like it."

"Did he ever say we must not have a bull-fight?"

"No, I don't think he ever did," admitted Demi.

"Then hold your tongue. Drive on, Tom, and here's a red rag to flap at the old thing. I'll help you to stir her up," and over the wall went Dan, full of the new game, and the rest followed like a flock of sheep; even Demi, who sat upon the bars, and watched the fun with interest.

Poor Buttercup was not in a very good mood, for she had been lately bereft of her calf, and mourned for the little thing most dismally. Just now she regarded all mankind as her enemies (and I do not blame her), so when the matadore came prancing towards her with the red hand-kerchief flying at the end of his long lance, she threw up her head, and gave a most appropriate "Moo!" Tommy rode gallantly at her, and Toby recognizing an old friend, was quite willing to approach; but when the lance came down on her back with a loud whack, both cow and donkey were surprised and disgusted. Toby backed with a bray of remonstrance, and Buttercup lowered her horns angrily.

"At her again, Tom; she's jolly cross, and will do it capitally!" called Dan coming up behind with another rod, while Jack and Ned followed his example.

Seeing herself thus beset, and treated with such disrespect, Buttercup trotted round the field, getting more and more bewildered and excited every moment, for whichever way she turned, there was a dreadful boy, yelling and brandishing a new and very disagreeable sort of whip. It was great fun for them, but real misery for her, till she lost patience and turned the tables in the most unexpected manner. All at once she wheeled short round, and charged full at her old friend Toby, whose conduct cut her to the heart. Poor slow Toby backed so precipitately, that he tripped over a stone, and down went horse, matadore, and all, in one ignominious heap, while distracted Buttercup took a surprising leap over the wall, and galloped wildly out of sight down the road.

"Catch her, stop her, head her off! Run, boys, run!" shouted Dan, tearing after her at his best pace, for she was Mr. Bhaer's pet Alderney, and if any thing happened to her, Dan feared it would be all over with him. Such a running and racing and bawling and puffing as there was before she was caught! The fish-poles were left behind; Toby was trotted nearly off his legs in the chase; and every boy was red, breathless, and scared. They found poor Buttercup at last in a flower garden, where she had taken refuge, worn out with the long run. Borrowing a rope for a halter, Dan led her home, followed by a party of very sober young gentlemen, for the cow was in a sad state, having strained her shoulder in jumping, so that she limped, her eyes looked wild, and her glossy coat was wet and muddy.

"You'll catch it this time, Dan," said Tommy, as he led the wheezing donkey beside the maltreated cow.

"So will you, for you helped."

"We all did, but Demi," added Jack.

"He put it into our heads," said Ned.

"I told you not to do it," cried Demi, who was most broken-hearted at poor Buttercup's state.

"Old Bhaer will send me off, I guess. Don't care if he does," muttered Dan, looking worried in spite of his words.

"We'll ask him not to, all of us," said Demi, and the others assented with the exception of Stuffy, who cherished the hope that all the punishment might fall on one guilty head. Dan only said, "Don't bother about me." But he never forgot it, even though he led the lads astray again, as soon as the temptation came.

When Mr. Bhaer saw the animal, and heard the story, he said very little, evidently fearing that he should say too much in the first moments of impatience. Buttercup was made comfortable in her stall, and the boys sent to their rooms till supper-time. This brief respite gave them time to think the matter over, to wonder what the penalty would be, and to try to imagine where Dan would be sent. He whistled briskly in his room, so that no one should think he cared a bit; but while he waited to know his fate, the longing to stay grew stronger and stronger, the more he recalled the comfort and kindness he had known here, the hardship and neglect he had felt elsewhere. He knew they tried to help him, and at the bottom of his heart he was grateful, but his rough life had made him hard and careless, suspicious and wilful. He hated restraint of any sort, and fought against it like an untamed creature, even while he knew it was kindly meant, and dimly felt that he would be the better for it. He made up his mind to be turned adrift again, to knock about the city as he had done nearly all his life; a prospect that made him knit his black brows, and look about the cosy little room with a wistful expression that would have touched a much harder heart than Mr. Bhaer's if he had seen it. It vanished instantly, however, when the good man came in, and said in his accustomed grave way—

"I have heard all about it, Dan, and though you have broken the rules again, I am going to give you one more trial, to please Mother Bhaer."

Dan flushed up to his forehead at this unexpected reprieve, but he only said in his gruff way—

"I didn't know there was any rule about bull fighting."

"As I never expected to have any at Plumfield, I never did make such a rule," answered Mr. Bhaer, smiling in spite of himself at the boy's excuse. Then he added gravely, "But one of the first and most important of our few laws is the law of kindness to every dumb creature on the place. I want everybody and every thing to be happy here, to love, and trust, and serve us, as we try to love and trust and serve them faithfully and willingly. I have often said that you were kinder to the animals than any of the other boys, and Mrs. Bhaer liked that trait in you very much,

Tommy rode gallantly at her.

because she thought it showed a good heart. But you have disappointed
us in that, and we are sorry, for we hoped to make you quite one of us.
Shall we try again?"

Dan's eyes had been on the floor, and his hands nervously picking at
the bit of wood he had been whittling as Mr. Bhaer came in, but when
he heard the kind voice ask that question, he looked up quickly, and
said in a more respectful tone than he had ever used before—

"Yes, please."

"Very well then, we will say no more, only you will stay at home from
the walk tomorrow, as the other boys will, and all of you must wait on
poor Buttercup till she is well again."

"I will."

"Now, go down to supper, and do your best, my boy, more for your
own sake than for ours." Then Mr. Bhaer shook hands with him, and
Dan went down more tamed by kindness, than he would have been by
the good whipping which Asia had strongly recommended.

Dan did try for a day or two, but not being used to it, he soon tired
and relapsed into his old wilful ways. Mr. Bhaer was called from home
on business one day, and the boys had no lessons. They liked this, and
played hard till bed-time, when most of them turned in and slept like
dormice. Dan, however, had a plan in his head, and when he and Nat
were alone, he unfolded it.

"Look here!" he said, taking from under his bed a bottle, a cigar, and
a pack of cards "I'm going to have some fun, and do as I used to with
the fellows in town. Here's some beer, I got it off the old man at the
station, and this cigar; you can pay for 'em, or Tommy will, he's got
heaps of money, and I haven't a cent. I'm going to ask him in; no, you
go, they won't mind you."

"The folks won't like it," began Nat.

"They won't know. Daddy Bhaer is away, and Mrs. Bhaer's busy with
Ted; he's got croup or something, and she can't leave him. We shan't
sit up late or make any noise, so where's the harm?"

"Asia will know if we burn the lamp long, she always does."

"No, she won't, I've got the dark lantern on purpose, it don't give
much light, and we can shut it quick if we hear any one coming," said
Dan.

This idea struck Nat as a fine one, and lent an air of romance to the
thing. He started off to tell Tommy, but put his head in again to say—

"You want Demi, too, don't you?"

"No, I don't; the Deacon will roll up eyes and preach if you tell him.
He will be asleep, so just tip the wink to Tom and cut back again."

Nat obeyed, and returned in a minute with Tommy half dressed,
rather tousled about the head and very sleepy, but quite ready for fun
as usual.

"Now, keep quiet, and I'll show you how to play a first-rate game
called 'Poker,' " said Dan, as the three revellers gathered round the table,
on which were set forth the bottle, the cigar, and the cards. "First we'll
all have a drink, then we'll take a go at the 'weed,' and then we'll play.
That's the way men do, and it's jolly fun."

The beer circulated in a mug, and all three smacked their lips over it, though Nat and Tommy did not like the bitter stuff. The cigar was worse still, but they dared not say so, and each puffed away till he was dizzy or choked, when he passed the "weed" on to his neighbor. Dan liked it, for it seemed like old times when he now and then had a chance to imitate the low men who surrounded him. He drank, and smoked, and swaggered as much like them as he could, and, getting into the spirit the part he assumed, he soon began to swear under his breath for fear someone should hear him. "You mustn't; it's wicked to say 'Damn!' " cried Tommy, who had followed his leader so far.

"Oh, hang! Don't you preach, but play away; it's part of the fun to swear."

"I'd rather say 'thunder—turtles,' " said Tommy, who had composed this interesting exclamation and was very proud of it.

"And I'll say 'The Devil;' that sounds well," added Nat, much impressed by Dan's manly ways.

Dan scoffed at their "nonsense," and swore stoutly as he tried to teach them the new game.

But Tommy was very sleepy, and Nat's head began to ache with the beer and the smoke, so neither of them was very quick to learn, and the game dragged. The room was nearly dark, for the lantern burned badly; they could not laugh loud nor move about much, for Silas slept next door in the shed-chamber, and altogether the party was dull. In the middle of a deal Dan stopped suddenly, called out, "Who's that?" in a startled tone, and at the same moment drew the slide over the light. A voice in the darkness said, tremulously, "I can't find Tommy," and then there was the quick patter of bare feet running away down the entry that led from the wing to the main house.

"It's Demi! He's gone to call some one; cut into bed, Tom, and don't tell!" cried Dan, whisking all signs of the revel out of sight, and beginning to tear off his clothes, while Nat did the same.

Tommy flew to his room and dived into bed, where he lay laughing till something burned his hand, when he discovered that he was still clutching the stump of the festive cigar, which he happened to be smoking when the revel broke up.

It was nearly out, and he was about to extinguish it carefully when Nursey's voice was heard, and fearing it would betray him if he hid it in the bed, he threw it underneath, after a final pinch which he thought finished it.

Nursey came in with Demi, who looked much amazed to see the red face of Tommy reposing peacefully upon his pillow.

"He wasn't there just now, because I woke up and could not find him anywhere," said Demi, pouncing on him.

"What mischief are you at now, bad child?" asked Nursey, with a good-natured shake, which made the sleeper open his eyes to say, meekly,—

"I only ran into Nat's room to see him about something. Go away, and let me alone; I'm awful sleepy."

Nursey tucked Demi in, and went off to reconnoitre, but only found two boys slumbering peacefully in Dan's room. "Some little frolic," she thought, and as there was no harm done she said nothing to Mrs. Bhaer, who was busy and worried over little Teddy.

Tommy was sleepy and telling Demi to mind his own business and not ask questions, he was snoring in ten minutes, little dreaming what was going on under his bed. The cigar did not go out, but smouldered away on the straw carpet till it was nicely on fire, and a hungry little flame went creeping along till the dimity bedcover caught, then the sheets, and then the bed itself. The beer made Tommy sleep heavily, and the smoke stupefied Demi, so they slept on till the fire began to scorch them, and they were in danger of being burned to death.

Franz was sitting up to study, and as he left the school-room he smelt the smoke, dashed up-stairs and saw it coming in a cloud from the left wing of the house. Without stopping to call anyone, he ran into the room, dragged the boys from the blazing bed, and splashed all the water he could find at hand on to the flames. It checked but did not quench the fire, and the children, wakened on being tumbled topsy-turvy into a cold hall, began to roar at the top of their voices. Mrs. Bhaer instantly appeared, and a minute after Silas burst out of his room shouting "Fire!" in a tone that raised the whole house. A flock of white goblins with scared faces crowded into the hall, and for a minute everyone was panic-stricken.

Then Mrs. Bhaer found her wits, bade Nursey see to the burnt boys, and sent Franz and Silas down-stairs for some tubs of wet clothes which she flung on to the bed, over the carpet, and up against the curtains, now burning finely, and threatening to kindle the walls.

Most of the boys stood dumbly looking on, but Dan and Emil worked bravely, running to and fro with water from the bath-room, and helping to pull down the dangerous curtains.

The peril was soon over, and ordering the boys all back to bed, and leaving Silas to watch lest the fire broke out again, Mrs. Bhaer and Franz went to see how the poor boys got on. Demi had escaped with one burn and a grand scare, but Tommy had not only most of his hair scorched off his head, but a great burn on his arm, that made him half crazy with the pain. Demi was soon made cosy, and Franz took him away to his own bed, where the kind lad soothed his fright and hummed him to sleep as cosily as a woman. Nursey watched over poor Tommy all night, trying to ease his misery, and Mrs. Bhaer vibrated between him and little Teddy with oil and cotton, paregoric and squills, saying to herself from time to time, as if she found great amusement in the thought, "I always *knew* Tommy would set the house on fire, and now he has done it!"

When Mr. Bhaer got home next morning he found a nice state of things. Tommy in bed, Teddy wheezing like a little grampus, Mrs. Jo quite used up, and the whole flock of boys so excited that they all talked at once, and almost dragged him by main force to view the ruins. Under his quiet management things soon fell into order, for every one felt that he was equal to a dozen conflagrations, and worked with a will at whatever task he gave them.

There was no school that morning, but by afternoon the damaged room was put to rights, the invalids were better, and there was time to hear and judge the little culprits quietly. Nat and Tommy told their parts in the mischief, and were honestly sorry for the danger they had brought to the dear old house and all in it. But Dan put on his devil-may-care look, and would not own that there was much harm done.

Now, of all things, Mr. Bhaer hated drinking, gambling, and swearing; smoking he had given up that the lads might not be tempted to try it, and it grieved and angered him deeply to find that the boy, with whom he had tried to be most forbearing, should take advantage of his absence to introduce these forbidden vices, and teach his innocent little lads to think it manly and pleasant to indulge in them. He talked long and earnestly to the assembled boys, and ended by saying, with an air of mingled firmness and regret—

"I think Tommy is punished enough, and that scar on his arm will remind him for a long time to let these things alone. Nat's fright will do for him, for he is really sorry, and does try to obey me. But you, Dan, have been many times forgiven, and yet it does no good. I cannot have my boys hurt by your bad example, nor my time wasted in talking to deaf ears, so you can say good-by to them all, and tell Nursey to put up your things in my little black bag."

"Oh! sir, where is he going?" cried Nat.

"To a pleasant place up in the country, where I sometimes send boys when they don't do well here. Mr. Page is a kind man, and Dan will be happy there if he chooses to do his best."

"Will he ever come back?" asked Demi.

"That will depend on himself; I hope so."

As he spoke, Mr. Bhaer left the room to write his letter to Mr. Page, and the boys crowded round Dan very much as people do about a man who is going on a long and perilous journey to unknown regions.

"I wonder if you'll like it," began Jack.

"Shan't stay if I don't," said Dan, coolly.

"Where will you go?" asked Nat.

"I may go to sea, or out west, or take a look at California," answered Dan, with a reckless air that quite took away the breath of the little boys.

"Oh, don't! Stay with Mr. Page awhile and then come back here; do, Dan," pleaded Nat, much affected at the whole affair.

"I don't care where I go, or how long I stay, and I'll be hanged if I ever come back here," with which wrathful speech Dan went away to put up his things, every one of which Mr. Bhaer had given him.

That was the only good-by he gave the boys, for they were all talking the matter over in the barn when he came down, and he told Nat not to call them. The wagon stood at the door, and Mrs. Bhaer came out to speak to Dan, looking so sad that his heart smote him, and he said in a low tone—

"May I say good-by to Teddy?"

"Yes, dear; go in and kiss him, he will miss his Danny very much."

No one saw the look in Dan's eyes as he stooped over the crib, and saw the little face light up at first sight of him, but he heard Mrs. Bhaer say pleadingly—

"Can't we give the poor lad *one* more trial, Fritz?" and Mr. Bhaer answer in his steady way—

"My dear, it is not best, so let him go where he can do no harm to others, while they do good to him, and by and by he shall come back, I promise you."

"He's the only boy we ever failed with, and I am so grieved, for I thought there was the making of a fine man in him, spite of his faults."

Dan heard Mrs. Bhaer sigh, and he wanted to ask for *one more* trial himself, but his pride would not let him, and he came out with the hard look on his face, shook hands without a word, and drove away with Mr. Bhaer, leaving Nat and Mrs. Jo to look after him with tears in their eyes.

A few days afterwards they received a letter from Mr. Page, saying that Dan was doing well, whereat they all rejoiced. But three weeks later came another letter, saying that Dan had run away, and nothing had been heard of him, whereat they all looked sober, and Mr. Bhaer said—

"Perhaps I ought to have given him another chance."

Mrs. Bhaer, however, nodded wisely and answered, "Don't be troubled, Fritz; the boy will come back to us, I'm sure of it."

But time went on and no Dan came.


# CHAPTER VII

## NAUGHTY NAN

"Fritz, I've got a new idea," cried Mrs. Bhaer, as she met her husband one day after school.

"Well, my dear, what is it?" And he waited willingly to hear the new plan, for some of Mrs. Jo's ideas were so droll, it was impossible to help laughing at them, though usually they were quite sensible, and he was glad to carry them out.

"Daisy needs a companion, and the boys would be all the better for another girl among them; you know we believe in bringing up little men and women together, and it is high time we acted up to our belief. They pet and tyrannize over Daisy by turns, and she is getting spoilt. Then they must learn gentle ways, and improve their manners, and having girls about will do it better than anything else."

"You are right, as usual. Now, who shall we have?" asked Mr Bhaer, seeing by the look in her eye that Mrs. Jo had someone all ready to propose.

"Little Annie Harding."

"What! Naughty Nan, as the lads call her?" cried Mr. Bhaer, looking very much amused.

"Yes, she is running wild at home since her mother died, and is too bright a child to be spoilt by servants, I have had my eye on her for some time, and when I met her father in town the other day I asked him why he did not send her to school. He said he would gladly if he could find as good a school for girls, as ours was for boys. I know he would rejoice to have her come; so suppose we drive over this afternoon and see about it."

"Have not you cares enough now, my Jo, without this little gypsy to torment you?" asked Mr. Bhaer, patting the hand that lay on his arm.

"Oh dear, no," said Mother Bhaer, briskly. "I like it, and never was happier than since I had my wilderness of boys. You see, Fritz, I feel a great sympathy for Nan, because I was such a naughty child myself that I know all about it. She is full of spirits, and only needs to be taught what to do with them to be as nice a little girl as Daisy. Those quick wits of hers would enjoy lessons if they were rightly directed, and what is now a tricksy midget would soon become a busy happy child. I know how to manage her, for I remember how my blessed mother managed me, and"—

"And if you succeed half as well as she did, you will have done a magnificent work," interrupted Mr. Bhaer, who labored under the delusion that Mrs. B. was the best and most charming woman alive.

"Now, if you make fun of my plan I'll give you bad coffee for a week, and then where are you, sir?" cried Mrs. Jo, tweaking him by the ear just as if he was one of the boys.

"Won't Daisy's hair stand erect with horror at Nan's wild ways?" asked Mr. Bhaer, presently, when Teddy had swarmed up his waistcoat, and Rob up his back, for they always flew at their father the minute school was done."

"At first, perhaps, but it will do Posy good. She is getting prim and Bettyish, and needs stirring up a bit. She always has a good time when Nan comes over to play, and the two will help each other without knowing it. Dear me, half the science of teaching is knowing how much children do for one another, and when to mix them."

"I only hope she won't turn out another firebrand."

"My poor Dan! I never can quite forgive myself for letting him go," sighed Mrs. Bhaer.

At the sound of the name, little Teddy, who had never forgotten his friend, struggled down from his father's arms, and trotted to the door, looked out over the sunny lawn with a wistful face, and then trotted back again, saying, as he always did when disappointed of the longed-for sight—

"My Danny's tummin' soon."

"I really think we ought to have kept him, if only for Teddy's sake, he was so fond of him, and perhaps baby's love would have done for him what we failed to do."

"I've sometimes felt that myself; but after keeping the boys in a ferment, and nearly burning up the whole family, I thought it safer to remove the firebrand, for a time at least," said Mr. Bhaer.

"Dinner's ready, let me ring the bell," and Rob began a solo upon that instrument which made it impossible to hear one's self speak.

"Then, I may have Nan, may I?" asked Mrs. Jo.

"A dozen Nans if you want them, my dear," answered Mr. Bhaer, who had room in his fatherly heart for all the naughty neglected children in the world.

When Mrs. Bhaer returned from her drive that afternoon, before she could unpack the load of little boys, without whom she seldom moved, a small girl of ten skipped out at the back of the carry-all, and ran into the house, shouting—

"Hi, Daisy! Where are you?"

Daisy came, and looked pleased to see her guest, but also a trifle alarmed, when Nan said, still prancing, as if it was impossible to keep still—

"I'm going to stay here always, papa says I may, and my box is coming tomorrow, all my things had to be washed and mended, and your aunt came and carried me off. Isn't it great fun?"

"Why, yes. Did you bring your big doll?" asked Daisy, hoping she had, for on the last visit Nan had ravaged the baby house, and insisted on washing Blanche Matilda's plaster face, which spoilt the poor dear's complexion forever.

"Yes, she's somewhere round," returned Nan, with most unmaternal carelessness. "I made you a ring coming along, and pulled the hairs out of Dobbin's tail. Don't you want it?" and Nan presented a horse-hair ring in token of friendship, as they had both vowed they would never speak to one another again when they last parted.

Won by the beauty of the offering, Daisy grew more cordial, and proposed retiring to the nursery, but Nan said, "No, I want to see the boys, and the barn," and ran off, swinging her hat by one string till it broke, when she left it to its fate on the grass.

"Hullo! Nan!" cried the boys as she bounced in among them with the announcement—

"I'm going to stay."

"Hooray!" bawled Tommy from the wall on which he was perched, for Nan was a kindred spirit, and he foresaw "larks" in the future.

"I can bat; let me play," said Nan, who could turn her hand to anything, and did not mind hard knocks.

"We ain't playing now, and our side beat without you."

"I can beat you in running, anyway," returned Nan, falling back on her strong point.

"Can she?" asked Nat of Jack.

"She runs very well for a girl," answered Jack, who looked down upon Nan with condescending approval.

"Will you try?" said Nan, longing to display her powers.

"It's too hot," and Tommy languished against the wall as if quite exhausted.

"What's the matter with Stuffy?" asked Nan, whose quick eyes were roving from face to face.

"Ball hurt his hand; he howls at everything," answered Jack, scornfully.

"I don't, I never cry, no matter how much I'm hurt; it's babyish," said Nan, loftily.

"Pooh! I could make you cry in two minutes," returned Stuffy, rousing up.

"See if you can."

"Go and pick that bunch of nettles then," and Stuffy pointed to a sturdy specimen of that prickly plant growing by the wall.

Nan instantly "grasped the nettle," pulled it up, and held it with a defiant gesture, in spite of the almost unbearable sting.

"Good for you," cried the boys, quick to acknowledge courage even in one of the weaker sex.

More nettled than she was, Stuffy determined to get a cry out of her somehow, and he said tauntingly, "You are used to poking your hands into everything, so that isn't fair. Now go and bump your head real hard against the barn, and see if you don't howl then."

"Don't do it," said Nat, who hated cruelty.

But Nan was off, and running straight at the barn, she gave her head a blow that knocked her flat, and sounded like a battering-ram. Dizzy, but undaunted she staggered up, saying stoutly, though her face was drawn with pain.

"That hurt, but I don't cry."

"Do it again," said Stuffy, angrily; and Nan *would* have done it, but Nat held her; and Tommy, forgetting the heat, flew at Stuffy like a little game-cock, roaring out—

"Stop it, or I'll throw you over the barn!" And so shook and hustled poor Stuffy, that for a minute he did not know whether he was on his head or his heels.

"She told me to," was all he could say, when Tommy let him alone.

"Never mind if she did; it is awfully mean to hurt a little girl," said Demi, reproachfully.

"Ho! I don't mind; I ain't a little girl, I'm older than you and Daisy; so now," cried Nan, ungratefully.

"Don't preach, Deacon, you bully Posy every day of your life," called out the Commodore, who just then hove in sight.

"I don't hurt her; do I Daisy?" and Demi turned to his sister, who was "pooring" Nan's tingling hands, and recommending water for the purple lump rapidly developing itself on her forehead.

"You are the best boy in the world," promptly answered Daisy; adding, as truth compelled her to do, "You do hurt me sometimes, but you don't mean to."

"Put away the bats and things, and mind what you are about, my hearties. No fighting allowed aboard this ship," said Emil, who rather lorded it over the others.

"How do you do, Madge Wildfire?" said Mr. Bhaer, as Nan came in with the rest to supper. "Give the right hand, little daughter, and mind thy manners," he added, as Nan offered him her left.

"The other hurts me."

"The poor little hand! What has it been doing to get those blisters?" he asked, drawing it from behind her back, where she had put it with a look which made him think she had been in mischief.

Before Nan could think of any excuse, Daisy burst out with the whole story, during which Stuffy tried to hide his face in a bowl of bread and milk. When the tale was finished, Mr. Bhaer looked down the long table towards his wife, and said with a laugh in his eyes—

"This rather belongs to your side of the house, so I won't meddle with it, my dear."

Mrs. Jo knew what he meant, but she liked her little black sheep all the better for her pluck, though she only said in her soberest way—

"Do you know why I asked Nan to come here?"

"To plague me," muttered Stuffy, with his mouth full.

"To help me make little gentlemen of you, and I think you have shown that some of you need it."

Here Stuffy retired into his bowl again, and did not emerge till Demi made them all laugh by saying, in his slow wondering way—

"How can she, when she's such a tom-boy!"

"That's just it, she needs help as much as you, and I expect you to set her an example of good manners."

"Is she going to be a little gentleman too?" asked Rob.

"She'd like it; wouldn't you, Nan?" added Tommy.

"No, I shouldn't; I hate boys!" said Nan, fiercely for her hand still smarted, and she began to think that she might have shown her courage in some wiser way.

"I am sorry you hate my boys, because they *can* be well-mannered, and most agreeable when they choose. Kindness in looks and words and ways is true politeness, and anyone can have it if they only try to treat other people as they like to be treated themselves."

Mrs. Bhaer had addressed herself to Nan, but the boys nudged one another, and appeared to take the hint, for that time at least, and passed the butter; said "please," and "thank you," "yes, sir," and "no, ma'am," with unusual elegance and respect. Nan said nothing, but kept herself quiet and refrained from tickling Demi, though strongly tempted to do so, because of the dignified airs he put on. She also appeared to have forgotten her hatred of boys, and played "I spy" with them till dark. Stuffy was observed to offer her frequent sucks of his candy-ball during the game which evidently sweetened her temper, for the last thing she said on going to bed was—

"When my battledore and shuttle-cock comes, I'll let you all play with 'em."

Her first remark in the morning was, "Has my box come?" And when told that it would arrive sometime during the day, she fretted and fumed, and whipped her doll, till Daisy was shocked. She managed to exist, however, till five o'clock, when she disappeared, and was not missed till supper-time, because those at home thought she had gone to the hill with Tommy and Demi.

"I saw her going down the avenue alone as hard as she could pelt," said Mary Anne, coming in with the hasty-pudding, and finding every one asking, "Where is Nan?"

"She has run home, little gypsy!" cried Mrs. Bhaer, looking anxious.

"Perhaps she has gone to the station to look after her luggage," suggested Franz.

"That is impossible, she does not know the way, and if she found it she could never carry the box a mile," said Mrs. Bhaer, beginning to think that her new idea might be rather a hard one to carry out.

"It would be like her," and Mr. Bhaer caught up his hat to go and find the child, when a shout from Jack, who was at the window, made every one hurry to the door.

There was Miss Nan, to be sure, tugging along a large band-box tied up in a linen bag. Very hot and dusty and tired did she look, but marched stoutly along, and came puffing up to the steps, where she dropped her load with a sigh of relief, and sat down upon it, observing as she crossed her tired arms—

"I couldn't wait any longer, so I went and got it."

"I couldn't wait any longer, so I went and got it."

"But you did not know the way," said Tommy, while the rest stood round enjoying the joke.

"Oh, I found it, I never get lost."

"It's a mile, how could you go so far?"

"Well, it was pretty far, but I rested a good deal."

"Wasn't that thing very heavy?"

"It's so round, I couldn't get hold of it good, and I thought my arms would break right off."

"I don't see how the station-master let you have it," said Tommy.

"I didn't say anything to him. He was in the little ticket place, and didn't see me, so I just took it off the platform."

"Run down and tell him it is all right, Franz, or old Dodd will think it is stolen," said Mr. Bhaer, joining in the shout of laughter at Nan's coolness.

"I told you we would send for it if it did not come. Another time you must wait, for you will get into trouble if you run away. Promise me this, or I shall not dare to trust you out of my sight," said Mrs. Bhaer, wiping the dust off Nan's little hot face.

"Well, I won't, only papa tells me not to put off doing things, so I don't."

"That is rather a poser; I think you had better give her some supper now, and a private lecture by and by," said Mr. Bhaer, too much amused to be angry at the young lady's exploit.

The boys thought it "great fun," and Nan entertained them at supper-time with an account of her adventures; for a big dog had barked at her, a man had laughed at her, a woman had given her a doughnut, and her hat had fallen into the brook when she stopped to drink, exhausted with her exertion.

"I fancy you will have your hands full now, my dear, Tommy and Nan are quite enough for one woman," said Mr. Bhaer, half an hour later.

"I know it will take some time to tame the child, but she is such a generous, warm-hearted little thing, I should love her even if she were twice as naughty," answered Mrs. Jo, pointing to the merry group, in the middle of which stood Nan, giving away her things right and left, as lavishly as if the big band-box had no bottom.

It was those good traits that soon made little "Giddy gaddy," as they called her, a favorite with every one. Daisy never complained of being dull again, for Nan invented the most delightful plays, and her pranks rivalled Tommy's, to the amusement of the whole school. She buried her big doll and forgot it for a week, and found it well mildewed when she dug it up. Daisy was in despair, but Nan took it to the painter who was at work about the house, got him to paint it brick red, with staring black eyes, then she dressed it up with feathers, and scarlet flannel, and one of Ned's leaden hatchets; and in the character of an Indian chief, the late Poppydilla tomahawked all the other dolls, and caused the nursery to run red with imaginary gore. She gave away her new shoes to a beggar child, hoping to be allowed to go barefoot, but found it impossible to combine charity and comfort, and was ordered to ask leave before disposing of her clothes. She delighted the boys by making a fire-ship out of a shingle with two large sails wet with turpentine, which she lighted, and then sent the little vessel floating down the brook at dusk. She harnessed the old turkey-cock to a straw wagon, and made him trot round the house at a tremendous pace. She gave her coral necklace for four unhappy kittens, which had been tormented by some heartless lads, and tended them for days as gently as a mother, dressing their wounds with cold cream, feeding them with a doll's spoon, and mourning over them when they died, till she was consoled by one of Demi's best turtles. She made Silas tattoo an anchor on her arm like his, and begged hard to have a blue star on each cheek, but he dared not do it, though she coaxed and scolded till the soft-hearted fellow longed to give in. She rode every animal on the place, from the big horse Andy to the cross pig, from whom she was rescued with difficulty. Whatever the boys dared her to do she instantly attempted, no matter how dangerous it might be, and they were never tired of testing her courage.

Mr. Bhaer suggested that they should see who would study best, and Nan found as much pleasure in using her quick wits and fine memory as her active feet and merry tongue, while the lads had to do their best to keep their places, for Nan showed them that girls could do most things as well as boys, and some things better. There were no rewards in school, but Mr. Bhaer's "Well done!" and Mrs. Bhaer's good report on the conscience book, taught them to love duty for its own sake, and try to do it faithfully, sure that sooner or later the recompense would come. Little Nan was quick to feel the new atmosphere, to enjoy it, to show that it was what she needed; for this little garden was full of sweet flowers, half hidden by the weeds; and when kind hands gently began to cultivate it, all sorts of green shoots sprung up, promising to blossom beautifully in the warmth of love and care, the best climate for young hearts and souls all the world over.

# CHAPTER VIII

## PRANKS AND PLAYS

As there is no particular plan to this story, except to describe a few scenes in the life at Plumfield for the amusement of certain little persons, we will gently ramble along in this chapter and tell some of the pastimes of Mrs. Jo's boys. I beg leave to assure my honored readers that most of the incidents are taken from real life, and that the oddest are the truest; for no person, no matter how vivid an imagination he may have, can invent anything half so droll as the freaks and fancies that originate in the lively brains of little people.

Daisy and Demi were full of these whims, and lived in a world of their own, peopled with lovely or grotesque creatures, to whom they gave the queerest names, and with whom they played the queerest games. One of these nursery inventions was an invisible sprite called "The Naughty Kitty-mouse," whom the children had believed in, feared, and served for a long time. They seldom spoke of it to any one else, kept their rites as private as possible; and, as they never tried to describe it even to themselves, this being had a vague mysterious charm very agreeable to Demi, who delighted in elves and goblins. A most whimsical and tyrannical imp was the Naughty Kitty-mouse, and Daisy found a fearful pleasure in its service, blindly obeying its most absurd demands, which were usually proclaimed from the lips of Demi, whose powers of invention were great. Rob and Teddy sometimes joined in these ceremonies, and considered them excellent fun, although they did not understand half that went on.

One day after school Demi whispered to his sister, with an ominous wag of the head—

"The Kitty-mouse wants us this afternoon."

"What for?" asked Daisy, anxiously.

"A *sackerryfice*," answered Demi, solemnly. "There must be a fire behind the big rock at two o'clock, and we must all bring the things we like best, and burn them!" he added, with an awful emphasis on the last words.

"Oh, dear! I love the new paper dollies Aunt Amy painted for me best of anything, must I burn them up?" cried Daisy, who never thought of denying the unseen tyrant anything it demanded.

"Every one. I shall burn my boat, my best scrapbook, and *all* my soldiers," said Demi, firmly.

"Well, I will; but it's too bad of Kitty-mouse to want our very nicest things," sighed Daisy.

"A *sackerryfice* means to give up what you are fond of, so we *must*," explained Demi, to whom the new idea had been suggested by hearing Uncle Fritz describe the customs of the Greeks to the big boys who were reading about them in school.

"Is Rob coming too?" asked Daisy.

"Yes, and he is going to bring his toy village; it is all made of wood, you know, and will burn nicely. We'll have a grand bonfire, and see them blaze up, won't we?"

This brilliant prospect consoled Daisy, and she ate her dinner with a row of paper dolls before her, as a sort of farewell banquet.

At the appointed hour the sacrificial train set forth, each child bearing the treasures demanded by the insatiable Kitty-mouse. Teddy insisted on going also, and seeing that all the others had toys, he tucked a squeaking lamb under one arm, and old Annabella under the other, little dreaming what anguish the latter idol was to give him.

"Where are you going, my chickens?" asked Mrs. Jo, as the flock passed her door.

"To play by the big rock; can't we?"

"Yes, only don't go near the pond, and take good care of baby."

"I always do," said Daisy, leading forth her charge with a capable air.

"Now, you must all sit round, and not move till I tell you. This flat stone is an altar, and I am going to make a fire on it."

Demi then proceeded to kindle up a small blaze, as he had seen the boys do at picnics. When the flame burned well, he ordered the company to march round it three times and then stand in a circle.

"I shall begin, and as fast as my things are burnt, you must bring yours."

With that he solemnly laid on a little paper book full of pictures, pasted in by himself; this was followed by a dilapidated boat, and then one by one the unhappy leaden soldiers marched to death. Not one faltered or hung back, from the splendid red and yellow captain, to the small drummer who had lost his legs; all vanished in the flames and mingled in one common pool of melted lead.

"Now, Daisy!" called the high priest of Kitty-mouse, when his rich offerings had been consumed, to the great satisfaction of the children.

"My dear dollies, how *can* I let them go?" moaned Daisy, hugging the entire dozen with a face full of maternal woe.

"You must," commanded Demi; and with a farewell kiss to each, Daisy laid her blooming dolls upon the coals.

"Let me keep one, the dear blue thing, she is *so* sweet," besought the poor little mamma, clutching her last in despair.

"More! More!" growled an awful voice, and Demi cried, "That's the Kitty-mouse! She must have every one, quick or she will scratch us!"

In went the precious blue belle, flounces, rosy hat, and all, and nothing but a few black flakes remained of that bright band.

"Stand the houses and trees round, and let them catch themselves; it will be like a real fire then," said Demi, who liked variety even in his "sackerryfices."

Charmed by this suggestion, the children arranged the doomed village, laid a line of coals along the main street, and then sat down to watch the conflagration. It was somewhat slow to kindle owing to the paint, but at last one ambitious little cottage blazed up, fired a tree of the palm species, which fell onto the roof of a large family mansion, and in a few minutes the entire town was burning merrily. The wooden population stood and stared at the destruction like blockheads, as they were, till they also caught and blazed away without a cry. It took some time to reduce the town to ashes, and the lookers-on enjoyed the spectacle immensely, cheering as each house fell, dancing like wild Indians when the steeple flamed aloft, and actually casting one wretched little churn-shaped lady, who had escaped to the suburbs, into the very heart of the fire.

The superb success of this last offering excited Teddy to such a degree, that he first threw his lamb into the conflagration, and before it had time even to roast, he planted poor dear Annabella on the funeral pyre. Of course she did not like it, and expressed her anguish and resentment in a way that terrified her infant destroyer. Being covered with kid, she did not blaze, but did what was worse, she *squirmed*. First one leg curled up, then the other, in a very awful and lifelike manner; next she flung her arms over her head as if in great agony; her head itself turned on her shoulders, her glass eyes fell out, and with one final writhe of her whole body, she sank down a blackened mass on the ruins of the town. This unexpected demonstration startled every one and frightened Teddy half out of his little wits. He looked, then screamed and fled toward the house, roaring "Marmar," at the top of his voice.

Mrs. Bhaer heard the outcry and ran to the rescue, but Teddy could only cling to her and pour out in his broken way something about, "poor Bella hurted," "a dreat fire," and "all the dollies dorn." Fearing some dire mishap, his mother caught him up and hurried to the scene of action, where she found the blind worshippers of Kitty-mouse mourning over the charred remains of the lost darling.

"What have you been at? Tell me all about it," said Mrs. Jo, composing herself to listen patiently, for the culprits looked so penitent, she forgave them beforehand.

With some reluctance Demi explained their play, and Aunt Jo laughed till the tears ran down her cheeks, the children were so solemn, and the play was so absurd.

"I thought you were too sensible to play such a silly game as this. If I had any Kitty-mouse I'd have a good one who liked you to play in safe pleasant ways, and not destroy and frighten. Just see what a ruin you have made; all Daisy's pretty dolls, Demi's soldiers, and Rob's new village, besides poor Teddy's pet lamb, and dear old Annabella. I shall have to write up in the nursery the verse that used to come in the boxes of toys—

*'The children of Holland take pleasure in making,*
*What the children of Boston take pleasure in breaking.'*

Only I shall put Plumfield instead of Boston."

"We never will again, truly, truly!" cried the repentant little sinners, much abashed at this reproof.

"Demi told us to," said Rob.

"Well, I heard Uncle tell about the Greece people, who had altars and things, and so I wanted to be like them, only I hadn't any live creatures to sackerryfice, so we burnt up our toys."

"Dear me, that is something like the bean store," said Aunt Jo, laughing again.

"Tell about it," suggested Daisy, to change the subject.

"Once there was a poor woman who had three or four little children, and she used to lock them up in her room when she went out to work, to keep them safe. One day when she was going away she said, 'Now, my dears, don't let baby fall out of window, don't play with the matches, and don't put beans up your noses.' Now the children had never dreamed of doing that last thing, but she put it into their heads, and the minute she was gone, they ran and stuffed their naughty little noses full of beans, just to see how it felt, and she found them all crying when she came home."

"Did it hurt?" asked Rob, with such intense interest that his mother hastily added a warning sequel, lest a new edition of the bean story should appear in her own family.

"Very much, as I know, for when *my* mother told me this story, I was so silly that I went and tried it myself. I had no beans, so I took some little pebbles, and poked several into my nose. I did not like it at all, and wanted to take them out again very soon, but one would not come, and I was so ashamed to tell what a goose I had been that I went for hours with the stone hurting me very much. At last the pain got so bad I had to tell, and when my mother could not get it out the doctor came. Then I was put in a chair and held tight, Rob, while he used his ugly little pincers till the stone hopped out. Dear me! How my wretched little nose did ache, and how people laughed at me!" and Mrs. Jo shook her head in a dismal way, as if the memory of her sufferings was too much for her.

Rob looked deeply impressed and I am glad to say took the warning to heart. Demi proposed that they should bury poor Annabella, and in the interest of the funeral Teddy forgot his fright. Daisy was soon consoled by another batch of dolls from Aunt Amy, and the Naughty Kitty-mouse seemed to be appeased by the last offerings, for she tormented them no more.

"Brops" was the name of a new and absorbing play, invented by Bangs. As this interesting animal is not to be found in any Zoölogical Garden, unless Du Chaillu has recently brought one from the wilds of Africa, I will mention a few of its peculiar habits and traits, for the benefit of inquiring minds. The Brop is a winged quadruped, with a human face of a youthful and merry aspect. When it walks the earth it grunts, when it soars it gives a shrill hoot, occasionally it goes erect, and talks good English. Its body is usually covered with a substance much resembling a shawl, sometimes red, sometimes blue, often plaid, and, strange to say, they frequently change skins with one another. On their heads they have a horn very like a stiff brown paper lamp-lighter. Wings of the same substance flap upon their shoulders when they fly; this is never very far from the ground, as they usually fall with violence if they attempt any lofty flights. They browse over the earth, but can sit up and eat like the squirrel. Their favorite nourishment is the seed-cake; apples also are freely taken, and sometimes raw carrots are nibbled when food is scarce. They live in dens, where they have a sort of nest, much like a clothes-basket, in which the little Brops play till their wings are grown. These singular animals quarrel at times, and it is on these occasions that they burst into human speech, call each other names, cry, scold, and sometimes tear off horns and skin, declaring fiercely that they "won't play." The few privileged persons who have studied them are inclined to think them a remarkable mixture of the monkey, the sphinx, the roc, and the queer creatures seen by the famous Peter Wilkins.

This game was a great favorite, and the younger children beguiled many a rainy afternoon flapping or creeping about the nursery, acting like little bedlamites and being as merry as little grigs. To be sure, it was rather hard upon clothes, particularly trouser-knees and jacket-elbows; but Mrs. Bhaer only said, as she patched and darned—

"We do things just as foolish, and not half so harmless. If I could get as much happiness out of it as the little dears do, I'd be a Brop myself."

Nat's favorite amusements were working in his garden, and sitting in the willow-tree with his violin, for that green nest was a fairy world to him, and there he loved to perch, making music like a happy bird. The lads called him "Old Chirper," because he was always humming, whistling, or fiddling, and they often stopped a minute in their work or play to listen to the soft tones of the violin, which seemed to lead a little orchestra of summer sounds. The birds appeared to regard him as one of themselves, and fearlessly sat on the fence or lit among the boughs to watch him with their quick bright eyes. The robins in the apple-tree near by evidently considered him a friend, for the father bird hunted insects close beside him, and the little mother brooded as confidingly over her blue eggs as if the boy was only a new sort of blackbird, who cheered her patient watch with his song. The brown brook babbled and sparkled below him, the bees haunted the clover fields on either side, friendly faces peeped at him as they passed, the old house stretched its wide wings hospitably toward him, and with a blessed sense of rest and love, and happiness, Nat dreamed for hours in this nook, unconscious what healthful miracles were being wrought upon him.

One listener he had who never tired, and to whom he was more than a mere schoolmate. Poor Billy's chief delight was to lie beside the brook, watching leaves and bits of foam dance by, listening dreamily to the music in the willow-tree. He seemed to think Nat a sort of angel who sat aloft and sang, for a few baby memories still lingered in his mind and seemed to grow brighter at these times. Seeing the interest he took in Nat, Mr. Bhaer begged him to help them lift the cloud from the feeble brain by this gentle spell. Glad to do any thing to show his gratitude, Nat always smiled on Billy when he followed him about, and let him listen undisturbed to the music which seemed to speak a language he could understand. "Help one another," was a favorite Plumfield motto, and Nat learned how much sweetness is added to life by trying to live up to it.

Jack Ford's peculiar pastime was buying and selling; and he bid fair to follow in the footsteps of his uncle, a country merchant, who sold a little of everything and made money fast. Jack had seen the sugar sanded, the molasses watered, the butter mixed with lard, and things of that kind, and labored under the delusion that it was all a proper part of the business. His stock in trade was of a different sort, but he made as much as he could out of every worm he sold, and always got the best of the bargain when he traded with the boys for string, knives, fish-hooks, or whatever the article might be. The boys, who all had nicknames, called him "Skinflint," but Jack did not care as long as the old tobacco-pouch in which he kept his money grew heavier and heavier.

He established a sort of auction-room, and now and then sold off all the odds and ends he had collected, or helped the lads exchange things with one another. He got bats, balls, hockey-sticks, etc., cheap, from one set of mates, furbished them up, and let them for a few cents a time to another set, often extending his business beyond the gates of Plumfield in spite of the rules. Mr. Bhaer put a stop to some of his speculations, and tried to give him a better idea of business talent than mere sharpness in overreaching his neighbors. Now and then Jack made a bad bargain, and felt worse about it than about any failure in lessons or conduct, and took his revenge on the next innocent customer who came along. His account-book was a curiosity; and his quickness at figures quite remarkable. Mr. Bhaer praised him for this, and tried to make his sense of honesty and honor as quick; and, by and by, when Jack found that he could not get on without these virtues, he owned that his teacher was right.

Cricket and football the boys had of course—but, after the stirring accounts of these games in the immortal "Tom Brown at Rugby," no feeble female pen may venture to do more than respectfully allude to them.

There he loved to perch, making music like a happy bird.

Emil spent his holidays on the river or the pond, and drilled the elder lads for a race with certain town boys, who now and then invaded their territory. The race duly came off, but as it ended in a general shipwreck, it was not mentioned in public; and the Commodore had serious thoughts of retiring to a desert island, so disgusted was he with his kind for a time. No desert island being convenient, he was forced to remain among his friends, and found consolation in building a boat-house.

The little girls indulged in the usual plays of their age, improving upon them somewhat as their lively fancies suggested. The chief and most absorbing play was called "Mrs. Shakespeare Smith." The name was provided by Aunt Jo, but the trials of the poor lady were quite original. Daisy was Mrs. S. S., and Nan by turns her daughter or a neighbor, Mrs. Giddygaddy.

No pen can describe the adventures of these ladies, for in one short afternoon their family was the scene of births, marriages, deaths, floods, earthquakes, tea-parties, and balloon ascensions. Millions of miles did these energetic women travel, dressed in hats and habits never seen before by mortal eye, perched on the bed, driving the posts like mettlesome steeds, and bouncing up and down till their heads spun. Fits and fires were the pet afflictions, with a general massacre now and then by way of change. Nan was never tired of inventing fresh combinations, and Daisy followed her leader with blind admiration. Poor Teddy was a frequent victim, and was often rescued from real danger, for the excited ladies were apt to forget that he was not of the same stuff as their long-suffering dolls. Once he was shut into a closet for a dungeon, and forgotten by the girls, who ran off to some out-of-door game. Another time he was half drowned in the bath-tub, playing be a "cunning little whale." And, worst of all, he was cut down just in time after being hung up for a robber.

But the institution most patronized by all was the Club. It had no other name, and it needed none, being the only one in the neighborhood. The elder lads got it up, and the younger were occasionally admitted if they behaved well. Tommy and Demi were honorary members, but were always obliged to retire unpleasantly early, owing to circumstances over which they had no control. The proceedings of this club were somewhat peculiar, for it met at all sorts of places and hours, had all manner of queer ceremonies and amusements, and now and then was broken up tempestuously, only to be re-established, however, on a firmer basis.

Rainy evenings the members met in the school-room, and passed the time in games: chess, morris, backgammon, fencing matches, recitations, debates, or dramatic performances of a darkly tragical nature. In summer the barn was the rendezvous, and what went on there no uninitiated mortal knows. On sultry evenings the Club adjourned to the brook for aquatic exercises, and the members sat about in airy attire, frog-like and cool. On such occasions the speeches were unusually eloquent, quite flowing, as one might say; and if any orator's remarks displeased the audience, cold water was thrown upon him till his ardor was effectually quenched. Franz was president, and maintained order admirably, considering the unruly nature of the members. Mr. Bhaer never interfered with their affairs, and was rewarded for this wise forbearance by being invited now and then to behold the mysteries unveiled, which he appeared to enjoy much.

When Nan came she wished to join the Club, and caused great excitement and division among the gentlemen by presenting endless petitions, both written and spoken, disturbing their solemnities by insulting them through the keyhole, performing vigorous solos on the door, and writing up derisive remarks on walls and fences, for she belonged to the "Irrepressibles." Finding these appeals vain, the girls, by the advice of Mrs. Jo, got up an institution of their own, which they called the Cosy Club. To this they magnanimously invited the gentlemen whose youth excluded them from the other one, and entertained these favored beings so well with little suppers, new games devised by Nan, and other pleasing festivities, that, one by one, the elder boys confessed a desire to partake of these more elegant enjoyments, and, after much consultation, finally decided to propose an interchange of civilities.

The members of the Cosy Club were invited to adorn the rival establishment on certain evenings, and to the surprise of the gentlemen their presence was not found to be a restraint upon the conversation or amusement of the regular frequenters; which could not be said of all Clubs, I fancy. The ladies responded handsomely and hospitably to these overtures of peace, and both institutions flourished long and happily.

# CHAPTER IX

## DAISEY'S BALL

"MRS. SHAKESPEARE SMITH would like to have Mr. John Brooke, Mr. Thomas Bangs, and Mr. Nathaniel Blake to come to her ball at three o'clock today.

"*P.S.*—Nat must bring his fiddle, so we can dance, and all the boys must be good, or they cannot have any of the nice things we have cooked."

This elegant invitation would, I fear, have been declined, but for the hint given in the last line of the postscript.

"They *have* been cooking lots of goodies. I smelt 'em. Let's go," said Tommy.

"We needn't stay after the feast, you know," added Demi.

"I never went to a ball. What do you have to do?" asked Nat.

"Oh, we just play be men, and sit round stiff and stupid like grown-up folks, and dance to please the girls. Then we eat up everything, and come away as soon as we can."

"I think I could do that," said Nat, after considering Tommy's description for a minute.

"I'll write and say we'll come." And Demi despatched the following gentlemanly reply—

"We will all come. Please have lots to eat.—J. B. Esquire."

Great was the anxiety of the ladies about their first ball, because if everything went well they intended to give a dinner-party to the chosen few.

"Aunt Jo likes to have the boys play with us, if they are not rough; so we must make them like our balls, then they will do them good," said Daisy, with her maternal air, as she set the table and surveyed the store of refreshments with an anxious eye.

"Demi and Nat will be good, but Tommy will do something bad, I know he will," replied Nan, shaking her head over the little cake-basket which she was arranging.

"Then I shall send him right home," said Daisy, with decision.

"People don't do so at parties, it isn't proper."

"I shall never ask him any more."

"That would do. He'd be sorry not to come to the dinner-ball, wouldn't he?"

"I guess he would! We'll have the splendidest things ever seen, won't we? Real soup with a ladle and a tureem (she meant *tureen*) and a little bird for turkey, and gravy, and all kinds of nice vegytubbles." Daisy never *could* say vegetables properly, and had given up trying.

"It is 'most three, and we ought to dress," said Nan, who had arranged a fine costume for the occasion, and was anxious to wear it.

"I am the mother, so I shan't dress up much," said Daisy, putting on a night-cap ornamented with a red bow, one of her Aunt's long skirts, and a shawl; a pair of spectacles, and a large pocket handkerchief completed her toilette, making a plump, rosy, little matron of her.

Nan had a wreath of artificial flowers, a pair of old pink slippers, a yellow scarf, a green muslin skirt, and a fan made of feathers from the duster; also, as a last touch of elegance, a smelling-bottle without any smell in it.

"I am the daughter, so I rig up a good deal, and I must sing and dance, and talk more than you do. The mothers only get the tea and be proper, you know."

A sudden very loud knock caused Miss Smith to fly into a chair, and fan herself violently, while her mamma sat bolt upright on the sofa, and tried to look quite calm and "proper." Little Bess, who was on a visit, acted the part of maid, and opened the door, saying with a smile, "Wart in gemplemun, it's all weady."

In honor of the occasion, the boys wore high paper collars, tall black hats, and gloves of every color and material, for they were an afterthought, and not a boy among them had a perfect pair.

"Good day, mum," said Demi, in a deep voice, which was so hard to keep up that his remarks had to be extremely brief.

Everyone shook hands and then sat down, looking so funny, yet so sober, that the gentlemen forgot their manners, and rolled in their chairs with laughter.

"Oh don't!" cried Mrs. Smith, much distressed.

"You can't ever come again if you act so," added Miss Smith, rapping Mr. Bangs with her bottle because he laughed loudest.

"I can't help it, you look so like fury," gasped Mr. Bangs, with most uncourteous candor.

"So do you, but I shouldn't be so rude as to say so. He shan't come to the dinner-ball, shall he, Daisy?" cried Nan, indignantly.

"I think we had better dance now. Did you bring your fiddle, sir?" asked Mrs. Smith, trying to preserve her polite composure.

"It is outside the door," and Nat went to get it.

"Better have tea first," proposed the unabashed Tommy, winking openly at Demi to remind him that the sooner the refreshments were secured the sooner they could escape.

"No, we never have supper first; and if you don't dance well you won't have any supper at all, *not one bit, sir*," said Mrs. Smith, so sternly that her wild guests saw she was not to be trifled with, and grew overwhelmingly civil all at once.

"*I* will take Mr. Bangs and teach him the polka, for he does not know it fit to be seen," added the hostess, with a reproachful look that sobered Tommy at once.

Nat struck up, and the ball opened with two couples, who went conscientiously through a somewhat varied dance. The ladies did well, because they liked it, but the gentlemen exerted themselves from more selfish motives, for each felt that he must earn his supper, and labored manfully toward that end. When everyone was out of breath they were allowed to rest; and, indeed, poor Mrs. Smith needed it, for her long dress had tripped her up many times. The little maid passed round molasses and water in such small cups that one guest actually emptied nine. I refrain from mentioning his name, because this mild beverage affected him so much that he put cup and all into his mouth at the ninth round, and choked himself publicly.

"You must ask Nan to play and sing now," said Daisy to her brother, who sat looking very much like an owl, as he gravely regarded the festive scene between his high collars.

"Give us a song, mum," said the obedient guest, secretly wondering where the piano was.

Miss Smith sailed up to an old secretary which stood in the room, threw back the lid of the writing-desk, and sitting down before it, accompanied herself with a vigor which made the old desk rattle as she sang that new and lovely song, beginning—

> *"Gaily the troubadour*
> *Touched his guitar,*
> *As he was hastening*
> *Home from the war."*

The gentlemen applauded so enthusiastically that she gave them "Bounding Billows," "Little Bo-Peep," and other gems of song, till they were obliged to hint that they had had enough. Grateful for the praises bestowed upon her daughter, Mrs. Smith graciously announced—

"*Now* we will have tea. Sit down carefully, and don't grab."

It was beautiful to see the air of pride with which the good lady did the honors of her table, and the calmness with which she bore the little mishaps that occurred. The best pie flew wildly on to the floor when she tried to cut it with a very dull knife; the bread and butter vanished with a rapidity calculated to dismay a housekeeper's soul; and, worst of all, the custards were so soft that they had to be drunk up, instead of being eaten elegantly with the new tin spoons.

I grieve to state that Miss Smith squabbled with the maid for the best jumble, which caused Bess to toss the whole dish into the air, and burst out crying amid a rain of falling cakes. She was comforted by a seat at the table, and the sugar-bowl to empty; but during this flurry a large plate of patties was mysteriously lost, and could not be found. They were the chief ornament of the feast, and Mrs. Smith was indignant at the loss, for she had made them herself, and they were beautiful to behold. I put it to any lady if it was not hard to have one dozen delicious patties (made of flour, salt, and water, with a large raisin in the middle of each, and much sugar over the whole) swept away at one fell swoop?

"You hid them, Tommy; I know you did!" cried the outraged hostess, threatening her suspected guest with the milk-pot.

"I didn't!"

"You did!"

"It isn't proper to contradict," said Nan, who was hastily eating up the jelly during the fray.

"Give them back, Demi," said Tommy.

"That's a fib, you've got them in your own pocket," bawled Demi, roused by the false accusation.

"Let's take 'em away from him. It's too bad to make Daisy cry," suggested Nat, who found his first ball more exciting than he expected.

Daisy was already weeping, Bess like a devoted servant mingled her tears with those of her mistress, and Nan denounced the entire race of boys as "plaguey things." Meanwhile the battle raged among the gentlemen, for, when the two defenders of innocence fell upon the foe, that hardened youth intrenched himself behind a table and pelted them with the stolen tarts which were very effective missiles, being nearly as hard as bullets. While his ammunition held out the besieged prospered, but the moment the last patty flew over the parapet, the villain was seized, dragged howling from the room, and cast upon the hall floor in an ignominious heap. The conquerors then returned flushed with victory, and while Demi consoled poor Mrs. Smith, Nat and Nan collected the scattered tarts, replaced each raisin in its proper bed, and rearranged the dish so that it really looked almost as well as ever. But their glory had departed, for the sugar was gone, and no one cared to eat them after the insult offered to them.

"I guess we had better go," said Demi, suddenly, as Aunt Jo's voice was heard on the stairs.

"P'raps we had," and Nat hastily dropped a stray jumble that he had just picked up.

But Mrs. Jo was among them before the retreat was accomplished, and into her sympathietic ear the young ladies poured the story of their woes.

"No more balls for these boys till they have atoned for this bad behavior by doing something kind to you," said Mrs. Jo, shaking her head at the three culprits.

"We were only in fun," began Demi.

*"Gaily the troubadour*
*Touched his guitar."*

"I don't like fun that makes other people unhappy, I am disappointed in you, Demi, for I hoped you would never learn to tease Daisy. Such a kind little sister as she is to you."

"Boys always tease their sisters; Tom says so," muttered Demi.

"I don't intend that *my* boys shall, and I must send Daisy home if you cannot play happily together," said Aunt Jo, soberly.

At this awful threat, Demi sidled up to his sister, and Daisy hastily dried her tears, for to be separated was the worst misfortune that could happen to the twins.

"Nat was bad too, and Tommy was baddest of all," observed Nan, fearing that two of the sinners would not get their fair share of punishment.

"I am sorry," said Nat, much ashamed.

"I ain't!" bawled Tommy through the keyhole, where he was listening, with all his might.

Mrs. Jo wanted very much to laugh, but kept her countenance, and said impressively, as she pointed to the door—

"You can go, boys, but remember, you are not to speak to or play with the little girls till I give you leave. You don't deserve the pleasure, so I forbid it."

The ill-mannered young gentlemen hastily retired to be received outside with derision and scorn by the unrepentant Bangs, who would not associate with them for at least fifteen minutes. Daisy was soon consoled for the failure of her ball, but lamented the edict that parted her from her brother, and mourned over his short-comings in her tender little heart. Nat rather enjoyed the trouble, and went about turning up her pug nose at the three, especially Tommy, who pretended not to care, and loudly proclaimed his satisfaction at being rid of those "stupid girls." But in his secret soul he soon repented of the rash act that caused this banishment from the society he loved, and every hour of separation taught him the value of the "stupid girls."

The others gave in very soon, and longed to be friends, for now there was no Daisy to pet and cook for them; no Nan to amuse and doctor them; and, worst of all, no Mrs. Jo to make home pleasant and life easy for them. To their great affliction, Mrs. Jo seemed to consider herself one of the offended girls, for she hardly spoke to the outcasts, looked as if she did not see them when she passed, and was always too busy now to attend to their requests. This sudden and entire exile from favor cast a gloom over their souls, for when Mother Bhaer deserted them, their sun had set at noon-day, as it were, and they had no refuge left.

This unnatural state of things actually lasted for three days, then they could bear it no longer, and fearing that the eclipse might become total, went to Mr. Bhaer for help and counsel.

It is my private opinion that he had received instructions how to behave if the case should be laid before him. But no one suspected it, and he gave the afflicted boys some advice, which they gratefully accepted and carried out in the following manner:—

Secluding themselves in the garret, they devoted several play-hours to the manufacture of some mysterious machine, which took so much paste that Asia grumbled, and the little girls wondered mightily. Nan nearly got her inquisitive nose pinched in the door, trying to see what was going on and Daisy sat about openly lamenting that they could not all play nicely together, and not have any dreadful secrets. Wednesday afternoon was fine, and after a good deal of consultation about wind and weather, Nat and Tommy went off, bearing an immense flat parcel hidden under many newspapers. Nan nearly died with suppressed curiosity, Daisy nearly cried with vexation, and both quite trembled with interest when Demi marched into Mrs. Bhaer's room, hat in hand, and said, in the politest tone possible to a mortal boy of his years,—

"Please, Aunt Jo, would you and the girls come out to a surprise party we have made for you? Do, it's a *very* nice one."

"Thank you, we will come with pleasure; only, I must take Teddy with me," replied Mrs. Bhaer, with a smile that cheered Demi like sunshine after rain.

"We'd like to have him. The little wagon is all ready for the girls; and you won't mind walking just up to Pennyroyal Mill, will you, Aunty?"

"I should like it exceedingly; but are you quite sure I shall not be in the way?"

"Oh no, indeed! We want you very much; and the party will be spoilt if you don't come," cried Demi, with great earnestness.

"Thank you kindly, sir;" and Aunt Jo made him a grand curtsey, for she liked frolics as well as any of them.

"Now, young ladies, we must not keep them waiting; on with the hats, and let us be off at once. I'm all impatience to know what the surprise is."

As Mrs. Bhaer spoke every one bustled about and in five minutes the three little girls and Teddy were packed into the "clothes-basket," as they called the wicker wagon which Toby drew. Demi walked at the head of the procession, and Mrs. Jo brought up the rear, escorted by Kit. It was a most imposing party, I assure you, for Toby had a red feather-duster in his head, two remarkable flags waved over the carriage, Kit had a blue bow on his neck, which nearly drove him wild, Demi wore a nosegay of dandelions in his buttonhole, and Mrs. Jo carried the queer Japanese umbrella in honor of the occasion.

The girls had little flutters of excitement all the way; and Teddy was so charmed with the drive that he kept dropping his hat overboard, and when it was taken from him he prepared to tumble out himself, evidently feeling that it behooved him to do something for the amusement of the party.

When they came to the hill "nothing was to be seen but the grass blowing in the wind," as the fairy books say, and the children looked disappointed. But Demi said, in his most impressive manner,—

"Now, you all get out and stand still, and the surprise party will come in;" with which remark he retired behind a rock, over which heads had been bobbing at intervals for the last half-hour.

A short pause of intense suspense, and then Nat, Demi, and Tommy marched forth, each bearing a new kite, which they presented to the three young ladies. Shrieks of delight arose, but were silenced by the boys, who said, with faces brimful of merriment, "That isn't all the surprise;" and, running behind the rock again, emerged bearing a fourth kite of superb size, on which was printed, in bright yellow letters, "For Mother Bhaer."

"We thought you'd like one too, because you were angry with us, and took the girls' part," cried all three, shaking with laughter, for this part of the affair evidently *was* a surprise to Mrs. Jo.

She clapped her hands, and joined in the laugh, looking thoroughly tickled at the joke.

"Now boys, that is regularly splendid! Who did think of it?" she asked, receiving the monster kite with as much pleasure as the little girls did theirs.

"Uncle Fritz proposed it when we planned to make the others; he said you'd like it, so we made a bouncer," answered Demi, beaming with satisfaction at the success of the plot.

"Uncle Fritz knows what I like. Yes, these are magnificent kites, and we were wishing we had some the other day when you were flying yours, weren't we, girls?"

"That's why we made them for you," cried Tommy, standing on his head as the most appropriate way of expressing his emotions.

"Let us fly them," said energetic Nan.

"I don't know how," began Daisy.

"We'll show you, we want to!" cried all the boys in a burst of devotion, as Demi took Daisy's, Tommy Nan's, and Nat, with difficulty, persuaded Bess to let go her little blue one.

"Aunty, if you will wait a minute, we'll pitch yours for you," said Demi, feeling that Mrs. Bhaer's favor must not be lost again by any neglect of theirs.

"Bless your buttons, dear, I know all about it; and here is a boy who will toss up for me," added Mrs. Jo, as the professor peeped over the rock with a face full of fun.

He came out at once, tossed up the big kite, and Mrs. Jo ran off with it in fine style, while the children stood and enjoyed the spectacle. One by one all the kites went up, and floated far overhead like gay birds, balancing themselves on the fresh breeze that blew steadily over the hill. Such a merry time as they had! Running and shouting, sending up the kites or pulling them down, watching their antics in the air, and feeling them tug at the string like live creatures trying to escape. Nan was quite wild with the fun, Daisy thought the new play nearly as interesting as dolls, and little Bess was so fond of her "boo tite," that she would only let it go on very short flights, preferring to hold it in her lap and look at the remarkable pictures painted on it by Tommy's dashing brush. Mrs. Jo enjoyed hers immensely, and it acted as if it knew who owned it, for it came tumbling down head first when least expected, caught on trees, nearly pitched into the river, and finally darted away to such a height that it looked a mere speck among the clouds.

By and by every one got tired, and fastening the kite strings to trees and fences, all sat down to rest, except Mr. Bhaer, who went off to look at the cows, with Teddy on his shoulder.

"Did you ever have such a good time as this before?" asked Nat, as they lay about on the grass, nibbling pennyroyal like a flock of sheep.

"Not since I last flew a kite, years ago, when I was a girl," answered Mrs. Jo.

"I'd like to have known you when you were a girl, you must have been so jolly," said Nat.

"I was a naughty little girl, I am sorry to say."

"I like naughty little girls," observed Tommy, looking at Nan, who made a frightful grimace at him in return for the compliment.

"Why don't I remember you then, Aunty? Was I too young?" asked Demi.

"Rather, dear."

"I suppose my memory hadn't come then. Grandpa says that different parts of the mind unfold as we grow up, and the memory part of my mind hadn't unfolded when you were little, so I can't remember how you looked," explained Demi.

"Now, little Socrates, you had better keep that question for grandpa, it is beyond me," said Aunt Jo, putting on the extinguisher.

"Well, I will, *he* knows about those things, and *you* don't," returned Demi, feeling that on the whole kites were better adapted to the comprehension of the present company.

"Tell about the last time you flew a kite," said Nat, for Mrs. Jo had laughed as she spoke of it, and he thought it might be interesting.

"Oh, it was only rather funny, for I was a great girl of fifteen, and was ashamed to be seen at such a play. So Uncle Teddy and I privately made our kites, and stole away to fly them. We had a capital time, and were resting as we are now, when suddenly we heard voices, and saw a party of young ladies and gentlemen coming back from a picnic. Teddy did not mind, though he was rather a large boy to be playing with a kite, but I was in a great flurry, for I knew I should be sadly laughed at, and never hear the last of it, because my wild ways amused the neighbors as much as Nan's do us.

" 'What shall I do?' I whispered to Teddy, as the voices drew nearer and nearer.

" 'I'll show you,' he said, and whipping out his knife he cut the strings. Away flew the kites, and when the people came up we were picking flowers as properly as you please. They never suspected us, and we had a grand laugh over our narrow escape."

"Were the kites lost, Aunty?" asked Daisy.

"Quite lost, but I did not care, for I made up my mind that it would be best to wait till I was an old lady before I played with kites again; and you see I have waited," said Mrs. Jo, beginning to pull in the big kite, for it was getting late.

"Must we go now?"

"I must, or you won't have any supper; and that sort of surprise party would not suit you, I think, my chickens."

"Hasn't our party been a nice one?" asked Tommy, complacently.

"Splendid!" answered everyone.

"Do you know why? It is because *your* guests have behaved themselves, and tried to make every thing go well. You understand what I mean, don't you?"

"Yes 'm," was all the boys said, but they stole a shamefaced look at one another, as they meekly shouldered their kites and walked home, thinking of another party where the guests had *not* behaved themselves, and things had gone badly on account of it.

# CHAPTER X

## HOME AGAIN

JULY had come, and haying begun; the little gardens were doing finely, and the long summer days were full of pleasant hours. The house stood open from morning till night, and the lads lived out of doors, except at school time. The lessons were short, and there were many holidays, for the Bhaers believed in cultivating healthy bodies by much exercise, and our short summers are best used in out-of-door work. Such a rosy, sunburnt, hearty set as the boys became; such appetites as they had; such sturdy arms and legs, as outgrew jackets and trousers; such laughing and racing all over the place; such antics in house and barn; such adventures in the tramps over hill and dale; and such satisfaction in the hearts of the worthy Bhaers, as they saw their flock prospering in mind and body, I cannot begin to describe. Only one thing was needed to make them quite happy, and it came when they least expected it.

One balmy night when the little lads were in bed, the elder ones bathing down at the brook, and Mrs. Bhaer undressing Teddy in her parlor, he suddenly cried out, "Oh, my Danny!" and pointed to the window where the moon shone brightly.

"No, lovey, he is not there, it was the pretty moon," said his mother.

"No, no, Danny at a window; Teddy saw him," persisted baby, much excited.

"It might have been," and Mrs. Bhaer hurried to the window, hoping it would prove true. But the face was gone, and nowhere appeared any signs of a mortal boy; she called his name, ran to the front door with Teddy in his little shirt, and made him call too, thinking the baby voice might have more effect than her own. No one answered, nothing appeared, and they went back much disappointed. Teddy would not be satisfied with the moon, and after he was in his crib kept popping up his head to ask if Danny was not "tummin' soon."

By and by he fell asleep, the lads trooped up to bed, the house grew still, and nothing but the chirp of the crickets broke the soft silence of the summer night, Mrs. Bhaer sat sewing, for the big basket was always piled with socks, full of portentous holes, and thinking of the lost boy. She had decided that baby had been mistaken, and did not even disturb Mr. Bhaer by telling him of the child's fancy, for the poor man got little time to himself till the boys were abed, and he was busy writing letters. It was past ten when she rose to shut up the house. As she paused a minute to enjoy the lovely scene from the steps, something white caught her eye on one of the hay-cocks scattered over the lawn. The children had been playing there all the afternoon, and, fancying that Nan had left her hat as usual, Mrs. Bhaer went out to get it. But as she approached, she saw that it was neither hat nor handkerchief, but a shirt sleeve with a brown hand sticking out of it. She hurried round the hay-cock, and there lay Dan, fast asleep.

Ragged, dirty, thin, and worn-out he looked; one foot was bare, the other tied up in the old gingham jacket which he had taken from his own back to use as a clumsy bandage for some hurt. He seemed to have hidden himself behind the hay-cock, but in his sleep had thrown out the arm that had betrayed him. He sighed and muttered as if his dreams disturbed him, and once when he moved, he groaned as if in pain, but still slept on quite spent with weariness.

"He must not lie here," said Mrs. Bhaer, and stooping over him she gently called his name. He opened his eyes and looked at her, as if she was a part of his dream, for he smiled and said drowsily, "Mother Bhaer, I've come home."

The look, the words touched her very much, and she put her hand under his head to lift him up, saying in her cordial way—

"I thought you would, and I'm so glad to see you, Dan." He seemed to wake thoroughly then, and started up looking about him as if he suddenly remembered where he was, and doubted even that kind welcome. His face changed, and he said in his old rough way—

"I was going off in the morning. I only stopped to peek in, as I went by."

"But why not come in, Dan? Didn't you hear us call you? Teddy saw, and cried for you."

"Didn't suppose you'd let me in," he said, fumbling with a little bundle which he had taken up as if going immediately.

"Try and see," was all Mrs. Bhaer answered, holding out her hand and pointing to the door, where the light shone hospitably.

With a long breath, as if a load was off his mind, Dan took up a stout stick, and began to limp towards the house, but stopped suddenly, to say inquiringly—

"Mr. Bhaer won't like it. I ran away from Page."

"He knows it, and was sorry, but it will make no difference. Are you lame?" asked Mrs. Jo, as he limped on again.

"Getting over a wall a stone fell on my foot and smashed it. I don't mind," and he did his best to hide the pain each step cost him.

Mrs. Bhaer helped him into her own room, and, once there, he dropped into a chair, and laid his head back, white and faint with weariness and suffering.

"My poor Dan! Drink this, and then eat a little; you are at home now, and Mother Bhaer will take good care of you."

He only looked up at her with eyes full of gratitude, as he drank the wine she held to his lips, and then began slowly to eat the food she brought him. Each mouthful seemed to put heart into him, and presently he began to talk as if anxious to have her know all about him.

"Where have you been, Dan?" she asked, beginning to get out some bandages.

"I ran off more 'n a month ago. Page was good enough, but too strict. I didn't like it, so I cut away down the river with a man who was going in his boat. That's why they couldn't tell where I'd gone. When I left the man, I worked for a couple of weeks with a farmer, but I thrashed his boy, and then the old man thrashed me, and I ran off again and walked here."

"All the way?"

"Yes, the man didn't pay me, and I wouldn't ask for it. Took it out in beating the boy," and Dan laughed, yet looked ashamed, as he glanced at his ragged clothes and dirty hands.

"How did you live? It was a long, long tramp for a boy like you."

"Oh, I got on well enough, till I hurt my foot. Folks gave me things to eat, and I slept in barns and tramped by day. I got lost trying to make a short cut, or I'd have been here sooner."

"But if you did not mean to come in and stay with us, what were you going to do?"

"I thought I'd like to see Teddy again, and you; and then I was going back to my old work in the city, only I was so tired I went to sleep on the hay. I'd have been gone in the morning, if you hadn't found me."

"Are you sorry I did?" and Mrs. Jo looked at him with a half merry, half reproachful look, as she knelt down to look at his wounded foot.

The color came up into Dan's face, and he kept his eyes fixed on his plate, as he said very low, "No, ma'am, I'm glad, I wanted to stay, but I was afraid you"—

He did not finish, for Mrs. Bhaer interrupted him by an exclamation of pity, as she saw his foot, for it was seriously hurt.

"When did you do it?"

"Three days ago."

"And you have walked on it in this state?"

"I had a stick, and I washed it at every brook I came to, and one woman gave me a rag to put on it."

"Mr. Bhaer must see and dress it at once," and Mrs. Jo hastened into the next room, leaving the door ajar behind her, so that Dan heard all that passed.

"Fritz, that boy has come back."

"Who? Dan?"

"Yes, Teddy saw him at the window, and we called to him, but he went away and hid behind the hay-cocks on the lawn. I found him there just now fast asleep, and half dead with weariness and pain. He ran away from Page a month ago, and has been making his way to us ever since. He pretends that he did not mean to let us see him, but go on to the city, and his old work, after a look at us. It is evident, however, that the hope of being taken in has led him here through everything, and there he is waiting to know if you will forgive and take him back."

"Did he say so?"

"His eyes did, and when I waked him, he said, like a lost child, 'Mother Bhaer, I've come home.' I hadn't the heart to scold him, and just took him in like a poor little black sheep come back to the fold. I may keep him, Fritz?"

"Of course you may! This proves to me that we have a hold on the boy's heart, and I would no more send him away now than I would my own Rob."

Dan heard a soft little sound, as if Mrs. Jo thanked her husband without words, and, in the instant's silence that followed, two great tears that had slowly gathered in the boy's eyes brimmed over and rolled down his dusty cheeks. No one saw them, for he brushed them hastily away; but in that little pause I think Dan's old distrust for these good people vanished forever, the soft spot in his heart was touched, and he felt an impetuous desire to prove himself worthy of the love and pity that was so patient and forgiving. He said nothing, he only wished the wish with all his might, resolved to try in his blind boyish way, and sealed his resolution with the tears which neither pain, fatigue, nor loneliness could wring from him.

"Come and see his foot. I am afraid it is badly hurt, for he has kept on three days through heat and dust, with nothing but water and an old jacket to bind it up with. I tell you, Fritz, that boy is a brave lad, and will make a fine man yet."

"I hope so, for your sake, enthusiastic woman, your faith deserves success. Now, I will go and see your little Spartan. Where is he?"

"In my room; but, dear, you'll be very kind to him, no matter how gruff he seems. I am sure that is the way to conquer him. He won't bear sternness nor much restraint, but a soft word and infinite patience will lead him as it used to lead me."

"As if you ever were like this little rascal!" cried Mr. Bhaer, laughing, yet half angry at the idea.

"I was in spirit, though I showed it in a different way. I seem to know by instinct how he feels, to understand what will win and touch him, and to sympathize with his temptations and faults. I am glad I do, for it will help me to help him; and if I can make a good man of this wild boy, it will be the best work of my life."

"God bless the work, and help the worker!"

Mr. Bhaer spoke now as earnestly as she had done and both came in together to find Dan's head down upon his arm, as if he was quite overcome by sleep. But he looked up quickly, and tried to rise as Mr. Bhaer said pleasantly—

"So you like Plumfield better than Page's farm. Well, let us see if we can get on more comfortably this time than we did before."

"Thanky, sir," said Dan, trying not to be gruff, and finding it easier than he expected.

"Now, the foot! Ach!—this is not well. We must have Dr. Firth tomorrow. Warm water, Jo, and old linen."

Mr. Bhaer bathed and bound up the wounded foot, while Mrs. Jo prepared the only empty bed in the house. It was in the little guest-chamber leading from the parlor, and often used when the lads were poorly, for it saved Mrs. Jo from running up and down, and the invalids could see what was going on. When it was ready, Mr. Bhaer took the boy in his arms, and carried him in, helped him undress, laid him on the little white bed, and left him with another hand-shake, and a fatherly "Good-night, my son."

Dan dropped asleep at once, and slept heavily for several hours; then his foot began to throb and ache, and he awoke to toss about uneasily, trying not to groan lest any one should hear him, for he *was* a brave lad, and did bear pain like "a little Spartan," as Mr. Bhaer called him.

Mrs. Jo had a way of flitting about the house at night, to shut the windows if the wind grew chilly, to draw mosquito curtains over Teddy, or look after Tommy, who occasionally walked in his sleep. The least noise waked her, and as she often heard imaginary robbers, cats, and conflagrations, the doors stood open all about, so her quick ear caught the sound of Dan's little moans, and she was up in a minute. He was just giving his hot pillow a despairing thump when a light came glimmering through the hall, and Mrs. Jo crept in, looking like a droll ghost, with her hair in a great knob on the top of her head, and a long gray dressing-gown trailing behind her.

"Are you in pain, Dan?"

"It's pretty bad; but I didn't mean to wake you."

"I'm a sort of owl, always flying about at night. Yes, your foot is like fire; the bandages must be wet again," and away flapped the maternal owl for more cooling stuff, and a great mug of ice water.

"Oh, that's *so* nice!" sighed Dan, as the wet bandages went on again, and a long draught of water cooled his thirsty throat.

"There, now, sleep your best, and don't be frightened if you see me again, for I'll slip down by and by, and give you another sprinkle."

As she spoke, Mrs. Jo stooped to turn the pillow and smooth the bed-clothes, when, to her great surprise, Dan put his arm round her neck, drew her face down to his, and kissed her, with a broken "Thank you, ma'am," which said more than the most eloquent speech could have done; for the hasty kiss, the muttered words, meant, "I'm sorry, I will try." She understood it, accepted the unspoken confession, and did not spoil it by any token of surprise. She only remembered that he had no mother, kissed the brown cheek half hidden on the pillow as if ashamed of that little touch of tenderness, and left him, saying, what he long remembered, "You are my boy now, and if you choose you can make me proud and glad to say so."

Once again just at dawn, she stole down to find him so fast asleep that he did not wake, and showed no sign of consciousness as she wet his foot, except that the lines of pain smoothed themselves away, and left his face quite peaceful.

The day was Sunday, and the house so still that he never waked till near noon, and, looking round him, saw an eager little face peering in at the door. He held out his arms, and Teddy tore across the room to cast himself bodily upon the bed, shouting, "My Danny's tum!" as he hugged and wriggled with delight. Mrs. Bhaer appeared next, bringing breakfast, and never seeming to see how shamefaced Dan looked at the memory of the little scene last night. Teddy insisted on giving him his "betfus," and fed him like a baby, which, as he was not very hungry, Dan enjoyed very much.

Then came the doctor, and the poor Spartan had a bad time of it, for some of the little bones of his foot were injured, and putting them to rights was such a painful job, that Dan's lips were white, and great drops stood on his forehead, though he never cried out, and only held Mrs. Jo's hand so tight that it was red long afterwards.

Mr. Bhaer bathed and bound up the wounded foot.

"You must keep this boy quiet, for a week at least, and not let him put his foot to the ground. By that time, I shall know whether he may hop a little with a crutch, or stick to his bed for a while longer," said Dr. Firth, putting up the shining instruments that Dan did not like to see.

"It will get well sometime, won't it?" he asked, looking alarmed at the word "crutches."

"I hope so"; and with that the doctor departed, leaving Dan much depressed; for the loss of a foot is a dreadful calamity to an active boy.

"Don't be troubled, I am a famous nurse, and we will have you tramping about as well as ever in a month," said Mrs. Jo, taking a hopeful view of the case.

But the fear of being lame haunted Dan, and even Teddy's caresses did not cheer him; so Mrs. Jo proposed that one or two of the boys should come in and pay him a little visit, and asked whom he would like to see.

"Nat and Demi; I'd like my hat too, there's something in it I guess they'd like to see. I suppose you threw away my bundle of plunder?" said Dan, looking rather anxious as he put the question.

"No, I kept it, for I thought they must be treasures of some kind, you took such care of them"; and Mrs. Jo brought him his old straw hat stuck full of butterflies and beetles, and a handkerchief containing a collection of odd things picked up on his way: birds' eggs, carefully done up in moss, curious shells and stones, bits of fungus, and several little crabs, in a state of great indignation at their imprisonment.

"Could I have something to put these fellers in? Mr. Hyde and I found 'em, and they are first-rate ones, so I'd like to keep and watch 'em; can I?" asked Dan, forgetting his foot, and laughing to see the crabs go sidling and backing over the bed.

"Of course you can; Polly's old cage will be just the thing. Don't let them nip Teddy's toes while I get it"; and away went Mrs. Jo, leaving Dan overjoyed to find that his treasures were not considered rubbish, and thrown away.

Nat, Demi, and the cage arrived together, and the crabs were settled in their new house, to the great delight of the boys, who, in the excitement of the performance, forgot any awkwardness they might otherwise have felt in greeting the runaway. To these admiring listeners Dan related his adventures much more fully than he had done to the Bhaers. Then he displayed his "plunder," and described each article so well, that Mrs. Jo, who had retired to the next room to leave them free, was surprised and interested, as well as amused, at their boyish chatter.

"How much the lad knows of these things! How absorbed he is in them! And what a mercy it is just now, for he cares so little for books, it would be hard to amuse him while he is laid up; but the boys can supply him with beetles and stones to any extent, and I am glad to find out this taste of his; it is a good one, and may perhaps prove the making of him. If he should turn out a great naturalist, and Nat a musician, I should have cause to be proud of this year's work;" and Mrs. Jo sat smiling over her book as she built castles in the air, just as she used to do when a girl, only then they were for herself, and now they were for other people, which is the reason perhaps that some of them came to pass in reality— for charity is an excellent foundation to build anything upon.

Nat was most interested in the adventures, but Demi enjoyed the beetles and butterflies immensely drinking in the history of their changeful little lives as if it were a new and lovely sort of fairy tale—for, even in his plain way, Dan told it well, and found great satisfaction in the thought that here at least the small philosopher could learn of him. So interested were they in the account of catching a musk rat, whose skin was among the treasures, that Mr. Bhaer had to come himself to tell Nat and Demi it was time for the walk. Dan looked so wistfully after them as they ran off, that Father Bhaer proposed carrying him to the sofa in the parlor for a little change of air and scene.

When he was established, and the house quiet, Mrs. Jo, who sat near by showing Teddy pictures, said, in an interested tone, as she nodded towards the treasures still in Dan's hands—

"Where did you learn so much about these things?"

"I always liked 'em, but didn't know much till Mr. Hyde told me."

"Who was Mr. Hyde?"

"Oh, he was a man who lived round in the woods studying these things—I don't know what you call him—and wrote about frogs, and fishes, and so on. He stayed at Page's, and used to want me to go and help him, and it was great fun, 'cause he told me ever so much, and was uncommon jolly and wise. Hope I'll see him again sometime."

"I hope you will," said Mrs. Jo, for Dan's face had brightened up, and he was so interested in the matter that he forgot his usual taciturnity.

"Why, he could make birds come to him, and rabbits and squirrels didn't mind him any more than if he was a tree. He never hurt 'em, and they seemed to know him. Did you ever tickle a lizard with a straw?" asked Dan, eagerly.

"No, but I should like to try it."

"Well, I've done it, and it's so funny to see 'em turn over and stretch out, they like it so much. Mr. Hyde used to do it; and he'd make snakes listen to him while he whistled, and he knew just when certain flowers would blow, and bees wouldn't sting him, and he'd tell the wonderfullest things about fish and flies, and the Indians and the rocks."

"I think you were so fond of going with Mr. Hyde, you rather neglected Mr. Page," said Mrs. Jo, slyly.

"Yes, I did; I hated to have to weed and hoe when I might be tramping round with Mr. Hyde. Page thought such things silly, and called Mr. Hyde crazy because he'd lay hours watching a trout or a bird."

"Suppose you say *lie* instead of *lay*, it is better grammar," said Mrs. Jo, very gently; and then added, "Yes, Page is a thorough farmer, and would not understand that a naturalist's work was just as interesting, and perhaps just as important as his own. Now, Dan, if you really love these things, as I think you do, and I am glad to see it, you shall have time to study them and books to help you; but I want you to do something besides, and to do it faithfully, else you will be sorry by and by, and find that you have got to begin again."

"Yes, ma'am," said Dan, meekly, and looked a little scared by the serious tone of the last remarks, for he hated books, yet had evidently made up his mind to study anything she proposed.

"Do you see that cabinet with twelve drawers in it?" was the next very unexpected question.

Dan did see two tall old-fashioned ones standing on either side of the piano; he knew them well, and had often seen nice bits of string, nails, brown paper, and such useful matters come out of the various drawers. He nodded and smiled. Mrs. Jo went on—

"Well, don't you think those drawers would be good places to put your eggs, and stones, and shells, and lichens?"

"Oh, splendid but you wouldn't like my things 'clutterin' round,' as Mr. Page used to say, would you?" cried Dan, sitting up to survey the old piece of furniture with sparkling eyes.

"I like litter of that sort; and if I didn't, I should give you the drawers, because I have a regard for children's little treasures, and think they should be treated respectfully. Now, I am going to make a bargain with you, Dan, and I hope you will keep it honorably. Here are twelve good-sized drawers, one for each month of the year, and they shall be yours as fast as you earn them, by doing the little duties that belong to you. I believe in rewards of a certain kind, especially for young folks; they help us along, and though we may begin by being good for the sake of the reward, if it is rightly used, we shall soon learn to love goodness for itself."

"Do you have 'em?" asked Dan, looking as if this was new talk for him.

"Yes, indeed! I haven't learnt to get on without them yet. My rewards are not drawers, or presents, or holidays, but they are things which I like as much as you do the others. The good behavior and success of my boys is one of the rewards I love best, and I work for it as I want you to work for your cabinet. Do what you dislike, and do it well, and you get two rewards—one, the prize you see and hold; the other, the satisfaction of a duty cheerfully performed. Do you understand that?"

"Yes, ma'am."

"We all need these little helps; so you shall try to do your lessons and your work, play kindly with all the boys, and use your holidays well; and if you bring me a good report, or if I see and know it without words— for I'm quick to spy out the good little efforts of my boys—you shall have a compartment in the drawer for your treasures. See, some are already divided into four parts, and I will have the others made in the same way, a place for each week; and when the drawer is filled with curious and pretty things, I shall be as proud of it as you are; prouder, I think—for in the pebbles, mosses, and gay butterflies, I shall see good resolutions carried out, conquered faults, and a promise well kept. Shall we do this, Dan?"

The boy answered with one of the looks which said much, for it showed that he felt and understood her wish and words, although he did not know how to express his interest and gratitude for such care and kindness. She understood the look, and seeing by the color that flushed up to his forehead that he was touched, as she wished him to be, she said no more about that side of the new plan, but pulled out the upper drawer, dusted it, and set it on two chairs before the sofa, saying briskly—

"Now, let us begin at once by putting those nice beetles in a safe place. These compartments will hold a good deal, you see. I'd pin the butterflies and bugs round the sides; they will be quite safe there, and leave room for the heavy things below. I'll give you some cotton wool, and clean paper and pins, and you can get ready for the week's work."

"But I can't go out to find any new things," said Dan, looking piteously at his foot.

"That's true; never mind, we'll let these treasures do for this week, and I dare say the boys will bring you loads of things if you ask them."

"They don't know the right sort; besides, if I lay, no, *lie* here all the time, I can't work and study, and earn my drawers."

"There are plenty of lessons you can learn lying there, and several little jobs of work you can do for me."

"Can I?" and Dan looked both surprised and pleased.

"You can learn to be patient and cheerful in spite of pain and no play. You can amuse Teddy for me, wind cotton, read to me when I sew, and do many things without hurting your foot, which will make the days pass quickly, and not be wasted ones."

Here Demi ran in with a great butterfly in one hand, and a very ugly little toad in the other.

"See, Dan, I found them, and ran back to give them to you; aren't they beautiful ones?" panted Demi, all out of breath.

Dan laughed at the toad, and said he had no place to put him, but the butterfly was a beauty, and if Mrs. Jo would give him a big pin, he would stick it right up in the drawer.

"I don't like to see the poor thing struggle on a pin; if it must be killed, let us put it out of pain at once with a drop of camphor," said Mrs. Jo, getting out the bottle.

"I know how to do it—Mr. Hyde always killed 'em that way—but I didn't have any camphor, so I use a pin," and Dan gently poured a drop on the insect's head, when the pale green wings fluttered an instant, and then grew still.

This dainty little execution was hardly over when Teddy shouted from the bedroom, "Oh, the little trabs are out, and the big one's eaten 'em all up." Demi and his aunt ran to the rescue, and found Teddy dancing excitedly in a chair, while two little crabs were scuttling about the floor, having got through the wires of the cage. A third was clinging to the top of the cage, evidently in terror of his life, for below appeared a sad yet funny sight. The big crab had wedged himself into the little recess where Polly's cup used to stand, and there he sat eating one of his relations in the coolest way. All the claws of the poor victim were pulled off, and he was turned upside down, his upper shell held in one claw close under the mouth of the big crab like a dish, while he leisurely ate out of it with the other claw, pausing now and then to turn his queer bulging eyes from side to side, and to put out a slender tongue and lick them in a way that made the children scream with laughter. Mrs. Jo carried the cage in for Dan to see the sight, while Demi caught and confined the wanderers under an inverted wash-bowl.

"I'll have to let these fellers go, for I can't keep 'em in the house," said Dan, with evident regret.

"I'll take care of them for you, if you will tell me how, and they can live in my turtle-tank just as well as not," said Demi, who found them more interesting even than his beloved slow turtles. So Dan gave him directions about the wants and habits of the crabs, and Demi bore them away to introduce them to their new home and neighbors. "What a good boy he is!" said Dan, carefully settling the first butterfly, and remembering that Demi had given up his walk to bring it to him.

"He ought to be, for a great deal has been done to make him so."

"He's had folks to tell him things, and to help him; I haven't," said Dan, with a sigh, thinking of his neglected childhood, a thing he seldom did, and feeling as if he had not had fair play somehow.

"I know it, dear, and for that reason I don't expect as much from you as from Demi, though he is younger; you shall have all the help that we can give you now, and I hope to teach you how to help yourself in the best way. Have you forgotten what Father Bhaer told you when you were here before, about wanting to be good, and asking God to help you?"

"No, ma'am," very low.

"Do you try that way still?"

"No, ma'am," lower still.

"Will you do it every night to please me?"

"Yes, ma'am," very soberly.

"I shall depend on it, and I think I shall know if you are faithful to your promise, for these things always show to people who believe in them, though not a word is said. Now here is a pleasant story about a boy who hurt his foot worse than you did yours; read it, and see how bravely he bore his trouble."

She put that charming little book, "The Crofton Boys," into his hands, and left him for an hour, passing in and out from time to time that he might not feel lonely. Dan did not love to read, but soon got so interested that he was surprised when the boys came home. Daisy brought him a nosegay of wild flowers, and Nan insisted on helping bring him his supper, as he lay on the sofa with the door open into the dining-room, so that he could see the lads at table, and they could nod sociably to him over their bread and butter.

Mr. Bhaer carried him away to his bed early, and Teddy came in his night-gown to say good-night, for he went to his little nest with the birds.

"I want to say my prayers to Danny; may I?" he asked; and when his mother said "Yes," the little fellow knelt down by Dan's bed, and folding his chubby hands, said softly—

"Pease Dod bess everybody, and hep me to be dood."

Then he went away smiling with sleepy sweetness over his mother's shoulder.

But after the evening talk was done, the evening song sung, and the house grew still with beautiful Sunday silence, Dan lay in his pleasant room wide awake, thinking new thoughts, feeling new hopes and desires stirring in his boyish heart, for two good angels had entered in: love and gratitude began the work which time and effort were to finish; and with an earnest wish to keep his first promise, Dan folded his hands together in the darkness, and softly whispered Teddy's little prayer—

"Please God bless every one, and help me to be good."

# CHAPTER XI

## UNCLE TEDDY

FOR a week Dan only moved from bed to sofa; a long week and a hard one, for the hurt foot was very painful at times, the quiet days very wearisome to the active lad, longing to be out enjoying the summer weather, and especially difficult was it to be patient. But Dan did his best, and everyone helped him in their various ways; so the time passed, and he was rewarded at last by hearing the doctor say, on Saturday morning—

"This foot is doing better than I expected. Give the lad the crutch this afternoon, and let him stump about the house a little."

"Hooray!" shouted Nat, and raced away to tell the other boys the good news.

Everybody was very glad, and after dinner the whole flock assembled to behold Dan crutch himself up and down the hall a few times before he settled in the porch to hold a sort of *levée*. He was much pleased at the interest and good-will shown him, and brightened up more and more every minute; for the boys came to pay their respects, the little girls fussed about him with stools and cushions, and Teddy watched over him as if he was a frail creature unable to do any thing for himself. They were still sitting and standing about the steps when a carriage stopped at the gate, a hat was waved from it, and with a shout of "Uncle Teddy! Uncle Teddy!" Rob scampered down the avenue as fast as his short legs would carry him. All the boys but Dan ran after him to see who should be first to open the gate, and in a moment the carriage drove up with boys swarming all over it, while Uncle Teddy sat laughing in the midst, with his little daughter on his knee.

"Stop the triumphal car and let Jupiter descend," he said, and jumping out ran up the steps to meet Mrs. Bhaer, who stood smiling and clapping her hands like a girl.

"How goes it, Teddy?"

"All right, Jo."

Then they shook hands, and Mr. Laurie put Bess into her aunt's arms, saying, as the child hugged her tight, "Goldilocks wanted to see you so much that I ran away with her, for I was quite pining for a sight of you myself. We want to play with your boys for an hour or so, and to see how 'the old woman who lived in a shoe, and had so many children she did not know what to do,' is getting on."

"I'm so glad! Play away, and don't get into mischief," answered Mrs. Jo, as the lads crowded round the pretty child, admiring her long golden hair, dainty dress, and lofty ways, for the little "Princess," as they called her, allowed no one to kiss her, but sat smiling down upon them, and graciously patting their heads with her little, white hands. They all adored her, especially Rob, who considered her a sort of doll, and dared not touch her lest she should break, but wrrshipped her at a respectful distance, made happy by an occasional mark of favor from her little highness. As she immediately demanded to see Daisy's kitchen, she was borne off by Mrs. Jo, with a train of small boys following. The others, all but Nat and Demi, ran away to the menagerie and gardens to have all in order; for Mr. Laurie always took a general survey, and looked disappointed if things were not flourishing.

Standing on the steps, he turned to Dan, saying like an old acquaintance, though he had only seen him once or twice before—

"How is the foot?"

"Better, sir."

"Rather tired of the house aren't you?"

"Guess I am!" and Dan's eyes roved away to the green hills and woods where he longed to be.

"Suppose we take a little turn before the others come back? That big, easy carriage will be quite safe and comfortable, and a breath of fresh air will do you good. Get a cushion and a shawl, Demi, and let's carry Dan off."

The boys thought it a capital joke, and Dan looked delighted, but asked, with an unexpected burst of virtue—

"Will Mrs. Bhaer like it?"

"Oh, yes; we settled all that a minute ago."

"You didn't say anything about it, so I don't see how you could," said Demi, inquisitively.

"We have a way of sending messages to one another, without any words. It is a great improvement on the telegraph."

"I know—it's eyes; I saw you lift your eyebrows, and nod toward the carriage, and Mrs. Bhaer laughed and nodded back again," cried Nat, who was quite at his ease with kind Mr. Laurie by this time.

"Right. Now then, come on," and in a minute Dan found himself settled in the carriage, his foot on a cushion on the seat opposite, nicely covered with a shawl, which fell down from the upper regions in a most mysterious manner, just when they wanted it. Demi climbed up to the box beside Peter, the black coachman. Nat sat next Dan in the place of honor, while Uncle Teddy would sit opposite,—to take care of the foot he said, but really that he might study the faces before him—both so happy, yet so different, for Dan's was square, and brown, and strong, while Nat's was long, and fair, and rather weak, but very amiable with its mild eyes and good forehead.

"By the way, I've got a book somewhere here that you may like to see," said the oldest boy of the party, diving under the seat and producing a book which made Dan exclaim—

"Oh! By George, isn't that a stunner?" as he turned the leaves, and saw fine plates of butterflies, and birds, and every sort of interesting insect, colored like life. He was so charmed that he forgot his thanks, but Mr. Laurie did not mind, and was quite satisfied to see the boy's eager delight, and to hear his exclamations over certain old friends as he came to them. Nat leaned on his shoulder to look, and Demi turned his back to the horses, and let his feet dangle inside the carriage, so that he might join in the conversation.

When they got among the beetles, Mr. Laurie took a curious little object out of his vest-pocket, and laying it in the palm of his hand, said—

"There's a beetle that is thousands of years old;" and then, while the lads examined the queer stone-bug, that looked so old and gray, he told them how it came out of the wrappings of a mummy, after lying for ages in a famous tomb. Finding them interested, he went on to tell about the Egyptians, and the strange and splendid ruins they have left behind them—the Nile, and how he sailed up the mighty river, with the handsome dark men to work his boat; how he shot alligators, saw wonderful beasts and birds; and afterwards crossed the desert on a camel, who pitched him about like a ship in a storm.

"Uncle Teddy tells stories 'most as well as Grandpa," said Demi, approvingly, when the tale was done, and the boys' eyes asked for more.

"Thank you," said Mr. Laurie, quite soberly, for he considered Demi's praise worth having, for children are good critics in such cases, and to suit them is an accomplishment that any one may be proud of.

"Here's another trifle or two that I tucked into my pocket as I was turning over my traps to see if I had any thing that would amuse Dan," and Uncle Teddy produced a fine arrow-head and a string of wampum.

"Oh! Tell about the Indians," cried Demi, who was fond of playing wigwam.

"Dan knows lots about them," added Nat.

"More than I do, I dare say. Tell us something," and Mr. Laurie looked as interested as the other two.

"Mr. Hyde told me; he's been among 'em, and can talk their talk, and likes 'em," began Dan, flattered by their attention, but rather embarrassed by having a grown-up listener.

"What is wampum for?" asked curious Demi, from his perch.

The others asked questions likewise, and, before he knew it, Dan was reeling off all Mr. Hyde had told him, as they sailed down the river a few weeks before. Mr. Laurie listened well, but found the boy more interesting than the Indians, for Mrs. Jo had told him about Dan, and he rather took a fancy to the wild lad, who ran away as he himself had often longed to do, and who was slowly getting tamed by pain and patience.

"I've been thinking that it would be a good plan for you fellows to have a museum of your own; a place in which to collect all the curious and interesting things that you find, and make, and have given you. Mrs. Jo is too kind to complain, but it is rather hard for her to have the house littered up with all sorts of rattletraps,—half-a-pint of dor-bugs in one of her best vases, for instance, a couple of dead bats nailed up in the back entry, wasps' nests tumbling down on people's heads, and stones lying round everywhere, enough to pave the avenue. There are not many women who would stand that sort of thing, are there, now?"

As Mr. Laurie spoke with a merry look in his eyes, the boys laughed and nudged one another, for it was evident that someone told tales out of school, else how could he know of the existence of these inconvenient treasures.

"Where can we put them, then?" said Demi, crossing his legs and leaning down to argue the question.

"In the old carriage-house."

"But it leaks and there isn't any window, nor any place to put things, and it's all dust and cobwebs," began Nat.

"Wait till Gibbs and I have touched it up a bit, and then see how you like it. He is to come over on Monday to get it ready; then next Saturday I shall come out, and we will fix it up, and make the beginning, at least, of a fine little museum. Everyone can bring his things and have a place for them; and Dan is to be the head man, because he knows most about such matters, and it will be quiet, pleasant work for him now that he can't knock about much."

"Won't that be jolly?" cried Nat, while Dan smiled all over his face and had not a word to say, but hugged his book, and looked at Mr. Laurie as if he thought him one of the greatest public benefactors that ever blessed the world.

"Shall I go round again, sir?" asked Peter, as they came to the gate, after two slow turns about the half-mile triangle.

"No, we must be prudent, else we can't come again. I must go over the premises, take a look at the carriage-house, and have a little talk with Mrs. Jo before I go;" and, having deposited Dan on his sofa to rest and enjoy his book, Uncle Teddy went off to have a frolic with the lads who were raging about the place in search of him. Leaving the little girls to mess up-stairs, Mrs. Bhaer sat down by Dan, and listened to his eager account of the drive till the flock returned, dusty, warm, and much excited about the new museum, which every one considered the most brilliant idea of the age.

"I always wanted to endow some sort of an institution, and I am going to begin with this," said Mr. Laurie, sitting down on a stool at Mrs. Jo's feet.

"You have endowed one already. What do you call this?" and Mrs. Jo pointed to the happy-faced lads, who had camped upon the floor about them.

"I call it a very promising Bhaer-garden, and I'm proud to be a member of it. Did you know I was the head boy in this school?" he asked, turning to Dan, and changing the subject skilfully, for he hated to be thanked for the generous things he did.

"I thought Franz was!" answered Dan, wondering what the man meant.

"Oh, dear no! I'm the first boy Mrs. Jo ever had to take care of, and I was such a bad one that she isn't done with me yet, though she has been working at me for years and years."

"How old she must be!" said Nat, innocently.

"She began early, you see. Poor thing! She was only fifteen when she took me, and I led her such a life, it's a wonder she isn't wrinkled and gray, and quite worn out," and Mr. Laurie looked up at her laughing.

"Don't, Teddy. I won't have you abuse yourself so;" and Mrs. Jo stroked the curly black head at her knee as affectionately as ever, for, in spite of every thing, Teddy was her boy still.

"If it hadn't been for you, there never would have been a Plumfield. It was my success with you, sir, that gave me courage to try my pet plan. So the boys may thank you for it, and name the new institution 'The Laurence Museum,' in honor of its founder,—won't we, boys?" she added, looking very like the lively Jo of old times.

"We will! We will!" shouted the boys throwing up their hats, for though they had taken them off on entering the house, according to rule, they had been in too much of a hurry to hang them up.

"I'm as hungry as a bear, can't I have a cookie?" asked Mr. Laurie, when the shout subsided and he had expressed his thanks by a splendid bow.

"Trot out and ask Asia for the gingerbread-box, Demi. It isn't in order to eat between meals, but, on this joyful occasion, we won't mind, and have a cookie all round," said Mrs. Jo; and when the box came she dealt them out with a liberal hand, every one munching away in a social circle.

Suddenly, in the midst of a bite, Mr. Laurie cried out, "Bless my heart, I forgot grandma's bundle!" and running out to the carriage, returned with an interesting white parcel, which, being opened, disclosed a choice collection of beasts, birds, and pretty things cut out of crisp sugary cake, and baked a lovely brown.

"There's one for each, and a letter to tell which is whose. Grandma and Hannah made them, and I tremble to think what would have happened to me if I had forgotten to leave them."

Then, amid much laughing and fun, the cakes were distributed. A fish for Dan, a fiddle for Nat, a book for Demi, a monkey for Tommy, a flower for Daisy, a hoop for Nan, who had driven twice round the triangle without stopping, a star for Emil, who put on airs because he studied astronomy, and, best of all, an omnibus for Franz, whose great delight was to drive the family bus. Stuffy got a fat pig, and the little folks had birds, and cats, and rabbits, with black currant eyes.

"Now I must go. Where is my Goldilocks? Mamma will come flying out to get her if I'm not back early," said Uncle Teddy, when the last crumb had vanished which it speedily did, you may be sure.

The young ladies had gone into the garden, and while they waited till Franz looked them up, Jo and Laurie stood at the door talking together.

"How does little Giddy-gaddy come on?" he asked, for Nan's pranks amused him very much, and he was never tired of teasing Jo about her.

"Nicely; she is getting quite mannerly, and begins to see the error of her wild ways."

"Don't the boys encourage her in them?"

"Yes; but I keep talking, and lately she has improved much. You saw how prettily she shook hands with you, and how gentle she was with Bess. Daisy's example has its effect upon her, and I'm quite sure that a few months will work wonders."

Here Mrs. Jo's remarks were cut short by the appearance of Nan tearing round the corner at a break-neck pace, driving a mettlesome team of four boys, and followed by Daisy trundling Bess in a wheelbarrow. Hats off, hair flying, whip cracking, and barrow bumping, up they came in a cloud of dust, looking as wild a set of little hoydens as one would wish to see.

"So these are the model children, are they? It's lucky I didn't bring Mrs. Curtis out to see your school for the cultivation of morals and manners; she would never have recovered from the shock of this spectacle," said Mr. Laurie, laughing at Mrs. Jo's premature rejoicing over Nan's improvement.

"Laugh away; I'll succeed yet. As you used to say at College, quoting some professor, 'Though the experiment has failed, the principle remains the same,' " said Mrs. Bhaer, joining in the merriment.

"I'm afraid Nan's example is taking effect upon Daisy, instead of the other way. Look at my little princess! She has utterly forgotten her dignity, and is screaming like the rest. Young ladies, what does this mean?" and Mr. Laurie rescued his small daughter from impending destruction, for the four horses were champing their bits and curvetting madly all about her, as she sat brandishing a great whip in both hands.

"We're having a race, and I beat," shouted Nan.

"I could have run faster, only I was afraid of spilling Bess," screamed Daisy.

"Hi! Go long!" cried the princess, giving such a flourish with her whip that the horses ran away, and were seen no more.

"My precious child! Come away from this ill-mannered crew before you are quite spoilt. Good-by, Jo! Next time I come, I shall expect to find the boys making patchwork."

"It wouldn't hurt them a bit. I don't give in, mind you; for my experiments always fail a few times before they succeed. Love to Amy and my blessed Marmee," called Mrs. Jo, as the carriage drove away; and the last Mr. Laurie saw of her, she was consoling Daisy for her failure by a ride in the wheelbarrow, and looking as if she liked it.

Great was the excitement all the week about the repairs in the carriage-house, which went briskly on in spite of the incessant questions, advice, and meddling of the boys. Old Gibbs was nearly driven wild with it all, but managed to do his work nevertheless; and by Friday night the place was all in order—roof mended, shelves up, walls whitewashed, a great window cut at the back which let in a flood of sunshine, and gave them a fine view of the brook, the meadows, and the distant hills; and over the great door, painted in red letters, was "The Laurence Museum."

All Saturday morning the boys were planning how it should be furnished with their spoils, and when Mr. Laurie arrived, bringing an aquarium which Mrs. Amy said she was tired of, their rapture was great.

The afternoon was spent in arranging things, and when the running and lugging aud hammering was over, the ladies were invited to behold the institution.

It certainly was a pleasant place, airy, clean, and bright. A hop-vine shook its green bells round the open window, the pretty aquarium stood in the middle of the room, with some delicate water plants rising above the water, and gold-fish showing their brightness as they floated to and fro below. On either side of the window were rows of shelves ready to receive the curiosities yet to be found. Dan's tall cabinet stood before the great door, which was fastened up, while the small door was to be used. On the cabinet stood a queer Indian idol, very ugly, but very interesting; old Mr. Laurence sent it, as well as a fine Chinese junk in full sail, which had a conspicuous place on the long table in the middle of the room. Above, swinging in a loop, and looking as if she was alive, hung Polly, who died at an advanced age, had been carefully stuffed, and was now presented by Mrs. Jo. The walls were decorated with all sorts of things. A snake's skin, a big wasp's nest, a birch-bark canoe, a string of birds' eggs, wreaths of gray moss from the South, and a bunch of cotton-pods. The dead bats had a place, also a large turtle-shell, and an ostrich-egg proudly presented by Demi, who volunteered to explain these rare curiosities to guests whenever they liked. There were so many stones that it was impossible to accept them all, so only a few of the best were arranged among the shells on the shelves, the rest were piled up in corners, to be exaimned by Dan at his leisure.

Every one was eager to give something, even Silas, who sent home for a stuffed wild-cat killed in his youth. It was rather moth-eaten and shabby, but on a high bracket and best side foremost the effect was fine, for the yellow glass eyes glared, and the mouth snarled so naturally, that Teddy shook in his little shoes at sight of it, when he came bringing his most cherished treasure, one cocoon, to lay upon the shrine of science.

"Isn't it beautiful? I'd no idea we had so many curious things. I gave that; don't it look well? We might make a lot by charging something for letting folks see it."

Jack added that last suggestion to the general chatter that went on as the family viewed the room.

"This is a free museum, and if there is any speculating on it I'll paint out the name over the door," said Mr. Laurie, turning so quickly that Jack wished he had held his tongue.

"Hear! Hear!" cried Mr. Bhaer.

"Speech! Speech!" added Mrs. Jo.

"Can't, I'm too bashful. You give them a lecture yourself—you are used to it," Mr. Laurie answered, retreating towards the window, meaning to escape. But she held him fast, and said, laughing as she looked at the dozen pairs of dirty hands about her,—

"If I did lecture, it would be on the chemical and cleansing properties of soap. Come now, as the founder of the institution, you really ought to give us a few moral remarks, and we will applaud tremendously."

Seeing that there was no way of escaping, Mr. Laurie looked up at Polly hanging overhead, seemed to find inspiration in the brilliant old bird, and sitting down upon the table, said, in his pleasant way,—

"There *is* one thing I'd like to suggest, boys, and that is, I want you to get some good as well as much pleasure out of this. Just putting curious or pretty things here won't do it; so suppose you read up about them, so that when anybody asks questions you can answer them, and understand the matter. I used to like these things myself, and should enjoy hearing about them now, for I've forgotten all I once knew. It wasn't much, was it, Jo? Here's Dan now, full of stories about birds, and bugs, and so on; let him take care of the museum, and once a week the rest of you take turns to read a composition, or tell about some animal, mineral, or vegetable. We should all like that, and I think it would put considerable useful knowledge into our heads. What do you say, Professor?"

"I'd like it much, and will give the lads all the help I can. But they will need books to read up these new subjects, and we have not many, I fear," began Mr. Bhaer, looking much pleased, and planning many fine lectures on geology, which he liked. "We should have a library for the special purpose."

"Is that a useful sort of book, Dan?" asked Mr. Laurie, pointing to the volume that lay open by the cabinet.

"Oh yes! It tells all I want to know about insects. I had it here to see how to fix the butterflies right. I covered it so it is not hurt;" and Dan caught it up, fearing the lender might think him careless.

"Give it here a minute;" and, pulling out his pencil, Mr. Laurie wrote Dan's name in it, saying, as he set the book up on one of the corner shelves, where nothing stood but a stuffed bird without a tail, "There, that is the beginning of the museum library. I'll hunt up some more books, and Demi shall keep them in order. Where are those jolly little books we used to read, Jo? 'Insect Architecture' or some such name— all about ants having battles, and bees having queens, and crickets eating holes in our clothes and stealing milk, and larks of that sort."

"In the garret at home. I'll have them sent out, and we will plunge into Natural History with a will," said Mrs. Jo, ready for anything.

"Won't it be hard to write about such things?" asked Nat, who hated compositions.

"At first, perhaps; but you will soon like it. If you think that hard, how would you like to have this subject given to you, as it was to a girl of thirteen:—A conversation between Themistocles, Aristides, and Pericles on the proposed appropriation of the funds of the confederacy of Delos for the ornamentation of Athens?" said Mrs. Jo.

The boys groaned at the mere sound of the long names, and the gentlemen laughed at the absurdity of the lesson.

"Did she write it?" asked Demi, in an awe-stricken tone.

"Yes, but you can imagine what a piece of work she made of it, though she was rather a bright child."

"I'd like to have seen it," said Mr. Bhaer.

"Perhaps I can find it for you; I went to school with her," and Mrs. Jo looked so wicked that every one knew who the little girl was.

Hearing of this fearful subject for a composition quite reconciled the boys to the thought of writing about familiar things. Wednesday afternoon was appointed for the lectures, as they preferred to call them, for some chose to talk instead of write. Mr. Bhaer promised a portfolio in which the written productions should be kept, and Mrs. Bhaer said she would attend the course with great pleasure.

Then the dirty-handed society went off to wash, followed by the Professor, trying to calm the anxiety of Rob, who had been told by Tommy that all water was full of invisible polywogs.

"I like your plan very much, only don't be too generous, Teddy," said Mrs. Bhaer, when they were left alone. "You know most of the boys have got to paddle their own canoes when they leave us, and too much sitting in the lap of luxury will unfit them for it."

"I'll be moderate, but do let me amuse myself. I get desperately tired of business sometimes, and nothing freshens me up like a good frolic with your boys. I like that Dan very much, Jo. He isn't demonstrative;

but he has the eye of a hawk, and when you have tamed him a little he will do you credit."

"I'm so glad you think so. Thank you very much for your kindness to him, especially for this museum affair; it will keep him happy while he is lame, give me a chance to soften and smooth this poor, rough lad, and make him love us. What did inspire you with such a beautiful, helpful idea, Teddy?" asked Mrs. Bhaer, glancing back at the pleasant room, as she turned to leave it.

Laurie took both her hands in his, and answered, with a look that made her eyes fill with happy tears—

"Dear Jo! I have known what it is to be a motherless boy, and I never can forget how much you and yours have done for me all these years."

# CHAPTER XII

## HUCKLEBERRIES

THERE was a great clashing of tin pails, much running to and fro, and frequent demands for something to eat, one August afternoon, for the boys were going huckleberrying, and made as much stir about it as if they were setting out to find the North-West Passage.

"Now, my lads, get off as quietly as you can, for Rob is safely out of the way, and won't see you," said Mrs. Bhaer, as she tied Daisy's broad-brimmed hat, and settled the great blue pinafore in which she had enveloped Nan.

But the plan did not succeed, for Rob had heard the bustle, decided to go, and prepared himself, without a thought of diappointment. The troop was just getting under way when the little man came marching down stairs with his best hat on, a bright tin pail in his hand, and a face beaming with satisfaction.

"Oh, dear! Now we shall have a scene," sighed Mrs. Bhaer, who found her eldest son very hard to manage at times.

"I'm all ready," said Rob, and took his place in the ranks with such perfect unconsciousness of his mistake, that it really was very hard to undeceive him.

"It's too far for you, my love; stay and take care of me, for I shall be all alone," began his mother.

"You've got Teddy. I'm a big boy, so I can go; you said I might when I was bigger, and I am now," persisted Rob, with a cloud beginning to dim the brightness of his happy face.

"We are going up to the great pasture, and it's ever so far; we don't want you tagging on," cried Jack, who did not admire the little boys.

"I won't tag, I'll run and keep up. O mamma! Let me go! I want to fill my new pail, and I'll bring 'em all to you. Please, please, I will be good!" prayed Robby, looking up at his mother, so grieved and disappointed that her heart began to fail her.

"But, my deary, you'll get so tired and hot you won't have a good time.

Wait till I go, and then we will stay all day, and pick as many berries as you want."

"You never do go, you are so busy, and I'm tired of waiting. I'd rather go and get the berries for you all myself. I love to pick 'em, and I want to fill my new pail dreffly," sobbed Rob.

The pathetic sight of great tears tinkling into the dear new pail, and threatening to fill it with salt water instead of huckleberries, touched all the ladies present. His mother patted the weeper on his back; Daisy offered to stay at home with him; and Nan said, in her decided way,—

"Let him come; I'll take care of him."

"If Franz was going I wouldn't mind, for he is very careful; but he is haying with the father, and I'm not sure about the rest of you," began Mrs. Bhaer.

"It's so far," put in Jack.

"I'd carry him if I was going—wish I was," said Dan, with a sigh.

"Thank you, dear, but you must take care of your foot. I wish I could go. Stop a minute, I think I can manage it after all;" and Mrs. Bhaer ran out to the steps, waving her apron wildly.

Silas was just driving away in the hay-cart, but turned back, and agreed at once, when Mrs. Jo proposed that he should take the whole party to the pasture, and go for them at five o'clock.

"It will delay your work a little, but never mind; we will pay you in huckleberry pies," said Mrs. Jo, knowing Silas's weak point.

His rough, brown face brightened up, and he said, with a cheery "Haw! Haw!"—"Wal now, Mis Bhaer, if you go to bribin' of me, I shall give in right away."

"Now, boys, I have arranged it so that you can all go," said Mrs. Bhaer, running back again, much relieved, for she loved to make them happy, and always felt miserable when she had disturbed the serenity of her little sons; for she believed that the small hopes and plans and pleasures of children should be tenderly respected by grown-up people, and never rudely thwarted or ridiculed.

"Can I go?" said Dan, delighted.

"I thought especially of you. Be careful, and never mind the berries, but sit about and enjoy the lovely things which you know how to find all about you," answered Mrs. Bhaer, who remembered his kind offer to her boy.

"Me too! Me too!" sung Rob, dancing with joy, and clapping his precious pail and cover like castanets.

"Yes, and Daisy and Nan must take good care of you. Be at the bars at five o'clock, and Silas will come for you all."

Robby cast himself upon his mother in a burst of gratitude, promising to bring her every berry he picked, and not eat one. Then they were all packed into the hay-cart, and went rattling away, the brightest face among the dozen being that of Rob, as he sat between his two temporary little mothers, beaming upon the whole world, and waving his best hat; for his indulgent mamma had not the heart to bereave him of it, since this was a gala-day to him.

Such a happy afternoon as they had, in spite of the mishaps which usually occur on such expeditions! Of course Tommy came to grief, tumbled upon a hornets' nest and got stung; but being used to woe, he bore the smart manfully, till Dan suggested the application of damp earth, which much assuaged the pain. Daisy saw a snake, and in flying from it lost half her berries; but Demi helped her to fill up again, and discussed reptiles most learnedly the while. Ned fell out of a tree, and split his jacket down the back, but suffered no other fracture. Emil and Jack established rival claims to a certain thick patch, and while they were squabbling about it, Stuffy quickly and quietly stripped the bushes and fled to the protection of Dan, who was enjoying himself immensely. The crutch was no longer necessary, and he was delighted to see how strong his foot felt as he roamed about the great pasture, full of interesting rocks and stumps, with familiar little creatures in the grass, and well-known insects dancing in the air.

But of all the adventures that happened on this afternoon that which befell Nan and Rob was the most exciting, and it long remained one of the favorite histories of the household. Having explored the country pretty generally, torn three rents in her frock, and scratched her face in a barberry-bush, Nan began to pick the berries that shone like big, black beads on the low, green bushes. Her nimble fingers flew, but still her basket did not fill up as rapidly as she desired, so she kept wandering here and there to search for better places, instead of picking contentedly and steadily as Daisy did. Rob followed Nan, for her energy suited him better than his cousin's patience, and he too was anxious to have the biggest and best berries for Marmar.

"I keep putting 'em in, but it don't fill up, and I'm so tired," said Rob, pausing a moment to rest his short legs, and beginning to think huckle-berrying was not all his fancy painted it; for the sun blazed, Nan skipped hither and thither like a grasshopper, and the berries fell out of his pail almost as fast as he put them in, because, in his struggles with the bushes, it was often upside-down.

"Last time we came they were ever so much thicker over that wall— great bouncers; and there is a cave there, where the boys made a fire. Let's go and fill our things quick, and then hide in the cave and let the others find us," proposed Nan, thirsting for adventures.

Rob consented, and away they went, scrambling over the wall and running down the sloping fields on the other side, till they were hidden among the rocks and underbrush. The berries were thick, and at last the pails were actually full. It was shady and cool down there, and a little spring gave the thirsty children a refreshing drink out of its mossy cup.

"Now we will go and rest in the cave, and eat our lunch," said Nan, well satisfied with her success so far.

"Do you know the way?" asked Rob.

" 'Course I do; I've been once, and I always remember. Didn't I go and get my box all right?"

That convinced Rob, and he followed blindly as Nan led him over stock and stone, and brought him, after much meandering, to a small recess in the rock, where the blackened stones showed that fires had been made.

"Now, isn't it nice?" asked Nan, as she took out a bit of bread-and-butter, rather damaged by being mixed up with nails, fishhooks, stones, and other foreign substances, in the young lady's pocket.

"Yes; do you think they will find us soon?" asked Rob, who found the shadowy glen rather dull, and began to long for more society.

"No, I don't; because if I hear them, I shall hide, and have fun making them find me."

"P'raps they won't come."

"Don't care; I can get home myself."

"Is it a great way?" asked Rob, looking at his little, stubby boots, scratched and wet with his long wandering.

"It's six miles, I guess." Nan's ideas of distance were vague, and her faith in her own powers great.

"I think we better go now," suggested Rob, presently.

"I shan't go till I have picked over my berries;" and Nan began what seemed to Rob an endless task.

"Oh, dear! You said you'd take good care of me," he sighed, as the sun seemed to drop behind the hill all of a sudden.

"Well, I *am* taking care of you as hard as I can. Don't be cross, child; I'll go in a minute," said Nan, who considered five-year-old Robby a mere infant compared to herself.

So little Rob sat looking anxiously about him, and waiting patiently, for, spite of some misgivings, he felt great confidence in Nan.

"I guess it's going to be night pretty soon," he observed, as if to himself, as a mosquito bit him, and the frogs in a neighboring marsh began to pipe up for the evening concert.

"My goodness me! So it is. Come right away this minute, or they will be gone," cried Nan, looking up from her work, and suddenly perceiving that the sun was down.

"I heard a horn about an hour ago; maybe they were blowing for us," said Rob, trudging after his guide as she scrambled up the steep hill.

"Where was it?" asked Nan, stopping short.

"Over that way;" he pointed with a dirty little finger in an entirely wrong direction.

"Let's go that way and meet them;" and Nan wheeled about, and began to trot through the bushes, feeling a trifle anxious, for there were so many cowpaths all about she could not remember which way they came.

On they went over stock and stone again, pausing now and then to listen for the horn, which did not blow any more, for it was only the moo of a cow on her way home.

"I don't remember seeing that pile of stones—do you?" asked Nan, as she sat on a wall to rest a moment and take an observation.

"I don't remember anything, but I want to go home," and Rob's voice had a little tremble in it that made Nan put her arms round him and lift him gently down, saying, in her most capable way,—

"I'm going just as fast as I can, dear. Don't cry, and when we come to the road, I'll carry you."

"Where is the road?" and Robby wiped his eyes to look for it.

"Over by that big tree. Don't you know that's the one Ned tumbled out of?"

"So it is. Maybe they waited for us; I'd like to ride home—wouldn't you?" and Robby brightened up as he plodded along toward the end of the great pasture.

"No, I'd rather walk," answered Nan, feeling quite sure that she would be obliged to do so, and preparing her mind for it.

Another long trudge through the fast-deepening twilight and another disappointment, for when they reached the tree, they found to their dismay that it was not the one Ned climbed, and no road anywhere appeared.

"Are we lost?" quavered Rob, clasping his pail in despair.

"Not much. I don't see which way to go, and I guess we'd better call."

So they both shouted till they were hoarse, yet nothing answered but the frogs in full chorus.

"There is another tall tree over there, perhaps that's the one," said Nan, whose heart sunk within her, though she still spoke bravely.

"I don't think I can go any more; my boots are so heavy I can't pull 'em"; and Robby sat down on a stone quite worn out.

"Then we must stay here all night. *I* don't care much, if snakes don't come."

"I'm frightened of snakes. I can't stay all night, Oh, dear! I don't like to be lost," and Rob puckered up his face to cry, when suddenly a thought occurred to him, and he said, in a tone of perfect confidence,—

"Marmar will come and find me—she always does; I ain't afraid now."

"She won't know where we are."

"She didn't know I was shut up in the ice-house, but she found me. I know she'll come," returned Robby, so trustfully that Nan felt relieved, and sat down by him, saying, with a remorseful sigh,—

"I wish we hadn't run away."

"You made me; but I don't mind much—Marmar will love me just the same," answered Rob, clinging to his sheet-anchor when all other hope was gone.

"I'm so hungry. Let's eat our berries," proposed Nan after a pause, during which Rob began to nod.

"So am I, but I can't eat mine, 'cause I told Marmar I'd keep them all for her."

"You'll have to eat them if no one comes for us," said Nan, who felt like contradicting everything just then. "If we stay here a great many days, we shall eat up all the berries in the field, and then we shall starve," she added, grimly.

"I shall eat sassafras. I know a big tree of it, and Dan told me how squirrels dig up the roots and eat them and I love to dig," returned Rob, undaunted by the prospect of starvation.

"Yes; and we can catch frogs, and cook them. My father ate some once, and he said they were nice," put in Nan beginning to find a spice of romance even in being lost in a huckleberry pasture.

"How could we cook frogs? We haven't got any fire."

"I don't know; next time I'll have matches in my pocket," said Nan, rather depressed by this obstacle to the experiment in frog-cookery.

"Couldn't we light a fire with a firefly?" asked Rob, hopefully, as he watched them flitting to and fro like winged sparks.

"Let's try;" and several minutes were pleasantly spent in catching the flies, and trying to make them kindle a green twig or two. "It's a lie to call them *fire*-flies when there isn't a fire in them," Nan said, throwing one unhappy insect away with scorn, though it shone its best, and obligingly walked up and down the twigs to please the innocent little experimenters.

"Marmar's a good while coming," said Rob, after another pause, during which they watched the stars overhead, smelt the sweet fern crushed under foot, and listened to the crickets' serenade.

"I don't see why God made any night; day is so much pleasanter," said Nan, thoughtfully.

"It's to sleep in," answered Rob, with a yawn.

"Then do go to sleep," said Nan, pettishly.

"I want my own bed. Oh, I wish I could see Teddy!" cried Rob, painfully reminded of home by the soft chirp of birds safe in their little nests.

"I don't believe your mother will ever find us," said Nan, who was becoming desperate, for she hated patient waiting of any sort. "It's so dark she won't see us."

"It was all black in the ice-house, and I was so scared I didn't call her, but she saw me; and she will see me now, no matter how dark it is," returned confiding Rob, standing up to peer into the gloom for the help which never failed him.

"I see her! I see her!" he cried, and ran as fast as his tired legs would take him toward a dark figure slowly approaching. Suddenly he stopped, then turned about, and came stumbling back, screaming, in a great panic,—

"No, it's a bear, a big black one!" and hid his face in Nan's skirts.

For a moment Nan quailed; even her courage gave out at thought of a real bear, and she was about to turn and flee in great disorder, when a mild "Moo!" changed her fear to merriment, as she said, laughing,—

"It's a cow, Robby! The nice, black cow we saw this afternoon."

The cow seemed to feel that it was not just the thing to meet two little people in her pasture after dark, and the amiable beast paused to inquire into the case. She let them stroke her, and stood regarding them with her soft eyes so mildly, that Nan, who feared no animal but a bear, was fired with a desire to milk her.

"Silas taught me how; and berries and milk would be so nice," she said, emptying the contents of her pail into her hat, and boldly beginning her new task, while Rob stood by and repeated, at her command, the poem from Mother Goose :—

> "Cushy cow, bonny, let down your milk,
>   Let down your milk to me,
>   And I will give you a gown of silk,
>   A gown of silk and a silver tee."

But the immortal rhyme had little effect, for the benevolent cow had already been milked, and had only half a gill to give the thirsty children.

"Shoo! Get away! You are an old cross patch," cried Nan, ungratefully, as she gave up the attempt in despair; and poor Mooly walked on with a gentle gurgle of surprise and reproof.

"Are we lost?" quavered Rob.

"Each can have a sip, and then we must take a walk. We shall go to sleep if we don't; and lost people mustn't sleep. Don't you know how Hannah Lee in the pretty story slept under the snow and died?"

"But there isn't any snow now, and it's nice and warm," said Rob, who was not blessed with as lively a fancy as Nan.

"No matter, we will poke about a little, and call some more; and then, if nobody comes, we will hide under the bushes, like Hop-o'-my-thumb and his brothers."

It was a very short walk, however, for Rob was so sleepy he could not get on, and tumbled down so often that Nan entirely lost patience, being half distracted by the responsibility she had taken upon herself.

"If you tumble down again, I'll shake you," she said, lifting the poor little man up very kindly as she spoke, for Nan's bark was much worse than her bite.

"Please don't. It's my boots—they keep slipping so"; and Rob manfully checked the sob just ready to break out, adding, with a plaintive patience that touched Nan's heart, "If the skeeters didn't bite me so, I could go to sleep till Marmar comes."

"Put your head on my lap, and I'll cover you up with my apron; I'm not afraid of the night," said Nan, sitting down and trying to persuade herself that she did not mind the shadow nor the mysterious rustlings all about her.

"Wake me up when she comes," said Rob, and was fast asleep in five minutes with his head in Nan's lap under the pinafore.

The little girl sat for some fifteen minutes, staring about her with anxious eyes, and feeling as if each second was an hour. Then a pale light began to glimmer over the hill-top, and she said to herself—

"I guess the night is over and morning is coming. I'd like to see the sun rise, so I'll watch, and when it comes up we can find our way right home."

But before the moon's round face peeped above the hill to destroy her hope, Nan had fallen asleep, leaning back in a little bower of tall ferns, and was deep in a midsummer night's dream of fireflies and blue aprons, mountains of huckleberries, and Robby wiping away the tears of a black cow, who sobbed, "I want to go home! I want to go home!"

While the children were sleeping, peacefully lulled by the drowsy hum of many neighborly mosquitoes, the family at home were in a great state of agitation. The hay-cart came at five, and all but Jack, Emil, Nan, and Rob were at the bars ready for it. Franz drove instead of Silas, and when the boys told him that the others were going home through the wood, he said, looking ill-pleased, "They ought to have left Rob to ride, he will be tired out by the long walk."

"It's shorter that way, and they will carry him," said Stuffy, who was in a hurry for his supper.

"You are sure Nan and Rob went with them?"

"Of course they did; I saw them getting over the wall, and sung out that it was most five, and Jack called back that they were going the other way," explained Tommy.

"Very well, pile in then," and away rattled the haycart with the tired children and the full pails.

Mrs. Jo looked sober when she heard of the division of the party, and sent Franz back with Toby to find and bring the little ones home. Supper was over, and the family sitting about in the cool hall as usual, when Franz came trotting back, hot, dusty, and anxious.

"Have they come?" he called out when half-way up the avenue.

"No!" and Mrs. Jo flew out of her chair looking so alarmed that every one jumped up and gathered round Franz.

"I can't find them anywhere," he began; but the words were hardly spoken when a loud "Hullo!" startled them all, and the next minute Jack and Emil came round the house.

"Where are Nan and Rob?" cried Mrs. Jo, clutching Emil in a way that caused him to think his aunt had suddenly lost her wits.

"I don't know. They came home with the others, didn't they?" he answered, quickly.

"No; George and Tommy said they went with you."

"Well, they didn't. Haven't seen them. We took a swim in the pond, and came by the wood," said Jack, looking alarmed, as well he might.

"Call Mr. Bhaer, get the lanterns, and tell Silas I want him."

That was all Mrs. Jo said, but they knew what she meant, and flew to obey orders. In ten minutes, Mr. Bhaer and Silas were off to the wood, and Franz tearing down the road on Old Andy to search the great pasture. Mrs. Jo caught up some food from the table, a little bottle of brandy from the medicine-closet, took a lantern, and bidding Jack and Emil come with her, and the rest not stir, she trotted away on Toby, never stopping for hat or shawl. She heard someone running after her, but said not a word till, as she paused to call and listen, the light of her lantern shone on Dan's face.

"You here! I told Jack to come," she said, half-inclined to send him back, much as she needed help.

"I wouldn't let him; he and Emil hadn't had any supper, and I wanted to come more than they did," he said, taking the lantern from her and smiling up in her face with the steady look in his eyes that made her feel as if, boy though he was, she had someone to depend on.

Off she jumped, and ordered him on to Toby, in spite of his pleading to walk; then they went on again along the dusty, solitary road, stopping every now and then to call and hearken breathlessly for little voices to reply.

When they came to the great pasture, other lights were already flitting to and fro like will-o'-the-wisps, and Mr. Bhaer's voice was heard shouting, "Nan! Rob! Rob! Nan!" in every part of the field. Silas whistled and roared, Dan plunged here and there on Toby, who seemed to understand the case, and went over the roughest places with unusual docility. Often Mrs. Jo hushed them all, saying, with a sob in her throat, "The noise may frighten them, let me call; Robby will know *my* voice;" and then she would cry out the beloved little name in every tone of tenderness, till the very echoes whispered it softly, and the winds seemed to waft it willingly; but still no answer came.

The sky was overcast now, and only brief glimpses of the moon were seen, heat-lightning darted out of the dark clouds now and then, and a faint far-off rumble as of thunder told that a summer-storm was brewing.

"O my Robby! My Robby!" mourned poor Mrs. Jo, wandering up and down like a pale ghost, while Dan kept beside her like a faithful firefly. "What shall I say to Nan's father if she comes to harm? Why did I ever trust my darling so far away? Fritz, do you hear anything?" And when a mournful "'No" came back, she wrung her hands so despairingly, that Dan sprung down from Toby's back, tied the bridle to the bars, and said, in his decided way,—

"They may have gone down to the spring—I'm going to look."

He was over the wall and away so fast that she could hardly follow him; but when she reached the spot, he lowered the lantern and showed her with joy the marks of little feet in the soft ground about the spring. She fell down on her knees to examine the tracks, and then sprung up, saying eagerly—

"Yes; that is the mark of my Robby's little boots! Come this way, they must have gone on."

Such a weary search! But now some inexplicable instinct seemed to lead the anxious mother, for presently Dan uttered a cry, and caught up a little shining object lying in the path. It was the cover of the new tin pail, dropped in the first alarm of being lost. Mrs. Jo hugged and kissed it as if it were a living thing; and when Dan was about to utter a glad shout to bring the others to the spot, she stopped him, saying, as she hurried on, "No, let *me* find them; I let Rob go, and I want to give him back to his father all myself."

A little farther on Nan's hat appeared, and after passing the place more than once, they came at last upon the babes in the wood, both sound asleep. Dan never forgot the little picture on which the light of his lantern shone that night. He thought Mrs. Jo would cry out, but she only whispered "Hush!" as she softly lifted away the apron, and saw the little ruddy face below. The berry-stained lips were half-open as the breath came and went, the yellow hair lay damp on the hot forehead, and both the chubby hands held fast the little pail still full.

The sight of the childish harvest, treasured through all the troubles of that night for her, seemed to touch Mrs. Jo to the heart, for suddenly she gathered up her boy, and began to cry over him, so tenderly, yet so heartily, that he woke up, and at first seemed bewildered. Then he remembered, and hugged her close, saying with a laugh of triumph—

"I knew you'd come! O Marmar! I did want you so!" For a moment they kissed and clung to one another, quite forgetting all the world; for no matter how lost and soiled and worn-out wandering sons may be, mothers can forgive and forget everything as they fold them in their fostering arms. Happy the son whose faith in his mother remains unchanged, and who, through all his wanderings, has kept some filial token to repay her brave and tender love.

Dan meantime picked Nan out of her bush, and, with a gentleness none but Teddy ever saw in him before, he soothed her first alarm at the sudden waking, and wiped away her tears; for Nan also began to cry for joy, it was so good to see a kind face and feel a strong arm round her after what seemed to her ages of loneliness and fear.

"My poor little girl, don't cry! You are all safe now, and no one shall say a word of blame tonight," said Mrs. Jo, taking Nan into her capacious

Dan never forgot the little picture on which the light of his lantern shone that night.

embrace, and cuddling both children as a hen might gather her lost chickens under her motherly wings.

"It was my fault; but I *am* sorry. I tried to take care of him, and I covered him up and let him sleep, and didn't touch his berries, though I was *so* hungry; and I never will do it again—truly never, never," sobbed Nan, quite lost in a sea of penitence and thankfulness.

"Call them now, and let us get home," said Mrs. Jo; and Dan, getting upon the wall, sent the joyful word "Found !" ringing over the field.

How the wandering lights came dancing from all sides, and gathered round the little group among the sweet fern bushes! Such a hugging, and kissing, and talking, and crying, as went on, must have amazed the glowworms, and evidently delighted the mosquitoes, for they hummed frantically, while the little moths came in flocks to the party, and the frogs croaked as if they could not express their satisfaction loudly enough.

Then they set out for home,—a queer party, for Franz rode on to tell the news; Dan and Toby led the way; then came Nan in the strong arms of Silas, who considered her "the smartest little baggage he ever saw," and teased her all the way home about her pranks. Mr. Bhaer would let no one carry Rob but himself, and the little fellow, refreshed by sleep, sat up, and chattered gayly, feeling himself a hero, while his mother went beside him holding on to any part of his precious little body that came handy, and never tired of hearing him say, "I *knew* Marmar would come," or seeing him lean down to kiss her, and put a plump berry into her mouth, " 'Cause he picked 'em all for her."

The moon shone out just as they reached the avenue, and all the boys came shouting to meet them, so the lost lambs were borne in triumph and safety, and landed in the dining-room, where the unromantic little things demanded supper instead of preferring kisses and caresses. They were set down to bread and milk, while the entire household stood round to gaze upon them. Nan soon recovered her spirits, and recounted her perils with a relish now that they were all over. Rob seemed absorbed in his food, but put down his spoon all of a sudden, and set up a doleful roar.

"My precious, why do you cry?" asked his mother, who still hung over him.

"I'm crying 'cause I was lost," bawled Rob, trying to squeeze out a tear, and failing entirely.

"But you are found now. Nan says you didn't cry out in the field, and I was glad you were such a brave boy."

"I was so busy being frightened I didn't have any time then. But I want to cry now, 'cause I don't like to be lost," explained Rob, struggling with sleep, emotion, and a mouthful of bread and milk.

The boys set up such a laugh at this funny way of making up for lost time, that Rob stopped to look at them, and the merriment was so infectious, that, after a surprised stare, he burst out into a merry "Ha, ha!" and beat his spoon upon the table as if he enjoyed the joke immensely.

"It is ten o'clock; into bed, every man of you," said Mr. Bhaer, looking at his watch.

"And, thank Heaven! There will be no empty ones tonight," added Mrs. Bhaer, watching, with full eyes, Robby going up in his father's arms, and Nan, escorted by Daisy and Demi, who considered her the most interesting heroine of their collection.

"Poor Aunt Jo is so tired she ought to be carried up herself," said gentle Franz, putting his arm round her as she paused at the stair-foot, looking quite exhausted by her fright and long walk.

"Let's make an arm-chair," proposed Tommy.

"No, thank you, my lads; but somebody may lend me a shoulder to lean on," answered Mrs. Jo.

"Me! Me!" and half-a-dozen jostled one another, all eager to be chosen, for there was something in the pale motherly face that touched the warm hearts under the round jackets.

Seeing that they considered it an honor, Mrs. Jo gave it to the one who had earned it, and nobody grumbled when she put her arm on Dan's broad shoulder, saying, with a look that made him color up with pride and pleasure, —

"He found the children; so I think he must help me up."

Dan felt richly rewarded for his evening's work, not only that he was chosen from all the rest to go proudly up bearing the lamp, but because Mrs. Jo said, heartily, "Good-night, my boy! God bless you!" as he left her at her door.

"I wish I *was* your boy," said Dan, who felt as if danger and trouble had somehow brought him nearer than ever to her.

"You shall be my oldest son," and she sealed her promise with a kiss that made Dan hers entirely.

Little Rob was all right next day, but Nan had a headache, and lay on Mother Bhaer's sofa with cold-cream upon her scratched face. Her remorse was quite gone, and she evidently thought being lost rather a fine amusement. Mrs. Jo was not pleased with this state of things, and had no desire to have her children led from the paths of virtue, or her pupils lying round loose in huckleberry fields. So she talked soberly to Nan, and tried to impress upon her mind the difference between liberty and license, telling several tales to enforce her lecture. She had not decided how to punish Nan, but one of these stories suggested a way, and as Mrs. Jo liked odd penalties she tried it.

"All children run away," pleaded Nan, as if it was as natural and necessary a thing as measles or whooping cough.

"Not all, and some who do run away don't get found again," answered Mrs. Jo.

"Didn't you do it yourself?" asked Nan, whose keen little eyes saw some traces of a kindred spirit in the serious lady who was sewing so morally before her.

Mrs. Jo laughed, and owned that she did.

"Tell about it," demanded Nan, feeling that she was getting the upper hand in the discussion.

Mrs. Jo saw that, and sobered down at once, saying, with a remorseful shake of the head,—

"I did it a good many times, and led my poor mother rather a hard life with my pranks, till she cured me."

"How?" and Nan sat up with a face full of interest.

"I had a new pair of shoes once, and wanted to show them; so, though

I was told not to leave the garden, I ran away and was wandering about all day. It was in the city, and why I wasn't killed I don't know. Such a time as I had. I frolicked in the park with dogs, sailed boats in the Back Bay with strange boys, dined with a little Irish beggar-girl on salt fish and potatoes, and was found at last fast asleep on a door-step with my arms round a great dog. It was late in the evening, and I was as dirty as a little pig, and the new shoes were worn out—I had travelled so far."

"How nice!" cried Nan, looking all ready to go and do it herself.

"It was *not* nice next day"; and Mrs. Jo tried to keep her eyes from betraying how much she enjoyed the memory of her early capers.

"Did your mother whip you?" asked Nan, curiously.

"She never whipped me but once, and then she begged my pardon, or I don't think I ever should have forgiven her, it hurt my feelings so much."

"Why did she beg your pardon?—my father don't."

"Because, when she had done it, I turned round and said, 'Well, you are mad yourself, and ought to be whipped as much as me.' She looked at me a minute, then her anger all died out, and she said, as if ashamed, 'You are right, Jo, *I am* angry; and why should I punish you for being in a passion when I set you such a bad example? Forgive me, dear, and let us try to help one another in a better way.' I never forgot it, and it did me more good than a dozen rods."

Nan sat thoughtfully turning the little cold-cream jar for a minute, and Mrs. Jo said nothing, but let that idea get well into the busy little mind that was so quick to see and feel what went on about her.

"I like that," said Nan, presently, and her face looked less elfish, with its sharp eyes, inquisitive nose, and mischievous mouth. "What did your mother do to you when you ran away that time?"

"She tied me up to the bed-post with a long string, so that I could not go out of the room, and there I stayed all day with the little worn-out shoes hanging up before me to remind me of my fault."

"I should think that *would* cure anybody," cried Nan, who loved her liberty above all things.

"It did cure me, and I think it will you, so I am going to try it," said Mrs. Jo, suddenly taking a ball of strong twine out of a drawer in her work-table.

Nan looked as if she was decidedly getting the worst of the argument now, and sat feeling much crestfallen while Mrs. Jo tied one end round her waist and the other to the arm of the sofa, saying, as she finished—

"I don't like to tie you up like a naughty little dog, but if you don't remember any better than a dog, I must treat you like one."

"I'd just as lief be tied up as not—I like to play dog;" and Nan put on a don't-care face, and began to growl and grovel on the floor.

Mrs. Jo took no notice, but leaving a book or two and a handkerchief to hem, she went away, and left Miss Nan to her own devices. This was not agreeable, and after sitting a moment she tried to untie the cord. But it was fastened in the belt of her apron behind, so she began on the knot at the other end. It soon came loose, and, gathering it up, Nan was about to get out of the window, when she heard Mrs. Jo say to somebody as she passed through the hall—

"No, I don't think she will run away now; she is an honorable little girl, and knows that I do it to help her."

In a minute Nan whisked back, tied herself up, and began to sew violently. Rob came in a moment after, and was so charmed with the new punishment, that he got a jump-rope and tethered himself to the other arm of the sofa in the most social manner.

"I got lost too, so I ought to be tied up as much as Nan," he explained to his mother when she saw the new captive.

"I'm not sure that you don't deserve a little punishment, for you knew it was wrong to go far away from the rest."

"Nan took me," began Rob, willing to enjoy the novel penalty, but not willing to take the blame.

"You needn't have gone. You have got a conscience, though you are a little boy, and you must learn to mind it."

"Well, my conscience didn't prick me a bit when she said 'Let's get over the wall,' " answered Rob, quoting one of Demi's expressions.

"Did you stop to see if it did?"

"No."

"Then you cannot tell."

"I guess it's such a little conscience that it don't prick hard enough for me to feel it," added Rob, after thinking over the matter for a minute.

"We must sharpen it up. It's bad to have a dull conscience; so you may stay here till dinner-time, and talk about it with Nan. I trust you both not to untie yourselves till I say the word."

"No, we won't," said both, feeling a certain sense of virtue in helping to punish themselves.

For an hour they were very good, then they grew tired of one room, and longed to get out. Never had the hall seemed so inviting; even the little bedroom acquired a sudden interest, and they would gladly have gone in and played tent with the curtains of the best bed. The open windows drove them wild because they could not reach them; and the outer world seemed so beautiful, they wondered how they ever found the heart to say it was dull. Nan pined for a race round the lawn, and Rob remembered with dismay that he had not fed his dog that morning, and wondered what poor Pollux would do. They watched the clock, and Nan did some nice calculations in minutes and seconds, while Rob learned to tell all the hours between eight and one so well that he never forgot them. It was maddening to smell the dinner, to know that there was to be succotash and huckleberry pudding, and to feel that they would not be on the spot to secure good helps of both. When Mary Ann began to set the table, they nearly cut themselves in two trying to see what meat there was to be; and Nan offered to help her make the beds, if she would only see that she had "lots of sauce on her pudding."

When the boys came bursting out of school, they found the children tugging at their halters like a pair of restive little colts, and were much edified, as well as amused, by the sequel to the exciting adventures of the night.

"Untie me now, Marmar; my conscience will prick like a pin next time, I know it will," said Rob, as the bell rang, and Teddy came to look at him with sorrowful surprise.

"We shall see," answered his mother, setting him free. He took a good run down the hall, back through the dining-room, and brought up beside Nan, quite beaming with virtuous satisfaction.

"I'll bring her dinner to her, may I?" he asked, pitying his fellow-captive.

"That's my kind little son! Yes, pull out the table, and get a chair;" and Mrs. Jo hurried away to quell the ardor of the others, who were always in a raging state of hunger at noon.

Nan ate alone, and spent a long afternoon attached to the sofa. Mrs. Bhaer lengthened her bonds so that she could look out of the window; and there she stood watching the boys play, and all the little summer creatures enjoying their liberty. Daisy had a pic-nic for the dolls on the lawn, so that Nan might see the fun if she could not join in it. Tommy turned his best somersaults to console her; Demi sat on the steps reading aloud to himself, which amused Nan a good deal; and Dan brought a little tree-toad to show her as the most delicate attention in his power.

But nothing atoned for the loss of freedom; and a few hours of confinement taught Nan how precious it was. A good many thoughts went through the little head that lay on the window-sill during the last quiet hour when all the children went to the brook to see Emil's new ship launched. She was to have christened it, and had depended on smashing a tiny bottle of currant-wine over the prow as it was named *Josephine* in honor of Mrs. Bhaer. Now she had lost her chance, and Daisy wouldn't do it half so well. Tears rose to her eyes as she remembered that it was all her own fault; and she said aloud, addressing a fat bee who was rolling about in the yellow heart of a rose just under the window—

"If you have run away, you'd better go right home, and tell your mother you are sorry, and never do so anymore."

"I am glad to hear you give him such good advice, and I think he has taken it," said Mrs. Jo, smiling, as the bee spread his dusty wings and flew away.

Nan brushed off a bright drop or two that shone on the window-sill, and nestled against her friend as she took her on her knee, adding kindly—for she had seen the little drops, and knew what they meant—

"Do you think my mother's cure for running away a good one?"

"Yes, ma'am," answered Nan, quite subdued by her quiet day.

"I hope I shall not have to try it again."

"I guess not"; and Nan looked up with such an earnest little face that Mrs. Jo felt satisfied, and said no more, for she liked to have her penalties do their own work, and did not spoil the effect by too much moralizing.

Here Rob appeared, bearing with infinite care what Asia called a "sarcer pie," meaning one baked in a saucer.

"It's made out of some of my berries, and I'm going to give you half at supper-time," he announced, with a flourish.

"What makes you, when I'm so naughty?" asked Nan, meekly.

"Because we got lost together. You ain't going to be naughty again, are you?"

"Never," said Nan, with great decision.

"Oh, goody! Now let's go and get Mary Ann to cut this for us all ready to eat; it's 'most tea-time"; and Rob beckoned with the delicious little pie.

Nan started to follow, then stopped, and said—

"I forgot, I can't go."

"Try and see," said Mrs. Bhaer, who had quietly untied the cord sash while she had been talking.

Nan saw that she was free, and with one tempestuous kiss to Mrs. Jo, she was off like a humming-bird, followed by Robby, dribbling huckleberry juice as he ran.

# CHAPTER XIII

## GOLDILOCKS

AFTER the last excitement peace descended upon Plumfield and reigned unbroken for several weeks, for the elder boys felt that the loss of Nan and Rob lay at their door, and all became so paternal in their care that they were rather wearying; while the little ones listened to Nan's recital of her perils so many times, that they regarded being lost as the greatest ill humanity was heir to, and hardly dared to put their little noses outside the great gate lest night should suddenly descend upon them, and ghostly black cows come looming through the dusk.

"It is too good to last," said Mrs. Jo; for years of boy-culture had taught her that such lulls were usually followed by outbreaks of some sort, and when less wise women would have thought that the boys had become confirmed saints, she prepared herself for a sudden erruption of the domestic volcano.

One cause of this welcome calm was a visit from little Bess, whose parents lent her for a week while they were away with Grandpa Laurence, who was poorly. The boys regarded Goldilocks as a mixture of child, angel, and fairy, for she was a lovely little creature, and the golden hair which she inherited from her blonde mamma enveloped her like a shining veil, behind which she smiled upon her worshippers when gracious, and hid herself when offended. Her father would not have it cut, and it hung below her waist, so soft and fine and bright, that Demi insisted that it was silk spun from a cocoon. Every one praised the little Princess, but it did not seem to do her harm, only to teach her that her presence brought sunshine, her smiles made answering smiles on other faces, and her baby griefs filled every heart with tenderest sympathy.

Unconsciously she did her young subjects more good than many a real sovereign, for her rule was very gentle and her power was felt rather than seen. Her natural refinement made her dainty in all things, and had a good effect upon the careless lads about her. She would let no one touch her roughly or with unclean hands, and more soap was used during her visits than at any other time, because the boys considered it the highest honor to be allowed to carry her highness, and the deepest disgrace to be repulsed with the disdainful command, "Do away, dirty boy!"

Loud voices displeased her and quarrelling frightened her; so gentler tones came into the boyish voices as they addressed her, and squabbles were promptly suppressed in her presence by lookers-on if the principals could not restrain themselves. She liked to be waited on, and the biggest boys did her little errands without a murmur, while the small lads were her devoted slaves in all things. They begged to be allowed to draw her carriage, bear her berry-basket, or pass her plate at table. No service was too humble, and Tommy and Ned came to blows before they could decide which should have the honor of blacking her little boots.

Nan was especially benefited by a week in the society of a well-bred lady, though such a very small one; for Bess would look at her with a mixture of wonder and alarm in her great blue eyes when the hoyden screamed and romped; and she shrunk from her as if she thought her a sort of wild animal. Warm-hearted Nan felt this very much. She said at first, "Pooh! I don't care!" But she did care, and was so hurt when Bess said, "I love my tuzzin best, tause she is twiet," that she shook poor Daisy till her teeth chattered in her head, and then fled to the barn to cry dismally. In that general refuge for perturbed spirits she found comfort and good counsel from some source or other. Perhaps the swallows from their mud-built nests overhead twittered her a little lecture on the beauty of gentleness. However that might have been, she came out quite subdued, and carefully searched the orchard for a certain kind of early apple that Bess liked because it was sweet and small and rosy. Armed with this peace-offering, she approached the Princess, and humbly presented it. To her great joy it was graciously accepted, and when Daisy gave Nan a forgiving kiss, Bess did likewise, as if she felt that she had been too severe and desired to apologize. After this they played pleasantly together, and Nan enjoyed the royal favor for days. To be sure she felt a little like a wild bird in a pretty cage at first, and occasionally had to slip out to stretch her wings in a long flight, or to sing at the top of her voice, where neither would disturb the plump turtle-dove Daisy, nor the dainty golden canary Bess. But it did her good; for, seeing how every one loved the little Princess for her small graces and virtues, she began to imitate her, because Nan wanted much love, and tried hard to win it.

Not a boy in the house but felt the pretty child's influence, and was improved by it without exactly knowing how or why, for babies can work miracles in the hearts that love them. Poor Billy found infinite satisfaction in staring at her, and though she did not like it she permitted it without a frown, after she had been made to understand that he was not quite like the others, and on that account must be more kindly treated. Dick and Dolly overwhelmed her with willow whistles, the only thing they knew how to make, and she accepted but never used them. Rob served her like a little lover, and Teddy followed her like a pet dog. Jack she did not like, because he was afflicted with warts and had a harsh voice. Stuffy displeased her because he did not eat tidily, and George tried hard not to gobble, that he might not disgust the dainty little lady opposite. Ned was banished from court in utter disgrace when he was discovered tormenting some unhappy field-mice. Goldilocks never could forget the sad spectacle, and retired behind her veil when he approached, waving him away with an imperious little hand, and crying, in a tone of mingled grief and anger,—

"No, I tarn't love him; he tut the poor mouses' little tails off, and they queeked!"

Daisy promptly abdicated when Bess came, and took the humble post of chief cook, while Nan was first maid of honor; Emil was chancellor of the exchequer, and spent the public moneys lavishly in getting up spectacles that cost whole ninepences. Franz was prime minister, and directed her affairs of state, planned royal progresses through the kingdom, and kept foreign powers in order. Demi was her philosopher, and fared much better than such gentlemen usually do among crowned heads. Dan was her standing army, and defended her territories gallantly; Tommy was court fool, and Nat a tuneful Rizzio to this innocent little Mary.

Uncle Fritz and Aunt Jo enjoyed this peaceful episode, and looked on at the pretty play in which the young folk unconsciously imitated their elders, without adding the tragedy that is so apt to spoil the dramas acted on the larger stage.

"They teach us quite as much as we teach them," said Mr. Bhaer.

"Bless the dears! They never guess how many hints they give us as to the best way of managing them," answered Mrs. Jo.

"I think you were right about the good effect of having girls among the boys. Nan *has* stirred up Daisy, and Bess is teaching the little bears how to behave better than we can. If this reformation goes on as it has begun, I shall soon feel like Dr. Blimber with his model young gentlemen," said Professor, laughing, as he saw Tommy not only remove his own hat, but knock off Ned's also, as they entered the hall where the Princess was taking a ride on the rocking-horse, attended by Rob and Teddy astride of chairs, and playing gallant knights to the best of their ability.

"You will never be a Blimber, Fritz, you couldn't do it if you tried; and our boys will never submit to the forcing process of that famous hot-bed. No fear that they will be too elegant: American boys like liberty too well. But good manners they cannot fail to have, if we give them the kindly spirit that shines through the simplest demeanor, making it courteous and cordial, like yours, my dear old boy."

"Tut! Tut! We will not compliment; for if I begin you will run away, and I have a wish to enjoy this happy half hour to the end;" yet Mr. Bhaer looked pleased with the compliment, for it was true, and Mrs. Jo felt that she had received the best her husband could give her, by saying that he found his truest rest and happiness in her society.

"To return to the children: I have just had another proof of Goldilocks' good influence," said Mrs. Jo, drawing her chair nearer the sofa, where the Professor lay resting after a long day's work in his various gardens. "Nan hates sewing, but for love of Bess has been toiling half the afternoon over a remarkable bag in which to present a dozen of our love-apples to her idol when she goes. I praised her for it, and she said, in her quick way, 'I like to sew for other people; it is stupid sewing for myself.' I took the hint, and shall give her some little shirts and aprons for Mrs. Carney's children. She is so generous, she will sew her fingers sore for them, and I shall not have to make a task of it."

"But needlework is not a fashionable accomplishment, my dear."

"Sorry for it. My girls shall learn all I can teach them about it, even if they give up the Latin, Algebra, and half-a-dozen ologies it is considered necessary for girls to muddle their poor brains over now-a-days. Amy means to make Bess an accomplished woman; but the dear's mite of a forefinger has little pricks on it already, and her mother has several specimens of needlework which she values more than the clay bird without a bill, that filled Laurie with such pride when Bess made it."

"I also have a proof of the Princess's power," said Mr. Bhaer, after he had watched Mrs. Jo sew on a button with an air of scorn for the whole system of fashionable education. "Jack is so unwilling to be classed with Stuffy and Ned, as distasteful to Bess, that he came to me a little while ago, and asked me to touch his warts with caustic. I have often proposed it, and he never would consent; but now he bore the smart manfully, and consoles his present discomfort by hopes of future favor, when he can show her fastidious ladyship a smooth hand."

Mrs. Bhaer laughed at the story, and just then Stuffy came in to ask if he might give Goldilocks some of the bonbons his mother had sent him.

"She is not allowed to eat sweeties; but if you like to give her the pretty box with the pink sugar-rose in it, she would like it very much," said Mrs. Jo, unwilling to spoil this unusual piece of self-denial, for the "fat boy" seldom offered to share his sugar-plums.

"Won't she eat it? I shouldn't like to make her sick," said Stuffy, eying the delicate sweetmeat lovingly, yet putting it into the box.

"Oh, no, she won't touch it, if I tell her it is to look at, not to eat. She will keep it for weeks, and never think of tasting it. Can you do as much?"

"I should hope so! I'm ever so much older than she is," cried Stuffy, indignantly.

"Well, suppose we try. Here, put your bonbons in this bag and see how long you can keep them. Let me count—two hearts, four red fishes, three barley-sugar horses, nine almonds, and a dozen chocolate drops. Do you agree to that?" asked sly Mrs. Jo, popping the sweeties into her little spool-bag.

"Yes," said Stuffy, with a sigh; and pocketing the forbidden fruit, he went away to give Bess the present, that won a smile from her, and permission to escort her round the garden.

"Poor Stuffy's heart has really got the better of his stomach at last, and his efforts will be much encouraged by the rewards Bess gives him," said Mrs. Jo.

"Happy the man who can put temptation in his pocket and learn self-denial from so sweet a little teacher!" added Mr. Bhaer, as the children passed the window, Stuffy's fat face full of placid satisfaction, and Goldilocks surveying her sugar-rose with polite interest, though she would have preferred a real flower with a "pitty smell."

When her father came to take her home, a universal wail arose, and the parting gifts showered upon her increased her luggage to such an extent that Mr. Laurie proposed having out the big wagon to take it into town. Every one had given her something; and it was found difficult to pack white mice, cake, a parcel of shells, apples, a rabbit kicking violently in a bag, a large cabbage for his refreshment, a bottle of minnows, and a mammoth bouquet. The farewell scene was moving, for the Princess sat upon the hall-table, surrounded by her subjects. She kissed her cousins, and held out her hand to the other boys, who shook it gently with various soft speeches, for they were taught not to be ashamed of showing their emotions.

"Come again, soon, little dear," whispered Dan, fastening his best green-and-gold beetle in her hat.

"Don't forgot me, Princess, whatever you do," said the engaging Tommy, taking a last stroke of the pretty hair.

"I am coming to your house next week, and then I shall see you, Bess," added Nat, as if he found consolation in the thought.

"Do shake hands now," cried Jack, offering a smooth paw.

"Here are two nice new ones to remember us by," said Dick and Dolly, presenting fresh whistles, quite unconscious that seven old ones had been privately deposited in the kitchen-stove.

"My little precious! I shall work you a book-mark right away, and you must keep it *always*," said Nan, with a warm embrace.

But of all the farewells, poor Billy's was the most pathetic, for the thought that she was really going became so unbearable that he cast himself down before her, hugging her little blue boots and blubbering despairingly, "Don't go away! Oh, don't!" Goldilocks was so touched by this burst of feeling, that she leaned over and lifting the poor lad's head, said, in her soft, little voice,—

"Don't cry, poor Billy! I will tiss you and tum adain soon."

This promise consoled Billy, and he fell back beaming with pride at the unusual honor conferred upon him.

"Me too! Me too!" clamored Dick and Dolly, feeling that their devotion deserved some return. The others looked as if they would like to join in the cry; and something in the kind, merry faces about her moved the Princess to stretch out her arms and say, with reckless condescension,—

"I will tiss evvybody!"

Like a swarm of bees about a very sweet flower, the affectionate lads surrounded their pretty playmate, and kissed her till she looked like a little rose, not roughly, but so enthusiastically that nothing but the crown of her hat was visible for a moment. Then her father rescued her, and she drove away still smiling and waving her hands, while the boys sat on the fence screaming like a flock of guinea-fowls, "Come back! Come back!" till she was out of sight.

They all missed her, and each dimly felt that he was better for having known a creature so lovely, delicate, and sweet; for little Bess appealed to the chivalrous instinct in them as something to love, admire, and protect with a tender sort of reverence. Many men remember some pretty child who has made a place in his heart and kept her memory alive by the simple magic of her innocence; these little men were just learning to feel this power, and to love it for its gentle influence, not ashamed to let the small hand lead them, nor to own their loyalty to womankind, even in the bud.

# CHAPTER XIV

## DAMON AND PYTHIAS

MRS. BHAER was right; peace was only a temporary lull, a storm was brewing, and two days after Bess left, a moral earthquake shook Plumfield to its centre.

Tommy's hens were at the bottom of the trouble, for if they had not persisted in laying so many eggs, he could not have sold them and made such sums. Money is the root of all evil, and yet it is such a useful root that we cannot get on without it any more than we can without potatoes. Tommy certainly could not, for he spent his income so recklessly, that Mr. Bhaer was obliged to insist on a savings-bank, and presented him with a private one—an imposing tin edifice, with the name over the door, and a tall chimney, down which the pennies were to go, there to rattle temptingly till leave was given to open a sort of trap-door in the floor.

The house increased in weight so rapidly, that Tommy soon became satisfied with his investment, and planned to buy unheard-of treasures with his capital. He kept account of the sums deposited, and was promised that he might break the bank as soon as he had five dollars, on condition that he spent the money wisely. Only one dollar was needed, and the day Mrs. Jo paid him for four dozen eggs, he was so delighted, that he raced off to the barn to display the bright quarters to Nat, who was also laying by money for the long-desired violin.

"I wish I had 'em to put with my three dollars, then I'd soon get enough to buy my fiddle," he said, looking wistfully at the money.

"P'raps I'll lend you some. I haven't decided yet what I'll do with mine," said Tommy, tossing up his quarters, and catching them as they fell.

"Hi! Boys! Come down to the brook and see what a jolly great snake Dan's got!" called a voice from behind the barn.

"Come on," said Tommy; and, laying his money inside the old winnowing machine, away he ran, followed by Nat.

The snake was very interesting, and then a long chase after a lame crow, and its capture, so absorbed Tommy's mind and time, that he never thought of his money till he was safely in bed that night.

"Never mind, no one but Nat knows where it is," said the easy-going lad, and fell asleep untroubled by any anxiety about his property.

Next morning, just as the boys assembled for school, Tommy rushed into the room breathlessly, demanding—

"I say, who has got my dollar?"

"What are you talking about?" asked Franz.

Tommy explained, and Nat corroborated his statement.

Every one else declared they knew nothing about it, and began to look suspiciously at Nat, who got more and more alarmed and confused with each denial.

"Somebody must have taken it," said Franz, as Tommy shook his fist at the whole party, and wrathfully declared that—

"By thunder turtles! If I get hold of the thief, I'll give him what he won't forget in a hurry."

"Keep cool, Tom; we shall find him out; thieves always come to grief," said Dan, as one who knew something of the matter.

"Maybe some tramp slept in the barn and took it," suggested Ned.

"No, Silas don't allow that; besides, a tramp wouldn't go looking in that old machine for money," said Emil, with scorn.

"Wasn't it Silas himself?" said Jack.

"Well, I like that! Old Si is as honest as daylight. You wouldn't catch him touching a penny of ours," said Tommy, handsomely defending his chief admirer from suspicion.

"Whoever it was had better tell, and not wait to be found out," said Demi, looking as if an awful misfortune had befallen the family.

"I know you think it's me," broke out Nat, red and excited.

"You are the only one who knew where it was," said Franz.

"I can't help it—I didn't take it. I tell you I didn't—I didn't!" cried Nat, in a desperate sort of way.

"Gently, gently, my son! What is all this noise about?" and Mr. Bhaer walked in among them.

Tommy repeated the story of his loss, and, as he listened, Mr. Bhaer's face grew graver and graver; for, with all their faults and follies, the lads till now had been honest.

"Take your seats," he said; and, when all were in their places, he added slowly, as his eye went from face to face with a grieved look, that was harder to bear than a storm of words,—

"Now, boys, I shall ask each one of you a single question, and I want an honest answer. I am not going to try to frighten, bribe, or surprise the truth out of you, for every one of you have got a conscience, and know what it is for. Now is the time to undo the wrong done to Tommy, and to set yourselves right before us all. I can forgive the yielding to a sudden temptation much easier than I can deceit. Don't add a lie to the theft, but confess frankly, and we will all try to help you make us forget and forgive."

He paused a moment, and one might have heard a pin drop, the room was so still; then slowly and impressively he put the question to each one, receiving the same answer in varying tones from all. Every face was flushed and excited, so that Mr. Bhaer could not take color as a witness, and some of the little boys were so frightened that they stammered over the two short words as if guilty, though it was evident that they could not be. When he came to Nat, his voice softened, for the poor lad looked so wretched, Mr. Bhaer felt for him. He believed him to be the culprit, and hoped to save the boy from another lie, by winning him to tell the truth without fear.

"Now, my son, give me an honest answer. Did you take the money?"

"No, sir!" and Nat looked up at him imploringly.

As the words fell from his trembling lips, somebody hissed.

"Stop that!" cried Mr. Bhaer, with a sharp rap on his desk, as he looked sternly toward the corner whence the sound came.

Ned, Jack, and Emil sat there, and the first two looked ashamed of themselves, but Emil called out—

"It wasn't me, uncle! I'd be ashamed to hit a fellow when he is down."

"Good for you!" cried Tommy, who was in a sad state of affliction at the trouble his unlucky dollar had made.

"Silence!" commanded Mr. Bhaer; and when it came, he said soberly—

"I am *very* sorry, Nat, but evidences are against you, and your old fault makes us more ready to doubt you than we should be if we could trust you as we do some of the boys, who never fib. But mind, my child, I do not charge you with this theft; I shall not punish you for it till I am *perfectly* sure, nor ask anything more about it. I shall leave it for you to settle with your own conscience. If you are guilty, come to me at any hour of the day or night and confess it, and I will forgive and help you to amend. If you are innocent, the truth will appear sooner or later, and the instant it does, I will be the first to beg your pardon for doubting you, and will so gladly do my best to clear your character before us all."

"I didn't! I didn't!" sobbed Nat, with his head down upon his arms, for he could not bear the look of distrust and dislike which he read in the many eyes fixed on him.

"I hope not." Mr. Bhaer paused a minute, as if to give the culprit, whoever he might be, one more chance. Nobody spoke, however, and only sniffs of sympathy from some of the little fellows broke the silence. Mr. Bhaer shook his head, and added, regretfully,—

"There is nothing more to be done, then, and I have but one thing to say: I shall not speak of this again, and I wish you all to follow my example. I cannot expect you to feel as kindly toward any one whom you suspect as before this happened, but I do expect and desire that you will not torment the suspected person in any way,—he will have a hard enough time without that. Now go to your lessons."

"Father Bhaer let Nat off too easy," muttered Ned to Emil, as they got out their books.

"Hold your tongue," growled Emil, who felt that this event was a blot upon the family honor.

Many of the boys agreed with Ned, but Mr. Bhaer was right, nevertheless; and Nat would have been wiser to confess on the spot and have the trouble over, for even the hardest whipping he ever received from his father was far easier to bear than the cold looks, the avoidance, and general suspicion that met him on all sides. If ever a boy was sent to Coventry and kept there, it was poor Nat; and he suffered a week of slow torture, though not a hand was raised against him, and hardly a word said.

That was the worst of it; if they would only have talked it out, or even have thrashed him all round, he could have stood it better than the silent distrust that made every face so terrible to meet. Even Mrs. Bhaer's showed traces of it, though her manner was nearly as kind as ever; but the sorrowful anxious look in Father Bhaer's eyes cut Nat to the heart, for he loved his teacher dearly, and knew that he had disappointed all his hopes by this double sin.

Only one person in the house entirely believed in him, and stood up for him stoutly against all the rest. This was Daisy. She could not explain why she trusted him against all appearances, she only felt that she could not doubt him, and her warm sympathy made her strong to take his part. She would not hear a word against him from anyone, and actually slapped her beloved Demi when he tried to convince her that it *must* have been Nat, because no one else knew where the money was.

"Maybe the hens ate it; they are greedy old things," she said; and when Demi laughed, she lost her temper, slapped the amazed boy, and then burst out crying and ran away, still declaring, "He didn't! He didn't! He didn't!"

Neither aunt nor uncle tried to shake the child's faith in her friend, but only hoped her innocent instinct might prove sure, and loved her all the better for it. Nat often said, after it was over, that he couldn't have stood it, if it had not been for Daisy. When the others shunned him, she clung to him closer than ever, and turned her back on the rest. She did not sit on the stairs now when he solaced himself with the old fiddle, but went in and sat beside him, listening with a face so full of confidence and affection, that Nat forgot disgrace for a time, and was happy. She asked him to help her with her lessons, she cooked him marvellous messes in her kitchen, which he ate manfully, no matter what they were, for gratitude gave a sweet flavor to the most distasteful. She proposed impossible games of cricket and ball, when she found that he shrank from joining the other boys. She put little nosegays from her garden on his desk, and tried in every way to show that *she* was not a fair-weather friend, but faithful through evil as well as good repute. Nan soon followed her example, in kindness at least; curbed her sharp tongue, and kept her scornful little nose from any demonstration of doubt or dislike, which was good of Madame Giddy-gaddy, for she firmly believed that Nat took the money.

Most of the boys let him severely alone, but Dan, though he said he despised him for being a coward, watched over him with a grim sort of protection, and promptly cuffed any lad who dared to molest his mate or make him afraid. His idea of friendship was as high as Daisy's, and, in his own rough way, he lived up to it as loyally.

Sitting by the brook one afternoon, absorbed in the study of the domestic habits of water-spiders, he overheard a bit of conversation on the other side of the wall. Ned, who was intensely inquisitive, had been on tenter-hooks to know *certainly* who was the culprit; for of late one or two of the boys had begun to think that they were wrong, Nat was so steadfast in his denials, and so meek in his endurance of their neglect. This doubt had teased Ned past bearing, and he had several times privately beset Nat with questions, regardless of Mr. Bhaer's express command. Finding Nat reading alone on the shady side of the wall, Ned could not resist stopping for a nibble at the forbidden subject. He had worried Nat for some ten minutes before Dan arrived, and the first word the spider-student heard were these, in Nat's patient, pleading voice,—

"Don't, Ned! Oh don't! I can't tell you, because I don't know, and it's mean of you to keep nagging at me on the sly, when Father Bhaer told you not to plague me. You wouldn't dare to if Dan was round."

"I ain't afraid of Dan; he's nothing but an old bully. Don't believe but what he took Tom's money, and you know it, and won't tell. Come, now!"

"He didn't, but, if he did, I *would* stand up for him, he has always been so good to me," said Nat, so earnestly, that Dan forgot his spiders, and rose quickly to thank him, but Ned's next words arrested him.

"I *know* Dan did it, and gave the money to you. Shouldn't wonder if he got his living picking pockets before he came here, for nobody knows anything about him but you," said Ned, not believing his own words, but hoping to get the truth out of Nat by making him angry.

He succeeded in a part of his ungenerous wish, for Nat cried out, fiercely,—

"If you say that again I'll go and tell Mr. Bhaer all about it. I don't want to tell tales, but, by George! I will, if you don't let Dan alone."

"Then you'll be a sneak, as well as a liar and a thief," began Ned, with a jeer, for Nat had borne insult to himself so meekly, the other did not believe he would dare to face the master just to stand up for Dan.

What he might have added I cannot tell, for the words were hardly out of his mouth when a long arm from behind took him by the collar, and, jerking him over the wall in a most promiscuous way, landed him with a splash in the middle of the brook.

"Say that again and I'll duck you till you can't see!" cried Dan, looking like a modern Colossus of Rhodes as he stood, with a foot on either side the narrow stream, glaring down at the discomfited youth in the water.

"I was only in fun," said Ned.

"You are a sneak yourself to badger Nat round the corner. Let me catch you at it again, and I'll souse you in the river next time. Get up, and clear out!" thundered Dan, in a rage.

Ned fled, dripping, and his impromptu sitz-bath evidently did him good, for he was very respectful to both the boys after that, and seemed to have left his curiosity in the brook. As he vanished Dan jumped over the wall, and found Nat lying as if quite worn out and bowed down with his troubles.

"He won't pester you again, I guess. If he does, just tell me, and I'll see to him," said Dan, trying to cool down.

"I don't mind what he says about me so much, I've got used to it," answered Nat, sadly; "but I hate to have him pitch into you."

"How do you know he isn't right?" asked Dan, turning his face away.

"What, about the money?" cried Nat, looking up with a startled air.

"Yes."

"But I don't believe it! *You* don't care for money; all you want is your old bugs and things," and Nat laughed, incredulously.

"I want a butterfly-net as much as you want a fiddle; why shouldn't I steal the money for it as much as you?" said Dan, still turning away, and busily punching holes in the turf with his stick.

"I don't think you would. You like to fight and knock folks round sometimes, but you don't lie, and I don't believe you'd steal," and Nat shook his head decidedly.

"I've done both. I used to fib like fury; it's too much trouble now; and I stole things to eat out of gardens when I ran away from Page, so you

Landed him with a splash in the middle of the brook.

see I *am* a bad lot," said Dan, speaking in the rough, reckless way which he had been learning to drop lately.

"O Dan! Don't say it's you! I'd rather have it any of the other boys," cried Nat, in such a distressed tone that Dan looked pleased, and showed that he did, by turning round with a queer expression in his face, though he only answered—

"I won't say anything about it. But don't you fret, and we'll pull through somehow, see if we don't."

Something in his face and manner gave Nat a new idea; and he said, pressing his hands together, in the eagerness of his appeal,—

"I think you know who did it. If you do, beg him to tell, Dan. It's so hard to have 'em all hate me for nothing. I don't think I *can* bear it much longer. If I had any place to go to, I'd run away, though I love Plumfield dearly; but I'm not brave and big like you, so I must stay and wait till someone shows them that I haven't lied."

As he spoke, Nat looked so broken and despairing, that Dan could not bear it, and, muttering huskily—

"You won't wait long," he walked rapidly away, and was seen no more for hours.

"What is the matter with Dan?" asked the boys of one another several times during the Sunday that followed a week which seemed as if it would *never* end. Dan was often moody, but that day he was so sober and silent that no one could get anything out of him. When they walked he strayed away from the rest, and came home late. He took no part in the evening conversation, but sat in the shadow, so busy with his own thoughts that he scarcely seemed to hear what was going on. When Mrs. Jo showed him an unusually good report in the Conscience Book, he looked at it without a smile, and said, wistfully,—

"You think I am getting on, don't you?"

"Excellently, Dan! And I am so pleased, because I always thought you only needed a little help to make you a boy to be proud of."

He looked up at her with a strange expression in his black eyes—an expression of mingled pride and love and sorrow which she could not understand then—but remembered afterward.

"I'm afraid you'll be disappointed, but I do try," he said, shutting the book without a sign of pleasure in the page that he usually liked so much to read over and talk about.

"Are you sick, dear?" asked Mrs. Jo, with her hand on his shoulder.

"My foot aches a little; I guess I'll go to bed. Good-night, mother," he added, and held the hand against his cheek a minute, then went away looking as if he had said good-by to something very dear.

"Poor Dan! He takes Nat's disgrace to heart sadly. He is a strange boy; I wonder if I ever shall understand him thoroughly?" said Mrs. Jo to herself, as she thought over Dan's late improvement with real satisfaction, yet felt that there was more in the lad than she had at first suspected.

One of the things which cut Nat most deeply was an act of Tommy's, for after his loss Tommy had said to him, kindly but firmly,—

"I don't wish to hurt you, Nat, but you see I can't afford to lose my money, so I guess we won't be partners any longer;" and with that Tommy rubbed out the sign, "T. Bangs & Co."

Nat had been very proud of the "Co.," and had hunted eggs industriously, kept his accounts all straight, and had added a good sum to his income from the sale of his share of stock in trade.

"O, Tom! Must you?" he said, feeling that his good name was gone forever in the business world if this was done.

"I must," returned Tommy, firmly. "Emil says that when one man 'bezzles (I believe that's the word—it means to take money and cut away with it) the property of a firm, the other one sues him, or pitches into him somehow, and won't have anything more to do with him. Now you have 'bezzled my property; I shan't sue you, and I shan't pitch into you, but I *must* dissolve the partnership, because I can't trust you, and I don't wish to fail."

"I can't make you believe me, and you won't take my money, though I'd be thankful to give all my dollars if you'd only say you don't think I took your money. Do let me hunt for you, I won't ask any wages, but do it for nothing. I know all the places, and I like it," pleaded Nat.

But Tommy shook his head, and his jolly round face looked suspicious and hard as he said, shortly, "Can't do it; wish you didn't know the places. Mind you don't go hunting on the sly, and speculate in my eggs."

Poor Nat was so hurt that he could not get over it. He felt that he had lost not only his partner and patron, but that he was bankrupt in honor, and an outlaw from the business community. No one trusted his word, written or spoken, in spite of his efforts to redeem the past falsehood; the sign was down, the firm broken up, and he a ruined man. The barn, which was the boys' Wall Street, knew him no more. Cockletop and her sisters cackled for him in vain, and really seemed to take his misfortune to heart, for eggs were fewer, and some of the biddies retired in disgust to new nests, which Tommy could not find.

"*They* trust me," said Nat, when he heard of it; and though the boys shouted at the idea, Nat found comfort in it, for when one is down in the world, the confidence of even a speckled hen is most consoling.

Tommy took no new partner, however, for distrust had entered in, and poisoned the peace of his once confiding soul. Ned offered to join him, but he declined, saying, with a sense of justice that did him honor—

"It might turn out that Nat didn't take my money, and then we could be partners again. I don't think it will happen, but I will give him a chance, and keep the place open a little longer."

Billy was the only person whom Bangs felt he could trust in his shop, and Billy was trained to hunt eggs, and hand them over unbroken, being quite satisfied with an apple or a sugar-plum for wages. The morning after Dan's gloomy Sunday, Billy said to his employer, as he displayed the results of a long hunt—

"Only two."

"It gets worse and worse; I never saw such provoking old hens," growled Tommy, thinking of the days when he often had six to rejoice over. "Well, put 'em in my hat and give me a new bit of chalk; I must mark 'em up, anyway."

Billy mounted a peck-measure, and looked into the top of the machine, where Tommy kept his writing materials.

"There's lots of money in here," said Billy.

"No, there isn't. Catch me leaving my cash round again," returned Tommy.

"I see 'em—one, four, eight, two dollars," persisted Billy, who had not yet mastered the figures correctly.

"What a jack you are!" and Tommy hopped up to get the chalk for himself, but nearly tumbled down again, for there actually were four bright quarters in a row, with a bit of paper on them directed to "Tom Bangs," that there might be no mistake.

"Thunder turtles!" cried Tommy, and seizing them he dashed into the house, bawling wildly, "It's all right! Got my money! Where's Nat?"

He was soon found, and his surprise and pleasure were so genuine that few doubted his word when he now denied all knowledge of the money.

"How could I put it back when I didn't take it? Do believe me now, and be good to me again," he said, so imploringly, that Emil slapped him on the back, and declared *he* would for one.

"So will I, and I'm jolly glad it's not you. But who the dickens is it?" said Tommy, after shaking hands heartily with Nat.

"Never mind, as long as it's found," said Dan, with his eyes fixed on Nat's happy face.

"Well, I like that! I'm not going to have my things hooked, and then brought back like the juggling man's tricks," cried Tommy, looking at his money as if he suspected witchcraft.

"We'll find him out somehow, though he was sly enough to print this so his writing wouldn't be known," said Franz, examining the paper.

"Demi prints tip-top," put in Rob, who had not a very clear idea what the fuss was all about.

"You can't make me believe it's him, not if you talk till you are blue," said Tommy, and the others hooted at the mere idea; for the little deacon, as they called him, was above suspicion.

Nat felt the difference in the way they spoke of Demi and himself, and would have given all he had or ever hoped to have, to be so trusted; for he had learned how easy it is to lose the confidence of others, how very, very hard to win it back, and truth became to him a precious thing since he had suffered from neglecting it.

Mr. Bhaer was very glad one step had been taken in the right direction, and waited hopefully for yet further revelations. They came sooner than he expected, and in a way that surprised and grieved him very much. As they sat at supper that night, a square parcel was handed to Mr. Bhaer from Mrs. Bates, a neighbor. A note accompanied the parcel, and, while Mr, Bhaer read it, Demi pulled off the wrapper, exclaiming, as he saw its contents,—

"Why, it's the book Uncle Teddy gave Dan!"

"The devil!" broke from Dan, for he had not yet quite cured himself of swearing, though he tried hard.

Mr. Bhaer looked up quickly at the sound. Dan tried to meet his eyes, but could not; his own fell, and he sat biting his lips, getting redder and redder till he was the picture of shame.

"What is it?" asked Mrs. Bhaer, anxiously.

"I should have preferred to talk about this in private, but Demi has spoilt that plan, so I may as well have it out now," said Mr. Bhaer, looking a little stern, as he always did when any meanness or deceit came up for judgment.

"The note is from Mrs. Bates, and she says that her boy Jimmy told her he bought this book of Dan last Saturday. She saw that it was worth much more than a dollar, and thinking there was some mistake, has sent it to me. Did you sell it, Dan?"

"Yes, sir," was the slow answer.

"Why?"

"Wanted money."

"For what?"

"To pay somebody."

"To whom did you owe it?"

"Tommy."

"Never borrowed a cent of me in his life," cried Tommy, looking scared, for he guessed what was coming now, and felt that on the whole he would have preferred witchcraft, for he admired Dan immensely.

"Perhaps he took it," cried Ned, who owed Dan a grudge for the ducking, and, being a mortal boy, liked to pay it off.

"O Dan!" cried Nat, clasping his hands, regardless of the bread and butter in them.

"It is a hard thing to do, but I must have this settled, for I cannot have you watching each other like detectives, and the whole school disturbed in this way. Did you put that dollar in the barn this morning?" asked Mr. Bhaer.

Dan looked him straight in the face, and answered steadily, "Yes, I did."

A murmur went round the table, Tommy dropped his mug with a crash; Daisy cried out, "I knew it wasn't Nat." Nan began to cry, and Mrs. Jo left the room, looking so disappointed, sorry, and ashamed that Dan could not bear it. He hid his face in his hands a moment, then threw up his head, squared his shoulders as if settling some load upon them, and said, with the dogged look, and half-resolute, half-reckless tone he had used when he first came—

"I did it; now you may do what you like to me, but I won't say another word about it."

"Not even that you are sorry?" asked Mr. Bhaer, troubled by the change in him.

"I ain't sorry."

"I'll forgive him without asking," said Tommy, feeling that it was harder somehow to see brave Dan disgraced than timid Nat.

"Don't want to be forgiven," returned Dan, gruffly.

"Perhaps you will when you have thought about it quietly by yourself. I won't tell you now how surprised and disappointed I am, but by and by I will come up and talk to you in your room."

"Won't make any difference," said Dan, trying to speak defiantly, but failing as he looked at Mr. Bhaer's sorrowful face; and, taking his words for a dismissal, Dan left the room, as if he found it impossible to stay.

It would have done him good if he had stayed; for the boys talked the matter over with such sincere regret, and pity, and wonder, it might have touched and won him to ask pardon. No one was glad to find that it was he, not even Nat; for, spite of all his faults, and they were many, everyone liked Dan now, because under his rough exterior lay some of the manly virtues which we most admire and love. Mrs. Jo had been the chief prop, as well as cultivator, of Dan; and she took it sadly to heart that her last and most interesting boy had turned out so ill. The theft was bad, but the lying about it, and allowing another to suffer so much from an unjust suspicion, was worse; and most discouraging of all was the attempt to restore the money in an underhand way, for it showed not only a want of courage, but a power of deceit that boded ill for the future. Still more trying was his steady refusal to talk of the matter, to ask pardon, or express any remorse. Days passed; and he went about his lessons and his work, silent, grim, and unrepentant. As if taking warning by their treatment of Nat, he asked no sympathy of anyone, rejected the advances of the boys, and spent his leisure hours roaming about the fields and woods, trying to find playmates in the birds and beasts, and succeeding better than most boys would have done, because he knew and loved them so well.

"If this goes on much longer, I'm afraid he will run away again, for he is too young to stand a life like this," said Mr. Bhaer, quite dejected at the failure of all his efforts.

"A little while ago I should have been quite sure that nothing would tempt him away, but now I am ready for anything, he is so changed," answered poor Mrs. Jo, who mourned over her boy, and could not be comforted, because he shunned her more than anyone else, and only looked at her with the half-fierce, half-imploring eyes of a wild animal caught in a trap, when she tried to talk to him alone.

Nat followed him about like a shadow, and Dan did not repulse him as rudely as he did others, but said, in his blunt way, "*You* are all right; don't worry about me. I can stand it better than you did."

"But I don't like to have you all alone," Nat would say, sorrowfully.

"I like it;" and Dan would tramp away, stifling a sigh sometimes, for he *was* lonely.

Passing through the birch grove one day, he came upon several of the boys, who were amusing themselves by climbing up the trees and swinging down again, as the slender elastic stems bent till their tops touched the ground. Dan paused a minute to watch the fun, without offering to join in it, and as he stood there Jack took his turn. He had unfortunately chosen too large a tree; for when he swung off, it only bent a little way, and left him hanging at a dangerous height.

"Go back; you can't do it!" called Ned from below.

Jack tried, but the twigs slipped from his hands, and he could not get his legs round the trunk. He kicked, and squirmed, and clutched in vain, then gave it up, and hung breathless, saying, helplessly,—

"Catch me! Help me! I must drop!"

"You'll be killed if you do," cried Ned frightened out of his wits.

"Hold on!" shouted Dan; and up the tree he went crashing his way along till he nearly reached Jack, whose face looked up at him, full of fear and hope.

"You'll both come down," said Ned, dancing with excitement on the slope underneath, while Nat held out his arms, in the wild hope of breaking the fall.

"That's what I want; stand from under," answered Dan, coolly; and, as he spoke, his added weight bent the tree many feet nearer the earth.

Jack dropped safely; but the birch, lightened of half its load, flew up again so suddenly, that Dan, in the act of swinging round to drop feet foremost, lost his hold and fell heavily.

"I'm not hurt, all right in a minute," he said, sitting up, a little pale and dizzy, as the boys gathered round him, full of admiration and alarm.

"You're a trump, Dan, and I'm ever so much obliged to you," cried Jack, gratefully.

"It wasn't anything," muttered Dan, rising slowly.

"I say it was, and I'll shake hands with you, though you are——" Ned checked the unlucky word on his tongue, and held out his hand, feeling that it was a handsome thing on his part.

"But *I* won't shake hands with a sneak;" and Dan turned his back with a look of scorn that caused Ned to remember the brook, and retire with undignified haste.

"Come home, old chap; I'll give you a lift;" and Nat walked away with him, leaving the others to talk over the feat together, to wonder when Dan would "come round," and to wish one and all that Tommy's "confounded money had been in Jericho before it made such a fuss."

When Mr. Bhaer came into school next morning, he looked so happy, that the boys wondered what had happened to him, and really thought he had lost his mind when they saw him go straight to Dan, and, taking him by both hands, say all in one breath, as he shook them heartily,—

"I know all about it, and I beg your pardon. It was like you to do it, and I love you for it, though it's never right to tell lies, even for a friend."

"What is it?" cried Nat, for Dan said not a word, only lifted up his head, as if a weight of some sort had fallen off his back.

"Dan did *not* take Tommy's money;" and Mr. Bhaer quite shouted it, he was so glad.

"Who did?" cried the boys in a chorus.

Mr. Bhaer pointed to one empty seat, and every eye followed his finger, yet no one spoke for a minute, they were so surprised.

"Jack went home early this morning, but he left this behind him;" and in the silence Mr. Bhaer read the note which he had found tied to his door-handle when he rose.

> "I took Tommy's dollar. I was peeking in through a crack, and saw him put it there. I was afraid to tell before, though I wanted to. I didn't care so much about Nat, but Dan is a trump, and I can't stand it any longer. I never spent the money; it's under the carpet in my room, right behind the washstand. I'm awful sorry. I am going home, and don't think I shall ever come back, so Dan may have my things.
>
> "JACK."

It was not an elegant confession, being badly written, much blotted, and very short; but it was a precious paper to Dan; and, when Mr. Bhaer paused, the boy went to him, saying, in rather a broken voice, but with clear eyes, and the frank, respectful manner they had tried to teach him—

"I'll say I'm sorry now, and ask you to forgive me, sir."

"It was a kind lie, Dan, and I can't help forgiving it; but you see it did no good," said Mr. Bhaer, with a hand on either shoulder, and a face full of relief and affection.

"It kept the boys from plaguing Nat. That's what I did it for. It made him right down miserable. I didn't care so much," explained Dan, as if glad to speak out after his hard silence.

"How could you do it? You are always *so* kind to me," faltered Nat, feeling a strong desire to hug his friend and cry. Two girlish performances, which would have scandalized Dan to the last degree.

"It's all right now, old fellow, so don't be a fool," he said, swallowing the lump in his throat, and laughing out as he had not done for weeks. "Does Mrs. Bhaer know?" he asked, eagerly.

"Yes; and she is so happy I don't know what she will do to you," began Mr. Bhaer, but got no farther, for here the boys came crowding about Dan in a tumult of pleasure and curiosity; but before he had answered more than a dozen questions, a voice cried out—

"Three cheers for Dan!" and there was Mrs. Jo in the doorway waving her dish-towel, and looking as if she wanted to dance a jig for joy, as she used to do when a girl.

"Now then," cried Mr. Bhaer, and led off a rousing hurrah, which startled Asia in the kitchen, and made old Mr. Roberts shake his head as he drove by, saying—

"Schools are not what they were when I was young!"

Dan stood it pretty well for a minute, but the sight of Mrs. Jo's delight upset him, and he suddenly bolted across the hall into the parlor, whither she instantly followed, and neither were seen for half an hour.

Mr. Bhaer found it very difficult to calm his excited flock; and, seeing that lessons were an impossibility for a time, he caught their attention by telling them the fine old story of the friends whose fidelity to one another has made their names immortal. The lads listened and remembered, for just then their hearts were touched by the loyalty of a humbler pair of friends. The lie was wrong, but the love that prompted it and the courage that bore in silence the disgrace which belonged to another, made Dan a hero in their eyes. Honesty and honor had a new meaning now; a good name was more precious than gold; for once lost money could not buy it back; and faith in one another made life smooth and happy as nothing else could do.

Tommy proudly restored the name of the firm; Nat was devoted to Dan; and all the boys tried to atone to both for former suspicion and neglect. Mrs. Jo rejoiced over her flock, and Mr. Bhaer was never tired of telling the story of his young Damon and Pythias.

"I'm not hurt, all right in a minute."

# CHAPTER XV

## IN THE WILLOW

THE old tree saw and heard a good many little scenes and confidences that summer, because it became the favorite retreat of all the children, and the willow seemed to enjoy it, for a pleasant welcome always met them, and the quiet hours spent in its arms did them all good. It had a great deal of company one Saturday afternoon, and some little bird reported what went on there.

First came Nan and Daisy with their small tubs and bits of soap, for now and then they were seized with a tidy fit, and washed up all their dolls' clothes in the brook. Asia would not have them "slopping round" in her kitchen, and the bath-room was forbidden since Nan forgot to turn off the water till it overflowed and came gently dripping down through the ceiling. Daisy went systematically to work, washing first the white and then the colored things, rinsing them nicely, and hanging them to dry on a cord fastened from one barberry-bush to another, and pinning them up with a set of tiny clothes-pins Ned had turned for her. But Nan put all her little things to soak in the same tub, and then forgot them while she collected thistledown to stuff a pillow for Semiramis, Queen of Babylon, as one doll was named. This took some time, and when Mrs. Giddy-gaddy came to take out her clothes, deep green stains appeared on everything, for she had forgotten the green silk lining of a certain cape, and its color had soaked nicely into the pink and blue gowns, the little chemises, and even the best ruffled petticoat.

"Oh me! What a mess!" sighed Nan.

"Lay them on the grass to bleach," said Daisy, with an air of experience.

"So I will, and we can sit up in the nest and watch that they don't blow away."

The Queen of Babylon's wardrobe was spread forth upon the bank, and, turning up their tubs to dry, the little washerwomen climbed into the nest, and fell to talking, as ladies are apt to do in the pauses of domestic labor.

"I'm going to have a feather-bed to go with my new pillow," said Mrs. Giddy-gaddy, as she transferred the thistledown from her pocket to her handkerchief, losing about half in the process.

"I wouldn't; Aunt Jo says feather-beds aren't healthy. I never let *my* children sleep on anything but a mattress," returned Mrs. Shakespeare Smith, decidedly.

"I don't care; my children are so strong they often sleep on the floor, and don't mind it" (which was quite true). "I can't afford nine mattresses, and I like to make beds myself."

"Won't Tommy charge for the feathers?"

"Maybe he will, but I shan't pay him, and he won't care," returned Mrs. G., taking a base advantage of the well-known good-nature of T. Bangs.

"I think the pink will fade out of that dress sooner than the green mark will," observed Mrs. S., looking down from her perch, and changing the subject, for she and her gossip differed on many points, and Mrs. Smith was a discreet lady.

"Never mind; I'm tired of dolls, and I guess I shall put them all away and attend to my farm; I like it rather better than playing house," said Mrs. G., unconsciously expressing the desire of many older ladies, who cannot dispose of their families so easily however.

"But you mustn't leave them; they will die without their mother," cried tender Mrs. Smith.

"Let 'em die then; I'm tired of fussing over babies, and I'm going to play with the boys; they need me to see to 'em," returned the strong-minded lady.

Daisy knew nothing about woman's rights; she quietly took all she wanted, and no one denied her claim, because she did not undertake what she could not carry out, but unconsciously used the all-powerful right of her own influence to win from others any privilege for which she had proved her fitness. Nan attempted all sorts of things, undaunted by direful failures, and clamored fiercely to be allowed to do everything that the boys did. They laughed at her, hustled her out of the way, and protested against her meddling with their affairs. But she would not be quenched and she would be heard, for her will was strong, and she had the spirit of a rampant reformer. Mrs. Bhaer sympathized with her, but tried to curb her frantic desire for entire liberty, showing her that she must wait a little, learn self-control, and be ready to use her freedom before she asked for it. Nan had meek moments when she agreed to this, and the influences at work upon her were gradually taking effect. She no longer declared that she would be engine-driver or a blacksmith, but turned her mind to farming, and found in it a vent for the energy bottled up in her active little body. It did not quite satisfy her, however; for her sage and sweet marjoram were dumb things, and could not thank her for her care. She wanted something human to love, work for, and protect, and was never happier than when the little boys brought their cut fingers, bumped heads, or bruised joints for her to "mend up." Seeing this, Mrs. Jo proposed that she should learn how to do it nicely, and Nursey had an apt pupil in bandaging, plastering, and fomenting. The boy's began to call her "Dr. Giddy-gaddy," and she liked it so well that Mrs. Jo one day said to the Professor—

"Fritz, I see what we can do for that child. She wants something to live for even now, and will be one of the sharp, strong, discontented women if she does not have it. Don't let us snub her restless little nature, but do our best to give her the work she likes, and by and by persuade her father to let her study medicine. She will make a capital doctor, for she has courage, strong nerves, a tender heart, and an intense love and pity for the weak and suffering."

Mr. Bhaer smiled at first, but agreed to try, and gave Nan an herb-garden, teaching her the various healing properties of the plants she tended, and letting her try their virtues on the children in the little illnesses they had from time to time. She learned fast, remembered well, and showed a sense and interest most encouraging to her Professor, who did not shut his door in her face because she was a little woman.

She was thinking of this, as she sat in the willow that day, and when Daisy said in her gentle way—

"I love to keep house, and mean to have a nice one for Demi when we grow up and live together."

Nan replied with decision—

"Well, I haven't got any brother, and I don't want any house to fuss over. I shall have an office, with lots of bottles and drawers and pestle things in it, and I shall drive round in a horse and chaise and cure sick people. That will be such fun."

"Ugh! How can you bear the bad-smelling stuff and the nasty little powders and castor-oil and senna and hive syrup?" cried Daisy, with a shudder.

"I shan't have to take any, so I don't care. Besides, they make people well, and I like to cure folks. Didn't my sage-tea make Mother Bhaer's headache go away, and my hops stop Ned's toothache in five hours? So now!"

"Shall you put leeches on people, and cut off legs and pull out teeth?" asked Daisy, quaking at the thought.

"Yes, I shall do everything; I don't care if the people are all smashed up, I shall mend them. My grandpa was a doctor and I saw him sew a great cut in a man's cheek, and I held the sponge, and wasn't frightened a bit, and Grandpa said I was a brave girl."

"How could you? I'm sorry for sick people, and I like to nurse them, but it makes my legs shake so I have to run away. I'm not a brave girl," sighed Daisy.

"Well, you can be my nurse, and cuddle my patients when I have given them the physic and cut off their legs," said Nan, whose practice was evidently to be of the heroic kind.

"Ship ahoy! Where are you, Nan?" called a voice from below.

"Here we are."

"Ay, ay!" said the voice, and Emil appeared holding one hand in the other, with his face puckered up as if in pain.

"Oh, what's the matter?" cried Daisy, anxiously.

"A confounded splinter in my thumb. Can't get it out. Take a pick at it, will you, Nanny?"

"It's in very deep, and I haven't any needle," said Nan, examining a tarry thumb with interest.

"Take a pin," said Emil, in a hurry.

"No, it's too big and hasn't got a sharp point."

Here Daisy, who had dived into her pocket, presented a neat little housewife with four needles in it.

"You are the Posy who always has what we want," said Emil; and Nan resolved to have a needle-book in her own pocket henceforth, for just such cases as this were always occurring in her practice.

Daisy covered her eyes, but Nan probed and picked with a steady hand, while Emil gave directions not down in any medical work or record.

"Starboard now! Steady, boys, steady! Try another tack. Heave ho! There she is!"

"Suck it," ordered the Doctor, surveying the splinter with an experienced eye.

"Too dirty," responded the patient, shaking his bleeding hand.

"Wait; I'll tie it up if you have got a handkerchief."

"Haven't; take one of those rags down there."

"Gracious! No, indeed; they are doll's clothes," cried Daisy, indignantly.

"Take one of mine; I'd like to have you," said Nan; and swinging himself down, Emil caught up the first "rag" he saw. It happened to be the frilled skirt; but Nan tore it up without a murmur; and when the royal petticoat was turned into a neat little bandage she dismissed her patient with the command—

"Keep it wet, and let it alone; then it will heal right up, and not be sore."

"What do you charge?" asked the Commodore, laughing.

"Nothing; I keep a 'spensary; that is a place where poor people are doctored free gratis for nothing," explained Nan, with an air.

"Thank you, Doctor Giddy-gaddy. I'll always call you in when I come to grief;" and Emil departed, but looked back to say—for one good turn deserved another—"Your duds are blowing away, Doctor."

Forgiving the disrespectful word, "duds," the ladies hastily descended, and, gathering up their wash, retired to the house to fire up the little stove, and go to ironing.

A passing breath of air shook the old willow, as if it laughed softly at the childish chatter which went on in the nest, and it had hardly composed itself when another pair of birds alighted for a confidential twitter.

"Now, I'll tell you the secret," began Tommy, who was "swellin' wisibly" with the importance of his news.

"Tell away," answered Nat, wishing he had brought his fiddle, it was so shady and quiet here.

"Well, we fellows were talking over the late interesting case of circumstantial evidence," said Tommy, quoting at random from a speech Franz had made at the club, "and I proposed giving Dan something to make up for our suspecting him, to show our respect, and so on, you know—something handsome and useful, that he could keep always, and be proud of. What do you think we chose?"

"A butterfly-net; he wants one ever so much," said Nat, looking a little disappointed, for he meant to get it himself.

"No, sir; it's to be a microscope, a real swell one, that we see what-do-you-call-ems in water with, and stars, and ant-eggs, and all sorts of games, you know. Won't it be a jolly good present?" said Tommy, rather confusing microscopes and telescopes in his remarks.

"Tip-top! I'm so glad! Won't it cost a heap, though?" cried Nat, feeling that his friend was beginning to be appreciated.

"Of course it will; but we are all going to give something. I headed the paper with my five dollars; for if it is done at all, it must be done handsome."

"What! All of it? I never did see such a generous chap as you are;" and Nat beamed upon him with sincere admiration.

"Well, you see, I've been so bothered with my property, that I'm tired of it, and don't mean to save up any more, but give it away as I go along, and then nobody will envy me, or want to steal it, and I shan't be suspecting folks, and worrying about my old cash," replied Tommy, on whom the cares and anxieties of a millionaire weighed heavily.

"Will Mr. Bhaer let you do it?"

"He thought it was a first-rate plan, and said that some of the best men he knew preferred to do good with their money, instead of laying it up to be squabbled over when they died."

"Your father is rich; does he do that way?"

"I'm not sure; he gives me all I want; I know that much. I'm going to talk to him about it when I go home. Anyhow, I shall set him a good example;" and Tommy was so serious, that Nat did not dare to laugh, but said, respectfully,—

"You will be able to do ever so much with your money, won't you?"

"So Mr. Bhaer said, and he promised to advise me about useful ways of spending it. I'm going to begin with Dan; and next time I get a dollar or so, I shall do something for Dick, he's such a good little chap, and only has a cent a week for pocket-money. He can't earn much, you know; so I'm going to kind of see to him;" and good-hearted Tommy quite longed to begin.

"I think that's a beautiful plan, and I'm not going to try to buy a fiddle anymore; I'm going to get Dan his net all myself, and if there is any money left, I'll do something to please poor Billy. He's fond of me, and though he isn't poor, he'd like some little thing from me, because I can make out what he wants better than the rest of you." And Nat fell to wondering how much happiness could be got out of his precious three dollars.

"So I would. Now come and ask Mr. Bhaer if you can't go in town with me on Monday afternoon, so you can get the net, while I get the microscope. Franz and Emil are going to, and we'll have a jolly time larking round among the shops."

The lads walked away arm-in-arm, discussing the new plans with droll importance, yet beginning already to feel the sweet satisfaction which comes to those who try, no matter how humbly, to be earthly providences to the poor and helpless, and gild their mite with the gold of charity before it is laid up where thieves cannot break through and steal.

"Come up and rest while we sort the leaves; it's so cool and pleasant here," said Demi, as he and Dan came sauntering home from a long walk in the woods.

"All right!" answered Dan, who was a boy of few words, and up they went.

"What makes the birch leaves shake so much more than the others?" asked inquiring Demi, who was always sure of an answer from Dan.

"They are hung differently. Don't you see the stem where it joins the leaf is sort of pinched one way, and where it joins the twig, it is pinched another. That makes it waggle with the least bit of wind, but the elm leaves hang straight, and keep stiller."

"How curious! Will this do so?" and Demi held up a sprig of acacia, which he had broken from a little tree on the lawn, because it was so pretty.

"No; that belongs to the sort that shuts up when you touch it. Draw your finger down the middle of the stem, and see if the leaves don't curl up," said Dan, who was examining a bit of mica.

Demi tried it, and presently the little leaves did fold together, till the spray showed a single instead of a double line of leaves.

"I like that; tell me about the others. What do these do?" asked Demi, taking up a new branch.

"Feed silk-worms; they live on mulberry leaves, till they begin to spin themselves up. I was in a silk-factory once, and there were rooms full of shelves all covered with leaves, and worms eating them so fast that it made a rustle. Sometimes they eat so much they die. Tell that to Stuffy," and Dan laughed, as he took up another bit of rock with a lichen on it.

"I know one thing about this mullein leaf: the fairies use them for blankets," said Demi, who had not quite given up his faith in the existence of the little folk in green.

"If I had a microscope, I'd show you something prettier than fairies," said Dan, wondering if he should ever own that coveted treasure. "I knew an old woman who used mullein leaves for a night-cap because she had face-ache. She sewed them together, and wore it all the time."

"How funny! Was she your grandmother?"

"Never had any. She was a queer old woman, and lived alone in a little tumble-down house with nineteen cats. Folks called her a witch, but she wasn't, though she looked like an old rag-bag. She was real kind to me when I lived in that place, and used to let me get warm at her fire when the folks at the poorhouse were hard on me."

"Did you live in a poorhouse?"

"A little while. Never mind that—I didn't mean to speak of it;" and Dan stopped short in his unusual fit of communicativeness.

"Tell about the cats, please," said Demi, feeling that he had asked an unpleasant question, and sorry for it.

"Nothing to tell; only she had a lot of 'em, and kept 'em in a barrel nights; and I used to go and tip over the barrel sometimes, and let 'em out all over the house, and then she'd scold, and chase 'em and put 'em in again, spitting and yowling like fury."

"Was she good to them?" asked Demi, with a hearty child's laugh, pleasant to hear.

"Guess she was. Poor old soul! She took in all the lost and sick cats in the town; and when anybody wanted one they went to Marm Webber, and she let 'em pick any kind and color they wanted, and only asked ninepence,—she was so glad to have her pussies get a good home."

"I should like to see Marm Webber. Could I, if I went to that place?"

"She's dead. All my folks are," said Dan, briefly.

"I'm sorry;" and Demi sat silent a minute, wondering what subject would be safe to try next. He felt delicate about speaking of the departed lady, but was very curious about the cats, and could not resist asking softly—

"Did she cure the sick ones?"

"Sometimes. One had a broken leg, and she tied it up to a stick, and it got well; and another had fits, and she doctored it with *yarbs* till it was cured. But some of 'em died, and she buried 'em; and when they couldn't get well, she killed 'em easy."

"How?" asked Demi, feeling that there was a peculiar charm about this old woman, and some sort of joke about the cats, because Dan was smiling to himself.

"A kind lady, who was fond of cats, told her how, and gave her some stuff, and sent all her own pussies to be killed that way. Marm used to put a sponge, wet with ether, in the bottom of an old boot, then poke puss in head downwards. The ether put her to sleep in a jiffy, and she was drowned in warm water before she woke up."

"I hope the cats didn't feel it. I shall tell Daisy about that. You have known a great many interesting things, haven't you?" asked Demi, and fell to meditating on the vast experience of a boy who had run away more than once, and taken care of himself in a big city.

"Wish I hadn't sometimes."

"Why? Don't remembering them feel good?"

"No."

"It's very singular how hard it is to manage your mind," said Demi, clasping his hands round his knees, and looking up at the sky as if for information upon his favorite topic.

"Devilish hard—no, I don't mean that;" and Dan bit his lips, for the forbidden word slipped out in spite of him, and he wanted to be more careful with Demi than with any of the other boys.

"I'll play I didn't hear it," said Demi; "and you won't do it again, I'm sure."

"Not if I can help it. That's one of the things I don't want to remember. I keep pegging away, but it don't seem to do much good;" and Dan looked discouraged.

"Yes, it does. You don't say half so many bad words as you used to; and Aunt Jo is pleased, because she said it was a hard habit to break up."

"Did she?" and Dan cheered up a bit.

"You must put swearing away in your fault-drawer, and lock it up; that's the way I do with my badness."

"What do you mean?" asked Dan, looking as if he found Demi almost as amusing as a new sort of cock-chafer or beetle.

"Well, it's one of my private plays, and I'll tell you, but I think you'll laugh at it," began Demi, glad to hold forth on this congenial subject. "I play that my mind is a round room, and my soul is a little sort of creature with wings that lives in it. The walls are full of shelves and drawers, and in them I keep my thoughts, and my goodness and badness, and all sorts of things. The goods I keep where I can see them, and the bads I lock up tight, but they get out, and I have to keep putting them in and squeezing them down, they are so strong. The thoughts I play with when I am alone or in bed, and I make up and do what I like with them. Every Sunday I put my room in order, and talk with the little spirit that lives there, and tell him what to do. He is very bad sometimes, and won't mind me, and I have to scold him, and take him to Grandpa. He always makes him behave, and be sorry for his faults, because Grandpa likes this play, and gives me nice things to put in the drawers, and tells me how to shut up the naughties. Hadn't you better try that way? It's a very good one;" and Demi looked so earnest and full of faith, that Dan did not laugh at his quaint fancy, but said, soberly,—

"I don't think there is a lock strong enough to keep my badness shut up. Anyway my room is in such a clutter I don't know how to clear it up."

"You keep your drawers in the cabinet all spandy nice; why can't you do the others?"

"I ain't used to it. Will you show me how?" and Dan looked as if inclined to try Demi's childish way of keeping a soul in order.

"I'd love to, but I don't know how, except to talk as Grandpa does. I can't do it good like him, but I'll try."

"Don't tell anyone; only now and then we'll come here and talk things over, and I'll pay you for it by telling all I know about my sort of things. Will that do?" and Dan held out his big, rough hand.

Demi gave his smooth, little hand readily, and the league was made; for in the happy, peaceful world where the younger boy lived, lions and lambs played together, and little children innocently taught their elders.

"Hush!" said Dan, pointing toward the house, as Demi was about to indulge in another discourse on the best way of getting badness down, and keeping it down; and peeping from their perch, they saw Mrs. Jo strolling slowly along, reading as she went, while Teddy trotted behind her, dragging a little cart upside down.

"Wait till they see us," whispered Demi, and both sat still as the pair came nearer, Mrs. Jo so absorbed in her book that she would have walked into the brook if Teddy had not stopped her by saying—

"Marmar, I wanter fis."

Mrs. Jo put down the charming book which she had been trying to read for a week, and looked about her for a fishing-pole, being used to making toys out of nothing. Before she had broken one from the hedge, a slender willow bough fell at her feet; and, looking up, she saw the boys laughing in the nest.

"Up! up!" cried Teddy, stretching his arms and flapping his skirts as if about to fly.

"I'll come down and you come up. I must go to Daisy now"; and Demi departed to rehearse the tale of the nineteen cats, with the exciting boot-and-barrel episodes.

Teddy was speedily whisked up; and then Dan said, laughing, "Come, too; there's plenty of room. I'll lend you a hand."

Mrs. Jo glanced over her shoulder, but no one was in sight; and, rather liking the joke of the thing, she laughed back, saying, "Well, if you won't mention it, I think I will;" and with two nimble steps was in the willow.

"I haven't climbed a tree since I was married. I used to be very fond of it when I was a girl," she said, looking well-pleased with her shady perch.

"Now, you read if you want to, and I'll take care of Teddy," proposed Dan, beginning to make a fishing-rod for impatient Baby.

"I don't think I care about it now. What were you and Demi at up here?" asked Mrs. Jo, thinking, from the sober look in Dan's face, that he had something on his mind.

"Oh! We were talking. I'd been telling him about leaves and things, and he was telling me some of his queer plays. Now, then, Major, fish away;" and Dan finished off his work by putting a big blue fly on the bent pin which hung at the end of the cord he had tied to the willow-rod.

Teddy leaned down from the tree, and was soon wrapt up in watching for the fish which he felt sure would come. Dan held him by his little petticoats, lest he should take a "header" into the brook, and Mrs. Jo soon won him to talk by doing so herself.

"I am so glad you told Demi about 'leaves and things;' it is just what he needs; and I wish you would teach him, and take him to walk with you."

"I'd like to, he is so bright; but"—

"But what?"

"I didn't think you'd trust me."

"Why not?"

"Well, Demi is so kind of precious, and so good, and I'm such a bad lot, I thought you'd keep him away from me."

"But you are *not* a 'bad lot,' as you say; and I do trust you, Dan, entirely, because you honestly try to improve, and do better and better every week."

"Really?" and Dan looked up at her with the cloud of despondency lifting from his face.

"Yes; don't you feel it?"

"I hoped so, but I didn't know."

"I have been waiting and watching quietly, for I thought I'd give you a good trial first; and if you stood it, I would give you the best reward I had. You *have* stood it well; and now I'm going to trust not only Demi, but my own boy, to you, because you can teach them some things better than any of us."

"Can I?" and Dan looked amazed at the idea.

"Demi has lived among older people so much that he needs just what you have—knowledge of common things, strength, and courage. He thinks you are the bravest boy he ever saw, and admires your strong way of doing things. Then you know a great deal about natural objects, and can tell him more wonderful tales of birds, and bees, and leaves, and animals, than his story-books give him; and, being true, these stories will teach and do him good. Don't you see now how much you can help him, and why I like to have him with you?"

"But I swear sometimes, and might tell him something wrong. I wouldn't mean to, but it might slip out, just as 'devil' did a few minutes ago," said Dan, anxious to do his duty, and let her know his shortcomings.

"I know you try not to say or do any thing to harm the little fellow, and here is where I think Demi will help *you*, because he is so innocent and wise in his small way, and has what I am trying to give you, dear— good principles. It is never too early to try and plant them in a child, and never too late to cultivate them in the most neglected person. You are only boys yet; you can teach one another. Demi will unconsciously strengthen your moral sense, you will strengthen his common sense, and I shall feel as if I had helped you both."

Words could not express how pleased and touched Dan was by this confidence and praise. No one had ever trusted him before, no one had cared to find out and foster the good in him, and no one had suspected how much there was hidden away in the breast of the neglected boy, going fast to ruin, yet quick to feel and value sympathy and help. No honor that he might earn hereafter would ever be half so precious as the right to teach his few virtues and his small store of learning to the child whom he most respected; and no more powerful restraint could have been imposed upon him than the innocent companion confided to his care. He found courage now to tell Mrs. Jo of the plan already made with Demi, and she was glad that the first step had been so naturally taken. Everything seemed working well for Dan, and she rejoiced over him, because it had seemed a hard task, yet, working on with a firm belief in the possibility of reformation in far older and worse subjects than he, there had come this quick and hopeful change to encourage her. He felt that he had friends now and a place in the world, something to live and work for, and, though he said little, all that was best and bravest in a character made old by a hard experience responded to the love and faith bestowed on him, and Dan's salvation was assured.

Their quiet talk was interrupted by a shout of delight from Teddy, who, to the surprise of everyone, did actually catch a trout where no trout had been seen for years. He was so enchanted with his splendid success that he insisted on showing his prize to the family before Asia cooked it for supper; so the three descended and went happily away together, all satisfied with the work of that half hour.

Ned was the next visitor to the tree, but he only made a short stay, sitting there at his ease while Dick and Dolly caught a pailful of grasshoppers and crickets for him. He wanted to play a joke on Tommy, and intended to tuck up a few dozen of the lively creatures in his bed, so that when Bangs got in he would speedily tumble out again, and pass a portion of the night in chasing "hopper-grasses" round the room. The hunt was soon over, and having paid the hunters with a few peppermints apiece Ned retired to make Tommy's bed.

For an hour the old willow sighed and sung to itself, talked with the brook, and watched the lengthening shadows as the sun went down. The first rosy color was touching its graceful branches when a boy came stealing up the avenue, across the lawn, and, spying Billy by the brookside, went to him, saying, in a mysterious tone,—

"Go and tell Mr. Bhaer I want to see him down here, please. Don't let anyone hear."

Billy nodded and ran off, while the boy swung himself up into the tree, and sat there looking anxious, yet evidently feeling the charm of the place and hour. In five minutes Mr. Bhaer appeared, and, stepping up on the fence, leaned into the nest, saying, kindly,—

"I am glad to see you, Jack; but why not come in and meet us all at once?"

"I wanted to see you first, please, sir. Uncle made me come back. I know I don't deserve anything, but I hope the fellows won't be hard upon me."

Poor Jack did not get on very well, but it was evident that he was sorry and ashamed, and wanted to be received as easily as possible; for his

Uncle had thrashed him well and scolded him soundly for following the example he himself set. Jack had begged not to be sent back, but the school was cheap, and Mr. Ford insisted, so the boy returned as quietly as possible, and took refuge behind Mr. Bhaer.

"I hope not, but I can't answer for them, though I will see that they are not unjust. I think, as Dan and Nat have suffered so much, being innocent, you should suffer something, being guilty. Don't you?" asked Mr. Bhaer, pitying Jack, yet feeling that he deserved punishment for a fault which had so little excuse.

"I suppose so, but I sent Tommy's money back, and I said I was sorry, isn't that enough?" said Jack, rather sullenly; for the boy who could do so mean a thing was not brave enough to bear the consequences well.

"No; I think you should ask pardon of all three boys, openly and honestly. You cannot expect them to respect and trust you for a time, but you *can* live down this disgrace if you try, and I will help you. Stealing and lying are detestable sins, and I hope this will be a lesson to you. I am glad you are ashamed, it is a good sign; bear it patiently, and do your best to earn a better reputation."

"I'll have an auction, and sell off all my goods dirt cheap," said Jack, showing his repentance in the most characteristic way.

"I think it would be better to *give* them away, and begin on a new foundation. Take 'Honesty is the best policy' for your motto, and live up to it in act, and word, and thought, and though you don't make a cent of money this summer, you will be a rich boy in the autumn," said Mr. Bhaer, earnestly.

It was hard, but Jack consented, for he really felt that cheating didn't pay, and wanted to win back the friendship of the boys. His heart clung to his possessions, and he groaned inwardly at the thought of actually giving away certain precious things. Asking pardon publicly was easy compared to this; but then be began to discover that certain other things, invisible, but most valuable, were better property than knives, fish-hooks, or even money itself. So he decided to buy up a little integrity, even at a high price, and secure the respect of his playmates, though it was not a salable article.

"Well, I'll do it," he said, with a sudden air of resolution, which pleased Mr. Bhaer.

"Good! And I'll stand by you. Now come and begin at once."

And Father Bhaer led the bankrupt boy back into the little world, which received him coldly at first, but slowly warmed to him, when he showed that he had profited by the lesson, and was sincerely anxious to go into a better business with a new stock-in-trade.

# CHAPTER XVI

## TAMING THE COLT

"WHAT in the world is that boy doing?" said Mrs. Jo to herself, as she watched Dan running round the half-mile triangle as if for a wager. He was all alone, and seemed possessed by some strange desire to run himself into a fever, or break his neck; for, after several rounds, he tried leaping walls, and turning somersaults up the avenue, and finally dropped down on the grass before the door as if exhausted.

"Are you training for a race, Dan?" asked Mrs. Jo, from the window where she sat.

He looked up quickly, and stopped panting to answer, with a laugh,—
"No; I'm only working off my steam."

"Can't you find a cooler way of doing it? You will be ill if you tear about so in such warm weather," said Mrs. Jo, laughing also, as she threw him out a great palm-leaf fan.

"Can't help it. I *must* run somewhere," answered Dan, with such an odd expression in his restless eyes, that Mrs. Jo was troubled, and asked, quickly,—

"Is Plumfield getting too narrow for you?"

"I wouldn't mind if it was a little bigger. I like it though; only the fact is the devil gets into me some times, and then I do want to bolt."

The words seemed to come against his will, for he looked sorry the minute they were spoken, and seemed to think he deserved a reproof for his ingratitude. But Mrs. Jo understood the feeling, and though sorry to see it she could not blame the boy for confessing it. She looked at him anxiously, seeing how tall and strong he had grown, how full of energy his face was, with its eager eyes and resolute mouth; and re-membering the utter freedom he had known for years before, she felt how even the gentle restraint of this home would weigh upon him at times when the old lawless spirit stirred in him. "Yes," she said to herself, "my wild hawk needs a larger cage; and yet, if I let him go, I am afraid he will be lost. I must try and find some lure strong enough to keep him safe."

"I know all about it," she added, aloud. "It is not 'the devil,' as you call it, but the very natural desire of all young people for liberty. I used to feel just so, and once, I really did think for a minute that I would bolt."

"Why didn't you?" said Dan, coming to lean on the low window-ledge, with an evident desire to continue the subject.

"I knew it was foolish, and love for my mother kept me at home."

"I haven't got any mother," began Dan.

"I thought you had *now*," said Mrs. Jo, gently stroking the rough hair off his hot forehead.

"You are no end good to me, and I can't ever thank you enough, but it isn't just the same, is it?" and Dan looked up at her with a wistful, hungry look that went to her heart.

"No, dear, it is not the same, and never can be. I think an own mother would have been a great deal to you. But as that cannot be, you must try to let me fill her place. I fear I have not done all I ought, or you would not want to leave me," she added, sorrowfully.

"Yes, you have!" cried Dan, eagerly. "I don't want to go, and I won't go, if I can help it; but every now and then I feel as if I must burst out somehow. I want to run straight ahead somewhere, to smash something, or pitch into somebody. Don't know why, but I do, and that's all about it."

Dan laughed as he spoke, but he meant what he said, for he knit his black brows, and brought down his fist on the ledge with such force, that Mrs. Jo's thimble flew off into the grass. He brought it back, and as she took it she held the big, brown hand a minute, saying, with a look that showed the words cost her something—

"Well, Dan, run if you must, but don't run far; and come back to me soon, for I want you very much."

He was rather taken aback by this unexpected permission to play truant, and somehow it seemed to lessen his desire to go. He did not understand why, but Mrs. Jo did, and, knowing the natural perversity of the human mind, counted on it to help her now. She felt instinctively that the more the boy was restrained the more he would fret against it; but leave him free, and the mere sense of liberty would content him, joined to the knowledge that his presence was dear to those whom he loved best. It was a little experiment, but it succeeded, for Dan stood silent a moment, unconsciously picking the fan to pieces and turning the matter over in his mind. He felt that she appealed to his heart and his honor, and owned that he understood it by saying presently, with a mixture of regret and resolution in his face,—

"I won't go yet awhile, and I'll give you warning before I bolt. That's fair, isn't it?"

"Yes, we will let it stand so. Now, I want to see if I can't find some way for you to work off your steam better than running about the place like a mad dog, spoiling my fans, or fighting with the boys. What can we invent?" and while Dan tried to repair the mischief he had done, Mrs. Jo racked her brain for some new device to keep her truant safe until he had learned to love his lessons better.

"How would you like to be my express-man?" she said, as a sudden thought popped into her head.

"Go into town, and do the errands?" asked Dan, looking interested at once.

"Yes; Franz is tired of it, Silas cannot be spared just now, and Mr. Bhaer has no time. Old Andy is a safe horse, you are a good driver, and know your way about the city as well as a postman. Suppose you try it, and see if it won't do most as well to drive away two or three times a week as to run away once a month."

"I'd like it ever so much, only I must go alone and do it all myself. I don't want any of the other fellows bothering round," said Dan, taking to the new idea so kindly that he began to put on business airs already.

"If Mr. Bhaer does not object you shall have it all your own way. I suppose Emil will growl, but he cannot be trusted with horses, and you can. By the way, tomorrow is market-day, and I must make out my list. You had better see that the wagon is in order, and tell Silas to have the fruit and vegetables ready for mother. You will have to be up early and get back in time for school, can you do that?"

"I'm always an early bird, so I don't mind," and Dan slung on his jacket with despatch.

"The early bird got the worm this time, I'm sure," said Mrs. Jo, merrily.

"And a jolly good worm it is," answered Dan, as he went laughing away to put a new lash to the whip, wash the wagon, and order Silas about with all the importance of a young express-man.

"Before he is tired of this I will find something else and have it ready when the next restless fit comes on," said Mrs. Jo to herself, as she wrote her list with a deep sense of gratitude that all her boys were not Dans.

Mr. Bhaer did not entirely approve of the new plan, but agreed to give it a trial, which put Dan on his mettle, and caused him to give up certain wild plans of his own, in which the new lash and the long hill were to have borne a part. He was up and away very early the next morning, heroically resisting the temptation to race with the milkmen going into town. Once there, he did his errands carefully, and came jogging home again in time for school, to Mr. Bhaer's surprise and Mrs. Jo's great satisfaction. The Commodore did growl at Dan's promotion, but was pacified by a superior padlock to his new boat-house, and the thought that seamen were meant for higher honors than driving market-wagons and doing family errands. So Dan filled his new office well and contentedly for weeks, and said no more about bolting. But one day Mr. Bhaer found him pummelling Jack, who was roaring for mercy under his knee.

"Why, Dan, I thought you had given up fighting," he said, as he went to the rescue.

"We ain't fighting, we are only wrestling," answered Dan, leaving off reluctantly.

"It looks very much like it, and feels like it, hey, Jack?" said Mr. Bhaer, as the defeated gentleman got upon his legs with difficulty.

"Catch me wrestling with him again. He's most knocked my head off," snarled Jack, holding on to that portion of his frame as if it really was loose upon his shoulders.

"The fact is, we began in fun, but when I got him down I couldn't help pounding him. Sorry I hurt you, old fellow," explained Dan, looking rather ashamed of himself.

"I understand. The longing to pitch into somebody was so strong you couldn't resist. You are a sort of Berserker, Dan, and something to tussle with is as necessary to you as music is to Nat," said Mr. Bhaer, who knew all about the conversation between the boy and Mrs. Jo.

"Can't help it. So if you don't want to be pounded you'd better keep out of the way," answered Dan, with a warning look in his black eyes that made Jack sheer off in haste.

"If you want something to wrestle with, I will give you a tougher specimen than Jack," said Mr. Bhaer; and, leading the way to the woodyard, he pointed out certain roots of trees that had been grubbed up in the spring, and had been lying there waiting to be split.

"There, when you feel inclined to maltreat the boys, just come and work off your energies here, and I'll thank you for it."

"So I will;" and, seizing the axe that lay near, Dan hauled out a tough root, and went at it so vigorously, that the chips flew far and wide, and Mr. Bhaer fled for his life.

To his great amusement, Dan took him at his word, and was often seen wrestling with the ungainly knots, hat and jacket off, red face, and wrathful eyes; for he got into royal rages over some of his adversaries, and swore at them under his breath till he had conquered them, when he exulted, and marched off to the shed with an armful of gnarled oak-wood in triumph. He blistered his hands, tired his back, and dulled the axe, but it did him good, and he got more comfort out of the ugly roots than anyone dreamed, for with each blow he worked off some of the pent-up power that would otherwise have been expended in some less harmless way.

"When this is gone I really don't know what I *shall* do," said Mrs. Jo to herself, for no inspiration came, and she was at the end of her resources.

But Dan found a new occupation for himself, and enjoyed it some time before anyone discovered the cause of his contentment. A fine young horse of Mr. Laurie's was kept at Plumfield that summer, running loose in a large pasture across the brook. The boys were all interested in the handsome, spirited creature, and for a time were fond of watching him gallop and frisk with his plumey tail flying and his handsome head in the air. But they soon got tired of it, and left Prince Charlie to himself. All but Dan, *he* never tired of looking at the horse, and seldom failed to visit him each day with a lump of sugar, a bit of bread, or an apple to make him welcome. Charlie was grateful, accepted his friendship, and the two loved one another as if they felt some tie between them, inexplicable but strong. In whatever part of the wide field he might be, Charlie always came at full speed when Dan whistled at the bars, and the boy was never happier than when the beautiful, fleet creature put its head on his shoulder, looking up at him with fine eyes full of intelligent affection.

"We understand one another without any palaver, don't we, old fellow?" Dan would say, proud of the horse's confidence, and so jealous of his regard, that he told no one how well the friendship prospered, and never asked anybody but Teddy to accompany him on these daily visits.

Mr. Laurie came now and then to see how Charlie got on, and spoke of having him broken to harness in the autumn.

"He won't need much taming, he is such a gentle, fine-tempered brute. I shall come out and try him with a saddle myself some day," he said, on one of these visits.

"He lets me put a halter on him, but I don't believe he will bear a saddle even if *you* put it on," answered Dan, who never failed to be present when Charlie and his master met.

"I shall coax him to bear it, and not mind a few tumbles at first. He has never been harshly treated, so, though he will be surprised at the new performances, I think he won't be frightened, and his antics will do no harm."

"I wonder what he *would* do," said Dan to himself, as Mr. Laurie went away with the Professor, and Charlie returned to the bars, from which he had retired when the gentlemen came up.

A daring fancy to try the experiment took possession of the boy as he sat on the topmost rail with the glossy back temptingly near him. Never thinking of danger, he obeyed the impulse, and while Charlie unsuspectingly nibbled at the apple he held, Dan quickly and quietly took his seat. He did not keep it long, however, for with an astonished snort, Charlie reared straight up, and deposited Dan on the ground. The fall did not hurt him, for the turf was soft, and he jumped up, saying, with a laugh,—

"I did it any way! Come here, you rascal, and I'll try it again."

But Charlie declined to approach, and Dan left him resolving to succeed in the end; for a struggle like this suited him exactly. Next time he took a halter, and having got it on, he played with the horse for a while, leading him to and fro, and putting him through various antics till he was a little tired; then Dan sat on the wall and gave him bread, but watched his chance, and getting a good grip of the halter, slipped on to his back. Charlie tried the old trick, but Dan held on, having had practice with Toby, who occasionally had an obstinate fit, and tried to shake off his rider. Charlie was both amazed and indignant; and after prancing for a minute, set off at a gallop, and away went Dan heels over head. If he had not belonged to the class of boys who go through all sorts of dangers unscathed, he would have broken his neck; as it was, he got a heavy fall, and lay still collecting his wits, while Charlie tore round the field tossing his head with every sign of satisfaction at the discomfiture of his rider. Presently it seemed to occur to him that something was wrong with Dan, and, being of a magnanimous nature, he went to see what the matter was. Dan let him sniff about and perplex himself for a few minutes; then he looked up at him, saying, as decidedly as if the horse could understand,—

"You think you have beaten, but you are mistaken, old boy; and I'll ride you yet—see if I don't."

He tried no more that day, but soon after attempted a new method of introducing Charlie to a burden. He strapped a folded blanket on his back, and then let him race, and rear, and roll, and fume as much as he liked. After a few fits of rebellion Charlie submitted, and in a few days permitted Dan to mount him, often stopping short to look round, as if he said, half patiently, half reproachfully, "I don't understand it, but I suppose you mean no harm, so I permit the liberty."

Dan patted and praised him, and took a short turn every day, getting frequent falls, but persisting in spite of them, and longing to try a saddle and bridle, but not daring to confess what he had done. He had his wish, however, for there had been a witness of his pranks who said a good word for him.

"Do you know what that chap has ben doin' lately?" asked Silas of his master, one evening, as he received his orders for the next day.

"Which boy?" said Mr. Bhaer, with an air of resignation, expecting some sad revelation.

"Dan, he's ben a breaking the colt, sir, and I wish I may die if he ain't done it," answered Silas, chuckling.

"How do you know?"

"Wal, I kinder keep an eye on the little fellers, and most gen'lly know what they're up to; so when Dan kep going off to the paster, and coming home black and blue, I mistrusted that *suthing* was goin' on. I didn't say nothin', but I crep up into the barn chamber, and from there I see him goin' through all manner of games with Charlie. Blest if he warn't throwed time and agin, and knocked round like a bag o' meal. But the pluck of the boy did beat all, and he 'peared to like it, and kep on as ef bound to beat."

"But, Silas, you should have stopped it—the boy might have been killed," said Mr. Bhaer, wondering what freak his irrepressibles would take into their heads next.

"S'pose I oughter; but there warn't no real danger, for Charlie ain't no tricks, and is as pretty a tempered horse as ever I see. Fact was, I couldn't bear to spile sport, for ef there's anything I do admire it's grit, and Dan is chock full on't. But now I know he's hankerin' after a saddle, and yet won't take even the old one on the sly; so I just thought I'd up and tell, and may be you'd let him try what he can do. Mr. Laurie won't mind, and Charlie's all the better for 't."

"We shall see;" and off went Mr. Bhaer to inquire into the matter.

Dan owned up at once, and proudly proved that Silas was right by showing off his power over Charlie; for by dint of much coaxing, many carrots, and infinite perseverance, he really had succeeded in riding the colt with a halter and blanket. Mr. Laurie was much amused, and well pleased with Dan's courage and skill, and let him have a hand in all future performances; for he set about Charlie's education at once, saying that he was not going to be outdone by a slip of a boy. Thanks to Dan, Charlie took kindly to the saddle and bridle when he had once reconciled himself to the indignity of the bit; and after Mr. Laurie had trained him a little, Dan was permitted to ride him, to the great envy and admiration of the other boys.

"Isn't he handsome? And don't he mind me like a lamb?" said Dan one day as he dismounted and stood with his arm round Charlie's neck.

"Yes, and isn't he a much more useful and agreeable animal than the wild colt who spent his days racing about the field, jumping fences, and running away now and then?" asked Mrs. Bhaer from the steps where she always appeared when Dan performed with Charlie.

"Of course he is. See he won't run away now, even if I don't hold him, and he comes to me the minute I whistle; I have tamed him well, haven't I?" and Dan looked both proud and pleased, as well he might, for, in spite of their struggles together, Charlie loved him better than his master.

"I am taming a colt too, and I think I shall succeed as well as you if I am as patient and persevering," said Mrs. Jo, smiling so significantly at him, that Dan understood and answered, laughing, yet in earnest,—

"We won't jump over the fence and run away, but stay and let them make a handsome, useful span of us, hey, Charlie?"

"Isn't he handsome?" said Dan.

# CHAPTER XVII

## COMPOSITION DAY

"HURRY up, boys, it's three o'clock, and Uncle Fritz likes us to be punctual, you know," said Franz one Wednesday afternoon as a bell rang, and a stream of literary-looking young gentlemen with books and paper in their hands were seen going toward the museum.

Tommy was in the school-room, bending over his desk, much bedaubed with ink, flushed with the ardor of inspiration, and in a great hurry as usual, for easy-going Bangs never was ready till the very last minute. As Franz passed the door looking up laggards, Tommy gave one last blot and flourish, and departed out of the window waving his paper to dry it as he went. Nan followed, looking very important, with a large roll in her hand, and Demi escorted Daisy, both evidently brimful of some delightful secret.

The museum was all in order, and the sunshine among the hop-vines made pretty shadows on the floor as it peeped through the great window. On one side sat Mr. and Mrs. Bhaer, on the other was a little table on which the compositions were laid as soon as read, and in a large semicircle sat the children on camp-stools, which occasionally shut up and let the sitter down, thus preventing any stiffness in the assembly. As it took too much time to have all read, they took turns, and on this Wednesday the younger pupils were the chief performers, while the elder ones listened with condescension and criticised freely.

"Ladies first; so Nan may begin," said Mr. Bhaer, when the settling of stools and rustling of papers had subsided.

Nan took her place beside the little table, and, with a preliminary giggle, read the following interesting essay on

### "THE SPONGE

"The sponge, my friends, is a most useful and interesting plant. It grows on rocks under the water, and is a kind of sea-weed, I believe. People go and pick it and dry it and wash it, because little fish and insects live in the holes of the sponge; I found shells in my new one, and sand. Some are very fine and soft; babies are washed with them. The sponge has many uses. I will relate some of them, and I hope my friends will remember what I say. One use is to wash the face; I don't like it myself, but I do it because I wish to be clean. Some people *don't*, and they are dirty." Here the eye of the reader rested sternly upon Dick and Dolly, who quailed under it, and instantly resolved to scrub themselves virtuously on all occasions. "Another use is to wake people up; I allude to *boys* par-*tic*-u-lar-ly." Another pause after the long word to enjoy the smothered laugh that went round the room. "Some boys do not get up when called, and Mary Ann squeezes the water out of a wet sponge on their faces, and it makes them so mad they wake up." Here the laugh broke out, and Emil said, as if he had been hit,—

"Seems to me you are wandering from the subject."

"No, I ain't; we are to write about vegetables or animals, and I'm doing both: for boys are animals, aren't they?" cried Nan; and, undaunted by the indignant "No!" shouted at her, she calmly proceeded—

"One more interesting thing is done with sponges, and this is when doctors put ether on it, and hold it to people's noses when they have teeth out. *I* shall do this when I am bigger, and give ether to the sick, so they will go to sleep and not feel me cut off their legs and arms."

"I know somebody who killed cats with it," called out Demi, but was promptly crushed by Dan, who upset his camp-stool and put a hat over his face.

"I will *not* be interruckted," said Nan, frowning upon the unseemly scrimmagers. Order was instantly restored, and the young lady closed her remarks as follows:—

"My composition has three morals, my friends." Somebody groaned, but no notice was taken of the insult. "First, is keep your faces clean—second, get up early—third, when the ether sponge is put over your nose, breathe hard and don't kick, and your teeth will come out easy. I have no more to say." And Miss Nan sat down amid tumultuous applause.

"That is a very remarkable composition; its tone is high, and there is a good deal of humor in it. Very well done, Nan. Now Daisy," and Mr. Bhaer smiled at one young lady as he beckoned to the other.

Daisy colored prettily as she took her place, and said in her modest little voice,—

"I'm afraid you won't like mine; it isn't nice and funny like Nan's. But I couldn't do any better."

"We always like yours, Posy," said Uncle Fritz, and a gentle murmur from the boys seemed to confirm the remark. Thus encouraged, Daisy read her little paper, which was listened to with respectful attention.

"THE CAT

"The cat is a sweet animal. I love them very much. They are clean and pretty, and catch rats and mice, and let you pet them, and are fond of you if you are kind. They are very wise, and can find their way anywhere. Little cats are called kittens, and are dear things. I have two, named Huz and Buz, and their mother is Topaz, because she has yellow eyes. Uncle told me a pretty story about a man named Ma-ho-met. He had a nice cat, and when she was asleep on his sleeve, and he wanted to go away, he cut off the sleeve so as not to wake her up. I think he was a kind man. Some cats catch fish."

"So do I!" cried Teddy, jumping up eager to tell about his trout.

"Hush!" said his mother, setting him down again as quickly as possible, for orderly Daisy hated to be "interruckted" as Nan expressed it.

"I read about one who used to do it very slyly. I tried to make Topaz, but she did not like the water, and scratched me. She does like tea, and when I play in my kitchen she pats the teapot with her paw, till I give her some. She is a fine cat, she eats apple-pudding and molasses. Most cats do not."

"That's a first-rater," called out Nat, and Daisy retired, pleased with the praise of her friend.

"Demi looks so impatient we must have him up at once or he won't hold out," said Uncle Fritz, and Demi skipped up with alacrity.

"Mine is a poem!" he announced in a tone of triumph, and read his first effort in a loud and solemn voice:—

> *"I write about the butterfly,*
> *It is a pretty thing;*
> *And flies about like the birds,*
> *But it does not sing.*
>
> *"First it is a little grub,*
> *And then it is a nice yellow cocoon,*
> *And then the butterfly*
> *Eats its way out soon.*
>
> *"They live on dew and honey,*
> *They do not have any hive,*
> *They do not sting like wasps, and bees, and hornets,*
> *And to be as good as they are we should strive.*
>
> *"I should like to be a beautiful butterfly,*
> *All yellow, and blue, and green, and red;*
> *But I should not like*
> *To have Dan put camphor on my poor little head."*

This unusual burst of genius brought down the house, and Demi was obliged to read it again, a somewhat difficult task, as there was no punctuation whatever, and the little poet's breath gave out before he got to the end of some of the long lines.

"He will be a Shakspeare yet," said Aunt Jo, laughing as if she would die, for this poetic gem reminded her of one of her own, written at the age of ten, and beginning gloomily—

> *"I wish I had a quiet tomb,*
> *Beside a little rill;*
> *Where birds, and bees, and butterflies,*
> *Would sing upon the hill."*

"Come on, Tommy. If there is as much ink inside your paper as there is outside, it will be a long composition," said Mr. Bhaer, when Demi had been induced to tear himself from his poem and sit down.

"It isn't a composition, it's a letter. You see, I forgot all about its being my turn till after school, and then I didn't know what to have, and there wasn't time to read up; so I thought you wouldn't mind my taking a letter that I wrote to my Grandma. It's got something about birds in it, so I thought it would do."

With this long excuse, Tommy plunged into a sea of ink and floundered through, pausing now and then to decipher one of his own flourishes.

"My dear Grandma,—

I hope you are well. Uncle James sent me a pocket rifle. It is a beautiful little instrument of killing, shaped like this—[Here Tommy displayed a remarkable sketch of what looked like an intricate pump, or the inside of a small steam-engine]—44 are the sights; 6 is a false stock that fits in at A; 3 is the trigger, and 2 is the cock. It loads at the breech, and fires with great force and straightness. I am going out shooting squirrels soon. I shot several fine birds for the museum. They had speckled breasts, and Dan liked them very much. He stuffed them tip-top, and they sit on the tree quite natural, only one looks a little tipsy. We had a Frenchman working here the other day, and Asia called his name so funnily that I will tell you about it. His name was Germain: first she called him Jerry, but we laughed at her, and she changed it to Jeremiah; but ridicule was the result, so it became Mr. Germany; but ridicule having been again resumed, it became Garrymon, which it has remained ever since. I do not write often, I am so busy; but I think of you often, and sympathize with you, and sincerely hope you get on as well as can be expected without me.—Your affectionate grandson,

"Thomas Buckminster Bangs."

"*P.S.*—If you come across any postage-stamps, remember me.

"*N.B.*—Love to all, and a great deal to Aunt Almira. Does she make any nice plum-cakes now?

"*P.S.*—Mrs. Bhaer sends her respects.

"*P.S.*—And so would Mr. B. if he knew I was in act to write.

"*N.B.*—Father is going to give me a watch on my birthday. I am glad, as at present I have no means of telling time, and am often late at school.

"*P.S.*—I hope to see you soon. Don't you wish to send for me?

T. B. B."

As each postscript was received with a fresh laugh from the boys, by the time he came to the sixth and last, Tommy was so exhausted that he was glad to sit down and wipe his ruddy face.

"I hope the dear old lady will live through it," said Mr. Bhaer, under cover of the noise.

"We won't take any notice of the broad hint given in that last *P.S.* The letter will be quite as much as she can bear without a visit from Tommy," answered Mrs. Jo, remembering that the old lady usually took to her bed after a visitation from her irrepressible grandson.

"Now, me," said Teddy, who had learned a bit of poetry, and was so eager to say it that he had been bobbing up and down during the reading, and could no longer be restrained.

"I'm afraid he will forget it if he waits; and I have had a deal of trouble in teaching him," said his mother.

Teddy trotted to the rostrum, dropped a curtsey and nodded his head at the same time, as if anxious to suit every one; then, in his baby voice, and putting the emphasis on the wrong words, he said his verse all in one breath:—

> "Little drops *of* water,
>     Little drains of sand,
>     Mate a mighty okum (ocean),
>     *And* a peasant land.
>     Little wrts *of* kindness,
>     Pokin evvy day,
>     Make *a* home a hebbin,
>     And hep us *on* a way."

Clapping his hands at the end, he made another double salutation, and then ran to hide his head in his mother's lap, quite overcome by the success of his "piece," for the applause was tremendous.

Dick and Dolly did not write, but were encouraged to observe the habits of animals and insects, and report what they saw. Dick liked this, and always had a great deal to say; so, when his name was called, he marched up, and, looking at the audience with his bright confiding eyes, told his little story so earnestly that no one smiled at his crooked body, because the "straight soul" shone through it beautifully.

"I've been watching dragonflies, and I read about them in Dan's book, and I'll try and tell you what I remember. There's lots of them flying round on the pond, all blue, with big eyes, and sort of lace wings, very pretty. I caught one, and looked at him, and I think he was the handsomest inseck I ever saw. They catch littler creatures than they are to eat, and have a queer kind of hook thing that folds up when they ain't hunting. It likes the sunshine, and dances round all day. Let me see! What else was there to tell about? Oh, I know! The eggs are laid in the water, and go down to the bottom, and are hatched in the mud. Little ugly things come out of 'em; I can't say the name, but they are brown, and keep having new skins, and getting bigger and bigger. Only think! It takes them two years to be a dragonfly! Now *this* is the curious*est* part of it, so you listen tight, for I don't believe you know it. When it is ready it knows somehow, and the ugly, grubby thing climbs up out of the water on a flag or a bulrush, and bursts open its back."

"Come, I don't believe that," said Tommy, who was not an observing boy, and really thought Dick was "making up."

"It does burst open its back, don't it?" and Dick appealed to Mr. Bhaer, who nodded a very decided affirmative, to the little speaker's great satisfaction.

"Well, out comes the dragonfly, all whole, and he sits in the sun—sort of coming alive, you know; and he gets strong, and then he spreads his pretty wings, and flies away up in the air, and never is a grub any more. That's all I know; but I shall watch and try and see him do it, for I think it's splendid to turn into a beautiful dragonfly, don't you?"

Dick had told his story well, and, when he described the flight of the new-born insect, had waved his hands, and looked up as if he saw, and wanted to follow it. Something in his face suggested to the minds of the elder listeners the thought that some day little Dick would have his wish, and after years of helplessness and pain would climb up into the sun some happy day, and, leaving his poor little body behind him, find a new and lovely shape in a fairer world than this. Mrs. Jo drew him to her side, and said, with a kiss on his thin cheek,—

"That is a sweet little story, dear, and you remembered wonderfully well. I shall write and tell your mother all about it;" and Dick sat on her knee, contentedly smiling at the praise, and resolving to watch well, and catch the dragonfly in the act of leaving its old body for the new, and see how he did it. Dolly had a few remarks to make upon the "Duck," and made them in a sing-song tone, for he had learned it by heart, and thought it a great plague to do it at all.

"Wild ducks are hard to kill; men hide and shoot at them, and have tame ducks to quack and make the wild ones come where the men can fire at them. They have wooden ducks made too, and they sail round, and the wild ones come to see them; they are stupid, I think. Our ducks are very tame. They eat a great deal, and go poking round in the mud and water. They don't take good care of their eggs, but let them spoil, and"—

"Mine don't!" cried Tommy.

"Well, some people's do; Silas said so. Hens take good care of little ducks, only they don't like to have them go in the water, and make a great fuss. But the little ones don't care a bit. I like to eat ducks with stuffing in them, and lots of apple-sauce."

"I have something to say about owls," began Nat, who had carefully prepared a paper upon this subject with some help from Dan.

"Owls have big heads, round eyes, hooked bills, and strong claws. Some are gray, some white, some black and yellowish. Their feathers are very soft, and stick out a great deal. They fly very quietly, and hunt bats, mice, little birds, and such things. They build nests in barns, hollow trees, and some take the nests of other birds. The great horned owl has two eggs bigger than a hen's, and reddish brown. The tawny owl has five eggs, white and smooth; and this is the kind that hoots at night. Another kind sounds like a child crying. They eat mice and bats whole, and the parts that they cannot digest they make into little balls and spit out."

"My gracious! How funny!" Nan was heard to observe.

"They cannot see by day; and if they get out into the light, they go flapping round half blind, and the other birds chase and peck at them as if they were making fun. The horned owl is very big, 'most as big as the eagle. It eats rabbits, rats, snakes, and birds; and lives in rocks and old tumble-down houses. They have a good many cries, and scream like a person being choked, and say, 'Waugh O! Waugh O!' And it scares people at night in the woods. The white owl lives by the sea, and in cold places, and looks something like a hawk. There is a kind of owl that makes holes to live in like moles. It is called the burrowing owl, and is very small. The barn-owl is the commonest kind; and I have watched one sitting in a hole in a tree, looking like a little gray cat, with one eye shut and the other open. He comes out at dusk, and sits round waiting for the bats. I caught one, and here he is."

With that Nat suddenly produced from inside his jacket a little downy bird, who blinked and ruffled up his feathers, looking very plump and sleepy and scared.

"Don't touch him! He is going to show off," said Nat, displaying his new pet with great pride. First he put a cocked hat on the bird's head, and the boys laughed at the funny effect; then he added a pair of paper spectacles, and that gave the owl such a wise look that they shouted with merriment. The performance closed with making the bird angry, and seeing him cling to a handkerchief upside down, pecking and "clucking," as Rob called it. He was allowed to fly after that, and settled himself on the bunch of pine-cones over the door, where he sat staring down at the company with an air of sleepy dignity that amused them very much.

"Have you any thing for us, George?" asked Mr. Bhaer, when the room was still again.

"Well, I read and learned ever so much about moles, but I declare I've forgotten every bit of it, except that they dig holes to live in, that you catch them by pouring water down, and that they can't possibly live without eating very often;" and Stuffy sat down, wishing he had not been too lazy to write out his valuable observations, for a general smile went round when he mentioned the last of the three facts which lingered in his memory.

"Then we are done for today," began Mr. Bhaer, but Tommy called out, in a great hurry,—

"No, we ain't. Don't you know? We must give the thing;" and he winked violently as he made an eye-glass of his fingers.

"Bless my heart, I forgot! Now is your time, Tom;" and Mr. Bhaer dropped into his seat again, while all the boys but Dan looked mightily tickled at something.

Nat, Tommy, and Demi left the room, and speedily returned with a little red morocco box set forth in state on Mrs. Jo's best silver salver. Tommy bore it, and, still escorted by Nat and Demi, marched up to unsuspecting Dan, who stared at them as if he thought they were going to make fun of him. Tommy had prepared an elegant and impressive speech for the occasion, but when the minute came, it all went out of his head, and he just said, straight from his kindly boyish heart,—

"Here, old fellow, we all wanted to give you something to kind of pay for what happened awhile ago, and to show how much we liked you for being such a trump. Please take it, and have a jolly good time with it."

Dan was so surprised he could only get as red as the little box, and mutter "Thanky, boys!" as he fumbled to open it. But when he saw what was inside, his face lighted up, and he seized the long desired treasure, saying, so enthusiastically that every one was satisfied, though his language was any thing but polished,—

"What a stunner! I say, you fellows are regular bricks to give me this; it's just what I wanted. Give us your paw, Tommy."

Many paws were given, and heartily shaken, for the boys were charmed with Dan's pleasure, and crowded round him to shake hands and expatiate on the beauties of their gift. In the midst of this pleasant chatter, Dan's eye went to Mrs. Jo, who stood outside the group enjoying the scene with all her heart.

"No, I had nothing to do with it. The boys got it up all themselves," she said, answering the grateful look that seemed to thank her for that happy moment. Dan smiled, and said, in a tone that only she could understand,—

"It's you all the same;" and making his way through the boys, he held out his hand first to her and then to the good Professor, who was beaming benevolently on his flock.

He thanked them both with the silent, hearty squeeze he gave the kind hands that had held him up and led him into the safe refuge of a happy home. Not a word was spoken, but they felt all he would say, and little Teddy expressed their pleasure for them as he leaned from his father's arm to hug the boy, and say, in his baby way,—

"My dood Danny! Everybody loves him now."

"Come here, show off your spy-glass, Dan, and let us see some of your magnified pollywogs and annymalcumisms as you call 'em," said Jack, who felt so uncomfortable during this scene that he would have slipped away if Emil had not kept him.

"So I will, take a squint at that and see what you think of it," said Dan, glad to show off his precious microscope.

He held it over a beetle that happened to be lying on the table, and Jack bent down to take his squint, but looked up with an amazed face, saying,—

"My eye! What nippers the old thing has got! I see now why it hurts so confoundedly when you grab a dorbug and he grabs back again."

"He winked at me," cried Nan, who had poked her head under Jack's elbow and got the second peep.

Every one took a look, and then Dan showed them the lovely plumage on a moth's wing, the four feathery corners to a hair, the veins on a leaf, hardly visible to the naked eye, but like a thick net through the wonderful little glass; the skin on their own fingers, looking like queer hills and valleys; a cobweb like a bit of coarse sewing silk, and the sting of a bee.

"It's like the fairy spectacles in my story-book, only more curious," said Demi, enchanted with the wonders he saw.

"Dan is a magician now, and he can show you many miracles going on all round you; for he has two things needful—patience and a love of nature. We live in a beautiful and wonderful world, Demi, and the more you know about it the wiser and the better you will be. This little glass will give you a new set of teachers, and you may learn fine lessons from them if you will," said Mr. Bhaer, glad to see how interested the boys were in the matter.

"Could I see anybody's soul with this microscope if I looked hard?" asked Demi, who was much impressed with the power of the bit of glass.

"No, dear; it's not powerful enough for that, and never can be made so. You must wait a long while before your eyes are clear enough to see the most invisible of God's wonders. But looking at the lovely things you can see will help you to understand the lovelier things you can *not* see," answered Uncle Fritz, with his hand on the boy's head.

"Well, Daisy and I both think that if there *are* any angels, their wings look like that butterfly's as we see it through the glass, only more soft and gold."

"Believe it if you like, and keep your own little wings as bright and beautiful, only don't fly away for a long time yet."

"No, I won't," and Demi kept his word.

"Good-by, my boys; I must go now, but I leave you with our new Professor of Natural History"; and Mrs. Jo went away well pleased with that composition-day.

# CHAPTER XVIII

## CROPS

THE gardens did well that summer, and in September the little crops were gathered in with much rejoicing. Jack and Ned joined their farms and raised potatoes, those being a good salable article. They got twelve bushels, counting little ones and all, and sold them to Mr. Bhaer at a fair price, for potatoes went fast in that house. Emil and Franz devoted themselves to corn, and had a jolly little husking in the barn, after which they took their corn to the mill, and came proudly home with meal enough to supply the family with hasty-pudding and Johnny-cake for a long time. They would not take money for their crop; because, as Franz said, "We never can pay Uncle for all he has done for us if we raised corn for the rest of our days."

Nat had beans in such abundance that he despaired of ever shelling them, till Mrs. Jo proposed a new way, which succeeded admirably. The dry pods were spread upon the barn-floor, Nat fiddled, and the boys danced quadrilles on them, till they were thrashed out with much merriment and very little labor.

Tommy's six weeks' beans were a failure; for a dry spell early in the season hurt them, because he gave them no water; and after that he was so sure that they could take care of themselves, he let the poor things struggle with bugs and weeds till they were exhausted, and died a lingering death. So Tommy had to dig his farm over again, and plant peas. But they were late; the birds ate many; the bushes, not being firmly planted, blew down, and when the poor peas came at last, no one cared for them, as their day was over, and spring-lamb had grown into mutton. Tommy consoled himself with a charitable effort; for he transplanted all the thistles he could find, and tended them carefully for Toby, who was fond of the prickly delicacy, and had eaten all he could find on the place. The boys had great fun over Tom's thistle bed; but he insisted that it was better to care for poor Toby than for himself, and declared that he would devote his entire farm next year to thistles, worms, and snails, that Demi's turtles and Nat's pet owl might have the food they loved, as well as the donkey. So like shiftless, kind-hearted, happy-go-lucky Tommy!

Demi had supplied his grandmother with lettuce all summer, and in the autumn sent his grandfather a basket of turnips, each one scrubbed up till it looked like a great white egg. His Grandma was fond of salad, and one of his Grandpa's favorite quotations was—

*"Lucullus, whom frugality could charm,*
*Ate roasted turnips at the Sabine farm."*

Therefore these vegetable offerings to the dear domestic god and goddess were affectionate, appropriate, and classical.

Daisy had nothing but flowers in her little plot, and it bloomed all summer long with a succession of gay or fragrant posies. She was very fond of her garden, and delved away in it at all hours, watching over her roses, and pansies, sweet-peas, and mignonette, as faithfully and tenderly as she did over her dolls or her friends. Little nosegays were sent into town on all occasions, and certain vases about the house were her especial care. She had all sorts of pretty fancies about her flowers, and loved to tell the children the story of the pansy, and show them how the step-mother-leaf sat up in her green chair in purple and gold; how the two own children in gay yellow had each its little seat, while the step children, in dull colors, both sat on one small stool, and the poor little father, in his red nightcap, was kept out of sight in the middle of the flower; that a monk's dark face looked out of the monk's-hood larkspur; that the flowers of the canary-vine were so like dainty birds fluttering their yellow wings, that one almost expected to see them fly away, and the snapdragons that went off like little pistol-shots when you cracked them. Splendid dollies did she make out of scarlet and white poppies, with ruffled robes tied round the waist with grass blade sashes, and astonishing hats of coriopsis on their green heads. Pea-pod boats, with rose-leaf sails, received these flower-people, and floated them about a placid pool in the most charming style; for finding that there were no elves, Daisy made her own, and loved the fanciful little friends who played their parts in her summer-life.

Nan went in for herbs, and had a fine display of useful plants, which she tended with steadily increasing interest and care. Very busy was she in September cutting, drying, and tying up her sweet harvest, and writing down in a little book how the different herbs are to be used. She had tried several experiments, and made several mistakes; so she wished to be particular lest she should give little Huz another fit by administering wormwood instead of catnip.

Dick, Dolly, and Rob each grubbed away on his small farm, and made more stir about it than all the rest put together. Parsnips and carrots were the crops of the two D.'s; and they longed for it to be late enough to pull up the precious vegetables. Dick did privately examine his carrots, and plant them again, feeling that Silas was right in saying it was too soon for them yet.

Rob's crop was four small squashes and one immense pumpkin. It really was a "bouncer," as every one said; and I assure you that two small persons could sit on it side by side. It seemed to have absorbed all the goodness of the little garden, and all the sunshine that shone down on it, and lay there a great round, golden ball, full of rich suggestions of pumpkin-pies for weeks to come. Robby was so proud of his mammoth vegetable that he took every one to see it, and, when frosts began to nip, covered it up each night with an old bedquilt, tucking it round as if the pumpkin was a well-beloved baby. The day it was gathered he would let no one touch it but himself, and nearly broke his back tugging it to the barn in his little wheelbarrow, with Dick and Dolly harnessed in front to give a heave up the path. His mother promised him that the Thanksgiving-pies should be made from it, and hinted vaguely that she had a plan in her head which would cover the prize pumpkin and its owner with glory.

Poor Billy had planted cucumbers, but unfortunately hoed them up and left the pig-weed. This mistake grieved him very much for ten minutes, then he forgot all about it, and sowed a handful of bright buttons which he had collected, evidently thinking in his feeble mind that they were money, and would come up and multiply, so that he might make many quarters, as Tommy did. No one disturbed him, and he did what he liked with his plot, which soon looked as if a series of small earthquakes had stirred it up. When the general harvest-day came, he would have had nothing but stones and weeds to show, if kind old Asia had not hung half a dozen oranges on the dead tree he had stuck up in the middle. Billy was delighted with his crop; and no one spoiled his pleasure in the little miracle which pity wrought for him, by making withered branches bear strange fruit.

Stuffy had various trials with his melons; for, being impatient to taste them, he had a solitary revel before they were ripe, and made himself so ill, that for a day or two it seemed doubtful if he would ever eat any more. But he pulled through it, and served up his first cantelope without tasting a mouthful himself. They were excellent melons, for he had a warm slope for them, and they ripened fast. The last and best were lingering on the vines, and Stuffy had announced that he should sell them to a neighbor. This disappointed the boys, who had hoped to eat the melons themselves, and they expressed their displeasure in a new and striking manner. Going one morning to gaze upon the three fine watermelons which he had kept for the market, Stuffy was horrified to find the word "PIG" cut in white letters on the green rind, staring at him from every one. He was in a great rage, and flew to Mrs. Jo for redress. She listened, condoled with him, and then said—

"If you want to turn the laugh, I'll tell you how, but you must give up the melons."

"Well, I will; for I can't thrash all the boys, but I'd like to give them something to remember, the mean sneaks," growled Stuffy, still in a fume.

Now Mrs. Jo was pretty sure who had done the trick, for she had seen three heads suspiciously near to one another in the sofa-corner the evening before; and when these heads had nodded with chuckles and whispers, this experienced woman knew that mischief was afoot. A moonlight night, a rustling in the old cherry-tree near Emil's window, a cut on Tommy's finger, all helped to confirm her suspicions; and having cooled Stuffy's wrath a little, she bade him bring his maltreated melons to her room, and say not a word to anyone of what had happened. He did so, and the three wags were amazed to find their joke so quietly taken. It spoilt the fun, and the entire disappearance of the melons made them uneasy. So did Stuffy's good-nature, for he looked more placid and plump than ever, and surveyed them with an air of calm pity that perplexed them much.

At dinner-time they discovered why; for then Stuffy's vengeance fell upon them, and the laugh *was* turned against them. When the pudding was eaten, and the fruit was put on, Mary Ann re-appeared in a high state of giggle, bearing a large water-melon; Silas followed with another; and Dan brought up the rear with a third. One was placed before each of the three guilty lads; and they read on the smooth green skin this addition to their own work, "With the compliments of the PIG." Everyone else read it also, and the whole table was in a roar, for the trick had been whispered about; so every one understood the sequel. Emil, Ned, and Tommy did not know where to look, and had not a word to say for themselves; so they wisely joined in the laugh, cut up the melons, and handed them round, saying, what all the rest agreed to, that Stuffy had taken a wise and merry way to return good for evil.

Dan had no garden, for he was away or lame the greater part of the summer; so he had helped Silas wherever he could, chopped wood for Asia, and taken care of the lawn so well, that Mrs. Jo always had smooth paths and nicely shaven turf before her door.

When the others got in their crops, he looked sorry that he had so little to show; but as autumn went on, he bethought him of a woodland harvest which no one would dispute with him, and which was peculiarly his own. Every Saturday he was away alone to forests, fields, and hills, and always came back loaded with spoils; for he seemed to know the meadows where the best flag-root grew, the thicket where the sassafras was spiciest, the haunts where the squirrels went for nuts, the white oak whose bark was most valuable, and the little gold-thread vine that Nursey liked to cure the canker with. All sorts of splendid red and yellow leaves did Dan bring home for Mrs. Jo to dress her parlor with,—graceful-seeded grasses, clematis tassels, downy, soft, yellow wax-work berries, and mosses, red-brimmed, white, or emerald green.

"I need not sigh for the woods now, because Dan brings the woods to me," Mrs. Jo used to say, as she glorified the walls with yellow maple boughs and scarlet woodbine wreaths, or filled her vases with russet ferns, hemlock sprays full of delicate cones, and hardy autumn flowers; for Dan's crop suited her well.

The great garret was full of the children's little stores, and for a time was one of the sights of the house. Daisy's flower seeds in neat little paper bags, all labelled, lay in the drawer of a three-legged table. Nan's herbs hung in bunches against the wall, filling the air with their aromatic breath. Tommy had a basket of thistledown with the tiny seeds attached, for he meant to plant them next year, if they did not all fly away before that time. Emil had bunches of pop-corn hanging there to dry, and Demi laid up acorns and different sorts of grain for the pets. But Dan's crop made the best show, for fully one half of the floor was covered with the nuts he brought. All kinds were there, for he ranged the woods for miles round, climbed the tallest trees, and forced his way into the thickest hedges for his plunder. Walnuts, chestnuts, hazelnuts, and beechnuts lay in separate compartments, getting brown, and dry, and sweet, ready for winter revels.

There was one butternut-tree on the place, and Rob and Teddy called it theirs. It bore well this year, and the great dingy nuts came dropping down to hide among the dead leaves, where the busy squirrels found them better than the lazy Bhaers. Their father had told them (the boys, not the squirrels) they should have the nuts if they would pick them up, but no one was to help. It was easy work, and Teddy liked it, only he soon got tired, and left his little basket half full for another day. But the other day was slow to arrive, and, meantime, the sly squirrels were hard at work scampering up and down the old elm-trees stowing the nuts away till their holes were full, then all about in the crotches of the boughs, to be removed at their leisure. Their funny little ways amused the boys, till one day Silas said—

"Hev you sold them nuts to the squirrels?"

"No," answered Rob, wondering what Silas meant.

"Wal, then, you'd better fly round, or them spry little fellers won't leave you none."

"Oh, we can beat them when we begin. There are such lots of nuts we shall have a plenty."

"There ain't many more to come down, and they have cleared the ground pretty well, see if they hain't."

Robby ran to look, and was alarmed to find how few remained. He called Teddy, and they worked hard all one afternoon, while the squirrels sat on the fence and scolded.

"Now, Ted, we must keep watch, and pick up just as fast as they fall, or we shan't have more than a bushel, and every one will laugh at us if we don't."

"The naughty quillies tarn't have 'em. I'll pick fast and run and put 'em in the barn twick," said Teddy, frowning at little Frisky, who chattered and whisked his tail indignantly.

That night a high wind blew down hundreds of nuts, and when Mrs. Jo came to wake her little sons, she said, briskly,—

"Come, my laddies, the squirrels are hard at it, and you will have to work well today, or they will have every nut on the ground."

"No, they won't," and Robby tumbled up in a great hurry, gobbled his breakfast, and rushed out to save his property.

Teddy went too, and worked like a little beaver, trotting to and fro with full and empty baskets. Another bushel was soon put away in the corn barn, and they were scrambling among the leaves for more nuts when the bell rang for school.

"O father! Let me stay out and pick. Those horrid squirrels will have my nuts if you don't. I'll do my lessons by and by," cried Rob, running into the school-room, flushed and tousled by the fresh cold wind and his eager work.

"If you had been up early and done a little every morning there would be no hurry now. I told you that, Rob, and you never minded. I cannot have the lessons neglected as the work has been. The squirrels will get more than their share this year, and they deserve it, for they have worked best. You may go an hour earlier, but that is all," and Mr. Bhaer led

Rob to his place, where the little man dashed at his books as if bent on making sure of the precious hour promised him.

It was almost maddening to sit still and see the wind shaking down the last nuts, and the lively thieves flying about, pausing now and then to eat one in his face, and flirt their tails, as if they said, saucily, "We'll have them in spite of you, lazy Rob." The only thing that sustained the poor child in this trying moment was the sight of Teddy working away all alone. It was really splendid the pluck and perseverance of the little lad. He picked and picked till his back ached; he trudged to and fro till his small legs were tired; and he defied wind, weariness, and wicked "quillies," till his mother left her work and did the carrying for him, full of admiration for the kind little fellow who tried to help his brother. When Rob was dismissed he found Teddy reposing in the bushel-basket quite used up, but unwilling to quit the field; for he flapped his hat at the thieves with one grubby little hand, while he refreshed himself with the big apple held in the other.

Rob fell to work and the ground was cleared before two o'clock, the nuts safely in the corn-barn loft, and the weary workers exulted in their success. But Frisky and his wife were not to be vanquished so easily; and when Rob went up to look at his nuts a few days later he was amazed to see how many had vanished. None of the boys could have stolen them, because the door had been locked; the doves could not have eaten them, and there were no rats about. There was great lamentation among the young Bhaers till Dick said—

"I saw Frisky on the roof of the corn-barn, maybe he took them."

"I know he did! I'll have a trap, and kill him dead," cried Rob, disgusted with Frisky's grasping nature.

"Perhaps, if you watch, you can find out where he puts them, and I may be able to get them back for you," said Dan, who was much amused by the fight between the boys and squirrels.

So Rob watched and saw Mr. and Mrs. Frisky drop from the drooping elm boughs on to the roof of the corn-barn, dodge in at one of the little doors, much to the disturbance of the doves, and come out with a nut in each mouth. So laden they could not get back the way they came, but ran down the low roof, along the wall, and leaping off at a corner they vanished a minute and re-appeared without their plunder. Rob ran to the place, and in a hollow under the leaves found a heap of the stolen property hidden away to be carried off to the holes by and by.

"Oh, you little villains! I'll cheat *you* now, and not leave one," said Rob. So he cleared the corner and the corn-barn, and put the contested nuts in the garret, making sure that no broken window-pane could anywhere let in the unprincipled squirrels. They seemed to feel that the contest was over, and retired to their hole, but now and then could not resist throwing down nut-shells on Rob's head, and scolding violently as if they could not forgive him nor forget that he had the best of the battle.

Father and Mother Bhaer's crop was of a different sort, and not so easily described; but they were satisfied with it, felt that their summer work had prospered well, and by and by had a harvest that made them very happy.

# CHAPTER XIX

## JOHN BROOKE

"WAKE up, Demi, dear! I want you."

"Why, I've just gone to bed; it can't be morning yet"; and Demi blinked like a little owl as he waked from his first sound sleep.

"It's only ten, but your father is ill, and we must go to him. O my little John! My poor little John!" And Aunt Jo laid her head down on the pillow with a sob that scared sleep from Demi's eyes and filled his heart with fear and wonder; for he dimly felt why Aunt Jo called him "John," and wept over him as if some loss had come that left him poor. He clung to her without a word, and in a minute she was quite steady again, and said with a tender kiss as she saw his troubled face,—

"We are going to say good-by to him, my darling, and there is no time to lose; so dress quickly and come to me in my room. I must go to Daisy."

"Yes, I will"; and when Aunt Jo was gone, little Demi got up quietly, dressed as if in a dream, and leaving Tommy fast asleep went away through the silent house, feeling that something new and sorrowful was going to happen—something that set him apart from the other boys for a time, and made the world seem as dark and still and strange as those familiar rooms did in the night. A carriage sent by Mr. Laurie stood before the door. Daisy was soon ready, and the brother and sister held each other by the hand all the way into town, as they drove swiftly and silently with aunt and uncle through the shadowy roads to say good-by to father.

None of the boys but Franz and Emil knew what had happened, and when they came down next morning, great was their wonderment and discomfort, for the house seemed forlorn without its master and mistress. Breakfast was a dismal meal with no cheery Mrs. Jo behind the teapots; and when school-time came, Father Bhaer's place was empty. They wandered about in a disconsolate kind of way for an hour, waiting for news and hoping it would be all right with Demi's father, for good John Brooke was much beloved by the boys. Ten o'clock came, and no one arrived to relieve their anxiety. They did not feel like playing, yet the time dragged heavily, and they sat about listless and sober. All at once, Franz got up, and said, in his persuasive way,—

"Look here, boys! Let's go into school and do our lessons just as if Uncle was here. It will make the day go faster, and will please him, I know."

"But who will hear us say them?" asked Jack.

"I will; I don't know much more than you do, but I'm the oldest here, and I'll try to fill Uncle's place till he comes, if you don't mind."

Something in the modest, serious way Franz said this impressed the boys, for, though the poor lad's eyes were red with quiet crying for Uncle John in that long sad night, there was a new manliness about him, as if he had already begun to feel the cares and troubles of life, and tried to take them bravely.

"I will, for one," and Emil went to his seat, remembering that obedience to his superior officer is a seaman's first duty.

The others followed; Franz took his uncle's seat, and for an hour order reigned. Lessons were learned and paid, and Franz made a patient, pleasant teacher, wisely omitting such lessons as he was not equal to, and keeping order more by the unconscious dignity that sorrow gave him than by any words of his own. The little boys were reading when a step was heard in the hall, and every one looked up to read the news in Mr. Bhaer's face as he came in. The kind face told them instantly that Demi had no father now, for it was worn and pale, and full of tender grief, which left him no words with which to answer Rob, as he ran to him saying, reproachfully,—

"What made you go and leave me in the night, papa?"

The memory of the other father who had left his children in the night, never to return, made Mr. Bhaer hold his own boy close, and, for a minute, hide his face in Robby's curly hair. Emil laid his head down on his arms, Franz went to put his hand on his uncle's shoulder, his boyish face pale with sympathy and sorrow, and the others sat so still that the soft rustle of the falling leaves outside was distinctly heard.

Rob did not clearly understand what had happened, but he hated to see papa unhappy, so he lifted up the bent head, and said, in his chirpy little voice,—

"Don't cry, mein Vater! We are all so good, we did our lessons without you, and Franz was the master."

Mr. Bhaer looked up then, tried to smile, and said in a grateful tone that made the lads feel like saints, "I thank you very much, my boys. It was a beautiful way to help and comfort me. I shall not forget it, I assure you."

"Franz proposed it, and was a first-rate master, too," said Nat; and the others gave a murmur of assent most gratifying to the young dominie.

Mr. Bhaer put Rob down, and, standing up, put his arm round his tall nephew's shoulder, as he said, with a look of genuine pleasure,—

"This makes my hard day easier, and gives me confidence in you all. I am needed there in town, and must leave you for some hours. I thought to give you a holiday, or send some of you home, but if you like to stay and go on as you have begun, I shall be glad and proud of my good boys."

"We'll stay"; "We'd rather"; "Franz can see to us"; cried several, delighted with the confidence shown in them.

"Isn't Marmar coming home?" asked Rob, wistfully; for home without "Marmar" was the world without the sun to him.

"We shall both come tonight; but dear Aunt Meg needs Mother more than you do now, and I know you like to lend her for a little while."

"Well, I will; but Teddy's been crying for her, and he slapped Nursey, and was dreadful naughty," answered Rob, as if the news might bring mother home.

"Where is my little man?" asked Mr. Bhaer.

"Dan took him out, to keep him quiet. He's all right now," said Franz pointing to the window, through which they could see Dan drawing baby in his little wagon, with the dogs frolicking about him.

"I won't see him, it would only upset him again; but tell Dan I leave Teddy in his care. You older boys I trust to manage yourselves for a day. Franz will direct you, and Silas is here to oversee matters. So good-by till tonight."

"Just tell me a word about Uncle John," said Emil, detaining Mr. Bhaer, as he was about hurrying away again.

"He was only ill a few hours, and died as he has lived, so cheerfully, so peacefully, that it seems a sin to mar the beauty of it with any violent or selfish grief. We were in time to say good-by; and Daisy and Demi were in his arms as he fell asleep on Aunt Meg's breast. No more now, I cannot bear it," and Mr. Bhaer went hastily away quite bowed with grief, for in John Brooke he had lost both friend and brother, and there was no one left to take his place.

All that day the house was very still; the small boys played quietly in the nursery; the others, feeling as if Sunday had come in the middle of the week, spent it in walking, sitting in the willow, or among their pets, all talking much of "Uncle John," and feeling that something gentle, just, and strong, had gone out of their little world, leaving a sense of loss that deepened every hour. At dusk, Mr. and Mrs. Bhaer came home alone, for Demi and Daisy were their mother's best comfort now, and could not leave her. Poor Mrs. Jo seemed quite spent, and evidently needed the same sort of comfort, for her first words, as she came up the stairs, were, "Where is my baby?"

"Here I is," answered a little voice, as Dan put Teddy into her arms, adding, as she hugged him close, "My Danny tooked tare of me all day, and I was dood."

Mrs. Jo turned to thank the faithful nurse, but Dan was waving off the boys, who had gathered in the hall to meet her, and was saying, in a low voice, "Keep back; she don't want to be bothered with us now."

"No, don't keep back. I want you all. Come in and see me, my boys. I've neglected you all day;" and Mrs. Jo held out her hands to them as they gathered round and escorted her into her own room, saying little, but expressing much by affectionate looks and clumsy little efforts to show their sorrow and sympathy.

"I am so tired, I will lie here and cuddle Teddy, and you shall bring me in some tea," she said, trying to speak cheerfully for their sakes.

A general stampede into the dining-room followed, and the supper-table would have been ravaged if Mr. Bhaer had not interfered. It was agreed that one squad should carry in the mother's tea, and another bring it out. The four nearest and dearest claimed the first honor, so Franz bore the teapot, Emil the bread, Rob the milk, and Teddy insisted on carrying the sugar-basin, which was lighter by several lumps when it arrived than when it started. Some women might have found it annoying at such a time to have boys creaking in and out, upsetting cups and rattling spoons in violent efforts to be quiet and helpful; but it suited Mrs. Jo, because just then her heart was very tender; and remembering that many of her boys were fatherless or motherless, she yearned over them, and found comfort in their blundering affection. It was the sort

The memory of the other father . . . made Mr. Bhaer hold
his own boy close.

of food that did her more good than the very thick bread-and-butter that they gave her, and the rough Commodore's broken whisper—

"Bear up, Aunty, it's a hard blow; but we'll weather it somehow," cheered her more than the sloppy cup he brought her, full of tea as bitter as if some salt tear of his own had dropped into it on the way. When supper was over, a second deputation removed the tray; and Dan said, holding out his arms for sleepy little Teddy,—

"Let me put him to bed, you're so tired, Mother."

"Will you go with him, lovey?" asked Mrs. Jo of her small lord and master, who lay on her arm among the sofa-pillows.

"Torse I will;" and he was proudly carried off by his faithful bearer.

"I wish *I* could do something," said Nat, with a sigh, as Franz leaned over the sofa, and softly stroked Aunt Jo's hot forehead.

"You can, dear. Go and get your violin, and play me the sweet little airs Uncle Teddy sent you last. Music will comfort me better than any thing else tonight."

Nat flew for his fiddle, and, sitting just outside her door, played as he had never done before, for now his heart was in it, and seemed to magnetize his fingers. The other lads sat quietly upon the steps, keeping watch that no new-comer should disturb the house; Franz lingered at his post; and so, soothed, served, and guarded by her boys, poor Mrs. Jo slept at last, and forgot her sorrow for an hour.

Two quiet days, and on the third Mr. Bhaer came in, just after school, with a note in his hand, looking both moved and pleased.

"I want to read you something, boys," he said; and as they stood round him he read this:—

> "DEAR BROTHER FRITZ,—
>
> I hear that you do not mean to bring your flock today, thinking that I may not like it. Please do. The sight of his friends will help Demi through the hard hour, and I want the boys to hear what father says of my John. It will do them good, I know. If they would sing one of the sweet old hymns you have taught them so well, I should like it better than any other music, and feel that it was beautifully suited to the occasion. Please ask them, with my love.
>
> MEG."

"Will you go?" and Mr. Bhaer looked at the lads, who were greatly touched by Mrs. Brooke's kind words and wishes.

"Yes," they answered, like one boy; and an hour later they went away with Franz to bear their part in John Brooke's simple funeral.

The little house looked as quiet, sunny, and home-like as when Meg entered it a bride, ten years ago, only then it was early summer, and roses blossomed everywhere; now it was early autumn, and dead leaves rustled softly down, leaving the branches bare. The bride was a widow now; but the same beautiful serenity shone in her face, and the sweet resignation of a truly pious soul made her presence a consolation to those who came to comfort her.

"O Meg! How *can* you bear it so?" whispered Jo, as she met them at the door with a smile of welcome, and no change in her gentle manner, except more gentleness.

"Dear Jo, the love that has blest me for ten happy years supports me still. It could not die, and John is more my own than ever," whispered Meg; and in her eyes the tender trust was so beautiful and bright, that Jo believed her, and thanked God for the immortality of love like hers.

They were all there—father and mother, Uncle Teddy, and Aunt Amy, old Mr. Laurence, white-haired and feeble now, Mr. and Mrs. Bhaer, with their flock, and many friends, come to do honor to the dead. One would have said that modest John Brooke, in his busy, quiet, humble life, had had little time to make friends; but now they seemed to start up everywhere,—old and young, rich and poor, high and low; for all unconsciously his influence had made itself widely felt, his virtues were remembered, and his hidden charities rose up to bless him. The group about his coffin was a far more eloquent eulogy than any Mr. March could utter. There were the rich men whom he had served faithfully for years; the poor old women whom he cherished with his little store, in memory of his mother; the wife to whom he had given such happiness that death could not mar it utterly; the brothers and sisters in whose hearts he had made a place forever; the little son and daughter, who already felt the loss of his strong arm and tender voice; the young children, sobbing for their kindest playmate, and the tall lads, watching with softened faces a scene which they never could forget. A very simple service, and very short; for the fatherly voice that had faltered in the marriage-sacrament now failed entirely as Mr. March endeavored to pay his tribute of reverence and love to the son whom he most honored. Nothing but the soft coo of Baby Josy's voice up-stairs broke the long hush that followed the last Amen, till, at a sign from Mr. Bhaer, the well-trained boyish voices broke out in a hymn, so full of lofty cheer, that one by one all joined in it, singing with full hearts, and finding their troubled spirits lifted into peace on the wings of that brave, sweet psalm.

As Meg listened, she felt that she had done well; for not only did the moment comfort her with the assurance that John's last lullaby was sung by the young voices he loved so well, but in the faces of the boys she saw that they had caught a glimpse of the beauty of virtue in its most impressive form, and that the memory of the good man lying dead before them would live long and helpfully in their remembrance. Daisy's head lay in her lap, and Demi held her hand, looking often at her, with eyes so like his father's, and a little gesture that seemed to say, "Don't be troubled, mother; I am here"; and all about her were friends to lean upon and love; so patient, pious Meg put by her heavy grief, feeling that her best help would be to live for others, as her John had done.

That evening, as the Plumfield boys sat on the steps, as usual, in the mild September moonlight, they naturally fell to talking of the event of the day.

Emil began by breaking out, in his impetuous way, "Uncle Fritz is the wisest, and Uncle Laurie the jolliest, but Uncle John was the *best*; and I'd rather be like him than any man I ever saw."

"So would I. Did you hear what those gentlemen said to Grandpa today? I would like to have that said of me when I was dead"; and Franz felt with regret that he had not appreciated Uncle John enough.

"What did they say?" asked Jack, who had been much impressed by the scenes of the day.

"Why, one of the partners of Mr. Laurence, where Uncle John has been ever so long, was saying that he was conscientious almost to a fault as a business man, and above reproach in all things. Another gentleman said no money could repay the fidelity and honesty with which Uncle John had served him, and then Grandpa told them the best of all. Uncle John once had a place in the office of a man who cheated, and when this man wanted uncle to help him do it, uncle wouldn't, though he was offered a big salary. The man was angry and said, 'You will never get on in business with such strict principles'; and uncle answered back, 'I *never* will try to get on *without* them,' and left the place for a much harder and poorer one."

"Good!" cried several of the boys warmly, for they were in the mood to understand and value the little story as never before.

"He wasn't rich, was he?" asked Jack.

"No."

"He never did any thing to make a stir in the world, did he?"

"No."

"He was only good?"

"That's all"; and Franz found himself wishing that Uncle John *had* done something to boast of, for it was evident that Jack was disappointed by his replies.

"Only good. That is *all* and every thing," said Mr. Bhaer, who had overheard the last few words, and guessed what was going on in the minds of the lads.

"Let me tell you a little about John Brooke, and you will see why men honor him, and why he was satisfied to be good rather than rich or famous. He simply did his duty in all things, and did it so cheerfully, so faithfully, that it kept him patient, brave, and happy through poverty and loneliness and years of hard work. He was a good son, and gave up his own plans to stay and live with his mother while she needed him. He was a good friend, and taught Laurie much beside his Greek and Latin, did it unconsciously, perhaps, by showing him an example of an upright man. He was a faithful servant, and made himself so valuable to those who employed him that they will find it hard to fill his place. He was a good husband and father, so tender, wise, and thoughtful, that Laurie and I learned much of him, and only knew how well he loved his family, when we discovered all he had done for them, unsuspected and unassisted."

Mr. Bhaer stopped a minute, and the boys sat like statues in the moonlight until he went on again, in a subdued, but earnest voice: "As he lay dying, I said to him, 'Have no care for Meg and the little ones; I will see that they never want.' Then he smiled and pressed my hand, and answered, in his cheerful way, 'No need of that; I have cared for them.' And so he had, for when we looked among his papers, all was in order, not a debt remained; and safely put away was enough to keep Meg comfortable and independent. Then we knew why he had lived so plainly, denied himself so many pleasures, except that of charity, and worked so hard that I fear he shortened his good life. He never asked help for himself, though often for others, but bore his own burden and worked out his own task bravely and quietly. No one can say a word of complaint against him, so just and generous and kind was he; and now, when he is gone, all find so much to love and praise and honor, that I am proud to have been his friend, and would rather leave my children the legacy he leaves his than the largest fortune ever made. Yes! Simple, genuine goodness is the best capital to found the business of this life upon. It lasts when fame and money fail, and is the only riches we can take out of this world with us. Remember that, my boys; and if you want to earn respect and confidence and love follow in the footsteps of John Brooke."

When Demi returned to school, after some weeks at home, he seemed to have recovered from his loss with the blessed elasticity of childhood, and so he had in a measure; but he did not forget, for his was a nature into which things sank deeply, to be pondered over, and absorbed into the soil where the small virtues were growing fast. He played and studied, worked and sang, just as before, and few suspected any change; but there was one—and Aunt Jo saw it—for she watched over the boy with her whole heart, trying to fill John's place in her poor way. He seldom spoke of his loss, but Aunt Jo often heard a stifled sobbing in the little bed at night; and when she went to comfort him, all his cry was, "I want my father! Oh, I want my father!"—for the tie between the two had been a very tender one, and the child's heart bled when it was broken. But time was kind to him, and slowly he came to feel that father was not lost, only invisible for a while, and sure to be found again, well and strong and fond as ever, even though his little son should see the purple asters blossom on his grave many, many times before they met. To this belief Demi held fast, and in it found both help and comfort, because it led him unconsciously through a tender longing for the father whom he had seen to a childlike trust in the Father whom he had not seen. Both were in heaven, and he prayed to both, trying to be good for love of them.

The outward change corresponded to the inward, for in those few weeks Demi seemed to have grown tall, and began to drop his childish plays, not as if ashamed of them, as some boys do, but as if he had outgrown them, and wanted something manlier. He took to the hated arithmetic, and held on so steadily that his uncle was charmed, though he could not understand the whim, until Demi said—

"I am going to be a bookkeeper when I grow up, like papa, and I must know about figures and things, else I can't have nice, neat ledgers like his."

At another time he came to his aunt with a very serious face, and said—

"What can a small boy do to earn money?"

"Why do you ask, my deary?"

"My father told me to take care of mother and the little girls, and I want to, but I don't know how to begin."

"He did not mean now, Demi, but by and by, when you are large."

"But I wish to begin *now*, if I can, because I think I ought to make some money to buy things for the family. I am ten, and other boys no bigger than I earn pennies sometimes."

"Well, then, suppose you rake up all the dead leaves and cover the strawberry bed. I'll pay you a dollar for the job," said Aunt Jo.

"Isn't that a great deal? I could do it in one day. You must be fair, and not pay too much, because I want to truly earn it."

"My little John, I will be fair, and not pay a penny too much. Don't work too hard; and when that is done I will have something else for you to do," said Mrs. Jo, much touched by his desire to help, and his sense of justice, so like his scrupulous father.

When the leaves were done, many barrowloads of chips were wheeled from the wood to the shed, and another dollar earned. Then Demi helped cover the school-books, working in the evenings, under Franz's direction, tugging patiently away at each book, letting no one help, and receiving his wages with such satisfaction that the dingy bills became quite glorified in his sight.

"Now, I have a dollar for each of them, and I should like to take my money to mother all myself, so she can see that I have minded my father."

So Demi made a duteous pilgrimage to his mother, who received his little earnings as a treasure of great worth, and would have kept it untouched, if Demi had not begged her to buy some *useful* thing for herself and the women-children, whom he felt were left to his care.

This made him very happy, and, though he often forgot his responsibilities for a time, the desire to help was still there, strengthening with his years. He always uttered the words "my father" with an air of gentle pride, and often said, as if he claimed a title full of honor, "Don't call me Demi any more. I am John Brooke now." So, strengthened by a purpose and a hope, the little lad of ten bravely began the world, and entered into his inheritance,—the memory of a wise and tender father, the legacy of an honest name.

# CHAPTER XX

## ROUND THE FIRE

WITH the October frosts came the cheery fires in the great fireplaces; and Demi's dry pine-chips helped Dan's oak-knots to blaze royally, and go roaring up the chimney with a jolly sound. All were glad to gather round the hearth, as the evenings grew longer, to play games, read, or lay plans for the winter. But the favorite amusement was story-telling, and Mr. and Mrs. Bhaer were expected to have a store of lively tales always on hand. Their supply occasionally gave out, and then the boys were thrown upon their own resources, which were not always successful. Ghost-parties were the rage at one time; for the fun of the thing consisted in putting out the lights, letting the fire die down, and then sitting in the dark, and telling the most awful tales they could invent. As this resulted in scares of all sorts among the boys, Tommy's walking in his sleep on the shed roof, and a general state of nervousness in the little ones, it was forbidden, and they fell back on more harmless amusements.

One evening, when the small boys were snugly tucked in bed, and the older lads were lounging about the school-room fire, trying to decide what they should do, Demi suggested a new way of settling the question.

Seizing the hearth-brush, he marched up and down the room, saying, "Row, row, row"; and when the boys, laughing and pushing, had got into line, he said, "Now, I'll give you two minutes to think of a play." Franz was writing, and Emil reading the Life of Lord Nelson, and neither joined the party, but the others thought hard, and when the time was up were ready to reply.

"Now, Tom!" and the poker softly rapped him on the head.

"Blind-man's Buff."

"Jack!"

"Commerce; a good round game, and have cents for the pool."

"Uncle forbids our playing for money. Dan, what do you want?"

"Let's have a battle between the Greeks and Romans."

"Stuffy?"

"Roast apples, pop corn, and crack nuts."

"Good! Good!" cried several; and when the vote was taken, Stuffy's proposal carried the day.

Some went to the cellar for apples, some to the garret for nuts, and others looked up the popper and the corn.

"We had better ask the girls to come in, hadn't we?" said Demi, in a sudden fit of politeness.

"Daisy pricks chestnuts beautifully," put in Nat, who wanted his little friend to share the fun.

"Nan pops corn tip-top we must have her," added Tommy.

"Bring in your sweethearts then, we don't mind," said Jack, who laughed at the innocent regard the little people had for one another.

"You shan't call my sister a sweetheart; it is so silly!" cried Demi, in a way that made Jack laugh.

"She *is* Nat's darling, isn't she, old chirper?"

"Yes, if Demi don't mind. I can't help being fond of her, she is so good to me," answered Nat, with bashful earnestness, for Jack's rough ways disturbed him.

"Nan is my sweetheart, and I shall marry her in about a year, so don't you get in the way, any of you," said Tommy, stoutly; for he and Nan had settled their future, child-fashion, and were to live in the willow, lower down a basket for food, and do other charmingly impossible things.

Demi was quenched by the decision of Bangs, who took him by the arm and walked him off to get the ladies. Nan and Daisy were sewing with Aunt Jo on certain small garments for Mrs. Carney's newest baby.

"Please, ma'am, could you lend us the girls for a little while? We'll be very careful of them," said Tommy, winking one eye to express apples, snapping his fingers to signify pop-corn, and gnashing his teeth to convey the idea of nut-cracking.

The girls understood this pantomime at once, and began to pull off their thimbles before Mrs. Jo could decide whether Tommy was going into convulsions or was brewing some unusual piece of mischief. Demi explained with elaboration, permission was readily granted, and the boys departed with their prize.

"Don't you speak to Jack," whispered Tommy, as he and Nan promenaded down the hall to get a fork to prick the apples.

"Why not?"

"He laughs at me, so I don't wish you to have any thing to do with him."

"Shall, if I like," said Nan, promptly resenting this premature assumption of authority on the part of her lord.

"Then I won't have you for my sweetheart."

"I don't care."

"Why, Nan, I thought you were fond of me!" and Tommy's voice was full of tender reproach.

"If you mind Jack's laughing I don't care for you one bit."

"Then you may take back your old ring; I won't wear it any longer"; and Tommy plucked off a horse-hair pledge of affection which Nan had given him in return for one made of a lobster's feeler.

"I shall give it to Ned," was her cruel reply; for Ned liked Mrs. Giddy-gaddy, and had turned her clothes-pins, boxes, and spools enough to set up housekeeping with.

Tommy said, "Thunder-turtles!" as the only vent equal to the pent-up anguish of the moment, and, dropping Nan's arm, retired in high dudgeon, leaving her to follow with the fork,—a neglect which naughty Nan punished by proceeding to prick his heart with jealousy as if it were another sort of apple.

The hearth was swept, and the rosy Baldwins put down to roast. A shovel was heated, and the chestnuts danced merrily upon it, while the corn poppd wildly in its wire prison. Dan cracked his best walnuts, and every one chattered and laughed, while the rain beat on the window-pane and the wind howled round the house.

"Why is Billy like this nut?" asked Emil, who was frequently inspired with bad conundrums.

"Because he is cracked," answered Ned.

"That's not fair; you mustn't make fun of Billy, because he can't hit back again. It's mean," cried Dan, smashing a nut wrathfully.

"To what family of insects does Blake belong?" asked peacemaker Franz, seeing that Emil looked ashamed and Dan lowering.

"Gnats," answered Jack.

"Why is Daisy like a bee?" cried Nat, who had been wrapt in thought for several minutes.

"Because she is queen of the hive," said Dan.

"No."

"Because she is sweet."

"Bees are not sweet."

"Give it up."

"Because she makes sweet things, is always busy, and likes flowers," said Nat, piling up his boyish compliments till Daisy blushed like a rosy clover.

"Why is Nan like a hornet?" demanded Tommy, glowering at her,

All were glad to gather round the hearth . . . to play games.

and adding, without giving any one time to answer, "Because she *isn't* sweet, makes a great buzzing about nothing, and stings like fury."

"Tommy's mad, and I'm glad," cried Ned, as Nan tossed her head and answered quickly—

"What thing in the china-closet is Tom like?"

"A pepper pot," answered Ned, giving Nan a nut meat with a tantalizing laugh that made Tommy feel as if he would like to bounce up like a hot chestnut and hit somebody.

Seeing that ill-humor was getting the better of the small supply of wit in the company, Franz cast himself into the breach again.

"Let's make a law that the first person who comes into the room shall tell us a story. No matter who it is, he must do it, and it will be fun to see who comes first."

The others agreed, and did not have to wait long, for a heavy step soon came clumping through the hall, and Silas appeared, bearing an armful of wood. He was greeted by a general shout, and stood staring about him with a bewildered grin on his big red face, till Franz explained the joke.

"Sho! I can't tell a story," he said, putting down his load and preparing to leave the room. But the boys fell upon him, forced him into a seat, and held him there, laughing and clamoring for their story, till the good-natured giant was overpowered.

"I don't know but jest one story, and that's about a horse," he said, much flattered by the reception he received.

"Tell it! Tell it!" cried the boys.

"Wal," began Silas, tipping his chair back against the wall, and putting his thumbs in the arm-holes of his waistcoat, "I jined a cavalry regiment durin' the war, and see a consid'able amount of fightin'. My horse, Major, was a fust-rate animal, and I was as fond on him as ef he'd ben a human critter. He warn't harnsome, but he was the best-tempered, stiddyest, lovenest brute I ever see. The fust battle we went into, he give me a lesson that I didn't forgit in a hurry, and I'll tell you how it was. It ain't no use tryin' to picter the noise and hurry, and general horridness of a battle to you young fellers, for I ain't no words to do it in; but I'm free to confess that I got so sort of confused and upset at the fust on it, that I didn't know what I was about. We was ordered to charge, and went ahead like good ones, never stoppin' to pick up them that went down in the scrimmage. I got a shot in the arm, and was pitched out of the saddle—don't know how, but there I was left behind with two or three others, dead and wounded, for the rest went on, as I say. Wal, I picked myself up and looked round for Major, feeling as ef I'd had about enough for that spell. I didn't see him nowhere, and was kinder walking back to camp, when I heard a whinny that sounded nateral. I looked round, and there was Major stopping for me a long way off, and lookin' as ef he didn't understand why I was loiterin' behind. I whistled, and he trotted up to me as I'd trained him to do. I mounted as well as I could with my left arm bleedin' and was for going on to camp, for I declare I felt as sick and wimbly as a woman; folks often do in their fust battle. But, no, sir! Major was the bravest of the two, and he wouldn't go, not a peg; he jest rared up, and danced, and snorted, and acted as ef the smell of powder and the noise had drove him half wild. I done my best, but he wouldn't give in, so I did; and what do you think that plucky brute done? He wheeled slap round, and galloped back like a hurricane, right into the thickest of the scrimmage!"

"Good for him!" cried Dan excitedly, while the other boys forgot apples and nuts in their interest.

"I wish I may die ef I warn't ashamed of myself," continued Silas, warming up at the recollection of that day. "I was as mad as a hornet, and I forgot my waound, and jest pitched in, rampagin' raound like fury till there come a shell into the midst of us, and in bustin' knocked a lot of us flat. I didn't know nothin' for a spell, and when I come-to, the fight was over jest there, and I found myself layin' by a wall with poor Major long-side wuss wounded than I was. My leg was broke, and I had a ball in my shoulder, but he, poor old feller! Was all tore in the side with a piece of that blasted shell."

"O Silas! What did you do?" cried Nan, pressing close to him with a face full of eager sympathy and interest.

"I dragged myself nigher, and tried to stop the bleedin' with sech rags as I could tear off of me with one hand. But it warn't no use, and he lay moanin' with horrid pain, and lookin' at me with them lovin' eyes of his, till I thought I couldn't bear it. I give him all the help I could, and when the sun got hotter and hotter, and he began to lap out his tongue, I tried to get to a brook that was a good piece away, but I couldn't do it, being stiff and faint, so I give it up and fanned him with my hat. Now you listen to this, and when you hear folks comin' down on the rebs, you jest remember what one on 'em did, and give him the credit of it. A poor feller in gray laid not fur off, shot through the lungs, and dying fast. I'd offered him my handkerchief to keep the sun off his face, and he'd thanked me kindly, for in sech times as that men don't stop to think on which side they belong, but jest buckle-to and help one another. When he see me mournin' over Major and tryin' to ease his pain, he looked up with his face all damp and white with sufferin', and sez he, 'There's water in my canteen; take it, for it can't help me,' and he flung it to me. I couldn't have took it ef I hadn't had a little brandy in a pocket flask, and I made him drink it. It done him good, and I felt as much set up as if I'd drunk it myself. It's surprisin' the good sech little things do folks sometimes;" and Silas paused as if he felt again the comfort of that moment when he and his enemy forgot their feud, and helped one another like brothers.

"Tell about Major," cried the boys, impatient for the catastrophe.

"I poured the water over his poor pantin' tongue, and ef ever a dumb critter looked grateful, he did then. But it warn't of much use, for the dreadful waound kep on tormentin' him, till I couldn't bear it any longer. It was hard, but I done it in mercy, and I know he forgive me."

"What did you do?" asked Emil, as Silas stopped abruptly with a loud "hem," and a look in his rough face that made Daisy go and stand by him with her little hand on his knee.

"I shot him."

Quite a thrill went through the listeners as Silas said that, for Major seemed a hero in their eyes, and his tragic end roused all their sympathy.

"Yes, I shot him, and put him out of his misery. I patted him fust, and said, 'Good-by'; then I laid his head easy on the grass, give a last look into his lovin' eyes, and sent a bullet through his head. He hardly stirred, I aimed so true, and when I see him quite still, with no more moanin' and pain, I was glad, and yet—wal, I don't know as I need be ashamed on't—I jest put my arms raound his neck and boo-hooed like a great baby. Sho! I didn't know I was such a fool"; and Silas drew his sleeve across his eyes, as much touched by Daisy's sob, as by the memory of faithful Major.

No one spoke for a minute, because the boys were as quick to feel the pathos of the little story as tender-hearted Daisy, though they did not show it by crying.

"I'd like a horse like that," said Dan, half-aloud.

"Did the rebel man die too?" asked Nan, anxiously.

"Not then. We laid there all day, and at night some of our fellers came to look after the missing ones. They nat'rally wanted to take me fust, but I knew I could wait, and the rebel had but one chance, maybe, so I made them carry him off right away. He had jest strength enough to hold out his hand to me and say, 'Thanky, comrade!' and them was the last words he spoke, for he died an hour after he got to the hospital-tent."

"How glad you must have been that you were kind to him!" said Demi, who was deeply impressed by this story.

"Wal, I did take comfort thinkin' of it, as I laid there alone for a number of hours with my head on Major's neck, and see the moon come up. I'd like to have buried the poor beast decent, but it warn't possible; so I cut off a bit of his mane, and I've kep it ever sence. Want to see it, sissy?"

"Oh, yes, please," answered Daisy, wiping away her tears to look.

Silas took out an old "wallet," as he called his pocket-book, and produced from an inner fold a bit of brown paper, in which was a rough lock of white horse-hair. The children looked at it silently, as it lay in the broad palm, and no one found any thing to ridicule in the love Silas bore his good horse Major.

"That is a sweet story, and I like it, though it did make me cry. Thank you very much, Si," and Daisy helped him fold and put away his little relic; while Nan stuffed a handful of pop-corn into his pocket, and the boys loudly expressed their flattering opinions of his story, feeling that there had been two heroes in it.

He departed, quite overcome by his honors, and the little conspirators talked the tale over while they waited for their next victim. It was Mrs. Jo, who came in to measure Nan for some new pinafores she was making for her. They let her get well in, and then pounced upon her, telling her the law, and demanding the story. Mrs. Jo was very much amused at the new trap, and consented at once, for the sound of the happy voices had been coming across the hall so pleasantly that she quite longed to join them, and forget her own anxious thoughts of Sister Meg.

"Am I the first mouse you have caught, you sly pussies-in-boots?" she asked, as she was conducted to the big chair, supplied with refreshments, and surrounded by a flock of merry-faced listeners.

They told her about Silas and his contribution, and she slapped her forehead in despair, for she was quite at her wits' end, being called upon so unexpectedly for a bran new tale.

"What *shall* I tell about?" she said.

"Boys," was the general answer.

"Have a party in it," said Daisy.

"And something good to eat," added Stuffy.

"That reminds me of a story, written years ago by a dear old lady. I used to be very fond of it, and I fancy you will like it, for it has both boys, and 'something good to eat' in it."

"What is it called?" asked Demi.

" ' The Suspected Boy.' "

Nat looked up from the nuts he was picking, and Mrs. Jo smiled at him, guessing what was in his mind.

"Miss Crane kept a school for boys in a quiet little town, and a very good school it was, of the old-fashioned sort. Six boys lived in her house, and four or five more came in from the town. Among those who lived with her was one named Lewis White. Lewis was not a bad boy, but rather timid, and now and then he told a lie. One day a neighbor sent Miss Crane a basket of gooseberries. There were not enough to go round, so kind Miss Crane, who liked to please her boys, went to work and made a dozen nice little gooseberry tarts.

"I'd like to try gooseberry tarts. I wonder if she made them as I do my raspberry ones," said Daisy, whose interest in cooking had lately revived.

"Mush," said Nat, tucking a plump pop-corn into her mouth to silence her, for he felt a peculiar interest in this tale, and thought it opened well.

"When the tarts were done, Miss Crane put them away in the best parlor closet and said not a word about them, for she wanted to surprise the boys at tea-time. When the minute came and all were seated at table, she went to get her tarts, but came back looking much troubled, for what do you think had happened?"

"Somebody had hooked them!" cried Ned.

"No, there they were, but some one *had* stolen all the fruit out of them by lifting up the upper crust and then putting it down after the gooseberry had been scraped out."

"What a mean trick!" and Nan looked at Tommy, as if to imply that he would do the same.

"When she told the boys her plan and showed them the poor little patties all robbed of their sweetness, the boys were much grieved and disappointed, and all declared that they knew nothing about the matter. 'Perhaps the rats did it,' said Lewis, who was among the loudest to deny any knowledge of the tarts. 'No, rats would have nibbled crust and all, and never lifted it up and scooped out the fruit. Hands did that,' said Miss Crane, who was more troubled about the lie that some one must have told than about her lost patties. Well, they had supper and went to bed, but in the night Miss Crane heard some one groaning, and going to see who it was she found Lewis in great pain. He had evidently eaten something that disagreed with him, and was so sick that Miss Crane was alarmed, and was going to send for the doctor, when Lewis moaned out, 'It's the gooseberries; I ate them, and I *must* tell before I die,' for the thought of a doctor frightened him. 'If that is all, I'll give you an emetic and you will soon get over it,' said Miss Crane. So Lewis had a good dose, and by morning was quite comfortable. 'Oh, don't tell the boys; they will laugh at me so,' begged the invalid. Kind Miss Crane promised not to, but Sally, the girl, told the story, and poor Lewis had no peace for a long time. His mates called him Old Gooseberry, and were never tired of asking him the price of tarts."

"Served him right," said Emil.

"Badness always gets found out," added Demi, morally.

"No, it don't," muttered Jack, who was tending the apples with great devotion, so that he might keep his back to the rest and account for his red face.

"Is that all?" asked Dan.

"No, that is only the first part; the second part is more interesting. Some time after this a peddler came by one day and stopped to show his things to the boys, several of whom bought pocket-combs, jew's-harps, and various trifles of that sort. Among the knives was a little white-handled penknife that Lewis wanted very much, but he had spent all his pocket-money, and no one had any to lend him. He held the knife in his hand, admiring and longing for it, till the man packed up his goods to go, then he reluctantly laid it down, and the man went on his way. The next day, however, the peddler returned to say that he could not find that very knife, and thought he must have left it at Miss Crane's. It was a very nice one with a pearl handle, and he could not afford to lose it. Every one looked, and every one declared they knew nothing about it. This young gentleman had it last, and seemed to want it very much. 'Are you quite sure you put it back?' said the man to Lewis, who was much troubled at the loss, and vowed over and over again that he did return it. His denials seemed to do no good, however, for every one was sure he had taken it, and after a stormy scene Miss Crane paid for it, and the man went grumbling away."

"Did Lewis have it?" cried Nat, much excited.

"You will see. Now poor Lewis had another trial to bear, for the boys were constantly saying, 'Lend me your pearl-handled knife, Gooseberry,' and things of that sort, till Lewis was so unhappy he begged to be sent home. Miss Crane did her best to keep the boys quiet, but it was hard work, for they would tease, and she could not be with them all the time. That is one of the hardest things to teach boys; they won't 'hit a fellow when he is down,' as they say, but they will torment him in little ways till he would thank them to fight it out all round."

"I know that," said Dan.

"So do I," added Nat, softly.

Jack said nothing, but he quite agreed; for he knew that the elder boys despised him, and let him alone for that very reason.

"Do go on about poor Lewis, Aunt Jo. I don't believe he took the knife, but I want to be sure," said Daisy, in great anxiety.

"Well, week after week went on and the matter was not cleared up. The boys avoided Lewis, and he, poor fellow, was almost sick with the trouble he had brought upon himself. He resolved never to tell another lie, and tried so hard that Miss Crane pitied and helped him, and really came at last to believe that he did not take the knife. Two months after the peddler's first visit, he came again, and the first thing he said was—

" 'Well, ma'am, I found that knife after all. It had slipped behind the lining of my valise, and fell out the other day when I was putting in a new stock of goods. I thought I'd call and let you know, as you paid for it, and maybe would like it, so here it is.'

"The boys had all gathered round, and at these words they felt much ashamed, and begged Lewis' pardon so heartily that he could not refuse to give it. Miss Crane presented the knife to him, and he kept it many years to remind him of the fault that had brought him so much trouble."

"I wonder why it is that things you eat on the sly hurt you, and don't when you eat them at table," observed Stuffy, thoughtfully.

"Perhaps your conscience affects your stomach," said Mrs. Jo, smiling at his speech.

"He is thinking of the cucumbers," said Ned, and a gale of merriment followed the words, for Stuffy's last mishap had been a funny one.

He ate two large cucumbers in private, felt very ill, and confided his anguish to Ned, imploring him to do something, Ned good-naturedly recommended a mustard plaster and a hot flat iron to the feet; only in applying these remedies he reversed the order of things, and put the plaster on the feet, the flat iron on the stomach, and poor Stuffy was found in the barn with blistered soles and a scorched jacket.

"Suppose you tell another story, that was such an interesting one," said Nat, as the laughter subsided.

Before Mrs. Jo could refuse these insatiable Oliver Twists, Rob walked into the room trailing his little bedcover after him, and wearing an expression of great sweetness as he said, steering straight to his mother as a sure haven of refuge,—

"I heard a great noise, and I thought sumfin dreffle might have happened, so I came to see."

"Did you think I would forget you, naughty boy?" asked his mother, trying to look stern.

"No; but I thought you'd feel better to see me right here," responded the insinuating little party.

"I had much rather see you in bed, so march straight up again, Robin."

"Everybody that comes in here has to tell a story, and you can't, so you'd better cut and run," said Emil.

"Yes, I can! I tell Teddy lots of ones, all about bears and moons, and little flies that say things when they buzz," protested Rob, bound to stay at any price.

"Tell one now, then, right away," said Dan, preparing to shoulder and bear him off.

"Well, I will; let me fink a minute," and Rob climbed into his mother's lap, where he was cuddled, with the remark—

"It is a family failing, this getting out of bed at wrong times. Demi used to do it; and as for me, I was hopping in and out all night long. Meg used to think the house was on fire, and send me down to see, and I used to stay and enjoy myself, as you mean to, my bad son."

"I've finked now," observed Rob, quite at his ease, and eager to win the *entrée* into this delightful circle.

Every one looked and listened with faces full of suppressed merriment as Rob, perched on his mother's knee and wrapped in the gay coverlet, told the following brief but tragic tale with an earnestness that made it very funny:—

"Once a lady had a million children, and one nice little boy. She went up-stairs and said, 'You mustn't go in the yard.' But he wented, and fell into the pump, and was drowned dead."

"Is that all?" asked Franz, as Rob paused out of breath with this startling beginning.

"No there is another piece of it," and Rob knit his downy eyebrows in the effort to evolve another inspiration.

"What did the lady do when he fell into the pump?" asked his mother, to help him on.

"Oh, she pumped him up, and wrapped him in a newspaper, and put him on a shelf to dry for seed."

A general explosion of laughter greeted this surprising conclusion, and Mrs. Jo patted the curly head, as she said, solemnly,—

"My son, you inherit your mother's gift of story-telling. Go where glory waits thee."

"Now I can stay, can't I? Wasn't it a good story?" cried Rob, in high feather at his superb success.

"You can stay till you have eaten these twelve pop-corns," said his mother, expecting to see them vanish at one mouthful.

But Rob was a shrewd little man, and got the better her by eating them one by one very slowly, and enjoying every minute with all his might.

"Hadn't you better tell the other story, while you wait for him?" said Demi, anxious that no time should be lost.

"I really have nothing but a little tale about a wood-box," said Mrs. Jo, seeing that Rob had still seven corns to eat.

"Is there a boy in it?"

"It is all boy."

"Is it true?" asked Demi.

"Every bit of it."

"Goody! Tell on, please."

"James Snow and his mother lived in a little house, up in New Hampshire. They were poor, and James had to work to help his mother, but he loved books so well he hated work, and just wanted to sit and study all day long."

"How could he! I hate books, and like work," said Dan, objecting to James at the very outset.

"It takes all sorts of people to make a world; workers and students both are needed, and there is room for all. But I think the workers should study some, and the students should know how to work if necessary," answered Mrs. Jo, looking from Dan to Demi with a significant expression.

"I'm sure I do work," and Demi showed three small hard spots in his little palm, with pride.

"And I'm sure I study," added Dan, nodding with a groan toward the blackboard full of neat figures.

"See what James did. He did not mean to be selfish, but his mother was proud of him, and let him do as he liked, working away by herself that he might have books and time to read them. One autumn James wanted to go to school, and went to the minister to see if he would help him, about decent clothes and books. Now the minister had heard the gossip about James's idleness, and was not inclined to do much for him, thinking that a boy who neglected his mother, and let her slave for him, was not likely to do very well even at school. But the good man felt more interested when he found how earnest James was, and being rather an odd man, he made this proposal to the boy, to try how sincere he was.

" 'I will give you clothes and books on one condition, James.'

" 'What is that, sir?' and the boy brightened up at once.

" 'You are to keep your mother's wood-box full all winter long, and do it yourself. If you fail, school stops.' James laughed at the queer condition and readily agreed to it, thinking it a very easy one.

"He began school, and for a time got on capitally with the wood-box, for it was autumn, and chips and brush-wood were plentiful. He ran out morning and evening and got a basket full, or chopped up the cat sticks for the little cooking stove, and as his mother was careful and saving, the task was not hard. But in November the frost came, the days were dull and cold, and wood went fast. His mother bought a load with her own earnings, but it seemed to melt away, and was nearly gone, before James remembered that *he* was to get the next. Mrs. Snow was feeble and lame with rheumatism, and unable to work as she had done, so James had to put down his books, and see what he could do.

"It was hard, for he was going on well, and so interested in his lessons that he hated to stop except for food and sleep. But he knew the minister would keep his word, and much against his will James set about earning money in his spare hours, lest the wood-box should get empty. He did all sorts of things, ran errands, took care of a neighbor's cow, helped the old sexton dust and warm the church on Sundays, and in these ways got enough to buy fuel in small quantities. But it was hard work; the days were short, the winter was bitterly cold, the precious time went fast, and the dear books were so fascinating, that it was sad to leave them, for dull duties that never seemed done.

"The minister watched him quietly, and seeing that he was in earnest helped him without his knowledge. He met him often driving the wood sleds from the forest, where the men were chopping, and as James plodded beside the slow oxen, he read or studied, anxious to use every minute. 'The boy is worth helping, this lesson will do him good, and when he has learned it, I will give him an easier one,' said the minister to himself, and on Christmas eve a splendid load of wood was quietly dropped at the door of the little house, with a new saw and a bit of paper, saying only—

" 'The Lord helps those who help themselves.'

"Poor James expected nothing, but when he woke on that cold Christmas morning, he found a pair of warm mittens, knit by his mother, with her stiff painful fingers. This gift pleased him very much, but her kiss and

tender look as she called him her 'good son,' was better still. In trying
to keep her warm, he had warmed his own heart, you see, and in filling
the wood-box he had also filled those months with duties faithfully done.
He began to see this, to feel that there was something better than books,
and to try to learn the lessons God set him, as well as those his school-
master gave.

"When he saw the great pile of oak and pine logs at his door, and
read the little paper, he knew who sent it, and understood the minister's
plan; thanked him for it, and fell to work with all his might. Other boys
frolicked that day, but James sawed wood, and I think of all the lads in
the town the happiest was the one in the new mittens, who whistled like
a blackbird as he filled his mother's wood-box."

"That's a first rater!" cried Dan, who enjoyed a simple matter-of-fact
story better than the finest fairy tale; "I like that fellow after all."

"I could saw wood for you, Aunt Jo!" said Demi, feeling as if a new
means of earning money for his mother was suggested by the story.

"Tell about a bad boy. I like them best," said Nan.

"You'd better tell about a naughty cross-patch of a girl," said Tommy,
whose evening had been spoilt by Nan's unkindness. It made his apple
taste bitter, his pop-corn was insipid, his nuts were hard to crack, and
the sight of Ned and Nan on one bench made him feel his life a burden.

But there were no more stories from Mrs. Jo, for on looking down at
Rob he was discovered to be fast asleep with his last corn firmly clasped
in his chubby hand. Bundling him up in his coverlet, his mother carried
him away and tucked him up with no fear of his popping out again.

"Now let's see who will come next," said Emil, setting the door temptingly
ajar.

Mary Ann passed first, and he called out to her, but Silas had warned
her, and she only laughed and hurried on in spite of their enticements.
Presently a door opened, and a strong voice was heard humming in the
hall—

> *"Ich weiss nicht was soll es bedeuten*
> *Dass ich so traurig bin."*

"It's Uncle Fritz; all laugh loud and he will be sure to come in," said
Emil.

A wild burst of laughter followed, and in came Uncle Fritz, asking,
"What is the joke, my lads?"

"Caught! Caught! You can't go out till you've told a story," cried the
boys, slamming the door.

"So! That is the joke then? Well, I have no wish to go, it is so pleasant
here, and I pay my forfeit at once," which he did by sitting down and
beginning instantly—

"A long time ago your Grandfather, Demi, went to lecture in a great
town, hoping to get some money for a home for little orphans that some
good people were getting up. His lecture did well, and he put a considerable
sum of money in his pocket, feeling very happy about it. As he was
driving in a chaise to another town, he came to a lonely bit of road, late
in the afternoon, and was just thinking what a good place it was for

robbers when he saw a bad-looking man come out of the woods in front of him and go slowly along as if waiting till he came up. The thought of the money made Grandfather rather anxious, and at first he had a mind to turn round and drive away. But the horse was tired, and then he did not like to suspect the man, so he kept on, and when he got nearer and saw how poor and sick and ragged the stranger looked, his heart reproached him, and stopping, he said in his kind voice—

" 'My friend, you look tired; let me give you a lift.' The man seemed surprised, hesitated a minute, and then got in. He did not seem inclined to talk, but Grandfather kept on in his wise, cheerful way, speaking of what a hard year it had been, how much the poor had suffered, and how difficult it was to get on sometimes. The man slowly softened a little, and, won by the kind chat, told his story. How he had been sick, could get no work, had a family of children, and was almost in despair. Grandfather was so full of pity that he forgot his fear, and, asking the man his name, said he would try and get him work in the next town, as he had friends there. Wishing to get at pencil and paper, to write down the address, Grandfather took out his plump pocket-book, and the minute he did so, the man's eye was on it. Then Grandfather remembered what was in it and trembled for his money, but said quietly—

" 'Yes, I have a little sum here for some poor orphans. I wish it was my own, I would so gladly give you some of it. I am not rich, but I know many of the trials of the poor; this five dollars *is* mine, and I want to give it to you for your children.'

"The hard, hungry look in the man's eyes changed to a grateful one as he took the small sum, freely given, and left the orphans' money untouched. He rode on with Grandfather till they approached the town, then he asked to be set down. Grandpa shook hands with him, and was about to drive on, when the man said, as if something made him, 'I was desperate when we met, and I meant to rob you, but you were so kind I couldn't do it. God bless you, sir, for keeping me from it!' "

"Did Grandpa ever see him again?" asked Daisy, eagerly.

"No; but I believe the man found work, and did not try robbery any more."

"That was a curious way to treat him; I'd have knocked him down," said Dan.

"Kindness is always better than force. Try it and see," answered Mr. Bhaer, rising.

"Tell another, please," cried Daisy.

"You must, Aunt Jo did," added Demi.

"Then I certainly won't, but keep my others for next time. Too many tales are as bad as too many bonbons. I have paid my forfeit and I go," and Mr. Bhaer ran for his life, with the whole flock in full pursuit. He had the start, however, and escaped safely into his study, leaving the boys to go rioting back again.

They were so stirred up by the race that they could not settle to their former quiet, and a lively game of Blindman's Bluff followed, in which Tommy showed that he had taken the moral of the last story to heart, for, when he caught Nan, he whispered in her ear, "I'm sorry I called you a cross-patch."

Nan was not to be outdone in kindness, so, when they played "Button, button, who's got the button?" and it was her turn to go round, she said, "Hold fast all I give you," with such a friendly smile at Tommy, that he was not surprised to find the horse-hair ring in his hand instead of the button. He only smiled back at her then, but when they were going to bed, he offered Nan the best bite of his last apple; she saw the ring on his stumpy little finger, accepted the bite, and peace was declared. Both were sorry for the temporary coldness, neither was ashamed to say, "I was wrong, forgive me," so the childish friendship remained unbroken, and the home in the willow lasted long, a pleasant little castle in the air.

# CHAPTER XXI

## THANKSGIVING

THIS yearly festival was always kept at Plumfield in the good old-fashioned way, and nothing was allowed to interfere with it. For days beforehand, the little girls helped Asia and Mrs. Jo in store-room and kitchen, making pies and puddings, sorting fruit, dusting dishes, and being very busy and immensely important. The boys hovered on the outskirts of the forbidden ground, sniffing the savory odors, peeping in at the mysterious performances, and occasionally being permitted to taste some delicacy in the process of preparation.

Something more than usual seemed to be on foot this year for the girls were as busy up-stairs as down, so were the boys in school-room and barn, and a general air of bustle pervaded the house. There was a great hunting up of old ribbons and finery, much cutting and pasting of gold paper, and the most remarkable quantity of straw, gray cotton, flannel, and big black beads, used by Franz and Mrs. Jo. Ned hammered at strange machines in the workshop, Demi and Tommy went about murmuring to themselves as if learning something. A fearful racket was heard in Emil's room at intervals, and peals of laughter from the nursery when Rob and Teddy were sent for and hidden from sight whole hours at a time. But the thing that puzzled Mr. Bhaer the most was what became of Rob's big pumpkin. It had been borne in triumph to the kitchen, where a dozen golden-tinted pies soon after appeared. It would not have taken more than a quarter of the mammoth vegetable to make them, yet where was the rest? It disappeared, and Rob never seemed to care, only chuckled, when it was mentioned, and told his father, "To wait and see," for the fun of the whole thing was to surprise Father Bhaer at the end, and not let him know a bit about what was to happen.

He obediently shut eyes, ears, and mouth, and went about trying not to see what was in plain sight, not to hear the tell-tale sounds that filled the air, not to understand any of the perfectly transparent mysteries going on all about him. Being a German, he loved these simple domestic festivals, and encouraged them with all his heart, for they made home so pleasant that the boys did not care to go elsewhere for fun.

When at last the day came, the boys went off for a long walk, that they might have good appetites for dinner; as if they ever needed them! The girls remained at home to help set the table, and give last touches to various affairs which filled their busy little souls with anxiety. The school-room had been shut up since the night before, and Mr. Bhaer was forbidden to enter it on pain of a beating from Teddy, who guarded the door like a small dragon, though he was dying to tell about it, and nothing but his father's heroic self-denial in not listening, kept him from betraying the grand secret.

"It's all done, and it's perfectly splendid," cried Nan, coming out at last with an air of triumph.

"The—you know—goes beautifully, and Silas knows just what to do now," added Daisy, skipping with delight at some unspeakable success.

"I'm blest if it ain't the 'cutest thing I ever see, them critters in particular," and Silas, who had been let into the secret, went off laughing like a great boy.

"They are coming; I hear Emil roaring 'Land lubbers lying down below,' so we must run and dress," cried Nan, and up-stairs they scampered in a great hurry.

The boys came trooping home with appetites that would have made the big turkey tremble, if it had not been past all fear. They also retired to dress; and for half-an-hour there was a washing, brushing, and prinking that would have done any tidy woman's heart good to see. When the bell rang, a troop of fresh-faced lads with shiny hair, clean collars, and Sunday jackets on, filed into the dining-room, where Mrs. Jo, in her one black silk, with a knot of her favorite white chrysanthemums in her bosom, sat at the head of the table, "looking splendid," as the boys said, whenever she got herself up. Daisy and Nan were as gay as a posy bed in their new winter dresses, with bright sashes and hair ribbons. Teddy was gorgeous to behold in a crimson merino blouse, and his best button boots, which absorbed and distracted him as much as Mr. Toot's wristbands did on one occasion.

As Mr. and Mrs. Bhaer glanced at each other down the long table, with those rows of happy faces on either side, they had a little thanksgiving, all to themselves, and without a word, for one heart said to the other,— "Our work has prospered, let us be grateful and go on."

The clatter of knives and forks prevented much conversation for a few minutes, and Mary Ann with an amazing pink bow in her hair "flew round" briskly, handing plates and ladling out gravy. Nearly every one had contributed to the feast, so the dinner was a peculiarly interesting one to the eaters of it, who beguiled the pauses by remarks on their own productions.

"If these are not good potatoes I never saw any," observed Jack, as he received his fourth big mealy one.

"Some of my herbs are in the stuffing of the turkey, that's why it's so nice," said Nan, taking a mouthful with intense satisfaction.

"My ducks are prime any way; Asia said she never cooked such fat ones," added Tommy.

"Well, our carrots are beautiful, ain't they, and our parsnips will be ever so good when we dig them," put in Dick, and Dolly murmured his assent from behind the bone he was picking.

"I helped make the pies with my pumpkin," called out Robby, with a laugh which he stopped by retiring into his mug.

"I picked some of the apples that the cider is made of," said Demi.

"I raked the cranberries for the sauce," cried Nat.

"I got the nuts," added Dan, and so it went on all round the table.

"Who made up Thanksgiving?" asked Rob, for being lately promoted to jacket and trousers he felt a new and manly interest in the institutions of his country.

"See who can answer that question," and Mr. Bhaer nodded to one or two of his best history boys.

"I know," said Demi, "the Pilgrims made it."

"What for?" asked Rob, without waiting to learn who the Pilgrims were.

"I forget," and Demi subsided,

"I believe it was because they were not starved once, and so when they had a good harvest, they said, 'We will thank God for it,' and they had a day and called it Thanksgiving," said Dan, who liked the story of the brave men who suffered so nobly for their faith.

"Good! I didn't think you would remember any thing but natural history," and Mr. Bhaer tapped gently on the table as applause for his pupil.

Dan looked pleased; and Mrs. Jo said to her son, "Now do you understand about it, Robby?"

"No, I don't. I thought pil-grins were a sort of big bird that lived on rocks, and I saw pictures of them in Demi's book."

"He means penguins. Oh, isn't he a little goosey!" and Demi laid back in his chair and laughed aloud.

"Don't laugh at him, but tell him all about it if you can," said Mrs. Bhaer, consoling Rob with more cranberry sauce for the general smile that went round the table at his mistake.

"Well, I will;" and, after a pause to collect his ideas, Demi delivered the following sketch of the Pilgrim Fathers, which would have made even those grave gentlemen smile if they could have heard it.

"You see, Rob, some of the people in England didn't like the king, or something, so they got into ships and sailed away to this country. It was all full of Indians, and bears, and wild creatures, and they lived in forts, and had a dreadful time."

"The bears?" asked Robby, with interest.

"No; the Pilgrims, because the Indians troubled them. They hadn't enough to eat, and they went to church with guns, and ever so many died, and they got out of the ships on a rock, and it's called Plymouth Rock, and Aunt Jo saw it and touched it. The Pilgrims killed all the Indians, and got rich; and hung the witches, and were very good; and some of my greatest great-grandpas came in the ships. One was the Mayflower; and they made Thanksgiving, and we have it always, and I like it. Some more turkey, please."

"I think Demi will be an historian, there is such order and clearness in his account of events;" and Uncle Fritz's eyes laughed at Aunt Jo, as he helped the descendant of the Pilgrims to his third bit of turkey.

"I thought you must eat as much as ever you could on Thanksgiving. But Franz says you mustn't even then;" and Stuffy looked as if he had received bad news.

"Franz is right, so mind your knife and fork, and be moderate, or else you won't be able to help in the surprise by and by," said Mrs. Jo.

"I'll be careful; but everybody does eat lots, and I like it better than being moderate," said Stuffy, who leaned to the popular belief that Thanksgiving must be kept by coming as near apoplexy as possible, and escaping with merely a fit of indigestion or a headache.

"Now, my 'pilgrims' amuse yourselves quietly till tea-time, for you will have enough excitement this evening," said Mrs. Jo, as they rose from the table after a protracted sitting, finished by drinking every one's health in cider.

"I think I will take the whole flock for a drive, it is so pleasant; then you can rest, my dear, or you will be worn out this evening," added Mr. Bhaer; and as soon as coats and hats could be put on, the great omnibus was packed full, and away they went for a long gay drive, leaving Mrs. Jo to rest and finish sundry small affairs in peace.

An early and light tea was followed by more brushing of hair and washing of hands; then the flock waited impatiently for the company to come. Only the family was expected; for these small revels were strictly domestic, and such being the case, sorrow was not allowed to sadden the present festival. All came; Mr. and Mrs. March, with Aunt Meg, so sweet and lovely, in spite of her black dress and the little widow's cap that encircled her tranquil face. Uncle Teddy and Aunt Amy, with the Princess looking more fairy-like than ever, in a sky-blue gown, and a great bouquet of hot-house flowers, which she divided among the boys, sticking one in each button-hole, making them feel peculiarly elegant and festive. One strange face appeared, and Uncle Teddy led the unknown gentleman up to the Bhaers, saying—

"This is Mr. Hyde; he has been inquiring about Dan, and I ventured to bring him tonight, that he might see how much the boy has improved."

The Bhaers received him cordially, for Dan's sake, pleased that the lad had been remembered. But, after a few minutes' chat, they were glad to know Mr. Hyde for his own sake, so genial, simple, and interesting was he. It was pleasant to see the boy's face light up when he caught sight of his friend; pleasanter still to see Mr. Hyde's surprise and satisfaction in Dan's improved manners and appearance, and pleasantest of all to watch the two sit talking in a corner, forgetting the differences of age, culture, and position, in the one subject which interested both, as man and boy compared notes, and told the story of their summer life.

"The performances must begin soon, or the actors will go to sleep," said Mrs. Jo, when the first greetings were over.

So every one went into the school-room, and took seats before a curtain made of two big bed-covers. The children had already vanished; but stifled laughter, and funny little exclamations from behind the curtain, betrayed their whereabouts. The entertainment began with a spirited exhibition of gymnastics, led by Franz. The six elder lads, in blue trousers and red shirts, made a fine display of muscle with dumb-bells, clubs, and weights, keeping time to the music of the piano, played by Mrs. Jo behind the scenes. Dan was so energetic in this exercise, that there was some danger of his knocking down his neighbors, like so many nine-pins, or sending his bean-bags whizzing among the audience; for he was excited by Mr. Hyde's presence, and a burning desire to do honor to his teachers.

"A fine, strong lad. If I go on my trip to South America, in a year or two, I shall be tempted to ask you to lend him to me, Mr. Bhaer," said Mr. Hyde, whose interest in Dan was much increased by the report he had just heard of him.

"You shall have him, and welcome, though we shall miss our young Hercules very much. It would do him a world of good, and I am sure he would serve his friend faithfully."

Dan heard both question and answer, and his heart leaped with joy at the thought of travelling in a new country with Mr. Hyde, and swelled with gratitude for the kindly commendation which rewarded his efforts to be all these friends desired to see him.

After the gymnastics, Demi and Tommy spoke the old school dialogue, "Money makes the mare go." Demi did very well, but Tommy was capital as the old farmer; for he imitated Silas in a way that convulsed the audience, and caused Silas himself to laugh so hard that Asia had to slap him on the back, as they stood in the hall enjoying the fun immensely.

Then Emil, who had got his breath by this time, gave them a sea-song in costume, with a great deal about "stormy winds," "lee shores," and a rousing chorus of "Luff, boys, luff," which made the room ring; after which Ned performed a funny Chinese dance, and hopped about like a large frog in a pagoda hat. As this was the only public exhibition ever had at Plumfield, a few exercises in lightening—arithmetic, spelling, and reading—were given. Jack quite amazed the public by his rapid calculations on the blackboard. Tommy won in the spelling match, and Demi read a little French fable so well that uncle Teddy was charmed.

"Where are the other children?" asked every one as the curtain fell, and none of the little ones appeared.

"Oh, that is the surprise. It's *so* lovely, I pity you because you don't know it," said Demi, who had gone to get his mother's kiss, and stayed by her to explain the mystery when it should be revealed.

Goldilocks had been carried off by Aunt Jo, to the great amazement of her papa, who quite outdid Mr. Bhaer in acting wonder, suspense, and wild impatience to know "what was going to happen."

At last, after much rustling, hammering, and very audible directions from the stage manager, the curtain rose to soft music, and Bess was discovered sitting on a stool beside a brown paper fire-place. A dearer little Cinderella was never seen; for the gray gown was very ragged, the tiny shoes all worn, the face so pretty under the bright hair, and the attitude so dejected, it brought tears as well as smiles, to the fond eyes looking at the baby actress. She sat quite still, till a voice whispered, "Now!"—then she sighed a funny little sigh, and said, "Oh, I wish I tood go to the ball!" so naturally, that her father clapped frantically, and her mother called out, "Little darling!" These highly improper expressions of feeling caused Cinderella to forget herself, and shake her head at them, saying, reprovingly, 'You mustn't 'peak to me."

Silence instantly prevailed, and three taps were heard on the wall. Cinderella looked alarmed, but before she could remember to say, "What is dat?" the back of the brown paper fire-place opened like a door, and, with some difficulty, the fairy godmother got herself and her pointed hat through. It was Nan, in a red cloak, a cap, and a wand, which she waved as she said decidedly—

"You *shall* go to the ball, my dear."

"Now you must pull and show my pretty dess," returned Cinderella, tugging at her brown gown.

"No, no; you must say, 'How can I go in my rags?' " said the godmother in her own voice.

"Oh yes, so I mus"; and the Princess said it, quite undisturbed at her forgetfulness.

"I change your rags into a splendid dress, because you are good," said the godmother in her stage tones; and deliberately unbuttoning the brown pinafore, she displayed a gorgeous sight.

The little Princess really was pretty enough to turn the heads of any number of small princes, for her mamma had dressed her like a tiny court lady, in a rosy silk train with satin under-skirt, and bits of bouquets here and there, quite lovely to behold. The godmother put a crown, with pink and white feathers drooping from it, on her head, and gave her a pair of silver paper slippers, which she put on, and then stood up, lifting her skirts to show them to the audience, saying, with pride, "My dlass ones, ain't they pitty?"

She was so charmed with them, that she was with difficulty recalled to her part, and made to say—

"But I have no toach, Dodmother."

"Behold it!" and Nan waved her wand with such a flourish, that she nearly knocked off the crown of the Princess.

Then appeared the grand triumph of the piece. First, a rope was seen to flap on the floor, to tighten with a twitch as Emil's voice was heard to say, "Heave, a hoy!" and Silas's gruff one to reply, "Stiddy, now, stiddy!" A shout of laughter followed, for four large gray rats appeared, rather shaky as to their legs and queer as to their tails, but quite fine about the head, where black beads shone in the most lifelike manner. They drew, or were intended to appear as if they did, a magnificent coach made of half the mammoth pumpkin, mounted on the wheels of Teddy's wagon, painted yellow to match the gay carriage. Perched on a seat in front sat a jolly little coachman in a white cotton-wool wig, cocked hat, scarlet breeches, and laced coat, who cracked a long whip and jerked the red reins so energetically, that the gray steeds reared finely. It was Teddy, and he beamed upon the company so affably that they gave him a round all to himself; and Uncle Laurie said, "If I could find as sober a coachman as that one, I would engage him on the spot." The coach stopped, the godmother lifted in the Princess, and she was trundled away in state, kissing her hand to the public, with her glass shoes sticking up in front, and her pink train sweeping the ground behind, for, elegant as the coach was, I regret to say that her Highness was rather a tight fit.

The next scene was the ball, and here Nan and Daisy appeared as gay as peacocks in all sorts of finery. Nan was especially good as the proud sister, and crushed many imaginary ladies as she swept about the palace-hall. The Prince, in solitary state upon a somewhat unsteady throne, sat gazing about him from under an imposing crown, as he played with his sword and admired the rosettes in his shoes. When Cinderella came in he jumped up, and exclaimed, with more warmth than elegance,—

"My gracious! Who is that?" and immediately led the lady out to dance, while the sisters scowled and turned up their noses in the corner.

The stately jig executed by the little couple was very pretty, for the childish faces were so earnest, the costumes so gay, and the steps so peculiar, that they looked like the dainty quaint figures painted on a Watteau fan. The Princess's train was very much in her way, and the sword of Prince Rob nearly tripped him up several times. But they overcame these obstacles remarkably well, and finished the dance with much grace and spirit, considering that neither knew what the other was about.

"Drop your shoe," whispered Mrs. Jo's voice as the lady was about to sit down.

"Oh, I fordot!" and, taking off one of the silvery slippers, Cinderella planted it carefully in the middle of the stage, said to Rob, "Now you must try and tatch me," and ran away, while the Prince, picking up the shoe, obediently trotted after her.

The third scene, as everybody knows, is where the herald comes to try on the shoe. Teddy, still in coachman's dress, came in blowing a tin fish-horn melodiously, and the proud sisters each tried to put on the slipper. Nan insisted on playing cut off her toe with a carving-knife, and performed that operation so well that the herald was alarmed, and begged to be "welly keerful." Cinderella then was called, and came in with the pinafore half on, slipped her foot into the slipper, and announced, with satisfaction,—

"I am the Pinsiss."

Daisy wept, and begged pardon; but Nan, who liked tragedy, improved upon the story, and fell in a fainting-fit upon the floor, where she remained comfortably enjoying the rest of the play. It was not long, for the Prince ran in, dropped upon his knees, and kissed the hand of Goldilocks with great ardor, while the herald blew a blast that nearly deafened the audience. The curtain had no chance to fall, for the Princess ran off the stage to her father, crying, "Didn't I do it well?' while the Prince and herald had a fencing-match with the tin horn and wooden sword.

"It was beautiful!" said every one; and, when the raptures had a little subsided, Nat came out with his violin in his hand.

"Hush! Hush!" cried all the children, and silence followed, for something in the boy's bashful manner and appealing eyes made every one listen kindly.

The Bhaers thought he would play some of the old airs he knew so well, but, to their surprise, they heard a new and lovely melody, so softly, sweetly played, that they could hardly believe it could be Nat. It was one of those songs without words that touch the heart, and sing of all tender home-like hopes and joys, soothing and cheering those who listen to its simple music. Aunt Meg leaned her head on Demi's shoulder, Grandmother wiped her eyes, and Mrs. Jo looked up at Mr. Laurie, saying, in a choky whisper,—

"You composed that."

"I wanted your boy to do you honor, and thank you in his own way," answered Laurie, leaning down to answer her.

When Nat made his bow and was about to go, he was called back by many hands, and had to play again. He did so with such a happy face, that it was good to see him, for he did his best, and gave them the gay old tunes that set the feet to dancing, and made quietude impossible.

"Clear the floor!" cried Emil; and in a minute the chairs were pushed back, the older people put safely in corners, and the children gathered on the stage.

"Show your manners!" called Emil; and the boys pranced up to the ladies, old and young, with polite invitations to "tread the mazy," as dear Dick Swiveller has it. The small lads nearly came to blows for the Princess, but she chose Dick, like a kind, little gentle-woman as she was, and let him lead her proudly to her place. Mrs. Jo was not allowed to decline; and Aunt Amy filled Dan with unspeakable delight by refusing Franz and taking him. Of course Nan and Tommy, Nat and Daisy, paired off, while Uncle Teddy went and got Asia, who was longing to "jig it," and felt much elated by the honor done her. Silas and Mary Ann had a private dance in the hall; and for half-an-hour Plumfield was at its merriest.

The party wound up with a grand promenade of all the young folks, headed by the pumpkin-coach with the Princess and driver inside, and the rats in a wildly frisky state.

While the children enjoyed this final frolic, the elders sat in the parlor looking on as they talked together of the little people with the interest of parents and friends.

"What are you thinking of, all by yourself, with such a happy face, sister Jo?" asked Laurie, sitting down beside her on the sofa.

"My summer's work, Teddy, and amusing myself by imagining the future of my boys," she answered, smiling, as she made room for him.

"They are all to be poets, painters, and statesmen, famous soldiers, or at least merchant princes, I suppose."

"No, I am not as aspiring as I once was, and I shall be satisfied if they are honest men. But I will confess that I do expect a little glory and a career for some of them. Demi is not a common child, and I think he will blossom into something good and great in the best sense of the word. The others will do well, I hope, especially my last two boys, for, after hearing Nat play tonight, I really think he has genius."

"Too soon to say; talent he certainly has, and there is no doubt that the boy can soon earn his bread by the work he loves. Build him up for another year or so, and then I will take him off your hands, and launch him properly."

"That is such a pleasant prospect for poor Nat, who came to me six months ago so friendless and forlorn. Dan's future is already plain to me. Mr. Hyde will want him soon, and I mean to give him a brave and faithful little servant. Dan is one who *can* serve well if the wages are love and confidence, and he has the energy to carve out his own future in his own way. Yes, I am very happy over our success with these boys— one so weak, and one so wild; both so much better now, and so full of promise."

"What magic did you use, Jo?"

"I only loved them, and let them see it. Fritz did the rest."

"Dear soul! You look as if 'only loving' had been rather hard work sometimes," said Laurie, stroking her thin cheek with a look of more tender admiration than he had ever given her as a girl.

"I'm a faded old woman, but I'm a very happy one; so don't pity me, Teddy;" and she glanced about the room with eyes full of a sincere content.

"Yes, your plan seems to work better and better every year," he said, with an emphatic nod of approval toward the cheery scene before him.

"How can it fail to work well when I have so much help from you all?" answered Mrs. Jo, looking gratefully at her most generous patron.

"It is the best joke of the family, this school of yours and its success. So unlike the future we planned for you, and yet so suited to you after all. It was a regular inspiration, Jo," said Laurie, dodging her thanks as usual.

"Ah! But you laughed at it in the beginning, and still make all manner of fun of me and my inspirations. Didn't you predict that having girls with the boys would prove a dead failure? Now see how well it works"; and she pointed to the happy group of lads and lassies dancing, singing, and chattering together with every sign of kindly good fellowship.

"I give in, and when my Goldilocks is old enough I'll send her to you. Can I say more than that?"

"I shall be so proud to have your little treasure trusted to me. But really, Teddy, the effect of these girls has been excellent. I know you will laugh at me, but I don't mind, I'm used to it; so I'll tell you that one of my favorite fancies is to look at my family as a small world, to watch the progress of my little men, and, lately, to see how well the influence of my little women works upon them. Daisy is the domestic element, and they all feel the charm of her quiet, womanly ways. Nan is the restless, energetic, strong-minded one; they admire her courage, and give her a fair chance to work out her will, seeing that she has sympathy as well as strength, and the power to do much in their small world. Your Bess is the lady, full of natural refinement, grace, and beauty. She polishes them unconsciously, and fills her place as any lovely woman may, using her gentle influence to lift and hold them above the coarse, rough things of life, and keep them gentlemen in the best sense of the fine old word."

"It is not always the ladies who do that best, Jo. It is sometimes the strong brave woman who stirs up the boy and makes a man of him"; and Laurie bowed to her with a significant laugh.

"No; I think the graceful woman, whom the boy you allude to married, has done more for him than the wild Nan of his youth; or, better still, the wise, motherly woman who watched over him, as Daisy watches over Demi, did most to make him what he is"; and Jo turned toward her mother, who sat a little apart with Meg, looking so full of the sweet dignity and beauty of old age, that Laurie gave her a glance of filial respect and love as he replied, in serious earnest,—

"All three did much for him, and I can understand how well these little girls will help your lads."

"Not more than the lads help them; it is mutual, I assure you. Nat does much for Daisy with his music; Dan can manage Nan better than any of us; and Demi teaches your Goldilocks so easily and well that Fritz calls them Roger Ascham and Lady Jane Grey. Dear me! If men and women would only trust, understand, and help one another as my children do, what a capital place the world would be!" and Mrs. Jo's eyes grew absent, as if she was looking at a new and charming state of society in which people lived as happily and innocently as her flock at Plumfield.

"You are doing your best to help on the good time, my dear. Continue to believe in it, to work for it, and to prove its possibility by the success of your small experiment," said Mr. March, pausing as he passed to say an encouraging word, for the good man never lost his faith in humanity, and still hoped to see peace, good-will, and happiness reign upon the earth.

"I am not so ambitious as that, father. I only want to give these children a home in which they can be taught the few simple things which will help to make life less hard to them when they go out to fight their battles in the world. Honesty, courage, industry, faith in God, their fellow-creatures, and themselves; that is all I try for."

"That is every thing. Give them these helps, then let them go to work out their life as men and women; and whatever their success or failure is, I think they will remember and bless your efforts, my good son and daughter."

The Professor had joined them, and as Mr. March spoke he gave a hand to each, and left them with a look that was a blessing. As Jo and her husband stood together for a moment talking quietly, and feeling that their summer work had been well done if father approved, Mr. Laurie slipped into the hall, said a word to the children, and all of a sudden the whole flock pranced into the room, joined hands and danced about Father and Mother Bhaer, singing blithely—

> "Summer days are over,
>    Summer work is done;
> Harvests have been gathered
>    Gayly one by one.
> Now the feast is eaten,
>    Finished is the play;
> But one rite remains for
>    Our Thanksgiving-day.
>
> "Best of all the harvest
>    In the dear God's sight,
> Are the happy children
>    In the home tonight;
> And we come to offer
>    Thanks where thanks are due,

*With grateful hearts and voices,*
*Father, mother, unto you."*

With the last words the circle narrowed till the good Professor and his wife were taken prisoner by many arms and half hidden by the bouquet of laughing young faces which surrounded them, proving that one plant had taken root and blossomed beautifully in all the little gardens. For love is a flower that grows in any soil, works its sweet miracles undaunted by autumn frost or winter snow, blooming fair and fragrant all the year, and blessing those who give and those who receive.

# Short Stories

*Illustrated by Frank T. Merrill,*
*Addie Ledyard, and Others*

# TESSA'S SURPRISES

## I

LITTLE TESSA sat alone by the fire, waiting for her father to come home from work. The children were fast asleep, all four in the big bed behind the curtain; the wind blew hard outside, and the snow beat on the window-panes; the room was large, and the fire so small and feeble that it didn't half warm the little bare toes peeping out of the old shoes on the hearth.

Tessa's father was an Italian plaster-worker, very poor, but kind and honest. The mother had died not long ago, and left twelve-year old Tessa to take care of the little children. She tried to be very wise and motherly, and worked for them like any little woman; but it was so hard to keep the small bodies warm and fed, and the small souls good and happy, that poor Tessa was often at her wits' end. She always waited for her father, no matter how tired she was, so that he might find his supper warm, a bit of fire, and a loving little face to welcome him. Tessa thought over her troubles at these quiet times, and made her plans; for her father left things to her a good deal, and she had no friends but Tommo, the harp-boy upstairs, and the lively cricket who lived in the chimney. Tonight her face was very sober, and her pretty brown eyes very thoughtful as she stared at the fire and knit her brows, as if perplexed. She was not thinking of her old shoes, nor the empty closet, nor the boys' ragged clothes just then. No; she had a fine plan in her good little head, and was trying to discover how she could carry it out.

You see, Christmas was coming in a week; and she had set her heart on putting something in the children's stockings, as the mother used to do, for while she lived things were comfortable. Now Tessa had not a penny in the world, and didn't know how to get one, for all the father's earnings had to go for food, fire, and rent.

"If there were only fairies, ah! How heavenly that would be; for then,

I should tell them all I wish, and, pop! Behold the fine things in my lap!" said Tessa to herself. "I must earn the money; there is no one to give it to me, and I cannot beg. But what can I do, so small and stupid and shy as I am? I *must* find some way to give the little ones a nice Christmas. I *must!* I *must!*" and Tessa pulled her long hair, as if that would help her think.

But it didn't, and her heart got heavier and heavier; for it did seem hard that in a great city full of fine things, there should be none for poor Nono, Sep, and little Speranza. Just as Tessa's tears began to tumble off her eyelashes on to her brown cheeks, the cricket began to chirp. Of course, he didn't say a word; but it really did seem as if he had answered her question almost as well as a fairy; for, before he had piped a dozen shrill notes, an idea popped into Tessa's head,—such a truly splendid idea that she clapped her hands and burst out laughing. "I'll do it! I'll do it! If father will let me," she said to herself, smiling and nodding at the fire. "Tommo will like to have me go with him and sing, while he plays his harp in the streets. I know many songs, and may get money if I am not frightened; for people throw pennies to other little girls who only play the tambourine. Yes, I will try; and then, if I do well, the little ones shall have a Merry Christmas."

So full of her plan was Tessa, that she ran upstairs at once, and asked Tommo if he would take her with him on the morrow. Her friend was delighted, for he thought Tessa's songs very sweet, and was sure she would get money if she tried.

"But see, then, it is cold in the streets; the wind bites, and the snow freezes one's fingers. The day is very long, people are cross, and at night one is ready to die with weariness. Thou art so small, Tessa, I am afraid it will go badly with thee," said Tommo, who was a merry, black-eyed boy of fourteen, with the kindest heart in the world under his old jacket.

"I do not mind cold and wet and cross people, if I can get the pennies," answered Tessa, feeling very brave with such a friend to help her. She thanked Tommo, and ran away to get ready, for she felt sure her father would not refuse her anything. She sewed up the holes in her shoes as well as she could, for she had much of that sort of cobbling to do; she mended her only gown, and laid ready the old hood and shawl which had been her mother's. Then she washed out little Ranza's frock and put it to dry, because she would not be able to do it the next day. She set the table and got things ready for breakfast, for Tommo went out early, and must not be kept waiting for her. She longed to make the beds and dress the children over night, she was in such a hurry to have all in order; but, as that could not be, she sat down again, and tried over all the songs she knew. Six pretty ones were chosen; and she sung away with all her heart in a fresh little voice so sweetly that the children smiled in their sleep, and her father's tired face brightened as he entered, for Tessa was his cheery cricket on the hearth. When she had told her plan, Peter Benari shook his head, and thought it would never do; but Tessa begged so hard, he consented at last that she should try it for one week, and sent her to bed the happiest little girl in New York.

Next morning the sun shone, but the cold wind blew, and the snow lay thick in the streets. As soon as her father was gone, Tessa flew about and put everything in nice order, telling the children she was going out for the day, and they were to mind Tommo's mother, who would see about the fire and the dinner; for the good woman loved Tessa, and entered into her little plans with all her heart. Nono and Guiseppe, or Sep, as they called him, wondered what she was going away for, and little Ranza cried at being left; but Tessa told them they would know all about it in a week, and have a fine time if they were good; so they kissed her all round and let her go.

Poor Tessa's heart beat fast as she trudged away with Tommo, who slung his harp over his shoulder, and gave her his hand. It was rather a dirty hand, but so kind that Tessa clung to it, and kept looking up at the friendly brown face for encouragement.

"We go first to the *café*, where many French and Italians eat the breakfast. They like my music, and often give me sips of hot coffee, which I like much. You too shall have the sips, and perhaps the pennies, for these people are greatly kind," said Tommo, leading her into a large smoky place, where many people sat at little tables, eating and drinking. "See, now, have no fear, give them 'Bella Monica;' that is merry and will make the laugh," whispered Tommo, tuning his harp.

For a moment Tessa felt so frightened that she wanted to run away; but she remembered the empty stockings at home, and the fine plan, and she resolved *not* to give it up. One fat old Frenchman nodded to her, and it seemed to help her very much; for she began to sing before she thought, and that was the hardest part of it. Her voice trembled, and her cheeks grew redder and redder as she went on; but she kept her eyes fixed on her old shoes, and so got through without breaking down, which was very nice. The people laughed, for the song *was* merry; and the fat man smiled and nodded again. This gave her courage to try another, and she sung better and better each time; for Tommo played his best, and kept whispering to her, "Yes; we go well; this is fine. They will give the money and the blessed coffee."

So they did; for, when the little concert was over, several men put pennies in the cap Tessa offered, and the fat man took her on his knee, and ordered a mug of coffee, and some bread and butter for them both. This quite won her heart; and when they left the *café*, she kissed her hand to the old Frenchman, and said to her friend, "How kind they are! I like this very much; and now it is not hard."

But Tommo shook his curly head, and answered, soberly, "Yes, I took you there first, for they love music, and are of our country; but up among the great houses we shall not always do well. The people there are busy or hard or idle, and care nothing for harps and songs. Do not skip and laugh too soon; for the day is long, and we have but twelve pennies yet."

Tessa walked more quietly, and rubbed her cold hands, feeling that the world was a very big place, and wondering how the children got on at home without the little mother. Till noon they did not earn much, for everyone seemed in a hurry, and the noise of many sleigh-bells drowned the music. Slowly they made their way up to the great squares where the big houses were, with fine ladies and pretty children at the windows. Here Tessa sung all her best songs, and Tommo played as fast as his fingers could fly; but it was too cold to have the windows open, so the pretty children could not listen long, and the ladies tossed out a little money, and soon went back to their own affairs.

All the afternoon the two friends wandered about, singing and playing, and gathering up their small harvest. At dusk they went home,—Tessa so hoarse she could hardly speak, and so tired she fell asleep over her supper. But she had made half a dollar, for Tommo divided the money fairly, and she felt rich with her share. The other days were very much like this; sometimes they made more, sometimes less, but Tommo always "went halves;" and Tessa kept on, in spite of cold and weariness, for her plans grew as her earnings increased, and now she hoped to get useful things, instead of candy and toys alone.

On the day before Christmas she made herself as tidy as she could, for she hoped to earn a good deal. She tied a bright scarlet handkerchief over the old hood, and the brilliant color set off her brown cheeks and bright eyes, as well as the pretty black braids of her hair. Tommo's mother lent her a pair of boots so big that they turned up at the toes, but there were no holes in them, and Tessa felt quite elegant in whole boots. Her hands were covered with chilblains, for she had no mittens; but she put them under her shawl, and scuffled merrily away in her big boots, feeling so glad that the week was over, and nearly three dollars safe in her pocket. How gay the streets were that day! How brisk everyone was, and how bright the faces looked, as people trotted about with big baskets, holly-wreaths, and young evergreens going to blossom into splendid Christmas trees!

"If I could have a tree for the children, I'd never want anything again. But I can't; so I'll fill the socks all full, and be happy," said Tessa, as she looked wistfully into the gay stores, and saw the heavy baskets go by.

"Who knows what may happen if we do well?" returned Tommo, nodding wisely, for he had a plan as well as Tessa, and kept chuckling over it as he trudged through the mud. They did *not* do well, somehow, for everyone seemed so full of their own affairs they could not stop to listen, even to "Bella Monica," but bustled away to spend their money in turkeys, toys, and trees. In the afternoon it began to rain, and poor Tessa's heart to fail her; for the big boots tired her feet, the cold wind made her hands ache, and the rain spoilt the fine red handkerchief. Even Tommo looked sober, and didn't whistle as he walked, for he also was disappointed, and his plan looked rather doubtful, the pennies came in so slowly.

"We'll try one more street, and then go home, thou art so tired, little one. Come; let me wipe thy face, and give me thy hand here in my jacket pocket; there it will be as warm as any kitten;" and kind Tommo brushed away the drops which were not *all* rain from Tessa's cheeks, tucked the poor hand into his ragged pocket, and led her carefully along the slippery streets, for the boots nearly tripped her up.

## II

AT the first house, a cross old gentleman flapped his newspaper at them; at the second, a young gentleman and lady were so busy talking, that they never turned their heads; and at the third, a servant came out and told them to go away, because someone was sick. At the fourth, some people let them sing all their songs, and gave nothing. The next three houses were empty; and the last of all showed not a single face, as they looked up anxiously. It was so cold, so dark and discouraging, that Tessa couldn't help one sob; and, as he glanced down at the little red nose and wet figure beside him, Tommo gave his harp an angry thump, and said something very fierce in Italian. They were just going to turn away; but they didn't, for that angry thump happened to be the best thing they could have done. All of a sudden a little head appeared at the window, as if the sound had brought it; then another and another, till there were five, of all heights and colors, and five eager faces peeped out, smiling and nodding to the two below.

"Sing, Tessa; sing! Quick! Quick!" cried Tommo, twanging away with all his might, and showing his white teeth, as he smiled back at the little gentle-folk.

Bless us! How Tessa did tune up at that! She chirped away like a real bird, forgetting all about the tears on her cheeks, the ache in her hands, and the heaviness at her heart. The children laughed, and clapped their hands, and cried "More! More! Sing another, little girl! Please, do!" And away they went again, piping and playing, till Tessa's breath was gone, and Tommo's stout fingers tingled well.

"Mamma says, come to the door; it's too muddy to throw the money in the street!" cried out a kindly child's voice, as Tessa held up the old cap, with beseeching eyes.

Up the wide stone steps went the street musicians, and the whole flock came running down to give a handful of silver, and ask all sorts of questions. Tessa felt so grateful, that, without waiting for Tommo, she sang her sweetest little song all alone. It was about a lost lamb, and her heart was in the song; therefore, she sang it well, so well, that a pretty young lady came down to listen, and stood watching the bright-eyed child, who looked about her as she sang, evidently enjoying the light and warmth of the fine hall, and the sight of the lovely children with their gay dresses, shining hair, and dainty little shoes.

"You have a charming voice, child. Who taught you to sing?" asked the young lady, kindly.

"My mother. She is dead now; but I do not forget," answered Tessa, in her pretty broken English.

"I wish she could sing at our tree, since Bella is ill," cried one of the children, peeping through the banisters.

"She is not fair enough for the angel, and too large to go up in the tree. But she sings sweetly, and looks as if she would like to see a tree," said the young lady.

"Oh, so much!" exclaimed Tessa; adding eagerly, "my sister Ranza is small and pretty as a baby-angel. She could sit up in the fine tree, and I could sing for her from under the table."

"Sit down and warm yourself, and tell me about Ranza," said the kind elder sister, who liked the confiding little girl, in spite of her shabby clothes.

So Tessa sat down and dried the big boots over the furnace, and told her story, while Tommo stood modestly in the background, and the children listened with faces full of interest.

"O Rose! Let us see the little girl; and if she will do, let us have her, and Tessa can learn our song, and it will be splendid!" cried the biggest boy, who sat astride of a chair, and stared at the harp with round eyes.

"I'll ask mamma," said Rose; and away she went into the dining-room close by. As the door opened, Tessa saw what looked to her like a fairy feast,—all silver mugs and flowery plates and oranges and nuts and rosy wine in tall glass pitchers, and smoking dishes that smelt so deliciously she could not restrain a little sniff of satisfaction.

"Are you hungry?" asked the boy, in a grand tone.

"Yes, sir," meekly answered Tessa.

"I say, mamma; she wants something to eat. Can I give her an orange?" called the boy, prancing away into the splendid room, quite like a fairy prince, Tessa thought.

A plump, motherly lady came out and looked at Tessa, asked a few questions, and then told her to come tomorrow with Ranza, and they would see what could be done. Tessa clapped her hands for joy,—she didn't mind the chilblains now,—and Tommo played a lively march, he was so pleased.

"Will you come, too, and bring your harp? You shall be paid, and shall have something from the tree, likewise," said the motherly lady, who liked what Tessa gratefully told about his kindness to her.

"Ah, yes; I shall come with much gladness, and play as never in my life before," cried Tommo, with a flourish of the old cap that made the children laugh.

"Give these to your brothers," said the fairy prince, stuffing nuts and oranges into Tessa's hands.

"And these to the little girl," added one of the young princesses, flying out of the dining-room with cakes and rosy apples for Ranza.

Tessa didn't know what to say; but her eyes were full, and she just took the mother's white hand in both her little grimy ones, and kissed it many times in her pretty Italian fashion. The lady understood her, and stroked her cheek softly, saying to her elder daughter, "We must take care of this good little creature. Freddy, bring me your mittens; these poor hands must be covered. Alice, get your play-hood; this hand-kerchief is all wet; and, Maud, bring the old chinchilla tippet."

The children ran, and in a minute there were lovely blue mittens on the red hands, a warm hood over the black braids, and a soft "pussy" round the sore throat.

"Ah! So kind, so very kind! I have no way to say 'thank you;' but Ranza shall be for you a heavenly angel, and I will sing my heart out for your tree!" cried Tessa, folding the mittens as if she would say a prayer of thankfulness if she knew how.

Then they went away, and the pretty children called after them, "Come again, Tessa! Come again, Tommo!" Now the rain didn't seem dismal, the wind cold, nor the way long, as they bought their gifts and hurried home, for kind words and the sweet magic of charity had changed all the world to them.

I think the good spirits who fly about on Christmas Eve, to help the

"Sing, Tessa; sing!" cried Tommo.
Tessa's Surprises

loving fillers of little stockings, smiled very kindly on Tessa as she brooded joyfully over the small store of presents that seemed so magnificent to her. All the goodies were divided evenly into three parts and stowed away in father's three big socks, which hung against the curtain. With her three dollars, she had got a pair of shoes for Nono, a knit cap for Sep, and a pair of white stockings for Ranza; to her she also gave the new hood; to Nono the mittens; and to Sep the tippet.

"Now the dear boys can go out, and my Ranza will be ready for the lady to see, in her nice new things," said Tessa, quite sighing with pleasure to see how well the gifts looked pinned up beside the bulging socks, which wouldn't hold them all. The little mother kept nothing for herself but the pleasure of giving everything away; yet, I think, she was both richer and happier than if she had kept them all. Her father laughed as he had not done since the mother died, when he saw how comically the old curtain had broken out into boots and hoods, stockings and tippets.

"I wish I had a gold gown and a silver hat for thee, my Tessa, thou art so good. May the saints bless and keep thee always!" said Peter Benari tenderly, as he held his little daughter close, and gave her the good-night kiss.

Tessa felt very rich as she crept under the faded counterpane, feeling as if she had received a lovely gift, and fell happily asleep with chubby Ranza in her arms, and the two rough black heads peeping out at the foot of the bed. She dreamed wonderful dreams that night, and woke in the morning to find real wonders before her eyes. She got up early, to see if the socks were all right, and there she found the most astonishing sight. Four socks, instead of three; and by the fourth, pinned out quite elegantly, was a little dress, evidently meant for her,—a warm, woollen dress, all made, and actually with bright buttons on it. It nearly took her breath away; so did the new boots on the floor, and the funny long stocking like a gray sausage, with a wooden doll staring out at the top, as if she said, politely, "A Merry Christmas, ma'am!" Tessa screamed and danced in her delight, and up tumbled all the children to scream and dance with her, making a regular carnival on a small scale. Everybody hugged and kissed everybody else, offered sucks of orange, bites of cake, and exchanges of candy; everyone tried on the new things, and pranced about in them like a flock of peacocks. Ranza skipped to and fro airily, dressed in her white socks and the red hood; the boys promenaded in their little shirts, one with his creaking new shoes and mittens, the other in his gay cap and fine tippet; and Tessa put her dress straight on, feeling that her father's "gold gown" was not all a joke. In her long stocking she found all sorts of treasures; for Tommo had stuffed it full of queer things, and his mother had made gingerbread into every imaginable shape, from fat pigs to full omnibuses.

Dear me! What happy little souls they were that morning; and when they were quiet again, how like a fairy tale did Tessa's story sound to them. Ranza was quite ready to be an angel; and the boys promised to be marvellously good, if they were only allowed to see the tree at the "palace," as they called the great house.

Little Ranza was accepted with delight by the kind lady and her children, and Tessa learned the song quite easily. The boys *were* asked; and, after a happy day, the young Italians all returned, to play their parts at the fine Christmas party. Mamma and Miss Rose drilled them all; and, when the folding-doors flew open, one rapturous "Oh!" arose from the crowd of children gathered to the festival. I assure you, it was splendid; the great tree glittering with lights and gifts; and, on her invisible perch, up among the green boughs, sat the little golden-haired angel, all in white, with downy wings, a shining crown on her head, and the most serene satisfaction in her blue eyes, as she stretched her chubby arms to those below, and smiled her baby smile at them. Before anyone could speak, a voice, as fresh and sweet as a lark's, sang the Christmas Carol so blithely, that everyone stood still to hear, and then clapped till the little angel shook on her perch, and cried out, "Be' till, or me'll fall!" How they laughed at that; and what fun they had talking to Ranza, while Miss Rose stripped the tree, for the angel could not resist temptation, and amused herself by eating all the bonbons she could reach, till she was taken down, to dance about like a fairy in a white frock and red shoes. Tessa and her friends had many presents; the boys were perfect lambs, Tommo played for the little folks to dance, and everyone said something friendly to the strangers, so that they did not feel shy, in spite of shabby clothes. It was a happy night; and all their lives they remembered it as something too beautiful and bright to be quite true. Before they went home, the kind mamma told Tessa she should be her friend, and gave her a motherly kiss, which warmed the child's heart and seemed to set a seal upon that promise. It was faithfully kept, for the rich lady had been touched by Tessa's patient struggles and sacrifices; and for many years, thanks to her benevolence, there was no end to Tessa's Surprises.

# CLAMS

## A GHOST STORY

"I HAVEN'T a room in the house, ma'am, but if you don't mind going down to the cottage, and coming up here to your meals, I can accommodate you, and would be glad to," said Mrs. Grant, in answer to my demand for board.

"Where is the cottage?" and I looked about me, feeling ready to accept anything in the way of shelter, after the long, hot journey from broiling Boston, to breezy York Harbor.

"Right down there, just a step, you see. It's all in order, and next week it will be full, for many folks prefer it because of the quiet."

At the end of a precipitous path, which offered every facility for accidents of all sorts, from a sprained ankle to a broken neck, stood the cottage, a little white building with a pretty woodbine over the porch, gay flowers in the garden, and the blue Atlantic rolling up at the foot of the cliff.

"A regular 'Cottage by the Sea.' It will suit me exactly if I can have that front upper room. I don't mind being alone, so have my trunk taken down, please, and I'll get ready for tea," said I, congratulating myself on my good luck. Alas, how little I knew what a night of terror I was to pass in that picturesque abode!

An hour later, refreshed by my tea and invigorated by the delicious coolness, I plunged recklessly into the gayeties of the season, and accepted two invitations for the evening,—one to a stroll on Sunset Hill, the other to a clam-bake on the beach.

The stroll came first, and while my friend paused at one of the fishily-fragrant houses by the way, to interview her washerwoman, I went on to the hilltop, where a nautical old gentleman with a spy-glass welcomed me with the amiable remark,—

"Pretty likely place for a prospeck."

Entering into a conversation with this ancient mariner, I asked if he knew any legend or stories concerning the old houses all about us.

"Sights of em; but it aint allers the *old* places as has the most stories concernin' 'em. Why, that cottage down yonder aint more'n fifty year old, and they say there's been a lot of ghosts seen there, owin' to a man's killin' of himself in the back bedroom."

"What, that house at the end of the lane?" I asked, with sudden interest.

"Jes' so; nice place, but lonesome and dampish. Ghosts and toadstools is apt to locate in houses of that sort," placidly responded the venerable tar.

The dampness scared me more than the goblins, for I never saw a ghost yet, but I had been haunted by rheumatism, and found it a hard fiend to exorcise.

"I've taken a room there, so I'm rather interested in knowing what company I'm to have."

"Took a room, hev you? Wal, I dare say you won't be troubled. Some folks have a knack of seeing sperrits, and then agin some hasn't. My wife is uncommon powerful that way, but I aint; my sight's dreadful poor for that sort of critter."

There was such a sly twinkle in the starboard eye of the old fellow as he spoke, that I laughed outright, and asked, sociably,—

"Has she ever seen the ghosts of the cottage? I think *I* have rather a knack that way, and I'd like to know what to expect."

"No, her sort is the rappin' kind. Down yonder the only ghost I take much stock in is old Bezee Tucker's. He killed himself in the back bedroom, and some folks say they've heard him groanin' there nights, and a drippin' sound; he bled to death, you know. It was kep' quiet at the time, and is forgotten now by all but a few old chaps like me. Bezee was allers civil to the ladies, so I guess he won't bother you, ma'am"; and the old fellow laughed.

"If he does, I'll let you know"; and with that I departed, for my friend called to me that the beach party was clamoring for our company.

In the delights of that festive hour, I forgot the croaking of the ancient mariner, for I was about to taste a clam for the first time in my life, and it was a most absorbing moment. Perched about on the rocks like hungry penguins, we watched the jovial cooks with breathless interest, as they struggled with refractory frying-pans, fish that stubbornly refused to brown, steaming seaweed and hot stones.

A certain captivating little Margie waited upon me so prettily that I should have been tempted to try a sea porcupine unskinned if she had offered it, so irresistible was her chirping way of saying, "Oh, here's a perfectly lovely one! Do take him by his little black head and eat him quick."

So beguiled, I indulged recklessly in clams, served hot between two shells, little dreaming what a price I was to pay for that marine banquet.

We kept up till late, and then I was left at my own door by my friend, who informed me that York was a very primitive, safe place, where people slept with unlocked doors, and nothing ever went amiss o' nights.

I said nothing of the ghosts, being ashamed to own that I quaked a little at the idea of the "back bedroom," as I shut out the friendly faces and bolted myself in.

A lamp and matches stood in the hall, and lighting the lamp, I whisked up stairs with suspicious rapidity, locked my door and retired to bed, firmly refusing to own even to myself that I had ever heard the name of Bezee Tucker.

Being very tired, I soon fell asleep; but fried potatoes and a dozen or two of hot clams are not viands best fitted to insure quiet repose, so a fit of nightmare brought me to a realizing sense of my indiscretion.

From a chaos of wild dreams was finally evolved a gigantic clam, whose mission it was to devour me as I had devoured its relatives. The sharp shells gaped before me, a solemn voice said, "Take her by her little head and eat her quick." Retribution was at hand, and, with a despairing effort to escape by diving, I bumped my head smartly against the wall, and woke up feeling as if there was an earthquake under the bed.

Collecting my scattered wits, I tried to compose myself to slumber again; but alas! That fatal feast had murdered sleep, and I vainly tried to lull my wakeful senses with the rustle of woodbine leaves about the window, and the breaking waves upon the beach.

In one of the pauses between the ebb and flow of the waves, I heard a curious sound in the house,—a muffled sort of moan, coming at regular intervals. And, as I sat up to make out where it was, another sound caught my attentive ear. Drip, drip, drip, went something out in the hall, and in an instant the tale told me on Sunset Hill came back with unpleasant vividness.

"Nonsense! It is raining, and the roof leaks," I said to myself, while a disagreeable thrill went through me, and fancy, aided by indigestion, began to people the house with uncanny inmates.

No rain had fallen for weeks, and peeping through my curtain I saw the big, bright stars shining in a cloudless sky; so that explanation failed, and still the drip, drip, drip went on. Likewise the moaning, so distinctly now that it was evident the little back bedroom was next the chamber in which I was quaking at that identical moment.

"Some one is sleeping there," I said, and then recollected that all the rooms were locked, and all the keys but mine in Mrs. Grant's pocket up at the house.

"Well, let the goblins enjoy themselves; I won't disturb them if they let me alone. Some of the ladies thought me brave to dare to sleep here, and it will never do to own I was scared by a foolish story and an odd sound."

So down I lay, and said the multiplication table industriously for several minutes, trying to turn a deaf ear to the outer world, and curb my unruly thoughts. But it was a failure, and, when I found myself saying over and over "Four times twelve is twenty-four," I gave up affecting courage, and went in for a good honest scare.

As a cheerful subject for midnight meditation I kept thinking of B. Tucker, in spite of every effort to abstain. In vain I recalled the fact that the departed gentleman was "allers civil to the ladies." I still was in mortal fear lest he might think it necessary to come and apologize in person for "bothering" me.

Presently a clock struck three, and I involuntarily gave a groan that beat the ghost's all hollow, so full of anguish was I at the thought of several hours of weary waiting in such awesome suspense.

I was not sure at what time the daylight would appear, and bitterly regretted not gathering useful information about sunrise, tides, and such things, instead of listening to the foolish gossip of Uncle Peter on the hill-top.

Minute after minute dragged slowly on, and I was just thinking that I should be obliged to shout "Fire!" as the only means of relief in my power, when a stealthy step under the window gave me a new sensation.

This was a start, not a scare, for the new visitor was a human foe, and I had little fear of such, being possessed of good lungs, strong arms, and a Roman dagger nearly as big as a carving-knife. That step broke the spell, and, creeping noiselessly to the window, I peeped out to see a dark figure coming up the stem of the tall tree close by, hand over hand, like a sailor or a monkey.

"Two can play at that game, my friend; you scare me, and I'll scare you"; and with an actual sense of relief in breaking the oppressive silence, I suddenly flung up the curtain, and, leaning out, brandished my dagger with what I intended to be an awe-inspiring screech, but, owing to the flutter of my breath, the effort ended in a curious mixture of howl and bray.

A most effective sound nevertheless; for the rascal dropped as if shot, and, with one upward glance at the white figure dimly seen in the star light, fled as if a legion of goblins were at his heels.

"What next?" thought I, wondering whether tragedy or comedy would close this eventful night.

I sat and waited, chilly, but valiant, while the weird sounds went on within, and silence reigned without, till the cheerful crow of the punctual "cockadoo," as Margie called him, announced the dawn and laid the ghosts. A red glow in the east banished my last fear, and, wrapping the drapery of my couch about me, I soon lay down to quiet slumber, quite worn out.

The sun shining in my face waked me; a bell ringing spasmodically warned me to hurry, and a childish voice calling out, "Bet-fast is most weady, Miss Wee," assured me that sweet little spirits haunted the cottage as well as ghostly ones.

As I left my room to join Margie, who was waiting in the porch, and looking like a rosy morning glory half-way up the woodbine trellis, I saw two things which caused me to feel that the horrors of the night were not all imaginary.

Just outside the back bedroom door was a damp place, as if that part of the floor had been newly washed; and when, goaded by curiosity, I peeped through the keyhole of the haunted chamber, my eye distinctly saw an open razor lying on a dusty table.

My vision was limited to that one object, but it was quite enough, and I went up the hill brooding darkly over the secret hidden in my breast. I longed to tell some one, but was ashamed, and, when asked why so pale and absent-minded, I answered, with a gloomy smile,—

"It is the clams."

All day I hid my sufferings pretty well, but as night approached, and I thought of another lonely vigil in the haunted cottage, my heart began to fail, and, when we sat telling stories in the dusk, a brilliant idea came into my head.

I would relate my ghost story, and rouse the curiosity of the listeners to such a pitch that some of them would offer to share my quarters, in hopes of seeing the spirit of the restless Tucker.

Cheered by this delusive fancy, when my turn came I made a thrilling tale of the night's adventures, and, having worked my audience up to a flattering state of excitement, paused for applause.

It came in a most unexpected form, however, for Mrs. Grant burst out laughing, and the two boys, Johnny and Joe rolled off the piazza in convulsions of merriment.

Much disgusted at this unseemly demonstration, I demanded the cause of it, and involuntarily joined in the general shout when Mrs. Grant demolished my ghost by informing me that Bezee Tucker lived, died in, and haunted the tumble-down house at the *other* end of the lane.

"Then who or what made those mysterious noises?" I asked, relieved but rather nettled at the downfall of my romance.

"My brother Seth," replied Mrs. Grant, still laughing. "I thought you might be afraid to be there all alone, so he slipped into the bedroom, and I forgot to tell you. He's a powerful snorer, and that's one of the awful sounds. The other was the dripping of salt water; for you wanted some, and the girl got it in a leaky pail. Seth wiped up the slops when he came out early in the morning."

I said nothing about the keyhole view of the harmless razor, but, feeling that I did deserve some credit for my heroic reception of the burglar, I mildly asked if it was the custom in York for men as well as turkeys to roost in trees.

An explosion from the boys extinguished my last hope of glory, for as soon as he could speak Joe answered, unable to resist the joke, though telling it betrayed his own transgressions.

"Johnny planned to be up awful early, and pick the last cherries off that tree. I wanted to get ahead of him, so I sneaked down before light to humbug him, for I was going a-fishing, and we have to be off by four."

"Did you get your cherries?" I asked, bound to have some of the laugh on my side.

"Guess I didn't," grumbled Joe, rubbing his knees, while Johnny added, with an exulting chuckle,—

"He got a horrid scare and a right good scraping, for he didn't know any one was down there. Couldn't go fishing either, he was so lame, and I had the cherries after all. Served him right, didn't it?"

No answer was necessary, for the two lads indulged in a friendly scuffle among the hay-cocks, while Mrs. Grant went off to repeat the tale in the kitchen, whence the sound of a muffled roar soon assured me that Seth was enjoying the joke as well as the rest of us.

# ONAWANDAH

LONG ago,—when hostile Indians haunted the great forests, and every settlement had its fort for the protection of the inhabitants,—in one of the towns on the Connecticut River, lived Parson Bain and his little son and daughter. The wife and mother was dead; but an old servant took care of them, and did her best to make Reuben and Eunice good children. Her direst threat, when they were naughty, was, "The Indians will come and fetch you, if you don't behave." So they grew up in great fear of the red men. Even the friendly Indians, who sometimes came for food or powder, were regarded with suspicion by the people. No man went to work without his gun near by. On Sundays, when they trudged to the rude meeting-house, all carried the trusty rifle on the shoulder; and while the pastor preached, a sentinel mounted guard at the door, to give warning if canoes came down the river or a dark face peered from the wood.

One autumn night, when the first heavy rains were falling and a cold wind whistled through the valley, a knock came at the minister's door, and, opening it, he found an Indian boy, ragged, hungry, and foot-sore, who begged for food and shelter. In his broken way, he told how he had fallen ill, and been left to die by enemies who had taken him from his own people, months before; how he had wandered for days till almost sinking; and that he had come now to ask for help, led by the hospitable light in the parsonage window.

"Send him away, master, or harm will come of it. He is a spy, and we shall all be scalped by the murdering Injuns who are waiting in the wood," said old Becky, harshly; while little Eunice hid in the old servant's ample skirts, and twelve-year-old Reuben laid his hand on his cross-bow, ready to defend his sister if need be.

But the good man drew the poor lad in, saying, with his friendly smile: "Shall not a Christian be as hospitable as a godless savage? Come in, child, and be fed: you sorely need rest and shelter."

Leaving his face to express the gratitude he had no words to tell, the boy sat by the comfortable fire and ate like a famished wolf, while Becky muttered her forebodings and the children eyed the dark youth at a safe distance. Something in his pinched face, wounded foot, and eyes full of dumb pain and patience, touched the little girl's tender heart, and, yielding to a pitiful impulse, she brought her own basin of new milk and, setting it beside the stranger, ran to hide behind her father, suddenly remembering that this was one of the dreaded Indians.

"That was well done, little daughter. Thou shalt love thine enemies, and share thy bread with the needy. See, he is smiling; that pleased him, and he wishes us to be his friends."

But Eunice ventured no more that night, and quaked in her little bed at the thought of the strange boy sleeping on a blanket before the fire below. Reuben hid his fears better, and resolved to watch while others slept; but was of as soon as his curly head touched the pillow, and dreamed of tomahawks aud war-whoops till morning.

Next day, neighbors came to see the waif, and one and all advised sending him away as soon as possible, since he was doubtless a spy, as Becky said, and would bring trouble of some sort.

"When he is well, he may go whithersoever he will; but while he is too lame to walk, weak with hunger, and worn out with weariness, I will harbor him. He cannot feign suffering and starvation like this. I shall do my duty, and leave the consequences to the Lord," answered the parson, with such pious firmness that the neighbors said no more.

But they kept a close watch upon Onawandah, when he went among them, silent and submissive, but with the proud air of a captive prince, and sometimes a fierce flash in his black eyes when the other lads taunted him with his red skin. He was very lame for weeks, and could only sit in the sun, weaving pretty baskets for Eunice, and shaping bows and arrows for Reuben. The children were soon his friends, for with them he was always gentle, trying in his soft language and expressive gestures to show his good-will and gratitude; for they defended him against their ruder playmates, and, following their father's example, trusted and cherished the homeless youth.

When he was able to walk, he taught the boy to shoot and trap the wild creatures of the wood, to find fish where others failed, and to guide himself in the wilderness by star and sun, wind and water. To Eunice he brought little offerings of bark and feathers; taught her to make moccasins of skin, belts of shells, or pouches gay with porcupine quills and colored grass. He would not work for old Becky,—who plainly showed her distrust,—saying: "A brave does not grind corn and bring wood; that is squaw's work. Onawandah will hunt and fish and fight for you, but no more." And even the request of the parson could not win obedience in this, though the boy would have died for the good man.

"We can not tame an eagle as we can a barnyard fowl. Let him remember only kindness of us, and so we turn a foe into a friend," said Parson Bain, stroking the sleek, dark head, that always bowed before him, with a docile reverence shown to no other living creature.

Winter came, and the settlers fared hardly through the long months, when the drifts rose to the eaves of their low cabins, and the stores, carefully harvested, failed to supply even their simple wants. But the minister's family never lacked wild meat, for Onawandah proved himself a better hunter than any man in the town; and the boy of sixteen led the way on his snow-shoes when they went to track a bear to its den, chase the deer for miles, or shoot the wolves that howled about their homes in the winter nights.

But he never joined in their games, and sat apart when the young folk made merry, as if he scorned such childish pastimes and longed to be a man in all things. Why he stayed when he was well again, no one could tell, unless he waited for spring to make his way to his own people. But Reuben and Eunice rejoiced to keep him; for while he taught them many things, he was their pupil also, learning English rapidly, and proving himself a very affectionate and devoted friend and servant, in his own quiet way.

"Be of good cheer, little daughter; I shall be gone but three days, and our brave Onawandah will guard you well," said the parson, one April morning, as he mounted his horse to visit a distant settlement, where the bitter winter had brought sickness and death to more than one household.

The boy showed his white teeth in a bright smile as he stood beside the children, while Becky croaked, with a shake of the head:—

"I hope you mayn't find you've warmed a viper in your bosom, master."

Two days later, it seemed as if Becky was a true prophet, and that the confiding minister *had* been terribly deceived; for Onawandah went away to hunt, and that night the awful war-whoop woke the sleeping villagers, to find their houses burning, while the hidden Indians shot at them by the light of the fires kindled by dusky scouts. In terror and confusion the whites flew to the fort; and, while the men fought bravely, the women held blankets to catch arrows and bullets, or bound up the hurts of their defenders.

It was all over by daylight, and the red men sped away up the river, with several prisoners, and such booty as they could plunder from the deserted houses. Not till all fear of a return of their enemies was over, did the poor people venture to leave the fort and seek their ruined homes. Then it was discovered that Becky and the parson's children were gone, and great was the bewailing, for the good man was much beloved by all his flock.

Suddenly the smothered voice of Becky was heard by a party of visitors, calling dolefully:—

"I am here, betwixt the beds. Pull me out, neighbors, for I am half dead with fright and smothering."

The old woman was quickly extricated from her hiding-place, and with much energy declared that she had seen Onawandah, disguised with war-paint, among the Indians, and that he had torn away the children from her arms before she could fly from the house.

"He chose his time well, when they were defenseless, dear lambs! Spite of all my warnings, master trusted him, and this is the thanks we get. Oh, my poor master! How can I tell him this heavy news?"

There was no need to tell it; for, as Becky sat moaning and beating her breast on the fireless hearth, and the sympathizing neighbors stood about her, the sound of a horse's hoofs was heard, and the parson came down the hilly road like one riding for his life. He had seen the smoke afar off, guessed the sad truth, and hurried on, to find his home in ruins, and to learn by his first glance at the faces around him that his children were gone.

When he had heard all there was to tell, he sat down upon his door-stone with his head in his hands, praying for strength to bear a grief too deep for words. The wounded and weary men tried to comfort him with hope, and the women wept with him as they hugged their own babies closer to the hearts that ached for the lost children. Suddenly a stir went through the mournful group, as Onawandah came from the wood with a young deer upon his shoulders, and amazement in his face as he saw the desolation before him. Dropping his burden, he stood an instant looking with eyes that kindled fiercely; then he came bounding toward them, undaunted by the hatred, suspicion, and surprise plainly written on the countenances before him. He missed his playmates, and asked but one question:—

"The boy, the little squaw,—where gone?"

His answer was a rough one, for the men seized him and poured forth the tale, heaping reproaches upon him for such treachery and ingratitude. He bore it all in proud silence till they pointed to the poor father, whose dumb sorrow was more eloquent than all their wrath. Onawandah looked at him, and the fire died out of his eyes as if quenched by the tears he would not shed. Shaking off the hands that held him, he went to his good friend, saying with passionate earnestness:—

"Onawandah is *not* traitor! Onawandah remembers! Onawandah grateful! You believe?"

The poor parson looked up at him, and could not doubt his truth; for genuine love and sorrow ennobled the dark face, and he had never known the boy to lie.

"I believe and trust you still, but others will not. Go, you are no longer safe here, and I have no home to offer you," said the parson, sadly, feeling that he cared for none, unless his children were restored to him.

"Onawandah has no fear. He goes; but he comes again to bring the boy, the little squaw."

Few words, but they were so solemnly spoken that the most unbelieving were impressed; for the youth laid one hand on the gray head bowed before him, and lifted the other toward heaven, as if calling the Great Spirit to hear his vow.

A relenting murmur went through the crowd, but the boy paid no heed, as he turned away, and with no arms but his hunting knife and bow, no food but such as he could find, no guide but the sun by day, the stars by night, plunged into the pathless forest and was gone.

Then the people drew a long breath, and muttered to one another:—

"He will never do it, yet he is a brave lad for his years."

"Only a shift to get off with a whole skin, I warrant you. These varlets are as cunning as foxes," added Becky, sourly.

The parson alone believed and hoped, though weeks and months went by, and his children did not come.

Meantime, Reuben and Eunice were far away in an Indian camp, resting as best they could, after the long journey that followed that dreadful night. Their captors were not cruel to them, for Reuben was a stout fellow, and, thanks to Onawandah, could hold his own with the boys who would have tormented him if he had been feeble or cowardly. Eunice also was a hardy creature for her years, and when her first fright and fatigue were over, made herself useful in many ways among the squaws, who did not let the pretty child suffer greatly; though she was neglected, because they knew no better.

Life in a wigwam was not a life of ease, and fortunately the children were accustomed to simple habits and the hardships that all endured in those early times. But they mourned for home till their young faces were pathetic with the longing, and their pillows of dry leaves were often wet with tears in the night. Their clothes grew ragged, their hair unkempt, their faces tanned by sun and wind. Scanty food and exposure to all weathers tried the strength of their bodies, and uncertainty as to their fate saddened their spirits; yet they bore up bravely, and said their prayers faithfully, feeling sure that God would bring them home to father in His own good time.

One day, when Reuben was snaring birds in the wood,—for the Indians had no fear of such young children venturing to escape,—he heard the cry of a quail, and followed it deeper and deeper into the forest, till it ceased, and, with a sudden rustle, Onawandah rose up from the brakes, his finger on his lips to prevent any exclamation that might betray him to other ears and eyes.

"I come for you and little Laroka" (the name he gave Eunice, meaning "Wild Rose"). "I take you home. Not know me yet. Go and wait."

He spoke low and fast; but the joy in his face told how glad he was to find the boy after his long search, and Reuben clung to him, trying not to disgrace himself by crying like a girl, in his surprise and delight.

Lying hidden in the tall brakes they talked in whispers, while one told of the capture, and the other of a plan of escape; for, though a friendly tribe, these Indians were not Onawandah's people, and they must not suspect that he knew the children, else they might be separated at once.

"Little squaw betray me. You watch her. Tell her not to cry out, not speak me any time. When I say come we go—fast—in the night. Not ready yet."

These were the orders Reuben received, and, when he could compose himself, he went back to the wigwams, leaving his friend in the wood, while he told the good news to Eunice, and prepared her for the part she must play.

Fear had taught her self-control, and the poor child stood the test well, working off her relief and rapture by pounding corn on the stone mortar till her little hands were blistered, and her arms ached for hours afterward.

Not till the next day did Onawandah make his appearance, and then he came limping into the village, weary, lame, and half starved, after his long wandering in the wilderness. He was kindly welcomed, and his story believed; for he told only the first part, and said nothing of his life among the white men. He hardly glanced at the children when they were pointed out to him by their captors, and scowled at poor Eunice, who forgot her part in her joy, and smiled as she met the dark eyes that till now had always looked kindly at her. A touch from Reuben warned her, and she was glad to hide her confusion by shaking her long hair over her face, as if afraid of the stranger.

Onawandah took no further notice of them, but seemed to be very

lame with the old wound in his foot, which prevented his being obliged
to hunt with the men. He was resting and slowly gathering strength for
the hard task he had set himself, while he waited for a safe time to save
the children. They understood, but the suspense proved too much for
little Eunice, and she pined with impatience to be gone. She lost appetite
and color, and cast such appealing glances at Onawandah, that he could
not seem quite indifferent, and gave her a soft word now and then, or
did such acts of kindness as he could perform unsuspected. When she
lay awake at night thinking of home, a cricket would chirp outside the
wigwam, and a hand slip in a leaf full of berries, or a bark-cup of fresh
water for the feverish little mouth. Sometimes it was only a caress or a
whisper of encouragement, that re-assured the childish heart, and sent
her to sleep with a comfortable sense of love and protection, like a
sheltering wing over a motherless bird.

Reuben stood it better, and entered heartily into the excitement of
the plot; for he had grown tall and strong in these trying months, and
felt that he must prove himself a man to sustain and defend his sister.
Quietly he put away each day a bit of dried meat, a handful of parched
corn, or a well-sharpened arrowhead, as provision for the journey; while
Onawandah seemed to be amusing himself with making moccasins and
a little vest of deer-skin for an Indian child about the age of Eunice.

At last, in the early autumn, all the men went off on the war-path,
leaving only boys and women behind. Then Onawandah's eyes began
to kindle, and Reuben's heart to beat fast, for both felt that their time
for escape had come.

All was ready, and one moonless night the signal was given. A cricket
chirped shrilly outside the tent where the children slept with one old
squaw. A strong hand cut the skin beside their bed of fir-boughs, and
two trembling creatures crept out to follow the tall shadow that flitted
noiselessly before them into the darkness of the wood. Not a broken
twig, a careless step, or a whispered word betrayed them, and they
vanished as swiftly and silently as hunted deer flying for their lives.

Till dawn they hurried on, Onawandah carrying Eunice, whose strength
soon failed, and Reuben manfully shouldering the hatchet and the pouch
of food. At sunrise they hid in a thicket by a spring and rested, while
waiting for the friendly night to come again. Then they pushed on, and
fear gave wings to their feet, so that by another morning they were far
enough away to venture to travel more slowly and sleep at night.

If the children had learned to love and trust the Indian boy in happier
times, they adored him now, and came to regard him as an earthly
Providence; so faithful, brave, and tender was he,—so forgetful of himself,
so bent on saving them. He never seemed to sleep, ate the poorest
morsels, or went without any food when provision failed; let no danger
daunt him, no hardship wring complaint from him, but went on through
the wild forest, led by guides invisible to them, till they began to hope
that home was near.

Twice he saved their lives. Once, when he went in search of food,
leaving Reuben to guard his sister, the children, being very hungry,
ignorantly ate some poisonous berries which looked like wild cherries,
and were deliciously sweet. The boy generously gave most of them to

Eunice, and soon was terror-stricken to see her grow pale, and cold, and deathly ill. Not knowing what to do, he could only rub her hands and call wildly for Onawandah.

The name echoed through the silent wood, and, though far away, the keen ear of the Indian heard it, his fleet feet brought him back in time, and his knowledge of wild roots and herbs made it possible to save the child when no other help was at hand.

"Make fire. Keep warm. I soon come," he said, after hearing the story and examining Eunice, who could only lift her eyes to him, full of childish confidence and patience.

Then he was off again, scouring the woods like a hound on the scent, searching everywhere for the precious little herb that would counteract the poison. Any one watching him would have thought him crazy, as he rushed hither and thither, tearing up the leaves, creeping on his hands and knees that it might not escape him, and when he found it, springing up with a cry that startled the birds, and carried hope to poor Reuben, who was trying to forget his own pain in his anxiety for Eunice, whom he thought dying.

"Eat, eat, while I make drink. All safe now," cried Onawandah, as he came leaping toward them with his hands full of green leaves, and his dark face shining with joy.

The boy was soon relieved, but for hours they hung over the girl, who suffered sadly, till she grew unconscious and lay as if dead. Reuben's courage failed then, and he cried bitterly, thinking how hard it would be to leave the dear little creature under the pines and go home alone to father. Even Onawandah lost hope for a while, and sat like a bronze statue of despair, with his eyes fixed on his Wild Rose, who seemed fading away too soon.

Suddenly he rose, stretched his arms to the west, where the sun was setting splendidly, and in his own musical language prayed to the Great Spirit. The Christian boy fell upon his knees, feeling that the only help was in the Father who saw and heard them even in the wilderness. Both were comforted, and when they turned to Eunice there was a faint tinge of color on the pale cheeks, as if the evening red kissed her; the look of pain was gone, and she slept quietly, without the moans that had made their hearts ache before.

"He hears! He hears!" cried Onawandah, and for the first time Reuben saw tears in his keen eyes, as the Indian boy turned his face to the sky, full of a gratitude that no words were sweet enough to tell.

All night Eunice lay peacefully sleeping, and the moon lighted Onawandah's lonely watch, for Reuben was worn out with suspense, and slept beside his sister.

In the morning she was safe, and great was the rejoicing; but for two days the little invalid was not allowed to continue the journey, much as they longed to hurry on. It was a pretty sight, the bed of hemlock boughs spread under a green tent of woven branches, and on the pillow of moss the pale child watching the flicker of sunshine through the leaves, listening to the babble of a brook close by, or sleeping tranquilly, lulled by the murmur of the pines. Patient, loving, and grateful, it was a pleasure to serve her, and both the lads were faithful nurses. Onawandah cooked birds for her to eat, and made a pleasant drink of the wild-raspberry leaves to quench her thirst. Reuben snared rabbits, that she might have nourishing food, and longed to shoot a deer for provision, that she might not suffer hunger again on their journey. This boyish desire led him deeper into the wood than it was wise for him to go alone, for it was near nightfall, and wild creatures haunted the forest in those days. The fire, which Onawandah kept constantly burning, guarded their little camp where Eunice lay; but Reuben, with no weapon but his bow and hunting knife, was beyond this protection when he at last gave up his vain hunt and turned homeward. Suddenly, the sound of stealthy steps startled him, but he could see nothing through the dusk at first, and hurried on, fearing that some treacherous Indian was following him. Then he remembered his sister, and resolved not to betray her resting-place if he could help it, for he had learned courage of Onawandah, and longed to be as brave and generous as his dusky hero.

So he paused to watch and wait, and soon saw the gleam of two fiery eyes, not behind, but above him, in a tree. Then he knew that it was an "Indian devil," as they called a species of fierce animal that lurked in the thickets and sprang on its prey like a small tiger.

"If I could only kill it alone, how proud Onawandah would be of me," thought Reuben, burning for the good opinion of his friend.

It would have been wiser to hurry on and give the beast no time to spring; but the boy was over bold, and, fitting an arrow to the string, aimed at the bright eye-ball and let fly. A sharp snarl showed that some harm was done, and, rather daunted by the savage sound, Reuben raced away, meaning to come back next day for the prize he hoped he had secured.

But soon he heard the creature bounding after him, and he uttered one ringing shout for help, feeling too late that he had been foolhardy. Fortunately, he was nearer camp than he thought. Onawandah heard him, and was there in time to receive the beast, as, mad with the pain of the wound, it sprung at Reuben. There was no time for words, and the boy could only watch in breathless interest and anxiety the fight which went on between the brute and the Indian.

It was sharp but short; for Onawandah had his knife, and as soon as he could get the snarling, struggling creature down, he killed it with a skilful stroke. But not before it had torn and bitten him more dangerously than he knew; for the dusk hid the wounds, and excitement kept him from feeling them at first. Reuben thanked him heartily, and accepted his few words of warning with grateful docility; then both hurried back to Eunice, who till next day knew nothing of her brother's danger.

Onawandah made light of his scratches, as he called them, got their supper, and sent Reuben early to bed for tomorrow they were to start again.

Excited by his adventure, the boy slept lightly, and waking in the night, saw by the flicker of the fire Onawandah binding up a deep wound in his breast with wet moss and his own belt. A stifled groan betrayed how much he suffered; but when Reuben went to him, he would accept no help, said it was nothing, and sent him back to bed, preferring to endure the pain in stern silence, with true Indian pride and courage.

Next morning, they set out and pushed on as fast as Eunice's strength allowed. But it was evident that Onawandah suffered much, though he would not rest, forbade the children to speak of his wounds, and pressed on with feverish haste, as if he feared that his strength might not hold out. Reuben watched him anxiously, for there was a look in his face that troubled the boy and filled him with alarm, as well as with remorse and love. Eunice would not let him carry her as before, but trudged bravely behind him, though her feet ached and her breath often failed as she tried to keep up; and both children did all they could to comfort and sustain their friend, who seemed glad to give his life for them.

In three days they reached the river, and, as if Heaven helped them in their greatest need, found a canoe, left by some hunter, near the shore. In they sprang, and let the swift current bear them along, Eunice kneeling in the bow like a little figure-head of Hope, Reuben steering with his paddle, and Onawandah sitting with arms tightly folded over his breast, as if to control the sharp anguish of the neglected wound. He knew that it was past help now, and only cared to see the children safe; then, worn out but happy, he was proud to die, having paid his debt to the good parson, and proved that he was not a liar nor a traitor.

Hour after hour they floated down the great river, looking eagerly for signs of home, and when at last they entered the familiar valley, while the little girl cried for joy, and the boy paddled as he had never done before, Onawandah sat erect, with his haggard eyes fixed on the dim distance, and sang his death-song in a clear, strong voice,—though every breath was pain,—bent on dying like a brave, without complaint or fear.

At last they saw the smoke from the cabins on the hillside, and, hastily mooring the canoe, all sprang out, eager to be at home after their long and perilous wandering. But as his foot touched the land, Onawandah felt that he could do no more, and stretching his arms toward the parsonage, the windows of which glimmered as hospitably as they had done when he first saw them, he said, with a pathetic sort of triumph in his broken voice: "Go. I cannot. Tell the good father, Onawandah not lie, not forget. He keep his promise."

Then he dropped upon the grass and lay as if dead, while Reuben, bidding Eunice keep watch, ran as fast as his tired legs could carry him to tell the tale and bring help.

The little girl did her part tenderly, carrying water in her hands to wet the white lips, tearing up her ragged skirt to lay fresh bandages on the wound that had been bleeding the brave boy's life away, and, sitting by him, gathered his head into her arms, begging him to wait till father came.

But poor Onawandah had waited too long; now he could only look up into the dear, loving, little face bent over him, and whisper wistfully: "Wild Rose will remember Onawandah?" as the light went out of his eyes, and his last breath was a smile for her.

When the parson and his people came hurrying up full of wonder, joy, and good-will, they found Eunice weeping bitterly, and the Indian boy lying like a young warrior smiling at death.

"Ah, my neighbors, the savage has taught us a lesson we never can forget. Let us imitate his virtues, and do honor to his memory," said the pastor, as he held his little daughter close and looked down at the pathetic figure at his feet, whose silence was more eloquent than any words.

All felt it, and even old Becky had a remorseful sigh for the boy who had kept his word so well and given back her darlings safe.

They buried him where he lay; and for years the lonely mound under the great oak was kept green by loving hands. Wild roses bloomed there, and the murmur of the Long River of Pines was a fit lullaby for faithful Onawandah.

# AN OLD-FASHIONED THANKSGIVING

SIXTY years ago, up among the New Hampshire hills, lived Farmer Bassett, with a house full of sturdy sons and daughters growing up about him. They were poor in money, but rich in land and love, for the wide acres of wood, corn, and pasture land fed, warmed, and clothed the flock, while mutual patience, affection, and courage made the old farm-house a very happy home.

November had come; the crops were in, and barn, buttery, and bin were overflowing with the harvest that rewarded the summer's hard work. The big kitchen was a jolly place just now, for in the great fire-place roared a cheerful fire; on the walls hung garlands of dried apples, onions, and corn; up aloft from the beams shone crook-necked squashes, juicy hams, and dried venison—for in those days deer still haunted the deep forests, and hunters flourished. Savory smells were in the air; on the crane hung steaming kettles, and down among the red embers copper sauce-pans simmered, all suggestive of some approaching feast.

A white-headed baby lay in the old blue cradle that had rocked seven other babies, now and then lifting his head to look out, like a round, full moon, then subsided to kick and crow contentedly, and suck the rosy apple he had no teeth to bite. Two small boys sat on the wooden settle shelling corn for popping, and picking out the biggest nuts from the goodly store their own hands had gathered in October. Four young girls stood at the long dresser, busily chopping meat, pounding spice, and slicing apples; and the tongues of Tilly, Prue, Roxy, and Rhody went as fast as their hands. Farmer Bassett, and Eph, the oldest boy, were "chorin' 'round" outside, for Thanksgiving was at hand, and all must be in order for that time-honored day.

To and fro, from table to hearth, bustled buxom Mrs. Bassett, flushed and floury, but busy and blithe as the queen bee of this busy little hive should be.

"I do like to begin seasonable and have things to my mind. Thanksgivin' dinners can't be drove, and it does take a sight of victuals to fill all these hungry stomicks," said the good woman, as she gave a vigorous stir to the great kettle of cider apple-sauce, and cast a glance of housewifely pride at the fine array of pies set forth on the buttery shelves.

"Only one more day and then it will be time to eat. I didn't take but one bowl of hasty pudding this morning, so I shall have plenty of room when the nice things come," confided Seth to Sol, as he cracked a large hazel-nut as easily as a squirrel.

"No need of my starvin' beforehand. *I always* have room enough, and I'd like to have Thanksgiving every day," answered Solomon, gloating like a young ogre over the little pig that lay near by, ready for roasting.

"Sakes alive, I don't, boys! It's a marcy it don' come but once a year. I should be worn to a thread-paper with all this extra work atop of my winter weavin' and spinnin'," laughed their mother, as she plunged her plump arms into the long bread-trough and began to knead the dough as if a famine was at hand.

Tilly, the oldest girl, a red-cheeked, black-eyed lass of fourteen, was grinding briskly at the mortar, for spices were costly, and not a grain must be wasted. Prue kept time with the chopper, and the twins sliced away at the apples till their little brown arms ached, for all knew how to work, and did so now with a will.

"I think it's real fun to have Thanksgiving at home. I'm sorry Gran'ma is sick, so we can't go there as usual, but I like to mess 'round here, don't you, girls?" asked Tilly, pausing to take a sniff at the spicy pestle.

"It will be kind of lonesome with only our own folks." "I like to see all the cousins and aunts, and have games, and sing," cried the twins, who were regular little romps, and could run, swim, coast and shout as well as their brothers.

"I don't care a mite for all that. It will be so nice to eat dinner together, warm and comfortable at home," said quiet Prue, who loved her own cozy nooks like a cat.

"Come, girls, fly 'round and get your chores done, so we can clear away for dinner jest as soon as I clap my bread into the oven," called Mrs. Bassett presently, as she rounded off the last loaf of brown bread which was to feed the hungry mouths that seldom tasted any other.

"Here's a man comin' up the hill, lively!" "Guess it's Gad Hopkins. Pa told him to bring a dezzen oranges, if they warn't too high!" shouted Sol and Seth, running to the door, while the girls smacked their lips at the thought of this rare treat, and Baby threw his apple overboard, as if getting ready for a new cargo.

But all were doomed to disappointment, for it was not Gad, with the much-desired fruit. It was a stranger, who threw himself off his horse and hurried up to Mr. Bassett in the yard, with some brief message that made the farmer drop his ax and look so sober that his wife guessed at once some bad news had come; and crying, "Mother's wuss! I know she is!" out ran the good woman, forgetful of the flour on her arms and the oven waiting for its most important batch.

The man said old Mr. Chadwick, down to Keene, stopped him as he passed, and told him to tell Mrs. Bassett her mother was failin' fast, and she'd better come today. He knew no more, and having delivered his errand he rode away, saying it looked like snow and he must be jogging, or he wouldn't get home till night.

"We must go right off, Eldad. Hitch up, and I'll be ready in less'n no time," said Mrs. Bassett, wasting not a minute in tears and lamentations, but pulling off her apron as she went in, with her mind in a sad jumble of bread, anxiety, turkey, sorrow, haste, and cider apple-sauce.

A few words told the story, and the children left their work to help her get ready, mingling their grief for "Gran'ma" with regrets for the lost dinner.

"I'm dreadful sorry, dears, but it can't be helped. I couldn't cook nor eat no way, now, and if that blessed woman gets better sudden, as she has before, we'll have cause for thanksgivin', and I'll give you a dinner you won't forget in a hurry," said Mrs. Bassett, as she tied on her brown silk pumpkin-hood, with a sob for the good old mother who had made it for her.

Not a child complained after that, but ran about helpfully, bringing moccasins, heating the footstone, and getting ready for a long drive, because Gran'ma lived twenty miles away, and there were no railroads in those parts to whisk people to and fro like magic. By the time the old yellow sleigh was at the door, the bread was in the oven, and Mrs. Bassett was waiting, with her camlet cloak on, and the baby done up like a small bale of blankets.

"Now, Eph, you must look after the cattle like a man, and keep up the fires, for there's a storm brewin', and neither the children nor dumb critters must suffer," said Mr. Bassett, as he turned up the collar of his rough coat and put on his blue mittens, while the old mare shook her bells as if she preferred a trip to Keene to hauling wood all day.

"Tilly, put extry comfortables on the beds tonight, the wind is so searchin' up chamber. Have the baked beans and Injun-puddin' for dinner, and whatever you do, don't let the boys git at the mince-pies, or you'll have them down sick. I shall come back the minute I can leave Mother. Pa will come tomorrer, anyway, so keep snug and be good. I depend on you, my darter; use your jedgment, and don't let nothin' happen while Mother's away."

"Yes'm, yes'm—good-bye, good-bye!" called the children, as Mrs. Bassett was packed into the sleigh and driven away, leaving a stream of directions behind her.

Eph, the sixteen-year-old boy, immediately put on his biggest boots, assumed a sober, responsible manner, and surveyed his little responsibilities with a paternal air, drolly like his father's. Tilly tied on her mother's bunch of keys, rolled up the sleeves of her homespun gown, and began to order about the younger girls. They soon forgot poor Granny, and found it great fun to keep house all alone, for Mother seldom left home, but ruled her family in the good old-fashioned way. There were no servants, for the little daughters were Mrs. Bassett's only maids, and the stout boys helped their father, all working happily together with no wages but love; learning in the best manner the use of the heads and hands with which they were to make their own way in the world.

The few flakes that caused the farmer to predict bad weather soon increased to a regular snow-storm, with gusts of wind, for up among the hills winter came early and lingered long. But the children were busy, gay, and warm in-doors, and never minded the rising gale nor the whirling white storm outside.

Tilly got them a good dinner, and when it was over the two elder girls went to their spinning, for in the kitchen stood the big and little wheels, and baskets of wool-rolls, ready to be twisted into yarn for the winter's knitting, and each day brought its stint of work to the daughters, who hoped to be as thrifty as their mother.

Eph kept up a glorious fire, and superintended the small boys, who popped corn and whittled boats on the hearth; while Roxy and Rhody dressed corn-cob dolls in the settle corner, and Bose, the brindled mastiff, lay on the braided mat, luxuriously warming his old legs. Thus employed, they made a pretty picture, these rosy boys and girls, in their homespun suits, with the rustic toys or tasks which most children nowadays would find very poor or tiresome.

Tilly and Prue sang, as they stepped to and fro, drawing out the smoothly twisted threads to the musical hum of the great spinning-wheels. The little girls chattered like magpies over their dolls and the new bed-spread they were planning to make, all white dimity stars on a blue calico ground, as a Christmas present to Ma. The boys roared at Eph's jokes, and had rough and tumble games over Bose, who didn't mind them in the least; and so the afternoon wore pleasantly away.

At sunset the boys went out to feed the cattle, bring in heaps of wood, and lock up for the night, as the lonely farm-house seldom had visitors after dark. The girls got the simple supper of brown bread and milk, baked apples, and a doughnut all 'round as a treat. Then they sat before the fire, the sisters knitting, the brothers with books or games, for Eph loved reading, and Sol and Seth never failed to play a few games of Morris with barley corns, on the little board they had made themselves at one corner of the dresser.

"Read out a piece," said Tilly, from Mother's chair, where she sat in state, finishing off the sixth woolen sock she had knit that month.

"It's the old history book, but here's a bit you may like, since it's about our folks," answered Eph, turning the yellow page to look at a picture of two quaintly dressed children in some ancient castle.

"Yes, read that. I always like to hear about the Lady Matildy I was named for, and Lord Bassett, Pa's great-great-great-grandpa. He's only a farmer now, but it's nice to know that we were somebody two or three hundred years ago," said Tilly, bridling and tossing her curly head as she fancied the Lady Matilda might have done.

"Don't read the queer words, 'cause we don't understand 'em. Tell it," commanded Roxy, from the cradle, where she was drowsily cuddled with Rhody.

"Well, a long time ago, when Charles the First was in prison, Lord Bassett was a true friend to him," began Eph, plunging into his story without delay. "The lord had some papers that would have hung a lot of people if the king's enemies got hold of 'em, so when he heard one day, all of a sudden, that soldiers were at the castle-gate to carry him off, he had just time to call his girl to him, and say: 'I may be going to my death, but I wont betray my master. There is no time to burn the papers, and I can not take them with me; they are hidden in the old leathern chair where I sit. No one knows this but you, and you must guard them till I come or send you a safe messenger to take them away. Promise me to be brave and silent, and I can go without fear.' You see, he wasn't afraid to die, but he *was* to seem a traitor. Lady Matildy promised solemnly, and the words were hardly out of her mouth when the men came in, and her father was carried away a prisoner and sent off to the Tower.

"But she didn't cry; she just called her brother, and sat down in that chair, with her head leaning back on those papers, like a queen, and waited while the soldiers hunted the house over for 'em: wasn't that a smart girl?" cried Tilly, beaming with pride, for she was named for this ancestress, and knew the story by heart.

"I reckon she was scared, though, when the men came swearin' in and asked her if she knew anything about it. The boy did his part then, for *he* didn't know, and fired up and stood before his sister; and he says, says he, as bold as a lion: 'If my lord had told us where the papers be, we would die before we would betray him. But we are children and know nothing, and it is cowardly of you to try to fright us with oaths and drawn swords!' "

As Eph quoted from the book, Seth planted himself before Tilly, with the long poker in his hand, saying, as he flourished it valiantly:

"Why didn't the boy take his father's sword and lay about him? I would, if any one was ha'sh to Tilly."

"You bantam! He was only a bit of a boy, and couldn't do anything. Sit down and hear the rest of it," commanded Tilly, with a pat on the yellow head, and a private resolve that Seth should have the largest piece of pie at dinner next day, as reward for his chivalry.

"Well, the men went off after turning the castle out of window, but they said they should come again; so faithful Matildy was full of trouble, and hardly dared to leave the room where the chair stood. All day she sat there, and at night her sleep was so full of fear about it, that she often got up and went to see that all was safe. The servants thought the fright had hurt her wits, and let her be, but Rupert, the boy, stood by her and never was afraid of her queer ways. She was 'a pious maid,' the book says, and often spent the long evenings reading the Bible, with her brother by her, all alone in the great room, with no one to help her bear her secret, and no good news of her father. At last, word came that the king was dead and his friends banished out of England. Then the poor children were in a sad plight, for they had no mother, and the servants all ran away, leaving only one faithful old man to help them."

"But the father did come?" cried Roxy, eagerly.

"You'll see," continued Eph, half telling, half reading.

"Matilda was sure he would, so she sat on in the big chair, guarding the papers, and no one could get her away, till one day a man came with her father's ring and told her to give up the secret. She knew the ring, but would not tell until she had asked many questions, so as to be very sure, and while the man answered all about her father and the king, she looked at him sharply. Then she stood up and said, in a tremble, for there was something strange about the man: 'Sir, I doubt you in spite of the ring, and I will not answer till you pull off the false beard you wear, that I may see your face and know if you are my father's friend or foe.' Off came the disguise, and Matilda found it was my lord himself, come to take them with him out of England. He was very proud of that faithful girl, I guess, for the old chair still stands in the castle, and the name keeps in the family, Pa says, even over here, where some of the Bassetts came along with the Pilgrims."

"Our Tilly would have been as brave, I know, and she looks like the old picter down to Grandma's don't she, Eph?" cried Prue, who admired her bold, bright sister very much.

"Well, I think you'd do the settin' part best, Prue, you are so patient. Till would fight like a wild cat, but she can't hold her tongue worth a cent," answered Eph; whereat Tilly pulled his hair, and the story ended with a general frolic.

When the moon-faced clock behind the door struck nine, Tilly tucked up the children under the "extry comfortables," and having kissed them all around, as Mother did, crept into her own nest, never minding the little drifts of snow that sifted in upon her coverlet between the shingles of the roof, nor the storm that raged without.

As if he felt the need of unusual vigilance, old Bose lay down on the mat before the door, and pussy had the warm hearth all to herself. If any late wanderer had looked in at midnight, he would have seen the fire blazing up again, and in the cheerful glow the old cat blinking her yellow eyes, as she sat bolt upright beside the spinning-wheel, like some sort of household goblin, guarding the children while they slept.

When they woke, like early birds, it still snowed, but up the little Bassetts jumped, broke the ice in their pitchers, and went down with cheeks glowing like winter apples, after a brisk scrub and scramble into their clothes. Eph was off to the barn, and Tilly soon had a great kettle of mush ready, which, with milk warm from the cows, made a wholesome breakfast for the seven hearty children.

"Now about dinner," said the young housekeeper, as the pewter spoons stopped clattering, and the earthen bowls stood empty.

"Ma said, have what we liked, but she didn't expect us to have a real Thanksgiving dinner, because she wont be here to cook it, and we don't know how," began Prue, doubtfully.

"I can roast a turkey and make a pudding as well as anybody, I guess. The pies are all ready, and if we can't boil vegetables and so on, we don't deserve any dinner," cried Tilly, burning to distinguish herself, and bound to enjoy to the utmost her brief authority.

"Yes, yes!" cried all the boys, "let's have a dinner anyway; Ma wont care, and the good victuals will spoil if they aint eaten right up."

"Pa is coming tonight, so we wont have dinner till late; that will be real genteel and give us plenty of time," added Tilly, suddenly realizing the novelty of the task she had undertaken.

"Did you ever roast a turkey?" asked Roxy, with an air of deep interest.

"Should you darst to try?" said Rhody, in an awe-stricken tone.

"You will see what I can do. Ma said I was to use my jedgment about things, and I'm going to. All you children have got to do is to keep out of the way and let Prue and me work. Eph, I wish you'd put a fire in the best room, so the little ones can play in there. We shall want the settin'-room for the table, and I wont have 'em pickin' 'round when we get things fixed," commanded Tilly, bound to make her short reign a brilliant one.

"I don't know about that. Ma didn't tell us to," began cautious Eph, who felt that this invasion of the sacred best parlor was a daring step.

"Don't we always do it Sundays and Thanksgivings? Wouldn't Ma wish the children kept safe and warm anyhow? Can I get up a nice dinner with four rascals under my feet all the time? Come, now, if you want roast turkey and onions, plum-puddin' and mince-pie, you'll have to do as I tell you, and be lively about it."

Tilly spoke with such spirit, and her last suggestion was so irresistible, that Eph gave in, and, laughing good-naturedly, tramped away to heat up the best room, devoutly hoping that nothing serious would happen to punish such audacity.

The young folks delightedly trooped in to destroy the order of that prim apartment with housekeeping under the black horse-hair sofa, "horseback riders" on the arms of the best rocking-chair, and an Indian war-dance all over the well-waxed furniture. Eph, finding the society of the peaceful sheep and cows more to his mind than that of two excited sisters, lingered over his chores in the barn as long as possible, and left the girls in peace.

Now Tilly and Prue were in their glory, and as soon as the breakfast things were out of the way, they prepared for a grand cooking-time. They were handy girls, though they had never heard of a cooking-school, never touched a piano, and knew nothing of embroidery beyond the samplers which hung framed in the parlor; one ornamented with a pink mourner under a blue weeping-willow, the other with this pleasing verse, each word being done in a different color, which gave the effect of a distracted rainbow:

> *"This sampler neat was worked by me,*
> *In my twelfth year, Prudence B."*

Both rolled up their sleeves, put on their largest aprons, and got out all the spoons, dishes, pots, and pans they could find, "so as to have everything handy," as Prue said.

"Now, sister, we'll have dinner at five; Pa will be here by that time if he is coming tonight, and be so surprised to find us all ready, for he wont have had any very nice victuals if Gran'ma is so sick," said Tilly importantly. "I shall give the children a piece at noon" (Tilly meant luncheon); "doughnuts and cheese, with apple-pie and cider will please 'em. There's beans for Eph; he likes cold pork, so we wont stop to warm it up, for there's lots to do and I don't mind saying to you I'm dreadful dubersome about the turkey."

"It's all ready but the stuffing, and roasting is as easy as can be. I can baste first rate. Ma always likes to have me, I'm so patient and stiddy, she says," answered Prue, for the responsibility of this great undertaking did not rest upon her, so she took a cheerful view of things.

"I know, but it's the stuffin' that troubles me," said Tilly, rubbing her round elbows as she eyed the immense fowl laid out on a platter before her. "I don't know how much I want, nor what sort of yarbs to put in, and he's so awful big, I'm kind of afraid of him."

"I aint! I fed him all summer, and he never gobbled at *me*. I feel real mean to be thinking of gobbling him, poor old chap," laughed Prue, patting her departed pet with an air of mingled affection and appetite.

"Well, I'll get the puddin' off my mind fust, for it ought to bile all day. Put the big kettle on, and see that the spit is clean, while I get ready."

Prue obediently tugged away at the crane, with its black hooks, from which hung the iron tea-kettle and three-legged pot; then she settled the long spit in the grooves made for it in the tall andirons, and put the dripping-pan underneath, for in those days meat was roasted as it should be, not baked in ovens.

Meantime Tilly attacked the plum-pudding. She felt pretty sure of coming out right, here, for she had seen her mother do it so many times, it looked very easy. So in went suet and fruit; all sorts of spice, to be sure she got the right ones, and brandy instead of wine. But she forgot both sugar and salt, and tied it in the cloth so tightly that it had no room to swell, so it would come out as heavy as lead and as hard as a cannon-ball, if the bag did not burst and spoil it all. Happily unconscious of these mistakes, Tilly popped it into the pot, and proudly watched it bobbing about before she put the cover on and left it to its fate.

"I can't remember what flavorin' Ma puts in," she said, when she had got her bread well soaked for the stuffing. "Sage and onions and apple-sauce go with goose, but I can't feel sure of anything but pepper and salt for a turkey."

"Ma puts in some kind of mint, I know, but I forget whether it is spearmint, peppermint, or penny-royal," answered Prue, in a tone of doubt, but trying to show her knowledge of "yarbs," or, at least, of their names.

"Seems to me it's sweet marjoram or summer savory. I guess we'll put both in, and then we are sure to be right. The best is up garret; you run and get some, while I mash the bread," commanded Tilly, diving into the mess.

Away trotted Prue, but in her haste she got catnip and wormwood, for the garret was darkish, and Prue's little nose was so full of the smell of the onions she had been peeling, that everything smelt of them. Eager to be of use, she pounded up the herbs and scattered the mixture with a liberal hand into the bowl.

"It doesn't smell just right, but I suppose it will when it is cooked," said Tilly, as she filled the empty stomach, that seemed aching for food, and sewed it up with the blue yarn, which happened to be handy. She forgot to tie down his legs and wings, but she set him by till his hour came, well satisfied with her work.

"Shall we roast the little pig, too? I think he'd look nice with a necklace of sausages, as Ma fixed one last Christmas," asked Prue, elated with their success.

"I couldn't do it. I loved that little pig, and cried when he was killed. I should feel as if I was roasting the baby," answered Tilly, glancing toward the buttery where piggy hung, looking so pink and pretty it certainly did seem cruel to eat him.

It took a long time to get all the vegetables ready, for, as the cellar was full, the girls thought they would have every sort. Eph helped, and by noon all was ready for cooking, and the cranberry-sauce, a good deal scorched, was cooling in the lean-to.

Luncheon was a lively meal, and doughnuts and cheese vanished in such quantities that Tilly feared no one would have an appetite for her sumptuous dinner. The boys assured her they would be starving by fve o'clock, and Sol mourned bitterly over the little pig that was not to be served up.

"Now you all go and coast, while Prue and I set the table and get out the best chiny," said Tilly, bent on having her dinner look well, no matter what its other failings might be.

Out came the rough sleds, on went the round hoods, old hats, red cloaks, and moccasins, and away trudged the four younger Bassetts, to disport themselves in the snow, and try the ice down by the old mill, where the great wheel turned and splashed so merrily in the summer-time.

Eph took his fiddle and scraped away to his heart's content in the parlor, while the girls, after a short rest, set the table and made all ready to dish up the dinner when that exciting moment came. It was not at all the sort of table we see now, but would look very plain and countrified to us, with its green-handled knives and two-pronged steel forks; its red-and-white china, and pewter platters, scoured till they shone, with mugs and spoons to match, and a brown jug for the cider. The cloth was coarse, but white as snow, and the little maids had seen the blue-eyed flax grow, out of which their mother wove the linen they had watched and watered while it bleached in the green meadow. They had no napkins and little silver; but the best tankard and Ma's few wedding spoons were set forth in state. Nuts and apples at the corners gave an air, and the place of honor was left in the middle for the oranges yet to come.

"Don't it look beautiful?" said Prue, when they paused to admire the general efect.

"Pretty nice, I think. I wish Ma could see how well we can do it," began Tilly, when a loud howling startled both girls, and sent them flying to the window. The short afternoon had passed so quickly that twilight had come before they knew it, and now, as they looked out through the gathering dusk, they saw four small black figures tearing up the road, to come bursting in, all screaming at once: "The bear, the bear! Eph, get the gun! He's coming, he's coming!"

Eph had dropped his fiddle, and got down his gun before the girls could calm the children enough to tell their story, which they did in a somewhat incoherent manner. "Down in the holler, coastin', we heard a growl," began Sol, with his eyes as big as saucers. "I see him fust lookin' over the wall," roared Seth, eager to get his share of honor.

"Awful big and shaggy," quavered Roxy, clinging to Tilly, while Rhody hid in Prue's skirts, and piped out: "His great paws kept clawing at us, and I was so scared my legs would hardly go."

"We ran away as fast as we could go, and he come growling after us. He's awful hungry, and he'll eat every one of us if he gets in;" continued Sol, looking about him for a safe retreat.

"Oh, Eph, don't let him eat us," cried both little girls, flying up stairs to hide under their mother's bed, as their surest shelter.

"No danger of that, you little geese. I'll shoot him as soon as he comes. Get out of the way, boys," and Eph raised the window to get good aim.

"There he is! Fire away, and don't miss!" cried Seth, hastily following Sol, who had climbed to the top of the dresser as a good perch from which to view the approaching fray.

Prue retired to the hearth as if bent on dying at her post rather than desert the turkey, now "browning beautiful," as she expressed it. But Tilly boldly stood at the open window, ready to lend a hand if the enemy proved too much for Eph.

All had seen bears, but none had ever come so near before, and even brave Eph felt that the big brown beast slowly trotting up the door-yard was an unusually formidable specimen. He was growling horribly, and stopped now and then as if to rest and shake himself.

"Get the ax, Tilly, and if I should miss, stand ready to keep him off while I load again," said Eph, anxious to kill his first bear in style and alone; a girl's help didn't count.

Tilly flew for the ax, and was at her brother's side by the time the bear was near enough to be dangerous. He stood on his hind legs, and seemed to sniff with relish the savory odors that poured out of the window.

"Fire, Eph!" cried Tilly, firmly.

"Wait till he rears again. I'll get a better shot, then," answered the boy, while Prue covered her ears to shut out the bang, and the small boys cheered from their dusty refuge up among the pumpkins.

But a very singular thing happened next, and all who saw it stood amazed, for suddenly Tilly threw down the ax, flung open the door, and ran straight into the arms of the bear, who stood erect to receive her, while his growlings changed to a loud "Haw, haw!" that startled the children more than the report of a gun.

"It's Gad Hopkins, tryin' to fool us!" cried Eph, much disgusted at the loss of his prey, for these hardy boys loved to hunt, and prided themselves on the number of wild animals and birds they could shoot in a year.

"Oh, Gad, how could you scare us so?" laughed Tilly, still held fast in one shaggy arm of the bear, while the other drew a dozen oranges from some deep pocket in the buffalo-skin coat, and fired them into the kitchen with such good aim that Eph ducked, Prue screamed, and Sol and Seth came down much quicker than they went up.

"Wal, you see I got upsot over yonder, and the old horse went home while I was floundering in a drift, so I tied on the buffalers to tote 'em easy, and come along till I see the children playin' in the holler. I jest meant to give 'em a little scare, but they run like partridges, and I kep' up the joke to see how Eph would like this sort of company," and Gad haw-hawed again.

"You'd have had a warm welcome if we hadn't found you out. I'd have put a bullet through you in a jiffy, old chap," said Eph, coming out to shake hands with the young giant, who was only a year or two older than himself.

"Come in and set up to dinner with us. Prue and I have done it all ourselves, and Pa will be along soon, I reckon," cried Tilly, trying to escape.

Suddenly Tilly ran straight into the arms of the bear.
An Old-Fashioned Thanksgiving

"Couldn't, no ways. My folks will think I'm dead ef I don't get along home, sence the horse and sleigh have gone ahead empty. I've done my arrant and had my joke; now I want my pay, Tilly," and Gad took a hearty kiss from the rosy cheeks of his "little sweetheart," as he called her. His own cheeks tingled with the smart slap she gave him as she ran away, calling out that she hated bears and would bring her ax next time.

"I aint afeared; your sharp eyes found me out; and ef you run into a bear's arms you must expect a hug," answered Gad, as he pushed back the robe and settled his fur cap more becomingly.

"I should have known you in a minute if I hadn't been asleep when the girls squalled. You did it well, though, and I advise you not to try it again in a hurry, or you'll get shot," said Eph, as they parted, he rather crestfallen and Gad in high glee.

"My sakes alive—the turkey is burnt one side, and the kettles have biled over so the pies I put to warm are all ashes!" scolded Tilly, as the flurry subsided and she remembered her dinner.

"Well, I can't help it. I couldn't think of victuals when I expected to be eaten alive myself, could I?" pleaded poor Prue, who had tumbled into the cradle when the rain of oranges began.

Tilly laughed, and all the rest joined in, so good humor was restored, and the spirits of the younger ones were revived by sucks from the one orange which passed from hand to hand with great rapidity, while the older girls dished up the dinner. They were just struggling to get the pudding out of the cloth when Roxy called out, "Here's Pa!"

"There's folks with him," added Rhody.

"Lots of 'em! I see two big sleighs chock full," shouted Seth, peering through the dusk.

"It looks like a seminary. Guess Gramma's dead and come up to be buried here," said Sol in a solemn tone. This startling suggestion made Tilly, Prue, and Eph hasten to look out, full of dismay at such an ending of their festival.

"If that is a funeral; the mourners are uncommon jolly," said Eph, drily, as merry voices and loud laughter broke the white silence without.

"I see Aunt Cinthy, and Cousin Hetty—and there's Mose and Amos. I do declare, Pa's bringin' 'em all home to have some fun here," cried Prue, as she recognized one familiar face after another.

"Oh, my patience! Aint I glad I got dinner, and don't I hope it will turn out good!" exclaimed Tilly, while the twins pranced with delight, and the small boys roared:

"Hooray for Pa! Hooray for Thanksgivin'!"

The cheer was answered heartily, and in came Father, Mother, Baby, aunts and cousins, all in great spirits, and all much surprised to find such a festive welcome awaiting them.

"Aint Gran'ma dead at all?" asked Sol, in the midst of the kissing and hand-shaking.

"Bless your heart, no! It was all a mistake of old Mr. Chadwick's. He's as deaf as an adder, and when Mrs. Brooks told him Mother was mendin' fast, and she wanted me to come down today, certain sure, he got the message all wrong, and give it to the fust person passin' in such a way as to scare me 'most to death, and send us down in a hurry. Mother was sittin' up as chirk as you please, and dreadful sorry you didn't all come."

"So, to keep the house quiet for her, and give you a taste of the fun, your Pa fetched us all up to spend the evenin', and we are goin' to have a jolly time on't, to jedge by the looks of things," said Aunt Cinthy, briskly finishing the tale when Mrs. Bassett paused for want of breath.

"What in the world put it into your head we was comin', and set you to gettin' up such a supper?" asked Mr. Bassett, looking about him, well pleased and much surprised at the plentiful table.

Tilly modestly began to tell, but the others broke in and sang her praises in a sort of chorus, in which bears, pigs, pies, and oranges were oddly mixed. Great satisfaction was expressed by all, and Tilly and Prue were so elated by the commendation of Ma and the aunts, that they set forth their dinner, sure everything was perfect.

But when the eating began, which it did the moment wraps were off, then their pride got a fall; for the first person who tasted the stuffing (it was big Cousin Mose, and that made it harder to bear) nearly choked over the bitter morsel.

"Tilly Bassett, whatever made you put wormwood and catnip in your stuffin'?" demanded Ma, trying not to be severe, for all the rest were laughing, and Tilly looked ready to cry.

"I did it," said Prue, nobly taking all the blame, which caused Pa to kiss her on the spot, and declare that it didn't do a might of harm, for the turkey was all right.

"I never see onions cooked better. All the vegetables is well done, and the dinner a credit to you, my dears," declared Aunt Cinthy, with her mouth full of the fragrant vegetable she praised.

The pudding was an utter failure, in spite of the blazing brandy in which it lay—as hard and heavy as one of the stone balls on Squire Dunkin's great gate. It was speedily whisked out of sight, and all fell upon the pies, which were perfect. But Tilly and Prue were much depressed, and didn't recover their spirits till the dinner was over and the evening fun well under way.

"Blind-man's buff," "Hunt the slipper," "Come, Philander," and other lively games soon set every one bubbling over with jollity, and when Eph struck up "Money Musk" on his fiddle, old and young fell into their places for a dance. All down the long kitchen they stood, Mr. and Mrs. Bassett at the top, the twins at the bottom, and then away they went, heeling and toeing, cutting pigeon-wings, and taking their steps in a way that would convulse modern children with their new-fangled romps called dancing. Mose and Tilly covered themselves with glory by the vigor with which they kept it up, till fat Aunt Cinthy fell into a chair, breathlessly declaring that a very little of such exercise was enough for a woman of her "heft."

Apples and cider, chat and singing, finished the evening, and after a grand kissing all round, the guests drove away in the clear moonlight which came just in time to cheer their long drive.

When the jingle of the last bell had died away, Mr. Bassett said soberly, as they stood together on the hearth: "Children, we have special cause to be thankful that the sorrow we expected was changed into joy, so we'll read a chapter 'fore we go to bed, and give thanks where thanks is due."

Then Tilly set out the light-stand with the big Bible on it, and a candle on each side, and all sat quietly in the fire-light, smiling as they listened with happy hearts to the sweet old words that fit all times and seasons so beautifully.

When the good-nights were over, and the children in bed, Prue put her arm around Tilly and whispered tenderly, for she felt her shake, and was sure she was crying:

"Don't mind about the old stuffin' and puddin', deary—nobody cared, and Ma said we really did do surprisin' well for such young girls."

The laughter Tilly was trying to smother broke out then, and was so infectious, Prue could not help joining her, even before she knew the cause of the merriment.

"I was mad about the mistakes, but don't care enough to cry. I'm laughing to think how Gad fooled Eph and I found him out. I thought Mose and Amos would have died over it when I told them, it was so funny," explained Tilly, when she got her breath.

"I was so scared that when the first orange hit me, I thought it was a bullet, and scrabbled into the cradle as fast as I could. It was real mean to frighten the little ones so," laughed Prue, as Tilly gave a growl.

Here a smart rap on the wall of the next room caused a sudden lull in the fun, and Mrs. Bassett's voice was heard, saying warningly, "Girls, go to sleep immediate, or you'll wake the baby."

"Yes'm," answered two meek voices, and after a few irrepressible giggles, silence reigned, broken only by an occasional snore from the boys, or the soft scurry of mice in the buttery, taking their part in this old-fashioned Thanksgiving.

# HOW IT ALL HAPPENED

IT was a small room with nothing in it but a bed, two chairs, and a big chest. A few little gowns hung on the wall, and the only picture was the wintry sky, sparkling with stars, framed by the uncurtained window. But the moon, pausing to peep, saw something pretty and heard something pleasant. Two heads in little round night-caps lay on one pillow, two pairs of wide-awake blue eyes stared up at the light, and two tongues were going like mill clappers.

"I'm so glad we got our shirts done in time! It seemed as if we never should, and I don't think six cents is half enough for a great red flannel thing with four button-holes—do you?" said one little voice, rather wearily.

"No; but then we each made four, and fifty cents is a good deal of money. Are you sorry we didn't keep our quarters for ourselves?" asked the other voice, with an under-tone of regret in it.

"Yes, I am, till I think how pleased the children will be with our tree, for they don't expect anything, and will be so surprised. I wish we had more toys to put on it, for it looks so small and mean with only three or four things."

"It won't hold any more, so I wouldn't worry about it. The toys are very red and yellow, and I guess the babies won't know how cheap they are, but like them as much as if they cost heaps of money."

This was a cheery voice, and as it spoke the four blue eyes turned toward the chest under the window, and the kind moon did her best to light up the tiny tree standing there. A very pitiful little tree it was—only a branch of hemlock in an old flower-pot, propped up with bits of coal, and hung with a few penny toys earned by the patient fingers of the elder sisters, that the little ones should not be disappointed.

But in spite of the magical moonlight the broken branch, with its scanty supply of fruit, looked pathetically poor, and one pair of eyes filled slowly with tears, while the other pair lost their happy look, as if a cloud had come over the sunshine.

"Are you crying, Dolly?"

"Not much, Polly."

"What makes you, dear?"

"I didn't know how poor we were till I saw the tree, and then I couldn't help it," sobbed the elder sister, for at twelve she already knew something of the cares of poverty, and missed the happiness that seemed to vanish out of all their lives when father died.

"It's dreadful! I never thought we'd have to earn our tree, and only be able to get a broken branch, after all, with nothing on it but three sticks of candy, two squeaking dogs, a red cow, and an ugly bird with one feather in its tail;" and overcome by a sudden sense of destitution, Polly sobbed even more despairingly than Dolly.

"Hush, dear; we must cry softly, or mother will hear, and come up, and then we shall have to tell. You know we said we wouldn't seem to mind not having any Christmas, she felt so sorry about it."

"I *must* cry, but I'll be quiet."

So the two heads went under the pillow for a few minutes, and not a sound betrayed them as the little sisters cried softly in one another's arms, lest mother should discover that they were no longer careless children, but brave young creatures trying to bear their share of the burden cheerfully.

When the shower was over, the faces came out shining like roses after rain, and the voices went on again as before.

"Don't you wish there really was a Santa Claus, who knew what we wanted, and would come and put two silver half-dollars in our stockings, so we could go and see *Puss in Boots* at the Museum tomorrow afternoon?"

"Yes, indeed; but we didn't hang up any stockings, you know, because mother had nothing to put in them. It does seem as if rich people might think of poor people now and then. Such little bits of things would make us happy, and it couldn't be much trouble to take two small girls to the play, and give them candy now and then."

"*I* shall when I'm rich, like Mr. Chrome and Miss Kent. I shall go round every Christmas with a big basket of goodies, and give *all* the poor children some."

"P'r'aps if we sew ever so many flannel shirts we may be rich by-and-by. I should give mother a new bonnet first of all, for I heard Miss Kent say no lady would wear such a shabby one. Mrs. Smith said fine bonnets didn't make real ladies. I like her best, but I do want a locket like Miss Kent's."

"I should give mother some new rubbers, and then I should buy a white apron, with frills like Miss Kent's, and bring home nice bunches of grapes and good things to eat, as Mr. Chrome does. I often smell them, but he never gives *me* any; he only says, 'Hullo, chick!' and I'd rather have oranges any time."

"It will take us a long while to get rich, I'm afraid. It makes me tired to think of it. I guess we'd better go to sleep now, dear."

"Good-night, Dolly."

"Good-night, Polly."

Two soft kisses were heard, a nestling sound followed, and presently the little sisters lay fast asleep cheek against cheek, on the pillow wet with their tears, never dreaming what was going to happen to them tomorrow.

Now Miss Kent's room was next to theirs, and as she sat sewing she could hear the children's talk, for they soon forgot to whisper. At first she smiled, then she looked sober, and when the prattle ceased she said to herself, as she glanced about her pleasant chamber:

"Poor little things! They think I'm rich, and envy me, when I'm only a milliner earning my living. I ought to have taken more notice of them, for their mother has a hard time, I fancy, but never complains. I'm sorry they heard what I said, and if I knew how to do it without offending her, I'd trim a nice bonnet for a Christmas gift, for she *is* a lady, in spite of her old clothes. I can give the children some of the things they want anyhow, and I will. The idea of those mites making a fortune out of shirts at six cents apiece!"

Miss Kent laughed at the innocent delusion, but sympathized with her little neighbors, for she knew all about hard times. She had good wages now, but spent them on herself, and liked to be fine rather than neat. Still, she was a good-hearted girl, and what she had overheard set her to thinking soberly, then to acting kindly, as we shall see.

"If I hadn't spent all my money on my dress for the party to-morrow night, I'd give each of them a half-dollar. As I can not, I'll hunt up the other things they wanted, for it's a shame they shouldn't have a bit of Christmas, when they tried so hard to please the little ones."

As she spoke she stirred about her room, and soon had a white apron, an old carnelian heart on a fresh blue ribbon, and two papers of bonbons ready. As no stockings were hung up, she laid a clean towel on the floor before the door, and spread forth the small gifts to look their best.

Miss Kent was so busy that she did not hear a step come quietly up stairs, and Mr. Chrome, the artist, peeped at her through the balusters, wondering what she was about. He soon saw, and watched her with pleasure, thinking that she never looked prettier than now.

Presently she caught him at it, and hastened to explain, telling what she had heard, and how she was trying to atone for her past neglect of these young neighbors. Then she said good-night, and both went into their rooms, she to sleep happily, and he to smoke as usual.

But his eye kept turning to some of the "nice little bundles" that lay on his table, as if the story he had heard suggested how he might follow

Miss Kent's example. I rather think he would not have disturbed himself if he had not heard the story told in such a soft voice, with a pair of bright eyes full of pity looking into his, for little girls were not particularly interesting to him, and he was usually too tired to notice the industrious creatures toiling up and down stairs on various errands, or sewing at the long red seams.

Now that he knew something of their small troubles, he felt as if it would please Miss Kent, and be a good joke, to do his share of the pretty work she had begun.

So presently he jumped up, and, opening his parcels, took out two oranges and two bunches of grapes, then he looked up two silver half-dollars, and stealing into the hall, laid the fruit upon the towel, and the money atop of the oranges. This addition improved the display very much, and Mr. Chrome was stealing back, well pleased, when his eye fell on Miss Kent's door, and he said to himself, "She too shall have a little surprise, for she is a dear, kind-hearted soul."

In his room was a prettily painted plate, and this he filled with green and purple grapes, tucked a sentimental note underneath, and leaving it on her threshold, crept away as stealthily as a burglar.

The house was very quiet when Mrs. Smith, the landlady, came up to turn off the gas. "Well, upon my word, here's fine doings, to be sure!" she said, when she saw the state of the upper hall, "Now I wouldn't have thought it of Miss Kent, she is such a giddy girl, nor of Mr. Chrome, he is so busy with his own affairs. I meant to give those children each a cake tomorrow, they are such good little things. I'll run down and get them now, as my contribution to this fine set out."

Away trotted Mrs. Smith to her pantry, and picked out a couple of tempting cakes, shaped like hearts and full of plums. There was a goodly array of pies on the shelves, and she took two of them, saying, as she climbed the stairs again, "They remembered the children, so I'll remember them, and have my share of the fun."

So up went the pies, for Mrs. Smith had not much to give, and her spirit was generous, though her pastry was not of the best. It looked very droll to see pies sitting about on the thresholds of closed doors, but the cakes were quite elegant, and filled up the corners of the towel handsomely, for the apron lay in the middle, with the oranges right and left, like two sentinels in yellow uniforms.

It was very late when the flicker of a candle came up stairs, and a pale lady, with a sweet sad face, appeared, bringing a pair of red and a pair of blue mittens for her Dolly and Polly. Poor Mrs. Blake did have a hard time, for she stood all day in a great store that she might earn bread for the poor children who staid at home and took care of one another. Her heart was very heavy that night, because it was the first Christmas she had ever known without gifts and festivity of some sort. But Petkin, the youngest child, had been ill, times were very hard, the little mouths gaped for food like the bills of hungry birds, and there was no tender mate to help fill them.

If any elves had been hovering about the dingy hall just then, they would have seen the mother's tired face brighten beautifully when she discovered the gifts, and found that her little girls had been so kindly remembered. Something more brilliant than the mock diamonds in Miss Kent's best ear-rings fell and glittered on the dusty floor as Mrs. Blake added the mittens to the other things, and went to her lonely room again, smiling as she thought how she could thank them all in a sweet and simple way.

Her windows were full of flowers, for the delicate tastes of the poor lady found great comfort in their beauty. "I have nothing else to give, and these will show how grateful I am," she said, as she rejoiced that the scarlet geraniums were so full of gay clusters, the white chrysanthemum stars were all out, and the pink roses at their loveliest.

They slept now, dreaming of a sunny morrow as they sat safely sheltered from the bitter cold. But that night was their last, for a gentle hand cut them all, and soon three pretty nosegays stood in a glass, waiting for dawn, to be laid at three doors, with a few grateful words which would surprise and delight the receivers, for flowers were rare in those hard-working lives, and kind deeds often come back to the givers in fairer shapes than they go.

Now one would think that there had been gifts enough, and no more could possibly arrive, since all had added his or her mite except Betsey, the maid, who was off on a holiday, and the babies fast asleep in their trundle-bed, with nothing to give but love and kisses. Nobody dreamed that the old cat would take it into her head that her kittens were in danger, because Mrs. Smith had said she thought they were nearly old enough to be given away. But she must have understood, for when all was dark and still, the anxious mother went patting up stairs to the children's door, meaning to hide her babies under their bed, sure they would save them from destruction. Mrs. Blake had shut the door, however, so poor Puss was disappointed; but finding a soft, clean spot among a variety of curious articles, she laid her kits there, and kept them warm all night with her head pillowed on the blue mittens.

In the cold morning Dolly and Polly got up and scrambled into their clothes, not with joyful haste to see what their stockings held, for they had none, but because they had the little ones to dress while mother got the breakfast.

Dolly opened the door, and started back with a cry of astonishment at the lovely spectacle before her. The other people had taken in their gifts, so nothing destroyed the magnificent effect of the treasures so curiously collected in the night. Puss had left her kits asleep, and gone down to get her own breakfast, and there, in the middle of the ruffled apron, as if in a dainty cradle, lay the two Maltese darlings, with white bibs and boots on, and white tips to the tiny tails curled round their little noses in the sweetest way.

Polly and Dolly could only clasp their hands and look in rapturous silence for a minute; then they went down on their knees and revelled in the unexpected richness before them.

"I do believe there *is* a Santa Claus, and that he heard us, for here is everything we wanted," said Dolly, holding the carnelian heart in one hand and the plummy one in the other.

"It must have been some kind of a fairy, for we didn't mention kittens, but we wanted one, and here are two darlings," cried Polly, almost purring

Dolly opened the door, and started back with a cry of
astonishment.

## How It All Happened

with delight as the downy bunches unrolled and gaped till their bits of pink tongues were visible.

"Mrs. Smith was one fairy, I guess, and Miss Kent was another, for that is her apron. I shouldn't wonder if Mr. Chrome gave us the oranges and the money: men always have lots, and his name is on this bit of paper," said Dolly.

"Oh, I'm *so* glad! Now we shall have a Christmas like other people and I'll never say again that rich folks don't remember poor folks. Come and show all our treasures to mother and the babies; they must have some," answered Polly, feeling that the world was all right, and life not half as hard as she thought it last night.

Shrieks of delight greeted the sisters, and all that morning there was joy and feasting in Mrs. Blake's room, and in the afternoon Dolly and Polly went to the Museum, and actually saw *Puss in Boots;* for their mother insisted on their going, having discovered how the hard-earned quarters had been spent. This was such unhoped-for bliss that they could hardly believe it, and kept smiling at one another so brightly that people wondered who the happy little girls in shabby cloaks could be who clapped their new mittens so heartily, and laughed till it was better than music to hear them.

This was a very remarkable Christmas-day, and they long remembered it; for while they were absorbed in the fortunes of the Marquis of Carabas and the funny cat, who tucked his tail in his belt, washed his face so awkwardly, and didn't know how to purr, strange things were happening at home, and more surprises were in store for our little friends. You see, when people once begin to do kindnesses, it is so easy and pleasant they find it hard to leave off; and sometimes it beautifies them so that they find they love one another very much—as Mr. Chrome and Miss Kent did, though we have nothing to do with that except to tell how they made the poor little tree grow and blossom.

They were very jolly at dinner, and talked a good deal about the Blakes, who ate in their own rooms. Miss Kent told what the children said, and it touched the soft spot in all their hearts to hear about the red shirts, though they laughed at Polly's lament over the bird with only one feather in its tail.

"I'd give them a better tree if I had any place to put it, and knew how to trim it up," said Mr. Chrome, with a sudden burst of generosity, which so pleased Miss Kent that her eyes shone like Christmas candles.

"Put it in the back parlor. All the Browns are away for a week, and we'll help you trim it—won't we, my dear?" cried Mrs. Smith, warmly; for she saw that he was in a sociable mood, and thought it a pity that the Blakes should not profit by it.

"Yes, indeed; I should like it of all things, and it needn't cost much, for I have some skill in trimmings, as you know." And Miss Kent looked so gay and pretty as she spoke that Mr. Chrome made up his mind that millinery must be a delightful occupation.

"Come on then, ladies, and we'll have a little frolic. I'm a lonely old bachelor, with nowhere to go today, and I'd like some fun."

They had it, I assure you; for they all fell to work as busy as bees, flying and buzzing about with much laughter as they worked their pleasant miracle. Mr. Chrome acted more like the father of a large family than a crusty bachelor, Miss Kent's skillful fingers flew as they never did before, and Mrs. Smith trotted up and down as briskly as if she were sixteen instead of being a stout old woman of sixty.

The children were so full of the play, and telling all about it, that they forgot their tree till after supper; but when they went to look for it they found it gone, and in its place a great paper hand with one finger pointing down stairs, and on it these mysterious words in red ink:

"Look in the Browns' back parlor!"

At the door of that interesting apartment they found their mother with Will and Petkin, for another hand had suddenly appeared to them pointing up. The door flew open quite as if it were a fairy play and they went in to find a pretty tree planted in a red box on the centre table, lighted with candles, hung with gilded nuts, red apples, gay bonbons, and a gift for each.

Mr. Chrome was hidden behind one folding-door, and fat Mrs. Smith squeezed behind the other, and they both thought it a great improvement upon the old-fashioned Santa Claus to have Miss Kent, in the white dress she made for the party, with Mrs. Blake's roses in her hair, step forward as the children gazed in silent rapture, and with a few sweet words welcome them to the little surprise their friends had made.

There were many Christmas trees in the city that night, but none which gave such hearty pleasure as the one which so magically took the place of the broken branch and its few poor toys. They were all there, however, and Dolly and Polly were immensely pleased to see that of all her gifts Petkin chose the forlorn bird to carry to bed with her, the one yellow feather being just to her taste.

Mrs. Blake put on her neat bonnet, and was so gratified that Miss Kent thought it the most successful one she ever trimmed. She was well paid for it by the thanks of one neighbor and the admiration of another; for when she went to her party Mr. Chrome went with her, and said something on the way which made her heart dance more lightly than her feet that night.

Good Mrs. Smith felt that her house had covered itself with glory by this event, and Dolly and Polly declared that it was the most perfect and delightful surprise party ever seen.

It was all over by nine o'clock, and with good-night kisses for every one the little girls climbed up to bed laden with treasures and too happy for many words. But as they tied their round caps Dolly said, thoughtfully:

"On the whole, I think it's rather nice to be poor when people are kind to you."

"Well, I'd *rather* be rich; but if I can't be, it is very good fun to have Christmas trees like this one," answered truthful Polly, never guessing that they had planted the seed from which the little pine-tree grew so quickly and beautifully.

When the moon came to look in at the window on her nightly round, two smiling faces lay on the pillow, which was no longer wet with tears, but rather knobby with the mine of riches hidden underneath,—first fruits of the neighborly friendship which flourished in that house until another and a merrier Christmas came.

# MY MAY-DAY AMONG CURIOUS BIRDS AND BEASTS

BEING alone in London, yet wishing to celebrate the day, I decided to pay my respects to the lions at the Zoological Gardens. A lovely place it was, and I enjoyed myself immensely; for Mayday in England is just what it should be, mild, sunny, flowery, and spring-like. As I walked along the well-kept paths, between white and rosy hawthorn hedges, I kept coming upon new and curious sights; for the birds and beasts are so skilfully arranged, that it is more like travelling through a strange and pleasant country than visiting a menagerie.

The first thing I saw was a great American bison; and I was so glad to meet with anyone from home, that I'd have patted him with pleasure, if he had shown any cordiality toward me. He didn't, however, but stared savagely with his fiery eyes, and put down his immense head with a sullen snort, as if he'd have tossed me with great satisfaction. I did not blame him, for the poor fellow was homesick, doubtless, for his own wide prairies and the free life he had lost. So I threw him some fresh clover, and went on to the pelicans.

I never knew before what handsome birds they were; not graceful, but with such snowy plumage, tinged with pale pink and faint yellow. They had just had their bath, and stood arranging their feathers with their great bills, uttering a queer cry now and then, and nodding to one another sociably. When fed, they gobbled up the fish, never stopping to swallow it till the pouches under their bills were full; then they leisurely emptied them, and seemed to enjoy their lunch with the grave deliberation of regular Englishmen.

Being in a hurry to see the lions, I went on to the long row of cages, and there found a splendid sight. Six lions and lionesses, in three or four different cages, sitting or standing in dignified attitudes, and eying the spectators with a mild expression in their fine eyes. One lioness was ill, and lay on her bed, looking very pensive, while her mate moved restlessly about her, evidently anxious to do something for her, and much afflicted by her suffering. I liked this lion very much, for, though the biggest, he was very gentle, and had a noble face.

The tigers were rushing about, as tigers usually are; some creeping noiselessly to and fro, some leaping up and down, and some washing their faces with their velvet paws. All looked and acted so like cats, that I wasn't at all surprised to hear one of them purr when the keeper scratched her head. It was a very loud and large purr, but no fireside pussy could have done it better, and everyone laughed at the sound.

There were pretty spotted leopards, panthers, and smaller varieties of the same species. I sat watching them a long time, longing to let some of the wild things out for a good run, they seemed so unhappy barred in those small dens.

Suddenly the lions began to roar, the tigers to snarl, and all to get very much excited about something, sniffing at the openings, thrusting their paws through the bars, and lashing their tails impatiently. I couldn't imagine what the trouble was, till, far down the line, I saw a man with a barrow full of lumps of raw meat. This was their dinner; and, as they were fed but once a day, they were ravenous. Such roars and howls and cries as arose, while the man went slowly down the line, gave one a good idea of the sounds to be heard in Indian forests and jungles. The lions behaved best, for they only paced up and down, with an occasional cry; but the tigers were quite frantic; for they tumbled one over the other, shook the cages, and tried to reach the bystanders, just out of reach behind the bar that kept us at a safe distance. One lady had a fright, for the wind blew the end of her shawl within reach of a tiger's great claw, and he clutched it, trying to drag her nearer. The shawl came off, and the poor lady ran away screaming, as if a whole family of wild beasts were after her.

When the lumps of meat were thrown in, it was curious to see how differently the anmials behaved. The tigers snarled and fought and tore and got so savage I was very grateful that they were safely shut up. In a few minutes, nothing but white bones remained, and then they howled for more. One little leopard was better bred than the others, for he went up on a shelf in the cage, and ate his dinner in a quiet, proper manner, which was an example to the rest.

The lions ate in dignified silence, all but my favorite, who carried his share to his sick mate, and by every gentle means in his power tried to make her eat. She was too ill, however, and turned away with a plaintive moan which seemed to grieve him sadly. He wouldn't touch his dinner, but lay down near her, with the lump between his paws, as if guarding it for her; and there I left him patiently waiting, in spite of his hunger, till his mate could share it with him. As I took a last look at his fine old face, I named him Douglas, and walked away, humming to myself the lines of the ballad,—

> "Douglas, Douglas,
> Tender and true."

As a contrast to the wild beasts, I went to see the monkeys who lived in a fine large house, all to themselves. Here was every variety, from the great ugly chimpanzee to the funny little fellows who played like boys, and cut up all sorts of capers. A mamma sat tending her baby, and looking so like a little old woman that I laughed till the gray monkey with the blue nose scolded at me. He was a cross old party, and sat huddled up in the straw, scowling at everyone, like an ill-tempered old bachelor. Half a dozen little ones teased him capitally by dropping bits of bread, nut-shells, and straws down on him from above, as they climbed about the perches or swung by their tails. One poor little chap had lost the curly end of his tail,—I'm afraid the gray one bit it off,—and kept trying to swing like the others, forgetting that the strong, curly end was what he held on with. He would run up the bare boughs, and give a jump, expecting to catch and swing, but the lame tail wouldn't hold him, and down he'd go, bounce on to the straw. At first he'd sit and stare about him, as if much amazed to find himself there; then he'd scratch his little round head, and begin to scold violently, which seemed to delight the other monkeys; and finally, he'd examine his poor little tail, and appear to understand the misfortune which had befallen him. The funny expression of his face was irresistible, and I enjoyed seeing him very much, and gave him a bun to comfort him when I went away.

The snake-house came next, and I went in, on my way to visit the rhinoceros family. I rather like snakes, since I had a tame green one, who lived under the doorstep, and would come out and play with me on sunny days. These snakes I found very interesting, only they got under their blankets and wouldn't come out, and I wasn't allowed to poke them; so I missed seeing several of the most curious. An ugly cobra laid and blinked at me through the glass, looking quite as dangerous as he was. There were big and little snakes,—black, brown, and speckled, lively and lazy, pretty and plain ones,—but I liked the great boa best.

When I came to his cage, I didn't see anything but the branch of a tree, such as I had seen in other cages, for the snakes to wind up and down. "Where is he, I wonder? I hope he hasn't got out," I said to myself, thinking of a story I read once of a person in a menagerie, who turned suddenly and saw a great boa gliding toward him. As I stood wondering if the big worm could be under the little flat blanket before me, the branch began to move all at once, and with a start, I saw a limb swing down to stare at me with the boa's glittering eyes. He was so exactly the color of the bare bough, and lay so still, I had not seen him till he came to take a look at me. A very villainous looking reptile he was, and I felt grateful that I didn't live in a country where such unpleasant neighbors might pop in upon you unexpectedly. He was kind enough to take a promenade and show me his size, which seemed immense, as he stretched himself, and then knotted his rough, grayish body into a great loop, with the fiery-eyed head in the middle. He was not one of the largest kind, but I was quite satisfied, and left him to his dinner of rabbits, which I hadn't the heart to stay and see him devour alive.

I was walking toward the camel's pagoda, when, all of a sudden a long, dark, curling thing came over my shoulder, and I felt warm breath in my face. "It's the boa!" I thought, and gave a skip which carried me into the hedge, where I stuck, much to the amusement of some children riding on the elephant whose trunk had frightened me. He had politely tried to tell me to clear the way, which I certainly had done with all speed. Picking myself out of the hedge, I walked beside him, examining his clumsy feet, and peering up at his small, intelligent eye. I'm very sure he winked at me, as if enjoying the joke, and kept poking his trunk into my pocket, hoping to find something eatable.

I felt as if I had got into a foreign country as I looked about me and saw elephants and camels walking among the trees; flocks of snow-white cranes stalking over the grass, on their long scarlet legs; striped zebras racing in their paddock; queer kangaroos hopping about, with little ones in their pouches; pretty antelopes chasing one another; and, in an immense wire-covered aviary, all sorts of brilliant birds were flying about, as gaily as if at home.

One of the curiosities was a sea-cow, who lived in a tank of salt water, and came at the keeper's call to kiss him, and flounder on its flippers along the margin of the tank after a fish. It was very like a seal, only much larger, and had four fins instead of two. Its eyes were lovely, so dark and soft and liquid; but its mouth was not pretty, and I declined one of the damp kisses which it was ready to dispense at word of command.

The great polar bear lived next door, and spent his time splashing in and out of a pool of water, or sitting on a block of ice, panting, as if the mild spring day was blazing midsummer. He looked very unhappy, and I thought it a pity that they didn't invent a big refrigerator for him.

These are not half of the wonderful creatures I saw, but I have not room to tell more; only I advise all who can to pay a visit to the Zoological Gardens when they go to London, for it is one of the most interesting sights in that fine old city.

# HOW THEY CAMPED OUT

"IT looks so much like snow I think it would be wiser to put off your sleighing party, Gwen," said Mrs. Arnold, looking anxiously out at the heavy sky and streets still drifted by the last winter storm.

"Not before night, mamma; we don't mind its being cloudy, we like it, because the sun makes the snow so dazzling when we get out of town. We can't give it up now, for here comes Patrick with the boys." And Gwen ran down to welcome the big sleigh, which just then drove up with four jolly lads skirmishing about inside.

"Come on!" called Mark, her brother, knocking his friends right and left, to make room for the four girls who were to complete the party.

"What do you think of the weather, Patrick?" asked Mrs. Arnold from the window, still undecided about the wisdom of letting her flock go off alone, papa having been called away after the plan was made.

"Faith, ma'm, it's an illigant day barring the wind, that's a thrifle could to the nose. I'll have me eye on the childer, ma'm, and there'll be no throuble at all, at all," replied the old coachman, lifting a round red face out of his muffler, and patting little Gus on the shoulder, as he sat proudly on the high seat holding the whip.

"Be careful, dears, and come home early."

With which parting caution mamma shut the window, and watched the young folks drive gayly away, little dreaming what would happen before they got back.

The wind was more than a "thrifle could," for when they got out of the city it blew across the open country in bitter blasts, and made the eight little noses almost as red as old Pat's, who had been up all night at a wake, and was still heavy-headed with too much whiskey, though no one suspected it.

The lads enjoyed themselves immensely snowballing one another; for the drifts were still fresh enough to furnish soft snow, and Mark, Bob, and Tony had many a friendly tussle in it as they went up hills, or paused to breathe the horses after a swift trot along a level bit of road. Little Gus helped drive till his hands were benumbed in spite of the new red mittens, and he had to descend among the girls, who were cuddled cosily under the warm robes, telling secrets, eating candy, and laughing at the older boys' pranks.

Sixteen-year-old Gwendoline was matron of the party, and kept excellent order among the girls; for Ruth and Alice were nearly her own age, and Rita a most obedient younger sister.

"I say, Gwen, we are going to stop at the old house on the way home and get some nuts for this evening. Papa said we might, and some of the big Baldwins too. I've got baskets, and while we fellows fill them you girls can look round the house," said Mark, when the exhausted young gentlemen returned to their seats.

"That will be nice. I want to get some books, and Rita has been very anxious about one of her dolls, which she is sure was left in the nursery closet. If we are going to stop we ought to be turning back, Pat, for it is beginning to snow and will be dark early," answered Gwen, suddenly realizing that great flakes were fast whitening the roads and the wind had risen to a gale.

"Shure and I will, miss dear, as soon as iver I can; but it's round a good bit we must go, for I couldn't be turning here widout upsettin' the whole of yez, it's that drifted. Rest aisy, and I'll fetch up at the ould place in half an hour, plaze the powers," said Pat, who had lost his way and wouldn't own it, being stupid with a sup or two he had privately taken on the way, to keep the chill out of his bones he said.

On they went again, with the wind at their backs, caring little for the snow that now fell fast, or the gathering twilight, since they were going toward home they thought. It was a very long half-hour before Pat brought them to the country-house, which was shut up for the winter. With difficulty they ploughed their way up to the steps, and scrambled on to the piazza, where they danced about to warm their feet till Mark unlocked the door and let them in, leaving Pat to enjoy a doze on his seat.

"Make haste, boys; it is cold and dark here, and we must get home. Mamma will be so anxious, and it really is going to be a bad storm," said Gwen, whose spirits were damped by the gloom of the old house, and who felt her responsibility, having promised to be home early.

Off went the boys to attic and cellar, being obliged to light the lantern left here for the use of whoever came now and then to inspect the premises. The girls, having found books and doll, sat upon the rolled-up carpets, or peeped about at the once gay and hospitable rooms, now looking very empty and desolate with piled-up furniture, shuttered windows, and fireless hearths.

"If we were going to stay long I'd have a fire in the library. Papa often does when he comes out, to keep the books from moulding," began Gwen, but was interrupted by a shout from without, and, running to the door, saw Pat picking himself out of a drift while the horses were galloping down the avenue at full speed.

"Be jabbers, them villains give a jump when that fallin' branch struck 'em, and out I wint, bein' tuk unknownst, just thinkin' of me poor cousin Mike. May his bed above be aisy the day! Whist now, miss dear! I'll fetch 'em back in a jiffy. Stop still till I come, and kape them b'ys quite."

With a blow to settle his hat, Patrick trotted gallantly away into the storm, and the girls went in to tell the exciting news to the lads, who came whooping back from their search, with baskets of nuts and apples.

"Here's a go!" cried Mark. "Old Pat will run half-way to town before he catches the horses, and we are in for an hour or two at least."

"Then do make a fire, for we shall die of cold if we have to wait long," begged Gwen, rubbing Rita's cold hands, and looking anxiously at little Gus, who was about making up his mind to roar.

"So we will, and be jolly till the blunderbuss gets back. Camp down, girls, and you fellows, come and hold the lantern while I get wood and stuff. It is so confoundedly dark, I shall break my neck down the shed steps." And Mark led the way to the library, where the carpet still remained, and comfortable chairs and sofas invited the chilly visitors to rest.

"How can you light your fire when you get the wood?" asked Ruth, a practical damsel, who looked well after her own creature comforts and was longing for a warm supper.

"Papa hides the matches in a tin box, so the rats won't get at them. Here they are, and two or three bits of candle for the sticks on the chimney-piece, if he forgets to have the lantern trimmed. Now we will light up, and look cosey when the boys come back."

And producing the box from under a sofa-cushion, Gwen cheered the hearts of all by lighting two candles, rolling up the chairs, and making ready to be comfortable. Thoughtful Alice went to see if Pat was returning, and found a buffalo-robe lying on the steps. Returning with this, she reported that there was no sign of the runaways, and advised making ready for a long stay.

"How mamma will worry!" thought Gwen, but made light of the affair, because she saw Rita looked timid, and Gus shivered till his teeth chattered.

"We will have a nice time, and play we are shipwrecked people or Arctic explorers. Here comes Dr. Kane and the sailors with supplies of wood, so we can thaw our pemmican and warm our feet. Gus shall be the little Esquimaux boy, all dressed in fur, as he is in the picture we have at home," she said, wrapping the child in the robe, and putting her own sealskin cap on his head to divert his mind.

"Here we are! Now for a jolly blaze, boys; and if Pat doesn't come back we can have our fun here instead of at home," cried Mark, well pleased with the adventure, as were his mates.

So they fell to work, and soon a bright fire was lighting up the room with its cheerful shine, and the children gathered about it, quite careless of the storm raging without, and sure that Pat would come in time.

"I'm hungry," complained Gus as soon as he was warm.

"So am I," added Rita from the rug, where the two little ones sat toasting themselves.

"Eat an apple," said Mark.

"They are so hard and cold I don't like them," began Gus,

"Roast some!" cried Ruth.

"And crack nuts," suggested Alice. "Pity we can't cook something in real camp style , it would be such fun," said Tony, who had spent weeks on Monadnock, living upon the supplies he and his party tugged up the mountain on their backs.

"We shall not have time for anything but what we have. Put down your apples and crack away, or we shall be obliged to leave them," advised Gwen, coming back from an observation at the front door with an anxious line on her forehead; for the storm was rapidly increasing, and there was no sign of Pat or the horses.

The rest were in high glee, and an hour or two slipped quickly away as they enjoyed the impromptu feast and played games. Gus recalled them to the discomforts of their situation by saying with a yawn and a whimper,—

"I'm so sleepy! I want my own bed and mamma."

"So do I!" echoed Rita, who had been nodding for some time, and longed to lie down and sleep comfortably anywhere.

"Almost eight o'clock! By jove, that old Pat *is* taking his time, I think. Wonder if he has got into trouble? We can't do anything, and may as well keep quiet here," said Mark, looking at his watch and beginning to understand that the joke was rather a serious one.

"Better make a night of it and all go to sleep. Pat can wake us up when he comes. The cold makes a fellow *so* drowsy." And Bob gave a stretch that nearly rent him asunder.

"I will let the children nap on the sofa. They are so tired of waiting, and may as well amuse themselves in that way as in fretting. Come, Gus and Rita, each take a pillow, and I'll cover you up with my shawl."

Gwen made the little ones comfortable, and they were off in five minutes. The others kept up bravely till nine o'clock, then the bits of candles were burnt out, the stories all told, nuts and apples had lost their charm, and weariness and hunger caused spirits to fail perceptibly.

"I've eaten five Baldwins, and yet I want more. Something filling and good. Can't we catch a rat and roast him?" proposed Bob, who was a hearty lad and was ravenous by this time.

"Isn't there anything in the house?" asked Ruth, who dared not eat nuts for fear of indigestion.

"Not a thing that I know of except a few pickles in the storeroom; we had so many, mamma left some here," answered Gwen, resolving to provision the house before she left it another autumn.

"Pickles alone are rather sour feed. If we only had a biscuit now, they wouldn't be bad for a relish," said Tony, with the air of a man who had known what it was to live on burnt bean-soup and rye flapjacks for a week.

"I saw a keg of soft-soap in the shed. How would that go with the pickles?" suggested Bob, who felt equal to the biggest and acidest cucumber ever grown.

"Mamma knew an old lady who actually did eat soft-soap and cream for her complexion," put in Alice, whose own fresh face looked as if she had tried the same distasteful remedy with success.

The boys laughed, and Mark, who felt that hospitality required him to do something for his guests, said briskly,—

"Let us go on a foraging expedition while the lamp holds out to burn, for the old lantern is almost gone and then we are done for. Come on, Bob; your sharp nose will smell out food if there is any."

"Don't set the house afire, and bring more wood when you come, for we must have light of some kind in this poky place," called Gwen, with a sigh, wishing every one of them were safely at home and abed.

A great tramping of boots, slamming of doors, and shouting of voices followed the departure of the boys, as well as a crash, a howl, and then a roar of laughter, as Bob fell down the cellar stairs, having opened the door in search of food and poked his nose in too far. Presently they came back, very dusty, cobwebby, and cold, but triumphantly bearing a droll collection of trophies. Mark had a piece of board and the lantern, Tony a big wooden box and a tin pail, Bob fondly embraced a pickle jar and a tumbler of jelly which had been forgotten on a high shelf in the storeroom.

"Meal, pickles, jam, and boards. What a mess and what are we to do with it all?" cried the girls, much amused at the result of the expedition.

"Can any of you make a hoe cake?" demanded Mark.

"No, indeed! I can make caramels and cocoanut-cakes," said Ruth, proudly.

"I can make good toast and tea," added Alice.

"I can't cook anything," confessed Gwen, who was unusually accomplished in French, German, and music.

"Girls aren't worth much in the hour of need. Take hold, Tony, you are the chap for me." And Mark disrespectfully turned his back on the young ladies, who could only sit and watch the lads work.

"He can't do it without water," whispered Ruth,

"Or salt," answered Alice.

"Or a pan to bake it in," added Gwen; and then all smiled at the dilemma they foresaw.

But Tony was equal to the occasion, and calmly went on with his task, while Mark arranged the fire and Bob opened the pickles. First the new cook filled the pail with snow till enough was melted to wet the meal; this mixture was stirred with a pine stick till thick enough, then spread on the board and set up before the bed of coals to brown.

"It never will bake in the world." "He can't turn it, so it won't be done on both sides." "Won't be fit to eat any way!" And with these dark hints the girls consoled themselves for their want of skill.

But the cake did bake a nice brown, Tony did turn it neatly with his jack-knife and the stick, and when it was done cut it into bits, added jelly, and passed it round on an old atlas; and every one said,—

"It really does taste good!"

Two more were baked, and eaten with pickles for a change, thea all were satisfied, and after a vote of thanks to Tony they began to think of sleep.

"Pat has gone home and told them we are all right, and mamma knows we can manage here well enough for one night, so don't worry, Gwen, but take a nap, and I'll lie on the rug and see to the fire."

Mark's happy-go-lucky way of taking things did not convince his sister; but as she could do nothing, she submitted and made her friends as comfortable as she could.

All had plenty of wraps, so the girls nestled into the three large chairs, Bob and Tony rolled themselves up in the robe, with their feet to the fire, and were soon snoring like weary hunters. Mark pillowed his head on a log, and was sound asleep in ten minutes in spite of his promise to be sentinel.

Gwen's chair was the least easy of the three, and she could not forget herself like the rest, but sat wide awake, watching the blaze, counting the hours, and wondering why no one came to them.

The wind blew fiercely, the snow beat against the blinds, rats scuttled about the walls, and now and then a branch fell upon the roof with a crash. Weary, yet excited, the poor girl imagined all sorts of mishaps to Pat and the horses, recalled various ghost stories she had heard, and wondered if it was on such a night as this that a neighbor's house had been robbed. So nervous did she get at last that she covered up her face and resolutely began to count a thousand, feeling that anything was better than having to wake Mark and own she was frightened.

Before she knew it she fell into a drowse and dreamed that they were all cast away on an iceberg and a polar bear was coming up to devour Gus, who innocently called to the big white dog and waited to caress him.

"A bear! A bear! Oh, boys, save him!" murmured Gwen in her sleep, and the sound of her own distressed voice waked her.

The fire was nearly out, for she had slept longer than she knew, the room was full of shadows, and the storm seemed to have died away. In the silence which now reigned, unbroken even by a snore, Gwen heard a sound that made her start and tremble. Some one was coming softly up the back stairs. All the outer doors were locked, she was sure; all the boys lay in their places, for she could see and count the three long figures and little Gus in a bunch on the sofa. The girls had not stirred, and this was no rat's scamper, but a slow and careful tread, stealing nearer and nearer to the study door, left ajar when the last load of wood was brought in.

"Pat would knock or ring, and papa would speak, so that we might not be scared. I want to scream, but I won't till I see that it really is some one," thought Gwen, while her heart beat fast and her eyes were fixed on the door, straining to see through the gloom.

The steps drew nearer, paused on the threshold, and then a head appeared as the door noiselessly swung wider open. A man's head in a fur cap, but it was neither papa nor Pat nor Uncle Ed. Poor Gwen would have called out then, but her voice was gone, and she could only lie back, looking, mute and motionless. A tiny spire of flame sprung up and flickered for a moment on the tall dark figure in the doorway, a big man with a beard, and in his hand something that glittered. Was it a pistol or a dagger or a dark lantern? thought the girl, as the glimmer died away, and the shadows returned to terrify her.

The man seemed to look about him keenly for a moment, then vanished, and the steps went down the hall to the front door, which was opened from within and some one admitted quietly. Whispers were heard, and then feet approached again, accompanied by a gleam of light.

"Now I must scream!" thought Gwen; and scream she did with all her might, as two men entered, one carrying a lantern, the other a bright tin can.

"Boys! Robbers! Fire! Tramps! Oh, do wake up!" cried Gwen, frantically pulling Mark by the hair, and Bob and Tony by the legs, as the quickest way of rousing them.

Then there was a scene! The boys sprung up and rubbed their eyes, the girls hid theirs and began to shriek, while the burglars laughed aloud, and poor Gwen, quite worn out, fainted away on the rug. It was all over in a minute, however; for Mark had his wits about him, and his first glance at the man with the lantern allayed his fears.

"Hullo, Uncle Ed! We are all right. Got tired of waiting for you, so we went to sleep."

"Stop screaming, girls, and quiet those children! Poor little Gwen is badly frightened. Get some snow, Tom, while I pick her up," commanded the uncle, and order was soon established.

The boys were all right at once, and Ruth and Alice devoted themselves to the children, who were very cross and sleepy in spite of their fright. Gwen was herself in a moment, and so ashamed of her scare that she was glad there was no more light to betray her pale cheeks.

"I should have known you, uncle, at once, but to see a strange man startled me, and he didn't speak, and I thought that can was a pistol," stammered Gwen, when she had collected her wits a little.

"Why, that's my old friend and captain, Tom May. Don't you remember him, child? He thought you were all asleep, so crept out to tell me and let me in."

"How did he get in himself?" asked Gwen, glad to turn the conversation.

"Found the shed door open, and surprised the camp by a flank movement. You wouldn't do for picket duty, boys," laughed Captain Tom, enjoying the dismay of the lads.

"Oh, thunder! I forgot to bolt it when we first went for the wood. Had to open it, the place was so plaguy dark," muttered Bob, much disgusted.

"Where's Pat?" asked Tony, with great presence of mind, feeling anxious to shift all blame to his broad shoulders.

Uncle Ed shook the snow from his hair and clothes, and, poking up the fire, leisurely sat down and took Gus on his knee before he replied,—"Serve out the grog, Tom, while I spin my yarn."

Round went the can of hot coffee, and a few sips brightened up the young folks immensely, so that they listened with great interest to the tale of Pat's mishaps.

"The scamp was half-seas over when he started, and deserves all he got. In the first place he lost his way, then tumbled overboard, and let the horses go. He floundered after them a mile or two, then lost his bearings in the storm, pitched into a ditch, broke his head, and lay there till found. The fellows carried him to a house off the road, and there he is in a nice state; for, being his countrymen, they dosed him with whiskey till he was 'quite and aisy,' and went to sleep, forgetting all about you, the horses, and his distracted mistress at home. The animals were stopped at the cross-roads, and there we found them after a lively cruise round the country. Then we hunted up Pat; but what with the blow and too many drops of 'the crayther,' his head was in a muddle, and we could get nothing out of him. So we went home again, and then your mother remembered that you had mentioned stopping here, and we fitted out a new craft and set sail, prepared for a long voyage. Your father was away, so Tom volunteered, and here we are."

"A jolly lark! Now let us go home and go to bed," proposed Mark, with a gape.

"Isn't it most morning?" asked Tony, who had been sleeping like a dormouse.

"Just eleven. Now pack up and let us be off. The storm is over, the moon coming out, and we shall find a good supper waiting for the loved and lost. Bear a hand, Tom, and ship this little duffer, for he's off again."

Uncle Ed put Gus into the captain's arms, and, taking Rita himself, led the way to the sleigh which stood at the door. In they all bundled, and after making the house safe, off they went, feeling that they had had a pretty good time on the whole.

"I will learn cooking and courage, before I try camping out again," resolved Gwen, as she went jingling homeward; and she kept her word.

# JIMMY'S CRUISE IN THE PINAFORE

## HOW HE SHIPPED

A BOY sat on a door-step in a despondent attitude, with his eyes fixed on a pair of very shabby shoes, and his elbows resting on his knees, as if to hide the big patches there. But it was not the fact that his toes were nearly out and his clothes dilapidated which brought the wrinkles to his forehead and the tears to his eyes, for he was used to that state of things, and bore it without complaint. The prospect was a dull one for a lively lad full of the spring longings which sunny April weather always brings. But it was not the narrow backstreet where noisy children played and two or three dusty trees tried to bud without sunshine, that made him look so dismal. Nor was it the knowledge that a pile of vests was nearly ready for him to trudge away with before he could really rest after doing many errands to save mother's weary feet.

No, it was a burden that lay very heavily on his heart, and made it impossible to even whistle as he waited. Above the sounds that filled the street he heard a patient moan from the room within; and no matter what object his eyes rested on, he saw with sorrowful distinctness a small white face turned wistfully toward the window, as if weary of the pillow where it had laid so long.

Merry little Kitty, who used to sing and dance from morning till night, was now so feeble and wasted that he could carry her about like a baby. All day she lay moaning softly, and her one comfort was when "brother" could come and sing to her. That night he could not sing; his heart was so full, because the doctor had said that the poor child must have country air as soon as possible, else she never would recover from the fever which left her such a sad little ghost of her former self. But, alas, there was no money for the trip, and mother was sewing day and night to earn enough for a week at least of blessed country air and quiet. Jimmy did his best to help, but could find very little to do, and the pennies came in so slowly he was almost in despair.

There was no father to lend a strong hand, and Mrs. Nelson was one of the "silent poor," who cannot ask for charity, no matter how much they may need it. The twelve-year-old boy considered himself the man of the family, and manfully carried as many burdens as his young shoulders would bear; but this was a very heavy one, so it is no wonder that he looked sober. Holding his curly head in his hands, as if to keep it from flying asunder with the various plans working inside, he sat staring at the dusty bricks in a desperate frame of mind.

Warm days were coming, and every hour was precious, for poor Kitty pined in the close room, and all he could do was to bring her dandelions and bits of green grass from the Common when she begged to go in the fields and pick "pretties" for herself. He loved the little sister dearly, and, as he remembered her longing, his eyes filled, and he doubled up both fists with an air of determination, muttering to himself,—

"She *shall* go! I don't see any other way, and I'll do it!"

The plan which had been uppermost lately was this. His father had been a sailor, and Jimmy proposed to run way to sea as cabin boy. His wages were to be paid before he went, so mother and Kitty could be in the country while he was gone, and in a few months he would come sailing gayly home to find the child her rosy self again. A very boyish and impossible plan, but he meant it, and was in just the mood to carry it out,—for every other attempt to make money had failed.

"I'll do it as sure as my name is Jim Nelson. I'll take a look at the ships this very night, and go in the first one that will have me," he said, with a resolute nod of the head, though his heart sank within him at the thought. "I wonder which kind of captains pay boys best? I guess I'll try a steamer; they make short trips. I heard the cannon today, so one is in, and I'll try for a place before I go to bed."

Little did desperate Jimmy guess what ship he would really sail in, nor what a prosperous voyage he was about to make; for help was coming that very minute, as it generally does, sooner or later, to generous people who are very much in earnest.

First a shrill whistle was heard, at the sound of which he looked up quickly; then a rosy-faced girl of about his own age came skipping down the street, swinging her hat by one string; and, as Jimmy watched her approach, a smile began to soften the grim look he wore, for Willy Bryant was his best friend and neighbor, being full of courage, fun, and kindness. He nodded, and made room for her on the step,—the place she usually occupied at spare moments when they got lessons and recounted their scrapes to each other.

But tonight Willy seemed possessed of some unusually good piece of news which she chose to tell in her own lively fashion, for, instead of sitting down, she began to dance a sailor's hornpipe, singing gayly, "I'm little Buttercup, sweet little Buttercup," till her breath gave out.

"What makes you so jolly, Will?" asked Jimmy as she dropped down beside him and fanned herself with the ill-used hat.

"Such fun—you'll never guess—just what we wanted—if your mother only will! You'll dance, too, when you know," panted the girl, smiling like a substantial sort of fairy come to bring good luck.

"Fire away, then. It will have to be extra nice to set me off. I don't feel a bit like jigs now," answered Jimmy, as the gloom obscured his face again, like a cloud over the sun.

"You know 'Pinafore'?" began Will, and getting a quick nod for an answer, she poured forth the following tale with great rapidity: "Well, some folks are going to get it up with children to do it, and they want any boys and girls that can sing to go and be looked at tomorrow, and the good ones will be picked out, and dressed up, and taught how to act, and have the nicest time that ever was. Some of our girls are going, and so am I, and you sing and must come, too, and have some fun. Won't it be jolly?"

"I guess it would; but I can't. Mother needs me every minute out of school," began Jimmy, with a shake of the head, having made up his mind some time ago that he must learn to do without fun.

"But we shall be paid for it," cried Will, clapping her hands with the double delight of telling the best part of her story, and seeing Jimmy's sober face clear suddenly as if the sun had burst forth with great brilliancy.

"Really? How much? Can I sing well enough?" and he clutched her arm excitedly, for this unexpected ray of hope dazzled him.

"Some of them will have ten dollars a week, and some more,—the real nice ones, like Lee, the singing boy, who is a wonder," answered Will, in the tone of one well informed on such points.

"Ten dollars!" gasped Jimmy, for the immensity of the sum took his breath away. "Could *I* get that? How long? Where do we go? Do they really want us fellows? Are you sure it's all true?"

"It was all in the paper, and Miss Pym, the teacher who boards at our house, told Ma about it. The folks advertised for school-children, sixty of 'em, and will really pay; and Ma said I could go and try, and all the money I get I'm going to put in a bank and have for my own. Don't you believe me now?"

Miss Pym and the newspapers settled the matter in Jimmy's mind, and made him more anxious than before about the other point.

"Do you think *I* would have any chance?" he asked, still holding Will, who seemed inclined for another dance.

"I know you would. Don't you do splendidly at school? And didn't they want you for a choir boy, only your mother couldn't spare you?" answered Will, decidedly; for Jimmy did love music, and had a sweet little pipe of his own, as she well knew.

"Mother will have to spare me now, if they pay like that. I can work all day and do without sleep to earn money this way. Oh, Will, I'm so glad you came, for I was just ready to run away to sea. There didn't seem anything else to do," whispered Jimmy in a choky sort of tone, as hopes and fears struggled together in his boyish mind.

"Run as fast as you like, and I'll go too. We'll sail in the 'Pinafore,' and come home with our pockets full of money.

"*'Sing, hey, the merry maiden and the tar !'*"

burst out Will, who was so full of spirits she could not keep still another minute.

Jimmy joined in, and the fresh voices echoed through the street so pleasantly that Mrs. Peters stopped scolding her six squabbling children, while Kitty's moaning changed to a feeble little sound of satisfaction, for "brother's" lullabies were her chief comfort and delight.

"We shall lose school, you know, for we act in the afternoon, not the evening. I don't care; but you will, you like to study so well. Miss Pym didn't like it at first, but Ma said it would help the poor folks, and a little fun wouldn't hurt the children. I thought of you right away, and if you don't get as much money as I do, you shall have some of mine, so Kitty can go away soon."

Will's merry face grew very sweet and kind as she said that, and Jimmy was glad his mother called him just then, because he did not know how to thank this friend in need. When he came out with the parcel of vests he looked like a different boy, for Mrs. Nelson had told him to go and find out all about it, and had seemed as much dazzled by the prospect as he did, sewing was such weary work.

Their interview with Miss Pym was a most encouraging one, and it was soon settled that Jimmy should go with Will to try for a place on the morrow.

"And I'll get it, too!" he said to himself, as he kissed Kitty's thin cheek, full of the sweet hope that he might be the means of bringing back life and color to the little face he loved so well.

He was so excited he could not sleep, and beguiled the long hours by humming under his breath all the airs he knew belonging to the already popular opera. Next morning he flew about his work as if for a wager, and when Will came for him there was not a happier heart in all the city than the hopeful one that thumped under Jimmy's threadbare best jacket.

Such a crowd of girls and boys as they found at the hall where they were told to apply for inspection; such a chirping and piping went on there, it sounded like a big cage full of larks and linnets; and by and by, when the trial was over, such a smiling troop of children as was left to be drilled by the energetic gentlemen who had the matter in hand. Among this happy band stood our Jimmy, chosen for his good voice, and Will, because of her bright face and lively, self-possessed manners. They could hardly wait to be dismissed, and it was a race home to see who should be first to tell the good news. Jimmy tried to be quiet on Kitty's account, but failed entirely; and it was a pleasant sight to see the boy run into his mother's arms, crying joyfully,—

"I'm in! I'm in! Ten dollars a week! Hurrah!"

"I can hardly believe it!" And weary Mrs. Nelson dropped her needle to indulge in a few moments of delightful repose.

"If it goes well they may want us for a month or six weeks," the man said. "Just think, maybe I'll get fifty or sixty dollars! And Baby will get well right off," cried Jimmy, in an arithmetical sort of rapture, as he leaned above Kitty, who tried to clap her little hands without quite knowing what the joy was all about.

## HOW HE SAILED

After that day Jimmy led a very happy life, for he loved music and enjoyed the daily drill with his mates, though it was long before he saw the inside of the theatre. Will knew a good deal about it, for an actor's family had boarded with her mother, and the little girl had been behind the scenes. But to Jimmy, who had only seen one fairy play, all was very strange when at last he went upon the stage; for the glittering world he expected was gone, and all was dusty, dark, and queer, with trap-doors underfoot, machinery overhead, and a wilderness of scenery jumbled together in the drollest way. He was all eyes and ears, and enjoyed himself immensely as he came and went, sung and acted, with the troop of lads who made up the sailor chorus. It was a real ship to him, in spite of painted cannon, shaky masts, and cabin doors that led nowhere. He longed to run up the rigging; but as that was forbidden, for fear of danger, he contented himself by obeying orders with nautical obedience, singing with all his might, and taking great satisfaction in his blue suit with the magical letters "H. M. S. Pinafore" round his cap.

Day by day all grew more and more interesting. His mother was never tired of hearing his adventures, he sung Kitty to sleep with the new songs, and the neighbors took such a friendly interest in his success that they called him Lord Nelson, and predicted that he would be as famous as his great namesake.

When the grand day came at last, and the crew of jolly young tars stood ready to burst forth with the opening chorus,

> *"We sail the ocean blue,*
> *Our saucy ship's a beauty,*
> *We're gallant men and true,*
> *And bound to do our duty!"*

Jimmy hardly knew whether he stood on his head or his heels at first, for, in spite of many rehearsals, everything seemed changed. Instead of daylight gas shone everywhere, the empty seats were full, the orchestra playing splendidly, and when the curtain rose, a sea of friendly faces welcomed them, and the pleasant sound of applause made the hearts under the blue jackets dance gayly.

How those boys did sing! How their eyes shone, and their feet kept time to the familiar strains! With what a relish they hitched up their trousers and lurched about, or saluted and cheered as the play demanded. With what interest they watched the microscopic midshipmite, listened to Rafe as his sweet voice melodiously told the story of his hapless love, and smiled on pretty Josephine, who was a regular bluebird without the scream.

"Ain't this fun?" whispered Jimmy's next neighbor, taking advantage of a general burst of laughter, as the inimitable little bumboat woman advertised her wares with captivating drollery.

"Right down jolly!" answered Jimmy, feeling that a series of somersaults across the stage would be an immense relief to the pent-up emotions of his boyish soul. For under all the natural excitement of the hour deep down lay the sweet certainty that he was earning health for Kitty, and it made his heart sing for joy more blithely than any jovial chorus to which he lent his happy voice.

But his bliss was not complete till the stately Sir Joseph, K. C. B., had come aboard, followed by "his sisters and his cousins and his aunts;" for among that flock of devoted relatives in white muslin and gay ribbons was Will. Standing in the front row, her bright face was good to see, for her black eyes sparkled, every hair on her head curled its best, her cherry bows streamed in the breeze, and her feet pranced irresistibly at the lively parts of the music. She longed to dance the hornpipe which the little Quaker aunt did so capitally, but, being denied that honor, distinguished herself by the comic vigor with which she "polished up the handle of the big front door," and did the other "business" recorded by the gallant "ruler of the Queen's Navee."

She and Jimmy nodded to each other behind the Admiral's august back, and while Captain Corcoran was singing to the moon, and Buttercup suffering the pangs of "Wemorse," the young people had a gay time behind the scenes. Jimmy and Will sat upon a green baize bank to compare notes, while the relatives flew about like butterflies, and the sailors talked base-ball, jack-knives, and other congenial topics, when not envying Sir Joseph his cocked hat, and the Captain his epaulettes.

It was a very successful launch, and the merry little crew set sail with a fair wind and every prospect of a prosperous voyage. When the first performance was over, our two children left their fine feathers behind them, like Cinderella when the magic hour struck, and went gayly home, feeling much elated, for they knew they should go back to fresh triumphs, and were earning money by their voices like Jenny Lind and Mario. How they pitied other boys and girls who could not go in at that mysterious little door; how important they felt as parts of the spectacle about which every one was talking, and what millionaires they considered themselves as they discussed their earnings and planned what to do with the prospective fortunes.

That was the beginning of many busy, happy weeks for both the children,—weeks which they long remembered with great pleasure, as did older and wiser people; for that merry, innocent little opera proved that theatres can be made the scenes of harmless amusement, and opened to a certain class of young people a new and profitable field for their talents. So popular did this small company become that the piece went on through the summer vacation, and was played in the morning as well as afternoon to satisfy the crowds who wished to see and hear it.

Never had the dear old Boston Museum, which so many of us have loved and haunted for years, seen such a pretty sight as one of those morning performances. It was the perfection of harmless merry-making, and the audience was as pleasant a spectacle as that upon the stage. Fathers and mothers stole an hour from their busy lives to come and be children with their children, irresistibly attracted and charmed by the innocent fun, the gay music that bewitched the ear one could hardly tell why, and the artless acting of those who are always playing parts, whether the nursery or the theatre is their stage.

The windows stood open, and sunshine and fresh air came in to join the revel. Babies crowed and prattled, mammas chatted together, old people found they had not forgotten how to laugh, and boys and girls rejoiced over the discovery of a new delight for holidays. It was good to be there, and in spite of all the discussion in papers and parlors, no harm came to the young mariners, but much careful training of various sorts, and well-earned wages that went into pockets which sorely needed a silver lining.

## HOW THE VOYAGE ENDED

So the good ship "Pinafore" sailed and sailed for many prosperous weeks, and when at last she came into port and dropped anchor for the season she was received with a salute of general approbation for the successful engagement out of which she came with her flags flying and not one of her gallant crew killed or wounded. Well pleased with their share of the glory, officers and men went ashore to spend their prize money with true sailor generosity, all eager to ship again for another cruise in the autumn.

But long before that time Able Seaman James Nelson had sent his family into the country, mother begging Will to take good care of her dear boy till he could join them, and Kitty throwing kisses as she smiled good-by, with cheeks already the rosier for the comforts "brother" had earned for her. Jimmy would not desert his ship while she floated, but managed to spend his Sundays out of town, often taking Will with him as first mate; and, thanks to her lively tongue, friends were soon made for the new-comers. Mrs. Nelson found plenty of sewing, Kitty grew strong and well in the fine air, and the farmer with whom they lived, seeing what a handy lad the boy was, offered him work and wages for the autumn, so all could be independent and together. With this comfortable prospect before him, Jimmy sang away like a contented blackbird, never tiring of his duty, for he was a general favorite, and Kitty literally strewed his way with flowers gathered by her own grateful little hands.

When the last day came, he was in such spirits that he was found doing double-shuffles in corners, hugging the midshipmite, who was a little girl of about Kitty's age, and treating his messmates to peanuts with a lavish hand. Will had her hornpipe, also, when the curtain was down, kissed every one of the other "sisters, cousins, and aunts," and joined lustily in the rousing farewell cheers given by the crew.

A few hours later, a cheerful-looking boy might have been seen trudging toward one of the railway-stations. A new hat, brave in blue streamers, was on his head; a red balloon struggled to escape from one hand; a shabby carpet-bag, stuffed full, was in the other; and a pair of shiny shoes creaked briskly, as if the feet inside were going on a very pleasant errand.

About this young traveller, who walked with a sailor-like roll and lurch, revolved a little girl chattering like a magpie, and occasionally breaking into song, as if she couldn't help it.

"Be sure you come next Saturday; it won't be half such fun if you don't go halves," said the boy, beaming at her as he hauled down the impatient balloon, which seemed inclined to break from its moorings

> " *Yes, I know*
> *That is so!*' "

hummed the girl with a skip to starboard, that she might bear a hand

*Clockwise, from top left:* Sir Joseph Porter, K.C.B., Cousin
Hebe, Josephine, Ralph Rackstraw.

Jimmy's Cruise in the *Pinafore*

with the bag. "Keep some cherries for me, and don't forget to give Kit the doll I dressed for her."

"I shouldn't have been going myself if it hadn't been for you, Will. I never shall forget that," said Jimmy, whom intense satisfaction rendered rather more sedate than his friend.

"Running away to sea is great fun,

> *'With a tar that ploughs the water!'* "

sung Will in spite of herself.

> " ' *And a gallant captain's daughter,'* "

echoed Jimmy, smiling across the carpet-bag. Then both joined in an irrepressible chorus of "Dash it! Dash it!" as a big man nearly upset them and a dog barked madly at the balloon.

Being safely landed in the train, Jimmy hung out of the window till the last minute, discussing his new prospects with Will, who stood on tiptoe outside, bubbling over with fun.

"I'll teach you to make butter and cheese, and you shall be my dairy-woman, for I mean to be a farmer," he said, just as the bell rang.

"All right, I'd like that ever so much." And then the irrepressible madcap burst out, to the great amusement of the passengers,—

> " '*For you might have been a Roosian,*
> *A Frenchman, Turk or Proosian,*
> *Or an Ital-i-an.'* "

*Clockwise, from top left:* Little Buttercup, Captain Corcoran,
Dick Deadeye, Bill Bobstay, the Bos'n.

### Jimmy's Cruise in the *Pinafore*

And Jimmy could not resist shouting back, as the train began to move,—

"'*But in spite of all temptations*
*To belong to other nations,*
*I'm an Amer-i-can.*'"

Then he subsided, to think over the happy holiday before him and the rich cargo of comfort, independence, and pleasure he had brought home from his successful cruise in the "Pinafore."

# THE WHALE'S STORY

FREDDY sat thinking on the seat under the trees. It was a wide, white seat, about four feet long, sloping from the sides to the middle, something like a swing; and was not only comfortable but curious, for it was made of a whale's bone. Freddy often sat there, and thought about it for he was very much interested in it, and nobody could tell him anything of it, except that it had been there a long time.

"Poor old whale, I wonder how you got here, where you came from, and if you were a good and happy creature while you lived," said Freddy, patting the old bone with his little hand.

It gave a great creak; and a sudden gust of air stirred the trees, as if some monster groaned and sighed. Then Freddy heard a strange voice, very loud, yet cracked and queer, as if some one tried to talk with a broken jaw.

"Freddy ahoy!" called the big voice. "I'll tell you all about it; for you are the only person who ever pitied me, or cared to know any thing about me."

"Why, can you talk?" asked Freddy, very much astonished and a little frightened.

"Of course I can, for this is a part of my jaw-bone. I should talk better if my whole mouth was here; but I'm afraid my voice would then be so loud you wouldn't be able to hear it. I don't think any one but you would understand me, any way. It isn't every one that can, you know; but you are a thoughtful little chap, with a lively fancy as well as a kind heart, so you shall hear my story."

"Thank you, I should like it very much, if you would please to speak a little lower, and not sigh; for your voice almost stuns me, and your breath nearly blows me away," said Freddy.

"I'll try: but it's hard to suit my tone to such a mite, or to help groaning when I think of my sad fate; though I deserve it, perhaps," said the bone, more gently.

"Were you a naughty whale?" asked Freddy.

"I was proud, very proud, and foolish; and so I suffered for it. I dare say you know a good deal about us. I see you reading often, and you seem a sensible child."

"No: I haven't read about you yet, and I only know that you are the biggest fish there is," replied Freddy.

The bone creaked and shook, as if it was laughing, and said in a tone that showed it hadn't got over its pride yet:

"You're wrong there, my dear; we are not fishes at all, though stupid mortals have called us so for a long time. We can't live without air; we have warm, red blood; and we don't lay eggs,—so we are *not* fishes. We certainly *are* the biggest creatures in the sea and out of it. Why, bless you! Some of us are nearly a hundred feet long; our tails alone are fifteen or twenty feet wide; the biggest of us weigh five hundred thousand pounds, and have in them the fat, bone, and muscle of a thousand cattle. The lower jaw of one of my family made an arch large enough for a man on horseback to ride under easily, and my cousins of the sperm-family usually yield eighty barrels of oil."

"Gracious me, what monsters you are!" cried Freddy, taking a long breath, while his eyes got bigger and bigger as he listened.

"Ah! You may well say so; we are a very wonderful and interesting family. All our branches are famous in one way or another. Fin-backs, sperms, and rights are the largest; then come the norwhals, the dolphins, and porpoises,—which last, I dare say, you've seen."

"Yes: but tell me about the big ones, please. Which were you?" cried Freddy.

"I was a Right whale, from Greenland. The Sperms live in warm places; but to us the torrid zone is like a sea of fire, and we don't pass it. Our cousins do; and go to the East Indies by way of the North Pole, which is more than your famous Parrys and Franklins could do."

"I don't know about that; but I'd like to hear what you eat, and how you live, and why you came here," said Freddy, who thought the whale rather inclined to boast.

"Well, we haven't got any teeth,—our branch of the family; and we live on creatures so small, that you could only see them with a microscope. Yes, you may stare; but it's true, my dear. The roofs of our mouths are made of whalebone, in broad pieces from six to eight feet long, arranged one against the other; so they make an immense sieve. The tongue, which makes about five barrels of oil, lies below, like a cushion of white satin. When we want to feed, we rush through the water, which is full of the little things we eat, and catch them in our sieve, spurting the water through two holes in our heads. Then we collect the food with our tongue, and swallow it; for, though we are so big, our throats are small. We roam about in the ocean, leaping and floating, feeding and spouting, flying from our enemies, or fighting bravely to defend our young ones."

"Have you got any enemies? I shouldn't think you could have, you are so large," said Freddy.

"But we have, and many too,—three who attack us in the water, and several more that men use against us. The killer, the sword-fish, and the thrasher trouble us at home. The killer fastens to us, and won't be shaken off till he has worried us to death; the sword-fish stabs us with his sword; and the thrasher whips us to death with his own slender, but strong and heavy body. Then, men harpoon us, shoot or entrap us; and make us into oil and candles and seats, and stiffening for gowns and umbrellas," said the bone, in a tone of scorn.

Freddy laughed at the idea, and asked, "How about candles? I know about oil and seats and umbrellas; but I thought candles were made of wax."

"I can't say much on that point: I only know that, when a sperm whale is killed, they make oil out of the fat part as they do of ours; but the Sperms have a sort of cistern in their heads, full of stuff like cream, and rose-colored. They cut a hole in the skull, and dip it out; and sometimes get sixteen or twenty barrels. This is made into what you call spermaceti candles. *We* don't have any such nonsense about us; but the Sperms always were a light-headed set."

Here the bone laughed, in a cracked sort of roar, which sent Freddy flying off the seat on to the grass, where he stayed, laughing also, though he didn't see any joke.

"I beg your pardon, child. It isn't often that I laugh; for I've a heavy heart somewhere, and have known trouble enough to make me as sad as the sea is sometimes."

"Tell me about your troubles; I pity you very much, and like to hear you talk," said Freddy, kindly.

"Unfortunately we are very easily killed, in spite of our size; and have various afflictions besides death. We grow blind; our jaws are deformed sometimes; our tails, with which we swim, get hurt; and we have dyspepsia."

Freddy shouted at that; for he knew what dyspepsia was, because at the sea-side there were many sickly people who were always groaning about that disease.

"It's no laughing matter, I assure you," said the whale's bone. "We suffer a great deal, and get thin and weak and miserable. I've sometimes thought that's the reason we are blue."

"Perhaps, as you have no teeth, you don't chew your food enough, and so have dyspepsia, like an old gentleman I know," said Freddy.

"That's not the reason; my cousins, the Sperms. have teeth, and dyspepsia also."

"Are they blue?"

"No, black and white. But I was going to tell you my troubles. My father was harpooned when I was very young, and I remember how bravely he died. The Rights usually run away when they see a whaler coming; not from cowardice,—oh, dear, no!—but discretion. The Sperms stay and fight, and are killed off very fast; for they are a very headstrong family. We fight when we can't help it; and my father died like a hero. They chased him five hours before they stuck him; he tried to get away, and dragged three or four boats and sixteen hundred fathoms of line from eight in the morning till four at night. Then they got out another line, and he towed the ship itself for more than an hour. There were fifteen harpoons in him: he chewed up a boat, pitched several men overboard, and damaged the vessel, before they killed him. Ah! He was a father to be proud of."

Freddy sat respectfully silent for a few minutes, as the old bone seemed to feel a great deal on the subject. Presently he went on again:

"The Sperms live in herds; but the Rights go in pairs, and are very fond of one another. My wife was a charming creature, and we were very happy, till one sad day, when she was playing with our child,—a sweet little whaleling only twelve feet long, and weighing but a ton,—

my son was harpooned. His mamma, instead of flying, wrapped her fins round him, and dived as far as the line allowed. Then she came up, and dashed at the boats in great rage and anguish, entirely regardless of the danger she was in. The men struck my son, in order to get her and they soon succeeded; but even then, in spite of her suffering, she did not try to escape, but clung to little Spouter till both were killed. Alas! Alas!"

Here the poor bone creaked so dismally, Freddy feared it would tumble to pieces, and bring the story to an end too soon.

"Don't think of those sorrowful things," he said; "tell me how you came to be here. Were you harpooned?"

"Not I; for I've been very careful all my life to keep out of the way of danger: I'm not like one of my relations, who attacked a ship, gave it such a dreadful blow that he made a great hole, the water rushed in, and the vessel was wrecked. But he paid dearly for that prank; for a few months afterward another ship harpooned him very easily, finding two spears still in him, and a wound in his head. I forgot to mention, that the Sperms have fine ivory teeth, and make ambergris,—a sort of stuff that smells very nice, and costs a great deal. I give you these little facts about my family, as you seem interested, and it's always well to improve the minds of young people."

"You are very kind; but will you be good enough to tell about yourself?" said Freddy again; for the bone seemed to avoid that part of the story, as if he didn't want to tell it.

"Well, if I must, I must; but I'm sorry to confess what a fool I've been. You know what coral is, don't you?"

"No," said Freddy, wondering why it asked.

"Then I must tell you, I suppose. There is a bit in the house there,— that rough, white, stony stuff on the table in the parlor. It's full of little holes, you know. Well, those holes are the front doors of hundreds of little polypes, or coral worms, who build the great branches of coral, and live there. They are of various shapes and colors,—some like stars; some fine as a thread, and blue or yellow; others like snails and tiny lobsters. Some people say the real coral-makers are shaped like little oblong bags of jelly, closed at one end, the other open, with six or eight little feelers, like a star, all around it. The other creatures are boarders or visitors: these are the real workers, and, when they sit in their cells and put out their feelers, they make all manner of lovely colors under the water,—crimson, green, orange, and violet. But if they are taken up or touched, the coral people go in doors, and the beautiful hues disappear. They say there are many coral reefs and islands built by these industrious people, in the South Seas; but I can't go there to see, and I am contented with those I find in the northern latitudes. I knew such a community of coral builders, and used to watch them long ago, when they began to work. It was a charming spot down under the sea; for all manner of lovely plants grew there; splendid fishes sailed to and fro; wonderful shells lay about; crimson and yellow prawns, long, gliding green worms, and purple sea-urchins, were there. When I asked the polypes what they were doing, and they answered, 'Building an island,' I laughed at them; for the idea that these tiny, soft atoms could make any thing was ridiculous. 'You may roar; but you'll see that we are right, if you live long enough,' said they. 'Our family have built thousands of islands and long reefs, that the sea can't get over, strong as it is.' That amused me immensely; but I wouldn't believe it, and laughed more than ever."

"It does seem very strange," said Freddy, looking at the branch of coral which he had brought out to examine.

"Doesn't it? And isn't it hard to believe? I used to go, now and then, to see how the little fellows got on, and always found them hard at it. For a long while there was only a little plant without leaves, growing slowly taller and taller; for they always build upward toward the light. By and by, the small shrub was a tree: flying-fish roosted in its branches; sea-cows lay under its shadow; and thousands of jolly little polypes lived and worked in its white chambers. I was glad to see them getting on so well; but still I didn't believe in the island story and used to joke them about their ambition. They were very good-natured, and only answered me, 'Wait a little longer, Friend Right.' I had my own affairs to attend to; so, for years at a time, I forgot the coral-workers, and spent most of my life up Greenland way, for warm climates don't agree with my constitution. When I came back, after a long absence, I was astonished to see the tree grown into a large umbrella-shaped thing, rising above the water. Sea-weed had washed up and clung there; sea-birds had made nests there; land-birds and the winds had carried seeds there, which had sprung up; trunks of trees had been cast there by the sea; lizards, insects, and little animals came with the trees, and were the first inhabitants; and, behold! It *was* an island."

"What did you say then?" asked Freddy.

"I was angry, and didn't want to own that I was wrong; so I insisted that it wasn't a real island, without people on it. 'Wait a little longer,' answered the polypes; and went on, building broader and broader foundations. I flounced away in a rage, and didn't go back for a great while. I hoped something would happen to the coral builders and their island; but I was so curious that I couldn't keep away, and, on going back there, I found a settlement of fishermen, and the beginning of a thriving town. Now I should have been in a towering passion at this, if in my travels I hadn't discovered a race of little creatures as much smaller than polypes as a mouse is smaller than an elephant. I heard two learned men talking about diatoms, as they sailed to Labrador; and I listened. They said these people lived in both salt and fresh water, and were found in all parts of the world. They were a glassy shell, holding a soft, golden-yellow substance, and that they were so countless that banks were made of them, and that a town here in these United States was founded on them. They were the food of many little sea-animals, who, in turn, fed us big creatures, and were very interesting and wonderful. I saved up this story; and, when the polypes asked if they hadn't done what they intended, I told them I didn't think it so very remarkable, for the tiny diatoms made cities, and were far more astonishing animals than they. I thought that would silence them; but they just turned round, and informed me that my diatoms were plants, not animals,—so my story was all humbug. Then I *was* mad; and couldn't get over the fact that these little rascals had done what we, the kings of the sea, couldn't do. I wasn't content with being the biggest creature there: I wanted to be the most skilful also. I didn't remember that every thing has its own place and use, and should be happy in doing the work for which it was made. I fretted over the matter a long while, and at last decided to make an island myself."

"How could you?" asked Freddy.

"I had my plans; and thought them very wise ones. I was so bent on outdoing the polypes that I didn't much care what happened; and so I went to work in my clumsy way. I couldn't pile up stones, or build millions of cells; so I just made an island of myself. I swam up into the harbor yonder one night; covered my back with sea-weed; and lay still on the top of the water. In the morning the gulls came to see what it was, and pecked away at the weeds, telling me very soon that they knew what I was after, and that I couldn't gull them. All the people on shore turned out to see the wonder also; for a fisherman had carried the tidings, and every one was wild to behold the new island. After staring and chattering a long while, boats came off to examine the mystery. Loads of scientific gentlemen worked away at me with microscopes, hammers, acids, and all sorts of tests, to decide what I was; and kept up such a fire of long words that I was 'most dead. They couldn't make up their minds; and meanwhile news of the strange thing spread, and every sort of person came to see me. The gulls kept telling them the joke; but they didn't understand, and I got on capitally. Every night I dined and fed and frolicked till dawn; then put on my sea-weeds, and lay still to be stared at. I wanted some one to come and live on me; then I should be equal to the island of the polypes. But no one came, and I was beginning to be tired of fooling people, when I was fooled myself. An old sailor came to visit me: he had been a whaler, and he soon guessed the secret. But he said nothing till he was safely out of danger; then he got all ready, and one day, as I lay placidly in the sun, a horrible harpoon came flying through the air, and sunk deep into my back. I forgot every thing but the pain, and dived for my life. Alas! The tide was low; the harbor-bar couldn't be passed; and I found hundreds of boats chasing me, till I was driven ashore down there on the flats. Big and strong as we are, once out of water, and we are perfectly helpless. I was soon despatched; and my bones left to whiten on the sand. This was long ago; and, one by one, all my relics have been carried off or washed away. My jaw-bone has been used as a seat here, till it's worn out; but I couldn't crumble away till I'd told some one my story. Remember, child, pride goeth before a fall."

Then, with a great creak, the bone tumbled to pieces; and found a peaceful grave in the long green grass.

# MY BOYS

FEELING that I have been unusually fortunate in my knowledge of a choice and pleasing variety of this least appreciated portion of the human race, I have a fancy to record some of my experiences, hoping that it may awaken an interest in other minds, and cause other people to cultivate the delightful, but too often neglected boys, who now run to waste, so to speak.

I have often wondered what they thought of the peculiar treatment they receive, even at the hands of their nearest friends. While they are rosy, roly-poly little fellows they are petted and praised, adorned and adored, till it is a miracle that they are not utterly ruined. But the moment they outgrow their babyhood their trials begin, and they are regarded as nuisances till they are twenty-one, when they are again received into favor.

Yet that very time of neglect is the period when they most need all manner of helps, and ought to have them. I like boys and oysters raw; so, though good manners are always pleasing, I don't mind the rough outside burr which repels most people, and perhaps that is the reason why the burrs open and let me see the soft lining and taste the sweet nut hidden inside.

My first well-beloved boy was a certain Frank, to whom I clung at the age of seven with a devotion which I fear he did not appreciate. There were six girls in the house, but I would have nothing to say to them, preferring to tag after Frank, and perfectly happy when he allowed me to play with him. I regret to say that the small youth was something of a tyrant, and one of his favorite amusements was trying to make me cry by slapping my hands with books, hoop-sticks, shoes, anything that came along capable of giving a good stinging blow. I believe I endured these marks of friendship with the fortitude of a young Indian, and felt fully repaid for a blistered palm by hearing Frank tell the other boys "She's a brave little thing, and you can't make her cry."

My chief joy was in romping with him in the long galleries of a piano manufactory behind our house. What bliss it was to mount one of the cars on which the workmen rolled heavy loads from room to room, and to go thundering down the inclined planes, regardless of the crash that usually awaited us at the bottom! If I could have played foot-ball on the Common with my Frank and Billy Babcock, life could have offered me no greater joy at that period. As the prejudices of society forbid this sport, I revenged myself by driving hoop all around the mall without stopping, which the boys could *not* do.

I can remember certain happy evenings, when we snuggled in sofa corners and planned tricks and ate stolen goodies, and sometimes Frank would put his curly head in my lap and let me stroke it when he was tired. What the girls did I don't recollect; their domestic plays were not to my taste, and the only figure that stands out from the dimness of the past is that jolly boy with a twinkling eye. This memory would be quite radiant but for one sad thing,—a deed that cut me to the soul then, and which I have never quite forgiven in all these years.

On one occasion I did something very naughty, and when called up for judgment fled to the dining-room, locked the door, and from my stronghold defied the whole world. I could have made my own terms, for it was near dinner-time and the family must eat; but, alas, for the treachery of the human heart! Frank betrayed me. He climbed in at the window, unlocked the door, and delivered me up to the foe. Nay, he even defended the base act, and helped bear the struggling culprit to imprisonment. That nearly broke my heart, for I believed *he* would stand by me as staunchly as I always stood by him. It was a sad blow, and I couldn't love or trust him any more. Peanuts and candy, ginger-snaps and car-rides were unavailing; even foot-ball could not reunite the broken friendship, and to this day I recollect the pang that entered my little heart when I lost my faith in the loyalty of my first boy.

The second attachment was of quite a different sort, and had a happier ending. At the mature age of ten, I left home for my first visit to a family of gay and kindly people in—well, why not say right out?—Providence. There were no children, and at first I did not mind this, as everyone petted me, especially one of the young men named Christopher. So kind and patient, yet so merry was this good Christy that I took him for my private and particular boy, and loved him dearly, for he got me out of innumerable scrapes, and never was tired of amusing the restless little girl who kept the family in a fever of anxiety by her pranks. *He* never laughed at her mishaps and mistakes, never played tricks upon her like a certain William who composed the most trying nicknames, and wickedly goaded the wild visitor into all manner of naughtiness. Christy stood up for her through everything; let her ride the cows, feed the pigs, bang on the piano, and race all over the spice mill, feasting on cinnamon and cloves; brought her down from housetops and fished her out of brooks; never scolded, and never seemed tired of the troublesome friendship of little Torment.

In a week I had exhausted every amusement and was desperately homesick. It has always been my opinion that I should have been speedily restored to the bosom of my family but for Christy, and but for him I should assuredly have ran away before the second week was out. He kept me, and in the hour of my disgrace stood by me like a man and a brother.

One afternoon, inspired by a spirit of benevolence, enthusiastic but short-sighted, I collected several poor children in the barn and regaled them on cake and figs, helping myself freely to the treasures of the pantry without asking leave, meaning to explain afterward. Being discovered before the supplies were entirely exhausted, the patience of the long-suffering matron gave out, and I was ordered up to the garret to reflect upon my sins, and the pleasing prospect of being sent home with the character of the worst child ever known.

My sufferings were deep as I sat upon a fuzzy little trunk all alone in the dull garret, thinking how hard it was to do right, and wondering why I was scolded for feeding the poor when we were expressly bidden to do so. I felt myself an outcast, and bewailed the disgrace I had brought upon my family. Nobody conld possibly love such a bad child; and if the mice were to come and eat me then and there,—a la Bishop Hatto,— it would only be a relief to my friends. At this dark moment I heard Christy say below, "She meant it kindly, so I wouldn't mind, Fanny;" and then up came my boy full of sympathy and comfort. Seeing the tragic expression of my face, he said not a word, but, sitting down in an old chair, took me on his knee and held me close and quietly, letting the action speak for itself. It did most eloquently; for the kind arm seemed to take me back from that dreadful exile, and the friendly face to assure me without words that I had not sinned beyond forgiveness.

I had not shed a tear before, but now I cried tempestuously, and clung to him like a shipwrecked little mariner in a storm. Neither spoke, but he held me fast and let me cry myself to sleep; for, when the shower was over, a pensive peace fell upon me, and the dim old garret seemed not a prison, but a haven of refuge, since my boy came to share it with me. How long I slept I don't know, but it must have been an hour, at least; yet my good Christy never stirred, only waited patiently till I woke up in the twilight and was not afraid because he was there. He took me down as meek as a mouse, and kept me by him all that trying evening, screening me from jokes, rebukes, and sober looks; and when I went to bed he came up to kiss me, and to assure me that this awful circumstance should not be reported at home. This took a load off my heart, and I remember fervently thanking him, and telling him I never would forget it.

I never have, though he died long ago, and others have probably forgotten all about the naughty prank. I often longed to ask him how he knew the surest way to win a child's heart by the patience, sympathy, and tender little acts that have kept his memory green for nearly thirty years.

Cy was a comrade after my own heart, and for a summer or two we kept the neighborhood in a ferment by our adventures and hair-breadth escapes. I think I never knew a boy so full of mischief, and my opportunities of judging have been manifold. He did not get into scrapes himself, but possessed a splendid talent for deluding others into them, and then morally remarking, "There, I told you so!" His way of saying "You dars'nt do this or that," was like fire to powder; and why I still live in the possession of all my limbs and senses is a miracle to those who know my youthful friendship with Cy. It was he who incited me to jump off of the highest beam in the barn to be borne home on a board with a pair of sprained ankles. It was he who dared me to rub my eyes with red peppers, and then sympathizingly led me home blind and roaring with pain. It was he who solemnly assured me that all the little pigs would die in agony if their tails were not cut off, and won me to hold thirteen little squealers while the operation was performed. Those thirteen innocent pink tails haunt me yet, and the memory of that deed has given me a truly Jewish aversion to pork.

I did not know him long, but he was a kindred soul, and must have a place in my list of boys. He is a big, brown man now, and having done his part in the war, is at work on his farm. We meet sometimes, and though we try to be dignified and proper, it is quite impossible; there is a sly twinkle in Cy's eye that upsets my gravity, and we always burst out laughing at the memory of our early frolics.

My Augustus! Oh, my Augustus! My first little lover, and the most romantic of my boys. At fifteen I met this charming youth, and thought I had found my fate. It was at a spelling school in a little country town where I, as a stranger and visitor from the city, was an object of interest. Painfully conscious of this fact, I sat in a corner trying to look easy and elegant, with a large red bow under my chin, and a carnelian ring in

The memory of those thirteen pink tails has haunted me
ever since.

My Boys

full view. Among the boys and girls who frolicked about me, I saw one lad of seventeen with "large blue eyes, a noble brow, and a beautiful straight nose," as I described him in a letter to my sister. This attractive youth had a certain air of refinement and ease of manner that the others lacked; and when I found he was the minister's son, I felt that I might admire him without loss of dignity. "Imagine my sensations," as Miss Burney's Evelina says, when this boy came and talked to me, a little bashfully at first, but soon quite freely, and invited me to a huckleberry party next day. I had observed that he was one of the best spellers. I also observed that his language was quite elegant; he even quoted Byron, and rolled his eyes in a most engaging manner, not to mention that he asked who gave me my ring, and said he depended on escorting me to the berry pasture.

Dear me, how interesting it was! And when I found myself, next day, sitting under a tree in the sunny field (full of boys and girls, all more or less lovering), with the amiable Augustus at my feet, gallantly supplying me with bushes to strip while we talked about books and poetry, I really felt as if I had got into a novel, and enjoyed it immensely. I believe a dim idea that Gus was sentimental hovered in my mind, but I would not encourage it, though I laughed in my sleeve when he was spouting Latin for my benefit, and was uncertain whether to box his ears or simper later in the day, when he languished over the gate, and said he thought chestnut hair the loveliest in the world.

Poor, dear boy! How innocent and soft-hearted and full of splendid dreams he was, and what deliciously romantic times we had floating on the pond, while the frogs sung to his accordion, as he tried to say un-utterable things with his honest blue eyes. It makes me shiver now to think of the mosquitoes and the damp; but it was Pauline and Claude Melnotte then, and when I went home we promised to be true to one another, and write every week during the year he was away at school.

We parted,—not in tears by any means; that sort of nonsense comes later, when the romance is less childish,—but quite jolly and comfortable, and I hastened to pour forth the thrilling tale to my faithful sister, who approved of the match, being a perfect "mush of sentiment" herself.

I fear it was not a very ardent flame, however, for Gus did not write every week, and I did not care a bit; nevertheless, I kept his picture and gave it a sentimental sigh when I happened to think of it, while he sent messages now and then, and devoted himself to his studies like an ambitious boy as he was. I hardly expected to see him again, but soon after the year was out, to my great surprise he called. I was so fluttered by the appearance of his card that I rather lost my head, and did such a silly thing that it makes me laugh even now. He liked chestnut hair, and, pulling out my combs, I rushed down, theatrically dishevelled, hoping to impress my lover with my ardor and my charms.

I expected to find little Gus; but, to my great confusion, a tall being with a beaver in his hand rose to meet me, looking so big and handsome and generally imposing, that I could not recover myself for several minutes, and mentally wailed for my combs, feeling like an untidy simpleton.

I don't know whether he thought me a little cracked or not, but he was very friendly and pleasant, and told me his plans, and hoped I would make another visit, and smoothed his beaver, and let me see his tail-coat, and behaved himself like a dear, conceited, clever boy. He did not allude to our love-passages, being shy, and I blessed him for it; for really, I don't know what rash thing I might have done under the exciting circumstances. Just as he was going, however, he forgot his cherished hat for a minute, put out both hands, and said heartily, with his old boyish laugh,—

"Now you will come, and we'll go boating and berrying, and all the rest of it again, won't we?"

The blue eyes were full of fun and feeling, too, I fancied, as I blushingly retired behind my locks and gave the promise. But I never went, and never saw my little lover any more, for in a few weeks he was dead of a fever, brought on by too much study,—and so ended the sad history of my fourth boy.

After this, for many years, I was a boyless being; but was so busy I did not feel my destitute condition till I went to the hospital during the war, and found my little sergeant. His story has been told elsewhere, but the sequel to it is a pleasant one, for Baby B. still writes to me now and then, asks advice about his future, and gladdens me with good news of his success as a business man in Kansas.

As if to atone for the former dearth, a sudden shower of most superior boys fell upon me, after I recovered from my campaign. Some of the very best sort it was my fortune to know and like,—real gentlemen, yet boys still,—and jolly times they had, stirring up the quiet old town with their energetic society.

There was W., a stout, amiable youth, who would stand in the middle of a strawberry patch, with his hands in his pockets, and let us feed him luxuriously. B., a delightful scapegrace, who came once a week to confess his sins, beat his breast in despair, vow awful vows of repentance, and then cheerfully depart, to break every one of them in the next twenty-four hours. S. the gentle-hearted giant; J. the dandy; sober, sensible B.; and E., the young knight without reproach or fear.

But my especial boy of the batch was A.,—proud and cold and shy to other people, sad and serious sometimes when his good heart and tender conscience showed him his short-comings, but so grateful for sympathy and a kind word.

I could not get at him as easily as I could the other lads, but, thanks to Dickens, I found him out at last.

We played Dolphus and Sophy Tetterby in the "Haunted Man," at one of the school festivals; and during the rehearsals I discovered that my Dolphus was—permit the expression, oh, well-bred readers!—a trump. What fun we had, to be sure, acting the droll and pathetic scenes together, with a swarm of little Tetterbys skirmishing about us! From that time he has been my Dolphus and I his Sophy, and my yellow-haired laddie don't forget me, though he has a younger Sophy now, and some small Tetterbys of his own. He writes just the same affectionate letters as he used to do, though I, less faithful, am too busy to answer them.

But the best and dearest of all my flock was my Polish boy, Ladislas Wisniewski,—two hiccoughs and a sneeze will give you the name perfectly. Six years ago, as I went down to my early breakfast at our Pension in

Vevey, I saw that a stranger had arrived. He was a tall youth, of eighteen or twenty, with a thin, intelligent face, and the charmingly polite manners of a foreigner. As the other boarders came in, one by one, they left the door open, and a draught of cold autumn air blew in from the stone corridor, making the new comer cough, shiver, and cast wistful glances toward the warm corner by the stove. My place was there, and the heat often oppressed me, so I was glad of an opportunity to move.

A word to Madame Vodoz effected the change; and at dinner I was rewarded by a grateful smile from the poor fellow, as he nestled into his warm seat, after a pause of surprise and a flush of pleasure at the small kindness from a stranger. We were too far apart to talk much, but, as he filled his glass, the Pole bowed to me, and said low in French,—

"I drink the good health to Mademoiselle."

I returned the wish, but he shook his head with a sudden shadow on his face, as if the words meant more than mere compliment to him.

"That boy is sick and needs care. I must see to him," said I to myself, as I met him in the afternoon, and observed the military look of his blue and white suit, as he touched his cap and smiled pleasantly. I have a weakness for brave boys in blue, and having discovered that he had been in the late Polish Revolution, my heart warmed to him at once.

That evening he came to me in the salon, and expressed his thanks in the prettiest broken English I ever heard. So simple, frank, and grateful was he that a few words of interest won his little story from him, and in half an hour we were friends. With his fellow-students he had fought through the last outbreak, had suffered imprisonment and hardship rather than submit, had lost many friends, his fortune and his health, and at twenty, lonely, poor, and ill, was trying bravely to cure the malady which seemed fatal.

"If I recover myself of this affair in the chest, I teach the music to acquire my bread in this so hospitable country. At Paris, my friends, all two, find a refuge, and I go to them in spring if I die not here. Yes, it is solitary, and my memories are not gay, but I have my work, and the good God remains always to me, so I content myself with much hope, and I wait."

Such genuine piety and courage increased my respect and regard immensely, and a few minutes later he added to both by one of the little acts that show character better than words.

He told me about the massacre, when five hundred Poles were shot down by Cossacks in the marketplace, merely because they sung their national hymn.

"Play me that forbidden air," I said, wishing to judge of his skill, for I had heard him practicing softly in the afternoon.

He rose willingly, then glanced about the room and gave a little shrug which made me ask what he wanted.

"I look to see if the Baron is here. He is Russian, and to him my national air will not be pleasing."

"Then play it. He dare not forbid it here, and I should rather enjoy that little insult to your bitter enemy," said I, feeling very indignant with everything Russian just then.

"Ah, mademoiselle, it is true we are enemies, but we are also gentlemen," returned the boy, proving that *he* at least was one.

I thanked him for his lesson in politeness, and as the Baron was not there he played the beautiful hymn, singing it enthusiastically in spite of the danger to his weak lungs. A true musician evidently, for, as he sung his pale face glowed, his eyes shone, and his lost vigor seemed restored to him.

From that evening we were fast friends; for the memory of certain dear lads at home made my heart open to this lonely boy, who gave me in return the most grateful affection and service. He begged me to call him "Varjo," as his mother did. He constituted himself my escort, errand-boy, French teacher, and private musician, making those weeks infinitely pleasant by his winning ways, his charming little confidences, and faithful friendship.

We had much fun over our lessons, for I helped him about his English. With a great interest in free America, and an intense longing to hear about our war, the barrier of an unknown tongue did not long stand between us. Beginning with my bad French and his broken English, we got on capitally; but he outdid me entirely, making astonishing progress, though he often slapped his forehead with the despairing exclamation,—

"I am imbecile! I never can will shall to have learn this beast of English!"

But he did, and in a month had added a new language to the five he already possessed.

His music was the delight of the house; and he often gave us little concerts with the help of Madam Teiblin, a German St. Cecelia, with a cropped head and a gentlemanly sack, cravat, and collar. Both were enthusiasts, and the longer they played the more inspired they got. The piano vibrated, the stools creaked, the candles danced in their sockets, and everyone sat mute while the four white hands chased one another up and down the keys, and the two fine faces beamed with such ecstasy that we almost expected to see instrument and performers disappear in a musical whirlwind.

Lake Leman will never seem so lovely again as when Laddie and I roamed about its shores, floated on its bosom, or laid splendid plans for the future in the sunny garden of the old chateau. I tried it again last year, but the charm was gone, for I missed my boy with his fun, his music, and the frank, fresh affection he gave his "little mamma," as he insisted on calling the lofty spinster who loved him like half a dozen grandmothers rolled into one.

December roses blossomed in the gardens then, and Laddie never failed to have a posy ready for me at dinner. Few evenings passed without "confidences" in my corner of the salon, and I still have a pile of merry little notes which I used to find tucked under my door. He called them chapters of a great history we were to write together, and being a "*polisson*" he illustrated it with droll pictures, and a funny mixture of French and English romance.

It was very pleasant, but like all pleasant things in this world of change it soon came to an end. When I left for Italy we jokingly agreed to meet in Paris the next May, but neither really felt that we should ever meet again, for Laddie hardly expected to outlive the winter, and I felt sure

I should soon be forgotten. As he kissed my hand there were tears in my boy's eyes, and a choke in the voice that tried to say cheerfully,—

"*Bon voyage*, dear and good little mamma. I do not say adieu, but *au revoir*."

Then the carriage rolled away, the wistful face vanished, and nothing remained to me but the memory of Laddie, and a little stain on my glove where a drop had fallen.

As I drew near Paris six months later, and found myself wishing that I might meet Varjo in the great, gay city, and wondering if there was any chance of my doing it, I never dreamed of seeing him so soon; but, as I made my way among the crowd of passengers that poured through the station, feeling tired, bewildered, and homesick, I suddenly saw a blue and white cap wave wildly in the air, then Laddie's beaming face appeared, and Laddie's eager hands grasped mine so cordially that I began to laugh at once, and felt that Paris was almost as good as home.

"Ah, ha! Behold the little mamma, who did not thought to see again her bad son! Yes, I am greatly glad that I make the fine surprise for you as you come all weary to this place of noise. Give to me the billets, for I am still mademoiselle's servant and go to find the coffers."

He got my trunks, put me into a carriage, and as we rolled merrily away I asked how he chanced to meet me so unexpectedly. Knowing where I intended to stay, he had called occasionally till I notified Madame D. of the day and hour of my arrival, and then he had come to "make the fine surprise." He enjoyed the joke like a true boy, and I was glad to see how well he looked, and how gay he seemed.

"You are better?" I said.

"I truly hope so. The winter was good to me and I cough less. It is a small hope, but I do not enlarge my fear by a sad face. I yet work and save a little purse, so that I may not be a heaviness to those who have the charity to finish me if I fall back and yet die."

I would not hear of that, and told him he looked as well and happy as if he had found a fortune.

He laughed, and answered with his fine bow, "I have. Behold, you come to make the fête for me. I find also here my friends Joseph and Napoleon. Poor as mouses of the church, as you say, but brave boys, and we work together with much gayety."

When I asked if he had leisure to be my guide about Paris, for my time was short and I wanted to see *everything*, he pranced, and told me he had promised himself a holiday, and had planned many excursions the most wonderful, charming, and gay. Then, having settled me at Madame's, he went blithely away to what I afterward discovered were very poor lodgings, across the river.

Next day began the pleasantest fortnight in all my year of travel. Laddie appeared early, elegant to behold in a new hat and buff gloves, and was immensely amused because the servant informed me that my big son had arrived.

I believe the first thing a woman does in Paris is to buy a new bonnet. I did, or rather stood by and let "my son" do it in the best of French, only whispering when he proposed gorgeous *chapeaus* full of flowers and feathers, that I could not afford it.

"Ah! We must make our economies, must we? See, then, this modest, pearl-colored one, with the crape rose. Yes, we will have that, and be most elegant for the Sunday promenade."

I fear I should have bought a pea-green hat with a yellow plume if he had urged it, so wheedlesome and droll were his ways and words. His good taste saved me, however, and the modest one was sent home for the morrow, when we were to meet Joseph and Napoleon and go to the concert in the Tuileries garden.

Then we set off on our day of sight-seeing, and Laddie proved himself an excellent guide. We had a charming trip about the enchanted city, a gay lunch at a café, and a first brief glimpse of the Louvre. At dinner-time I found a posy at my place; and afterward Laddie came and spent the evening in my little salon, playing to me, and having what he called "babblings and pleasantries." I found that he was translating "Vanity Fair" into Polish, and intended to sell it at home. He convulsed me with his struggles to put cockney English and slang into good Polish, for he had saved up a list of words for me to explain to him. Haystack and bean-pot were among them, I remember; and when he had mastered the meanings he fell upon the sofa exhausted.

Other days like this followed, and we led a happy life together; for my twelve years' seniority made our adventures quite proper, and I fearlessly went anywhere on the arm of my big son. Not to theaters or balls, however, for heated rooms were bad for Laddie, but pleasant trips out of the city in the bright spring weather, quiet strolls in the gardens, moonlight concerts in the Champs Elysées; or, best of all, long talks with music in the little red salon, with the gas turned low, and the ever-changing scenes of the Rue de Rivoli under the balcony.

Never were pleasures more cheaply purchased or more thoroughly enjoyed, for our hearts were as light as our purses, and our "little economies" gave zest to our amusements.

Joseph and Napoleon sometimes joined us, and I felt in my element with the three invalid soldier boys, for Napoleon still limped with a wound received in the war, Joseph had never recovered from his two years' imprisonment in an Austrian dungeon, and Laddie's loyalty might yet cost him his life.

Thanks to them, I discovered a joke played upon me by my "*polisson*." He told me to call him "ma drogha," saying it meant "my friend," in Polish. I innocently did so, and he seemed to find great pleasure in it, for his eyes always laughed when I said it. Using it one day before the other lads, I saw a queer twinkle in their eyes, and, suspecting mischief, demanded the real meaning of the words. Laddie tried to silence them, but the joke was too good to keep, and I found to my dismay that I had been calling him "my darling" in the tenderest manner.

How the three rascals shouted, and what a vain struggle it was to try and preserve my dignity when Laddie clasped his hands and begged pardon, explaining that jokes were necessary to his health, and he never meant me to know the full baseness of this "pleasantrie!" I revenged myself by giving him some bad English for his translation, and telling him of it just as I left Paris.

It was not all fun with my boy, however; he had his troubles, and in spite of his cheerfulness he knew what heartache was. Walking in the quaint garden of the Luxembourg one day, he confided to me the little romance of his life. A very touching little romance as he told it, with eloquent eyes and voice and frequent pauses for breath. I cannot give his words, but the simple facts were these:—

He had grown up with a pretty cousin, and at eighteen was desperately in love with her. She returned his affection, but they could not be happy, for her father wished her to marry a richer man. In Poland, to marry without the consent of parents is to incur lasting disgrace; so Leonore obeyed, and the young pair parted. This had been a heavy sorrow to Laddie, and he rushed into the war hoping to end his trouble.

"Do you ever hear from your cousin?" I asked, as he walked beside me, looking sadly down the green aisles where kings and queens had loved and parted years ago.

"I only know that she suffers still, for she remembers. Her husband submits to the Russians, and I despise him as I have no English to tell;" and he clenched his hands with the flash of the eye and sudden kindling of the whole face that made him handsome.

He showed me a faded little picture, and when I tried to comfort him, he laid his head down on the pedestal of one of the marble queens who guard the walk, as if he never cared to lift it up again.

But he was all right in a minute, and bravely put away his sorrow with the little picture. He never spoke of it again, and I saw no more shadows on his face till we came to say good-by.

"You have been so kind to me, I wish I had something beautiful to give you, Laddie," I said, feeling that it would be hard to get on without my boy.

"This time it is for always; so, as a parting souvenir, give to me the sweet English good-by."

As he said this, with a despairing sort of look, as if he could not spare even so humble a friend as myself, my heart was quite rent within me, and, regardless of several prim English ladies, I drew down his tall head and kissed him tenderly, feeling that in this world there were no more meetings for us. Then I ran away and buried myself in an empty railway carriage, hugging the little cologne bottle he had given me.

He promised to write, and for five years he has kept his word, sending me from Paris and Poland cheery, bright letters in English, at my desire, so that he might not forget. Here is one as a specimen.

"MY DEAR AND GOOD FRIEND,—What do you think of me that I do not write so long time? Excuse me, my good mamma, for I was so busy in these days I could not do this pleasant thing. I write English without the fear that you laugh at it, because I know it is more agreeable to read the own language, and I think you are not excepted of this rule. It is good of me, for the expressions of love and regard, made with faults, take the funny appearance; they are *ridicule*, and instead to go to the heart, they make the laugh. Never mind, I do it.

"You cannot imagine yourself how *stupide* is Paris when you are gone. I fly to my work, and make no more fêtes,—it is too sad alone. I tie myself to my table and my Vanity (not of mine, for I am not vain, am I?). I wish some chapters to finish themselfs *vite*, that I send them to Pologne and know the end. I have a little question to ask you (of Vanity as always). I cannot translate this, no one of *dictionnaires* makes me the words, and I think it is *jàrgon de prison*, this little period. Behold:—

> '*Mopy, is that your snum?*'
> '*Nubble your dad and gully the dog,*' *&c.*

"So funny things I cannot explain myself, so I send to you, and you reply sooner than without it, for you have so kind interest in my work you do not stay to wait. So this is a little hook for you to make you write some words to your son who likes it so much and is fond of you.

"My doctor tells me my lungs are soon to be reestablished; so you may imagine yourself how glad I am, and of more courage in my future. You may one day see your Varjo in Amerique, if I study commerce as I wish. So then the last time of seeing ourselves is *not* the last. Is that to please you? I suppose the grand *histoire* is finished, *n'est ce pas?* You will then send it to me care of M. Gryhomski Austriche, and he will give to me in clandestine way at Varsovie, otherwise it will be confiscated at the frontier by the stupide Russians.

"Now we are dispersed in two sides of world far apart, for soon I go home to Pologne and am no more '*juif errant.*' It is now time I work at my life in some useful way, and I do it.

"As I am your *grand fils*, it is proper that I make you my compliment of happy Christmas and New Year, is it not? I wish for you so many as they may fulfil long human life. May this year bring you more and more good hearts to love you (the only real happiness in the hard life), and may I be as now, yours for always,

"VARJO."

A year ago he sent me his photograph and a few lines. I acknowledged the receipt of it, but since then not a word has come, and I begin to fear that my boy is dead. Others have appeared to take his place, but they don't suit, and I keep his corner always ready for him if he lives. If he is dead, I am glad to have known so sweet and brave a character, for it does one good to see even as short-lived and obscure a hero as my Polish boy, whose dead December rose embalms for me the memory of Varjo, the last and dearest of my boys.

It is hardly necessary to add, for the satisfaction of inquisitive little women, that Laddie was the original of Laurie, as far as a pale pen and ink sketch could embody a living, loving boy.

# A CURIOUS CALL

I HAVE often wondered what the various statues standing about the city think of all day, and what criticisms they would make upon us and our doings, if they could speak. I frequently stop and stare at them, wondering if they don't feel lonely; if they wouldn't be glad of a nod as we go by; and I always long to offer my umbrella to shield their uncovered heads on a rainy day, especially to good Ben Franklin, when the snow lies white on his benevolent forehead. I was always fond of this old gentleman; and one of my favorite stories when a little girl, was that of his early life, and the time when he was so poor he walked about Philadelphia with a roll of bread under each arm, eating a third as he went. I never pass without giving him a respectful look, and wishing he could know how grateful I am for all he had done in the printing line; for, without types and presses, where would the books be?

Well, I never imagined that he understood why the tall woman in the big bonnet stared at him; but he did, and he liked it, and managed to let me know it in a very curious manner, as you shall hear.

As I look out, the first thing I see is the great gilt eagle on the City-Hall dome. There he sits, with open wings, all day long, looking down on the people, who must appear like ants scampering busily to and fro about an ant-hill. The sun shines on him splendidly in the morning; the gay flag waves and rustles in the wind above him sometimes; and the moonlight turns him to silver when she comes glittering up the sky. When it rains, he never shakes his feathers; snow beats on him without disturbing his stately repose; and he never puts his head under his wing at night, but keeps guard in darkness as in day, like a faithful sentinel. I like the big, lonely bird, call him my particular fowl, and often wish he'd turn his head and speak to me. One night he did actually do it, or seemed to; for I've never been able to decide whether I dreamed what I'm going to tell you, or whether it really happened.

It was a stormy night; and, as I drew down my curtain, I said to myself, after peering through the driving snow to catch a glimpse of my neighbor, "Poor Goldy! He'll have a rough time of it. I hope this northeaster won't blow him off his perch." Then I sat down by my fire, took my knitting, and began to meditate. I'm sure I didn't fall asleep; but I can't prove it, so we'll say no more about it. All at once there came a tap at my door, as I thought; and I said "Come in," just as Mr. Poe did when that unpleasant raven paid him a call. No one came, so I went to see who it was. Not a sign of a human soul in the long hall, only little Jessie, the poodle, asleep on her mat. Down I sat; but in a minute the tap came again; this time so loud that I knew it was at the window, and went to open it, thinking that one of my doves wanted to come in perhaps. Up went the sash, and in bounced something so big and so bright that it dazzled and scared me.

"Don't be frightened, ma'am; it's only me," said a hoarse voice. So I collected my wits, rubbed my eyes, and looked at my visitor. It was the gold eagle off the City Hall! I don't expect to be believed; but I wish you'd been here to see, for I give you my word, it was a sight to behold. How he ever got in at such a small window I can't tell; but there he was, strutting majestically up and down the room, his golden plumage rustling, and his keen eyes flashing as he walked. I really didn't know what to do. I couldn't imagine what he came for; I had my doubts about the propriety of offering him a chair; and he was so much bigger than I

expected that I was afraid he might fly away with me, as the roc did
with Sinbad; so I did nothing but sidle to the door, ready to whisk out,
if my strange guest appeared to be peckishly inclined. My respectful
silence seemed to suit him; for, after a turn or two, he paused, nodded
gravely, and said affably, "Good-evening, ma'am. I stepped over to bring
you old Ben's respects, and to see how you were getting on."

"I'm very much obliged, sir. May I inquire who Mr. Old-Ben is? I'm
afraid I haven't the honor of his acquaintance."

"Yes, you have; it's Ben Franklin, of City-Hall yard. You know him;
and he wished me to thank you for your interest in him."

"Dear me! How very odd! Will you sit down, sir?"

"Never sit! I'll perch here"; and the great fowl took his accustomed
attitude just in front of the fire, looking so very splendid that I couldn't
keep my eyes off of him.

"Ah! You often do that. Never mind; I rather like it," said the eagle,
graciously, as he turned his brilliant eye upon me. I was rather abashed;
but being very curious, I ventured to ask a few questions, as he seemed
in a friendly mood.

"Being a woman, sir, I'm naturally of an inquiring turn; and I must
confess that I have a strong desire to know how it happens that you take
your walks abroad, when you are supposed to be permanently engaged
at home?"

He shrugged his shoulders, and actually winked at me, as he replied,
"That's all people know of what goes on under, or rather over, their
noses. Bless you, ma'am! I leave my roost every night, and enjoy myself
in all sorts of larks. Excuse the expression; but, being ornithological, it
is more proper for me than for some people who use it."

"What a gay old bird!" thought I, feeling quite at home after that.
"Please tell me what you do, when the shades of evening prevail, and
you go out for a frolic?"

"I am a gentleman; therefore I behave myself," returned the eagle,
with a stately air. "I must confess, I smoke a great deal: but that's not
my fault, it's the fault of the chimneys. They keep it up all day, and I
have to take it; just as you poor ladies have to take cigar smoke, whether
you like it or not. My amusements are of a wholesome kind. I usually
begin by taking a long flight down the harbor, for a look at the lighthouses,
the islands, the shipping, and the sea. My friends, the gulls, bring their
reports to me; for they are the harbor-police, and I take notes of their
doings. The school-ship is an object of interest to me, and I often perch
on the mast-head, to see how the lads are getting on. Then I take a turn
over the city, gossip with the weathercocks, pay my compliments to the
bells, inspect the fire-alarm, and pick up information by listening at the
telegraph wires. People often talk about 'a little bird' who spreads news;
but they don't know how that figure of speech originated. It is the
sparrows sitting on the wires, who receive the electric shock, and, being
hollow-boned, the news go straight to their heads; they then fly about,
chirping it on the housetops, and the air carries it everywhere. That's
the way rumors rise and news spread."

"If you'll allow, I'll make a note of that interesting fact," said I, wondering
if I might believe him. He appeared to fall into a reverie, while I jotted

down the sparrow story, and it occurred to me that perhaps I ought to offer my distinguished guest some refreshment; but, when I modestly alluded to it, he said, with an aldermanic air, "No, thank you; I've just dined at the Parker House."

Now, I really could *not* swallow that; and so plainly betrayed my incredulity, that the eagle explained. "The savory smells which rise to my nostrils from that excellent hotel, with an occasional sniff from the Tremont, are quite sufficient to satisfy my appetite; for, having no stomach, I don't need much food, and I drink nothing but water."

"I wish others would follow your example in that latter habit," said I, respectfully, for I was beginning to see that there was something in my bird, though he *was* hollow. "Will you allow me to ask if the other statues in the city fly by night?"

"They promenade in the parks; and occasionally have social gatherings, when they discuss politics, education, medicine, or any of the subjects in which they are interested. Ah! We have grand times when you are all asleep. It quite repays me for being obliged to make an owl of myself."

"Do the statues come from the shops to these parties?" I asked, resolving to take a late walk the next moonlight night.

"Sometimes; but they get lazy and delicate, living in close, warm places. We laugh at cold and bad weather, and are so strong and hearty that I shouldn't be surprised if I saw Webster and Everett flying round the Common on the new-fashioned velocipedes, for they believed in exercise. Goethe and Schiller often step over from De Vries's window, to flirt with the goddesses, who come down from their niches on Horticultural Hall. Nice, robust young women are Pomona and Flora. If your niminy-piminy girls could see them run, they would stop tilting through the streets, and learn that the true Grecian Bend is the line of beauty always found in straight shoulders, well-opened chest, and an upright figure, firmly planted on active feet."

"In your rambles don't you find a great deal of misery?" said I, to change the subject, for he was evidently old-fashioned in his notions.

"Many sad sights!" And he shook his head with a sigh; then added, briskly, "But there is a deal of charity in our city, and it does its work beautifully. By the by, I heard of a very sweet charity the other day,— a church whose Sunday school is open to all the poor children who will come; and there, in pleasant rooms, with books, pictures, kindly teachers, and a fatherly minister to welcome them, the poor little creatures find refreshment for their hungry souls. I like that; it's a lovely illustration of the text, 'Suffer little children to come unto me;' and *I* call it practical Christianity."

He did like it, my benevolent old bird; for he rustled his great wings, as if he wanted to clap them, if there had only been room; and every feather shone as if a clearer light than that of my little fire had fallen on it as he spoke.

"You are a literary woman, hey?" he said suddenly, as if he'd got a new idea, and was going to pounce upon me with it.

"Ahem! I do a little in that line," I answered, with a modest cough.

"Then tell people about that place; write some stories for the children; go and help teach them; do something, and make others do what they can to increase the Sabbath sunshine that brightens one day in the week for the poor babies who live in shady places.''

"I should be glad to do my best; and, if I'd known before"—I began.

"You might have known, if you'd looked about you. People are so wrapped up in their own affairs they don't do half they might. Now, then, hand me a bit of paper, and I'll give you the address, so you won't have any excuse for forgetting what I tell you."

"Mercy on us! What will he do next?" thought I, as he tweaked a feather out of his breast, gave the nib a peck, and then coolly wrote these words on the card I handed him: "*Church of the Disciples. Knock, and it shall be opened!*" There it was, in letters of gold; and, while I looked at it, feeling reproached that I hadn't known it sooner, my friend,—he didn't seem a stranger any more,—said in a business-like tone, as he put back his pen, "Now I must be off. Old Ben reads an article on the 'Abuses of the Press at the present day,' and I must be there to report."

"It must be very interesting. I suppose you don't allow mortals at your meetings?" said I, burning to go, in spite of the storm.

"No, ma'am. We meet on the Common; and, in the present state of the weather, I don't think flesh and blood would stand it. Bronze, marble, and wood, are sterner stuff, and can defy the elements."

"Good evening; pray, call again," I said, hospitably.

"I will; your eyrie suits me; but don't expect me to call in the daytime. I'm on duty then, and can't take my eye off my charge. The city needs a deal of watching, my dear. Bless me! It's striking eight. Your watch is seven minutes slow by the Old South. Good-night, good-night!"

And as I opened the window, the great bird soared away like a flash of light through the storm, leaving me so astonished at the whole performance that I haven't got over it yet.

# BACK WINDOWS

As I sit working at my back window, I look out on a long row of other people's back windows; and it is quite impossible for me to help seeing and being interested in my neighbors. There are a good many children in those houses; and though I don't know one of their names, I know them a great deal better than they think I do. I never spoke a word to any of them, and never expect to do so; yet, I have my likes and dislikes among them, and could tell them things that they have said and done, which would astonish them very much, I assure you.

First, the babies,—for there are three: the aristocratic baby, the happy-go-lucky baby, and the forlorn baby. The aristocratic baby lives in a fine, well-furnished room, has a pretty little mamma, who wears white gowns, and pink ribbons in her cap; likewise, a fond young papa, who evidently thinks *this* the most wonderful baby in Boston. There is a stout, motherly lady, who is the grandma, I fancy, for she is always hovering about "the dear" with cups, blankets, or a gorgeous red worsted bird to amuse it. Baby is a plump, rosy, sweet-faced little creature, always smiling and kissing its hand to the world in general. In its pretty white frocks, with its own little pink or blue ribbons, and its young mamma proudly holding it up to see and be seen, my aristocratic neighbor has an easy life of it, and is evidently one of the little lilies who do nothing but blossom in the sunshine.

The happy-go-lucky baby is just able to toddle; and I seldom pull up my curtain in the morning without seeing him at his window in his yellow flannel night-gown, taking a look at the weather. No matter whether it rains or shines, there he is, smiling and nodding, and looking so merry, that it is evident he has plenty of sunshine bottled up in his own little heart for private use. I depend on seeing him, and feel as if the world was not right until this golden little sun rises to shine upon me. He don't seem to have any one to take care of him, but trots about all day, and takes care of himself. Sometimes he is up in the chambers with the girl, while she makes beds, and he helps; then he takes a stroll into the parlor, and spins the gay curtain tassels to his heart's content; next, he dives into the kitchen (I hope he does not tumble downstairs, but I dare say he wouldn't mind if he did), and he gets pushed about by all the busy women, as they "fly round." I rather think it gets too hot for him there about dinner-time; for he often comes out into the yard for a walk at noon, and seems to find endless wonders and delights in the ash-barrel, the water-butt, two old flower-pots, and a little grass plat, in which he plants a choice variety of articles, in the firm faith they will come up in full bloom. I hope the big spoon and his own red shoe *will* sprout and appear before any trouble is made about their mysterious disappearance. At night I see a little shadow bobbing about on the curtain, and watch it, till, with a parting glimpse at a sleepy face at the window, my small sun sets, and I leave him to his dreams.

The forlorn baby roars all day, and I don't blame him; for he is trotted, shaken, spanked, and scolded by a very cross nurse, who treats him like a mealbag. I pity that little neighbor, and don't believe he will stand it long; for I see him double up his tiny fists, and spar away at nothing, as if getting ready for a good tussle with the world by and by, if he lives to try it.

Then the boys,—bless their buttons!—how amusing they are. One young man, aged about ten, keeps hens; and the trials of that boy are really pathetic. The biddies get out every day or two, and fly away all over the neighborhood, like feathers when you shake a pillow. They cackle and crow, and get up on sheds and fences, and trot down the streets, all at once, and that poor fellow spins round after them like a distracted top. One by one he gets them and comes lugging them back, upside down, in the most undignified attitude, and shuts them up, and hammers away, and thinks they are all safe, and sits down to rest, when a triumphant crow from some neighboring shed tells him that that rascally black rooster is out again for another promenade. I'm not bloodthirsty; but I really do long for Thanksgiving, that my neighbor Hen-ry may find rest for the sole of his foot; for, not till his poultry are safely eaten will he ever know where they are.

Another boy has a circus about once a week, and tries to break his neck jumping through hoops, hanging to a rope by his heels, turning somersaults in the air, and frightening his mother out of her wits by his pranks. I suspect that he has been to see Leotard, and I admire his energy, for he is never discouraged; and, after tumbling flat, half-a-dozen times, he merely rubs his elbows and knees, and then up and takes another.

There is a good, domestic boy, who brushes and curls his three little sisters' hair every morning, and must do it very gently, for they seem to like it; and I often see them watch at the back gate for him, and clap their hands, and run to meet him, sure of being welcomed as little sisters like to be met by the big brothers whom they love. I respect that virtuous boy.

The naughty boy is very funny; and the running fight he keeps up with the cross cook is as good as a farce. He *is* a torment, but I think she could tame him, if she took the right way. The other day she wouldn't let him in because she had washed up her kitchen and his boots were muddy. He wiped them on the grass, but that wouldn't do; and, after going at her with his head down, like a battering-ram, he gave it up, or seemed to; for, the minute she locked the door behind her and came out to take in her clothes, that sly dog whipped up one of the low windows, scrambled in, and danced a hornpipe all over the kitchen, while the fat cook scolded and fumbled for her key, for *she* couldn't follow through the window. Of course he was off upstairs by the time she got in; but I'm afraid he had a shaking, for I saw him glowering fiercely as he came out later with a basket, going some "confounded errand." Occasionally his father brings him out and whips him for some extra bad offense, during which performance he howls dismally; but when he is left sitting despondently and miraculously on an old chair without any seat, he soon cheers up, boos at a strange cat, whistles to his dog,—who is just like him,—or falls back on that standing cure for all the ills that boys are heir to, and whittles vigorously. I know I ought to frown upon this reprehensible young person, and morally close my eyes to his pranks; but I really can't do it, and am afraid I find this little black sheep the most interesting of the flock.

The girls have tea-parties, make calls, and play mother, of course; and the sisters of the good boy have capital times up in a big nursery, with such large dollies that I can hardly tell which are the babies and which the mammas. One little girl plays about at home with a dirty face, tumbled hair, and an old pinafore on. She won't be made tidy, and I see her kick and cry when they try to make her neat. Now and then there is a great dressing and curling; and then I see her prancing away in her light boots, smart hat, and pretty dress, looking as fresh as a daisy. But I don't admire her; for I've been behind the scenes, you see, and I know that she likes to be fine rather than neat.

So is the girl who torments her kitty, slaps her sister, and runs away when her mother tells her not to go out of the yard. But the housewifely little girl who tends the baby, washes the cups, and goes to school early with a sunshiny face and kiss all round, *she*, now, is a neighbor worth having, and I'd put a good mark against her name if I knew it.

I don't know as it would be proper for me to mention the grown-up people over the way. They go on very much as the children do; for there is the lazy, dandified man, who gets up late, and prinks; the cross man, who swears at the shed-door when it won't shut; the fatherly man, who sits among his children every evening; and the cheery old man up in the attic, who has a flower in his window, and looks out at the world with very much the same serene smile as my orange-colored baby.

The women, too, keep house, make calls, and play mother; and some don't do it well either. The forlorn baby's mamma never seems to cuddle and comfort him; and some day, when the little fist lies cold and quiet, I'm afraid she'll wish she had. Then the naughty boy's mother. I'm very sure, if she put her arms round him sometimes, and smoothed that rough head of his, and spoke to him as only mothers can speak, that it would tame him far better than the scoldings and thrashings; for I know there is a true boy's heart, warm and tender, somewhere under the jacket that gets dusted so often. As for the fine lady who lets her children do as they can, while she trims her bonnet, or makes panniers, I wouldn't be introduced to her on any account. But as some might think it was unjustifiable curiosity on my part to see these things, and an actionable offense to speak of them, I won't mention them.

I sometimes wonder if the kind spirits who feel an interest in mortals ever take a look at us on the shady side which we don't show the world, seeing the trouble, vanities, and sins which we think no one knows. If they love, pity, or condemn us? What records they keep, and what rewards they prepare for those who are so busy with their work and play that they forget who may be watching their back windows with clearer eyes and truer charity than any inquisitive old lady with a pen in her hand?

# LITTLE MARIE OF LEHON

"HERE comes our pretty little girl," I said to Kate, as we sat resting on the seat beside the footpath that leads from Dinan on the hill to Lehon in the valley.

Yes, there she was, trotting toward us in her round cap, blue woollen gown, white apron, and wooden shoes. On her head was a loaf of buckwheat bread as big as a small wheel, in one hand a basket full of green stuff, while the other led an old goat, who seemed in no hurry to get home. We had often seen this rosy, bright-eyed child, had nodded to her, but never spoken, for she looked rather shy and always seemed in haste. Now the sight of the goat reminded us of an excuse for addressing her, and as she was about to pass with the respectful little curtsey of the country, my friend said in French:—

"Stay, please. I want to speak to you." She stopped at once and stood looking at us under her long eyelashes in a timid, yet confiding way, very pretty to see.

"We want to drink goat's milk every morning: can you let us have it, little one?"

"Oh, yes, mademoiselle! Nannette gives fine milk, and no one has yet engaged her," answered the child, her whole face brightening at the prospect.

"What name have you?"

"Marie Rosier, mademoiselle."

"And you live at Lehon?"

"Yes, mademoiselle."

"Have you parents?"

"Truly, yes, of the best. My father has a loom, my mother works in the field and mill with brother Yvon, and I go to school and care for Nannette and nurse little Bebe."

"What school?"

"At the convent, mademoiselle. The good sisters teach us the catechism, also to write and read and sew. I like it much," and Marie glanced at the little prayer in her apron pocket, as if proud to show she could read it.

"What age have you?"

"Ten years, mademoiselle."

"You are young to do so much, for we often see you in the market buying and selling, and sometimes digging in your garden there below, and bringing water from the river. Do you love work as well as school?"

"Ah, no; but mademoiselle knows it is necessary to work; every one does, and I am glad to do my part. Yvon works much harder than I, and the father sits all day at his loom, yet he is sick and suffers much. Yes, I am truly glad to help," and little Marie settled the big loaf as if quite ready to bear her share of the burdens.

"Shall we go and see your father about the goat? And if he agrees will you bring the milk fresh and warm every morning?" I asked, thinking that a sight of that blooming face would brighten our days for us.

"Oh, yes! I always do it for the ladies, and you will find the milk quite fresh and warm, hey, Nannette?" and Marie laughed as she pulled the goat from the hedge where she was nibbling the young leaves.

We followed the child as she went clattering down the stony path, and soon came into the narrow street bounded on one side by the row of low, stone houses, and on the other by the green, wet meadow full of willows, and the rapid millstream. All along this side of the road sat women and children, stripping the bark from willow twigs to be used in basket-making. A busy sight and a cheerful one; for the women gossiped in their high, clear voices, the children sang and laughed, and the babies crept about as freely as young lambs.

We found Marie's home a very poor one. Only two rooms in the little hut, the lower one with its earthern floor, beds in the wall, smoky fire, and single window where the loom stood. At it sat a pale, dark man who stopped work as we entered, and seemed glad to rest while we talked to him, or rather while Kate did, for I could not understand his odd French, and preferred to watch Marie during the making of the bargain.

Yvon, a stout lad of twelve, was cutting up brush with an old sickle, and little Bebe, looking like a Dutch doll in her tiny round cap, tight blue gown, and bits of sabots, clung to Marie as she got the supper.

I wondered what the children at home would have said to such a supper. A few cabbage leaves made the soup, and this, with the dry black bread and a sip of sour wine, was all they had. There were no plates or bowls, but little hollow places in the heavy wooden table near the edge, and into these fixed cups Marie ladled the soup, giving each a wooden spoon from a queer rack in the middle; the kettle stood at one end, the big loaf lay at the other, and all stood round eating out of their little troughs, with Nannette and a rough dog close by to receive any crusts that might be left.

Presently the mother came in, a true Breton woman; rosy and robust, neat and cheery, though her poor clothes were patched all over, her hands more rough and worn with hard work than any I ever saw, and the fine hair under her picturesque cap gray at thirty with much care.

I saw then where Marie got the brightness that seemed to shine in every feature of her little face, for the mother's coming was like a ray of sunshine in that dark place, and she had a friendly word and look for every one.

Our little arrangement was soon made, and we left them all smiling and nodding as if the few francs we were to pay would be a fortune to them.

Early next morning we were wakened by Françoise the maid, who came up to announce that the goat's milk had arrived. Then we heard a queer, quick, tapping sound on the stairs, and to our great amusement, Nannette walked into the room, straight up to my bedside, and stood there looking at me with her mild yellow eyes as if she was quite used to seeing night-caps. Marie followed with a pretty little bowl in her hand, and said, laughing at our surprise, "See, dear mademoiselle; in this way I make sure that the milk is quite fresh and warm;" and kneeling down, she milked the bowl full in a twinkling, while Nannette quietly chewed her cud and sniffed at a plate of rolls on the table.

The warm draught was delicious, and we drank each our portion with much merriment.

"It is our custom," said Françoise; who stood by with her arms folded, and looked on in a lofty manner.

"What had you for your own breakfast?" I asked, as I caught Marie's eye hungrily fixed on the rolls and some tempting little cakes of chocolate left from our lunch the day before.

"My good bread, as usual, mademoiselle, also sorrel salad and—and water," answered Marie, as if trying to make the most of her scanty meal.

"Will you eat the rolls and put the chocolate in your pocket to nibble at school? You must be tired with this long walk so early."

She hesitated, but could not resist; and said in a low tone, as she held the bread in her hand without eating it,—

"Would mademoiselle be angry if I took it to Bebe? She has never tasted the beautiful white bread, and it would please her much."

I emptied the plate into her basket, tucked in the chocolate, and added a gay picture for baby, which unexpected treasures caused Marie to clasp her hands and turn quite red with delight.

After that she came daily, and we had merry times with old Nannette and her little mistress, whom we soon learned to love, so busy, blithe, and grateful was she.

We soon found a new way to employ her, for the boy who drove our donkey did not suit us, and we got the donkey-woman to let us have Marie in the afternoon when her lessons were done. She liked that, and so did we; for she seemed to understand the nature of donkeys, and could manage them without so much beating and shouting as the boy thought necessary. Such pleasant drives as we had, we two big women in the droll wagon, drawn by the little gray donkey that looked as if made of an old trunk, so rusty and rough was he as he went trotting along, his long ears wagging, and his small hoofs clattering over the fine, hard road, while Marie sat on the shaft with a long whip, talking and laughing, and giving Andrè a poke now and then, crying "E! E! houp la!" to make him go.

We found her a capital little guide and story-teller, for her grandmother had told her all the tales and legends of the neighborhood, and it was very pleasant to hear her repeat them in pretty peasant French, as we sat among the ruins, while Kate sketched, I took notes, and Marie held the big parasol over us.

Some of these stories were charming; at least as *she* told them, with her little face changing from gay to sad as she gesticulated most dramatically.

The romance of "Gilles de Bretagne" was one of her favorites. How he carried off his child-wife when she was only twelve, how he was imprisoned and poisoned, and at last left to starve in a dungeon, and would stand at his window crying, "Bread, bread; for the love of God!" yet no one dared to give him any, till a poor peasant woman went in the night and gave him half her black loaf. Not once, but every night, for six months, though she robbed her children to do it. And when he was dying, it was she who took a priest to him that he might confess through the bars of his cell.

"So good, ah, so good, this poor woman! It is beautiful to hear of that, mademoiscllc!" little Marie would say, with her black eyes full, and her lips trembling.

But the story she liked best of all was about the peasant girl and her grandmother.

"See then, dear ladies, it was in this way. In the time of the great war many poor people were shot because it was feared they would burn the chateaus. In one of these so sad parties being driven to St. Malo to be shot, was this young girl. Only fifteen, dear ladies, behold how young is this! And see the brave thing she did! With her went the old grandmother whom she loved next the good God. They went slowly, she was so old, and one of the officers who guarded them had pity on the pretty girl, and said to her as they were a little apart from the rest, 'Come, you are young and can run. I will save you; it is a pity so fine a little girl be shot.'

"Then she was glad and thanked him much, saying, 'And the grandmother also? You will save her with me?' 'It is impossible,' says the officer. 'She is too old to run. I can save but one, and her life is nearly over; let her go, and do you fly into the next wood. I will not betray you, and when we come up with the gang it will be too late to find you.'

"Then the great temptation of Satan came to this girl. She had no wish to suffer, but she could not leave the good old grandmere to die alone. She wept, she prayed, and the saints gave her courage.

" 'No, I will not go,' she said; and in the morning at St. Malo she was shot with the old mother in her arms."

"Could you do that for your grandmere?" I once asked, as she stopped for breath, because this tale always excited her. She crossed herself devoutly, and answered with fire in her eyes and a resolute gesture of her little brown hands,—

"I should try, mademoiselle."

I think she would, and succeed, too, for she was a brave and tender-hearted child, as she soon after proved.

A long drought parched the whole country that summer, and the gardens suffered much, especially the little plats in Lehon, for most of them were on the steep hillside behind the huts, and unless it rained water had to be carried up from the stream below. The cabbages and onions on which these poor people depend, when fresh salads are gone, were dying in the baked earth, and a hard winter was before them if this little store failed.

The priests prayed for rain in thc churches, and long processions streamed out of the gates to visit the old stone cross called the "Croix de Saint Esprit," and, kneeling there in crowds, the people implored the blessing of rain to save their harvest. We felt great pity for them, but liked little Marie's way of praying best.

She did not come one morning, but sent her brother, who only laughed, and said Marie had hurt her foot, when we inquired for her. Anxious to know if she was really ill we went to see her in the afternoon, and heard a pretty little story of practical Christianity.

Marie lay asleep on her mother's bed in the wall, and her father, sitting by her, told the tale in a low voice, pausing now and then to look at her, as if his little daughter had done something to be proud of.

It seems that in the village there was an old woman, frightfully disfigured by fire, and not quite sane as the people thought. She was harmless, but never showed herself by day, and only came out at night to work in her garden or take the air. Many of the ignorant peasants feared her, however, for the country abounds in fairy legends, and strange tales of ghosts and goblins. But the more charitable left bread at her door, and took in return the hose she knit or the thread she spun.

During the drought it was observed that *her* garden, though the steepest and stoniest, was never dry; *her* cabbages flourished when her neighbors' withered, and *her* onions stood up green and tall as if some special rain-spirit watched over them. People wondered and shook their heads, but could not explain it, for Mother Lobineau was too infirm to carry much water up the steep path, and who would help her unless some of her own goblin friends did it?

This idea was suggested by the story of a peasant returning late at night, who had seen something white flitting to and fro in the garden-patch, and when he called to it saw it vanish most mysteriously. This made quite a stir in the town; others watched also, saw the white phantom in the starlight, and could not tell where it went when it vanished behind the chestnut trees on the hill, till one man, braver than the rest, hid himself behind these trees and discovered the mystery. The sprite was Marie, in her little shift, who stepped out of the window of the loft where she slept on to a bough of the tree, and thence to the hill, for the house was built so close against the bank that it was "but a step from garret to garden," as they say in Morlaix.

In trying to escape from this inquisitive neighbor, Marie hurt her foot, but was caught, and confessed that it was she who went at night to water poor Mother Lobineau's cabbages; because if they failed the old woman might starve, and no one else remembered her destitute and helpless state.

The good-hearted people were much touched by this silent sermon on loving one's neighbor as one's self, and Marie was called the "little saint," and tended carefully by all the good women. Just as the story ended, she woke up, and at first seemed inclined to hide under the bedclothes. But we had her out in a minute, and presently she was laughing over her good deed, with a true child's enjoyment of a bit of roguery, saying in her simple way,—

"Yes; it was so droll to go running about *en chemise*, like the girl in the tale of the 'Midsummer Eve,' where she pulls the Saint Johnswort flower, and has her wish to hear all the creatures talk. I liked it much, and Yvon slept so like the dormouse that he never heard me creep in and out. It was hard to bring much water, but the poor cabbages were *so* glad, and Mother Lobineau felt that all had not forgotten her."

We took care that little Saint Marie was not forgotten, but quite well, and all ready for her confirmation when the day came. This is a pretty sight, and for her sake we went to the old church of St. Sauveur to see it. It was a bright spring day, and the gardens were full of early flowers, the quaint streets gay with proud fathers and mothers in holiday dress, and flocks of strangers pausing to see the long procession of little girls with white caps and veils, gloves and gowns, prayer-books and rosaries, winding through the sunny square into the shadowy church with chanting and candles, garlands and crosses.

The old priest was too ill to perform the service, but the young one who took his place announced, after it was over, that if they would pass the house the good old man would bless them from his balcony. That was the best of all, and a sweet sight, as the feeble, fatherly old priest leaned from his easy-chair to stretch his trembling hands over the little flock so like a bed of snowdrops, while the bright eyes and rosy faces looked reverently up at him, and the fresh voices chanted the responses as the curly heads under the long veils bowed and passed by.

We learned afterward that our Marie had been called in and praised for her secret charity,—a great honor, because the good priest was much beloved by all his flock, and took a most paternal interest in the little ones.

That was almost the last we saw of our little friend, for we left Dinan soon after, bidding the Lehon family good-by, and leaving certain warm souvenirs for winter-time. Marie cried and clung to us at parting, then smiled like an April day, and waved her hand as we went away, never expecting to see her any more.

But the next morning, just as we were stepping on board the steamer to go down the Rance to St. Malo, we saw a little white cap come bobbing through the market-place, down the steep street, and presently Marie appeared with two great bunches of pale yellow primroses and wild blue hyacinths in one hand, while the other held her sabots that she might run the faster. Rosy and smiling and breathless with haste she came racing up to us, crying,—

"Behold my souvenir for the dear ladies. I do not cry now. No; I am glad the day is so fine. *Bon voyage! bon voyage!*"

We thanked and kissed and left her on the shore, bravely trying not to cry, as she waved her wooden shoes and kissed her hand till we were out of sight, and had nothing but the soft colors and sweet breath of our nosegays to remind us of Little Marie of Lehon.

# CUPID AND CHOW-CHOW

MAMMA began it by calling her rosy, dimpled, year-old baby Cupid, and as he grew up the name became more and more appropriate, for the pretty boy loved everyone, everyone loved him, and he made those about him fond of one another, like a regular little god of love.

Especially beautiful and attractive did he look as he pranced on the door-steps one afternoon while waiting the arrival of a little cousin. Our Cupid's costume was modernized out of regard to the prejudices of society, and instead of wings, bandage, bow and arrow, he was gorgeous to behold in small buckled shoes, purple silk hose, black velvet knickerbockers, and jacket with a lace collar, which, with his yellow hair cut straight across the forehead, and falling in long, curling love-locks behind, made him look like an old picture of a young cavalier.

It was impossible for the little sprig to help being a trifle vain when every one praised his comeliness, and every mirror showed him a rosy face, with big blue eyes, smiling lips, white teeth, a cunning nose, and a dimple in the chin, not to mention the golden mane that hung about his neck.

Yes, Cupid was vain; and as he waited, he pranced, arranged the dear buckled shoes in the first position, practised his best bow, felt of his dimple, and smiled affably as he pictured to himself the pleasure and surprise of the little cousin when he embraced her in the ardent yet gentle way which made his greetings particularly agreeable to those who liked such tender demonstrations.

Cupid had made up his mind to love Chow-chow very much, both because she was his cousin, and because she must be interesting if all papa's stories of her were true. Her very name was pleasing to him, for it suggested Indian sweetmeats, though papa said it was given to her because she was such a mixture of sweet and sour that one never knew whether he would get his tongue bitten by a hot bit of ginger, or find a candied plum melting in his mouth when he tried that little jar of Chow-chow.

"I know I shall like her, and of course she will like me lots, 'cause everybody does," thought Cupid, settling his love-locks and surveying his purple legs like a contented young peacock.

Just then a carriage drove up the avenue, stopped at the foot of the steps, and out skipped a tall, brown man, a small, pale lady, and a child, who whisked away to the pond so rapidly that no one could see what she was like.

A great kissing and hand-shaking went on between the papas and mammas, and Cupid came in for a large share, but did not enjoy it as much as usual, for the little girl had fled and he *must* get at her. So the instant Aunt Susan let him go he ran after the truant, quite panting with eagerness and all aglow with amiable intentions, for he was a hospitable little soul, and loved to do the honors of his pleasant home like a gentleman.

A little figure, dressed in a brown linen frock, with dusty boots below it, and above it a head of wild black hair, tied up with a large scarlet bow, stood by the pond throwing stones at the swans, who ruffled their feathers in stately anger at such treatment. Suddenly a pair of velvet arms embraced her, and half turning she looked up into a rosy, smiling face, with two red lips suggestively puckered for a hearty kiss.

Chow-chow's black eyes sparkled, and her little brown face flushed as red as her ribbon as she tried to push the boy away with a shrill scream.

"Don't be frightened. I'm Cupid. I must kiss you. I truly must. I always do when people come, and I like you very much."

With this soothing remark, the velvet arms pressed her firmly, and the lips gave her several soft kisses, which, owing to her struggles, lit upon her nose, chin, top-knot, and ear; for, having begun, Cupid did not know when to leave off.

But Chow-chow's wrath was great, her vengeance swift, and getting one hand free she flung the gravel it held full in the flushed and smiling face of this bold boy who had dared to kiss her without leave.

Poor Cupid fell back blinded and heart-broken at such a return for his warm welcome, and while he stood trying to clear his smarting eyes, a fierce little voice said close by,—

"Does it hurt?"

"Oh! Dreadfully!"

"I'm glad of it."

"Then you don't love me?"

"I hate you!"

"I don't see why."

"I don't like to be hugged and kissed. I don't let anybody but papa and mamma do it, ever,—so, now!"

"But I'm your cousin, and you *must* love me. Won't you, please?" besought Cupid, with one eye open and a great tear on his nose.

"I'll see about it. I don't like crying boys," returned the hard-hearted damsel.

"Well, you made me; but I forgive you," and Cupid magnanimously put out his hand for a friendly shake. But Chow-chow was off like a startled deer, and vanished into the house, singing at the top of her voice a nursery rhyme to this effect,—

> *"And she bids you to come in,*
> *With a dimple in your chin,*
> *Billy boy, Billy boy."*

When Cupid, with red eyes and a sad countenance, made his appearance, he found Chow-chow on her father's knee eating cake, while the elders talked. She had told the story, and now from the safe stronghold of papa's arm condescended to smile upon the conquered youth.

Cupid went to mamma, and in one long whisper told his woes; then sat upon the cushion at her feet, and soon forgot them all in the mingled joys of eating macaroons and giving Chow-chow smile for smile across the hearth-rug.

"I predict that we shall be much amused and edified by the progress of the friendship just begun," said Cupid's papa, a quiet man, who loved children and observed them with affectionate interest.

"And I predict a hard time of it for your young man, if he attempts to tame my strong-minded little woman here. Her mother's ideas are peculiar, and she wants to bring Chow-chow up according to the new lights,—with contempt for dress and all frivolous pursuits; to make her hardy, independent, and quite above caring for such trifles as love, domestic life, or the feminine accomplishments we used to find so charming."

As Chow-chow's papa spoke, he looked from the child in her ugly gray frock, thick boots, and mop of hair tied up in a style neither pretty nor becoming, to his wife in *her* plain dress, with *her* knob of hair, decided mouth, sarcastic nose, and restless eyes that seemed always on the watch to find some new wrong and protest against it.

"Now, George, how can you misrepresent my views and principles so? But it's no use trying to convince or out-talk you. We never get a chance, and our only hope is to bring up our girls so that they may not be put down as we are," returned Mrs. Susan, with a decided air.

"Show us how you are going to defend your sex and conquer ours, Chow-chow; give us your views generally. Now, then, who is in favor of the Elective Franchise?" said Uncle George, with a twinkle of the eye.

Up went Aunt Susan's hand, and to the great amusement of all up went Chow-chow's also; and, scrambling to her feet on papa's knee, she burst into a harangue which convulsed her hearers, for in it the child's voice made queer work with the long words, and the red bow wagged belligerently as she laid down the law with energy, and defined her views, closing with a stamp of her foot.

"This is our platform: Free speech, free love, free soil, free every thing; and Woman's Puckerage for ever!"

Even Aunt Susan had to laugh at that burst, for it was delivered with such vigor that the speaker would have fallen on her nose if she had not been sustained by a strong arm.

Cupid laughed because the rest did, and then turned his big eyes full of wonder on his mother, asking what it all meant.

"Only fun, my dear."

"Now, Ellen, that's very wrong. Why don't you explain this great subject to him, and prepare him to take a nobler part in the coming struggle than those who have gone before him have done?" said Mrs. Susan, with a stern look at her husband, who was petting the little daughter, who evidently loved him best.

"I don't care to disturb his happy childhood with quarrels beyond his comprehension. I shall teach him to be as good and just a man as his father, and feel quite sure that no woman will suffer wrong at his hands," returned Mrs. Ellen, smiling at Cupid's papa, who nodded back as if they quite understood each other.

"We never did agree and we never shall, so I will say no more; but we shall see what a good effect my girl's strength of character will have upon your boy, who has been petted and spoiled by too much tenderness."

So Aunt Susan settled the matter; and as the days went on, the elder people fell into the way of observing how the little pair got on together, and were much amused by the vicissitudes of that nursery romance.

In the beginning Chow-chow rode over Cupid rough-shod, quite trampled upon him in fact; and he bore it, because he wanted her to like him, and had been taught that the utmost courtesy was due a guest. But when he got no reward for his long-suffering patience he was sometimes tempted to rebel, and probably would have done so if he had not had mamma to comfort and sustain him. Chow-chow was very quick at spying out the weaknesses of her friends and alarmingly frank in proclaiming her discoveries; so poor Cupid's little faults were seen and proclaimed very soon, and life made a burden to him, until he found out the best way of silencing his tormentor was by mending the faults.

"My papa says you are a dandy-prat, and you are," said Chow-chow, one day when the desire to improve her race was very strong upon her.

"What is a dandy-prat?" asked Cupid, looking troubled at the new accusation.

"I asked him, and he said a vain fellow; and you are vain,—so now!"

"Am I?" and Cupid stopped to think it over.

"Yes; you're horrid vain of your hair, and your velvet clothes, and the dimple in your chin. I know it, 'cause you always look in the glass when you are dressed up, and keep feeling of that ugly hole in your chin, and I see you brush your hair ever so much."

Poor Cupid colored up with shame, and turn his back to the mirror, as the sharp-tongued young monitor went on:—

"My mamma said if you were her boy she'd cut off your curls, put you in a plain suit, and stick some court-plaster over that place till you forgot all about it."

Chow-chow expected an explosion of grief or anger after that last slap; but to her amazement the boy walked out of the room without a word. Going up to his mother as she sat busy with a letter, he asked in a very earnest voice,—

"Mamma, am I vain?"

"I'm afraid you are a little, my dear," answered mamma, deep in her letter.

With a sad but resolute face Cupid went back to Chow-chow, bearing a pair of shears in one hand and a bit of court-plaster in the other.

"You may cut my hair off, if you want to. I ain't going to be a dandy-prat any more," he said, offering the fatal shears with the calmness of a hero.

Chow-chow was much surprised, but charmed with the idea of shearing this meek sheep, so she snipped and slashed until the golden locks lay shining on the floor, and Cupid's head looked as if rats had been gnawing his hair.

"Do you like me better now?" he asked, looking in her eyes as his only mirror, and seeing there the most approving glance they had ever vouchsafed him.

"Yes, I do; girl-boys are hateful."

He might have retorted, "So are boy-girls," but he was a gentleman, so he only smiled and held up his chin for her to cover the offending dimple, which she did with half a square of black plaster.

"I shall never wear my velvet clothes any more unless mamma makes me, and I don't think she will when I tell her about it, 'cause she likes to have me cure my faults," said Cupid when the sacrifice was complete, and even stern Chow-chow was touched by the sweetness with which he bore the rebuke, the courage with which he began the atonement for his little folly.

When he appeared at dinner, great was the outcry; and when the story was told, great was the effect produced. Aunt Susan said with satisfaction,—

"You see what an excellent effect my girl's Spartan training has on her, and how fine her influence is on your effeminate boy."

Uncle George laughed heartily, but whispered something to Chow-chow that made her look ashamed and cast repentant glances at her victim. Cupid's papa shook hands with the boy, and said, smiling, "I am rather proud of my 'dandy-prat,' after all."

But mamma grieved for the lost glory of her little Absalom, and found it hard to pardon naughty Chow-chow, until Cupid looked up at her with a grave, clear look which even the big patch could not spoil, and said manfully,—

"You know I *was* vain, mamma, but I won't be any more, and you'll be glad, because you love *me* better than my hair, don't you?"

Then she hugged the cropped head close, and kissed the hidden dimple without a word of reproach; but she laid the yellow locks away as if she *did* love them after all, and often followed the little lad in the rough gray suit, as if his sacrifice had only made him more beautiful in her eyes.

Chow-chow was quite affable for some days after this prank, and treated her slave with more gentleness, evidently feeling that, though belonging to an inferior race, he deserved a trifle of regard for his obedience to her teachings. But her love of power grew by what it fed on and soon brought fresh woe to faithful Cupid, who adored her, though she frowned upon his little passion and gave him no hope.

"You are a 'fraid-cat," asserted her majesty, one afternoon as they played in the stable, and Cupid declined to be kicked by the horse Chow-chow was teasing.

"No, I ain't; but I don't like to be hurt, and it's wrong to fret Charley, and I won't poke him with my hoe."

"Well, it isn't wrong to turn this thing, but you don't dare to put your finger on that wheel and let me pinch it a little bit," added Chow-chow, pointing to some sort of hay-cutting machine that stood near by.

"What for?" asked Cupid, who did object to being hurt in any way.

"To show you ain't a 'fraid-cat. I know you are. I'm not, see there," and Chow-chow gave her own finger a very gentle squeeze.

"I can bear it harder than that," and devoted Cupid laid his plump forefinger between two wheels, bent on proving his courage at all costs.

Chow-chow gave a brisk turn to the handle, slipped in doing so, and brought the whole weight of the cruel cogs on the tender little finger, crushing the top quite flat. Blood flowed, Chow-chow stopped aghast; and Cupid, with one cry of pain, caught and reversed the handle, drew out the poor finger, walked unsteadily in to mamma, saying, with dizzy eyes and white lips, "She didn't mean to do it," and then fainted quite away in a little heap at her feet.

The doctor came flying, shook his head over the wound, and drew out a case of dreadful instruments that made even strong-minded Aunt Susan turn away her head, and bound up the little hand that might never be whole and strong again. Chow-chow stood by quite white and still until it was all over and Cupid asleep in his mother's arms; then she dived under the sofa and sobbed there, refusing to be comforted until her father came home. What that misguided man said to her no one ever knew, but when Cupid was propped up on the couch at tea-time, Chow-chow begged piteously to be allowed to feed him.

The wounded hero, with his arm in a sling, permitted her to minister to him; and she did it so gently, so patiently, that her father said low to Mrs. Ellen,—

"I have hopes of her yet, for all the woman is not taken out of her, in spite of the new lights."

When they parted for the evening, Cupid, who had often sued for a good-night kiss and sued in vain, was charmed to see the red top-knot bending over him, and to hear Chow-chow whisper, with a penitent kiss, "I truly didn't mean to, Coopy."

The well arm held her fast as the martyr whispered back, "Just say I ain't a 'fraid-cat, and I don't mind smashing my finger."

Chow-chow said it that night and thought it next day and for many following days, for each morning, when the doctor came to dress the "smashed" finger, she insisted on being by as a sort of penance. She forced herself to watch the bright instruments without shivering, she ran for warm water, she begged to spread the salve on the bandage, to hold the smelling-bottle, and to pick all the lint that was used.

And while she performed these small labors of love, she learned a little lesson that did her more good than many of mamma's lectures. For Cupid showed her the difference between the rash daring that runs foolish risks, and the steady courage that bears pain without complaint. Every day the same scene took place; Chow-chow would watch for and announce the doctor; would bustle out the salve-box, bandage, and basin, set the chair, and call Cupid from his book with a new gentleness in her voice.

The boy would answer at once, take his place, and submit the poor swollen hand to the ten minutes' torture of little probes and scissors, caustic and bathing, without a word, a tear, or sound of suffering. He only turned his head away, grew white about the lips, damp on the forehead, and when it was all over would lean against his mother for a minute, faint and still.

Then Chow-chow would press her hands together with a sigh of mingled pity, admiration, and remorse, and when the boy looked up to say stoutly, "It didn't hurt very much," she would put his sling on for him, and run before to settle the pillows, carry him the little glass of wine and water he was to take, and hover round him until he was quite himself again, when she would subside close by, and pick lint or hem sails while he read aloud to her from one of his dear books.

"It is a good lesson in surgery and nursing for her. I intend to have her study medicine if she shows any fondness for it," said Aunt Susan.

"It is a good lesson in true courage, and I am glad to have her learn it early," added Uncle George, who now called Cupid a "trump" instead of a "dandy-prat."

"It is a good lesson in loving and serving others for love's sake, as all women must learn to do soon or late," said gentle Mrs. Ellen.

"It is teaching them both how to bear and forbear, to teach and help, and comfort one another, and take the pains and pleasures of life as they should do together," concluded Cupid's papa, watching the little couple with the wise kind eyes that saw a pretty story in their daily lives.

Slowly the finger healed, and to every one's surprise was not much disfigured, which Cupid insisted was entirely owing to Chow-chow's superior skill in spreading salve and picking lint. Before this time, however, Chow-chow, touched by his brave patience, his generous refusal to blame her for the mishap, and his faithful affection, had in a tender moment confessed to her little lover that she did "like him a great deal," and consented to go and live in the old swan-house on the island in the pond as soon as he was well enough.

But no sooner had she enraptured him by these promises than she dashed his joy by adding certain worldly conditions which she had heard discussed by her mamma and her friends.

"But we can't be married until we have a lot of money. Nobody does, and we *must* have ever so much to buy things with."

"Yes, but papa said he'd give us some little furniture to put in our house, and mamma will let us have as much cake and milk-tea as we want, and I shall be very fond of you, and what's the use of money?" asked the enamoured Cupid, who believed in love in a cottage, or swan-house rather.

"I shan't marry a poor boy, so now!" was the mercenary Chow-chow's decision.

"Well, I'll see how much I've got; but I should think you would like me just as well without," and Cupid went away to inspect his property with as much anxiety as any man preparing for matrimony.

But Cupid's finances were in a bad state, for he spent his pocket-money as fast as he got it, and had lavished gifts upon his sweetheart with princely prodigality. So he punched a hole in his savings-bank and counted his small hoard, much afflicted to find it only amounted to seventy-eight cents, and a button put in for fun. Bent on winning his mistress, no sacrifice seemed too great, so he sold his livestock, consisting of one lame hen, a rabbit, and a choice collection of caterpillars. But though he drove sharp bargains, these sales only brought him in a dollar or two. Then he went about among his friends, and begged and borrowed small sums, telling no one his secret lest they should laugh at him but, pleading for a temporary accommodation so earnestly and prettily that no one could refuse.

When he had strained every nerve and tried every wile, he counted up his gains and found that he had four dollars and a half. That seemed a fortune to the innocent; and, getting it all in bright pennies, he placed it in a new red purse, and with pardonable pride laid his offering at Chow-chow's feet.

But alas for love's labor lost! The cruel fair crushed all his hopes by saying coldly,—

"That isn't half enough. We ought to have ten dollars, and I won't like you until you get it."

"O Chow-chow! I tried so hard; do play it's enough," pleaded poor Cupid.

"No, I shan't. I don't care much for the old swan-house now, and you ain't half so pretty as you used to be."

"*You* made me cut my hair off, and now you don't love me 'cause I'm ugly," cried the afflicted little swain, indignant at such injustice.

But Chow-chow was in a naughty mood, so she swung on the gate, and would not relent in spite of prayers and blandishments.

"I'll get some more money somehow, if you will wait. Will you, please?"

"I'll see 'bout it."

And with that awful uncertainty weighing upon his soul, poor Cupid went away to wrestle with circumstances. Feeling that matters had now reached a serious point, he confided his anxieties to mamma; and she, finding that it was impossible to laugh or reason him out of his untimely passion, comforted him by promising to buy at high prices all the nosegays he could gather out of his own little garden.

"But it will take a long time to make ten dollars that way. Don't you think Chow-chow might come now, when it is all warm and pleasant, and not stop until summer is gone, and no birds and flowers and nice things to play with? It's so hard to wait," sighed Cupid, holding his cropped head in his hands, and looking the image of childish despair.

"So it is, and *I* think Chow is a little goose not to go at once and enjoy love's young dream without wasting precious time trying to make money. Tell her papa said so, and he ought to know," added Uncle George, under his breath, for he *had* tried it, and found that it did not work well.

Cupid did tell her, but little madam had got the whim into her perverse head; and the more she was urged to give in, the more decided she grew. So Cupid accepted his fate like a man, and delved away in his garden, watering his pinks, weeding his mignonette, and begging his roses to bloom as fast and fair as they could, so that he might be happy before the summer was gone. Rather a pathetic little lover, mamma thought, as she watched him tugging away with the lame hand, or saw him come beaming in with his posies to receive the precious money that was to buy a return for his loyal love.

Tender-hearted Mrs. Ellen tried to soften Chow-chow and teach her sundry feminine arts against the time she went to housekeeping on the island, for Mrs. Susan was so busy hearing lectures, reading reports, and attending to the education of other people's children that her own ran wild. In her good moods, Chow-chow took kindly to the new lessons, and began to hem a table-cloth for the domestic board at which she was to preside; also swept and dusted now and then, and once cooked a remarkable mess, which she called "Coopy's favorite pudding," and intended to surprise him with it soon after the wedding. But these virtuous efforts soon flagged, the table-cloth was not finished, the duster was converted into a fly-killer, and her dolls lay unheeded in corners after a few attempts at dressing and nursing had ended in *ennui*.

How long matters would have gone on in this unsatisfactory way no one knows; but a rainy day came, and the experiences it gave the little pair brought things to a crisis.

The morning was devoted to pasting pictures and playing horse all over the house, with frequent pauses for refreshment and an occasional squabble. After dinner, as the mammas sat sewing and the papas talking or reading in one room, the children played in the other, quite unconscious that they were affording both amusement and instruction to their elders.

"Let's play house," suggested Cupid, who was of a domestic turn, and thought a little rehearsal would not be amiss.

"Well, I will," consented Chow-chow, who was rather subdued by the violent exercises of the morning.

So a palatial mansion was made of chairs, the dolls' furniture arranged, the stores laid in, and housekeeping begun.

"Now, you must go off to your business while I 'tend to my work," said Chow-chow, after they had breakfasted off a seed-cake and sugar and water tea in the bosom of their family.

Cupid obediently put on papa's hat, took a large book under his arm, and went away to look at pictures behind the curtains, while Mrs. C. bestirred herself at home in a most energetic manner, spanking her nine dolls until their cries rent the air, rattling her dishes with perilous activity, and going to market with the coal-hod for her purchases.

Mr. Cupid returned to dinner rather early, and was scolded for so doing, but pacified his spouse by praising her dessert,—a sandwich of sliced apple, bread, and salt, which he ate like a martyr.

A ride on the rocking-horse with his entire family about him filled the soul of Mr. Cupid with joy, though the trip was rendered a little fatiguing by his having to dismount frequently to pick up the various darlings as they fell out of his pockets or their mother's arms as she sat behind him on a pillion.

"Isn't this beautiful?" he asked, as they swung to and fro,—Mrs. Cupid leaning her head on his shoulder, and dear little Claribel Maud peeping out of his breast-pocket, while Walter Hornblower and Rosie Ruth, the twins, sat up between the horse's ears, their china faces beaming in a way to fill a father's heart with pride.

"It will be much nicer if the horse runs away and we all go smash. I'll pull out his tail, then he'll rear, and we must tumble off," proposed the restless Mrs. C., whose dramatic soul delighted in tragic adventures.

So the little papa's happy moment was speedily banished as he dutifully precipitated himself and blooming family upon the floor, to be gathered up and doctored with chalk and ink, and plasters of paper stuck all over their faces.

When this excitement subsided, it was evening, and Mrs. Cupid bundled her children off to bed, saying,—

"Now, you must go to your club, and I am going to my lecture."

"But I thought you'd sew now and let me read to you, and have our little candles burn, and be all cosey, like papa and mamma," answered Cupid, who already felt the discomfort of a strong-minded wife.

"My papa and mamma don't do so. He always goes to the club, and smokes and reads papers and plays chess, and mamma goes to Woman's Puckerage meetings,— so I must."

"Let me go too; I never saw a Puckerage lecture, and I'd like to," said Cupid, who felt that a walk arm-in-arm with his idol would make any sort of meeting endurable.

"No, you can't! Papa *never* goes; he says they are all gabble and nonsense, and mamma says his club is all smoke and slang, and they *never* go together."

So Chow-chow locked the door, and the little pair went their separate ways; while the older pair in the other room laughed at the joke, yet felt that Cupid's plan was the best, and wondered how Ellen and her husband managed to get on so well.

Chow-chow's lecture did not seem to be very interesting, for she was soon at home again. But Mr. Cupid, after smoking a lamp-lighter with his feet up, fell to reading a story that interested him, and forgot to go home until he finished it. Then, to his great surprise, he was told that it was morning, that he had been out all night, and couldn't have any breakfast. This ruffled him, and he told madam she was a bad wife, and he wouldn't love her if she did not instantly give him his share of the little pie presented by cook, as a bribe to keep them out of the kitchen.

Mrs. C. sternly refused, and locked up the pie, declaring that she hated housekeeping and wouldn't live with him any more, which threat she made good by quitting the house, vowing not to speak to him again that day, but to play alone, free and happy.

The deserted husband sat down among his infants with despair in his soul, while the spirited wife, in an immense bonnet, pranced about the room, waving the key of the pie-closet and rejoicing in her freedom. Yes, it was truly pathetic to see poor Mr. Cupid's efforts at housekeeping and baby-tending; for, feeling that they had a double claim upon him now, he tried to do his duty by his children. But he soon gave it up, piled them all into one bed, and covered them with a black cloth, saying mournfully, "I'll play they all died of mumps, then I can sell the house and go away. I can't bear to stay here when *she* is gone."

The house was sold, the dead infants buried under the sofa, and then the forsaken man was a homeless wanderer. He tried in many ways to amuse himself. He travelled to China on the tailless horse, went to California in a balloon, and sailed around the world on a raft made of two chairs and the hearth-brush. But these wanderings always ended near the ruins of his home, and he always sat down for a moment to watch the erratic movements of his wife.

That sprightly lady fared better than he, for her inventive fancy kept her supplied with interesting plays, though a secret sense of remorse for her naughtiness weighed upon her spirits at times. She had a concert, and sang surprising medleys, with drum accompaniments. She rode five horses in a circus, and jumped over chairs and foot-stools in the most approved manner. She had a fair, a fire, and a shipwreck; hunted lions, fished for crocodiles, and played be a monkey in a style that would have charmed Darwin.

But somehow none of these festive games had their usual relish. There was no ardent admirer to applaud her music, no two-legged horse to help her circus with wild prancings and life-like neighs, no devoted friend and defender to save her from the perils of flood and fire, no comrade to hunt with her, no fellow-monkey to skip from perch to perch with social jabberings, as they cracked their cocoa-nuts among imaginary palms. All was dull and tiresome.

A strong sense of loneliness fell upon her, and for the first time she appreciated her faithful little friend. Then the pie weighed upon her conscience; there it was, wasting its sweetness in the closet, and no one ate it. She had not the face to devour it alone; she could not make up her mind to give it to Cupid; and after her fierce renunciation of him, how could she ask him to forgive her? Gradually her spirits declined, and about the time that the other wanderer got back from his last trip she sat down to consider her position.

Hearing no noise in the other room, Uncle George peeped in and saw the divided pair sitting in opposite corners, looking askance at each other, evidently feeling that a wide gulf lay between them, and longing to cross it, yet not quite knowing how. A solemn and yet a comical sight, so Uncle George beckoned the others to come and look.

"My boy will give in first. See how beseechingly he looks at the little witch!" whispered Mrs. Ellen, laughing softly.

"No, he won't; she hurt his feelings very much by leaving him, and he won't relent until she goes back; then he'll forgive and forget like a man," said Cupid's papa.

"I hope my girl will remain true to her principles," began Aunt Susan.

"She'll be a miserable baby if she does," muttered Uncle George.

"I was going on to say that, finding she has done wrong, I hope she will have the courage to say so, hard as it is, and so expiate her fault and try to do better," added Aunt Susan, fast and low, with a soft look in her eyes, as she watched the little girl sitting alone, while so much honest affection was waiting for her close by, if pride would let her take it.

Somehow Uncle George's arm went round her waist when she said that, and he gave a quick nod, as if something pleased him very much.

"Shall I speak, and help the dears bridge over their little trouble?" asked Mrs. Ellen, pretending not to see the older children making up their differences behind her.

"No; let them work it out for themselves. I'm curious to see how they will manage," said papa, hoping that his boy's first little love would prosper in spite of thorns among the roses.

So they waited, and presently the affair was settled in a way no one expected. As if she could not bear the silence any longer, Chow-chow suddenly bustled up, saying to herself,—

"I haven't played lecture. I always like that, and here's a nice place."

Pulling out the drawers of a secretary like steps, she slowly mounted to the wide ledge atop, and began the droll preachment her father had taught her in ridicule of mamma's hobby.

"Do stop her, George; it's so absurd," whispered Mrs. Susan.

"Glad you think so, my dear," laughed Uncle George.

"There is some sense in it, and I have no doubt the real and true will come to pass when we women learn how far to go, and how to fit ourselves for the new duties by doing the old ones well," said Mrs. Ellen, who found good in all things, and kept herself so womanly sweet and strong that no one could deny her any right she chose to claim.

"She is like so many of those who mount your hobby, Susan, and ride away into confusions of all sorts, leaving empty homes behind them. The happy, womanly women will have the most influence after all, and do the most to help the bitter, sour, discontented ones. They need help, God knows, and I shall be glad to lend a hand toward giving them their rights in all things."

As papa spoke, Chow-chow, who had caught sight of the peeping faces, and was excited thereby, burst into a tremendous harangue, waving her hands, stamping her feet, and dancing about on her perch as if her wrongs had upset her wits. All of a sudden the whole secretary lurched forward, out fell the drawers, open flew the doors, down went Chow-chow with a screech, and the marble slab came sliding after, as if to silence the irrepressible little orator forever. How he did it no one knew, but before the top fell Cupid was under it, received it on his shoulders, and held it up with all his might, while Chow-chow scrambled out from the ruins with no hurt but a bump on the forehead. Papa had his boy out in a twinkling, and both mammas fell upon their rescued darlings with equal alarm and tenderness; for Mrs. Susan got her little girl in her arms before Mr. George could reach her, and Chow-chow clung there, sobbing away her fright and pain as if the maternal purring was a new and pleasant solace.

"I'll never play that nasty old puckerage any more," she declared, feeling of the purple lump on her brow.

"Nor I either, in that way," whispered her mamma, with a look that made Chow-chow ask curiously,—

"Why, did you hurt yourself too?"

"I am afraid I did."

"Be sure that your platform is all right before you try again, Poppet, else it will let you down when you least expect it, and damage your best friends as well as yourself," said Mr. George, setting up the fallen rostrum.

"I'm not going to have any flatporm; I'm going to be good and play with Coopy, if he'll let me," added the penitent Chow-chow, glancing with shy, wet eyes at Cupid, who stood near with a torn jacket and a bruise on the already wounded hand.

His only answer was to draw her out of her mother's arms, embrace her warmly, and seat her beside him on the little bench he loved to share with her. This ready and eloquent forgiveness touched Chow-chow's heart, and the lofty top-knot went down upon Cupid's shoulder as if the little fortress lowered its colors in token of entire surrender. Cupid's only sign of triumph was a gentle pat on the wild, black head, and a nod towards the spectators, as he said, smiling all over his chubby face,—

"Every thing is nice and happy now, and we don't mind the bumps."

"Let us sheer off, we are only in the way," said Mr. George, and the elders retired, but found it impossible to resist occasional peeps at the little pair, as the reconciliation scene went on.

"0 Coopy! I *was* so bad, I don't think you *can* love me any more," began the repentant one with a sob.

"Oh, yes I can; and just as soon as I get money enough, we'll go and live in the swan-house, won't we?" returned the faithful lover, making the most of this melting mood.

"I'll go right away tomorrow, I don't care about the money. I like the nice bright pennies, and we don't need much, and I've got my new saucepan to begin with," cried Chow-chow in a burst of generosity, for, like a true woman, though she demanded impossibilities at first, yet when her heart was won she asked nothing but love, and was content with a saucepan.

"O Goody! And I've got my drum," returned the enraptured Cupid, as ready as the immortal Traddles to go to housekeeping with a toasting fork and a bird-cage, or some such useful trifles.

"But I *was* bad about the pie," cried Chow-chow as her sins kept rising before her; and, burning to make atonement for this one, she ran to the closet, tore out the pie, and, thrusting it into Cupid's hands, said in a tone of heroic resolution, "There, you eat it *all*, and I won't taste a bit."

"No, *you* eat it all, I'd like to see you. I don't care for it, truly, 'cause I love you more than a million pies," protested Cupid, offering back the treasure in a somewhat ruinous state after its various vicissitudes.

"Then give me a tiny bit, and you have the rest," said Chow-chow, bent on self-chastisement.

"The fairest way is to cut it 'zactly in halves, and each have a piece. Mamma says that's the right thing to do always." And Cupid, producing a jack-knive, proceeded to settle the matter with masculine justice.

So side by side they devoured the little bone of contention, chattering amicably about their plans; and as the last crumb vanished, Cupid said persuasively, as if the league was not quite perfect without that childish ceremony,—

"Now let's kiss and be friends, and never quarrel any more."

As the rosy mouths met in a kiss of peace, the sound was echoed from the other room, for Mr. George's eyes made the same proposal, and his wife answered it as tenderly as Chow-chow did Cupid. Not a word was said, for grown people do not " 'fess" and forgive with the sweet frankness of children; but both felt that the future would be happier than the past, thanks to the lesson they had learned from the little romance of Cupid and Chow-chow.

# PATTY'S PLACE

## I

### HOW SHE FOUND IT

PATTY stood at one of the windows of the Asylum, looking thoughtfully down into the yard, where twenty girls were playing.

All had cropped heads, all wore brown gowns and blue aprons, and all were orphans like herself. Some were pretty and some plain, some rosy and gay, some pale and feeble, but all seemed happy and having a good time in spite of many drawbacks.

More than once one of them nodded and beckoned to Patty, but she shook her head decidedly, and still stood, listlessly watching them, and thinking to herself with a child's impatient spirit,—

"Oh, if some one would only come and take me away! I'm so tired of living here I don't think I *can* bear it much longer."

Poor Patty might well wish for a change; for she had been in the Asylum ever since she could remember; but though every one was kind to her, she was heartily tired of the place, and longed to find a home as many of the girls did.

The children were nursed and taught until old enough to help themselves, then were adopted by people or went out to service. Now and then some forlorn child was claimed by relatives who had discovered it, and once the relatives of a little girl proved to be rich and generous people, who came for Katy in a fine carriage, treated all the other girls in honor of the happy day, and from time to time let Katy visit them with hands full of gifts for her former playmates and friends.

This event had made a great stir in the Asylum, and the children were never tired of talking it over and telling it to new comers as a modern sort of fairy tale. For a time, each hoped to be claimed in the same way, and stories of what they would do when their turn came was one of the favorite amusements of the house.

By and by Katy ceased to come, and gradually new girls took the place of those that left, and her good fortune was forgotten by all but Patty. To her it always remained a splendid possibility, and she comforted her loneliness by visions of the day when her "folks" would come for her, and bear her away to a future of luxury and pleasure, rest and love.

But no one came, and year after year Patty worked and waited, saw others chosen and herself left to the many duties and few pleasures of her dull life. The reason why she was not taken was because of her pale face, her short figure, with one shoulder higher than the other, and her shy ways. She was not ill now, but looked so, and was a sober, quiet little woman at thirteen.

People who came for pets chose the pretty little ones; and those who wanted servants took the tall, strong, merry-faced girls, who spoke up brightly and promised to learn and do any thing required of them.

The good matron often recommended Patty as a neat, capable, gentle little person, but no one seemed to want her, and after every failure her heart grew heavier and her face sadder, for the thought of spending her life there was unbearable.

Nobody guessed what a world of hopes and thoughts and feelings was hidden under that blue pinafore, what dreams the solitary child enjoyed, or what a hungry, aspiring young soul lived in that crooked little body.

But God knew; and when the time came He remembered Patty and sent her the help best fitted for her needs. Sometimes, when we least expect it, a small cross proves a lovely crown, a seemingly unimportant event becomes a life-long experience, or a stranger changes into a friend.

It happened so now; for as Patty said aloud with a great sigh, "I don't think I *can* bear it any longer!" a hand touched her shoulder, and a voice said, gently,—

"Bear what, my child?"

The touch was so light and the voice so kind that Patty answered before she had time to feel shy.

"Living here, ma'am, and never being chosen out like the other girls are."

"Tell me all about it, dear. I'm waiting for a friend, and I'd like to hear your troubles," sitting down in the window-seat and drawing Patty beside her.

She was not young, nor pretty, nor finely dressed, only a gray-haired woman in plain black; but her face was so motherly, her eyes so cheerful, and her voice so soothing, that Patty felt at ease in a minute, and nestled up to her as she told her little woes in a few simple words.

"You don't know any thing about your parents?" asked the lady.

"No, ma'am; I was left here a baby without even a name pinned to me, and no one has come to find me. But I shouldn't wonder if they did yet, so I keep ready all the time and learn as hard as I can, so they won't be ashamed of me, for I guess my folks is respectable," and Patty lifted her head with an air of pride that made the lady ask, with a smile,—

"What makes you think so?"

"Well, I heard the matron tell a lady who chose Nelly Brian that she always thought *I* came of high folks because I was so different from the others, and my ways was nice, and my feet so small,—see if they ain't,"— and, slipping them out of the rough shoes she wore, Patty held up two slender little feet with the arched insteps that tell of good birth.

Miss Murry laughed right out at the innocent vanity of the poor child, and said, heartily, "They *are* small, and so are your hands in spite of work, and your hair is fine, and your eyes are soft and clear, and you are a good child I'm sure, which is best of all."

Pleased and touched by the praise that is so pleasant to us all, yet half ashamed of herself, Patty blushed and smiled, put on her shoes, and said, with unusual animation,—'

'I'm pretty good, I believe, and I know I'd be much better if I only could get out. I do so long to see trees and grass, and sit in the sun and hear birds. I'd work real hard and be happy if I could live in the country."

"What can you do?" asked Miss Murry, stroking the smooth head and looking down into the wistful eyes fixed upon her.

Modestly, but with a flutter of hope at her heart, Patty told over her domestic accomplishments, s good list for a thirteen-year-older, but Patty had been drilling so long she was unusually clever at all sorts of house-work as well as needle-work.

As she ended, she asked, timidly,—

"Did you come for a girl, ma'am?"

"My sister did; but she has found one she likes, and is going to take her on trial," was the answer that made the light fade out of Patty's eyes and the hope die in her heart.

"Who is it, please?"

"Lizzie Brown, a tall, nice-looking girl of fourteen."

You won't like her I know, for Lizzie is a real——;" there Patty stopped short, turned red, and looked down, as if ashamed to meet the keen, kind eyes fixed on her.

"A real what?"

"Please, ma'am, don't ask; it was mean of me to say that, and I mustn't go on. Lizzie can't help being good with you, and I am glad she's got a chance to go away."

Miss Murry asked no more questions; but she liked the little glimpse of character, and tried to brighten Patty's face again by talking of something she liked.

"Suppose your 'folks,' as you say, never come for you, and you never find your fortune, as some girls do, can't you make friends and fortune for yourself?"

"How can I?" questioned Patty, wonderingly.

"By taking cheerfully whatever comes, by being helpful and affectionate to all, and wasting no time in dreaming about what may happen, but bravely making each day a comfort and a pleasure to yourself and others. Can you do that?"

"I can try, ma'am," answered Patty, meekly.

"I wish you would; and when I come again you can tell me how you get on. I think you will succeed; and when you do, you will have found a fine fortune, and be sure of friends. Now I must go; cheer up, deary, your turn must come some day."

With a kiss that won Patty's heart, Miss Murry went away, casting more than one look of pity at the little figure in the window-seat, sobbing, with a blue pinafore over its face.

This disappointment was doubly hard to Patty; because Lizzie was not a good girl, and deserved nothing, and Patty had taken a great fancy to the lady who spoke so kindly to her.

For a week after this she went about her work with a sad face, and all her day-dreams were of living with Miss Murry in the country.

Monday afternoon, as she stood sprinkling clothes, one of the girls burst in saying, all in a breath,—

"Somebody's come for you, and you are to go right up to the parlor. It's Mrs. Murry, and she 's brought Liz back, 'cause she told fibs, and was lazy, and Liz is as mad as hops, for it is a real nice place, with cows, and pigs, and children; and the work ain't hard and she wanted to stay. Do hurry, and don't stand staring at me that way."

"It can't be me—no one ever wants me—it's some mistake"—stammered Patty, so startled and excited, she did not know what to say or do.

"No, it isn't. Mrs. Murry won't have any one but *you*, and the matron says you are to come right up. Go along; I'll finish here. I'm *so* glad you have got a chance at last;" and with a good-natured hug, the girl pushed Patty out of the kitchen.

In a few minutes Patty came flying back, all in a twitter of delight, to report that she was going at once, and must say good-by all round. Every one was pleased, and when the flurry was over, the carriage drove away with the happiest little girl ever seen inside, for at last some one *did* want her, and Patty *had* found a place.

## II

## HOW SHE FILLED IT

For a year Patty lived with the Murrys, industrious, docile, and faithful, but not yet happy, because she had not found all she expected. They were kind to her, as far as plenty of food and not too much work went. They clothed her comfortably, let her go to church, and did not scold her very often. But no one showed that they loved her, no one praised her efforts, no one seemed to think that she had any hope or wish beyond her daily work, and no one saw in the shy, quiet little maid-servant, a lonely, tender-hearted girl longing for a crumb of the love so freely given to the children of the house.

The Murrys were busy people; the farm was large, and the master and his eldest son were hard at it all summer. Mrs. Murry was a brisk, smart housewife, who "flew round" herself, and expected others to do likewise. Pretty Ella, the daughter, was about Patty's age, and busy with her school, her little pleasures, and all the bright plans young girls love and live in. Two or three small lads rioted about the house, making much work, and doing very little.

One of these boys was lame, and this fact seemed to establish a sort of friendly understanding between him and Patty, for he was the only one who ever expressed any regard for her. She was very good to him, always ready to help him, always patient with his fretfulness, and always quick to understand his sensitive nature.

"She's only a servant, a charity girl who works for her board, and wears my old duds. She's good enough in her place, but of course she can't expect to be like one of us," Ella said to a young friend once, and Patty heard her.

"Only a servant"—that was the hard part, and it never occurred to any one to make it softer; so Patty plodded on, still hoping and dreaming about friends and fortune.

If it had not been for Miss Murry I fear the child would not have got on at all. But Aunt Jane never forgot her, though she lived twenty miles away, and seldom came to the farm. She wrote once a month, and always put in a little note to Patty, which she expected to have answered.

So Patty wrote a neat reply, very stiff and short at first; but after a time she quite poured out her heart to this one friend who sent her encouraging words, cheered her with praise now and then, and made her anxious to be all Miss Jane seemed to expect. No one took much notice of this correspondence, for Aunt Jane was odd, and Patty used to post her replies herself, being kindly provided with stamps by her friend.

This was Patty's anchor in her little sea of troubles, and she clung to it, hoping that some time, when she had earned such a beautiful reward, she would go and live with Miss Murry.

Christmas was coming, and great fun was expected; for the family were to pass the day before at Aunt Jane's, and bring her home for the dinner and dance next day. For a week beforehand, Mrs. Murry flew round with more than her accustomed speed, and Patty trotted from morning till night, lending a hand at all the least agreeable jobs. Ella did the light, pretty work, and spent much time over her new dress, and the gifts she was making for the boys.

Every thing was done at last, and Mrs. Murry declared that she should drop if she had another thing to do but go to Jane's and rest.

Patty had lived on the hope of going with them, but nothing was said about it, and they all trooped gayly away to the station, leaving her to take care of the house, and see that the cat did not touch one of the dozen pies stored away in the pantry.

Patty kept up bravely till they were gone; then she sat down like Cinderella, and cried, and cried until she couldn't cry any more, for it did seem as if she never was to have any fun, and no fairy godmother came to help her. The shower did her good, and she went about her work with a meek, patient face that would have touched a heart of stone.

All the morning she finished up the odd jobs left her to do, and in the afternoon, as the only approach to a holiday she dared venture, she sat at the parlor window and watched other people go to and fro, intent on merry-makings in which she had no part.

One pleasant little task she had, and that was arranging gifts for the small boys. Miss Jane had given her a bit of money now and then, and out of her meagre store the affectionate child had made presents for the lads; poor ones, but full of good-will and the desire to win some in return.

The evening was very long, for the family did not return as early as they expected to do, so Patty got out her treasure-box, and, sitting on the warm kitchen hearth, tried to amuse herself, while the wind howled outside and snow fell fast.

There we must leave her for a little while, quite unconscious of the happy surprise that was being prepared for her.

When Aunt Jane welcomed the family, her first word, as she emerged from a chaos of small boys' arms and legs, was "Why, where is Patty?"

"At home, of course; where should she be?" answered Mrs. Murry.

"Here with you. I said '*all come*' in my letter; didn't you understand it?"

"Goodness, Jane, you didn't mean bring her too, I hope."

"Yes, I did, and I'm so disappointed I'd go and get her if I had time."

Miss Jane knit her brows and looked vexed, as Ella laughed at the idea of a servant's going pleasuring with the family.

"It can't be helped now, so we'll say no more, and make it up to Patty tomorrow, if we can." And Aunt Jane smiled her own pleasant smile, and kissed the little lads all round, as if to sweeten her temper as soon as possible.

They had a capital time, and no one observed that Aunty now and then led the talk to Patty, asked a question about her, caught up every little hint dropped by the boys concerning her patience and kindness, and when Mrs. Murry said, as she sat resting, with a cushion at her back, a stool at her feet, and a cup of tea steaming deliciously under her nose,— "Afraid to leave her there in charge? Oh, dear no! I've entire confidence in her, and she is equal to taking care of the house for a week if need be. On the whole, Jane, I consider her a pretty promising girl. She isn't very quick, but she *is* faithful, steady, and honest as daylight."

"High praise from you, Maria; I hope she knows your good opinion of her."

"No, indeed; it don't do to pamper up a girl's pride by praising her. I say, 'Very well, Patty,' when I'm satisfied, and that 's enough."

"Ah, but *you* wouldn't be satisfied if George only said, 'Very well, Maria,' when you had done your very best to please him in some way."

"That 's a different thing," began Mrs. Murry, but Miss Jane shook her head, and Ella said, laughing,—

"It's no use to try and convince Aunty on that point, she has taken a fancy to Pat, and won't see any fault in her. She's a good child enough; but I can't get anything out of her, she is so odd and shy."

"I can; she's first rate, and takes care of me better than any one else," said Harry, the lame boy, with sudden warmth, for Patty had quite won his selfish little heart by many services.

"She'll make mother a nice helper as she grows up, and I consider it a good speculation. In four years she'll be eighteen, and if she goes on doing so well, I shan't begrudge her wages," added Mr. Murry, who sat near by, with a small son on each knee.

"She'd be quite pretty if she was straight, and plump, and jolly. But she is as sober as a deacon, and when her work is done, sits in a corner, watching us with her big eyes, as shy and mute as a mouse," said Ned, the big brother, lounging on the sofa.

"A dull, steady-going girl, just fitted for a servant, and no more," concluded Mrs. Murry, setting down her cup as if the subject was ended.

"You are quite mistaken, and I'll prove it!" and up jumped Aunt Jane so energetically, that the boys laughed and the elders looked annoyed. Pulling out a portfolio, Aunt Jane untied a little bundle of letters, saying impressively,—

"Now listen, all of you, and see what has been going on under Patty's blue pinafore this year."

Then Miss Jane read the little letters one by one, and it was curious to see how the faces of the listeners woke up, grew attentive first, then touched, then self-reproachful, and finally how full of interest, and respect, and something very like affection for little Patty.

These letters were pathetic to read, as Aunty read them to listeners who could supply much that the writer generously left unsaid, and the involuntary comments of the hearers proved the truth of Patty's words.

"*Does* she envy me because I'm 'pretty and gay, and have a good time?' I never thought how hard it must be for her to see me have all the fun, and she all the work. She's a girl like me, though she does grub; and I might have done more for her than give her my old clothes, and let her help dress me when I go to a party," said Ella, hastily, as Aunt Jane laid down one letter in which poor Patty told of many "good times and she not in 'em."

"Sakes alive, if I'd known the child wanted me to kiss her now and then, as I do the rest, I'd have done it in a minute," said Mrs. Murry, with sudden softness in her sharp eyes, as Aunt Jane read this little bit,— "I *am* grateful, but, oh! I'm so lonely, and it's so hard not to have any mother like the children. If Mrs. Murry would only kiss me good-night sometimes, it would do me more good than pretty clothes or nice victuals."

"I've been thinking I'd let her go to school a spell, ever since I heard her showing Bob how to do his lessons. But mother didn't think she could spare her," broke in Mr. Murry, apologetically.

"If Ella would help a little, I guess I could. Anyway, we might try a while, since she is so eager to learn," added his wife, anxious not to seem unjust to sister Jane.

"Well, Joe laughed at her as well as me, when the boys hunched up their shoulders the way she does," cried conscience-stricken Bob, as he heard a sad little paragraph about her crooked figure, and learned that it came from lugging heavy babies at the Asylum.

"I cuffed 'em both for it, and *I* have always liked Patty," said Harry, in a moral tone, which moved Ned to say,—

"You'd be a selfish little rascal if you didn't, when she slaves so for you and gets no thanks for it. Now that I know how it tires her poor little back to carry wood and water, I shall do it of course. If she'd only told me, I'd have done it all the time."

And so it went on till the letters were done, and they knew Patty as she was, and each felt sorry that he or she had not found her out before. Aunt Jane freed her mind upon the subject, and they talked it over till quite an enthusiastic state of feeling set in, and Patty was in danger of being killed with kindness.

It is astonishing how generous and kind people are when once waked up to a duty, a charity or a wrong. Now, every one was eager to repair past neglect, and if Aunt Jane had not wisely restrained them, the young folks would have done something absurd.

They laid many nice little plans to surprise Patty, and each privately resolved not only to give her a Christmas gift, but, what was better, to turn over a new leaf for the new year.

All the way home they talked over their various projects, and the boys kept bouncing into Aunt Jane's seat, to ask advice about their funny ideas.

"It must have been rather lonesome for the poor little soul all day. I declare I wish we'd taken her along," said Mrs. Murry, as they approached the house, through the softly-falling snow.

"She's got a jolly good fire all ready for us, and that's a mercy, for I'm half frozen," said Harry, hopping up the step.

"Don't you think if I touch up my blue merino it would fit Patty, and make a nice dress for tomorrow, with one of my white aprons?" whispered Ella, as she helped Aunt Jane out of the sleigh.

"Hope the child isn't sick or scared; it's two hours later than I expected to be at home," added Mr. Murry, stepping up to peep in at the kitchen window, for no one came to open the door, and no light but the blaze of the fire shone out.

"Come softly and look in; it's a pretty little sight, if it is in a kitchen," he whispered, beckoning to the rest.

Quietly creeping to the two low windows, they all looked in, and no one said a word, for the lonely little figure was both pretty and pathetic, when they remembered the letters lately read. Flat on the old rug lay Patty fast asleep; one arm pillowed her head, and in the other lay Puss in a cosy bunch, as if she had crept there to be sociable, since there was no one else to share Patty's long vigil. A row of slippers, large and small, stood warming on the hearth, two little nightgowns hung over a chair, the tea-pot stood in a warm nook, and through the open door they could see the lamp burning brightly in the sitting-room, the table ready, and all things in order,

"Faithful little creature! She's thought of every blessed thing, and I'll go right in and wake her up with a good kiss!" cried Mrs. Murry, making a dart at the door.

But Aunt Jane drew her back, begging her not to frighten the child by any sudden demonstrations. So they all went softly in, so softly that tired Patty did not wake, even though Puss pricked up her ears and opened her moony eyes with a lazy purr.

"Look here," whispered Bob, pointing to the poor little gifts half tumbling out of Patty's apron. She had been pinning names on them when she fell asleep, and so her secret was known too soon.

No one laughed at the presents, and Ella covered them up with a look of tender pity at the few humble treasures in Patty's box, remembering as she laid back what she had once called "rubbish," how full her own boxes were of the pretty things girls love, and how easy it would have been to add to Patty's store.

No one exactly knew how to wake up the sleeper, for she was something more than a servant in their eyes now. Aunt Jane settled the matter by stooping down and taking Patty in her arms. The big eyes opened at once and stared up at the face above them for a moment, then a smile so bright, so glad, shone all over the child's face that it was transfigured, as Patty clung to Aunt Jane, crying joyously,—

"Is it really you? I was so afraid you wouldn't come that I cried myself to sleep about it."

Never had any of them seen such love and happiness in Patty's face before, heard such a glad, tender sound in her voice, or guessed what an ardent soul lay in her quiet body.

She was herself again in a minute, and, jumping up, slipped away to see that every thing was ready, should any one want supper after the cold drive.

They all went to bed so soon that there was no time to let out the secret, and though Patty *was* surprised at the kind good-nights all said to her, she thought it was because Miss Jane brought a warmer atmosphere with her.

Patty's surprises began early next day, for the first thing she saw on opening her eyes was a pair of new stockings hanging at the foot of her bed, crammed full of gifts, and several parcels lying on the table.

Didn't she have a good time opening the delightful bundles? Didn't she laugh and cry at the droll things the boys gave, the comfortable and pretty things the elders sent? And wasn't she a happy child when she tried to say her prayers and couldn't find words beautiful enough to express her gratitude for so much kindness?

A new Patty went down stairs that morning,—a bright-faced girl with smiles on the mouth that used to be so sad and silent, confidence in the timid eyes, and the magic of the heartiest good-will to make her step light, her hand skilful, her labor a joy, and service no burden.

"They do care for me, after all, and I never will complain again," she thought, with a glad flutter at her heart, and sudden color in her cheeks, as every one welcomed her with a friendly "Merry Christmas, Patty!"

It *was* a merry Christmas, and when the bountiful dinner was spread and Patty stood ready to wait, you can imagine her feelings as Mr. Murry pointed to a seat near Miss Jane and said, in a fatherly tone that made his bluff voice sweet,—

"Sit down and enjoy it with us, my girl; nobody has more right to it, and we are all one family to day."

Patty could not eat much, her heart was so full; but it was a splendid feast to her, and when healths were drank she was overwhelmed by the honor Harry did her, for he bounced up and exclaimed,—

"Now we must drink 'Our Patty, long life and good luck to her!' "

That really *was* too much, and she fairly ran away to hide her blushes in the kitchen roller, and work off her excitement washing dishes.

More surprises came that evening; when she went to put on her clean calico she found the pretty blue dress and white apron laid ready on her bed "with Ella's love." -

"It's like a fairy story, and keeps getting nicer and nicer since the godmother came," whispered Patty, as she shyly looked up at Aunt Jane, when passing ice-cream at the party several hours later.

"Christmas is the time for all sorts of pleasant miracles, for the good fairies fly about just then, and give good-luck pennies to the faithful workers who have earned them," answered Miss Jane, smiling back at her little handmaid, who looked so neat and blithe in her new suit and happy face.

Patty thought nothing farther in the way of bliss *could* happen to her that night, but it did when Ned, anxious to atone for his past neglect, pranced up to her, as a final contra-dance was forming, and said heartily,—

"Come, Patty, every one is to dance this, even Harry and the cat," and before she could collect her wits enough to say "No," she was leading off and flying down the middle with the young master in great style.

That was the crowning honor; for she was a girl with all a girl's innocent hopes, fears, desires and delights, and it *had* been rather hard to stand by while all the young neighbors were frolicking together.

When every one was gone, the tired children asleep, and the elders on their way up to bed, Mrs. Murry suddenly remembered she had not covered the kitchen fire. Aunt Jane said she would do it, and went down so softly that she did not disturb faithful Patty, who had gone to see that all was safe.

Aunt Jane stopped to watch the little figure standing on the hearth alone, looking into the embers with thoughtful eyes. If Patty could have seen her future there, she would have found a long life spent in glad service to those she loved and who loved her. Not a splendid future, but a useful happy one; "only a servant," yet a good and faithful woman, blessed with the confidence, respect and affection of those who knew her genuine worth.

As a smile broke over Patty's face, Miss Jane said, with an arm round the little blue-gowned figure,—

"What are you dreaming and smiling about, deary? The friends that are to come for you some day, with a fine fortune in their pockets?"

"No, ma'am, I feel as if I'd found my folks, and I don't want any finer fortune than the love they've given me today. I'm trying to think how I can deserve it, and smiling because it's so beautiful and I'm so happy," answered Patty, looking up at her first friend with full eyes and a glad, grateful glance that made her lovely.

# LITTLE BUTTON-ROSE

"IF you please, I've come," said a small girl, as she walked into a large room where three ladies sat at work.

One of the ladies was very thin, one very stout, and the youngest very pretty. The eldest put on her glasses, the stout one dropped her sewing, and the pretty one exclaimed,—

"Why, it must be little Rosamond!"

"Yes, I've come; the man is taking my trunk upstairs, and I've got a letter for Cousin Penelope," said the child, with the sweet composure of one always sure of a welcome.

The stout lady held out her hand for the letter; but the little girl, after a keen look at the three faces, went to the old lady, who received her with a kiss, saying,—

"That's right; but how did you know, dear?"

"Oh, Papa said Cousin Penny is old, Cousin Henny fat, and Cousin Cicely rather pretty; so I knew in one minute," replied Rosamond, in a tone of innocent satisfaction at her own cleverness, and quite unconscious of the effect of her speech.

Miss Penelope hastily retired behind the letter, Miss Henrietta frowned so heavily that the gold-rimmed eye-glasses flew off her nose with a clash, and Cicely laughed outright, as she exclaimed,—

"I'm afraid we have got an *enfant terrible* among us, though I can't complain of my share of the compliments."

"I never expected to find Clara's child well mannered, and I see I was quite right. Take your hat off, Rosamond, and sit down. It tires Sister to lean on her in that way," said Miss Henny in a severe tone, with no offer of any warmer welcome.

Seeing that something was amiss, the child quietly obeyed, and perching herself in an ancient arm-chair crossed her short legs, folded her plump hands over the diminutive travelling-bag she carried, and sat looking about the room with a pair of very large blue eyes, quite unabashed, though rather pensive, as if the memory of some tender parting were still fresh in her little heart.

While Miss Penny slowly reads the letter, Miss Henny works daisies on a bit of canvas with pettish jerks of her silk, and Miss Cicely leans in the sofa-corner, staring at the newcomer, we will briefly introduce our small heroine. Her father was cousin to the elder ladies, and being called suddenly across the water on business, took his wife with him, leaving the little girl to the care of these relatives, thinking her too young for so long a journey. Cicely, an orphan niece who lived with the old ladies, was to have the care of Rosy; and a summer in the quiet country town would do her good, while change of scene would console her for this first separation from her mother. How she fared remains to be seen; and we need only add that the child had been well trained, made the companion of a sweet and tender woman, and was very anxious to please the parents whom she passionately loved, by keeping the promises she had made them, and being "as brave as Papa, as patient and kind as dear Mamma."

"Well, what do you think of it, Missy?" asked Cicely, as the blue eyes came back to her, after roving round the spacious, old-fashioned, and rather gloomy room.

"It's a pretty large, dark place for a little girl to be all alone in;" and there was a suspicious quiver in the childish voice, as Rosy opened her bag to produce a very small handkerchief, evidently feeling that she might have sudden need of it if some one did not speak to her very soon.

"We keep it dark on account of Sister's eyes. When *I* was a little girl, it wasn't considered polite to say rude things about other people's houses, especially if they were very handsome ones," said Miss Henny, with a stern glance over the eye-glasses at the young offender, whose second remark was even more unfortunate than her first.

"I didn't mean to be rude, but I *must* tell the truth. Little girls like bright places. I'm sorry about Cousin Penny's eyes. I will read to her; I do to Mamma, and she says it is very well for a child only eight years old."

The gentle answer and the full eyes seemed to calm Miss Henny's wrath, for her size was her tender point, and the old house her especial pride; so she dropped the awe-inspiring glasses, and said more kindly,—

"There is a nice little room ready for you upstairs, and a garden to play in. Cicely will hear you read every day, and I will teach you to sew, for of course that *most* useful part of your education has been neglected."

"No, ma'am, I sew my four patches every day, and make little wee stitches, and I can hem Papa's hank'chifs, and I was learning to darn his socks with a big needle when—when they went away."

Rosy paused with a sudden choke; but too proud to break down, she only wiped two drops off her cheek with the long ends of her little gray silk glove, set her lips, and remained mistress of herself, privately planning to cry all she liked when she was safely in the "nice little room" promised her.

Cicely, though a lazy, selfish young lady, was touched by the child's pathetic face, and said in a friendly tone, as she patted the couch where she lay,—

"Come here, dear, and sit by me, and tell me what kind of a kitten you'd like best. I know of a sweet yellow one, and two grays. Our Tabby is too old to play with you; so you will want a kitty, I'm sure."

"Oh yes, if I may!" and Rosy skipped to the new seat with a smile which plainly proved that this sort of welcome was just what she liked.

"Now, Cicely, why will you put such an idea into Rosamond's head when you know we can't have kittens round the house for Sister to stumble over, not to mention the mischief the horried things always do? Tabby is all the child needs, with her doll. Of course you have a doll?" and Miss Henny asked the question as solemnly as if she had said, "Have you a soul?"

"Oh yes, I have nine in my trunk, and two little ones in my bag, and Mamma is going to send me a big, big one from London, as soon as she gets there, to sleep with me and be my little comfort," cried Rosy, rapidly producing from her bag a tiny bride and groom, three seedcakes, a smelling-bottle, and a purse out of which fell a shower of bright cents, also crumbs all over the immaculate carpet.

"Mercy on us, what a mess! Pick it all up, child, and don't unpack any more in the parlor. One doll is quite enough for me," said Miss Henny, with a sigh of resignation as if asking patience to bear this new calamity.

Rosy echoed the sigh as she crept about reclaiming her precious pennies, and eating the crumbs as the only way of disposing of them.

"Never mind, it's only her way; the heat makes her a little cross, you see," whispered Cicely, bending down to hold the bag, into which Rosy bundled her treasures in hot haste.

"I thought fat people were always pleasant. I'm glad *you* ain't fat," answered the little girl, in a tone which was perfectly audible.

What would have happened I tremble to think, if Miss Penny had not finished the letter at that moment and handed it to her sister, saying as she held out her arms to the child,—

"Now I know all about it, and you are to be my baby; so come and give me some sweet kisses, darling."

Down dropped the bag, and with a little sob of joy the child nestled close to the kind old heart that welcomed her so tenderly at last.

"Papa calls me his button-rose, 'cause I'm so small and pink and sweet, and thorny too sometimes," she said, looking up brightly, after a few moments of the fond and foolish cuddling all little creatures love and need so much when they leave the nest, and miss the brooding of motherly wings.

"We'll call you anything you like, darling; but Rosamond is a pretty old name, and I'm fond of it, for it was your grandmamma's, and a sweeter woman never lived," said Miss Penny, stroking the fresh cheeks, where the tears shone like dew on pink rose-leaves.

"I shall call you Chicken Little, because we have Henny and Penny; and the girls and Tab downstairs can be Goosey-Loosey, Turkey-Lurkey, and Cocky-Locky. I'll be Ducky-Lucky, and I'm sure Foxy-Loxy lives next door," said Cicely, laughing at her own wit, while Miss Henny looked up saying, with the first smile Rosy had seen,—

"That's true enough! And I hope Chicken Little will keep out of his way, no matter if the sky does fall."

"Who is it? A truly fox? I never saw one. Could I peep at him some time?" cried the child, much interested at once.

"No, dear; it's only a neighbor of ours who has treated us badly, at least we think so, and we don't speak, though we used to be good friends some years ago. It's sad to live so, but we don't quite see how to help it yet. We are ready to do our part; but Mr. Dover should take the first step, as he was in the wrong."

"Please tell about it. I have horrid quarrels with Mamie Parsons sometimes, but we always kiss and make up, and feel all happy again. Can't you, Cousin Penny?" asked the child, softly touching the little white curls under the lace cap.

"Well, no, dear; grown people cannot settle differences in that pretty way. We must wait till he apologizes, and then we shall gladly be friends again. You see Mr. Dover was a missionary in India for many years, and we were very intimate with his mother. Our gardens join, and a gate in our fence led across their field to the back street, and was most convenient when we wanted to walk by the river or send the maids on errands in a hurry. The old lady was very neighborly, and we were quite comfortable till Thomas came home and made trouble. He'd lost his wife and children, poor man, and his liver was out of order, and living among the heathen so long had made him melancholy and queer; so he tried to amuse himself with gardening and keeping hens."

"I'm glad! I love flowers and biddies," murmured Rosy, listening with deep interest to this delightful mixture of quarrels and heathen, sorrow, poultry, mysterious diseases, and gardens.

"He had no right to shut up our gate and forbid our crossing that little field, and no *gentleman* would have *dared* to do it after all our kindness to his mother," exclaimed Miss Henny, so suddenly and violently that Rosamond nearly fell off the old lady's lap with the start she gave.

"No, sister, I don't agree there. Mr. Thomas had a perfect *right* to do as he liked with his own land; but I think we should have had no trouble if you had been willing to sell him the corner of our garden where the old summer-house is, for his hens," began Miss Penny in a mild tone.

"Sister! You know the tender memories connected with that bower, and how terrible it would have been to *me* to see it torn down, and noisy fowls clucking and pecking where I and my poor Calvin once sat together," cried Miss Henny, trying to look sentimental, which was an impossible feat for a stout lady in a flowery muslin gown, and a fly-away cap full of blue ribbons, on a head once flaxen and now gray.

"We won't discuss the point, Henrietta," said the elder lady with dignity; whereupon the other returned to the letter, bridling and tossing her head in a way which caused Rosy to stare, and resolve to imitate it when she played be a proud princess with her dolls.

"Well, dear, that was the beginning of the trouble," continued Miss Penny; "and now we don't speak, and the old lady misses us, I'm sure, and I often long to run in and see her, and I'm so sorry you can't enjoy the wonders of that house, for it's full of beautiful and curious things, most instructive for children to observe. Mr. Thomas has been a great traveller, and has a tiger skin in the parlor so natural it's quite startling to behold; also spears and arrows, and necklaces of shark's teeth, from the Cannibal Islands, and the loveliest stuffed birds, my dear, all over the place, and pretty shells and baskets, and ivory toys, and odd dresses, and no end of wonderful treasures. Such a sad pity you can't see them!" and Miss Penny looked quite distressed at the child's loss.

"Oh, but I guess I will see 'em! Every one is good to me, and old gentlemen like little girls. Papa says so, and *he* always does what I want when I say 'Please' with my wheedulin smile, as he calls it," said Rosy, giving them a sample of the most engaging sort.

"You funny little thing, do try it, and soften the heart of that tiresome man! He has the finest roses in town and the most delicious fruit, and we never get any, though he sends quantities everywhere else. Such a fuss over an old earwiggy arbor! It is perfectly provoking, when we might enjoy so much over there; and who knows what might happen!"

As Cicely spoke, she smoothed her brown curls and glanced at the mirror, quite conscious that a very pretty young lady of twenty was wasting her sweetness in the great gloomy house, with two elderly spinsters.

"I'll get some for you," answered Rosy, with a nod of such calm conviction of her own power, that Cicely laughed again, and proposed that she should go at once and view the battle-field.

"Could I *run* in the garden? I'd love to, after riding so long," asked

Rosy, eager to be off; for her active legs ached for exercise, and the close, shady room oppressed her.

"Yes, dear; but don't get into mischief, or worry Tabby, or pick the flowers. Of course you wouldn't touch green fruit, or climb trees, or soil your little frock. I'll ring the bell for you to come in and be dressed for tea when it is time."

With these directions and a kiss, Miss Penny, as Cicely did not stir, let the child out at the back door of the long hall, and watched her walk demurely down the main path of the prim old garden, where no child had played for years, and even the toads and fat robins behaved in the most decorous manner.

"It's pretty dull, but it's better than the parlor with all the staring pictures," said Rosy to herself, after a voyage of discovery had shown her the few charms of the place. The sight of a large yellow cat reposing in the sun cheered her eyes at that moment, and she hastened to scrape acquaintance with the stately animal; for the snails were not social, and the toads stared even more fixedly at her than the painted eyes of her respected ancestors.

But Tabby disliked children as much as her mistress, and after submitting ungraciously to a few caresses from the eager little hands, she rose and retired majestically to a safer perch on the top of the high wall which enclosed the garden. Being too lazy to jump, she walked up the shelves of an old flower-stand moulding in a corner, and by so doing, gave Rosy a brilliant idea, which she at once put into action by following Tabby's example. Up this new sort of ladder she went, and peeped over the wall, delighted at this unexpected chance to behold the enemy's territory.

"Oh, what a pretty place!" she cried, clasping her grubby little hands with rapture, as the beauties of the forbidden land burst upon her view.

It was indeed a paradise to a child's eyes,—for flowers bloomed along the winding paths; ripening fruit lay rosy and tempting in the beds below; behind the wire walls that confined them clucked and strutted various sorts of poultry; cages of gay birds hung on the piazza; and through the open windows of the house one caught glimpses of curious curtains, bright weapons, and mysterious objects in the rooms beyond.

A gray-headed gentleman in a queer nankeen coat lay asleep on a bamboo lounge under the great cherry tree, with a purple silk handkerchief half over his face.

"That's the missionary man, I s'pose. he doesn't look cross at all. If I could only get down there, I'd go and wake him with a softly kiss, as I do Papa, and ask to see his pretty things."

Being quite unconscious of fear, Rosy certainly would have carried out her daring plan, had it been possible; but no way of descending on the other side appeared, so she sighed and sat gazing wistfully, till Cousin Henny appeared for a breath of fresh air, and ordered her down at once.

"Come and see if my balsam-seeds have started yet. I keep planting them, but they *won't* come up," she said, pointing out a mound of earth newly dug and watered.

Rosy obediently scrambled up, and was trying to decide whether some green sprouts were chickweed or the dilatory balsams when a sudden uproar in the next garden made her stop to listen, while Miss Henny said in a tone of great satisfaction, as the cackle of hens arose,—

"Some trouble with those horrid fowls of his. I detest them, crowing in the night, and waking us at dawn with their noise. I wish some thief would steal every one of them. Nobody has a right to annoy their neighbors with troublesome pets."

Before Rosy could describe the beauties of the white bantams or the size of the big golden cock, a loud voice cried,—

"You rascal! I'll hang you if I catch you here again. Go home quicker than you came, and tell your mistress to teach you better manners, if she values your life."

It's that man! Such language! I wonder who he's caught? That bad boy who steals our plums, perhaps."

The words were hardly out of Miss Henny's mouth when her question was answered in a sudden and dreadful way; for over the wall, hurled by a strong arm, flew Tabby, high in the air, to fall with a thump directly in the middle of the bed where they stood. Miss Henny uttered a shrill scream, caught up her stunned treasure, and rushed into the house as fast as her size and flounces permitted, leaving Rosy breathless with surprise and indignation.

Burning to resent this terrible outrage, she climbed quickly up the steps, and astonished the irate old gentleman on the other side by the sudden apparition of a golden head, a red childish face, and a dirty little finger pointed sternly at him, as this small avening angel demanded,—

"Missionary man, how *could* you kill my cousin's cat?"

"Bless my soul! Who are you?" said the old gentleman, staring at this unexpected actor on the field of battle.

"I'm Button-Rose, and I hate cruel people! Tabby's dead, and now there isn't any one to play with over here."

This sad prospect made the blue eyes fill with sudden tears; and the application of the dirty fingers added streaks of mud to the red cheeks, which much damaged the appearance of the angel, though it added pathos to the child's reproach.

"Cats have nine lives, and Tabby's used to being chucked over the wall. I've done it several times, and it seems to agree with her, for she comes back to kill my chicks as bold as brass. See that!" and the old gentleman held up a downy dead chicken, as proof of Tabby's sin.

"Poor little chicky!" groaned Rosy, yearning to mourn over the dear departed and bury it with tender care. "It *was* naughty of Tab; but, sir, you know cats are made to catch things, and they can't help it."

"They will have to help it, or I'll drown the lot. This is a rare breed, and I've but two left after all my trouble, thanks to that rascal of yours! What are you going to do about it?" demanded Mr. Dover, in a tone that made Rosy feel as if she had committee the murder herself.

"I'll talk to Tabby and try to make her good, and I'll shut her up in the old rabbit-house over here; then I hope she will be sorry and never do it any more," she said, in such a remorseful tone that the old gentleman relented at once, ashamed to afflict such a tender little soul.

"Try it," he said, with a smile that made his yellow face pleasant all at

once. Then, as if ready to change the subject, he asked, looking curiously
at the little figure perched on the wall,—

"Where did you come from? Never saw any children over there before.
They don't allow 'em."

Rosy introduced herself in a few words, and seeing that her new
acquaintance seemed interested, she added with the wheedling smile
Papa found so engaging,—

"It's pretty lonely here, I guess; so p'r'aps you'll let me peep at your
nice garden sometimes if it doesn't trouble you, Sir?"

"Poor little soul! It must be desperately dull with those three tabbies,"
he said to himself, as he stroked the dead chicken in his hand, and
watched the little face bent toward him.

"Peep as much as you like, child; or, better still, come over and run
about. *I* like little girls," he added aloud, with a nod and a wave of
welcome.

"I told 'em I was sure you did! I'd love to come, but they wouldn't let
me, I know. I'm so sorry about the fight. Couldn't you make it up, and
be pleasant again?" asked Rosy, clasping her hands with a beseeching
gesture as her bright face grew sad and serious remembering the feud.

"So they've told you that nonsense already, have they? Nice neighbors
*they* are," said the old gentleman, frowning as if ill pleased at the news.

"I'm glad I know; p'r'aps I can be a peace-maker. Mamma says they
are good to have in families, and I'd like to be one if I could. Would
you mind if I tried to peace-make a little, so I could come over? I do
want to see the red birds and the tiger skin awfully, if you please."

"What do you know about 'em?" asked the old gentleman, sitting down
on a garden chair, as if he didn't mind continuing the chat with this new
neighbor.

Nearly tumbling off the wall in her earnestness, Rosy repeated all that
Cousin Penny had said; and something in the reasonable words, the
flattering description of his treasures, and the sincere regret of the old
lady seemed to have a good effect upon Mr. Dover, for when Rosy paused
out of breath, he said in such an altered tone that it was evident the
peace-making had already begun,—

"Miss Carey is a gentlewoman! I always thought so. You tell her, with
my compliments, that I'd be glad to see you any time if she has no
objection. I'll put my step-ladder there, and you can come over instead
of the cat. But mind you don't meddle, or I might give you a toss like
Tabby."

"I'm not afraid," laughed Rosy. "I'll go and ask right away, and I won't
touch a thing, and I know you'll like me for a friend. Papa says I'm a
dear little one. Thank you very much, sir. Good'by till I come again;"
and with a kiss of the hand, the yellow head sunk out of sight like the
sun going down, leaving a sense of darkness behind when the beaming
little face disappeared, though fresh stains of green mould from the wall
made it rather like the tattooed countenances Mr. Dover used to see
among his cannibal friends in Africa.

He sat musing with the dead chicken in his hand, forgetful of time,
till a ring of his own door-bell called him in to receive a note from Miss

Penelope, thanking him for his invitation to little Rosamond, but declining it in the most polite and formal words.

"I expected it! Bless the silly old souls! Why can't they be reasonable, and accept the olive branch when I offer it? I'll be hanged if I do again! The fat one is at the bottom of this. Miss Pen would give in if that absurd Henrietta didn't hold her back. Well, I'm sorry for the child, but that's not my fault;" and throwing down the note, Mr. Dover went out to water his roses.

For a week or two, Button-Rose hardly dared glance toward the forbidden spot from her window, as she was ordered to play in the front garden, and sent to take sober walks with Cicely, who loved to stop and gossip with her friends, while the poor child waited patiently till the long tales were told.

Nursing Tabby was her chief consolation; and so kind was she, that the heart of the old cat softened to her, and she actually purred her thanks at last, for all the saucers of cream, bits of chicken, soft pats, and tender words bestowed upon her by the little girl.

"Well, I declare! Tab won't do that even for me," said Miss Henny, one day, when she came upon the child sitting alone in the hall with a picture-book and the cat comfortably asleep in her lap.

"Ammals always love me, if people don't," answered Button-Rose, soberly; for she had not yet forgiven the stout lady for denying her the delights offered by the "missionary man."

"That's because *an-i-mals* can't see how naughty you are sometimes," said Miss henny tartly, not having recovered her temper even after many days.

"I shall make *every* one love me before I go away. Mamma told me to, and I shall. I know how;" and Button smiled with a wise little nod that was pretty to see, as she proudly cuddled her first conquest.

"We shall see;" and Miss Henny ponderously departed, wondering what odd fancy the little thing would take into her head next.

It was soon evident; for when she came down from her long nap, later in the afternoon, Miss Henny found Rosamond reading aloud to her sister in the great dim parlor. They made a curious contrast,—the pale white-haired, feeble old lady, with her prim dress, high cap, knitting, and shaded eyes; and the child, rosy and round, quaint and sweet, a pretty little ornament for the old-fashioned room, as she sat among the tea-poys and samplers, ancient china and furniture, with the portraits of great grandfathers and grandmothers simpering and staring at her, as if pleased and surprised to see such a charming little descendant among them.

"Bless the baby! What is she at now?" asked Miss Henny, feeling more amiable after her sleep.

"I'm reading to Cousin Penny, 'cause no one else does, and her poor eyes hurt her, and she likes stories, and so do I," answered Button, with one chubby finger on the place in her book, and eyes full of pride at the grown-up employment she had found for herself.

"So kind of the little dear! She found me alone and wanted to amuse me; so I proposed a story to suit us both, and she does very well with a little help now and then. I haven't read 'Simple Susan' for years, and really enjoy it. Maria Edgeworth was always a favorite of mine, and I still think her far superior to any modern writer for the young," said Miss Penny, looking quite animated and happy in the new entertainment provided for her.

"Go on, child; let me hear how well you can read;" and Miss Henny settled herself in the sofa-corner with her embroidery.

So Button started bravely off, and tried so hard that she was soon out of breath. As she paused, she said with a gasp,—

"Isn't Susan a dear girl? She gives *all* the best things to other people, and is kind to the old harper. She didn't send him away, as you did the music-man today, and tell him to be still."

"Organs are a nuisance, and I never allow them here. Go on, and don't criticise your elders, Rosamond."

"Mamma and I always talk over stories, and pick out the morals of 'em. *She* likes it;" with which remark, made sweetly not pertly, Button went on to the end, with an occasional lift over a long word; and the old ladies were interested, in spite of themselves, in the simple tale read in that childish voice.

"Thank you, dear, it is very nice, and we will have one every day. Now, what can I do for you?" asked Miss Penny, as the little girl pushed the curls off her forehead, with a sigh of mingled weariness and satisfaction.

"Let me go in the back garden and peep through the knot-hole at the pretty roses. I do long to see if the moss ones are out, and the cherries ripe," said Rosy, clasping her hands imploringly.

"It can do not harm, Henrietta. Yes, dear, run away and get some catnip for Tabby, and see if the balsams are up yet."

That last suggestion won Miss Henny's consent; and Button was off at once, skipping like a young colt all over the garden, which now seemed delightful to her.

At the back of the summer-house was a narrow space between it and the fence where certain plump toads lived; peeping in to watch them, Rosy had spied a large knot-hole in the old boards, and through it found she could get a fine view of several rose bushes, a tree, and one window of the "missionary man's" house. She had longed for another peep since the flower stand was gone, and climbing trees forbidden; now with joy she slipped into the damp nook, regardless of the speckled gentlemen who stared at her with dismay, and took a good look at the forbidden paradise beyond.

Yes, the "moss ones" were in bloom, the cherries quite red, and at the window was the gray head of Mr. Dover, as he sat reading in his queer yellow dressing-gown.

Button yearned to get in, and leaned so hard against the hateful fence that the rotten board cracked, a long bit fell out, and she nearly went after it, as it dropped upon the green bank below. Now the full splendor of the roses burst upon her, and a delightful gooseberry bush stood close by with purplish berries temptingly bobbing within reach. This obliging bush hid the hole, but left fine openings to see through; so the child popped her curly head out, and gazed delightedly at the chickens, the flowers, the fruit, and the unconscious old gentleman not far away.

"I'll have it for my secret; or maybe I'll tell Cousin Penny, and beg her to let me peep if I truly promise never to go in," thought Button, knowing well who her best friend was.

At bedtime, when the dear old lady came to give the good-night kiss, which the others forgot, Rosy, as Miss Penny called her, made her request; and it was granted, for Miss Penny had a feeling that the little peacemaker would sooner or later heal the breach with her pretty magic, and so she was very ready to lend a hand in a quite way.

Next day at play-time, Button was hurrying down her last bit of gingerbread, which she was obliged to eat properly in the dining room, instead of enjoying out-of-doors, when she heard a sudden flurry in the garden, and running to the window saw Roxy the maid chasing a chicken to and fro, while Miss Henny stood flapping her skirts on the steps, and crying, "Shoo!" till she was red in the face.

"It's the white banty, and it must have come in my hole! Oh dear, I hope they won't catch it! Cousin Henny said she'd wring the neck of the first one that flied over the wall."

Away went Rosy, to join in the hunt; for Miss Henny was too fat to run, and Roxy found the lively fowl too much for her. It was a long and hard chase; feathers flew, the maid lost her breath, Rosy tumbled down, and Miss Henny screamed and scolded till she was forced to sit down and watch in silence.

At last poor, hunted Banty ran into the arbor, for its clipped wings would not lift it over the wall. Button rushed after it, and dismal squalls plainly proclaimed that the naughty chicken was caught.

Miss Henny waddled down the path, declaring that she *would* wring its neck; and Roxy went puffing after her, glad to rest. But the old summer house was empty. No little girl, no ruffled bantam, appeared. Both had vanished like magic; and mistress and maid stared at each other in amazement, till they saw that the long-disused window was open, and a gleam of light came in from the narrow opening behind.

"My patience! If that child hasn't crept out there, and bolted through that hole in the fence! Did you ever, Miss?" exclaimed Roxy, trying not to look pleased at being spared the distasteful task of killing the poor chicken.

"Naughty girl!" began Miss Henny, when the sound of voices made both listen. "Slip in there, and see what is going on," said the mistress, well knowing that her stout person never could be squeezed into the small space between house and fence.

Roxy, being thin, easily obeyed, and in a whisper telephoned what went on beyond the hole, causing Miss Henny much vexation, surprise, and at last real pleasure, as the child performed her little part in the mission she had undertaken.

"Oh, please, it's all my fault! I kept the hole open, Mr. Thomas, and so Banty flied in. But it isn't hurt a bit, and I've brought it home all safe, 'cause I know you love your chickies, and Tabby ate lots of 'em," said the childish voice in its most conciliatory tone.

"Why didn't you fling it over the wall, as I did the cat?" asked Mr. Dover, smiling, as he shut up the truant fowl, and turned to look at the rosy, breathless child, whose pink frock bore the marks of many a tumble on grass and gravel.

"It would hurt Banty's feelings, and yours too, and not be polite. So I came myself, to make some pollygies, and say it was my fault. But, please, could I keep the hole to peep through, if I always put up a board when I go away? It is so dull in there, and *so* sweet in here!"

"Don't you think a little gate would be nicer,—one just big enough for you, with a hook to fasten it? We'll call it a button-hole," laughed Mr. Dover. "Then you could peep; or perhaps the ladies will think better of it, and show that they pardon my ill-treatment of Tabby by letting you come in and pick some cherries and roses now and then."

This charming proposal caused the little girl to clasp her hands and cry aloud,—

"That would be perfully sp'endid! I know Cousin Penny would like it, and let me. P'r'aps she'd come herself; she's so thin, she could, and she loves your mother and wants to see her. Only, Cousin Henny won't let us be nice and friendly. S'pose you send *her* some cherries; she loves good things to eat, and maybe she will say yes, if you send lots."

Mr. Dover laughed at this artless proposal, and Miss Henny smiled at the prospect of a gift of the luscious black-heart cherries she had been longing for. Roxy wisely repeated only the agreeable parts of the conversation; so nothing ruffled the lady's temper. Now, whether Mr. Dover's sharp eye caught a glimpse of the face among the gooseberry bushes, and suspected eavesdroppers, or whether the child's earnest desire to make peace touched him, who shall say? Certain it is that his eyes twinkled like a boy's, as he said rather loudly, in his most affable tone,—

"I shall be most happy to send Miss Henrietta a basket of fruit. She used to be a charming young woman. It's a pity she shuts herself up so much; but that sad little romance of hers has darkened her life, I suppose. Ah, well, I can sympathize with her!"

Rosy stared at the sudden change in his manner, and was rather bewildered by his grown-up way of talking to her. But being intent on securing something nice to carry home, she stuck to the cherries, which she *did* understand, and point to the piazza said with a business-like air,—

"There's a basket; so we might pick 'em right away. I love to go up in trees and throw 'em down; and I know Cousin Henny will like cherries ever so much, and not scold a bit when I take some to her."

"Then come on," cried Mr. Thomas, relapsing into the hearty manner she liked so much; and away he went, quite briskly, down the path, with his yellow skirts waving in the wind, and Button skipping after him in great glee.

"They actucally *are* a-picking cherries, Miss, up in the tree like a couple of robins a-chirpin' and laughin' as gay as can be," reported Roxy, from her peep-hole.

"Rip off the rest of that board, then I can see," whispered Miss Henny, quivering with interest now; for she had heard Mr. Dover's words, and her wrath was appeased by that flattering allusion to herself.

Off came the rest of the board, and from the window, half hidden in woodbine, she could now see over the bushes into the next garden. The peep-hole commanded the tree, and she watched with eager eyes the filling of the basket to be sent her, planning the while a charming note of thanks.

"Do look, Miss; they are resting now, and she's on his knee. Ain't it a pretty picter?" whispered Roxy, unmindful of the earwigs, ants, and daddy-long-legs promenading over her as she crouched in her mouldy corner, intent on the view beyond.

"Very pretty! He lost several children in India and I suppose Rosy reminds him of them. Ah, poor man! I can sympathize with him, for *I* too have loved and lost," sighed Miss Henny, pensively surveying the group on the rustic seat.

They were playing cherry-bob; and the child's laughter made pleasant music in the usually quiet place, while the man's face lost its sad, stern look, and was both gay and tender, as he held the little creature close, and popped the ripe fruit into the red, laughing mouth.

As the last sweet morsel disappeared Rosy said, with a long breath of perfect content,—

"It's *almost* as good as having Papa to play with. I do hope the cousins *will* let me come again! If they don't, I think my heart will break, 'cause I get so homesick over there, and have so many trials, and no one but Cousin Penny ever cuddles me."

"Bless her heart! We'll send her some flowers for that. You tell her that Mrs. Dover is poorly, and would like very much to see her; and so would Mr. Thomas, who enjoys her little niece immensely. Can you remember that?"

"Every word! *She* is very nice to me, and I love her, and I guess she will be glad to come. She likes *moss*-roses, and so do I," added the unblushing little beggar, as Mr. Dover took out his knife and began to make the bouquet which was to be Miss Penny's bribe. He could not bear to give up his little playmate, and was quite ready to try again, with this persistent and charming ally to help him heal the breach.

"Shall you send anything to Cis? You needn't mind about it, 'cause she can't keep me at home, but it might please her, and make her stop rapping my head with her thimble when I ask questions, and slapping my fingers when I touch any of her pretty things," suggested Button, as the flowers were added to the fruit, making a fine display.

"I never send presents to *young* ladies," said Mr. Thomas shortly, adding, with both hand out, and his most inviting smile, "But I *always* kiss nice little girls if they will allow me?"

Button threw both arms about his neck and gave him a shower of grateful kisses, which were sweeter to the lonely old man than all the cherries that ever grew, or the finest flowers in his garden. Then Miss Rosamond proudly marched home, finding no trace of the watchers, for both had fled while the "cuddling" went on. Roxy was soberly setting the dinner table, and Miss Henny in the parlor breathing hard behind a newspaper. Miss Penny and Cicely were spending the day out, so the roses had to wait; but the basket was most graciously received, also the carefully delivered message, and the child's heart was rejoiced by free permission to go and see "our kind neighbor now and then, if Sister does not object."

Rosy was in great spirits, and prattled away as they sat at dinner, emboldened by the lady's unusual amiability to ask all sorts of questions, some of which proved rather embarrassing to Miss Henny, and very amusing to Roxy, listening in the china closet.

"I wish *I* had 'spepsia," was the abrupt remark of the small person as her plate of drumsticks was removed and the pudding appeared, accompanied by the cherries.

"Why, dear?" asked Miss Henny, busily arranging the small dish of delicate tidbits, which left little but the skeleton of the roast fowl for the kitchen.

"Then I could have the nicest bits of chicken, and heaps of sauce on my pudding, and the butteryest slices of toast, and *all* the cream for my tea, as you do. It isn't a *very* bad pain, is it?" asked Rosy, in such perfect good faith that Miss Henny's sudden flush and Roxy's hasty dive into the closet never suggested to her that this innocent speech was bringing the old lady's besetting sin to light in the most open manner.

"Yes, child, it is *very* bad, and you may thank your stars that I try to keep you from it by feeding you on plain food. At my age, and suffering as I do, the best of everything is needed to keep up my strength," said Miss Henny, tartly. But the largest plate of pudding, with "heaps of sauce," went to the child this day, and when the fruit was served, an unusually small portion was put away for the invalid, who was obliged to sustain nature with frequent lunches through the day and evening.

"I'm s'prised that you suffer much, Cousin Henny. How brave you must be, not to cry about it, and go round in horrid pain, as you do, and dress so nicely, and see people, and work 'broidering, and make calls! I hope I shall be brave if I ever *do* have 'spepsia; but I guess I shan't, you take such care to give me small pieces every time."

With which cheerful remark Rosy closed that part of the conversation and returned to the delights of her new friend's garden. But from that day, among other changes which began about this time, the child's cup and plate were well filled, and the dread of adding to her own sufferings seemed to curb the dyspeptic's voracious appetite. "A cheild was amang them takin' notes," and every one involuntarily dreaded those clear eyes and that frank tongue, so innocently observing and criticising all that went on. Cicely had already been reminded of a neglected duty by Rosy's reading to Miss Penny, and tried to be more faithful in that, as in other services which she owed the old lady. So the little missionary was evidently getting on, though quite unconscious of her work at home, so absorbed was she in her foreign mission; for, like many another missionary, the savage over the way was more interesting than the selfish, slothful, or neglected souls at home.

Miss Penny was charmed with her flowers and the friendly message sent her, and to Rosy's great delight went next day, in best bonnet and gown, to make a call upon the old lady "who was poorly," for that appeal could not be resisted. Rosy also, in honor of the great occasion, wore *her* best hat, and a white frock so stiff that she looked like a little opera dancer as the long black legs skipped along the street; for this was far too grand a visit to be paid through a hole in the wall.

In the basket were certain delicacies for the old lady, and a card had been prepared, with the names of Miss Carey and Miss Rosamond Carey beautifully written on it by Cis, who was dying to go, but dared not after Rosy had told her Mr. Dover's remark about young ladies.

As the procession of two paused at the door, both the young and the old heart fluttered a little, for. this was the first decided step toward reconciliation, and any check might spoil it all. The maid stared, but civilly led these unexpected guests in and departed with the card. Miss Penny settled herself in a large chair and looked about with pensive interest at the familiar room. But Rosy made a bee-line for the great tiger-skin, and regardless of her clean frock lay down on it to examine the head, which glared at her with yellow eyes, showing all its sharp teeth in the most delightfully natural manner.

Mr. Dover came in with a formal bow, but Miss Penny put out both hands, and said in her sweet old voice,—

"Let us be friends again for the sake of your mother."

That settled the matter at once, and Mr. Thomas was so eager to do his part that he not only shook the hands heartily, but kept them in his as he said like an honest man,—

"My dear neighbor, I beg your pardon! *I* was wrong, but I'm not too proud to own it and say I'm glad to let bygones be bygones for the sake of all. Now come and see my mother; she is longing for you."

What went on in the next room Rosy never knew or cared, for Mr. Thomas soon returned, and amused her so well, showing his treasures, that she forgot where she was till the maid came to say tea was ready.

"Are we going to stay?" cried the little girl, beaming from under a Feejee crown of feathers, which produced as comical an effect upon her curly head as did the collar of shark's teeth round her plump neck or the great Japanese war-fan in her hand.

"Yes, we have tea at five; come and turn it out. I've ordered the little cups especially for you," said her host, as he changed the small Amazon to a pretty child again and led her away to preside at the table, where the quaint china and silver, and the dainty cake and bread and butter proved much more attractive than the little old lady in a big cap who patted her head and smiled at her.

Never had Rosy enjoyed such a delicious meal; for the rapture of pouring real tea out of a pot shaped like a silver melon, into cups as thin as egg-shells, and putting in sugar with tongs like claws, not to mention much thick cream, also spicy, plummy cakes that melted in one's mouth, was too great for words.

The little maid was so absorbed in her new duties that she never minded what the elders talked about, till the plates were empty, the pot ran dry, and no one could be prevailed on to have any more tea. Then she leaned back in her chair and remarked with an air of calm satisfaction, as she looked from one to the other, and smiled that engaging smile of hers,—

"Isn't being friends a great deal nicer than fighting and throwing cats over walls and calling bad names?"

It was impossible not to laugh, and that cheerful sound seemed to tune every one to the sweetest harmony, while the little peacemaker was passed round as if a last course of kisses was absolutely necessary.

Then the party broke up, and Mr. Dover escorted his guests to their own gate, to the great amazement of the neighbors and the very visible pride of Miss Button-Rose, who went up the walk with her head as high as if the wreath of daisies on her little hat had been a conqueror's crown.

Now that the first step had been taken, all would have gone smoothly if Cicely, offended because Mr. Thomas took no notice of *her*, had not put it into Miss Henny's head that as the original quarrel began between her and their neighbor, it would not be dignified to give in till Mr. Dover had come and begged pardon of *her* as well as of Miss Penny. This suited the foolish old lady, who never could forget certain plain words spoken in the heat of battle, though the kindly ones lately heard had much softened her heart toward the offender.

"No, I shall not forget my dignity nor humble myself by going over there to apologize as Penelope has. *She* can do as she likes; and now that he has asked to be forgiven, there is perhaps no harm in *her* seeing the old lady. But with me it is different. *I* was insulted, and till Thomas Dover comes here and solemnly asks my pardon I will *not* cross his threshold, no matter what bribes he sends," said Miss Henny, with an air of heroic firmness.

But it did cost her a pang when her sister went every now and then to take tea with the old lady and came home full of pleasant news; while Rosy prattled of the fine things she saw, the nice things she had to eat, and never failed to bring some gift to share, or to display to the exiles from Paradise. They ate the "bribes," however, as they called the fruit, admired the pretty trinkets and toys, and longed to share in the mild festivities of the pleasant house over the way, but stood firm in spite of all Rosy's wiles, till something unexpected happened to touch their hearts, conquer their foolish pride, and crown the little peacemaker's efforts with success.

One August afternoon Cicely was discontentedly looking over her small store of ornaments as she made ready for a party. She loved gayety, and went about a great deal, leaving many duties undone, or asking the little girl to attend to them for her, neglecting, however, to show any gratitude for these small services so cheerfully done.

As she sat tossing over her boxes, Button-Rose came in looking tired and listless, for it was a hot day, and she had been out twice to do errands for Cicely, besides trotting busily up and down to wait on the old ladies while the young one put fresh ribbons on her dress and curled her hair for the evening.

"Could I lie on your sofa, please, Cis? My head aches, and my legs are *so* tired," said little Button, when her tap had been answered by a sharp "What do you want, child?"

"No, I'm going to lie there myself and have a nap as soon as I'm done here. It's cooler than the bed, and I must be fresh for tonight," said Cicely, too intent on her own affairs to see how used up Rosy looked.

"Then could I look at your pretty things if I don't touch 'em?" asked the child, longing to peep into the interesting boxes scattered on the table.

"No, you can't! I'm busy, and don't want you asking questions and meddling. Go away and let me alone."

Cicely spoke crossly, and waved her hand with a warning gesture, thereby upsetting the tray which held the beads of the necklace she had decided to wear for want of something better.

"There, now see what you've done! Pick up every one, and be quick, for I'm in a hurry."

"But I didn't touch 'em," began poor Button, as she crept about hunting for the black and white beads that looked like very ugly marbles.

"Don't talk; pick them up and then scamper; you are always in mischief!" scolded Cis, vexed with herself, and the heat, and the accident, and the whole world just then.

Rosy said no more, but several great tears dropped on the carpet as she groped in corners, under the bed, and behind the chairs for the runaways; and when the last was found she put it in her tyrant's hand, saying, with a wistful look,—

"I'm very sorry I troubled you. Seems to me if *I* had a little cousin, I'd love to have her play with my things, and I wouldn't be cross to her. Now I'll go and try to *amoose* myself with Bella; *she* is always good to me."

"Run along then. Thank goodness that doll came when it did, for I'm tried of 'amoosing' small girls as well as old ladies," said Cis, busy with her beads, yet sorry she had been so petulant with patient little Button, who seldom reproached her, being a cheery child, and blessed with a sweet temper.

Rosy felt too languid to play; so when she had told Bella, the London doll, her trials, and comforted herself with some kisses on the waxen cheeks, she roamed away to the summer house, which was cool and quiet, longing for some one to caress her; for the little heart was homesick and the little head ached badly.

The "button-hole" had been made, the alley swept out, to the great dismay of the spiders, earwigs, and toads, who had fled to quieter quarters, and Rosy had leave to go and come when she like if Mr. Dover did not object. He never did; and it was her greatest delight to walk in the pretty garden at her own sweet will, always with the hope of meeting its kindly owner, for now they were firm friends. She had been too busy for a run there that day; and now, as she peeped in, it looked so shady and inviting, and it seemed so natural to turn to her dear "missionary man" for entertainment, that she went straight up to his study window and peeped in.

He too seemed out of sorts that hot afternoon, for he sat leaning his head on both hands at the desk strewn with piles of old letters. Button-Rose's tender heart yearned over him at once, and stepping quietly in at the long open window she went to him, saying in her tenderest tone,—

"Does your head ache, Sir? Let me soft it as I do Papa's; he says that always makes it more better. Please let me? I'd love to dearly."

"Ah, my darling, I wish you could. But the pain is in my heart, and nothing will ever cure it," sighed Mr. Thomas, as he drew her close and put his wrinkled yellow cheek to her soft one, which looked more like a damask rose than usual.

"You have trials too, I s'pose. Mine trouble me today, so I came over to see you. Shall I go away?" asked Rosy with a sigh and the wistful look again.

"No, stay, and we will comfort each other. Tell me your troubles, Button, and perhaps I can help them," the kind old gentleman said as he took her on his knee and stroked the curly head with a paternal touch.

So Rosy told her latest grief, and never saw the smile that crept about the lips that asked in a tone of deep interest,—

"Well, what do you mean to do to that unkind Cicely?"

"For a minute I wanted to slap her back when she tried to spat my hands. Then I 'membered that Mamma said a kiss for a blow was a good thing, so I picked up the beads and planned to do it; but Cis looked *so* cross I couldn't. If I had a pretty necklace I'd go and give it to her, and then maybe she'd love me better."

"My dear little missionary, you *shall* have beads to win the heart of *your* heathen, if that is all you need. See here; take anything you like, and give it with the kiss."

As he spoke, Mr. Dover pulled open a drawer in the desk and displayed a delightful collection of pretty, quaint, and curious trinkets picked up in foreign lands, and kept for keepsakes, since no little daughters of his own lived to wear them.

"How perf'ly dorgeous!" cried Rosy, who often fell into baby talk when excited; and plunging in her hands, she revelled for some minutes in sandal-wood cases, carved ivory fans, silver bangles, barbaric brooches, and necklaces of coral, shells, amber, and golden coins, that jingled musically.

"What *shall* I take for her?" cried the little maid, bewildered by such a mine of wealth. "You pick out one, Mr. Thomas, that will please her so much, 'cause you never send her anything, and she don't like it," said Rosy, fearing that her own taste was not to be trusted, as she liked the shells and shark's teeth ornaments best.

"No, I'll give *you* one, and you shall do as you like about giving it to her. This, now, is really valuable and pretty, and any young lady would like to wear it. It makes me think of you, my Button, for it is like sunshine, and the word cut on the little heart means peace."

Mr. Dover held up a string of amber beads with its carved amulet, and swung it to and fro where the light shone through it till each bead looked like a drop of golden wine.

"Yes, that is lovely, and it smells nice, too. She will be so s'prised and pleased; I'll go and take it to her right away," cried Rosy, forgetting to ask anything for herself, in her delight at this fine gift for Cis.

But as she lifted her head after he had fastened the clasp about her neck, something in his face recalled the look it wore when she first came in, and putting both hands upon his shoulders, she said in her sweet little way,—

"You've made my troubles go away, can't I make yours? You are *so* kind to me, I'd love to help you if I could."

"You do, my child, more than you know; for when I get you in my arms it seems as if one of my poor babies had come back to me, and for a minute I forget the three little graves far away in India."

"Three!" cried Button, like a sad, soft echo; and she clung to the poor man as if trying to fill the empty arms with the love and pity that overflowed the childish soul in her small body.

This was the comfort Mr. Thomas wanted, and for a few moments he just cradled her on his hungry heart, crooning a Hindostanee lullaby, while a few slow tears came dropping down upon the yellow head, so like those hidden for years under the Indian flowers. Presently he seemed to come back from the happy past to which the old letters had carried him. He wiped his eyes, and Rosy's also, with the big purple silk handkerchief, and pressing some very grateful kisses on the hot cheeks, said cheerfully again,—

"God bless you, child, that's done me good! But don't let it sadden you, dear; forget all about it, and tell no one what a sentimental old fool I am."

"I never truly will! Only when you feel sorry about the poor little babies, let me come and give you cuddlings. They always make people feel more better, and I love 'em, and don't get any now my dear people are away."

So the two made a tender little plan to comfort each other when hearts were heavy with longings for the absent, and parted at the small gate, both much cheered, and faster friends than ever.

Rosy hastened in with her peace-offering, forgetful now of headache or loneliness as she sat patiently in the wide entry window-seat listening till some sound in Cicely's room should show that she was awake. Before that happened, however, poor Button fell asleep herself, lulled by the quiet of the house,—for everyone was napping,—and dreamed that Mr. Dover stood waving a rainbow over his head, while several Indian gods and three little girls were dancing round him, hand in hand, to the tune of "Ring around a rosy."

A loud yawn roused her, and there was Cis peeping out of her door to see what time it was by the old-fashioned clock on the landing. Up scrambled the child, feeling dizzy and heavy-eyed, but so eager to give pleasure that she lost no time in saying, as she swung the necklace in the sunshine,—

"See! this is for you, if you like it more better than the thunder-and-lightning marbles, as Cousin Penny calls the one you were going to wear."

"How lovely! Where *did* you get it, child?" cried Cis, wide awake at once, as she ran to the glass to try the effect of the new ornament on her white neck.

"My dear Mr. Thomas gave it to me; but he said I could give it away if I liked, and I want you to have it, 'cause it's ever so much prettier than any you've got."

"That's very kind of you, Chicken, but why not keep it yourself? You like nice things as well as I do," said Cicely, much impressed by the value of the gift, for it was real amber, and the clasp of gold.

"Well, I've talked with Mr. Thomas about missionarying a great deal, and he told me how he made the *savinges* good by giving them beads, and things to eat, and being patient and kind to them. So I thought I'd play be a missionary, and call this house Africa, and try to make the people here behave more better," answered Rosy, with such engaging earnestness, as well as frankness, that Cis laughed, and exclaimed,—

"You impertinent monkey, to call us heathen and try to convert us! How do you expect to do it?"

Poor Button fell asleep.
Little Button-Rose

"Oh, I'm getting on pretty well, only you don't *convert* as quick as some of the *savinges* did. I'll tell you about it;" and Button went on eagerly. "Cousin Penny is the good old one, but rather fussy and slow, so I'm kind and patient, and now she loves me and lets me do things I like. *She* is my best one. Cousin Henny is my cannybel, 'cause she eats so much, and I please *her* by bringing nice things and getting her cushions ready. You are my baddest one, who is cross to me, and fights, and raps my head, and slaps my hands; so I thought some beads would be nice for you, and I bringed these beauties. Mr. Thomas gave 'em to me when I told him my trials."

Cicely looked angry, amused, and ashamed, as she listened to the funny yet rather pathetic little play with which the lonely child had tried to cheer herself and win the hearts of those about her. She had the grace to blush, and offer back the necklace, saying in a self-reproachful tone,—

"Keep your beads, little missionary, I'll be converted without them, and try to be kinder to you. I *am* a selfish wretch, but you shall play my little sister, and not have to go to strangers for comfort in your trials any more. Come, kiss me, dear, and we'll begin now."

Rosy was in her arms at once, and clung there, saying with a face all smiles,—

"That's what I wanted! I thought I'd make a good *savinge* of you if I tried *very* hard. Please be kind to me just till Mamma comes back, and I'll be the best little sister that ever was."

"Why didn't you tell me all about it before?" asied Cicely, smoothing the tired head on her shoulder with a new gentleness; for this last innocent confession had touched her heart as well as her conscience.

"You never seemed to care about my plays, and always said, 'Don't chatter, child; run away and take care of yourself.' So I did; but it was pretty dull, with only Tabby to tell secrets to and Bella to kiss. Mr. Thomas said people over here didn't like children very well, and I found they didn't. *He* does, dearly, so I went to him; but I like you now, you are so soft and kind to me."

"How hot your cheeks are! Come and let me cool them, and brush your hair for tea," said Cis, as she touched the child's feverish skin, and saw how heavy her eyes were.

"I'm all burning up, and my head is *so* funny. I don't want any tea. I want to lie on your sofa and go to sleep again. Can I?" asked Rosy, with a dizzy look about the room, and a shiver at the idea of eating.

"Yes, dear, I'll put on your little wrapper, and make you all comfortable, and bring you some ice-water, for your lips are very dry."

As she spoke, Cicely bustled about the room, and soon had Rosy nicely settled with her best cologne-bottle and a fan; then she hastened down to report that something was wrong, with a fear in her own heart that if any harm did come to the child it would be her fault. Some days before Cicely had sent Button-Rose with a note to a friend's house where she knew some of the younger children were ill. Since then she had heard that it was scarlet fever; but though Rosy had waited some time for an answer to the note, and seen one of the invalids, Cis had never mentioned the fact, being ashamed to confess her carelessness, hoping no harm was done. Now she felt that it *had* come, and went to tell gentle Cousin Penny with tears of vain regret.

Great was the lamentation when the doctor, who was sent for in hot haste, pronounced it scarlet fever; and deep was the self-reproach of the two older women for their blindness in not before remarking the languid air and want of appetite in the child. But Cicely was full of remorse; for every quick word, every rap of the hateful thimble, every service accepted without thanks, weighed heavily on her conscience now, as such things have an inconvenient way of doing when it is too late to undo them. Every one was devoted to the child, even lazy Miss Henny gave up her naps to sit by her at all hours, Miss Penny hovered over the little bed like a grandmother, and Cicely refused to think of pleasure till the danger was over.

For soon Button-Rose was very ill, and the old house haunted by the dreadful fear that death would rob them of the little creature who grew so precious when the thought of losing her made their hearts stand still. How could they live without the sound of that sweet voice chirping about the house, the busy feet tripping up and down, the willing hands trying to help, the sunny face smiling at every one, and going away into corners to hide the tears that sometimes came to dim its brightness? What would comfort the absent mother for such a loss as this, and how could they answer to the father for the carelessness that risked the child's life for a girl's errand? No one dared to think, and all prayed heartily for Rosy's life, as they watched and waited by the little bed where she lay so patiently, till the fever grew high and she began to babble about many things. Her childish trials were all told, her longings for Mamma, whose place no one could fill, her quaint little criticisms upon those about her, and her plans for making peace. These innocent revelations caused many tears, and wrought some changes in those who heard; for Miss Penny quite forgot her infirmities to live in the sick-room as the most experienced nurse and tenderest watcher. Miss Henny cooked her daintiest gruel, brewed her coolest drinks, and lost many pounds in weight by her indefatigable trotting up and down to minister to the invalid's least caprice. Cicely was kept away for fear of infection, but *her* penance was to wander about the great house, more silent than ever now, to answer the inquiries and listen to the sad forebodings of the neighbors, who came to offer help and sympathy; for all loved little Button-Rose, and grieved to think of any blight falling on the pretty blossom. To wile away the long hours, Cicely fell to dusting the empty rooms, setting closets and drawers to rights, and keeping all fresh and clean, to the great relief of the old cousins, who felt that everything would go to destruction in their absence. She read and sewed now, having no heart for jaunting about; and as she made the long neglected white pinafores, for Rosy, she thought much of the little girl who might never live to wear them.

Meantime the fever took its course, and came at last to the fateful day when a few hours would settle the question of life or death. The hot flush died out of the cheeks that had lost their soft roundness now, the lips were parched, the half-shut eyes looked like sick violets, and all the pretty curls were tangled on the pillow. Rosy no longer sung to Bella, talked of "three dear little girls" and Mr. Thomas, tigers and bangles,

Cis and necklaces, hens and gates. She ceased to call for Mamma, asked no more why her "missionary man" never came, and took no notice of the anxious old faces bending over her. She lay in a stupor, and the doctor held the little wasted hand, and tried to see the face of his watch with dim eyes as he counted the faint pulse, whispering solemnly,—

"We can only hope and wait now. Sleep alone can save her."

As the sisters sat, one on either side the narrow bed that day, and Cicely walked restlessly up and down the long hall below, where both doors stood open to let in the cool evening air, as the sun went down, a quick but quiet step came up the steps, and Mr. Dover walked in without ringing. He had been away, and coming home an hour ago, heard the sad news. Losing not a moment, he hurried to ask about his little Button, and his face showed how great his love and fear were, as he said in a broken whisper,—

"Will she live? My mother never told me how serious it was, or I should have returned at once."

"We hope so, Sir, but—" And there Cicely's voice failed, as she hid her face and sobbed.

"My dear girl, don't give way. Keep up your heart, hope, pray, will that the darling *shall* live, and that may do some good. We can't let her go! We won't let her go! Let me see her; I know much of fevers far worse than this, and might be able to suggest something," begged Mr. Dover, throwing down his hat, and waving an immense fan with such an air of resolution and cheery good-will that tired Cis felt comforted at once, and led the way upstairs entirely forgetting the great feud, as he did.

At the threshold of the door he paused, till the girl had whispered his name. Miss Penny, always a gentlewoman, rose at once and went to meet him, but Miss Henny did not even seem to see him, for just then, as if dimly feeling that her friend was near, Rosy stirred, and gave a long sigh.

Silently the three stood and looked at the beloved little creature lying there in the mysterious shadow of death, and they so helpless to keep her if the hour for departure had come.

"God help us!" sighed pious Miss Penny, folding her old hands, as if they did that often now.

"Drifting away, I fear;" and Miss Henny's plump face looked almost beautiful, with the tears on it, as she leaned nearer to listen to the faint breath at the child's lips.

"No; we will keep her, please the Lord! If we can make her sleep quietly for the next few hours she is safe. Let me try. Fan slowly with this, Miss Henrietta, and you, dear lady, pray that the precious little life may be given us."

As he spoke, Mr. Dover gave the great fan to Miss Henny, took the small cold hands in his, and sitting on the bedside held them close in his large warm ones, as if trying to pour life and strength into the frail body, as his eyes, fixed on the half-opened ones, seemed to call back the innocent soul hovering on the threshold of its prison, like the butterfly poised upon the chrysalis before it soars away.

Miss Penny knelt down near by, and laying her white head on the other pillow, again besought God to spare this treasure to the father and mother over the sea. How long they remained so none of them ever knew, silent and motionless but for the slow waving of the noiseless fan, which went to and fro like the wing of a great white bird, as if Miss Henny's stout arm could never tire. Miss Penny was so still she seemed to be asleep. Mr. Dover never stirred, but grew paler as the minutes passed; and Cicely, creeping now and then to look in and steal away, saw strange power in the black eyes that seemed to hold the fluttering spirit of the little child by the love and longing that made them both tender and commanding.

A level ray of sunlight stole through the curtain at last and turned the tangles of bright hair to pure gold. Miss Henny rose to shut it out, and as if her movement broke the spell, Rosy took a long full breath, turned on the pillow, and putting one hand under her cheek, seemed to fall asleep as naturally as she used to do when well. Miss Penny looked up, touched the child's forehead, and whispered, with a look of gratitude as bright as if the sunshine had touched her also,—

"It is moist! This is real sleep! Oh, my baby! Oh, my baby!" And the old head went down again with a stifled sob, for her experienced eye told her that the danger was passing by and Rosy would live.

"The prayers of the righteous avail much," murmured Mr. Dover, turning to the other lady, who stood beside her sister looking down at the little figure now lying so restfully between them.

"How can we thank you?" she whispered, offering her hand, with the smile which had once made her pretty, and still touched the old face with something better than beauty.

Mr. Dover took the hand and answered, with an eloquent look at the child,—

"Let not the sun go down upon our wrath. Forgive me and be friends again, for her sake."

"I will!" And the plump hands gave the thin ones a hearty shake as the great feud ended forever over the bed of the little peace-maker whose childish play had turned to happy earnest.

# ROSA'S TALE

"Now, I believe every one has had a Christmas present and a good time. Nobody has been forgotten, not even the cat," said Mrs. Ward to her daughter, as she looked at Pobbylinda, purring on the rug, with a new ribbon round her neck and the remains of a chicken bone between her paws.

It was very late, for the Christmas-tree was stripped, the little folks abed, the baskets and bundles left at poor neighbors' doors, and everything ready for the happy day which would begin as the clock struck twelve. They were resting after their labors, while the yule log burned down; but the mother's words reminded Belinda of one good friend who had received no gift that night.

"We've forgotten Rosa! Her mistress is away, but she *shall* have a present nevertheless. Late as it is, she will like some apples and cake and a Merry Christmas from the family."

Belinda jumped up as she spoke, and, having collected such remnants of the feast as a horse would relish, she put on her hood, lighted a lantern, and trotted off to the barn.

As she opened the door of the loose box in which Rosa was kept, she saw her eyes shining in the dark as she lifted her head with a startled air. Then, recognizing a friend, she rose and came rustling through the straw to greet her late visitor. She was evidently much pleased with the attention, and rubbed her nose against Miss Belinda gratefully, but seemed rather dainty, and poked over the contents of the basket, as if a little suspicious, though apples were her favorite treat.

Knowing that she would enjoy the little feast more if she had company while she ate it, for Rosa was a very social beast, Miss Belinda hung up the lantern, and, sitting down on an inverted bucket, watched her as she munched contentedly.

"Now really'," said Miss Belinda, when telling her story afterwards, "I am not sure whether I took a nap and dreamed what follows, or whether it actually happened, for strange things do occur at Christmas time, as every one knows.

"As I sat there the town clock struck twelve, and the sound reminded me of the legend which affirms that all dumb animals are endowed with speech for one hour after midnight on Christmas eve, in memory of the animals about the manger when the blessed Child was born.

" 'I wish the pretty fancy was a fact, and our Rosa could speak, if only for an hour, because I am sure she has an interesting history, and I long to know it.'

"I said this aloud, and to my utter amazement the bay mare stopped eating, fixed her intelligent eyes upon my face, and answered in a language I understood perfectly well,—

" 'You shall know it, for whether the legend is true or not I feel as if I could confide in you and tell you all I feel. I was lying awake listening to the fun in the house, thinking of my dear mistress over the sea and feeling very sad, for I heard you say I was to be sold. That nearly broke my heart, for no one has ever been so kind to me as Miss Merry, and nowhere shall I be taken care of, nursed, and loved as I have been since she bought me. I know I am getting old, and stiff in the knees, and my forefoot is lame, and sometimes I'm cross when my shoulder aches; but I do try to be a patient, grateful beast. I've got fat with good living, my work is not hard, I dearly love to carry those who have done so much for me, and I'll tug for them till I die in harness, if they will only keep me.'

"I was so astonished at this address that I tumbled off the pail, and sat among the straw staring up at Rosa, as dumb as if I had lost the power she had gained. She seemed to enjoy my surprise, and added to it by letting me hear a genuine *horse laugh*, hearty, shrill, and clear, as she shook her pretty head, and went on talking rapidly in the language which I now perceived to be a mixture of English and the peculiar dialect of the horse-country Gulliver visited.

" 'Thank you for remembering me tonight, and in return for the goodies you bring I'll tell my story as fast as I can, for I have often longed to recount the trials and triumphs of my life. Miss Merry came last Christmas eve to bring me sugar, and I wanted to speak, but it was too early and I could not say a word, though my heart was full.'

"Rosa paused an instant, and her fine eyes dimmed as if with tender tears at the recollection of the happy year which had followed the day she was bought from the drudgery of a livery-stable to be a lady's pet. I stroked her neck as she stooped to sniff affectionately at my hood, and said eagerly,—

" ' Tell away, dear, I'm full of interest, and understand every word you say.'

"Thus encouraged, Rosa threw up her head, and began with an air of pride which plainly proved, what we had always suspected, that she belonged to a good family.

" 'My father was a famous racer, and I am very like him; the same color, spirit, and grace, and but for the cruelty of man I might have been as renowned as he. I was a very happy colt, petted by my master, tamed by love, and never struck a blow while he lived. I gained one race for him, and promised so well that when he died I brought a great price. I mourned for him, but was glad to be sent to my new owner's racing-stable and made much of, for people predicted that I should be another Goldsmith Maid or Flora Temple. Ah, how ambitious and proud I was in those days! Vain of my good blood, my speed, and my beauty; for indeed I *was* handsome then, though you may find it hard to believe now.' And Rosa sighed regretfully as she stole a look at me, and took the attitude which showed to advantage the fine lines about her head and neck.

" 'I do not find it hard, for we have always said you had splendid points about you. Miss Merry saw them, though you were a skeleton, when she bought you; so did the skilful Cornish blacksmith when he shod you. And it is easy to see that you belong to a good family by the way you hold your head without a check-rein and carry your tail like a plume,' I said, with a look of admiration which comforted her as much as if she had been a *passée* belle.

" 'I must hurry over this part of my story, because, though brilliant, it was very brief, and ended in a way which made it the bitterest portion of my life,' continued Rosa. 'I won several races, and great fame was predicted for me. You may guess how high my reputation was when I tell you that before my last fatal trial thousands were bet on me, and my rival trembled in his shoes. I was full of spirit, eager to show my speed and sure of success. Alas, how little I knew of the wickedness of human nature then, how dearly I bought the knowledge, and how it has changed my whole life! You do not know much about such matters, of course, and I won't digress to tell you all the tricks of the trade; only beware of jockeys and never bet.

" 'I was kept carefully out of every one's way for weeks, and only taken out for exercise by my trainer. Poor Bill! I was fond of him, and he was so good to me that I never have forgotten him, though he broke his neck years ago. A few nights before the great race, as I was getting a good sleep, carefully tucked away in my roomy stall, some one stole in and gave me a warm mash. It was dark. I was half awake, and I ate it like a fool, though I knew by instinct that it was not Bill who fed it to me. I was a confiding creature then, and as all sorts of queer things had been done to prepare me I thought it was all right. But it was not, and that deceit has caused me to be suspicious about my food ever since, for the mash was dosed in some way; it made me very ill, and my enemies nearly triumphed, thanks to this cowardly trick.

" 'Bill worked over me day and night, that I might be fit to run. I did my best to seem well and gay, but there was not time for me to regain my lost strength and spirit, and pride alone kept me up. "I'll win for my master if I die in doing it," I said to myself, and when the hour came pranced to my place trying to look as well as ever, though my heart was very heavy and I trembled with excitement. "Courage, my lass, and we'll beat in spite of their black tricks," whispered Bill, as he sprung to his place.

" 'I lost the first heat, but won the second, and the sound of the cheering gave me strength to walk away without staggering, though my legs shook under me. What a splendid minute that was when, encouraged and refreshed by my faithful Bill, I came on the track again! I knew my enemies began to fear, for I had borne myself so bravely they fancied I was quite well, and now, excited by that first success, I was mad with impatience to be off and cover myself with glory.'

"Rosa looked as if the 'splendid minute' had come again, for she arched her neck, opened wide her red nostrils, and pawed the straw with one little foot, while her eyes shone with sudden fire, and her ears were pricked up as if to catch again the shouts she heard that day.

" 'I wish I had been there to see you!' I exclaimed, quite carried away by her ardor.

" 'I wish you had, for I won, I won! The big black horse did his best, but I had vowed to win or die, and I kept my word, for I beat him by a head, and then dropped as if dead. I might as well have died then, people thought, for the poison, the exertion, and the fall ruined me for a racer. My master cared no more for me, and would have had me shot if Bill had not saved my life. I was pronounced good for nothing, and he bought me cheap. I was lame and useless for a long time, but his patient care did wonders, and just as I was able to be of use to him he was killed.

" 'A gentleman in want of a saddle-horse purchased me because my easy gait and quiet temper suited him; for I was meek enough now, and my size fitted me to carry his delicate daughter.

" 'For more than a year I served little Miss Alice, rejoicing to see how rosy her pale cheeks became, how upright her feeble figure grew, thanks to the hours spent with me; for my canter rocked her as gently as if she were in a cradle, and fresh air was the medicine she needed. She often said she owed her life to me, and I liked to think so, for she made *my* life a very easy one.

" 'But somehow my good times never lasted long, and when Miss Alice went West I was sold. I had been so well treated that I *looked* as handsome and gay as ever, though my shoulder never was strong again, and I often had despondent moods, longing for the excitement of the race-course with the instinct of my kind so I was glad when, attracted by my spirit and beauty, a young army officer bought me and I went to the war. Ah! You never guessed that, did you? Yes, I did my part gallantly and saved my master's life more than once. You have observed how martial music delights me, but you don't know that it is because it reminds me of the proudest hour of my life. I've told you about the saddest; let me relate this also, and give me a pat for the brave action which won my master his promotion, though I got no praise for my part of the achievement.

" 'In one of the hottest battles my captain was ordered to lead his men to a most perilous exploit. They hesitated, so did he; for it must cost many lives, and, brave as they were, they paused an instant. But *I* settled the point, for I was wild with the sound of drums, the smell of powder, the excitement of the hour, and, finding myself sharply reined in, I rebelled, took the bit between my teeth, and dashed straight away into the midst of the fight, spite of all my rider could do. The men thought their captain led them on, and with a cheer they followed, carrying all before them.

" 'What happened just after that I never could remember, except that I got a wound here in my neck and a cut on my flank; the scar is there still, and I'm proud of it, though buyers always consider it a blemish. But when the battle was won my master was promoted on the field, and I carried him up to the general as he sat among his officers under the torn flags.

" 'Both of us were weary and wounded, both were full of pride at what we had done; but *he* got all the praise and the honor, *I* only a careless word and a better supper than usual.

" 'I thought no one knew what I had done, and resented the ingratitude of your race; for it was the horse, not the man, who led that forlorn hope, and I did think I should have a rosette at least, when others got stars and bars for far less dangerous deeds. Never mind, my master knew the truth, and thanked me for my help by keeping me always with him till the sad day when he was shot in a skirmish, and lay for hours with none to watch and mourn over him but his faithful horse.

" 'Then I knew how much he loved and thanked me, for his hand stroked me while it had the strength his eye turned to me till it grew too dim for seeing, and when help came, among the last words he whispered to a comrade were these, "Be kind to Rosa and send her safely home; she has earned her rest."

" 'I *had* earned it, but I did not get it, for when I was sent home the old mother's heart was broken at the loss of her son, and she did not live long to cherish me. Then my hard times began, for my next owner was a fast young man, who ill used me in many ways, till the spirit of my father rose within me, and I gave my brutal master a grand runaway and smash-up.

" 'To tame me down, I was sold for a car horse; and that almost killed me, for it was dreadful drudgery to tug, day after day, over the hard pavement with heavy loads behind me, uncongenial companions beside me, and no affection to cheer my life.

" 'I have often longed to ask why Mr. Bergh does not try to prevent such crowds from piling into those cars; and now I beg you to do what you can to stop such an unmerciful abuse.

" 'In snow-storms it was awful, and more than one of my mates dropped dead with overwork and discouragement. I used to wish I could do the same, for my poor feet, badly shod, became so lame I could hardly walk at times, and the constant strain on the up grades brought back the old trouble in my shoulder worse than ever.

" 'Why they did not kill me I don't know, for I was a miserable creature then; but there must be something attractive about me, I fancy, for people always seem to think me worth saving. What can it be, ma'am?'

" 'Now, Rosa, don't be affected; you know you are a very engaging little animal, and if you live to be forty will still have certain pretty ways about you, that win the hearts of women, if not of men. *They* see your weak points, and take a money view of the case; bnt *we* sympathize with your afflictions, are amused with your coquettish airs, and like your affectionate nature. Now hurry up and finish, for I find it a trifle cold out here.'

"I laughed as I spoke, for Rosa eyed me with a sidelong glance and gently waved the docked tail, which was her delight; for the sly thing liked to be flattered and was as fond of compliments as a girl.

" 'Many thanks. I will come now to the most interesting portion of my narrative. As I was saying, instead of knocking me on the head I was packed off to New Hampshire, and had a fine rest among the green hills, with a dozen or so of weary friends. It was during this holiday that I acquired the love of nature which Miss Merry detected and liked in me, when she found me ready to study sunsets with her, to admire new landscapes, and enjoy bright summer weather.

" 'In the autumn a livery-stable keeper bought me, and through the winter fed me up till I was quite presentable in the spring. It was a small town, but through the summer many city people visited there, so I was kept on the trot while the season lasted, because ladies could drive me. You, Miss Belinda, were one of the ladies, and I never shall forget, though I have long ago forgiven it, how you laughed at my queer gait the day you hired me.

" 'My tender feet and stiff knees made me tread very gingerly, and amble along with short mincing steps, which contrasted oddly, I know, with my proudly waving tail and high-carried head. You liked me nevertheless, because I didn't rattle you down the steep hills, was not afraid of locomotives, and stood patiently while you gathered flowers and enjoyed the lovely prospects.

" 'I have always felt a regard for you since you did not whip me, and admired my eyes, which, I may say without vanity, have always been considered unusually fine. But no one ever won my whole heart like Miss Merry, and I never shall forget the happy day when she came to the stable to order a saddle-horse. Her cheery voice made me prick up my ears, and when she said, after looking at several showy beasts, "No, they don't suit me. This one now has the right air; can I ride her?" My heart danced within me and I looked round with a whinny of delight. She understood my welcome, and came right up to me, patted me, peered into my face, rubbed my nose, and looked at my feet with an air of interest and sympathy, that made me feel as if I'd like to carry her round the world.

" 'Ah, what rides we had after that! What happy hours trotting gayly through the green woods, galloping over the breezy hills, or pacing slowly along quiet lanes, where I often lunched luxuriously on clover-tops, while Miss Merry took a sketch of some picturesque bit with me in the foreground.

" 'I liked that, and we had long chats at such times, for she seemed to understand me perfectly. She was never frightened when I danced for pleasure on the soft turf, never chid me when I snatched a bite from the young trees as we passed through sylvan ways, never thought it a trouble to let me wet my tired feet in babbling brooks, or to dismount and take out the stones that plagued me.

" 'Then how well she rode! So firm yet light a seat, so steady a hand, so agile a foot to spring on and off, and such infectious spirits, that no matter how despondent or cross I might be, in five minutes I felt gay and young again when dear Miss Merry was on my back.'

"Here Rosa gave a frisk that sent the straw flying, and made me shrink into a corner, while she pranced about the box with a neigh which waked the big brown colt next door, and set poor Buttercup to lowing for her calf, the loss of which she had forgotten for a little while in sleep.

" 'Ah, Miss Merry never ran away from me! She knew my heels were to be trusted, and she let me caper as I would, glad to see me lively. Never mind, Miss Belinda, come out and I'll be sober, as befits my years,' laughed Rosa, composing herself, and adding, so like a woman that I could not help smiling in the dark,—

" 'When I say "years" I beg you to understand that I am *not* as old as that base man declared, but just in the prime of life for a horse. Hard usage has made me seem old before my time, and I am good for years of service yet.'

" 'Few people have been through as much as you have, Rosa, and you certainly *have* earned the right to rest,' I said consolingly, for her little whims and vanities amused me much.

" 'You know what happened next,' she continued; 'but I must seize this opportunity to express my thanks for all the kindness I've received since Miss Merry bought me, in spite of the ridicule and dissuasion of all her friends.

" 'I know I didn't look like a good bargain, for I *was* very thin and lame and shabby; but she saw and loved the willing spirit in me, pitied my hard lot, and felt that it would be a good deed to buy me even if she never got much work out of me.

" 'I shall always remember that, and whatever happens to me hereafter, I never shall be as proud again as I was the day she put my new saddle and bridle on, and I was led out, sleek, plump, and handsome, with blue rosettes at my ears, my tail cut in the English style, and on my back Miss Merry in her London hat and habit, all ready to head a cavalcade of eighteen horsemen and horsewomen. *We* were the most perfect pair of all, and when the troop caracoled down the wide street six abreast, *my* head was the highest, *my* rider the straightest, and *our* two hearts the friendliest in all the goodly company.

" 'Nor is it pride and love alone that binds me to her, it is gratitude as well, for did not she often bathe my feet herself, rub me down, water me, blanket me, and daily come to see me when I was here alone for weeks in the winter time? Didn't she study horses' feet and shoes, that I might be cured if possible? Didn't she write to the famous friend of my race for advice, and drive me seven miles to get a good smith to shoe me well? Have not my poor contracted feet grown much better, thanks to the weeks of rest without shoes which she gave me? Am I not fat and handsome, and, barring the stiff knees, a very presentable horse? If I am, it is all owing to her; and for that reason I want to live and die in her service.

" '*She* doesn't want to sell me, and only bade you do it because you didn't want the care of me while she is gone. Dear Miss Belinda, please keep me! I'll eat as little as I can. I won't ask for a new blanket, though your old army one is very thin and shabby. I'll trot for you all winter, and try not to show it if I am lame. I'll do anything a horse can, no matter how humble, to earn my living, only don't, pray don't send me away among strangers who have neither interest nor pity for me!'

"Rosa had spoken rapidly, feeling that her plea must be made now or never, for before another Christmas she might be far away and speech of no use to win her wish. I was much touched, though she was only a horse; for she was looking earnestly at me as she spoke, and made the last words very eloquent by preparing to bend her stiff knees and lie down at my feet. I stopped her, and answered with an arm about her neck and her soft nose in my hand,—

" 'You shall *not* be sold, Rosa! You shall go and board at Mr. Town's great stable, where you will have pleasant society among the eighty horses who usually pass the winter there. Your shoes shall be taken off, and you shall rest till March at least. The best care will be taken of you, dear, and I will come and see you; and in the spring you shall return to us, even if Miss Merry is not here to welcome you.'

" 'Thanks, many, many thanks! But I wish I could do something to earn my board. I hate to be idle, though rest *is* delicious. Is there nothing I can do to repay you, Miss Belinda? Please answer quickly, for I know the hour is almost over,' cried Rosa, stamping with anxiety; for, like all her sex, she wanted the last word.

"Yes, you can,' I cried, as a sudden idea popped into my head. 'I'll write down what you have told me, and send the little story to a certain paper I know of, and the money I get for it will pay your board. So rest in peace, my dear; you *will* have earned your living, and may feel that your debt is paid.'

"Before she could reply the clock struck one, and a long sigh of satisfaction was all the response in her power. But we understood each other now, and, cutting a lock from her mane for Miss Merry, I gave Rosa a farewell caress and went away, wondering if I had made it all up, or if she had really broken a year's silence and freed her mind.

"However that may be, here is the tale, and the sequel to it is, that the bay mare has really gone to board at a first-class stable," concluded Miss Belinda. "I call occasionally and leave my card in the shape of an apple, finding Madam Rosa living like an independent lady, with her large box and private yard on the sunny side of the barn, a kind ostler to wait upon her, and much genteel society from the city when she is inclined for company.

"What more could any reasonable horse desire?"


# LUNCH

"SISTER Jerusha, it really does wear upon me to see those dear boys eat such bad pies and stuff day after day when they ought to have good wholesome things for lunch. I actually ache to go and give each one of 'em a nice piece of bread-and-butter or one of our big cookies," said kind Miss Mehitable Plummer, taking up her knitting after a long look at the swarm of boys pouring out of the grammar school opposite, to lark about the yard, sit on the posts, or dive into a dingy little shop close by, where piles of greasy tarts and cakes lay in the window. They would not have allured any but hungry school-boys, and ought to have been labelled Dyspepsia and Headache, so unwholesome were they.

Miss Jerusha looked up from her seventeenth patchwork quilt, and answered, with a sympathetic glance over the way,—

"If we had enough to go round I'd do it myself, and save these poor deluded dears from the bilious turns that will surely take them down before vacation comes. That fat boy is as yellow as a lemon now, and no wonder, for I've seen him eat half a dozen dreadful turnovers for one lunch."

Both old ladies shook their heads and sighed, for they led a very quiet life in the narrow house that stood end to the street, squeezed in between two stores, looking as out of place as the good spinsters would have done among the merry lads opposite. Sitting at the front windows day after day, the old ladies had learned to enjoy watching the boys, who came and went, like bees to a hive, month by month. They had their favorites, and beguiled many a long hour speculating on the looks, manners, and probable station of the lads. One lame boy was Miss Jerusha's pet, though she never spoke to him, and a tall bright-faced fellow, who rather lorded it over the rest, quite won Miss Hetty's old heart by helping her across the street on a slippery day. They longed to mend some of the shabby clothes, to cheer up the dull discouraged ones, advise the sickly, reprove the rude, and, most of all, feed those who persisted in buying lunch at the dirty bake-shop over the way.

The good souls were famous cooks, and had many books full of all manner of nice receipts, which they seldom used, as they lived simply and saw little company. A certain kind of molasses cookie made by their honored mother,—a renowned housewife in her time,—and eaten by the sisters as children, had a peculiar charm for them. A tin box was always kept full, though they only now and then nibbled one, and preferred to give them away to poor children, as they trotted to market each day. Many a time had Miss Hetty felt sorely tempted to treat the boys, but was a little timid, for they were rough fellows, and she regarded them much as a benevolent tabby would a party of frisky puppies.

Today the box was full of fresh cookies, crisp, brown, and sweet; their spicy odor pervaded the room, and the china-closet door stood suggestively open. Miss Hetty's spectacles turned that way, then went back to the busy scene in the street, as if trying to get courage for the deed. Something happened just then which decided her, and sealed the doom of the bilious tarts and their maker.

Several of the younger lads were playing marbles on the sidewalk,for Hop Scotch, Leap Frog, and friendly scuffles were going on in the yard, and no quiet spot could be found. The fat boy sat on a post near by, and, having eaten his last turnover, fell to teasing the small fellows peacefully playing at his feet. One was the shabby lame boy, who hopped to and fro with his crutch, munching a dry cracker, with now and then a trip to the pump to wash it down. He seldom brought any lunch, and seemed to enjoy this poor treat so much that the big bright-faced chap tossed him a red apple as he came out of the yard to get his hat, thrown there by the mate he had been playfully thrashing.

The lame child eyed the pretty apple lovingly, and was preparing to take the first delicious bite, when the fat youth with a dexterous kick sent it flying into the middle of the street, where a passing wheel crushed it down into the mud.

"It's a shame! He *shall* have something good! The scamp!" And with this somewhat confused exclamation Miss Hetty threw down her work, ran to the closet, then darted to the front door, embracing the tin box, as if the house was on fire and that contained her dearest treasures.

"Sakes alive, what *is* the matter with sister?" ejaculated Miss Jerusha, going to the window just in time to see the fat boy tumble off the post as the tall lad came to the rescue, while the cripple went hopping across the street in answer to a kindly quavering voice that called out to him,—

"Come here, boy, and get a cookie,—a dozen if you want 'em."

"Sister's done it at last!" And, inspired by this heroic example, Miss Jerusha threw up the window, saying, as she beckoned to the avenger,—

"You too, because you stood by that poor little boy. Come right over and help yourself."

Charley Howe laughed at the indignant old ladies, but, being a gentleman, took off his hat and ran across to thank them for their interest in the fray. Several other lads followed as irresistibly as flies to a honeypot, for the tin box was suggestive of cake, and they waited for no invitation.

Miss Hetty was truly a noble yet a droll sight, as she stood there, a trim little old lady, with her cap-strings flying in the wind, her rosy old face shining with good-will, as she dealt out cookies with a lavish hand, and a kind word to all.

"Here's a nice big one for you, my dear. I don't know your name, but I do your face, and I like to see a big boy stand up for the little ones," she said, beaming at Charley as he came up.

"Thank you ma'am. That's a splendid one. We don't get anything so nice over there." And Charley gratefully bolted the cake in three mouthfuls, having given away his own lunch.

"No, indeed! One of these is worth a dozen of those nasty pies. I hate to see you eating them, and I don't believe your mothers know how bad they are," said Miss Hetty, diving for another handful into the depths of the box, which was half empty already.

"Wish you'd teach old Peck how you make 'em. We'd be glad enough to buy these and let the cockroach pies alone," said Charley, accepting another and enjoying the fun, for half the fellows were watching the scene from over the way.

"Cockroach pies! You don't mean to say?" cried Miss Hetty, nearly dropping her load in her horror at the idea, for she had heard of fricasseed frogs and roasted locusts, and thought a new delicacy had been found.

"We find 'em in the apple-sauce sometimes, and nails and bits of barrel in the cake, so some of us don't patronize Peck," replied Charley; and little Briggs the cripple added eagerly,—

"I never do; my mother won't let me."

"He never has any money, that's why," bawled Dickson, the fat boy, dodging behind the fence as he spoke.

"Never you mind, sonny, you come here every day, and *I'll* see that you have a good lunch. Apples too, *red ones,* if you like them, with your cake," answered Miss Hetty, patting his head and sending an indignant glance across the street.

"Cry-baby! Molly-coddle! Grandma's darling!" jeered Dickson, and then fled, for Charley fired a ball at him with such good aim it narrowly escaped his nose.

"That boy will have the jaundice as sure as fate, and he deserves it," said Miss Hetty, sternly, as she dropped the lid on the now empty box; for while she was talking the free-and-easy young gentlemen had been helping themselves.

"Thank you very much, ma'am, for my cookie. I won't forget to call tomorrow." And little Briggs shook hands with as innocent a face as if his jacket pocket was not bulging in a most suspicious manner.

"You'll get your death a cold, Hetty," called Miss Jerusha, and, taking the hint, Charley promptly ended the visit.

"Sheer off, fellows. We are no end obliged, ma'am, and I'll see that Briggs isn't put upon by sneaks."

Then the boys ran off, and the old lady retired to her parlor to sink into her easy-chair, as much excited by this little feat as if she had led a forlorn hope to storm a battery.

"I'll fill both those big tins tomorrow, and treat every one of the small boys, if I'm spared," she panted, with a decided nod, as she settled her cap and composed her neat black skirts, with which the wind had taken liberties, as she stood on the steps.

"I'm not sure it isn't our duty to make and sell good, wholesome lunches to those boys. We can afford to do it cheap, and it wouldn't be much trouble. Just put the long table across the front entry for half an hour every day, and let them come and get a bun, a cookie, or a buttered biscuit. It could be done, sister," said Miss Jerusha, longing to distinguish herself in some way also.

"It *shall* be done, sister!" And Miss Hetty made up her mind at that moment to devote some of her time and skill to rescuing those blessed boys from the unprincipled Peck and his cockroach pies.

It was pleasant, as well as droll, to see how heartily the good souls threw themselves into the new enterprise, how bravely they kept each other up when courage showed signs of failing, and how rapidly they became convinced that it was a duty to provide better food for the future defenders and rulers of their native land.

"You can't expect the dears to study with clear heads if they are not fed properly, and half the women in the world never think that what goes into children's stomachs affects their brains," declared Miss Hetty, as she rolled out vast sheets of dough next day, emphasizing her remarks with vigorous flourishes of the rolling-pin.

"Our blessed mother understood how to feed a family. Fourteen stout boys and girls, all alive and well, and you and I as smart at seventy one and two, as most folks at forty. Good, plain victuals and plenty of 'em is the secret of firm health," responded Miss Jerusha, rattling a pan of buns briskly into the oven.

"We'd better make some Brighton Rock. It is gone out of fashion, but our brothers used to be dreadful fond of it, and boys are about alike all the world over. Ma's *resate* never fails, and it will be a new treat for the little dears."

"S'pose we have an extra can of milk left and give 'em a good mugful? Some of those poor things look as if they never got a drop. Peck sells beer, and milk is a deal better. Shall we, sister?"

"We'll try it, Jerushy. In for a penny, in for a pound."

And upon that principle the old ladies did the thing handsomely, deferring the great event till Monday, that all might be in apple-pie order. They said nothing of it when the lads came on Friday morning, and all Saturday, which was a holiday at school, was a very busy one with them.

"Hullo! Miss Hetty *has* done it now, hasn't she? Look at that, old Peck, and tremble!" exclaimed Charley to his mates, as he came down the street on Monday morning, and espied a neat little sign on the sisters' door, setting forth the agreeable fact that certain delectable articles of food and drink could be had within at reasonable prices during recess.

No caps were at the windows, but behind the drawn curtains two beaming old faces were peeping out to see how the boys took the great announcement. Whoever remembers Hawthorne's half-comic, half-pathetic description of poor Hepsibah Pyncheon's hopes and fears, when arranging her gingerbread wares in the little shop, can understand something of the excitement of the sisters that day, as the time drew near when the first attempt was to be made.

"Who will set the door open?" said Miss Hetty when the fateful moment came, and boys began to pour out into the yard.

"I will!" And, nerving herself to the task, Miss Jerusha marched boldly round the table, set wide the door, and then, as the first joyful whoop from the boys told that the feast was in view, she whisked back into the parlor panic-stricken.

"There they come,—hundreds of them, I should think by the sound!" she whispered, as the tramp of feet came nearer, and the clamor of voices exclaiming,—

"What bully buns!" "Ain't those cookies rousers?" "New stuff too, looks first-rate." "I told you it wasn't a joke." "Wonder how Peck likes it?" "Dickson sha'n't come in." "You go first, Charley." "Here's a cent for you, Briggs; come on and trade like the rest of us."

"I'm so flurried I couldn't make change to save my life," gasped Miss Jerusba from behind the sofa, whither she had fled.

"It is *my* turn now. Be calm, and we shall soon get used to it."

Bracing herself to meet the merry chaff of the boys, as new and trying to the old lady as real danger would have been, Miss Hetty stepped forth into the hall to be greeted by a cheer, and then a chorus of demands for everything so temptingly set forth upon her table. Intrenched behind a barricade of buns, she dealt out her wares with rapidly increasing speed and skill, for as fast as one relay of lads were satisfied another came up, till the table was bare, the milk-can ran dry, and nothing was left to tell the tale but an empty water-pail and a pile of five-cent pieces.

"I hope I didn't cheat any one, but I was flurried, sister, they were so very noisy and so hungry. Bless their dear hearts; they are full now, I trust." And Miss Hetty looked over her glasses at the crumby countenances opposite, meeting many nods and smiles in return, as her late customers enthusiastically recommended her establishment to the patronage of those who had preferred Peck's questionable dainties.

"The Brighton Rock was a success; we must have a good store for tomorrow, and more milk. Briggs drank it like a baby, and your nice boy proposed my health like a little gentleman, as he is," replied Miss Jerusha, who had ventured out before it was too late, and done the honors of the can with great dignity, in spite of some inward trepidation at the astonishing feats performed with the mug.

"Peck's nose is out of joint, if I may use so vulgar an expression, and *our* lunch a triumphant success. Boys know what is good, and we need not fear to lose their custom as long as we can supply them. I shall order a barrel of flour at once, and heat up the big oven. We have put our hand to the work and must not turn back, for our honor is pledged now."

With which lofty remark Miss Hetty closed the door, trying to look utterly unconscious of the anxious Peck, who was flattening his nose against his dingy window-pane to survey his rivals over piles of unsold pastry.

The little venture *was* a success, and all that winter the old ladies did their part faithfully, finding the task more to their taste than everlasting patchwork and knitting, and receiving a fair profit on their outlay, being shrewd managers, and rich in old-fashioned thrift, energy, and industry.

The boys revelled in wholesome fare, and soon learned to love "the Aunties," as they were called, while such of the parents as took an interest in the matter showed their approval in many ways most gratifying to the old ladies.

The final triumph, however, was the closing of Peck's shop for want of custom, for few besides the boys patronized him. None mourned for him, and Dickson proved the truth of Miss Hetty's prophecy by actually having a bilious fever in the spring.

But a new surprise awaited the boys; for when they came flocking back after the summer vacation, there stood the little shop, brave in new paint and fittings, full of all the old goodies, and over the door a smart sign, "Plummer & Co."

"By Jove, the Aunties are bound to cover themselves with glory. Let's go in and hear all about it. Behave now, you fellows, or I'll see about it afterward," commanded Charley, as he paused to peer in through the clean windows at the tempting display.

In they trooped, and, tapping on the counter, stood ready to greet the old ladies as usual, but to their great surprise a pretty young woman appeared, and smilingly asked what they would have.

"We want the Aunties, if you please. Isn't this their shop?" said little Briggs, bitterly disappointed at not finding his good friends.

"You will find them over there at home as usual. Yes, this is their shop, and I'm their niece. My husband is the Co., and we run the shop for the aunts. I hope you'll patronize us, gentlemen."

"We will! We will! Three cheers for Plummer & Co.!" cried Charley, leading off three rousers, that made the little shop ring again, and brought two caps to the opposite windows, as two cheery old faces smiled and nodded, full of satisfaction at the revolution so successfully planned and carried out.

# A NIGHT

## From *Hospital Sketches*

BEING fond of the night side of nature, I was soon promoted to the post of night nurse, with every facility for indulging in my favorite pastime of "owling." My colleague, a black-eyed widow, relieved me at dawn, we two taking care of the ward between us, like regular nurses, turn and turn about. I usually found my boys in the jolliest state of mind their condition allowed; for it was a known fact that Nurse Periwinkle objected to blue devils, and entertained a belief that he who laughed most was surest of recovery. At the beginning of my reign, dumps and dismals prevailed; the nurses looked anxious and tired, the men gloomy or sad; and a general "Hark!-from-the-tombs-a-doleful-sound" style of conversation seemed to be the fashion: a state of things which caused one coming from a merry, social New England town, to feel as if she had got into an exhausted receiver; and the instinct of self-preservation, to say nothing of a philanthropic desire to serve the race, caused a speedy change in Ward No. 1.

More flattering than the most gracefully turned compliment, more grateful than the most admiring glance, was the sight of those rows of faces, all strange to me a little while ago, now lighting up, with smiles of welcome, as I came among them, enjoying that moment heartily, with a womanly pride in their regard, a motherly affection for them all. The evenings were spent in reading aloud, writing letters, waiting on and amusing the men, going the rounds with Dr. P., as he made his second daily survey, dressing my dozen wounds afresh, giving last doses, and making them cozy for the long hours to come, till the nine o'clock bell rang, the gas was turned down, the day nurses went off duty, the night watch came on, and my nocturnal adventures began.

My ward was now divided into three rooms; and, under favor of the matron, I had managed to sort out the patients in such a way that I had what I called, "my duty room," my "pleasure room," and my "pathetic room," and worked for each a different way. One, I visited, armed with a dressing tray, full of rollers, plasters, and pins; another, with books, flowers, games, and gossip; a third, with teapots, lullabies, consolation, and, sometimes, a shroud.

Wherever the sickest or most helpless man chanced to be, there I had my watch, often visiting the other rooms, to see that the general watchman of the ward did his duty by the fires and the wounds, the latter needing constant wetting. Not only on this account did I meander, but also to get fresher air than the close rooms afforded; for, owing to the stupidity of that mysterious "somebody" who does all the damage in the world, the windows had been carefully nailed down above, and the lower sashes could only be raised in the mildest weather, for the men lay just below. I had suggested a summary smashing of a few panes here and there, when frequent appeals to headquarters had proved unavailing, and daily orders to lazy attendants had come to nothing. No one seconded the motion, however, and the nails were far beyond my reach; for, though belonging to the sisterhood of "ministering angels," I had no wings, and might as well have asked for a suspension bridge, as a pair of steps, in that charitable chaos.

One of the harmless ghosts who bore me company during the haunted hours, was Dan, the watchman, whom I regarded with a certain awe; for, though so much together, I never fairly saw his face, and, but for his legs, should never have recognized him, as we seldom met by day. These legs were remarkable, as was his whole figure, for his body was short, rotund, and done up in a big jacket, and muffler; his beard hid the lower part of his face, his hat-brim the upper; and all I ever discovered was a pair of sleepy eyes, and a very mild voice. But the legs!—very long, very thin, very crooked and feeble, looking like gray sausages in their tight coverings, and finished off with a pair of expansive, green cloth shoes, very like Chinese junks with the sails down. This figure, gliding noiselessly about the dimly-lighted rooms, was strongly suggestive of the spirit of a beer-barrel mounted on cork-screws, haunting the old hotel in search of its lost mates, emptied and staved in long ago.

Another goblin who frequently appeared to me, was the attendant of "the pathetic room," who, being a faithful soul, was often up to tend two or three men, weak and wandering as babies, after the fever had gone. The amiable creature beguiled the watches of the night by brewing jorums of a fearful beverage, which he called coffee, and insisted on sharing with me; coming in with a great bowl of something like mud soup, scalding hot, guiltless of cream, rich in an all-pervading flavor of molasses, scorch and tin pot. Such an amount of good will and neighborly kindness also went into the mess, that I never could find the heart to refuse, but always received it with thanks, sipped it with hypocritical relish while he remained, and whipped it into the slop-jar the instant he departed, thereby gratifying him, securing one rousing laugh in the doziest hour of the night, and no one was the worse for the transaction but the pigs. Whether they were "cut off untimely in their sins," or not, I carefully abstained from inquiring.

It was a strange life—asleep half the day, exploring Washington the other half, and all night hovering, like a massive cherubim, in a red rigolette, over the slumbering sons of man. I liked it, and found many things to amuse, instruct, and interest me. The snores alone were quite a study, varying from the mild sniff to the stentorian snort, which startled the echoes and hoised the performer erect to accuse his neighbor of the deed, magnanimously forgive him, and, wrapping the drapery of his couch about him, lie down to vocal slumber. After listening for a week to this band of wind instruments, I indulged in the belief that I could recognize each by the snore alone, and was tempted to join the chorus by breaking out with John Brown's favorite hymn:

*"Blow ye the trumpet, blow!"*

I would have given much to have possessed the art of sketching, for many of the faces became wonderfully interesting when un-conscious. Some grew stern and grim, the men evidently dreaming of war, as they gave orders, groaned over their wounds, or damned the rebels vigorously; some grew sad and infinitely pathetic, as if the pain borne silently all day, revenged itself by now betraying what the man's pride had concealed so well. Often the roughest grew young and pleasant when sleep smoothed the hard lines away, letting the real nature assert itself; many almost seemed to speak, and I learned to know these men better by night than through any intercourse by day. Sometimes they disappointed me, for faces that looked merry and good in the light, grew bad and sly when the shadows came; and though they made no confidences in words, I read their lives, leaving them to wonder at the change of manner this midnight magic wrought in their nurse. A few talked busily; one drummer boy sang sweetly, though no persuasions could win a note from him by day; and several depended on being told what they had talked of in the morning. Even my constitutionals in the chilly halls, possessed a certain charm, for the house was never still. Sentinels tramped round it all night long, their muskets glittering in the wintry moonlight as they walked, or stood before the doors, straight and silent, as figures of stone, causing one to conjure up romantic visions of guarded forts, sudden surprises, and daring deeds; for in these war times the hum drum life of Yankeedom has vanished, and the most prosaic feel some thrill of that excitement which stirs the nation's heart, and makes its capital a camp of hospitals. Wandering up and down these lower halls, I often heard cries from above, steps hurrying to and fro, saw surgeons passing up, or men coming down carrying a stretcher, where lay a long white figure, whose face was shrouded and whose fight was done. Sometimes I stopped to watch the passers in the street, the moonlight shining on the spire opposite, or the gleam of some vessel floating, like a white-winged sea-gull, down the broad Potomac, whose fullest flow can never wash away the red stain of the land.

The night whose events I have a fancy to record, opened with a little comedy, and closed with a great tragedy; for a virtuous and useful life untimely ended is always tragical to those who see not as God sees. My headquarters were beside the bed of a New Jersey boy, crazed by the horrors of that dreadful Saturday. A slight wound in the knee brought him there; but his mind had suffered more than his body; some string of that delicate machine was over strained, and, for days, he had been re-living in imagination, the scenes he could not forget, till his distress broke out in incoherent ravings, pitiful to hear. As I sat by him, endeavoring to soothe his poor distracted brain by the constant touch of wet hands over his hot forehead, he lay cheering his comrades on, hurrying them back, then counting them as they fell around him, often clutching my arm, to drag me from the vicinity of a bursting shell, or covering up his head to screen himself from a shower of shot; his face brilliant with fever; his eyes restless; his head never still; every muscle strained and rigid; while an incessant stream of defiant shouts, whispered warnings, and broken laments, poured from his lips with that forceful bewilderment which makes such wanderings so hard to overhear.

It was past eleven, and my patient was slowly wearying himself into fitful intervals of quietude, when, in one of these pauses, a curious sound arrested my attention. Looking over my shoulder, I saw a one-legged phantom hopping nimbly down the room; and, going to meet it, recognized a certain Pennsylvania gentleman, whose wound-fever had taken a turn for the worse, and, depriving him of the few wits a drunken campaign had left him, set him literally tripping on the light, fantastic toe "toward home," as he blandly informed me, touching the military cap which formed a striking contrast to the severe simplicity of the rest of his *undress* uniform. When sane, the least movement produced a roar of pain or a volley of oaths; but the departure of reason seemed to have wrought an agreeable change, both in the man and his manners; for, balancing himself on one leg, like a meditative stork, he plunged into an animated discussion of the war, the President, lager beer, and Enfield rifles, regardless of any suggestions of mine as to the propriety of returning to bed, lest he be court-martialed for desertion.

Any thing more supremely ridiculous can hardly be imagined than this figure, all draped in white, its one foot covered with a big blue sock, a dingy cap set rakingly askew on its shaven head, and placid satisfaction beaming in its broad red face, as it flourished a mug in one hand, an old boot in the other, calling them canteen and knapsack, while it skipped and fluttered in the most unearthly fashion. What to do with the creature I didn't know; Dan was absent, and if I went to find him, the perambulator might festoon himself out of the window, set his toga on fire, or do some of his neighbors a mischief. The attendant of the room was sleeping like a near relative of the celebrated Seven, and nothing short of pins would rouse him; for he had been out that day, and whiskey asserted its supremacy in balmy whiffs. Still declaiming, in a fine flow of eloquence, the demented gentleman hopped on, blind and deaf to my graspings and entreaties; and I was about to slam the door in his face, and run for help, when a second and saner phantom came to the rescue, in the likeness of a big Prussian, who spoke no English, but divined the crisis, and put an end to it, by bundling the lively monoped into his bed, like a baby, with an authoritative command to "stay put," which received added weight from being delivered in an odd conglomeration of French and German, accompanied by warning wags of a head decorated with a yellow cotton night cap, rendered most imposing by a tassel like a bell-pull. Rather exhausted by his excursion, the member from Pennsylvania subsided; and, after an irrepressible laugh together, my Prussian ally and myself were returning to our places, when the echo of a sob caused us to glance along the beds. It came from one in the corner—such a little bed!—and such a tearful little face looked up at us, as we stopped beside it! The twelve years old drummer boy was not singing now, but sobbing, with a manly effort all the while to stifle the distressful sounds that would break out.

"What is it, Billy?" I asked, as he rubbed the tears away, and checked himself in the middle of a great sob to answer plaintively:

"I've got a chill, ma'am, but I aint cryin' for that, 'cause I'm used to it. I dreamed Kit was here, and when I waked up he wasn't, and I couldn't help it, then."

The boy came in with the rest, and the man who was taken dead from the ambulance was the Kit he mourned. Well he might; for, when the wounded were brought from Fredericksburg, the child lay in one of the camps thereabout, and this good friend, though sorely hurt himself, would not leave him to the exposure and neglect of such a time and place; but, wrapping him in his own blanket, carried him in his arms to the transport, tended him during the passage, and only yielded up his charge when Death met him at the door of the hospital which promised care and comfort for the boy. For ten days, Billy had burned or shivered with fever and ague, pining the while for Kit, and refusing to be comforted, because he had not been able to thank him for the generous protection, which, perhaps, had cost the giver's life. The vivid dream had wrung the childish heart with a fresh pang, and when I tried the solace fitted for his years, the remorseful fear that haunted him found vent in a fresh burst of tears, as he looked at the wasted hands I was endeavoring to warm:

"Oh! If I'd only been as thin when Kit carried me as I am now, maybe he wouldn't have died; but I was heavy, he was hurt worser than we knew, and so it killed him; and I didn't see him, to say good bye."

This thought had troubled him in secret; and my assurances that his friend would probably have died at all events, hardly assuaged the bitterness of his regretful grief.

At this juncture, the delirious man began to shout; the one-legged rose up in his bed, as if preparing for another dart, Billy bewailed himself more piteously than before: and if ever a woman was at her wit's end, that distracted female was Nurse Periwinkle, during the space of two or three minutes, as she vibrated between the three beds, like an agitated pendulum. Like a most opportune reinforcement, Dan, the bandy, appeared, and devoted himself to the lively party, leaving me free to return to my post; for the Prussian, with a nod and a smile, took the lad away to his own bed, and lulled him to sleep with a soothing murmur, like a mammoth humble bee. I liked that in Fritz, and if he ever wondered afterward at the dainties which sometimes found their way into his rations, or the extra comforts of his bed, he might have found a solution of the mystery in sundry persons' knowledge of the fatherly action of that night.

Hardly was I settled again, when the inevitable bowl appeared, and its bearer delivered a message I had expected, yet dreaded to receive:

"John is going, ma'am, and wants to see you, if you can come."

"The moment this boy is asleep; tell him so, and let me know if I am in danger of being too late."

My Ganymede departed, and while I quieted poor Shaw, I thought of John. He came in a day or two after the others; and, one evening, when I entered my "pathetic room," I found a lately emptied bed occupied by a large, fair man, with a fine face, and the serenest eyes I ever met. One of the earlier comers had often spoken of a friend, who had remained behind, that those apparently worse wounded than himself might reach a shelter first. It seemed a David and Jonathan sort of friendship. The man fretted for his mate, and was never tired of praising John—his courage, sobriety, self-denial, and unfailing kindliness of heart; always winding up with: "He's an out an' out fine feller, ma'am; you see if he aint."

I had some curiosity to behold this piece of excellence, and when he came, watched him for a night or two, before I made friends with him; for, to tell the truth, I was a little afraid of the stately looking man, whose bed had to be lengthened to accommodate his commanding stature; who seldom spoke, uttered no complaint, asked no sympathy, but tranquilly observed waht went on about him; and, as he lay high upon his pillows, no picture of dying statesman or warrior was ever fuller of real dignity than this Virginia blacksmith. A most attractive face he had, framed in brown hair and beard, comely featured and full of vigor, as yet unsubdued by pain; thoughtful and often beautifully mild while watching the afflictions of others, as if entirely forgetful of his own. His mouth was grave and firm, with plenty of will and courage in its lines, but a smile could make it as sweet as any woman's; and his eyes were child's eyes, looking one fairly in the face, with a clear, straightforward glance, which promised well for such as placed their faith in him. He seemed to cling to life, as if it were rich in duties and delights, and he had learned the secret of content. The only time I saw his composure disturbed, was when my surgeon brought another to examine John, who scrutinized their faces with an anxious look, asking of the elder: "Do you think I shall pull through, sir?" "I hope so, my man." And, as the two passed on, John's eye still followed them, with an intentness which would have won a truer answer from them, had they seen it. A momentay shadow flitted over his face; then came the usual serenity, as if, in that brief eclipse, he had acknowledged the existence of some hard possibility, and, asking nothing yet hoping all things, left the issue in God's hands, with that submission which is true piety.

The next night, as I went my rounds with Dr. P., I happened to ask which man in the room probably suffered most; and, to my great surprise, he glanced at John:

"Every breath he draws is like a stab; for the ball pierced the left lung, broke a rib, and did no end of damage here and there; so the poor lad can find neither forgetfulness nor ease, because he must lie on his wounded back or suffocate. It will be a hard struggle, and a long one, for he possesses great vitality; but even his temperate life can't save him; I wish it could.'

"You don't mean he must die, Doctor?"

"Bless you, there's not the slightest hope for him; and you'd better tell him so before long; women have a way of doing such things comfortably, so I leave it to you. He won't last more than a day or two, at furthest."

I could have sat down on the spot and cried heartily, if I had not learned the wisdom of bottling up one's tears for leisure moments. Such an end seemed very hard for such a man, when half a dozen worn out, worthless bodies round him, were gathering up the remnants of wasted lives, to linger on for years perhaps, burdens to others, daily reproaches to themselves. The army needed men like John, earnest, brave, an faithful; fighting for liberty and justice with both heart and hand, true soldiers of the Lord. I could not give him up so soon, or think with any patience of so excellent a nature robbed of its fulfilment, and blundered into eternity by the rashness or stupidity of those at whose hands so many lives may be required. It was an easy thing for Dr. P. to say: "Tell him he must die,' but a cruelly hard thing to do, and by no means as "comfortable" as he politely suggested. I had not the heart to do it then, and privately indulged the hope that some change for the better might take place, in spite of gloomy prophesies; so, rendering my task unnecessary.

A few minutes later, as I came in again, with fresh rollers, I saw John sitting erect, with no one to support him, while the surgeon dressed his back. I had never hitherto seen it done; for, having simpler wounds to attend to, and knowing the fidelity of the attendant, I had left John to him, thinking it might be more aggreable and safe; for both strength and experience were needed in his case. I had forgotten that the strong man might long for the gentle tendance of a woman's hands, the sympathetic magnetism of a woman's presence, as well as the feebler souls about him. The Doctor's words caused me to reproach myself with neglect, not of any real duty perhaps, but of those little cares and kindnesses that solace homesick spirits, and make the heavy hours pass easier. John looked lonely and forsaken just then, as he sat with bent head, hands folded on his knee, and no outwad sign of suffering, till, looking nearer, I saw great tears roll down and drop upon the floor. It was a new sight there; for, though I had seen many suffer, some swore, some groaned, most endured silently, but none wept. Yet it did not seem weak, only very touching, and straightway my fear vanished, my heart opened wide and took him in, as, gathering the bent head in my arms, as freely as if he had been a little child, I said, "Let me help you bear it, John."

Never, on any human countenance, have I seen so swift and beautiful a look of gratitude, surprise and comfort, as that which answered me more eloquently than the whispered—

"Thank you, ma'am, this is right good! This is what I wanted!"

"Then why not ask for it before?"

"I didn't like to be a trouble; you seemed so busy, and I could manage to get on alone."

"You shall not want it any more, John."

Nor did he; for now I understood the wistful look that sometimes followed me, as I went out, after a brief pause beside his bed, or merely a passing nod, while busied with those who seemed to need me more than he, because more urgent in their demands. Now I knew that to him, as to so many, I was the poor substitute for mother, wife, or sister, and in his eyes no stranger, but a friend who hitherto had seemed neglectful; for, in his modesty, he had never guessed the truth. This was changed now; and, through the tedious operation of probing, bathing, and dressing his wounds, he leaned against me, holding my hand fast, and, if pain wrung further tears from him, no one saw them fall but me. When he was laid down again, I hovered about him, in a remorseful state of mind that would not let me rest, till I had bathed his face, brushed his bonny brown hair, set all things smooth about him, and laid a knot of heath and heliotrope on his clean pillow. While doing this, he watched me with the satisfied expression I so liked to see; and when I offered the little nosegay, held it carefully in his great hand, smoothed a ruffled leaf or two, surveyed and smelt it with an air of genuine delight, and lay contentedly regarding the glimmer of the sunshine on the green. Although the manliest man among my forty, he said, "Yes, ma'am," like a little boy; received suggestions for his comfort with the quick smile that brightened his whole face; and now and then, as I stood tidying the table by his bed, I felt him softly touch my gown, as if to assure himself that I was there. Anything more natural and frank I never saw, and found this brave John as bashful as brave, yet full of excellencies and fine aspirations, which, having no power to express themselves in words, seemed to have bloomed into his character and made him what he was.

After that night, an hour of each evening that remained to him was devoted to his ease or pleasure. He could not talk much, for breath was precious, and he spoke in whispers; but from occasional conversations, I gleaned scraps of private history which only added to the affection and respect I felt for him. Once he asked me to write a letter, and as I settled pen and paper, I said, with an irrepressible glimmer of feminine curiosity, "Shall it be addressed to wife, or mother, John?"

"Neither, ma'am; I've got no wife, and will write to mother myself when I get better. Did you think I was married because of this?" he asked, touching a plain ring he wore, and often turned thoughtfully on his finger when he lay alone.

"Partly that, but more from a settled sort of look you have; a look which young men seldom get until they marry."

"I didn't know that; but I'm not so very young, ma'am, thirty in May, and have been what you might call settled this ten years. Mother's a widow, I'm the oldest child she has, and it wouldn't do for me to marry until Lizzy has a home of her own, and Jack's learned his trade; for we're not rich, and I must be father to the children and husband to the dear old woman, if I can."

"No doubt but you are both, John; yet how came you to go to war, if you felt so? Wasn't enlisting as bad as marrying?"

"No, ma'am, not as I see it, for one is helping my neighbor, the other pleasing myself. I went because I couldn't help it. I didn't want the glory or the pay; I wanted the right thing done, and people kept saying the men who were in earnest ought to fight. I was in earnest, the Lord knows! But I held off as long as I could, not knowing which was my duty. Mother saw the case, gave me her ring to keep me steady, and said 'Go:' so I went."

A short story and a simple one, but the man and the mother were portrayed better than pages of fine writing could have done it.

"Do you ever regret that you came, when you lie here suffering so much?"

"Never, ma'am; I haven't helped a great deal, but I've shown I was willing to give my life, and perhaps I've got to; but I don't blame anybody, and if it was to do over again, I'd do it. I'm a little sorry I wasn't wounded in front; it looks cowardly to be hit in the back, but I obeyed orders, and it don't matter in the end, I know."

Poor John! It did not matter now, except that a shot in front might have spared the long agony in store for him. He seemed to read the thought that troubled me, as he spoke so hopefully when there was no hope, for he suddenly added:

"This is my first battle; do they think it's going to be my last?"

"I'm afraid they do, John."

It was the hardest question I had ever been called upon to answer; doubly hard with those clear eyes fixed on mine, forcing a truthful answer by their own truth. He seemed a little startled at first, pondered over the fateful fact a moment, then shook his head, with a glance at the broad chest and muscular limbs stretched out before him:

"I'm not afraid, but it's difficult to believe all at once. I'm so strong it don't seem possible for such a little wound to kill me."

Merry Mercutio's dying words glanced through my memory as he spoke: " 'Tis not so deep as a well, nor so wide as a church door, but 'tis enough." And John would have said the same could he have seen the ominous black holes between his shoulders; he never had, but, seeing the ghastly sights about him, could not believe his own wound more fatal than these, for all the suffering it caused him.

"Shall I write to your mother, now?" I asked, thinking that these sudden tidings might change all plans and purposes. But they did not; for the man received the order of the Divine Commander to march with the same unquestioning obedience with which the soldier had received that of the human one; doubtless remembering that the first led him to life, and the last to death.

"No, ma'am; to Jack just the same; he'll break it to her best, and I'll add a line to her myself when you get done."

So I wrote the letter which he dictated, finding it better than any I had sent; for, though here and there a little ungrammatical or inelegant, each sentence came to me briefly worded, but most expressive; full of excellent counsel to the boy, tenderly bequeathing "mother and Lizzie" to his care, and bidding him good bye in words the sadder for their simplicity. He added a few lines, with steady hand, and, as I sealed it, said, with a patient sort of sigh, "I hope the answer will come in time for me to see it;" then, turning away his face, laid the flowers against his lips, as if to hide some quiver of emotion at the thought of such a sudden sundering of all the dear home ties.

These things had happened two days before; now John was dying,

John—the manliest man among my forty.

A Night

and the letter had not come. I had been summoned to many death beds in my life, but to none that made my heart ache as it did then, since my mother called me to watch the departure of a spirit akin to this in its gentleness and patient strength. As I went in, John stretched out both hands:

"I knew you'd come! I guess I'm moving on, ma'am."

He was; and so rapidly that, even while he spoke, over his face I saw the grey veil falling that no human hand can lift. I sat down by him, wiped the drops from his forehead, stirred the air about him with the slow wave of a fan, and waited to help him die. He stood in sore need of help—and I could do so little; for, as the doctor had foretold, the strong body rebelled against death, and fought every inch of the way, forcing him to draw each breath with a spasm, and clench his hands with an imploring look, as if he asked, "How long must I endure this, and be still!" For hours he suffered dumbly, without a moment's respite, or a moment's murmuring; his limbs grew cold, his face damp, his lips white, and, again and again, he tore the covering off his breast, as if the lightest weight added to his agony; yet through it all, his eyes never lost their perfect serenity, and the man's soul seemed to sit therein, undaunted by the ills that vexed his flesh.

One by one, the men woke, and round the room appeared a circle of pale faces and watchful eyes, full of awe and pity; for, though a stranger, John was beloved by all. Each man there had wondered at his patience, respected his piety, admired his fortitude, and now lamented his hard death; for the influence of an upright nature had made itself deeply felt, even in one little week. Presently, the Jonathan who so loved this comely David, came creeping from his bed for a last look and word. The kind soul was full of trouble, as the choke in his voice, the grasp of his hand, betrayed; but there were no tears, and the farewell of the friends was the more touching for its brevity.

"Old boy, how are you?" faltered the one.

"Most through, thank heaven!" whispered the other.

"Can I say or do anything for you anywheres?"

"Take my things home, and tell them that I did my best."

"I will! I will!"

"Good bye, Ned."

"Good bye, John, good bye!"

They kissed each other, tenderly as women, and so parted, for poor Ned could not stay to see his comrade die. For a little while, there was no sound in the room but the drip of water, from a stump or two, and John's distressful gasps, as he slowly breathed his life away. I thought him nearly gone, and had just laid down the fan, believing its help to be no longer needed, when suddenly he rose up in his bed, and cried out with a bitter cry that broke the silence, sharply startling every one with its agonized appeal:

"For God's sake, give me air!"

It was the only cry pain or death had wrung from him, the only boon he had asked; and none of us could grant it, for all the airs that blew were useless now. Dan flung up the window. The first red streak of dawn was warming the grey east, a herald of the coming sun; John saw it, and with the love of light which lingers in us to the end, seemed to read in it a sign of hope of help, for, over his whole face there broke that mysterious expression, brighter than any smile, which often comes to eyes that look their last. He laid himself gently down; and, stretching out his strong right arm, as if to grasp and bring the blessed air to his lips in a fuller flow, lapsed into a merciful unconsciousness, which assured us that for him suffering was forever past. He died then; for, though the heavy breaths still tore their way up for a little longer, they were but the waves of an ebbing tide that beat unfelt against the wreck, which an immortal voyager had deserted with a smile. He never spoke again, but to the end held my hand close, so close that when he was asleep at last, I could not draw it away. Dan helped me, warning me as he did so that it was unsafe for dead and living flesh to lie so long together; but though my hand was strangely cold and stiff, and four white marks remained across its back, even when warmth and color had returned elsewhere, I could not but be glad that, through its touch, the presence of human sympathy, perhaps, had lightened that hard hour.

When they had made him ready for the grave, John lay in state for half an hour, a thing which seldom happened in that busy place; but a universal sentiment of reverence and affection seemed to fill the hearts of all who had known or heard of him; and when the rumor of his death went through the house, always astir, many came to see him, and I felt a tender sort of pride in my lost patient; for he looked a most heroic figure, lying there stately and still as the statue of some young knight asleep upon his tomb. The lovely expression which so often beautifies dead faces, soon replaced the marks of pain, and I longed for those who loved him best to see him when half an hour's acquaintance with Death had made them friends. As we stood looking at him, the ward master handed me a letter, saying it had been forgotten the night before. It was John's letter, come just an hour too late to gladden the eyes that had longed and looked for it so eagerly! But he had it; for, after I had cut some brown locks for his mother, and taken off the ring to send her, telling how well the talisman had done its work, I kissed this good son for her sake, and laid the letter in his hand, still folded as when I drew my own away, feeling that its place was there, and making myself happy with the thought, that, even in his solitary grave in the "Government Lot," he would not be without some token of the love which makes life beautiful and outlives death. Then I left him, glad to have known so genuine a man, and carrying with me an enduring memory of the brave Virginia blacksmith, as he lay serenely waiting for the dawn of that long day which knows no night.

# A HAPPY BIRTHDAY

A CERTAIN fine old lady was seventy-three on the 8th of October. The day was always celebrated with splendor by her children and grandchildren; but on this occasion they felt that something unusually interesting and festive should be done, because grandma had lately been so very ill that no one thought she would ever see another birthday. It pleased God to spare her, however, and here she was, almost as well and gay as ever.

Some families do not celebrate these days, and so miss a great deal of pleasure, I think. But the people of whom I write always made a great deal of such occasions, and often got up very funny amusements, as you will see.

As grandma was not very strong, some quiet fun must be devised this time, and the surprises sprinkled along through the day, lest they should be too much for her if they all burst upon her at once.

The morning was fine and clear, and the first thing that happened was the appearance of two little ghosts, "all in white," who came prancing into the old lady's room, while she lay placidly watching the sun rise, and thinking of the many years she had seen.

"A happy birthday, gramma!" cried the little ghosts, scrambling up to kiss the smiling old face in the ruffled night-cap.

There was a great laughing, and cuddling, and nestling among the pillows, before the small arms and legs subsided, and two round, rosy faces appeared, listening attentively to the stories grandma told them till it was time to dress.

Now you must know that there were only two grandchildren in this family, but they were equal to half a dozen, being lively, droll little chaps, full of all manner of pranks, and considered by their relatives the *most* remarkable boys alive.

These two fellows were quite bursting with the great secrets of the day, and had to rush out as soon as breakfast was done, in order to keep from "letting the cat out of the bag."

A fine dinner was cooked, and grandma's favorite niece came to eat it with her, bringing a bag full of goodies, and a heart full of love and kind wishes to the old lady.

All the afternoon, friends and presents kept coming, and Madam, in her best gown and most imposing cap, sat in state to receive them. A poet came with some lovely flowers; the doctor brought a fine picture; one neighbor sent her a basket of grapes; another took her for a drive; and some poor children, whom grandma had clothed and helped, sent her some nuts they had picked all themselves, while their grateful mother brought a bottle of cream and a dozen eggs.

It was very pleasant, and the bright autumn day was a little harvest time for the old lady, who had sowed love and charity broadcast with no thought of any reward.

The tea-table was ornamented with a splendid cake, white as snow outside, but rich and plummy inside, with a gay posy stuck atop of the little Mont Blanc. Mrs. Trot, the housekeeper, made and presented it, and it was so pretty all voted not to cut it till evening, for the table was full of other good things.

Grandma's tea was extra strong, and tasted unusually nice with Mrs. Hosy's rich cream in it. She felt that she needed this refreshment to prepare her for the grand surprise to come; for the family gifts were not yet given.

The boys vanished directly after tea, and shouts of laughter were heard from Aunt Tribulation's room. What larks as they had up there no one knew; but every one was sure they were preparing some fun in honor of the occasion.

Grandma was not allowed to go into the study, and much tacking and rummaging went on for a time. Then all the lamps were collected there, leaving grandma and grandpa to sit in the parlor, talking tenderly together by the soft glimmer of fire-light, as they used to do forty years ago.

Presently something scarlet and gold, feathery and strange, flitted by the door and vanished in the study. Queer little yells and the sound of dancing feet were heard. Then there was a hunt for the cat; next, Mrs. Trot was called from the kitchen, and all but the boys came to escort grandma to the scene of glory.

Leaning on grandpa's arm, she marched first; then came Mrs. Coobiddy, the mother of the boys, bearing Aunt Carmine's picture; for this auntie was over the water and could not come, so, at grandma's desire, her portrait was borne in the procession.

Aunt Trib followed, escorted by Thomas Pib, the great cat, with his best red bow on. Mrs. Trot and Belinda, the little maid, brought up the rear. A music-box in the hall played the "Grand March" from "Norma"; and, with great dignity, all filed into the study to behold an imposing spectacle.

A fire burned brightly on the hearth, making the old-fashioned andirons shine like gold. All the lamps illuminated the room, which was trimmed with scarlet and yellow leaves. An arch of red woodbine, evergreen and ferns from the White Mountains was made over the recess which held the journals, letters and books of the family; for their name was Penn, and they all wrote so much that blots were found everywhere about the house, and a flock of geese lived in the back yard, all ready to have their quills tweaked out at a minute's notice.

Before this recess stood a great arm-chair, in which the father of grandma had been laid, a newborn baby, and nearly smothered by being sat upon by the fat nurse. This thrilling fact gave it a peculiar interest to the boys; for, if great-grandpa had been smashed, where would they have been?

In front of this ancient seat stood a round table loaded with gifts, and on each side stood an Indian chief in full costume, bearing lighted Chinese lanterns on the ends of their spears, and war-clubs on their shoulders.

The arranging of these costumes had caused much labor and fun; for the splendid crowns, a foot high, were made of hen's feathers, carefully collected and sewed on to paper by Aunt Trib; the red shirts were fringed and bedecked with old devices; leather leggings went above the warriors' knees, and all the family breast-pins were stuck about them.

Daggers, hatchets, clubs, and spears were made by the lads themselves, and red army blankets hung gracefully from their shoulders. They had planned to paint their faces blue and red, like the Feejee Islanders at Barnum's show; but Mrs. Coobiddy would not consent to have her handsome boys disfigure themselves; so the only paint they wore was nature's red in their cheeks, and heaven's blue in their eyes, as they stood by grandma's throne, smiling like a pair of very mild and happy little chiefs.

It really was a fine sight, I assure you, and grandma was quite overcome by the spectacle. So she was introduced to her gifts as quickly as possible, to divert her mind from the tender thought that all these fond and foolish adornments were to please her.

Every gift had a poem attached, and as the presents were of every description, the verses possessed an agreeable variety. Here are a few as a sample. A small tea-kettle was one gift, and this pleasing verse seemed to be bubbling out of its spout:——

> "A little kettle, fat and fair,
>     To sit on grandma's stove,
> To simmer softly, and to sing
>     A song of Freddie's love."

Another was this brief warning tucked into a match-box:—

> "On this you scratch
> Your little match.
> When the spark flies
> Look out for your eyes!
> When the lucifer goes
> Look out for your nose!
> Little Jack gives you this
> With a birthday kiss."

A third was rather sentimental, from Mrs. Coobiddy:—

> "Within doth lie
> A silken tie,
> Your dress to deck;
> Soft and warm
> As daughter's arm
> Round mother's neck."

Mr. Pib presented a mouse-trap all set; and in order to explain his poem, I must relate an incident in his varied career.

Pib had long been one of the family, and was much respected and beloved by them all. In fact, he was so petted and stuffed that he grew as fat and big as a small dog, and so clumsy that he could no longer catch the mice who dodged about among the dishes in the kitchen closets.

In vain had Mrs. Trot shut him up there; in vain had Aunt Trib told him it was his duty to clear the cupboards of such small deer. Poor fat Pib only bounced about, broke the china, rattled down the pans, to come out with empty paws, while the saucy mice squeaked scornfully, and pranced about under his very nose.

One day Trib saw Pib catch a squirrel, and having eaten it he brought the tail to her as a trophy of his skill. This displeased his mistress, and she gave him away, after a good scolding for killing squirrels and letting mice, his lawful prey, go free.

Pib was so depressed that he went into the bag without a mew or a scratch, and was borne away to his new home in another part of the town.

But he had no intention of staying; and after a day under the sofa, passed in deep thought, and without food or drink, he made up his mind to go home. Slipping out, he travelled all night, and appeared next morning, joyfully waving his tail, and purring like a small organ.

Aunt Trib was glad to see him, and when he had explained that he really did do his best about the mice, she forgave him, and got the trap for him to give grandma, that she might no longer be annoyed by having her private stores nibbled at.

> "Dear madam with respect
>     My offering I bring;
> The hooks all baited well,
>     And ready for a spring.
> No more the cunning mice
>     Your biscuits shall abuse,
> Nor put their babes to sleep
>     Within your fur-lined shoes.
> The trap myp work must do;
>     Forgive your portly cat,
> For he, like you, has grown
>     For lively work too fat.
> All larger, fiercer game
>     I galantly defy,
> And squirrel, rat and mole
>     Beneath my paw shall die.
> So, with this solemn vow,
>     T. Pib his gift presents,
> And sprawling at your feet
>     Purrs forth his compliments.

Which he actually did, and then sat bolt upright on the rug, surveying the scene with the dignity of a judge and the gravity of an owl.

Such funny presents! A wood-box and a water-carrier; a blue and gold gruel-bowl, and a black silk apron; a new diary, and a pound of remarkably choice tea; a pretty letter on birch bark, sealed with a tiny red leaf; and a bust of the wisest man in America, were some of them.

How the dear old lady did enjoy it all, and how grateful she was for the smallest trifle! An old friend sent her a lock of her mother's hair, and the sight of the little brown curl made her forget how white her own was, as she went back to the time when she last kissed that tender little mother fifty years ago.

Fearing that tears would follow the smiles too soon, Aunt Trib announced that the famous Indian chiefs, Chingchangpopocattepattle and Pockeyhockeyclutteryar, would now give a war-dance and other striking performances to represent Indian customs.

Then all sat round, and the warriors leaped into the middle of the room with a war-whoop that caused Mr. Pib to leave precipitately. It was a most exciting spectacle; for after the dance came a fight, and one chief tomahawked, scalped, and buried the other in the space of two minutes.

But the ladies mourned so for the blond little Pockeyhockeyclutteryar that he had to come alive and join in a hunting expedition, during which they shot all the chairs for buffaloes and deer, and came home to roast a sofa pillow over their fire, and feast thereupon with the relish of hungry hunters.

These exploits were brought to an end by the arrival of more friends with more gifts, and the introduction of the birthday cake. This was out by the queen of the *fête*, and the panting chiefs handed it round with much scuffling of big moccasins and tripping over disarranged blankets.

Then all filled their glasses with water, and drank the toast,"Grandma, God bless her!" After which the entire company took hands and danced about the big chair, singing in chorus:—

> *"Long may she wave, and may we all*
> *Her dear face to see,*
> *As bright and well at seventy-four*
> *As now at seventy-three."*

The clock struck ten, and every one went home leaving the family to end the day as they began it, round grandma's bed, with good-night kisses and the sound of her last words in their ears:—

"It has been a beautiful and happy day, my dears, and if I never see another you may always remember that I thought this one my best and brightest birthday."

# BUZZ

I LIVE high up in a city house all alone. My room is a cosy little place, though there is nothing very splendid in it,—only my pictures and books, my flowers and my little friend. When I began to live there, I was very busy and therefore very happy; but by and by, when my hurry was over and I had more time to myself, I often felt lonely. When I ate my meals I used to wish for a pleasant companion to eat with me; and when I sat by the fire evenings, I thought how much more social it would be if someone sat opposite. I had many friends and callers through the day, but the evenings were often rather dull; for I couldn't read much, and didn't care to go out in the stormy weather.

I was wishing for a cheerful friend one night, when all of a sudden I found one; for, sitting on my hand, I saw a plump, jolly-looking fly. He sat quietly staring at me, with a mild little hum, as if to say,—

"How are you? You wanted a friend, and here I am. Will you have me?"

Of course I would, for I liked him directly, he was so cheery and confiding, and seemed as glad to see me as I was to see him. All his mates were dead and gone, and he was alone, like myself. So I waggled one finger, by way of welcome, fearing to shake my hand, lest he should tumble off and feel hurt at my reception. He seemed to understand me, and buzzed again, evidently saying,—

"Thank you, ma'am. I should like to stay in your warm room, and amuse you for my board. I won't disturb you, but do my best to be a good little friend."

So the bargain was struck, and he stopped to tea. I found that his manners had been neglected; for he was inclined to walk over the butter, drink out of the cream-pot, and put his fingers in the jelly. A few taps with my spoon taught him to behave with more propriety, and he sipped a drop of milk from the waiter with a crumb of sugar, as a well-bred fly should do.

On account of his fine voice, I named him Buzz, and we soon got on excellently together. He seemed to like his new quarters, and, after exploring every corner of the room, he chose his favorite haunts and began to enjoy himself. I always knew where he was, for he kept up a constant song, humming and buzzing, like a little kettle getting ready to boil.

On sunny days, he amused himself by bumping his head against the window, and watching what went on outside. It would have given me a headache, but he seemed to enjoy it immensely. Up in my hanging basket of ivy he made his bower, and sat there on the moss basking in the sunshine, as luxuriously as any gentleman in his conservatory. He was interested in the plants, and examined them daily with great care, walking over the ivy leaves, grubbing under the moss, and poking his head into the unfolding hyacinth buds to see how they got on.

The pictures, also, seemed to attract his attention, for he spent much time skating over the glasses and studying the designs. Sometimes I would find him staring at my Madonna, as if he said, "What in the world are all those topsy-turvy children about?" Then he'd sit in the middle of a brook, in a watercolor sketch by Vautin, as if bathing his feet, or seem to be eating the cherry which one little duck politely offers another little duck, in Oscar Pletch's Summer Party. He frequently kissed my mother's portrait, and sat on my father's bald head, as if trying to get out some of the wisdom stored up there, like honey in an ill-thatched bee-hive. My bronze Mercury rather puzzled him, for he could not understand why the young gentleman didn't fly off when he had four wings and seemed in such a hurry.

I'm afraid he was a trifle vain, for he sat before the glass a great deal, and I often saw him cleaning his proboscis, and twiddling his feelers, and I know he was "prinking," as we say. The books pleased him, too, and he used to run them over, as if trying to choose which he would read, and never seemed able to decide. He would have nothing to say to the fat French Dictionary, or my English Plays, but liked Goethe and Schiller, Emerson and Browning, as well as I did. Carlyle didn't suit him, and Richter evidently made his head ache. But Jean Ingelow's Poems delighted him, and so did her "Stories Told to a Child." "Fairy Bells" he often listened to, and was very fond of the pictures in a photograph book of foreign places and great people.

He frequently promenaded on the piazza of a little Swiss chalet, standing on the mantel-piece, and thought it a charming residence for a single gentleman like himself. The closet delighted him extremely, and he buzzed in the most joyful manner when he got among the provisions,—for we kept house together. Such revels as he had in the sugarbowl; such feasts of gingerbread and grapes; such long sips of milk, and sly peeps into every uncovered box and dish! Once I'm afraid he took too much cider, for I found him lying on his back, kicking and humming like a crazy top, and he was very queer all the rest of that day; so I kept the bottle corked after that. But his favorite nook was among the ferns in the vase which a Parian dancing-girl carried. She stood just over the stove on one little toe, rattling some castanets, which made no sound, and never getting a step farther for all her prancing. This was a warm and pretty retreat for Buzz, and there he spent much of his time, swinging on the ferns, sleeping snugly in the vase, or warming his feet in the hot air that blew up, like a south wind, from the stove.

I don't believe there was a happier fly in Boston than my friend Buzz, and I grew fonder and fonder of him every day; for he never got into mischief, but sung his cheery song, no matter what the weather was, and made himself agreeable. Then he was so interested in all I did, it was delightful to have him round. When I wrote he came and walked about over my paper to see that it was right, peeped into my ink-stand, and ran after my pen. He never made silly or sharp criticisms on my stories, but appeared to admire them very much; so I am sure he was a good judge. When I sewed, he sat in my basket, or played hide-and-seek in the folds of my work, talking away all the while in the most sociable manner. He often flew up all of a sudden, and danced about in the air, as if he was in such a jolly mood he couldn't keep still, and wanted me to come and play with him. But, alas! I had no wings, and could only sit stupidly still, and laugh at his pranks. That was his exercise, for he never went out, and only took a sniff of air now and then when I opened the windows.

Well, little Buzz and I lived together many weeks, and never got tired of one another, which is saying a good deal. At Christmas I went home for a week and left my room to take care of itself. I put the hyacinths into the closet to be warm, and dropped the curtain, so the frost should not nip my ivy; but I forgot Buzz. I really would have taken him with me, or carried him down to a neighbor's room to be taken care of while I was away, but I never thought of him in the hurry of getting my presents and myself ready. Off I went without even saying "goodby," and never thought of my little friend till Freddy, my small nephew, said to me one evening at dusk,—

"Aunt Jo, tell me a story."

So I began to tell him about Buzz, and all of a sudden I cried out,—

"Mercy on me! I'm afraid he'll die of cold while I'm gone."

It troubled me a good deal, and I wanted to know how the poor little fellow was so much that I would have gone to see if I had not been so far away. But it would be rather silly to hurry away twenty miles to look after one fly: so I finished my visit, and then went back to my room, hoping to find Buzz alive and well in spite of the cold.

Alas, no! my little friend was gone. There he lay on his back on the mantel-piece, his legs meekly folded, and his wings stiff and still. He had evidently gone to the warm place, and been surprised when the heat died out and left him to freeze. My poor little Buzz had sung his last song, danced his last dance, and gone where the good flies go. I was very sorry, and buried him among the ivy roots, where the moss lay green above him, the sun shone warmly on him, and the bitter cold could never come. I miss him very much; when I sit writing, I miss his cheerful voice and busy wings; at meals there is no tidy little body to drink up spilt drops and eat the crumbs; in the evenings, when I sit alone, I want him more than ever, and every day as I water my plants, I say, softly,— "Grow green, ivy, lie lightly, moss, shine warmly, sun, and make his last bed pleasant to my little friend."

# A STRANGE ISLAND

ONE day I lay rocking in my boat, reading a very famous book, which all children know and love; and the name of which I'll tell you by and by. So busily was I reading, that I never minded the tide; and presently discovered that I was floating out to sea, with neither sail nor oar. At first I was very much frightened; for there was no one in sight on land or sea, and I didn't know where I might drift to. But the water was calm, the sky clear, and the wind blew balmily; so I waited for what should happen.

Presently I saw a speck on the sea, and eagerly watched it; for it drew rapidly near, and seemed to be going my way. When it came closer, I was much amazed; for, of all the queer boats I ever saw, this was the queerest. It was a great wooden bowl, very cracked and old; and in it sat three gray-headed little gentlemen with spectacles, all reading busily, and letting the boat go where it pleased. Now, right in their way was a rock; and I called out, "Sir, sir, take care."

But my call came too late: crash went the bowl, out came the bottom, and down plumped all the little gentlemen into the sea. I tried not to laugh, as the books, wigs, and spectacles flew about; and, urging my boat nearer, I managed to fish them up, dripping and sneezing, and looking like drowned kittens. When the flurry was over, and they had got their breath, I asked who they were, and where they were going.

"We are from Gotham, ma'am," said the fattest one wiping a very wet face on a very wet handkerchief. "We were going to that island yonder. We have often tried, but never got there: it's always so, and I begin to think the thing can't be done."

I looked where he pointed; and, sure enough, there was an island where I had never seen one before. I rubbed my eyes, and looked again. Yes: there it was,—a little island, with trees and people on it; for I saw smoke coming out of the chimney of a queerly-shaped house on the shore.

"What is the name of it?" I asked.

The little old gentleman put his finger on his lips, and said, with a mysterious nod:

"I couldn't tell you, ma'am. It's a secret; but, if you manage to land there, you will soon know."

The other old men nodded at the same time; and then all went to reading again, with the water still dropping off the ends of their noses.

This made me very curious; and, as the tide drifted us nearer and nearer, I looked well about me, and saw several things that filled me with a strong desire to land on the island. The odd house, I found, was built like a high-heeled shoe; and at every window I saw children's heads. Some were eating broth; some were crying; and some had nightcaps on. I caught sight of a distracted old lady flying about, with a ladle in one hand, and a rod in the other; but the house was so full of children (even up to the sky-light,—out of which they popped their heads, and nodded at me) that I couldn't see much of the mamma of this large family: one seldom can, you know.

I had hardly got over my surprise at this queer sight, when I saw a cow fly up through the air, over the new moon that hung there, and come down and disappear in the woods. I really didn't know what to make of this, but had no time to ask the old men what it meant; for a cat, playing a fiddle, was seen on the shore. A little dog stood by, listening and laughing; while a dish and a spoon ran away over the beach with all their might. If the boat had not floated up to the land, I think I should have swam there,—I was so anxious to see what was going on; for there was a great racket on the island, and such a remarkable collection of creatures, it was impossible to help staring.

As soon as we landed, three other gentlemen came to welcome the ones I had saved, and seemed very glad to see them. They appeared to have just landed from a tub in which was a drum, rub-a-dub-dubbing all by itself. One of the new men had a white frock on, and carried a large knife; the second had dough on his hands, flour on his coat, and a hot-looking face; the third was very greasy, had a bundle of candles under his arm, and a ball of wicking half out of his pocket. The six shook hands, and walked away together, talking about a fair; and left me to take care of myself.

I walked on through a pleasant meadow, where a pretty little girl was looking sadly up at a row of sheep's tails hung on a tree. I also saw a little boy in blue, asleep by a hay-cock; and another boy taking aim at a cock-sparrow, who clapped his wings and flew away. Presently I saw two more little girls: one sat by a fire warming her toes; and, when I asked what her name was, she said pleasantly:

"Polly Flinders, ma'am."

The other one sat on a tuft of grass, eating some thing that looked very nice; but, all of a sudden, she dropped her bowl, and ran away, looking very much frightened.

"What's the matter with her?" I asked of a gay young frog who came tripping along with his hat under his arm.

"Miss Muffit is a fashionable lady, and afraid of spiders, madam; also of frogs." And he puffed himself angrily up, till his eyes quite goggled in his head.

"And, pray, who are you, sir?" I asked, staring at his white vest, green coat, and fine cravat.

"Excuse me, if I don't give my name, ma'am. My false friend, the rat, got me into a sad scrape once; and Rowley insists upon it that a duck destroyed me, which is all gammon, ma'am,—all gammon."

With that, the frog skipped away; and I turned into a narrow lane, which seemed to lead toward some music. I had not gone far, when I heard the rumbling of a wheelbarrow, and saw a little man wheeling a little woman along. The little man looked very hot and tired; but the little woman looked very nice, in a smart bonnet and shawl, and kept looking at a new gold ring on her finger, as she rode along under her little umbrella. I was wondering who they were, when down went the wheelbarrow; and the little lady screamed so dismally that I ran away, lest I should get into trouble,—being a stranger.

Turning a corner, I came upon a very charming scene, and slipped into a quiet nook to see what was going on. It was evidently a wedding; and I was just in time to see it, for the procession was passing at that moment. First came a splendid cock-a-doodle, all in black and gold, like a herald, blowing his trumpet, and marching with a very dignified step. Then came a rook, in black, like a minister, with spectacles and white cravat. A lark and bullfinch followed,—friends, I suppose; and then the bride and bridegroom. Miss Wren was evidently a Quakeress; for she wore a sober dress, and a little white veil, through which her bright eyes shone. The bridegroom was a military man, in his scarlet uniform,—a plump, bold-looking bird, very happy and proud just then. A goldfinch gave away the bride, and a linnet was bridemaid. The ceremony was very fine; and, as soon as it was over, the blackbird, thrush and nightingale burst out in a lovely song.

A splendid dinner followed, at which was nearly every bird that flies; so you may imagine the music there was. They had currant-pie in abundance; and cherry-wine, which excited a cuckoo so much, that he became quite rude, and so far forgot himself as to pull the bride about. This made the groom so angry that he begged his friend, the sparrow, to bring his bow and arrow, and punish the ruffian. But, alas! Sparrow had also taken a drop too much: he aimed wrong, and, with a dreadful cry, Mr. Robin sank dying into the arms of his wife, little Jane.

It was too much for me; and, taking advantage of the confusion that followed, I left the tragical scene as fast as possible.

A little farther on, I was shocked to see a goose dragging an old man down some steps that led to a little house.

"Dear me! What's the matter here?" I cried.

"He won't say his prayers," screamed the goose.

"But perhaps he was never taught," said I.

"It's never too late to learn: he's had his chance; he won't be pious and good, so away with him. Don't interfere, whatever you do: hold your tongue, and go about your business," scolded the goose who certainly had a dreadful temper.

I dared say no more; and, when the poor old man had been driven away by this foul proceeding, I went up the steps and peeped in; for I heard some one crying, and thought the cross bird, perhaps, had hurt some one else. A little old woman stood there, wringing her hands in great distress; while a small dog was barking at her with all his might.

"Bless me! The fashions have got even here," thought I; for the old woman was dressed in the latest style,—or, rather, she had overdone it sadly; for her gown was nearly up to her knees, and she was nearly as ridiculous an object as some of the young ladies I had seen at home.

She had a respectable bonnet on, however, instead of a straw saucer; and her hair was neatly put under a cap,—not made into a knob on the top of her head.

"My dear soul, what's the trouble?" said I, quite touched by her tears.

"Lud a mercy, ma'am! I've been to market with my butter and eggs,— for the price of both is so high, one can soon get rich now-a-days,—and, being tired, I stopped to rest a bit, but fell asleep by the road. Somebody— I think it's a rogue of a peddler who sold me wooden nutmegs, and a clock that wouldn't go, and some pans that came to bits the first time I used them—somebody cut my new gown and petticoat off all round, in the shameful way you see. I thought I never should get home; for I was such a fright, I actually didn't know myself. But, thinks I, my doggy will know me; and then I shall be sure I'm I, and not some boldfaced creature in short skirts. But, oh, ma'am! Doggy *don't* know me; and I ain't myself, and I don't know what to do."

"He's a foolish little beast; so don't mind him, but have a cup of tea, and go to bed. You can make your gown decent to-morrow; and, if I see the tricksy peddler, I'll give him a scolding."

This seemed to comfort the old woman; though doggy still barked.

"My next neighbor has a dog who never behaves in this way," she said, as she put her teapot on the coals. "He's a remarkable beast; and you'd better stop to see him as you pass, ma'am. He's always up to some funny prank or other."

I said I would; and, as I went by the next house, I took a look in at the window. The closet was empty, I observed; but the dog sat smoking a pipe, looking as grave as a judge.

"Where is your mistress?" asked I.

"Gone for some tripe," answered the dog, politely taking the pipe out of his mouth, and adding, "I hope the smoke doesn't annoy you."

"I don't approve of smoking," said I.

"Sorry to hear it," said the dog, coolly.

I was going to lecture him on this bad habit; but I saw his mistress coming with a dish in her hand, and, fearing she might think me rude to peep in at her windows, I walked on, wondering what we were coming to when even four-legged puppies smoked.

At the door of the next little house, I saw a market-wagon loaded with vegetables, and a smart young pig just driving it away. I had heard of this interesting family, and took a look as I passed by. A second tidy pig sat blowing the fire; and a third was eating roast-beef, as if he had just come in from his work. The fourth, I was grieved to see, looked very sulky; for it was evident he had been naughty, and so lost his dinner. The little pig was at the door, crying to get in; and it was sweet to see how kindly the others let him in, wiped his tears, tied on his bib, and brought him his bread and milk. I was very glad to see these young orphans doing so well, and I knew my friends at home would enjoy hearing from them.

A loud scream made me jump; and the sudden splash of water made me run along, without stopping to pick up a boy and girl who came tumbling down the hill with an empty pail, bumping their heads as they rolled. Smelling something nice, and feeling hungry, I stepped into a large room near by,—a sort of eating-house, I fancy; for various parties seemed to be enjoying themselves in their different ways. A small boy sat near the door, eating a large pie; and he gave me a fine plum which he had just pulled out. At one table was a fat gentleman cutting another pie, which had a dark crust, through which appeared the heads of a flock of birds, all singing gayly.

"There's no end to the improvements in cooking, and no accounting for tastes," I added, looking at a handsomely-dressed lady, who sat near, eating bread and honey.

As I passed this party, I saw behind the lady's chair a maid, with a clothes-pin in her hand, and no nose. She sobbingly told me a bird had nipped it off; and I gave her a bit of court-plaster, which I fortunately had in my pocket.

Another couple were dividing their meat in a queer way; for one took all the fat, and the other all the lean. The next people were odder still; for the man looked rather guilty, and seemed to be hiding a three-peck measure under his chair, while he waited for his wife to bring on some cold barley-pudding, which, to my surprise, she was frying herself. I also saw a queer moonstruck-looking man inquiring the way to Norridge; and another man making wry faces over some plum-pudding, with which he had burnt his mouth, because his friend came down too soon.

I ordered pease-porridge hot, and they brought it cold; but I didn't wait for any thing else, being in a hurry to see all there was to be seen on this strange island. Feeling refreshed, I strolled on, passing a jolly old gentleman smoking and drinking, while three fiddlers played before him. As I turned into a road that led toward a hill, a little boy, riding a dapple-gray pony, and an old lady on a white horse, with bells ringing somewhere, trotted by me, followed by a little girl, who wished to know where she could buy a penny bun. I told her the best were at Newmarch's, in Bedford Street, and she ran on, much pleased; but I'm afraid she never found that best of bake-shops. I was going quietly along, when the sound of another horse coming made me look round; and there I saw a dreadful sight,—a wild horse, tearing over the ground, with fiery eyes and streaming tail. On his back sat a crazy man, beating him with a broom; a crazy woman was behind him, with her bonnet on wrong side before, holding one crazy child in her lap, while another stood on the horse; a third was hanging on by one foot, and all were howling at the top of their voices as they rushed by. I scrambled over the wall to get out of the way, and there I saw more curious sights. Two blind men were sitting on the grass, trying to see two lame men who were hobbling along as hard as they could; and, near by, a bull was fighting a bee in the most violent manner. This rather alarmed me; and I scrambled back into the road again, just as a very fine lady jumped over a barberry-bush near by, and a gentleman went flying after, with a ring in one hand and a stick in the other.

"What very odd people they have here!" I thought. Close by was a tidy little house under the hill, and in it a tidy little woman who sold things to eat. Being rather hungry, in spite of my porridge, I bought a baked apple and a cranberry-pie; for she said they were good, and I found she told the truth. As I sat eating my pie, some dogs began to bark; and by came a troop of beggars, some in rags, and some in old velvet gowns. A drunken grenadier was with them, who wanted a pot of beer; but as he had no money, the old woman sent him about his business.

On my way up the hill, I saw a little boy crying over a dead pig, and his sister, who seemed to be dead also. I asked his name, and he sobbed out, "Johnny Pringle, ma'am;" and went on crying so hard I could do nothing to comfort him. While I stood talking to him, a sudden gust of wind blew up the road, and down came the bough of a tree; and, to my surprise, a cradle with a baby in it also. The baby screamed dreadfully, and I didn't know how to quiet it; so I ran back to the old woman, and left it with her, asking if that was the way babies were taken care of there.

"Bless you, my dear! It's ma is making patty-cakes; and put it up there to be out of the way of Tom Tinker's dog. I'll soon hush it up," said the old woman; and, trotting it on her knee, she began to sing:

> *"Hey! My kitten, my kitten,*
> *Hey! My kitten, my deary."*

Feeling that the child was in good hands, I hurried away, for I saw something was going on upon the hill-top. When I got to the hill-top, I was shocked to find some people tossing an old woman in a blanket. I begged them to stop; but one of the men, who, I found, was a Welchman, by the name of Taffy, told me the old lady liked it.

"But why does she like it?" I asked in great surprise.

"Tom, the piper's son, will tell you: it's my turn to toss now," said the man.

"Why, you see, ma'am," said Tom, "she is one of those dreadfully nice old women, who are always fussing and scrubbing, and worrying people to death, with everlastingly cleaning house. Now and then we get so tired out with her that we propose to her to clean the sky itself. She likes that; and, as this is the only way we can get her up, we toss till she sticks somewhere, and then leave her to sweep cobwebs till she is ready to come back and behave herself."

"Well, that is the oddest thing I ever heard. I know just such an old lady, and when I go home I'll try your plan. It seems to me that you have a great many queer old ladies on this island," I said to another man, whom they called Peter, and who stood eating pumpkin all the time.

"Well, we do have rather a nice collection; but you haven't seen the best of all. We expect her every minute; and Margery Daw is to let us know the minute she lights on the island," replied Peter, with his mouth full.

"Lights?" said I, "you speak as if she flew."

"She rides on a bird. Hurrah! The old sweeper has lit. Now the cobwebs will fly. Don't hurry back," shouted the man; and a faint, far-off voice answered, "I shall be back again by and by."

The people folded up the blanket, looking much relieved; and I was examining a very odd house which was built by an ancient king called

Boggen, when Margery Daw, a dirty little girl, came up the hill, screaming, at the top of her voice:

"She's come! She's come!"

Every one looked up; and I saw a large white bird slowly flying over the island. On its back sat the nicest old woman that ever was seen: all the others were nothing compared to her. She had a pointed hat on over her cap, a red cloak, high-heeled shoes, and a crutch in her hand. She smiled and nodded as the bird approached; and every one ran and nodded, and screamed, "Welcome! Welcome, mother!"

As soon as she touched the ground, she was so surrounded that I could only see the top of her hat; for hundreds and hundreds of little children suddenly appeared, like a great flock of birds,—rosy, happy, pretty children; but all looked unreal, and among them I saw some who looked like little people I had known long ago.

"Who are they?" I asked of a bonny lass, who was sitting on a cushion, eating strawberries and cream.

"They are the phantoms of all the little people who ever read and loved our mother's songs," said the maid.

"What did she write?" I asked, feeling very queer, and as if I was going to remember something.

"Songs that are immortal; and you have them in your hand," replied the bonny maid, smiling at my stupidity.

I looked; and there, on the cover of the book I had been reading so busily when the tide carried me away, I saw the words "Mother Goose's Melodies." I was so delighted that I had seen her I gave a shout, and tried to get near enough to hug and kiss the dear old soul, as the swarm of children were doing; but my cry woke me, and I was *so* sorry to find it all a dream!

# ROSES AND FORGET-ME-NOTS

## I

### ROSES

IT was a cold November storm, and every thing looked forlorn. Even the pert sparrows were draggle-tailed and too much out of spirits to fight for crumbs with the fat pigeons who tripped through the mud with their little red boots as if in haste to get back to their cosy home in the dove-cot.

But the most forlorn creature out that day was a small errand girl, with a bonnet-box on each arm, and both hands struggling to hold a big broken umbrella. A pair of worn-out boots let in the wet upon her tired feet; a thin cotton dress and an old shawl poorly protected her from the storm; and a faded hood covered her head.

The face that looked out from this hood was too pale and anxious for one so young; and when a sudden gust turned the old umbrella inside out with a crash, despair fell upon poor Lizzie, and she was so miserable she could have sat down in the rain and cried.

But there was no time for tears; so, dragging the dilapidated umbrella along, she spread her shawl over the bonnet-boxes and hurried down the broad street, eager to hide her misfortunes from a pretty young girl who stood at a window laughing at her.

She could not find the number of the house where one of the fine hats was to be left; and after hunting all down one side of the street, she crossed over, and came at last to the very house where the pretty girl lived. She was no longer to be seen; and, with a sigh of relief, Lizzie rang the bell, and was told to wait in the hall while Miss Belle tried the hat on.

Glad to rest, she warmed her feet, righted her umbrella, and then sat looking about her with eyes quick to see the beauty and the comfort that made the place so homelike and delightful. A small waiting-room opened from the hall, and in it stood many blooming plants, whose fragrance attracted Lizzie as irresistibly as if she had been a butterfly or bee.

Slipping in, she stood enjoying the lovely colors, sweet odors, and delicate shapes of these household spirits; for Lizzie loved flowers passionately; and just then they possessed a peculiar charm for her.

One particularly captivating little rose won her heart, and made her long for it with a longing that became a temptation too strong to resist. It was so perfect; so like a rosy face smiling out from the green leaves, that Lizzie could *not* keep her hands off it, and having smelt, touched, and kissed it, she suddenly broke the stem and hid it in her pocket. Then, frightened at what she had done, she crept back to her place in the hall, and sat there, burdened with remorse.

A servant came just then to lead her upstairs; for Miss Belle wished the hat altered, and must give directions. With her heart in a flutter, and pinker roses in her cheeks than the one in her pocket, Lizzie followed to a handsome room, where a pretty girl stood before a long mirror with the hat in her hand.

"Tell Madame Tifany that I don't like it at all, for she hasn't put in the blue plume mamma ordered; and I won't have rose-buds, they are so common," said the young lady, in a dissatisfied tone, as she twirled the hat about.

"Yes, miss," was all Lizzie could say; for *she* considered that hat the loveliest thing a girl could possibly own.

"You had better ask your mamma about it, Miss Belle, before you give any orders. She will be up in a few moments, and the girl can wait," put in a maid, who was sewing in the anteroom.

"I suppose I must; but I *won't* have roses," answered Belle, crossly. Then she glanced at Lizzie, snd said more gently, "You look very cold; come and sit by the fire while you wait."

"I'm afraid I'll wet the pretty rug, miss; my feet are sopping," said Lizzie, gratefully, but timidly.

"So they are! Why didn't you wear rubber boots?"

"I haven't got any."

"I'll give you mine, then, for I hate them; and as I never go out in wet weather, they are of no earthly use to me. Marie, bring them here; I shall be glad to get rid of them, and I'm sure they'll be useful to you."

"Oh, thank you, miss! I'd like 'em ever so much, for I'm out in the rain half the time, and get bad colds because my boots are old," said Lizzie, smiling brightly at the thought of the welcome gift.

"I should think your mother would get you warmer things," began Belle, who found something rather interesting in the shabby girl, with shy bright eyes, and curly hair bursting out of the old hood.

"I haven't got any mother," said Lizzie, with a pathetic glance at her poor clothes.

"I'm so sorry! Have you brothers and sisters?" asked Belle, hoping to find something pleasant to talk about; for she was a kind little soul.

"No, miss; I've got no folks at all."

"Oh, dear; how sad! Why, who takes care of you?" cried Belle, looking quite distressed.

"No one; I take care of myself. I work for Madame, and she pays me a dollar a week. I stay with Mrs. Brown, and chore round to pay for my keep. My dollar don't get many clothes, so I can't be as neat as I'd like." And the forlorn look came back to poor Lizzie's face.

Belle said nothing, but sat among the sofa cushions, where she had thrown herself, looking soberly at this other girl, no older than she was, who took care of herself and was all alone in the world. It was a new idea to Belle, who was loved and petted as an only child is apt to be. She often saw beggars and pitied them, but knew very little about their wants and lives; so it was like turning a new page in her happy life to be brought so near to poverty as this chance meeting with the milliner's girl.

"Aren't you afraid and lonely and unhappy?" she said, slowly, trying to understand and put herself in Lizzie's place.

"Yes; but it's no use. I can't help it, and may be things will get better by and by, and I'll have my wish," answered Lizzie, more hopefully, because Belle's pity warmed her heart and made her troubles seem lighter.

"What is your wish?" asked Belle, hoping mamma wouldn't come just yet, for she was getting interested in the stranger.

"To have a nice little room, and make flowers, like a French girl I know. It's such pretty work, and she gets lots of money, for every one likes her flowers. She shows me how, sometimes, and I can do leaves first-rate; but"—

There Lizzie stopped suddenly, and the color rushed up to her forehead; for she remembered the little rose in her pocket and it weighed upon her conscience like a stone.

Before Belle could ask what was the matter, Marie came in with a tray of cake and fruit saying:

"Here's your lunch, Miss Belle."

"Put it down, please; I'm not ready for it yet." And Belle shook her head as she glanced at Lizzie, who was staring hard at the fire with such a troubled face that Belle could not bear to see it.

Jumping out of her nest of cushions, she heaped a plate with good things, and going to Lizzie, offered it, saying, with a gentle courtesy that made the act doubly sweet:

"Please have some; you must be tired of waiting."

But Lizzie could not take it; she could only cover her face and cry; for this kindness rent her heart and made the stolen flower a burden too heavy to be borne.

"Oh, don't cry so! Are you sick? Have I been rude? Tell me all about it; and if I can't do any thing, mamma can," said Belle, surprised and troubled.

"No; I'm not sick; I'm bad, and I can't bear it when you are so good to me," sobbed Lizzie, quite overcome with penitence; and taking out the crumpled rose, she confessed her fault with many tears.

"Don't feel so much about such a little thing as that," began Belle, warmly; then checked herself, and added, more soberly, "It *was* wrong to take it without leave; but it's all right now, and I'll give you as many roses as you want, for I know you are a good girl."

"Thank you. I didn't want it only because it was pretty, but I wanted to copy it. I can't get any for myself, and so I can't do my make-believe ones well. Madame won't even lend me the old ones in the store, and Estelle has none to spare for me, because I can't pay her for teaching me. She gives me bits of muslin and wire and things, and shows me now and then. But I know if I had a real flower I could copy it; so she'd see I did know something, for I try real hard. I'm *so* tired of slopping round the streets, I'd do any thing to earn my living some other way."

Lizzie had poured out her trouble rapidly; and the little story was quite affecting when one saw the tears on her cheeks, the poor clothes, and the thin hands that held the stolen rose. Belle was much touched, and, in her impetuous way, set about mending matters as fast as possible.

"Put on those boots and that pair of dry stockings right away. Then tuck as much cake and fruit into your pocket as it will hold. I'm going to get you some flowers, and see if mamma is too busy to attend to me."

With a nod and a smile, Belle flew about the room a minute; then vanished, leaving Lizzie to her comfortable task, feeling as if fairies still haunted the world as in the good old times.

When Belle came back with a handful of roses she found Lizzie absorbed in admiring contemplation of her new boots, as she ate sponge-cake in a blissful sort of waking-dream.

"Mamma can't come; but I don't care about the hat. It will do very well, and isn't worth fussing about. There, will those be of any use to you?" And she offered the nosegay with a much happier face than the one Lizzie first saw.

"Oh, miss, they're just lovely! I'll copy that pink rose as soon as ever I can, and when I've learned how to do 'em tip-top, I'd like to bring you some, if you don't mind," answered Lizzie, smiling all over her face as she buried her nose luxuriously in the fragrant mass.

"I'd like it very much, for I should think you'd have to be very clever to make such pretty things. I really quite fancy those rose-buds in my hat, now I know that you're going to learn how to make them. Put an orange in your pocket, and the flowers in water as soon as you can, so they'll be fresh when you want them. Good by. Bring home our hats every time and tell me how you get on."

With kind words like these, Belle dismissed Lizzie, who ran downstairs, feeling as rich as if she had found a fortune. Away to the next place she hurried, anxious to get her errands done and the precious posy safely into fresh water. But Mrs. Turretville was not at home, and the bonnet could not be left till paid for. So Lizzie turned to go down the high steps, glad that she need not wait. She stopped one instant to take a delicious sniff at her flowers, and that was the last happy moment that poor Lizzie knew for many weary months.

The new boots were large for her, the steps slippery with sleet, and down went the little errand girl, from top to bottom, till she landed in the gutter directly upon Mrs. Turretville's costly bonnet.

"I've saved my posies, anyway," sighed Lizzie, as she picked herself up, bruised, wet, and faint with pain; "but, oh, my heart! Won't Madame scold when she sees that band-box smashed flat," groaned the poor child, sitting on the curbstone to get her breath and view the disaster.

The rain poured, the wind blew, the sparrows on the park railing chirped derisively, and no one came along to help Lizzie out of her troubles. Slowly she gathered up her burdens; painfully she limped away in the big boots; and the last the naughty sparrows saw of her was a shabby little figure going round the corner, with a pale, tearful face held lovingly over the bright bouquet that was her one treasure and her only comfort in the moment which brought to her the great misfortune of her life.

## II

## FORGET-ME-NOTS

"Oh, mamma, I am so relieved that the box has come at last! If it had not, I do believe I should have died of disappointment," cried pretty Belle, five years later, on the morning before her eighteenth birthday.

"It would have been a serious disappointment, darling; for I had set my heart on your wearing my gift tomorrow night, and when the steamers kept coming in without my trunk from Paris, I was very anxious. I hope you will like it."

"Dear mama, I know I shall like it; your taste is so good and you know what suits me so well. Make haste, Marie; I'm dying to see it," said Belle, dancing about the great trunk, as the maid carefully unfolded tissue papers and muslin wrappers.

A young girl's first ball-dress is a grand affair,—in her eyes, at least; and Belle soon stopped dancing, to stand with clasped hands, eager eyes and parted lips before the snowy pile of illusion that was at last daintily lifted out upon the bed. Then, as Marie displayed its loveliness, little cries of delight were heard, and when the whole delicate dress was arranged to the best effect she threw herself upon her mother's neck and actually cried with pleasure.

"Mamma, it is too lovely! And you are very kind to do so much for me. How shall I ever thank you?"

"By putting it right on to see if it fits; and when you wear it look your happiest, that I may be proud of my pretty daughter."

Mamma got no further, for Marie uttered a French shriek, wrung her hands, and then began to burrow wildly in the trunk and among the papers, crying distractedly:

"Great heavens, madame! The wreath has been forgotten! What an affliction! Mademoiselle's enchanting toilette is destroyed without the wreath, and nowhere do I find it."

In vain they searched; in vain Marie wailed and Belle declared it must be somewhere; no wreath appeared. It was duly set down in the bill, and a fine sum charged for a head-dress to match the dainty forget-me-nots that looped the fleecy skirts and ornamented the bosom of the dress. It had evidently been forgotten; and mamma despatched Marie at once to try and match the flowers, for Belle would not hear of any other decoration for her beautiful blonde hair.

The dress fitted to a charm, and was pronounced by all beholders the loveliest thing ever seen. Nothing was wanted but the wreath to make it quite perfect, and when Marie returned, after a long search, with no forget-me-nots, Belle was in despair.

"Wear natural ones," suggested a sympathizing friend.

But another hunt among greenhouses was as fruitless as that among the milliners' rooms. No forget-me-nots could be found, and Marie fell exhausted into a chair, desolated at what she felt to be an awful calamity.

"Let me have the carriage, and I'll ransack the city till I find some," cried Belle, growing more resolute with each failure.

Mamma was deep in preparations for the ball, and could not help her afflicted daughter, though she was much disappointed at the mishap. So Belle drove off, resolved to have her flowers whether there were any or not.

Any one who has ever tried to match a ribbon, find a certain fabric, or get any thing done in a hurry, knows what a wearisome task it sometimes is, and can imagine Belle's state of mind after repeated disappointments. She was about to give up in despair, when some one suggested that perhaps the Frenchwoman, Estelle Valnor, might make the desired wreath, if there was time.

Away drove Belle, and, on entering the room, gave a sigh of satisfaction, for a whole boxful of the loveliest forget-me-nots stood upon the table. As fast as possible, she told her tale and demanded the flowers, no matter what the price might be. Imagine her feelings when the Frenchwoman, with a shrug, announced that it was impossible to give mademoiselle a single spray. All were engaged to trim a bridesmaid's dress, and must be sent away at once.

It really was too bad! And Belle lost her temper entirely, for no persuasion or bribes would win a spray from Estelle. The provoking part of it was that the wedding would not come off for several days, and there was time enough to make more flowers for that dress, since Belle only wanted a few for her hair. Neither would Estelle make her any, as her hands were full, and so small an order was not worth deranging one's self for; but observing Belle's sorrowful face, she said, affably:

"Mademoiselle may, perhaps, find the flowers she desires at Miss Berton's. She has been helping me with these garlands, and may have some left. Here is her address."

Belle took the card with thanks, and hurried away with a last hope faintly stirring in her girlish heart, for Belle had an unusually ardent wish to look her best at this party, since Somebody was to be there, and Somebody considered forget-me-nots the sweetest flowers in the world. Mamma knew this, and the kiss Belle gave her when the dress came had a more tender meaning than gratified vanity or daughterly love.

Up many stairs she climbed, and came at last to a little room, very poor but very neat, where, at the one window, sat a young girl, with crutches by her side and her lap full of flower-leaves and petals. She rose slowly as Belle came in, and then stood looking at her, with such a wistful expression in her shy, bright eyes, that Belle's anxious face cleared involuntarily, and her voice lost its impatient tone.

As she spoke, she glanced about the room, hoping to see some blue blossoms awaiting her. But none appeared; and she was about to despond again, when the girl said, gently:

"I have none by me now, but I may be able to find you some."

"Thank you very much; but I have been everywhere in vain. Still, if you do get any, please send them to me as soon as possible. Here is my card."

Miss Berton glanced at it, then cast a quick look at the sweet, anxious face before her, and smiled so brightly that Belle smiled also, and asked wonderingly:

"What is it? What do you see?"

"I see the dear young lady who was so kind to me long ago. You don't remember me, and never knew my name; but I never have forgotten you all these years. I always hoped I could do something to show how grateful I was, and now I can, for you shall have your flowers if I sit up all night to make them."

But Belle still shook her head and watched the smiling face before her with wondering eyes, till the girl added, with sudden color in her cheeks:

"Ah, you've done so many kind things in your life, you don't remember the little errand girl from Madame Tifany's who stole a rose in your hall, and how you gave her rubber boots and cake and flowers, and were so good to her she couldn't forget it if she lived to be a hundred."

"But you are so changed," began Belle, who did faintly recollect that little incident in her happy life.

"Yes, I had a fall and hurt myself so that I shall always be lame."

And Lizzie went on to tell how Madame had dismissed her in a rage; how she lay ill till Mrs. Brown sent her to the hospital; and how for a year she had suffered much alone, in that great house of pain, before one of the kind visitors had befriended her.

While hearing the story of the five years, that had been so full of pleasure, ease and love for herself, Belle forgot her errand, and, sitting beside Lizzie, listened with pitying eyes to all she told of her endeavors to support herself by the delicate handiwork she loved.

"I'm very happy now," ended Lizzie, looking about the little bare room with a face full of the sweetest content. "I get nearly work enough to pay my way, and Estelle sends me some when she has more than she can do. I've learned to do it nicely, and it is so pleasant to sit here and make flowers instead of trudging about in the wet with other people's hats. Though I do sometimes wish I was able to trudge, one gets on so slowly with crutches."

A little sigh followed the words, and Belle put her own plump hand on the delicate one that held the crutch, saying, in her cordial young voice:

"I'll come and take you to drive sometimes, for you are too pale, and you'll get ill sitting here at work day after day. Please let me; I'd love to; for I feel so idle and wicked when I see busy people like you that I reproach myself for neglecting my duty and having more than my share of happiness."

Lizzie thanked her with a look, and then said, in a tone of interest that was delightful to hear:

"Tell about the wreath you want; I should so love to do it for you, if I can."

Belle had forgotten all about it in listening to this sad little story of a girl's life. Now she felt half ashamed to talk of so frivolous a matter till she remembered that it would help Lizzie; and, resolving to pay for it as never garland was paid for before, she entered upon the subject with renewed interest.

"You shall have the flowers in time for your ball tomorrow night. I will engage to make a wreath that will please you, only it may take longer than I think. Don't be troubled if I don't send it till evening; it will surely come in time. I can work fast, and this will be the happiest job I ever did," said Lizzie, beginning to lay out mysterious little tools and bend delicate wires.

"You are altogether too grateful for the little I have done. It makes me feel ashamed to think I did not find you out before and do something better worth thanks."

"Ah, it wasn't the boots or the cake or the roses, dear Miss Belle. It was the kind looks, the gentle words, the way it was done, that went right to my heart, and did me more good than a million of money. I never stole a pin after that day, for the little rose wouldn't let me forget how you forgave me so sweetly. I sometimes think it kept me from greater temptations, for I was a poor, forlorn child, with no one to keep me good."

Pretty Belle looked prettier than ever as she listened, and a bright tear stood in either eye like a drop of dew on a blue flower. It touched her very much to learn that her little act of childish charity had been so sweet and helpful to this lonely girl, and now lived so freshly in her grateful memory. It showed her, suddenly, how precious little deeds of love and sympathy are; how strong to bless, how easy to perform, how comfortable to recall. Her heart was very full and tender just then, and the lesson sunk deep into it never to be forgotten.

She sat a long time watching flowers bud and blossom under Lizzie's skilful fingers, and then hurried home to tell all her glad news to mamma.

If the next day had not been full of most delightfully exciting events, Belle might have felt some anxiety about her wreath, for hour after hour went by and nothing arrived from Lizzie.

Evening came, and all was ready. Belle was dressed, and looked so lovely that mamma declared she needed nothing more. But Marie insisted

"Promise that I may make the flowers you wear on your wedding-day," whispered Lizzie.

### Roses and Forget-Me-Nots

that the grand effect would be ruined without the garland among the sunshiny hair. Belle had time now to be anxious, and waited with growing impatience for the finishing touch to her charming toilette.

"I must be downstairs to receive, and can't wait another moment; so put in the blue pompon and let me go," she said at last, with a sigh of disappointment, for the desire to look beautiful that night in Somebody's eyes had increased four-fold.

With a tragic gesture, Marie was about to adjust the pompon when the quick tap of a crutch came down the hall, and Lizzie hurried in, flushed and breathless, but smiling happily as she uncovered the box she carried with a look of proud satisfaction.

A general "Ah!" of admiration arose as Belle, mamma, and Marie surveyed the lovely wreath that lay before them; and when it was carefully arranged on the bright head that was to wear it, Belle blushed with pleasure. Mamma said: "It is more beautiful than any Paris could have sent us;" and Marie clasped her hands theatrically, sighing, with her head on one side:

"Truly, yes; mademoiselle is now adorable!"

"I am so glad you like it. I did my very best and worked all night, but I had to beg one spray from Estelle, or, with all my haste, I could not have finished in time," said Lizzie, refreshing her weary eyes with a long, affectionate gaze at the pretty figure before her.

A fold of the airy skirt was caught on one of the blue clusters, and Lizzie knelt down to arrange it as she spoke. Belle leaned toward her and said softly: "Money alone can't pay you for this kindness; so tell me how I can best serve you. This is the happiest night of my life, and I want to make every one feel glad also."

"Then don't talk of paying me, but promise that I may make the flowers you wear on your wedding-day," whispered Lizzie, kissing the kind hand held out to help her rise, for on it she saw a brilliant ring, and in the blooming, blushing face bent over her she read the tender little story that Somebody had told Belle that day.

"So you shall! And I'll keep this wreath all my life for your sake, dear," answered Belle, as her full heart bubbled over with pitying affection for the poor girl who would never make a bridal garland for herself.

Belle kept her word, even when she was in a happy home of her own; for out of the dead roses bloomed a friendship that brightened Lizzie's life; and long after the blue garland was faded Belle remembered the helpful little lesson that taught her to read the faces poverty touches with a pathetic eloquence, which says to those who look, "Forget-me-not."

# MAMMA'S PLOT

"IT'S the meanest thing I ever heard of, and I won't bear it!" cried Kitty, sitting down on her half-packed trunk, with a most rebellious expression.

"You must, my dear: it is the rule of the school, and you must submit. I'm very sorry, for I expected great comfort and pleasure from your little letters; but if madam has to read and correct them all, of course they will be compositions, and not particularly interesting," said mamma, with a sigh, as she folded up the small garments as tenderly as if her little girl had been inside of them.

"I didn't mind much about it when I read the rules, but now that I'm really going it seems like a prison; and I shall be just wild to tell you every thing. How can I, if that old lady has got to see what I write? I know I shan't like the food, and I can't ask you to send me any goodies without her knowing it. If I'm homesick, I shall want to tell you, and of course there will be lots of funny things you'd enjoy, but for this disgusting rule. I do declare I won't go!" and Kitty cast her new boots sternly on the floor.

"Yes, you will, Puss, because papa and I want you to. This is an excellent school; old-fashioned in some things, and I like it for that, though this rule is not a wise one, I fancy. You must do the best you can, and perhaps madam won't be very particular about what you write to me, if you are a good child."

"I know she will. I saw fussiness in her face. She's sure to be strict and prim, and I shall be so miserable." Here Kitty began to cry over her woes.

It was a habit of hers to have a great many troubles, and to be very much afflicted about trifles, for she had not a real trial in the world except her own fidgety little self. As she sat on her trunk, with all her possessions scattered about her, and one great tear on the end of her nose (she couldn't squeeze out another to save her life), she was a very pathetic object; and mamma felt so tender about losing her that she could not make light of this grief, as she often did when Kitty wept over some trifle.

All of a sudden a bright idea came into her head, for mothers' wits are usually sharper than other people's where their children are concerned. Up she got, and hurrying to her desk pulled out a box of many-colored note-paper, with envelopes to match, saying, as she showed them, with a smile,—

"I've thought of a nice plan, a sort of joke between us. Come here, and I'll tell you about it."

So Kitty wiped away her one tear, and ran to hear the new plan, full of curiosity and interest; for pretty papers are always attractive, and mamma looked as if the joke was going to be a funny one.

"I will fill your little portfolio with these, and for each color we will have a different meaning, which I shall understand. Let me see. When you are well and happy, use this pink paper; when you are homesick, take the blue; if you want goodies, use the green; and if you don't feel well, take the violet. How do you like the idea, Puss?"

"It's regularly splendid! I do love to have secrets, and this will be such a nice one, all private between our two selves. Mamma, you are a perfect dear, and I'll send you a letter every week. It will be such fun to write it all prim and proper, and let madam see it, and then have it tell you all about me by the color."

And Kitty danced about the room till the little blue bow on the top of her head stood straight up as if with excitement.

So the portfolio was fitted out in great style, and Kitty felt as proud as you please; for other girls didn't have colored note-papers, much less private jokes with their mammas. The new arrangement made her quite willing to go; and all that day she kept looking at her mother with twinkling eyes, and the last thing she said, as the carriage drove away, was,—

"Don't forget what pink, blue, green, and violet means, mamma."

The first week was a hard one, for every thing was new, and the rules *were* rather strict. Kitty did her best for the honor of her family, but sometimes her woes did seem heavier than she could bear, especially French verbs, and getting up very early.

So when Saturday came, and the home letters were to be written, she longed to pour out her full heart to dear mamma, but did not dare to do it, for madam went about among the girls, suggesting, correcting, and overseeing their productions as if they were nothing but compositions.

"Remember, my dears, these three rules when you are writing letters. Always put in something about your heavenly Father, the progress of your studies, and your duty to parents and teachers. None of these important points have been touched upon in your epistle, Miss Catherine; therefore, as it is much blotted, and badly spelled, I desire you to rewrite it, making these additions. Here is an excellent sample of the proper style;" and madam laid a model letter before poor Kitty, who muttered to herself, as she read it,—

"I might as well write a sermon, and done with it. Papa will laugh, and mamma won't get one bit of news from it. I'll let her know how unhappy I am, any way."

So Kitty took out her bluest paper (the homesick color, you know), and produced the following letter, which madam approved and sent:—

MY DEAR MAMMA,— With every sentiment which affection can suggest, I hasten to inform you that I am well, and trust you also and my honored father are enjoying that best of blessings, robust health.

I am endeavoring to prove by diligence and good conduct my gratitude for the advantages now offered me, and trust that my progress may be a source of satisfaction to my parents and teachers, as well as profitable to myself in years to come.

Madam is most kind to me, and my schoolmates are agreeable and friendly young ladies. That I may merit their affection and respect is the sincere wish of my heart, for friendship adds a charm to life, and strengthens the most amiable sentiments of the youthful mind.

As Monday is your birthday, please accept this little picture as a token of my love, with best wishes for many happy returns of the day. May our heavenly Father, in his infinite goodness, long preserve you to us, and, when this earthly pilgrimage is over, may your landing be on that happy shore where naught but bliss can meet you, and where your virtues will receive the recompense which they deserve.

I desire much to see you, but do not repine, since you deem it best to send me from you for a time. Our meeting will be the more delightful for this separation, and time soon flies when profitably employed.

Please give my love to all, especially my papa, and believe me, dear
mamma,
        Your ever dutiful and affectionate daughter,
                                CATHERINE AUGUSTA MURRY

"It's perfectly awful," said Kitty to herelf, as she read it over; and so
it was, but madam was an old-fashioned lady, and had been brought up
to honor her parents in the old-fashioned way. Letters like that were
wrtten in her youth, and she saw no occasion to change the style for
what she called the modern slipshod mixture of gossip and slang.

The good lady never thought there might be a middle course, and
that it was a better way to teach composition to let the children write
their own natural little letters, with hints as to spelling, grammar, and
other necessary matters, than to make them copy the Grandisonian style
of her own youth.

Poor Kitty rebelled sadly, but submitted, and found her only comfort
in the thought that mamma would find something in the letter besides
what this disrespectful little person called "madam's old rubbish."

Mamma did find it, and sent back such a tender reply that Kitty's
heart reproached her for causing so much anxiety, when things were
not very bad after one got used to them.

So the next letter was a cheerful pink one, and though the contents
were not a bit more interesting than the first one it gave great satisfaction.

A green one went next, for as Kitty's spirits improved she felt the
need of a few home goodies to sweeten her studies and enliven her play
hours. As only sensible dainties came, and madam was propitiated by a
particularly delicate cake, presented with all due respect, she made no
objection to an occasional box from home.

Kitty therefore found herself a great favorite, and all the girls were
very fond of her, especially when the "sweeties" arrived.

"I think your mother is perfectly splendid to send such nice things
without your saying a word. I have to tease mine when I go home on a
visit, and she always forgets, and I can't remind her because the griffin
sees my letters, and cuts out all requests for food, 'as if you were not
properly supplied with the best in the market.' "

Fanny said that,—the wag and romp of the school,—and as she imitated
the "griffln," as she had naughtily named madam, there was a general
giggle, in which Kitty was glad to join, for she did get goodies without
"saying a word," and the idea tickled her immensely.

But she told her secret to no one, and, finding that the pink notes
made mamma very happy, she tried not to think of her "woes" when
she sat down to write. This little bit of self-denial was its own reward;
for, as the woes only existed in her own imagination, when she resolutely
stopped thinking of them they vanished.

Plenty of work and play, young society, and the affectionate desire to
please her mother did for Kitty just what mamma had hoped. At home
she was too much petted and pitied, as the youngest is apt to be; and
so she had the "fidgets," which are to little people what "nerves" are to
the elders. Now she had no time to dawdle and bemoan herself: if she

did, other girls went to the head of the class, led the games, and got the best marks.

So Kitty bestirred herself, and in three months was quite another child. Madam praised her, the girls loved her, mamma was both pleased and proud, and papa quite decided that Puss should have a little gold watch on her next birthday.

The pink paper was soon used up, since there was no call for any of the other colors, except an occasional green sheet; and a new stock was gladly sent by mamma, who was quite satisfied with the success of her little plot.

But mamma had been rather troubled about one thing, and that was the breaking of the rule. It had seemed a foolish one to her, and she had taught Kitty how to escape it. That was a bad example, and so she wrote to madam and "'fessed," like an honest mamma as she was.

She did it so prettily and penitently that old madam was not angry; indeed, when the matter was sensibly and respectfully put before her, she saw the justice of it, forgave the little plot, and amazed her pupils by gradually omitting to watch over them as they wrote.

When saucy Fanny spoke of it, she answered that she trusted them to write only what was true and modest, and, finding that the times had changed a little since her young days, she meant to relax some of her rules.

That pleased the girls, and they proved their gratitude by honorably forbearing to put into their letters any thing disrespectful toward the dear old griffin. Some of the most affectionate freely took their letters to her for correction; and when she had read a few, and laughed over them till her spectacles were dim, she quite depended on seeing them, and found what used to be a dull task now changed to a very pleasant amusement.

As a contrast to the model letter already inserted (and which I beg leave to state was really written from school by a little girl of twelve), I will only add one which Kitty wrote after the old rule was set aside:—

MY DEAR LITTLE MAMMA,—Now that I can tell you every thing, I will answer the questions you asked in your last, and please, please don't think I am a vain thing because I seem to praise myself. It is truly what people say and do, and I never should have told if you had not asked me.

You want to know if I am liked. Why, mamma, I'm a leading girl. Others fight to walk with me, and bribe me with their nice things to sit by them. I'm at the head most of the time, and try not to be grand about it; so I help the others, and am as kind and generous as I know how to be.

Madam is just as dear and clever as she can be, and I'm actually fond of her. Don't tell, but I fancy I'm her favorite, for she lets me do ever so many things that she once forbid, and isn't half so strict as she was.

I'm truly glad I came, for I do get on, and haven't had a woe this ever so long. Isn't that nice? I'm homesick sometimes, and look at my blue paper, but I won't use it; so I go and have a good run, or chatter French with madam, and get cheered up before I write.

I miss you most at night, mamma dear, for then I have no one to tell my goods and bads to, and so get right. But not having you, I remember what you told me, that I always have God, and to him I open my heart as I never did before. Prayers mean something to me now, and I say them so earnestly that sometimes I cry, and that makes me feel so fresh and strong, and ready to go on again.

I do try to be good, and don't ask for any reward but to see you look proud and pleased when I come home. I'd give any thing if I could hug you now and then, because *you* don't mind if I tumble your collar: madam does, and that spoils the fun of it. Kissing is a kind of inspiration, you know; and one doesn't stop to think of clothes when one is so full of love, it must spill over in kisses.

That sounds sentimental, but I'm not going to take it out, because you'll understand what I mean, and won't laugh. That's the comfort of private letters, isn't it?

Now, good-by, my dearest mother. Lots of love to papa, and do both write soon to your own little

Puss.

Just as Kitty was folding it up, madam came by, and quite mechanically held out her hand for it, as she used to do.

Kitty caught it back, and then blushed and looked distressed; for madam said gravely, as she remembered the new rule,—

"I beg your pardon, I forgot. Seal it up, my dear; I won't ask to read your secrets any more."

Kitty saw that she was hurt, and with an impulsive gesture thrust the letter into madam's hand, saying bravely, though she quaked a little at some of the things she had written,—

"Please read it. There are no secrets in it, only foolish things that mamma likes to know because they are about me. You'll think I'm a vain goose, but I'd rather you did that than think I told tales, or did any thing sly."

Thus urged, madam read the letter; and Kitty stood by, with cheeks much pinker than the paper, expecting a lecture when the last word came. But, to her great amazement, the old lady kissed her as she gave it back, and said, in a voice as gentle as if speaking to one of her own little daughters, lost long ago,—

"It is a good letter, my dear, and a true one. Give my regards to your mamma, and tell her that your suspicion about my favorite is quite correct."